THE COMPLETE
NOVELS OF
JAMES JOYCE

THE COMPLETE NOVELS OF

JAMES JOYCE

*Dubliners, A Portrait of the
Artist as a Young Man,
Ulysses & Finnegans Wake*

WORDSWORTH EDITIONS

For my husband
ANTHONY JOHN RANSON
with love from your wife, the publisher.
Eternally grateful for your unconditional love,
not just for me but for our children,
Simon, Andrew and Nichola Trayler

Readers who are interested in other titles from
Wordsworth Editions are invited to visit our website at
www.wordsworth-editions.com

For our latest list and a full mail-order service, contact
Bibliophile Books, 5 Datapoint, South Crescent, London E16 4TL
TEL: +44 (0)20 7474 2474 FAX: +44 (0)20 7474 8589
ORDERS: orders@bibliophilebooks.com
WEBSITE: www.bibliophilebooks.com

First published in 2012 by Wordsworth Editions Limited
8B East Street, Ware, Hertfordshire SG12 9HJ

ISBN 978 1 84022 677 5

Typeset in Great Britain by Antony Gray
Printed and bound by Clays Ltd, St Ives plc

CONTENTS

DUBLINERS

Contents

The Sisters

There was no hope for him this time: it was the third stroke. Night after night I had passed the house (it was vacation time) and studied the lighted square of window: and night after night I had found it lighted in the same way, faintly and evenly. If he was dead, I thought, I would see the reflection of candles on the darkened blind for I knew that two candles must be set at the head of a corpse. He had often said to me: 'I am not long for this world,' and I had thought his words idle. Now I knew they were true. Every night as I gazed up at the window I said softly to myself the word paralysis. It had always sounded strangely in my ears, like the word gnomon in the Euclid and the word simony in the Catechism. But now it sounded to me like the name of some maleficent and sinful being. It filled me with fear, and yet I longed to be nearer to it and to look upon its deadly work.

Old Cotter was sitting at the fire, smoking, when I came downstairs to supper. While my aunt was ladling out my stirabout he said, as if returning to some former remark of his: 'No, I wouldn't say he was exactly . . . but there was something queer . . . there was something uncanny about him. I'll tell you my opinion . . . '

He began to puff at his pipe, no doubt arranging his opinion in his mind. Tiresome old fool! When we knew him first he used to be rather interesting, talking of faints and worms; but I soon grew tired of him and his endless stories about the distillery.

'I have my own theory about it,' he said. 'I think it was one of those . . . peculiar cases . . . But it's hard to say . . . '

He began to puff again at his pipe without giving us his theory. My uncle saw me staring and said to me: 'Well, so your old friend is gone, you'll be sorry to hear.'

'Who?' said I.

'Father Flynn.'

'Is he dead?'

'Mr Cotter here has just told us. He was passing by the house.'

I knew that I was under observation so I continued eating as if the news had not interested me. My uncle explained to old Cotter.

'The youngster and he were great friends. The old chap taught him a great deal, mind you; and they say he had a great wish for him.'

'God have mercy on his soul,' said my aunt piously.

Old Cotter looked at me for a while. I felt that his little beady black eyes were examining me but I would not satisfy him by looking up from my plate. He returned to his pipe and finally spat rudely into the grate.

'I wouldn't like children of mine,' he said, 'to have too much to say to a man like that.'

'How do you mean, Mr Cotter?' asked my aunt.

'What I mean is,' said old Cotter, 'it's bad for children. My idea is: let a young lad run about and play with young lads of his own age and not be . . . Am I right, Jack?'

'That's my principle, too,' said my uncle. 'Let him learn to box his corner. That's what I'm always saying to that Rosicrucian there: take exercise. Why, when I was a nipper every morning of my life I had a cold bath, winter and summer. And that's what stands to me now. Education is all very fine and large . . . Mr Cotter might take a pick of that leg of mutton,' he added to my aunt.

'No, no, not for me,' said old Cotter.

My aunt brought the dish from the safe and put it on the table.

'But why do you think it's not good for children, Mr Cotter?' she asked.

'It's bad for children,' said old Cotter, 'because their minds are so impressionable. When children see things like that, you know, it has an effect . . . '

I crammed my mouth with stirabout for fear I might give utterance to my anger. Tiresome old red-nosed imbecile!

It was late when I fell asleep. Though I was angry with old Cotter for alluding to me as a child, I puzzled my head to extract meaning from his unfinished sentences. In the dark of my room I imagined that I saw again the heavy grey face of the paralytic. I drew the blankets over my head and tried to think of Christmas. But the grey face still followed me. It murmured; and I understood that it desired to confess something. I felt my soul receding into some pleasant and vicious region; and there again I found it waiting for me. It began to confess to me in a murmuring voice and I wondered why it smiled continually and why the lips were so moist with spittle. But then I remembered that it had died of paralysis and I felt that I too was smiling feebly as if to absolve the simoniac of his sin.

The next morning after breakfast I went down to look at the little house in Great Britain Street. It was an unassuming shop, registered under the vague name of *Drapery*. The drapery consisted mainly of children's bootees and umbrellas; and on ordinary days a notice used to hang in the window, saying: *Umbrellas Re-covered.* No notice was visible now for the shutters were up. A crape bouquet was tied to the door-knocker with ribbon. Two poor women and a telegram boy were reading the card pinned on the crape. I also approached and read:

July 1st, 1895
The Revd James Flynn (formerly of S. Catherine's Church,
Meath Street), aged sixty-five years.
R. I. P.

The reading of the card persuaded me that he was dead and I was disturbed to find myself at check. Had he not been dead I would have gone into the little dark room behind the shop to find him sitting in his armchair by the fire, nearly smothered in his greatcoat. Perhaps my aunt would have given me a packet of High Toast for him and this present would have roused him from his stupefied doze. It was always I who emptied the packet into his black snuff-box for his hands trembled too much to allow him to do this without spilling half the snuff about the floor. Even as he raised his large trembling hand to his nose little clouds of smoke dribbled through his fingers over the front of his coat. It may have been these constant showers of snuff which gave his ancient priestly garments their green faded look for the red handkerchief, blackened, as it always was, with the snuff-stains of a week, with which he tried to brush away the fallen grains, was quite inefficacious.

I wished to go in and look at him but I had not the courage to knock. I walked away slowly along the sunny side of the street, reading all the theatrical advertisements in the shop-windows as I went. I found it strange that neither I nor the day seemed in a mourning mood and I felt even annoyed at discovering in myself a sensation of freedom as if I had been freed from something by his death. I wondered at this for, as my uncle had said the night before, he had taught me a great deal. He had studied in the Irish college in Rome and he had taught me to pronounce Latin properly. He had told me stories about the catacombs and about Napoleon Bonaparte, and he had explained to me the meaning of the different ceremonies of the mass and of the different vestments worn by the priest. Sometimes he had amused himself by putting difficult questions to me, asking me what one should do in certain circumstances or whether such and such sins were mortal or venial or only imperfections. His questions showed me how complex and mysterious were certain institutions of the Church which I had always regarded as the simplest acts. The duties of the priest towards the Eucharist and towards the secrecy of the confessional seemed so grave to me that I wondered how anybody had ever found in himself the courage to undertake them; and I was not surprised when he told me that the fathers of the Church had written books as thick as the *Post Office Directory* and as closely printed as the law notices in the newspaper, elucidating all these intricate questions. Often when I thought of this I could make no answer or only a very foolish and halting one upon which he used to smile and nod his head twice or thrice. Sometimes he used to put me through the responses of the mass which he had made me learn by heart; and, as I pattered, he used to smile pensively and nod his head, now and then pushing huge pinches of snuff up each nostril alternately. When he smiled he used to uncover his big discoloured teeth and let his tongue lie upon his lower lip – a habit which had made me feel uneasy in the beginning of our acquaintance before I knew him well.

As I walked along in the sun I remembered old Cotter's words and tried to remember what had happened afterwards in the dream. I remembered that I had noticed long velvet curtains and a swinging lamp of antique fashion. I felt that I had been very far away, in some land where the customs were strange – in Persia, I thought . . . But I could not remember the end of the dream.

In the evening my aunt took me with her to visit the house of mourning. It was after sunset; but the window-panes of the houses that looked to the west reflected the tawny gold of a great bank of clouds. Nannie received us in the hall; and, as it would have been unseemly to have shouted at her, my aunt shook hands with her for all. The old woman pointed upwards interrogatively and, on my aunt's nodding, proceeded to toil up the narrow staircase before us, her bowed head being scarcely above the level of the banister-rail. At the first landing she stopped and beckoned us forward encouragingly towards the open door of the dead-room. My aunt went in and the old woman, seeing that I hesitated to enter, began to beckon to me again repeatedly with her hand.

I went in on tiptoe. The room through the lace end of the blind was suffused with dusky golden light amid which the candles looked like pale thin flames. He had been coffined. Nannie gave the lead and we three knelt down at the foot of the bed. I pretended to pray but I could not gather my thoughts because the old woman's mutterings distracted me. I noticed how clumsily her skirt was hooked at the back and how the heels of her cloth boots were trodden down all to one side. The fancy came to me that the old priest was smiling as he lay there in his coffin.

But no. When we rose and went up to the head of the bed I saw that he was not smiling. There he lay, solemn and copious, vested as for the altar, his large hands loosely retaining a chalice. His face was very truculent, grey and massive, with black cavernous nostrils and circled by a scanty white fur. There was a heavy odour in the room – the flowers.

We crossed ourselves and came away. In the little room downstairs we found Eliza seated in his armchair in state. I groped my way towards my usual chair in the corner while Nannie went to the sideboard and brought out a decanter of sherry and some wine-glasses. She set these on the table and invited us to take a little glass of wine. Then, at her sister's bidding, she filled out the sherry into the glasses and passed them to us. She pressed me to take some cream crackers also but I declined because I thought I would make too much noise eating them. She seemed to be somewhat disappointed at my refusal and went over quietly to the sofa where she sat down behind her sister. No one spoke: we all gazed at the empty fireplace.

My aunt waited until Eliza sighed and then said: 'Ah, well, he's gone to a better world.'

Eliza sighed again and bowed her head in assent. My aunt fingered the stem of her wineglass before sipping a little.

'Did he . . . peacefully?' she asked.

'Oh, quite peacefully, ma'am,' said Eliza 'You couldn't tell when the breath went out of him. He had a beautiful death, God be praised.'

'And everything . . . ? '

'Father O'Rourke was in with him a Tuesday and anointed him and prepared him and all.'

'He knew then?'

'He was quite resigned.'

'He looks quite resigned,' said my aunt.

'That's what the woman we had in to wash him said. She said he just looked as if he was asleep, he looked that peaceful and resigned. No one would think he'd make such a beautiful corpse.'

'Yes, indeed,' said my aunt.

She sipped a little more from her glass and said: 'Well, Miss Flynn, at any rate it must be a great comfort for you to know that you did all you could for him. You were both very kind to him, I must say.'

Eliza smoothed her dress over her knees.

'Ah, poor James!' she said. 'God knows we done all we could, as poor as we are – we wouldn't see him want anything while he was in it.'

Nannie had leaned her head against the sofa-pillow and seemed about to fall asleep.

'There's poor Nannie,' said Eliza, looking at her, 'she's wore out. All the work we had, she and me, getting in the woman to wash him and then laying him out and then the coffin and then arranging about the mass in the chapel. Only for Father O'Rourke I don't know what we'd done at all. It was him brought us all them flowers and them two candlesticks out of the chapel and wrote out the notice for the *Freeman's General* and took charge of all the papers for the cemetery and poor James's insurance.'

'Wasn't that good of him?' said my aunt.

Eliza closed her eyes and shook her head slowly.

'Ah, there's no friends like the old friends,' she said, 'when all is said and done, no friends that a body can trust.'

'Indeed, that's true,' said my aunt. 'And I'm sure now that he's gone to his eternal reward he won't forget you and all your kindness to him.'

'Ah, poor James!' said Eliza. 'He was no great trouble to us. You wouldn't hear him in the house any more than now. Still, I know he's gone and all to that . . .'

'It's when it's all over that you'll miss him,' said my aunt.

'I know that,' said Eliza. 'I won't be bringing him in his cup of beef-tea any more, nor you, ma'am, sending him his snuff. Ah, poor James!'

She stopped, as if she were communing with the past and then said shrewdly: 'Mind you, I noticed there was something queer coming over him latterly. Whenever I'd bring in his soup to him there I'd find him with his breviary fallen to the floor, lying back in the chair and his mouth open.'

She laid a finger against her nose and frowned: then she continued: 'But still and all he kept on saying that before the summer was over he'd go out for a drive one fine day just to see the old house again where we were all born down in Irishtown and take me and Nannie with him. If we could only get one of them new-fangled carriages that makes no noise that Father O'Rourke told him about, them with the rheumatic wheels, for the day cheap – he said, at Johnny Rush's over the way there and drive out the three of us together of a Sunday evening. He had his mind set on that . . . Poor James!'

'The Lord have mercy on his soul!' said my aunt.

Eliza took out her handkerchief and wiped her eyes with it. Then she put it back again in her pocket and gazed into the empty grate for some time without speaking.

'He was too scrupulous always,' she said. 'The duties of the priesthood was too much for him. And then his life was, you might say, crossed.'

'Yes,' said my aunt. 'He was a disappointed man. You could see that.'

A silence took possession of the little room and, under cover of it, I approached the table and tasted my sherry and then returned quietly to my chair in the corner. Eliza seemed to have fallen into a deep reverie. We waited respectfully for her to break the silence: and after a long pause she said slowly: 'It was that chalice he broke . . . That was the beginning of it. Of course, they say it was all right, that it contained nothing, I mean. But still . . . They say it was the boy's fault. But poor James was so nervous, God be merciful to him!'

'And was that it?' said my aunt. 'I heard something . . .'

Eliza nodded.

'That affected his mind,' she said. 'After that he began to mope by himself, talking to no one and wandering about by himself. So one night he was wanted for to go on a call and they couldn't find him anywhere. They looked high up and low down; and still they couldn't see a sight of him anywhere. So then the clerk suggested to try the chapel. So then they got the keys and opened the chapel and the clerk and Father O'Rourke and another priest that was there brought in a light for to look for him . . . And what do you think but there he was, sitting up by himself in the dark in his confession-box, wide-awake and laughing-like softly to himself?'

She stopped suddenly as if to listen. I too listened; but there was no sound in the house: and I knew that the old priest was lying still in his coffin as we had seen him, solemn and truculent in death, an idle chalice on his breast.

Eliza resumed: 'Wide-awake and laughing-like to himself . . . So then, of course, when they saw that, that made them think that there was something gone wrong with him . . .'

An Encounter

It was Joe Dillon who introduced the Wild West to us. He had a little library made up of old numbers of *The Union Jack, Pluck* and *The Halfpenny Marvel*. Every evening after school we met in his back garden and arranged Indian battles. He and his fat young brother Leo, the idler, held the loft of the stable while we tried to carry it by storm; or we fought a pitched battle on the grass. But, however well we fought, we never won siege or battle and all our bouts ended with Joe Dillon's war dance of victory. His parents went to eight-o'clock mass every morning in Gardiner Street and the peaceful odour of Mrs Dillon was prevalent in the hall of the house. But he played too fiercely for us who were younger and more timid. He looked like some kind of an Indian when he capered round the garden, an old tea-cosy on his head, beating a tin with his fist and yelling: 'Ya! yaka, yaka, yaka!'

Everyone was incredulous when it was reported that he had a vocation for the priesthood. Nevertheless it was true.

A spirit of unruliness diffused itself among us and, under its influence, differences of culture and constitution were waived. We banded ourselves together, some boldly, some in jest and some almost in fear: and of the number of these latter, the reluctant Indians who were afraid to seem studious or lacking in robustness, I was one. The adventures related in the literature of the Wild West were remote from my nature but, at least, they opened doors of escape. I liked better some American detective stories which were traversed from time to time by unkempt fierce and beautiful girls. Though there was nothing wrong in these stories and though their intention was sometimes literary they were circulated secretly at school. One day when Father Butler was hearing the four pages of Roman History, clumsy Leo Dillon was discovered with a copy of *The Halfpenny Marvel.*

'This page or this page? This page? Now, Dillon, up! *"Hardly had the day"* . . . Go on! What day? *"Hardly had the day dawned"*. . . Have you studied it? What have you there in your pocket?'

Everyone's heart palpitated as Leo Dillon handed up the paper and everyone assumed an innocent face. Father Butler turned over the pages, frowning.

'What is this rubbish?' he said. *'The Apache Chief!* Is this what you read instead of studying your Roman History? Let me not find any more of this wretched stuff in this college. The man who wrote it, I suppose, was some wretched fellow who writes these things for a drink. I'm surprised at boys like you, educated, reading such stuff. I could understand it if you were . . . National School boys. Now, Dillon, I advise you strongly, get at your work or . . . '

This rebuke during the sober hours of school paled much of the glory of the Wild West for me, and the confused puffy face of Leo Dillon awakened one of my consciences. But when the restraining influence of the school was at a distance I began to hunger again for wild sensations, for the escape which those chronicles of disorder alone seemed to offer me. The mimic warfare of the evening became at last as wearisome to me as the routine of school in the morning because I wanted real adventures to happen to myself. But real adventures, I reflected, do not happen to people who remain at home: they must be sought abroad.

The summer holidays were near at hand when I made up my mind to break out of the weariness of school-life for one day at least. With Leo Dillon and a boy named Mahony I planned a day's miching. Each of us saved up sixpence. We were to meet at ten in the morning on the Canal Bridge. Mahony's big sister was to write an excuse for him and Leo Dillon was to tell his brother to say he was sick. We arranged to go along the Wharf Road until we came to the ships, then to cross in the ferryboat and

walk out to see the Pigeon House. Leo Dillon was afraid we might meet
Father Butler or someone out of the college; but Mahony asked, very
sensibly, what would Father Butler be doing out at the Pigeon House. We
were reassured: and I brought the first stage of the plot to an end by
collecting sixpence from the other two, at the same time showing them my
own sixpence. When we were making the last arrangements on the eve we
were all vaguely excited. We shook hands, laughing, and Mahony said: 'Till
tomorrow, mates!'

That night I slept badly. In the morning I was first-comer to the bridge
as I lived nearest. I hid my books in the long grass near the ashpit at the end
of the garden where nobody ever came and hurried along the canal bank. It
was a mild sunny morning in the first week of June. I sat up on the coping
of the bridge admiring my frail canvas shoes which I had diligently pipe-
clayed overnight and watching the docile horses pulling a tramload of
business people up the hill. All the branches of the tall trees which lined the
mall were gay with little light green leaves and the sunlight slanted through
them on to the water. The granite stone of the bridge was beginning to be
warm and I began to pat it with my hands in time to an air in my head. I was
very happy.

When I had been sitting there for five or ten minutes I saw Mahony's
grey suit approaching. He came up the hill, smiling, and clambered up
beside me on the bridge. While we were waiting he brought out the catapult
which bulged from his inner pocket and explained some improvements
which he had made in it. I asked him why he had brought it and he told me
he had brought it to have some gas with the birds. Mahony used slang
freely, and spoke of Father Butler as Old Bunser. We waited on for a
quarter of an hour more but still there was no sign of Leo Dillon. Mahony,
at last, jumped down and said: 'Come along. I knew Fatty'd funk it.'

'And his sixpence . . . ?' I said.

'That's forfeit,' said Mahony. 'And so much the better for us – a bob and
a tanner instead of a bob.'

We walked along the North Strand Road till we came to the Vitriol
Works and then turned to the right along the Wharf Road. Mahony began
to play the Indian as soon as we were out of public sight. He chased a crowd
of ragged girls, brandishing his unloaded catapult and, when two ragged
boys began, out of chivalry, to fling stones at us, he proposed that we should
charge them. I objected that the boys were too small, and so we walked on,
the ragged troop screaming after us: '*Swaddlers! Swaddlers!*' thinking that we
were Protestants because Mahony, who was dark-complexioned, wore the
silver badge of a cricket club in his cap. When we came to the Smoothing

Iron we arranged a siege; but it was a failure because you must have at least three. We revenged ourselves on Leo Dillon by saying what a funk he was and guessing how many he would get at three o'clock from Mr Ryan.

We came then near the river. We spent a long time walking about the noisy streets flanked by high stone walls, watching the working of cranes and engines and often being shouted at for our immobility by the drivers of groaning carts. It was noon when we reached the quays and, as all the labourers seemed to be eating their lunches, we bought two big currant buns and sat down to eat them on some metal piping beside the river. We pleased ourselves with the spectacle of Dublin's commerce – the barges signalled from far away by their curls of woolly smoke, the brown fishing fleet beyond Ringsend, the big white sailing-vessel which was being discharged on the opposite quay. Mahony said it would be right skit to run away to sea on one of those big ships and even I, looking at the high masts, saw, or imagined, the geography which had been scantily dosed to me at school gradually taking substance under my eyes. School and home seemed to recede from us and their influences upon us seemed to wane.

We crossed the Liffey in the ferryboat, paying our toll to be transported in the company of two labourers and a little Jew with a bag. We were serious to the point of solemnity, but once during the short voyage our eyes met and we laughed. When we landed we watched the discharging of the graceful three-master which we had observed from the other quay. Some bystander said that she was a Norwegian vessel. I went to the stern and tried to decipher the legend upon it but, failing to do so, I came back and examined the foreign sailors to see had any of them green eyes for I had some confused notion . . . The sailors' eyes were blue and grey and even black. The only sailor whose eyes could have been called green was a tall man who amused the crowd on the quay by calling out cheerfully every time the planks fell: 'All right! All right!'

When we were tired of this sight we wandered slowly into Ringsend. The day had grown sultry, and in the windows of the grocers' shops musty biscuits lay bleaching. We bought some biscuits and chocolate which we ate sedulously as we wandered through the squalid streets where the families of the fishermen live. We could find no dairy and so we went into a huckster's shop and bought a bottle of raspberry lemonade each. Refreshed by this, Mahony chased a cat down a lane, but the cat escaped into a wide field. We both felt rather tired and when we reached the field we made at once for a sloping bank over the ridge of which we could see the Dodder.

It was too late and we were too tired to carry out our project of visiting the Pigeon House. We had to be home before four o'clock lest our adventure should be discovered. Mahony looked regretfully at his catapult and I had to suggest going home by train before he regained any cheerfulness. The sun went in behind some clouds and left us to our jaded thoughts and the crumbs of our provisions.

There was nobody but ourselves in the field. When we had lain on the bank for some time without speaking I saw a man approaching from the far end of the field. I watched him lazily as I chewed one of those green stems on which girls tell fortunes. He came along by the bank slowly. He walked with one hand upon his hip and in the other hand he held a stick with which he tapped the turf lightly. He was shabbily dressed in a suit of greenish-black and wore what we used to call a jerry hat with a high crown. He seemed to be fairly old for his moustache was ashen-grey. When he passed at our feet he glanced up at us quickly and then continued his way. We followed him with our eyes and saw that when he had gone on for perhaps fifty paces he turned about and began to retrace his steps. He walked towards us very slowly, always tapping the ground with his stick, so slowly that I thought he was looking for something in the grass.

He stopped when he came level with us and bade us good-day. We answered him and he sat down beside us on the slope slowly and with great care. He began to talk of the weather, saying that it would be a very hot summer and adding that the seasons had changed greatly since he was a boy – a long time ago. He said that the happiest time of one's life was undoubtedly one's schoolboy days and that he would give anything to be young again. While he expressed these sentiments which bored us a little we kept silent. Then he began to talk of school and of books. He asked us whether we had read the poetry of Thomas Moore or the works of Sir Walter Scott and Lord Lytton. I pretended that I had read every book he mentioned so that in the end he said: 'Ah, I can see you are a bookworm like myself. Now,' he added, pointing to Mahony who was regarding us with open eyes, 'he is different; he goes in for games.'

He said he had all Sir Walter Scott's works and all Lord Lytton's works at home and never tired of reading them. 'Of course,' he said, 'there were some of Lord Lytton's works which boys couldn't read.' Mahony asked why couldn't boys read them – a question which agitated and pained me because I was afraid the man would think I was as stupid as Mahony. The man, however, only smiled. I saw that he had great gaps in his mouth between his yellow teeth. Then he asked us which of us had the most sweethearts. Mahony mentioned lightly that he had three totties. The man asked me how many I had. I answered that I had none. He did not believe me and said he was sure I must have one. I was silent.

'Tell us,' said Mahony pertly to the man, 'how many have you yourself?'

The man smiled as before and said that when he was our age he had lots of sweethearts.

'Every boy,' he said, 'has a little sweetheart.'

His attitude on this point struck me as strangely liberal in a man of his age. In my heart I thought that what he said about boys and sweethearts was reasonable. But I disliked the words in his mouth and I wondered why he shivered once or twice as if he feared something or felt a sudden chill. As he proceeded I noticed that his accent was good. He began to speak to us about girls, saying what nice soft hair they had and how soft their hands were and how all girls were not so good as they seemed to be if one only knew. There was nothing he liked, he said, so much as looking at a nice young girl, at her nice white hands and her beautiful soft hair. He gave me the impression that he was repeating something which he had learned by heart or that, magnetised by some words of his own speech, his mind was slowly circling round and round in the same orbit. At times he spoke as if he were simply alluding to some fact that everybody knew, and at times he lowered his voice and spoke mysteriously as if he were telling us something secret which he did not wish others to overhear. He repeated his phrases over and over again, varying them and surrounding them with his mono- tonous voice. I continued to gaze towards the foot of the slope, listening to him.

After a long while his monologue paused. He stood up slowly, saying that he had to leave us for a minute or so, a few minutes, and, without changing the direction of my gaze, I saw him walking slowly away from us towards the near end of the field. We remained silent when he had gone. After a silence of a few minutes I heard Mahony exclaim: 'I say! Look what he's doing!'

As I neither answered nor raised my eyes Mahony exclaimed again: 'I say . . . He's a queer old josser!'

'In case he asks us for our names,' I said, 'let you be Murphy and I'll be Smith.'

We said nothing further to each other. I was still considering whether I would go away or not when the man came back and sat down beside us again. Hardly had he sat down when Mahony, catching sight of the cat which had escaped him, sprang up and pursued her across the field. The man and I watched the chase. The cat escaped once more and Mahony began to throw stones at the wall she had escaladed. Desisting from this, he began to wander about the far end of the field, aimlessly.

After an interval the man spoke to me. He said that my friend was a very rough boy and asked did he get whipped often at school. I was going to reply indignantly that we were not National School boys to be whipped, as he called it; but I remained silent. He began to speak on the subject of chastising boys. His mind, as if magnetised again by his speech, seemed to circle slowly round and round its new centre. He said that when boys were that kind they ought to be whipped and well whipped. When a boy was rough and unruly there was nothing would do him any good but a good sound whipping. A slap on the hand or a box on the ear was no good: what he wanted was to get a nice warm whipping. I was surprised at this sentiment and involuntarily glanced up at his face. As I did so I met the gaze of a pair of bottle-green eyes peering at me from under a twitching forehead. I turned my eyes away again.

The man continued his monologue. He seemed to have forgotten his recent liberalism. He said that if ever he found a boy talking to girls or having a girl for a sweetheart he would whip him and whip him; and that would teach him not to be talking to girls. And if a boy had a girl for a sweetheart and told lies about it then he would give him such a whipping as no boy ever got in this world. He said that there was nothing in this world he would like so well as that. He described to me how he would whip such a boy as if he were unfolding some elaborate mystery. He would love that, he said, better than anything in this world; and his voice, as he led me monotonously through the mystery, grew almost affectionate and seemed to plead with me that I should understand him.

I waited till his monologue paused again. Then I stood up abruptly. Lest I should betray my agitation I delayed a few moments pretending to fix my shoe properly and then, saying that I was obliged to go, I bade him good-day. I went up the slope calmly but my heart was beating quickly with fear that he would seize me by the ankles. When I reached the top of the slope I turned round and, without looking at him, called loudly across the field: 'Murphy!'

My voice had an accent of forced bravery in it and I was ashamed of my paltry stratagem. I had to call the name again before Mahony saw me and hallooed in answer. How my heart beat as he came running across the field to me! He ran as if to bring me aid. And I was penitent; for in my heart I had always despised him a little.

Araby

North Richmond Street, being blind, was a quiet street except at the hour when the Christian Brothers' School set the boys free. An uninhabited house of two storeys stood at the blind end, detached from its neighbours in a square ground. The other houses of the street, conscious of decent lives within them, gazed at one another with brown imperturbable faces.

The former tenant of our house, a priest, had died in the back drawing-room. Air, musty from having been long enclosed, hung in all the rooms, and the waste room behind the kitchen was littered with old useless papers. Among these I found a few paper-covered books, the pages of which were curled and damp: *The Abbot*, by Walter Scott, *The Devout Communicant* and *The Memoirs of Vidocq*. I liked the last best because its leaves were yellow. The wild garden behind the house contained a central apple-tree and a few straggling bushes, under one of which I found the late tenant's rusty bicycle-pump. He had been a very charitable priest; in his will he had left all his money to institutions and the furniture of his house to his sister.

When the short days of winter came dusk fell before we had well eaten our dinners. When we met in the street the houses had grown sombre. The space of sky above us was the colour of ever-changing violet and towards it the lamps of the street lifted their feeble lanterns. The cold air stung us and we played till our bodies glowed. Our shouts echoed in the silent street. The career of our play brought us through the dark muddy lanes behind the houses where we ran the gauntlet of the rough tribes from the cottages, to the back doors of the dark dripping gardens where odours arose from the ashpits, to the dark odorous stables where a coachman smoothed and combed the horse or shook music from the buckled harness. When we returned to the street, light from the kitchen windows had filled the areas. If my uncle was seen turning the corner we hid in the shadow until we had seen him safely housed. Or if Mangan's sister came out on the doorstep to call her brother in to his tea we watched her from our shadow peer up and down the street. We waited to see whether she would remain or go in and, if she remained, we left our shadow and walked up to Mangan's steps resignedly. She was waiting for us, her figure defined by the light from the half-opened door. Her brother always teased her before he obeyed and I stood by the railings looking at her. Her dress swung as she moved her body and the soft rope of her hair tossed from side to side.

Every morning I lay on the floor in the front parlour watching her door. The blind was pulled down to within an inch of the sash so that I could not be seen. When she came out on the door-step my heart leaped. I ran to the hall, seized my books and followed her. I kept her brown figure always in my eye and, when we came near the point at which our ways diverged, I quickened my pace and passed her. This happened morning after morning. I had never spoken to her, except for a few casual words, and yet her name was like a summons to all my foolish blood. Her image accompanied me even in places the most hostile to romance. On Saturday evenings when my aunt went marketing I had to go to carry some of the parcels. We walked through the flaring streets, jostled by drunken men and bargaining women, amid the curses of labourers, the shrill litanies of shop-boys who stood on guard by the barrels of pigs' cheeks, the nasal chanting of street-singers, who sang a *come-all-you* about O'Donovan Rossa, or a ballad about the troubles in our native land. These noises converged in a single sensation of life for me: I imagined that I bore my chalice safely through a throng of foes. Her name sprang to my lips at moments in strange prayers and praises which I myself did not understand. My eyes were often full of tears (I could not tell why) and at times a flood from my heart seemed to pour itself out into my bosom. I thought little of the future. I did not know whether I would ever speak to her or not or, if I spoke to her, how I could tell her of my confused adoration. But my body was like a harp and her words and gestures were like fingers running upon the wires.

One evening I went into the back drawing-room in which the priest had died. It was a dark rainy evening and there was no sound in the house. Through one of the broken panes I heard the rain impinge upon the earth, the fine incessant needles of water playing in the sodden beds. Some distant lamp or lighted window gleamed below me. I was thankful that I could see so little. All my senses seemed to desire to veil themselves and, feeling that I was about to slip from them, I pressed the palms of my hands together until they trembled, murmuring: '*O love! O love!*' many times.

At last she spoke to me. When she addressed the first words to me I was so confused that I did not know what to answer. She asked me was I going to *Araby*. I forgot whether I answered yes or no. It would be a splendid bazaar, she said she would love to go.

'And why can't you?' I asked.

While she spoke she turned a silver bracelet round and round her wrist. She could not go, she said, because there would be a retreat that week in her convent. Her brother and two other boys were fighting for their caps and I was alone at the railings. She held one of the spikes, bowing her head towards me. The light from the lamp opposite our door caught the white curve of her neck, lit up her hair that rested there and, falling, lit up the hand upon the railing. It fell over one side of her dress and caught the white border of a petticoat, just visible as she stood at ease.

'It's well for you,' she said.

'If I go,' I said, 'I will bring you something.'

What innumerable follies laid waste my waking and sleeping thoughts after that evening! I wished to annihilate the tedious intervening days. I chafed against the work of school. At night in my bedroom and by day in the classroom her image came between me and the page I strove to read. The syllables of the word *Araby* were called to me through the silence in which my soul luxuriated and cast an Eastern enchantment over me. I asked for leave to go to the bazaar on Saturday night. My aunt was surprised and hoped it was not some Freemason affair. I answered few questions in class. I watched my master's face pass from amiability to sternness; he hoped I was not beginning to idle. I could not call my wandering thoughts together. I had hardly any patience with the serious work of life which, now that it stood between me and my desire, seemed to me child's play, ugly monotonous child's play.

On Saturday morning I reminded my uncle that I wished to go to the bazaar in the evening. He was fussing at the hallstand, looking for the hat-brush, and answered me curtly: 'Yes, boy, I know.'

As he was in the hall I could not go into the front parlour and lie at the window. I felt the house in bad humour and walked slowly towards the school. The air was pitilessly raw and already my heart misgave me.

When I came home to dinner my uncle had not yet been home. Still it was early. I sat staring at the clock for some time and, when its ticking began to irritate me, I left the room. I mounted the staircase and gained the upper part of the house. The high cold empty gloomy rooms liberated me and I went from room to room singing. From the front window I saw my companions playing below in the street. Their cries reached me weakened and indistinct and, leaning my forehead against the cool glass, I looked over at the dark house where she lived. I may have stood there for an hour, seeing nothing but the brown-clad figure cast by my imagination, touched discreetly by the lamplight at the curved neck, at the hand upon the railings and at the border below the dress.

When I came downstairs again I found Mrs Mercer sitting at the fire. She was an old garrulous woman, a pawnbroker's widow, who collected used stamps for some pious purpose. I had to endure the gossip of the tea-table. The meal was prolonged beyond an hour and still my uncle did not come. Mrs Mercer stood up to go: she was sorry she couldn't wait any longer, but it was after eight o'clock and she did not like to be out late, as the night air was bad for her. When she had gone I began to walk up and down the room, clenching my fists. My aunt said: 'I'm afraid you may put off your bazaar for this night of Our Lord.'

At nine o'clock I heard my uncle's latchkey in the halldoor. I heard him talking to himself and heard the hallstand rocking when it had received the weight of his overcoat. I could interpret these signs. When he was midway through his dinner I asked him to give me the money to go to the bazaar. He had forgotten.

'The people are in bed and after their first sleep now,' he said.

I did not smile. My aunt said to him energetically: 'Can't you give him the money and let him go? You've kept him late enough as it is.'

My uncle said he was very sorry he had forgotten. He said he believed in the old saying: 'All work and no play makes Jack a dull boy.' He asked me where I was going and, when I had told him a second time he asked me did I know *The Arab's Farewell to his Steed*. When I left the kitchen he was about to recite the opening lines of the piece to my aunt.

I held a florin tightly in my hand as I strode down Buckingham Street towards the station. The sight of the streets thronged with buyers and glaring with gas recalled to me the purpose of my journey. I took my seat in a third-class carriage of a deserted train. After an intolerable delay the train moved out of the station slowly. It crept onward among ruinous houses and over the twinkling river. At Westland Row Station a crowd of people pressed to the carriage doors; but the porters moved them back, saying that it was a special train for the bazaar. I remained alone in the bare carriage. In a few minutes the train drew up beside an improvised wooden platform. I passed out on to the road and saw by the lighted dial of a clock that it was ten minutes to ten. In front of me was a large building which displayed the magical name.

I could not find any sixpenny entrance and, fearing that the bazaar would be closed, I passed in quickly through a turnstile, handing a shilling to a weary-looking man. I found myself in a big hall girdled at half its height by a gallery. Nearly all the stalls were closed and the greater part of the hall was in darkness. I recognised a silence like that which pervades a church after a service. I walked into the centre of the bazaar timidly. A few people were gathered about the stalls which were still open. Before a curtain, over which the words *Café Chantant* were written in coloured lamps, two men were counting money on a salver. I listened to the fall of the coins.

Remembering with difficulty why I had come I went over to one of the stalls and examined porcelain vases and flowered tea-sets. At the door of the stall a young lady was talking and laughing with two young gentlemen. I remarked their English accents and listened vaguely to their conversation.

'O, I never said such a thing!'

'O, but you did!'

'O, but I didn't!'

'Didn't she say that?'

'Yes. I heard her.'

'O, there's a . . . fib!'

Observing me the young lady came over and asked me did I wish to buy anything. The tone of her voice was not encouraging; she seemed to have spoken to me out of a sense of duty. I looked humbly at the great jars that stood like eastern guards at either side of the dark entrance to the stall and murmured: 'No, thank you.'

The young lady changed the position of one of the vases and went back to the two young men. They began to talk of the same subject. Once or twice the young lady glanced at me over her shoulder.

I lingered before her stall, though I knew my stay was useless, to make my interest in her wares seem the more real. Then I turned away slowly and walked down the middle of the bazaar. I allowed the two pennies to fall against the sixpence in my pocket. I heard a voice call from one end of the gallery that the light was out. The upper part of the hall was now completely dark.

Gazing up into the darkness I saw myself as a creature driven and derided by vanity; and my eyes burned with anguish and anger.

Eveline

She sat at the window watching the evening invade the avenue. Her head was leaned against the window curtains and in her nostrils was the odour of dusty cretonne. She was tired.

Few people passed. The man out of the last house passed on his way home; she heard his footsteps clacking along the concrete pavement and afterwards crunching on the cinder path before the new red houses. One time there used to be a field there in which they used to play every evening with other people's children. Then a man from Belfast bought the field and built houses in it – not like their little brown houses but bright brick houses with shining roofs. The children of the avenue used to play together in that field – the Devines, the Waters, the Dunns, little Keogh the cripple, she and her brothers and sisters. Ernest, however, never played: he was too grown up. Her father used often to hunt them in out of the field with his blackthorn stick; but usually little Keogh used to keep *nix* and call out when he saw her father coming. Still they seemed to have been rather happy then. Her father was not so bad then; and besides, her mother was alive. That was a long time ago; she and her brothers and sisters were all grown up; her mother was dead. Tizzie Dunn was dead, too, and the Waters had gone back to England. Everything changes. Now she was going to go away like the others, to leave her home.

Home! She looked round the room, reviewing all its familiar objects which she had dusted once a week for so many years, wondering where on earth all the dust came from. Perhaps she would never see again those familiar objects from which she had never dreamed of being divided. And yet during all those years she had never found out the name of the priest whose yellowing photograph hung on the wall above the broken harmonium beside the coloured print of the promises made to Blessed Margaret Mary Alacoque. He had been a school friend of her father. Whenever he showed the photograph to a visitor her father used to pass it with a casual word: 'He is in Melbourne now.'

She had consented to go away, to leave her home. Was that wise? She tried to weigh each side of the question. In her home anyway she had shelter and food; she had those whom she had known all her life about her. Of course she had to work hard, both in the house and at business. What would they say of her in the Stores when they found out that she had run away with a fellow? Say she was a fool, perhaps; and her place would be filled up by advertisement. Miss Gavan would be glad. She had always had an edge on her, especially whenever there were people listening.

'Miss Hill, don't you see these ladies are waiting?'

'Look lively, Miss Hill, please.'

She would not cry many tears at leaving the Stores.

But in her new home, in a distant unknown country, it would not be like that. Then she would be married – she, Eveline. People would treat her with respect then. She would not be treated as her mother had been. Even now, though she was over nineteen, she sometimes felt herself in danger of her father's violence. She knew it was that that had given her the palpitations. When they were growing up he had never gone for her, like he used to go for Harry and Ernest, because she was a girl; but latterly he had begun to threaten her and say what he would do to her only for her dead mother's sake. And now she had nobody to protect her. Ernest was dead and Harry, who was in the church decorating business, was nearly always down somewhere in the country. Besides, the invariable squabble for money on Saturday nights had begun to weary her unspeakably. She always gave her entire wages – seven shillings – and Harry always sent up what he could but the trouble was to get any money from her father. He said she used to squander the money, that she had no head, that he wasn't going to give her his hard-earned money to throw about the streets, and much more, for he was usually fairly bad on Saturday night. In the end he would give her the money and ask her had she any intention of buying Sunday's dinner. Then she had to rush out as quickly as she could and do her marketing, holding her black leather purse tightly in her hand as she elbowed her way through the crowds and returning home late under her load of provisions. She had hard work to keep the house together and to see that the two young children who had been left to her charge went to school regularly and got their meals regularly. It was hard work – a hard life – but now that she was about to leave it she did not find it a wholly undesirable life.

She was about to explore another life with Frank. Frank was very kind, manly, open-hearted. She was to go away with him by the night-boat to be his wife and to live with him in Buenos Aires where he had a home waiting for her. How well she remembered the first time she had seen him; he was lodging in a house on the main road where she used to visit. It seemed a few weeks ago. He was standing at the gate, his peaked cap pushed back on his head and his hair tumbled forward over a face of bronze. Then they had come to know each other. He used to meet her outside the Stores every evening and see her home. He took her to see *The Bohemian Girl* and she felt elated as she sat in an unaccustomed part of the theatre with him. He was awfully fond of music and sang a little. People knew that they were courting and, when he sang about the lass that loves a sailor, she always felt pleasantly confused. He used to call her Poppens out of fun. First of all it had been an excitement for her to have a fellow and then she had begun to like him. He had tales of distant countries. He had started as a deck boy at a pound a month on a ship of the Allan Line going out to Canada. He told her the names of the ships he had been on and the names of the different services. He had sailed through the Straits of Magellan and he told her stories of the terrible Patagonians. He had fallen on his feet in Buenos Aires, he said, and had come over to the old country just for a holiday. Of course, her father had found out the affair and had forbidden her to have anything to say to him.

'I know these sailor chaps,' he said.

One day he had quarrelled with Frank and after that she had to meet her lover secretly.

The evening deepened in the avenue. The white of two letters in her lap grew indistinct. One was to Harry; the other was to her father. Ernest had been her favourite but she liked Harry too. Her father was becoming old lately, she noticed; he would miss her. Sometimes he could be very nice. Not long before, when she had been laid up for a day, he had read her out a ghost story and made toast for her at the fire. Another day, when their mother was alive, they had all gone for a picnic to the Hill of Howth. She remembered her father putting on her mother's bonnet to make the children laugh.

Her time was running out but she continued to sit by the window, leaning her head against the window curtain, inhaling the odour of dusty cretonne. Down far in the avenue she could hear a street organ playing; she knew the air. Strange that it should come that very night to remind her of the promise to her mother, her promise to keep the home together as long as she could. She remembered the last night of her mother's illness; she was again in the close dark room at the other side of the hall and outside she heard a melancholy air of Italy. The organ-player had been ordered to go away and given sixpence. She remembered her father strutting back into the sickroom saying: 'Damned Italians! coming over here!'

As she mused the pitiful vision of her mother's life laid its spell on the very quick of her being – that life of commonplace sacrifices closing in final craziness. She trembled as she heard again her mother's voice saying constantly with foolish insistence: 'Derevaun Seraun! Derevaun Seraun!'

She stood up in a sudden impulse of terror. Escape! She must escape! Frank would have her. He would give her life, perhaps love, too. But she wanted to live. Why should she be unhappy? She had a right to happiness. Frank would take her in his arms, fold her in his arms. He would save her.

She stood among the swaying crowd in the station at the North Wall. He held her hand and she knew that he was speaking to her, saying something about the passage over and over again.

The station was full of soldiers with brown baggages. Through the wide doors of the sheds she caught a glimpse of the black mass of the boat, lying in beside the quay wall, with illumined portholes. She answered nothing. She felt her cheek pale and cold and, out of a maze of distress, she prayed to God to direct her, to show her what was her duty. The boat blew a long mournful whistle into the mist. If she went, tomorrow she would be on the sea with Frank, steaming towards Buenos Aires. Their passage had been booked. Could she still draw back after all he had done for her? Her distress awoke a nausea in her body and she kept moving her lips in silent fervent prayer.

A bell clanged upon her heart. She felt him seize her hand: 'Come!'

All the seas of the world tumbled about her heart. He was drawing her into them: he would drown her. She gripped with both hands at the iron railing.

'Come!'

No! No! No! It was impossible. Her hands clutched the iron in frenzy. Amid the seas she sent a cry of anguish!

'Eveline! Evvy!'

He rushed beyond the barrier and called to her to follow. He was shouted at to go on but he still called to her. She set her white face to him, passive, like a helpless animal. Her eyes gave him no sign of love or farewell or recognition.

After the Race

The cars came scudding in towards Dublin, running evenly like pellets in the groove of the Naas Road. At the crest of the hill at Inchicore sightseers had gathered in clumps to watch the cars careering homeward, and through this channel of poverty and inaction the Continent sped its wealth and industry. Now and again the clumps of people raised the cheer of the gratefully oppressed. Their sympathy, however, was for the blue cars – the cars of their friends, the French.

The French, moreover, were virtual victors. Their team had finished solidly; they had been placed second and third and the driver of the winning German car was reported a Belgian. Each blue car, therefore, received a double measure of welcome as it topped the crest of the hill and each cheer of welcome was acknowledged with smiles and nods by those in the car. In one of these trimly built cars was a party of four young men whose spirits seemed to be at present well above the level of successful Gallicism: in fact, these four young men were almost hilarious. They were Charles Ségouin, the owner of the car; André Rivière, a young electrician of Canadian birth; a huge Hungarian named Villona and a neatly groomed young man named Doyle. Ségouin was in good humour because he had unexpectedly received some orders in advance (he was about to start a motor establishment in Paris) and Rivière was in good humour because he was to be appointed manager of the establishment; these two young men (who were cousins) were also in good humour because of the success of the French cars. Villona was in good humour because he had had a very satisfactory luncheon; and besides he was an optimist by nature. The fourth member of the party, however, was too excited to be genuinely happy.

He was about twenty-six years of age, with a soft, light brown moustache and rather innocent-looking grey eyes. His father, who had begun life as an advanced Nationalist, had modified his views early. He had made his money as a butcher in Kingstown and by opening shops in Dublin and in the suburbs he had made his money many times over. He had also been fortunate enough to secure some of the police contracts and in the end he had become rich enough to be alluded to in the Dublin newspapers as a merchant prince. He had sent his son to England to be educated in a big Catholic college and had afterwards sent him to Dublin University to study law. Jimmy did not study very earnestly and took to bad courses for a while. He had money and he was popular; and he divided his time curiously between musical and motoring circles. Then he had been sent for a term to Cambridge to see a little life. His father, remonstrative, but covertly proud of the excess, had paid his bills and brought him home. It was at Cambridge that he had met Ségouin. They were not much more than acquaintances as yet but Jimmy found great pleasure in the society of one who had seen so much of the world and was reputed to own some of the biggest hotels in France. Such a person (as his father agreed) was well worth knowing, even if he had not been the charming companion he was. Villona was entertaining also – a brilliant pianist – but, unfortunately, very poor.

The car ran on merrily with its cargo of hilarious youth. The two cousins sat on the front seat; Jimmy and his Hungarian friend sat behind. Decidedly Villona was in excellent spirits; he kept up a deep bass hum of melody for miles of the road. The Frenchmen sung their laughter and light words over their shoulders and often Jimmy had to strain forward to catch the quick phrase. This was not altogether pleasant for him, as he had nearly always to make a deft guess at the meaning and shout back a suitable answer in the face of a high wind. Besides Villona's humming would confuse anybody; the noise of the car, too.

Rapid motion through space elates one; so does notoriety; so does the possession of money. These were three good reasons for Jimmy's excitement. He had been seen by many of his friends that day in the company of these Continentals. At the control Ségouin had presented him to one of the French competitors and, in answer to his confused murmur of compliment, the swarthy face of the driver had disclosed a line of shining white teeth. It was pleasant after that honour to return to the profane world of spectators amid nudges and significant looks. Then as to money – he really had a great sum under his control. Ségouin, perhaps, would not think it a great sum but Jimmy who, in spite of temporary errors, was at heart the inheritor of solid instincts knew well with what difficulty it had been got together. This knowledge had previously kept his bills within the limits of reasonable recklessness and, if he had been so conscious of the labour latent in money when there had been question merely of some freak of the higher intelligence, how much more so now when he was about to stake the greater part of his substance! It was a serious thing for him.

Of course, the investment was a good one and Ségouin had managed to give the impression that it was by a favour of friendship the mite of Irish money was to be included in the capital of the concern. Jimmy had a respect for his father's shrewdness in business matters and in this case it had been his father who had first suggested the investment; money to be made in the motor business, pots of money. Moreover Ségouin had the unmistakable air of wealth. Jimmy set out to translate into days' work that lordly car in which he sat. How smoothly it ran. In what style they had come careering along the country roads! The journey laid a magical finger on the genuine pulse of life and gallantly the machinery of human nerves strove to answer the bounding courses of the swift blue animal.

They drove down Dame Street. The street was busy with unusual traffic, loud with the horns of motorists and the gongs of impatient tram-drivers. Near the Bank Ségouin drew up and Jimmy and his friend alighted. A little knot of people collected on the footpath to pay homage to the snorting motor. The party was to dine together that evening in Ségouin's hotel and, meanwhile, Jimmy and his friend, who was staying with him, were to go home to dress. The car steered out slowly for Grafton Street while the two young men pushed their way through the knot of gazers. They walked northward with a curious feeling of disappointment in the exercise, while the city hung its pale globes of light above them in a haze of summer evening.

In Jimmy's house this dinner had been pronounced an occasion. A certain pride mingled with his parents' trepidation, a certain eagerness, also, to play fast and loose, for the names of great foreign cities have at least this virtue. Jimmy, too, looked very well when he was dressed and, as he stood in the hall giving a last equation to the bows of his dress tie, his father may have felt even commercially satisfied at having secured for his son qualities often unpurchaseable. His father, therefore, was unusually friendly with Villona and his manner expressed a real respect for foreign accomplishments; but this subtlety of his host was probably lost upon the Hungarian, who was beginning to have a sharp desire for his dinner.

The dinner was excellent, exquisite. Ségouin, Jimmy decided, had a very refined taste. The party was increased by a young Englishman named Routh whom Jimmy had seen with Ségouin at Cambridge. The young men supped in a snug room lit by electric candle lamps. They talked volubly and with little reserve. Jimmy, whose imagination was kindling, conceived the lively youth of the Frenchmen twined elegantly upon the firm framework of the Englishman's manner. A graceful image of his, he thought, and a just one. He admired the dexterity with which their host directed the conversation. The five young men had various tastes and their tongues had been loosened. Villona, with immense respect, began to discover to the mildly surprised Englishman the beauties of the English madrigal, deploring the loss of old instruments. Rivière, not wholly ingenuously, undertook to explain to Jimmy the triumph of the French mechanicians. The resonant voice of the Hungarian was about to prevail in ridicule of the spurious lutes of the romantic painters when Ségouin shepherded his party into politics. Here was congenial ground for all. Jimmy, under generous influences, felt the buried zeal of his father wake to life within him: he aroused the torpid Routh at last. The room grew doubly hot and Ségouin's task grew harder each moment: there was even danger of personal spite. The alert host at an opportunity lifted his glass to Humanity and, when the toast had been drunk, he threw open a window significantly.

That night the city wore the mask of a capital. The five young men strolled along Stephen's Green in a faint cloud of aromatic smoke. They talked loudly and gaily and their cloaks dangled from their shoulders. The people made way for them. At the corner of Grafton Street a short fat man was putting two handsome ladies on a car in charge of another fat man. The car drove off and the short fat man caught sight of the party.

'André.'

'It's Farley!'

A torrent of talk followed. Farley was an American. No one knew very well what the talk was about. Villona and Rivière were the noisiest, but all the men were excited. They got up on a car, squeezing themselves together amid much laughter. They drove by the crowd, blended now into soft colours, to a music of merry bells. They took the train at Westland Row and in a few seconds, as it seemed to Jimmy, they were walking out of Kingstown Station. The ticket-collector saluted Jimmy; he was an old man: 'Fine night, sir!'

It was a serene summer night; the harbour lay like a darkened mirror at their feet. They proceeded towards it with linked arms, singing *Cadet Roussel* in chorus, stamping their feet at every: '*Ho! Ho! Hohé, vraiment!*'

They got into a rowboat at the slip and made out for the American's yacht. There was to be supper, music, cards. Villona said with conviction: 'It is delightful!'

There was a yacht piano in the cabin. Villona played a waltz for Farley and Rivière, Farley acting as cavalier and Rivière as lady. Then an impromptu square dance, the men devising original figures. What merriment! Jimmy took his part with a will; this was seeing life, at least. Then Farley got out of breath and cried '*Stop!*' A man brought in a light supper, and the young men sat down to it for form's sake. They drank, however: it was Bohemian. They drank Ireland, England, France, Hungary, the United States of America. Jimmy made a speech, a long speech, Villona saying: '*Hear! hear!*' whenever there was a pause. There was a great clapping of hands when he sat down. It must have been a good speech. Farley clapped him on the back and laughed loudly. What jovial fellows! What good company they were!

Cards! cards! The table was cleared. Villona returned quietly to his piano and played voluntaries for them. The other men played game after game, flinging themselves boldly into the adventure. They drank the health of the Queen of Hearts and of the Queen of Diamonds.

Jimmy felt obscurely the lack of an audience: the wit was flashing. Play ran very high and paper began to pass. Jimmy did not know exactly who was winning but he knew that he was losing. But it was his own fault for he frequently mistook his cards and the other men had to calculate his I.O.U.'s for him. They were devils of fellows but he wished they would stop: it was getting late. Someone gave the toast of the yacht *The Belle of Newport* and then someone proposed one great game for a finish.

The piano had stopped; Villona must have gone up on deck. It was a terrible game. They stopped just before the end of it to drink for luck. Jimmy understood that the game lay between Routh and Ségouin. What excitement! Jimmy was excited too; he would lose, of course. How much had he written away? The men rose to their feet to play the last tricks, talking and gesticulating. Routh won. The cabin shook with the young men's cheering and the cards were bundled together. They began then to gather in what they had won. Farley and Jimmy were the heaviest losers.

He knew that he would regret in the morning but at present he was glad of the rest, glad of the dark stupor that would cover up his folly. He leaned his elbows on the table and rested his head between his hands, counting the beats of his temples. The cabin door opened and he saw the Hungarian standing in a shaft of grey light: 'Daybreak, gentlemen!'

Two Gallants

The grey warm evening of August had descended upon the city and a mild warm air, a memory of summer, circulated in the streets. The streets, shuttered for the repose of Sunday, swarmed with a gaily coloured crowd. Like illumined pearls the lamps shone from the summits of their tall poles upon the living texture below which, changing shape and hue unceasingly, sent up into the warm grey evening air an unchanging, unceasing murmur.

Two young men came down the hill of Rutland Square. One of them was just bringing a long monologue to a close. The other, who walked on the verge of the path and was at times obliged to step on to the road, owing to his companion's rudeness, wore an amused listening face. He was squat and ruddy. A yachting cap was shoved far back from his forehead and the narrative to which he listened made constant waves of expression break forth over his face from the corners of his nose and eyes and mouth. Little jets of wheezing laughter followed one another out of his convulsed body. His eyes, twinkling with cunning enjoyment, glanced at every moment towards his companion's face. Once or twice he rearranged the light waterproof which he had slung over one shoulder in toreador fashion. His breeches, his white rubber shoes and his jauntily slung waterproof expressed youth. But his figure fell into rotundity at the waist, his hair was scant and grey and his face, when the waves of expression had passed over it, had a ravaged look.

When he was quite sure that the narrative had ended he laughed noiselessly for fully half a minute. Then he said: 'Well! . . . That takes the biscuit!'

His voice seemed winnowed of vigour; and to enforce his words he added with humour: 'That takes the solitary, unique, and, if I may so call it, *recherché* biscuit!'

He became serious and silent when he had said this. His tongue was tired for he had been talking all the afternoon in a public-house in Dorset Street. Most people considered Lenehan a leech but, in spite of this reputation, his adroitness and eloquence had always prevented his friends from forming any general policy against him. He had a brave manner of coming up to a party of them in a bar and of holding himself nimbly at the borders of the company until he was included in a round. He was a sporting vagrant armed with a vast stock of stories, limericks and riddles. He was insensitive to all kinds of discourtesy. No one knew how he achieved the stern task of living, but his name was vaguely associated with racing tissues.

'And where did you pick her up, Corley?' he asked.

Corley ran his tongue swiftly along his upper lip.

'One night, man,' he said, 'I was going along Dame Street and I spotted a fine tart under Waterhouse's clock and said good-night, you know. So we went for a walk round by the canal and she told me she was a slavey in a house in Baggot Street. I put my arm round her and squeezed her a bit that night. Then next Sunday, man, I met her by appointment. We went out to Donnybrook and I brought her into a field there. She told me she used to go with a dairyman . . . It was fine, man. Cigarettes every night she'd bring me and paying the tram out and back. And one night she brought me two bloody fine cigars – O, the real cheese, you know, that the old fellow used to smoke . . . I was afraid, man, she'd get in the family way. But she's up to the dodge.'

'Maybe she thinks you'll marry her,' said Lenehan.

'I told her I was out of a job,' said Corley. 'I told her I was in Pim's. She doesn't know my name. I was too hairyto tell her that. But she thinks I'm a bit of class, you know.'

Lenehan laughed again, noiselessly.

'Of all the good ones ever I heard,' he said, 'that emphatically takes the biscuit.'

Corley's stride acknowledged the compliment. The swing of his burly body made his friend execute a few light skips from the path to the roadway and back again. Corley was the son of an inspector of police and he had inherited his father's frame and gait. He walked with his hands by his sides, holding himself erect and swaying his head from side to side. His head was large, globular and oily; it sweated in all weathers; and his large round hat, set upon it sideways, looked like a bulb which had grown out of another. He always stared straight before him as if he were on parade and, when he wished to gaze after someone in the street, it was necessary for him to move his body from the hips. At present he was about town. Whenever any job was vacant a friend was always ready to give him the hard word. He was often to be seen walking with policemen in plain clothes, talking earnestly. He knew the inner side of all affairs and was fond of delivering final judgments. He spoke without listening to the speech of his companions. His conversation was mainly about himself: what he had said to such a person and what such a person had said to him and what he had said to settle the matter. When he reported these dialogues he aspirated the first letter of his name after the manner of Florentines.

Lenehan offered his friend a cigarette. As the two young men walked on through the crowd Corley occasionally turned to smile at some of the passing girls but Lenehan's gaze was fixed on the large faint moon circled with a double halo. He watched earnestly the passing of the grey web of twilight across its face. At length he said: 'Well . . . tell me, Corley, I suppose you'll be able to pull it off all right, eh?'

Corley closed one eye expressively as an answer.

'Is she game for that?' asked Lenehan dubiously. 'You can never know women.'

'She's all right,' said Corley. 'I know the way to get around her, man. She's a bit gone on me.'

'You're what I call a gay Lothario,' said Lenehan. 'And the proper kind of a Lothario, too!'

A shade of mockery relieved the servility of his manner. To save himself he had the habit of leaving his flattery open to the interpretation of raillery. But Corley had not a subtle mind.

'There's nothing to touch a good slavey,' he affirmed. 'Take my tip for it.'

'By one who has tried them all,' said Lenehan.

'First I used to go with girls, you know,' said Corley, unbosoming; 'girls off the South Circular. I used to take them out, man, on the tram somewhere and pay the tram or take them to a band or a play at the theatre or buy them chocolate and sweets or something that way. I used to spend money on them right enough,' he added, in a convincing tone, as if he was conscious of being disbelieved.

But Lenehan could well believe it; he nodded gravely.

'I know that game, ' he said, 'and it's a mug's game.'

'And damn the thing I ever got out of it,' said Corley.

'Ditto here,' said Lenehan.

'Only off of one of them,' said Corley.

He moistened his upper lip by running his tongue along it. The recollection brightened his eyes. He too gazed at the pale disc of the moon, now nearly veiled, and seemed to meditate.

'She was . . . a bit of all right,' he said regretfully.

He was silent again. Then he added: 'She's on the turf now. I saw her driving down Earl Street one night with two fellows with her on a car.'

'I suppose that's your doing,' said Lenehan.

'There was others at her before me,' said Corley philosophically.

This time Lenehan was inclined to disbelieve. He shook his head to and fro and smiled.

'You know you can't kid me, Corley,' he said.

'Honest to God!' said Corley. 'Didn't she tell me herself?'

Lenehan made a tragic gesture.

'Base betrayer!' he said.

As they passed along the railings of Trinity College, Lenehan skipped out into the road and peered up at the clock.

'Twenty after,' he said.

'Time enough,' said Corley. 'She'll be there all right. I always let her wait a bit.'

Lenehan laughed quietly.

'Ecod! Corley, you know how to take them,' he said.

'I'm up to all their little tricks,' Corley confessed.

'But tell me,' said Lenehan again, 'are you sure you can bring it off all right? You know it's a ticklish job. They're damn close on that point. Eh?. . . What?'

His bright, small eyes searched his companion's face for reassurance. Corley swung his head to and fro as if to toss aside an insistent insect, and his brows gathered.

'I'll pull it off,' he said. 'Leave it to me, can't you?'

Lenehan said no more. He did not wish to ruffle his friend's temper, to be sent to the devil and told that his advice was not wanted. A little tact was necessary. But Corley's brow was soon smooth again. His thoughts were running another way.

'She's a fine decent tart,' he said, with appreciation; 'that's what she is.'

They walked along Nassau Street and then turned into Kildare Street. Not far from the porch of the club a harpist stood in the roadway, playing to a little ring of listeners. He plucked at the wires heedlessly, glancing quickly from time to time at the face of each new-comer and from time to time, wearily also, at the sky. His harp, too, heedless that her coverings had fallen about her knees, seemed weary alike of the eyes of strangers and of her master's hands. One hand played in the bass the melody of *Silent, O Moyle*, while the other hand careered in the treble after each group of notes. The notes of the air sounded deep and full.

The two young men walked up the street without speaking, the mournful music following them. When they reached Stephen's Green they crossed the road. Here the noise of trams, the lights and the crowd released them from their silence.

'There she is!' said Corley.

At the corner of Hume Street a young woman was standing. She wore a blue dress and a white sailor hat. She stood on the curbstone, swinging a sunshade in one hand. Lenehan grew lively.

'Let's have a look at her, Corley,' he said.

Corley glanced sideways at his friend and an unpleasant grin appeared on his face.

'Are you trying to get inside me?' he asked.

'Damn it!' said Lenehan boldly, 'I don't want an introduction. All I want is to have a look at her. I'm not going to eat her.'

'O . . . A look at her?' said Corley, more amiably. 'Well . . . I'll tell you what. I'll go over and talk to her and you can pass by.'

'Right!' said Lenehan.

Corley had already thrown one leg over the chains when Lenehan called out: 'And after? Where will we meet?'

'Half ten,' answered Corley, bringing over his other leg.

'Where?'

'Corner of Merrion Street. We'll be coming back.'

'Work it all right now,' said Lenehan in farewell.

Corley did not answer. He sauntered across the road swaying his head from side to side. His bulk, his easy pace, and the solid sound of his boots had something of the conqueror in them. He approached the young woman and, without saluting, began at once to converse with her. She swung her umbrella more quickly and executed half turns on her heels. Once or twice when he spoke to her at close quarters she laughed and bent her head.

Lenehan observed them for a few minutes. Then he walked rapidly along beside the chains at some distance and crossed the road obliquely. As he approached Hume Street corner he found the air heavily scented and his eyes made a swift anxious scrutiny of the young woman's appearance. She had her Sunday finery on. Her blue serge skirt was held at the waist by a belt of black leather. The great silver buckle of her belt seemed to depress the centre of her body, catching the light stuff of her white blouse like a clip. She wore a short black jacket with mother-of-pearl buttons and a ragged black boa. The ends of her tulle collarette had been carefully disordered and a big bunch of red flowers was pinned in her bosom stems upwards. Lenehan's eyes noted approvingly her stout short muscular body. Frank rude health glowed in her face, on her fat red cheeks and in her unabashed blue eyes. Her features were blunt. She had broad nostrils, a straggling mouth which lay open in a contented leer, and two projecting front teeth. As he passed Lenehan took off his cap and, after about ten seconds, Corley returned a salute to the air. This he did by raising his hand vaguely and pensively changing the angle of position of his hat.

Lenehan walked as far as the Shelbourne Hotel where he halted and waited. After waiting for a little time he saw them coming towards him and, when they turned to the right, he followed them, stepping lightly in his white shoes, down one side of Merrion Square. As he walked on slowly, timing his pace to theirs, he watched Corley's head which turned at every moment towards the young woman's face like a big ball revolving on a pivot. He kept the pair in view until he had seen them climbing the stairs of the Donnybrook tram; then he turned about and went back the way he had come.

Now that he was alone his face looked older. He gaiety seemed to forsake him and, as he came by the railings of the Duke's Lawn, he allowed his hand to run along them. The air which the harpist had played began to control his movements. His softly padded feet played the melody while his fingers swept a scale of variations idly along the railings after each group of notes.

He walked listlessly round Stephen's Green and then down Grafton Street. Though his eyes took note of many elements of the crowd through which he passed they did so morosely. He found trivial all that was meant to charm him and did not answer the glances which invited him to be bold. He knew that he would have to speak a great deal, to invent and to amuse, and his brain and throat were too dry for such a task. The problem of how he could pass the hours till he met Corley again troubled him a little. He could think of no way of passing them but to keep on walking. He turned to the left when he came to the corner of Rutland Square and felt more at ease in the dark quiet street, the sombre look of which suited his mood. He paused at last before the window of a poor-looking shop over which the words *Refreshment Bar* were printed in white letters. On the glass of the window were two flying inscriptions: *Ginger Beer* and *Ginger Ale*. A cut ham was exposed on a great blue dish while near it on a plate lay a segment of very light plum-pudding. He eyed this food earnestly for some time and then, after glancing warily up and down the street, went into the shop quickly.

He was hungry for, except some biscuits which he had asked two grudging curates to bring him, he had eaten nothing since breakfast-time. He sat down at an uncovered wooden table opposite two work-girls and a mechanic. A slatternly girl waited on him.

'How much is a plate of peas?' he asked.

'Three halfpence, sir,' said the girl.

'Bring me a plate of peas,' he said, 'and a bottle of ginger beer.'

He spoke roughly in order to belie his air of gentility for his entry had been followed by a pause of talk. His face was heated. To appear natural he pushed his cap back on his head and planted his elbows on the table. The mechanic and the two work-girls examined him point by point before resuming their conversation in a subdued voice. The girl brought him a plate of grocer's hot peas, seasoned with pepper and vinegar, a fork and his ginger beer. He ate his food greedily and found it so good that he made a note of the shop mentally. When he had eaten all the peas he sipped his ginger beer and sat for some time thinking of Corley's adventure. In his imagination he beheld the pair of lovers walking along some dark road; he heard Corley's voice in deep energetic gallantries and saw again the leer of the young woman's mouth. This vision made him feel keenly his own poverty of purse and spirit. He was tired of knocking about, of pulling the devil by the tail, of shifts and intrigues. He would be thirty-one in November. Would he never get a good job? Would he never have a home of his own? He thought how pleasant it would be to have a warm fire to sit by and a good dinner to sit down to. He had walked the streets long enough with friends and with girls. He knew what those friends were worth: he knew the girls too. Experience had embittered his heart against the world. But all hope had not left him. He felt better after having eaten than he had felt before, less weary of his life, less vanquished in spirit. He might yet be able to settle down in some snug corner and live happily if he could only come across some good simple-minded girl with a little of the ready.

He paid twopence halfpenny to the slatternly girl and went out of the shop to begin his wandering again. He went into Capel Street and walked along towards the City Hall. Then he turned into Dame Street. At the corner of George's Street he met two friends of his and stopped to converse with them. He was glad that he could rest from all his walking. His friends asked him had he seen Corley and what was the latest. He replied that he had spent the day with Corley. His friends talked very little. They looked vacantly after some figures in the crowd and sometimes made a critical remark. One said that he had seen Mac an hour before in Westmoreland Street. At this Lenehan said that he had been with Mac the night before in Egan's. The young man who had seen Mac in Westmoreland Street asked was it true that Mac had won a bit over a billiard match. Lenehan did not know: he said that Holohan had stood them drinks in Egan's.

He left his friends at a quarter to ten and went up George's Street. He turned to the left at the City Markets and walked on into Grafton Street. The crowd of girls and young men had thinned and on his way up the street he heard many groups and couples bidding one another good-night. He went as far as the clock of the College of Surgeons: it was on the stroke of ten. He set off briskly along the northern side of the Green hurrying for fear Corley should return too soon. When he reached the corner of Merrion Street he took his stand in the shadow of a lamp and brought out one of the cigarettes which he had reserved and lit it. He leaned against the lamp-post and kept his gaze fixed on the part from which he expected to see Corley and the young woman return.

His mind became active again. He wondered had Corley managed it successfully. He wondered if he had asked her yet or if he would leave it to the last. He suffered all the pangs and thrills of his friend's situation as well as those of his own. But the memory of Corley's slowly revolving head calmed him somewhat: he was sure Corley would pull it off all right. All at once the idea struck him that perhaps Corley had seen her home by another way and given him the slip. His eyes searched the street: there was no sign of them, yet it was surely half an hour since he had seen the clock of the College of Surgeons. Would Corley do a thing like that? He lit his last cigarette and began to smoke it nervously. He strained his eyes as each tram stopped at the far corner of the square. They must have gone home by another way. The paper of his cigarette broke and he flung it into the road with a curse.

Suddenly he saw them coming towards him. He started with delight and keeping close to his lamp-post tried to read the result in their walk. They were walking quickly, the young woman taking quick short steps, while Corley kept beside her with his long stride. They did not seem to be speaking. An intimation of the result pricked him like the point of a sharp instrument. He knew Corley would fail; he knew it was no go.

They turned down Baggot Street and he followed them at once, taking the other footpath. When they stopped he stopped too. They talked for a few moments and then the young woman went down the steps into the area of a house. Corley remained standing at the edge of the path, a little distance from the front steps. Some minutes passed. Then the hall-door was opened slowly and cautiously. A woman came running down the front steps and coughed. Corley turned and went towards her. His broad figure hid hers from view for a few seconds and then she reappeared running up the steps. The door closed on her and Corley began to walk swiftly towards Stephen's Green.

Lenehan hurried on in the same direction. Some drops of light rain fell. He took them as a warning and, glancing back towards the house which the young woman had entered to see that he was not observed, he ran eagerly across the road. Anxiety and his swift run made him pant. He called out: 'Hallo, Corley!'

Corley turned his head to see who had called him, and then continued walking as before. Lenehan ran after him, settling the waterproof on his shoulders with one hand.

'Hallo, Corley!' he cried again.

He came level with his friend and looked keenly in his face. He could see nothing there.

'Well?' he said. 'Did it come off?'

They had reached the corner of Ely Place. Still without answering Corley swerved to the left and went up the side street. His features were composed in stern calm. Lenehan kept up with his friend, breathing uneasily. He was baffled and a note of menace pierced through his voice.

'Can't you tell us?' he said. 'Did you try her?'

Corley halted at the first lamp and stared grimly before him. Then with a grave gesture he extended a hand towards the light and, smiling, opened it slowly to the gaze of his disciple. A small gold coin shone in the palm.

The Boarding House

Mrs Mooney was a butcher's daughter. She was a woman who was quite able to keep things to herself: a determined woman. She had married her father's foreman and opened a butcher's shop near Spring Gardens. But as soon as his father-in-law was dead Mr Mooney began to go to the devil. He drank, plundered the till, ran headlong into debt. It was no use making him take the pledge: he was sure to break out again a few days after. By fighting his wife in the presence of customers and by buying bad meat he ruined his business. One night he went for his wife with the cleaver and she had to sleep in a neighbour's house.

After that they lived apart. She went to the priest and got a separation from him with care of the children. She would give him neither money nor food nor house-room; and so he was obliged to enlist himself as a sheriff's man. He was a shabby stooped little drunkard with a white face and a white moustache and white eyebrows, pencilled above his little eyes, which were pink-veined and raw; and all day long he sat in the bailiff's room, waiting to be put on a job. Mrs Mooney, who had taken what remained of her money out of the butcher business and set up a boarding house in Hardwicke Street, was a big imposing woman. Her house had a floating population made up of tourists from Liverpool and the Isle of Man and, occasionally, *artistes* from the music halls. Its resident population was made up of clerks from the city. She governed the house cunningly and firmly, knew when to give credit, when to be stern and when to let things pass. All the resident young men spoke of her as *The Madam*.

Mrs Mooney's young men paid fifteen shillings a week for board and lodgings (beer or stout at dinner excluded). They shared in common tastes and occupations and for this reason they were very chummy with one another. They discussed with one another the chances of favourites and outsiders. Jack Mooney, the Madam's son, who was clerk to a commission agent in Fleet Street, had the reputation of being a hard case. He was fond of using soldiers' obscenities: usually he came home in the small hours. When he met his friends he had always a good one to tell them and he was always sure to be on to a good thing – that is to say, a likely horse or a likely *artiste*. He was also handy with the mits and sang comic songs. On Sunday nights there would often be a reunion in Mrs Mooney's front drawing-room. The music-hall *artistes* would oblige; and Sheridan played waltzes and polkas and vamped accompaniments. Polly Mooney, the Madam's daughter, would also sing. She sang:

> 'I'm a . . . naughty girl.
> You needn't sham:
> You know I am.'

Polly was a slim girl of nineteen; she had light soft hair and a small full mouth. Her eyes, which were grey with a shade of green through them, had a habit of glancing upwards when she spoke with anyone, which made her look like a little perverse madonna. Mrs Mooney had first sent her daughter to be a typist in a corn-factor's office but, as a disreputable sheriff's man used to come every other day to the office, asking to be allowed to say a word to his daughter, she had taken her daughter home again and set her to do housework. As Polly was very lively the intention was to give her the run of the young men. Besides, young men like to feel that there is a young woman not very far away. Polly, of course, flirted with the young men but Mrs Mooney, who was a shrewd judge, knew that the young men were only passing the time away: none of them meant business. Things went on so for a long time and Mrs Mooney began to think of sending Polly back to typewriting when she noticed that something was going on between Polly and one of the young men. She watched the pair and kept her own counsel.

Polly knew that she was being watched, but still her mother's persistent silence could not be misunderstood. There had been no open complicity between mother and daughter, no open understanding but, though people in the house began to talk of the affair, still Mrs Mooney did not intervene. Polly began to grow a little strange in her manner and the young man was evidently perturbed. At last, when she judged it to be the right moment, Mrs Mooney intervened. She dealt with moral problems as a cleaver deals with meat: and in this case she had made up her mind. It was a bright Sunday morning of early summer, promising heat, but with a fresh breeze blowing. All the windows of the boarding house were open and the lace curtains ballooned gently towards the street beneath the raised sashes. The belfry of George's Church sent out constant peals and worshippers, singly or in groups, traversed the little circus before the church, revealing their purpose by their self-contained demeanour no less than by the little volumes in their gloved hands. Breakfast was over in the boarding house and the table of the breakfast-room was covered with plates on which lay yellow streaks of eggs with morsels of bacon-fat and bacon-rind. Mrs Mooney sat in the straw armchair and watched the servant Mary remove the breakfast things. She made Mary collect the crusts and pieces of broken bread to help to make Tuesday's bread-pudding. When the table was cleared, the broken bread collected, the sugar and butter safe under lock and key, she began to reconstruct the interview which she had had the night before with Polly. Things were as she had suspected: she had been frank in her questions and Polly had been frank in her answers. Both had been somewhat awkward, of course. She had been made awkward by her not wishing to receive the news in too cavalier a fashion or to seem to have connived and Polly had been made awkward not merely because allusions of that kind always made her awkward but also because she did not wish it to be thought that in her wise innocence she had divined the intention behind her mother's tolerance.

Mrs Mooney glanced instinctively at the little gilt clock on the mantel-piece as soon as she had become aware through her reverie that the bells of George's Church had stopped ringing. It was seventeen minutes past eleven: she would have lots of time to have the matter out with Mr Doran and then catch short twelve at Marlborough Street. She was sure she would win. To begin with she had all the weight of social opinion on her side: she was an outraged mother. She had allowed him to live beneath her roof, assuming that he was a man of honour, and he had simply abused her hospitality. He was thirty-four or thirty-five years of age, so that youth could not be pleaded as his excuse; nor could ignorance be his excuse since he was a man who had seen something of the world. He had simply taken advantage of Polly's youth and inexperience: that was evident. The question was: What reparation would he make?

There must be reparation made in such case. It is all very well for the man: he can go his ways as if nothing had happened, having had his moment of pleasure, but the girl has to bear the brunt. Some mothers would be content to patch up such an affair for a sum of money; she had known cases of it. But she would not do so. For her only one reparation could make up for the loss of her daughter's honour: marriage.

She counted all her cards again before sending Mary up to Mr Doran's room to say that she wished to speak with him. She felt sure she would win. He was a serious young man, not rakish or loud-voiced like the others. If it had been Mr Sheridan or Mr Meade or Bantam Lyons her task would have been much harder. She did not think he would face publicity. All the lodgers in the house knew something of the affair; details had been invented by some. Besides, he had been employed for thirteen years in a great Catholic wine-merchant's office and publicity would mean for him, perhaps, the loss of his job. Whereas if he agreed all might be well. She knew he had a good screw for one thing and she suspected he had a bit of stuff put by.

Nearly the half-hour! She stood up and surveyed herself in the pier-glass. The decisive expression of her great florid face satisfied her and she thought of some mothers she knew who could not get their daughters off their hands.

Mr Doran was very anxious indeed this Sunday morning. He had made two attempts to shave but his hand had been so unsteady that he had been obliged to desist. Three days' reddish beard fringed his jaws and every two or three minutes a mist gathered on his glasses so that he had to take them off and polish them with his pocket-handkerchief. The recollection of his confession of the night before was a cause of acute pain to him; the priest had drawn out every ridiculous detail of the affair and in the end had so magnified his sin that he was almost thankful at being afforded a loophole of reparation. The harm was done. What could he do now but marry her or run away? He could not brazen it out. The affair would be sure to be talked of and his employer would be certain to hear of it. Dublin is such a small city: everyone knows everyone else's business. He felt his heart leap warmly in his throat as he heard in his excited imagination old Mr Leonard calling out in his rasping voice: 'Send Mr Doran here, please.'

All his long years of service gone for nothing! All his industry and diligence thrown away! As a young man he had sown his wild oats, of course; he had boasted of his free-thinking and denied the existence of God to his companions in public-houses. But that was all passed and done with . . . nearly. He still bought a copy of *Reynolds's Newspaper* every week but he attended to his religious duties and for nine-tenths of the year lived a regular life. He had money enough to settle down on; it was not that. But the family would look down on her. First of all there was her disreputable father and then her mother's boarding house was beginning to get a certain fame. He had a notion that he was being had. He could imagine his friends talking of the affair and laughing. She *was* a little vulgar; sometimes she said 'I seen' and 'If I had've known.' But what would grammar matter if he really loved her? He could not make up his mind whether to like her or despise her for what she had done. Of course he had done it too. His instinct urged him to remain free, not to marry. Once you are married you are done for, it said.

While he was sitting helplessly on the side of the bed in shirt and trousers she tapped lightly at his door and entered. She told him all, that she had made a clean breast of it to her mother and that her mother would speak with him that morning. She cried and threw her arms round his neck, saying: 'O Bob! Bob! What am I to do? What am I to do at all?'

She would put an end to herself, she said.

He comforted her feebly, telling her not to cry, that it would be all right, never fear. He felt against his shirt the agitation of her bosom.

It was not altogether his fault that it had happened. He remembered well, with the curious patient memory of the celibate, the first casual caresses her dress, her breath, her fingers had given him. Then late one night as he was undressing for bed she had tapped at his door, timidly. She wanted to relight her candle at his for hers had been blown out by a gust. It was her bath night. She wore a loose open combing-jacket of printed flannel. Her white instep shone in the opening of her furry slippers and the blood glowed warmly behind her perfumed skin. From her hands and wrists too as she lit and steadied her candle a faint perfume arose.

On nights when he came in very late it was she who warmed up his dinner. He scarcely knew what he was eating feeling her beside him alone, at night, in the sleeping house. And her thoughtfulness! If the night was anyway cold or wet or windy there was sure to be a little tumbler of punch ready for him. Perhaps they could be happy together . . .

They used to go upstairs together on tiptoe, each with a candle, and on the third landing exchange reluctant good-nights. They used to kiss. He remembered well her eyes, the touch of her hand and his delirium . . .

But delirium passes. He echoed her phrase, applying it to himself: '*What am I to do?*' The instinct of the celibate warned him to hold back. But the sin was there; even his sense of honour told him that reparation must be made for such a sin.

While he was sitting with her on the side of the bed Mary came to the door and said that the missus wanted to see him in the parlour. He stood up to put on his coat and waistcoat, more helpless than ever. When he was dressed he went over to her to comfort her. It would be all right, never fear. He left her crying on the bed and moaning softly: '*O my God!*'

Going down the stairs his glasses became so dimmed with moisture that he had to take them off and polish them. He longed to ascend through the roof and fly away to another country where he would never hear again of his trouble, and yet a force pushed him downstairs step by step. The implacable faces of his employer and of the Madam stared upon his discomfiture. On the last flight of stairs he passed Jack Mooney who was coming up from the pantry nursing two bottles of *Bass*. They saluted coldly; and the lover's eyes rested for a second or two on a thick bulldog face and a pair of thick short arms. When he reached the foot of the staircase he glanced up and saw Jack regarding him from the door of the return-room.

Suddenly he remembered the night when one of the music-hall *artistes*, a little blond Londoner, had made a rather free allusion to Polly. The reunion had been almost broken up on account of Jack's violence. Everyone tried to quiet him. The music-hall *artiste*, a little paler than usual, kept smiling and saying that there was no harm meant: but Jack kept shouting at him that if any fellow tried that sort of a game on with his sister he'd bloody well put his teeth down his throat, so he would.

Polly sat for a little time on the side of the bed, crying. Then she dried her eyes and went over to the looking-glass. She dipped the end of the towel in the water-jug and refreshed her eyes with the cool water. She looked at herself in profile and readjusted a hairpin above her ear. Then she went back to the bed again and sat at the foot. She regarded the pillows for a long time and the sight of them awakened in her mind secret, amiable memories. She rested the nape of her neck against the cool iron bed-rail and fell into a reverie. There was no longer any perturbation visible on her face.

She waited on patiently, almost cheerfully, without alarm, her memories gradually giving place to hopes and visions of the future. Her hopes and visions were so intricate that she no longer saw the white pillows on which her gaze was fixed or remembered that she was waiting for anything.

At last she heard her mother calling. She started to her feet and ran to the banisters.

'Polly! Polly!'

'Yes, mamma?'

'Come down, dear. Mr Doran wants to speak to you.'

Then she remembered what she had been waiting for.

A Little Cloud

Eight years before he had seen his friend off at the North Wall and wished him godspeed. Gallaher had got on. You could tell that at once by his travelled air, his well-cut tweed suit, and fearless accent. Few fellows had talents like his and fewer still could remain unspoiled by such success. Gallaher's heart was in the right place and he had deserved to win. It was something to have a friend like that.

Little Chandler's thoughts ever since lunchtime had been of his meeting with Gallaher, of Gallaher's invitation and of the great city London where Gallaher lived. He was called Little Chandler because, though he was but slightly under the average stature, he gave one the idea of being a little man. His hands were white and small, his frame was fragile, his voice was quiet and his manners were refined. He took the greatest care of his fair silken hair and moustache and used perfume discreetly on his handkerchief. The half-moons of his nails were perfect and when he smiled you caught a glimpse of a row of childish white teeth.

As he sat at his desk in the King's Inns he thought what changes those eight years had brought. The friend whom he had known under a shabby and necessitous guise had become a brilliant figure on the London Press. He turned often from his tiresome writing to gaze out of the office window. The glow of a late autumn sunset covered the grass plots and walks. It cast a shower of kindly golden dust on the untidy nurses and decrepit old men who drowsed on the benches; it flickered upon all the moving figures – on the children who ran screaming along the gravel paths and on everyone who passed through the gardens. He watched the scene and thought of life; and (as always happened when he thought of life) he became sad. A gentle melancholy took possession of him. He felt how useless it was to struggle against fortune, this being the burden of wisdom which the ages had bequeathed to him.

He remembered the books of poetry upon his shelves at home. He had bought them in his bachelor days and many an evening, as he sat in the little room off the hall, he had been tempted to take one down from the bookshelf and read out something to his wife. But shyness had always held him back; and so the books had remained on their shelves. At times he repeated lines to himself and this consoled him.

When his hour had struck he stood up and took leave of his desk and of his fellow-clerks punctiliously. He emerged from under the feudal arch of the King's Inns, a neat modest figure, and walked swiftly down Henrietta Street. The golden sunset was waning and the air had grown sharp. A horde of grimy children populated the street. They stood or ran in the roadway or crawled up the steps before the gaping doors or squatted like mice upon the thresholds. Little Chandler gave them no thought. He picked his way deftly through all that minute vermin-like life and under the shadow of the gaunt spectral mansions in which the old nobility of Dublin had roystered. No memory of the past touched him, for his mind was full of a present joy.

He had never been in Corless's but he knew the value of the name. He knew that people went there after the theatre to eat oysters and drink liqueurs; and he had heard that the waiters there spoke French and German. Walking swiftly by at night he had seen cabs drawn up before the door and richly dressed ladies, escorted by cavaliers, alight and enter quickly. They wore noisy dresses and many wraps. Their faces were powdered and they caught up their dresses, when they touched earth, like alarmed Atalantas. He had always passed without turning his head to look. It was his habit to walk swiftly in the street even by day and whenever he found himself in the city late at night he hurried on his way apprehensively and excitedly. Sometimes, however, he courted the causes of his fear. He chose the darkest and narrowest streets and, as he walked boldly forward, the silence that was spread about his footsteps troubled him, the wandering, silent figures troubled him; and at times a sound of low fugitive laughter made him tremble like a leaf.

He turned to the right towards Capel Street. Ignatius Gallaher on the London Press! Who would have thought it possible eight years before? Still, now that he reviewed the past, Little Chandler could remember many signs of future greatness in his friend. People used to say that Ignatius Gallaher was wild. Of course, he did mix with a rakish set of fellows at that time, drank freely and borrowed money on all sides. In the end he had got mixed up in some shady affair, some money transaction: at least, that was one version of his flight. But nobody denied him talent. There was always a certain . . . something in Ignatius Gallaher that impressed you in spite of yourself. Even when he was out at elbows and at his wits' end for money he kept up a bold face. Little Chandler remembered (and the remembrance brought a slight flush of pride to his cheek) one of Ignatius Gallaher's sayings when he was in a tight corner: 'Half time now, boys,' he used to say light-heartedly. 'Where's my considering cap?'

That was Ignatius Gallaher all out; and, damn it, you couldn't but admire him for it.

Little Chandler quickened his pace. For the first time in his life he felt himself superior to the people he passed. For the first time his soul revolted against the dull inelegance of Capel Street. There was no doubt about it: if you wanted to succeed you had to go away. You could do nothing in Dublin. As he crossed Grattan Bridge he looked down the river towards the lower quays and pitied the poor stunted houses. They seemed to him a band of tramps, huddled together along the river-banks, their old coats covered with dust and soot, stupefied by the panorama of sunset and waiting for the first chill of night to bid them arise, shake themselves and begone. He wondered whether he could write a poem to express his idea. Perhaps Gallaher might be able to get it into some London paper for him. Could he write something original? He was not sure what idea he wished to express but the thought that a poetic moment had touched him took life within him like an infant hope. He stepped onward bravely.

Every step brought him nearer to London, farther from his own sober inartistic life. A light began to tremble on the horizon of his mind. He was not so old – thirty-two. His temperament might be said to be just at the point of maturity. There were so many different moods and impressions that he wished to express in verse. He felt them within him. He tried to weigh his soul to see if it was a poet's soul. Melancholy was the dominant note of his temperament, he thought, but it was a melancholy tempered by recurrences of faith and resignation and simple joy. If he could give expression to it in a book of poems perhaps men would listen. He would never be popular: he saw that. He could not sway the crowd but he might appeal to a little circle of kindred minds. The English critics, perhaps, would recognise him as one of the Celtic school by reason of the melancholy tone of his poems; besides that, he would put in allusions. He began to invent sentences and phrases from the notice which his book would get. 'Mr Chandler has the gift of easy and graceful verse'. . . 'A wistful sadness pervades these poems' . . . 'The Celtic note.' It was a pity his name was not more Irish-looking. Perhaps it would be better to insert his mother's name before the surname: Thomas Malone Chandler, or better still: T. Malone Chandler. He would speak to Gallaher about it.

He pursued his reverie so ardently that he passed his street and had to turn back. As he came near Corless's his former agitation began to over-master him and he halted before the door in indecision. Finally he opened the door and entered.

The light and noise of the bar held him at the doorways for a few moments. He looked about him, but his sight was confused by the shining of many red and green wine-glasses. The bar seemed to him to be full of people and he felt that the people were observing him curiously. He glanced quickly to right and left (frowning slightly to make his errand appear serious), but when his sight cleared a little he saw that nobody had turned to look at him: and there, sure enough, was Ignatius Gallaher leaning with his back against the counter and his feet planted far apart.

'Hallo, Tommy, old hero, here you are! What is it to be? What will you have? I'm taking whiskey: better stuff than we get across the water. Soda? Lithia? No mineral? I'm the same. Spoils the flavour . . . Here, *garçon*, bring us two halves of malt whiskey, like a good fellow . . . Well, and how have you been pulling along since I saw you last? Dear God, how old we're getting! Do you see any signs of ageing in me – eh, what? A little grey and thin on the top – what?'

Ignatius Gallaher took off his hat and displayed a large closely cropped head. His face was heavy, pale and clean-shaven. His eyes, which were of bluish slate-colour, relieved his unhealthy pallor and shone out plainly above the vivid orange tie he wore. Between these rival features the lips appeared very long and shapeless and colourless. He bent his head and felt with two sympathetic fingers the thin hair at the crown. Little Chandler shook his head as a denial. Ignatius Gallaher put on his hat again.

'It pulls you down,' he said, 'Press life. Always hurry and scurry, looking for copy and sometimes not finding it: and then, always to have something new in your stuff. Damn proofs and printers, I say, for a few days. I'm deuced glad, I can tell you, to get back to the old country. Does a fellow good, a bit of a holiday. I feel a ton better since I landed again in dear dirty Dublin . . . Here you are, Tommy. Water? Say when.'

Little Chandler allowed his whiskey to be very much diluted.

'You don't know what's good for you, my boy,' said Ignatius Gallaher. 'I drink mine neat.'

'I drink very little as a rule,' said Little Chandler modestly. 'An odd half-one or so when I meet any of the old crowd: that's all.'

'Ah, well,' said Ignatius Gallaher, cheerfully, 'here's to us and to old times and old acquaintance.'

They clinked glasses and drank the toast.

'I met some of the old gang today,' said Ignatius Gallaher. 'O'Hara seems to be in a bad way. What's he doing?'

'Nothing,' said Little Chandler. 'He's gone to the dogs.'

'But Hogan has a good sit, hasn't he?'

'Yes; he's in the Land Commission.'

'I met him one night in London and he seemed to be very flush . . . Poor O'Hara! Booze, I suppose?'

'Other things, too,' said Little Chandler shortly.

Ignatius Gallaher laughed.

'Tommy,' he said, 'I see you haven't changed an atom. You're the very same serious person that used to lecture me on Sunday mornings when I had a sore head and a fur on my tongue. You'd want to knock about a bit in the world. Have you never been anywhere even for a trip?'

'I've been to the Isle of Man,' said Little Chandler.

Ignatius Gallaher laughed.

'The Isle of Man!' he said. 'Go to London or Paris: Paris, for choice. That'd do you good.'

'Have you seen Paris?'

'I should think I have! I've knocked about there a little.'

'And is it really so beautiful as they say?' asked Little Chandler.

He sipped a little of his drink while Ignatius Gallaher finished his boldly.

'Beautiful?' said Ignatius Gallaher, pausing on the word and on the flavour of his drink. 'It's not so beautiful, you know. Of course, it is beautiful . . . But it's the life of Paris; that's the thing. Ah, there's no city like Paris for gaiety, movement, excitement . . .'

Little Chandler finished his whiskey and, after some trouble, succeeded in catching the barman's eye. He ordered the same again.

'I've been to the Moulin Rouge,' Ignatius Gallaher continued when the barman had removed their glasses, 'and I've been to all the Bohemian cafés. Hot stuff! Not for a pious chap like you, Tommy.'

Little Chandler said nothing until the barman returned with two glasses: then he touched his friend's glass lightly and reciprocated the former toast. He was beginning to feel somewhat disillusioned. Gallaher's accent and way of expressing himself did not please him. There was something vulgar in his friend which he had not observed before. But perhaps it was only the result of living in London amid the bustle and competition of the Press. The old personal charm was still there under this new gaudy manner. And, after all, Gallaher had lived, he had seen the world. Little Chandler looked at his friend enviously.

'Everything in Paris is gay,' said Ignatius Gallaher. 'They believe in enjoying life – and don't you think they're right? If you want to enjoy yourself properly you must go to Paris. And, mind you, they've a great feeling for the Irish there. When they heard I was from Ireland they were ready to eat me, man.'

Little Chandler took four or five sips from his glass.

'Tell me,' he said, 'is it true that Paris is so . . . immoral as they say?'

Ignatius Gallaher made a catholic gesture with his right arm.

'Every place is immoral,' he said. 'Of course you do find spicy bits in Paris. Go to one of the students' balls, for instance. That's lively, if you like, when the *cocottes* begin to let themselves loose. You know what they are, I suppose?'

'I've heard of them,' said Little Chandler.

Ignatius Gallaher drank off his whiskey and shook his head.

'Ah,' he said, 'you may say what you like. There's no woman like the Parisienne – for style, for go.'

'Then it is an immoral city,' said Little Chandler, with timid insistence – 'I mean, compared with London or Dublin?'

'London!' said Ignatius Gallaher. 'It's six of one and half a dozen of the other. You ask Hogan, my boy. I showed him a bit about London when he was over there. He'd open your eye . . . I say, Tommy, don't make punch of that whiskey: liquor up.'

'No, really . . . '

'O, come on, another one won't do you any harm. What is it? The same again, I suppose?'

'Well . . . all right.'

'*François*, the same again . . . Will you smoke, Tommy?'

Ignatius Gallaher produced his cigar-case. The two friends lit their cigars and puffed at them in silence until their drinks were served.

'I'll tell you my opinion,' said Ignatius Gallaher, emerging after some time from the clouds of smoke in which he had taken refuge, 'it's a rum world. Talk of immorality! I've heard of cases – what am I saying? – I've known them: cases of – immorality . . . '

Ignatius Gallaher puffed thoughtfully at his cigar and then, in a calm historian's tone, he proceeded to sketch for his friend some pictures of the corruption which was rife abroad. He summarised the vices of many capitals and seemed inclined to award the palm to Berlin. Some things he could not vouch for (his friends had told him), but of others he had had personal experience. He spared neither rank nor caste. He revealed many of the secrets of religious houses on the Continent and described some of the practices which were fashionable in high society and ended by telling, with details, a story about an English duchess – a story which he knew to be true. Little Chandler was astonished.

'Ah, well,' said Ignatius Gallaher, 'here we are in old jog-along Dublin where nothing is known of such things.'

'How dull you must find it,' said Little Chandler, 'after all the other places you've seen!'

'Well,' said Ignatius Gallaher, 'it's a relaxation to come over here, you know. And, after all, it's the old country, as they say, isn't it? You can't help having a certain feeling for it. That's human nature . . . But tell me something about yourself. Hogan told me you had . . . tasted the joys of connubial bliss. Two years ago, wasn't it?'

Little Chandler blushed and smiled.

'Yes,' he said. 'I was married last May twelve months.'

'I hope it's not too late in the day to offer my best wishes,' said Ignatius Gallaher. 'I didn't know your address or I'd have done so at the time.'

He extended his hand, which Little Chandler took.

'Well, Tommy,' he said, 'I wish you and yours every joy in life, old chap, and tons of money, and may you never die till I shoot you. And that's the wish of a sincere friend, an old friend. You know that?'

'I know that,' said Little Chandler.

'Any youngsters?' said Ignatius Gallaher.

Little Chandler blushed again.

'We have one child,' he said.

'Son or daughter?'

'A little boy.'

Ignatius Gallaher slapped his friend sonorously on the back.

'Bravo,' he said, 'I wouldn't doubt you, Tommy.'

Little Chandler smiled, looked confusedly at his glass and bit his lower lip with three childishly white front teeth.

'I hope you'll spend an evening with us,' he said, 'before you go back. My wife will be delighted to meet you. We can have a little music and – '

'Thanks awfully, old chap,' said Ignatius Gallaher, 'I'm sorry we didn't meet earlier. But I must leave tomorrow night.'

'Tonight, perhaps . . . ?'

'I'm awfully sorry, old man. You see I'm over here with another fellow, clever young chap he is too, and we arranged to go to a little card-party. Only for that . . . '

'O, in that case . . . '

'But who knows?' said Ignatius Gallaher considerately. 'Next year I may take a little skip over here now that I've broken the ice. It's only a pleasure deferred.'

'Very well,' said Little Chandler, 'the next time you come we must have an evening together. That's agreed now, isn't it?'

'Yes, that's agreed,' said Ignatius Gallaher. 'Next year if I come, *parole d' honneur.*'

'And to clinch the bargain,' said Little Chandler, 'we'll just have one more now.'

Ignatius Gallaher took out a large gold watch and looked at it.

'Is it to be the last?' he said. 'Because you know, I have an a.p.'

'O, yes, positively,' said Little Chandler.

'Very well, then,' said Ignatius Gallaher, 'let us have another one as a *deoc an doruis* – that's good vernacular for a small whiskey, I believe.'

Little Chandler ordered the drinks. The blush which had risen to his face a few moments before was establishing itself. A trifle made him blush at any time: and now he felt warm and excited. Three small whiskies had gone to his head and Gallaher's strong cigar had confused his mind, for he was a delicate and abstinent person. The adventure of meeting Gallaher after eight years, of finding himself with Gallaher in Corless's surrounded by lights and noise, of listening to Gallaher's stories and of sharing for a brief space Gallaher's vagrant and triumphant life, upset the equipoise of his sensitive nature. He felt acutely the contrast between his own life and his friend's, and it seemed to him unjust. Gallaher was his inferior in birth and education. He was sure that he could do something better than his friend had ever done, or could ever do, something higher than mere tawdry journalism if he only got the chance. What was it that stood in his way? His unfortunate timidity! He wished to vindicate himself in some way, to assert his manhood. He saw behind Gallaher's refusal of his invitation. Gallaher was only patronising him by his friendliness just as he was patronising Ireland by his visit.

The barman brought their drinks. Little Chandler pushed one glass towards his friend and took up the other boldly.

'Who knows?' he said, as they lifted their glasses. 'When you come next year I may have the pleasure of wishing long life and happiness to Mr and Mrs Ignatius Gallaher.'

Ignatius Gallaher in the act of drinking closed one eye expressively over the rim of his glass. When he had drunk he smacked his lips decisively, set down his glass and said: 'No blooming fear of that, my boy. I'm going to have my fling first and see a bit of life and the world before I put my head in the sack – if I ever do.'

'Someday you will,' said Little Chandler calmly.

Ignatius Gallaher turned his orange tie and slate-blue eyes full upon his friend.

'You think so?' he said.

'You'll put your head in the sack,' repeated Little Chandler stoutly, 'like everyone else if you can find the girl.'

He had slightly emphasised his tone and he was aware that he had betrayed himself; but, though the colour had heightened in his cheek, he did not flinch from his friend's gaze. Ignatius Gallaher watched him for a few moments and then said: 'If ever it occurs, you may bet your bottom dollar there'll be no mooning and spooning about it. I mean to marry money. She'll have a good fat account at the bank or she won't do for me.'

Little Chandler shook his head.

'Why, man alive,' said Ignatius Gallaher, vehemently, 'do you know what it is? I've only to say the word and tomorrow I can have the woman and the cash. You don't believe it? Well, I know it. There are hundreds – what am I saying? – thousands of rich Germans and Jews, rotten with money, that'd only be too glad . . . You wait a while, my boy. See if I don't play my cards properly. When I go about a thing I mean business, I tell you. You just wait.'

He tossed his glass to his mouth, finished his drink and laughed loudly. Then he looked thoughtfully before him and said in a calmer tone: 'But I'm in no hurry. They can wait. I don't fancy tying myself up to one woman, you know.'

He imitated with his mouth the act of tasting and made a wry face.

'Must get a bit stale, I should think,' he said.

Little Chandler sat in the room off the hall, holding a child in his arms. To save money they kept no servant but Annie's young sister Monica came for an hour or so in the morning and an hour or so in the evening to help. But Monica had gone home long ago. It was a quarter to nine. Little Chandler had come home late for tea and, moreover, he had forgotten to bring Annie home the parcel of coffee from Bewley's. Of course she was in a bad humour and gave him short answers. She said she would do without any tea but when it came near the time at which the shop at the corner closed she decided to go out herself for a quarter of a pound of tea and two pounds of sugar. She put the sleeping child deftly in his arms and said: 'Here. Don't waken him.'

A little lamp with a white china shade stood upon the table and its light fell over a photograph which was enclosed in a frame of crumpled horn. It was Annie's photograph. Little Chandler looked at it, pausing at the thin tight lips. She wore the pale blue summer blouse which he had brought her home as a present one Saturday. It had cost him ten and elevenpence; but what an agony of nervousness it had cost him! How he had suffered that day, waiting at the shop door until the shop was empty, standing at the counter and trying to appear at his ease while the girl piled ladies' blouses before him, paying at the desk and forgetting to take up the odd penny of his change, being called back by the cashier, and finally, striving to hide his blushes as he left the shop by examining the parcel to see if it was securely tied. When he brought the blouse home Annie kissed him and said it was very pretty and stylish; but when she heard the price she threw the blouse on the table and said it was a regular swindle to charge ten and elevenpence for it. At first she wanted to take it back but when she tried it on she was delighted with it, especially with the make of the sleeves, and kissed him and said he was very good to think of her.

Hm! . . .

He looked coldly into the eyes of the photograph and they answered coldly. Certainly they were pretty and the face itself was pretty. But he found something mean in it. Why was it so unconscious and ladylike? The composure of the eyes irritated him. They repelled him and defied him: there was no passion in them, no rapture. He thought of what Gallaher had said about rich Jewesses. Those dark Oriental eyes, he thought, how full they are of passion, of voluptuous longing! . . . Why had he married the eyes in the photograph?

He caught himself up at the question and glanced nervously round the room. He found something mean in the pretty furniture which he had bought for his house on the hire system. Annie had chosen it herself and it reminded him of her. It too was prim and pretty. A dull resentment against his life awoke within him. Could he not escape from his little house? Was it too late for him to try to live bravely like Gallaher? Could he go to London? There was the furniture still to be paid for. If he could only write a book and get it published, that might open the way for him.

A volume of Byron's poems lay before him on the table. He opened it cautiously with his left hand lest he should waken the child and began to read the first poem in the book:

> Hushed are the winds and still the evening gloom,
> Not e'en a Zephyr wanders through the grove,
> Whilst I return to view my Margaret's tomb
> And scatter flowers on the dust I love.

He paused. He felt the rhythm of the verse about him in the room. How melancholy it was! Could he, too, write like that, express the melancholy of his soul in verse? There were so many things he wanted to describe: his sensation of a few hours before on Grattan Bridge, for example. If he could get back again into that mood . . .

The child awoke and began to cry. He turned from the page and tried to hush it: but it would not be hushed. He began to rock it to and fro in his arms but its wailing cry grew keener. He rocked it faster while his eyes began to read the second stanza:

> Within this narrow cell reclines her clay,
> That clay where once . . .

It was useless. He couldn't read. He couldn't do anything. The wailing of the child pierced the drum of his ear. It was useless, useless! He was a prisoner for life. His arms trembled with anger and suddenly bending to the child's face he shouted: 'Stop!'

The child stopped for an instant, had a spasm of fright and began to scream. He jumped up from his chair and walked hastily up and down the room with the child in his arms. It began to sob piteously, losing its breath for four or five seconds, and then bursting out anew. The thin walls of the room echoed the sound. He tried to soothe it but it sobbed more convulsively. He looked at the contracted and quivering face of the child and began to be alarmed. He counted seven sobs without a break between them and caught the child to his breast in fright. If it died! . . .

The door was burst open and a young woman ran in, panting.

'What is it? What is it?' she cried.

The child, hearing its mother's voice, broke out into a paroxysm of sobbing.

'It's nothing, Annie . . . it's nothing . . . He began to cry . . . '

She flung her parcels on the floor and snatched the child from him.

'What have you done to him?' she cried, glaring into his face.

Little Chandler sustained for one moment the gaze of her eyes and his heart closed together as he met the hatred in them. He began to stammer: 'It's nothing . . . He . . . he began to cry . . . I couldn't . . . I didn't do anything . . . What?'

Giving no heed to him she began to walk up and down the room, clasping the child tightly in her arms and murmuring: 'My little man! My little mannie! was 'ou frightened, love? . . . There now, love! There now! . . . Lambabaun! Mamma's little lamb of the world! . . . There now!'

Little Chandler felt his cheeks suffused with shame and he stood back out of the lamplight. He listened while the paroxysm of the child's sobbing grew less and less; and tears of remorse started to his eyes.

Counterparts

The bell rang furiously and, when Miss Parker went to the tube, a furious voice called out in a piercing North of Ireland accent: 'Send Farrington here!'

Miss Parker returned to her machine, saying to a man who was writing at a desk: 'Mr Alleyne wants you upstairs.'

The man muttered *'Blast* him!' under his breath and pushed back his chair to stand up. When he stood up he was tall and of great bulk. He had a hanging face, dark wine-coloured, with fair eyebrows and moustache: his eyes bulged forward slightly and the whites of them were dirty. He lifted up the counter and, passing by the clients, went out of the office with a heavy step.

He went heavily upstairs until he came to the second landing, where a door bore a brass plate with the inscription *Mr Alleyne.* Here he halted, puffing with labour and vexation, and knocked. The shrill voice cried: 'Come in!'

The man entered Mr Alleyne's room. Simultaneously Mr Alleyne, a little man wearing gold-rimmed glasses on a clean-shaven face, shot his head up over a pile of documents. The head itself was so pink and hairless it seemed like a large egg reposing on the papers. Mr Alleyne did not lose a moment: 'Farrington? What is the meaning of this? Why have I always to complain of you? May I ask you why you haven't made a copy of that contract between Bodley and Kirwan? I told you it must be ready by four o'clock.'

'But Mr Shelley said, sir – '

'*Mr Shelley said, sir* . . . Kindly attend to what I say and not to what *Mr Shelley says sir.* You have always some excuse or another for shirking work. Let me tell you that if the contract is not copied before this evening I'll lay the matter before Mr Crosbie . . . Do you hear me now?'

'Yes, sir.'

'Do you hear me now? . . . Ay and another little matter! I might as well be talking to the wall as talking to you. Understand once for all that you get a half an hour for your lunch and not an hour and a half. How many courses do you want, I'd like to know . . . Do you mind me now?'

'Yes, sir.'

Mr Alleyne bent his head again upon his pile of papers. The man stared fixedly at the polished skull which directed the affairs of Crosbie & Alleyne, gauging its fragility. A spasm of rage gripped his throat for a few moments and then passed, leaving after it a sharp sensation of thirst. The man recognised the sensation and felt that he must have a good night's drinking. The middle of the month was passed and, if he could get the copy done in time, Mr Alleyne might give him an order on the cashier. He stood still, gazing fixedly at the head upon the pile of papers. Suddenly Mr Alleyne began to upset all the papers, searching for something. Then, as if he had been unaware of the man's presence till that moment, he shot up his head again, saying: 'Eh? Are you going to stand there all day? Upon my word, Farrington, you take things easy!'

'I was waiting to see . . .'

'Very good, you needn't wait to see. Go downstairs and do your work.'

The man walked heavily towards the door and, as he went out of the room, he heard Mr Alleyne cry after him that if the contract was not copied by evening Mr Crosbie would hear of the matter.

He returned to his desk in the lower office and counted the sheets which remained to be copied. He took up his pen and dipped it in the ink but he continued to stare stupidly at the last words he had written: *In no case shall the said Bernard Bodley be*. . . The evening was falling and in a few minutes they would be lighting the gas: then he could write. He felt that he must slake the thirst in his throat. He stood up from his desk and, lifting the counter as before, passed out of the office. As he was passing out the chief clerk looked at him inquiringly.

'It's all right, Mr Shelley,' said the man, pointing with his finger to indicate the objective of his journey.

The chief clerk glanced at the hat-rack, but, seeing the row complete, offered no remark. As soon as he was on the landing the man pulled a shepherd's plaid cap out of his pocket, put it on his head and ran quickly down the rickety stairs. From the street door he walked on furtively on the inner side of the path towards the corner and all at once dived into a doorway. He was now safe in the dark snug of O'Neill's shop, and, filling up the little window that looked into the bar with his inflamed face, the colour of dark wine or dark meat, he called out: 'Here, Pat, give us a g.p., like a good fellow.'

The curate brought him a glass of plain porter. The man drank it at a gulp and asked for a caraway seed. He put his penny on the counter and, leaving the curate to grope for it in the gloom, retreated out of the snug as furtively as he had entered it.

Darkness, accompanied by a thick fog, was gaining upon the dusk of

February and the lamps in Eustace Street had been lit. The man went up by the houses until he reached the door of the office, wondering whether he could finish his copy in time. On the stairs a moist pungent odour of perfumes saluted his nose: evidently Miss Delacour had come while he was out in O'Neill's. He crammed his cap back again into his pocket and re-entered the office, assuming an air of absent-mindedness.

'Mr Alleyne has been calling for you,' said the chief clerk severely. 'Where were you?'

The man glanced at the two clients who were standing at the counter as if to intimate that their presence prevented him from answering. As the clients were both male the chief clerk allowed himself a laugh.

'I know that game,' he said. 'Five times in one day is a little bit . . . Well, you better look sharp and get a copy of our correspondence in the Delacour case for Mr Alleyne.'

This address in the presence of the public, his run upstairs and the porter he had gulped down so hastily confused the man and, as he sat down at his desk to get what was required, he realised how hopeless was the task of finishing his copy of the contract before half past five. The dark damp night was coming and he longed to spend it in the bars, drinking with his friends amid the glare of gas and the clatter of glasses. He got out the Delacour correspondence and passed out of the office. He hoped Mr Alleyne would not discover that the last two letters were missing.

The moist pungent perfume lay all the way up to Mr Alleyne's room. Miss Delacour was a middle-aged woman of Jewish appearance. Mr Alleyne was said to be sweet on her or on her money. She came to the office often and stayed a long time when she came. She was sitting beside his desk now in an aroma of perfumes, smoothing the handle of her umbrella and nodding the great black feather in her hat. Mr Alleyne had swivelled his chair round to face her and thrown his right foot jauntily upon his left knee. The man put the correspondence on the desk and bowed respectfully but neither Mr Alleyne nor Miss Delacour took any notice of his bow. Mr Alleyne tapped a finger on the correspondence and then flicked it towards him as if to say: *That's all right: you can go.*

The man returned to the lower office and sat down again at his desk. He stared intently at the incomplete phrase: *In no case shall the said Bernard Bodley be* . . . and thought how strange it was that the last three words began with the same letter. The chief clerk began to hurry Miss Parker, saying she would never have the letters typed in time for post. The man listened to the clicking of the machine for a few minutes and then set to work to finish his copy. But his head was not clear and his mind wandered away to the glare and rattle of the public-house. It was a night for hot punches. He struggled on with his copy, but when the clock struck five he had still fourteen pages to write. Blast it! He couldn't finish it in time. He longed to execrate aloud, to bring his fist down on something violently. He was so enraged that he wrote *Bernard Bernard* instead of *Bernard Bodley* and had to begin again on a clean sheet.

He felt strong enough to clear out the whole office single-handed. His body ached to do something, to rush out and revel in violence. All the indignities of his life enraged him . . . Could he ask the cashier privately for an advance? No, the cashier was no good, no damn good: he wouldn't give an advance . . . He knew where he would meet the boys: Leonard and O'Halloran and Nosey Flynn. The barometer of his emotional nature was set for a spell of riot.

His imagination had so abstracted him that his name was called twice before he answered. Mr Alleyne and Miss Delacour were standing outside the counter and all the clerks had turned round in anticipation of something. The man got up from his desk. Mr Alleyne began a tirade of abuse, saying that two letters were missing. The man answered that he knew nothing about them, that he had made a faithful copy. The tirade continued: it was so bitter and violent that the man could hardly restrain his fist from descending upon the head of the manikin before him: 'I know nothing about any other two letters,' he said stupidly.

'*You – know – nothing.* Of course you know nothing,' said Mr Alleyne. 'Tell me,' he added, glancing first for approval to the lady beside him, 'do you take me for a fool? Do you think me an utter fool?'

The man glanced from the lady's face to the little egg-shaped head and back again; and, almost before he was aware of it, his tongue had found a felicitous moment: 'I don't think, sir,' he said, 'that that's a fair question to put to me.'

There was a pause in the very breathing of the clerks. Everyone was astounded (the author of the witticism no less than his neighbours) and Miss Delacour, who was a stout amiable person, began to smile broadly. Mr Alleyne blushed to the hue of a wild rose and his mouth twitched with a dwarf's passion. He shook his fist in the man's face till it seemed to vibrate like the knob of some electric machine: 'You impertinent ruffian! You impertinent ruffian! I'll make short work of you! Wait till you see! You'll apologise to me for your impertinence or you'll quit the office instanter! You'll quit this, I'm telling you, or you'll apologise to me!'

He stood in a doorway opposite the office watching to see if the cashier would come out alone. All the clerks passed out and finally the cashier came out with the chief clerk. It was no use trying to say a word to him when he was with the chief clerk. The man felt that his position was bad enough. He had been obliged to offer an abject apology to Mr Alleyne for his impertinence but he knew what a hornet's nest the office would be for him. He could remember the way in which Mr Alleyne had hounded little Peake out of the office in order to make room for his own nephew. He felt savage and thirsty and revengeful, annoyed with himself and with everyone else. Mr Alleyne would never give him an hour's rest; his life would be a hell to him. He had made a proper fool of himself this time. Could he not keep his tongue in his cheek? But they had never pulled together from the first, he and Mr Alleyne, ever since the day Mr Alleyne had overheard him mimicking his North of Ireland accent to amuse Higgins and Miss Parker: that had been the beginning of it. He might have tried Higgins for the money, but sure Higgins never had anything for himself. A man with two establishments to keep up, of course he couldn't . . .

He felt his great body again aching for the comfort of the public-house. The fog had begun to chill him and he wondered could he touch Pat in O'Neill's. He could not touch him for more than a bob – and a bob was no use. Yet he must get money somewhere or other: he had spent his last penny for the g.p. and soon it would be too late for getting money anywhere. Suddenly, as he was fingering his watch-chain, he thought of Terry Kelly's pawn-office in Fleet Street. That was the dart! Why didn't he think of it sooner?

He went through the narrow alley of Temple Bar quickly, muttering to himself that they could all go to hell because he was going to have a good night of it. The clerk in Terry Kelly's said *A crown?* but the consignor held out for six shillings; and in the end the six shillings was allowed him literally. He came out of the pawn-office joyfully, making a little cylinder of the coins between his thumb and fingers. In Westmoreland Street the footpaths were crowded with young men and women returning from business and ragged urchins ran here and there yelling out the names of the evening editions. The man passed through the crowd, looking on the spectacle generally with proud satisfaction and staring masterfully at the office-girls. His head was full of the noises of tram-gongs and swishing trolleys and his nose already sniffed the curling fumes of punch. As he walked on he pre-considered the terms in which he would narrate the incident to the boys: 'So, I just looked at him – coolly, you know, and looked at her. Then I looked back at him again – taking my time, you know. "I don't think that that's a fair question to put to me," says I.'

Nosey Flynn was sitting up in his usual corner of Davy Byrne's and, when he heard the story, he stood Farrington a half-one, saying it was as smart a thing as ever he heard. Farrington stood a drink in his turn. After a while O'Halloran and Paddy Leonard came in and the story was repeated to them. O'Halloran stood tailors of malt, hot, all round and told the story of the retort he had made to the chief clerk when he was in Callan's of Fownes's Street; but, as the retort was after the manner of the liberal shepherds in the eclogues, he had to admit that it was not as clever as Farrington's retort. At this Farrington told the boys to polish off that and have another.

Just as they were naming their poisons who should come in but Higgins! Of course he had to join in with the others. The men asked him to give his version of it, and he did so with great vivacity for the sight of five small hot whiskies was very exhilarating. Everyone roared laughing when he showed the way in which Mr Alleyne shook his fist in Farrington's face. Then he imitated Farrington, saying, '*And here was my nabs, as cool as you please,*' while Farrington looked at the company out of his heavy dirty eyes, smiling and at times drawing forth stray drops of liquor from his moustache with the aid of his lower lip.

When that round was over there was a pause. O'Halloran had money but neither of the other two seemed to have any; so the whole party left the shop somewhat regretfully. At the corner of Duke Street Higgins and Nosey Flynn bevelled off to the left while the other three turned back towards the city. Rain was drizzling down on the cold streets and, when they reached the Ballast Office, Farrington suggested the Scotch House. The bar was full of men and loud with the noise of tongues and glasses. The three men pushed past the whining match-sellers at the door and formed a little party at the corner of the counter. They began to exchange stories. Leonard introduced them to a young fellow named Weathers who was performing at the Tivoli as an acrobat and knockabout *artiste*. Farrington stood a drink all round. Weathers said he would take a small Irish and Apollinaris. Farrington, who had definite notions of what was what, asked the boys would they have an Apollinaris too; but the boys told Tim to make theirs hot. The talk became theatrical. O'Halloran stood a round and then Farrington stood another round, Weathers protesting that the hospitality was too Irish. He promised to get them in behind the scenes and introduce them to some nice girls. O'Halloran said that he and Leonard would go, but that Farrington wouldn't go because he was a married man; and Farrington's heavy dirty eyes leered at the company in token that he understood he was being chaffed. Weathers made them all have just one little tincture at his expense and promised to meet them later on at Mulligan's in Poolbeg Street.

When the Scotch House closed they went round to Mulligan's. They went into the parlour at the back and O'Halloran ordered small hot specials all round. They were all beginning to feel mellow. Farrington was just standing another round when Weathers came back. Much to Farrington's relief he drank a glass of bitter this time. Funds were getting low but they had enough to keep them going. Presently two young women with big hats and a young man in a check suit came in and sat at a table close by. Weathers saluted them and told the company that they were out of the Tivoli. Farrington's eyes wandered at every moment in the direction of one of the young women. There was something striking in her appearance. An immense scarf of peacock-blue muslin was wound round her hat and knotted in a great bow under her chin; and she wore bright yellow gloves, reaching to the elbow. Farrington gazed admiringly at the plump arm which she moved very often and with much grace; and when, after a little time, she answered his gaze he admired still more her large dark brown eyes. The oblique staring expression in them fascinated him. She glanced at him once or twice and, when the party was leaving the room, she brushed against his chair and said '*O, pardon!*' in a London accent. He watched her leave the room in the hope that she would look back at him, but he was disappointed. He cursed his want of money and cursed all the rounds he had stood, particularly all the whiskies and Apollinaris which he had stood to Weathers. If there was one thing that he hated it was a sponge. He was so angry that he lost count of the conversation of his friends.

When Paddy Leonard called him he found that they were talking about feats of strength. Weathers was showing his biceps muscle to the company and boasting so much that the other two had called on Farrington to uphold the national honour. Farrington pulled up his sleeve accordingly and showed his biceps muscle to the company. The two arms were examined and compared and finally it was agreed to have a trial of strength. The table was cleared and the two men rested their elbows on it, clasping hands. When Paddy Leonard said 'Go!' each was to try to bring down the other's hand on to the table. Farrington looked very serious and determined. The trial began. After about thirty seconds Weathers brought his opponent's hand slowly down on to the table. Farrington's dark wine-coloured face flushed darker still with anger and humiliation at having been defeated by such a stripling.

'You're not to put the weight of your body behind it. Play fair,' he said.

'Who's not playing fair?' said the other.

'Come on again. The two best out of three.'

The trial began again. The veins stood out on Farrington's forehead, and the pallor of Weathers' complexion changed to peony. Their hands and arms trembled under the stress. After a long struggle Weathers again brought his opponent's hand slowly on to the table. There was a murmur of applause from the spectators. The curate, who was standing beside the table, nodded his red head towards the victor and said with stupid familiarity: 'Ah! that's the knack!'

'What the hell do you know about it?' said Farrington fiercely, turning on the man. 'What do you put in your gab for?'

'Sh, sh!' said O'Halloran, observing the violent expression of Farrington's face. 'Pony up, boys. We'll have just one little smahan more and then we'll be off.'

A very sullen-faced man stood at the corner of O'Connell Bridge waiting for the little Sandymount tram to take him home. He was full of smouldering anger and revengefulness. He felt humiliated and discontented; he did not even feel drunk; and he had only twopence in his pocket. He cursed everything. He had done for himself in the office, pawned his watch, spent all his money; and he had not even got drunk. He began to feel thirsty again and he longed to be back again in the hot reeking public-house. He had lost his reputation as a strong man, having been defeated twice by a mere boy. His heart swelled with fury and, when he thought of the woman in the big hat who had brushed against him and said *Pardon!* his fury nearly choked him.

His tram let him down at Shelbourne Road and he steered his great body along in the shadow of the wall of the barracks. He loathed returning to his home. When he went in by the side-door he found the kitchen empty and the kitchen fire nearly out. He bawled upstairs: 'Ada! Ada!'

His wife was a little sharp-faced woman who bullied her husband when he was sober and was bullied by him when he was drunk. They had five children. A little boy came running down the stairs.

'Who is that?' said the man, peering through the darkness.

'Me, pa.'

'Who are you? Charlie?'

'No, pa. Tom.'

'Where's your mother?'

'She's out at the chapel.'

'That's right . . . Did she think of leaving any dinner for me?'

'Yes, pa. I – '

'Light the lamp. What do you mean by having the place in darkness? Are the other children in bed?'

The man sat down heavily on one of the chairs while the little boy lit the lamp. He began to mimic his son's flat accent, saying half to himself: '*At the chapel. At the chapel, if you please!*' When the lamp was lit he banged his fist on the table and shouted: 'What's for my dinner?'

'I'm going . . . to cook it, pa,' said the little boy.

The man jumped up furiously and pointed to the fire.

'On that fire! You let the fire out! By God, I'll teach you to do that again!'

He took a step to the door and seized the walking-stick which was standing behind it.

'I'll teach you to let the fire out!' he said, rolling up his sleeve in order to give his arm free play.

The little boy cried '*O, pa!*' and ran whimpering round the table, but the man followed him and caught him by the coat. The little boy looked about him wildly but, seeing no way of escape, fell upon his knees.

'Now, you'll let the fire out the next time!' said the man, striking at him vigorously with the stick. 'Take that, you little whelp!'

The boy uttered a squeal of pain as the stick cut his thigh. He clasped his hands together in the air and his voice shook with fright.

'O, pa!' he cried. 'Don't beat me, pa! And I'll . . . I'll say a *Hail Mary* for you . . . I'll say a *Hail Mary* for you, pa, if you don't beat me . . . I'll say a *Hail Mary* . . .'

Clay

The matron had given her leave to go out as soon as the women's tea was over and Maria looked forward to her evening out. The kitchen was spick and span: the cook said you could see yourself in the big copper boilers. The fire was nice and bright and on one of the side-tables were four very big barmbracks. These barmbracks seemed uncut; but if you went closer you would see that they had been cut into long thick even slices and were ready to be handed round at tea. Maria had cut them herself.

Maria was a very, very small person indeed but she had a very long nose and a very long chin. She talked a little through her nose, always soothingly: '*Yes, my dear,*' and '*No, my dear.*' She was always sent for when the women quarrelled over their tubs and always succeeded in making peace. One day the matron had said to her: 'Maria, you are a veritable peace-maker!'

And the sub-matron and two of the Board ladies had heard the compliment. And Ginger Mooney was always saying what she wouldn't do to the dummy who had charge of the irons if it wasn't for Maria. Everyone was so fond of Maria.

The women would have their tea at six o'clock and she would be able to get away before seven. From Ballsbridge to the Pillar, twenty minutes; from the Pillar to Drumcondra, twenty minutes; and twenty minutes to buy the things. She would be there before eight. She took out her purse with the silver clasps and read again the words *A Present from Belfast*. She was very fond of that purse because Joe had brought it to her five years before when he and Alphy had gone to Belfast on a Whit-Monday trip. In the purse were two half-crowns and some coppers. She would have five shillings clear after paying tram fare. What a nice evening they would have, all the children singing! Only she hoped that Joe wouldn't come in drunk. He was so different when he took any drink.

Often he had wanted her to go and live with them; but she would have felt herself in the way (though Joe's wife was ever so nice with her) and she had become accustomed to the life of the laundry. Joe was a good fellow. She had nursed him and Alphy too; and Joe used often to say: 'Mamma is mamma but Maria is my proper mother.'

After the break-up at home the boys had got her that position in the Dublin by Lamplight laundry, and she liked it. She used to have such a bad opinion of Protestants but now she thought they were very nice people, a little quiet and serious, but still very nice people to live with. Then she had her plants in the conservatory and she liked looking after them. She had lovely ferns and wax-plants and, whenever anyone came to visit her, she always gave the visitor one or two slips from her conservatory. There was one thing she didn't like and that was the tracts on the walls; but the matron was such a nice person to deal with, so genteel.

When the cook told her everything was ready she went into the women's room and began to pull the big bell. In a few minutes the women began to come in by twos and threes, wiping their steaming hands in their petticoats and pulling down the sleeves of their blouses over their red steaming arms. They settled down before their huge mugs which the cook and the dummy filled up with hot tea, already mixed with milk and sugar in huge tin cans. Maria superintended the distribution of the barmbrack and saw that every woman got her four slices. There was a great deal of laughing and joking during the meal. Lizzie Fleming said Maria was sure to get the ring and, though Fleming had said that for so many Hallow Eves, Maria had to laugh and say she didn't want any ring or man either; and when she laughed her grey-green eyes sparkled with disappointed shyness and the tip of her nose nearly met the tip of her chin. Then Ginger Mooney lifted up her mug of tea and proposed Maria's health while all the other women clattered with their mugs on the table, and said she was sorry she hadn't a sup of porter to drink it in. And Maria laughed again till the tip of her nose nearly met the tip of her chin and till her minute body nearly shook itself asunder because she knew that Mooney meant well though, of course, she had the notions of a common woman.

But wasn't Maria glad when the women had finished their tea and the cook and the dummy had begun to clear away the tea-things! She went into her little bedroom and, remembering that the next morning was a mass morning, changed the hand of the alarm from seven to six. Then she took off her working skirt and her house-boots and laid her best skirt out on the bed and her tiny dress-boots beside the foot of the bed. She changed her blouse too and, as she stood before the mirror, she thought of how she used to dress for mass on Sunday morning when she was a young girl; and she looked with quaint affection at the diminutive body which she had so often adorned. In spite of its years she found it a nice tidy little body.

When she got outside the streets were shining with rain and she was glad of her old brown waterproof. The tram was full and she had to sit on the little stool at the end of the car, facing all the people, with her toes barely touching the floor. She arranged in her mind all she was going to do and thought how much better it was to be independent and to have your own money in your pocket. She hoped they would have a nice evening. She was sure they would but she could not help thinking what a pity it was Alphy and Joe were not speaking. They were always falling out now but when they were boys together they used to be the best of friends: but such was life.

She got out of her tram at the Pillar and ferreted her way quickly among the crowds. She went into Downes's cake-shop but the shop was so full of people that it was a long time before she could get herself attended to. She bought a dozen of mixed penny cakes, and at last came out of the shop laden with a big bag. Then she thought what else would she buy: she wanted to buy something really nice. They would be sure to have plenty of apples and nuts. It was hard to know what to buy and all she could think of was cake. She decided to buy some plumcake but Downes's plumcake had not enough almond icing on top of it so she went over to a shop in Henry Street. Here she was a long time in suiting herself and the stylish young lady behind the counter, who was evidently a little annoyed by her, asked her was it wedding-cake she wanted to buy. That made Maria blush and smile at the young lady; but the young lady took it all very seriously and finally cut a thick slice of plumcake, parcelled it up and said: 'Two-and-four, please.'

She thought she would have to stand in the Drumcondra tram because none of the young men seemed to notice her but an elderly gentleman made room for her. He was a stout gentleman and he wore a brown hard hat; he had a square red face and a greyish moustache. Maria thought he was a colonel-looking gentleman and she reflected how much more polite he was than the young men who simply stared straight before them. The gentleman began to chat with her about Hallow Eve and the rainy weather. He supposed the bag was full of good things for the little ones and said it was only right that the youngsters should enjoy themselves while they were young. Maria agreed with him and favoured him with demure nods and hems. He was very nice with her, and when she was getting out at the Canal Bridge she thanked him and bowed, and he bowed to her and raised his hat and smiled agreeably; and while she was going up along the terrace, bending her tiny head under the rain, she thought how easy it was to know a gentleman even when he has a drop taken.

Everybody said: 'O, *here's Maria!*' when she came to Joe's house. Joe was there, having come home from business, and all the children had their Sunday dresses on. There were two big girls in from next door and games were going on. Maria gave the bag of cakes to the eldest boy, Alphy, to divide and Mrs Donnelly said it was too good of her to bring such a big bag of cakes and made all the children say: 'Thanks, Maria.'

But Maria said she had brought something special for papa and mamma, something they would be sure to like, and she began to look for her plumcake. She tried in Downes's bag and then in the pockets of her water-proof and then on the hallstand but nowhere could she find it. Then she asked all the children had any of them eaten it – by mistake, of course – but the children all said no and looked as if they did not like to eat cakes if they were to be accused of stealing. Everybody had a solution for the mystery and Mrs Donnelly said it was plain that Maria had left it behind her in the tram. Maria, remembering how confused the gentleman with the greyish moustache had made her, coloured with shame and vexation and dis-appointment. At the thought of the failure of her little surprise and of the two and four-pence she had thrown away for nothing she nearly cried outright.

But Joe said it didn't matter and made her sit down by the fire. He was very nice with her. He told her all that went on in his office, repeating for her a smart answer which he had made to the manager. Maria did not understand why Joe laughed so much over the answer he had made but she said that the manager must have been a very overbearing person to deal with. Joe said he wasn't so bad when you knew how to take him, that he was a decent sort so long as you didn't rub him the wrong way. Mrs Donnelly played the piano for the children and they danced and sang. Then the two next-door girls handed round the nuts. Nobody could find the nutcrackers and Joe was nearly getting cross over it and asked how did they expect Maria to crack nuts without a nutcracker. But Maria said she didn't like nuts and that they weren't to bother about her. Then Joe asked would she take a bottle of stout and Mrs Donnelly said there was port wine too in the house if she would prefer that. Maria said she would rather they didn't ask her to take anything: but Joe insisted.

So Maria let him have his way and they sat by the fire talking over old times and Maria thought she would put in a good word for Alphy. But Joe cried that God might strike him stone dead if ever he spoke a word to his brother again and Maria said she was sorry she had mentioned the matter. Mrs Donnelly told her husband it was a great shame for him to speak that way of his own flesh and blood but Joe said that Alphy was no brother of his and there was nearly being a row on the head of it. But Joe said he would not lose his temper on account of the night it was and asked his wife to open some more stout. The two next-door girls had arranged some Hallow Eve games and soon everything was merry again. Maria was delighted to see the children so merry and Joe and his wife in such good spirits. The next-door girls put some saucers on the table and then led the children up to the table, blindfold. One got the prayer-book and the other three got the water; and when one of the next-door girls got the ring Mrs Donnelly shook her finger at the blushing girl as much as to say: *O, I know all about it!* They insisted then on blindfolding Maria and leading her up to the table to see what she would get; and, while they were putting on the bandage, Maria laughed and laughed again till the tip of her nose nearly met the tip of her chin.

They led her up to the table amid laughing and joking and she put her hand out in the air as she was told to do. She moved her hand about here and there in the air and descended on one of the saucers. She felt a soft wet substance with her fingers and was surprised that nobody spoke or took off her bandage. There was a pause for a few seconds; and then a great deal of scuffling and whispering. Somebody said something about the garden, and at last Mrs Donnelly said something very cross to one of the next-door girls and told her to throw it out at once: that was no play. Maria understood that it was wrong that time and so she had to do it over again: and this time she got the prayer-book.

After that Mrs Donnelly played Miss McCloud's Reel for the children and Joe made Maria take a glass of wine. Soon they were all quite merry again and Mrs Donnelly said Maria would enter a convent before the year was out because she had got the prayer-book. Maria had never seen Joe so nice to her as he was that night, so full of pleasant talk and reminiscences. She said they were all very good to her.

At last the children grew tired and sleepy and Joe asked Maria would she not sing some little song before she went, one of the old songs. Mrs Donnelly said '*Do, please, Maria!*' and so Maria had to get up and stand beside the piano. Mrs Donnelly bade the children be quiet and listen to Maria's song. Then she played the prelude and said '*Now, Maria!*' and Maria, blushing very much, began to sing in a tiny quavering voice. She sang *I Dreamt that I Dwelt*, and when she came to the second verse she sang again:

> 'I dreamt that I dwelt in marble halls
>   With vassals and serfs at my side
> And of all who assembled within those walls
>   That I was the hope and the pride.

> 'I had riches too great to count, could boast
>   Of a high ancestral name,
> But I also dreamt, which pleased me most,
>   That you loved me still the same.'

But no one tried to show her her mistake; and when she had ended her song Joe was very much moved. He said that there was no time like the long ago and no music for him like poor old Balfe, whatever other people might say; and his eyes filled up so much with tears that he could not find what he was looking for and in the end he had to ask his wife to tell him where the corkscrew was.

A Painful Case

Mr James Duffy lived in Chapelizod because he wished to live as far as possible from the city of which he was a citizen and because he found all the other suburbs of Dublin mean, modern and pretentious. He lived in an old sombre house and from his windows he could look into the disused distillery or upwards along the shallow river on which Dublin is built. The lofty walls of his uncarpeted room were free from pictures. He had himself bought every article of furniture in the room: a black iron bedstead, an iron washstand, four cane chairs, a clothes-rack, a coal-scuttle, a fender and irons and a square table on which lay a double desk. A bookcase had been made in an alcove by means of shelves of white wood. The bed was clothed with white bedclothes and a black and scarlet rug covered the foot. A little hand-mirror hung above the wash-stand and during the day a white-shaded lamp stood as the sole ornament of the mantelpiece. The books on the white wooden shelves were arranged from below upwards according to bulk. A complete Wordsworth stood at one end of the lowest shelf and a copy of the *Maynooth Catechism*, sewn into the cloth cover of a notebook, stood at one end of the top shelf. Writing materials were always on the desk. In the desk lay a manuscript translation of Hauptmann's *Michael Kramer*, the stage directions of which were written in purple ink, and a little sheaf of papers held together by a brass pin. In these sheets a sentence was inscribed from time to time and, in an ironical moment, the headline of an advertisement for *Bile Beans* had been pasted on to the first sheet. On lifting the lid of the desk a faint fragrance escaped – the fragrance of new cedar-wood pencils or of a bottle of gum or of an over-ripe apple which might have been left there and forgotten.

Mr Duffy abhorred anything which betokened physical or mental disorder. A mediaeval doctor would have called him saturnine. His face, which carried the entire tale of his years, was of the brown tint of Dublin streets. On his long and rather large head grew dry black hair and a tawny moustache did not quite cover an unamiable mouth. His cheekbones also gave his face a harsh character; but there was no harshness in the eyes which, looking at the world from under their tawny eyebrows, gave the impression of a man ever alert to greet a redeeming instinct in others but often disappointed. He lived at a little distance from his body, regarding his own acts with doubtful side-glances. He had an odd autobiographical habit which led him to compose in his mind from time to time a short sentence about himself containing a subject in the third person and a predicate in the past tense. He never gave alms to beggars and walked firmly, carrying a stout hazel.

He had been for many years cashier of a private bank in Baggot Street. Every morning he came in from Chapelizod by tram. At midday he went to Dan Burke's and took his lunch – a bottle of lager beer and a small trayful of arrowroot biscuits. At four o'clock he was set free. He dined in an eating-house in George's Street where he felt himself safe from the society of Dublin's gilded youth and where there was a certain plain honesty in the bill of fare. His evenings were spent either before his landlady's piano or roaming about the outskirts of the city. His liking for Mozart's music brought him sometimes to an opera or a concert: these were the only dissipations of his life.

He had neither companions nor friends, church nor creed. He lived his spiritual life without any communion with others, visiting his relatives at Christmas and escorting them to the cemetery when they died. He performed these two social duties for old dignity's sake but conceded nothing further to the conventions which regulate the civic life. He allowed himself to think that in certain circumstances he would rob his bank but, as these circumstances never arose, his life rolled out evenly – an adventureless tale.

One evening he found himself sitting beside two ladies in the Rotunda. The house, thinly peopled and silent, gave distressing prophecy of failure. The lady who sat next him looked round at the deserted house once or twice and then said: 'What a pity there is such a poor house tonight! It's so hard on people to have to sing to empty benches.'

He took the remark as an invitation to talk. He was surprised that she seemed so little awkward. While they talked he tried to fix her permanently in his memory. When he learned that the young girl beside her was her daughter he judged her to be a year or so younger than himself. Her face, which must have been handsome, had remained intelligent. It was an oval face with strongly marked features. The eyes were very dark blue and steady. Their gaze began with a defiant note but was confused by what seemed a deliberate swoon of the pupil into the iris, revealing for an instant a temperament of great sensibility. The pupil reasserted itself quickly, this half-disclosed nature fell again under the reign of prudence, and her astrakhan jacket, moulding a bosom of a certain fullness, struck the note of defiance more definitely.

He met her again a few weeks afterwards at a concert in Earlsfort Terrace and seized the moments when her daughter's attention was diverted to become intimate. She alluded once or twice to her husband but her tone was not such as to make the allusion a warning. Her name was Mrs Sinico. Her husband's great-great-grandfather had come from Leghorn. Her husband was captain of a mercantile boat plying between Dublin and Holland; and they had one child.

Meeting her a third time by accident he found courage to make an appointment. She came. This was the first of many meetings; they met always in the evening and chose the most quiet quarters for their walks together. Mr Duffy, however, had a distaste for underhand ways and, finding that they were compelled to meet stealthily, he forced her to ask him to her house. Captain Sinico encouraged his visits, thinking that his daughter's hand was in question. He had dismissed his wife so sincerely from his gallery of pleasures that he did not suspect that anyone else would take an interest in her. As the husband was often away and the daughter out giving music lessons Mr Duffy had many opportunities of enjoying the lady's society. Neither he nor she had had any such adventure before and neither was conscious of any incongruity. Little by little he entangled his thoughts with hers. He lent her books, provided her with ideas, shared his intellectual life with her. She listened to all.

Sometimes in return for his theories she gave out some fact of her own life. With almost maternal solicitude she urged him to let his nature open to the full: she became his confessor. He told her that for some time he had assisted at the meetings of an Irish Socialist Party where he had felt himself a unique figure amidst a score of sober workmen in a garret lit by an inefficient oil-lamp. When the party had divided into three sections, each under its own leader and in its own garret, he had discontinued his attendances. The workmen's discussions, he said, were too timorous; the interest they took in the question of wages was inordinate. He felt that they were hard-featured realists and that they resented an exactitude which was the produce of a leisure not within their reach. No social revolution, he told her, would be likely to strike Dublin for some centuries.

She asked him why did he not write out his thoughts. For what, he asked her, with careful scorn. To compete with phrase-mongers, incapable of thinking consecutively for sixty seconds? To submit himself to the criticisms of an obtuse middle class which entrusted its morality to policemen and its fine arts to impresarios?

He went often to her little cottage outside Dublin; often they spent their evenings alone. Little by little, as their thoughts entangled, they spoke of subjects less remote. Her companionship was like a warm soil about an exotic. Many times she allowed the dark to fall upon them, refraining from lighting the lamp. The dark discreet room, their isolation, the music that still vibrated in their ears united them. This union exalted him, wore away the rough edges of his character, emotionalised his mental life. Sometimes he caught himself listening to the sound of his own voice. He thought that in her eyes he would ascend to an angelical stature; and, as he attached the fervent nature of his companion more and more closely to him, he heard the strange impersonal voice which he recognised as his own, insisting on the soul's incurable loneliness. We cannot give ourselves, it said: we are our own. The end of these discourses was that one night during which she had shown every sign of unusual excitement, Mrs Sinico caught up his hand passionately and pressed it to her cheek.

Mr Duffy was very much surprised. Her interpretation of his words disillusioned him. He did not visit her for a week; then he wrote to her asking her to meet him. As he did not wish their last interview to be troubled by the influence of their ruined confessional they met in a little cake-shop near the Parkgate. It was cold autumn weather but in spite of the cold they wandered up and down the roads of the Park for nearly three hours. They agreed to break off their intercourse: every bond, he said, is a bond to sorrow. When they came out of the Park they walked in silence towards the tram; but here she began to tremble so violently that, fearing another collapse on her part, he bade her goodbye quickly and left her. A few days later he received a parcel containing his books and music.

Four years passed. Mr Duffy returned to his even way of life. His room still bore witness of the orderliness of his mind. Some new pieces of music encumbered the music-stand in the lower room and on his shelves stood two volumes by Nietzsche: *Thus Spake Zarathustra* and *The Gay Science*.He wrote seldom in the sheaf of papers which lay in his desk. One of his sentences, written two months after his last interview with Mrs Sinico, read: Love between man and man is impossible because there must not be sexual intercourse and friendship between man and woman is impossible because there must be sexual intercourse. He kept away from concerts lest he should meet her. His father died; the junior partner of the bank retired. And still every morning he went into the city by tram and every evening walked home from the city after having dined moderately in George's Street and read the evening paper for dessert.

One evening as he was about to put a morsel of corned beef and cabbage into his mouth his hand stopped. His eyes fixed themselves on a paragraph in the evening paper which he had propped against the water-carafe. He replaced the morsel of food on his plate and read the paragraph attentively. Then he drank a glass of water, pushed his plate to one side, doubled the paper down before him between his elbows and read the paragraph over and over again. The cabbage began to deposit a cold white grease on his plate. The girl came over to him to ask was his dinner not properly cooked. He said it was very good and ate a few mouthfuls of it with difficulty. Then he paid his bill and went out.

He walked along quickly through the November twilight, his stout hazel stick striking the ground regularly, the fringe of the buff *Mail* peeping out of a side-pocket of his tight reefer overcoat. On the lonely road which leads from the Parkgate to Chapelizod he slackened his pace. His stick struck the ground less emphatically and his breath, issuing irregularly, almost with a sighing sound, condensed in the wintry air. When he reached his house he went up at once to his bedroom and, taking the paper from his pocket, read the paragraph again by the failing light of the window. He read it not aloud, but moving his lips as a priest does when he reads the prayers *Secreto*. This was the paragraph:

DEATH OF A LADY AT SYDNEY PARADE
a painful case

Today at the City of Dublin Hospital the Deputy Coroner (in the absence of Mr Leverett) held an inquest on the body of Mrs Emily Sinico, aged forty-three years, who was killed at Sydney Parade Station yesterday evening. The evidence showed that the deceased lady, while attempting to cross the line, was knocked down by the engine of the ten o'clock slow train from Kingstown, thereby sustaining injuries of the head and right side which led to her death.

James Lennon, driver of the engine, stated that he had been in the employment of the railway company for fifteen years. On hearing the guard's whistle he set the train in motion and a second or two afterwards brought it to rest in response to loud cries. The train was going slowly.

P. Dunne, railway porter, stated that as the train was about to start he observed a woman attempting to cross the lines. He ran towards her and shouted, but, before he could reach her, she was caught by the buffer of the engine and fell to the ground.

A juror. 'You saw the lady fall?'

Witness. 'Yes.'

Police Sergeant Croly deposed that when he arrived he found the deceased lying on the platform apparently dead. He had the body taken to the waiting-room pending the arrival of the ambulance.

Constable 57E corroborated.

Dr Halpin, assistant house surgeon of the City of Dublin Hospital, stated that the deceased had two lower ribs fractured and had sustained severe contusions of the right shoulder. The right side of the head had been injured in the fall. The injuries were not sufficient to have caused death in a normal person. Death, in his opinion, had been probably due to shock and sudden failure of the heart's action.

Mr H. B. Patterson Finlay, on behalf of the railway company, expressed his deep regret at the accident. The company had always taken every precaution to prevent people crossing the lines except by the bridges, both by placing notices in every station and by the use of patent spring gates at level crossings. The deceased had been in the habit of crossing the lines late at night from platform to platform and, in view of certain other circumstances of the case, he did not think the railway officials were to blame.

Captain Sinico, of Leoville, Sydney Parade, husband of the deceased, also gave evidence. He stated that the deceased was his wife. He was not in Dublin at the time of the accident as he had arrived only that morning from Rotterdam. They had been married for twenty-two years and had lived happily until about two years ago when his wife began to be rather intemperate in her habits.

Miss Mary Sinico said that of late her mother had been in the habit of going out at night to buy spirits. She, witness, had often tried to reason with her mother and had induced her to join a League. She was not at home until an hour after the accident.

The jury returned a verdict in accordance with the medical evidence and exonerated Lennon from all blame.

The Deputy Coroner said it was a most painful case, and expressed great sympathy with Captain Sinico and his daughter. He urged on the railway company to take strong measures to prevent the possibility of similar accidents in the future. No blame attached to anyone.

Mr Duffy raised his eyes from the paper and gazed out of his window on the cheerless evening landscape. The river lay quiet beside the empty distillery and from time to time a light appeared in some house on the Lucan road. What an end! The whole narrative of her death revolted him and it revolted him to think that he had ever spoken to her of what he held sacred. The threadbare phrases, the inane expressions of sympathy, the cautious words of a reporter won over to conceal the details of a common-place vulgar death attacked his stomach. Not merely had she degraded herself; she had degraded him. He saw the squalid tract of her vice, miserable and malodorous. His soul's companion! He thought of the hobbling wretches whom he had seen carrying cans and bottles to be filled by the barman. Just God, what an end! Evidently she had been unfit to live, without any strength of purpose, an easy prey to habits, one of the wrecks on which civilisation has been reared. But that she could have sunk so low! Was it possible he had deceived himself so utterly about her? He remembered her outburst of that night and interpreted it in a harsher sense than he had ever done. He had no difficulty now in approving of the course he had taken.

As the light failed and his memory began to wander he thought her hand touched his. The shock which had first attacked his stomach was now attacking his nerves. He put on his overcoat and hat quickly and went out. The cold air met him on the threshold; it crept into the sleeves of his coat. When he came to the public-house at Chapelizod Bridge he went in and ordered a hot punch.

The proprietor served him obsequiously but did not venture to talk. There were five or six workingmen in the shop discussing the value of a gentleman's estate in County Kildare. They drank at intervals from their huge pint tumblers and smoked, spitting often on the floor and sometimes dragging the sawdust over their spits with their heavy boots. Mr Duffy sat on his stool and gazed at them, without seeing or hearing them. After a while they went out and he called for another punch. He sat a long time over it. The shop was very quiet. The proprietor sprawled on the counter reading the *Herald* and yawning. Now and again a tram was heard swishing along the lonely road outside.

As he sat there, living over his life with her and evoking alternately the two images in which he now conceived her, he realised that she was dead, that she had ceased to exist, that she had become a memory. He began to feel ill at ease. He asked himself what else could he have done. He could not have carried on a comedy of deception with her; he could not have lived with her openly. He had done what seemed to him best. How was he to blame? Now that she was gone he understood how lonely her life must have been, sitting night after night alone in that room. His life would be lonely too until he, too, died, ceased to exist, became a memory – if anyone remembered him.

It was after nine o'clock when he left the shop. The night was cold and gloomy. He entered the Park by the first gate and walked along under the gaunt trees. He walked through the bleak alleys where they had walked four years before. She seemed to be near him in the darkness. At moments he seemed to feel her voice touch his ear, her hand touch his. He stood still to listen. Why had he withheld life from her? Why had he sentenced her to death? He felt his moral nature falling to pieces.

When he gained the crest of the Magazine Hill he halted and looked along the river towards Dublin, the lights of which burned redly and hospitably in the cold night. He looked down the slope and, at the base, in the shadow of the wall of the Park, he saw some human figures lying. Those venal and furtive loves filled him with despair. He gnawed the rectitude of his life; he felt that he had been outcast from life's feast. One human being had seemed to love him and he had denied her life and happiness: he had sentenced her to ignominy, a death of shame. He knew that the prostrate creatures down by the wall were watching him and wished him gone. No one wanted him; he was outcast from life's feast. He turned his eyes to the grey gleaming river, winding along towards Dublin. Beyond the river he saw a goods train winding out of Kingsbridge Station, like a worm with a fiery head winding through the darkness, obstinately and laboriously. It passed slowly out of sight; but still he heard in his ears the laborious drone of the engine reiterating the syllables of her name.

He turned back the way he had come, the rhythm of the engine pounding in his ears He began to doubt the reality of what memory told him. He halted under a tree and allowed the rhythm to die away. He could not feel her near him in the darkness nor her voice touch his ear. He waited for some minutes listening. He could hear nothing: the night was perfectly silent. He listened again: perfectly silent. He felt that he was alone.

Ivy Day in the Committee Room

Old Jack raked the cinders together with a piece of cardboard and spread them judiciously over the whitening dome of coals. When the dome was thinly covered his face lapsed into darkness but, as he set himself to fan the fire again, his crouching shadow ascended the opposite wall and his face slowly re-emerged into light. It was an old man's face, very bony and hairy. The moist blue eyes blinked at the fire and the moist mouth fell open at times, munching once or twice mechanically when it closed. When the cinders had caught he laid the piece of cardboard against the wall, sighed and said: 'That's better now, Mr O'Connor.'

Mr O'Connor, a grey-haired young man, whose face was disfigured by many blotches and pimples, had just brought the tobacco for a cigarette into a shapely cylinder but when spoken to he undid his handiwork meditatively. Then he began to roll the tobacco again meditatively and after a moment's thought decided to lick the paper.

'Did Mr Tierney say when he'd be back?' he asked in a husky falsetto.

'He didn't say.'

Mr O'Connor put his cigarette into his mouth and began to search his pockets. He took out a pack of thin pasteboard cards.

'I'll get you a match,' said the old man.

'Never mind, this'll do,' said Mr O'Connor.

He selected one of the cards and read what was printed on it:

Municipal Elections
ROYAL EXCHANGE WARD
Mr Richard J. Tierney, P.L.G., respectfully solicits the favour of your vote and influence at the coming election in the Royal Exchange Ward.

Mr O'Connor had been engaged by Tierney's agent to canvass one part of the ward but, as the weather was inclement and his boots let in the wet, he spent a great part of the day sitting by the fire in the Committee Room in Wicklow Street with Jack, the old caretaker. They had been sitting thus since the short day had grown dark. It was the sixth of October, dismal and cold out of doors.

Mr O'Connor tore a strip off the card and, lighting it, lit his cigarette. As he did so the flame lit up a leaf of dark glossy ivy in the lapel of his coat. The old man watched him attentively and then, taking up the piece of cardboard again, began to fan the fire slowly while his companion smoked.

'Ah, yes,' he said, continuing, 'it's hard to know what way to bring up children. Now who'd think he'd turn out like that! I sent him to the Christian Brothers and I done what I could for him, and there he goes boozing about. I tried to make him someway decent.'

He replaced the cardboard wearily.

'Only I'm an old man now I'd change his tune for him. I'd take the stick to his back and beat him while I could stand over him – as I done many a time before. The mother, you know, she cocks him up with this and that . . . '

'That's what ruins children,' said Mr O'Connor.

'To be sure it is,' said the old man. 'And little thanks you get for it, only impudence. He takes th'upper hand of me whenever he sees I've a sup taken. What's the world coming to when sons speaks that way to their fathers?'

'What age is he?' said Mr O'Connor.

'Nineteen,' said the old man.

'Why don't you put him to something?'

'Sure, amn't I never done at the drunken bowsy ever since he left school? "I won't keep you," I says. "You must get a job for yourself." But, sure, it's worse whenever he gets a job; he drinks it all.'

Mr O'Connor shook his head in sympathy, and the old man fell silent, gazing into the fire. Someone opened the door of the room and called out : 'Hello! Is this a Freemasons' meeting?'

'Who's that?' said the old man.

'What are you doing in the dark?' asked a voice.

'Is that you, Hynes?' asked Mr O'Connor.

'Yes. What are you doing in the dark?' said Mr Hynes, advancing into the light of the fire.

He was a tall, slender young man with a light brown moustache. Imminent little drops of rain hung at the brim of his hat and the collar of his jacket-coat was turned up.

'Well, Mat,' he said to Mr O'Connor, 'how goes it?'

Mr O'Connor shook his head. The old man left the hearth, and after stumbling about the room returned with two candlesticks which he thrust one after the other into the fire and carried to the table. A denuded room came into view and the fire lost all its cheerful colour. The walls of the room were bare except for a copy of an election address. In the middle of the room was a small table on which papers were heaped.

Mr Hynes leaned against the mantelpiece and asked: 'Has he paid you yet?'

'Not yet,' said Mr O'Connor. 'I hope to God he'll not leave us in the lurch tonight.'

Mr Hynes laughed.

'O, he'll pay you. Never fear,' he said.

'I hope he'll look smart about it if he means business,' said Mr O'Connor.

'What do you think, Jack?' said Mr Hynes satirically to the old man.

The old man returned to his seat by the fire, saying: 'It isn't but he has it, anyway. Not like the other tinker.'

'What other tinker?' said Mr Hynes.

'Colgan,' said the old man scornfully.

'It is because Colgan's a working-man you say that? What's the difference between a good honest bricklayer and a publican – eh? Hasn't the working-man as good a right to be in the Corporation as anyone else – ay, and a better right than those shoneens that are always hat in hand before any fellow with a handle to his name? Isn't that so, Mat?' said Mr Hynes, addressing Mr O'Connor.

'I think you're right,' said Mr O'Connor.

'One man is a plain honest man with no hunker-sliding about him. He goes in to represent the labour classes. This fellow you're working for only wants to get some job or other.'

'Of course, the working-classes should be represented,' said the old man.

'The working-man,' said Mr Hynes, 'gets all kicks and no halfpence. But it's labour produces everything. The working-man is not looking for fat jobs for his sons and nephews and cousins. The working-man is not going to drag the honour of Dublin in the mud to please a German monarch.'

'How's that?' said the old man.

'Don't you know they want to present an address of welcome to Edward Rex if he comes here next year? What do we want kowtowing to a foreign king?'

'Our man won't vote for the address,' said Mr O'Connor. 'He goes in on the Nationalist ticket.'

'Won't he?' said Mr Hynes. 'Wait till you see whether he will or not. I know him. Is it Tricky Dicky Tierney?'

'By God! perhaps you're right, Joe,' said Mr O'Connor. 'Anyway, I wish he'd turn up with the spondulics.'

The three men fell silent. The old man began to rake more cinders together. Mr Hynes took off his hat, shook it and then turned down the collar of his coat, displaying, as he did so, an ivy leaf in the lapel.

'If this man was alive,' he said, pointing to the leaf, 'we'd have no talk of an address of welcome.'

'That's true,' said Mr O'Connor.

'Musha, God be with them times!' said the old man. 'There was some life in it then.'

The room was silent again. Then a bustling little man with a snuffling nose and very cold ears pushed in the door. He walked over quickly to the fire, rubbing his hands as if he intended to produce a spark from them.

'No money, boys,' he said.

'Sit down here, Mr Henchy,' said the old man, offering him his chair.

'O, don't stir, Jack, don't stir,' said Mr Henchy.

He nodded curtly to Mr Hynes and sat down on the chair which the old man vacated.

'Did you serve Aungier Street?' he asked Mr O'Connor.

'Yes,' said Mr O'Connor, beginning to search his pockets for memoranda.

'Did you call on Grimes?'

'I did.'

'Well? How does he stand?'

'He wouldn't promise. He said: "I won't tell anyone what way I'm going to vote." But I think he'll be all right.'

'Why so?'

'He asked me who the nominators were; and I told him. I mentioned Father Burke's name. I think it'll be all right.'

Mr Henchy began to snuffle and to rub his hands over the fire at a terrific speed. Then he said: 'For the love of God, Jack, bring us a bit of coal. There must be some left.'

The old man went out of the room.

'It's no go,' said Mr Henchy, shaking his head. 'I asked the little shoeboy, but he said: "O, now, Mr Henchy, when I see the work going on properly I won't forget you, you may be sure." Mean little tinker! 'Usha, how could he be anything else?'

'What did I tell you, Mat?' said Mr Hynes. 'Tricky Dicky Tierney.'

'O, he was tricky as they make 'em,' said Mr Henchy. 'He hasn't got those little pigs' eyes for nothing. Blast his soul! Couldn't he pay up like a man instead of: "O, now, Mr Henchy, I must speak to Mr Fanning . . . I've spent a lot of money"? Mean little schoolboy of hell! I suppose he forgets the time his little old father kept the hand-me-down shop in Mary's Lane.'

'But is that a fact?' asked Mr O'Connor.

'God, yes,' said Mr Henchy. 'Did you never hear that? And the men used to go in on Sunday morning before the houses were open to buy a waistcoat or a trousers – moya! But Tricky Dicky's little old father always had a tricky little black bottle up in a corner. Do you mind now? That's that. That's where he first saw the light.'

The old man returned with a few lumps of coal which he placed here and there on the fire.

'That's a nice how-do-you-do,' said Mr O'Connor. 'How does he expect us to work for him if he won't stump up?' 'I can't help it,' said Mr Henchy. 'I expect to find the bailiffs in the hall when I go home.'

Mr Hynes laughed and, shoving himself away from the mantelpiece with the aid of his shoulders, made ready to leave.

'It'll be all right when King Eddie comes,' he said. 'Well, boys, I'm off for the present. See you later. 'Bye, 'bye.'

He went out of the room slowly. Neither Mr Henchy nor the old man said anything, but, just as the door was closing, Mr O'Connor, who had been staring moodily into the fire, called out suddenly: ' 'Bye, Joe.'

Mr Henchy waited a few moments, and then nodded in the direction of the door.

'Tell me,' he said across the fire, 'what brings our friend in here? What does he want?'

' 'Usha, poor Joe!' said Mr O'Connor, throwing the end of his cigarette into the fire, 'he's hard up, like the rest of us.'

Mr Henchy snuffled vigorously and spat so copiously that he nearly put out the fire, which uttered a hissing protest.

'To tell you my private and candid opinion,' he said, 'I think he's a man from the other camp. He's a spy of Colgan's, if you ask me. Just go round and try and find out how they're getting on. They won't suspect you. Do you twig?'

'Ah, poor Joe is a decent skin,' said Mr O'Connor.

'His father was a decent, respectable man,' Mr Henchy admitted. 'Poor old Larry Hynes! Many a good turn he did in his day! But I'm greatly afraid our friend is not nineteen carat. Damn it, I can understand a fellow being hard up, but what I can't understand is a fellow sponging. Couldn't he have some spark of manhood about him?'

'He doesn't get a warm welcome from me when he comes,' said the old man. 'Let him work for his own side and not come spying around here.'

'I don't know,' said Mr O'Connor dubiously, as he took out cigarette-papers and tobacco. 'I think Joe Hynes is a straight man. He's a clever chap, too, with the pen. Do you remember that thing he wrote . . . ?'

'Some of these hillsiders and fenians are a bit too clever if you ask me,' said Mr Henchy. 'Do you know what my private and candid opinion is about some of those little jokers? I believe half of them are in the pay of the Castle.'

'There's no knowing,' said the old man.

'O, but I know it for a fact,' said Mr Henchy. 'They're Castle hacks . . . I don't say Hynes . . . No, damn it, I think he's a stroke above that . . . But there's a certain little nobleman with a cock-eye – you know the patriot I'm alluding to?'

Mr O'Connor nodded.

'There's a lineal descendant of Major Sirr for you if you like! O, the heart's blood of a patriot! That's a fellow now that'd sell his country for fourpence – ay – and go down on his bended knees and thank the Almighty Christ he had a country to sell.'

There was a knock at the door.

'Come in!' said Mr Henchy.

A person resembling a poor clergyman or a poor actor appeared in the doorway. His black clothes were tightly buttoned on his short body and it was impossible to say whether he wore a clergyman's collar or a layman's, because the collar of his shabby frock-coat, the uncovered buttons of which reflected the candlelight, was turned up about his neck. He wore a round hat of hard black felt. His face, shining with raindrops, had the appearance of damp yellow cheese save where two rosy spots indicated the cheekbones. He opened his very long mouth suddenly to express disappointment and at the same time opened wide his very bright blue eyes to express pleasure and surprise.

'O Father Keon!' said Mr Henchy, jumping up from his chair. 'Is that you? Come in!'

'O, no, no, no!' said Father Keon quickly, pursing his lips as if he were addressing a child.

'Won't you come in and sit down?'

'No, no, no!' said Father Keon, speaking in a discreet, indulgent, velvety voice. 'Don't let me disturb you now! I'm just looking for Mr Fanning . . .'

'He's round at the *Black Eagle*,' said Mr Henchy. 'But won't you come in and sit down a minute?'

'No, no, thank you. It was just a little business matter,' said Father Keon. 'Thank you, indeed.'

He retreated from the doorway and Mr Henchy, seizing one of the candlesticks, went to the door to light him downstairs.

'O, don't trouble, I beg!'

'No, but the stairs is so dark.'

'No, no, I can see . . . Thank you, indeed.'

'Are you right now?'

'All right, thanks . . . Thanks.'

Mr Henchy returned with the candlestick and put it on the table. He sat down again at the fire. There was silence for a few moments.

'Tell me, John,' said Mr O'Connor, lighting his cigarette with another pasteboard card.

'Hm?'

'What he is exactly?'

'Ask me an easier one,' said Mr Henchy.

'Fanning and himself seem to me very thick. They're often in Cavanagh's together. Is he a priest at all?'

' 'Mmmyes, I believe so . . . I think he's what you call a black sheep. We haven't many of them, thank God! but we have a few . . . He's an unfortunate man of some kind . . . '

'And how does he knock it out?' asked Mr O'Connor.

'That's another mystery.'

'Is he attached to any chapel or church or institution or – '

'No,' said Mr Henchy, 'I think he's travelling on his own account . . . God forgive me,' he added, 'I thought he was the dozen of stout.'

'Is there any chance of a drink itself?' asked Mr O'Connor.

'I'm dry too,' said the old man.

'I asked that little shoeboy three times,' said Mr Henchy, 'would he send up a dozen of stout. I asked him again now, but he was leaning on the counter in his shirt-sleeves having a deep goster with Alderman Cowley.'

'Why didn't you remind him?' said Mr O'Connor.

'Well, I couldn't go over while he was talking to Alderman Cowley. I just waited till I caught his eye, and said: "About that little matter I was speaking to you about . . . " "That'll be all right, Mr H.," he said. Yerra, sure the little hop-o'-my thumb has forgotten all about it.'

'There's some deal on in that quarter,' said Mr O'Connor thoughtfully. 'I saw the three of them hard at it yesterday at Suffolk Street corner.'

'I think I know the little game they're at,' said Mr Henchy. 'You must owe the City Fathers money nowadays if you want to be made Lord Mayor. Then they'll make you Lord Mayor. By God! I'm thinking seriously of becoming a City Father myself. What do you think? Would I do for the job?'

Mr O'Connor laughed.

'So far as owing money goes . . .'

'Driving out of the Mansion House,' said Mr Henchy, 'in all my vermin, with Jack here standing up behind me in a powdered wig – eh?'

'And make me your private secretary, John.'

'Yes. And I'll make Father Keon my private chaplain. We'll have a family party.'

'Faith, Mr Henchy,' said the old man, 'you'd keep up better style than some of them. I was talking one day to old Keegan, the porter. "And how do you like your new master, Pat?" says I to him. "You haven't much entertaining now," says I. "Entertaining!" says he. "He'd live on the smell of an oil-rag." And do you know what he told me? Now, I declare to God, I didn't believe him.'

'What?' said Mr Henchy and Mr O'Connor.

'He told me: "What do you think of a Lord Mayor of Dublin sending out for a pound of chops for his dinner? How's that for high living?" says he. "Wisha! wisha," says I. "A pound of chops," says he, "coming into the Mansion House." "Wisha!" says I, "what kind of people is going at all now?" '

At this point there was a knock at the door, and a boy put in his head.

'What is it?' said the old man.

'From the *Black Eagle*,' said the boy, walking in sideways and depositing a basket on the floor with a noise of shaken bottles.

The old man helped the boy to transfer the bottles from the basket to the table and counted the full tally. After the transfer the boy put his basket on his arm and asked: 'Any bottles?'

'What bottles?' said the old man.

'Won't you let us drink them first?' said Mr Henchy.

'I was told to ask for bottles.'

'Come back tomorrow,' said the old man.

'Here, boy!' said Mr Henchy, 'will you run over to O'Farrell's and ask him to lend us a corkscrew – for Mr Henchy, say. Tell him we won't keep it a minute. Leave the basket there.'

The boy went out and Mr Henchy began to rub his hands cheerfully, saying: 'Ah, well, he's not so bad after all. He's as good as his word, anyhow.'

'There's no tumblers,' said the old man.

'O, don't let that trouble you, Jack,' said Mr Henchy. 'Many's the good man before now drank out of the bottle.'

'Anyway, it's better than nothing,' said Mr O'Connor.

'He's not a bad sort,' said Mr Henchy, 'only Fanning has such a loan of him. He means well, you know, in his own tinpot way.'

The boy came back with the corkscrew. The old man opened three bottles and was handing back the corkscrew when Mr Henchy said to the boy,

'Would you like a drink, boy?'

'If you please, sir,' said the boy.

The old man opened another bottle grudgingly, and handed it to the boy.

'What age are you?' he asked.

'Seventeen,' said the boy.

As the old man said nothing further, the boy took the bottle, said: 'Here's my best respects, sir, to Mr Henchy,' drank the contents, put the bottle back on the table and wiped his mouth with his sleeve. Then he took up the corkscrew and went out of the door sideways, muttering some form of salutation.

'That's the way it begins,' said the old man.

'The thin edge of the wedge,' said Mr Henchy. The old man distributed the three bottles which he had opened and the men drank from them simultaneously. After having drank each placed his bottle on the mantelpiece within hand's reach and drew in a long breath of satisfaction.

'Well, I did a good day's work today,' said Mr Henchy, after a pause.

'That so, John?'

'Yes. I got him one or two sure things in Dawson Street, Crofton and myself. Between ourselves, you know, Crofton (he's a decent chap, of course), but he's not worth a damn as a canvasser. He hasn't a word to throw to a dog. He stands and looks at the people while I do the talking.'

Here two men entered the room. One of them was a very fat man, whose blue serge clothes seemed to be in danger of falling from his sloping figure. He had a big face which resembled a young ox's face in expression, staring blue eyes and a grizzled moustache. The other man, who was much younger and frailer, had a thin, clean-shaven face. He wore a very high double collar and a wide-brimmed bowler hat.

'Hello, Crofton!' said Mr Henchy to the fat man. 'Talk of the devil . . . '

'Where did the booze come from?' asked the young man. 'Did the cow calve?'

'O, of course, Lyons spots the drink first thing!' said Mr O'Connor, laughing.

'Is that the way you chaps canvas,' said Mr Lyons, 'and Crofton and I out in the cold and rain looking for votes?'

'Why, blast your soul,' said Mr Henchy, 'I'd get more votes in five minutes than you two'd get in a week.'

'Open two bottles of stout, Jack,' said Mr O'Connor.

'How can I?' said the old man, 'when there's no corkscrew?'

'Wait now, wait now!' said Mr Henchy, getting up quickly. 'Did you ever see this little trick?'

He took two bottles from the table and, carrying them to the fire, put them on the hob. Then he sat down again by the fire and took another drink from his bottle. Mr Lyons sat on the edge of the table, pushed his hat towards the nape of his neck and began to swing his legs.

'Which is my bottle?' he asked.

'This, lad,' said Mr Henchy.

Mr Crofton sat down on a box and looked fixedly at the other bottle on the hob. He was silent for two reasons. The first reason, sufficient in itself, was that he had nothing to say; the second reason was that he considered his companions beneath him. He had been a canvasser for Wilkins, the Conservative, but when the Conservatives had withdrawn their man and, choosing the lesser of two evils, given their support to the Nationalist candidate, he had been engaged to work for Mr Tierney.

In a few minutes an apologetic 'Pok!' was heard as the cork flew out of Mr Lyons' bottle. Mr Lyons jumped off the table, went to the fire, took his bottle and carried it back to the table.

'I was just telling them, Crofton,' said Mr Henchy, 'that we got a good few votes today.'

'Who did you get?' asked Mr Lyons.

'Well, I got Parkes for one, and I got Atkinson for two, and I got Ward of Dawson Street. Fine old chap he is, too – regular old toff, old Conservative! "But isn't your candidate a Nationalist? " said he. "He's a respectable man," said I. "He's in favour of whatever will benefit this country. He's a big ratepayer," I said. "He has extensive house property in the city and three places of business and isn't it to his own advantage to keep down the rates? He's a prominent and respected citizen," said I, "and a Poor Law Guardian, and he doesn't belong to any party, good, bad, or indifferent." That's the way to talk to 'em.'

'And what about the address to the King?' said Mr Lyons, after drinking and smacking his lips.

'Listen to me,' said Mr Henchy. 'What we want in this country, as I said to old Ward, is capital. The King's coming here will mean an influx of money into this country. The citizens of Dublin will benefit by it. Look at all the factories down by the quays there, idle! Look at all the money there is in the country if we only worked the old industries, the mills, the ship-building yards and factories. It's capital we want.'

'But look here, John,' said Mr O'Connor. 'Why should we welcome the King of England? Didn't Parnell himself . . . '

'Parnell,' said Mr Henchy, 'is dead. Now, here's the way I look at it. Here's this chap come to the throne after his old mother keeping him out of it till the man was grey. He's a man of the world, and he means well by us. He's a jolly fine decent fellow, if you ask me, and no damn nonsense about him. He just says to himself: "The old one never went to see these wild Irish. By Christ, I'll go myself and see what they're like." And are we going to insult the man when he comes over here on a friendly visit? Eh? Isn't that right, Crofton?'

Mr Crofton nodded his head.

'But after all now,' said Mr Lyons argumentatively, 'King Edward's life, you know, is not the very . . . '

'Let bygones be bygones,' said Mr Henchy. 'I admire the man personally. He's just an ordinary knockabout like you and me. He's fond of his glass of grog and he's a bit of a rake, perhaps, and he's a good sportsman. Damn it, can't we Irish play fair?'

'That's all very fine,' said Mr Lyons. 'But look at the case of Parnell now.'

'In the name of God,' said Mr Henchy, 'where's the analogy between the two cases?'

'What I mean,' said Mr Lyons, 'is we have our ideals. Why, now, would we welcome a man like that? Do you think now after what he did Parnell was a fit man to lead us? And why, then, would we do it for Edward the Seventh?'

'This is Parnell's anniversary,' said Mr O'Connor, 'and don't let us stir up any bad blood. We all respect him now that he's dead and gone – even the Conservatives,' he added, turning to Mr Crofton.

Pok! The tardy cork flew out of Mr Crofton's bottle. Mr Crofton got up from his box and went to the fire. As he returned with his capture he said in a deep voice: 'Our side of the house respects him, because he was a gentleman.'

'Right you are, Crofton!' said Mr Henchy fiercely. 'He was the only man that could keep that bag of cats in order. "Down, ye dogs! Lie down, ye curs! " That's the way he treated them. Come in Joe! Come in!' he called out, catching sight of Mr Hynes in the doorway.

Mr Hynes came in slowly.

'Open another bottle of stout, Jack,' said Mr Henchy. 'O, I forgot there's no corkscrew! Here, show me one here and I'll put it at the fire.'

The old man handed him another bottle and he placed it on the hob.

'Sit down, Joe,' said Mr O'Connor, 'we're just talking about the Chief.'

'Ay,' said Mr Henchy.

Mr Hynes sat on the side of the table near Mr Lyons, but said nothing.

'There's one of them, anyhow,' said Mr Henchy, 'that didn't renege him. By God, I'll say for you, Joe! No, by God, you stuck to him like a man!'

'O, Joe,' said Mr O'Connor suddenly. 'Give us that thing you wrote – do you remember? Have you got it on you?'

'O, ay!' said Mr Henchy. 'Give us that. Did you ever hear that, Crofton? Listen to this now: splendid thing.'

'Go on,' said Mr O'Connor. 'Fire away, Joe.'

Mr Hynes did not seem to remember at once the piece to which they were alluding, but, after reflecting a while, he said: 'O, that thing is it . . . Sure, that's old now.'

'Out with it, man!' said Mr O'Connor.

' 'Sh, 'sh,' said Mr Henchy. 'Now, Joe!'

Mr Hynes hesitated a little longer. Then amid the silence he took off his hat, laid it on the table and stood up. He seemed to be rehearsing the piece in his mind. After a rather long pause he announced:

The Death of Parnell
6th October, 1891

He cleared his throat once or twice and then began to recite:

> 'He is dead. Our Uncrowned King is dead.
>   O, Erin, mourn with grief and woe
> For he lies dead whom the fell gang
>   Of modern hypocrites laid low.
>
> He lies slain by the coward hounds
>   He raised to glory from the mire;
> And Erin's hopes and Erin's dreams
>   Perish upon her monarch's pyre.
>
> In palace, cabin or in cot
>   The Irish heart where'er it be
> Is bowed with woe – for he is gone
>   Who would have wrought her destiny.

He would have had his Erin famed,
   The green flag gloriously unfurled,
Her statesmen, bards and warriors raised
   Before the nations of the World.

He dreamed (alas, 'twas but a dream!)
   Of Liberty: but as he strove
To clutch that idol, treachery
   Sundered him from the thing he loved.

Shame on the coward, caitiff hands
   That smote their Lord or with a kiss
Betrayed him to the rabble-rout
   Of fawning priests – no friends of his.

May everlasting shame consume
   The memory of those who tried
To befoul and smear the exalted name
   Of one who spurned them in his pride.

He fell as fall the mighty ones,
   Nobly undaunted to the last,
And death has now united him
   With Erin's heroes of the past.

No sound of strife disturb his sleep!
   Calmly he rests: no human pain
Or high ambition spurs him now
   The peaks of glory to attain.

They had their way: they laid him low.
   But Erin, list, his spirit may
Rise, like the Phoenix from the flames,
   When breaks the dawning of the day,

The day that brings us Freedom's reign
   And on that day may Erin well
Pledge in the cup she lifts to Joy
   One grief – the memory of Parnell.'

Mr Hynes sat down again on the table. When he had finished his recitation there was a silence and then a burst of clapping: even Mr Lyons clapped. The applause continued for a little time. When it had ceased all the auditors drank from their bottles in silence.

Pok! The cork flew out of Mr Hynes' bottle, but Mr Hynes remained sitting flushed and bareheaded on the table. He did not seem to have heard the invitation.

'Good man, Joe!' said Mr O'Connor, taking out his cigarette papers and pouch the better to hide his emotion.

'What do you think of that, Crofton?' cried Mr Henchy. 'Isn't that fine? What?'

Mr Crofton said that it was a very fine piece of writing.

A Mother

Mr Holohan, assistant secretary of the *Eire Abu* Society, had been walking up and down Dublin for nearly a month, with his hands and pockets full of dirty pieces of paper, arranging about the series of concerts. He had a game leg and for this his friends called him Hoppy Holohan. He walked up and down constantly, stood by the hour at street corners arguing the point and made notes; but in the end it was Mrs Kearney who arranged everything.

Miss Devlin had become Mrs Kearney out of spite. She had been educated in a high-class convent, where she had learned French and music. As she was naturally pale and unbending in manner she made few friends at school. When she came to the age of marriage she was sent out to many houses, where her playing and ivory manners were much admired. She sat amid the chilly circle of her accomplishments, waiting for some suitor to brave it and offer her a brilliant life. But the young men whom she met were ordinary and she gave them no encouragement, trying to console her romantic desires by eating a great deal of Turkish Delight in secret. However, when she drew near the limit and her friends began to loosen their tongues about her, she silenced them by marrying Mr Kearney, who was a bootmaker on Ormond Quay.

He was much older than she. His conversation, which was serious, took place at intervals in his great brown beard. After the first year of married life, Mrs Kearney perceived that such a man would wear better than a romantic person, but she never put her own romantic ideas away. He was sober, thrifty and pious; he went to the altar every first Friday, sometimes with her, oftener by himself. But she never weakened in her religion and was a good wife to him. At some party in a strange house when she lifted her eyebrow ever so slightly, he stood up to take his leave and, when his cough troubled him, she put the eider-down quilt over his feet and made a strong rum punch. For his part, he was a model father. By paying a small sum every week into a society, he ensured for both his daughters a dowry of one hundred pounds each when they came to the age of twenty-four. He sent the older daughter, Kathleen, to a good convent, where she learned French and music, and afterward paid her fees at the Academy. Every year in the month of July Mrs Kearney found occasion to say to some friend: 'My good man is packing us off to Skerries for a few weeks.'

If it was not Skerries it was Howth or Greystones.

When the Irish Revival began to be appreciable Mrs Kearney determined to take advantage of her daughter's name and brought an Irish teacher to the house. Kathleen and her sister sent Irish picture postcards to their friends and these friends sent back other Irish picture postcards. On special Sundays, when Mr Kearney went with his family to the pro-cathedral, a little crowd of people would assemble after mass at the corner of Cathedral Street. They were all friends of the Kearneys – musical friends or Nationalist friends; and, when they had played every little counter of gossip, they shook hands with one another all together, laughing at the crossing of so many hands, and said goodbye to one another in Irish. Soon the name of Miss Kathleen Kearney began to be heard often on people's lips. People said that she was very clever at music and a very nice girl and, moreover, that she was a believer in the language movement. Mrs Kearney was well content at this. Therefore she was not surprised when one day Mr Holohan came to her and proposed that her daughter should be the accompanist at a series of four grand concerts which his Society was going to give in the Antient Concert Rooms. She brought him into the drawing-room, made him sit down and brought out the decanter and the silver biscuit-barrel. She entered heart and soul into the details of the enterprise, advised and dissuaded: and finally a contract was drawn up by which Kathleen was to receive eight guineas for her services as accompanist at the four grand concerts.

As Mr Holohan was a novice in such delicate matters as the wording of bills and the disposing of items for a programme, Mrs Kearney helped him. She had tact. She knew what *artistes* should go into capitals and what *artistes* should go into small type. She knew that the first tenor would not like to come on after Mr Meade's comic turn. To keep the audience continually diverted she slipped the doubtful items in between the old favourites. Mr Holohan called to see her every day to have her advice on some point. She was invariably friendly and advising – homely, in fact. She pushed the decanter towards him, saying: 'Now, help yourself, Mr Holohan!'

And while he was helping himself she said: 'Don't be afraid! Don't be afraid of it!'

Everything went on smoothly. Mrs Kearney bought some lovely blush-pink charmeuse in Brown Thomas's to let into the front of Kathleen's dress. It cost a pretty penny; but there are occasions when a little expense is justifiable. She took a dozen of two-shilling tickets for the final concert and sent them to those friends who could not be trusted to come otherwise. She forgot nothing, and, thanks to her, everything that was to be done was done.

The concerts were to be on Wednesday, Thursday, Friday and Saturday. When Mrs Kearney arrived with her daughter at the Antient Concert Rooms on Wednesday night she did not like the look of things. A few young men, wearing bright blue badges in their coats, stood idle in the vestibule; none of them wore evening dress. She passed by with her daughter and a quick glance through the open door of the hall showed her the cause of the stewards' idleness. At first she wondered had she mistaken the hour. No, it was twenty minutes to eight.

In the dressing-room behind the stage she was introduced to the secretary of the Society, Mr Fitzpatrick. She smiled and shook his hand. He was a little man, with a white, vacant face. She noticed that he wore his soft brown hat carelessly on the side of his head and that his accent was flat. He held a programme in his hand, and, while he was talking to her, he chewed one end of it into a moist pulp. He seemed to bear disappointments lightly. Mr Holohan came into the dressing-room every few minutes with reports from the box-office. The *artistes* talked among themselves nervously, glanced from time to time at the mirror and rolled and unrolled their music. When it was nearly half-past eight, the few people in the hall began to express their desire to be entertained. Mr Fitzpatrick came in, smiled vacantly at the room, and said: 'Well now, ladies and gentlemen. I suppose we'd better open the ball.'

Mrs Kearney rewarded his very flat final syllable with a quick stare of contempt, and then said to her daughter encouragingly: 'Are you ready, dear?'

When she had an opportunity, she called Mr Holohan aside and asked him to tell her what it meant. Mr Holohan did not know what it meant. He said that the committee had made a mistake in arranging for four concerts: four was too many.

'And the *artistes!*' said Mrs Kearney. 'Of course they are doing their best, but really they are not good.'

Mr Holohan admitted that the *artistes* were no good but the committee, he said, had decided to let the first three concerts go as they pleased and reserve all the talent for Saturday night. Mrs Kearney said nothing, but, as the mediocre items followed one another on the platform and the few people in the hall grew fewer and fewer, she began to regret that she had put herself to any expense for such a concert. There was something she didn't like in the look of things and Mr Fitzpatrick's vacant smile irritated her very much. However, she said nothing and waited to see how it would end. The concert expired shortly before ten, and everyone went home quickly.

The concert on Thursday night was better attended, but Mrs Kearney saw at once that the house was filled with paper. The audience behaved indecorously, as if the concert were an informal dress rehearsal. Mr Fitzpatrick seemed to enjoy himself; he was quite unconscious that Mrs Kearney was taking angry note of his conduct. He stood at the edge of the screen, from time to time jutting out his head and exchanging a laugh with two friends in the corner of the balcony. In the course of the evening, Mrs Kearney learned that the Friday concert was to be abandoned and that the committee was going to move heaven and earth to secure a bumper house on Saturday night. When she heard this, she sought out Mr Holohan. She buttonholed him as he was limping out quickly with a glass of lemonade for a young lady and asked him was it true. Yes, it was true.

'But, of course, that doesn't alter the contract,' she said. 'The contract was for four concerts.'

Mr Holohan seemed to be in a hurry; he advised her to speak to Mr Fitzpatrick. Mrs Kearney was now beginning to be alarmed. She called Mr Fitzpatrick away from his screen and told him that her daughter had signed for four concerts and that, of course, according to the terms of the contract, she should receive the sum originally stipulated for, whether the society gave the four concerts or not. Mr Fitzpatrick, who did not catch the point at issue very quickly, seemed unable to resolve the difficulty and said that he would bring the matter before the committee. Mrs Kearney's anger began to flutter in her cheek and she had all she could do to keep from asking: 'And who is the *Cometty* pray?'

But she knew that it would not be ladylike to do that: so she was silent.

Little boys were sent out into the principal streets of Dublin early on Friday morning with bundles of handbills. Special puffs appeared in all the evening papers, reminding the music-loving public of the treat which was in store for it on the following evening. Mrs Kearney was somewhat reassured, but she thought well to tell her husband part of her suspicions. He listened carefully and said that perhaps it would be better if he went with her on Saturday night. She agreed. She respected her husband in the same way as she respected the General Post Office, as something large, secure and fixed; and though she knew the small number of his talents, she appreciated his abstract value as a male. She was glad that he had suggested coming with her. She thought her plans over.

The night of the grand concert came. Mrs Kearney, with her husband and daughter, arrived at the Antient Concert Rooms three-quarters of an hour before the time at which the concert was to begin. By ill luck it was a rainy evening. Mrs Kearney placed her daughter's clothes and music in charge of her husband and went all over the building looking for Mr Holohan or Mr Fitzpatrick. She could find neither. She asked the stewards was any member of the committee in the hall and, after a great deal of trouble, a steward brought out a little woman named Miss Beirne to whom Mrs Kearney explained that she wanted to see one of the secretaries. Miss Beirne expected them any minute and asked could she do anything. Mrs Kearney looked searchingly at the oldish face which was screwed into an expression of trustfulness and enthusiasm and answered: 'No, thank you!'

The little woman hoped they would have a good house. She looked out at the rain until the melancholy of the wet street effaced all the trustfulness and enthusiasm from her twisted features. Then she gave a little sigh and said: 'Ah, well! We did our best, the dear knows.'

Mrs Kearney had to go back to the dressing-room.

The *artistes* were arriving. The bass and the second tenor had already come. The bass, Mr Duggan, was a slender young man with a scattered black moustache. He was the son of a hall porter in an office in the city and, as a boy, he had sung prolonged bass notes in the resounding hall. From this humble state he had raised himself until he had become a first-rate *artiste*. He had appeared in grand opera. One night, when an operatic *artiste* had fallen ill, he had undertaken the part of the king in the opera of *Maritana* at the Queen's Theatre. He sang his music with great feeling and volume and was warmly welcomed by the gallery; but, unfortunately, he marred the good impression by wiping his nose in his gloved hand once or twice out of thoughtlessness. He was unassuming and spoke little. He said *yous* so softly that it passed unnoticed and he never drank anything stronger than milk for his voice's sake. Mr Bell, the second tenor, was a fair-haired little man who competed every year for prizes at the Feis Ceoil. On his fourth trial he had been awarded a bronze medal. He was extremely nervous and extremely jealous of other tenors and he covered his nervous jealousy with an ebullient friendliness. It was his humour to have people know what an ordeal a concert was to him. Therefore when he saw Mr Duggan he went over to him and asked: 'Are you in it too?'

'Yes,' said Mr Duggan.

Mr Bell laughed at his fellow-sufferer, held out his hand and said: 'Shake!'

Mrs Kearney passed by these two young men and went to the edge of the screen to view the house. The seats were being filled up rapidly and a pleasant noise circulated in the auditorium. She came back and spoke to her husband privately. Their conversation was evidently about Kathleen for they both glanced at her often as she stood chatting to one of her Nationalist friends, Miss Healy, the contralto. An unknown solitary woman with a pale face walked through the room. The women followed with keen eyes the faded blue dress which was stretched upon a meagre body. Someone said that she was Madam Glynn, the soprano.

'I wonder where did they dig her up,' said Kathleen to Miss Healy. 'I'm sure I never heard of her.'

Miss Healy had to smile. Mr Holohan limped into the dressing-room at that moment and the two young ladies asked him who was the unknown woman. Mr Holohan said that she was Madam Glynn from London. Madam Glynn took her stand in a corner of the room, holding a roll of music stiffly before her and from time to time changing the direction of her startled gaze. The shadow took her faded dress into shelter but fell revengefully into the little cup behind her collar-bone. The noise of the hall became more audible. The first tenor and the baritone arrived together. They were both well dressed, stout and complacent and they brought a breath of opulence among the company.

Mrs Kearney brought her daughter over to them, and talked to them amiably. She wanted to be on good terms with them but, while she strove to be polite, her eyes followed Mr Holohan in his limping and devious courses. As soon as she could she excused herself and went out after him.

'Mr Holohan, I want to speak to you for a moment,' she said.

They went down to a discreet part of the corridor. Mrs Kearney asked him when was her daughter going to be paid. Mr Holohan said that Mr Fitzpatrick had charge of that. Mrs Kearney said that she didn't know anything about Mr Fitzpatrick. Her daughter had signed a contract for eight guineas and she would have to be paid. Mr Holohan said that it wasn't his business.

'Why isn't it your business?' asked Mrs Kearney. 'Didn't you yourself bring her the contract? Anyway, if it's not your business it's my business and I mean to see to it.'

'You'd better speak to Mr Fitzpatrick,' said Mr Holohan distantly.

'I don't know anything about Mr Fitzpatrick,' repeated Mrs Kearney. 'I have my contract, and I intend to see that it is carried out.'

When she came back to the dressing-room her cheeks were slightly suffused. The room was lively. Two men in outdoor dress had taken possession of the fireplace and were chatting familiarly with Miss Healy and the baritone. They were the *Freeman* man and Mr O'Madden Burke. The *Freeman* man had come in to say that he could not wait for the concert as he had to report the lecture which an American priest was giving in the Mansion House. He said they were to leave the report for him at the *Freeman* office and he would see that it went in. He was a grey-haired man, with a plausible voice and careful manners. He held an extinguished cigar in his hand and the aroma of cigar smoke floated near him. He had not intended to stay a moment because concerts and *artistes* bored him considerably but he remained leaning against the mantelpiece. Miss Healy stood in front of him, talking and laughing. He was old enough to suspect one reason for her politeness but young enough in spirit to turn the moment to account. The warmth, fragrance and colour of her body appealed to his senses. He was pleasantly conscious that the bosom which he saw rise and fall slowly beneath him rose and fell at that moment for him, that the laughter and fragrance and wilful glances were his tribute. When he could stay no longer he took leave of her regretfully.

'O'Madden Burke will write the notice,' he explained to Mr Holohan, 'and I'll see it in.'

'Thank you very much, Mr Hendrick,' said Mr Holohan. 'You'll see it in, I know. Now, won't you have a little something before you go?'

'I don't mind,' said Mr Hendrick.

The two men went along some tortuous passages and up a dark staircase and came to a secluded room where one of the stewards was uncorking bottles for a few gentlemen. One of these gentlemen was Mr O'Madden Burke, who had found out the room by instinct. He was a suave, elderly man who balanced his imposing body, when at rest, upon a large silk umbrella. His magniloquent western name was the moral umbrella upon which he balanced the fine problem of his finances. He was widely respected.

While Mr Holohan was entertaining the *Freeman* man Mrs Kearney was speaking so animatedly to her husband that he had to ask her to lower her voice. The conversation of the others in the dressing-room had become strained. Mr Bell, the first item, stood ready with his music but the accompanist made no sign. Evidently something was wrong. Mr Kearney looked straight before him, stroking his beard, while Mrs Kearney spoke into Kathleen's ear with subdued emphasis. From the hall came sounds of encouragement, clapping and stamping of feet. The first tenor and the baritone and Miss Healy stood together, waiting tranquilly, but Mr Bell's nerves were greatly agitated because he was afraid the audience would think that he had come late.

Mr Holohan and Mr O'Madden Burke came into the room. In a moment Mr Holohan perceived the hush. He went over to Mrs Kearney and spoke with her earnestly. While they were speaking the noise in the hall grew louder. Mr Holohan became very red and excited. He spoke volubly, but Mrs Kearney said curtly at intervals: 'She won't go on. She must get her eight guineas.'

Mr Holohan pointed desperately towards the hall where the audience was clapping and stamping. He appealed to Mr Kearney and to Kathleen. But Mr Kearney continued to stroke his beard and Kathleen looked down, moving the point of her new shoe: it was not her fault. Mrs Kearney repeated: 'She won't go on without her money.'

After a swift struggle of tongues Mr Holohan hobbled out in haste. The room was silent. When the strain of the silence had become somewhat painful Miss Healy said to the baritone: 'Have you seen Mrs Pat Campbell this week?'

The baritone had not seen her but he had been told that she was very fine. The conversation went no further. The first tenor bent his head and began to count the links of the gold chain which was extended across his waist, smiling and humming random notes to observe the effect on the frontal sinus. From time to time everyone glanced at Mrs Kearney.

The noise in the auditorium had risen to a clamour when Mr Fitzpatrick burst into the room, followed by Mr Holohan, who was panting. The clapping and stamping in the hall were punctuated by whistling. Mr Fitzpatrick held a few bank-notes in his hand. He counted out four into Mrs Kearney's hand and said she would get the other half at the interval. Mrs Kearney said: 'This is four shillings short.'

But Kathleen gathered in her skirt and said: 'Now, Mr Bell,' to the first item, who was shaking like an aspen. The singer and the accompanist went out together. The noise in the hall died away. There was a pause of a few seconds: and then the piano was heard.

The first part of the concert was very successful except for Madam Glynn's item. The poor lady sang *Killarney* in a bodiless gasping voice, with all the old-fashioned mannerisms of intonation and pronunciation which she believed lent elegance to her singing. She looked as if she had been resurrected from an old stage-wardrobe and the cheaper parts of the hall made fun of her high wailing notes. The first tenor and the contralto, however, brought down the house. Kathleen played a selection of Irish airs which was generously applauded. The first part closed with a stirring patriotic recitation delivered by a young lady who arranged amateur theatricals. It was deservedly applauded; and, when it was ended, the men went out for the interval, content.

All this time the dressing-room was a hive of excitement. In one corner were Mr Holohan, Mr Fitzpatrick, Miss Beirne, two of the stewards, the baritone, the bass, and Mr O'Madden Burke. Mr O'Madden Burke said it was the most scandalous exhibition he had ever witnessed. Miss Kathleen Kearney's musical career was ended in Dublin after that, he said. The baritone was asked what did he think of Mrs Kearney's conduct. He did not like to say anything. He had been paid his money and wished to be at peace with men. However, he said that Mrs Kearney might have taken the *artistes* into consideration. The stewards and the secretaries debated hotly as to what should be done when the interval came.

'I agree with Miss Beirne,' said Mr O'Madden Burke. 'Pay her nothing.'

In another corner of the room were Mrs Kearney and her husband, Mr Bell, Miss Healy and the young lady who had to recite the patriotic piece. Mrs Kearney said that the committee had treated her scandalously. She had spared neither trouble nor expense and this was how she was repaid.

They thought they had only a girl to deal with and that, therefore, they could ride roughshod over her. But she would show them their mistake. They wouldn't have dared to have treated her like that if she had been a man. But she would see that her daughter got her rights: she wouldn't be fooled. If they didn't pay her to the last farthing she would make Dublin ring. Of course she was sorry for the sake of the *artistes*. But what else could she do? She appealed to the second tenor, who said he thought she had not been well treated. Then she appealed to Miss Healy. Miss Healy wanted to join the other group but she did not like to do so because she was a great friend of Kathleen's and the Kearneys had often invited her to their house.

As soon as the first part was ended Mr Fitzpatrick and Mr Holohan went over to Mrs Kearney and told her that the other four guineas would be paid after the committee meeting on the following Tuesday and that, in case her daughter did not play for the second part, the committee would consider the contract broken and would pay nothing.

'I haven't seen any committee,' said Mrs Kearney angrily. 'My daughter has her contract. She will get four pounds eight into her hand or a foot she won't put on that platform.'

'I'm surprised at you, Mrs Kearney,' said Mr Holohan. 'I never thought you would treat us this way.'

'And what way did you treat me?' asked Mrs Kearney.

Her face was inundated with an angry colour and she looked as if she would attack someone with her hands.

'I'm asking for my rights,' she said.

'You might have some sense of decency,' said Mr Holohan.

'Might I, indeed? . . . And when I ask when my daughter is going to be paid I can't get a civil answer.'

She tossed her head and assumed a haughty voice: 'You must speak to the secretary. It's not my business. I'm a great fellow fol-the-diddle-I-do.'

'I thought you were a lady,' said Mr Holohan, walking away from her abruptly.

After that Mrs Kearney's conduct was condemned on all hands: everyone approved of what the committee had done. She stood at the door, haggard with rage, arguing with her husband and daughter, gesticulating with them. She waited until it was time for the second part to begin in the hope that the secretaries would approach her. But Miss Healy had kindly consented to play one or two accompaniments. Mrs Kearney had to stand aside to allow the baritone and his accompanist to pass up to the platform. She stood still for an instant like an angry stone image and, when the first notes of the song struck her ear, she caught up her daughter's cloak and said to her husband: 'Get a cab!'

He went out at once. Mrs Kearney wrapped the cloak round her daughter and followed him. As she passed through the doorway she stopped and glared into Mr Holohan's face.

'I'm not done with you yet,' she said.

'But I'm done with you,' said Mr Holohan.

Kathleen followed her mother meekly. Mr Holohan began to pace up and down the room, in order to cool himself for he felt his skin on fire.

'That's a nice lady!' he said. 'O, she's a nice lady!'

'You did the proper thing, Holohan,' said Mr O'Madden Burke, poised upon his umbrella in approval.

Grace

Two gentlemen who were in the lavatory at the time tried to lift him up: but he was quite helpless. He lay curled up at the foot of the stairs down which he had fallen. They succeeded in turning him over. His hat had rolled a few yards away and his clothes were smeared with the filth and ooze of the floor on which he had lain, face downwards. His eyes were closed and he breathed with a grunting noise. A thin stream of blood trickled from the corner of his mouth.

These two gentlemen and one of the curates carried him up the stairs and laid him down again on the floor of the bar. In two minutes he was surrounded by a ring of men. The manager of the bar asked everyone who he was and who was with him. No one knew who he was but one of the curates said he had served the gentleman with a small rum.

'Was he by himself?' asked the manager.

'No, sir. There was two gentlemen with him.'

'And where are they?'

No one knew; a voice said: 'Give him air. He's fainted.'

The ring of onlookers distended and closed again elastically. A dark medal of blood had formed itself near the man's head on the tessellated floor. The manager, alarmed by the grey pallor of the man's face, sent for a policeman.

His collar was unfastened and his necktie undone. He opened his eyes for an instant, sighed and closed them again. One of the gentlemen who had carried him upstairs held a dinged silk hat in his hand. The manager asked repeatedly did no one know who the injured man was or where had his friends gone. The door of the bar opened and an immense constable entered. A crowd which had followed him down the laneway collected outside the door, struggling to look in through the glass panels.

The manager at once began to narrate what he knew. The constable, a young man with thick immobile features, listened. He moved his head slowly to right and left and from the manager to the person on the floor, as if he feared to be the victim of some delusion. Then he drew off his glove, produced a small book from his waist, licked the lead of his pencil and made ready to indite. He asked in a suspicious provincial accent: 'Who is the man? What's his name and address?'

A young man in a cycling-suit cleared his way through the ring of bystanders. He knelt down promptly beside the injured man and called for

water. The constable knelt down also to help. The young man washed the
blood from the injured man's mouth and then called for some brandy.
The constable repeated the order in an authoritative voice until a curate
came running with the glass. The brandy was forced down the man's
throat. In a few seconds he opened his eyes and looked about him.
He looked at the circle of faces and then, understanding, strove to rise to
his feet.

'You're all right now?' asked the young man in the cycling-suit.

'Sha, 's nothing,' said the injured man, trying to stand up.

He was helped to his feet. The manager said something about a hospital
and some of the bystanders gave advice. The battered silk hat was placed on
the man's head. The constable asked: 'Where do you live?'

The man, without answering, began to twirl the ends of his moustache.
He made light of his accident. It was nothing, he said: only a little accident.
He spoke very thickly.

'Where do you live?' repeated the constable.

The man said they were to get a cab for him. While the point was being
debated a tall agile gentleman of fair complexion, wearing a long yellow
ulster, came from the far end of the bar. Seeing the spectacle, he called out:
'Hallo, Tom, old man! What's the trouble?'

'Sha, 's nothing,' said the man.

The new-comer surveyed the deplorable figure before him and then
turned to the constable, saying: 'It's all right, constable. I'll see him home.'

The constable touched his helmet and answered: 'All right, Mr Power!'

'Come now, Tom,' said Mr Power, taking his friend by the arm. 'No
bones broken. What? Can you walk?'

The young man in the cycling-suit took the man by the other arm and
the crowd divided.

'How did you get yourself into this mess?' asked Mr Power.

'The gentleman fell down the stairs,' said the young man.

'I' 'ery 'uch o'liged to you, sir,' said the injured man.

'Not at all.'

' 'ant' we have a little . . . ? '

'Not now. Not now.'

The three men left the bar and the crowd sifted through the doors in to
the laneway. The manager brought the constable to the stairs to inspect the
scene of the accident. They agreed that the gentleman must have missed his
footing. The customers returned to the counter and a curate set about
removing the traces of blood from the floor.

When they came out into Grafton Street, Mr Power whistled for an

outsider. The injured man said again as well as he could: 'I' 'ery 'uch o'liged
to you, sir. I hope we'll 'eet again. 'y na'e is Kernan.'

The shock and the incipient pain had partly sobered him.

'Don't mention it,' said the young man.

They shook hands. Mr Kernan was hoisted on to the car and, while Mr
Power was giving directions to the carman, he expressed his gratitude to
the young man and regretted that they could not have a little drink together.

'Another time,' said the young man.

The car drove off towards Westmoreland Street. As it passed the Ballast
Office the clock showed half-past nine. A keen east wind hit them, blowing
from the mouth of the river. Mr Kernan was huddled together with cold.
His friend asked him to tell how the accident had happened.

'I 'an't 'an,' he answered, ' 'y 'ongue is hurt.'

'Show.'

The other leaned over the well of the car and peered into Mr Kernan's
mouth but he could not see. He struck a match and, sheltering it in the
shell of his hands, peered again into the mouth which Mr Kernan opened
obediently. The swaying movement of the car brought the match to and
from the opened mouth. The lower teeth and gums were covered with
clotted blood and a minute piece of the tongue seemed to have been bitten
off. The match was blown out.

'That's ugly,' said Mr Power.

'Sha, 's nothing,' said Mr Kernan, closing his mouth and pulling the
collar of his filthy coat across his neck.

Mr Kernan was a commercial traveller of the old school which believed
in the dignity of its calling. He had never been seen in the city without a silk
hat of some decency and a pair of gaiters. By grace of these two articles
of clothing, he said, a man could always pass muster. He carried on the
tradition of his Napoleon, the great Black-white, whose memory he evoked
at times by legend and mimicry. Modern business methods had spared him
only so far as to allow him a little office in Crowe Street, on the window
blind of which was written the name of his firm with the address – London,
E. C. On the mantelpiece of this little office a little leaden battalion of
canisters was drawn up and on the table before the window stood four or
five china bowls which were usually half full of a black liquid. From these
bowls Mr Kernan tasted tea. He took a mouthful, drew it up, saturated his
palate with it and then spat it forth into the grate. Then he paused to judge.

Mr Power, a much younger man, was employed in the Royal Irish
Constabulary Office in Dublin Castle. The arc of his social rise intersected
the arc of his friend's decline, but Mr Kernan's decline was mitigated by the

fact that certain of those friends who had known him at his highest point of success still esteemed him as a character. Mr Power was one of these friends. His inexplicable debts were a byword in his circle; he was a debonair young man.

The car halted before a small house on the Glasnevin road and Mr Kernan was helped into the house. His wife put him to bed, while Mr Power sat downstairs in the kitchen asking the children where they went to school and what book they were in. The children – two girls and a boy, conscious of their father's helplessness and of their mother's absence, began some horseplay with him. He was surprised at their manners and at their accents, and his brow grew thoughtful. After a while Mrs Kernan entered the kitchen, exclaiming: 'Such a sight! O, he'll do for himself one day and that's the holy alls of it. He's been drinking since Friday.'

Mr Power was careful to explain to her that he was not responsible, that he had come on the scene by the merest accident. Mrs Kernan, remembering Mr Power's good offices during domestic quarrels, as well as many small, but opportune loans, said: 'O, you needn't tell me that, Mr Power. I know you're a friend of his, not like some of the others he does be with. They're all right so long as he has money in his pocket to keep him out from his wife and family. Nice friends! Who was he with tonight, I'd like to know?'

Mr Power shook his head but said nothing.

'I'm so sorry,' she continued, 'that I've nothing in the house to offer you. But if you wait a minute I'll send round to Fogarty's, at the corner.'

Mr Power stood up.

'We were waiting for him to come home with the money. He never seems to think he has a home at all.'

'O, now, Mrs Kernan,' said Mr Power, 'we'll make him turn over a new leaf. I'll talk to Martin. He's the man. We'll come here one of these nights and talk it over.'

She saw him to the door. The carman was stamping up and down the footpath, and swinging his arms to warm himself.

'It's very kind of you to bring him home,' she said.

'Not at all,' said Mr Power.

He got up on the car. As it drove off he raised his hat to her gaily.

'We'll make a new man of him,' he said. 'Good-night, Mrs Kernan.'

Mrs Kernan's puzzled eyes watched the car till it was out of sight. Then she withdrew them, went into the house and emptied her husband's pockets.

She was an active, practical woman of middle age. Not long before she had celebrated her silver wedding and renewed her intimacy with her husband by waltzing with him to Mr Power's accompaniment. In her days of courtship, Mr Kernan had seemed to her a not ungallant figure: and she still hurried to the chapel door whenever a wedding was reported and, seeing the bridal pair, recalled with vivid pleasure how she had passed out of the Star of the Sea Church in Sandymount, leaning on the arm of a jovial well-fed man, who was dressed smartly in a frock-coat and lavender trousers and carried a silk hat gracefully balanced upon his other arm. After three weeks she had found a wife's life irksome and, later on, when she was beginning to find it unbearable, she had become a mother. The part of mother presented to her no insuperable difficulties and for twenty-five years she had kept house shrewdly for her husband. Her two eldest sons were launched. One was in a draper's shop in Glasgow and the other was clerk to a tea-merchant in Belfast. They were good sons, wrote regularly and sometimes sent home money. The other children were still at school.

Mr Kernan sent a letter to his office next day and remained in bed. She made beef-tea for him and scolded him roundly. She accepted his frequent intemperance as part of the climate, healed him dutifully whenever he was sick and always tried to make him eat a breakfast. There were worse husbands. He had never been violent since the boys had grown up, and she knew that he would walk to the end of Thomas Street and back again to book even a small order.

Two nights after, his friends came to see him. She brought them up to his bedroom, the air of which was impregnated with a personal odour, and gave them chairs at the fire. Mr Kernan's tongue, the occasional stinging pain of which had made him somewhat irritable during the day, became more polite. He sat propped up in the bed by pillows and the little colour in his puffy cheeks made them resemble warm cinders. He apologised to his guests for the disorder of the room, but at the same time looked at them a little proudly, with a veteran's pride.

He was quite unconscious that he was the victim of a plot which his friends, Mr Cunningham, Mr M'Coy and Mr Power had disclosed to Mrs Kernan in the parlour. The idea had been Mr Power's, but its development was entrusted to Mr Cunningham. Mr Kernan came of Protestant stock and, though he had been converted to the Catholic faith at the time of his marriage, he had not been in the pale of the Church for twenty years. He was fond, moreover, of giving side-thrusts at Catholicism.

Mr Cunningham was the very man for such a case. He was an elder colleague of Mr Power. His own domestic life was not very happy. People had great sympathy with him, for it was known that he had married an unpresentable woman who was an incurable drunkard. He had set up house for her six times; and each time she had pawned the furniture on him.

Everyone had respect for poor Martin Cunningham. He was a thoroughly sensible man, influential and intelligent. His blade of human knowledge, natural astuteness particularised by long association with cases in the police courts, had been tempered by brief immersions in the waters of general philosophy. He was well informed. His friends bowed to his opinions and considered that his face was like Shakespeare's. When the plot had been disclosed to her, Mrs Kernan had said: 'I leave it all in your hands, Mr Cunningham.'

After a quarter of a century of married life, she had very few illusions left. Religion for her was a habit, and she suspected that a man of her husband's age would not change greatly before death. She was tempted to see a curious appropriateness in his accident and, but that she did not wish to seem bloody-minded, she would have told the gentlemen that Mr Kernan's tongue would not suffer by being shortened. However, Mr Cunningham was a capable man; and religion was religion. The scheme might do good and, at least, it could do no harm. Her beliefs were not extravagant. She believed steadily in the Sacred Heart as the most generally useful of all Catholic devotions and approved of the sacraments. Her faith was bounded by her kitchen, but, if she was put to it, she could believe also in the banshee and in the Holy Ghost.

The gentlemen began to talk of the accident. Mr Cunningham said that he had once known a similar case. A man of seventy had bitten off a piece of his tongue during an epileptic fit and the tongue had filled in again, so that no one could see a trace of the bite.

'Well, I'm not seventy,' said the invalid.

'God forbid,' said Mr Cunningham.

'It doesn't pain you now?' asked Mr M'Coy.

Mr M'Coy had been at one time a tenor of some reputation. His wife, who had been a soprano, still taught young children to play the piano at low terms. His line of life had not been the shortest distance between two points and for short periods he had been driven to live by his wits. He had been a clerk in the Midland Railway, a canvasser for advertisements for The Irish Times and for The Freeman's Journal, a town traveller for a coal firm on commission, a private inquiry agent, a clerk in the office of the Sub-Sheriff, and he had recently become secretary to the City Coroner. His new office made him professionally interested in Mr Kernan's case.

'Pain? Not much,' answered Mr Kernan. 'But it's so sickening. I feel as if I wanted to retch off.'

'That's the booze,' said Mr Cunningham firmly.

'No,' said Mr Kernan. 'I think I caught cold on the car. There's something keeps coming into my throat, phlegm or – '

'Mucus,' said Mr M'Coy.

'It keeps coming like from down in my throat; sickening thing.'

'Yes, yes,' said Mr M'Coy, 'that's the thorax.'

He looked at Mr Cunningham and Mr Power at the same time with an air of challenge. Mr Cunningham nodded his head rapidly and Mr Power said: 'Ah, well, all's well that ends well.'

'I'm very much obliged to you, old man,' said the invalid.

Mr Power waved his hand.

'Those other two fellows I was with – '

'Who were you with?' asked Mr Cunningham.

'A chap. I don't know his name. Damn it now, what's his name? Little chap with sandy hair . . . '

'And who else?'

'Harford.'

'Hm,' said Mr Cunningham.

When Mr Cunningham made that remark, people were silent. It was known that the speaker had secret sources of information. In this case the monosyllable had a moral intention. Mr Harford sometimes formed one of a little detachment which left the city shortly after noon on Sunday with the purpose of arriving as soon as possible at some public-house on the outskirts of the city where its members duly qualified themselves as *bona fide* travellers. But his fellow-travellers had never consented to overlook his origin. He had begun life as an obscure financier by lending small sums of money to workmen at usurious interest. Later on he had become the partner of a very fat, short gentleman, Mr Goldberg, in the Liffey Loan Bank. Though he had never embraced more than the Jewish ethical code, his fellow-Catholics, whenever they had smarted in person or by proxy under his exactions, spoke of him bitterly as an Irish Jew and an illiterate, and saw divine disapproval of usury made manifest through the person of his idiot son. At other times they remembered his good points.

'I wonder where did he go to,' said Mr Kernan.

He wished the details of the incident to remain vague. He wished his friends to think there had been some mistake, that Mr Harford and he had missed each other. His friends, who knew quite well Mr Harford's manners in drinking, were silent. Mr Power said again: 'All's well that ends well.'

Mr Kernan changed the subject at once.

'That was a decent young chap, that medical fellow,' he said. 'Only for him – '

'O, only for him,' said Mr Power, 'it might have been a case of seven days, without the option of a fine.'

'Yes, yes,' said Mr Kernan, trying to remember. 'I remember now there was a policeman. Decent young fellow, he seemed. How did it happen at all?'

'It happened that you were peloothered, Tom,' said Mr Cunningham gravely.

'True bill,' said Mr Kernan, equally gravely.

'I suppose you squared the constable, Jack,' said Mr M'Coy.

Mr Power did not relish the use of his Christian name. He was not straight-laced, but he could not forget that Mr M'Coy had recently made a crusade in search of valises and portmanteaus to enable Mrs M'Coy to fulfil imaginary engagements in the country. More than he resented the fact that he had been victimised he resented such low playing of the game. He answered the question, therefore, as if Mr Kernan had asked it.

The narrative made Mr Kernan indignant. He was keenly conscious of his citizenship, wished to live with his city on terms mutually honourable and resented any affront put upon him by those whom he called country bumpkins.

'Is this what we pay rates for?' he asked. 'To feed and clothe these ignorant bostooms . . . and they're nothing else.'

Mr Cunningham laughed. He was a Castle official only during office hours.

'How could they be anything else, Tom?' he said.

He assumed a thick, provincial accent and said in a tone of command: '65, catch your cabbage!'

Everyone laughed. Mr M'Coy, who wanted to enter the conversation by any door, pretended that he had never heard the story. Mr Cunningham said: 'It is supposed – they say, you know – to take place in the depot where they get these thundering big country fellows, omadhauns, you know, to drill. The sergeant makes them stand in a row against the wall and hold up their plates.'

He illustrated the story by grotesque gestures. 'At dinner, you know. Then he has a bloody big bowl of cabbage before him on the table and a bloody big spoon like a shovel. He takes up a wad of cabbage on the spoon and pegs it across the room and the poor devils have to try and catch it on their plates: *65, catch your cabbage.*'

Everyone laughed again: but Mr Kernan was somewhat indignant still. He talked of writing a letter to the papers.

'These yahoos coming up here,' he said, 'think they can boss the people. I needn't tell you, Martin, what kind of men they are.'

Mr Cunningham gave a qualified assent.

'It's like everything else in this world,' he said. 'You get some bad ones and you get some good ones.'

'O yes, you get some good ones, I admit,' said Mr Kernan, satisfied.

'It's better to have nothing to say to them,' said Mr M'Coy. 'That's my opinion!'

Mrs Kernan entered the room and, placing a tray on the table, said: 'Help yourselves, gentlemen.'

Mr Power stood up to officiate, offering her his chair. She declined it, saying she was ironing downstairs, and, after having exchanged a nod with Mr Cunningham behind Mr Power's back, prepared to leave the room. Her husband called out to her: 'And have you nothing for me, duckie?'

'O, you! The back of my hand to you!' said Mrs Kernan tartly.

Her husband called after her: 'Nothing for poor little hubby!'

He assumed such a comical face and voice that the distribution of the bottles of stout took place amid general merriment.

The gentlemen drank from their glasses, set the glasses again on the table and paused. Then Mr Cunningham turned towards Mr Power and said casually: 'On Thursday night, you said, Jack?'

'Thursday, yes,' said Mr Power.

'Righto!' said Mr Cunningham promptly.

'We can meet in M'Auley's,' said Mr M'Coy. 'That'll be the most convenient place.'

'But we mustn't be late,' said Mr Power earnestly, 'because it is sure to be crammed to the doors.'

'We can meet at half-seven,' said Mr M'Coy.

'Righto!' said Mr Cunningham.

'Half-seven at M'Auley's be it!'

There was a short silence. Mr Kernan waited to see whether he would be taken into his friends' confidence. Then he asked: 'What's in the wind?'

'O, it's nothing,' said Mr Cunningham. 'It's only a little matter that we're arranging about for Thursday.'

'The opera, is it?' said Mr Kernan.

'No, no,' said Mr Cunningham in an evasive tone, 'it's just a little . . . spiritual matter.'

'O,' said Mr Kernan.

There was silence again. Then Mr Power said, point blank: 'To tell you the truth, Tom, we're going to make a retreat.'

'Yes, that's it,' said Mr Cunningham, 'Jack and I and M'Coy here – we're all going to wash the pot.'

He uttered the metaphor with a certain homely energy and, encouraged by his own voice, proceeded: 'You see, we may as well all admit we're a nice collection of scoundrels, one and all. I say, one and all,' he added with gruff charity and turning to Mr Power. 'Own up now!'

'I own up,' said Mr Power.

'And I own up,' said Mr M'Coy.

'So we're going to wash the pot together,' said Mr Cunningham.

A thought seemed to strike him. He turned suddenly to the invalid and said: 'D'ye know what, Tom, has just occurred to me? You might join in and we'd have a four-handed reel.'

'Good idea,' said Mr Power. 'The four of us together.'

Mr Kernan was silent. The proposal conveyed very little meaning to his mind, but, understanding that some spiritual agencies were about to concern themselves on his behalf, he thought he owed it to his dignity to show a stiff neck. He took no part in the conversation for a long while, but listened, with an air of calm enmity, while his friends discussed the Jesuits.

'I haven't such a bad opinion of the Jesuits,' he said, intervening at length. 'They're an educated order. I believe they mean well, too.'

'They're the grandest order in the Church, Tom,' said Mr Cunningham, with enthusiasm. 'The General of the Jesuits stands next to the Pope.'

'There's no mistake about it,' said Mr M'Coy, 'if you want a thing well done and no flies about, you go to a Jesuit. They're the boyos have influence. I'll tell you a case in point . . . '

'The Jesuits are a fine body of men,' said Mr Power.

'It's a curious thing,' said Mr Cunningham, 'about the Jesuit Order. Every other order of the Church had to be reformed at some time or other but the Jesuit Order was never once reformed. It never fell away.'

'Is that so?' asked Mr M'Coy.

'That's a fact,' said Mr Cunningham. 'That's history.'

'Look at their church, too,' said Mr Power. 'Look at the congregation they have.'

'The Jesuits cater for the upper classes,' said Mr M'Coy.

'Of course,' said Mr Power.

'Yes,' said Mr Kernan. 'That's why I have a feeling for them. It's some of those secular priests, ignorant, bumptious – '

'They're all good men,' said Mr Cunningham, 'each in his own way. The Irish priesthood is honoured all the world over.'

'O yes,' said Mr Power.

'Not like some of the other priesthoods on the continent,' said Mr M'Coy, 'unworthy of the name.'

'Perhaps you're right,' said Mr Kernan, relenting.

'Of course I'm right,' said Mr Cunningham. 'I haven't been in the world all this time and seen most sides of it without being a judge of character.'

The gentlemen drank again, one following another's example. Mr Kernan seemed to be weighing something in his mind. He was impressed. He had a high opinion of Mr Cunningham as a judge of character and as a reader of faces. He asked for particulars.

'O, it's just a retreat, you know,' said Mr Cunningham. 'Father Purdon is giving it. It's for business men, you know.'

'He won't be too hard on us, Tom,' said Mr Power persuasively.

'Father Purdon? Father Purdon?' said the invalid.

'O, you must know him, Tom,' said Mr Cunningham stoutly. 'Fine, jolly fellow! He's a man of the world like ourselves.'

'Ah . . . yes. I think I know him. Rather red face; tall.'

'That's the man.'

'And tell me, Martin . . . Is he a good preacher?'

'Munno . . . It's not exactly a sermon, you know. It's just a kind of a friendly talk, you know, in a common-sense way.'

Mr Kernan deliberated. Mr M'Coy said: 'Father Tom Burke, that was the boy!'

'O, Father Tom Burke,' said Mr Cunningham, 'that was a born orator. Did you ever hear him, Tom?'

'Did I ever hear him!' said the invalid, nettled. 'Rather! I heard him . . .'

'And yet they say he wasn't much of a theologian,' said Mr Cunningham.

'Is that so?' said Mr M'Coy.

'O, of course, nothing wrong, you know. Only sometimes, they say, he didn't preach what was quite orthodox.'

'Ah! . . . he was a splendid man,' said Mr M'Coy.

'I heard him once,' Mr Kernan continued. 'I forget the subject of his discourse now. Crofton and I were in the back of the . . . pit, you know . . . the – '

'The body,' said Mr Cunningham.

'Yes, in the back near the door. I forget now what . . . O yes, it was on the Pope, the late Pope. I remember it well. Upon my word it was magnificent, the style of the oratory. And his voice! God! hadn't he a voice! *The Prisoner of the Vatican*, he called him. I remember Crofton saying to me when we came out – '

'But he's an Orangeman, Crofton, isn't he?' said Mr Power.

' 'Course he is,' said Mr Kernan, 'and a damned decent Orangeman, too. We went into Butler's in Moore Street – faith, I was genuinely moved, tell you the God's truth – and I remember well his very words. *Kernan*, he said, *we worship at different altars*, he said, *but our belief is the same*. Struck me as very well put.'

'There's a good deal in that,' said Mr Power. 'There used always be crowds of Protestants in the chapel when Father Tom was preaching.'

'There's not much difference between us,' said Mr M'Coy. 'We both believe in – '

He hesitated for a moment.

'. . . in the Redeemer. Only they don't believe in the Pope and in the mother of God.'

'But, of course,' said Mr Cunningham quietly and effectively, 'our religion is *the* religion, the old, original faith.'

'Not a doubt of it,' said Mr Kernan warmly.

Mrs Kernan came to the door of the bedroom and announced: 'Here's a visitor for you!'

'Who is it?'

'Mr Fogarty.'

'O, come in! come in!'

A pale, oval face came forward into the light. The arch of its fair trailing moustache was repeated in the fair eyebrows looped above pleasantly astonished eyes. Mr Fogarty was a modest grocer. He had failed in business in a licensed house in the city because his financial condition had constrained him to tie himself to second-class distillers and brewers. He had opened a small shop on Glasnevin Road where, he flattered himself, his manners would ingratiate him with the housewives of the district. He bore himself with a certain grace, complimented little children and spoke with a neat enunciation. He was not without culture.

Mr Fogarty brought a gift with him, a half-pint of special whiskey. He inquired politely for Mr Kernan, placed his gift on the table and sat down with the company on equal terms. Mr Kernan appreciated the gift all the more since he was aware that there was a small account for groceries unsettled between him and Mr Fogarty. He said: 'I wouldn't doubt you, old man. Open that, Jack, will you?'

Mr Power again officiated. Glasses were rinsed and five small measures of whiskey were poured out. This new influence enlivened the conversation. Mr Fogarty, sitting on a small area of the chair, was specially interested.

'Pope Leo XIII,' said Mr Cunningham, 'was one of the lights of the age.

His great idea, you know, was the union of the Latin and Greek Churches. That was the aim of his life.'

'I often heard he was one of the most intellectual men in Europe,' said Mr Power. 'I mean, apart from his being Pope.'

'So he was,' said Mr Cunningham, 'if not *the* most so. His motto, you know, as Pope, was *Lux upon Lux* – *Light upon Light*.'

'No, no,' said Mr Fogarty eagerly. 'I think you're wrong there. It was *Lux in Tenebris*, I think – *Light in Darkness*.'

'O yes,' said Mr M'Coy, '*Tenebrae*.'

'Allow me,' said Mr Cunningham positively, 'it was *Lux upon Lux*. And Pius IX his predecessor's motto was *Crux upon Crux* – that is, *Cross upon Cross* – to show the difference between their two pontificates.'

The inference was allowed. Mr Cunningham continued.

'Pope Leo, you know, was a great scholar and a poet.'

'He had a strong face,' said Mr Kernan.

'Yes,' said Mr Cunningham. 'He wrote Latin poetry.'

'Is that so?' said Mr Fogarty.

Mr M'Coy tasted his whiskey contentedly and shook his head with a double intention, saying: 'That's no joke, I can tell you.'

'We didn't learn that, Tom,' said Mr Power, following Mr M'Coy's example, 'when we went to the penny-a-week school.'

'There was many a good man went to the penny-a-week school with a sod of turf under his oxter,' said Mr Kernan sententiously. 'The old system was the best: plain honest education. None of your modern trumpery . . . '

'Quite right,' said Mr Power.

'No superfluities,' said Mr Fogarty.

He enunciated the word and then drank gravely.

'I remember reading,' said Mr Cunningham, 'that one of Pope Leo's poems was on the invention of the photograph – in Latin, of course.'

'On the photograph!' exclaimed Mr Kernan.

'Yes,' said Mr Cunningham.

He also drank from his glass.

'Well, you know,' said Mr M'Coy, 'isn't the photograph wonderful when you come to think of it?'

'O, of course,' said Mr Power, 'great minds can see things.'

'As the poet says: *Great minds are very near to madness*,' said Mr Fogarty.

Mr Kernan seemed to be troubled in mind. He made an effort to recall the Protestant theology on some thorny points and in the end addressed Mr Cunningham.

'Tell me, Martin,' he said. 'Weren't some of the popes – of course, not our present man, or his predecessor, but some of the old popes – not exactly . . . you know . . . up to the knocker?'

There was a silence. Mr Cunningham said: 'O, of course, there were some bad lots . . . But the astonishing thing is this. Not one of them, not the biggest drunkard, not the most . . . out-and-out ruffian, not one of them ever preached *ex cathedra* a word of false doctrine. Now isn't that an astonishing thing?'

'That is,' said Mr Kernan.

'Yes, because when the Pope speaks *ex cathedra*,' Mr Fogarty explained, 'he is infallible.'

'Yes,' said Mr Cunningham.

'O, I know about the infallibility of the Pope. I remember I was younger then . . . Or was it that – ?'

Mr Fogarty interrupted. He took up the bottle and helped the others to a little more. Mr M'Coy, seeing that there was not enough to go round, pleaded that he had not finished his first measure. The others accepted under protest. The light music of whiskey falling into glasses made an agreeable interlude.

'What's that you were saying, Tom?' asked Mr M'Coy.

'Papal infallibility,' said Mr Cunningham, 'that was the greatest scene in the whole history of the Church.'

'How was that, Martin?' asked Mr Power.

Mr Cunningham held up two thick fingers.

'In the sacred college, you know, of cardinals and archbishops and bishops there were two men who held out against it while the others were all for it. The whole conclave except these two was unanimous. No! They wouldn't have it!'

'Ha!' said Mr M'Coy.

'And they were a German cardinal by the name of Dolling . . . or Dowling . . . or – '

'Dowling was no German, and that's a sure five,' said Mr Power, laughing.

'Well, this great German cardinal, whatever his name was, was one; and the other was John MacHale.'

'What?' cried Mr Kernan. 'Is it John of Tuam?'

'Are you sure of that now?' asked Mr Fogarty dubiously. 'I thought it was some Italian or American.'

'John of Tuam,' repeated Mr Cunningham, 'was the man.'

He drank and the other gentlemen followed his lead. Then he resumed: 'There they were at it, all the cardinals and bishops and archbishops from all the ends of the earth and these two fighting dog and devil until at last the

Pope himself stood up and declared infallibility a dogma of the Church *ex cathedra*. On the very moment John MacHale, who had been arguing and arguing against it, stood up and shouted out with the voice of a lion: "*Credo!*" '

'*I believe!*' said Mr Fogarty.

'*Credo!*' said Mr Cunningham. 'That showed the faith he had. He submitted the moment the Pope spoke.'

'And what about Dowling?' asked Mr M'Coy.

'The German cardinal wouldn't submit. He left the church.'

Mr Cunningham's words had built up the vast image of the church in the minds of his hearers. His deep, raucous voice had thrilled them as it uttered the word of belief and submission. When Mrs Kernan came into the room, drying her hands, she came into a solemn company. She did not disturb the silence, but leaned over the rail at the foot of the bed.

'I once saw John MacHale,' said Mr Kernan, 'and I'll never forget it as long as I live.'

He turned towards his wife to be confirmed.

'I often told you that?'

Mrs Kernan nodded.

'It was at the unveiling of Sir John Gray's statue. Edmund Dwyer Gray was speaking, blathering away, and here was this old fellow, crabbed-looking old chap, looking at him from under his bushy eyebrows.'

Mr Kernan knitted his brows and, lowering his head like an angry bull, glared at his wife.

'God!' he exclaimed, resuming his natural face, 'I never saw such an eye in a man's head. It was as much as to say: *I have you properly taped, my lad.* He had an eye like a hawk.'

'None of the Grays was any good,' said Mr Power.

There was a pause again. Mr Power turned to Mrs Kernan and said with abrupt joviality: 'Well, Mrs Kernan, we're going to make your man here a good holy pious and God-fearing Roman Catholic.'

He swept his arm round the company inclusively.

'We're all going to make a retreat together and confess our sins – and God knows we want it badly.'

'I don't mind,' said Mr Kernan, smiling a little nervously.

Mrs Kernan thought it would be wiser to conceal her satisfaction. So she said: 'I pity the poor priest that has to listen to your tale.'

Mr Kernan's expression changed.

'If he doesn't like it,' he said bluntly, 'he can . . . do the other thing. I'll just tell him my little tale of woe. I'm not such a bad fellow – '

Mr Cunningham intervened promptly.

'We'll all renounce the devil,' he said, 'together, not forgetting his works and pomps.'

'Get behind me, Satan!' said Mr Fogarty, laughing and looking at the others.

Mr Power said nothing. He felt completely out-generalled. But a pleased expression flickered across his face.

'All we have to do,' said Mr Cunningham, 'is to stand up with lighted candles in our hands and renew our baptismal vows.'

'O, don't forget the candle, Tom,' said Mr M'Coy, 'whatever you do.'

'What?' said Mr Kernan. 'Must I have a candle?'

'O yes,' said Mr Cunningham.

'No, damn it all,' said Mr Kernan sensibly, 'I draw the line there. I'll do the job right enough. I'll do the retreat business and confession, and . . . all that business. But . . . no candles! No, damn it all, I bar the candles!'

He shook his head with farcical gravity.

'Listen to that!' said his wife.

'I bar the candles,' said Mr Kernan, conscious of having created an effect on his audience and continuing to shake his head to and fro. 'I bar the magic-lantern business.'

Everyone laughed heartily.

'There's a nice Catholic for you!' said his wife.

'No candles!' repeated Mr Kernan obdurately. 'That's off!'

The transept of the Jesuit Church in Gardiner Street was almost full; and still at every moment gentlemen entered from the side door and, directed by the lay-brother, walked on tiptoe along the aisles until they found seating accommodation. The gentlemen were all well dressed and orderly. The light of the lamps of the church fell upon an assembly of black clothes and white collars, relieved here and there by tweeds, on dark mottled pillars of green marble and on lugubrious canvases. The gentlemen sat in the benches, having hitched their trousers slightly above their knees and laid their hats in security. They sat well back and gazed formally at the distant speck of red light which was suspended before the high altar.

In one of the benches near the pulpit sat Mr Cunningham and Mr Kernan. In the bench behind sat Mr M'Coy alone: and in the bench behind him sat Mr Power and Mr Fogarty. Mr M'Coy had tried unsuccessfully to find a place in the bench with the others, and, when the party had settled down in the form of a quincunx, he had tried unsuccessfully to make comic remarks. As these had not been well received, he had desisted. Even he was sensible of the decorous atmosphere and even he began to respond to the religious stimulus. In a whisper, Mr Cunningham drew Mr Kernan's attention to Mr Harford, the moneylender, who sat some distance off, and to Mr Fanning, the registration agent and mayor maker of the city, who was sitting immediately under the pulpit beside one of the newly elected councillors of the ward. To the right sat old Michael Grimes, the owner of three pawnbroker's shops, and Dan Hogan's nephew, who was up for the job in the Town Clerk's office. Farther in front sat Mr Hendrick, the chief reporter of *The Freeman's Journal*, and poor O'Carroll, an old friend of Mr Kernan's, who had been at one time a considerable commercial figure. Gradually, as he recognised familiar faces, Mr Kernan began to feel more at home. His hat, which had been rehabilitated by his wife, rested upon his knees. Once or twice he pulled down his cuffs with one hand while he held the brim of his hat lightly, but firmly, with the other hand.

A powerful-looking figure, the upper part of which was draped with a white surplice, was observed to be struggling up into the pulpit. Simultaneously the congregation unsettled, produced handkerchiefs and knelt upon them with care. Mr Kernan followed the general example. The priest's figure now stood upright in the pulpit, two-thirds of its bulk, crowned by a massive red face, appearing above the balustrade.

Father Purdon knelt down, turned towards the red speck of light and, covering his face with his hands, prayed. After an interval, he uncovered his face and rose. The congregation rose also and settled again on its benches. Mr Kernan restored his hat to its original position on his knee and presented an attentive face to the preacher. The preacher turned back each wide sleeve of his surplice with an elaborate large gesture and slowly surveyed the array of faces. Then he said:

'For the children of this world are wiser in their generation than the children of light. Wherefore make unto yourselves friends out of the mammon of iniquity so that when you die they may receive you into everlasting dwellings.'

Father Purdon developed the text with resonant assurance. It was one of the most difficult texts in all the Scriptures, he said, to interpret properly. It was a text which might seem to the casual observer at variance with the lofty morality elsewhere preached by Jesus Christ. But, he told his hearers, the text had seemed to him specially adapted for the guidance of those whose lot it was to lead the life of the world and who yet wished to lead that life not in the manner of worldlings. It was a text for business men and professional men. Jesus Christ, with His divine understanding of every cranny of our human nature, understood that all men were not called to the religious life, that by far the vast majority were forced to live in the world, and, to a certain extent, for the world: and in this sentence He designed to give them a word of counsel, setting before them as exemplars in the religious life those very worshippers of Mammon who were of all men the least solicitous in matters religious.

He told his hearers that he was there that evening for no terrifying, no extravagant purpose; but as a man of the world speaking to his fellow-men. He came to speak to business men and he would speak to them in a businesslike way. If he might use the metaphor, he said, he was their spiritual accountant; and he wished each and every one of his hearers to open his books, the books of his spiritual life, and see if they tallied accurately with conscience.

Jesus Christ was not a hard taskmaster. He understood our little failings, understood the weakness of our poor fallen nature, understood the tempt-ations of this life. We might have had, we all had from time to time, our temptations: we might have, we all had, our failings. But one thing only, he said, he would ask of his hearers. And that was: to be straight and manly with God. If their accounts tallied in every point to say: 'Well, I have verified my accounts. I find all well.'

But if, as might happen, there were some discrepancies, to admit the truth, to be frank and say like a man: 'Well, I have looked into my accounts. I find this wrong and this wrong. But, with God's grace, I will rectify this and this. I will set right my accounts.'

The Dead

Lily, the caretaker's daughter, was literally run off her feet. Hardly had she brought one gentleman into the little pantry behind the office on the ground floor and helped him off with his overcoat than the wheezy hall-door bell clanged again and she had to scamper along the bare hallway to let in another guest. It was well for her she had not to attend to the ladies also. But Miss Kate and Miss Julia had thought of that and had converted the bathroom upstairs into a ladies' dressing-room. Miss Kate and Miss Julia were there, gossiping and laughing and fussing, walking after each other to the head of the stairs, peering down over the banisters and calling down to Lily to ask her who had come.

It was always a great affair, the Misses Morkan's annual dance. Everybody who knew them came to it, members of the family, old friends of the family, the members of Julia's choir, any of Kate's pupils that were grown up enough, and even some of Mary Jane's pupils too. Never once had it fallen flat. For years and years it had gone off in splendid style, as long as anyone could remember; ever since Kate and Julia, after the death of their brother Pat, had left the house in Stoney Batter and taken Mary Jane, their only niece, to live with them in the dark, gaunt house on Usher's Island, the upper part of which they had rented from Mr Fulham, the corn-factor on the ground floor. That was a good thirty years ago if it was a day. Mary Jane, who was then a little girl in short clothes, was now the main prop of the household, for she had the organ in Haddington Road. She had been through the Academy and gave a pupils' concert every year in the upper room of the Antient Concert Rooms. Many of her pupils belonged to the better-class families on the Kingstown and Dalkey line. Old as they were, her aunts also did their share. Julia, though she was quite grey, was still the leading soprano in Adam and Eve's, and Kate, being too feeble to go about much, gave music lessons to beginners on the old square piano in the back room. Lily, the caretaker's daughter, did housemaid's work for them. Though their life was modest, they believed in eating well; the best of everything: diamond-bone sirloins, three-shilling tea and the best bottled stout. But Lily seldom made a mistake in the orders, so that she got on well with her three mistresses. They were fussy, that was all. But the only thing they would not stand was back answers.

Of course, they had good reason to be fussy on such a night. And then it was long after ten o'clock and yet there was no sign of Gabriel and his wife. Besides they were dreadfully afraid that Freddy Malins might turn up screwed. They would not wish for worlds that any of Mary Jane's pupils should see him under the influence; and when he was like that it was sometimes very hard to manage him. Freddy Malins always came late, but they wondered what could be keeping Gabriel: and that was what brought them every two minutes to the banisters to ask Lily had Gabriel or Freddy come.

'O, Mr Conroy,' said Lily to Gabriel when she opened the door for him, 'Miss Kate and Miss Julia thought you were never coming. Good-night, Mrs Conroy.'

'I'll engage they did,' said Gabriel, 'but they forget that my wife here takes three mortal hours to dress herself.'

He stood on the mat, scraping the snow from his goloshes, while Lily led his wife to the foot of the stairs and called out: 'Miss Kate, here's Mrs Conroy.'

Kate and Julia came toddling down the dark stairs at once. Both of them kissed Gabriel's wife, said she must be perished alive, and asked was Gabriel with her.

'Here I am as right as the mail, Aunt Kate! Go on up. I'll follow,' called out Gabriel from the dark.

He continued scraping his feet vigorously while the three women went upstairs, laughing, to the ladies' dressing-room. A light fringe of snow lay like a cape on the shoulders of his overcoat and like toecaps on the toes of his goloshes; and, as the buttons of his overcoat slipped with a squeaking noise through the snow-stiffened frieze, a cold, fragrant air from out-of-doors escaped from crevices and folds.

'Is it snowing again, Mr Conroy?' asked Lily.

She had preceded him into the pantry to help him off with his overcoat. Gabriel smiled at the three syllables she had given his surname and glanced at her. She was a slim, growing girl, pale in complexion and with hay-coloured hair. The gas in the pantry made her look still paler. Gabriel had known her when she was a child and used to sit on the lowest step nursing a rag doll.

'Yes, Lily,' he answered, 'and I think we're in for a night of it.'

He looked up at the pantry ceiling, which was shaking with the stamping and shuffling of feet on the floor above, listened for a moment to the piano and then glanced at the girl, who was folding his overcoat carefully at the end of a shelf.

'Tell me, Lily,' he said in a friendly tone, 'do you still go to school?'

'O no, sir,' she answered. 'I'm done schooling this year and more.'

'O, then,' said Gabriel gaily, 'I suppose we'll be going to your wedding one of these fine days with your young man, eh?'

The girl glanced back at him over her shoulder and said with great bitterness: 'The men that is now is only all palaver and what they can get out of you.'

Gabriel coloured, as if he felt he had made a mistake and, without looking at her, kicked off his goloshes and flicked actively with his muffler at his patent-leather shoes.

He was a stout, tallish young man. The high colour of his cheeks pushed upwards even to his forehead, where it scattered itself in a few formless patches of pale red; and on his hairless face there scintillated restlessly the polished lenses and the bright gilt rims of the glasses which screened his delicate and restless eyes. His glossy black hair was parted in the middle and brushed in a long curve behind his ears where it curled slightly beneath the groove left by his hat.

When he had flicked lustre into his shoes he stood up and pulled his waistcoat down more tightly on his plump body. Then he took a coin rapidly from his pocket.

'O Lily,' he said, thrusting it into her hands, 'it's Christmas-time, isn't it? Just . . . here's a little . . . '

He walked rapidly towards the door.

'O no, sir!' cried the girl, following him. 'Really, sir, I wouldn't take it.'

'Christmas-time! Christmas-time!' said Gabriel, almost trotting to the stairs and waving his hand to her in deprecation.

The girl, seeing that he had gained the stairs, called out after him: 'Well, thank you, sir.'

He waited outside the drawing-room door until the waltz should finish, listening to the skirts that swept against it and to the shuffling of feet. He was still discomposed by the girl's bitter and sudden retort. It had cast a gloom over him which he tried to dispel by arranging his cuffs and the bows of his tie. He then took from his waistcoat pocket a little paper and glanced at the headings he had made for his speech. He was undecided about the lines from Robert Browning, for he feared they would be above the heads of his hearers. Some quotation that they would recognise from Shakespeare or from the Melodies would be better. The indelicate clacking of the men's heels and the shuffling of their soles reminded him that their grade of culture differed from his. He would only make himself ridiculous by quoting poetry to them which they could not understand. They would think that he was airing his superior education. He would fail with them just as he had failed with the girl in the pantry. He had taken up a wrong tone. His whole speech was a mistake from first to last, an utter failure.

Just then his aunts and his wife came out of the ladies' dressing-room. His aunts were two small, plainly dressed old women. Aunt Julia was an inch or so the taller. Her hair, drawn low over the tops of her ears, was grey; and grey also, with darker shadows, was her large flaccid face. Though she was stout in build and stood erect, her slow eyes and parted lips gave her the appearance of a woman who did not know where she was or where she was going. Aunt Kate was more vivacious. Her face, healthier than her sister's, was all puckers and creases, like a shrivelled red apple, and her hair, braided in the same old-fashioned way, had not lost its ripe nut colour.

They both kissed Gabriel frankly. He was their favourite nephew, the son of their dead elder sister, Ellen, who had married T. J. Conroy of the Port and Docks.

'Gretta tells me you're not going to take a cab back to Monkstown tonight, Gabriel,' said Aunt Kate.

'No,' said Gabriel, turning to his wife, 'we had quite enough of that last year, hadn't we? Don't you remember, Aunt Kate, what a cold Gretta got out of it? Cab windows rattling all the way, and the east wind blowing in after we passed Merrion. Very jolly it was. Gretta caught a dreadful cold.'

Aunt Kate frowned severely and nodded her head at every word.

'Quite right, Gabriel, quite right,' she said. 'You can't be too careful.'

'But as for Gretta there,' said Gabriel, 'she'd walk home in the snow if she were let.'

Mrs Conroy laughed.

'Don't mind him, Aunt Kate,' she said. 'He's really an awful bother, what with green shades for Tom's eyes at night and making him do the dumb-bells, and forcing Eva to eat the stirabout. The poor child! And she simply hates the sight of it! . . . O, but you'll never guess what he makes me wear now!'

She broke out into a peal of laughter and glanced at her husband, whose admiring and happy eyes had been wandering from her dress to her face and hair. The two aunts laughed heartily, too, for Gabriel's solicitude was a standing joke with them.

'Goloshes!' said Mrs Conroy. 'That's the latest. Whenever it's wet under-foot I must put on my goloshes. Tonight even, he wanted me to put them on, but I wouldn't. The next thing he'll buy me will be a diving suit.'

Gabriel laughed nervously and patted his tie reassuringly, while Aunt Kate nearly doubled herself, so heartily did she enjoy the joke. The smile soon faded from Aunt Julia's face and her mirthless eyes were directed towards her nephew's face. After a pause she asked: 'And what are goloshes, Gabriel?'

'Goloshes, Julia!' exclaimed her sister. 'Goodness me, don't you know what goloshes are? You wear them over your . . . over your boots, Gretta, isn't it?'

'Yes,' said Mrs Conroy. 'Guttapercha things. We both have a pair now. Gabriel says everyone wears them on the continent.'

'O, on the continent,' murmured Aunt Julia, nodding her head slowly.

Gabriel knitted his brows and said, as if he were slightly angered: 'It's nothing very wonderful, but Gretta thinks it very funny because she says the word reminds her of Christy Minstrels.'

'But tell me, Gabriel,' said Aunt Kate, with brisk tact. 'Of course, you've seen about the room. Gretta was saying . . .'

'O, the room is all right,' replied Gabriel. 'I've taken one in the Gresham.'

'To be sure,' said Aunt Kate, 'by far the best thing to do. And the children, Gretta, you're not anxious about them?'

'O, for one night,' said Mrs Conroy. 'Besides, Bessie will look after them.'

'To be sure,' said Aunt Kate again. 'What a comfort it is to have a girl like that, one you can depend on! There's that Lily, I'm sure I don't know what has come over her lately. She's not the girl she was at all.'

Gabriel was about to ask his aunt some questions on this point, but she broke off suddenly to gaze after her sister, who had wandered down the stairs and was craning her neck over the banisters.

'Now, I ask you,' she said almost testily, 'where is Julia going? Julia! Julia! Where are you going?'

Julia, who had gone half way down one flight, came back and announced blandly: 'Here's Freddy.'

At the same moment a clapping of hands and a final flourish of the pianist told that the waltz had ended. The drawing-room door was opened from within and some couples came out. Aunt Kate drew Gabriel aside hurriedly and whispered into his ear: 'Slip down, Gabriel, like a good fellow and see if he's all right, and don't let him up if he's screwed. I'm sure he's screwed. I'm sure he is.'

Gabriel went to the stairs and listened over the banisters. He could hear two persons talking in the pantry. Then he recognised Freddy Malins' laugh. He went down the stairs noisily.

'It's such a relief,' said Aunt Kate to Mrs Conroy, 'that Gabriel is here. I always feel easier in my mind when he's here . . . Julia, there's Miss Daly and Miss Power will take some refreshment. Thanks for your beautiful waltz, Miss Daly. It made lovely time.'

A tall wizen-faced man, with a stiff grizzled moustache and swarthy skin, who was passing out with his partner, said: 'And may we have some refreshment, too, Miss Morkan?'

'Julia,' said Aunt Kate summarily, 'and here's Mr Browne and Miss Furlong. Take them in, Julia, with Miss Daly and Miss Power.'

'I'm the man for the ladies,' said Mr Browne, pursing his lips until his moustache bristled and smiling in all his wrinkles. 'You know, Miss Morkan, the reason they are so fond of me is – '

He did not finish his sentence, but, seeing that Aunt Kate was out of earshot, at once led the three young ladies into the back room. The middle of the room was occupied by two square tables placed end to end, and on these Aunt Julia and the caretaker were straightening and smoothing a large cloth. On the sideboard were arrayed dishes and plates, and glasses and bundles of knives and forks and spoons. The top of the closed square piano served also as a sideboard for viands and sweets. At a smaller sideboard in one corner two young men were standing, drinking hop-bitters.

Mr Browne led his charges thither and invited them all, in jest, to some ladies' punch, hot, strong and sweet. As they said they never took anything strong, he opened three bottles of lemonade for them. Then he asked one of the young men to move aside, and, taking hold of the decanter, filled out for himself a goodly measure of whiskey. The young men eyed him respectfully while he took a trial sip.

'God help me,' he said, smiling, 'it's the doctor's orders.'

His wizened face broke into a broader smile, and the three young ladies laughed in musical echo to his pleasantry, swaying their bodies to and fro, with nervous jerks of their shoulders. The boldest said: 'O, now, Mr Browne, I'm sure the doctor never ordered anything of the kind.'

Mr Browne took another sip of his whiskey and said, with sidling mimicry: 'Well, you see, I'm like the famous Mrs Cassidy, who is reported to have said: "Now, Mary Grimes, if I don't take it, make me take it, for I feel I want it." '

His hot face had leaned forward a little too confidentially and he had assumed a very low Dublin accent so that the young ladies, with one instinct, received his speech in silence. Miss Furlong, who was one of Mary Jane's pupils, asked Miss Daly what was the name of the pretty waltz she had played; and Mr Browne, seeing that he was ignored, turned promptly to the two young men who were more appreciative.

A red-faced young woman, dressed in pansy, came into the room, excitedly clapping her hands and crying: 'Quadrilles! Quadrilles!'

Close on her heels came Aunt Kate, crying: 'Two gentlemen and three ladies, Mary Jane!'

'O, here's Mr Bergin and Mr Kerrigan,' said Mary Jane. 'Mr Kerrigan, will you take Miss Power? Miss Furlong, may I get you a partner, Mr Bergin. O, that'll just do now.'

'Three ladies, Mary Jane,' said Aunt Kate.

The two young gentlemen asked the ladies if they might have the pleasure, and Mary Jane turned to Miss Daly.

'O, Miss Daly, you're really awfully good, after playing for the last two dances, but really we're so short of ladies tonight.'

'I don't mind in the least, Miss Morkan.'

'But I've a nice partner for you, Mr Bartell D'Arcy, the tenor. I'll get him to sing later on. All Dublin is raving about him.'

'Lovely voice, lovely voice!' said Aunt Kate.

As the piano had twice begun the prelude to the first figure Mary Jane led her recruits quickly from the room. They had hardly gone when Aunt Julia wandered slowly into the room, looking behind her at something.

'What is the matter, Julia?' asked Aunt Kate anxiously. 'Who is it?'

Julia, who was carrying in a column of table-napkins, turned to her sister and said, simply, as if the question had surprised her: 'It's only Freddy, Kate, and Gabriel with him.'

In fact right behind her Gabriel could be seen piloting Freddy Malins across the landing. The latter, a young man of about forty, was of Gabriel's size and build, with very round shoulders. His face was fleshy and pallid, touched with colour only at the thick hanging lobes of his ears and at the wide wings of his nose. He had coarse features, a blunt nose, a convex and receding brow, tumid and protruded lips. His heavy-lidded eyes and the disorder of his scanty hair made him look sleepy. He was laughing heartily in a high key at a story which he had been telling Gabriel on the stairs and at the same time rubbing the knuckles of his left fist backwards and forwards into his left eye.

'Good-evening, Freddy,' said Aunt Julia.

Freddy Malins bade the Misses Morkan good-evening in what seemed an offhand fashion by reason of the habitual catch in his voice and then, seeing that Mr Browne was grinning at him from the sideboard, crossed the room on rather shaky legs and began to repeat in an undertone the story he had just told to Gabriel.

'He's not so bad, is he?' said Aunt Kate to Gabriel.

Gabriel's brows were dark but he raised them quickly and answered: 'O, no, hardly noticeable.'

'Now, isn't he a terrible fellow!' she said. 'And his poor mother made him take the pledge on New Year's Eve. But come on, Gabriel, into the drawing-room.'

Before leaving the room with Gabriel she signalled to Mr Browne by frowning and shaking her forefinger in warning to and fro. Mr Browne nodded in answer and, when she had gone, said to Freddy Malins: 'Now, then, Teddy, I'm going to fill you out a good glass of lemonade just to buck you up.'

Freddy Malins, who was nearing the climax of his story, waved the offer aside impatiently but Mr Browne, having first called Freddy Malins' attention to a disarray in his dress, filled out and handed him a full glass of lemonade. Freddy Malins' left hand accepted the glass mechanically, his right hand being engaged in the mechanical readjustment of his dress. Mr Browne, whose face was once more wrinkling with mirth, poured out for himself a glass of whiskey while Freddy Malins exploded, before he had well reached the climax of his story, in a kink of high-pitched bronchitic laughter and, setting down his untasted and overflowing glass, began to rub the knuckles of his left fist backwards and forwards into his left eye, repeating words of his last phrase as well as his fit of laughter would allow him.

Gabriel could not listen while Mary Jane was playing her Academy piece, full of runs and difficult passages, to the hushed drawing-room. He liked music but the piece she was playing had no melody for him and he doubted whether it had any melody for the other listeners, though they had begged Mary Jane to play something. Four young men, who had come from the refreshment-room to stand in the doorway at the sound of the piano, had gone away quietly in couples after a few minutes. The only persons who seemed to follow the music were Mary Jane herself, her hands racing along the key-board or lifted from it at the pauses like those of a priestess in momentary imprecation, and Aunt Kate standing at her elbow to turn the page.

Gabriel's eyes, irritated by the floor, which glittered with beeswax under the heavy chandelier, wandered to the wall above the piano. A picture of the balcony scene in *Romeo and Juliet* hung there and beside it was a picture of the two murdered princes in the Tower which Aunt Julia had worked in red, blue and brown wools when she was a girl. Probably in the school they had gone to as girls that kind of work had been taught for one year. His mother had worked for him as a birthday present a waistcoat of purple tabinet, with little foxes' heads upon it, lined with brown satin and having round mulberry buttons. It was strange that his mother had had no musical talent though Aunt Kate used to call her the brains carrier of the Morkan family. Both she and Julia had always seemed a little proud of their serious and matronly Sister. Her photograph stood before the pier-glass. She held an open book on her knees and was pointing out something in it to Constantine who, dressed in a man-o'-war suit, lay at her feet. It was she who had chosen the names of her sons for she was very sensible of the dignity of family life. Thanks to her, Constantine was now senior curate in Balbriggan and, thanks to her, Gabriel himself had taken his degree in the Royal University. A shadow passed over his face as he remembered her sullen opposition to his marriage. Some slighting phrases she had used still rankled in his memory; she had once spoken of Gretta as being country cute and that was not true of Gretta at all. It was Gretta who had nursed her during all her last long illness in their house at Monkstown.

He knew that Mary Jane must be near the end of her piece for she was playing again the opening melody with runs of scales after every bar and while he waited for the end the resentment died down in his heart. The piece ended with a trill of octaves in the treble and a final deep octave in the bass. Great applause greeted Mary Jane as, blushing and rolling up her music nervously, she escaped from the room. The most vigorous clapping came from the four young men in the doorway who had gone away to the refreshment-room at the beginning of the piece but had come back when the piano had stopped.

Lancers were arranged. Gabriel found himself partnered with Miss Ivors. She was a frank-mannered talkative young lady, with a freckled face and prominent brown eyes. She did not wear a low-cut bodice and the large brooch which was fixed in the front of her collar bore on it an Irish device and motto.

When they had taken their places she said abruptly: 'I have a crow to pluck with you.'

'With me?' said Gabriel.

She nodded her head gravely.

'What is it?' asked Gabriel, smiling at her solemn manner.

'Who is G.C.?' answered Miss Ivors, turning her eyes upon him.

Gabriel coloured and was about to knit his brows, as if he did not understand, when she said bluntly: 'O, innocent Amy! I have found out that you write for *The Daily Express*. Now, aren't you ashamed of yourself?'

'Why should I be ashamed of myself?' asked Gabriel, blinking his eyes and trying to smile.

'Well, I'm ashamed of you,' said Miss Ivors frankly. 'To say you'd write for a paper like that. I didn't think you were a West Briton.' A look of perplexity appeared on Gabriel's face. It was true that he wrote a literary column every Wednesday in *The Daily Express*, for which he was paid fifteen shillings. But that did not make him a West Briton surely. The books he received for review were almost more welcome than the paltry cheque. He loved to feel the covers and turn over the pages of newly printed books. Nearly every day when his teaching in the college was ended he used to wander down the quays to the second-hand booksellers, to Hickey's on Bachelor's Walk, to Webb's or Massey's on Aston's Quay, or to O'Clohissey's in the by street. He did not know how to meet her charge. He wanted to say that literature was above politics. But they were friends of many years' standing and their careers had been parallel, first at the University and then as teachers: he could not risk a grandiose phrase with her. He continued blinking his eyes and trying to smile and murmured lamely that he saw nothing political in writing reviews of books.

When their turn to cross had come he was still perplexed and inattentive.

Miss Ivors promptly took his hand in a warm grasp and said in a soft friendly tone: 'Of course, I was only joking. Come, we cross now.'

When they were together again she spoke of the University question and Gabriel felt more at ease. A friend of hers had shown her his review of Browning's poems. That was how she had found out the secret: but she liked the review immensely. Then she said suddenly: 'O, Mr Conroy, will you come for an excursion to the Aran Isles this summer? We're going to stay there a whole month. It will be splendid out in the Atlantic. You ought to come. Mr Clancy is coming, and Mr Kilkelly and Kathleen Kearney. It would be splendid for Gretta too if she'd come. She's from Connacht, isn't she?'

'Her people are,' said Gabriel shortly.

'But you will come, won't you?' said Miss Ivors, laying her warm hand eagerly on his arm.

'The fact is,' said Gabriel, 'I have just arranged to go – '

'Go where?' asked Miss Ivors.

'Well, you know, every year I go for a cycling tour with some fellows and so – '

'But where?' asked Miss Ivors.

'Well, we usually go to France or Belgium or perhaps Germany,' said Gabriel awkwardly.

'And why do you go to France and Belgium,' said Miss Ivors, 'instead of visiting your own land?'

'Well,' said Gabriel, 'it's partly to keep in touch with the languages and partly for a change.'

'And haven't you your own language to keep in touch with – Irish?' asked Miss Ivors.

'Well,' said Gabriel, 'if it comes to that, you know, Irish is not my language.'

Their neighbours had turned to listen to the cross-examination. Gabriel glanced right and left nervously and tried to keep his good humour under the ordeal which was making a blush invade his forehead.

'And haven't you your own land to visit,' continued Miss Ivors, 'that you know nothing of, your own people, and your own country?'

'O, to tell you the truth,' retorted Gabriel suddenly, 'I'm sick of my own country, sick of it!'

'Why?' asked Miss Ivors.

Gabriel did not answer for his retort had heated him.

'Why?' repeated Miss Ivors.

They had to go visiting together and, as he had not answered her, Miss Ivors said warmly: 'Of course, you've no answer.'

Gabriel tried to cover his agitation by taking part in the dance with great energy. He avoided her eyes for he had seen a sour expression on her face. But when they met in the long chain he was surprised to feel his hand firmly pressed. She looked at him from under her brows for a moment quizzically until he smiled. Then, just as the chain was about to start again, she stood on tiptoe and whispered into his ear: 'West Briton!'

When the lancers were over Gabriel went away to a remote corner of the room where Freddy Malins' mother was sitting. She was a stout feeble old woman with white hair. Her voice had a catch in it like her son's and she stuttered slightly. She had been told that Freddy had come and that he was nearly all right. Gabriel asked her whether she had had a good crossing. She lived with her married daughter in Glasgow and came to Dublin on a visit once a year. She answered placidly that she had had a beautiful crossing and that the captain had been most attentive to her. She spoke also of the beautiful house her daughter kept in Glasgow, and of all the friends they had there. While her tongue rambled on Gabriel tried to banish from his mind all memory of the unpleasant incident with Miss Ivors. Of course the girl or woman, or whatever she was, was an enthusiast but there was a time for all things. Perhaps he ought not to have answered her like that. But she had no right to call him a West Briton before people, even in joke. She had tried to make him ridiculous before people, heckling him and staring at him with her rabbit's eyes.

He saw his wife making her way towards him through the waltzing couples. When she reached him she said into his ear: 'Gabriel, Aunt Kate wants to know won't you carve the goose as usual. Miss Daly will carve the ham and I'll do the pudding.'

'All right,' said Gabriel.

'She's sending in the younger ones first as soon as this waltz is over so that we'll have the table to ourselves.'

'Were you dancing?' asked Gabriel.

'Of course I was. Didn't you see me? What row had you with Molly Ivors?'

'No row. Why? Did she say so?'

'Something like that. I'm trying to get that Mr D'Arcy to sing. He's full of conceit, I think.'

'There was no row,' said Gabriel moodily, 'only she wanted me to go for a trip to the west of Ireland and I said I wouldn't.'

His wife clasped her hands excitedly and gave a little jump.

'O, do go, Gabriel,' she cried. 'I'd love to see Galway again.'

'You can go if you like,' said Gabriel coldly.

She looked at him for a moment, then turned to Mrs Malins and said: 'There's a nice husband for you, Mrs Malins.'

While she was threading her way back across the room Mrs Malins, without adverting to the interruption, went on to tell Gabriel what beautiful places there were in Scotland and beautiful scenery. Her son-in-law brought them every year to the lakes and they used to go fishing. Her son-in-law was a splendid fisher. One day he caught a beautiful big fish and the man in the hotel cooked it for their dinner.

Gabriel hardly heard what she said. Now that supper was coming near he began to think again about his speech and about the quotation. When he saw Freddy Malins coming across the room to visit his mother Gabriel left the chair free for him and retired into the embrasure of the window. The room had already cleared and from the back room came the clatter of plates and knives. Those who still remained in the drawing-room seemed tired of dancing and were conversing quietly in little groups. Gabriel's warm trembling fingers tapped the cold pane of the window. How cool it must be outside! How pleasant it would be to walk out alone, first along by the river and then through the park! The snow would be lying on the branches of the trees and forming a bright cap on the top of the Wellington Monument. How much more pleasant it would be there than at the supper-table!

He ran over the headings of his speech: Irish hospitality, sad memories, the Three Graces, Paris, the quotation from Browning. He repeated to himself a phrase he had written in his review: 'One feels that one is listening to a thought-tormented music.' Miss Ivors had praised the review. Was she sincere? Had she really any life of her own behind all her propagandism? There had never been any ill-feeling between them until that night. It unnerved him to think that she would be at the supper-table, looking up at him while he spoke with her critical quizzing eyes. Perhaps she would not be sorry to see him fail in his speech. An idea came into his mind and gave him courage. He would say, alluding to Aunt Kate and Aunt Julia: 'Ladies and Gentlemen, the generation which is now on the wane among us may have had its faults but for my part I think it had certain qualities of hospitality, of humour, of humanity, which the new and very serious and hyper-educated generation that is growing up around us seems to me to lack.' Very good: that was one for Miss Ivors. What did he care that his aunts were only two ignorant old women?

A murmur in the room attracted his attention. Mr Browne was advancing from the door, gallantly escorting Aunt Julia, who leaned upon his arm, smiling and hanging her head. An irregular musketry of applause escorted her also as far as the piano and then, as Mary Jane seated herself on the stool, and Aunt Julia, no longer smiling, half turned so as to pitch her voice fairly into the room, gradually ceased. Gabriel recognised the prelude. It was that of an old song of Aunt Julia's – *Arrayed for the Bridal*. Her voice, strong and clear in tone, attacked with great spirit the runs which embellish the air and though she sang very rapidly she did not miss even the smallest of the grace notes. To follow the voice, without looking at the singer's face, was to feel and share the excitement of swift and secure flight. Gabriel applauded loudly with all the others at the close of the song and loud applause was borne in from the invisible supper-table. It sounded so genuine that a little colour struggled into Aunt Julia's face as she bent to replace in the music-stand the old leather-bound song-book that had her initials on the cover. Freddy Malins, who had listened with his head perched sideways to hear her better, was still applauding when everyone else had ceased and talking animatedly to his mother who nodded her head gravely and slowly in acquiescence. At last, when he could clap no more, he stood up suddenly and hurried across the room to Aunt Julia whose hand he seized and held in both his hands, shaking it when words failed him or the catch in his voice proved too much for him.

'I was just telling my mother,' he said, 'I never heard you sing so well, never. No, I never heard your voice so good as it is tonight. Now! Would you believe that now? That's the truth. Upon my word and honour that's the truth. I never heard your voice sound so fresh and so . . . so clear and fresh, never.'

Aunt Julia smiled broadly and murmured something about compliments as she released her hand from his grasp. Mr Browne extended his open hand towards her and said to those who were near him in the manner of a showman introducing a prodigy to an audience: 'Miss Julia Morkan, my latest discovery!'

He was laughing very heartily at this himself when Freddy Malins turned to him and said: 'Well, Browne, if you're serious you might make a worse discovery. All I can say is I never heard her sing half so well as long as I am coming here. And that's the honest truth.'

'Neither did I,' said Mr Browne. 'I think her voice has greatly improved.'

Aunt Julia shrugged her shoulders and said with meek pride: 'Thirty years ago I hadn't a bad voice as voices go.'

'I often told Julia,' said Aunt Kate emphatically, 'that she was simply thrown away in that choir. But she never would be said by me.'

She turned as if to appeal to the good sense of the others against a refractory child while Aunt Julia gazed in front of her, a vague smile of reminiscence playing on her face.

'No,' continued Aunt Kate, 'she wouldn't be said or led by anyone, slaving there in that choir night and day, night and day. Six o'clock on Christmas morning! And all for what?'

'Well, isn't it for the honour of God, Aunt Kate?' asked Mary Jane, twisting round on the piano-stool and smiling.

Aunt Kate turned fiercely on her niece and said: 'I know all about the honour of God, Mary Jane, but I think it's not at all honourable for the pope to turn out the women out of the choirs that have slaved there all their lives and put little whipper-snappers of boys over their heads. I suppose it is for the good of the church if the pope does it. But it's not just, Mary Jane, and it's not right.'

She had worked herself into a passion and would have continued in defence of her sister for it was a sore subject with her but Mary Jane, seeing that all the dancers had come back, intervened pacifically: 'Now, Aunt Kate, you're giving scandal to Mr Browne who is of the other persuasion.' Aunt Kate turned to Mr Browne, who was grinning at this allusion to his religion, and said hastily: 'O, I don't question the pope's being right. I'm only a stupid old woman and I wouldn't presume to do such a thing. But there's such a thing as common everyday politeness and gratitude. And if I were in Julia's place I'd tell that Father Healey straight up to his face . . .'

'And besides, Aunt Kate,' said Mary Jane, 'we really are all hungry and when we are hungry we are all very quarrelsome.'

'And when we are thirsty we are also quarrelsome,' added Mr Browne.

'So that we had better go to supper,' said Mary Jane, 'and finish the discussion afterwards.'

On the landing outside the drawing-room Gabriel found his wife and Mary Jane trying to persuade Miss Ivors to stay for supper. But Miss Ivors, who had put on her hat and was buttoning her cloak, would not stay. She did not feel in the least hungry and she had already overstayed her time.

'But only for ten minutes, Molly,' said Mrs Conroy. 'That won't delay you.'

'To take a pick itself,' said Mary Jane, 'after all your dancing.'

'I really couldn't,' said Miss Ivors.

'I am afraid you didn't enjoy yourself at all,' said Mary Jane hopelessly.

'Ever so much, I assure you,' said Miss Ivors, 'but you really must let me run off now.'

'But how can you get home?' asked Mrs Conroy.

'O, it's only two steps up the quay.'

Gabriel hesitated a moment and said: 'If you will allow me, Miss Ivors, I'll see you home if you are really obliged to go.'

But Miss Ivors broke away from them.

'I won't hear of it,' she cried. 'For goodness' sake go in to your suppers and don't mind me. I'm quite well able to take care of myself.'

'Well, you're the comical girl, Molly,' said Mrs Conroy frankly.

'*Beannacht libh*,' cried Miss Ivors, with a laugh, as she ran down the staircase.

Mary Jane gazed after her, a moody puzzled expression on her face, while Mrs Conroy leaned over the banisters to listen for the hall-door. Gabriel asked himself was he the cause of her abrupt departure. But she did not seem to be in ill humour: she had gone away laughing. He stared blankly down the staircase.

At the moment Aunt Kate came toddling out of the supper-room, almost wringing her hands in despair.

'Where is Gabriel?' she cried. 'Where on earth is Gabriel? There's everyone waiting in there, stage to let, and nobody to carve the goose!'

'Here I am, Aunt Kate!' cried Gabriel, with sudden animation, 'ready to carve a flock of geese, if necessary.'

A fat brown goose lay at one end of the table and at the other end, on a bed of creased paper strewn with sprigs of parsley, lay a great ham, stripped of its outer skin and peppered over with crust crumbs, a neat paper frill round its shin and beside this was a round of spiced beef. Between these rival ends ran parallel lines of side-dishes: two little minsters of jelly, red and yellow; a shallow dish full of blocks of blancmange and red jam, a large green leaf-shaped dish with a stalk-shaped handle, on which lay bunches of purple raisins and peeled almonds, a companion dish on which lay a solid rectangle of Smyrna figs, a dish of custard topped with grated nutmeg, a small bowl full of chocolates and sweets wrapped in gold and silver papers and a glass vase in which stood some tall celery stalks. In the centre of the table there stood, as sentries to a fruit-stand which upheld a pyramid of oranges and American apples, two squat old-fashioned decanters of cut glass, one containing port and the other dark sherry. On the closed square piano a pudding in a huge yellow dish lay in waiting and behind it were three squads of bottles of stout and ale and minerals, drawn up according to the colours of their uniforms, the first two black, with brown and red labels, the third and smallest squad white, with transverse green sashes.

Gabriel took his seat boldly at the head of the table and, having looked to the edge of the carver, plunged his fork firmly into the goose. He felt quite at ease now for he was an expert carver and liked nothing better than to find himself at the head of a well-laden table.

'Miss Furlong, what shall I send you?' he asked. 'A wing or a slice of the breast?'

'Just a small slice of the breast.'

'Miss Higgins, what for you?'

'O, anything at all, Mr Conroy.'

While Gabriel and Miss Daly exchanged plates of goose and plates of ham and spiced beef Lily went from guest to guest with a dish of hot floury potatoes wrapped in a white napkin. This was Mary Jane's idea and she had also suggested apple sauce for the goose but Aunt Kate had said that plain roast goose without any apple sauce had always been good enough for her and she hoped she might never eat worse. Mary Jane waited on her pupils and saw that they got the best slices and Aunt Kate and Aunt Julia opened and carried across from the piano bottles of stout and ale for the gentlemen and bottles of minerals for the ladies. There was a great deal of confusion and laughter and noise, the noise of orders and counter-orders, of knives and forks, of corks and glass-stoppers. Gabriel began to carve second helpings as soon as he had finished the first round without serving himself. Everyone protested loudly so that he compromised by taking a long draught of stout for he had found the carving hot work. Mary Jane settled down quietly to her supper but Aunt Kate and Aunt Julia were still toddling round the table, walking on each other's heels, getting in each other's way and giving each other unheeded orders. Mr Browne begged of them to sit down and eat their suppers and so did Gabriel but they said there was time enough, so that, at last, Freddy Malins stood up and, capturing Aunt Kate, plumped her down on her chair amid general laughter.

When everyone had been well served Gabriel said, smiling: 'Now, if anyone wants a little more of what vulgar people call stuffing let him or her speak.'

A chorus of voices invited him to begin his own supper and Lily came forward with three potatoes which she had reserved for him.

'Very well,' said Gabriel amiably, as he took another preparatory draught, 'kindly forget my existence, ladies and gentlemen, for a few minutes.'

He set to his supper and took no part in the conversation with which the table covered Lily's removal of the plates. The subject of talk was the opera company which was then at the Theatre Royal. Mr Bartell D'Arcy, the tenor, a dark-complexioned young man with a smart moustache, praised very highly the leading contralto of the company but Miss Furlong thought she had a rather vulgar style of production. Freddy Malins said there was a negro chieftain singing in the second part of the Gaiety pantomime who had one of the finest tenor voices he had ever heard.

'Have you heard him?' he asked Mr Bartell D'Arcy across the table.

'No,' answered Mr Bartell D'Arcy carelessly.

'Because,' Freddy Malins explained, 'now I'd be curious to hear your opinion of him. I think he has a grand voice.'

'It takes Teddy to find out the really good things,' said Mr Browne familiarly to the table.

'And why couldn't he have a voice too?' asked Freddy Malins sharply. 'Is it because he's only a black?'

Nobody answered this question and Mary Jane led the table back to the legitimate opera. One of her pupils had given her a pass for *Mignon*. Of course it was very fine, she said, but it made her think of poor Georgina Burns. Mr Browne could go back farther still, to the old Italian companies that used to come to Dublin – Tietjens, Ilma de Murzka, Campanini, the great Trebelli Giuglini, Ravelli, Aramburo. Those were the days, he said, when there was something like singing to be heard in Dublin. He told too of how the top gallery of the old Royal used to be packed night after night, of how one night an Italian tenor had sung five encores to *Let me like a Soldier fall*, introducing a high C every time, and of how the gallery boys would sometimes in their enthusiasm unyoke the horses from the carriage of some great *prima donna* and pull her themselves through the streets to her hotel. Why did they never play the grand old operas now, he asked, *Dinorah, Lucrezia Borgia*? Because they could not get the voices to sing them: that was why.

'O, well,' said Mr Bartell D'Arcy, 'I presume there are as good singers today as there were then.'

'Where are they?' asked Mr Browne defiantly.

'In London, Paris, Milan,' said Mr Bartell D'Arcy warmly. 'I suppose Caruso, for example, is quite as good, if not better than any of the men you have mentioned.'

'Maybe so,' said Mr Browne. 'but I may tell you I doubt it strongly.'

'O, I'd give anything to hear Caruso sing,' said Mary Jane.

'For me,' said Aunt Kate, who had been picking a bone, 'there was only one tenor. To please me, I mean. But I suppose none of you ever heard of him.'

'Who was he, Miss Morkan?' asked Mr Bartell D'Arcy politely.

'His name,' said Aunt Kate, 'was Parkinson. I heard him when he was in his prime and I think he had then the purest tenor voice that was ever put into a man's throat.'

'Strange,' said Mr Bartell D'Arcy. 'I never even heard of him.'

'Yes, yes, Miss Morkan is right,' said Mr Browne. 'I remember hearing of old Parkinson but he's too far back for me.'

'A beautiful, pure, sweet, mellow English tenor,' said Aunt Kate with enthusiasm.

Gabriel having finished, the huge pudding was transferred to the table. The clatter of forks and spoons began again. Gabriel's wife served out spoonfuls of the pudding and passed the plates down the table. Midway down they were held up by Mary Jane, who replenished them with raspberry or orange jelly or with blancmange and jam. The pudding was of Aunt Julia's making and she received praises for it from all quarters. she herself said that it was not quite brown enough.

'Well, I hope, Miss Morkan,' said Mr Browne, 'that I'm brown enough for you because, you know, I'm all brown.'

All the gentlemen, except Gabriel, ate some of the pudding out of compliment to Aunt Julia. As Gabriel never ate sweets the celery had been left for him. Freddy Malins also took a stalk of celery and ate it with his pudding. He had been told that celery was a capital thing for the blood and he was just then under doctor's care. Mrs Malins, who had been silent all through the supper, said that her son was going down to Mount Melleray in a week or so. The table then spoke of Mount Melleray, how bracing the air was down there, how hospitable the monks were and how they never asked for a penny-piece from their guests.

'And do you mean to say,' asked Mr Browne incredulously, 'that a chap can go down there and put up there as if it were a hotel and live on the fat of the land and then come away without paying anything?'

'O, most people give some donation to the monastery when they leave,' said Mary Jane.

'I wish we had an institution like that in our church,' said Mr Browne candidly.

He was astonished to hear that the monks never spoke, got up at two in the morning and slept in their coffins. He asked what they did it for.

'That's the rule of the order,' said Aunt Kate firmly.

'Yes, but why?' asked Mr Browne.

Aunt Kate repeated that it was the rule, that was all. Mr Browne still seemed not to understand. Freddy Malins explained to him, as best he could, that the monks were trying to make up for the sins committed by all the sinners in the outside world. The explanation was not very clear for Mr Browne grinned and said: 'I like that idea very much but wouldn't a comfortable spring bed do them as well as a coffin?'

'The coffin,' said Mary Jane, 'is to remind them of their last end.'

As the subject had grown lugubrious it was buried in a silence of the table during which Mrs Malins could be heard saying to her neighbour in an indistinct undertone: 'They are very good men, the monks, very pious men.'

The raisins and almonds and figs and apples and oranges and chocolates and sweets were now passed about the table and Aunt Julia invited all the guests to have either port or sherry. At first Mr Bartell D'Arcy refused to take either but one of his neighbours nudged him and whispered something to him upon which he allowed his glass to be filled. Gradually as the last glasses were being filled the conversation ceased. A pause followed, broken only by the noise of the wine and by unsettlings of chairs. The Misses Morkan, all three, looked down at the tablecloth. Someone coughed once or twice and then a few gentlemen patted the table gently as a signal for silence. The silence came and Gabriel pushed back his chair and stood up.

The patting at once grew louder in encouragement and then ceased altogether. Gabriel leaned his ten trembling fingers on the tablecloth and smiled nervously at the company. Meeting a row of upturned faces he raised his eyes to the chandelier. The piano was playing a waltz tune and he could hear the skirts sweeping against the drawing-room door. People, perhaps, were standing in the snow on the quay outside, gazing up at the lighted windows and listening to the waltz music. The air was pure there. In the distance lay the park where the trees were weighted with snow. The Wellington Monument wore a gleaming cap of snow that flashed westward over the white field of Fifteen Acres.

He began: 'Ladies and Gentlemen,

'It has fallen to my lot this evening, as in years past, to perform a very pleasing task but a task for which I am afraid my poor powers as a speaker are all too inadequate.'

'No, no!' said Mr Browne.

'But, however that may be, I can only ask you tonight to take the will for the deed and to lend me your attention for a few moments while I endeavour to express to you in words what my feelings are on this occasion.

'Ladies and Gentlemen, it is not the first time that we have gathered together under this hospitable roof, around this hospitable board. It is not the first time that we have been the recipients – or perhaps, I had better say, the victims – of the hospitality of certain good ladies.'

He made a circle in the air with his arm and paused. Everyone laughed or smiled at Aunt Kate and Aunt Julia and Mary Jane who all turned crimson with pleasure. Gabriel went on more boldly: 'I feel more strongly with every recurring year that our country has no tradition which does it so

much honour and which it should guard so jealously as that of its hospitality.
It is a tradition that is unique as far as my experience goes (and I have visited
not a few places abroad) among the modern nations. Some would say,
perhaps, that with us it is rather a failing than anything to be boasted of. But
granted even that, it is, to my mind, a princely failing, and one that I trust
will long be cultivated among us. Of one thing, at least, I am sure. As long
as this one roof shelters the good ladies aforesaid – and I wish from my
heart it may do so for many and many a long year to come – the tradition of
genuine warm-hearted courteous Irish hospitality, which our forefathers
have handed down to us and which we in turn must hand down to our
descendants, is still alive among us.'

A hearty murmur of assent ran round the table. It shot through Gabriel's
mind that Miss Ivors was not there and that she had gone away dis-
courteously: and he said with confidence in himself: 'Ladies and Gentlemen,

'A new generation is growing up in our midst, a generation actuated by
new ideas and new principles. It is serious and enthusiastic for these new
ideas and its enthusiasm, even when it is misdirected, is, I believe, in the
main sincere. But we are living in a sceptical and, if I may use the phrase, a
thought-tormented age: and sometimes I fear that this new generation,
educated or hyper-educated as it is, will lack those qualities of humanity, of
hospitality, of kindly humour which belonged to an older day. Listening
tonight to the names of all those great singers of the past it seemed to me,
I must confess, that we were living in a less spacious age. Those days
might, without exaggeration, be called spacious days: and if they are gone
beyond recall let us hope, at least, that in gatherings such as this we shall
still speak of them with pride and affection, still cherish in our hearts the
memory of those dead and gone great ones whose fame the world will not
willingly let die.'

'Hear, hear!' said Mr Browne loudly.

'But yet,' continued Gabriel, his voice falling into a softer inflection,
'there are always in gatherings such as this sadder thoughts that will recur
to our minds: thoughts of the past, of youth, of changes, of absent faces
that we miss here tonight. Our path through life is strewn with many such
sad memories: and were we to brood upon them always we could not find
the heart to go on bravely with our work among the living. We have all of
us living duties and living affections which claim, and rightly claim, our
strenuous endeavours.

'Therefore, I will not linger on the past. I will not let any gloomy
moralising intrude upon us here tonight. Here we are gathered together for
a brief moment from the bustle and rush of our everyday routine. We are

met here as friends, in the spirit of good-fellowship, as colleagues, also to a certain extent, in the true spirit of *camaraderie*, and as the guests of – what shall I call them? – the Three Graces of the Dublin musical world.'

The table burst into applause and laughter at this allusion. Aunt Julia vainly asked each of her neighbours in turn to tell her what Gabriel had said.

'He says we are the Three Graces, Aunt Julia,' said Mary Jane.

Aunt Julia did not understand but she looked up, smiling, at Gabriel, who continued in the same vein: 'Ladies and Gentlemen,

'I will not attempt to play tonight the part that Paris played on another occasion. I will not attempt to choose between them. The task would be an invidious one and one beyond my poor powers. For when I view them in turn, whether it be our chief hostess herself, whose good heart, whose too good heart, has become a byword with all who know her, or her sister, who seems to be gifted with perennial youth and whose singing must have been a surprise and a revelation to us all tonight, or, last but not least, when I consider our youngest hostess, talented, cheerful, hard-working and the best of nieces, I confess, Ladies and Gentlemen, that I do not know to which of them I should award the prize.'

Gabriel glanced down at his aunts and, seeing the large smile on Aunt Julia's face and the tears which had risen to Aunt Kate's eyes, hastened to his close. He raised his glass of port gallantly, while every member of the company fingered a glass expectantly, and said loudly: 'Let us toast them all three together. Let us drink to their health, wealth, long life, happiness and prosperity and may they long continue to hold the proud and self-won position which they hold in their profession and the position of honour and affection which they hold in our hearts.'

All the guests stood up, glass in hand, and turning towards the three seated ladies, sang in unison, with Mr Browne as leader:

> 'For they are jolly gay fellows,
> For they are jolly gay fellows,
> For they are jolly gay fellows,
>   Which nobody can deny.'

Aunt Kate was making frank use of her handkerchief and even Aunt Julia seemed moved. Freddy Malins beat time with his pudding-fork and the singers turned towards one another, as if in melodious conference, while they sang with emphasis:

> 'Unless he tells a lie,
> Unless he tells a lie,'

Then, turning once more towards their hostesses, they sang:

> 'For they are jolly gay fellows,
> For they are jolly gay fellows,
> For they are jolly gay fellows,
>   Which nobody can deny.'

The acclamation which followed was taken up beyond the door of the supper-room by many of the other guests and renewed time after time, Freddy Malins acting as officer with his fork on high.

The piercing morning air came into the hall where they were standing so that Aunt Kate said: 'Close the door, somebody. Mrs Malins will get her death of cold.'

'Browne is out there, Aunt Kate,' said Mary Jane.

'Browne is everywhere,' said Aunt Kate, lowering her voice.

Mary Jane laughed at her tone.

'Really,' she said archly, 'he is very attentive.'

'He has been laid on here like the gas,' said Aunt Kate in the same tone, 'all during the Christmas.'

She laughed herself this time good-humouredly and then added quickly: 'But tell him to come in, Mary Jane, and close the door. I hope to goodness he didn't hear me.'

At that moment the hall-door was opened and Mr Browne came in from the doorstep, laughing as if his heart would break. He was dressed in a long green overcoat with mock astrakhan cuffs and collar and wore on his head an oval fur cap. He pointed down the snow-covered quay from where the sound of shrill prolonged whistling was borne in.

'Teddy will have all the cabs in Dublin out,' he said.

Gabriel advanced from the little pantry behind the office, struggling into his overcoat and, looking round the hall, said: 'Gretta not down yet?'

'She's getting on her things, Gabriel,' said Aunt Kate.

'Who's playing up there?' asked Gabriel.

'Nobody. They're all gone.'

'O no, Aunt Kate,' said Mary Jane. 'Bartell D'Arcy and Miss O'Callaghan aren't gone yet.'

'Someone is fooling at the piano anyhow,' said Gabriel.

Mary Jane glanced at Gabriel and Mr Browne and said with a shiver: 'It makes me feel cold to look at you two gentlemen muffled up like that. I wouldn't like to face your journey home at this hour.'

'I'd like nothing better this minute,' said Mr Browne stoutly, 'than a rattling fine walk in the country or a fast drive with a good spanking goer between the shafts.'

'We used to have a very good horse and trap at home,' said Aunt Julia sadly.

'The never-to-be-forgotten Johnny,' said Mary Jane, laughing.

Aunt Kate and Gabriel laughed too.

'Why, what was wonderful about Johnny?' asked Mr Browne.

'The late lamented Patrick Morkan, our grandfather, that is,' explained Gabriel, 'commonly known in his later years as the old gentleman, was a glue-boiler.'

'O, now, Gabriel,' said Aunt Kate, laughing, 'he had a starch mill.'

'Well, glue or starch,' said Gabriel, 'the old gentleman had a horse by the name of Johnny. And Johnny used to work in the old gentleman's mill, walking round and round in order to drive the mill. That was all very well; but now comes the tragic part about Johnny. One fine day the old gentleman thought he'd like to drive out with the quality to a military review in the park.'

'The Lord have mercy on his soul,' said Aunt Kate compassionately.

'Amen,' said Gabriel. 'So the old gentleman, as I said, harnessed Johnny and put on his very best tall hat and his very best stock collar and drove out in grand style from his ancestral mansion somewhere near Back Lane, I think.'

Everyone laughed, even Mrs Malins, at Gabriel's manner and Aunt Kate said: 'O, now, Gabriel, he didn't live in Back Lane, really. Only the mill was there.'

'Out from the mansion of his forefathers,' continued Gabriel, 'he drove with Johnny. And everything went on beautifully until Johnny came in sight of King Billy's statue: and whether he fell in love with the horse King Billy sits on or whether he thought he was back again in the mill, anyhow he began to walk round the statue.'

Gabriel paced in a circle round the hall in his goloshes amid the laughter of the others.

'Round and round he went,' said Gabriel, 'and the old gentleman, who was a very pompous old gentleman, was highly indignant. "Go on, sir! What do you mean, sir? Johnny! Johnny! Most extraordinary conduct! Can't understand the horse!" '

The peals of laughter which followed Gabriel's imitation of the incident was interrupted by a resounding knock at the hall door. Mary Jane ran to open it and let in Freddy Malins. Freddy Malins, with his hat well back on his head and his shoulders humped with cold, was puffing and steaming after his exertions.

'I could only get one cab,' he said.

'O, we'll find another along the quay,' said Gabriel.

'Yes,' said Aunt Kate. 'Better not keep Mrs Malins standing in the draught.'

Mrs Malins was helped down the front steps by her son and Mr Browne and, after many manoeuvres, hoisted into the cab. Freddy Malins clambered in after her and spent a long time settling her on the seat, Mr Browne helping him with advice. At last she was settled comfortably and Freddy Malins invited Mr Browne into the cab. There was a good deal of confused talk, and then Mr Browne got into the cab. The cabman settled his rug over his knees, and bent down for the address. The confusion grew greater and the cabman was directed differently by Freddy Malins and Mr Browne, each of whom had his head out through a window of the cab. The difficulty was to know where to drop Mr Browne along the route, and Aunt Kate, Aunt Julia and Mary Jane helped the discussion from the doorstep with cross-directions and contradictions and abundance of laughter. As for Freddy Malins he was speechless with laughter. He popped his head in and out of the window every moment to the great danger of his hat, and told his mother how the discussion was progressing, till at last Mr Browne shouted to the bewildered cabman above the din of everybody's laughter: 'Do you know Trinity College?'

'Yes, sir,' said the cabman.

'Well, drive bang up against Trinity College gates,' said Mr Browne, 'and then we'll tell you where to go. You understand now?'

'Yes, sir,' said the cabman.

'Make like a bird for Trinity College.'

'Right, sir,' said the cabman.

The horse was whipped up and the cab rattled off along the quay amid a chorus of laughter and adieus.

Gabriel had not gone to the door with the others. He was in a dark part of the hall gazing up the staircase. A woman was standing near the top of the first flight, in the shadow also. He could not see her face but he could see the terracotta and salmon-pink panels of her skirt which the shadow made appear black and white. It was his wife. She was leaning on the banisters, listening to something. Gabriel was surprised at her stillness and strained his ear to listen also. But he could hear little save the noise of laughter and dispute on the front steps, a few chords struck on the piano and a few notes of a man's voice singing.

He stood still in the gloom of the hall, trying to catch the air that the voice was singing and gazing up at his wife. There was grace and mystery in her attitude as if she were a symbol of something. He asked himself what is a woman standing on the stairs in the shadow, listening to distant music, a symbol of. If he were a painter he would paint her in that attitude. Her blue felt hat would show off the bronze of her hair against the darkness and the dark panels of her skirt would show off the light ones. *Distant Music* he would call the picture if he were a painter.

The hall-door was closed; and Aunt Kate, Aunt Julia and Mary Jane came down the hall, still laughing.

'Well, isn't Freddy terrible?' said Mary Jane. 'He's really terrible.'

Gabriel said nothing but pointed up the stairs towards where his wife was standing. Now that the hall-door was closed the voice and the piano could be heard more clearly. Gabriel held up his hand for them to be silent. The song seemed to be in the old Irish tonality and the singer seemed uncertain both of his words and of his voice. The voice, made plaintive by distance and by the singer's hoarseness, faintly illuminated the cadence of the air with words expressing grief:

> 'O, the rain falls on my heavy locks
> And the dew wets my skin,
> My babe lies cold . . . '

'O,' exclaimed Mary Jane. 'It's Bartell D'Arcy singing and he wouldn't sing all the night. O, I'll get him to sing a song before he goes.'

'O, do, Mary Jane,' said Aunt Kate.

Mary Jane brushed past the others and ran to the staircase, but before she reached it the singing stopped and the piano was closed abruptly.

'O, what a pity!' she cried. 'Is he coming down, Gretta?'

Gabriel heard his wife answer yes and saw her come down towards them. A few steps behind her were Mr Bartell D'Arcy and Miss O'Callaghan.

'O, Mr D'Arcy,' cried Mary Jane, 'it's downright mean of you to break off like that when we were all in raptures listening to you.'

'I have been at him all the evening,' said Miss O'Callaghan, 'and Mrs Conroy, too, and he told us he had a dreadful cold and couldn't sing.'

'O, Mr D'Arcy,' said Aunt Kate, 'now that was a great fib to tell.'

'Can't you see that I'm as hoarse as a crow?' said Mr D'Arcy roughly.

He went into the pantry hastily and put on his overcoat. The others, taken aback by his rude speech, could find nothing to say. Aunt Kate wrinkled her brows and made signs to the others to drop the subject. Mr D'Arcy stood swathing his neck carefully and frowning.

'It's the weather,' said Aunt Julia, after a pause.

'Yes, everybody has colds,' said Aunt Kate readily, 'everybody.'

'They say,' said Mary Jane, 'we haven't had snow like it for thirty years; and I read this morning in the newspapers that the snow is general all over Ireland.'

'I love the look of snow,' said Aunt Julia sadly.

'So do I,' said Miss O'Callaghan. 'I think Christmas is never really Christmas unless we have the snow on the ground.'

'But poor Mr D'Arcy doesn't like the snow,' said Aunt Kate, smiling.

Mr D'Arcy came from the pantry, fully swathed and buttoned, and in a repentant tone told them the history of his cold. Everyone gave him advice and said it was a great pity and urged him to be very careful of his throat in the night air. Gabriel watched his wife, who did not join in the conversation. She was standing right under the dusty fanlight and the flame of the gas lit up the rich bronze of her hair, which he had seen her drying at the fire a few days before. She was in the same attitude and seemed unaware of the talk about her. At last she turned towards them and Gabriel saw that there was colour on her cheeks and that her eyes were shining. A sudden tide of joy went leaping out of his heart.

'Mr D'Arcy,' she said, 'what is the name of that song you were singing?'

'It's called *The Lass of Aughrim*,' said Mr D'Arcy, 'but I couldn't remember it properly. Why? Do you know it?'

'*The Lass of Aughrim*,' she repeated. 'I couldn't think of the name.'

'It's a very nice air,' said Mary Jane. 'I'm sorry you were not in voice tonight.'

'Now, Mary Jane,' said Aunt Kate, 'don't annoy Mr D'Arcy. I won't have him annoyed.'

Seeing that all were ready to start she shepherded them to the door, where good-night was said: 'Well, good-night, Aunt Kate, and thanks for the pleasant evening.'

'Good-night, Gabriel. Good-night, Gretta!'

'Good-night, Aunt Kate, and thanks ever so much. Good-night, Aunt Julia.'

'O, good-night, Gretta, I didn't see you.'

'Good-night, Mr D'Arcy. Good-night, Miss O'Callaghan.'

'Good-night, Miss Morkan.'

'Good-night, again.'

'Good-night, all. Safe home.'

'Good-night. Good-night.'

The morning was still dark. A dull, yellow light brooded over the houses and the river; and the sky seemed to be descending. It was slushy underfoot; and only streaks and patches of snow lay on the roofs, on the parapets of the quay and on the area railings. The lamps were still burning redly in the murky air and, across the river, the palace of the Four Courts stood out menacingly against the heavy sky.

She was walking on before him with Mr Bartell D'Arcy, her shoes in a brown parcel tucked under one arm and her hands holding her skirt up from the slush. She had no longer any grace of attitude, but Gabriel's eyes were still bright with happiness. The blood went bounding along his veins; and the thoughts went rioting through his brain, proud, joyful, tender, valorous.

She was walking on before him so lightly and so erect that he longed to run after her noiselessly, catch her by the shoulders and say something foolish and affectionate into her ear. She seemed to him so frail that he longed to defend her against something and then to be alone with her. Moments of their secret life together burst like stars upon his memory. A heliotrope envelope was lying beside his breakfast-cup and he was caressing it with his hand. Birds were twittering in the ivy and the sunny web of the curtain was shimmering along the floor: he could not eat for happiness. They were standing on the crowded platform and he was placing a ticket inside the warm palm of her glove. He was standing with her in the cold, looking in through a grated window at a man making bottles in a roaring furnace. It was very cold. Her face, fragrant in the cold air, was quite close to his; and suddenly he called out to the man at the furnace: 'Is the fire hot, sir?'

But the man could not hear with the noise of the furnace. It was just as well. He might have answered rudely.

A wave of yet more tender joy escaped from his heart and went coursing in warm blood along his arteries. Like the tender fire of stars moments of their life together, that no one knew of or would ever know of, broke upon and illumined his memory. He longed to recall to her those moments, to make her forget the years of their dull existence together and remember only their moments of ecstasy. For the years, he felt, had not quenched his soul or hers. Their children, his writing, her household cares had not quenched all their souls' tender fire. In one letter that he had written to her then he had said: 'Why is it that words like these seem to me so dull and cold? Is it because there is no word tender enough to be your name?'

Like distant music these words that he had written years before were borne towards him from the past. He longed to be alone with her. When the others had gone away, when he and she were in the room in the hotel, then they would be alone together. He would call her softly: 'Gretta!'

Perhaps she would not hear at once: she would be undressing. Then something in his voice would strike her. She would turn and look at him . . .

At the corner of Winetavern Street they met a cab. He was glad of its rattling noise as it saved him from conversation. She was looking out of the window and seemed tired. The others spoke only a few words, pointing out some building or street. The horse galloped along wearily under the murky morning sky, dragging his old rattling box after his heels, and Gabriel was again in a cab with her, galloping to catch the boat, galloping to their honeymoon.

As the cab drove across O'Connell Bridge Miss O'Callaghan said: 'They say you never cross O'Connell Bridge without seeing a white horse.'

'I see a white man this time,' said Gabriel.

'Where?' asked Mr Bartell D'Arcy.

Gabriel pointed to the statue, on which lay patches of snow. Then he nodded familiarly to it and waved his hand.

'Good-night, Dan,' he said gaily.

When the cab drew up before the hotel, Gabriel jumped out and, in spite of Mr Bartell D'Arcy's protest, paid the driver. He gave the man a shilling over his fare. The man saluted and said: 'A prosperous New Year to you, sir.'

'The same to you,' said Gabriel cordially.

She leaned for a moment on his arm in getting out of the cab and while standing at the curb-stone, bidding the others good-night. She leaned lightly on his arm, as lightly as when she had danced with him a few hours before. He had felt proud and happy then, happy that she was his, proud of her grace and wifely carriage. But now, after the kindling again of so many memories, the first touch of her body, musical and strange and perfumed, sent through him a keen pang of lust. Under cover of her silence he pressed her arm closely to his side; and, as they stood at the hotel door, he felt that they had escaped from their lives and duties, escaped from home and friends and run away together with wild and radiant hearts to a new adventure.

An old man was dozing in a great hooded chair in the hall. He lit a candle in the office and went before them to the stairs. They followed him in silence, their feet falling in soft thuds on the thickly carpeted stairs. She mounted the stairs behind the porter, her head bowed in the ascent, her frail shoulders curved as with a burden, her skirt girt tightly about her. He could have flung his arms about her hips and held her still, for his arms were trembling with desire to seize her and only the stress of his nails against the palms of his hands held the wild impulse of his body in check. The porter halted on the stairs to settle his guttering candle. They halted, too, on the steps below him. In the silence Gabriel could hear the falling of the molten wax into the tray and the thumping of his own heart against his ribs.

The porter led them along a corridor and opened a door. Then he set his unstable candle down on a toilet-table and asked at what hour they were to be called in the morning.

'Eight,' said Gabriel.

The porter pointed to the tap of the electric-light and began a muttered apology, but Gabriel cut him short.

'We don't want any light. We have light enough from the street. And I say,' he added, pointing to the candle, 'you might remove that handsome article, like a good man.'

The porter took up his candle again, but slowly, for he was surprised by such a novel idea. Then he mumbled good-night and went out. Gabriel shot the lock to.

A ghastly light from the street lamp lay in a long shaft from one window to the door. Gabriel threw his overcoat and hat on a couch and crossed the room towards the window. He looked down into the street in order that his emotion might calm a little. Then he turned and leaned against a chest of drawers with his back to the light. She had taken off her hat and cloak and was standing before a large swinging mirror, unhooking her waist. Gabriel paused for a few moments, watching her, and then said: 'Gretta!'

She turned away from the mirror slowly and walked along the shaft of light towards him. Her face looked so serious and weary that the words would not pass Gabriel's lips. No, it was not the moment yet.

'You looked tired,' he said.

'I am a little,' she answered.

'You don't feel ill or weak?'

'No, tired: that's all.'

She went on to the window and stood there, looking out. Gabriel waited again and then, fearing that diffidence was about to conquer him, he said abruptly: 'By the way, Gretta!'

'What is it?'

'You know that poor fellow Malins?' he said quickly.

'Yes. What about him?'

'Well, poor fellow, he's a decent sort of chap, after all,' continued Gabriel in a false voice. 'He gave me back that sovereign I lent him, and I didn't expect it, really. It's a pity he wouldn't keep away from that Browne, because he's not a bad fellow, really.'

He was trembling now with annoyance. Why did she seem so abstracted? He did not know how he could begin. Was she annoyed, too, about something? If she would only turn to him or come to him of her own accord! To take her as she was would be brutal. No, he must see some ardour in her eyes first. He longed to be master of her strange mood.

'When did you lend him the pound?' she asked, after a pause.

Gabriel strove to restrain himself from breaking out into brutal language about the sottish Malins and his pound. He longed to cry to her from his soul, to crush her body against his, to overmaster her. But he said: 'O, at Christmas, when he opened that little Christmas-card shop in Henry Street.'

He was in such a fever of rage and desire that he did not hear her come from the window. She stood before him for an instant, looking at him strangely. Then, suddenly raising herself on tiptoe and resting her hands lightly on his shoulders, she kissed him.

'You are a very generous person, Gabriel,' she said.

Gabriel, trembling with delight at her sudden kiss and at the quaintness of her phrase, put his hands on her hair and began smoothing it back, scarcely touching it with his fingers. The washing had made it fine and brilliant. His heart was brimming over with happiness. Just when he was wishing for it she had come to him of her own accord. Perhaps her thoughts had been running with his. Perhaps she had felt the impetuous desire that was in him, and then the yielding mood had come upon her. Now that she had fallen to him so easily, he wondered why he had been so diffident.

He stood, holding her head between his hands. Then, slipping one arm swiftly about her body and drawing her towards him, he said softly: 'Gretta, dear, what are you thinking about?'

She did not answer nor yield wholly to his arm. He said again, softly: 'Tell me what it is, Gretta. I think I know what is the matter. Do I know?'

She did not answer at once. Then she said in an outburst of tears: 'O, I am thinking about that song, *The Lass of Aughrim*.'

She broke loose from him and ran to the bed and, throwing her arms across the bed-rail, hid her face. Gabriel stood stock-still for a moment in astonishment and then followed her. As he passed in the way of the cheval-glass he caught sight of himself in full length, his broad, well-filled shirt-front, the face whose expression always puzzled him when he saw it in a mirror, and his glimmering gilt-rimmed eyeglasses. He halted a few paces from her and said: 'What about the song? Why does that make you cry?'

She raised her head from her arms and dried her eyes with the back of her hand like a child. A kinder note than he had intended went into his voice.

'Why, Gretta?' he asked.

'I am thinking about a person long ago who used to sing that song.'

'And who was the person long ago?' asked Gabriel, smiling.

'It was a person I used to know in Galway when I was living with my grandmother,' she said.

The smile passed away from Gabriel's face. A dull anger began to gather again at the back of his mind and the dull fires of his lust began to glow angrily in his veins.

'Someone you were in love with?' he asked ironically.

'It was a young boy I used to know,' she answered, 'named Michael Furey. He used to sing that song, *The Lass of Aughrim*. He was very delicate.'

Gabriel was silent. He did not wish her to think that he was interested in this delicate boy.

'I can see him so plainly,' she said, after a moment. 'Such eyes as he had: big, dark eyes! And such an expression in them – an expression!'

'O, then, you are in love with him?' said Gabriel.

'I used to go out walking with him,' she said, 'when I was in Galway.'

A thought flew across Gabriel's mind.

'Perhaps that was why you wanted to go to Galway with that Ivors girl?' he said coldly.

She looked at him and asked in surprise: 'What for?'

Her eyes made Gabriel feel awkward. He shrugged his shoulders and said: 'How do I know? To see him, perhaps.'

She looked away from him along the shaft of light towards the window in silence.

'He is dead,' she said at length. 'He died when he was only seventeen. Isn't it a terrible thing to die so young as that?'

'What was he?' asked Gabriel, still ironically.

'He was in the gasworks,' she said.

Gabriel felt humiliated by the failure of his irony and by the evocation of this figure from the dead, a boy in the gasworks. While he had been full of memories of their secret life together, full of tenderness and joy and desire, she had been comparing him in her mind with another. A shameful consciousness of his own person assailed him. He saw himself as a ludicrous figure, acting as a pennyboy for his aunts, a nervous, well-meaning sentimentalist, orating to vulgarians and idealising his own clownish lusts, the pitiable fatuous fellow he had caught a glimpse of in the mirror. Instinctively he turned his back more to the light lest she might see the shame that burned upon his forehead.

He tried to keep up his tone of cold interrogation, but his voice when he spoke was humble and indifferent.

'I suppose you were in love with this Michael Furey, Gretta,' he said.

'I was great with him at that time,' she said.

Her voice was veiled and sad. Gabriel, feeling now how vain it would be to try to lead her whither he had purposed, caressed one of her hands and said, also sadly: 'And what did he die of so young, Gretta? Consumption, was it?'

'I think he died for me,' she answered.

A vague terror seized Gabriel at this answer, as if, at that hour when he had hoped to triumph, some impalpable and vindictive being was coming against him, gathering forces against him in its vague world. But he shook himself free of it with an effort of reason and continued to caress her hand. He did not question her again, for he felt that she would tell him of herself. Her hand was warm and moist: it did not respond to his touch, but he continued to caress it just as he had caressed her first letter to him that spring morning.

'It was in the winter,' she said, 'about the beginning of the winter when I was going to leave my grandmother's and come up here to the convent. And he was ill at the time in his lodgings in Galway and wouldn't be let out, and his people in Oughterard were written to. He was in decline, they said, or something like that. I never knew rightly.'

She paused for a moment and sighed.

'Poor fellow,' she said. 'He was very fond of me and he was such a gentle boy. We used to go out together, walking, you know, Gabriel, like the way they do in the country. He was going to study singing only for his health. He had a very good voice, poor Michael Furey.'

'Well; and then?' asked Gabriel.

'And then when it came to the time for me to leave Galway and come up to the convent he was much worse and I wouldn't be let see him so I wrote him a letter saying I was going up to Dublin and would be back in the summer, and hoping he would be better then.'

She paused for a moment to get her voice under control, and then went on: 'Then the night before I left, I was in my grandmother's house in Nuns' Island, packing up, and I heard gravel thrown up against the window. The window was so wet I couldn't see, so I ran downstairs as I was and slipped out the back into the garden and there was the poor fellow at the end of the garden, shivering.'

'And did you not tell him to go back?' asked Gabriel.

'I implored of him to go home at once and told him he would get his death in the rain. But he said he did not want to live. I can see his eyes as well as well! He was standing at the end of the wall where there was a tree.'

'And did he go home?' asked Gabriel.

'Yes, he went home. And when I was only a week in the convent he died and he was buried in Oughterard, where his people came from. O, the day I heard that, that he was dead!'

She stopped, choking with sobs, and, overcome by emotion, flung herself face downward on the bed, sobbing in the quilt. Gabriel held her hand for a moment longer, irresolutely, and then, shy of intruding on her grief, let it fall gently and walked quietly to the window.

She was fast asleep.

Gabriel, leaning on his elbow, looked for a few moments unresentfully on her tangled hair and half-open mouth, listening to her deep-drawn breath. So she had that romance in her life: a man had died for her sake. It hardly pained him now to think how poor a part he, her husband, had played in her life. He watched her while she slept, as though he and she had never lived together as man and wife. His curious eyes rested long upon her face and on her hair: and, as he thought of what she must have been then, in that time of her first girlish beauty, a strange, friendly pity for her entered his soul. He did not like to say even to himself that her face was no longer beautiful, but he knew that it was no longer the face for which Michael Furey had braved death.

Perhaps she had not told him all the story. His eyes moved to the chair over which she had thrown some of her clothes. A petticoat string dangled to the floor. One boot stood upright, its limp upper fallen down: the fellow of it lay upon its side. He wondered at his riot of emotions of an hour before. From what had it proceeded? From his aunt's supper, from his own foolish speech, from the wine and dancing, the merrymaking when saying good-night in the hall, the pleasure of the walk along the river in the snow. Poor Aunt Julia! She, too, would soon be a shade with the shade of Patrick Morkan and his horse. He had caught that haggard look upon her face for a moment when she was singing *Arrayed for the Bridal*. Soon, perhaps, he would be sitting in that same drawing-room, dressed in black, his silk hat on his knees. The blinds would be drawn down and Aunt Kate would be sitting beside him, crying and blowing her nose and telling him how Julia had died. He would cast about in his mind for some words that might console her, and would find only lame and useless ones. Yes, yes: that would happen very soon.

The air of the room chilled his shoulders. He stretched himself cautiously along under the sheets and lay down beside his wife. One by one, they were all becoming shades. Better pass boldly into that other world, in the full glory of some passion, than fade and wither dismally with age. He thought of how she who lay beside him had locked in her heart for so many years that image of her lover's eyes when he had told her that he did not wish to live.

Generous tears filled Gabriel's eyes. He had never felt like that himself towards any woman, but he knew that such a feeling must be love. The tears gathered more thickly in his eyes and in the partial darkness he imagined he saw the form of a young man standing under a dripping tree. Other forms were near. His soul had approached that region where dwell the vast hosts of the dead. He was conscious of, but could not apprehend, their wayward and flickering existence. His own identity was fading out into a grey impalpable world: the solid world itself which these dead had one time reared and lived in, was dissolving and dwindling.

A few light taps upon the pane made him turn to the window. It had begun to snow again. He watched sleepily the flakes, silver and dark, falling obliquely against the lamplight. The time had come for him to set out on his journey westward. Yes, the newspapers were right: snow was general all over Ireland. It was falling on every part of the dark central plain, on the treeless hills, falling softly upon the Bog of Allen and, farther westward, softly falling into the dark mutinous Shannon waves. It was falling, too, upon every part of the lonely churchyard on the hill where Michael Furey lay buried. It lay thickly drifted on the crooked crosses and headstones, on the spears of the little gate, on the barren thorns. His soul swooned slowly as he heard the snow falling faintly through the universe and faintly falling, like the descent of their last end, upon all the living and the dead.

A PORTRAIT OF THE ARTIST AS A YOUNG MAN

It ignotas animum dimittit in artes
[And he applies his mind to unknown arts]

Ovid, *Metamorphosis* viii, 188

Chapter 1

Once upon a time and a very good time it was there was a moocow coming down along the road and this moocow that was coming down along the road met a nicens little boy named baby tuckoo . . .

His father told him that story: his father looked at him through a glass: he had a hairy face.

He was baby tuckoo. The moocow came down the road where Betty Byrne lived: she sold lemon platt.

> *O, the wild rose blossoms*
> *On the little green place.*

He sang that song. That was his song.

> *O, the green wothe botheth.*

When you wet the bed first it is warm then it gets cold. His mother put on the oilsheet. That had the queer smell.

His mother had a nicer smell than his father. She played on the piano the sailor's hornpipe for him to dance. He danced:

> *Tralala lala,*
> *Tralala tralaladdy,*
> *Tralala lala,*
> *Tralala lala.*

Uncle Charles and Dante clapped. They were older than his father and mother but uncle Charles was older than Dante.

Dante had two brushes in her press. The brush with the maroon velvet back was for Michael Davitt and the brush with the green velvet back was for Parnell. Dante gave him a cachou every time he brought her a piece of tissue paper,

The Vances lived in number seven. They had a different father and mother. They were Eileen's father and mother. When they were grown up he was going to marry Eileen. He hid under the table. His mother said:

– O, Stephen will apologize.

Dante said:

– O, if not, the eagles will come and pull out his eyes. –

Pull out his eyes,
Apologize,
Apologize,
Pull out his eyes.

Apologize,
Pull out his eyes,
Pull out his eyes,
Apologize.

The wide playgrounds were swarming with boys. All were shouting and the prefects urged them on with strong cries. The evening air was pale and chilly and after every charge and thud of the footballers the greasy leather orb flew like a heavy bird through the grey light. He kept on the fringe of his line, out of sight of his prefect, out of the reach of the rude feet, feigning to run now and then. He felt his body small and weak amid the throng of the players and his eyes were weak and watery. Rody Kickham was not like that: he would be captain of the third line all the fellows said.

Rody Kickham was a decent fellow but Nasty Roche was a stink. Rody Kickham had greaves in his number and a hamper in the refectory. Nasty Roche had big hands. He called the Friday pudding dog-in-the-blanket. And one day he had asked:

– What is your name?

Stephen had answered: Stephen Dedalus.

Then Nasty Roche had said:

– What kind of a name is that?

And when Stephen had not been able to answer Nasty Roche had asked:

– What is your father?

Stephen had answered:

– A gentleman.

Then Nasty Roche had asked:

– Is he a magistrate?

He crept about from point to point on the fringe of his line, making little runs now and then. But his hands were bluish with cold. He kept his hands in the side pockets of his belted grey suit. That was a belt round his pocket. And belt was also to give a fellow a belt. One day a fellow said to Cantwell:

– I'd give you such a belt in a second.

Cantwell had answered:

– Go and fight your match. Give Cecil Thunder a belt. I'd like to see you. He'd give you a toe in the rump for yourself.

That was not a nice expression. His mother had told him not to speak

with the rough boys in the college. Nice mother! The first day in the hall of
the castle when she had said goodbye she had put up her veil double to her
nose to kiss him: and her nose and eyes were red. But he had pretended not
to see that she was going to cry. She was a nice mother but she was not so
nice when she cried. And his father had given him two five-shilling pieces
for pocket money. And his father had told him if he wanted anything to
write home to him and, whatever he did, never to peach on a fellow. Then at
the door of the castle the rector had shaken hands with his father and mother,
his soutane fluttering in the breeze, and the car had driven off with his father
and mother on it. They had cried to him from the car, waving their hands:

– Goodbye, Stephen, goodbye!
– Goodbye, Stephen, goodbye!

He was caught in the whirl of a scrimmage and, fearful of the flashing
eyes and muddy boots, bent down to look through the legs. The fellows
were struggling and groaning and their legs were rubbing and kicking and
stamping. Then Jack Lawton's yellow boots dodged out the ball and all the
other boots and legs ran after. He ran after them a little way and then
stopped. It was useless to run on. Soon they would be going home for the
holidays. After supper in the study hall he would change the number pasted
up inside his desk from seventy-seven to seventy-six.

It would be better to be in the study hall than out there in the cold. The
sky was pale and cold but there were lights in the castle. He wondered from
which window Hamilton Rowan had thrown his hat on the ha-ha and had
there been flowerbeds at that time under the windows. One day when he had
been called to the castle the butler had shown him the marks of the soldiers'
slugs in the wood of the door and had given him a piece of shortbread that
the community ate. It was nice and warm to see the lights in the castle. It was
like something in a book. Perhaps Leicester Abbey was like that. And there
were nice sentences in Doctor Cornwell's Spelling Book. They were like
poetry but they were only sentences to learn the spelling from.

> *Wolsey died in Leicester Abbey*
> *Where the abbots buried him.*
> *Canker is a disease of plants,*
> *Cancer one of animals.*

It would be nice to lie on the hearthrug before the fire, leaning his head
upon his hands, and think on those sentences. He shivered as if he had cold
slimy water next his skin. That was mean of Wells to shoulder him into the
square ditch because he would not swop his little snuffbox for Wells's
seasoned hacking chestnut, the conqueror of forty. How cold and slimy the

water had been! A fellow had once seen a big rat jump into the scum. Mother was sitting at the fire with Dante waiting for Brigid to bring in the tea. She had her feet on the fender and her jewelly slippers were so hot and they had such a lovely warm smell! Dante knew a lot of things. She had taught him where the Mozambique Channel was and what was the longest river in America and what was the name of the highest mountain in the moon. Father Arnall knew more than Dante because he was a priest but both his father and uncle Charles said that Dante was a clever woman and a well-read woman. And when Dante made that noise after dinner and then put up her hand to her mouth: that was heartburn.

A voice cried far out on the playground:

– All in!

Then other voices cried from the lower and third lines:

– All in! All in!

The players closed around, flushed and muddy, and he went among them, glad to go in. Rody Kickham held the ball by its greasy lace. A fellow asked him to give it one last: but he walked on without even answering the fellow. Simon Moonan told him not to because the prefect was looking. The fellow turned to Simon Moonan and said:

– We all know why you speak. You are McGlade's suck.

Suck was a queer word. The fellow called Simon Moonan that name because Simon Moonan used to tie the prefect's false sleeves behind his back and the prefect used to let on to be angry. But the sound was ugly. Once he had washed his hands in the lavatory of the Wicklow Hotel and his father pulled the stopper up by the chain after and the dirty water went down through the hole in the basin. And when it had all gone down slowly the hole in the basin had made a sound like that: suck. Only louder.

To remember that and the white look of the lavatory made him feel cold and then hot. There were two cocks that you turned and water came out: cold and hot. He felt cold and then a little hot: and he could see the names printed on the cocks. That was a very queer thing.

And the air in the corridor chilled him too. It was queer and wettish. But soon the gas would be lit and in burning it made a light noise like a little song. Always the same: and when the fellows stopped talking in the play-room you could hear it.

It was the hour for sums. Father Arnall wrote a hard sum on the board and then said:

– Now then, who will win? Go ahead, York! Go ahead, Lancaster!

Stephen tried his best, but the sum was too hard and he felt confused. The little silk badge with the white rose on it that was pinned on the breast of his jacket began to flutter. He was no good at sums, but he tried his best so that York might not lose. Father Arnall's face looked very black, but he was not in a wax: he was laughing. Then Jack Lawton cracked his fingers and Father Arnall looked at his copybook and said:

– Right. Bravo Lancaster! The red rose wins. Come on now, York! Forge ahead!

Jack Lawton looked over from his side. The little silk badge with the red rose on it looked very rich because he had a blue sailor top on. Stephen felt his own face red too, thinking of all the bets about who would get first place in elements, Jack Lawton or he. Some weeks Jack Lawton got the card for first and some weeks he got the card for first. His white silk badge fluttered and fluttered as he worked at the next sum and heard Father Arnall's voice. Then all his eagerness passed away and he felt his face quite cool. He thought his face must be white because it felt so cool. He could not get out the answer for the sum but it did not matter. White roses and red roses: those were beautiful colours to think of. And the cards for first place and second place and third place were beautiful colours too: pink and cream and lavender. Lavender and cream and pink roses were beautiful to think of. Perhaps a wild rose might be like those colours and he remembered the song about the wild rose blossoms on the little green place. But you could not have a green rose. But perhaps somewhere in the world you could.

The bell rang and then the classes began to file out of the rooms and along the corridors towards the refectory. He sat looking at the two prints of butter on his plate but could not eat the damp bread. The tablecloth was damp and limp. But he drank off the hot weak tea which the clumsy scullion, girt with a white apron, poured into his cup. He wondered whether the scullion's apron was damp too or whether all white things were cold and damp. Nasty Roche and Saurin drank cocoa that their people sent them in tins. They said they could not drink the tea; that it was hogwash. Their fathers were magistrates, the fellows said.

All the boys seemed to him very strange. They had all fathers and mothers and different clothes and voices. He longed to be at home and lay his head on his mother's lap. But he could not: and so he longed for the play and study and prayers to be over and to be in bed.

He drank another cup of hot tea and Fleming said:

– What's up? Have you a pain or what's up with you?

– I don't know, Stephen said.

– Sick in your breadbasket, Fleming said, because your face looks white. It will go away.

– O yes, Stephen said.

But he was not sick there. He thought that he was sick in his heart if you could be sick in that place. Fleming was very decent to ask him. He wanted to cry. He leaned his elbows on the table and shut and opened the flaps of his ears. Then he heard the noise of the refectory every time he opened the flaps of his ears It made a roar like a train at night. And when he closed the flaps the roar was shut off like a train going into a tunnel. That night at Dalkey the train had roared like that and then, when it went into the tunnel, the roar stopped. He closed his eyes and the train went on, roaring and then stopping; roaring again, stopping. It was nice to hear it roar and stop and then roar out of the tunnel again and then stop.

Then the higher line fellows began to come down along the matting in the middle of the refectory, Paddy Rath and Jimmy Magee and the Spaniard who was allowed to smoke cigars and the little Portuguese who wore the woolly cap. And then the lower line tables and the tables of the third line. And every single fellow had a different way of walking.

He sat in a corner of the playroom pretending to watch a game of dominoes and once or twice he was able to hear for an instant the little song of the gas. The prefect was at the door with some boys and Simon Moonan was knotting his false sleeves. He was telling them something about Tullabeg.

Then he went away from the door and Wells came over to Stephen and said:

– Tell us, Dedalus, do you kiss your mother before you go to bed?

Stephen answered:

– I do.

Wells turned to the other fellows and said:

– O, I say, here's a fellow says he kisses his mother every night before he goes to bed.

The other fellows stopped their game and turned round, laughing. Stephen blushed under their eyes and said:

– I do not.

Wells said:

– O, I say, here's a fellow says he doesn't kiss his mother before he goes to bed.

They all laughed again. Stephen tried to laugh with them. He felt his whole body hot and confused in a moment. What was the right answer to the question? He had given two and still Wells laughed. But Wells must know the right answer for he was in third of grammar. He tried to think of Wells's mother but he did not dare to raise his eyes to Wells's face. He did not like Wells's face. It was Wells who had shouldered him into the square ditch the day before because he would not swop his little snuffbox for

Wells's seasoned hacking chestnut, the conqueror of forty. It was a mean thing to do; all the fellows said it was. And how cold and slimy the water had been! And a fellow had once seen a big rat jump plop into the scum.

The cold slime of the ditch covered his whole body; and, when the bell rang for study and the lines filed out of the playrooms, he felt the cold air of the corridor and staircase inside his clothes. He still tried to think what was the right answer. Was it right to kiss his mother or wrong to kiss his mother? What did that mean, to kiss? You put your face up like that to say good night and then his mother put her face down. That was to kiss. His mother put her lips on his cheek; her lips were soft and they wetted his cheek; and they made a tiny little noise: kiss. Why did people do that with their two faces?

Sitting in the study hall he opened the lid of his desk and changed the number pasted up inside from seventy-seven to seventy-six. But the Christmas vacation was very far away: but one time it would come because the earth moved round always.

There was a picture of the earth on the first page of his geography: a big ball in the middle of clouds. Fleming had a box of crayons and one night during free study he had coloured the earth green and the clouds maroon. That was like the two brushes in Dante's press, the brush with the green velvet back for Parnell and the brush with the maroon velvet back for Michael Davitt. But he had not told Fleming to colour them those colours. Fleming had done it himself.

He opened the geography to study the lesson; but he could not learn the names of places in America. Still they were all different places that had different names. They were all in different countries and the countries were in continents and the continents were in the world and the world was in the universe.

He turned to the flyleaf of the geography and read what he had written there: himself, his name and where he was.

Stephen Dedalus
Class of Elements
Clongowes Wood College
Sallins
County Kildare
Ireland
Europe
The World
The Universe

That was in his writing: and Fleming one night for a cod had written on the opposite page:

> *Stephen Dedalus is my name,*
> *Ireland is my nation.*
> *Clongowes is my dwelling place*
> *And heaven my expectation.*

He read the verses backwards but then they were not poetry. Then he read the flyleaf from the bottom to the top till he came to his own name. That was he: and he read down the page again. What was after the universe? Nothing. But was there anything round the universe to show where it stopped before the nothing place began? It could not be a wall; but there could be a thin thin line there all round everything. It was very big to think about everything and everywhere. Only God could do that. He tried to think what a big thought that must be; but he could only think of God. God was God's name just as his name was Stephen. *Dieu* was the French for God and that was God's name too; and when anyone prayed to God and said *Dieu* then God knew at once that it was a French person that was praying. But, though there were different names for God in all the different languages in the world and God understood what all the people who prayed said in their different languages, still God remained always the same God and God's real name was God.

It made him very tired to think that way. It made him feel his head very big. He turned over the flyleaf and looked wearily at the green round earth in the middle of the maroon clouds. He wondered which was right, to be for the green or for the maroon, because Dante had ripped the green velvet back off the brush that was for Parnell one day with her scissors and had told him that Parnell was a bad man. He wondered if they were arguing at home about that. That was called politics. There were two sides in it: Dante was on one side and his father and Mr Casey were on the other side but his mother and uncle Charles were on no side. Every day there was something in the paper about it.

It pained him that he did not know well what politics meant and that he did not know where the universe ended. He felt small and weak. When would he be like the fellows in poetry and rhetoric? They had big voices and big boots and they studied trigonometry. That was very far away. First came the vacation and then the next term and then vacation again and then again another term and then again the vacation. It was like a train going in and out of tunnels and that was like the noise of the boys eating in the refectory when you opened and closed the flaps of the ears. Term, vacation; tunnel, out; noise, stop. How far away it was! It was better to go to bed to sleep. Only prayers in the chapel and then bed. He shivered and yawned. It would be lovely in bed after the sheets got a bit hot. First they were so cold to get into. He shivered to think how cold they were first. But then they got hot and then he could sleep. It was lovely to be tired. He yawned again. Night prayers and then bed: he shivered and wanted to yawn. It would be lovely in a few minutes. He felt a warm glow creeping up from the cold shivering sheets, warmer and warmer till he felt warm all over, ever so warm and yet he shivered a little and still wanted to yawn.

The bell rang for night prayers and he filed out of the study hall after the others and down the staircase and along the corridors to the chapel. The corridors were darkly lit and the chapel was darkly lit. Soon all would be dark and sleeping. There was cold night air in the chapel and the marbles were the colour the sea was at night. The sea was cold day and night: but it was colder at night. It was cold and dark under the seawall beside his father's house. But the kettle would be on the hob to make punch.

The prefect of the chapel prayed above his head and his memory knew the responses:

> *O Lord, open our lips*
> *And our mouths shall announce Thy praise.*
> *Incline unto our aid, O God!*
> *O Lord, make haste to help us!*

There was a cold night smell in the chapel. But it was a holy smell. It was not like the smell of the old peasants who knelt at the back of the chapel at Sunday mass. That was a smell of air and rain and turf and corduroy. But they were very holy peasants. They breathed behind him on his neck and sighed as they prayed. They lived in Clane, a fellow said: there were little cottages there and he had seen a woman standing at the half-door of a cottage with a child in her arms as the cars had come past from Sallins. It would be lovely to sleep for one night in that cottage before the fire of smoking turf, in the dark lit by the fire, in the warm dark, breathing the smell of the peasants, air and rain and turf and corduroy. But O, the road there between the trees was dark! You would be lost in the dark. It made him afraid to think of how it was.

He heard the voice of the prefect of the chapel saying the last prayer. He prayed it too against the dark outside under the trees.

> *Visit, we beseech Thee, O Lord, this habitation and drive away from it all the*
> *snares of the enemy. May Thy holy angels dwell herein to preserve us in peace*
> *and may Thy blessings be always upon us through Christ our Lord.*
>
> *Amen.*

His fingers trembled as he undressed himself in the dormitory. He told his fingers to hurry up. He had to undress and then kneel and say his own prayers and be in bed before the gas was lowered so that he might not go to hell when he died. He rolled his stockings off and put on his nightshirt quickly and knelt trembling at his bedside and repeated his prayers quickly, fearing that the gas would go down. He felt his shoulders shaking as he murmured:

> *God bless my father and my mother and spare them to me!*
> *God bless my little brothers and sisters and spare them to me!*
> *God bless Dante and Uncle Charles and spare them to me!*

He blessed himself and climbed quickly into bed and, tucking the end of the nightshirt under his feet, curled himself together under the cold white sheets, shaking and trembling. But he would not go to hell when he died; and the shaking would stop. A voice bade the boys in the dormitory good night. He peered out for an instant over the coverlet and saw the yellow curtains round and before his bed that shut him off on all sides. The light was lowered quietly.

The prefect's shoes went away. Where? Down the staircase and along the corridors or to his room at the end? He saw the dark. Was it true about the black dog that walked there at night with eyes as big as carriage-lamps? They said it was the ghost of a murderer. A long shiver of fear flowed over his body. He saw the dark entrance hall of the castle. Old servants in old dress were in the ironing-room above the staircase. It was long ago. The old servants were quiet. There was a fire there, but the hall was still dark. A figure came up the staircase from the hall. He wore the white cloak of a marshal; his face was pale and strange; he held his hand pressed to his side. He looked out of strange eyes at the old servants. They looked at him and saw their master's face and cloak and knew that he had received his death-wound. But only the dark was where they looked: only dark silent air. Their master had received his death-wound on the battlefield of Prague far away over the sea. He was standing on the field; his hand was pressed to his side; his face was pale and strange and he wore the white cloak of a marshal.

O how cold and strange it was to think of that! All the dark was cold and strange. There were pale strange faces there, great eyes like carriage-lamps. They were the ghosts of murderers, the figures of marshals who had received their death-wound on battlefields far away over the sea. What did they wish to say that their faces were so strange?

Visit, we beseech Thee, O Lord, this habitation and drive away from it all . . .

Going home for the holidays! That would be lovely: the fellows had told him. Getting up on the cars in the early wintry morning outside the door of the castle. The cars were rolling on the gravel. Cheers for the rector!

Hurray! Hurray! Hurray!

The cars drove past the chapel and all caps were raised. They drove merrily along the country roads. The drivers pointed with their whips to Bodenstown. The fellows cheered. They passed the farmhouse of the Jolly Farmer. Cheer after cheer after cheer. Through Clane they drove, cheering and cheered. The peasant women stood at the half-doors, the men stood here and there. The lovely smell there was in the wintry air: the smell of Clane: rain and wintry air and turf smouldering and corduroy.

The train was full of fellows: a long long chocolate train with cream facings. The guards went to and fro opening, closing, locking, unlocking the doors. They were men in dark blue and silver; they had silvery whistles and their keys made a quick music: click, click: click, click.

And the train raced on over the flat lands and past the Hill of Allen. The telegraph poles were passing, passing. The train went on and on. It knew. There were lanterns in the hall of his father's house and ropes of green branches. There were holly and ivy round the pierglass and holly and ivy, green and red, twined round the chandeliers. There were red holly and green ivy round the old portraits on the walls. Holly and ivy for him and for Christmas.

Lovely . . .

All the people. Welcome home, Stephen! Noises of welcome. His mother kissed him. Was that right? His father was a marshal now: higher than a magistrate. Welcome home, Stephen!

Noises . . .

There was a noise of curtain-rings running back along the rods, of water being splashed in the basins. There was a noise of rising and dressing and washing in the dormitory: a noise of clapping of hands as the prefect went up and down telling the fellows to look sharp. A pale sunlight showed the yellow curtains drawn back, the tossed beds. His bed was very hot and his face and body were very hot.

He got up and sat on the side of his bed. He was weak. He tried to pull on his stocking. It had a horrid rough feel. The sunlight was queer and cold.

Fleming said:

– Are you not well?

He did not know; and Fleming said:

– Get back into bed. I'll tell McGlade you're not well.

– He's sick.

– Who is?

– Tell McGlade.

– Get back into bed.

– Is he sick?

A fellow held his arms while he loosened the stocking clinging to his foot and climbed back into the hot bed.

He crouched down between the sheets, glad of their tepid glow. He heard the fellows talk among themselves about him as they dressed for mass. It was a mean thing to do, to shoulder him into the square ditch, they were saying.

Then their voices ceased; they had gone. A voice at his bed said:

– Dedalus, don't spy on us, sure you won't?

Wells's face was there. He looked at it and saw that Wells was afraid.

– I didn't mean to. Sure you won't?

His father had told him, whatever he did, never to peach on a fellow. He shook his head and answered no and felt glad.

Wells said:

– I didn't mean to, honour bright. It was only for cod. I'm sorry.

The face and the voice went away. Sorry because he was afraid. Afraid that it was some disease. Canker was a disease of plants and cancer one of animals: or another different. That was a long time ago then out on the playgrounds in the evening light, creeping from point to point on the fringe of his line, a heavy bird flying low through the grey light. Leicester Abbey lit up. Wolsey died there. The abbots buried him themselves.

It was not Wells's face, it was the prefect's. He was not foxing. No, no: he was sick really. He was not foxing. And he felt the prefect's hand on his forehead; and he felt his forehead warm and damp against the prefect's cold damp hand. That was the way a rat felt, slimy and damp and cold. Every rat had two eyes to look out of. Sleek slimy coats, little little feet tucked up to jump, black slimy eyes to look out of. They could understand how to jump. But the minds of rats could not understand trigonometry. When they were dead they lay on their sides. Their coats dried then. They were only dead things.

The prefect was there again and it was his voice that was saying that he was to get up, that Father Minister had said he was to get up and dress and go to the infirmary. And while he was dressing himself as quickly as he could the prefect said:

– We must pack off to Brother Michael because we have the colly-wobbles!

He was very decent to say that. That was all to make him laugh. But he could not laugh because his cheeks and lips were all shivery: and then the prefect had to laugh by himself.

The prefect cried:

– Quick march! Hayfoot! Strawfoot!

They went together down the staircase and along the corridor and past the bath. As he passed the door he remembered with a vague fear the warm turf-coloured bogwater, the warm moist air, the noise of plunges, the smell of the towels, like medicine.

Brother Michael was standing at the door of the infirmary and from the door of the dark cabinet on his right came a smell like medicine. That came from the bottles on the shelves. The prefect spoke to Brother Michael and Brother Michael answered and called the prefect sir. He had reddish hair mixed with grey and a queer look. It was queer that he would always be a brother. It was queer too that you could not call him sir because he was a brother and had a different kind of look. Was he not holy enough or why could he not catch up on the others?

There were two beds in the room and in one bed there was a fellow: and when they went in he called out:

– Hello! It's young Dedalus! What's up?

– The sky is up, Brother Michael said.

He was a fellow out of the third of grammar and, while Stephen was undressing, he asked Brother Michael to bring him a round of buttered toast.

– Ah, do! he said.

– Butter you up! said Brother Michael. You'll get your walking papers in the morning when the doctor comes.

– Will I? the fellow said. I'm not well yet.

Brother Michael repeated:

– You'll get your walking papers. I tell you.

He bent down to rake the fire. He had a long back like the long back of a tramhorse. He shook the poker gravely and nodded his head at the fellow out of third of grammar

Then Brother Michael went away and after a while the fellow out of third of grammar turned in towards the wall and fell asleep.

That was the infirmary. He was sick then. Had they written home to tell his mother and father? But it would be quicker for one of the priests to go himself to tell them. Or he would write a letter for the priest to bring.

DEAR MOTHER – I am sick. I want to go home. Please come and take me home. I am in the infirmary.

Your fond son,   STEPHEN

How far away they were! There was cold sunlight outside the window. He wondered if he would die. You could die just the same on a sunny day. He might die before his mother came. Then he would have a dead mass in the chapel like the way the fellows had told him it was when Little had died. All the fellows would be at the mass, dressed in black, all with sad faces. Wells too would be there but no fellow would look at him. The rector would be there in a cope of black and gold and there would be tall yellow candles on the altar and round the catafalque. And they would carry the coffin out of the chapel slowly and he would be buried in the little graveyard of the community off the main avenue of limes. And Wells would be sorry then for what he had done. And the bell would toll slowly.

He could hear the tolling. He said over to himself the song that Brigid had taught him.

> *Dingdong! The castle bell!*
> *Farewell my mother!*
> *Bury me in the old churchyard*
> *Beside my oldest brother.*
> *My coffin shall be black,*
> *Six angels at my back,*
> *Two to sing and two to pray*
> *And two to carry my soul away.*

How beautiful and sad that was! How beautiful the words were where they said *Bury me in the old churchyard!* A tremor passed over his body. How sad and how beautiful! He wanted to cry quietly but not for himself: for the words, so beautiful and sad, like music. The bell! The bell! Farewell! O farewell!

The cold sunlight was weaker and Brother Michael was standing at his bedside with a bowl of beef-tea. He was glad for his mouth was hot and dry. He could hear them playing in the playgrounds. And the day was going on in the college just as if he were there.

Then Brother Michael was going away and the fellow out of the third of grammar told him to be sure and come back and tell him all the news in the paper. He told Stephen that his name was Athy and that his father kept a lot of racehorses that were spiffing jumpers and that his father would give a good tip to Brother Michael any time he wanted it because Brother Michael was very decent and always told him the news out of the paper they got every day up in the castle. There was every kind of news in the paper: accidents, shipwrecks, sports, and politics.

– Now it is all about politics in the papers, he said. Do your people talk about that too?

– Yes, Stephen said.

– Mine too, he said.

Then he thought for a moment and said:

– You have a queer name, Dedalus, and I have a queer name too, Athy. My name is the name of a town. Your name is like Latin.

Then he asked:

– Are you good at riddles?

Stephen answered:

– Not very good.

Then he said:

– Can you answer me this one? Why is the county of Kildare like the leg of a fellow's breeches?

Stephen thought what could be the answer and then said:

– I give it up.

– Because there is a thigh in it, he said. Do you see the joke? Athy is the town in the county Kildare and a thigh is the other thigh.

– Oh, I see, Stephen said.

– That's an old riddle, he said.

After a moment he said:

– I say!

– What? asked Stephen.

– You know, he said, you can ask that riddle another way.

– Can you? said Stephen.

– The same riddle, he said. Do you know the other was to ask it?

– No, said Stephen.

– Can you not think of the other way? he said.

He looked at Stephen over the bedclothes as he spoke. Then he lay back on the pillow and said:

– There is another way but I won't tell you what it is.

Why did he not tell it? His father, who kept the racehorses, must be a magistrate too like Saurin's father and Nasty Roche's father. He thought of his own father, of how he sang songs while his mother played and of how he always gave him a shilling when he asked for sixpence and he felt sorry for him that he was not a magistrate like the other boys' fathers. Then why was he sent to that place with them? But his father had told him that he would be no stranger there because his granduncle had presented an address to the liberator there fifty years before. You could know the people of that time by their old dress. It seemed to him a solemn time: and he wondered if that was the time when the fellows in Clongowes wore blue coats with brass buttons and yellow waistcoats and caps of rabbit-skin and drank beer like grownup people and kept greyhounds of their own to course the hares with.

He looked at the window and saw that the daylight had grown weaker. There would be cloudy grey light over the playgrounds. There was no noise on the playgrounds. The class must be doing the themes or perhaps Father Arnall was reading out of the book.

It was queer that they had not given him any medicine. Perhaps Brother Michael would bring it back when he came. They said you got stinking stuff to drink when you were in the infirmary. But he felt better now than before. It would be nice getting better slowly. You could get a book then. There was a book in the library about Holland. There were lovely foreign names in it and pictures of strange looking cities and ships. It made you feel so happy.

How pale the light was at the window! But that was nice. The fire rose and fell on the wall. It was like waves. Someone had put coal on and he heard voices. They were talking. It was the noise of the waves. Or the waves were talking among themselves as they rose and fell.

He saw the sea of waves, long dark waves rising and falling, dark under the moonless night. A tiny light twinkled at the pierhead where the ship was entering: and he saw a multitude of people gathered by the waters' edge to see the ship that was entering their harbour. A tall man stood on the deck, looking out towards the flat dark land: and by the light at the pierhead he saw his face, the sorrowful face of Brother Michael.

He saw him lift his hand towards the people and heard him say in a loud voice of sorrow over the waters:

– He is dead. We saw him lying upon the catafalque.

A wail of sorrow went up from the people.

– Parnell! Parnell! He is dead!

They fell upon their knees, moaning in sorrow.

And he saw Dante in a maroon velvet dress and with a green velvet mantle hanging from her shoulders walking proudly and silently past the people who knelt by the water's edge.

A great fire, banked high and red, flamed in the grate and under the ivy-twined branches of the chandelier the Christmas table was spread. They had come home a little late and still dinner was not ready: but it would be ready in a jiffy his mother had said. They were waiting for the door to open and for the servants to come in, holding the big dishes covered with their heavy metal covers.

All were waiting: uncle Charles, who sat far away in the shadow of the window, Dante and Mr Casey who sat in the easy-chairs at either side of the hearth, Stephen, seated on a chair between them, his feet resting on the toasted boss. Mr Dedalus looked at himself in the pierglass above the mantelpiece, waxed out his moustache ends and then, parting his coat-tails, stood with his back to the glowing fire: and still from time to time he withdrew a hand from his coat-tail to wax out one of his moustache ends. Mr Casey leaned his head to one side and, smiling, tapped the gland of his neck with his fingers. And Stephen smiled too for he knew now that it was not true that Mr Casey had a purse of silver in his throat. He smiled to think how the silvery noise which Mr Casey used to make had deceived him. And when he had tried to open Mr Casey's hand to see if the purse of silver was hidden there he had seen that the fingers could not be straightened out: and Mr Casey had told him that he had got those three cramped fingers making a birthday present for Queen Victoria. Mr Casey tapped the gland of his neck and smiled at Stephen with sleepy eyes: and Mr Dedalus said to him:

– Yes. Well now, that's all right. O, we had a good walk, hadn't we, John? Yes . . . I wonder if there's any likelihood of dinner this evening. Yes . . . O, well now, we got a good breath of ozone round the Head today. Ay, bedad.

He turned to Dante and said:

– You didn't stir out at all, Mrs Riordan?

Dante frowned and said shortly:

– No.

Mr Dedalus dropped his coat-tails and went over to the sideboard. He brought forth a great stone jar of whisky from the locker and filled the decanter slowly, bending now and then to see how much he had poured in. Then replacing the jar in the locker he poured a little of the whisky into two glasses, added a little water and came back with them to the fireplace.

– A thimbleful, John, he said, just to whet your appetite.

Mr Casey took the glass, drank, and placed it near him on the mantelpiece. Then he said:

– Well, I can't help thinking of our friend Christopher manufacturing . . .

He broke into a fit of laughter and coughing and added:

– . . . manufacturing that champagne for those fellows.

Mr Dedalus laughed loudly.

– Is it Christy? he said. There's more cunning in one of those warts on his bald head than in a pack of jack foxes.

He inclined his head, closed his eyes, and, licking his lips profusely, began to speak with the voice of the hotel keeper.

– And he has such a soft mouth when he's speaking to you, don't you know. He's very moist and watery about the dewlaps, God bless him.

Mr Casey was still struggling through his fit of coughing and laughter. Stephen, seeing and hearing the hotel keeper through his father's face and voice, laughed.

Mr Dedalus put up his eyeglass and, staring down at him, said quietly and kindly:

– What are you laughing at, you little puppy, you?

The servants entered and placed the dishes on the table. Mrs Dedalus followed and the places were arranged.

– Sit over, she said.

Mr Dedalus went to the end of the table and said:

– Now, Mrs Riordan, sit over. John, sit you down, my hearty.

He looked round to where uncle Charles sat and said:

– Now then, sir, there's a bird here waiting for you.

When all had taken their seats he laid his hand on the cover and then said quickly, withdrawing it:

– Now, Stephen.

Stephen stood up in his place to say the grace before meals:

Bless us, O Lord, and these Thy gifts which through Thy bounty we are about to receive through Christ our Lord. Amen.

All blessed themselves and Mr Dedalus with a sigh of pleasure lifted from the dish the heavy cover pearled around the edge with glistening drops.

Stephen looked at the plump turkey which had lain, trussed and skewered, on the kitchen table. He knew that his father had paid a guinea for it in Dunn's of D'Olier Street and that the man had prodded it often at the breastbone to show how good it was: and he remembered the man's voice when he had said:

– Take that one, sir. That's the real Ally Daly.

Why did Mr Barrett in Clongowes call his pandybat a turkey? But Clongowes was far away: and the warm heavy smell of turkey and ham and celery rose from the plates and dishes and the great fire was banked high and red in the grate and the green ivy and red holly made you feel so happy and when dinner was ended the big plum pudding would be carried in, studded with peeled almonds and sprigs of holly, with bluish fire running around it and a little green flag flying from the top.

It was his first Christmas dinner and he thought of his little brothers and sisters who were waiting in the nursery, as he had often waited, till the pudding came. The deep low collar and the Eton jacket made him feel queer and oldish: and that morning when his mother had brought him down to the parlour, dressed for mass, his father had cried. That was because he was thinking of his own father. And uncle Charles had said so too.

Mr Dedalus covered the dish and began to eat hungrily. Then he said:

– Poor old Christy, he's nearly lopsided now with roguery.

– Simon, said Mrs Dedalus, you haven't given Mrs Riordan any sauce.

Mr Dedalus seized the sauceboat.

– Haven't I? he cried. Mrs Riordan, pity the poor blind.

Dante covered her plate with her hands and said:

– No, thanks.

Mr Dedalus turned to uncle Charles.

– How are you off, sir?

– Right as the mail, Simon.

– You, John?

– I'm all right. Go on yourself.

– Mary? Here, Stephen, here's something to make your hair curl.

He poured sauce freely over Stephen's plate and set the boat again on the table. Then he asked uncle Charles was it tender. Uncle Charles could not speak because his mouth was full; but he nodded that it was.

– That was a good answer our friend made to the canon. What? said Mr Dedalus.

– I didn't think he had that much in him, said Mr Casey.

– *I'll pay your dues, father, when you cease turning the house of God into a polling-booth.*

– A nice answer, said Dante, for any man calling himself a catholic to give to his priest.

– They have only themselves to blame, said Mr Dedalus suavely. If they took a fool's advice they would confine their attention to religion.

– It is religion, Dante said. They are doing their duty in warning the people.

– We go to the house of God, Mr Casey said, in all humility to pray to our Maker and not to hear election addresses.

– It is religion, Dante said again. They are right. They must direct their flocks.

– And preach politics from the altar, is it? asked Mr Dedalus.

– Certainly, said Dante. It is a question of public morality. A priest would not be a priest if he did not tell his flock what is right and what is wrong.

Mrs Dedalus bid down her knife and fork, saying:

– For pity sake and for pity sake let us have no political discussion on this day of all days in the year.

– Quite right, ma'am, said uncle Charles. Now, Simon, that's quite enough now. Not another word now.

– Yes, yes, said Mr Dedalus quickly.

He uncovered the dish boldly and said:

– Now then, who's for more turkey?

Nobody answered. Dante said:

– Nice language for any catholic to use!

– Mrs Riordan, I appeal to you, said Mrs Dedalus, to let the matter drop now.

Dante turned on her and said:

– And am I to sit here and listen to the pastors of my church being flouted?

– Nobody is saying a word against them, said Mr Dedalus, so long as they don't meddle in politics.

– The bishops and priests of Ireland have spoken, said Dante, and they must be obeyed.

– Let them leave politics alone, said Mr Casey, or the people may leave their church alone.

– You hear? said Dante, turning to Mrs Dedalus.

– Mr Casey! Simon! said Mrs Dedalus, let it end now.

– Too bad! Too bad! said uncle Charles.

– What? cried Mr Dedalus. Were we to desert him at the bidding of the English people?

– He was no longer worthy to lead, said Dante. He was a public sinner.

– We are all sinners and black sinners, said Mr Casey coldly.

– *Woe be to the man by whom the scandal cometh!* said Mrs Riordan. *It would be better for him that a millstone were tied about his neck and that he were cast into the depths of the sea rather than that he should scandalize one of these, my least little ones.* That is the language of the Holy Ghost.

– And very bad language if you ask me, said Mr Dedalus coolly.

– Simon! Simon! said uncle Charles. The boy.

– Yes, yes, said Mr Dedalus. I meant about the . . . I was thinking about the bad language of the railway porter. Well now, that's all right. Here, Stephen, show me your plate, old chap. Eat away now. Here.

He heaped up the food on Stephen's plate and served uncle Charles and Mr Casey to large pieces of turkey and splashes of sauce. Mrs Dedalus was eating little and Dante sat with her hands in her lap. She was red in the face. Mr Dedalus rooted with the carvers at the end of the dish and said:

– There's a tasty bit here we call the pope's nose. If any lady or gentleman . . .

He held a piece of fowl up on the prong of the carving-fork. Nobody spoke. He put it on his own plate, saying:

– Well, you can't say but you were asked. I think I had better eat it myself because I'm not well in my health lately.

He winked at Stephen and, replacing the dish-cover, began to eat again.

There was a silence while he ate. Then he said:

– Well now, the day kept up fine after all. There were plenty of strangers down too.

Nobody spoke. He said again:

– I think there were more strangers down than last Christmas.

He looked round at the others whose faces were bent towards their plates and, receiving no reply, waited for a moment and said bitterly:

– Well, my Christmas dinner has been spoiled anyhow.

– There could be neither luck nor grace, Dante said, in a house where there is no respect for the pastors of the church.

Mr Dedalus threw his knife and fork noisily on his plate.

– Respect! he said. Is it for Billy with the lip or for the tub of guts up in Armagh? Respect!

– Princes of the church, said Mr Casey with slow scorn.

– Lord Leitrim's coachman, yes, said Mr Dedalus.

– They are the Lord's anointed, Dante said. They are an honour to their country.

– Tub of guts, said Mr Dedalus coarsely. He has a handsome face, mind you, in repose. You should see that fellow lapping up his bacon and cabbage of a cold winter's day. O Johnny!

He twisted his features into a grimace of heavy bestiality and made a lapping noise with his lips.

– Really, Simon, you should not speak that way before Stephen. It's not right.

– O, he'll remember all this when he grows up, said Dante hotly – the language he heard against God and religion and priests in his own home.

– Let him remember too, cried Mr Casey to her from across the table, the language with which the priests and the priests' pawns broke Parnell's heart and hounded him into his grave. Let him remember that too when he grows up.

– Sons of bitches! cried Mr Dedalus. When he was down they turned on him to betray him and rend him like rats in a sewer. Low-lived dogs! And they look it! By Christ, they look it!

– They behaved rightly, cried Dante. They obeyed their bishops and their priests. Honour to them!

– Well, it is perfectly dreadful to say that not even for one day in the year, said Mrs Dedalus, can we be free from these dreadful disputes!

Uncle Charles raised his hands mildly and said:

– Come now, come now, come now! Can we not have our opinions whatever they are without this bad temper and this bad language? It is too bad surely.

Mrs Dedalus spoke to Dante in a low voice but Dante said loudly:

– I will not say nothing. I will defend my church and my religion when it is insulted and spit on by renegade catholics.

Mr Casey pushed his plate rudely into the middle of the table and, resting his elbows before him, said in a hoarse voice to his host:

– Tell me, did I tell you that story about a very famous spit?

– You did not, John, said Mr Dedalus.

– Why then, said Mr Casey, it is a most instructive story. It happened not long ago in the County Wicklow where we are now.

He broke off and, turning towards Dante, said with quiet indignation:

– And I may tell you, ma'am, that I, if you mean me, am no renegade catholic. I am a catholic as my father was and his father before him and his father before him again, when we gave up our lives rather than sell our faith.

– The more shame to you now, Dante said, to speak as you do.

– The story, John, said Mr Dedalus smiling. Let us have the story anyhow.

– Catholic indeed! repeated Dante ironically. The blackest protestant in the land would not speak the language I have heard this evening

Mr Dedalus began to sway his head to and fro, crooning like a country singer.

– I am no protestant, I tell you again, said Mr Casey, flushing. Mr Dedalus, still crooning and swaying his head, began to sing in a grunting nasal tone:

> *O, come all you Roman catholics*
> *That never went to mass.*

He took up his knife and fork again in good humour and set to eating, saying to Mr Casey:

– Let us have the story, John. It will help us to digest.

Stephen looked with affection at Mr Casey's face which stared across the table over his joined hands. He liked to sit near him at the fire, looking up at his dark fierce face. But his dark eyes were never fierce and his slow voice was good to listen to. But why was he then against the priests? Because Dante must be right then. But he had heard his father say that she was a spoiled nun and that she had come out of the convent in the Alleghanies when her brother had got the money from the savages for the trinkets and the chainies. Perhaps that made her severe against Parnell. And she did not like him to play with Eileen because Eileen was a protestant and when she was young she knew children that used to play with protestants and the protestants used to make fun of the litany of the Blessed Virgin. *Tower of Ivory*, they used to say, *House of Gold!* How could a woman be a tower of ivory or a house of gold? Who was right then? And he remembered the evening in the infirmary in Clongowes, the dark waters, the light at the pierhead and the moan of sorrow from the people when they had heard.

Eileen had long white hands. One evening when playing tig she had put her hands over his eyes: long and white and thin and cold and soft. That was ivory: a cold white thing. That was the meaning of *Tower of Ivory*.

– The story is very short and sweet, Mr Casey said. It was one day down in Arklow, a cold bitter day, not long before the chief died. May God have mercy on him!

He closed his eyes wearily and paused. Mr Dedalus took a bone from his plate and tore some meat from it with his teeth, saying:

– Before he was killed, you mean.

Mr Casey opened his eyes, sighed and went on:

– It was down in Arklow one day. We were down there at a meeting and after the meeting was over we had to make our way to the railway station through the crowd. Such booing and baaing, man, you never heard. They called us all the names in the world. Well there was one old lady, and a drunken old harridan she was surely, that paid all her attention to me. She kept dancing along beside me in the mud bawling and screaming into my face: *Priest-hunter! The Paris Funds! Mr Fox! Kitty O'Shea!*

– And what did you do, John? asked Mr Dedalus.

– I let her bawl away, said Mr Casey. It was a cold day and to keep up my heart I had (saving your presence, ma'am) a quid of Tullamore in my mouth and sure I couldn't say a word in any case because my mouth was full of tobacco juice.

– Well, John?

– Well. I let her bawl away, to her heart's content, *Kitty O'Shea* and the rest of it till at last she called that lady a name that I won't sully this Christmas board nor your ears, ma'am, nor my own lips by repeating.

He paused. Mr Dedalus, lifting his head from the bone, asked:

– And what did you do, John?

– Do! said Mr Casey. She stuck her ugly old face up at me when she said it and I had my mouth full of tobacco juice. I bent down to her and *Phth!* says I to her like that.

He turned aside and made the act of spitting.

– *Phth!* says I to her like that, right into her eye.

He clapped his hand to his eye and gave a hoarse scream of pain.

– *O Jesus, Mary and Joseph!* says she. *I'm blinded! I'm blinded and drownded!*

He stopped in a fit of coughing and laughter, repeating:

– *I'm blinded entirely.*

Mr Dedalus laughed loudly and lay back in his chair while uncle Charles swayed his head to and fro.

Dante looked terribly angry and repeated while they laughed:

– Very nice! Ha! Very nice!

It was not nice about the spit in the woman's eye.

But what was the name the woman had called Kitty O'Shea that Mr Casey would not repeat? He thought of Mr Casey walking through the crowds of people and making speeches from a wagonette. That was what he had been in prison for and he remembered that one night Sergeant O'Neill had come to the house and had stood in the hall, talking in a low voice with his father and chewing nervously at the chinstrap of his cap. And that night Mr Casey had not gone to Dublin by tram but a car had come to the door and he had heard his father say something about the Cabinteely road.

He was for Ireland and Parnell and so was his father: and so was Dante too for one night at the band on the esplanade she had hit a gentleman on the head with her umbrella because he had taken off his hat when the band played *God save the Queen* at the end.

Mr Dedalus gave a snort of contempt.

– Ah, John, he said. It is true for them. We are an unfortunate priest-ridden race and always were and always will be till the end of the chapter.

Uncle Charles shook his head, saying:

– A bad business! A bad business!

Mr Dedalus repeated:

– A priestridden Godforsaken race!

He pointed to the portrait of his grandfather on the wall to his right.

– Do you see that old chap up there, John? he said. He was a good Irishman when there was no money in the job. He was condemned to death as a whiteboy. But he had a saying about our clerical friends, that he would never let one of them put his two feet under his mahogany.

Dante broke in angrily:

– If we are a priestridden race we ought to be proud of it! They are the apple of God's eye. *Touch them not*, says Christ, *for they are the apple of My eye.*

– And can we not love our country then? asked Mr Casey. Are we not to follow the man that was born to lead us?

– A traitor to his country! replied Dante. A traitor, an adulterer! The priests were right to abandon him. The priests were always the true friends of Ireland.

– Were they, faith? said Mr Casey.

He threw his fist on the table and, frowning angrily, protruded one finger after another.

– Didn't the bishops of Ireland betray us in the time of the union when Bishop Lanigan presented an address of loyalty to the Marquess Cornwallis? Didn't the bishops and priests sell the aspirations of their country in 1829 in return for catholic emancipation? Didn't they denounce the fenian movement from the pulpit and in the confession box? And didn't they dishonour the ashes of Terence Bellew MacManus?

His face was glowing with anger and Stephen felt the glow rise to his own cheek as the spoken words thrilled him. Mr Dedalus uttered a guffaw of coarse scorn.

– O, by God, he cried, I forgot little old Paul Cullen! Another apple of God's eye!

Dante bent across the table and cried to Mr Casey:

– Right! Right! They were always right! God and morality and religion come first.

Mrs Dedalus, seeing her excitement, said to her:

– Mrs Riordan, don't excite yourself answering them.

– God and religion before everything! Dante cried. God and religion before the world.

Mr Casey raised his clenched fist and brought it down on the table with a crash.

– Very well then, he shouted hoarsely, if it comes to that, no God for Ireland!

– John! John! cried Mr Dedalus, seizing his guest by the coat sleeve.

Dante stared across the table, her cheeks shaking. Mr Casey struggled up from his chair and bent across the table towards her, scraping the air from before his eyes with one hand as though he were tearing aside a cobweb.

– No God for Ireland! he cried. We have had too much God in Ireland. Away with God!

– Blasphemer! Devil! screamed Dante, starting to her feet and almost spitting in his face.

Uncle Charles and Mr Dedalus pulled Mr Casey back into his chair again, talking to him from both sides reasonably. He stared before him out of his dark flaming eyes, repeating:

– Away with God, I say!

Dante shoved her chair violently aside and left the table, upsetting her napkin-ring which rolled slowly along the carpet and came to rest against the foot of an easy-chair. Mr Dedalus rose quickly and followed her towards the door. At the door Dante turned round violently and shouted down the room, her cheeks flushed and quivering with rage:

– Devil out of hell! We won! We crushed him to death! Fiend!

The door slammed behind her.

Mr Casey, freeing his arms from his holders, suddenly bowed his head on his hands with a sob of pain.

– Poor Parnell! he cried loudly. My dead king!

He sobbed loudly and bitterly.

Stephen, raising his terror-stricken face, saw that his father's eyes were full of tears.

The fellows talked together in little groups.

One fellow said:

– They were caught near the Hill of Lyons.

– Who caught them?

– Mr Gleeson and the minister. They were on a car.

The same fellow added:

– A fellow in the higher line told me.

Fleming asked:

– But why did they run away, tell us?

– I know why, Cecil Thunder said. Because they had fecked cash out of the rector's room.

– Who fecked it?

– Kickham's brother. And they all went shares in it.

– But that was stealing. How could they have done that?

– A fat lot you know about it, Thunder! Wells said. I know why they scut.

– Tell us why.

– I was told not to, Wells said.

– O, go on, Wells, all said. You might tell us. We won't let it out.

Stephen bent forward his head to hear. Wells looked round to see if anyone was coming. Then he said secretly:

– You know the altar wine they keep in the press in the sacristy?

– Yes.

– Well, they drank that and it was found out who did it by the smell. And that's why they ran away, if you want to know.

And the fellow who had spoken first said:

– Yes, that's what I heard too from the fellow in the higher line.

The fellows all were silent. Stephen stood among them, afraid to speak, listening. A faint sickness of awe made him feel weak. How could they have done that? He thought of the dark silent sacristy. There were dark wooden presses there where the crimped surplices lay quietly folded. It was not the chapel but still you had to speak under your breath. It was a holy place. He remembered the summer evening he had been there to be dressed as boat-bearer, the evening of the procession to the little altar in the wood. A strange and holy place. The boy that held the censer had swung it lifted by the middle chain to keep the coals lighting. That was called charcoal: and it had burned quietly as the fellow had swung it gently and had given off a weak sour smell. And then when all were vested he had stood holding out the boat to the rector and the rector had put a spoonful of incense in it and it had hissed on the red coals.

The fellows were talking together in little groups here and there on the playground. The fellows seemed to him to have grown smaller: that was because a sprinter had knocked him down the day before, a fellow out of second of grammar. He had been thrown by the fellow's machine lightly on the cinder path and his spectacles had been broken in three pieces and some of the grit of the cinders had gone into his mouth.

That was why the fellows seemed to him smaller and farther away and the goalposts so thin and far and the soft grey sky so high up. But there was no play on the football grounds for cricket was coming: and some said that Barnes would be prof and some said it would be Flowers. And all over the playgrounds they were playing rounders and bowling twisters and lobs. And from here and from there came the sounds of the cricket bats through the soft grey air. They said: pick, pack, pock, puck: little drops of water in a fountain slowly falling in the brimming bowl.

Athy, who had been silent, said quietly:

– You are all wrong.

All turned towards him eagerly.

– Why?

– Do you know?

– Who told you?

– Tell us, Athy.

Athy pointed across the playground to where Simon Moonan was walking by himself kicking a stone before him.

– Ask him, he said.

The fellows looked there and then said:

– Why him?

– Is he in it?

Athy lowered his voice and said:

– Do you know why those fellows scut? I will tell you but you must not let on you know.

– Tell us, Athy. Go on. You might if you know.

He paused for a moment and then said mysteriously:

– They were caught with Simon Moonan and Tusker Boyle in the square one night.

The fellows looked at him and asked:

– Caught?

– What doing?

Athy said:

– Smugging.

All the fellows were silent: and Athy said:

– And that's why.

Stephen looked at the faces of the fellows but they were all looking across the playground. He wanted to ask somebody about it. What did that mean about the smugging in the square? Why did the five fellows out of the higher line run away for that? It was a joke, he thought. Simon Moonan had nice clothes and one night he had shown him a ball of creamy sweets that the fellows of the football fifteen had rolled down to him along the carpet in the middle of the refectory when he was at the door. It was the night of the match against the Bective Rangers; and the ball was made just like a red and green apple only it opened and it was full of the creamy sweets. And one day Boyle had said that an elephant had two tuskers instead of two tusks and that was why he was called Tusker Boyle but some fellows called him Lady Boyle because he was always at his nails, paring them.

Eileen had long thin cool white hands too because she was a girl. They were like ivory; only soft. That was the meaning of *Tower of Ivory* but protestants could not understand it and made fun of it. One day he had stood beside her looking into the hotel grounds. A waiter was running up a trail of bunting on the flagstaff and a fox terrier was scampering to and fro on the sunny lawn. She had put her hand into his pocket where his hand was and he had felt how cool and thin and soft her hand was. She had said that pockets were funny things to have: and then all of a sudden she had broken away and had run laughing down the sloping curve of the path. Her fair hair had streamed out behind her like gold in the sun. *Tower of Ivory. House of Gold.* By thinking of things you could understand them.

But why in the square? You went there when you wanted to do something. It was all thick slabs of slate and water trickled all day out of tiny pinholes and there was a queer smell of stale water there. And behind the door of one of the closets there was a drawing in red pencil of a bearded man in a Roman dress with a brick in each hand and underneath was the name of the drawing:

Balbus was building a wall.

Some fellow had drawn it there for a cod. It had a funny face but it was very like a man with a beard. And on the wall of another closet there was written in backhand in beautiful writing:

Julius Caesar wrote The Calico Belly

Perhaps that was why they were there because it was a place where some fellows wrote things for cod. But all the same it was queer what Athy said and the way he said it. It was not a cod because they had run away. He looked with others across the playground and began to feel afraid.

At last Fleming said:

– And we are all to be punished for what other fellows did?

– I won't come back, see if I do, Cecil Thunder said. Three days' silence in the refectory and sending us up for six and eight every minute.

– Yes, said Wells. And old Barrett has a new way of twisting the note so that you can't open it and fold it again to see how many ferulae you are to get. I won't come back too.

– Yes, said Cecil Thunder, and the prefect of studies was in second of grammar this morning.

– Let us get up a rebellion, Fleming said. Will we?

All the fellows were silent. The air was very silent and you could hear the cricket bats but more slowly than before: pick, pock.

Wells asked:

– What is going to be done to them?

– Simon Moonan and Tusker are going to be flogged, Athy said, and the fellows in the higher line got their choice of flogging or being expelled.

– And which are they taking? asked the fellow who had spoke first.

– All are taking expulsion except Corrigan, Athy answered. He's going to be flogged by Mr Gleeson.

– I know why, Cecil Thunder said. He is right and the other fellows are wrong because a flogging wears off after a bit but a fellow that has been expelled from college is known all his life on account of it. Besides Gleeson won't flog him hard.

– It's best of his play not to, Fleming said.

– I wouldn't like to be Simon Moonan and Tusker Cecil Thunder said. But I don't believe they will be flogged. Perhaps they will be sent up for twice nine.

– No, no, said Athy. They'll both get it on the vital spot.

Wells rubbed himself and said in a crying voice:

– Please, sir, let me off!

Athy grinned and turned up the sleeves of his jacket, saying:

> *It can't be helped;*
> *It must be done.*
> *So down with your breeches*
> *And out with your bum.*

The fellows laughed; but he felt that they were a little afraid. In the silence of the soft grey air he heard the cricket bats from here and from there: pock. That was a sound to hear but if you were hit then you would feel a pain. The pandybat made a sound too but not like that. The fellows said it was made of whalebone and leather with lead inside: and he wondered what was the pain like. There were different kinds of sounds. A long thin cane would have a high whistling sound and he wondered what was that pain like. It made him shivery to think of it and cold: and what Athy said too. But what was there to laugh at in it? It made him shivery: but that was because you always felt like a shiver when you let down your trousers. It was the same in the bath when you undressed yourself. He wondered who had to let them down, the master or the boy himself. O how could they laugh about it that way?

He looked at Athy's rolled-up sleeves and knuckly inky hands. He had rolled up his sleeves to show how Mr Gleeson would roll up his sleeves. But Mr Gleeson had round shiny cuffs and clean white wrists and fattish white hands and the nails of them were long and pointed. Perhaps he pared them too like Lady Boyle. But they were terribly long and pointed nails. So long and cruel they were, though the white fattish hands were not cruel but gentle. And though he trembled with cold and fright to think of the cruel long nails and of the high whistling sound of the cane and of the chill you felt at the end of your shirt when you undressed yourself yet he felt a feeling of queer quiet pleasure inside him to think of the white fattish hands, clean and strong and gentle. And he thought of what Cecil Thunder had said:

that Mr Gleeson would not flog Corrigan hard. And Fleming had said he would not because it was best of his play not to. But that was not why.

A voice from far out on the playground cried:

– All in!

And other voices cried:

– All in! All in!

During the writing lesson he sat with his arms folded, listening to the slow scraping of the pens. Mr Harford went to and fro making little signs in red pencil and sometimes sitting beside the boy to show him how to hold his pen. He had tried to spell out the headline for himself though he knew already what it was for it was the last of the book. *Zeal without prudence is like a ship adrift.* But the lines of the letters were like fine invisible threads and it was only by closing his right eye tight and staring out of the left eye that he could make out the full curves of the capital.

But Mr Harford was very decent and never got into a wax. All the other masters got into dreadful waxes. But why were they to suffer for what fellows in the higher line did? Wells had said that they had drunk some of the altar wine out of the press the sacristy and that it had been found out who had done it by the smell. Perhaps they had stolen a monstrance to run away with and sell it somewhere. That must have been a terrible sin, to go in there quietly at night, to open the dark press and steal the flashing gold thing into which God was put on the altar in the middle of flowers and candles at benediction while the incense went up in clouds at both sides as the fellow swung the censer and Dominic Kelly sang the first part by himself in the choir. But God was not in it of course when they stole it. But still it was a strange and a great sin even to touch it. He thought of it with deep awe; a terrible and strange sin: it thrilled him to think of it in the silence when the pens scraped lightly. But to drink the altar wine out of the press and be found out by the smell was a sin too: but it was not terrible and strange. It only made you feel a little sickish on account of the smell of the wine. Because on the day when he had made his first holy communion in the chapel he had shut his eyes and opened his mouth and put out his tongue a little: and when the rector had stooped down to give him the holy communion he had smelt a faint winy smell off the rector's breath after the wine of the mass. The word was beautiful: wine. It made you think of dark purple because the grapes were dark purple that grew in Greece outside houses like white temples. But the faint smell of the rector's breath had made him feel a sick feeling on the morning of his first communion. The day of your first communion was the happiest day of your life. And once a lot of generals had asked Napoleon what was the happiest day of his life.

They thought he would say the day he won some great battle or the day he was made an emperor. But he said:

– Gentlemen, the happiest day of my life was the day on which I made my first holy communion.

Father Arnall came in and the Latin lesson began and he remained still, leaning on the desk with his arms folded. Father Arnall gave out the theme-books and he said that they were scandalous and that they were all to be written out again with the corrections at once. But the worst of all was Fleming's theme because the pages were stuck together by a blot: and Father Arnall held it up by a corner and said it was an insult to any master to send him up such a theme. Then he asked Jack Lawton to decline the noun *mare* and Jack Lawton stopped at the ablative singular and could not go on with the plural.

– You should be ashamed of yourself, said Father Arnall sternly. You, the leader of the class!

Then he asked the next boy and the next and the next. Nobody knew. Father Arnall became very quiet, more and more quiet as each boy tried to answer it and could not. But his face was black-looking and his eyes were staring though his voice was so quiet. Then he asked Fleming and Fleming said that the word had no plural. Father Arnall suddenly shut the book and shouted at him:

– Kneel out there in the middle of the class. You are one of the idlest boys I ever met. Copy out your themes again the rest of you.

Fleming moved heavily out of his place and knelt between the two last benches. The other boys bent over their theme-books and began to write. A silence filled the classroom and Stephen, glancing timidly at Father Arnall's dark face, saw that it was a little red from the wax he was in.

Was that a sin for Father Arnall to be in a wax or was he allowed to get into a wax when the boys were idle because that made them study better or was he only letting on to be in a wax? It was because he was allowed, because a priest would know what a sin was and would not do it. But if he did it one time by mistake what would he do to go to confession? Perhaps he would go to confession to the minister. And if the minister did it he would go to the rector: and the rector to the provincial: and the provincial to the general of the jesuits. That was called the order: and he had heard his father say that they were all clever men. They could all have become high-up people in the world if they had not become jesuits. And he wondered what Father Arnall and Paddy Barrett would have become and what Mr McGlade and Mr Gleeson would have become if they had not become jesuits. It was hard to think what because you would have to think of them in a different way with different coloured coats and trousers and with beards and moustaches and different kinds of hats.

The door opened quietly and closed. A quick whisper ran through the class: the prefect of studies. There was an instant of dead silence and then the loud crack of a pandybat on the last desk. Stephen's heart leapt up in fear.

– Any boys want flogging here, Father Arnall? cried the prefect of studies. Any lazy idle loafers that want flogging in this class?

He came to the middle of the class and saw Fleming on his knees.

– Hoho! he cried. Who is this boy? Why is he on his knees? What is your name, boy?

– Fleming, sir.

– Hoho, Fleming! An idler of course. I can see it in your eye. Why is he on his knees, Father Arnall?

– He wrote a bad Latin theme, Father Arnall said, and he missed all the questions in grammar.

– Of course he did! cried the prefect of studies, of course he did! A born idler! I can see it in the corner of his eye.

He banged his pandybat down on the desk and cried:

– Up, Fleming! Up, my boy!

Fleming stood up slowly.

– Hold out! cried the prefect of studies.

Fleming held out his hand. The pandybat came down on it with a loud smacking sound: one, two, three, four, five, six.

– Other hand!

The pandybat came down again in six loud quick smacks.

– Kneel down! cried the prefect of studies.

Fleming knelt down, squeezing his hands under his armpits, his face contorted with pain; but Stephen knew how hard his hands were because Fleming was always rubbing rosin into them. But perhaps he was in great pain for the noise of the pandybat was terrible. Stephen's heart was beating and fluttering.

– At your work, all of you! shouted the prefect of studies. We want no lazy idle loafers here, lazy idle little schemers. At your work, I tell you. Father Dolan will be in to see you every day. Father Dolan will be in tomorrow.

He poked one of the boys in the side with his pandybat, saying:

– You, boy! When will Father Dolan be in again?

– Tomorrow, sir, said Tom Furlong's voice.

– Tomorrow and tomorrow and tomorrow, said the prefect of studies.

Make up your minds for that. Every day Father Dolan. Write away. You, boy, who are you?

Stephen's heart jumped suddenly.

– Dedalus, sir.

– Why are you not writing like the others?

– I . . . my . . .

He could not speak with fright.

– Why is he not writing, Father Arnall?

– He broke his glasses, said Father Arnall, and I exempted him from work.

– Broke? What is this I hear? What is this your name is! said the prefect of studies.

– Dedalus, sir.

– Out here, Dedalus. Lazy little schemer. I see schemer in your face. Where did you break your glasses?

Stephen stumbled into the middle of the class, blinded by fear and haste.

– Where did you break your glasses? repeated the prefect of studies.

– The cinder-path, sir.

– Hoho! The cinder-path! cried the prefect of studies. I know that trick.

Stephen lifted his eyes in wonder and saw for a moment Father Dolan's white-grey not young face, his baldy white-grey head with fluff at the sides of it, the steel rims of his spectacles and his no-coloured eyes looking through the glasses. Why did he say he knew that trick?

– Lazy idle little loafer! cried the prefect of studies. Broke my glasses! An old schoolboy trick! Out with your hand this moment!

Stephen closed his eyes and held out in the air his trembling hand with the palm upwards. He felt the prefect of studies touch it for a moment at the fingers to straighten it and then the swish of the sleeve of the soutane as the pandybat was lifted to strike. A hot burning stinging tingling blow like the loud crack of a broken stick made his trembling hand crumple together like a leaf in the fire: and at the sound and the pain scalding tears were driven into his eyes. His whole body was shaking with fright, his arm was shaking and his crumpled burning livid hand shook like a loose leaf in the air. A cry sprang to his lips, a prayer to be let off. But though the tears scalded his eyes and his limbs quivered with pain and fright he held back the hot tears and the cry that scalded his throat.

– Other hand! shouted the prefect of studies.

Stephen drew back his maimed and quivering right arm and held out his left hand. The soutane sleeve swished again as the pandybat was lifted and a loud crashing sound and a fierce maddening tingling burning pain made his

hand shrink together with the palms and fingers in a livid quivering mass.
The scalding water burst forth from his eyes and, burning with shame and
agony and fear, he drew back his shaking arm in terror and burst out into a
whine of pain. His body shook with a palsy of fright and in shame and rage
he felt the scalding cry come from his throat and the scalding tears falling
out of his eyes and down his flaming cheeks.

– Kneel down, cried the prefect of studies.

Stephen knelt down quickly pressing his beaten hands to his sides. To
think of them beaten and swollen with pain all in a moment made him feel
so sorry for them as if they were not his own but someone else's that he felt
sorry for. And as he knelt, calming the last sobs in his throat and feeling the
burning tingling pain pressed into his sides, he thought of the hands which
he had held out in the air with the palms up and of the firm touch of the
prefect of studies when he had steadied the shaking fingers and of the
beaten swollen reddened mass of palm and fingers that shook helplessly in
the air.

– Get at your work, all of you, cried the prefect of studies from the door.
Father Dolan will be in every day to see if any boy, any lazy idle little loafer
wants flogging. Every day. Every day.

The door closed behind him.

The hushed class continued to copy out the themes. Father Arnall rose
from his seat and went among them, helping the boys with gentle words
and telling them the mistakes they had made. His voice was very gentle and
soft. Then he returned to his seat and said to Fleming and Stephen:

– You may return to your places, you two.

Fleming and Stephen rose and, walking to their seats, sat down. Stephen,
scarlet with shame, opened a book quickly with one weak hand and bent
down upon it, his face close to the page.

It was unfair and cruel because the doctor had told him not to read
without glasses and he had written home to his father that morning to send
him a new pair. And Father Arnall had said that he need not study till the
new glasses came. Then to be called a schemer before the class and to be
pandied when he always got the card for first or second and was the leader
of the Yorkists! How could the prefect of studies know that it was a trick?
He felt the touch of the prefect's fingers as they had steadied his hand and
at first he had thought he was going to shake hands with him because the
fingers were soft and firm: but then in an instant he had heard the swish of
the soutane sleeve and the crash. It was cruel and unfair to make him kneel
in the middle of the class then: and Father Arnall had told them both that
they might return to their places without making any difference between

them. He listened to Father Arnall's low and gentle voice as he corrected the themes. Perhaps he was sorry now and wanted to be decent. But it was unfair and cruel. The prefect of studies was a priest but that was cruel and unfair. And his white-grey face and the no-coloured eyes behind the steel-rimmed spectacles were cruel looking because he had steadied the hand first with his firm soft fingers and that was to hit it better and louder.

– It's a stinking mean thing, that's what it is, said Fleming in the corridor as the classes were passing out in file to the refectory, to pandy a fellow for what is not his fault.

– You really broke your glasses by accident, didn't you? Nasty Roche asked.

Stephen felt his heart filled by Fleming's words and did not answer.

– Of course he did! said Fleming. I wouldn't stand it. I'd go up and tell the rector on him.

– Yes, said Cecil Thunder eagerly, and I saw him lift the pandybat over his shoulder and he's not allowed to do that.

– Did they hurt you much? Nasty Roche asked.

– Very much, Stephen said.

– I wouldn't stand it, Fleming repeated, from Baldyhead or any other Baldyhead. It's a stinking mean low trick, that's what it is. I'd go straight up to the rector and tell him about it after dinner.

– Yes, do. Yes, do, said Cecil Thunder.

– Yes, do. Yes, go up and tell the rector on him, Dedalus, said Nasty Roche, because he said that he'd come in tomorrow again and pandy you.

– Yes, yes. Tell the rector, all said.

And there were some fellows out of second of grammar listening and one of them said:

– The senate and the Roman people declared that Dedalus had been wrongly punished.

It was wrong; it was unfair and cruel; and, as he sat in the refectory, he suffered time after time in memory the same humiliation until he began to wonder whether it might not really be that there was something in his face which made him look like a schemer and he wished he had a little mirror to see. But there could not be; and it was unjust and cruel and unfair.

He could not eat the blackish fish fritters they got on Wednesdays in lent and one of his potatoes had the mark of the spade in it. Yes, he would do what the fellows had told him. He would go up and tell the rector that he had been wrongly punished. A thing like that had been done before by somebody in history, by some great person whose head was in the books of history And the rector would declare that he had been wrongly punished because the senate and the Roman people always declared that the men who did that had been wrongly punished. Those were the great men whose names were in Richmal Magnall's Questions. History was all about those men and what they did and that was what Peter Parley's Tales about Greece and Rome were all about. Peter Parley himself was on the first page in a picture. There was a road over a heath with grass at the side and little bushes: and Peter Parley had a broad hat like a protestant minister and a big stick and he was walking fast along the road to Greece and Rome.

It was easy what he had to do. All he had to do was when the dinner was over and he came out in his turn to go on walking but not out to the corridor but up the staircase on the right that led to the castle. He had nothing to do but that: to turn to the right and walk fast up the staircase and in half a minute he would be in the low dark narrow corridor that led through the castle to the rector's room. And every fellow had said that it was unfair, even the fellow out of second of grammar who had said that about the senate and the Roman people.

What would happen?

He heard the fellows of the higher line stand up at the top of the refectory and heard their steps as they came down the matting: Paddy Rath and Jimmy Magee and the Spaniard and the Portuguese and the fifth was big Corrigan who was going to be flogged by Mr Gleeson. That was why the prefect of studies had called him a schemer and pandied him for nothing: and, straining his weak eyes, tired with the tears, he watched big Corrigan's broad shoulders and big hanging black head passing in the file. But he had done something and besides Mr Gleeson would not flog him hard: and he remembered how big Corrigan looked in the bath. He had skin the same colour as the turf coloured bogwater in the shallow end of the bath and when he walked along the side his feet slapped loudly on the wet tiles and at every step his thighs shook a little because he was fat.

The refectory was half empty and the fellows were still passing out in file. He could go up the staircase because there was never a priest or a prefect outside the refectory door. But he could not go. The rector would side with the prefect of studies and think it was a schoolboy trick and then the prefect of studies would come in every day the same, only it would be worse because he would be dreadfully waxy at any fellow going up to the rector about him. The fellows had told him to go but they would not go themselves. They had forgotten all about it. No, it was best to forget all about it and perhaps the prefect of studies had only said he would come in. No, it was best to hide out of the way because when you were small and young you could often escape that way.

The fellows at his table stood up. He stood up and passed out among them in the file. He had to decide. He was coming near the door. If he went on with the fellows he could never go up to the rector because he could not leave the playground for that. And if he went and was pandied all the same all the fellows would make fun and talk about young Dedalus going up to the rector to tell on the prefect of studies.

He was walking down along the matting and he saw the door before him. It was impossible: he could not. He thought of the baldy head of the prefect of studies with the cruel no-coloured eyes looking at him and he heard the voice of the prefect of studies asking him twice what his name was. Why could he not remember the name when he was told the first time? Was he not listening the first time or was it to make fun out of the name? The great men in the history had names like that and nobody made fun of them. It was his own name that he should have made fun of if he wanted to make fun. Dolan: it was like the name of a woman who washed clothes.

He had reached the door and, turning quickly up to the right, walked up the stairs and, before he could make up his mind to come back, he had entered the low dark narrow corridor that led to the castle. And as he crossed the threshold of the door of the corridor he saw, without turning his head to look, that all the fellows were looking after him as they went filing by.

He passed along the narrow dark corridor, passing little doors that were the doors of the rooms of the community. He peered in front of him and right and left through the gloom and thought that those must be portraits. It was dark and silent and his eyes were weak and tired with tears so that he could not see. But he thought they were the portraits of the saints and great men of the order who were looking down on him silently as he passed: saint Ignatius Loyola holding an open book and pointing to the words *Ad Majorem Dei Gloriam* in it; saint Francis Xavier pointing to his chest; Lorenzo Ricci with his berretta on his head like one of the prefects of the lines, the three patrons of holy youth – saint Stanislaus Kostka, saint Aloysius Gonzaga, and Blessed John Berchmans, all with young faces because they died when they were young, and Father Peter Kenny sitting in a chair wrapped in a big cloak.

He came out on the landing above the entrance hall and looked about him. That was where Hamilton Rowan had passed and the marks of the soldiers' slugs were there. And it was there that the old servants had seen the ghost in the white cloak of a marshal.

An old servant was sweeping at the end of the landing. He asked him where was the rector's room and the old servant pointed to the door at the far end and looked after him as he went on to it and knocked.

There was no answer. He knocked again more loudly and his heart jumped when he heard a muffled voice say:

– Come in!

He turned the handle and opened the door and fumbled for the handle of the green baize door inside. He found it and pushed it open and went in.

He saw the rector sitting at a desk writing. There was a skull on the desk and a strange solemn smell in the room like the old leather of chairs.

His heart was beating fast on account of the solemn place he was in and the silence of the room: and he looked at the skull and at the rector's kind-looking face.

– Well, my little man, said the rector, what is it?

Stephen swallowed down the thing in his throat and said:

– I broke my glasses, sir.

The rector opened his mouth and said:

– O!

Then he smiled and said:

– Well, if we broke our glasses we must write home for a new pair.

– I wrote home, sir, said Stephen, and Father Arnall said I am not to study till they come.

– Quite right! said the rector.

Stephen swallowed down the thing again and tried to keep his legs and his voice from shaking.

– But, sir?

– Yes?

– Father Dolan came in today and pandied me because I was not writing my theme.

The rector looked at him in silence and he could feel the blood rising to his face and the tears about to rise to his eyes.

The rector said:

– Your name is Dedalus, isn't it?

– Yes, sir . . .

– And where did you break your glasses?

– On the cinder-path, sir. A fellow was coming out of the bicycle house and I fell and they got broken. I don't know the fellow's name.

The rector looked at him again in silence. Then he smiled and said:

– O, well, it was a mistake; I am sure Father Dolan did not know.

– But I told him I broke them, sir, and he pandied me.

– Did you tell him that you had written home for a new pair? the rector asked.

– No, sir.

– O well then, said the rector, Father Dolan did not understand. You can say that I excuse you from your lessons for a few days.

Stephen said quickly for fear his trembling would prevent him:

– Yes, sir, but Father Dolan said he will come in tomorrow to pandy me again for it.

– Very well, the rector said, it is a mistake and I shall speak to Father Dolan myself. Will that do now?

Stephen felt the tears wetting his eyes and murmured:

– O yes sir, thanks.

The rector held his hand across the side of the desk where the skull was and Stephen, placing his hand in it for a moment, felt a cool moist palm.

– Good day now, said the rector, withdrawing his hand and bowing.

– Good day, sir, said Stephen.

He bowed and walked quietly out of the room, closing the doors carefully and slowly.

But when he had passed the old servant on the landing and was again in the low narrow dark corridor he began to walk faster and faster. Faster and faster he hurried on through the gloom excitedly. He bumped his elbow against the door at the end and, hurrying down the staircase, walked quickly through the two corridors and out into the air.

He could hear the cries of the fellows on the playgrounds. He broke into a run and, running quicker and quicker, ran across the cinder-path and reached the third line playground, panting.

The fellows had seen him running. They closed round him in a ring, pushing one against another to hear.

– Tell us! Tell us!

– What did he say?

– Did you go in?

– What did he say?

– Tell us! Tell us!

He told them what he had said and what the rector had said and, when he had told them, all the fellows flung their caps spinning up into the air and cried:

– Hurroo!

They caught their caps and sent them up again spinning sky-high and cried again:

– Hurroo! Hurroo!

They made a cradle of their locked hands and hoisted him up among them and carried him along till he struggled to get free. And when he had escaped from them they broke away in all directions, flinging their caps again into the air and whistling as they went spinning up and crying:

– Hurroo!

And they gave three groans for Baldyhead Dolan and three cheers for Conmee and they said he was the decentest rector that was ever in Clongowes.

The cheers died away in the soft grey air. He was alone. He was happy and free; but he would not be anyway proud with Father Dolan. He would be very quiet and obedient: and he wished that he could do something kind for him to show him that he was not proud.

The air was soft and grey and mild and evening was coming. There was the smell of evening in the air, the smell of the fields in the country where they digged up turnips to peel them and eat them when they went out for a walk to Major Barton's, the smell there was in the little wood beyond the pavilion where the gallnuts were.

The fellows were practising long shies and bowling lobs and slow twisters. In the soft grey silence he could hear the bump of the balls: and from here and from there through the quiet air the sound of the cricket bats: pick, pack, pock, puck: like drops of water in a fountain falling softly in the brimming bowl.

Chapter 2

Uncle Charles smoked such black twist that at last his nephew suggested to him to enjoy his morning smoke in a little outhouse at the end of the garden.

– Very good, Simon. All serene, Simon, said the old man tranquilly. Anywhere you like. The outhouse will do me nicely: it will be more salubrious.

– Damn me, said Mr Dedalus frankly, if I know how you can smoke such villainous awful tobacco. It's like gunpowder, by God.

– It's very nice, Simon, replied the old man. Very cool and mollifying.

Every morning, therefore, uncle Charles repaired to his outhouse but not before he had greased and brushed scrupulously his back hair and brushed and put on his tall hat. While he smoked the brim of his tall hat and the bowl of his pipe were just visible beyond the jambs of the outhouse door. His arbour, as he called the reeking outhouse which he shared with the cat and the garden tools, served him also as a sounding-box: and every morning he hummed contentedly one of his favourite songs: O, *twine me a bower* or

Blue Eyes and Golden Hair or *The Groves of Blarney* while the grey and blue coils of smoke rose slowly from his pipe and vanished in the pure air.

During the first part of the summer in Blackrock uncle Charles was Stephen's constant companion. Uncle Charles was a hale old man with a well tanned skin, rugged features and white side whiskers. On week days he did messages between the house in Carysfort Avenue and those shops in the main street of the town with which the family dealt. Stephen was glad to go with him on these errands for uncle Charles helped him very liberally to handfuls of whatever was exposed in open boxes and barrels outside the counter. He would seize a handful of grapes and sawdust or three or four American apples and thrust them generously into his grandnephew's hand while the shopman smiled uneasily; and, on Stephen's feigning reluctance to take them, he would frown and say:

– Take them, sir. Do you hear me, sir? They're good for your bowels.

When the order list had been booked the two would go on to the park where an old friend of Stephen's father, Mike Flynn, would be found seated on a bench, waiting for them. Then would begin Stephen's run round the park. Mike Flynn would stand at the gate near the railway station, watch in hand, while Stephen ran round the track in the style Mike Flynn favoured, his head high lifted, his knees well lifted and his hands held straight down by his sides. When the morning practice was over the trainer would make his comments and sometimes illustrate them by shuffling along for a yard or so comically in an old pair of blue canvas shoes. A small ring of wonder-struck children and nursemaids would gather to watch him and linger even when he and uncle Charles had sat down again and were talking athletics and politics. Though he had heard his father say that Mike Flynn had put some of the best runners of modern times through his hands Stephen often glanced at his trainer's flabby stubble covered face, as it bent over the long stained fingers through which he rolled his cigarette, and with pity at the mild lustreless blue eyes which would look up suddenly from the task and gaze vaguely into the blue distance while the long swollen fingers ceased their rolling and grains and fibres of tobacco fell back into the pouch.

On the way home uncle Charles would often pay a visit to the chapel and, as the font was above Stephen's reach, the old man would dip his hand and then sprinkle the water briskly about Stephen's clothes and on the floor of the porch. While he prayed he knelt on his red handkerchief and read above his breath from a thumb blackened prayer book wherein catchwords were printed at the foot of every page. Stephen knelt at his side respecting, though he did not share, his piety. He often wondered what his grand-uncle prayed for so seriously. Perhaps he prayed for the souls in purgatory or for the grace of a happy death or perhaps he prayed that God might send him back a part of the big fortune he had squandered in Cork.

On Sundays Stephen with his father and his grand-uncle took their constitutional. The old man was a nimble walker in spite of his corns and often ten or twelve miles of the road were covered. The little village of Stillorgan was the parting of the ways. Either they went to the left towards the Dublin mountains or along the Goatstown road and thence into Dundrum, coming home by Sandyford. Trudging along the road or standing in some grimy wayside public house his elders spoke constantly of the subjects nearer their hearts, of Irish politics, of Munster and of the legends of their own family, to all of which Stephen lent an avid ear. Words which he did not understand he said over and over to himself till he had learnt them by heart: and through them he had glimpses of the real world about them. The hour when he too would take part in the life of that world seemed drawing near and in secret he began to make ready for the great part which he felt awaited him the nature of which he only dimly apprehended.

His evenings were his own; and he pored over a ragged translation of *The Count of Monte Cristo*. The figure of that dark avenger stood forth in his mind for whatever he had heard or divined in childhood of the strange and terrible. At night he built up on the parlour table an image of the wonderful island cave out of transfers and paper flowers and coloured tissue paper and strips of the silver and golden paper in which chocolate is wrapped. When he had broken up this scenery, weary of its tinsel, there would come to his mind the bright picture of Marseille, of sunny trellises, and of Mercedes.

Outside Blackrock, on the road that led to the mountains, stood a small whitewashed house in the garden of which grew many rosebushes: and in this house, he told himself, another Mercedes lived. Both on the outward and on the homeward journey he measured distance by this landmark: and in his imagination he lived through a long train of adventures, marvellous as those in the book itself, towards the close of which there appeared an image of himself, grown older and sadder, standing in a moonlit garden with Mercedes who had so many years before slighted his love, and with a sadly proud gesture of refusal, saying:

– Madam, I never eat muscatel grapes.

He became the ally of a boy named Aubrey Mills and founded with him a gang of adventurers in the avenue. Aubrey carried a whistle dangling from his buttonhole and a bicycle lamp attached to his belt while the others had short sticks thrust daggerwise through theirs. Stephen, who had read of Napoleon's plain style of dress, chose to remain unadorned and thereby heightened for himself the pleasure of taking counsel with his lieutenant before giving orders. The gang made forays into the gardens of old maids or went down to the castle and fought a battle on the shaggy weed-grown rocks, coming home after it weary stragglers with the stale odours of the foreshore in their nostrils and the rank oils of the seawrack upon their hands and in their hair.

Aubrey and Stephen had a common milkman and often they drove out in the milk-car to Carrickmines where the cows were at grass. While the men were milking the boys would take turns in riding the tractable mare round the field. But when autumn came the cows were driven home from the grass: and the first sight of the filthy cowyard at Stradbrook with its foul green puddles and clots of liquid dung and steaming bran troughs, sickened Stephen's heart. The cattle which had seemed so beautiful in the country on sunny days revolted him and he could not even look at the milk they yielded.

The coming of September did not trouble him this year for he was not to be sent back to Clongowes. The practice in the park came to an end when Mike Flynn went into hospital. Aubrey was at school and had only an hour or two free in the evening. The gang fell asunder and there were no more nightly forays or battles on the rocks. Stephen sometimes went round with the car which delivered the evening milk and these chilly drives blew away his memory of the filth of the cowyard and he felt no repugnance at seeing the cow hairs and hayseeds on the milkman's coat. Whenever the car drew up before a house he waited to catch a glimpse of a well scrubbed kitchen or of a softly lighted hall and to see how the servant would hold the jug and how she would close the door. He thought it should be a pleasant life enough, driving along the roads every evening to deliver milk, if he had warm gloves and a fat bag of gingernuts in his pocket to eat from. But the same foreknowledge which had sickened his heart and made his legs sag suddenly as he raced round the park, the same intuition which had made him glance with mistrust at his trainer's flabby stubble-covered face as it bent heavily over his long stained fingers, dissipated any vision of the future. In a vague way he understood that his father was in trouble and that this was the reason why he himself had not been sent back to Clongowes. For some time he had felt the slight change in his house; and those changes in what he had deemed unchangeable were so many slight shocks to his boyish conception of the world. The ambition which he felt astir at times in the darkness of his soul sought no outlet. A dusk like that of the outer world obscured his mind as he heard the mare's hoofs clattering along the tram-track on the Rock Road and the great can swaying and rattling behind him.

He returned to Mercedes and, as he brooded upon her image, a strange unrest crept into his blood. Sometimes a fever gathered within him and led him to rove alone in the evening along the quiet avenue. The peace of the gardens and the kindly lights in the windows poured a tender influence into his restless heart. The noise of children at play annoyed him and their silly voices made him feel, even more keenly than he had felt at Clongowes, that he was different from others. He did not want to play. He wanted to meet in the real world the unsubstantial image which his soul so constantly beheld. He did not know where to seek it or how, but a premonition which led him on told him that this image would, without any overt act of his, encounter him. They would meet quietly as if they had known each other and had made their tryst, perhaps at one of the gates or in some more secret place. They would be alone, surrounded by darkness and silence: and in that moment of supreme tenderness he would be transfigured. He would fade into something impalpable under her eyes and then in a moment he would be transfigured. Weakness and timidity and inexperience would fall from him in that magic moment.

Two great yellow caravans had halted one morning before the door and men had come tramping into the house to dismantle it. The furniture had been hustled out through the front garden which was strewn with wisps of straw and rope ends and into the huge vans at the gate. When all had been safely stowed the vans had set off noisily down the avenue: and from the window of the railway carriage, in which he had sat with his red-eyed mother, Stephen had seen them lumbering along the Merrion Road.

The parlour fire would not draw that evening and Mr Dedalus rested the poker against the bars of the grate to attract the flame. Uncle Charles dozed in a corner of the half furnished uncarpeted room and near him the family portraits leaned against the wall. The lamp on the table shed a weak light over the boarded floor, muddied by the feet of the van-men. Stephen sat on a footstool beside his father listening to a long and incoherent monologue. He understood little or nothing of it at first but he became slowly aware that his father had enemies and that some fight was going to take place. He felt, too, that he was being enlisted for the fight, that some duty was being laid upon his shoulders. The sudden flight from the comfort and revery of Blackrock, the passage through the gloomy foggy city, the thought of the bare cheerless house in which they were now to live made his heart heavy, and again an intuition, a foreknowledge of the future came to him. He understood also why the servants had often whispered together in the hall and why his father had often stood on the hearthrug with his back to the fire, talking loudly to uncle Charles who urged him to sit down and eat his dinner.

– There's a crack of the whip left in me yet, Stephen, old chap, said Mr Dedalus, poking at the dull fire with fierce energy. We're not dead yet, sonny. No, by the Lord Jesus (God forgive me) not half dead.

Dublin was a new and complex sensation. Uncle Charles had grown so witless that he could no longer be sent out on errands and the disorder in settling in the new house left Stephen freer than he had been in Blackrock. In the beginning he contented himself with circling timidly round the neighbouring square or, at most, going half way down one of the side streets but when he had made a skeleton map of the city in his mind he followed boldly one of its central lines until he reached the custom-house. He passed unchallenged among the docks and along the quays wondering at the multitude of corks that lay bobbing on the surface of the water in a thick yellow scum, at the crowds of quay porters and the rumbling carts and the ill-dressed bearded policeman. The vastness and strangeness of the life suggested to him by the bales of merchandise stocked along the walls or swung aloft out of the holds of steamers wakened again in him the unrest which had sent him wandering in the evening from garden to garden in search of Mercedes. And amid this new bustling life he might have fancied himself in another Marseille but that he missed the bright sky and the sun-warmed trellises of the wineshops. A vague dissatisfaction grew up within him as he looked on the quays and on the river and on the lowering skies and yet he continued to wander up and down day after day as if he really sought someone that eluded him.

He went once or twice with his mother to visit their relatives: and though they passed a jovial array of shops lit up and adorned for Christmas his mood of embittered silence did not leave him. The causes of his embitter-ment were many, remote and near. He was angry with himself for being young and the prey of restless foolish impulses, angry also with the change of fortune which was reshaping the world about him into a vision of squalor and insincerity. Yet his anger lent nothing to the vision. He chronicled with patience what he saw, detaching himself from it and tasting its mortifying flavour in secret.

He was sitting on the backless chair in his aunt's kitchen. A lamp with a reflector hung on the japanned wall of the fireplace and by its light his aunt was reading the evening paper that lay on her knees. She looked a long time at a smiling picture that was set in it and said musingly:

– The beautiful Mabel Hunter!

A ringletted girl stood on tiptoe to peer at the picture and said softly:

– What is she in, mud?

– In a pantomime, love.

The child leaned her ringletted head against her mother's sleeve, gazing on the picture, and murmured as if fascinated:

– The beautiful Mabel Hunter!

As if fascinated, her eyes rested long upon those demurely taunting eyes and she murmured devotedly:

– Isn't she an exquisite creature?

And the boy who came in from the street, stamping crookedly under his stone of coal, heard her words. He dropped his load promptly on the floor and hurried to her side to see. He mauled the edges of the paper with his reddened and blackened hands, shouldering her aside and complaining that he could not see.

He was sitting in the narrow breakfast room high up in the old dark-windowed house. The firelight flickered on the wall and beyond the window a spectral dusk was gathering upon the river. Before the fire an old woman was busy making tea and, as she bustled at the task, she told in a low voice of what the priest and the doctor had said. She told too of certain changes they had seen in her of late and of her odd ways and sayings. He sat listening to the words and following the ways of adventure that lay open in the coals, arches and vaults and winding galleries and jagged caverns.

Suddenly he became aware of something in the doorway. A skull appeared suspended in the gloom of the doorway. A feeble creature like a monkey was there, drawn thither by the sound of voices at the fire. A whining voice came from the door asking:

– Is that Josephine?

The old bustling woman answered cheerily from the fireplace:

– No, Ellen, it's Stephen.

– O . . . O, good evening, Stephen.

He answered the greeting and saw a silly smile break over the face in the doorway.

– Do you want anything, Ellen? asked the old woman at the fire.

But she did not answer the question and said:

– I thought it was Josephine. I thought you were Josephine, Stephen.

And, repeating this several times, she fell to laughing feebly.

He was sitting in the midst of a children's party at Harold's Cross. His silent watchful manner had grown upon him and he took little part in the games. The children, wearing the spoils of their crackers, danced and romped noisily and, though he tried to share their merriment, he felt himself a gloomy figure amid the gay cocked hats and sunbonnets.

But when he had sung his song and withdrawn into a snug corner of the room he began to taste the joy of his loneliness. The mirth, which in the beginning of the evening had seemed to him false and trivial, was like a soothing air to him, passing gaily by his senses, hiding from other eyes the feverish agitation of his blood while through the circling of the dancers and amid the music and laughter her glance travelled to his corner, flattering, taunting, searching, exciting his heart.

In the hall the children who had stayed latest were putting on their things: the party was over. She had thrown a shawl about her and, as they went together towards the tram, sprays of her fresh warm breath flew gaily above her cowled head and her shoes tapped blithely on the glassy road.

It was the last tram. The lank brown horses knew it and shook their bells to the clear night in admonition. The conductor talked with the driver, both nodding often in the green light of the lamp. On the empty seats of the tram were scattered a few coloured tickets. No sound of footsteps came up or down the road. No sound broke the peace of the night save when the lank brown horses rubbed their noses together and shook their bells.

They seemed to listen, he on the upper step and she on the lower. She came up to his step many times and went down to hers again between their phrases and once or twice stood close beside him for some moments on the upper step, forgetting to go down, and then went down. His heart danced upon her movements like a cork upon a tide. He heard what her eyes said to him from beneath their cowl and knew that in some dim past, whether in life or revery, he had heard their tale before. He saw her urge her vanities, her fine dress and sash and long black stocking, and knew that he had yielded to them a thousand times. Yet a voice within him spoke above the noise of his dancing heart, asking him would he take her gift to which he had only to stretch out his hand. And he remembered the day when he and Eileen had stood looking into the hotel grounds, watching the waiters running up a trail of bunting on the flagstaff and the fox terrier scampering to and fro on the sunny lawn and how, all of a sudden, she had broken out into a peal of laughter and had run down the sloping curve of the path. Now, as then, he stood listlessly in his place, seemingly a tranquil watcher of the scene before him.

– She too wants me to catch hold of her, he thought. That's why she came with me to the tram. I could easily catch hold of her when she comes up to my step: nobody is looking. I could hold her and kiss her.

But he did neither: and, when he was sitting alone in the deserted tram, he tore his ticket into shreds and stared gloomily at the corrugated footboard.

The next day he sat at his table in the bare upper room for many hours. Before him lay a new pen, a new bottle of ink and a new emerald exercise.

From force of habit he had written at the top of the first page the initial letters of the jesuit motto: A.M.D.G. On the first line of the page appeared the title of the verses he was trying to write: To E— C—. He knew it was right to begin so for he had seen similar titles in the collected poems of Lord Byron. When he had written this title and drawn an ornamental line underneath he fell into a daydream and began to draw diagrams on the cover of the book. He saw himself sitting at his table in Bray the morning after the discussion at the Christmas dinner table, trying to write a poem about Parnell on the back of one of his father's second moiety notices. But his brain had then refused to grapple with the theme and, desisting, he had covered the page with the names and addresses of certain of his classmates:

> *Roderick Kickham*
> *John Lawton*
> *Anthony MacSwiney*
> *Simon Moonan*

Now it seemed as if he would fail again but, by dint of brooding on the incident, he thought himself into confidence. During this process all those elements which he deemed common and insignificant fell out of the scene. There remained no trace of the tram itself nor of the tram-men nor of the horses: nor did he and she appear vividly. The verses told only of the night and the balmy breeze and the maiden lustre of the moon. Some undefined sorrow was hidden in the hearts of the protagonists as they stood in silence beneath the leafless trees and when the moment of farewell had come the kiss, which had been withheld by one, was given by both. After this the letters L. D. S. were written at the foot of the page, and, having hidden the book, he went into his mother's bedroom and gazed at his face for a long time in the mirror of her dressing-table.

But his long spell of leisure and liberty was drawing to its end. One evening his father came home full of news which kept his tongue busy all through dinner. Stephen had been awaiting his father's return for there had been mutton hash that day and he knew that his father would make him dip his bread in the gravy. But he did not relish the hash for the mention of Clongowes had coated his palate with a scum of disgust.

– I walked bang into him, said Mr Dedalus for the fourth time, just at the corner of the square.

– Then I suppose, said Mrs Dedalus, he will be able to arrange it. I mean about Belvedere.

– Of course he will, said Mr Dedalus. Don't I tell you he's provincial of the order now?

– I never liked the idea of sending him to the Christian brothers myself, said Mrs Dedalus.

– Christian brothers be damned! said Mr Dedalus. Is it with Paddy Stink and Micky Mud? No, let him stick to the jesuits in God's name since he began with them. They'll be of service to him in after years. Those are the fellows that can get you a position.

– And they're a very rich order, aren't they, Simon?

– Rather. They live well, I tell you. You saw their table at Clongowes. Fed up, by God, like gamecocks.

Mr Dedalus pushed his plate over to Stephen and bade him finish what was on it.

– Now then, Stephen, he said, you must put your shoulder to the wheel, old chap. You've had a fine long holiday.

– O, I'm sure he'll work very hard now, said Mrs Dedalus, especially when he has Maurice with him.

– O, Holy Paul, I forgot about Maurice, said Mr Dedalus. Here, Maurice! Come here, you thick-headed ruffian! Do you know I'm going to send you to a college where they'll teach you to spell c.a.t. cat. And I'll buy you a nice little penny handkerchief to keep your nose dry. Won't that be grand fun?

Maurice grinned at his father and then at his brother.

Mr Dedalus screwed his glass into his eye and stared hard at both his sons. Stephen mumbled his bread without answering his father's gaze.

– By the bye, said Mr Dedalus at length, the rector, or provincial rather, was telling me that story about you and Father Dolan. You're an impudent thief, he said.

– O, he didn't, Simon!

– Not he! said Mr Dedalus. But he gave me a great account of the whole affair. We were chatting, you know, and one word borrowed another. And, by the way, who do you think he told me will get that job in the corporation? But I'll tell you that after. Well, as I was saying, we were chatting away quite friendly and he asked me did our friend here wear glasses still, and then he told me the whole story.

– And was he annoyed, Simon?

– Annoyed? Not he! *Manly little chap!* he said.

Mr Dedalus imitated the mincing nasal tone of the provincial.

Father Dolan and I, when I told them all at dinner about it, Father Dolan and I had a great laugh over it. *You better mind yourself, Father Dolan,* said I, *or young Dedalus will send you up for twice nine.* We had a famous laugh together over it. Ha! Ha! Ha!

Mr Dedalus turned to his wife and interjected in his natural voice:

– Shows you the spirit in which they take the boys there. O, a jesuit for your life, for diplomacy!

He reassumed the provincial's voice and repeated:

– I told them all at dinner about it and Father Dolan and I and all of us we had a hearty laugh together over it. Ha! Ha! Ha!

The night of the Whitsuntide play had come and Stephen from the window of the dressing-room looked out on the small grass-plot across which lines of Chinese lanterns were stretched. He watched the visitors come down the steps from the house and pass into the theatre. Stewards in evening dress, old Belvedereans, loitered in groups about the entrance to the theatre and ushered in the visitors with ceremony. Under the sudden glow of a lantern he could recognize the smiling face of a priest.

The Blessed Sacrament had been removed from the tabernacle and the first benches had been driven back so as to leave the dais of the altar and the space before it free. Against the walls stood companies of barbells and Indian clubs; the dumbbells were piled in one corner: and in the midst of countless hillocks of gymnasium shoes and sweaters and singlets in untidy brown parcels there stood the stout leather-jacketed vaulting horse waiting its turn to be carried up on the stage and set in the middle of the winning team at the end of the gymnastic display.

Stephen, though in deference to his reputation for essay writing he had been elected secretary to the gymnasium, had had no part in the first section of the programme but in the play which formed the second section he had the chief part, that of a farcical pedagogue. He had been cast for it on account of his stature and grave manners for he was now at the end of his second year at Belvedere and in number two.

A score of the younger boys in white knickers and singlets came pattering down from the stage, through the vestry and into the chapel. The vestry and chapel were peopled with eager masters and boys. The plump bald sergeant major was testing with his foot the springboard of the vaulting horse. The lean young man in a long overcoat, who was to give a special display of intricate club swinging, stood near watching with interest, his silver-coated clubs peeping out of his deep sidepockets. The hollow rattle of the wooden dumbbells was heard as another team made ready to go up on the stage: and in another moment the excited prefect was hustling the boys through the vestry like a flock of geese, flapping the wings of his soutane nervously and crying to the laggards to make haste. A little troop of Neapolitan peasants were practising their steps at the end of the chapel, some circling their arms above their heads, some swaying their baskets of paper violets and curtsying. In a dark corner of the chapel at the gospel side of the altar a stout old lady knelt amid her copious black skirts. When she stood up a pink-dressed figure, wearing a curly golden wig and an old-fashioned straw sunbonnet, with black pencilled eyebrows and cheeks delicately rouged and powdered, was discovered. A low murmur of curiosity ran round the chapel at the discovery of this girlish figure. One of the prefects, smiling and nodding his head, approached the dark corner and, having bowed to the stout old lady, said pleasantly:

– Is this a beautiful young lady or a doll that you have here, Mr Tallon?

Then, bending down to peer at the smiling painted face under the leaf of the bonnet, he exclaimed:

– No! Upon my word I believe it's little Bertie Tallon after all!

Stephen at his post by the window heard the old lady and the priest laugh together and heard the boys' murmurs of admiration behind him as they passed forward to see the little boy who had to dance the sunbonnet dance by himself. A movement of impatience escaped him. He let the edge of the blind fall and, stepping down from the bench on which he had been standing, walked out of the chapel.

He passed out of the schoolhouse and halted under the shed that flanked the garden. From the theatre opposite came the muffled noise of the audience and sudden brazen clashes of the soldiers' band. The light spread upwards from the glass roof making the theatre seem a festive ark, anchored among the hulks of houses, her frail cables of lanterns looping her to her moorings. A side door of the theatre opened suddenly and a shaft of light flew across the grass plots. A sudden burst of music issued from the ark, the prelude of a waltz: and when the side door closed again the listener could hear the faint rhythm of the music. The sentiment of the opening bars, their languor and supple movement, evoked the incommunicable emotion which had been the cause of all his day's unrest and of his impatient movement of a moment before. His unrest issued from him like a wave of sound: and on the tide of flowing music the ark was journeying, trailing her cables of lanterns in her wake. Then a noise like dwarf artillery broke the movement. It was the clapping that greeted the entry of the dumbbell team on the stage.

At the far end of the shed near the street a speck of pink light showed in the darkness and as he walked towards it he became aware of a faint aromatic odour. Two boys were standing in the shelter of a doorway, smoking, and before he reached them he had recognized Heron by his voice.

– Here comes the noble Dedalus! cried a high throaty voice. Welcome to our trusty friend!

This welcome ended in a soft peal of mirthless laughter as Heron salaamed and then began to poke the ground with his cane.

– Here I am, said Stephen, halting and glancing from Heron to his friend.

The latter was a stranger to him but in the darkness, by the aid of the glowing cigarette tips, he could make out a pale dandyish face over which a smile was travelling slowly, a tall overcoated figure and a hard hat. Heron did not trouble himself about an introduction but said instead:

– I was just telling my friend Wallis what a lark it would be tonight if you took off the rector in the part of the schoolmaster. It would be a ripping good joke.

Heron made a poor attempt to imitate for his friend Wallis the rector's pedantic bass and then, laughing at his failure, asked Stephen to do it.

– Go on, Dedalus, he urged, you can take him off rippingly. *He that will not hear the churcha let him be to theea as the heathena and the publicana.*

The imitation was prevented by a mild expression of anger from Wallis in whose mouthpiece the cigarette had become too tightly wedged.

– Damn this blankety blank holder, he said, taking it from his mouth and smiling and frowning upon it tolerantly. It's always getting stuck like that. Do you use a holder?

– I don't smoke, answered Stephen.

– No, said Heron, Dedalus is a model youth. He doesn't smoke and he doesn't go to bazaars and he doesn't flirt and he doesn't damn anything or damn all.

Stephen shook his head and smiled in his rival's flushed and mobile face, beaked like a bird's. He had often thought it strange that Vincent Heron had a bird's face as well as a bird's name. A shock of pale hair lay on the forehead like a ruffled crest: the forehead was narrow and bony and a thin hooked nose stood out between the close-set prominent eyes which were light and inexpressive. The rivals were school friends. They sat together in class, knelt together in the chapel, talked together after beads over their lunches. As the fellows in number one were undistinguished dullards, Stephen and Heron had been during the year the virtual heads of the school. It was they who went up to the rector together to ask for a free day or to get a fellow off.

– O by the way, said Heron suddenly, I saw your governor going in.

The smile waned on Stephen's face. Any allusion made to his father by a fellow or by a master put his calm to rout in a moment. He waited in timorous silence to hear what Heron might say next. Heron, however, nudged him expressively with his elbow and said:

– You're a sly dog.

– Why so? said Stephen.

– You'd think butter wouldn't melt in your mouth, said Heron. But I'm afraid you're a sly dog.

– Might I ask you what you are talking about? said Stephen urbanely.

– Indeed you might, answered Heron. We saw her, Wallis, didn't we? And deucedly pretty she is too. And inquisitive! *And what part does Stephen take, Mr Dedalus? And will Stephen not sing, Mr Dedalus?* Your governor was staring at her through that eyeglass of his for all he was worth so that I think the old man has found you out too. I wouldn't care a bit, by Jove. She's ripping, isn't she, Wallis?

– Not half bad, answered Wallis quietly as he placed his holder once more in a corner of his mouth.

A shaft of momentary anger flew through Stephen's mind at these indelicate allusions in the hearing of a stranger. For him there was nothing amusing in a girl's interest and regard. All day he had thought of nothing but their leave-taking on the steps of the tram at Harold's Cross, the stream of moody emotions it had made to course through him and the poem he had written about it. All day he had imagined a new meeting with her for he knew that she was to come to the play. The old restless moodiness had again filled his breast as it had done on the night of the party, but had not found an outlet in verse. The growth and knowledge of two years of boyhood stood between then and now, forbidding such an outlet: and all day the stream of gloomy tenderness within him had started forth and returned upon itself in dark courses and eddies, wearying him in the end until the pleasantry of the perfect and the painted little boy had drawn from him a movement of impatience.

– So you may as well admit, Heron went on, that we've fairly found you out this time. You can't play the saint on me any more, that's one sure five.

A soft peal of mirthless laughter escaped from his lips and, bending down as before, he struck Stephen lightly across the calf of the leg with his cane, as if in jesting reproof.

Stephen's moment of anger had already passed. He was neither flattered nor confused, but simply wished the banter to end. He scarcely resented what had seemed to him a silly indelicateness for he knew that the adventure in his mind stood in no danger from these words: and his face mirrored his rival's false smile.

– Admit! repeated Heron, striking him again with his cane across the calf of the leg.

The stroke was playful but not so lightly given as the first one had been.

Stephen felt the skin tingle and glow slightly and almost painlessly; and, bowing submissively, as if to meet his companion's jesting mood, began to recite the *Confiteor*. The episode ended well, for both Heron and Wallis laughed indulgently at the irreverence.

The confession came only from Stephen's lips and, while they spoke the words, a sudden memory had carried him to another scene called up, as if by magic, at the moment when he had noted the faint cruel dimples at the corners of Heron's smiling lips and had felt the familiar stroke of the cane against his calf and had heard the familiar word of admonition:

– Admit.

It was towards the close of his first term in the college when he was in number six. His sensitive nature was still smarting under the lashes of an undivined and squalid way of life. His soul was still disquieted and cast down by the dull phenomenon of Dublin. He had emerged from a two years' spell of revery to find himself in the midst of a new scene, every event and figure of which affected him intimately, disheartened him or allured and, whether alluring or disheartening, filled him always with unrest and bitter thoughts. All the leisure which his school life left him was passed in the company of subversive writers whose jibes and violence of speech set up a ferment in his brain before they passed out of it into his crude writings.

The essay was for him the chief labour of his week and every Tuesday, as he marched from home to the school, he read his fate in the incidents of the way, pitting himself against some figure ahead of him and quickening his pace to outstrip it before a certain goal was reached or planting his steps scrupulously in the spaces of the patchwork of the pathway and telling himself that he would be first and not first in the weekly essay.

On a certain Tuesday the course of his triumphs was rudely broken. Mr Tate, the English master, pointed his finger at him and said bluntly:

– This fellow has heresy in his essay.

A hush fell on the class. Mr Tate did not break it but dug with his hand between his thighs while his heavily starched linen creaked about his neck and wrists. Stephen did not look up. It was a raw spring morning and his eyes were still smarting and weak. He was conscious of failure and of detection, of the squalor of his own mind and home, and felt against his neck the raw edge of his turned and jagged collar.

A short loud laugh from Mr Tate set the class more at ease.

– Perhaps you didn't know that, he said.

– Where? asked Stephen.

Mr Tate withdrew his delving hand and spread out the essay.

– Here. It's about the Creator and the soul. Rrm . . . rrm . . . rrm . . . Ah! *without a possibility of ever approaching nearer*. That's heresy.

Stephen murmured:

– I meant *without a possibility of ever reaching*.

It was a submission and Mr Tate, appeased, folded up the essay and passed it across to him, saying:

– O . . . Ah! *ever reaching*. That's another story.

But the class was not so soon appeased. Though nobody spoke to him of the affair after class he could feel about him a vague general malignant joy.

A few nights after this public chiding he was walking with a letter along the Drumcondra Road when he heard a voice cry:

– Halt!

He turned and saw three boys of his own class coming towards him in the dusk. It was Heron who had called out and, as he marched forward between his two attendants, he cleft the air before him with a thin cane in time to their steps. Boland, his friend, marched beside him, a large grin on his face, while Nash came on a few steps behind, blowing from the pace and wagging his great red head.

As soon as the boys had turned into Clonliffe Road together they began to speak about books and writers, saying what books they were reading and how many books there were in their fathers' bookcases at home. Stephen listened to them in some wonderment for Boland was the dunce and Nash the idler of the class. In fact, after some talk about their favourite writers, Nash declared for Captain Marryat who, he said, was the greatest writer.

– Fudge! said Heron. Ask Dedalus. Who is the greatest writer, Dedalus?

Stephen noted the mockery in the question and said:

– Of prose do you mean?

– Yes.

– Newman, I think.

– Is it Cardinal Newman? asked Boland.

– Yes, answered Stephen.

The grin broadened on Nash's freckled face as he turned to Stephen and said:

– And do you like Cardinal Newman, Dedalus?

– O, many say that Newman has the best prose style, Heron said to the other two in explanation, of course he's not a poet.

– And who is the best poet, Heron? asked Boland.

– Lord Tennyson, of course, answered Heron.

– O, yes, Lord Tennyson, said Nash. We have all his poetry at home in a book.

At this Stephen forgot the silent vows he had been making and burst out:

– Tennyson a poet! Why, he's only a rhymester!

– O, get out! said Heron. Everyone knows that Tennyson is the greatest poet.

– And who do you think is the greatest poet? asked Boland, nudging his neighbour.

– Byron, of course, answered Stephen.

Heron gave the lead and all three joined in a scornful laugh.

– What are you laughing at? asked Stephen.

– You, said Heron. Byron the greatest poet! He's only a poet for uneducated people.

– He must be a fine poet! said Boland.

– You may keep your mouth shut, said Stephen, turning on him boldly. All you know about poetry is what you wrote up on the slates in the yard and were going to be sent to the loft for.

Boland, in fact, was said to have written on the slates in the yard a couplet about a classmate of his who often rode home from the college on a pony:

As Tyson was riding into Jerusalem
He fell and hurt his Alec Kafoozelum.

This thrust put the two lieutenants to silence but Heron went on:

– In any case Byron was a heretic and immoral too.

– I don't care what he was, cried Stephen hotly.

– You don't care whether he was a heretic or not? said Nash.

– What do you know about it? shouted Stephen. You never read a line of anything in your life except a trans, or Boland either.

– I know that Byron was a bad man, said Boland.

– Here, catch hold of this heretic, Heron called out.

In a moment Stephen was a prisoner.

– Tate made you buck up the other day, Heron went on, about the heresy in your essay.

– I'll tell him tomorrow, said Boland.

– Will you? said Stephen. You'd be afraid to open your lips.

– Afraid?

– Ay. Afraid of your life.

– Behave yourself! cried Heron, cutting at Stephen's legs with his cane.

It was the signal for their onset. Nash pinioned his arms behind while Boland seized a long cabbage stump which was lying in the gutter. Struggling and kicking under the cuts of the cane and the blows of the knotty stump

Stephen was borne back against a barbed wire fence.

– Admit that Byron was no good.

– No.

– Admit.

– No.

– Admit.

– No. No.

At last after a fury of plunges he wrenched himself free. His tormentors set off towards Jones's Road, laughing and jeering at him, while he, half blinded with tears, stumbled on, clenching his fists madly and sobbing.

While he was still repeating the *Confiteor* amid the indulgent laughter of his hearers and while the scenes of that malignant episode were still passing sharply and swiftly before his mind he wondered why he bore no malice now to those who had tormented him. He had not forgotten a whit of their cowardice and cruelty but the memory of it called forth no anger from him. All the descriptions of fierce love and hatred which he had met in books had seemed to him therefore unreal. Even that night as he stumbled homewards along Jones's Road he had felt that some power was divesting him of that sudden-woven anger as easily as a fruit is divested of its soft ripe peel.

He remained standing with his two companions at the end of the shed listening idly to their talk or to the bursts of applause in the theatre. She was sitting there among the others perhaps waiting for him to appear. He tried to recall her appearance but could not. He could remember only that she had worn a shawl about her head like a cowl and that her dark eyes had invited and unnerved him. He wondered had he been in her thoughts as she had been in his. Then in the dark and unseen by the other two he rested the tips of the fingers of one hand upon the palm of the other hand, scarcely touching it lightly. But the pressure of her fingers had been lighter and steadier: and suddenly the memory of their touch traversed his brain and body like an invisible wave.

A boy came towards them, running along under the shed. He was excited and breathless.

– O, Dedalus, he cried, Doyle is in a great bake about you. You're to go in at once and get dressed for the play. Hurry up, you better.

– He's coming now, said Heron to the messenger with a haughty drawl, when he wants to.

The boy turned to Heron and repeated:

– But Doyle is in an awful bake.

– Will you tell Doyle with my best compliments that I damned his eyes? answered Heron.

– Well, I must go now, said Stephen, who cared little for such points of honour.

– I wouldn't, said Heron, damn me if I would. That's no way to send for one of the senior boys. In a bake, indeed! I think it's quite enough that you're taking a part in his bally old play.

This spirit of quarrelsome comradeship which he had observed lately in his rival had not seduced Stephen from his habits of quiet obedience. He mistrusted the turbulence and doubted the sincerity of such comradeship which seemed to him a sorry anticipation of manhood. The question of honour here raised was, like all such questions, trivial to him. While his mind had been pursuing its intangible phantoms and turning in irresolution from such pursuit he had heard about him the constant voices of his father and of his masters, urging him to be a gentleman above all things and urging him to be a good catholic above all things. These voices had now come to be hollow-sounding in his ears. When the gymnasium had been opened he had heard another voice urging him to be strong and manly and healthy and when the movement towards national revival had begun to be felt in the college yet another voice had bidden him be true to his country and help to raise up her language and tradition. In the profane world, as he foresaw, a worldly voice would bid him raise up his father's fallen state by his labours and, meanwhile, the voice of his school comrades urged him to be a decent fellow, to shield others from blame or to beg them off and to do his best to get free days for the school. And it was the din of all these hollow-sounding voices that made him halt irresolutely in the pursuit of phantoms. He gave them ear only for a time but he was happy only when he was far from them, beyond their call, alone or in the company of phantasmal comrades.

In the vestry a plump fresh-faced jesuit and an elderly man, in shabby blue clothes, were dabbling in a case of paints and chalks. The boys who had been painted walked about or stood still awkwardly, touching their faces in a gingerly fashion with their furtive fingertips. In the middle of the vestry a young jesuit, who was then on a visit to the college, stood rocking himself rhythmically from the tips of his toes to his heels and back again, his hands thrust well forward into his side-pockets. His small head set off with glossy red curls and his newly shaven face agreed well with the spotless decency of his soutane and with his spotless shoes.

As he watched this swaying form and tried to read for himself the legend of the priest's mocking smile there came into Stephen's memory a saying which he had heard from his father before he had been sent to Clongowes, that you could always tell a jesuit by the style of his clothes. At the same moment he thought he saw a likeness between his father's mind and that of this smiling well-dressed priest: and he was aware of some desecration of the priest's office or of the vestry itself whose silence was now routed by loud talk and joking and its air pungent with the smells of the gas-jets and the grease.

While his forehead was being wrinkled and his jaws painted black and blue by the elderly man, he listened distractedly to the voice of the plump young jesuit which bade him speak up and make his points clearly. He could hear the band playing *The Lily of Killarney* and knew that in a few moments the curtain would go up. He felt no stage fright but the thought of the part he had to play humiliated him. A remembrance of some of his lines made a sudden flush rise to his painted cheeks. He saw her serious alluring eyes watching him from among the audience and their image at once swept away his scruples, leaving his will compact. Another nature seemed to have been lent him: the infection of the excitement and youth about him entered into and transformed his moody mistrustfulness. For one rare moment he seemed to be clothed in the real apparel of boyhood: and, as he stood in the wings among the other players, he shared the common mirth amid which the drop scene was hauled upwards by two able-bodied priests with violent jerks and all awry.

A few moments after he found himself on the stage amid the garish gas and the dim scenery, acting before the innumerable faces of the void. It surprised him to see that the play which he had known at rehearsals for a disjointed lifeless thing had suddenly assumed a life of its own. It seemed now to play itself, he and his fellow actors aiding it with their parts. When the curtain fell on the last scene he heard the void filled with applause and, through a rift in a side scene, saw the simple body before which he had acted magically deformed, the void of faces breaking at all points and falling asunder into busy groups. He left the stage quickly and rid himself of his mummery and passed out through the chapel into the college garden. Now that the play was over his nerves cried for some further adventure. He hurried onwards as if to overtake it. The doors of the theatre were all open and the audience had emptied out. On the lines which he had fancied the moorings of an ark a few lanterns swung in the night breeze, flickering cheerlessly. He mounted the steps from the garden in haste, eager that some prey should not elude him, and forced his way through the crowd in the hall and past the two jesuits who stood watching the exodus and bowing and shaking hands with the visitors. He pushed onward nervously, feigning a still greater haste and faintly conscious of the smiles and stares and nudges which his powdered head left in its wake.

When he came out on the steps he saw his family waiting for him at the first lamp. In a glance he noted that every figure of the group was familiar and ran down the steps angrily.

– I have to leave a message down in George's Street, he said to his father quickly. I'll be home after you.

Without waiting for his father's questions he ran across the road and began to walk at breakneck speed down the hill. He hardly knew where he was walking. Pride and hope and desire like crushed herbs in his heart sent up vapours of maddening incense before the eyes of his mind. He strode down the hill amid the tumult of sudden-risen vapours of wounded pride and fallen hope and baffled desire. They streamed upwards before his anguished eyes in dense and maddening fumes and passed away above him till at last the air was clear and cold again.

A film still veiled his eyes but they burned no longer. A power, akin to that which had often made anger or resentment fall from him, brought his steps to rest. He stood still and gazed up at the sombre porch of the morgue and from that to the dark cobbled laneway at its side. He saw the word *Lotts* on the wall of the lane and breathed slowly the rank heavy air.

– That is horse piss and rotted straw, he thought. It is a good odour to breathe. It will calm my heart. My heart is quite calm now. I will go back.

Stephen was once again seated beside his father in the corner of a railway carriage at Kingsbridge. He was travelling with his father by the night mail to Cork. As the train steamed out of the station he recalled his childish wonder of years before and every event of his first day at Clongowes. But he felt no wonder now. He saw the darkening lands slipping away past him, the silent telegraph-poles passing his window swiftly every four seconds, the little glimmering stations, manned by a few silent sentries, flung by the mail behind her and twinkling for a moment in the darkness like fiery grains flung backwards by a runner.

He listened without sympathy to his father's evocation of Cork and of scenes of his youth, a tale broken by sighs or draughts from his pocket flask whenever the image of some dead friend appeared in it or whenever the evoker remembered suddenly the purpose of his actual visit. Stephen heard but could feel no pity. The images of the dead were all strangers to him save that of uncle Charles, an image which had lately been fading out of memory. He knew, however, that his father's property was going to be sold by auction, and in the manner of his own dispossession he felt the world give the lie rudely to his phantasy.

At Maryborough he fell asleep. When he awoke–the train had passed out of Mallow and his father was stretched asleep on the other seat. The cold light of the dawn lay over the country, over the unpeopled fields and the closed cottages. The terror of sleep fascinated his mind as he watched the silent country or heard from time to time his father's deep breath or sudden sleepy movement. The neighbourhood of unseen sleepers filled him with strange dread, as though they could harm him, and he prayed that the day might come quickly. His prayer, addressed neither to God nor saint, began with a shiver, as the chilly morning breeze crept through the chink of the carriage door to his feet, and ended in a trail of foolish words which he made to fit the insistent rhythm of the train; and silently, at intervals of four seconds, the telegraph-poles held the galloping notes of the music between punctual bars. This furious music allayed his dread and, leaning against the windowledge, he let his eyelids close again.

They drove in a jingle across Cork while it was still early morning and Stephen finished his sleep in a bedroom of the Victoria Hotel. The bright warm sunlight was streaming through the window and he could hear the din of traffic. His father was standing before the dressing-table, examining his hair and face and moustache with great care, craning his neck across the water jug and drawing it back sideways to see the better. While he did so he sang softly to himself with quaint accent and phrasing:

> ' 'Tis youth and folly
> Makes young men marry,
> So here, my love, I'll
>   No longer stay.
> What can't be cured, sure,
> Must be injured, sure,
> So I'll go to
>   Amerikay.
>
> 'My love she's handsome,
> My love she's bony:
> She's like good whisky
>   When it is new;
> But when 'tis old
> And growing cold
> It fades and dies like
>   The mountain dew.'

The consciousness of the warm sunny city outside his window and the tender tremors with which his father's voice festooned the strange sad happy air, drove off all the mists of the night's ill humour from Stephen's brain. He got up quickly to dress and, when the song had ended, said:

– That's much prettier than any of your other *come-all-yous*.

– Do you think so? asked Mr Dedalus.

– I like it, said Stephen.

– It's a pretty old air, said Mr Dedalus, twirling the points of his moustache. Ah, but you should have heard Mick Lacy sing it! Poor Mick Lacy! He had little turns for it, grace notes that he used to put in that I haven't got. That was the boy who could sing a *come-all-you*, if you like.

Mr Dedalus had ordered drisheens for breakfast and during the meal he cross-examined the waiter for local news. For the most part they spoke at cross purposes when a name was mentioned, the waiter having in mind the present holder and Mr Dedalus his father or perhaps his grandfather.

– Well, I hope they haven't moved the Queen's College anyhow, said Mr Dedalus, for I want to show it to this youngster of mine.

Along the Mardyke the trees were in bloom. They entered the grounds of the college and were led by the garrulous porter across the quadrangle. But their progress across the gravel was brought to a halt after every dozen or so paces by some reply of the porter's.

– Ah, do you tell me so? And is poor Pottlebelly dead?

– Yes, sir. Dead, sir.

During these halts Stephen stood awkwardly behind the two men, weary of the subject and waiting restlessly for the slow march to begin again. By the time they had crossed the quadrangle his restlessness had risen to fever. He wondered how his father, whom he knew for a shrewd suspicious man, could be duped by the servile manners of the porter; and the lively southern speech which had entertained him all the morning now irritated his ears.

They passed into the anatomy theatre where Mr Dedalus, the porter aiding him, searched the desks for his initials. Stephen remained in the background, depressed more than ever by the darkness and silence of the theatre and by the air it wore of jaded and formal study. On the desk he read the word *Foetus* cut several times in the dark stained wood. The sudden legend startled his blood: he seemed to feel the absent students of the college about him and to shrink from their company. A vision of their life, which his father's words had been powerless to evoke, sprang up before him out of the word cut in the desk. A broad-shouldered student with a moustache was cutting in the letters with a jack-knife, seriously. Other students stood or sat near him laughing at his handiwork. One jogged his elbow. The big student turned on him, frowning. He was dressed in loose grey clothes and had tan boots.

Stephen's name was called. He hurried down the steps of the theatre so as to be as far away from the vision as he could be and, peering closely at his father's initials, hid his flushed face.

But the word and the vision capered before his eyes as he walked back across the quadrangle and towards the college gate. It shocked him to find in the outer world a trace of what he had deemed till then a brutish and individual malady of his own mind. His monstrous reveries came thronging into his memory. They too had sprung up before him, suddenly and furiously, out of mere words. He had soon given in to them and allowed them to sweep across and abase his intellect, wondering always where they came from, from what den of monstrous images, and always weak and humble towards others, restless and sickened of himself when they had swept over him.

– Ay, bedad! And there's the Groceries sure enough! cried Mr Dedalus. You often heard me speak of the Groceries, didn't you, Stephen. Many's the time we went down there when our names had been marked, a crowd of us, Harry Peard and little Jack Mountain and Bob Dyas and Maurice Moriarty, the French man, and Tom O'Grady and Mick Lacy that I told you of this morning and Joey Corbet and poor little good-hearted Johnny Keevers of the Tantiles.

The leaves of the trees along the Mardyke were astir and whispering in the sunlight. A team of cricketers passed, agile young men in flannels and blazers, one of them carrying the long green wicket-bag. In a quiet bystreet a German band of five players in faded uniforms and with battered brass instruments was playing to an audience of street arabs and leisurely messenger boys. A maid in a white cap and apron was watering a box of plants on a sill which shone like a slab of limestone in the warm glare. From another window open to the air came the sound of a piano, scale after scale rising into the treble.

Stephen walked on at his father's side, listening to stories he had heard before, hearing again the names of the scattered and dead revellers who had been the companions of his father's youth. And a faint sickness sighed in his heart. He recalled his own equivocal position in Belvedere, a free boy, a leader afraid of his own authority, proud and sensitive and suspicious, battling against the squalor of his life and against the riot of his mind. The letters cut in the stained wood of the desk stared upon him, mocking his bodily weakness and futile enthusiasms and making him loathe himself for his own mad and filthy orgies. The spittle in his throat grew bitter and foul to swallow and the faint sickness climbed to his brain so that for a moment he closed his eyes and walked on in darkness.

He could still hear his father's voice

– When you kick out for yourself, Stephen – as I daresay you will one of these days – remember, whatever you do, to mix with gentlemen. When I was a young fellow I tell you I enjoyed myself. I mixed with fine decent fellows. Everyone of us could do something. One fellow had a good voice, another fellow was a good actor, another could sing a good comic song, another was a good oarsman or a good racket player, another could tell a good story and so on. We kept the ball rolling anyhow and enjoyed ourselves and saw a bit of life and we were none the worse of it either. But we were all gentlemen, Stephen – at least I hope we were – and bloody good honest Irishmen too. That's the kind of fellows I want you to associate with, fellows of the right kidney. I'm talking to you as a friend, Stephen. I don't believe a son should be afraid of his father. No, I treat you as your grandfather treated me when I was a young chap. We were more like brothers than father and son. I'll never forget the first day he caught me smoking. I was standing at the end of the South Terrace one day with some maneens like myself and sure we thought we were grand fellows because we had pipes stuck in the corners of our mouths. Suddenly the governor passed. He didn't say a word, or stop even. But the next day, Sunday, we were out for a walk together and when we were coming home he took out his cigar case and said:

– By the by, Simon, I didn't know you smoked, or something like that.

– Of course I tried to carry it off as best I could.

– If you want a good smoke, he said, try one of these cigars. An American captain made me a present of them last night in Queenstown.

Stephen heard his father's voice break into a laugh which was almost a sob.

– He was the handsomest man in Cork at that time, by God he was! The women used to stand to look after him in the street.

He heard the sob passing loudly down his father's throat and opened his eyes with a nervous impulse. The sunlight breaking suddenly on his sight turned the sky and clouds into a fantastic world of sombre masses with lakelike spaces of dark rosy light. His very brain was sick and powerless. He could scarcely interpret the letters of the signboards of the shops. By his monstrous way of life he seemed to have put himself beyond the limits of reality. Nothing moved him or spoke to him from the real world unless he heard in it an echo of the infuriated cries within him. He could respond to no earthly or human appeal, dumb and insensible to the call of summer and gladness and companionship, wearied and dejected by his father's voice. He could scarcely recognize as his own thoughts, and repeated slowly to himself:

– I am Stephen Dedalus. I am walking beside my father whose name is

Simon Dedalus. We are in Cork, in Ireland. Cork is a city. Our room is in the Victoria Hotel. Victoria and Stephen and Simon. Simon and Stephen and Victoria. Names.

The memory of his childhood suddenly grew dim. He tried to call forth some of its vivid moments but could not. He recalled only names. Dante, Parnell, Clane, Clongowes. A little boy had been taught geography by an old woman who kept two brushes in her wardrobe. Then he had been sent away from home to a college, he had made his first communion and eaten slim jim out of his cricket cap and watched the firelight leaping and dancing on the wall of a little bedroom in the infirmary and dreamed of being dead, of mass being said for him by the rector in a black and gold cope, of being buried then in the little graveyard of the community off the main avenue of limes. But he had not died then. Parnell had died. There had been no mass for the dead in the chapel and no procession. He had not died but he had faded out like a film in the sun. He had been lost or had wandered out of existence for he no longer existed. How strange to think of him passing out of existence in such a way, not by death but by fading out in the sun or by being lost and forgotten somewhere in the universe! It was strange to see his small body appear again for a moment: a little boy in a grey belted suit. His hands were in his side-pockets and his trousers were tucked in at the knees by elastic bands.

On the evening of the day on which the property was sold Stephen followed his father meekly about the city from bar to bar. To the sellers in the market, to the barmen and barmaids, to the beggars who importuned him for a lob Mr Dedalus told the same tale – that he was an old Corkonian, that he had been trying for thirty years to get rid of his Cork accent up in Dublin and that Peter Pickackafax beside him was his eldest son but that he was only a Dublin jackeen.

They had set out early in the morning from Newcombe's coffee-house, where Mr Dedalus's cup had rattled noisily against its saucer, and Stephen had tried to cover that shameful sign of his father's drinking bout of the night before by moving his chin and coughing. One humiliation had succeeded another – the false smiles of the market sellers, the curvetings and oglings of the barmaids with whom his father flirted, the compliments and encouraging words of his father's friends. They had told him that he had a great look of his grandfather and Mr Dedalus had agreed that he was an ugly likeness. They had unearthed traces of a Cork accent in his speech and made him admit that the Lee was a much finer river than the Liffey. One of them, in order to put his Latin to the proof, had made him translate short passages from Dilectus and asked him whether it was correct to say:

Tempora mutantur nos et mutamur in illis or *Tempora mutantur et nos mutamur in illis*. Another, a brisk old man, whom Mr Dedalus called Johnny Cashman, had covered him with confusion by asking him to say which were prettier, the Dublin girls or the Cork girls.

– He's not that way built, said Mr Dedalus. Leave him alone. He's a level-headed thinking boy who doesn't bother his head about that kind of nonsense.

– Then he's not his father's son, said the little old man.

– I don't know, I'm sure, said Mr Dedalus, smiling complacently.

– Your father, said the little old man to Stephen, was the boldest flirt in the city of Cork in his day. Do you know that?

Stephen looked down and studied the tiled floor of the bar into which they had drifted.

– Now don't be putting ideas into his head, said Mr Dedalus. Leave him to his Maker.

– Yerra, sure I wouldn't put any ideas into his head. I'm old enough to be his grandfather. And I am a grandfather, said the little old man to Stephen. Do you know that?

– Are you? asked Stephen.

– Bedad I am, said the little old man. I have two bouncing grandchildren out at Sunday's Well. Now, then! What age do you think I am? And I remember seeing your grandfather in his red coat riding out to hounds. That was before you were born.

– Ay, or thought of, said Mr Dedalus.

– Bedad I did, repeated the little old man. And, more than that, I can remember even your greatgrandfather, old John Stephen Dedalus, and a fierce old fire-eater he was. Now, then! There's a memory for you!

– That's three generations – four generations, said another of the company. Why, Johnny Cashman, you must be nearing the century.

– Well, I'll tell you the truth, said the little old man. I'm just twenty-seven years of age.

– We're as old as we feel, Johnny, said Mr Dedalus. And just finish what you have there and we'll have another. Here, Tim or Tom or whatever your name is, give us the same again here. By God, I don't feel more than eighteen myself. There's that son of mine there not half my age and I'm a better man than he is any day of the week.

– Draw it mild now, Dedalus. I think it's time for you to take a back seat, said the gentleman who had spoken before.

– No, by God! asserted Mr Dedalus. I'll sing at tenor song against him or I'll vault a five-barred gate against him or I'll run with him after the hounds across the country as I did thirty years ago along with the Kerry Boy and the best man for it.

– But he'll beat you here, said the little old man, tapping his forehead and raising his glass to drain it.

– Well, I hope he'll be as good a man as his father. That's all I can say, said Mr Dedalus.

– If he is, he'll do, said the little old man.

– And thanks be to God, Johnny, said Mr Dedalus, that we lived so long and did so little harm.

– But did so much good, Simon, said the little old man gravely. Thanks be to God we lived so long and did so much good.

Stephen watched the three glasses being raised from the counter as his father and his two cronies drank to the memory of their past. An abyss of fortune or of temperament sundered him from them. His mind seemed older than theirs: it shone coldly on their strifes and happiness and regrets like a moon upon a younger earth. No life or youth stirred in him as it had stirred in them. He had known neither the pleasure of companionship with others nor the vigour of rude male health nor filial piety. Nothing stirred within his soul but a cold and cruel and loveless lust. His childhood was dead or lost and with it his soul capable of simple joys and he was drifting amid life like the barren shell of the moon.

> *Art thou pale for weariness*
> *Of climbing heaven and gazing on the earth,*
> *Wandering companionless . . . ?*

He repeated to himself the lines of Shelley's fragment. Its alternation of sad human ineffectiveness with vast inhuman cycles of activity chilled him and he forgot his own human and ineffectual grieving.

Stephen's mother and his brother and one of his cousins waited at the corner of quiet Foster Place while he and his father went up the steps and along the colonnade where the Highland sentry was parading. When they had passed into the great hall and stood at the counter Stephen drew forth his orders on the governor of the bank of Ireland for thirty and three pounds; and these sums, the moneys of his exhibition and essay prize, were paid over to him rapidly by the teller in notes and in coin respectively. He bestowed them in his pockets with feigned composure and suffered the friendly teller, to whom his father chatted, to take his hand across the broad counter and wish him a brilliant career in after life. He was impatient of their voices and could not keep his feet at rest. But the teller still deferred the serving of others to say he was living in changed times and that there was nothing like giving a boy the best education that money could buy. Mr Dedalus lingered in the hall gazing about him and up at the roof and telling Stephen, who urged him to come out, that they were standing in the house of commons of the old Irish parliament.

– God help us! he said piously, to think of the men of those times, Stephen, Hely Hutchinson and Flood and Henry Grattan and Charles Kendal Bushe, and the noblemen we have now, leaders of the Irish people at home and abroad. Why, by God, they wouldn't be seen dead in a ten-acre field with them. No, Stephen, old chap, I'm sorry to say that they are only as I roved out one fine May morning in the merry month of sweet July.

A keen October wind was blowing round the bank. The three figures standing at the edge of the muddy path had pinched cheeks and watery eyes. Stephen looked at his thinly clad mother and remembered that a few days before he had seen a mantle priced at twenty guineas in the windows of Barnardo's.

– Well that's done, said Mr Dedalus.

– We had better go to dinner, said Stephen. Where?

– Dinner? said Mr Dedalus. Well, I suppose we had better, what?

– Some place that's not too dear, said Mrs Dedalus.

– Underdone's?

– Yes. Some quiet place.

– Come along, said Stephen quickly. It doesn't matter about the dearness.

He walked on before them with short nervous steps, smiling. They tried to keep up with him, smiling also at his eagerness.

– Take it easy like a good young fellow, said his father. We're not out for the half mile, are we?

For a swift season of merrymaking the money of his prizes ran through Stephen's fingers. Great parcels of groceries and delicacies and dried fruits arrived from the city. Every day he drew up a bill of fare for the family and every night led a party of three or four to the theatre to see *Ingomar* or *The Lady of Lyons*. In his coat pockets he carried squares of Vienna chocolate for his guests while his trousers' pocket bulged with masses of silver and copper coins. He bought presents for everyone, overhauled his room, wrote out resolutions, marshalled his books up and down their shelves, pored upon all kinds of price lists, drew up a form of commonwealth for the household by which every member of it held some office, opened a loan bank for his family and pressed loans on willing borrowers so that he might have the pleasure of making out receipts and reckoning the interests on the sums lent. When he could do no more he drove up and down the city in trams.

Then the season of pleasure came to an end. The pot of pink enamel paint gave out and the wainscot of his bedroom remained with its unfinished and ill-plastered coat.

His household returned to its usual way of life. His mother had no further occasion to upbraid him for squandering his money. He too returned to his old life at school and all his novel enterprises fell to pieces. The commonwealth fell, the loan bank closed its coffers and its books on a sensible loss, the rules of life which he had drawn about himself fell into desuetude.

How foolish his aim had been! He had tried to build a breakwater of order and elegance against the sordid tide of life without him and to dam up, by rules of conduct and active interests and new filial relations, the powerful recurrence of the tides within him. Useless. From without as from within the waters had flowed over his barriers: their tides began once more to jostle fiercely above the crumbled mole.

He saw clearly too his own futile isolation. He had not gone one step nearer the lives he had sought to approach nor bridged the restless shame and rancour that had divided him from mother and brother and sister. He felt that he was hardly of the one blood with them but stood to them rather in the mystical kinship of fosterage, fosterchild and fosterbrother.

He turned to appease the fierce longings of his heart before which everything else was idle and alien. He cared little that he was in mortal sin, that his life had grown to be a tissue of subterfuge and falsehood. Beside the savage desire within him to realize the enormities which he brooded on nothing was sacred. He bore cynically with the shameful details of his secret riots in which he exulted to defile with patience whatever image had attracted his eyes. By day and by night he moved among distorted images of the outer world. A figure that had seemed to him by day demure and innocent came towards him by night through the winding darkness of sleep, her face transfigured by a lecherous cunning, her eyes bright with brutish joy. Only the morning pained him with its dim memory of dark orgiastic riot, its keen and humiliating sense of transgression.

He returned to his wanderings. The veiled autumnal evenings led him from street to street as they had led him years before along the quiet avenues of Blackrock. But no vision of trim front gardens or of kindly lights in the windows poured a tender influence upon him now. Only at times, in the pauses of his desire, when the luxury that was wasting him gave room to a softer languor, the image of Mercedes traversed the background of his memory. He saw again the small white house and the garden of rose-bushes on the road that led to the mountains and he remembered the sadly proud gesture of refusal which he was to make there, standing with her in the moonlit garden after years of estrangement and adventure. At those moments the soft speeches of Claude Melnotte rose to his lips and eased his unrest. A tender premonition touched him of the tryst he had then looked forward to and, in spite of the horrible reality which lay between his hope of then and now, of the holy encounter he had then imagined at which weakness and timidity and inexperience were to fall from him.

Such moments passed and the wasting fires of lust sprang up again. The verses passed from his lips and the inarticulate cries and the unspoken brutal words rushed forth from his brain to force a passage. His blood was in revolt. He wandered up and down the dark slimy streets peering into the gloom of lanes and doorways, listening eagerly for any sound. He moaned to himself like some baffled prowling beast. He wanted to sin with another of his kind, to force another being to sin with him and to exult with her in sin. He felt some dark presence moving irresistibly upon him from the darkness, a presence subtle and murmurous as a flood filling him wholly with itself. Its murmur besieged his ears like the murmur of some multitude in sleep; its subtle streams penetrated his being. His hands clenched convulsively and his teeth set together as he suffered the agony of its penetration. He stretched out his arms in the street to hold fast the frail swooning form that eluded him and incited him: and the cry that he had strangled for so long in his throat issued from his lips. It broke from him like a wail of despair from a hell of sufferers and died in a wail of furious entreaty, a cry for an iniquitous abandonment, a cry which was but the echo of an obscene scrawl which he had read on the oozing wall of a urinal.

He had wandered into a maze of narrow and dirty streets. From the foul laneways he heard bursts of hoarse riot and wrangling and the drawling of drunken singers. He walked onward, dismayed, wondering whether he had strayed into the quarter of the Jews. Women and girls dressed in long vivid gowns traversed the street from house to house. They were leisurely and perfumed. A trembling seized him and his eyes grew dim. The yellow gas-flames arose before his troubled vision against the vapoury sky, burning as if before an altar. Before the doors and in the lighted halls groups were gathered arrayed as for some rite. He was in another world: he had awakened from a slumber of centuries.

He stood still in the middle of the roadway, his heart clamouring against his bosom in a tumult. A young woman dressed in a long pink gown laid her hand on his arm to detain him and gazed into his face. She said gaily:

– Good night, Willie dear!

Her room was warm and lightsome. A huge doll sat with her legs apart in the copious easy-chair beside the bed. He tried to bid his tongue speak that he might seem at ease, watching her as she undid her gown, noting the proud conscious movements of her perfumed head.

As he stood silent in the middle of the room she came over to him and embraced him gaily and gravely. Her round arms held him firmly to her and he, seeing her face lifted to him in serious calm and feeling the warm calm rise and fall of her breast, all but burst into hysterical weeping. Tears of joy and relief shone in his delighted eyes and his lips parted though they would not speak.

She passed her tinkling hand through his hair, calling him a little rascal.
– Give me a kiss, she said.

His lips would not bend to kiss her. He wanted to be held firmly in her arms, to be caressed slowly, slowly, slowly. In her arms he felt that he had suddenly become strong and fearless and sure of himself. But his lips would not bend to kiss her.

With a sudden movement she bowed his head and joined her lips to his and he read the meaning of her movements in her frank uplifted eyes. It was too much for him. He closed his eyes, surrendering himself to her, body and mind, conscious of nothing in the world but the dark pressure of her softly parting lips. They pressed upon his brain as upon his lips as though they were the vehicle of a vague speech; and between them he felt an unknown and timid pressure, darker than the swoon of sin, softer than sound or odour.

Chapter 3

The swift December dusk had come tumbling clownishly after its dull day and, as he stared through the dull square of the window of the schoolroom, he felt his belly crave for its food. He hoped there would be stew for dinner, turnips and carrots and bruised potatoes and fat mutton pieces to be ladled out in thick peppered flour-fattened sauce. Stuff it into you, his belly counselled him.

It would be a gloomy secret night. After early nightfall the yellow lamps would light up, here and there, the squalid quarter of the brothels. He would follow a devious course up and down the streets, circling always nearer and nearer in a tremor of fear and joy, until his feet led him suddenly round a dark corner. The whores would be just coming out of their houses making ready for the night, yawning lazily after their sleep and settling the hairpins in their clusters of hair. He would pass by them calmly waiting for a sudden movement of his own will or a sudden call to his sin-loving soul from their soft perfumed flesh. Yet as he prowled in quest of that call, his senses, stultified only by his desire, would note keenly all that wounded or shamed them; his eyes, a ring of porter froth on clothless table or a photograph of two soldiers standing to attention or a gaudy playbill; his ears, the drawling jargon of greeting:

– Hello, Bertie, any good in your mind?

– Is that you, pigeon?

– Number ten. Fresh Nelly is waiting on you.

– Good night, husband! Coming in to have a short time?

The equation on the page of his scribbler began to spread out a widening tail, eyed and starred like a peacock's; and, when the eyes and stars of its indices had been eliminated, began slowly to fold itself together again. The indices appearing and disappearing were eyes opening and closing; the eyes opening and closing were stars being born and being quenched. The vast cycle of starry life bore his weary mind outward to its verge and inward to its centre, a distant music accompanying him outward and inward. What music? The music came nearer and he recalled the words, the words of Shelley's fragment upon the moon wandering companionless, pale for weariness. The stars began to crumble and a cloud of fine stardust fell through space.

The dull light fell more faintly upon the page whereon another equation began to unfold itself slowly and to spread abroad its widening tail. It was his own soul going forth to experience, unfolding itself sin by sin, spreading abroad the bale-fire of its burning stars and folding back upon itself, fading slowly, quenching its own lights and fires. They were quenched: and the cold darkness filled chaos.

A cold lucid indifference reigned in his soul. At his first violent sin he had felt a wave of vitality pass out of him and had feared to find his body or his soul maimed by the excess. Instead the vital wave had carried him on its bosom out of himself and back again when it receded: and no part of body or soul had been maimed but a dark peace had been established between them. The chaos in which his ardour extinguished itself was a cold indifferent knowledge of himself. He had sinned mortally not once but many times and he knew that, while he stood in danger of eternal damnation for the first sin alone, by every succeeding sin he multiplied his guilt and his punishment. His days and works and thoughts could make no atonement for him, the fountains of sanctifying grace having ceased to refresh his soul. At most, by an alms given to a beggar whose blessing he fled from, he might hope wearily to win for himself some measure of actual grace. Devotion had gone by the board. What did it avail to pray when he knew that his soul lusted after its own destruction? A certain pride, a certain awe, withheld him from offering to God even one prayer at night, though he knew it was in God's power to take away his life while he slept and hurl his soul hellward ere he could beg for mercy. His pride in his own sin, his loveless awe of God, told him that his offence was too grievous to be atoned for in whole or in part by a false homage to the All-seeing and All-knowing.

– Well now, Ennis, I declare you have a head and so has my stick! Do you mean to say that you are not able to tell me what a surd is?

The blundering answer stirred the embers of his contempt of his fellows. Towards others he felt neither shame nor fear. On Sunday mornings as he passed the church door he glanced coldly at the worshippers who stood bareheaded, four deep, outside the church, morally present at the mass which they could neither see nor hear. Their dull piety and the sickly smell of the cheap hair-oil with which they had anointed their heads repelled him from the altar they prayed at. He stooped to the evil of hypocrisy with others, sceptical of their innocence which he could cajole so easily.

On the wall of his bedroom hung an illuminated scroll, the certificate of his prefecture in the college of the sodality of the Blessed Virgin Mary. On Saturday mornings when the sodality met in the chapel to recite the little office his place was a cushioned kneeling-desk at the right of the altar from which he led his wing of boys through the responses. The falsehood of his position did not pain him. If at moments he felt an impulse to rise from his post of honour and, confessing before them all his unworthiness, to leave the chapel, a glance at their faces restrained him. The imagery of the psalms of prophecy soothed his barren pride. The glories of Mary held his soul captive: spikenard and myrrh and frankincense, symbolising her royal lineage, her emblems, the late-flowering plant and late-blossoming tree, symbolising the age-long gradual growth of her cultus among men. When it fell to him to read the lesson towards the close of the office he read it in a veiled voice, lulling his conscience to its music.

Quasi cedrus exaltata sum in Libanon et quasi cupressus in monte Sion. Quasi palma exaltata sum in Gades et quasi plantatio rosae in Jericho. Quasi uliva speciosa in campis et quasi platanus exaltata sum juxta aquam in plateis. Sicut cinnamomum et balsamum aromatizans odorem dedi et quasi myrrha electa dedi suavitatem odoris.

His sin, which had covered him from the sight of God, had led him nearer to the refuge of sinners. Her eyes seemed to regard him with mild pity; her holiness, a strange light glowing faintly upon her frail flesh, did not humiliate the sinner who approached her. If ever he was impelled to cast sin from him and to repent the impulse that moved him was the wish to be her knight. If ever his soul, re-entering her dwelling shyly after the frenzy of his body's lust had spent itself, was turned towards her whose emblem is the morning star, *bright and musical, telling of heaven and infusing peace*, it was when her names were murmured softly by lips whereon there still lingered foul and shameful words, the savour itself of a lewd kiss.

That was strange. He tried to think how it could be. But the dusk, deepening in the schoolroom, covered over his thoughts. The bell rang. The master marked the sums and cuts to be done for the next lesson and went out. Heron, beside Stephen, began to hum tunelessly.

My excellent friend Bombados.

Ennis, who had gone to the yard, came back, saying:
– The boy from the house is coming up for the rector.
A tall boy behind Stephen rubbed his hands and said:
– That's game ball. We can scut the whole hour. He won't be in till after half two. Then you can ask him questions on the catechism, Dedalus.

Stephen, leaning back and drawing idly on his scribbler, listened to the talk about him which Heron checked from time to time by saying:
– Shut up, will you. Don't make such a bally racket!

It was strange too that he found an arid pleasure in following up to the end the rigid lines of the doctrines of the church and penetrating into obscure silences only to hear and feel the more deeply his own condemnation. The sentence of saint James which says that he who offends against one commandment becomes guilty of all, had seemed to him first a swollen phrase until he had begun to grope in the darkness of his own state. From the evil seed of lust all other deadly sins had sprung forth: pride in himself and contempt of others, covetousness in using money for the purchase of unlawful pleasures, envy of those whose vices he could not reach to and calumnious murmuring against the pious, gluttonous enjoyment of food, the dull glowering anger amid which he brooded upon his longing, the swamp of spiritual and bodily sloth in which his whole being had sunk.

As he sat in his bench gazing calmly at the rector's shrewd harsh face, his mind wound itself in and out of the curious questions proposed to it. If a man had stolen a pound in his youth and had used that pound to amass a huge fortune how much was he obliged to give back, the pound he had stolen only or the pound together with the compound interest accruing upon it or all his huge fortune? If a layman in giving baptism pour the water before saying the words is the child baptized? Is baptism with a mineral water valid? How comes it that while the first beatitude promises the kingdom of heaven to the poor of heart the second beatitude promises also to the meek that they shall possess the land? Why was the sacrament of the eucharist instituted under the two species of bread and wine if Jesus Christ be present body and blood, soul and divinity, in the bread alone and in the wine alone? Does a tiny particle of the consecrated bread contain all the body and blood of Jesus Christ or a part only of the body and blood? If the wine change into vinegar and the host crumble into corruption after they have been consecrated, is Jesus Christ still present under their species as God and as man?

– Here he is! Here he is!

A boy from his post at the window had seen the rector come from the house. All the catechisms were opened and all heads bent upon them silently. The rector entered and took his seat on the dais. A gentle kick from the tall boy in the bench behind urged Stephen to ask a difficult question.

The rector did not ask for a catechism to hear the lesson from. He clasped his hands on the desk and said:

– The retreat will begin on Wednesday afternoon in honour of saint Francis Xavier whose feast day is Saturday. The retreat will go on from Wednesday to Friday. On Friday confession will be heard all the afternoon after beads. If any boys have special confessors perhaps it will be better for them not to change. Mass will be on Saturday morning at nine o'clock and general communion for the whole college. Saturday will be a free day. But Saturday and Sunday being free days some boys might be inclined to think that Monday is a free day also. Beware of making that mistake. I think you, Lawless, are likely to make that mistake.

– I sir? Why, sir?

A little wave of quiet mirth broke forth over the class of boys from the rector's grim smile. Stephen's heart began slowly to fold and fade with fear like a withering flower.

The rector went on gravely:

– You are all familiar with the story of the life of saint Francis Xavier, I suppose, the patron of your college. He came of an old and illustrious Spanish family and you remember that he was one of the first followers of saint Ignatius. They met in Paris where Francis Xavier was professor of philosophy at the university. This young and brilliant nobleman and man of letters entered heart and soul into the ideas of our glorious founder and you know that he, at his own desire, was sent by saint Ignatius to preach to the Indians. He is called, as you know, the apostle of the Indies. He went from country to country in the east, from Africa to India, from India to Japan, baptising the people. He is said to have baptized as many as ten thousand idolaters in one month. It is said that his right arm had grown powerless from having been raised so often over the heads of those whom he baptized. He wished then to go to China to win still more souls for God but he died of over on the island of Sancian. A great saint, saint Francis Xavier! A great soldier of God!

The rector paused and then, shaking his clasped hands before him, went on:

– He had the faith in him that moves mountains. Ten thousand souls won for God in a single month! That is a true conqueror, true to the motto of our order: *ad majorem Dei gloriam!* A saint who has great power in heaven, remember: power to intercede for us in our grief; power to obtain whatever we pray for if it be for the good of our souls; power above all to obtain for us the grace to repent if we be in sin. A great saint, saint Francis Xavier! A great fisher of souls!

He ceased to shake his clasped hands and, resting them against his forehead, looked right and left of them keenly at his listeners out of his dark stern eyes.

In the silence their dark fire kindled the dusk into a tawny glow. Stephen's heart had withered up like a flower of the desert that feels the simoom coming from afar.

– *Remember only thy last things and thou shalt not sin for ever* – words taken, my dear little brothers in Christ, from the book of Ecclesiastes, seventh chapter, fortieth verse. In the name of the Father and of the Son and of the Holy Ghost. Amen.

Stephen sat in the front bench of the chapel. Father Arnall sat at a table to the left of the altar. He wore about his shoulders a heavy cloak; his pale face was drawn and his voice broken with rheum. The figure of his old master, so strangely re-arisen, brought back to Stephen's mind his life at Clongowes: the wide playgrounds, swarming with boys; the square ditch; the little cemetery off the main avenue of limes where he had dreamed of being buried; the firelight on the wall of the infirmary where he lay sick; the sorrowful face of Brother Michael. His soul, as these memories came back to him, became again a child's soul.

– We are assembled here today, my dear little brothers in Christ, for one brief moment far away from the busy bustle of the outer world to celebrate and to honour one of the greatest of saints, the apostle of the Indies, the patron saint also of your college, saint Francis Xavier. Year after year, for much longer than any of you, my dear little boys, can remember or than I can remember, the boys of this college have met in this very chapel to make their annual retreat before the feast day of their patron saint. Time has gone on and brought with it its changes. Even in the last few years what changes can most of you not remember? Many of the boys who sat in those front benches a few years ago are perhaps now in distant lands, in the burning tropics, or immersed in professional duties or in seminaries, or voyaging over the vast expanse of the deep or, it may be, already called by the great God to another life and to the rendering up of their stewardship. And still as the years roll by, bringing with them changes for good and bad, the memory of the great saint is honoured by the boys of this college who make every year their annual retreat on the days preceding the feast day set apart by our Holy Mother the Church to transmit to all the ages the name and fame of one of the greatest sons of catholic Spain.

– Now what is the meaning of this word *retreat* and why is it allowed on all hands to be a most salutary practice for all who desire to lead before God and in the eyes of men a truly christian life? A retreat, my dear boys, signifies a withdrawal for awhile from the cares of our life, the cares of this workaday world, in order to examine the state of our conscience, to reflect on the mysteries of holy religion and to understand better why we are here in this world. During these few days I intend to put before you some thoughts concerning the four last things. They are, as you know from your catechism, death, judgement, hell, and heaven. We shall try to understand them fully during these few days so that we may derive from the understanding of them a lasting benefit to our souls. And remember, my dear boys, that we have been sent into this world for one thing and for one thing alone: to do God's holy will and to save our immortal souls. All else is worthless. One thing alone is needful, the salvation of one's soul. What doth it profit a man to gain the whole world if he suffer the loss of his immortal soul? Ah, my dear boys, believe me there is nothing in this wretched world that can make up for such a loss.

– I will ask you, therefore, my dear boys, to put away from your minds during these few days all worldly thoughts, whether of study or pleasure or ambition, and to give all your attention to the state of your souls. I need hardly remind you that during the days of the retreat all boys are expected to preserve a quiet and pious demeanour and to shun all loud unseemly pleasure. The elder boys, of course, will see that this custom is not infringed and I look especially to the prefects and officers of the sodality of Our Blessed Lady and of the sodality of the holy angels to set a good example to their fellow-students.

– Let us try, therefore, to make this retreat in honour of saint Francis with our whole heart and our whole mind. God's blessing will then be upon all your year's studies. But, above and beyond all, let this retreat be one to which you can look back in after years when maybe you are far from this college and among very different surroundings, to which you can look back with joy and thankfulness and give thanks to God for having granted you this occasion of laying the first foundation of a pious honourable zealous christian life. And if, as may so happen, there be at this moment in these benches any poor soul who has had the unutterable misfortune to lose God's holy grace and to fall into grievous sin, I fervently trust and pray that this retreat may be the turning point in the life of that soul. I pray to God through the merits of His zealous servant Francis Xavier, that such a soul may be led to sincere repentance and that the holy communion on saint Francis's day of this year may be a lasting covenant between God and that soul. For just and unjust, for saint and sinner alike, may this retreat be a memorable one.

– Help me, my dear little brothers in Christ. Help me by your pious attention, by your own devotion, by your outward demeanour. Banish from your minds all worldly thoughts and think only of the last things, death, judgement, hell, and heaven. He who remembers these things, says Ecclesiastes, shall not sin for ever. He who remembers the last things will act and think with them always before his eyes. He will live a good life and die a good death, believing and knowing that, if he has sacrificed much in this earthly life, it will be given to him a hundredfold and a thousandfold more in the life to come, in the kingdom without end – a blessing, my dear boys, which I wish you from my heart, one and all, in the name of the Father and of the Son and of the Holy Ghost. Amen!

As he walked home with silent companions, a thick fog seemed to compass his mind. He waited in stupor of mind till it should lift and reveal what it had hidden. He ate his dinner with surly appetite and when the meal was over and the grease-strewn plates lay abandoned on the table, he rose and went to the window, clearing the thick scum from his mouth with his tongue and licking it from his lips. So he had sunk to the state of a beast that licks his chaps after meat. This was the end; and a faint glimmer of fear began to pierce the fog of his mind. He pressed his face against the pane of the window and gazed out into the darkening street. Forms passed this way and that through the dull light. And that was life. The letters of the name of Dublin lay heavily upon his mind, pushing one another surlily hither and thither with slow boorish insistence. His soul was fattening and congealing into a gross grease, plunging ever deeper in its dull fear into a sombre threatening dusk while the body that was his stood, listless and dishonoured, gazing out of darkened eyes, helpless, perturbed, and human for a bovine god to stare upon.

The next day brought death and judgement, stirring his soul slowly from its listless despair. The faint glimmer of fear became a terror of spirit as the hoarse voice of the preacher blew death into his soul. He suffered its agony. He felt the death chill touch the extremities and creep onward towards the heart, the film of death veiling the eyes, the bright centres of the brain extinguished one by one like lamps, the last sweat oozing upon the skin, the powerlessness of the dying limbs, the speech thickening and wandering and failing, the heart throbbing faintly and more faintly, all but vanquished, the breath, the poor breath, the poor helpless human spirit, sobbing and sighing, gurgling and rattling in the throat. No help! No help! He – he himself – his body to which he had yielded was dying. Into the grave with it. Nail it down into a wooden box, the corpse. Carry it out of the house on the shoulders of hirelings. Thrust it out of men's sight into a long hole in the ground, into the grave, to rot, to feed the masses of its creeping worms and to be devoured by scuttling plump-bellied rats.

And while the friends were still standing in tears by the bedside the soul of the sinner was judged. At the last moment of consciousness the whole earthly life passed before the vision of the soul and, ere it had time to reflect, the body had died and the soul stood terrified before the judgement seat. God, who had long been merciful, would then be just. He had long been patient, pleading with the sinful soul, giving it time to repent, sparing it yet awhile. But that time had gone. Time was to sin and to enjoy, time was to scoff at God and at the warnings of His holy church, time was to defy His majesty, to disobey His commands, to hoodwink one's fellow men, to commit sin after sin and to hide one's corruption from the sight of men. But that time was over. Now it was God's turn: and He was not to be hoodwinked or deceived. Every sin would then come forth from its lurking place, the most rebellious against the divine will and the most degrading to our poor corrupt nature, the tiniest imperfection and the most heinous atrocity. What did it avail then to have been a great emperor, a great general, a marvellous inventor, the most learned of the learned? All were as one before the judgement seat of God. He would reward the good and punish the wicked. One single instant was enough for the trial of a man's soul. One single instant after the body's death, the soul had been weighed in the balance. The particular judgment was over and the soul had passed to the abode of bliss or to the prison of purgatory or had been hurled howling into hell.

Nor was that all. God's justice had still to be vindicated before men: after the particular there still remained the general judgment. The last day had come. The doomsday was at hand. The stars of heaven were falling upon the earth like the figs cast by the fig-tree which the wind has shaken. The sun, the great luminary of the universe, had become as sackcloth of hair. The moon was blood-red. The firmament was as a scroll rolled away. The archangel Michael, the prince of the heavenly host, appeared glorious and terrible against the sky. With one foot on the sea and one foot on the land he blew from the arch-angelical trumpet the brazen death of time. The three blasts of the angel filled all the universe. Time is, time was, but time shall be no more. At the last blast the souls of universal humanity throng towards the valley of Jehoshaphat, rich and poor, gentle and simple, wise and foolish, good and wicked. The soul of every human being that has ever existed, the souls of all those who shall yet be born, all the sons and daughters of Adam, all are assembled on that supreme day. And lo, the supreme judge is coming! No longer the lowly Lamb of God, no longer the meek Jesus of Nazareth, no longer the Man of Sorrows, no longer the Good Shepherd, He is seen now coming upon the clouds, in great power and majesty, attended by nine choirs of angels, angels and archangels, principalities, powers and virtues, thrones and dominations, cherubim and seraphim, God Omnipotent, God Everlasting. He speaks: and His voice is heard even at the farthest limits of space, even in the bottomless abyss. Supreme Judge, from His sentence there will be and can be no appeal. He calls the just to His side, bidding them enter into the kingdom, the eternity of bliss prepared for them. The unjust He casts from Him, crying in His offended majesty: *Depart from me, ye cursed, into everlasting fire which was prepared for the devil and his angels.* O, what agony then for the miserable sinners! Friend is torn apart from friend, children are torn from their parents, husbands from their wives. The poor sinner holds out his arms to those who were dear to him in this earthly world, to those whose simple piety perhaps he made a mock of, to those who counselled him and tried to lead him on the right path, to a kind brother, to a loving sister, to the mother and father who loved him so dearly. But it is too late: the just turn away from the wretched damned souls which now appear before the eyes of all in their hideous and evil character. O you hypocrites, O, you whited sepulchres, O you who present a smooth smiling face to the world while your soul within is a foul swamp of sin, how will it fare with you in that terrible day?

And this day will come, shall come, must come: the day of death and the day of judgment. It is appointed unto man to die and after death the judgment. Death is certain. The time and manner are uncertain, whether from long disease or from some unexpected accident: the Son of God cometh at an hour when you little expect Him. Be therefore ready every moment, seeing that you may die at any moment. Death is the end of us all. Death and judgment, brought into the world by the sin of our first parents, are the dark portals that close our earthly existence, the portals that open into the unknown and the unseen, portals through which every soul must pass, alone, unaided save by its good works, without friend or brother or parent or master to help it, alone and trembling. Let that thought be ever before our minds and then we cannot sin. Death, a cause of terror to the sinner, is a blessed moment for him who has walked in the right path, fulfilling the duties of his station in life, attending to his morning and evening prayers, approaching the holy sacrament frequently and performing good and merciful works. For the pious and believing catholic, for the just man, death is no cause of terror. Was it not Addison, the great English writer, who, when on his deathbed, sent for the wicked young earl of Warwick to let him see how a christian can meet his end? He it is and he alone, the pious and believing-christian, who can say in his heart:

> *O grave, where is thy victory?*
> *O death, where is thy sting?*

Every word of it was for him. Against his sin, foul and secret, the whole wrath of God was aimed. The preacher's knife had probed deeply into his disclosed conscience and he felt now that his soul was festering in sin. Yes, the preacher was right. God's turn had come. Like a beast in its lair his soul had lain down in its own filth but the blasts of the angel's trumpet had driven him forth from the darkness of sin into the light. The words of doom cried by the angel shattered in an instant his presumptuous peace. The wind of the last day blew through his mind, his sins, the jewel-eyed harlots of his imagination, fled before the hurricane, squeaking like mice in their terror and huddled under a mane of hair.

As he crossed the square, walking homeward, the light laughter of a girl reached his burning ear. The frail gay sound smote his heart more strongly than a trumpet blast, and, not daring to lift his eyes, he turned aside and gazed, as he walked, into the shadow of the tangled shrubs. Shame rose from his smitten heart and flooded his whole being. The image of Emma appeared before him, and under her eyes the flood of shame rushed forth anew from his heart. If she knew to what his mind had subjected her or how his brute-like lust had torn and trampled upon her innocence! Was that boyish love? Was that chivalry? Was that poetry? The sordid details of his orgies stank under his very nostrils. The soot-coated packet of pictures which he had hidden in the flue of the fireplace and in the presence of whose shameless or bashful wantonness he lay for hours sinning in thought and deed; his monstrous dreams, peopled by ape-like creatures and by harlots with gleaming jewel eyes; the foul long letters he had written in the joy of guilty confession and carried secretly for days and days only to throw them under cover of night among the grass in the corner of a field or beneath some hingeless door in some niche in the hedges where a girl might come upon them as she walked by and read them secretly. Mad! Mad! Was it possible he had done these things? A cold sweat broke out upon his forehead as the foul memories condensed within his brain.

When the agony of shame had passed from him he tried to raise his soul from its abject powerlessness. God and the Blessed Virgin were too far from him: God was too great and stern and the Blessed Virgin too pure and holy. But he imagined that he stood near Emma in a wide land and, humbly and in tears, bent and kissed the elbow of her sleeve.

In the wide land under a tender lucid evening sky, a cloud drifting westward amid a pale green sea of heaven, they stood together, children that had erred. Their error had offended deeply God's majesty though it was the error of two children; but it had not offended her whose beauty *is not like earthly beauty, dangerous to look upon, but like the morning star which is its emblem, bright and musical.* The eyes were not offended which she turned upon him nor reproachful. She placed their hands together, hand in hand, and said, speaking to their hearts:

– Take hands, Stephen and Emma. It is a beautiful evening now in heaven. You have erred but you are always my children. It is one heart that loves another heart. Take hands together, my dear children, and you will be happy together and your hearts will love each other.

The chapel was flooded by the dull scarlet light that filtered through the lowered blinds; and through the fissure between the last blind and the sash a shaft of wan light entered like a spear and touched the embossed brasses of the candlestick upon the altar that gleamed like the battle worn mail armour of angels.

Rain was falling on the chapel, on the garden, on the college. It would rain for ever, noiselessly. The water would rise inch by inch, covering the grass and shrubs, covering the trees and houses, covering the monuments and the mountain tops. All life would be choked off, noiselessly: birds, men, elephants, pigs, children: noiselessly floating corpses amid the litter of the wreckage of the world. Forty days and forty nights the rain would fall till the waters covered the face of the earth.

It might be. Why not?

– *Hell has enlarged its soul and opened its mouth without any limits* – words taken, my dear little brothers in Christ Jesus, from the book of Isaias, fifth chapter, fourteenth verse. In the name of the Father and of the Son and of the Holy Ghost. Amen.

The preacher took a chainless watch from a pocket within his soutane and, having considered its dial for a moment in silence, placed it silently before him on the table.

He began to speak in a quiet tone.

– Adam and Eve, my dear boys, were, as you know, our first parents, and you will remember that they were created by God in order that the seats in heaven left vacant by the fall of Lucifer and his rebellious angels might be filled again. Lucifer, we are told, was a son of the morning, a radiant and mighty angel; yet he fell: he fell and there fell with him a third part of the host of heaven: he fell and was hurled with his rebellious angels into hell. What his sin was we cannot say. Theologians consider that it was the sin of pride, the sinful thought conceived in an instant: *non serviam: I will not serve.* That instant was his ruin.

He offended the majesty of God by the sinful thought of one instant and God cast him out of heaven into hell for ever.

– Adam and Eve were then created by God and placed in Eden, in the plain of Damascus, that lovely garden resplendent with sunlight and colour, teaming with luxuriant vegetation. The fruitful earth gave them her bounty: beasts and birds were their willing servants: they knew not the ills our flesh is heir to, disease and poverty and death: all that a great and generous God could do for them was done. But there was one condition imposed on them by God: obedience to His word. They were not to eat of the fruit of the forbidden tree.

– Alas, my dear little boys, they too fell. The devil, once a shining angel, a son of the morning, now a foul fiend came in the shape of a serpent, the subtlest of all the beasts of the field. He envied them. He, the fallen great one, could not bear to think that man, a being of clay, should possess the inheritance which he by his sin had forfeited for ever. He came to the woman, the weaker vessel, and poured the poison of his eloquence into her ear, promising her – O, the blasphemy of that promise! – that if she and Adam ate of the forbidden fruit they would become as gods, nay as God

Himself. Eve yielded to the wiles of the archtempter. She ate the apple and gave it also to Adam who had not the moral courage to resist her. The poison tongue of Satan had done its work. They fell.

– And then the voice of God was heard in that garden, calling His creature man to account: and Michael, prince of the heavenly host, with a sword of flame in his hand, appeared before the guilty pair and drove them forth from Eden into the world, the world of sickness and striving, of cruelty and disappointment, of labour and hardship, to earn their bread in the sweat of their brow. But even then how merciful was God! He took pity on our poor degraded parents and promised that in the fullness of time He would send down from heaven One who would redeem them, make them once more children of God and heirs to the kingdom of heaven: and that One, that Redeemer of fallen man, was to be God's only begotten Son, the Second Person of the Most Blessed Trinity, the Eternal Word.

– He came. He was born of a virgin pure, Mary the virgin mother. He was born in a poor cowhouse in Judea and lived as a humble carpenter for thirty years until the hour of His mission had come. And then, filled with love for men, He went forth and called to men to hear the new gospel.

– Did they listen? Yes, they listened but would not hear. He was seized and bound like a common criminal, mocked at as a fool, set aside to give place to a public robber, scourged with five thousand lashes, crowned with a crown of thorns, hustled through the streets by the jewish rabble and the Roman soldiery, stripped of His garments and hanged upon a gibbet and His side was pierced with a lance and from the wounded body of our Lord water and blood issued continually.

– Yet even then, in that hour of supreme agony, Our Merciful Redeemer had pity for mankind. Yet even there, on the hill of Calvary, He founded the holy catholic church against which, it is promised, the gates of hell shall not prevail. He founded it upon the rock of ages, and endowed it with His grace, with sacraments and sacrifice, and promised that if men would obey the word of His church they would still enter into eternal life; but if, after all that had been done for them, they still persisted in their wickedness, there remained for them an eternity of torment: hell.

The preacher's voice sank. He paused, joined his palms for an instant, parted them. Then he resumed:

– Now let us try for a moment to realize, as far as we can, the nature of that abode of the damned which the justice of an offended God has called into existence for the eternal punishment of sinners. Hell is a strait and dark and foul-smelling prison, an abode of demons and lost souls, filled with fire and smoke. The straitness of this prison house is expressly designed by God to punish those who refused to be bound by His laws. In earthly prisons the poor captive had at least some liberty of movement, were it only within the four walls of his cell or is the gloomy yard of his prison. Not so in hell. There, by reason of the great number of the damned, the prisoners are heaped together in their awful prison, the walls of which are said to be four thousand miles thick: and the damned are so utterly bound and helpless that, as a blessed saint, saint Anselm, writes in his book on similitudes, they are not even able to remove from the eye a worm that gnaws it.

– They lie in exterior darkness. For, remember, the fire of hell gives forth no light. As, at the command of God, the fire of the Babylonian furnace lost its heat but not its light, so, at the command of God, the fire of hell, while retaining the intensity of its heat, burns eternally in darkness. It is a never ending storm of darkness, dark flames and dark smoke of burning brimstone, amid which the bodies are heaped one upon another without even a glimpse of air. Of all the plagues with which the land of the Pharaohs were smitten one plague alone, that of darkness, was called horrible. What name, then, shall we give to the darkness of hell which is to last not for three days alone but for all eternity?

– The horror of this strait and dark prison is increased by its awful stench. All the filth of the world, all the offal and scum of the world, we are told, shall run there as to a vast reeking sewer when the terrible conflagration of the last day has purged the world. The brimstone, too, which burns there in such prodigious quantity fills all hell with its intolerable stench; and the bodies of the damned themselves exhale such a pestilential odour that, as saint Bonaventure says, one of them alone would suffice to infect the whole world. The very air of this world, that pure element, becomes foul and unbreathable when it has been long enclosed. Consider then what must be the foulness of the air of hell. Imagine some foul and putrid corpse that has lain rotting and decomposing in the grave, a jelly-like mass of liquid corruption. Imagine such a corpse a prey to flames, devoured by the fire of burning brimstone and giving off dense choking fumes of nauseous loathsome decomposition. And then imagine this sickening stench, multiplied a millionfold and a millionfold again from the millions upon millions of fetid carcasses massed together in the reeking darkness, a huge and rotting human fungus. Imagine all this, and you will have some idea of the horror of the stench of hell.

– But this stench is not, horrible though it is, the greatest physical torment to which the damned are subjected. The torment of fire is the greatest torment to which the tyrant has ever subjected his fellow creatures. Place your finger for a moment in the flame of a candle and you will feel the pain of fire. But our earthly fire was created by God for the benefit of man, to maintain in him the spark of life and to help him in the useful arts, whereas the fire of hell is of another quality and was created by God to torture and punish the unrepentant sinner. Our earthly fire also consumes more or less rapidly according as the object which it attacks is more or less combustible, so that human ingenuity has even succeeded in inventing chemical preparations to check or frustrate its action. But the sulphurous brimstone which burns in hell is a substance which is specially designed to burn for ever and for ever with unspeakable fury. Moreover, our earthly fire destroys at the same time as it burns, so that the more intense it is the shorter is its duration; but the fire of hell has this property, that it preserves that which it burns, and, though it rages with incredible intensity, it rages for ever.

– Our earthly fire again, no matter how fierce or widespread it may be, is always of a limited extent; but the lake of fire in hell is boundless, shoreless and bottomless. It is on record that the devil himself, when asked the question by a certain soldier, was obliged to confess that if a whole mountain were thrown into the burning ocean of hell it would be burned up in an instant like a piece of wax. And this terrible fire will not afflict the bodies of the damned only from without, but each lost soul will be a hell unto itself, the boundless fire raging in its very vitals. O, how terrible is the lot of those wretched beings! The blood seethes and boils in the veins, the brains are boiling in the skull, the heart in the breast glowing and bursting, the bowels a red-hot mass of burning pulp, the tender eyes flaming like molten balls.

– And yet what I have said as to the strength and quality and bound-lessness of this fire is as nothing when compared to its intensity, an intensity which it has as being the instrument chosen by divine design for the punishment of soul and body alike. It is a fire which proceeds directly from the ire of God, working not of its own activity but as an instrument of Divine vengeance. As the waters of baptism cleanse the soul with the body, so do the fires of punishment torture the spirit with the flesh. Every sense of the flesh is tortured and every faculty of the soul therewith: the eyes with impenetrable utter darkness, the nose with noisome odours, the ears with yells and howls and execrations, the taste with foul matter, leprous corruption, nameless suffocating filth, the touch with red-hot goads and spikes, with cruel tongues of flame. And through the several torments of the senses the immortal soul is tortured eternally in its very essence amid the leagues upon leagues of glowing fires kindled in the abyss by the offended majesty of the Omnipotent God and fanned into everlasting and ever-increasing fury by the breath of the anger of the God-head.

– Consider finally that the torment of this infernal prison is increased by the company of the damned themselves. Evil company on earth is so noxious that the plants, as if by instinct, withdraw from the company of whatsoever is deadly or hurtful to them. In hell all laws are overturned – there is no thought of family or country, of ties, of relationships. The damned howl and scream at one another, their torture and rage intensified by the presence of beings tortured and raging like themselves. All sense of humanity is forgotten. The yells of the suffering sinners fill the remotest corners of the vast abyss. The mouths of the damned are full of blasphemies against God and of hatred for their fellow sufferers and of curses against those which were their accomplices in sin. In olden times it was the custom to punish the parricide, the man who had raised his murderous hand against his father, by casting him into the depths of the sea in a sack in which were placed a cock, a monkey, and a serpent. The intention of those law-givers who framed such a law, which seems cruel in our times, was to punish the criminal by the company of hurtful and hateful beasts. But what is the fury of those dumb beasts compared with the fury of execration which bursts from the parched lips and aching throats of the damned in hell when they behold in their companions in misery those who aided and abetted them in sin, those whose words sowed the first seeds of evil thinking and evil living in their minds, those whose immodest suggestions led them on to sin, those whose eyes tempted and allured them from the path of virtue. They turn upon those accomplices and upbraid them and curse them. But they are helpless and hopeless: it is too late now for repentance.

– Last of all consider the frightful torment to those damned souls, tempters and tempted alike, of the company of the devils. These devils will afflict the damned in two ways, by their presence and by their reproaches. We can have no idea of how horrible these devils are. Saint Catherine of Siena once saw a devil and she has written that, rather than look again for one single instant on such a frightful monster, she would prefer to walk until the end of her life along a track of red coals. These devils, who were once beautiful angels, have become as hideous and ugly as they once were beautiful. They mock and jeer at the lost souls whom they dragged down to ruin. It is they, the foul demons, who are made in hell the voices of conscience. Why did you sin? Why did you lend an ear to the temptings of friends? Why did you turn aside from your pious practices and good works? Why did you not shun the occasions of sin? Why did you not leave that evil companion? Why did you not give up that lewd habit, that impure habit? Why did you not listen to the counsels of your confessor? Why did you not, even after you had fallen the first or the second or the third or the fourth or the hundredth time, repent of your evil ways and turn to God who only waited for your repentance to absolve you of your sins? Now the time for repentance has gone by. Time is, time was, but time shall be no more! Time was to sin in secrecy, to indulge in that sloth and pride, to covet the unlawful, to yield to the promptings of your lower nature, to live like the beasts of the field, nay worse than the beasts of the field, for they, at least, are but brutes and have no reason to guide them: time was, but time shall be no more. God spoke to you by so many voices, but you would not hear. You would not crush out that pride and anger in your heart, you would not restore those ill-gotten goods, you would not obey the precepts of your holy church nor attend to your religious duties, you would not abandon those wicked companions, you would not avoid those dangerous temptations. Such is the language of those fiendish tormentors, words of taunting and of reproach, of hatred and of disgust. Of disgust, yes! For even they, the very devils, when they sinned, sinned by such a sin as alone was compatible with such angelical natures, a rebellion of the intellect: and they, even they, the foul devils must turn away, revolted and disgusted, from the contemplation of those unspeakable sins by which degraded man outrages and defiles the temple of the Holy Ghost, defiles and pollutes himself.

– O, my dear little brothers in Christ, may it never be our lot to hear that language! May it never be our lot, I say! In the last day of terrible reckoning I pray fequently to God that not a single soul of those who are in this chapel today may be found among those miserable beings whom the Great Judge shall command to depart for ever from His sight, that not one of us may ever hear ringing in his ears the awful sentence of rejection: *Depart from me, ye cursed, into everlasting fire which was prepared for the devil and his angels!*

He came down the aisle of the chapel, his legs shaking and the scalp of his head trembling as though it had been touched by ghostly fingers. He passed up the staircase and into the corridor along the walls of which the overcoats and waterproofs hung like gibbeted malefactors, headless and dripping and shapeless. And at every step he feared that he had already died, that his soul had been wrenched forth of the sheath of his body, that he was plunging headlong through space.

He could not grip the floor with his feet and sat heavily at his desk, opening one of his books at random and poring over it. Every word for him. It was true. God was almighty. God could call him now, call him as he sat at his desk, before he had time to be conscious of the summons. God had called him. Yes? What? Yes? His flesh shrank together as it felt the approach of the ravenous tongues of flames, dried up as it felt about it the swirl of stifling air. He had died. Yes. He was judged. A wave of fire swept through his body: the first. Again a wave. His brain began to glow. Another.

His brain was simmering and bubbling within the cracking tenement of the skull. Flames burst forth from his skull like a corolla, shrieking like voices: – Hell! Hell! Hell! Hell! Hell!

Voices spoke near him:

– On hell.

– I suppose he rubbed it into you well.

– You bet he did. He put us all into a blue funk.

– That's what you fellows want: and plenty of it to make you work.

He leaned back weakly in his desk. He had not died. God had spared him still. He was still in the familiar world of the school. Mr Tate and Vincent Heron stood at the window, talking, jesting, gazing out at the bleak rain, moving their heads.

– I wish it would clear up. I had arranged to go for a spin on the bike with some fellows out by Malahide. But the roads must be knee-deep.

– It might clear up, sir.

The voices that he knew so well, the common words, the quiet of the classroom when the voices paused and the silence was filled by the sound of softly browsing cattle as the other boys munched their lunches tranquilly, lulled his aching soul.

There was still time. O Mary, refuge of sinners, intercede for him! O Virgin Undefiled, save him from the gulf of death!

The English lesson began with the hearing of the history. Royal persons, favourites, intriguers, bishops, passed like mute phantoms behind their veil of names. All had died: all had been judged. What did it profit a man to gain the whole world if he lost his soul? At last he had understood: and human life lay around him, a plain of peace whereon ant-like men laboured in brotherhood, their dead sleeping under quiet mounds. The elbow of his companion touched him and his heart was touched: and when he spoke to answer a question of his master he heard his own voice full of the quietude of humility and contrition.

His soul sank back deeper into depths of contrite peace, no longer able to suffer the pain of dread, and sending forth, as he sank, a faint prayer. Ah yes, he would still be spared; he would repent in his heart and be forgiven; and then those above, those in heaven, would see what he would do to make up for the past: a whole life, every hour of life. Only wait.

– All, God! All, all!

A messenger came to the door to say that confessions were being heard in the chapel. Four boys left the room; and he heard others passing down the corridor. A tremulous chill blew round his heart, no stronger than a little wind, and yet, listening and suffering silently, he seemed to have laid an ear against the muscle of his own heart, feeling it close and quail, listening to the flutter of its ventricles.

No escape. He had to confess, to speak out in words what he had done and thought, sin after sin. How? How?

– Father, I . . .

The thought slid like a cold shining rapier into his tender flesh: confession. But not there in the chapel of the college. He would confess all, every sin of deed and thought, sincerely; but not there among his school companions. Far away from there in some dark place he would murmur out his own shame; and he besought God humbly not to be offended with him if he did not dare to confess in the college chapel and in utter abjection of spirit he craved forgiveness mutely of the boyish hearts about him.

Time passed.

He sat again in the front bench of the chapel. The daylight without was already failing and, as it fell slowly through the dull red blinds, it seemed that the sun of the last day was going down and that all souls were being gathered for the judgment. – *I am cast away from the sight of Thine eyes:* words taken, my dear little brothers in Christ, from the Book of Psalms, thirtieth chapter, twenty-third verse. In the name of the Father and of the Son and of the Holy Ghost. Amen.

The preacher began to speak in a quiet friendly tone. His face was kind and he joined gently the fingers of each hand, forming a frail cage by the union of their tips.

– This morning we endeavoured, in our reflection upon hell, to make what our holy founder calls in his book of spiritual exercises, the composition of place. We endeavoured, that is, to imagine with the senses of the mind, in our imagination, the material character of that awful place and of the physical torments which all who are in hell endure. This evening we shall consider for a few moments the nature of the spiritual torments of hell.

– Sin, remember, is a twofold enormity. It is a base consent to the promptings of our corrupt nature to the lower instincts, to that which is gross and beast-like; and it is also a turning away from the counsel of our higher nature, from all that is pure and holy, from the Holy God Himself. For this reason mortal sin is punished in hell by two different forms of punishment, physical and spiritual.

Now of all these spiritual pains by far the greatest is the pain of loss, so great, in fact, that in itself it is a torment greater than all the others. Saint Thomas, the greatest doctor of the church, the angelic doctor, as he is called, says that the worst damnation consists in this, that the understanding of man is totally deprived of divine light and his affection obstinately turned away from the goodness of God. God, remember, is a being infinitely good, and therefore the loss of such a being must be a loss infinitely painful. In this life we have not a very clear idea of what such a loss must be, but the damned in hell, for their greater torment, have a full understanding of that which they have lost, and understand that they have lost it through their own sins and have lost it for ever. At the very instant of death the bonds of the flesh are broken asunder and the soul at once flies towards God as towards the centre of her existence. Remember, my dear little boys, our souls long to be with God. We come from God, we live by God, we belong to God: we are His, inalienably His. God loves with a divine love every human soul, and every human soul lives in that love. How could it be otherwise? Every breath that we draw, every thought of our brain, every instant of life proceeds from God's inexhaustible goodness. And if it be pain for a mother to be parted from her child, for a man to be exiled from hearth and home, for friend to be sundered from friend, O think what pains what anguish it must be for the poor soul to be spurned from the presence of the supremely good and loving Creator Who has called that soul into existence from nothingness and sustained it in life and loved it with an immeasurable love. This, then, to be separated for ever from its greatest good, from God, and to feel the anguish of that separation, knowing full well that it is unchangeable: this is the greatest torment which the created soul is capable of bearing, *poena damni*, the pain of loss.

The second pain which will afflict the souls of the damned in hell is the pain of conscience. Just as in dead bodies worms are engendered by putre-faction, so in the souls of the lost there arises a perpetual remorse from the putrefaction of sin, the sting of conscience, the worm, as Pope Innocent the Third calls it, of the triple sting. The first sting inflicted by this cruel worm will be the memory of past pleasures. O what a dreadful memory will that be! In the lake of all-devouring flame the proud king will remember the pomps of his court, the wise but wicked man his libraries and instruments of research, the lover of artistic pleasures his marbles and pictures and other art treasures, he who delighted in the pleasures of the table his gorgeous feasts, his dishes prepared with such delicacy, his choice wines; the miser will remember his hoard of gold, the robber his ill-gotten wealth, the angry and revengeful and merciless murderers their deeds of blood and violence in which they revelled, the impure and adulterous the unspeakable and filthy pleasures in which they delighted. They will remember all this and loathe themselves and their sins. For how miserable will all those pleasures seem to the soul condemned to suffer in hellfire for ages and ages. How they will rage and fume to think that they have lost the bliss of heaven for the dross of earth, for a few pieces of metal, for vain honours, for bodily comforts, for a tingling of the nerves. They will repent indeed: and this is the second sting of the worm of conscience, a late and fruitless sorrow for sins committed. Divine justice insists that the understanding of those miserable wretches be fixed continually on the sins of which they were guilty, and moreover, as saint Augustine points out, God will impart to them His own knowledge of sin, so that sin will appear to them in all its hideous malice as it appears to the eyes of God Himself. They will behold their sins in all their foulness and repent but it will be too late and then they will bewail the good occasions which they neglected. This is the last and deepest and most cruel sting of the worm of conscience. The conscience will say: You had time and opportunity to repent and would not. You were brought up religiously by your parents. You had the sacraments and grace and indulgences of the church to aid you. You had the minister of God to preach to you, to call you back when you had strayed, to forgive you your sins, no matter how many, how abominable, if only you had confessed and repented. No. You would not. You flouted the ministers of holy religion, you turned your back on the confessional, you wallowed deeper and deeper in the mire of sin. God appealed to you, threatened you, entreated you to return to Him. O, what shame, what misery! The Ruler of the universe entreated you, a creature of clay, to love Him Who made you and to keep His law. No. You would not. And now, though you were to flood all hell with your tears if you could still weep, all that sea of repentance would not gain for you what a single tear of true repentance shed during your mortal life would have gained for you. You implore now a moment of earthly life wherein to repent: in vain. That time is gone: gone for ever.

– Such is the threefold sting of conscience, the viper which gnaws the very heart's core of the wretches in hell, so that filled with hellish fury they curse themselves for their folly and curse the evil companions who have brought them to such ruin and curse the devils who tempted them in life and now mock them in eternity and even revile and curse the Supreme Being Whose goodness and patience they scorned and slighted but Whose justice and power they cannot evade.

– The next spiritual pain to which the damned are subjected is the pain of extension. Man, in this earthly life, though he be capable of many evils, is not capable of them all at once, in as much as one evil corrects and counteracts another just as one poison frequently corrects another. In hell, on the contrary, one torment, instead of counteracting another, lends it still greater force: and, moreover, as the internal faculties are more perfect than the external senses, so are they more capable of suffering. Just as every sense is afflicted with a fitting torment, so is every spiritual faculty; the fancy with horrible images, the sensitive faculty with alternate longing and rage, the mind and understanding with an interior darkness more terrible even than the exterior darkness which reigns in that dreadful prison. The malice, impotent though it be, which possesses these demon souls is an evil of boundless extension, of limitless duration, a frightful state of wickedness which we can scarcely realize unless we bear in mind the enormity of sin and the hatred God bears to it.

– Opposed to this pain of extension and yet coexistent with it we have the pain of intensity. Hell is the centre of evils and, as you know, things are more intense at their centres than at their remotest points. There are no contraries or admixtures of any kind to temper or soften in the least the pains of hell. Nay, things which are good in themselves become evil in hell. Company, elsewhere a source of comfort to the afflicted, will be there a continual torment: knowledge, so much longed for as the chief good of the intellect, will there be hated worse than ignorance: light, so much coveted by all creatures from the lord of creation down to the humblest plant in the forest, will be loathed intensely. In this life our sorrows are either not very long or not very great because nature either overcomes them by habits or puts an end to them by sinking under their weight. But in hell the torments cannot be overcome by habit, for while they are of terrible intensity they are at the same time of continual variety, each pain, so to speak, taking fire from another and re-endowing that which has enkindled it with a still fiercer flame. Nor can nature escape from these intense and various tortures by succumbing to them for the soul is sustained and maintained in evil so that its suffering may be the greater. Boundless extension of torment, incredible intensity of suffering, unceasing variety of torture – this is what the divine majesty, so outraged by sinners, demands; this is what the holiness of heaven, slighted and set aside for the lustful and low pleasures of the corrupt flesh, requires; this is what the blood of the innocent Lamb of God, shed for the redemption of sinners, trampled upon by the vilest of the vile, insists upon.

– Last and crowning torture of all the tortures of that awful place is the eternity of hell. Eternity! O, dread and dire word. Eternity! What mind of man can understand it? And remember, it is an eternity of pain. Even though the pains of hell were not so terrible as they are, yet they would become infinite, as they are destined to last for ever. But while they are everlasting they are at the same time, as you know, intolerably intense, unbearably extensive. To bear even the sting of an insect for all eternity would be a dreadful torment. What must it be, then, to bear the manifold tortures of hell for ever? For ever! For all eternity! Not for a year or for an age but for ever. Try to imagine the awful meaning of this. You have often seen the sand on the seashore. How fine are its tiny grains! And how many of those tiny little grains go to make up the small handful which a child grasps in its play. Now imagine a mountain of that sand, a million miles high, reaching from the earth to the farthest heavens, and a million miles broad, extending to remotest space, and a million miles in thickness; and imagine such an enormous mass of countless particles of sand multiplied as often as there are leaves in the forest, drops of water in the mighty ocean, feathers on birds, scales on fish, hairs on animals, atoms in the vast expanse of the air: and imagine that at the end of every million years a little bird came to that mountain and carried away in its beak a tiny grain of that sand. How many millions upon millions of centuries would pass before that bird had carried away even a square foot of that mountain, how many eons upon eons of ages before it had carried away all? Yet at the end of that immense stretch of time not even one instant of eternity could be said to have ended. At the end of all those billions and trillions of years eternity would have scarcely begun. And if that mountain rose again after it had been all carried away, and if the bird came again and carried it all away again grain by grain, and if it so rose and sank as many times as there are stars in the sky, atoms in the air, drops of water in the sea, leaves on the trees, feathers upon birds, scales upon fish, hairs upon animals, at the end of all those innumerable risings and sinkings of that immeasurably vast mountain not one single instant of eternity could be said to have ended; even then, at the end of such a period, after that eon of time the mere thought of which makes our very brain reel dizzily, eternity would scarcely have begun.

– A holy saint (one of our own fathers I believe it was) was once vouchsafed a vision of hell. It seemed to him that he stood in the midst of a great hall, dark and silent save for the ticking of a great clock. The ticking went on unceasingly; and it seemed to this saint that the sound of the ticking was the ceaseless repetition of the words – ever, never; ever, never. Ever to be in hell, never to be in heaven; ever to be shut off from the presence of God, never to enjoy the beatific vision; ever to be eaten with flames, gnawed by vermin, goaded with burning spikes, never to be free from those pains; ever to have the conscience upbraid one, the memory enrage, the mind filled with darkness and despair, never to escape; ever to curse and revile the foul demons who gloat fiendishly over the misery of their dupes, never to behold the shining raiment of the blessed spirits; ever to cry out of the abyss of fire to God for an instant, a single instant, of respite from such awful agony, never to receive, even for an instant, God's pardon; ever to suffer, never to enjoy; ever to be damned, never to be saved; ever, never; ever, never. O, what a dreadful punishment! An eternity of endless agony, of endless bodily and spiritual torment, without one ray of hope, without one moment of cessation, of agony limitless in intensity, of torment infinitely varied, of torture that sustains eternally that which it eternally devours, of anguish that everlastingly preys upon the spirit while it racks the flesh, an eternity, every instant of which is itself an eternity of woe. Such is the terrible punishment decreed for those who die in mortal sin by an almighty and a just God.

– Yes, a just God! Men, reasoning always as men, are astonished that God should mete out an everlasting and infinite punishment in the fires of hell for a single grievous sin. They reason thus because, blinded by the gross illusion of the flesh and the darkness of human understanding, they are unable to comprehend the hideous malice of mortal sin. They reason thus because they are unable to comprehend that even venial sin is of such a foul and hideous nature that even if the omnipotent Creator could end all the evil and misery in the world, the wars, the diseases, the robberies, the crimes, the deaths, the murders, on condition that he allowed a single venial sin to pass unpunished, a single venial sin, a lie, an angry look, a moment of wilful sloth, He, the great omnipotent God could not do so because sin, be it in thought or deeds is a transgression of His law and God would not be God if He did not punish the transgressor.

– A sin, an instant of rebellious pride of the intellect, made Lucifer and a third part of the cohort of angels fall from their glory. A sin, an instant of folly and weakness, drove Adam and Eve out of Eden and brought death and suffering into the world. To retrieve the consequences of that sin the Only Begotten Son of God came down to earth, lived and suffered and died a most painful death, hanging for three hours on the cross.

– O, my dear little brethren in Christ Jesus, will we then offend that good Redeemer and provoke His anger? Will we trample again upon that torn and mangled corpse? Will we spit upon that face so full of sorrow and love? Will we too, like the cruel jews and the brutal soldiers, mock that gentle and compassionate Saviour Who trod alone for our sake the awful winepress of sorrow? Every word of sin is a wound in His tender side. Every sinful act is a thorn piercing His head. Every impure thought, deliberately yielded to, is a keen lance transfixing that sacred and loving heart. No, no. It is impossible for any human being to do that which offends so deeply the divine majesty, that which is punished by an eternity of agony, that which crucifies again the Son of God and makes a mockery of Him.

– I pray to God that my poor words may have availed today to confirm in holiness those who are in a state of grace, to strengthen the wavering, to lead back to the state of grace the poor soul that has strayed if any such be among you. I pray to God, and do you pray with me, that we may repent of our sins. I will ask you now, all of you, to repeat after me the act of contrition, kneeling here in this humble chapel in the presence of God. He is there in the tabernacle burning with love for mankind, ready to comfort the afflicted. Be not afraid. No matter how many or how foul the sins if you only repent of them they will be forgiven you. Let no worldly shame hold you back. God is still the merciful Lord who wishes not the eternal death of the sinner but rather that he be converted and live.

– He calls you to Him. You are His. He made you out of nothing. He loved you as only a God can love. His arms are open to receive you even though you have sinned against Him. Come to Him, poor sinner, poor vain and erring sinner. Now is the acceptable time. Now is the hour.

The priest rose and, turning towards the altar, knelt upon the step before the tabernacle in the fallen gloom. He waited till all in the chapel had knelt and every least noise was still. Then, raising his head, he repeated the act of contrition, phrase by phrase, with fervour. The boys answered him phrase by phrase. Stephen, his tongue cleaving to his palate, bowed his head, praying with his heart.

– *O my God!* –

– *O my God!* –

– *I am heartily sorry* –

– *I am heartily sorry* –

– *for having offended Thee* –

– *for having offended Thee* –

– *and I detest my sins* –

– *and I detest my sins* –

– *above every other evil* –

– *above every other evil* –

– *because they displease Thee, my God* –

– *because they displease Thee, my God* –

– *Who art so deserving* –

– *Who art so deserving* –

– *of all my love* –

– *of all my love* –

– *and I firmly purpose* –

– *and I firmly purpose* –

– *by Thy holy grace* –

– by Thy holy grace –
– never more to offend Thee –
– never more to offend Thee –
– and to amend my life –
– and to amend my life –

He went up to his room after dinner in order to be alone with his soul, and at every step his soul seemed to sigh; at every step his soul mounted with his feet, sighing in the ascent, through a region of viscid gloom.

He halted on the landing before the door and then, grasping the porcelain knob, opened the door quickly. He waited in fear, his soul pining within him, praying silently that death might not touch his brow as he passed over the threshold, that the fiends that inhabit darkness might not be given power over him. He waited still at the threshold as at the entrance to some dark cave. Faces were there; eyes: they waited and watched.

– We knew perfectly well of course that though it was bound to come to the light he would find considerable difficulty in endeavouring to try to induce himself to try to endeavour to ascertain the spiritual plenipotentiary and so we knew of course perfectly well –

Murmuring faces waited and watched; murmurous voices filled the dark shell of the cave. He feared intensely in spirit and in flesh but, raising his head bravely, he strode into the room firmly. A doorway, a room, the same room, same window. He told himself calmly that those words had absolutely no sense which had seemed to rise murmurously from the dark. He told himself that it was simply his room with the door open.

He closed the door and, walking swiftly to the bed, knelt beside it and covered his face with his hands. His hands were cold and damp and his limbs ached with chill. Bodily unrest and chill and weariness beset him, routing his thoughts. Why was he kneeling there like a child saying his evening prayers? To be alone with his soul, to examine his conscience, to meet his sins face to face, to recall their times and manners and circumstances, to weep over them. He could not weep. He could not summon them to his memory. He felt only an ache of soul and body, his whole being, memory, will, understanding, flesh, benumbed and weary.

That was the work of devils, to scatter his thoughts and overcloud his conscience, assailing him at the gates of the cowardly and sin-corrupted flesh: and, praying God timidly to forgive him his weakness, he crawled up on to the bed and, wrapping the blankets closely about him, covered his face again with his hands. He had sinned. He had sinned so deeply against heaven and before God that he was not worthy to be called God's child.

Could it be that he, Stephen Dedalus, had done those things? His conscience sighed in answer. Yes, he had done them, secretly, filthily, time after time, and, hardened in sinful impenitence, he had dared to wear the mask of holiness before the tabernacle itself while his soul within was a living mass of corruption. How came it that God had not struck him dead? The leprous company of his sins closed about him, breathing upon him, bending over him from all sides. He strove to forget them in an act of prayer, huddling his limbs closer together and binding down his eyelids: but the senses of his soul would not be bound and, though his eyes were shut fast, he saw the places where he had sinned and, though his ears were tightly covered, he heard. He desired with all his will not to hear or see. He desired till his frame shook under the strain of his desire and until the senses of his soul closed. They closed for an instant and then opened. He saw.

A field of stiff weeds and thistles and tufted nettle-bunches. Thick among the tufts of rank stiff growth lay battered canisters and clots and coils of solid excrement. A faint marshlight struggling upwards from all the ordure through the bristling grey-green weeds. An evil smell, faint and foul as the light, curled upwards sluggishly out of the canisters and from the stale crusted dung.

Creatures were in the field: one, three, six: creatures were moving in the field, hither and thither. Goatish creatures with human faces, hornybrowed, lightly bearded and grey as india-rubber. The malice of evil glittered in their hard eyes, as they moved hither and thither, trailing their long tails behind them. A rictus of cruel malignity lit up greyly their old bony faces. One was clasping about his ribs a torn flannel waistcoat, another complained monotonously as his beard stuck in the tufted weeds. Soft language issued from their spittleless lips as they swished in slow circles round and round the field, winding hither and thither through the weeds, dragging their long tails amid the rattling canisters. They moved in slow circles, circling closer and closer to enclose, to enclose, soft language issuing from their lips, their long swishing tails besmeared with stale shite, thrusting upwards their terrific faces . . .

Help!

He flung the blankets from him madly to free his face and neck. That was his hell. God had allowed him to see the hell reserved for his sins: stinking, bestial, malignant, a hell of lecherous goatish fiends. For him! For him!

He sprang from the bed, the reeking odour pouring down his throat, clogging and revolting his entrails. Air! The air of heaven! He stumbled towards the window, groaning and almost fainting with sickness. At the washstand a convulsion seized him within; and, clasping his cold forehead wildly, he vomited profusely in agony.

When the fit had spent itself he walked weakly to the window and, lifting the sash, sat in a corner of the embrasure and leaned his elbow upon the sill. The rain had drawn off; and amid the moving vapours from point to point of light the city was spinning about herself a soft cocoon of yellowish haze. Heaven was still and faintly luminous and the air sweet to breathe, as in a thicket drenched with showers; and amid peace and shimmering lights and quiet fragrance he made a covenant with his heart.

He prayed:

– He once had meant to come on earth in heavenly glory but we sinned; and then He could not safely visit us but with a shrouded majesty and a bedimmed radiance for He was God. So He came Himself in weakness not in power and He sent thee, a creature in His stead, with a creature's comeliness and lustre suited to our state. And now thy very face and form, dear mother, speak to us of the Eternal; not like earthly beauty, dangerous to look upon, but like the morning star which is thy emblem, bright and musical, breathing purity, telling of heaven and infusing peace. O harbinger of day! O light of the pilgrim! Lead us still as thou hast led. In the dark night, across the bleak wilderness guide us on to our Lord Jesus, guide us home.

His eyes were dimmed with tears and, looking humbly up to heaven, he wept for the innocence he had lost.

When evening had fallen he left the house, and the first touch of the damp dark air and the noise of the door as it closed behind him made ache again his conscience, lulled by prayer and tears. Confess! Confess! It was not enough to lull the conscience with a tear and a prayer. He had to kneel before the minister of the Holy Ghost and tell over his hidden sins truly and repentantly. Before he heard again the footboard of the housedoor trail over the threshold as it opened to let him in, before he saw again the table in the kitchen set for supper he would have knelt and confessed. It was quite simple.

The ache of conscience ceased and he walked onward swiftly through the dark streets. There were so many flagstones on the footpath of that street and so many streets in that city and so many cities in the world. Yet eternity had no end. He was in mortal sin. Even once was a mortal sin. It could happen in an instant. But how so quickly? By seeing or by thinking of seeing. The eyes see the thing, without having wished first to see. Then in an instant it happens. But does that part of the body understand or what? The serpent, the most subtle beast of the field. It must understand when it desires in one instant and then prolongs its own desire instant after instant, sinfully. It feels and understands and desires. What a horrible thing! Who made it to be like that, a bestial part of the body able to understand bestially and desire bestially? Was that then he or an inhuman thing moved by a lower soul? His soul sickened at the thought of a torpid snaky life feeding itself out of the tender marrow of his life and fattening upon the slime of lust. O why was that so? O why?

He cowered in the shadow of the thought, abasing himself in the awe of God Who had made all things and all men. Madness. Who could think such a thought? And, cowering in darkness and abject, he prayed mutely to his guardian angel to drive away with his sword the demon that was whispering to his brain.

The whisper ceased and he knew then clearly that his own soul had sinned in thought and word and deed wilfully through his own body. Confess! He had to confess every sin. How could he utter in words to the priest what he had done? Must, must. Or how could he explain without dying of shame? Or how could he have done such things without shame? A madman! Confess! O he would indeed to be free and sinless again! Perhaps the priest would know. O dear God!

He walked on and on through ill-lit streets, fearing to stand still for a moment lest it might seem that he held back from what awaited him, fearing to arrive at that towards which he still turned with longing. How beautiful must be a soul in the state of grace when God looked upon it with love!

Frowsy girls sat along the curbstones before their baskets. Their dank hair hung trailed over their brows. They were not beautiful to see as they crouched in the mire. But their souls were seen by God; and if their souls were in a state of grace they were radiant to see: and God loved them, seeing them.

A wasting breath of humiliation blew bleakly over his soul to think of how he had fallen, to feel that those souls were dearer to God than his. The wind blew over him and passed on to the myriads and myriads of other souls on whom God's favour shone now more and now less, stars now brighter and now dimmer sustained and failing. And the glimmering souls passed away, sustained and failing, merged in a moving breath. One soul was lost; a tiny soul: his. It flickered once and went out, forgotten, lost. The end: black, cold, void waste.

Consciousness of place came ebbing back to him slowly over a vast tract of time unlit, unfelt, unlived. The squalid scene composed itself around him; the common accents, the burning gas-jets in the shops, odours of fish and spirits and wet sawdust, moving men and women. An old woman was about to cross the street, an oilcan in her hand. He bent down and asked her was there a chapel near.

– A chapel, sir? Yes, sir. Church Street chapel.

– Church?

She shifted the can to her other hand and directed him; and, as she held out her reeking withered right hand under its fringe of shawl, he bent lower towards her, saddened and soothed by her voice.

– Thank you.

– You are quite welcome, sir.

The candles on the high altar had been extinguished but the fragrance of incense still floated down the dim nave. Bearded workmen with pious faces were guiding a canopy out through a side door, the sacristan aiding them with quiet gestures and words. A few of the faithful still lingered praying before one of the side-altars or kneeling in the benches near the confessionals. He approached timidly and knelt at the last bench in the body, thankful for the peace and silence and fragrant shadow of the church. The board on which he knelt was narrow and worn and those who knelt near him were humble followers of Jesus. Jesus too had been born in poverty and had worked in the shop of a carpenter, cutting boards and planing them, and had first spoken of the kingdom of God to poor fishermen, teaching all men to be meek and humble of heart.

He bowed his head upon his hands, bidding his heart be meek and humble that he might be like those who knelt beside him and his prayer as acceptable as theirs. He prayed beside them but it was hard. His soul was foul with sin and he dared not ask forgiveness with the simple trust of those whom Jesus, in the mysterious ways of God, had called first to His side, the carpenters, the fishermen, poor and simple people following a lowly trade, handling and shaping the wood of trees, mending their nets with patience.

A tall figure came down the aisle and the penitents stirred; and at the last moment, glancing up swiftly, he saw a long grey beard and the brown habit of a capuchin. The priest entered the box and was hidden. Two penitents rose and entered the confessional at either side. The wooden slide was drawn back and the faint murmur of a voice troubled the silence.

His blood began to murmur in his veins, murmuring like a sinful city summoned from its sleep to hear its doom. Little flakes of fire fell and powdery ashes fell softly, alighting on the houses of men. They stirred, waking from sleep, troubled by the heated air.

The slide was shot back. The penitent emerged from the side of the box. The farther side was drawn. A woman entered quietly and deftly where the first penitent had knelt. The faint murmur began again.

He could still leave the chapel. He could stand up, put one foot before the other and walk out softly and then run, run, run swiftly through the dark streets. He could still escape from the shame. Had it been any terrible crime but that one sin! Had it been murder! Little fiery flakes fell and touched him at all points, shameful thoughts, shameful words, shameful acts. Shame covered him wholly like fine glowing ashes falling continually. To say it in words! His soul, stifling and helpless, would cease to be.

The slide was shot back. A penitent emerged from the farther side of the box. The near slide was drawn. A penitent entered where the other penitent had come out. A soft whispering noise floated in vaporous cloudlets out of the box. It was the woman: soft whispering cloudlets, soft whispering vapour, whispering and vanishing.

He beat his breast with his fist humbly, secretly under cover of the wooden armrest. He would be at one with others and with God. He would love his neighbour. He would love God who had made and loved him. He would kneel and pray with others and be happy. God would look down on him and on them and would love them all.

It was easy to be good. God's yoke was sweet and light. It was better never to have sinned, to have remained always a child, for God loved little children and suffered them to come to Him. It was a terrible and a sad thing to sin. But God was merciful to poor sinners who were truly sorry. How true that was! That was indeed goodness.

The slide was shot to suddenly. The penitent came out. He was next. He stood up in terror and walked blindly into the box.

At last it had come. He knelt in the silent gloom and raised his eyes to the white crucifix suspended above him. God could see that he was sorry. He would tell all his sins. His confession would be long, long. Everybody in the chapel would know then what a sinner he had been. Let them know. It was true. But God had promised to forgive him if he was sorry. He was sorry. He clasped his hands and raised them towards the white form, praying with his darkened eyes, praying with all his trembling body, swaying his head to and fro like a lost creature, praying with whimpering lips.

– Sorry! Sorry! O sorry!

The slide clicked back and his heart bounded in his breast. The face of an old priest was at the grating, averted from him, leaning upon a hand. He made the sign of the cross and prayed of the priest to bless him for he had sinned. Then, bowing his head, he repeated the *Confiteor* in fright. At the words *my most grievous fault* he ceased, breathless.

– How long is it since your last confession, my child?

– A long time, father.

– A month, my child?

– Longer, father.

– Three months, my child?

– Longer, father.

– Six months?

– Eight months, father.

He had begun. The priest asked:

– And what do you remember since that time?

He began to confess his sins: masses missed, prayers not said, lies.

– Anything else, my child?

Sins of anger, envy of others, gluttony, vanity, disobedience.

– Anything else, my child?

There was no help. He murmured:

– I . . . committed sins of impurity, father.

The priest did not turn his head.

– With yourself, my child?

– And . . . with others.

– With women, my child?

– Yes, father.

– Were they married women, my child?

He did not know. His sins trickled from his lips, one by one, trickled in shameful drops from his soul, festering and oozing like a sore, a squalid stream of vice. The last sins oozed forth, sluggish, filthy. There was no more to tell. He bowed his head, overcome.

The priest was silent. Then he asked:

– How old are you, my child?

– Sixteen, father.

The priest passed his hand several times over his face. Then, resting his forehead against his hand, he leaned towards the grating and, with eyes still averted, spoke slowly. His voice was weary and old.

– You are very young, my child, he said, and let me implore of you to give up that sin. It is a terrible sin. It kills the body and it kills the soul. It is the cause of many crimes and misfortunes. Give it up, my child, for God's sake. It is dishonourable and unmanly. You cannot know where that wretched habit will lead you or where it will come against you. As long as you commit that sin, my poor child, you will never be worth one farthing to God. Pray to our mother Mary to help you. She will help you, my child. Pray to Our Blessed Lady when that sin comes into your mind. I am sure you will do that, will you not? You repent of all those sins. I am sure you do. And you will promise God now that by His holy grace you will never offend Him any more by that wicked sin. You will make that solemn promise to God, will you not?

– Yes, father.

The old and weary voice fell like sweet rain upon his quaking parching heart. How sweet and sad!

– Do so, my poor child. The devil has led you astray. Drive him back to hell when he tempts you to dishonour your body in that way – the foul spirit who hates our Lord. Promise God now that you will give up that sin, that wretched wretched sin.

Blinded by his tears and by the light of God's mercifulness he bent his head and heard the grave words of absolution spoken and saw the priest's hand raised above him in token of forgiveness.

– God bless you, my child. Pray for me.

He knelt to say his penance, playing in a corner of the dark nave; and his prayers ascended to heaven from his purified heart like perfume streaming upwards from a heart of white rose.

The muddy streets were gay. He strode homeward, conscious of an invisible grace pervading and making light his limbs. In spite of all he had done it. He had confessed and God had pardoned him. His soul was made fair and holy once more, holy and happy.

It would be beautiful to die if God so willed. It was beautiful to live in grace a life of peace and virtue and forbearance with others.

He sat by the fire in the kitchen, not daring to speak for happiness. Till that moment he had not known how beautiful and peaceful life could be. The green square of paper pinned round the lamp cast down a tender shade. On the dresser was a plate of sausages and white pudding and on the shelf there were eggs. They would be for the breakfast in the morning after the communion in the college chapel. White pudding and eggs and sausages and cups of tea. How simple and beautiful was life after all! And life lay all before him.

In a dream he fell asleep. In a dream he rose and saw that it was morning. In a waking dream he went through the quiet morning towards the college.

The boys were all there, kneeling in their places. He knelt among them, happy and shy. The altar was heaped with fragrant masses of white flowers; and in the morning light the pale flames of the candles among the white flowers were clear and silent as his own soul.

He knelt before the altar with his classmates, holding the altar cloth with them over a living rail of hands. His hands were trembling and his soul trembled as he heard the priest pass with the ciborium from communicant to communicant.

– *Corpus Domini nostri.*

Could it be? He knelt there sinless and timid; and he would hold upon his tongue the host and God would enter his purified body.

– *In vitam eternam. Amen.*

Another life! A life of grace and virtue and happiness! It was true. It was not a dream from which he would wake. The past was past.

– *Corpus Domini nostri.*

The ciborium had come to him.

Chapter 4

Sunday was dedicated to the mystery of the Holy Trinity, Monday to the Holy Ghost, Tuesday to the Guardian Angels, Wednesday to saint Joseph, Thursday to the Most Blessed Sacrament of the Altar, Friday to the Suffering Jesus, Saturday to the Blessed Virgin Mary.

Every morning he hallowed himself anew in the presence of some holy image or mystery. His day began with an heroic offering of its every moment of thought or action for the intentions of the sovereign pontiff and with an early mass. The raw morning air whetted his resolute piety; and often as he knelt among the few worshippers at the side-altar, following with his interleaved prayer-book the murmur of the priest, he glanced up for an instant towards the vested figure standing in the gloom between the two candles, which were the old and the new testaments, and imagined that he was kneeling at mass in the catacombs.

His daily life was laid out in devotional areas. By means of ejaculations and prayers he stored up ungrudgingly for the souls in purgatory centuries of days and quarantines and years: yet the spiritual triumph which he felt in achieving with ease so many fabulous ages of canonical penances did not wholly reward his zeal of prayer, since he could never know how much temporal punishment he had remitted by way of suffrage for the agonising soul; and, fearful lest in the midst of the purgatorial fire, which differed from the infernal only in that it was not everlasting, his penance might avail no more than a drop of moisture, he drove his soul daily through an increasing circle of works of supererogation.

Every part of his day, divided by what he regarded now as the duties of his station in life, circled about its own centre of spiritual energy. His life seemed to have drawn near to eternity; every thought, word, and deed, every instance of consciousness could be made to revibrate radiantly in heaven; and at times his sense of such immediate repercussion was so lively that he seemed to feel his soul in devotion pressing like fingers the keyboard of a great cash register and to see the amount of his purchase start forth immediately in heaven, not as a number but as a frail column of incense or as a slender flower.

The rosaries, too, which he said constantly – for he carried his beads loose in his trousers' pockets that he might tell them as he walked the streets – transformed themselves into coronals of flowers of such vague unearthly texture that they seemed to him as hueless and odourless as they were nameless. He offered up each of his three daily chaplets that his soul might grow strong in each of the three theological virtues, in faith in the Father Who had created him, in hope in the Son Who had redeemed him and in love of the Holy Ghost Who had sanctified him; and this thrice triple prayer he offered to the Three Persons through Mary in the name of her joyful and sorrowful and glorious mysteries.

On each of the seven days of the week he further prayed that one of the seven gifts of the Holy Ghost might descend upon his soul and drive out of it day by day the seven deadly sins which had defiled it in the past; and he prayed for each gift on its appointed day, confident that it would descend upon him, though it seemed strange to him at times that wisdom and understanding and knowledge were so distinct in their nature that each should be prayed for apart from the others. Yet he believed that at some future stage of his spiritual progress this difficulty would be removed when his sinful soul had been raised up from its weakness and enlightened by the Third Person of the Most Blessed Trinity. He believed this all the more, and with trepidation, because of the divine gloom and silence wherein dwelt the unseen Paraclete, Whose symbols were a dove and a mighty wind, to sin against Whom was a sin beyond forgiveness, the eternal mysterious secret Being to Whom, as God, the priests offered up mass once a year, robed in the scarlet of the tongues of fire.

The imagery through which the nature and kinship of the Three Persons of the Trinity were darkly shadowed forth in the books of devotion which he read – the Father contemplating from all eternity as in a mirror His Divine Perfections and thereby begetting eternally the Eternal Son and the Holy Spirit proceeding out of Father and Son from all eternity – were easier of acceptance by his mind by reason of their august incomprehensibility than was the simple fact that God had loved his soul from all eternity, for ages before he had been born into the world, for ages before the world itself had existed.

He had heard the names of the passions of love and hate pronounced solemnly on the stage and in the pulpit, had found them set forth solemnly in books and had wondered why his soul was unable to harbour them for any time or to force his lips to utter their names with conviction. A brief anger had often invested him but he had never been able to make it an abiding passion and had always felt himself passing out of it as if his very body were being divested with ease of some outer skin or peel. He had felt a subtle, dark, and murmurous presence penetrate his being and fire him with a brief iniquitous lust: it, too, had slipped beyond his grasp leaving his mind lucid and indifferent. This, it seemed, was the only love and that the only hate his soul would harbour.

But he could no longer disbelieve in the reality of love, since God Himself had loved his individual soul with divine love from all eternity. Gradually, as his soul was enriched with spiritual knowledge, he saw the whole world forming one vast symmetrical expression of God's power and love. Life became a divine gift for every moment and sensation of which, were it even the sight of a single leaf hanging on the twig of a tree, his soul should praise and thank the Giver. The world for all its solid substance and complexity no longer existed for his soul save as a theorem of divine power and love and universality. So entire and unquestionable was this sense of the divine meaning in all nature granted to his soul that he could scarcely understand why it was in any way necessary that he should continue to live. Yet that was part of the divine purpose and he dared not question its use, he above all others who had sinned so deeply and so foully against the divine purpose. Meek and abased by this consciousness of the one eternal omnipresent perfect reality his soul took up again her burden of pieties, masses and prayers and sacraments and mortifications, and only then for the first time since he had brooded on the great mystery of love did he feel within him a warm movement like that of some newly born life or virtue of the soul itself. The attitude of rapture in sacred art, the raised and parted hands, the parted lips and eyes as of one about to swoon, became for him an image of the soul in prayer, humiliated and faint before her Creator.

But he had been forewarned of the dangers of spiritual exaltation and did not allow himself to desist from even the least or lowliest devotion, striving also by constant mortification to undo the sinful past rather than to achieve a saintliness fraught with peril. Each of his senses was brought under a rigorous discipline. In order to mortify the sense of sight he made it his rule to walk in the street with downcast eyes, glancing neither to right nor left and never behind him. His eyes shunned every encounter with the eyes of women. From time to time also he balked them by a sudden effort of the will, as by lifting them suddenly in the middle of an unfinished sentence and closing the book. To mortify his hearing he exerted no control over his voice which was then breaking, neither sang nor whistled, and made no attempt to flee from noises which caused him painful nervous irritation such as the sharpening of knives on the knifeboard, the gathering of cinders on the fire-shovel and the twigging of the carpet. To mortify his smell was more difficult as he found in himself no instinctive repugnance to bad odours whether they were the odours of the outdoor world, such as those of dung or tar, or the odours of his own person among which he had made many curious comparisons and experiments. He found in the end that the only odour against which his sense of smell revolted was a certain stale fishy stink like that of longstanding urine; and whenever it was possible he subjected himself to this unpleasant odour. To mortify the taste he practised strict habits at table, observed to the letter all the fasts of the church and sought by distraction to divert his mind from the savours of different foods. But it was to the mortification of touch he brought the most assiduous ingenuity of inventiveness. He never consciously changed his position in bed, sat in the most uncomfortable positions, suffered patiently every itch and pain, kept away from the fire, remained on his knees all through the mass except at the gospels, left part of his neck and face undried so that air might sting them and, whenever he was not saying his beads, carried his arms stiffly at his sides like a runner and never in his pockets or clasped behind him.

He had no temptations to sin mortally. It surprised him however to find that at the end of his course of intricate piety and self-restraint he was so easily at the mercy of childish and unworthy imperfections. His prayers and fasts availed him little for the suppression of anger at hearing his mother sneeze or at being disturbed in his devotions. It needed an immense effort of his will to master the impulse which urged him to give outlet to such irritation. Images of the outbursts of trivial anger which he had often noted among his masters, their twitching mouths, close-shut lips and flushed cheeks, recurred to his memory, discouraging him, for all his practice of humility, by the comparison. To merge his life in the common tide of other lives was harder for him than any fasting or prayer and it was his constant failure to do this to his own satisfaction which caused in his soul at last a sensation of spiritual dryness together with a growth of doubts and scruples. His soul traversed a period of desolation in which the sacraments themselves seemed to have turned into dried-up sources. His confession became a channel for the escape of scrupulous and unrepented imperfections. His actual reception of the eucharist did not bring him the same dissolving moments of virginal self-surrender as did those spiritual communions made by him sometimes at the close of some visit to the Blessed Sacrament. The book which he used for these visits was an old neglected book written by saint Alphonsus Liguori, with fading characters and sere foxpapered leaves. A faded world of fervent love and virginal responses seemed to be evoked for his soul by the reading of its pages in which the imagery of the canticles was interwoven with the communicant's prayers. An inaudible voice seemed to caress the soul, telling her names and glories, bidding her arise as for espousal and come away, bidding her look forth, a spouse, from Amana and from the mountains of the leopards; and the soul seemed to answer with the same inaudible voice, surrendering herself: *Inter ubera mea commorabitur.*

This idea of surrender had a perilous attraction for his mind now that he felt his soul beset once again by the insistent voices of the flesh which began to murmur to him again during his prayers and meditations. It gave him an intense sense of power to know that he could, by a single act of consent, in a moment of thought, undo all that he had done. He seemed to feel a flood slowly advancing towards his naked feet and to be waiting for the first faint timid noiseless wavelet to touch his fevered skin. Then, almost at the instant of that touch, almost at the verge of sinful consent, he found himself standing far away from the flood upon a dry shore, saved by a sudden act of the will or a sudden ejaculation; and, seeing the silver line of the flood far away and beginning again its slow advance towards his feet, a new thrill of power and satisfaction shook his soul to know that he had not yielded nor undone all.

When he had eluded the flood of temptation many times in this way he grew troubled and wondered whether the grace which he had refused to lose was not being filched from him little by little. The clear certitude of his own immunity grew dim and to it succeeded a vague fear that his soul had really fallen unawares. It was with difficulty that he won back his old consciousness of his state of grace by telling himself that he had prayed to God at every temptation and that the grace which he had prayed for must have been given to him inasmuch as God was obliged to give it. The very frequency and violence of temptations showed him at last the truth of what he had heard about the trials of the saints. Frequent and violent temptations were a proof that the citadel of the soul had not fallen and that the devil raged to make it fall.

Often when he had confessed his doubts and scruples – some momentary inattention at prayer, a movement of trivial anger in his soul, or a subtle wilfulness in speech or act – he was bidden by his confessor to name some sin of his past life before absolution was given him. He named it with humility and shame and repented of it once more. It humiliated and shamed him to think that he would never be freed from it wholly, however holily he might live or whatever virtues or perfections he might attain. A restless feeling of guilt would always be present with him: he would confess and repent and be absolved, confess and repent again and be absolved again, fruitlessly. Perhaps that first hasty confession wrung from him by the fear of hell had not been good? Perhaps, concerned only for his imminent doom, he had not had sincere sorrow for his sin? But the surest sign that his confession had been good and that he had had sincere sorrow for his sin was, he knew, the amendment of his life.

– I have amended my life, have I not? he asked himself.

The director stood in the embrasure of the window, his back to the light, leaning an elbow on the brown crossblind, and, as he spoke and smiled, slowly dangling and looping the cord of the other blind, Stephen stood before him, following for a moment with his eyes the waning of the long summer daylight above the roofs or the slow deft movements of the priestly fingers. The priest's face was in total shadow, but the waning daylight from behind him touched the deeply grooved temples and the curves of the skull. Stephen followed also with his ears the accents and intervals of the priest's voice as he spoke gravely and cordially of indifferent themes, the vacation which had just ended, the colleges of the order abroad, the trans-ference of masters. The grave and cordial voice went on easily with its tale and in the pauses Stephen felt bound to set it on again with respectful questions. He knew that the tale was a prelude and his mind waited for the sequel. Ever since the message of summons had come for him from the director his mind had struggled to find the meaning of the message; and, during the long restless time he had sat in the college parlour waiting for the director to come in, his eyes had wandered from one sober picture to another around the walls and his mind wandered from one guess to another until the meaning of the summons had almost become clear. Then, just as he was wishing that some unforeseen cause might prevent the director from coming, he had heard the handle of the door turning and the swish of a soutane.

The director had begun to speak of the dominican and franciscan orders and of the friendship between saint Thomas and saint Bonaventure. The capuchin dress, he thought, was rather too . . .

Stephen's face gave back the priest's indulgent smile and, not being anxious to give an opinion, he made a slight dubitative movement with his lips.

– I believe, continued the director, that there is some talk now among the capuchins themselves of doing away with it and following the example of the other franciscans.

– I suppose they would retain it in the cloisters? said Stephen.

– O certainly, said the director. For the cloister it is all right but for the street I really think it would be better to do away with it, don't you?

– It must be troublesome, I imagine.

– Of course it is, of course. Just imagine when I was in Belgium I used to see them out cycling in all kinds of weather with this thing up about their knees! It was really ridiculous. *Les jupes*, they call them in Belgium.

The vowel was so modified as to be indistinct.

– What do they call them?

– *Les jupes.*

– O!

Stephen smiled again in answer to the smile which he could not see on the priest's shadowed face, its image or spectre only passing rapidly across his mind as the low discreet accent fell upon his ear. He gazed calmly before him at the waning sky, glad of the cool of the evening and of the faint yellow glow which hid the tiny flame kindling upon his cheek.

The names of articles of dress worn by women or of certain soft and delicate stuffs used in their making brought always to his mind a delicate and sinful perfume. As a boy he had imagined the reins by which horses are driven as slender silken bands and it shocked him to feel at Stradbrook the greasy leather of harness. It had shocked him, too, when he had felt for the first time beneath his tremulous fingers the brittle texture of a woman's stocking for, retaining nothing of all he read save that which seemed to him an echo or a prophecy of his own state, it was only amid soft-worded phrases or within rose-soft stuffs that he dared to conceive of the soul or body of a woman moving with tender life.

But the phrase on the priest's lips was disingenuous for he knew that a priest should not speak lightly on that theme. The phrase had been spoken lightly with design and he felt that his face was being searched by the eyes in the shadow. Whatever he had heard or read of the craft of jesuits he had put aside frankly as not borne out by his own experience. His masters, even when they had not attracted him, had seemed to him always intelligent and serious priests, athletic and high-spirited prefects. He thought of them as men who washed their bodies briskly with cold water and wore clean cold linen. During all the years he had lived among them in Clongowes and in Belvedere he had received only two pandies and, though these had been dealt him in the wrong, he knew that he had often escaped punishment. During all those years he had never heard from any of his masters a flippant

word: it was they who had taught him christian doctrine and urged him to
live a good life and, when he had fallen into grievous sin, it was they who
had led him back to grace. Their presence had made him diffident of himself
when he was a muff in Clongowes and it had made him diffident of himself
also while he had held his equivocal position in Belvedere. A constant sense
of this had remained with him up to the last year of his school life. He had
never once disobeyed or allowed turbulent companions to seduce him from
his habit of quiet obedience; and, even when he doubted some statement of
a master, he had never presumed to doubt openly. Lately some of their
judgments had sounded a little childish in his ears and had made him feel a
regret and pity as though he were slowly passing out of an accustomed
world and were hearing its language for the last time. One day when some
boys had gathered round a priest under the shed near the chapel, he had
heard the priest say:

– I believe that Lord Macaulay was a man who probably never committed
a mortal sin in his life, that is to say, a deliberate mortal sin.

Some of the boys had then asked the priest if Victor Hugo were not the
greatest French writer. The priest had answered that Victor Hugo had
never written half so well when he had turned against the church as he had
written when he was a catholic.

– But there are many eminent French critics, said the priest, who consider
that even Victor Hugo, great as he certainly was, had not so pure a French
style as Louis Veuillot.

The tiny flame which the priest's allusion had kindled upon Stephen's
cheek had sunk down again and his eyes were still fixed calmly on the
colourless sky. But an unresting doubt flew hither and thither before his
mind. Masked memories passed quickly before him: he recognized scenes
and persons yet he was conscious that he had failed to perceive some vital
circumstance in them. He saw himself walking about the grounds watching
the sports in Clongowes and eating slim jim out of his cricket cap. Some
jesuits were walking round the cycle-track in the company of ladies. The
echoes of certain expressions used in Clongowes sounded in remote caves
of his mind.

His ears were listening to these distant echoes amid the silence of the
parlour when he became aware that the priest was addressing him in a
different voice.

– I sent for you today, Stephen, because I wished to speak to you on a
very important subject.

– Yes, sir.

– Have you ever felt that you had a vocation?

Stephen parted his lips to answer yes and then withheld the word suddenly. The priest waited for the answer and added:

– I mean, have you ever felt within yourself, in your soul, a desire to join the order? Think.

– I have sometimes thought of it, said Stephen.

The priest let the blindcord fall to one side and, uniting his hands, leaned his chin gravely upon them, communing with himself.

– In a college like this, he said at length, there is one boy or perhaps two or three boys whom God calls to the religious life. Such a boy is marked off from his companions by his piety, by the good example he shows to others. He is looked up to by them; he is chosen perhaps as prefect by his fellow sodalists. And you, Stephen, have been such a boy in this college, prefect of Our Blessed Lady's sodality. Perhaps you are the boy in this college whom God designs to call to Himself.

A strong note of pride reinforcing the gravity of the priest's voice made Stephen's heart quicken in response.

To receive that call, Stephen, said the priest, is the greatest honour that the Almighty God can bestow upon a man. No king or emperor on this earth has the power of the priest of God. No angel or archangel in heaven, no saint, not even the Blessed Virgin herself, has the power of a priest of God: the power of the keys, the power to bind and to loose from sin, the power of exorcism, the power to cast out from the creatures of God the evil spirits that have power over them; the power, the authority, to make the great God of Heaven come down upon the altar and take the form of bread and wine. What an awful power, Stephen!

A flame began to flutter again on Stephen's cheek as he heard in this proud address an echo of his own proud musings. How often had he seen himself as a priest wielding calmly and humbly the awful power of which angels and saints stood in reverence! His soul had loved to muse in secret on this desire. He had seen himself, a young and silent-mannered priest, entering a confessional swiftly, ascending the altarsteps, incensing, genu-flecting, accomplishing the vague acts of the priesthood which pleased him by reason of their semblance of reality and of their distance from it. In that dim life which he had lived through in his musings he had assumed the voices and gestures which he had noted with various priests. He had bent his knee sideways like such a one, he had shaken the thurible only slightly like such a one, his chasuble had swung open like that of such another as he turned to the altar again after having blessed the people. And above all it had pleased him to fill the second place in those dim scenes of his imagining. He shrank from the dignity of celebrant because it displeased him to imagine that all the vague pomp should end in his own person or that the ritual should assign to him so clear and final an office. He longed for the minor sacred offices, to be vested with the tunicle of subdeacon at high mass, to stand aloof from the altar, forgotten by the people, his shoulders covered with a humeral veil, holding the paten within its folds or, when the sacrifice had been accomplished, to stand as deacon in a dalmatic of cloth of gold on the step below the celebrant, his hands joined and his face towards the people, and sing the chant *Ite missa est*. If ever he had seen himself celebrant it was as in the pictures of the mass in his child's massbook, in a church without worshippers, save for the angel of the sacrifice, at a bare altar, and served by an acolite scarcely more boyish than himself. In vague sacrificial or sacramental acts alone his will seemed drawn to go forth to encounter reality; and it was partly the absence of an appointed rite which had always constrained him to inaction whether he had allowed silence to cover his anger or pride or had suffered only an embrace he longed to give.

He listened in reverent silence now to the priest's appeal and through the words he heard even more distinctly a voice bidding him approach, offering him secret knowledge and secret power. He would know then what was the sin of Simon Magus and what the sin against the Holy Ghost for which there was no forgiveness. He would know obscure things, hidden from others, from those who were conceived and born children of wrath. He would know the sins, the sinful longings and sinful thoughts and sinful acts, of others, hearing them murmured into his ears in the confessional under the shame of a darkened chapel by the lips of women and of girls; but rendered immune mysteriously at his ordination by the imposition of hands, his soul would pass again uncontaminated to the white peace of the altar. No touch of sin would linger upon the hands with which he would elevate and break the host; no touch of sin would linger on his lips in prayer to make him eat and drink damnation to himself not discerning the body of the Lord. He would hold his secret knowledge and secret power, being as sinless as the innocent, and he would be a priest for ever according to the order of Melchisedec.

– I will offer up my mass tomorrow morning, said the director, that Almighty God may reveal to you His holy will. And let you, Stephen, make a novena to your holy patron saint, the first martyr, who is very powerful with God, that God may enlighten your mind. But you must be quite sure, Stephen, that you have a vocation because it would be terrible if you found afterwards that you had none. Once a priest always a priest, remember. Your catechism tells you that the sacrament of Holy Orders is one of those which can be received only once because it imprints on the soul an indelible spiritual mark which can never be effaced. It is before you must weigh well, not after. It is a solemn question, Stephen, because on it may depend the salvation of your eternal soul. But we will pray to God together.

He held open the heavy hall door and gave his hand as if already to a companion in the spiritual life. Stephen passed out on to the wide platform above the steps and was conscious of the caress of mild evening air. Towards Findlater's church a quartet of young men were striding along with linked arms, swaying their heads and stepping to the agile melody of their leader's concertina. The music passed in an instant, as the first bars of sudden music always did, over the fantastic fabrics of his mind, dissolving them painlessly and noiselessly as a sudden wave dissolves the sand-built turrets of children. Smiling at the trivial air he raised his eyes to the priest's face and, seeing in it a mirthless rejection of the sunken day, detached his hand slowly which had acquiesced faintly in the companionship.

As he descended the steps the impression which effaced his troubled self-communion was that of a mirthless mask reflecting a sunken day from the threshold of the college. The shadow, then, of the life of the college passed gravely over his consciousness. It was a grave and ordered and passionless life that awaited him, a life without material cares. He wondered how he would pass the first night in the novitiate and with what dismay he would wake the first morning in the dormitory. The troubling odour of the long corridors of Clongowes came back to him and he heard the discreet murmur of the burning gas-flames. At once from every part of his being unrest began to irradiate. A feverish quickening of his pulses followed, and a din of meaningless words drove his reasoned thoughts hither and thither con-fusedly. His lungs dilated and sank as if he were inhaling a warm moist unsustaining air and he smelt again the moist warm air which hung in the bath in Clongowes above the sluggish turf-coloured water.

Some instinct, waking at these memories, stronger than education or piety, quickened within him at every near approach to that life, an instinct subtle and hostile, and armed him against acquiescence. The chill and order of the life repelled him. He saw himself rising in the cold of the morning and filing down with the others to early mass and trying vainly to struggle with his prayers against the fainting sickness of his stomach. He saw himself sitting at dinner with the community of a college. What, then, had become of that deep-rooted shyness of his which had made him loth to eat or drink under a strange roof? What had come of the pride of his spirit which had always made him conceive himself as a being apart in every order?

The Reverend Stephen Dedalus, s.j.

His name in that new life leaped into characters before his eyes and to it there followed a mental sensation of an undefined face or colour of a face. The colour faded and became strong like a changing glow of pallid brick red. Was it the raw reddish glow he had so often seen on wintry mornings on the shaven gills of the priests? The face was eyeless and sour-favoured and devout, shot with pink tinges of suffocated anger. Was it not a mental spectre of the face of one of the jesuits whom some of the boys called Lantern Jaws and others Foxy Campbell?

He was passing at that moment before the jesuit house in Gardiner Street and wondered vaguely which window would be his if he ever joined the order. Then he wondered at the vagueness of his wonder, at the remoteness of his own soul from what he had hitherto imagined her sanctuary, at the frail hold which so many years of order and obedience had of him when once a definite and irrevocable act of his threatened to end for ever, in time and in eternity, his freedom. The voice of the director urging upon him the proud claims of the church and the mystery and power of the priestly office repeated itself idly in his memory. His soul was not there to hear and greet it and he knew now that the exhortation he had listened to had already fallen into an idle formal tale. He would never swing the thurible before the tabernacle as priest. His destiny was to be elusive of social or religious orders. The wisdom of the priest's appeal did not touch him to the quick. He was destined to learn his own wisdom apart from others or to learn the wisdom of others himself wandering among the snares of the world.

The snares of the world were its ways of sin. He would fall. He had not yet fallen but he would fall silently, in an instant. Not to fall was too hard, too hard; and he felt the silent lapse of his soul, as it would be at some instant to come, falling, falling, but not yet fallen, still unfallen, but about to fall.

He crossed the bridge over the stream of the Tolka and turned his eyes coldly for an instant towards the faded blue shrine of the Blessed Virgin which stood fowl-wise on a pole in the middle of a ham-shaped encampment of poor cottages. Then, bending to the left, he followed the lane which led up to his house. The faint sour stink of rotted cabbages came towards him from the kitchen gardens on the rising ground above the river. He smiled to think that it was this disorder, the misrule and confusion of his father's house and the stagnation of vegetable life, which was to win the day in his soul. Then a short laugh broke from his lips as he thought of that solitary farmhand in the kitchen gardens behind their house whom they had nick-named the man with the hat. A second laugh, taking rise from the first after a pause, broke from him involuntarily as he thought of how the man with the hat worked, considering in turn the four points of the sky and then regretfully plunging his spade in the earth.

He pushed open the latchless door of the porch and passed through the naked hallway into the kitchen. A group of his brothers and sisters was sitting round the table. Tea was nearly over and only the last of the second watered tea remained in the bottoms of the small glass jars and jampots which did service for teacups. Discarded crusts and lumps of sugared bread, turned brown by the tea which had been poured over them, lay scattered on the table. Little wells of tea lay here and there on the board, and a knife with a broken ivory handle was stuck through the pith of a ravaged turnover.

The sad quiet grey-blue glow of the dying day came through the window and the open door, covering over and allaying quietly a sudden instinct of remorse in Stephen's heart. All that had been denied them had been freely given to him, the eldest; but the quiet glow of evening showed him in their faces no sign of rancour.

He sat near them at the table and asked where his father and mother were. One answered:

– Goneboro toboro lookboro atboro aboro houseboro.

Still another removal! A boy named Fallon in Belvedere had often asked him with a silly laugh why they moved so often. A frown of scorn darkened quickly his forehead as he heard again the silly laugh of the questioner.

He asked:

– Why are we on the move again if it's a fair question?

– Becauseboro theboro landboro lordboro willboro putboro usboro outboro.

The voice of his youngest brother from the farther side of the fireplace began to sing the air *Oft in the Stilly Night*. One by one the others took up the air until a full choir of voices was singing. They would sing so for hours, melody after melody, glee after glee, till the last pale light died down on the horizon, till the first dark night clouds came forth and night fell.

He waited for some moments, listening, before he too took up the air with them. He was listening with pain of spirit to the overtone of weariness behind their frail fresh innocent voices. Even before they set out on life's journey they seemed weary already of the way.

He heard the choir of voices in the kitchen echoed and multiplied through an endless reverberation of the choirs of endless generations of children and heard in all the echoes an echo also of the recurring note of weariness and pain. All seemed weary of life even before entering upon it. And he remembered that Newman had heard this note also in the broken lines of Virgil, *giving utterance, like the voice of Nature herself, to that pain and weariness yet hope of better things which has been the experience of her children in every time.*

He could wait no longer.

From the door of Byron's public-house to the gate of Clontarf Chapel, from the gate of Clontarf Chapel to the door of Byron's public-house and then back again to the chapel and then back again to the public-house he had paced slowly at first, planting his steps scrupulously in the spaces of the patchwork of the footpath, then timing their fall to the fall of verses. A full hour had passed since his father had gone in with Dan Crosby, the tutor, to find out for him something about the university. For a full hour he had paced up and down, waiting: but he could wait no longer.

He set off abruptly for the Bull, walking rapidly lest his father's shrill whistle might call him back; and in a few moments he had rounded the curve at the police barrack and was safe.

Yes, his mother was hostile to the idea, as he had read from her listless silence. Yet her mistrust pricked him more keenly than his father's pride and he thought coldly how he had watched the faith which was fading down in his soul ageing and strengthening in her eyes. A dim antagonism gathered force within him and darkened his mind as a cloud against her disloyalty and when it passed, cloud-like, leaving his mind serene and dutiful towards her again, he was made aware dimly and without regret of a first noiseless sundering of their lives.

The university! So he had passed beyond the challenge of the sentries who had stood as guardians of his boyhood and had sought to keep him among them that he might be subject to them and serve their ends. Pride after satisfaction uplifted him like long slow waves. The end he had been born to serve yet did not see had led him to escape by an unseen path and now it beckoned to him once more and a new adventure was about to be opened to him. It seemed to him that he heard notes of fitful music leaping upwards a tone and downwards a diminished fourth, upwards a tone and downwards a major third, like triple-branching flames leaping fitfully, flame after flame, out of a midnight wood. It was an elfin prelude, endless and formless; and, as it grew wilder and faster, the flames leaping out of time, he seemed to hear from under the boughs and grasses wild creatures racing, their feet pattering like rain upon the leaves. Their feet passed in pattering tumult over his mind, the feet of hares and rabbits, the feet of harts and hinds and antelopes, until he heard them no more and remembered only a proud cadence from Newman:

– Whose feet are as the feet of harts and underneath the everlasting arms.

The pride of that dim image brought back to his mind the dignity of the office he had refused. All through his boyhood he had mused upon that which he had so often thought to be his destiny and when the moment had come for him to obey the call he had turned aside, obeying a wayward instinct. Now time lay between: the oils of ordination would never anoint his body. He had refused. Why?

He turned seaward from the road at Dollymount and as he passed on to the thin wooden bridge he felt the planks shaking with the tramp of heavily shod feet. A squad of christian brothers was on its way back from the Bull and had begun to pass, two by two, across the bridge. Soon the whole bridge was trembling and resounding. The uncouth faces passed him two by two, stained yellow or red or livid by the sea, and, as he strove to look at them with ease and indifference, a faint stain of personal shame and commiseration rose to his own face. Angry with himself he tried to hide his face from their eyes by gazing down sideways into the shallow swirling water under the bridge but he still saw a reflection therein of their top-heavy silk hats and humble tape-like collars and loosely-hanging clerical clothes.

– Brother Hickey.

Brother Quaid.

Brother MacArdle.

Brother Keogh. –

Their piety would be like their names, like their faces, like their clothes, and it was idle for him to tell himself that their humble and contrite hearts, it might be, paid a far richer tribute of devotion than his had ever been, a gift tenfold more acceptable than his elaborate adoration. It was idle for him to move himself to be generous towards them, to tell himself that if he ever came to their gates, stripped of his pride, beaten and in beggar's weeds, that they would be generous towards him, loving him as themselves. Idle and embittering, finally, to argue, against his own dispassionate certitude, that the commandment of love bade us not to love our neighbour as ourselves with the same amount and intensity of love but to love him as ourselves with the same kind of love.

He drew forth a phrase from his treasure and spoke it softly to himself:

– A day of dappled seaborne clouds.

The phrase and the day and the scene harmonised in a chord. Words. Was it their colours? He allowed them to glow and fade, hue after hue: sunrise gold, the russet and green of apple orchards, azure of waves, the grey-fringed fleece of clouds. No, it was not their colours: it was the poise and balance of the period itself. Did he then love the rhythmic rise and fall of words better than their associations of legend and colour? Or was it that, being as weak of sight as he was shy of mind, he drew less pleasure from the reflection of the glowing sensible world through the prism of a language many-coloured and richly storied than from the contemplation of an inner world of individual emotions mirrored perfectly in a lucid supple periodic prose?

He passed from the trembling bridge on to firm land again. At that instant, as it seemed to him, the air was chilled and, looking askance towards the water, he saw a flying squall darkening and crisping suddenly the tide. A faint click at his heart, a faint throb in his throat told him once more of how his flesh dreaded the cold infrahuman odour of the sea; yet he did not strike across the downs on his left but held straight on along the spine of rocks that pointed against the river's mouth.

A veiled sunlight lit up faintly the grey sheet of water where the river was embayed. In the distance along the course of the slow-flowing Liffey slender masts flecked the sky and, more distant still, the dim fabric of the city lay prone in haze. Like a scene on some vague arras, old as man's weariness, the image of the seventh city of christendom was visible to him across the timeless air, no older nor more weary nor less patient of subjection than in the days of the thingmote.

Disheartened, he raised his eyes towards the slow-drifting clouds, dappled and seaborne. They were voyaging across the deserts of the sky, a host of nomads on the march, voyaging high over Ireland, westward bound. The Europe they had come from lay out there beyond the Irish Sea, Europe of strange tongues and valleyed and woodbegirt and citadelled and of entrenched and marshalled races. He heard a confused music within him as of memories and names which he was almost conscious of but could not capture even for an instant; then the music seemed to recede, to recede, to recede, and from each receding trail of nebulous music there fell always one longdrawn calling note, piercing like a star the dusk of silence. Again! Again! Again! A voice from beyond the world was calling.

– Hello, Stephanos!

– Here comes The Dedalus!

– Ao! . . . Eh, give it over, Dwyer, I'm telling you, or I'll give you a stuff in the kisser for yourself . . . Ao!

– Good man, Towser! Duck him!

– Come along, Dedalus! Bous Stephanoumenos! Bous Stephaneforos!

– Duck him! Guzzle him now, Towser!

– Help! Help! . . . Ao!

He recognized their speech collectively before he distinguished their faces. The mere sight of that medley of wet nakedness chilled him to the bone. Their bodies, corpse-white or suffused with a pallid golden light or rawly tanned by the sun, gleamed with the wet of the sea. Their diving-stone, poised on its rude supports and rocking under their plunges, and the rough-hewn stones of the sloping breakwater over which they scrambled in their horseplay gleamed with cold wet lustre. The towels with which they smacked their bodies were heavy with cold seawater; and drenched with cold brine was their matted hair.

He stood still in deference to their calls and parried their banter with easy words. How characterless they looked: Shuley without his deep unbuttoned collar, Ennis without his scarlet belt with the snaky clasp, and Connolly without his Norfolk coat with the flapless side-pockets! It was a pain to see them, and a sword-like pain to see the signs of adolescence that made repellent their pitiable nakedness. Perhaps they had taken refuge in number and noise from the secret dread in their souls.

But he, apart from them and in silence, remembered in what dread he stood of the mystery of his own body.

– Stephanos Dedalos! Bous Stephanoumenos! Bous Stephaneforos!

Their banter was not new to him and now it flattered his mild proud sovereignty. Now, as never before, his strange name seemed to him a prophecy. So timeless seemed the grey warm air, so fluid and impersonal his own mood, that all ages were as one to him. A moment before the ghost of the ancient kingdom of the Danes had looked forth through the vesture of the haze-wrapped city. Now, at the name of the fabulous artificer, he seemed to hear the noise of dim waves and to see a winged form flying above the waves and slowly climbing the air. What did it mean? Was it a quaint device opening a page of some medieval book of prophecies and symbols, a hawk-like man flying sunward above the sea, a prophecy of the end he had been born to serve and had been following through the mists of childhood and boyhood, a symbol of the artist forging anew in his workshop out of the sluggish matter of the earth a new soaring impalpable imperishable being?

His heart trembled; his breath came faster and a wild spirit passed over his limbs as though he was soaring sunward. His heart trembled in an ecstasy of fear and his soul was in flight. His soul was soaring in an air beyond the world and the body he knew was purified in a breath and delivered of incertitude and made radiant and commingled with the element of the spirit. An ecstasy of flight made radiant his eyes and wild his breath and tremulous and wild and radiant his windswept limbs.

– One! Two! . . . Look out!

– Oh, Cripes, I'm drownded!

– One! Two! Three and away!

– The next! The next!

– One! . . . Uk!

– Stephaneforos!

His throat ached with a desire to cry aloud, the cry of a hawk or eagle on high, to cry piercingly of his deliverance to the winds. This was the call of life to his soul not the dull gross voice of the world of duties and despair, not the inhuman voice that had called him to the pale service of the altar. An instant of wild flight had delivered him and the cry of triumph which his lips withheld cleft his brain.

– Stephaneforos!

What were they now but cerements shaken from the body of death – the fear he had walked in night and day, the incertitude that had ringed him round, the shame that had abased him within and without cerements, the linens of the grave?

His soul had arisen from the grave of boyhood, spurning her grave-clothes. Yes! Yes! Yes! He would create proudly out of the freedom and power of his soul, as the great artificer whose name he bore, a living thing, new and soaring and beautiful, impalpable, imperishable.

He started up nervously from the stone-block for he could no longer quench the flame in his blood. He felt his cheeks aflame and his throat throbbing with song. There was a lust of wandering in his feet that burned to set out for the ends of the earth. On! On! his heart seemed to cry. Evening would deepen above the sea, night fall upon the plains, dawn glimmer before the wanderer and show him strange fields and hills and faces. Where?

He looked northward towards Howth. The sea had fallen below the line of seawrack on the shallow side of the breakwater and already the tide was running out fast along the foreshore. Already one long oval bank of sand lay warm and dry amid the wavelets. Here and there warm isles of sand gleamed above the shallow tide and about the isles and around the long bank and amid the shallow currents of the beach were lightclad figures, wading and delving.

In a few moments he was barefoot, his stockings folded in his pockets and his canvas shoes dangling by their knotted laces over his shoulders and, picking a pointed salt-eaten stick out of the jetsam among the rocks, he clambered down the slope of the breakwater.

There was a long rivulet in the strand and, as he waded slowly up its course, he wondered at the endless drift of seaweed. Emerald and black and russet and olive, it moved beneath the current, swaying and turning. The water of the rivulet was dark with endless drift and mirrored the high-drifting clouds. The clouds were drifting above him silently and silently the sea-tangle was drifting below him and the grey warm air was still and a new wild life was singing in his veins.

Where was his boyhood now? Where was the soul that had hung back from her destiny, to brood alone upon the shame of her wounds and in her house of squalor and subterfuge to queen it in faded cerements and in wreaths that withered at the touch? Or where was he?

He was alone. He was unheeded, happy and near to the wild heart of life. He was alone and young and wilful and wild-hearted, alone amid a waste of wild air and brackish waters and the sea-harvest of shells and tangle and veiled grey sunlight and gayclad lightclad figures of children and girls and voices childish and girlish in the air.

A girl stood before him in midstream, alone and still, gazing out to sea. She seemed like one whom magic had changed into the likeness of a strange and beautiful seabird. Her long slender bare legs were delicate as a crane's and pure save where an emerald trail of seaweed had fashioned itself as a sign upon the flesh. Her thighs, fuller and soft-hued as ivory, were bared almost to the hips, where the white fringes of her drawers were like feathering of soft white down. Her slate-blue skirts were kilted boldly about her waist and dovetailed behind her. Her bosom was as a bird's, soft and slight, slight and soft as the breast of some dark-plumaged dove. But her long fair hair was girlish: and girlish, and touched with the wonder of mortal beauty, her face.

She was alone and still, gazing out to sea; and when she felt his presence and the worship of his eyes her eyes turned to him in quiet sufferance of his gaze, without shame or wantonness. Long, long she suffered his gaze and then quietly withdrew her eyes from his and bent them towards the stream, gently stirring the water with her foot hither and thither. The first faint noise of gently moving water broke the silence, low and faint and whispering, faint as the bells of sleep; hither and thither, hither and thither; and a faint flame trembled on her cheek.

– Heavenly God! cried Stephen's soul, in an outburst of profane joy.

He turned away from her suddenly and set off across the strand. His cheeks were aflame; his body was aglow; his limbs were trembling. On and on and on and on he strode, far out over the sands, singing wildly to the sea, crying to greet the advent of the life that had cried to him.

Her image had passed into his soul for ever and no word had broken the holy silence of his ecstasy. Her eyes had called him and his soul had leaped at the call. To live, to err, to fall, to triumph, to recreate life out of life! A wild angel had appeared to him, the angel of mortal youth and beauty, an envoy from the fair courts of life, to throw open before him in an instant of ecstasy the gates of all the ways of error and glory. On and on and on and on!

He halted suddenly and heard his heart in the silence. How far had he walked? What hour was it?

There was no human figure near him nor any sound borne to him over the air. But the tide was near the turn and already the day was on the wane. He turned landward and ran towards the shore and, running up the sloping beach, reckless of the sharp shingle, found a sandy nook amid a ring of tufted sandknolls and lay down there that the peace and silence of the evening might still the riot of his blood.

He felt above him the vast indifferent dome and the calm processes of the heavenly bodies; and the earth beneath him, the earth that had borne him, had taken him to her breast.

He closed his eyes in the languor of sleep. His eyelids trembled as if they felt the vast cyclic movement of the earth and her watchers, trembled as if they felt the strange light of some new world. His soul was swooning into some new world, fantastic, dim, uncertain as under sea, traversed by cloudy shapes and beings. A world, a glimmer or a flower? Glimmering and trembling, trembling and unfolding, a breaking light, an opening flower, it spread in endless succession to itself, breaking in full crimson and unfolding and fading to palest rose, leaf by leaf and wave of light by wave of light, flooding all the heavens with its soft flushes, every flush deeper than the other.

Evening had fallen when he woke and the sand and arid grasses of his bed glowed no longer. He rose slowly and, recalling the rapture of his sleep, sighed at its joy.

He climbed to the crest of the sandhill and gazed about him. Evening had fallen. A rim of the young moon cleft the pale waste of skyline, the rim of a silver hoop embedded in grey sand; and the tide was flowing in fast to the land with a low whisper of her waves, islanding a few last figures in distant pools.

Chapter 5

He drained his third cup of watery tea to the dregs and set to chewing the crusts of fried bread that were scattered near him, staring into the dark pool of the jar. The yellow dripping had been scooped out like a boghole and the pool under it brought back to his memory the dark turf-coloured water of the bath in Clongowes. The box of pawn tickets at his elbow had just been rifled and he took up idly one after another in his greasy fingers the blue and white dockets, scrawled and sanded and creased and bearing the name of the pledger as Daly or MacEvoy.

1 Pair Buskins.

1 D. Coat.

3 Articles and White.

1 Man's Pants.

Then he put them aside and gazed thoughtfully at the lid of the box, speckled with louse marks, and asked vaguely:

– How much is the clock fast now?

His mother straightened the battered alarm clock that was lying on its side in the middle of the mantelpiece until its dial showed a quarter to twelve and then laid it once more on its side.

– An hour and twenty-five minutes, she said. The right time now is twenty past ten. The dear knows you might try to be in time for your lectures.

– Fill out the place for me to wash, said Stephen.

– Katey, fill out the place for Stephen to wash.

– Boody, fill out the place for Stephen to wash.

– I can't, I'm going for blue. Fill it out, you, Maggy.

When the enamelled basin had been fitted into the well of the sink and the old washing glove flung on the side of it he allowed his mother to scrub his neck and root into the folds of his ears and into the interstices at the wings of his nose.

– Well, it's a poor case, she said, when a university student is so dirty that his mother has to wash him.

– But it gives you pleasure, said Stephen calmly.

An ear-splitting whistle was heard from upstairs and his mother thrust a damp overall into his hands, saying:

– Dry yourself and hurry out for the love of goodness.

A second shrill whistle, prolonged angrily, brought one of the girls to the foot of the staircase.

– Yes, father?

– Is your lazy bitch of a brother gone out yet?

– Yes, father.

– Sure?

– Yes, father.

– Hm!

The girl came back, making signs to him to be quick and go out quietly by the back. Stephen laughed and said:

– He has a curious idea of genders if he thinks a bitch is masculine.

– Ah, it's a scandalous shame for you, Stephen, said his mother, and you'll live to rue the day you set your foot in that place. I know how it has changed you.

– Good morning, everybody, said Stephen, smiling and kissing the tips of his fingers in adieu.

The lane behind the terrace was waterlogged and as he went down it slowly, choosing his steps amid heaps of wet rubbish, he heard a mad nun screeching in the nuns' madhouse beyond the wall.

– Jesus! O Jesus! Jesus!

He shook the sound out of his ears by an angry toss of his head and hurried on, stumbling through the mouldering offal, his heart already bitten by an ache of loathing and bitterness. His father's whistle, his mother's mutterings, the screech of an unseen maniac were to him now so many voices offending and threatening to humble the pride of his youth. He drove their echoes even out of his heart with an execration; but, as he walked down the avenue and felt the grey morning light falling about him through the dripping trees and smelt the strange wild smell of the wet leaves and bark, his soul was loosed of her miseries.

The rain-laden trees of the avenue evoked in him, as always, memories of the girls and women in the plays of Gerhart Hauptmann; and the memory of their pale sorrows and the fragrance falling from the wet branches mingled in a mood of quiet joy. His morning walk across the city had begun, and he foreknew that as he passed the sloblands of Fairview he would think of the cloistral silver-veined prose of Newman; that as he walked along the North Strand Road, glancing idly at the windows of the provision shops, he would recall the dark humour of Guido Cavalcanti and smile; that as he went by Baird's stonecutting works in Talbot Place the spirit of Ibsen would blow through him like a keen wind, a spirit of wayward boyish beauty; and that passing a grimy marine dealer's shop beyond the Liffey he would repeat the song by Ben Jonson which begins:

I was not wearier where I lay.

His mind when wearied of its search for the essence of beauty amid the spectral words of Aristotle or Aquinas turned often for its pleasure to the dainty songs of the Elizabethans. His mind, in the vesture of a doubting monk, stood often in shadow under the windows of that age, to hear the grave and mocking music of the lutenists or the frank laughter of waist-coateers until a laugh too low, a phrase, tarnished by time, of chambering and false honour stung his monkish pride and drove him on from his lurking-place.

The lore which he was believed to pass his days brooding upon so that it had rapt him from the companionship of youth was only a garner of slender sentences from Aristotle's poetics and psychology and a *Synopsis Philosophiae Scholasticae ad mentem divi Thomae.* His thinking was a dusk of doubt and self-mistrust, lit up at moments by the lightnings of intuition, but lightnings of so clear a splendour that in those moment the world perished about his feet as if it had been fire-consumed; and thereafter his tongue grew heavy and he met the eyes of others with unanswering eyes, for he felt that the spirit of beauty had folded him round like a mantle and that in revery at least he had been acquainted with nobility. But when this brief pride of silence upheld him no longer he was glad to find himself still in the midst of common lives, passing on his way amid the squalor and noise and sloth of the city fearlessly and with a light heart.

Near the hoardings on the canal he met the consumptive man with the doll's face and the brimless hat coming towards him town the slope of the bridge with little steps, tightly buttoned into his chocolate overcoat, and holding his furled umbrella a span or two from him like a divining rod. It must be eleven, he thought, and peered into a dairy to see the time. The clock in the dairy told him that it was five minutes to five but, as he turned away, he heard a clock somewhere near him, but unseen, beating eleven strokes in swift precision. He laughed as he heard it for it made him think of McCann, and he saw him a squat figure in a shooting jacket and breeches and with a fair goatee, standing in the wind at Hopkins' corner, and heard him say:

– Dedalus, you're an antisocial being, wrapped up in yourself. I'm not. I'm a democrat and I'll work and act for social liberty and equality among all classes and sexes in the United States of the Europe of the future.

Eleven! Then he was late for that lecture too. What day of the week was it? He stopped at a newsagent's to read the headline of a placard. Thursday. Ten to eleven, English; eleven to twelve, French; twelve to one, physics. He fancied to himself the English lecture and felt, even at that distance, restless and helpless. He saw the heads of his classmates meekly bent as they wrote in their notebooks the points they were bidden to note, nominal definitions, essential definitions and examples or dates of birth or death, chief works, a favourable and an unfavourable criticism side by side. His own head was unbent for his thoughts wandered abroad and whether he looked around the little class of students or out of the window across the desolate gardens of the green an odour assailed him of cheerless cellar-damp and decay. Another head than his, right before him in the first benches, was poised squarely above its bending fellows like the head of a priest appealing without humility to the tabernacle for the humble worshippers about him. Why was it that when he thought of Cranly he could never raise before his mind the entire image of his body but only the image of the head and face? Even now against the grey curtain of the morning he saw it before him like the phantom of a dream, the face of a severed head or death-mask, crowned on the brows by its stiff black upright hair as by an iron crown. It was a priest-like face, priestlike in its palor, in the wide winged nose, in the shadowings below the eyes and along the jaws, priest-like in the lips that were long and bloodless and faintly smiling; and Stephen, remembering swiftly how he had told Cranly of all the tumults and unrest and longings in his soul, day after day and night by night, only to be answered by his friend's listening silence, would have told himself that it was the face of a guilty priest who heard confessions of those whom he had not power to absolve but that he felt again in memory the gaze of its dark womanish eyes.

Through this image he had a glimpse of a strange dark cavern of speculation but at once turned away from it, feeling that it was not yet the hour to enter it. But the nightshade of his friend's listlessness seemed to be diffusing in the air around him a tenuous and deadly exhalation and he found himself glancing from one casual word to another on his right or left in stolid wonder that they had been so silently emptied of instantaneous sense until every mean shop legend bound his mind like the words of a spell and his soul shrivelled up sighing with age as he walked on in a lane among heaps of dead language. His own consciousness of language was ebbing from his brain and trickling into the very words themselves which set to band and disband themselves in wayward rhythms:

> The ivy whines upon the wall,
> And whines and twines upon the wall,
> The yellow ivy upon the wall,
> Ivy, ivy up the wall.

Did anyone ever hear such drivel? Lord Almighty! Who ever heard of ivy whining on a wall? Yellow ivy; that was all right. Yellow ivory also. And what about ivory ivy?

The word now shone in his brain, clearer and brighter than any ivory sawn from the mottled tusks of elephants. *Ivory, ivoire, avorio, ebur*. One of the first examples that he had learnt in Latin had run: *India mittit ebur*; and he recalled the shrewd northern face of the rector who had taught him to construe the Metamorphoses of Ovid in a courtly English, made whimsical by the mention of porkers and potsherds and chines of bacon. He had learnt what little he knew of the laws of Latin verse from a ragged book written by a Portuguese priest.

Contrahit orator, variant in carmine vates.

The crises and victories and secessions in Roman history were handed on to him in the trite words *in tanto discrimine* and he had tried to peer into the social life of the city of cities through the words *implere ollam denariorum* which the rector had rendered sonorously as the filling of a pot with denaries. The pages of his time-worn Horace never felt cold to the touch even when his own fingers were cold; they were human pages and fifty years before they had been turned by the human fingers of John Duncan Inverarity and by his brother, William Malcolm Inverarity. Yes, those were noble names on the dusky flyleaf and, even for so poor a Latinist as he, the dusky verses were as fragrant as though they had lain all those years in myrtle and lavender and vervain; but yet it wounded him to think that he would never be but a shy guest at the feast of the world's culture and that the monkish learning, in terms of which he was striving to forge out an esthetic philosophy, was held no higher by the age he lived in than the subtle and curious jargons of heraldry and falconry.

The grey block of Trinity on his left, set heavily in the city's ignorance like a dull stone set in a cumbrous ring, pulled his mind downward and while he was striving this way and that to free his feet from the fetters of the reformed conscience he came upon the droll statue of the national poet of Ireland.

He looked at it without anger; for, though sloth of the body and of the soul crept over it like unseen vermin, over the shuffling feet and up the folds of the cloak and around the servile head, it seemed humbly conscious of its indignity. It was a Firbolg in the borrowed cloak of a Milesian; and he thought of his friend Davin, the peasant student. It was a jesting name between them, but the young peasant bore with it lightly:

– Go on, Stevie, I have a hard head, you tell me. Call me what you will.

The homely version of his christian name on the lips of his friend had touched Stephen pleasantly when first heard for he was as formal in speech with others as they were with him. Often, as he sat in Davin's rooms in Grantham Street, wondering at his friend's well-made boots that flanked the wall pair by pair and repeating for his friend's simple ear the verses and cadences of others which were the veils of his own longing and dejection, the rude Firbolg mind of his listener had drawn his mind towards it and flung it back again, drawing it by a quiet inbred courtesy of attention or by a quaint turn of old English speech or by the force of its delight in rude bodily skill – for Davin had sat at the feet of Michael Cusack, the Gael – repelling swiftly and suddenly by a grossness of intelligence or by a bluntness of feeling or by a dull stare of terror in the eyes, the terror of soul of a starving Irish village in which the curfew was still a nightly fear.

Side by side with his memory of the deeds of prowess of his uncle Mat Davin, the athlete, the young peasant worshipped the sorrowful legend of Ireland. The gossip of his fellow-students which strove to render the flat life of the college significant at any cost loved to think of him as a young fenian. His nurse had taught him Irish and shaped his rude imagination by the broken lights of Irish myth. He stood towards this myth upon which no individual mind had ever drawn out a line of beauty and to its unwieldy tales that divided against themselves as they moved down the cycles in the same attitude as towards the Roman catholic religion, the attitude of a dull-witted loyal serf. Whatsoever of thought or of feeling came to him from England or by way of English culture his mind stood armed against in obedience to a password; and of the world that lay beyond England he knew only the foreign legion of France in which he spoke of serving.

Coupling this ambition with the young man's humour Stephen had often called him one of the tame geese and there was even a point of irritation in the name pointed against that very reluctance of speech and deed in his friend which seemed so often to stand between Stephen's mind, eager of speculation, and the hidden ways of Irish life.

One night the young peasant, his spirit stung by the violent or luxurious language in which Stephen escaped from the cold silence of intellectual revolt, had called up before Stephen's mind a strange vision. The two were walking slowly towards Davin's rooms through the dark narrow streets of the poorer jews.

– A thing happened to myself, Stevie, last autumn, coming on winter, and I never told it to a living soul and you are the first person now I ever told it to. I disremember if it was October or November. It was October because it was before I came up here to join the matriculation class.

Stephen had turned his smiling eyes towards his friend's face, flattered by his confidence and won over to sympathy by the speaker's simple accent.

– I was away all that day from my own place over in Buttevant – I don't know if you know where that is – at a hurling match between the Croke's Own Boys and the Fearless Thurles and by God, Stevie, that was the hard fight. My first cousin, Fonsy Davin, was stripped to his buff that day minding cool for the Limericks but he was up with the forwards half the time and shouting like mad. I never will forget that day. One of the Crokes made a woeful wipe at him one time with his camann and I declare to God he was within an aim's ace of getting it at the side of his temple. Oh, honest to God, if the crook of it caught him that time he was done for.

– I am glad he escaped, Stephen had said with a laugh, but surely that's not the strange thing that happened you?

– Well, I suppose that doesn't interest you, but leastways there was such noise after the match that I missed the train home and I couldn't get any kind of a yoke to give me a lift for, as luck would have it, there was a mass meeting that same day over in Castletownroche and all the cars in the country were there. So there was nothing for it only to stay the night or to foot it out. Well, I started to walk and on I went and it was coming on night when I got into the Ballyhoura hills, that's better than ten miles from Kilmallock and there's a long lonely road after that. You wouldn't see the sign of a christian house along the road or hear a sound. It was pitch dark almost. Once or twice I stopped by the way under a bush to redden my pipe and only for the dew was thick I'd have stretched out there and slept. At last, after a bend of the road, I spied a little cottage with a light in the window. I went up and knocked at the door. A voice asked who was there and I answered I was over at the match in Buttevant and was walking back and that I'd be thankful for a glass of water. After a while a young woman opened the door and brought me out a big mug of milk. She was half undressed as if she was going to bed when I knocked and she had her hair hanging and I thought by her figure and by something in the look of her eyes that she must be carrying a child. She kept me in talk a long while at the door, and I thought it strange because her breast and her shoulders were bare. She asked me was I tired and would I like to stop the night there. She said she was all alone in the house and that her husband had gone that morning to Queenstown with his sister to see her off. And all the time she was talking, Stevie, she had her eyes fixed on my face and she stood so close to me I could hear her breathing. When I handed her back the mug at last she took my hand to draw me in over the threshold and said: '*Come in and stay the night here. You've no call to be frightened. There's no one in it but ourselves . . .* ' I didn't go in, Stevie. I thanked her and went on my way again, all in a fever. At the first bend of the road I looked back and she was standing at the door.

The last words of Davin's story sang in his memory and the figure of the woman in the story stood forth reflected in other figures of the peasant women whom he had seen standing in the doorways at Clane as the college cars drove by, as a type of her race and of his own, a bat-like soul waking to the consciousness of itself in darkness and secrecy and loneliness and, through the eyes and voice and gesture of a woman without guile, calling the stranger to her bed.

A hand was laid on his arm and a young voice cried:

– Ah, gentleman, your own girl, sir! The first handsel today, gentleman. Buy that lovely bunch. Will you, gentleman?

The blue flowers which she lifted towards him and her young blue eyes seemed to him at that instant images of guilelessness, and he halted till the image had vanished and he saw only her ragged dress and damp coarse hair and hoydenish face.

– Do, gentleman! Don't forget your own girl, sir!

– I have no money, said Stephen.

– Buy them lovely ones, will you, sir? Only a penny.

– Did you hear what I said? asked Stephen, bending towards her. I told you I had no money. I tell you again now.

– Well, sure, you will some day, sir, please God, the girl answered after an instant.

– Possibly, said Stephen, but I don't think it likely.

He left her quickly, fearing that her intimacy might turn to jibing and wishing to be out of the way before she offered her ware to another, a tourist from England or a student of Trinity. Grafton Street, along which he walked, prolonged that moment of discouraged poverty. In the roadway at the head of the street a slab was set to the memory of Wolfe Tone and he remembered having been present with his father at its laying. He remembered with bitterness that scene of tawdry tribute. There were four French delegates in a brake and one, a plump smiling young man, held, wedged on a stick, a card on which were printed the words: *Vive l'Irlande!*

But the trees in Stephen's Green were fragrant of rain and the rain-sodden earth gave forth its mortal odour, a faint incense rising upward through the mould from many hearts. The soul of the gallant venal city which his elders had told him of had shrunk with time to a faint mortal odour rising from the earth and he knew that in a moment when he entered the sombre college he would be conscious of a corruption other than that of Buck Egan and Burnchapel Whaley.

It was too late to go upstairs to the French class. He crossed the hall and took the corridor to the left which led to the physics theatre. The corridor was dark and silent but not unwatchful. Why did he feel that it was not unwatchful? Was it because he had heard that in Buck Whaley's time there was a secret staircase there? Or was the jesuit house extra-territorial and was he walking among aliens? The Ireland of Tone and of Parnell seemed to have receded in space.

He opened the door of the theatre and halted in the chilly grey light that struggled through the dusty windows. A figure was crouching before the large grate and by its leanness and greyness he knew that it was the dean of studies lighting the fire. Stephen closed the door quietly and approached the fireplace.

– Good morning, sir! Can I help you?

The priest looked up quickly and said:

– One moment now, Mr Dedalus, and you will see. There is an art in lighting a fire. We have the liberal arts and we have the useful arts. This is one of the useful arts.

– I will try to learn it, said Stephen.

– Not too much coal, said the dean, working briskly at his task, that is one of the secrets.

He produced four candle-butts from the side-pockets of his soutane and placed them deftly among the coals and twisted papers. Stephen watched him in silence. Kneeling thus on the flagstone to kindle the fire and busied with the disposition of his wisps of paper and candle-butts he seemed more than ever a humble server making ready the place of sacrifice in an empty temple, a levite of the Lord. Like a levite's robe of plain linen the faded worn soutane draped the kneeling figure of one whom the canonicals or the bell-bordered ephod would irk and trouble. His very body had waxed old in lowly service of the Lord – in tending the fire upon the altar, in bearing tidings secretly, in waiting upon worldlings, in striking swiftly when bidden – and yet had remained ungraced by aught of saintly or of prelatic beauty. Nay, his very soul had waxed old in that service without growing towards light and beauty or spreading abroad a sweet odour of her sanctity – a mortified will no more responsive to the thrill of its obedience than was to the thrill of love or combat his ageing body, spare and sinewy, greyed with a silver-pointed down.

The dean rested back on his hunkers and watched the sticks catch. Stephen, to fill the silence, said:

– I am sure I could not light a fire.

– You are an artist, are you not, Mr Dedalus? said the dean, glancing up and blinking his pale eyes. The object of the artist is the creation of the beautiful. What the beautiful is is another question.

He rubbed his hands slowly and drily over the difficulty.

– Can you solve that question now? he asked.

– Aquinas, answered Stephen, says *pulcra sunt quae visa placent.*

– This fire before us, said the dean, will be pleasing to the eye. Will it therefore be beautiful?

– In so far as it is apprehended by the sight, which I suppose means here esthetic intellection, it will be beautiful. But Aquinas also says *Bonum est in quod tendit appetitus.* In so far as it satisfies the animal craving for warmth fire is a good. In hell, however, it is an evil.

– Quite so, said the dean, you have certainly hit the nail on the head.

He rose nimbly and went towards the door, set it ajar and said:

– A draught is said to be a help in these matters.

As he came back to the hearth, limping slightly but with a brisk step, Stephen saw the silent soul of a jesuit look out at him from the pale loveless eyes. Like Ignatius he was lame but in his eyes burned no spark of Ignatius's enthusiasm. Even the legendary craft of the company, a craft subtler and more secret than its fabled books of secret subtle wisdom, had not fired his soul with the energy of apostleship. It seemed as if he used the shifts and lore and cunning of the world, as bidden to do, for the greater glory of God, without joy in their handling or hatred of that in them which was evil but turning them, with a firm gesture of obedience back upon themselves and for all this silent service it seemed as if he loved not at all the master and little, if at all, the ends he served. *Similiter atque senis baculus*, he was, as the founder would have had him, like a staff in an old man's hand, to be leaned on in the road at nightfall or in stress of weather, to lie with a lady's nosegay on a garden seat, to be raised in menace.

The dean returned to the hearth and began to stroke his chin.

– When may we expect to have something from you on the esthetic question? he asked.

– From me! said Stephen in astonishment. I stumble on an idea once a fortnight if I am lucky.

– These questions are very profound, Mr Dedalus, said the dean. It is like looking down from the cliffs of Moher into the depths. Many go down into the depths and never come up. Only the trained diver can go down into those depths and explore them and come to the surface again.

– If you mean speculation, sir, said Stephen, I also am sure that there is no such thing as free thinking inasmuch as all thinking must be bound by its own laws.

– Ha!

– For my purpose I can work on at present by the light of one or two ideas of Aristotle and Aquinas.

– I see. I quite see your point.

– I need them only for my own use and guidance until I have done something for myself by their light. If the lamp smokes or smells I shall try to trim it. If it does not give light enough I shall sell it and buy another.

– Epictetus also had a lamp, said the dean, which was sold for a fancy price after his death. It was the lamp he wrote his philosophical dissertations by. You know Epictetus?

– An old gentleman, said Stephen coarsely, who said that the soul is very like a bucketful of water.

– He tells us in his homely way, the dean went on, that he put an iron lamp before a statue of one of the gods and that a thief stole the lamp. What did the philosopher do? He reflected that it was in the character of a thief to steal and determined to buy an earthen lamp next day instead of the iron lamp.

A smell of molten tallow came up from the dean's candle butts and fused itself in Stephen's consciousness with the jingle of the words, bucket and lamp and lamp and bucket. The priest's voice, too, had a hard jingling tone. Stephen's mind halted by instinct, checked by the strange tone and the imagery and by the priest's face which seemed like an unlit lamp or a reflector hung in a false focus. What lay behind it or within it? A dull torpor of the soul or the dullness of the thundercloud, charged with intellection and capable of the gloom of God?

– I meant a different kind of lamp, sir, said Stephen.

– Undoubtedly, said the dean.

– One difficulty, said Stephen, in esthetic discussion is to know whether words are being used according to the literary tradition or according to the tradition of the marketplace. I remember a sentence of Newman's in which he says of the Blessed Virgin that she was detained in the full company of the saints. The use of the word in the marketplace is quite different. *I hope I am not detaining you.*

– Not in the least, said the dean politely.

– No, no, said Stephen, smiling, I mean –

– Yes, yes; I see, said the dean quickly, I quite catch the point: *detain.*

He thrust forward his under jaw and uttered a dry short cough.

– To return to the lamp, he said, the feeding of it is also a nice problem. You must choose the pure oil and you must be careful when you pour it in not to overflow it, not to pour in more than the funnel can hold.

– What funnel? asked Stephen.

– The funnel through which you pour the oil into your lamp.

– That? said Stephen. Is that called a funnel? Is it not a tundish?

– What is a tundish?

– That. The . . . funnel.

– Is that called a tundish in Ireland? asked the dean. I never heard the word in my life.

– It is called a tundish in Lower Drumcondra, said Stephen, laughing, where they speak the best English.

– A tundish, said the dean reflectively. That is a most interesting word. I must look that word up. Upon my word I must.

His courtesy of manner rang a little false and Stephen looked at the English convert with the same eyes as the elder brother in the parable may have turned on the prodigal. A humble follower in the wake of clamorous-conversions, a poor Englishman in Ireland, he seemed to have entered on the stage of jesuit history when that strange play of intrigue and suffering and envy and struggle and indignity had been all but given through – a late-comer, a tardy spirit. From what had he set out? Perhaps he had been born and bred among serious dissenters, seeing salvation in Jesus only and abhorring the vain pomps of the establishment. Had he felt the need of an implicit faith amid the welter of sectarianism and the jargon of its turbulent schisms, six principle men, peculiar people, seed and snake baptists, supra-lapsarian dogmatists? Had he found the true church all of a sudden in winding up to the end like a reel of cotton some fine-spun line of reasoning upon insufflation or the imposition of hands or the procession of the Holy Ghost? Or had Lord Christ touched him and bidden him follow, like that disciple who had sat at the receipt of custom, as he sat by the door of some zinc-roofed chapel, yawning and telling over his church pence?

The dean repeated the word yet again.

– Tundish! Well now, that is interesting!

– The question you asked me a moment ago seems to me more interesting. What is that beauty which the artist struggles to express from lumps of earth, said Stephen coldly.

The little word seemed to have turned a rapier point of his sensitiveness against this courteous and vigilant foe. He felt with a smart of dejection that the man to whom he was speaking was a countryman of Ben Jonson. He thought:

– The language in which we are speaking is his before it is mine. How different are the words *home*, *Christ*, *ale*, *master*, on his lips and on mine! I cannot speak or write these words without unrest of spirit. His language, so familiar and so foreign, will always be for me an acquired speech. I have not made or accepted its words. My voice holds them at bay. My soul frets in the shadow of his language.

– And to distinguish between the beautiful and the sublime, the dean added, to distinguish between moral beauty and material beauty. And to inquire what kind of beauty is proper to each of the various arts. These are some interesting points we might take up.

Stephen, disheartened suddenly by the dean's firm, dry tone, was silent; and through the silence a distant noise of many boots and confused voices came up the staircase.

– In pursuing these speculations, said the dean conclusively, there is, however, the danger of perishing of inanition. First you must take your degree. Set that before you as your first aim. Then, little by little, you will see your way. I mean in every sense, your way in life and in thinking. It may be uphill pedalling at first. Take Mr Moonan. He was a long time before he got to the top. But he got there.

– I may not have his talent, said Stephen quietly.

– You never know, said the dean brightly. We never can say what is in us. I most certainly should not be despondent. *Per aspera ad astra.*

He left the hearth quickly and went towards the landing to oversee the arrival of the first arts' class.

Leaning against the fireplace Stephen heard him greet briskly and impartially every student of the class and could almost see the frank smiles of the coarser students. A desolating pity began to fall like dew upon his easily embittered heart for this faithful serving man of the knightly Loyola, for this half brother of the clergy, more venal than they in speech, more steadfast of soul than they, one whom he would never call his ghostly father; and he thought how this man and his companions had earned the name of worldlings at the hands not of the unworldly only but of the worldly also for having pleaded, during all their history, at the bar of God's justice for the souls of the lax and the lukewarm and the prudent.

The entry of the professor was signalled by a few rounds of Kentish fire from the heavy boots of those students who sat on the highest tier of the gloomy theatre under the grey cobwebbed windows. The calling of the roll began and the responses to the names were given out in all tones until the name of Peter Byrne was reached.

– Here!

A deep bass note in response came from the upper tier, followed by coughs of protest along the other benches.

The professor paused in his reading and called the next name:

– Cranly!

No answer.

– Mr Cranly!

A smile flew across Stephen's face as he thought of his friend's studies.

– Try Leopardstown! said a voice from the bench behind.

Stephen glanced up quickly but Moynihan's snoutish face, outlined on the grey light, was impassive. A formula was given out. Amid the rustling of the notebooks Stephen turned back again and said:

– Give me some paper for God's sake.

– Are you as bad as that? asked Moynihan with a broad grin.

He tore a sheet from his scribbler and passed it down, whispering:

– In case of necessity any layman or woman can do it.

The formula which he wrote obediently on the sheet of paper, the coiling and uncoiling calculations of the professor, the spectre-like symbols of force and velocity fascinated and jaded Stephen's mind. He had heard some say that the old professor was an atheist freemason. O the grey dull day! It seemed a limbo of painless patient consciousness through which souls of mathematicians might wander, projecting long slender fabrics from plane to plane of ever rarer and paler twilight, radiating swift eddies to the last verges of a universe ever vaster, farther and more impalpable.

– So we must distinguish between elliptical and ellipsoidal. Perhaps some of you gentlemen may be familiar with the works of Mr W. S. Gilbert. In one of his songs he speaks of the billiard sharp who is condemned to play:

> On a cloth untrue
> With a twisted cue
> And elliptical billiard balls.

– He means a ball having the form of the ellipsoid of the principal axes of which I spoke a moment ago.

Moynihan leaned down towards Stephen's ear and murmured:

– What price ellipsoidal balls! chase me, ladies, I'm in the cavalry!

His fellow student's rude humour ran like a gust through the cloister of Stephen's mind, shaking into gay life limp priestly vestments that hung upon the walls, setting them to sway and caper in a sabbath of misrule. The forms of the community emerged from the gust-blown vestments, the dean of studies, the portly florid bursar with his cap of grey hair, the president, the little priest with feather hair who wrote devout verses, the squat peasant form of the professor of economics, the tall form of the young professor of mental science discussing on the landing a case of conscience with his class like a giraffe cropping high leafage among a herd of antelopes, the grave troubled prefect of the sodality, the plump round-headed professor of Italian with his rogue's eyes. They came ambling and stumbling, tumbling and capering, kilting their gowns for leap frog, holding one another back, shaken with deep false laughter, smacking one another behind and laughing at their rude malice, calling to one another by familiar nicknames, protesting with sudden dignity at some rough usage, whispering two and two behind their hands.

The professor had gone to the glass cases on the side wall, from a shelf of which he took down a set of coils, blew away the dust from many points and, bearing it carefully to the table, held a finger on it while he proceeded with his lecture. He explained that the wires in modern coils were of a compound called platinoid lately discovered by F. W. Martino.

He spoke clearly the initials and surname of the discovered. Moynihan whispered from behind:

– Good old Fresh Water Martin!

– Ask him, Stephen whispered back with weary humour, if he wants a subject for electrocution. He can have me.

Moynihan, seeing the professor bend over the coils, rose in his bench and, clacking noiselessly the fingers of his right hand, began to call with the voice of a slobbering urchin.

– Please, teacher! This boy is after saying a bad word, teacher.

– Platinoid, the professor said solemnly, is preferred to German silver because it has a lower coefficient of resistance by changes of temperature. The platinoid wire is insulated and the covering of silk that insulates it is wound on the ebonite bobbins just where my finger is. If it were wound single an extra current would be induced in the coils. The bobbins are saturated in hot paraffin wax . . .

A sharp Ulster voice said from the bench below Stephen:

– Are we likely to be asked questions on applied science?

The professor began to juggle gravely with the terms pure science and applied science. A heavy-built student, wearing gold spectacles, stared with some wonder at the questioner. Moynihan murmured from behind in his natural voice:

– Isn't MacAlister a devil for his pound of flesh?

Stephen looked coldly on the oblong skull beneath him overgrown with tangled twine-coloured hair. The voice, the accent, the mind of the questioner offended him and he allowed the offence to carry him towards wilful unkindness, bidding his mind think that the student's father would have done better had he sent his son to Belfast to study and have saved something on the train fare by so doing.

The oblong skull beneath did not turn to meet this shaft of thought and yet the shaft came back to its bowstring; for he saw in a moment the student's whey-pale face.

– That thought is not mine, he said to himself quickly. It came from the comic Irishman in the bench behind. Patience. Can you say with certitude by whom the soul of your race was bartered and its elect betrayed – by the questioner or by the mocker? Patience. Remember Epictetus. It is probably in his character to ask such a question at such a moment in such a tone and to pronounce the word *science* as a monosyllable.

The droning voice of the professor continued to wind itself slowly round and round the coils it spoke of, doubling, trebling, quadrupling its somnolent energy as the coil multiplied its ohms of resistance.

Moynihan's voice called from behind in echo to a distant bell:

– Closing time, gents!

The entrance hall was crowded and loud with talk. On a table near the door were two photographs in frames and between them a long roll of paper bearing an irregular tail of signatures. MacCann went briskly to and fro among the students, talking rapidly, answering rebuffs and leading one after another to the table. In the inner hall the dean of studies stood talking to a young professor, stroking his chin gravely and nodding his head.

Stephen, checked by the crowd at the door, halted irresolutely. From under the wide falling leaf of a soft hat Cranly's dark eyes were watching him.

– Have you signed? Stephen asked.

Cranly closed his long thin-lipped mouth, communed with himself an instant and answered:

– *Ego habeo.*

– What is it for?

– *Quod.*

– What is it for?

Cranly turned his pale face to Stephen and said blandly and bitterly:

– *Per pax universalis.*

Stephen pointed to the Tsar's photograph and said:

– He has the face of a besotted Christ.

The scorn and anger in his voice brought Cranly's eyes back from a calm survey of the walls of the hall.

– Are you annoyed? he asked.

– No, answered Stephen.

– Are you in bad humour?

– No.

– *Credo ut vos sanguinarius mendax estis*, said Cranly, *quia facies vostra monstrat ut vos in damno malo humore estis.*

Moynihan, on his way to the table, said in Stephen's ear:

– MacCann is in tiptop form. Ready to shed the last drop. Brand new world. No stimulants and votes for the bitches.

Stephen smiled at the manner of this confidence and, when Moynihan had passed, turned again to meet Cranly's eyes.

– Perhaps you can tell me, he said, why he pours his soul so freely into my ear. Can you?

A dull scowl appeared on Cranly's forehead. He stared at the table where Moynihan had bent to write his name on the roll, and then said flatly:

– A sugar!

– *Quis est in malo humore*, said Stephen, *ego aut vos?*

Cranly did not take up the taunt. He brooded sourly on his judgment and repeated with the same flat force:

– A flaming bloody sugar, that's what he is!

It was his epitaph for all dead friendships and Stephen wondered whether it would ever be spoken in the same tone over his memory. The heavy lumpish phrase sank slowly out of hearing like a stone through a quagmire. Stephen saw it sink as he had seen many another, feeling its heaviness depress his heart. Cranly's speech, unlike that of Davin, had neither rare phrases of Elizabethan English nor quaintly turned versions of Irish idioms. Its drawl was an echo of the quays of Dublin given back by a bleak decaying seaport, its energy an echo of the sacred eloquence of Dublin given back flatly by a Wicklow pulpit.

The heavy scowl faded from Cranly's face as MacCann marched briskly towards them from the other side of the hall.

– Here you are! said MacCann cheerily.

– Here I am! said Stephen.

– Late as usual. Can you not combine the progressive tendency with a respect for punctuality?

– That question is out of order, said Stephen. Next business.

His smiling eyes were fixed on a silver-wrapped tablet of milk chocolate which peeped out of the propagandist's breastpocket. A little ring of listeners closed round to hear the war of wits. A lean student with olive skin and lank black hair thrust his face between the two, glancing from one to the other at each phrase and seeming to try to catch each flying phrase in his open moist mouth. Cranly took a small grey handball from his pocket and began to examine it closely, turning it over and over.

– Next business? said MacCann. Hom!

He gave a loud cough of laughter, smiled broadly and tugged twice at the straw-coloured goatee which hung from his blunt chin.

– The next business is to sign the testimonial.

– Will you pay me anything if I sign? asked Stephen.

– I thought you were an idealist, said MacCann.

The gipsy-like student looked about him and addressed the onlookers in an indistinct bleating voice.

– By hell, that's a queer notion. I consider that notion to be a mercenary notion.

His voice faded into silence. No heed was paid to his words. He turned his olive face, equine in expression, towards Stephen, inviting him to speak again.

MacCann began to speak with fluent energy of the Tsar's rescript, of Stead, of general disarmament arbitration in cases of international disputes, of the signs of the times, of the new humanity and the new gospel of life which would make it the business of the community to secure as cheaply as possible the greatest possible happiness of the greatest possible number.

The gipsy student responded to the close of the period by crying:

– Three cheers for universal brotherhood!

– Go on, Temple, said a stout ruddy student near him. I'll stand you a pint after.

– I'm a believer in universal brotherhood, said Temple, glancing about him out of his dark oval eyes. Marx is only a bloody cod.

Cranly gripped his arm tightly to check his tongue, smiling uneasily, and repeated:

– Easy, easy, easy!

Temple struggled to free his arm but continued, his mouth flecked by a thin foam:

– Socialism was founded by an Irishman and the first man in Europe who preached the freedom of thought was Collins. Two hundred years ago. He denounced priestcraft, the philosopher of Middlesex. Three cheers for John Anthony Collins!

A thin voice from the verge of the ring replied:

– Pip! pip!

Moynihan murmured beside Stephen's ear:

– And what about John Anthony's poor little sister:

> Lottie Collins lost her drawers;
> Won't you kindly lend her yours?

Stephen laughed and Moynihan, pleased with the result, murmured again:

– We'll have five bob each way on John Anthony Collins.

– I am waiting for your answer, said MacCann briefly.

– The affair doesn't interest me in the least, said Stephen wearily. You know that well. Why do you make a scene about it?

– Good! said MacCann, smacking his lips. You are a reactionary, then?

– Do you think you impress me, Stephen asked, when you flourish your wooden sword?

– Metaphors! said MacCann bluntly. Come to facts.

Stephen blushed and turned aside. MacCann stood his ground and said with hostile humour:

– Minor poets, I suppose, are above such trivial questions as the question of universal peace.

Cranly raised his head and held the handball between the two students by way of a peace-offering, saying:

– *Pax super totum sanguinarium globum.*

Stephen, moving away the bystanders, jerked his shoulder angrily in the direction of the Tsar's image, saying:

– Keep your icon. If we must have a Jesus let us have a legitimate Jesus.

– By hell, that's a good one! said the gipsy student to those about him, that's a fine expression. I like that expression immensely.

He gulped down the spittle in his throat as if he were gulping down the phrase and, fumbling at the peak of his tweed cap, turned to Stephen, saying:

– Excuse me, sir, what do you mean by that expression you uttered just now?

Feeling himself jostled by the students near him, he said to them:

– I am curious to know now what he meant by that expression.

He turned again to Stephen and said in a whisper:

– Do you believe in Jesus? I believe in man. Of course, I don't know if you believe in man. I admire you, sir. I admire the mind of man independent of all religions. Is that your opinion about the mind of Jesus?

– Go on, Temple, said the stout ruddy student, returning, as was his wont, to his first idea, that pint is waiting for you.

– He thinks I'm an imbecile, Temple explained to Stephen, because I'm a believer in the power of mind.

Cranly linked his arms into those of Stephen and his admirer and said:

– *Nos ad manum ballum jocabimus.*

Stephen, in the act of being led away, caught sight of MacCann's flushed blunt-featured face.

– My signature is of no account, he said politely. You are right to go your way. Leave me to go mine.

– Dedalus, said MacCann crisply, I believe you're a good fellow but you have yet to learn the dignity of altruism and the responsibility of the human individual.

A voice said:

– Intellectual crankery is better out of this movement than in it.

Stephen, recognising the harsh tone of MacAlister's voice, did not turn in the direction of the voice. Cranly pushed solemnly through the throng of students, linking Stephen and Temple like a celebrant attended by his ministers on his way to the altar.

Temple bent eagerly across Cranly's breast and said:

– Did you hear MacAlister what he said? That youth is jealous of you. Did you see that? I bet Cranly didn't see that. By hell, I saw that at once.

As they crossed the inner hall, the dean of studies was in the act of escaping from the student with whom he had been conversing. He stood at the foot of the staircase, a foot on the lowest step, his threadbare soutane gathered about him for the ascent with womanish care, nodding his head often and repeating:

– Not a doubt of it, Mr Hackett! Very fine! Not a doubt of it!

In the middle of the hall the prefect of the college sodality was speaking earnestly, in a soft querulous voice, with a boarder. As he spoke he wrinkled a little his freckled brow and bit, between his phrases, at a tiny bone pencil.

– I hope the matric men will all come. The first arts' men are pretty sure. Second arts, too. We must make sure of the newcomers.

Temple bent again across Cranly, as they were passing through the doorway, and said in a swift whisper:

– Do you know that he is a married man? He was a married man before they converted him. He has a wife and children somewhere. By hell, I think that's the queerest notion I ever heard! Eh!

His whisper trailed off into sly cackling laughter. The moment they were through the doorway Cranly seized him rudely by the neck and shook him, saying:

– You flaming floundering fool! I'll take my dying bible there isn't a bigger bloody ape, do you know, than you in the whole flaming bloody world!

Temple wriggled in his grip, laughing still with sly content, while Cranly repeated flatly at every rude shake:

– A flaming flaring bloody idiot!

They crossed the weedy garden together. The president, wrapped in a heavy loose cloak, was coming towards them along one of the walks, reading his office. At the end of the walk he halted before turning and raised his eyes. The students saluted, Temple fumbling as before at the peak of his cap. They walked forward in silence. As they neared the alley Stephen could hear the thuds of the players' hands and the wet smacks of the ball and Davin's voice crying out excitedly at each stroke.

The three students halted round the box on which Davin sat to follow the game. Temple, after a few moments, sidled across to Stephen and said:

– Excuse me, I wanted to ask you, do you believe that Jean-Jacques Rousseau was a sincere man?

Stephen laughed outright. Cranly, picking up the broken stave of a cask from the grass at his feet, turned swiftly and said sternly:

– Temple, I declare to the living God if you say another word, do you know, to anybody on any subject, I'll kill you *super spottum*.

– He was like you, I fancy, said Stephen, an emotional man.

– Blast him, curse him! said Cranly broadly. Don't talk to him at all. Sure, you might as well be talking, do you know, to a flaming chamber-pot as talking to Temple. Go home, Temple. For God's sake, go home.

– I don't care a damn about you, Cranly, answered Temple, moving out of reach of the uplifted stave and pointing at Stephen. He's the only man I see in this institution that has an individual mind.

– Institution! Individual! cried Cranly. Go home, blast you, for you're a hopeless bloody man.

– I'm an emotional man, said Temple. That's quite rightly expressed. And I'm proud that I'm an emotionalist.

He sidled out of the alley, smiling slyly. Cranly watched him with a blank expressionless face.

– Look at him! he said. Did you ever see such a go-by-the-wall? His phrase was greeted by a strange laugh from a student who lounged against the wall, his peaked cap down on his eyes. The laugh, pitched in a high key and coming from a so muscular frame, seemed like the whinny of an elephant. The student's body shook all over and, to ease his mirth, he rubbed both his hands delightedly over his groins.

– Lynch is awake, said Cranly.

Lynch, for answer, straightened himself and thrust forward his chest.

– Lynch puts out his chest, said Stephen, as a criticism of life.

Lynch smote himself sonorously on the chest and said:

– Who has anything to say about my girth?

Cranly took him at the word and the two began to tussle. When their faces had flushed with the struggle they drew apart, panting. Stephen bent down towards Davin who, intent on the game, had paid no heed to the talk of the others.

– And how is my little tame goose? he asked. Did he sign, too?

Davin nodded and said:

– And you, Stevie?

Stephen shook his head.

– You're a terrible man, Stevie, said Davin, taking the short pipe from his mouth, always alone.

– Now that you have signed the petition for universal peace, said Stephen, I suppose you will burn that little copybook I saw in your room.

As Davin did not answer, Stephen began to quote:

– Long pace, fianna! Right incline, fianna! Fianna, by numbers, salute, one, two!

– That's a different question, said Davin. I'm an Irish nationalist, first and foremost. But that's you all out. You're a born sneerer, Stevie.

– When you make the next rebellion with hurleysticks, said Stephen, and want the indispensable informer, tell me. I can find you a few in this college.

– I can't understand you, said Davin. One time I hear you talk against English literature. Now you talk against the Irish informers. What with your name and your ideas – Are you Irish at all?

– Come with me now to the office of arms and I will show you the tree of my family, said Stephen.

– Then be one of us, said Davin. Why don't you learn Irish? Why did you drop out of the league class after the first lesson?

– You know one reason why, answered Stephen.

Davin tossed his head and laughed.

– Oh, come now, he said. Is it on account of that certain young lady and Father Moran? But that's all in your own mind, Stevie. They were only talking and laughing.

Stephen paused and laid a friendly hand upon Davin's shoulder.

– Do you remember, he said, when we knew each other first? The first morning we met you asked me to show you the way to the matriculation class, putting a very strong stress on the first syllable. You remember? Then you used to address the jesuits as father, you remember? I ask myself about you: *Is he as innocent as his speech?*

– I'm a simple person, said Davin. You know that. When you told me that night in Harcourt Street those things about your private life, honest to God, Stevie, I was not able to eat my dinner. I was quite bad. I was awake a long time that night. Why did you tell me those things?

– Thanks, said Stephen. You mean I am a monster.

– No, said Davin. But I wish you had not told me.

A tide began to surge beneath the calm surface of Stephen's friendliness.

– This race and this country and this life produced me, he said. I shall express myself as I am.

– Try to be one of us, repeated Davin. In heart you are an Irishman but your pride is too powerful.

– My ancestors threw off their language and took another, Stephen said. They allowed a handful of foreigners to subject them. Do you fancy I am going to pay in my own life and person debts they made? What for?

– For our freedom, said Davin.

– No honourable and sincere man, said Stephen, has given up to you his life and his youth and his affections from the days of Tone to those of Parnell, but you sold him to the enemy or failed him in need or reviled him and left him for another. And you invite me to be one of you. I'd see you damned first.

– They died for their ideals, Stevie, said Davin. Our day will come yet, believe me.

Stephen, following his own thought, was silent for an instant.

– The soul is born, he said vaguely, first in those moments I told you of. It has a slow and dark birth, more mysterious than the birth of the body. When the soul of a man is born in this country there are nets flung at it to hold it back from flight. You talk to me of nationality, language, religion. I shall try to fly by those nets.

Davin knocked the ashes from his pipe.

– Too deep for me, Stevie, he said. But a man's country comes first. Ireland first, Stevie. You can be a poet or a mystic after.

– Do you know what Ireland is? asked Stephen with cold violence. Ireland is the old sow that eats her farrow.

Davin rose from his box and went towards the players, shaking his head sadly. But in a moment his sadness left him and he was hotly disputing with Cranly and the two players who had finished their game. A match of four was arranged, Cranly insisting, however, that his ball should be used. He let it rebound twice or thrice to his hand and struck it strongly and swiftly towards the base of the alley, exclaiming in answer to its thud:

– Your soul!

Stephen stood with Lynch till the score began to rise. Then he plucked him by the sleeve to come away. Lynch obeyed, saying:

– Let us eke go, as Cranly has it.

Stephen smiled at this side-thrust.

They passed back through the garden and out through the hall where the doddering porter was pinning up a hall notice in the frame. At the foot of the steps they halted and Stephen took a packet of cigarettes from his pocket and offered it to his companion.

– I know you are poor, he said.

– Damn your yellow insolence, answered Lynch.

This second proof of Lynch's culture made Stephen smile again.

– It was a great day for European culture, he said, when you made up your mind to swear in yellow.

They lit their cigarettes and turned to the right. After a pause Stephen began:

– Aristotle has not defined pity and terror. I have. I say –

Lynch halted and said bluntly:

– Stop! I won't listen! I am sick. I was out last night on a yellow drunk with Horan and Goggins.

Stephen went on:

– Pity is the feeling which arrests the mind in the presence of whatsoever is grave and constant in human sufferings and unites it with the human sufferer. Terror is the feeling which arrests the mind in the presence of whatsoever is grave and constant in human sufferings and unites it with the secret cause.

– Repeat, said Lynch.

Stephen repeated the definitions slowly.

– A girl got into a hansom a few days ago, he went on, in London. She was on her way to meet her mother whom she had not seen for many years. At the corner of a street the shaft of a lorry shivered the window of the hansom in the shape of a star. A long fine needle of the shivered glass pierced her heart. She died on the instant. The reporter called it a tragic death. It is not. It is remote from terror and pity according to the terms of my definitions.

– The tragic emotion, in fact, is a face looking two ways, towards terror and towards pity, both of which are phases of it. You see I use the word *arrest*. I mean that the tragic emotion is static. Or rather the dramatic emotion is. The feelings excited by improper art are kinetic, desire or loathing. Desire urges us to possess, to go to something; loathing urges us to abandon, to go from something. The arts which excite them, pornographical or didactic, are therefore improper arts. The esthetic emotion (I used the general term) is therefore static. The mind is arrested and raised above desire and loathing.

– You say that art must not excite desire, said Lynch. I told you that one day I wrote my name in pencil on the backside of the Venus of Praxiteles in the Museum. Was that not desire?

– I speak of normal natures, said Stephen. You also told me that when you were a boy in that charming carmelite school you ate pieces of dried cowdung.

Lynch broke again into a whinny of laughter and again rubbed both his hands over his groins but without taking them from his pockets.

– O, I did! I did! he cried.

Stephen turned towards his companion and looked at him for a moment boldly in the eyes. Lynch, recovering from his laughter, answered his look from his humbled eyes. The long slender flattened skull beneath the long pointed cap brought before Stephen's mind the image of a hooded reptile. The eyes, too, were reptile-like in glint and gaze. Yet at that instant, humbled and alert in their look, they were lit by one tiny human point, the window of a shrivelled soul, poignant and self-embittered.

– As for that, Stephen said in polite parenthesis, we are all animals. I also am an animal.

– You are, said Lynch.

– But we are just now in a mental world, Stephen continued. The desire and loathing excited by improper esthetic means are really not esthetic emotions not only because they are kinetic in character but also because they are not more than physical. Our flesh shrinks from what it dreads and responds to the stimulus of what it desires by a purely reflex action of the nervous system. Our eyelid closes before we are aware that the fly is about to enter our eye.

– Not always, said Lynch critically.

– In the same way, said Stephen, your flesh responded to the stimulus of a naked statue, but it was, I say, simply a reflex action of the nerves. Beauty expressed by the artist cannot awaken in us an emotion which is kinetic or a sensation which is purely physical. It awakens, or ought to awaken, or induces, or ought to induce, an esthetic stasis, an ideal pity or an ideal terror, a stasis called forth, prolonged, and at last dissolved by what I call the rhythm of beauty.

– What is that exactly? asked Lynch.

– Rhythm, said Stephen, is the first formal esthetic relation of part to part in any esthetic whole or of an esthetic whole to its part or parts or of any part to the esthetic whole of which it is a part.

– If that is rhythm, said Lynch, let me hear what you call beauty; and, please remember, though I did eat a cake of cowdung once, that I admire only beauty.

Stephen raised his cap as if in greeting. Then, blushing slightly, he laid his hand on Lynch's thick tweed sleeve.

– We are right, he said, and the others are wrong. To speak of these things and to try to understand their nature and, having understood it, to try slowly and humbly and constantly to express, to press out again, from the gross earth or what it brings forth, from sound and shape and colour which are the prison gates of our soul, an image of the beauty we have come to understand – that is art.

They had reached the canal bridge and, turning from their course, went on by the trees. A crude grey light, mirrored in the sluggish water and a smell of wet branches over their head seemed to war against the course of Stephen's thought.

– But you have not answered my question, said Lynch. What is art? What is the beauty it expresses?

– That was the first definition I gave you, you sleepy-headed wretch, said Stephen, when I began to try to think out the matter for myself. Do you remember the night? Cranly lost his temper and began to talk about Wicklow bacon.

– I remember, said Lynch. He told us about them flaming fat devils of pigs.

– Art, said Stephen, is the human disposition of sensible or intelligible matter for an esthetic end. You remember the pigs and forget that. You are a distressing pair, you and Cranly.

Lynch made a grimace at the raw grey sky and said:

– If I am to listen to your esthetic philosophy give me at least another cigarette. I don't care about it. I don't even care about women. Damn you and damn everything. I want a job of five hundred a year. You can't get me one.

Stephen handed him the packet of cigarettes. Lynch took the last one that remained, saying simply:

– Proceed!

– Aquinas, said Stephen, says that is beautiful the apprehension or which pleases.

Lynch nodded.

– I remember that, he said, *Pulcra sunt quae visa placent.*

– He uses the word *visa*, said Stephen, to cover esthetic apprehensions of all kinds, whether through sight or hearing or through any other avenue of apprehension. This word, though it is vague, is clear enough to keep away good and evil which excite desire and loathing. It means certainly a stasis and not a kinesis. How about the true? It produces also a stasis of the mind.

You would not write your name in pencil across the hypotenuse of a right-angled triangle.

– No, said Lynch, give me the hypotenuse of the Venus of Praxiteles.

– Static therefore, said Stephen. Plato, I believe, said that beauty is the splendour of truth. I don't think that it has a meaning, but the true and the beautiful are akin. Truth is beheld by the intellect which is appeased by the most satisfying relations of the intelligible; beauty is beheld by the imagination which is appeased by the most satisfying relations of the sensible. The first step in the direction of truth is to understand the frame and scope of the intellect itself, to comprehend the act itself of intellection. Aristotle's entire system of philosophy rests upon his book of psychology and that, I think, rests on his statement that the same attribute cannot at the same time and in the same connexion belong to and not belong to the same subject. The first step in the direction of beauty is to understand the frame and scope of the imagination, to comprehend the act itself of esthetic apprehension. Is that clear?

– But what is beauty? asked Lynch impatiently. Out with an other definition. Something we see and like! Is that the best you and Aquinas can do?

– Let us take woman, said Stephen.

– Let us take her! said Lynch fervently.

– The Greek, the Turk, the Chinese, the Copt, the Hottentot, said Stephen, all admire a different type of female beauty. That seems to be a maze out of which we cannot escape. I see, however, two ways out. One is this hypothesis: that every physical quality admired by men in women is in direct connexion with the manifold functions of women for the propagation of the species. It may be so. The world, it seems, is drearier than even you, Lynch, imagined. For my part I dislike that way out. It leads to eugenics rather than to esthetic. It leads you out of the maze into a new gaudy lecture-room where MacCann, with one hand on *The Origin of Species* and the other hand on the new testament, tells you that you admired the great flanks of Venus because you felt that she would bear you burly offspring and admired her great breasts because you felt that she would give good milk to her children and yours.

– Then MacCann is a sulphur-yellow liar, said Lynch energetically.

– There remains another way out, said Stephen, laughing.

– To wit? said Lynch.

– This hypothesis, Stephen began.

A long dray laden with old iron came round the corner of Sir Patrick Dun's hospital covering the end of Stephen's speech with the harsh roar of jangled and rattling metal. Lynch closed his ears and gave out oath after oath till the dray had passed. Then he turned on his heel rudely. Stephen turned also and waited for a few moments till his companion's ill-humour had had its vent.

– This hypothesis, Stephen repeated, is the other way out: that, though the same object may not seem beautiful to all people, all people who admire a beautiful object find in it certain relations which satisfy and coincide with the stages themselves of all esthetic apprehension. These relations of the sensible, visible to you through one form and to me through another, must be therefore the necessary qualities of beauty. Now, we can return to our old friend saint Thomas for another pennyworth of wisdom.

Lynch laughed.

– It amuses me vastly, he said, to hear you quoting him time after time like a jolly round friar. Are you laughing in your sleeve?

– MacAlister, answered Stephen, would call my esthetic theory applied Aquinas. So far as this side of esthetic philosophy extends, Aquinas will carry me all along the line. When we come to the phenomena of artistic conception, artistic gestation, and artistic reproduction I require a new terminology and a new personal experience.

– Of course, said Lynch. After all Aquinas, in spite of his intellect, was exactly a good round friar. But you will tell me about the new personal experience and new terminology some other day. Hurry up and finish the first part.

– Who knows? said Stephen, smiling. Perhaps Aquinas would understand me better than you. He was a poet himself. He wrote a hymn for Maundy Thursday. It begins with the words *Pange lingua gloriosi*. They say it is the highest glory of the hymnal. It is an intricate and soothing hymn. I like it; but there is no hymn that can be put beside that mournful and majestic processional song, the *Vexilla Regis* of Venantius Fortunatus.

Lynch began to sing softly and solemnly in a deep bass voice:

> *Impleta sunt quae concinit*
> *David fideli carmine*
> *Dicendo nationibus*
> *Regnavit a ligno Deus.*

– That's great! he said, well pleased. Great music!

They turned into Lower Mount Street. A few steps from the corner a fat young man, wearing a silk neckcloth, saluted them and stopped.

– Did you hear the results of the exams? he asked. Griffin was plucked. Halpin and O'Flynn are through the home civil. Moonan got fifth place in the Indian. O'Shaughnessy got fourteenth. The Irish fellows in Clark's gave them a feed last night. They all ate curry.

His pallid bloated face expressed benevolent malice and, as he had advanced through his tidings of success, his small fat-encircled eyes vanished out of sight and his weak wheezing voice out of hearing.

In reply to a question of Stephen's his eyes and his voice came forth again from their lurking-places.

– Yes, MacCullagh and I, he said. He's taking pure mathematics and I'm taking constitutional history. There are twenty subjects. I'm taking botany too. You know I'm a member of the field club.

He drew back from the other two in a stately fashion and placed a plump woollen-gloved hand on his breast from which muttered wheezing laughter at once broke forth.

– Bring us a few turnips and onions the next time you go out, said Stephen drily, to make a stew.

The fat student laughed indulgently and said:

– We are all highly respectable people in the field club. Last Saturday we went out to Glenmalure, seven of us.

– With women, Donovan? said Lynch.

Donovan again laid his hand on his chest and said:

– Our end is the acquisition of knowledge.

Then he said quickly:

– I hear you are writing some essays about esthetics.

Stephen made a vague gesture of denial.

– Goethe and Lessing, said Donovan, have written a lot on that subject, the classical school and the romantic school and all that. The Laocoon interested me very much when I read it. Of course it is idealistic, German, ultra-profound.

Neither of the others spoke. Donovan took leave of them urbanely.

– I must go, he said softly and benevolently, I have a strong suspicion, amounting almost to a conviction, that my sister intended to make pancakes today for the dinner of the Donovan family.

– Goodbye, Stephen said in his wake. Don't forget the turnips for me and my mate.

Lynch gazed after him, his lip curling in slow scorn till his face resembled a devil's mask:

– To think that that yellow pancake-eating excrement can get a good job, he said at length, and I have to smoke cheap cigarettes!

They turned their faces towards Merrion Square and went for a little in silence.

– To finish what I was saying about beauty, said Stephen, the most satisfying relations of the sensible must therefore correspond to the necessary phases of artistic apprehension. Find these and you find the qualities of universal beauty. Aquinas says: *Ad pulcritudinem tria requiruntur integritas, consonantia, claritas.* I translate it so: *Three things are needed for beauty, wholeness, harmony, and radiance.* Do these correspond to the phases of apprehension? Are you following?

– Of course, I am, said Lynch. If you think I have an excrementitious intelligence run after Donovan and ask him to listen to you.

Stephen pointed to a basket which a butcher's boy had slung inverted on his head.

– Look at that basket, he said.

– I see it, said Lynch.

– In order to see that basket, said Stephen, your mind first of all separates the basket from the rest of the visible universe which is not the basket. The first phase of apprehension is a bounding line drawn about the object to be apprehended. An esthetic image is presented to us either in space or in time. What is audible is presented in time, what is visible is presented in space. But, temporal or spatial, the esthetic image is first luminously apprehended as selfbounded and selfcontained upon the immeasurable background of space or time which is not it. You apprehended it as *one* thing. You see it as one whole. You apprehend its wholeness. That is *integritas.*

– Bull's eye! said Lynch, laughing. Go on.

– Then, said Stephen, you pass from point to point, led by its formal lines; you apprehend it as balanced part against part within its limits; you feel the rhythm of its structure. In other words, the synthesis of immediate perception is followed by the analysis of apprehension. Having first felt that it is *one* thing you feel now that it is a *thing.* You apprehend it as complex, multiple, divisible, separable, made up of its parts, the result of its parts and their sum, harmonious. That is *consonantia.*

– Bull's eye again! said Lynch wittily. Tell me now what is *claritas* and you win the cigar.

– The connotation of the word, Stephen said, is rather vague. Aquinas uses a term which seems to be inexact. It baffled me for a long time. It would lead you to believe that he had in mind symbolism or idealism, the supreme quality of beauty being a light from some other world, the idea of which the matter is but the shadow, the reality of which it is but the symbol. I thought he might mean that *claritas* is the artistic discovery and representation of the divine purpose in anything or a force of generalisation which would make the esthetic image a universal one, make it outshine its proper conditions. But that is literary talk. I understand it so. When you have apprehended that basket as one thing and have then analysed it according to its form and apprehended it as a thing you make the only synthesis which is logically and esthetically permissible. You see that it is that thing which it is and no other thing. The radiance of which he speaks in the scholastic *quidditas*, the *whatness* of a thing. This supreme quality is felt by the artist when the esthetic image is first conceived in his imagination. The mind in that mysterious instant Shelley likened beautifully to a fading coal. The instant wherein that supreme quality of beauty, the dear radiance of the esthetic image, is apprehended luminously by the mind which has been arrested by its wholeness and fascinated by its harmony in the luminous silent stasis of esthetic pleasure, a spiritual state very like to that cardiac condition which the Italian physiologist Luigi Galvani, using a phrase almost as beautiful as Shelley's, called the enchantment of the heart.

Stephen paused and, though his companion did not speak, felt that his words had called up around them a thought-enchanted silence.

– What I have said, he began again, refers to beauty in the wider sense of the word, in the sense which the word has in the literary tradition. In the marketplace it has another sense. When we speak of beauty in the second sense of the term our judgment is influenced in the first place by the art itself and by the form of that art. The image, it is clear, must be set between the mind or senses of the artist himself and the mind or senses of others. If you bear this in memory you will see that art necessarily divides itself into three forms progressing from one to the next. These forms are: the lyrical form, the form wherein the artist presents his image in immediate relation to himself; the epical form, the form wherein he presents his image in mediate relation to himself and to others; the dramatic form, the form wherein he presents his image in immediate relation to others.

– That you told me a few nights ago, said Lynch, and we began the famous discussion.

– I have a book at home, said Stephen, in which I have written down questions which are more amusing than yours were. In finding the answers to them I found the theory of esthetic which I am trying to explain. Here are some questions I set myself: *Is a chair finely made tragic or comic? Is the portrait of Mona Lisa good if I desire to see it? Is the bust of Sir Philip Crampton lyrical, epical or dramatic? If not, why not?*

– Why not, indeed? said Lynch, laughing.

– *If a man hacking in fury at a block of wood, Stephen continued, make there an image of a cow, is that image a work of art? If not why not?*

– That's a lovely one, said Lynch, laughing again. That has the true scholastic stink.

– Lessing, said Stephen, should not have taken a group of statues to write of. The art, being inferior, does not present the forms I spoke of distinguished clearly one from another. Even in literature, the highest and most spiritual art, the forms are often confused. The lyrical form is in fact the simplest verbal vesture of an instant of emotion, a rhythmical cry such as ages ago cheered on the man who pulled at the oar or dragged stones up a slope. He who utters it is more conscious of the instant of emotion than of himself as feeling emotion. The simplest epical form is seen emerging out of lyrical literature when the artist prolongs and broods upon himself as the centre of an epical event and this form progresses till the centre of emotional gravity is equidistant from the artist himself and from others. The narrative is no longer purely personal. The personality of the artist passes into the narration itself, flowing round and round the persons and the action like a vital sea. This progress you will see easily in that old English ballad *Turpin Hero* which begins in the first person and ends in the third person. The dramatic form is reached when the vitality which has flowed and eddied round each person fills every person with such vital force that he or she assumes a proper and intangible esthetic life. The personality of the artist, at first a cry or a cadence or a mood and then a fluid and lambent narrative, finally refines itself out of existence, impersonalizes itself, so to speak. The esthetic image in the dramatic form is life purified in and reprojected from the human imagination. The mystery of esthetic, like that of material creation, is accomplished. The artist, like the God of creation, remains within or behind or beyond or above his handiwork, invisible, refined out of existence, indifferent, paring his fingernails.

– Trying to refine them also out of existence, said Lynch.

A fine rain began to fall from the high veiled sky and they turned into the duke's lawn to reach the national library before the shower came.

– What do you mean, Lynch asked surlily, by prating about beauty and the imagination in this miserable Godforsaken island? No wonder the artist retired within or behind his handiwork after having perpetrated this country.

The rain fell faster. When they passed through the passage beside the royal irish academy they found many students sheltering under the arcade of the library. Cranly, leaning against a pillar, was picking his teeth with a sharpened match, listening to some companions. Some girls stood near the entrance door. Lynch whispered to Stephen:

– Your beloved is here.

Stephen took his place silently on the step below the group of students, heedless of the rain which fell fast, turning his eyes towards her from time to time. She too stood silently among her companions. She has no priest to flirt with, he thought with conscious bitterness, remembering how he had seen her last. Lynch was right. His mind, emptied of theory and courage, lapsed back into a listless peace.

He heard the students talking among themselves. They spoke of two friends who had passed the final medical examination, of the chances of getting places on ocean liners, of poor and rich practices.

– That's all a bubble. An Irish country practice is better.

– Hynes was two years in Liverpool and he says the same. A frightful hole he said it was. Nothing but midwifery cases.

– Do you mean to say it is better to have a job here in the country than in a rich city like that? I know a fellow . . .

– Hynes has no brains. He got through by stewing, pure stewing.

– Don't mind him. There's plenty of money to be made in a big commercial city.

– Depends on the practice.

– *Ego credo ut vita pauperum est simpliciter atrox, simpliciter sanguinarius atrox, in Liverpoolio.*

Their voices reached his ears as if from a distance in interrupted pulsation. She was preparing to go away with her companions.

The quick light shower had drawn off, tarrying in clusters of diamonds among the shrubs of the quadrangle where an exhalation was breathed forth by the blackened earth. Their trim boots prattled as they stood on the steps of the colonnade, talking quietly and gaily, glancing at the clouds, holding their unbrellas at cunning angles against the few last raindrops, closing them again, holding their skirts demurely.

And if he had judged her harshly? If her life were a simple rosary of hours, her life simple and strange as a bird's life, gay in the morning, restless all day, tired at sundown? Her heart simple and wilful as a bird's heart?

Towards dawn he awoke. O what sweet music! His soul was all dewy wet. Over his limbs in sleep pale cool waves of light had passed. He lay still, as if his soul lay amid cool waters, conscious of faint sweet music. His mind was waking slowly to a tremulous morning knowledge, a morning inspiration. A spirit filled him, pure as the purest water, sweet as dew, moving as music. But how faintly it was inbreathed, how passionlessly, as if the seraphim themselves were breathing upon him! His soul was waking slowly, fearing to awake wholly. It was that windless hour of dawn when madness wakes and strange plants open to the light and the moth flies forth silently.

An enchantment of the heart! The night had been enchanted. In a dream or vision he had known the ecstasy of seraphic life. Was it an instant of enchantment only or long hours and years and ages?

The instant of inspiration seemed now to be reflected from all sides at once from a multitude of cloudy circumstances of what had happened or of what might have happened. The instant flashed forth like a point of light and now from cloud on cloud of vague circumstance confused form was veiling softly in afterglow. O! In the virgin womb of the imagination the word was made flesh. Gabriel the seraph had come to the virgin's chamber. An afterglow deepened within his spirit, whence the white flame had passed, deepening to a rose and ardent light. That rose and ardent light was her strange wilful heart, strange that no man had known or would know, wilful from before the beginning of the world; and lured by that ardent rose-like glow the choirs of the seraphim were falling from heaven.

> Are you not weary of ardent ways,
> Lure of the fallen seraphim?
> Tell no more of enchanted days.

The verses passed from his mind to his lips and, murmuring them over, he felt the rhythmic movement of a villanelle pass through them. The rose-like glow sent forth its rays of rhyme; ways, days, blaze, praise, raise. Its rays burned up the world, consumed the hearts of men and angels: the rays from the rose that was her wilful heart.

> Your eyes have set man's heart ablaze
> And you have had your will of him.
> Are you not weary of ardent ways?

And then? The rhythm died away, ceased, began again to move and beat. And then? Smoke, incense ascending from the altar of the world.

> Above the flame the smoke of praise
> Goes up from ocean rim to rim
> Tell no more of enchanted days.

Smoke went up from the whole earth, from the vapoury oceans, smoke of her praise. The earth was like a swinging swaying censer, a ball of incense, an ellipsoidal ball. The rhythm died out at once; the cry of his heart was broken. His lip began to murmur the first verses over and over; then went on stumbling through half verses, stammering and baffled; then stopped. The heart's cry was broken.

The veiled windless hour had passed and behind the panes of the naked window the morning light was gathering. A bell beat faintly very far away. A bird twittered; two birds, three. The bell and the bird ceased; and the dull white light spread itself east and west, covering the world, covering the roselight in his heart.

Fearing to lose all, he raised himself suddenly on his elbow to look for paper and pencil. There was neither on the table; only the soup plate he had eaten the rice from for supper and the candlestick with its tendrils of tallow and its paper socket, singed by the last flame. He stretched his arm wearily towards the foot of the bed, groping with his hand in the pockets of the coat that hung there. His fingers found a pencil and then a cigarette packet. He lay back and, tearing open the packet, placed the last cigarette on the window ledge and began to write out the stanzas of the villanelle in small neat letters on the rough cardboard surface.

Having written them out he lay back on the lumpy pillow, murmuring them again. The lumps of knotted flock under his head reminded him of the lumps of knotted horsehair in the sofa of her parlour on which he used to sit, smiling or serious, asking himself why he had come, displeased with her and with himself, confounded by the print of the Sacred Heart above the untenanted sideboard. He saw her approach him in a lull of the talk and beg him to sing one of his curious songs. Then he saw himself sitting at the old piano, striking chords softly from its speckled keys and singing, amid the talk which had risen again in the room, to her who leaned beside the mantelpiece a dainty song of the Elizabethans, a sad and sweet loth to depart, the victory chant of Agincourt, the happy air of Greensleeves. While he sang and she listened, or feigned to listen, his heart was at rest but when the quaint old songs had ended and he heard again the voices in the room he remembered his own sarcasm: the house where young men are called by their christian names a little too soon.

At certain instants her eyes seemed about to trust him but he had waited in vain. She passed now dancing lightly across his memory as she had been that night at the carnival ball, her white dress a little lifted, a white spray nodding in her hair. She danced lightly in the round. She was dancing towards him and, as she came, her eyes were a little averted and a faint glow was on her cheek. At the pause in the chain of hands her hand had lain in his an instant, a soft merchandise.

– You are a great stranger now.

– Yes. I was born to be a monk.

– I am afraid you are a heretic.

– Are you much afraid?

For answer she had danced away from him along the chain of hands, dancing lightly and discreetly, giving herself to none. The white spray nodded to her dancing and when she was in shadow the glow was deeper on her cheek.

A monk! His own image started forth a profaner of the cloister, a heretic franciscan, willing and willing not to serve, spinning like Gherardino da Borgo San Donnino, a lithe web of sophistry and whispering in her ear.

No, it was not his image. It was like the image of the young priest in whose company he had seen her last, looking at him out of dove's eyes, toying with the pages of her Irish phrasebook.

– Yes, yes, the ladies are coming round to us. I can see it every day. The ladies are with us. The best helpers the language has.

– And the church, Father Moran?

– The church too. Coming round too. The work is going ahead there too. Don't fret about the church.

Bah! he had done well to leave the room in disdain. He had done well not to salute her on the steps of the library! He had done well to leave her to flirt with her priest, to toy with a church which was the scullery-maid of christendom.

Rude brutal anger routed the last lingering instant of ecstasy from his soul. It broke up violently her fair image and flung the fragments on all sides. On all sides distorted reflections of her image started from his memory: the flower girl in the ragged dress with damp coarse hair and a hoyden's face who had called herself his own girl and begged his handsel, the kitchen-girl in the next house who sang over the clatter of her plates, with the drawl of a country singer, the first bars of *By Killarney's Lakes and Fells*, a girl who had laughed gaily to see him stumble when the iron grating in the footpath near Cork Hill had caught the broken sole of his shoe, a girl he had glanced at, attracted by her small ripe mouth, as she passed out of Jacob's biscuit factory, who had cried to him over her shoulder:

– Do you like what you seen of me, straight hair and curly eyebrows?

And yet he felt that, however he might revile and mock her image, his anger was also a form of homage. He had left the classroom in disdain that was not wholly sincere, feeling that perhaps the secret of her race lay behind those dark eyes upon which her long lashes flung a quick shadow. He had told himself bitterly as he walked through the streets that she was a figure of the womanhood of her country, a bat-like soul waking to the consciousness of itself in darkness and secrecy and loneliness, tarrying awhile, loveless and sinless, with her mild lover and leaving him to whisper of innocent transgressions in the latticed ear of a priest. His anger against her found vent in coarse railing at her paramour, whose name and, voice and features offended his baffled pride: a priested peasant, with a brother a policeman in Dublin and a brother a potboy in Moycullen. To him she would unveil her soul's shy nakedness, to one who was but schooled in the discharging of a formal rite rather than to him, a priest of the eternal imagination, transmuting the daily bread of experience into the radiant body of everliving life.

The radiant image of the eucharist united again in an instant his bitter and despairing thoughts, their cries arising unbroken in a hymn of thanksgiving.

> *Our broken cries and mournful lays*
> *Rise in one eucharistic hymn*
> *Are you not weary of ardent ways?*
>
> *While sacrificing hands upraise*
> *The chalice flowing to the brim.*
> *Tell no more of enchanted days.*

He spoke the verses aloud from the first lines till the music and rhythm suffused his mind, turning it to quiet indulgence; then copied them painfully to feel them the better by seeing them; then lay back on his bolster.

The full morning light had come. No sound was to be heard; but he knew that all around him life was about to awaken in common noises, hoarse voices, sleepy prayers. Shrinking from that life he turned towards the wall, making a cowl of the blanket and staring at the great overblown scarlet flowers of the tattered wallpaper. He tried to warm his perishing joy in their scarlet glow, imagining a roseway from where he lay upwards to heaven all strewn with scarlet flowers. Weary! Weary! He too was weary of ardent ways.

A gradual warmth, a languorous weariness passed over him descending along his spine from his closely cowled head. He felt it descend and, seeing himself as he lay, smiled. Soon he would sleep.

He had written verses for her again after ten years. Ten years before she had worn her shawl cowlwise about her head, sending sprays of her warm breath into the night air, tapping her foot upon the glassy road. It was the last tram; the lank brown horses knew it and shook their bells to the clear night in admonition. The conductor talked with the driver, both nodding often in the green light of the lamp. They stood on the steps of the tram, he on the upper, she on the lower. She came up to his step many times between their phrases and went down again and once or twice remained beside him forgetting to go down and then went down. Let be! Let be!

Ten years from that wisdom of children to his folly. If he sent her the verses? They would be read out at breakfast amid the tapping of egg-shells. Folly indeed! Her brothers would laugh and try to wrest the page from each other with their strong hard fingers. The suave priest, her uncle, seated in his arm-chair, would hold the page at arm's length, read it smiling and approve of the literary form.

No, no; that was folly. Even if he sent her the verses she would not show them to others. No, no; she could not.

He began to feel that he had wronged her. A sense of her innocence moved him almost to pity her, an innocence he had never understood till he had come to the knowledge of it through sin, an innocence which she too had not understood while she was innocent or before the strange humiliation of her nature had first come upon her. Then first her soul had begun to live as his soul had when he had first sinned, and a tender compassion filled his heart as he remembered her frail pallor and her eyes, humbled and saddened by the dark shame of womanhood.

While his soul had passed from ecstasy to languor where had she been? Might it be, in the mysterious ways of spiritual life, that her soul at those same moments had been conscious of his homage? It might be.

A glow of desire kindled again his soul and fired and fulfilled all his body. Conscious of his desire she was waking from odorous sleep, the temptress of his villanelle. Her eyes, dark and with a look of languor, were opening to his eyes. Her nakedness yielded to him, radiant, warm, odorous and lavish-limbed, enfolded him like a shining cloud, enfolded him like water with a liquid life; and like a cloud of vapour or like water circumfluent in space the liquid letters of speech, symbols of the element of mystery, flowed forth over his brain.

> *Are you not weary of ardent ways,*
> *Lure of the fallen seraphim?*
> *Tell no more of enchanted days.*
>
> *Your eyes have set man's heart ablaze*
> *And you have had your will of him.*
> *Are you not weary of ardent ways?*
>
> *Above the flame the smoke of praise*
> *Goes up from ocean rim to rim.*
> *Tell no more of enchanted days.*
>
> *Our broken cries and mournful lays*
> *Rise in one eucharistic hymn.*
> *Are you not weary of ardent ways?*

While sacrificing hands upraise
The chalice flowing to the brim.
Tell no more of enchanted days.

And still you hold our longing gaze
With languorous look and lavish limb!
Are you not weary of ardent ways?
Tell no more of enchanted days.

What birds were they? He stood on the steps of the library to look at them, leaning wearily on his ashplant. They flew round and round the jutting shoulder of a house in Molesworth Street. The air of the late March evening made clear their flight, their dark quivering bodies flying clearly against the sky as against a limp-hung cloth of smoky tenuous blue.

He watched their flight; bird after bird: a dark flash, a swerve, a flutter of wings. He tried to count them before all their darting quivering bodies passed: six, ten, eleven: and wondered were they odd or even in number. Twelve, thirteen: for two came wheeling down from the upper sky. They were flying high and low but ever round and round in straight and curving lines and ever flying from left to right, circling about a temple of air.

He listened to the cries: like the squeak of mice behind the wainscot: a shrill twofold note. But the notes were long and shrill and whirring, unlike the cry of vermin, falling a third or a fourth and trilled as the flying beaks clove the air. Their cry was shrill and clear and fine and falling like threads of silken light unwound from whirring spools.

The inhuman clamour soothed his ears in which his mother's sobs and reproaches murmured insistently and the dark frail quivering bodies wheeling and fluttering and swerving round an airy temple of the tenuous sky soothed his eyes which still saw the image of his mother's face.

Why was he gazing upwards from the steps of the porch, hearing their shrill twofold cry, watching their flight? For an augury of good or evil? A phrase of Cornelius Agrippa flew through his mind and then there flew hither and thither shapeless thoughts from Swedenborg on the correspondence of birds to things of the intellect and of how the creatures of the air have their knowledge and know their times and seasons because they, unlike man, are in the order of their life and have not perverted that order by reason.

And for ages men had gazed upward as he was gazing at birds in flight. The colonnade above him made him think vaguely of an ancient temple and the ashplant on which he leaned wearily of the curved stick of an augur. A sense of fear of the unknown moved in the heart of his weariness, a fear of symbols and portents, of the hawk-like man whose name he bore soaring out of his captivity on osier-woven wings, of Thoth, the god of writers, writing with a reed upon a tablet and bearing on his narrow ibis head the cusped moon.

He smiled as he thought of the god's image for it made him think of a bottle-nosed judge in a wig, putting commas into a document which he held at arm's length, and he knew that he would not have remembered the god's name but that it was like an Irish oath. It was folly. But was it for this folly that he was about to leave for ever the house of prayer and prudence into which he had been born and the order of life out of which he had come?

They came back with shrill cries over the jutting shoulder of the house, flying darkly against the fading air. What birds were they? He thought that they must be swallows who had come back from the south. Then he was to go away for they were birds ever going and coming, building ever an unlasting home under the eaves of men's houses and ever leaving the homes they had built to wander.

> *Bend down your faces, Oona and Aleel.*
> *I gaze upon them as the swallow gazes*
> *Upon the nest under the eave before*
> *He wander the loud waters.*

A soft liquid joy like the noise of many waters flowed over his memory and he felt in his heart the soft peace of silent spaces of fading tenuous sky above the waters, of oceanic silence, of swallows flying through the sea-dusk over the flowing waters.

A soft liquid joy flowed through the words where the soft long vowels hurtled noiselessly and fell away, lapping and flowing back and ever shaking the white bells of their waves in mute chime and mute peal, and soft low swooning cry; and he felt that the augury he had sought in the wheeling darting birds and in the pale space of sky above him had come forth from his heart like a bird from a turret, quietly and swiftly.

Symbol of departure or of loneliness? The verses crooned in the ear of his memory composed slowly before his remembering eyes the scene of the hall on the night of the opening of the national theatre. He was alone at the side of the balcony, looking out of jaded eyes at the culture of Dublin in the stalls and at the tawdry scene-cloths and human dolls framed by the garish lamps of the stage. A burly policeman sweated behind him and seemed at every moment about to act. The catcalls and hisses and mocking cries ran in rude gusts round the hall from his scattered fellow students.

– A libel on Ireland!

– Made in Germany.

– Blasphemy!

– We never sold our faith!

– No Irish woman ever did it!

– We want no amateur atheists.

– We want no budding buddhists.

A sudden swift hiss fell from the windows above him and he knew that the electric lamps had been switched on in the reader's room. He turned into the pillared hall, now calmly lit, went up the staircase and passed in through the clicking turnstile.

Cranly was sitting over near the dictionaries. A thick book, opened at the frontispiece, lay before him on the wooden rest. He leaned back in his chair, inclining his ear like that of a confessor to the face of the medical student who was reading to him a problem from the chess page of a journal. Stephen sat down at his right and the priest at the other side of the table closed his copy of *The Tablet* with an angry snap and stood up.

Cranly gazed after him blandly and vaguely. The medical student went on in a softer voice:

– Pawn to king's fourth.

– We had better go, Dixon, said Stephen in warning. He has gone to complain.

Dixon folded the journal and rose with dignity, saying:

– Our men retired in good order.

– With guns and cattle, added Stephen, pointing to the title page of Cranly's book on which was printed *Diseases of the Ox*.

As they passed through a lane of the tables Stephen said:

– Cranly, I want to speak to you.

Cranly did not answer or turn. He laid his book on the counter and passed out, his well-shod feet sounding flatly on the floor. On the staircase he paused and gazing absently at Dixon repeated:

– Pawn to king's bloody fourth.

– Put it that way if you like, Dixon said.

He had a quiet toneless voice and urbane manners and on a finger of his plump clean hand he displayed at moments a signet ring.

As they crossed the hall a man of dwarfish stature came towards them. Under the dome of his tiny hat his unshaven face began to smile with pleasure and he was heard to murmur. The eyes were melancholy as those of a monkey.

– Good evening, gentlemen, said the stubble-grown monkeyish face.

– Warm weather for March, said Cranly. They have the windows open upstairs.

Dixon smiled and turned his ring. The blackish, monkey-puckered face pursed its human mouth with gentle pleasure and its voice purred:

– Delightful weather for March. Simply delightful.

– There are two nice young ladies upstairs, captain, tired of waiting, Dixon said.

Cranly smiled and said kindly:

– The captain has only one love: sir Walter Scott. Isn't that so, captain?

– What are you reading now, captain? Dixon asked. *The Bride of Lammermoor?*

– I love old Scott, the flexible lips said, I think he writes something lovely. There is no writer can touch sir Walter Scott.

He moved a thin shrunken brown hand gently in the air in time to his praise and his thin quick eyelids beat often over his sad eyes.

Sadder to Stephen's ear was his speech: a genteel accent, low and moist, marred by errors, and, listening to it, he wondered was the story true and was the thin blood that flowed in his shrunken frame noble and come of an incestuous love?

The park trees were heavy with rain; and rain fell still and ever in the lake, lying grey like a shield. A game of swans flew there and the water and the shore beneath were fouled with their green-white slime. They embraced softly, impelled by the grey rainy light, the wet silent trees, the shield-like witnessing lake, the swans. They embraced without joy or passion, his arm about his sister's neck. A grey woollen cloak was wrapped athwart her from her shoulder to her waist and her fair head was bent in willing shame. He had loose red-brown hair and tender shapely strong freckled hands. Face? There was no face seen. The brother's face was bent upon her fair rain-fragrant hair. The hand freckled and strong and shapely and caressing was Davin's hand.

He frowned angrily upon his thought and on the shrivelled mannikin who had called it forth. His father's jibes at the Bantry gang leaped out of his memory. He held them at a distance and brooded uneasily on his own thought again. Why were they not Cranly's hands? Had Davin's simplicity and innocence stung him more secretly?

He walked on across the hall with Dixon, leaving Cranly to take leave elaborately of the dwarf.

Under the colonnade Temple was standing in the midst of a little group of students. One of them cried:

– Dixon, come over till you hear. Temple is in grand form.

Temple turned on him his dark gipsy eyes.

– You're a hypocrite, O'Keeffe, he said. And Dixon is a smiler. By hell, I think that's a good literary expression.

He laughed slyly, looking in Stephen's face, repeating:

– By hell, I'm delighted with that name. A smiler.

A stout student who stood below them on the steps said:

– Come back to the mistress, Temple. We want to hear about that.

– He had, faith, Temple said. And he was a married man too. And all the priests used to be dining there. By hell, I think they all had a touch.

– We shall call it riding a hack to spare the hunter, said Dixon.

– Tell us, Temple, O'Keeffe said, how may quarts of porter have you in you?

– All your intellectual soul is in that phrase, O'Keeffe, said Temple with open scorn.

He moved with a shambling gait round the group and spoke to Stephen.

– Did you know that the Forsters are the kings of Belgium? he asked.

Cranly came out through the door of the entrance hall, his hat thrust back on the nape of his neck and picking his teeth with care.

– And here's the wiseacre, said Temple. Do you know that about the Forsters?

He paused for an answer. Cranly dislodged a figseed from his teeth on the point of his rude toothpick and gazed at it intently.

– The Forster family, Temple said, is descended from Baldwin the first, king of Flanders. He was called the Forester. Forester and Forster are the same name. A descendant of Baldwin the First, captain Francis Forster, settled in Ireland and married the daughter of the last chieftain of Clanbrassil. Then there are the Blake Forsters. That's a different branch.

– From Baldhead, king of Flanders, Cranly repeated, rooting again deliberately at his gleaming uncovered teeth.

– Where did you pick up all that history? O'Keeffe asked.

– I know all the history of your family, too, Temple said, turning to Stephen. Do you know what Giraldus Cambrensis says about your family?

– Is he descended from Baldwin too? asked a tall consumptive student with dark eyes.

– Baldhead, Cranly repeated, sucking at a crevice in his teeth.

– *Pernobilis et pervetusta familia*, Temple said to Stephen.

The stout student who stood below them on the steps farted briefly. Dixon turned towards him, saying in a soft voice:

– Did an angel speak?

Cranly turned also and said vehemently but without anger:

– Goggins, you're the flamingest dirty devil I ever met, do you know.

– I had it on my mind to say that, Goggins answered firmly. It did no one any harm, did it?

– We hope, Dixon said suavely, that it was not of the kind known to science as a *paulo post futurum*.

– Didn't I tell you he was a smiler? said Temple, turning right and left. Didn't I give him that name?

– You did. We're not deaf, said the tall consumptive.

Cranly still frowned at the stout student below him. Then, with a snort of disgust, he shoved him violently down the steps.

– Go away from here, he said rudely. Go away, you stinkpot. And you are a stinkpot.

Goggins skipped down on to the gravel and at once returned to his place with good humour. Temple turned back to Stephen and asked:

– Do you believe in the law of heredity?

– Are you drunk or what are you or what are you trying to say? asked Cranly, facing round on him with an expression of wonder.

– The most profound sentence ever written, Temple said with enthusiasm, is the sentence at the end of the zoology. Reproduction is the beginning of death.

He touched Stephen timidly at the elbow and said eagerly:

– Do you feel how profound that is because you are a poet?

Cranly pointed his long forefinger.

– Look at him! he said with scorn to the others. Look at Ireland's hope!

They laughed at his words and gesture. Temple turned on him bravely, saying:

– Cranly, you're always sneering at me. I can see that. But I am as good as you any day. Do you know what I think about you now as compared with myself?

– My dear man, said Cranly urbanely, you are incapable, do you know, absolutely incapable of thinking.

– But do you know, Temple went on, what I think of you and of myself compared together?

– Out with it, Temple! the stout student cried from the steps. Get it out in bits!

Temple turned right and left, making sudden feeble gestures as he spoke.

– I'm a ballocks, he said, shaking his head in despair. I am and I know I am. And I admit it that I am.

Dixon patted him lightly on the shoulder and said mildly:

– And it does you every credit, Temple.

– But he, Temple said, pointing to Cranly, he is a ballocks, too, like me. Only he doesn't know it. And that's the only difference I see.

A burst of laughter covered his words. But he turned again to Stephen and said with a sudden eagerness:

– That word is a most interesting word. That's the only English dual number. Did you know?

– Is it? Stephen said vaguely.

He was watching Cranly's firm-featured suffering face, lit up now by a smile of false patience. The gross name had passed over it like foul water poured over an old stone image, patient of injuries; and, as he watched him, he saw him raise his hat in salute and uncover the black hair that stood stiffly from his fore head like an iron crown.

She passed out from the porch of the library and bowed across Stephen in reply to Cranly's greeting. He also? Was there not a slight flush on Cranly's cheek? Or had it come forth at Temple's words? The light had waned. He could not see.

Did that explain his friend's listless silence, his harsh comments, the sudden intrusions of rude speech with which he had shattered so often Stephen's ardent wayward confessions? Stephen had forgiven freely for he had found this rudeness also in himself. And he remembered an evening when he had dismounted from a borrowed creaking bicycle to pray to God in a wood near Malahide. He had lifted up his arms and spoken in ecstasy to the sombre nave of the trees, knowing that he stood on holy ground and in a holy hour. And when two constabulary men had come into sight round a bend in the gloomy road he had broken off his prayer to whistle loudly an air from the last pantomime.

He began to beat the frayed end of his ashplant against the base of a pillar. Had Cranly not heard him? Yet he could wait. The talk about him ceased for a moment and a soft hiss fell again from a window above. But no other sound was in the air and the swallows whose flight he had followed with idle eyes were sleeping.

She had passed through the dusk. And therefore the air was silent save for one soft hiss that fell. And therefore the tongues about him had ceased their babble. Darkness was falling.

Darkness falls from the air.

A trembling joy, lambent as a faint light, played like a fairy host around him. But why? Her passage through the darkening air or the verse with its black vowels and its opening sound, rich and lutelike?

He walked away slowly towards the deeper shadows at the end of the colonnade, beating the stone softly with his stick to hide his revery from the students whom he had left: and allowed his mind to summon back to itself the age of Dowland and Byrd and Nash.

Eyes, opening from the darkness of desire, eyes that dimmed the breaking east. What was their languid grace but the softness of chambering? And what was their shimmer but the shimmer of the scum that mantled the cesspool of the court of a slobbering Stuart. And he tasted in the language of memory ambered wines, dying fallings of sweet airs, the proud pavan, and saw with the eyes of memory kind gentlewomen in Covent Garden wooing from their balconies with sucking mouths and the pox-fouled wenches of the taverns and young wives that, gaily yielding to their ravishers, clipped and clipped again.

The images he had summoned gave him no pleasure. They were secret and inflaming but her image was not entangled by them. That was not the way to think of her. It was not even the way in which he thought of her. Could his mind then not trust itself? Old phrases, sweet only with a disinterred sweetness like the figseeds Cranly rooted out of his gleaming teeth.

It was not thought nor vision though he knew vaguely that her figure was passing homeward through the city. Vaguely first and then more sharply he smelt her body. A conscious unrest seethed in his blood. Yes, it was her body he smelt, a wild and languid smell, the tepid limbs over which his music had flowed desirously and the secret soft linen upon which her flesh distilled odour and a dew.

A louse crawled over the nape of his neck and, putting his thumb and forefinger deftly beneath his loose collar, he caught it. He rolled its body, tender yet brittle as a grain of rice, between thumb and finger for an instant before he let it fall from him and wondered would it live or die. There came to his mind a curious phrase from Cornelius à Lapide which said that the lice born of human sweat were not created by God with the other animals on the sixth day. But the tickling of the skin of his neck made his mind raw and red. The life of his body, ill clad, ill fed, louse-eaten, made him close his eyelids in a sudden spasm of despair and in the darkness he saw the brittle bright bodies of lice falling from the air and turning often as they fell. Yes, and it was not darkness that fell from the air. It was brightness.

Brightness falls from the air.

He had not even remembered rightly Nash's line. All the images it had awakened were false. His mind bred vermin. His thoughts were lice born of the sweat of sloth.

He came back quickly along the colonnade towards the group of students. Well then, let her go and be damned to her! She could love some clean athlete who washed himself every morning to the waist and had black hair on his chest. Let her.

Cranly had taken another dried fig from the supply in his pocket and was eating it slowly and noisily. Temple sat on the pediment of a pillar, leaning back, his cap pulled down on his sleepy eyes. A squat young man came out of the porch, a leather portfolio tucked under his armpit. He marched towards the group, striking the flags with the heels of his boots and with the ferrule of his heavy umbrella. Then, raising the umbrella in salute, he said to all:

– Good evening, sirs.

He struck the flags again and tittered while his head trembled with a slight nervous movement. The tall consumptive student and Dixon and O'Keeffe were speaking in Irish and did not answer him. Then, turning to Cranly, he said:

– Good evening, particularly to you.

He moved the umbrella in indication and tittered again. Cranly, who was still chewing the fig, answered with loud movements of his jaws.

– Good? Yes. It is a good evening.

The squat student looked at him seriously and shook his umbrella gently and reprovingly.

– I can see, he said, that you are about to make obvious remarks.

– Um, Cranly answered, holding out what remained of the half chewed fig and jerking it towards the squat student's mouth in sign that he should eat.

The squat student did not eat it but, indulging his special humour, said gravely, still tittering and prodding his phrase with his umbrella:

– Do you intend that . . . ?

He broke off, pointed bluntly to the munched pulp of the fig, and said loudly:

– I allude to that.

– Um, Cranly said as before.

– Do you intend that now, the squat student said, as *ipso facto* or, let us say, as so to speak?

Dixon turned aside from his group, saying:

– Goggins was waiting for you, Glynn. He has gone round to the Adelphi to look for you and Moynihan. What have you there? he asked, tapping the portfolio under Glynn's arm.

– Examination papers, Glynn answered. I give them monthly examinations to see that they are profiting by my tuition.

He also tapped the portfolio and coughed gently and smiled.

– Tuition! said Cranly rudely. I suppose you mean the barefooted children that are taught by a bloody ape like you. God help them!

He bit off the rest of the fig and flung away the butt.

– I suffer little children to come unto me, Glynn said amiably.

– A bloody ape, Cranly repeated with emphasis, and a blasphemous bloody ape!

Temple stood up and, pushing past Cranly, addressed Glynn:

– That phrase you said now, he said, is from the new testament about suffer the children to come to me.

– Go to sleep again, Temple, said O'Keeffe.

– Very well, then, Temple continued, still addressing Glynn, and if Jesus suffered the children to come why does the church send them all to hell if they die unbaptized? Why is that?

– Were you baptized yourself, Temple? the consumptive student asked.

– But why are they sent to hell if Jesus said they were all to come? Temple said, his eyes searching Glynn's eyes.

Glynn coughed and said gently, holding back with difficulty the nervous titter in his voice and moving his umbrella at every word:

– And, as you remark, if it is thus, I ask emphatically whence comes this thusness.

– Because the church is cruel like all old sinners, Temple said.

– Are you quite orthodox on that point, Temple? Dixon said suavely.

– Saint Augustine says that about unbaptized children going to hell, Temple answered, because he was a cruel old sinner too.

– I bow to you, Dixon said, but I had the impression that limbo existed for such cases.

– Don't argue with him, Dixon, Cranly said brutally. Don't talk to him or look at him. Lead him home with a sugan the way you'd lead a bleating goat.

– Limbo! Temple cried. That's a fine invention too. Like hell.

– But with the unpleasantness left out, Dixon said.

He turned smiling to the others and said:

– I think I am voicing the opinions of all present in saying so much.

– You are, Glynn said in a firm tone. On that point Ireland is united.

He struck the ferrule of his umbrella on the stone floor of the colonnade.

– Hell, Temple said. I can respect that invention of the grey spouse of Satan. Hell is Roman, like the walls of the Romans, strong and ugly. But what is limbo?

– Put him back into the perambulator, Cranly, O'Keeffe called out.

Cranly made a swift step towards Temple, halted, stamping his foot, crying as if to a fowl:

– Hoosh!

Temple moved away nimbly.

– Do you know what limbo is? he cried. Do you know what we call a notion like that in Roscommon?

– Hoosh! Blast you! Cranly cried, clapping his hands.

– Neither my arse nor my elbow! Temple cried out scornfully. And that's what I call limbo.

– Give us that stick here, Cranly said.

He snatched the ashplant roughly from Stephen's hand and sprang down the steps: but Temple, hearing him move in pursuit, fled through the dusk like a wild creature, nimble and fleet-footed. Cranly's heavy boots were heard loudly charging across the quadrangle and then returning heavily, foiled and spurning the gravel at each step.

His step was angry and with an angry abrupt gesture he thrust the stick back into Stephen's hand. Stephen felt that his anger had another cause but, feigning patience, touched his arm slightly and said quietly:

– Cranly, I told you I wanted to speak to you. Come away.

Cranly looked at him for a few moments and asked:

– Now?

– Yes, now, Stephen said. We can't speak here. Come away.

They crossed the quadrangle together without speaking. The bird call from *Siegfried* whistled softly followed them from the steps of the porch. Cranly turned, and Dixon, who had whistled, called out:

– Where are you fellows off to? What about that game, Cranly?

They parleyed in shouts across the still air about a game of billiards to be played in the Adelphi hotel. Stephen walked on alone and out into the quiet of Kildare Street opposite Maple's hotel he stood to wait, patient again. The name of the hotel, a colourless polished wood, and its colourless front stung him like a glance of polite disdain. He stared angrily back at the softly lit drawing-room of the hotel in which he imagined the sleek lives of the patricians of Ireland housed in calm. They thought of army commissions and land agents: peasants greeted them along the roads in the country; they knew the names of certain French dishes and gave orders to jarvies in high-pitched provincial voices which pierced through their skin-tight accents .

How could he hit their conscience or how cast his shadow over the imaginations of their daughters, before their squires begat upon them, that they might breed a race less ignoble than their own? And under the deepened dusk he felt the thoughts and desires of the race to which he belonged flitting like bats across the dark country lanes, under trees by the edges of streams and near the pool-mottled bogs. A woman had waited in the doorway as Davin had passed by at night and, offering him a cup of milk, had all but wooed him to her bed; for Davin had the mild eyes of one who could be secret. But him no woman's eyes had wooed.

His arm was taken in a strong grip and Cranly's voice said:

– Let us eke go.

They walked southward in silence. Then Cranly said:

– That blithering idiot, Temple! I swear to Moses, do you know, that I'll be the death of that fellow one time.

But his voice was no longer angry and Stephen wondered was he thinking of her greeting to him under the porch.

They turned to the left and walked on as before. When they had gone on so for some time Stephen said:

– Cranly, I had an unpleasant quarrel this evening.

– With your people? Cranly asked.

– With my mother.

– About religion?

– Yes, Stephen answered.

After a pause Cranly asked:

– What age is your mother?

– Not old, Stephen said. She wishes me to make my easter duty.

– And will you?

– I will not, Stephen said.

– Why not? Cranly said.

– I will not serve, answered Stephen.

– That remark was made before, Cranly said calmly.

– It is made behind now, said Stephen hotly.

Cranly pressed Stephen's arm, saying:

– Go easy, my dear man. You're an excitable bloody man, do you know.

He laughed nervously as he spoke and, looking up into Stephen's face with moved and friendly eyes, said:

– Do you know that you are an excitable man?

– I daresay I am, said Stephen, laughing also.

Their minds, lately estranged, seemed suddenly to have been drawn closer, one to the other.

– Do you believe in the eucharist? Cranly asked.

– I do not, Stephen said.

– Do you disbelieve then?

– I neither believe in it nor disbelieve in it, Stephen answered.

– Many persons have doubts, even religious persons, yet they overcome them or put them aside, Cranly said. Are your doubts on that point too strong?

– I do not wish to overcome them, Stephen answered.

Cranly, embarrassed for a moment, took another fig from his pocket and was about to eat it when Stephen said:

– Don't, please. You cannot discuss this question with your mouth full of chewed fig.

Cranly examined the fig by the light of a lamp under which he halted. Then he smelt it with both nostrils, bit a tiny piece, spat it out and threw the fig rudely into the gutter.

Addressing it as it lay, he said:

– Depart from me, ye cursed, into everlasting fire!

Taking Stephen's arm, he went on again and said:

– Do you not fear that those words may be spoken to you on the day of Judgment?

– What is offered me on the other hand? Stephen asked. An eternity of bliss in the company of the dean of studies?

– Remember, Cranly said, that he would be glorified.

– Ay, Stephen said somewhat bitterly, bright, agile, impassible and, above all, subtle.

– It is a curious thing, do you know, Cranly said dispassionately, how your mind is supersaturated with the religion in which you say you disbelieve. Did you believe in it when you were at school? I bet you did.

– I did, Stephen answered.

– And were you happier then? Cranly asked softly, happier than you are now, for instance?

– Often happy, Stephen said, and often unhappy. I was someone else then.

– How someone else? What do you mean by that statement?

– I mean, said Stephen, that I was not myself as I am now, as I had to become.

– Not as you are now, not as you had to become, Cranly repeated. Let me ask you a question. Do you love your mother?

Stephen shook his head slowly.

– I don't know what your words mean, he said simply.

– Have you never loved anyone? Cranly asked.

– Do you mean women?

– I am not speaking of that, Cranly said in a colder tone. I ask you if you ever felt love towards anyone or anything?

Stephen walked on beside his friend, staring gloomily at the footpath.

– I tried to love God, he said at length. It seems now I failed. It is very difficult. I tried to unite my will with the will of God instant by instant. In that I did not always fail. I could perhaps do that still –

Cranly cut him short by asking:

– Has your mother had a happy life?

– How do I know? Stephen said.

– How many children had she?

– Nine or ten, Stephen answered. Some died.

– Was your father . . . Cranly interrupted himself for an instant, and then said: I don't want to pry into your family affairs. But was your father what is called well-to-do? I mean, when you were growing up?

– Yes, Stephen said.

– What was he? Cranly asked after a pause

Stephen began to enumerate glibly his father's attributes.

– A medical student, all oarsman, a tenor, an amateur actor, a shouting politician, a small landlord, a small investor, a drinker, a good fellow, a story-teller, somebody's secretary, something in a distillery, a tax-gatherer, a bankrupt and at present a praiser of his own past.

Cranly laughed, tightening his grip on Stephen's arm, and said:

– The distillery is damn good.

– Is there anything else you want to know? Stephen asked.

– Are you in good circumstances at present?

– Do I look it? Stephen asked bluntly.

– So then, Cranly went on musingly, you were born in the lap of luxury.

He used the phrase broadly and loudly as he often used technical expressions, as if he wished his hearer to understand that they were used by him without conviction.

– Your mother must have gone through a good deal of suffering, he said then. Would you not try to save her from suffering more even if . . . or would you?

– If I could, Stephen said, that would cost me very little.

– Then do so, Cranly said. Do as she wishes you to do. What is it for you? You disbelieve in it. It is a form: nothing else. And you will set her mind at rest.

He ceased and, as Stephen did not reply, remained silent. Then, as if giving utterance to the process of his own thought, he said:

– Whatever else is unsure in this stinking dunghill of a world a mother's love is not. Your mother brings you into the world, carries you first in her body. What do we know about what she feels? But whatever she feels, it, at least, must be real. It must be. What are our ideas or ambitions? Play. Ideas! Why, this bloody bleating goat Temple has ideas. MacCann has ideas too. Every jackass going the roads thinks he has ideas.

Stephen, who had been listening to the unspoken speech behind the words, said with assumed carelessness:

– Pascal, if I remember rightly, would not suffer his mother to kiss him as he feared the contact of her sex.

– Pascal was a pig, said Cranly.

– Aloysius Gonzaga, I think, was of the same mind, Stephen said.

– And he was another pig then, said Cranly.

– The church calls him a saint, Stephen objected.

– I don't care a flaming damn what anyone calls him, Cranly said rudely and flatly. I call him a pig.

Stephen, preparing the words neatly in his mind, continued:

– Jesus, too, seems to have treated his mother with scant courtesy in public but Suarez, a jesuit theologian and Spanish gentleman, has apologized for him.

– Did the idea ever occur to you, Cranly asked, that Jesus was not what he pretended to be?

– The first person to whom that idea occurred, Stephen answered, was Jesus himself.

– I mean, Cranly said, hardening in his speech, did the idea ever occur to you that he was himself a conscious hypocrite, what he called the jews of his time, a whited sepulchre? Or, to put it more plainly, that he was a blackguard?

– That idea never occurred to me, Stephen answered. But I am curious to know are you trying to make a convert of me or a pervert of yourself?

He turned towards his friend's face and saw there a raw smile which some force of will strove to make finely significant.

Cranly asked suddenly in a plain sensible tone:

– Tell me the truth. Were you at all shocked by what I said?

– Somewhat, Stephen said.

– And why were you shocked, Cranly pressed on in the same tone, if you feel sure that our religion is false and that Jesus was not the son of God?

– I am not at all sure of it, Stephen said. He is more like a son of God than a son of Mary.

– And is that why you will not communicate, Cranly asked, because you are not sure of that too, because you feel that the host, too, may be the body and blood of the son of God and not a wafer of bread? And because you fear that it may be?

– Yes, Stephen said quietly, I feel that and I also fear it.

– I see, Cranly said

Stephen, struck by his tone of closure, reopened the discussion at once by saying:

– I fear many things: dogs, horses, fire-arms, the sea, thunderstorms, machinery, the country roads at night.

– But why do you fear a bit of bread?

– I imagine, Stephen said, that there is a malevolent reality behind those things I say I fear.

– Do you fear then, Cranly asked, that the God of the Roman catholics would strike you dead and damn you if you made a sacrilegious communion?

– The God of the Roman catholics could do that now, Stephen said. I fear more than that the chemical action which would be set up in my soul by a false homage to a symbol behind which are massed twenty centuries of authority and veneration.

– Would you, Cranly asked, in extreme danger, commit that particular sacrilege? For instance, if you lived in the penal days?

– I cannot answer for the past, Stephen replied. Possibly not.

– Then, said Cranby, you do not intend to become a protestant?

– I said that I had lost the faith, Stephen answered, but not that I had lost self-respect. What kind of liberation would that be to forsake an absurdity which is logical and coherent and to embrace one which is illogical and incoherent?

They had walked on towards the township of Pembroke and now, as they went on slowly along the avenues, the trees and the scattered lights in the villas soothed their minds. The air of wealth and repose diffused about them seemed to comfort their neediness. Behind a hedge of laurel a light glimmered in the window of a kitchen and the voice of a servant was heard singing as she sharpened knives. She sang, in short broken bars, *Rosie O'Grady.*

Cranly stopped to listen, saying:

– *Mulier cantat.*

The soft beauty of the Latin word touched with an enchanting touch the dark of the evening, with a touch fainter and more persuading than the touch of music or of a woman's hand. The strife of their minds was quelled. The figure of a woman as she appears in the liturgy of the church passed silently through the darkness: a white-robed figure, small and slender as a boy, and with a falling girdle. Her voice, frail and high as a boy's, was heard intoning from a distant choir the first words of a woman which pierce the gloom and clamour of the first chanting of the passion:

– *Et tu cum Jesu Galilaeo eras.*

And all hearts were touched and turned to her voice, shining like a young star, shining clearer as the voice intoned the proparoxyton and more faintly as the cadence died.

The singing ceased. They went on together, Cranly repeating in strongly stressed rhythm the end of the refrain:

> *And when we are married,*
> *O, how happy we'll be*
> *For I love sweet Rosie O'Grady*
> *And Rosie O'Grady loves me.*

– There's real poetry for you, he said. There's real love.

He glanced sideways at Stephen with a strange smile and said:

– Do you consider that poetry? Or do you know what the words mean?

– I want to see Rosie first, said Stephen

– She's easy to find, Cranly said.

His hat had come down on his forehead. He shoved it back and in the shadow of the trees Stephen saw his pale face, framed by the dark, and his large dark eyes. Yes. His face was handsome and his body was strong and hard. He had spoken of a mother's love. He felt then the sufferings of women, the weaknesses of their bodies and souls; and would shield them with a strong and resolute arm and bow his mind to them.

Away then: it is time to go. A voice spoke softly to Stephen's lonely heart, bidding him go and telling him that his friendship was coming to an end. Yes; he would go. He could not strive against another. He knew his part.

– Probably I shall go away, he said.

– Where? Cranly asked.

– Where I can, Stephen said.

– Yes, Cranly said. It might be difficult for you to live here now. But is it that makes you go?

– I have to go, Stephen answered.

– Because, Cranly continued, you need not look upon yourself as driven away if you do not wish to go or as a heretic or an outlaw. There are many good believers who think as you do. Would that surprise you? The church is not the stone building nor even the clergy and their dogmas. It is the whole mass of those born into it. I don't know what you wish to do in life. Is it what you told me the night we were standing outside Harcourt Street station?

– Yes, Stephen said, smiling in spite of himself at Cranly's way of remembering thoughts in connexion with places. The night you spent half an hour wrangling with Doherty about the shortest way from Sallygap to Larras.

– Pothead! Cranly said with calm contempt. What does he know about the way from Sallygap to Larras? Or what does he know about anything for that matter? And the big slobbering washing-pot head of him!

He broke into a loud long laugh.

– Well? Stephen said. Do you remember the rest?

– What you said, is it? Cranly asked. Yes, I remember it. To discover the mode of life or of art whereby your spirit could express itself in unfettered freedom.

Stephen raised his hat in acknowledgement.

– Freedom! Cranly repeated. But you are not free enough yet to commit a sacrilege. Tell me would you rob?

– I would beg first, Stephen said.

– And if you got nothing, would you rob?

– You wish me to say, Stephen answered, that the rights of property are provisional, and that in certain circumstances it is not unlawful to rob. Everyone would act in that belief. So I will not make you that answer. Apply to the jesuit theologian, Juan Mariana de Talavera, who will also explain to you in what circumstances you may lawfully kill your king and whether you had better hand him his poison in a goblet or smear it for him upon his robe or his saddlebow. Ask me rather would I suffer others to rob me, or if they did, would I call down upon them what I believe is called the chastisement of the secular arm?

– And would you?

– I think, Stephen said, it would pain me as much to do so as to be robbed.

– I see, Cranly said.

He produced his match and began to clean the crevice between two teeth. Then he said carelessly:

– Tell me, for example, would you deflower a virgin?

– Excuse me, Stephen said politely, is that not the ambition of most young gentlemen?

– What then is your point of view? Cranly asked.

His last phrase, sour smelling as the smoke of charcoal and disheartening, excited Stephen's brain, over which its fumes seemed to brood.

– Look here, Cranly, he said. You have asked me what I would do and what I would not do. I will tell you what I will do and what I will not do. I will not serve that in which I no longer believe, whether it call itself my home, my fatherland, or my church: and I will try to express myself in some mode of life or art as freely as I can and as wholly as I can, using for my defence the only arms I allow myself to use – silence, exile, and cunning.

Cranly seized his arm and steered him round so as to lead him back towards Leeson Park. He laughed almost slyly and pressed Stephen's arm with an elder's affection.

– Cunning indeed! he said. Is it you? You poor poet, you!

– And you made me confess to you, Stephen said, thrilled by his touch, as I have confessed to you so many other things, have I not?

– Yes, my child, Cranly said, still gaily.

– You made me confess the fears that I have. But I will tell you also what I do not fear. I do not fear to be alone or to be spurned for another or to leave whatever I have to leave. And I am not afraid to make a mistake, even a great mistake, a lifelong mistake, and perhaps as long as eternity too.

Cranly, now grave again, slowed his pace and said:

– Alone, quite alone. You have no fear of that. And you know what that word means? Not only to be separate from all others but to have not even one friend.

– I will take the risk, said Stephen.

– And not to have any one person, Cranly said, who would be more than a friend, more even than the noblest and truest friend a man ever had.

His words seemed to have struck some deep chord in his own nature. Had he spoken of himself, of himself as he was or wished to be? Stephen watched his face for some moments in silence. A cold sadness was there. He had spoken of himself, of his own loneliness which he feared.

– Of whom are you speaking? Stephen asked at length.

Cranly did not answer.

MARCH 20. Long talk with Cranly on the subject of my revolt. He had his grand manner on. I supple and suave. Attacked me on the score of love for one's mother. Tried to imagine his mother: cannot. Told me once, in a moment of thoughtlessness, his father was sixty-one when he was born. Can see him. Strong farmer type. Pepper and salt suit. Square feet. Unkempt, grizzled beard. Probably attends coursing matches. Pays his dues regularly but not plentifully to Father Dwyer of Larras. Sometimes talks to girls after nightfall. But his mother? Very young or very old? Hardly the first. If so, Cranly would not have spoken as he did. Old then. Probably, and neglected. Hence Cranly's despair of soul: the child of exhausted loins.

MARCH 21, MORNING. Thought this in bed last night but was too lazy and free to add to it. Free, yes. The exhausted loins are those of Elizabeth and Zacchary. Then he is the precursor. Item: he eats chiefly belly bacon and dried figs. Read locusts and wild honey. Also, when thinking of him, saw always a stern severed head or death mask as if outlined on a grey curtain or veronica. Decollation they call it in the fold. Puzzled for the moment by saint John at the Latin gate. What do I see? A decollated precursor trying to pick the lock.

MARCH 21, NIGHT. Free. Soul free and fancy free. Let the dead bury the dead. Ay. And let the dead marry the dead.

MARCH 22. In company with Lynch followed a sizeable hospital nurse. Lynch's idea. Dislike it. Two lean hungry greyhounds walking after a heifer.

MARCH 23. Have not seen her since that night. Unwell? Sits at the fire perhaps with mamma's shawl on her shoulders. But not peevish. A nice bowl of gruel? Won't you now?

MARCH 24. Began with a discussion with my mother. Subject: B.V.M. Handicapped by my sex and youth. To escape held up relations between Jesus and Papa against those between Mary and her son. Said religion was not a lying-in hospital. Mother indulgent. Said I have a queer mind and have read too much. Not true. Have read little and understood less. Then she said I would come back to faith because I had a restless mind. This means to leave church by back door of sin and re-enter through the skylight of repentance. Cannot repent. Told her so and asked for sixpence. Got threepence.

Then went to college. Other wrangle with little round head rogue's eye Ghezzi. This time about Bruno the Nolan. Began in Italian and ended in pidgin English. He said Bruno was a terrible heretic. I said he was terribly burned. He agreed to this with some sorrow. Then gave me recipe for what he calls *risotto alla bergamasca*. When he pronounces a soft *o* he protrudes his full carnal lips as if he kissed the vowel. Has he? And could he repent? Yes, he could: and cry two round rogue's tears, one from each eye.

Crossing Stephen's, that is, my green, remembered that his countrymen and not mine had invented what Cranly the other night called our religion. A quartet of them, soldiers of the ninety-seventh infantry regiment, sat at the foot of the cross and tossed up dice for the overcoat of the crucified.

Went to library. Tried to read three reviews. Useless. She is not out yet. Am I alarmed? About what? That she will never be out again.

Blake wrote:

> I wonder if William Bond will die
> For assuredly be is very ill.

Alas, poor William!

I was once at a diorama in Rotunda. At the end were pictures of big nobs. Among them William Ewart Gladstone, just then dead. Orchestra played *O Willie, we have missed you.*

A race of clodhoppers!

MARCH 25, MORNING. A troubled night of dreams. Want to get them off my chest.

A long curving gallery. From the floor ascend pillars of dark vapours. It is peopled by the images of fabulous kings, set in stone. Their hands are folded upon their knees in token of weariness and their eyes are darkened for the errors of men go up before them for ever as dark vapours.

Strange figures advance as from a cave. They are not as tall as men. One does not seem to stand quite apart from another. Their faces are phosphorescent, with darker streaks. They peer at me and their faces seem to ask me something. They do not speak.

MARCH 30. This evening Cranly was in the porch of the library, proposing a problem to Dixon and her brother. A mother let her child fall into the Nile. Still harping on the mother. A crocodile seized the child. Mother asked it back. Crocodile said all right if she told him what he was going to do with the child, eat it or not eat it.

This mentality, Lepidus would say, is indeed bred out of your mud by the operation of your sun.

And mine? Is it not too? Then into Nile mud with it!

APRIL 1. Disapprove of this last phase.

APRIL 2. Saw her drinking tea and eating cakes in Johnston's, Mooney and O'Brien's. Rather, lynx-eyed Lynch saw her as we passed. He tells me Cranly was invited there by brother. Did he bring his crocodile? Is he the shining light now? Well, I discovered him. I protest I did. Shining quietly behind a bushel of Wicklow bran.

APRIL 3. Met Davin at the cigar shop opposite Findlater's church. He was in a black sweater and had a hurley stick. Asked me was it true I was going away and why. Told him the shortest way to Tara was *via* Holyhead. Just then my father came up. Introduction. Father polite and observant. Asked Davin if he might offer him some refreshment. Davin could not, was going to a meeting. When we came away father told me he had a good honest eye. Asked me why I did join a rowing club. I pretended to think it over. Told me then how he broke Pennyfeather's heart. Wants me to read law. Says I was cut out for that. More mud, more crocodiles.

APRIL 5. Wild spring. Scudding clouds. O life! Dark stream of swirling bogwater on which apple-trees have cast down their delicate flowers. Eyes of girls among the leaves. Girls demure and romping. All fair or auburn: no dark ones. They blush better. Houpla!

APRIL 6. Certainly she remembers the past. Lynch says all women do. Then she remembers the time of her childhood – and mine, if I was ever a child. The past is consumed in the present and the present is living only because it brings forth the future. Statues of women, if Lynch be right, should always be fully draped, one hand of the woman feeling regretfully her own hinder parts.

APRIL 6, LATER. Michael Robartes remembers forgotten beauty and, when his arms wrap her round, he presses in his arms the loveliness which has long faded from the world. Not this. Not at all. I desire to press in my arms the loveliness which has not yet come into the world.

APRIL 10. Faintly, under the heavy night, through the silence of the city which has turned from dreams to dreamless sleep as a weary lover whom no caresses move, the sound of hoofs upon the road. Not so faintly now as they come near the bridge; and in a moment, as they pass the darkened windows, the silence is cloven by alarm as by an arrow. They are heard now far away, hoofs that shine amid the heavy night as gems, hurrying beyond the sleeping fields to what journey's end – what heart? – bearing what tidings?

APRIL 11. Read what I wrote last night. Vague words for a vague emotion. Would she like it? I think so. Then I should have to like it also.

APRIL 13. That tundish has been on my mind for a long time. I looked it up and find it English and good old blunt English too. Damn the dean of studies and his funnel! What did he come here for to teach us his own language or to learn it from us. Damn him one way or the other!

APRIL 14. John Alphonsus Mulrennan has just returned from the west of Ireland. European and Asiatic papers please copy. He told us he met an old man there in a mountain cabin. Old man had red eyed and short pipe. Old man spoke Irish. Mulrennan spoke Irish. Then old man and Mulrennan spoke English. Mulrennan spoke to him about universe and stars. Old man sat, listened, smoked, spat. Then said:

– Ah, there must be terrible queer creatures at the latter end of the world.

I fear him. I fear his red-rimmed horny eyes. It is with him I must struggle all through this night till day come, till he or I lie dead, gripping him by the sinewy throat till . . . Till what? Till he yield to me? No. I mean no harm.

APRIL 15. Met her today point blank in Grafton Street. The crowd brought us together. We both stopped. She asked me why I never came, said she had heard all sorts of stories about me. This was only to gain time.

Asked me was I writing poems? About whom? I asked her. This confused her more and I felt sorry and mean. Turned off that valve at once and opened the spiritual-heroic refrigerating apparatus, invented and patented in all countries by Dante Alighieri. Talked rapidly of myself and my plans. In the midst of it unluckily I made a sudden gesture of a revolutionary nature. I must have looked like a fellow throwing a handful of peas into the air. People began to look at us. She shook hands a moment after and, in going away, said she hoped I would do what I said.

Now I call that friendly, don't you?

Yes, I liked her today. A little or much? Don't know. I liked her and it seems a new feeling to me. Then, in that case, all the rest, all that I thought I thought and all that I felt I felt, all the rest before now, in fact ... O, give it up old chap! Sleep it off!

APRIL 16. Away! Away!

The spell of arms and voices: the white arms of roads, the promise of close embraces and the black arms of tall ships that stand against the moon, their tale of distant nations. They are held out to say: We are alone – come. And the voices say with them: We are your kinsmen. And the air is thick with their company as they call to me, their kinsman, making ready to go, shaking the wings of their exultant and terrible youth.

APRIL 26. Mother is putting my new secondhand clothes in order. She prays now, she says, that I may learn in my own life and away from home and friends what the heart is and what it feels. Amen. So be it. Welcome, O life! I go to encounter for the millionth time the reality of experience and to forge in the smithy of my soul the uncreated conscience of my race.

APRIL 27. Old father, old artificer, stand me now and ever in good stead.

Dublin, 1904
Trieste, 1914

ULYSSES

I

◀ STATELY, PLUMP BUCK MULLIGAN CAME FROM THE stairhead, bearing a bowl of lather on which a mirror and a razor lay crossed. A yellow dressinggown, ungirdled, was sustained gently behind him by the mild morning air. He held the bowl aloft and intoned:

– *Introibo ad altare Dei.*

Halted, he peered down the dark winding stairs and called up coarsely:

– Come up, Kinch. Come up, you fearful jesuit.

Solemnly he came forward and mounted the round gunrest. He faced about and blessed gravely thrice the tower, the surrounding country and the awaking mountains. Then, catching sight of Stephen Dedalus, he bent towards him and made rapid crosses in the air, gurgling in his throat and shaking his head. Stephen Dedalus, displeased and sleepy, leaned his arms on the top of the staircase and looked coldly at the shaking gurgling face that blessed him, equine in its length, and at the light untonsured hair, grained and hued like pale oak.

Buck Mulligan peeped an instant under the mirror and then covered the bowl smartly.

– Back to barracks, he said sternly.

He added in a preacher's tone:

– For this, O dearly beloved, is the genuine Christine: body and soul and blood and ouns. Slow music, please. Shut your eyes, gents. One moment. A little trouble about those white corpuscles. Silence, all.

He peered sideways up and gave a long low whistle of call, then paused awhile in rapt attention, his even white teeth glistening here and there with gold points. Chrysostomos. Two strong shrill whistles answered through the calm.

– Thanks, old chap, he cried briskly. That will do nicely. Switch off the current, will you?

He skipped off the gunrest and looked gravely at his watcher, gathering about his legs the loose folds of his gown. The plump shadowed face and sullen oval jowl recalled a prelate, patron of arts in the middle ages. A pleasant smile broke quietly over his lips.

– The mockery of it, he said gaily. Your absurd name, an ancient Greek.

He pointed his finger in friendly jest and went over to the parapet, laughing to himself. Stephen Dedalus stepped up, followed him wearily halfway and sat down on the edge of the gunrest, watching him still as he propped his mirror on the parapet, dipped the brush in the bowl and lathered cheeks and neck.

Buck Mulligan's gay voice went on.

– My name is absurd too: Malachi Mulligan, two dactyls. But it has a Hellenic ring, hasn't it? Tripping and sunny like the buck himself. We must go to Athens. Will you come if I can get the aunt to fork out twenty quid?

He laid the brush aside and, laughing with delight, cried:

– Will he come? The jejune jesuit.

Ceasing, he began to shave with care.

– Tell me, Mulligan, Stephen said quietly.

– Yes, my love?

– How long is Haines going to stay in this tower?

Buck Mulligan showed a shaven cheek over his right shoulder.

– God, isn't he dreadful? he said frankly. A ponderous Saxon. He thinks you're not a gentleman. God, these bloody English. Bursting with money and indigestion. Because he comes from Oxford. You know, Dedalus, you have the real Oxford manner. He can't make you out. O, my name for you is the best: Kinch, the knifeblade.

He shaved warily over his chin.

– He was raving all night about a black panther, Stephen said. Where is his guncase?

– A woful lunatic, Mulligan said. Were you in a funk?

– I was, Stephen said with energy and growing fear. Out here in the dark with a man I don't know raving and moaning to himself about shooting a black panther. You saved men from drowning. I'm not a hero, however. If he stays on here I am off.

Buck Mulligan frowned at the lather on his razorblade. He hopped down from his perch and began to search his trouser pockets hastily.

– Scutter, he cried thickly.

He came over to the gunrest and, thrusting a hand into Stephen's upper pocket, said:

– Lend us a loan of your noserag to wipe my razor.

Stephen suffered him to pull out and hold up on show by its corner a dirty crumpled handkerchief. Buck Mulligan wiped the razorblade neatly. Then, gazing over the handkerchief, he said:

– The bard's noserag. A new art colour for our Irish poets: snotgreen. You can almost taste it, can't you?

He mounted to the parapet again and gazed out over Dublin bay, his fair oakpale hair stirring slightly.

– God, he said quietly. Isn't the sea what Algy calls it: a grey sweet mother? The snotgreen sea. The scrotum-tightening sea. *Epi oinopa ponton.* Ah, Dedalus, the Greeks. I must teach you. You must read them in the original. *Thalatta! Thalatta!* She is our great sweet mother. Come and look.

Stephen stood up and went over to the parapet. Leaning on it he looked down on the water and on the mailboat clearing the harbour mouth of Kingstown.

– Our mighty mother, Buck Mulligan said.

He turned abruptly his great searching eyes from the sea to Stephen's face.

– The aunt thinks you killed your mother, he said. That's why she won't let me have anything to do with you.

– Someone killed her, Stephen said gloomily.

– You could have knelt down, damn it, Kinch, when your dying mother asked you, Buck Mulligan said. I'm hyperborean as much as you. But to think of your mother begging you with her last breath to kneel down and pray for her. And you refused. There is something sinister in you . . .

He broke off and lathered again lightly his farther cheek. A tolerant smile curled his lips.

– But a lovely mummer, he murmured to himself. Kinch, the loveliest mummer of them all.

He shaved evenly and with care, in silence, seriously.

Stephen, an elbow rested on the jagged granite, leaned his palm against his brow and gazed at the fraying edge of his shiny black coatsleeve. Pain, that was not yet the pain of love, fretted his heart. Silently, in a dream she had come to him after her death, her wasted body within its loose brown graveclothes giving off an odour of wax and rosewood, her breath, that had bent upon him, mute, reproachful, a faint odour of wetted ashes. Across the threadbare cuffedge he saw the sea hailed as a great sweet mother by the wellfed voice beside him. The ring of bay and skyline held a dull green mass of liquid. A bowl of white china had stood beside her deathbed holding the green sluggish bile which she had torn up from her rotting liver by fits of loud groaning vomiting.

Buck Mulligan wiped again his razorblade.

– Ah, poor dogsbody, he said in a kind voice. I must give you a shirt and a few noserags. How are the secondhand breeks?

– They fit well enough, Stephen answered.

Buck Mulligan attacked the hollow beneath his underlip.

– The mockery of it, he said contentedly, secondleg they should be. God knows what poxy bowsy left them off. I have a lovely pair with a hair stripe, grey. You'll look spiffing in them. I'm not joking, Kinch. You look damn well when you're dressed.

– Thanks, Stephen said. I can't wear them if they are grey.

– He can't wear them, Buck Mulligan told his face in the mirror. Etiquette is etiquette. He kills his mother but he can't wear grey trousers.'

He folded his razor neatly and with stroking palps of fingers felt the smooth skin.

Stephen turned his gaze from the sea and to the plump face with its smokeblue mobile eyes.

– That fellow I was with in the Ship last night, said Buck Mulligan, says you have g. p. i. He's up in Dottyville with Conolly Norman. General paralysis of the insane.

He swept the mirror a half circle in the air to flash the tidings abroad in sunlight now radiant on the sea. His curling shaven lips laughed and the edges of his white glittering teeth. Laughter seized all his strong wellknit trunk.

– Look at yourself, he said, you dreadful bard.

Stephen bent forward and peered at the mirror held out to him, cleft by a crooked crack, hair on end. As he and others see me. Who chose this face for me? This dogsbody to rid of vermin. It asks me too.

– I pinched it out of the skivvy's room, Buck Mulligan said. It does her all right. The aunt always keeps plainlooking servants for Malachi. Lead him not into temptation. And her name is Ursula.

Laughing again, he brought the mirror away from Stephen's peering eyes.

– The rage of Caliban at not seeing his face in a mirror, he said. If Wilde were only alive to see you.

Drawing back and pointing, Stephen said with bitterness:

– It is a symbol of Irish art. The cracked lookingglass of a servant.

Buck Mulligan suddenly linked his arm in Stephen's and walked with him round the tower, his razor and mirror clacking in the pocket where he had thrust them.

– It's not fair to tease you like that, Kinch, is it? he said kindly. God knows you have more spirit than any of them.

Parried again. He fears the lancet of my art as I fear that of his. The cold steelpen.

– Cracked lookingglass of a servant. Tell that to the oxy chap downstairs and touch him for a guinea. He's stinking with money and thinks you're not a gentleman. His old fellow made his tin by selling jalap to Zulus or some bloody swindle or other. God, Kinch, if you and I could only work together we might do something for the island. Hellenize it.

Cranly's arm. His arm.

– And to think of your having to beg from these swine. I'm the only one that knows what you are. Why don't you trust me more? What have you up your nose against me? Is it Haines? If he makes any noise here I'll bring down Seymour and we'll give him a ragging worse than they gave Clive Kempthorpe.

Young shouts of moneyed voices in Clive Kempthorpe's rooms. Pale-faces: they hold their ribs with laughter, one clasping another, O, I shall expire! Break the news to her gently, Aubrey! I shall die! With slit ribbons of his shirt whipping the air he hops and hobbles round the table, with trousers down at heels, chased by Ades of Magdalen with the tailor's shears. A scared calf's face gilded with marmalade. I don't want to be debagged! Don't you play the giddy ox with me!

Shouts from the open window startling evening in the quadrangle. A deaf gardener, aproned, masked with Matthew Arnold's face, pushes his mower on the sombre lawn watching narrowly the dancing motes of grass-halms.

To ourselves . . . new paganism . . . omphalos.

– Let him stay, Stephen said. There's nothing wrong with him except at night.

– Then what is it? Buck Mulligan asked impatiently. Cough it up. I'm quite frank with you. What have you against me now?

They halted, looking towards the blunt cape of Bray Head that lay on the water like the snout of a sleeping whale. Stephen freed his arm quietly.

– Do you wish me to tell you? he asked.

– Yes, what is it? Buck Mulligan answered. I don't remember anything.

He looked in Stephen's face as he spoke. A light wind passed his brow, fanning softly his fair uncombed hair and stirring silver points of anxiety in his eyes.

Stephen, depressed by his own voice, said:

– Do you remember the first day I went to your house after my mother's death?

Buck Mulligan frowned quickly and said:

– What? Where? I can't remember anything. I remember only ideas and sensations. Why? What happened in the name of God?

– You were making tea, Stephen said, and I went across the landing to get more hot water. Your mother and some visitor came out of the drawing-room. She asked you who was in your room.

– Yes? Buck Mulligan said. What did I say? I forget.

– You said, Stephen answered, O, *it's only Dedalus whose mother is beastly dead.*

A flush which made him seem younger and more engaging rose to Buck Mulligan's cheek.

– Did I say that? he asked. Well? What harm is that?

He shook his constraint from him nervously.

– And what is death, he asked, your mother's or yours or my own? You saw only your mother die. I see them pop off every day in the Mater and Richmond and cut up into tripes in the dissecting room. It's a beastly thing and nothing else. It simply doesn't matter. You wouldn't kneel down to pray for your mother on her deathbed when she asked you. Why? Because you have the cursed jesuit strain in you, only it's injected the wrong way. To me it's all a mockery and beastly. Her cerebral lobes are not functioning. She calls the doctor Sir Peter Teazle and picks buttercups off the quilt. Humour her till it's over. You crossed her last wish in death and yet you sulk with me because I don't whinge like some hired mute from Lalouette's. Absurd! I suppose I did say it. I didn't mean to offend the memory of your mother.

He had spoken himself into boldness. Stephen, shielding the gaping wounds which the words had left in his heart, said very coldly:

– I am not thinking of the offence to my mother.

– Of what, then? Buck Mulligan asked.

– Of the offence to me, Stephen answered.

Buck Mulligan swung round on his heel.

– O, an impossible person! he exclaimed.

He walked off quickly round the parapet. Stephen stood at his post, gazing over the calm sea towards the headland. Sea and headland now grew dim. Pulses were beating in his eyes, veiling their sight, and he felt the fever of his cheeks.

A voice within the tower called loudly:

– Are you up there, Mulligan?

– I'm coming, Buck Mulligan answered.

He turned towards Stephen and said:

– Look at the sea. What does it care about offences? Chuck Loyola, Kinch, and come on down. The Sassenach wants his morning rashers.

His head halted again for a moment at the top of the staircase, level with the roof.

– Don't mope over it all day, he said. I'm inconsequent. Give up the moody brooding.

His head vanished but the drone of his descending voice boomed out of the stairhead:

> *And no more turn aside and brood*
> *Upon love's bitter mystery*
> *For Fergus rules the brazen cars.*

Woodshadows floated silently by through the morning peace from the stairhead seaward where he gazed. Inshore and farther out the mirror of water whitened, spurned by lightshod hurrying feet. White breast of the dim sea. The twining stresses, two by two. A hand plucking the harpstrings merging their twining chords. Wavewhite wedded words shimmering on the dim tide.

A cloud began to cover the sun slowly, shadowing the bay in deeper green. It lay behind him, a bowl of bitter waters. Fergus' song: I sang it alone in the house, holding down the long dark chords. Her door was open: she wanted to hear my music. Silent with awe and pity I went to her bedside. She was crying in her wretched bed. For those words, Stephen: love's bitter mystery.

Where now?

Her secrets: old feather fans, tasselled dancecards, powdered with musk, a gaud of amber beads in her locked drawer. A birdcage hung in the sunny window of her house when she was a girl. She heard old Royce sing in the pantomime of Turko the terrible and laughed with others when he sang:

> *I am the boy*
> *That can enjoy*
> *Invisibility.*

Phantasmal mirth, folded away: muskperfumed.

> *And no more turn aside and brood.*

Folded away in the memory of nature with her toys. Memories beset his brooding brain. Her glass of water from the kitchen tap when she had approached the sacrament. A cored apple, filled with brown sugar, roasting for her at the hob on a dark autumn evening. Her shapely fingernails reddened by the blood of squashed lice from the children's shirts.

In a dream, silently, she had come to him, her wasted body within its loose graveclothes giving off an odour of wax and rosewood, her breath bent over him with mute secret words, a faint odour of wetted ashes.

Her glazing eyes, staring out of death, to shake and bend my soul. On me alone. The ghostcandle to light her agony. Ghostly light on the tortured face. Her hoarse loud breath rattling in horror, while all prayed on their knees. Her eyes on me to strike me down. *Liliata rutilantium te confessorum turma circumdet: iubilantium te virginum chorus excipiat.*

Ghoul! Chewer of corpses!

No, mother. Let me be and let me live.

– Kinch ahoy!

Buck Mulligan's voice sang from within the tower. It came nearer up the staircase, calling again. Stephen, still trembling at his soul's cry, heard warm running sunlight and in the air behind him friendly words.

– Dedalus, come down, like a good mosey. Breakfast is ready. Haines is apologizing for waking us last night. It's all right.

– I'm coming, Stephen said, turning.

– Do, for Jesus' sake, Buck Mulligan said. For my sake and for all our sakes.

His head disappeared and reappeared.

– I told him your symbol of Irish art. He says it's very clever. Touch him for a quid, will you? A guinea, I mean.

– I get paid this morning, Stephen said.

– The school kip? Buck Mulligan said. How much? Four quid? Lend us one.

– If you want it, Stephen said.

– Four shining sovereigns, Buck Mulligan cried with delight. We'll have a glorious drunk to astonish the druidy druids. Four omnipotent sovereigns.

He flung up his hands and tramped down the stone stairs, singing out of tune with a Cockney accent:

> *O, won't we have a merry time*
> *Drinking whisky, beer and wine,*
> *On coronation,*
> *Coronation day?*
> *O, won't we have a merry time*
> *On coronation day?*

Warm sunshine merrying over the sea. The nickel shavingbowl shone, forgotten, on the parapet. Why should I bring it down? Or leave it there all day, forgotten friendship?

He went over to it, held it in his hands awhile, feeling its coolness, smelling the clammy slaver of the lather in which the brush was stuck. So I carried the boat of incense then at Clongowes. I am another now and yet the same. A servant too. A server of a servant.

In the gloomy domed livingroom of the tower Buck Mulligan's gowned form moved briskly about the hearth to and fro, hiding and revealing its yellow glow. Two shafts of soft daylight fell across the flagged floor from the high barbicans: and at the meeting of their rays a cloud of coal-smoke and fumes of fried grease floated, turning.

– We'll be choked, Buck Mulligan said. Haines, open that door, will you?

Stephen laid the shavingbowl on the locker. A tall figure rose from the hammock where it had been sitting, went to the doorway and pulled open the inner doors.

– Have you the key? a voice asked.

– Dedalus has it, Buck Mulligan said. Janey Mack, I'm choked.

He howled without looking up from the fire:

– Kinch!

– It's in the lock, Stephen said, coming forward.

The key scraped round harshly twice and, when the heavy door had been set ajar, welcome light and bright air entered. Haines stood at the doorway, looking out. Stephen haled his upended valise to the table and sat down to wait. Buck Mulligan tossed the fry on to the dish beside him. Then he carried the dish and a large teapot over to the table, set them down heavily and sighed with relief.

– I'm melting, he said, as the candle remarked when . . . But hush. Not a word more on that subject. Kinch, wake up. Bread, butter, honey. Haines, come in. The grub is ready. Bless us, O Lord, and these thy gifts. Where's the sugar? O, jay, there's no milk.

Stephen fetched the loaf and the pot of honey and the buttercooler from the locker. Buck Mulligan sat down in a sudden pet.

– What sort of a kip is this? he said. I told her to come after eight.

– We can drink it black, Stephen said. There's a lemon in the locker.

– O, damn you and your Paris fads, Buck Mulligan said. I want Sandycove milk.

Haines came in from the doorway and said quietly:

– That woman is coming up with the milk.

– The blessings of God on you, Buck Mulligan cried, jumping up from his chair. Sit down. Pour out the tea there. The sugar is in the bag. Here, I can't go fumbling at the damned eggs. He hacked through the fry on the dish and slapped it out on three plates, saying:

– *In nomine Patris et Filii et Spiritus Sancti.*

Haines sat down to pour out the tea.

– I'm giving you two lumps each, he said. But, I say, Mulligan, you do make strong tea, don't you?

Buck Mulligan, hewing thick slices from the loaf said in an old woman's wheedling voice:

– When I makes tea I makes tea, as old mother Grogan said. And when I makes water I makes water.

– By Jove, it is tea, Haines said.

Buck Mulligan went on hewing and wheedling:

– *So I do, Mrs Cahill*, says she. *Begob, ma'am*, says Mrs Cahill, *God send you don't make them in the one pot.*

He lunged towards his messmates in turn a thick slice of bread, impaled on his knife.

– That's folk, he said very earnestly, for your book, Haines. Five lines of text and ten pages of notes about the folk and the fishgods of Dundrum. Printed by the weird sisters in the year of the big wind.

He turned to Stephen and asked in a fine puzzled voice, lifting his brows:

– Can you recall, brother, is mother Grogan's tea and water pot spoken of in the Mabinogion or is it in the Upanishads?

– I doubt it, said Stephen gravely.

– Do you now? Buck Mulligan said in the same tone. Your reasons, pray?

– I fancy, Stephen said as he ate, it did not exist in or out of the Mabinogion. Mother Grogan was, one imagines, a kinswoman of Mary Ann.

Buck Mulligan's face smiled with delight.

– Charming, he said in a finical sweet voice, showing his white teeth and blinking his eyes pleasantly. Do you think she was? Quite charming.

Then, suddenly overclouding all his features, he growled in a hoarsened rasping voice as he hewed again vigorously at the loaf:

> – *For old Mary Ann*
> *She doesn't care a damn,*
> *But, hising up her petticoats . . .*

He crammed his mouth with fry and munched and droned.

The doorway was darkened by an entering form.

– The milk, sir.

– Come in, ma'am, Mulligan said. Kinch, get the jug.

An old woman came forward and stood by Stephen's elbow.

– That's a lovely morning, sir, she said. Glory be to God.

– To whom? Mulligan said, glancing at her. Ah, to be sure.

Stephen reached back and took the milkjug from the locker.

– The islanders, Mulligan said to Haines casually, speak frequently of the collector of prepuces.

– How much, sir? asked the old woman.

– A quart, Stephen said.

He watched her pour into the measure and thence into the jug rich white milk, not hers. Old shrunken paps. She poured again a measureful and a tilly. Old and secret she had entered from a morning world, maybe a messenger. She praised the goodness of the milk, pouring it out. Crouching by a patient cow at daybreak in the lush field, a witch on her toadstool, her wrinkled fingers quick at the squirting dugs. They lowed about her whom they knew, dewsilky cattle. Silk of the kine and poor old woman, names given her in old times. A wandering crone, lowly form of an immortal serving her conqueror and her gay betrayer, their common cuckquean, a messenger from the secret morning. To serve or to upbraid, whether he could not tell: but scorned to beg her favour.

– It is indeed, ma'am, Buck Mulligan said, pouring milk into their cups.

– Taste it, sir, she said.

He drank at her bidding.

– If we could only live on good food like that, he said to her somewhat loudly, we wouldn't have the country full of rotten teeth and rotten guts. Living in a bogswamp, eating cheap food and the streets paved with dust, horsedung and consumptives' spits.

– Are you a medical student, sir? the old woman asked.

– I am, ma'am, Buck Mulligan answered.

Stephen listened in scornful silence. She bows her old head to a voice that speaks to her loudly, her bonesetter, her medicineman; me she slights. To the voice that will shrive and oil for the grave all there is of her but her woman's unclean loins, of man's flesh made not in God's likeness, the serpent's prey. And to the loud voice that now bids her be silent with wondering unsteady eyes.

– Do you understand what he says? Stephen asked her.

– Is it French you are talking, sir? the old woman said to Haines.

Haines spoke to her again a longer speech, confidently.

– Irish, Buck Mulligan said. Is there Gaelic on you?

– I thought it was Irish, she said, by the sound of it. Are you from west, sir?

– I am an Englishman, Haines answered.

– He's English, Buck Mulligan said, and he thinks we ought to speak Irish in Ireland.

– Sure we ought to, the old woman said, and I'm ashamed I don't speak the language myself. I'm told it's a grand language by them that knows.

– Grand is no name for it, said Buck Mulligan. Wonderful entirely. Fill us out some more tea, Kinch. Would you like a cup, ma'am?

– No, thank you, sir, the old woman said, slipping the ring of the milkcan on her forearm and about to go.

Haines said to her:

– Have you your bill? We had better pay her, Mulligan, hadn't we?

Stephen filled the three cups.

– Bill, sir? she said, halting. Well, it's seven mornings a pint at twopence is seven twos is a shilling and twopence over and these three mornings a quart at fourpence is three quarts is a shilling and one and two is two and two, sir.

Buck Mulligan sighed and having filled his mouth with a crust thickly buttered on both sides, stretched forth his legs and began to search his trouser pockets.

– Pay up and look pleasant, Haines said to him smiling.

Stephen filled a third cup, a spoonful of tea colouring faintly the thick rich milk. Buck Mulligan brought up a florin, twisted it round in his fingers and cried:

– A miracle!

He passed it along the table towards the old woman, saying:

– Ask nothing more of me, sweet. All I can give you I give.

Stephen laid the coin in her uneager hand.

– We'll owe twopence, he said.

– Time enough, sir, she said, taking the coin. Time enough. Good morning, sir.

She curtseyed and went out, followed by Buck Mulligan's tender chant:

> – *Heart of my heart, were it more,*
> *More would be laid at your feet.*

He turned to Stephen and said:

– Seriously, Dedalus. I'm stony. Hurry out to your school kip and bring us back some money. Today the bards must drink and junket. Ireland expects that every man this day will do his duty.

– That reminds me, Haines said, rising, that I have to visit your national library today.

– Our swim first, Buck Mulligan said.

He turned to Stephen and asked blandly:

– Is this the day for your monthly wash, Kinch?

Then he said to Haines:

– The unclean bard makes a point of washing once a month.

– All Ireland is washed by the gulfstream, Stephen said as he let honey trickle over a slice of the loaf.

Haines from the corner where he was knotting easily a scarf about the loose collar of his tennis shirt spoke:

– I intend to make a collection of your sayings if you will let me.

Speaking to me. They wash and tub and scrub. Agenbite of inwit. Conscience. Yet here's a spot.

– That one about the cracked lookingglass of a servant being the symbol of Irish art is deuced good.

Buck Mulligan kicked Stephen's foot under the table and said with warmth of tone:

– Wait till you hear him on Hamlet, Haines.

– Well, I mean it, Haines said, still speaking to Stephen. I was just thinking of it when that poor old creature came in.

– Would I make money by it? Stephen asked.

Haines laughed and, as he took his soft grey hat from the holdfast of the hammock, said:

– I don't know, I'm sure.

He strolled out to the doorway. Buck Mulligan bent across to Stephen and said with coarse vigour:

– You put your hoof in it now. What did you say that for?

– Well? Stephen said. The problem is to get money. From whom? From the milkwoman or from him. It's a toss up, I think.

– I blow him out about you, Buck Mulligan said, and then you come along with your lousy leer and your gloomy jesuit jibes.

– I see little hope, Stephen said, from her or from him.

Buck Mulligan sighed tragically and laid his hand on Stephen's arm.

– From me, Kinch, he said.

In a suddenly changed tone he added:

– To tell you the God's truth I think you're right. Damn all else they are good for. Why don't you play them as I do? To hell with them all. Let us get out of the kip.

He stood up, gravely ungirdled and disrobed himself of his gown, saying resignedly:

– Mulligan is stripped of his garments.

He emptied his pockets on to the table.

– There's your snotrag, he said.

And putting on his stiff collar and rebellious tie, he spoke to them, chiding them, and to his dangling watchchain. His hands plunged and rummaged in his trunk while he called for a clean handkerchief. Agenbite of inwit. God, we'll simply have to dress the character. I want puce gloves and green boots. Contradiction. Do I contradict myself? Very well then, I contradict myself. Mercurial Malachi. A limp black missile flew out of his talking hands.

– And there's your Latin quarter hat, he said.

Stephen picked it up and put it on. Haines called to them from the doorway:

– Are you coming, you fellows?

– I'm ready, Buck Mulligan answered, going towards the door. Come out, Kinch. You have eaten all we left, I suppose. Resigned he passed out with grave words and gait, saying, wellnigh with sorrow:

– And going forth he met Butterly.

Stephen, taking his ashplant from its leaningplace, followed them out and, as they went down the ladder, pulled to the slow iron door and locked it. He put the huge key in his inner pocket.

At the foot of the ladder Buck Mulligan asked:

– Did you bring the key?

– I have it, Stephen said, preceding them.

He walked on. Behind him he heard Buck Mulligan club with his heavy bathtowel the leader shoots of ferns or grasses.

– Down, sir. How dare you, sir?

Haines asked.

– Do you pay rent for this tower?

– Twelve quid, Buck Mulligan said.

– To the secretary of state for war, Stephen added over his shoulder.

They halted while Haines surveyed the tower and said at last:

– Rather bleak in wintertime, I should say. Martello you call it?

– Billy Pitt had them built, Buck Mulligan said, when the French were on the sea. But ours is the *omphalos*.

– What is your idea of Hamlet? Haines asked Stephen.

– No, no, Buck Mulligan shouted in pain. I'm not equal to Thomas Aquinas and the fiftyfive reasons he has made to prop it up. Wait till I have a few pints in me first.

He turned to Stephen, saying as he pulled down neatly the peaks of his primrose waistcoat:

– You couldn't manage it under three pints, Kinch, could you?

– It has waited so long, Stephen said listlessly, it can wait longer.

– You pique my curiosity, Haines said amiably. Is it some paradox?

– Pooh! Buck Mulligan said. We have grown out of Wilde and paradoxes. It's quite simple. He proves by algebra that Hamlet's grandson is Shakespeare's grandfather and that he himself is the ghost of his own father.

– What? Haines said, beginning to point at Stephen. He himself?

Buck Mulligan slung his towel stolewise round his neck and, bending in loose laughter, said to Stephen's ear:

– O, shade of Kinch the elder! Japhet in search of a father!

– We're always tired in the morning, Stephen said to Haines. And it is rather long to tell.

Buck Mulligan, walking forward again, raised his hands.

– The sacred pint alone can unbind the tongue of Dedalus, he said.

– I mean to say, Haines explained to Stephen as they followed, this tower and these cliffs here remind me somehow of Elsinore. *That beetles o'er his base into the sea*, isn't it?

Buck Mulligan turned suddenly for an instant towards Stephen but did not speak. In the bright silent instant Stephen saw his own image in cheap dusty mourning between their gay attires.

– It's a wonderful tale, Haines said, bringing them to halt again.

Eyes, pale as the sea the wind had freshened, paler, firm and prudent. The seas' ruler, he gazed southward over the bay, empty save for the smokeplume of the mailboat, vague on the bright skyline, and a sail tacking by the Muglins.

– I read a theological interpretation of it somewhere, he said bemused. The Father and the Son idea. The Son striving to be atoned with the Father.

Buck Mulligan at once put on a blithe broadly smiling face. He looked at them, his wellshaped mouth open happily, his eyes, from which he had suddenly withdrawn all shrewd sense, blinking with mad gaiety. He moved a doll's head to and fro, the brims of his Panama hat quivering, and began to chant in a quiet happy foolish voice:

> – *I'm the queerest young fellow that ever you heard.*
> *My mother's a jew, my father's a bird.*
> *With Joseph the joiner I cannot agree,*
> *So here's to disciples and Calvary.*

He held up a forefinger of warning.

> – *If anyone thinks that I amn't divine*
> *He'll get no free drinks when I'm making the wine*
> *But have to drink water and wish it were plain*
> *That I make when the wine becomes water again.*

He tugged swiftly at Stephen's ashplant in farewell and, running forward to a brow of the cliff, fluttered his hands at his sides like fins or wings of one about to rise in the air, and chanted:

> – *Goodbye, now, goodbye. Write down all I said*
> *And tell Tom, Dick and Harry I rose from the dead.*
> *What's bred in the bone cannot fail me to fly*
> *And Olivet's breezy . . . Goodbye, now, goodbye.*

He capered before them down towards the fortyfoot hole, fluttering his winglike hands, leaping nimbly, Mercury's hat quivering in the fresh wind that bore back to them his brief birdlike cries.

Haines, who had been laughing guardedly, walked on beside Stephen and said:

– We oughtn't to laugh, I suppose. He's rather blasphemous. I'm not a believer myself, that is to say. Still his gaiety takes the harm out of it somehow, doesn't it? What did he call it? Joseph the Joiner?

– The ballad of Joking Jesus, Stephen answered.

– O, Haines said, you have heard it before?

– Three times a day, after meals, Stephen said drily.

– You're not a believer, are you? Haines asked. I mean, a believer in the narrow sense of the word. Creation from nothing and miracles and a personal God.

– There's only one sense of the word, it seems to me, Stephen said.

Haines stopped to take out a smooth silver case in which twinkled a green stone. He sprang it open with his thumb and offered it.

– Thank you, Stephen said, taking a cigarette.

Haines helped himself and snapped the case to. He put it back in his sidepocket and took from his waistcoatpocket a nickel tinderbox, sprang it open too, and, having lit his cigarette, held the flaming spunk towards Stephen in the shell of his hands.

– Yes, of course, he said, as they went on again. Either you believe or you don't, isn't it? Personally I couldn't stomach that idea of a personal God. You don't stand for that, I suppose?

– You behold in me, Stephen said with grim displeasure, a horrible example of free thought.

He walked on, waiting to be spoken to, trailing his ashplant by his side. Its ferrule followed lightly on the path, squealing at his heels. My familiar, after me, calling Steeeeeeeeeephen. A wavering line along the path. They will walk on it tonight, coming here in the dark. He wants that key. It is mine, I paid the rent. Now I eat his salt bread. Give him the key too. All. He will ask for it. That was in his eyes.

– After all, Haines began . . .

Stephen turned and saw that the cold gaze which had measured him was not all unkind.

– After all, I should think you are able to free yourself. You are your own master, it seems to me.

– I am the servant of two masters, Stephen said, an English and an Italian.

– Italian? Haines said.

A crazy queen, old and jealous. Kneel down before me.

– And a third, Stephen said, there is who wants me for odd jobs.

– Italian? Haines said again. What do you mean?

– The imperial British state, Stephen answered, his colour rising, and the holy Roman catholic and apostolic church.

Haines detached from his underlip some fibres of tobacco before he spoke.

– I can quite understand that, he said calmly. An Irishman must think like that, I daresay. We feel in England that we have treated you rather unfairly. It seems history is to blame.

The proud potent titles clanged over Stephen's memory the triumph of their brazen bells: *et unam sanctam catholicam et apostolicam ecclesiam:* the slow growth and change of rite and dogma like his own rare thoughts, a chemistry of stars. Symbol of the apostles in the mass for pope Marcellus, the voices blended, singing alone loud in affirmation: and behind their chant the vigilant angel of the church militant disarmed and menaced her heresiarchs. A horde of heresies fleeing with mitres awry: Photius and the brood of mockers of whom Mulligan was one, and Arius, warring his life long upon the consubstantiality of the Son with the Father, and Valentine, spurning Christ's terrene body, and the subtle African heresiarch Sabellius who held that the Father was Himself His own Son. Words Mulligan had spoken a moment since in mockery to the stranger. Idle mockery. The void awaits surely all them that weave the wind: a menace, a disarming and a worsting from those embattled angels of the church, Michael's host, who defend her ever in the hour of conflict with their lances and their shields.

Hear, hear. Prolonged applause. *Zut! Nom de Dieu!*

– Of course I'm a Britisher, Haines' voice said, and I feel as one. I don't want to see my country fall into the hands of German jews either. That's our national problem, I'm afraid, just now.

Two men stood at the verge of the cliff, watching: businessman, boatman.

– She's making for Bullock harbour.

The boatman nodded towards the north of the bay with some disdain.

– There's five fathoms out there, he said. It'll be swept up that way when the tide comes in about one. It's nine days today.

The man that was drowned. A sail veering about the blank bay waiting for a swollen bundle to bob up, roll over to the sun a puffy face, salt white. Here I am.

They followed the winding path down to the creek. Buck Mulligan stood on a stone, in shirtsleeves, his unclipped tie rippling over his shoulder. A young man clinging to a spur of rock near him moved slowly frogwise his green legs in the deep jelly of the water.

– Is the brother with you, Malachi?

– Down in Westmeath. With the Bannons.

– Still there? I got a card from Bannon. Says he found a sweet young thing down there. Photo girl he calls her.

– Snapshot, eh? Brief exposure.

Buck Mulligan sat down to unlace his boots. An elderly man shot up near the spur of rock a blowing red face. He scrambled up by the stones, water glistening on his pate and on its garland of grey hair, water rilling over his chest and paunch and spilling jets out of his black sagging loincloth.

Buck Mulligan made way for him to scramble past and, glancing at Haines and Stephen, crossed himself piously with his thumbnail at brow and lips and breastbone.

– Seymour's back in town, the young man said, grasping again his spur of rock. Chucked medicine and going in for the army.

– Ah, go to God, Buck Mulligan said.

– Going over next week to stew. You know that red Carlisle girl, Lily?

– Yes.

– Spooning with him last night on the pier. The father is rotto with money.

– Is she up the pole?

– Better ask Seymour that.

– Seymour a bleeding officer, Buck Mulligan said.

He nodded to himself as he drew off his trousers and stood up, saying tritely:

– Redheaded women buck like goats.

He broke off in alarm, feeling his side under his flapping shirt.

– My twelfth rib is gone, he cried. I'm the *Uebermensch*. Toothless Kinch and I, the supermen.

He struggled out of his shirt and flung it behind him to where his clothes lay.

– Are you going in here, Malachi?

– Yes. Make room in the bed.

The young man shoved himself backward through the water and reached the middle of the creek in two long clean strokes. Haines sat down on a stone, smoking.

– Are you not coming in? Buck Mulligan asked.

– Later on, Haines said. Not on my breakfast.

Stephen turned away.

– I'm going, Mulligan, he said.

– Give us that key, Kinch, Buck Mulligan said, to keep my chemise flat.

Stephen handed him the key. Buck Mulligan laid it across his heaped clothes.

– And twopence, he said, for a pint. Throw it there.

Stephen threw two pennies on the soft heap. Dressing, undressing. Buck Mulligan erect, with joined hands before him, said solemnly:

– He who stealeth from the poor lendeth to the Lord. Thus spake Zarathustra.

His plump body plunged.

– We'll see you again, Haines said, turning as Stephen walked up the path and smiling at wild Irish.

Horn of a bull, hoof of a horse, smile of a Saxon.

– The Ship, Buck Mulligan cried. Half twelve.

– Good, Stephen said.

He walked along the upwardcurving path.

> *Liliata rutilantium.*
> *Turma circumdet.*
> *Iubilantium te virginum.*

The priest's grey nimbus in a niche where he dressed discreetly. I will not sleep here tonight. Home also I cannot go.

A voice, sweettoned and sustained, called to him from the sea. Turning the curve he waved his hand. It called again. A sleek brown head, a seal's, far out on the water, round.

Usurper.

*   *   *   *   *

◄ – YOU, COCHRANE, WHAT CITY SENT FOR HIM?

– Tarentum, sir.

– Very good. Well?

– There was a battle, sir.

– Very good. Where?

The boy's blank face asked the blank window.

Fabled by the daughters of memory. And yet it was in some way if not as memory fabled it. A phrase, then, of impatience, thud of Blake's wings of excess. I hear the ruin of all space, shattered glass and toppling masonry, and time one livid final flame. What's left us then?

– I forget the place, sir. 279 B.C.

– Asculum, Stephen said, glancing at the name and date in the gore-scarred book.

– Yes, sir. And he said: *Another victory like that and we are done for.*

That phrase the world had remembered. A dull ease of the mind. From a hill above a corpsestrewn plain a general speaking to his officers, leaned upon his spear. Any general to any officers. They lend ear.

– You, Armstrong, Stephen said. What was the end of Pyrrhus?

– End of Pyrrhus, sir?

– I know, sir. Ask me, sir, Comyn said.

– Wait. You, Armstrong. Do you know anything about Pyrrhus?

A bag of figrolls lay snugly in Armstrong's satchel. He curled them between his palms at whiles and swallowed them softly. Crumbs adhered to the tissues of his lips. A sweetened boy's breath. Welloff people, proud that their eldest son was in the navy. Vico Road, Dalkey.

– Pyrrhus, sir? Pyrrhus, a pier.

All laughed. Mirthless high malicious laughter. Armstrong looked round at his classmates, silly glee in profile. In a moment they will laugh more loudly, aware of my lack of rule and of the fees their papas pay.

– Tell me now, Stephen said, poking the boy's shoulder with the book, what is a pier.

– A pier, sir, Armstrong said. A thing out in the waves. A kind of bridge. Kingstown pier, sir.

Some laughed again: mirthless but with meaning. Two in the back bench whispered. Yes. They knew: had never learned nor ever been innocent. All. With envy he watched their faces. Edith, Ethel, Gerty, Lily. Their likes: their breaths, too, sweetened with tea and jam, their bracelets tittering in the struggle.

– Kingstown pier, Stephen said. Yes, a disappointed bridge.

The words troubled their gaze.

– How, sir? Comyn asked. A bridge is across a river.

For Haines's chapbook. No-one here to hear. Tonight deftly amid wild drink and talk, to pierce the polished mail of his mind. What then? A jester at the court of his master, indulged and disesteemed, winning a clement master's praise. Why had they chosen all that part? Not wholly for the smooth caress. For them too history was a tale like any other too often heard, their land a pawnshop.

Had Pyrrhus not fallen by a beldam's hand in Argos or Julius Caesar not been knifed to death. They are not to be thought away. Time has branded them and fettered they are lodged in the room of the infinite possibilities they have ousted. But can those have been possible seeing that they never were? Or was that only possible which came to pass? Weave, weaver of the wind.

– Tell us a story, sir.

– Oh, do, sir, A ghoststory.

– Where do you begin in this? Stephen asked, opening another book.

– *Weep no more,* Comyn said.

– Go on then, Talbot.

– And the history, sir?

– After, Stephen said. Go on, Talbot.

A swarthy boy opened a book and propped it nimbly under the breastwork of his satchel. He recited jerks of verse with odd glances at the text:

> – *Weep no more, woful shepherd, weep no more*
> *For Lycidas, your sorrow, is not dead,*
> *Sunk though he be beneath the watery floor . . .*

It must be a movement then, an actuality of the possible as possible. Aristotle's phrase formed itself within the gabbled verses and floated out into the studious silence of the library of Sainte Geneviève where he had read, sheltered from the sin of Paris, night by night. By his elbow a delicate Siamese conned a handbook of strategy. Fed and feeding brains about me: under glowlamps, impaled, with faintly beating feelers: and in my mind's darkness a sloth of the underworld, reluctant, shy of brightness, shifting her dragon scaly folds. Thought is the thought of thought. Tranquil brightness. The soul is in a manner all that is: the soul is the form of forms. Tranquillity sudden, vast, candescent: form of forms.

Talbot repeated:

> – *Through the dear might of Him that walked the waves,*
> *Through the dear might . . .*

– Turn over, Stephen said quietly. I don't see anything.

– What, sir? Talbot asked simply, bending forward.

His hand turned the page over. He leaned back and went on again having just remembered. Of him that walked the waves. Here also over these craven hearts his shadow lies and on the scoffer's heart and lips and on mine. It lies upon their eager faces who offered him a coin of the tribute. To Caesar what is Caesar's, to God what is God's. A long look from dark eyes, a riddling sentence to be woven and woven on the church's looms. Ay.

Riddle me, riddle me, randy ro.
My father gave me seeds to sow.

Talbot slid his closed book into his satchel.

– Have I heard all? Stephen asked.

– Yes, sir. Hockey at ten, sir.

– Half day, sir. Thursday.

– Who can answer a riddle? Stephen asked.

They bundled their books away, pencils clacking, pages rustling. Crowding together they strapped and buckled their satchels, all gabbling gaily:

– A riddle, sir? Ask me, sir.

– O, ask me, sir.

– A hard one, sir.

– This is the riddle, Stephen said:

The cock crew
The sky was blue:
The bells in heaven
Were striking eleven.
'Tis time for this poor soul
To go to heaven.

– What is that?

– What, sir?

– Again, sir. We didn't hear.

Their eyes grew bigger as the lines were repeated. After a silence Cochrane said:

– What is it, sir? We give it up.

Stephen, his throat itching, answered:

– The fox burying his grandmother under a hollybush.

He stood up and gave a shout of nervous laughter to which their cries echoed dismay.

A stick struck the door and a voice in the corridor called:

– Hockey!

They broke asunder, sidling out of their benches, leaping them. Quickly they were gone and from the lumberroom came the rattle of sticks and clamour of their boots and tongues.

Sargent who alone had lingered came forward slowly, showing an open copybook. His tangled hair and scraggy neck gave witness of unreadiness and through his misty glasses weak eyes looked up pleading. On his cheek, dull and bloodless, a soft stain of ink lay, dateshaped, recent and damp as a snail's bed.

He held out his copybook. The word *Sums* was written on the headline. Beneath were sloping figures and at the foot a crooked signature with blind loops and a blot. Cyril Sargent: his name and seal.

– Mr Deasy told me to write them out all again, he said, and show them to you, sir.

Stephen touched the edges of the book. Futility.

– Do you understand how to do them now? he asked.

– Numbers eleven to fifteen, Sargent answered. Mr Deasy said I was to copy them off the board, sir.

– Can you do them yourself? Stephen asked.

– No, sir.

Ugly and futile: lean neck and tangled hair and a stain of ink, a snail's bed. Yet someone had loved him, borne him in her arms and in her heart. But for her the race of the world would have trampled him under foot, a squashed boneless snail. She had loved his weak watery blood drained from her own. Was that then real? The only true thing in life? His mother's prostrate body the fiery Columbanus in holy zeal bestrode. She was no more: the trembling skeleton of a twig burnt in the fire, an odour of rosewood and wetted ashes. She had saved him from being trampled under foot and had gone, scarcely having been. A poor soul gone to heaven: and on a heath beneath winking stars a fox, red reek of rapine in his fur, with merciless bright eyes scraped in the earth, listened, scraped up the earth, listened, scraped and scraped.

Sitting at his side Stephen solved out the problem. He proves by algebra that Shakespeare's ghost is Hamlet's grandfather. Sargent peered askance through his slanted glasses. Hockeysticks rattled in the lumberroom: the hollow knock of a ball and calls from the field.

Across the page the symbols moved in grave morrice, in the mummery of their letters, wearing quaint caps of squares and cubes. Give hands, traverse, how to partner: so: imps of fancy of the Moors. Gone too from the world, Averroes and Moses Maimonides, dark men in mien and movement, flashing in their mocking mirrors the obscure soul of the world, a darkness shining in brightness which brightness could not comprehend.

– Do you understand now? Can you work the second for yourself?

– Yes, sir.

In long shady strokes Sargent copied the data. Waiting always for a word of help his hand moved faithfully the unsteady symbols, a faint hue of shame flickering behind his dull skin. *Amor matris:* subjective and objective genitive. With her weak blood and wheysour milk she had fed him and hid from sight of others his swaddling bands.

Like him was I, these sloping shoulders, this gracelessness. My childhood bends beside me. Too far for me to lay a hand there once or lightly. Mine is far and his secret as our eyes. Secrets, silent, stony sit in the dark palaces of both our hearts: secrets weary of their tyranny: tyrants willing to be dethroned.

The sum was done.

– It is very simple, Stephen said as he stood up.

– Yes, sir. Thanks, Sargent answered.

He dried the page with a sheet of thin blottingpaper and carried his copybook back to his desk.

– You had better get your stick and go out to the others, Stephen said as he followed towards the door the boy's graceless form.

– Yes, sir.

In the corridor his name was heard, called from the playfield.

– Sargent!

– Run on, Stephen said. Mr Deasy is calling you.

He stood in the porch and watched the laggard hurry towards the scrappy field where sharp voices were in strife. They were sorted in teams and Mr Deasy came stepping over wisps of grass with gaitered feet. When he had reached the schoolhouse voices again contending called to him. He turned his angry white moustache.

– What is it now? he cried continually without listening.

– Cochrane and Halliday are on the same side, sir, Stephen cried.

– Will you wait in my study for a moment, Mr Deasy said, till I restore order here.

And as he stepped fussily back across the field his old man's voice cried sternly:

– What is the matter? What is it now?

Their sharp voices cried about him on all sides: their many forms closed round him, the garish sunshine bleaching the honey of his illdyed head.

Stale smoky air hung in the study with the smell of drab abraded leather of its chairs. As on the first day he bargained with me here. As it was in the beginning, is now. On the sideboard the tray of Stuart coins, base treasure of a bog: and ever shall be. And snug in their spooncase of purple plush, faded, the twelve apostles having preached to all the gentiles: world without end.

A hasty step over the stone porch and in the corridor. Blowing out his rare moustache Mr Deasy halted at the table.

– First, our little financial settlement, he said.

He brought out of his coat a pocketbook bound by a leather thong. It slapped open and he took from it two notes, one of joined halves, and laid them carefully on the table.

– Two, he said, strapping and stowing his pocketbook away.

And now his strongroom for the gold. Stephen's embarrassed hand moved over the shells heaped in the cold stone mortar: whelks and money, cowries and leopard shells: and this, whorled as an emir's turban, and this, the scallop of Saint James. An old pilgrim's hoard, dead treasure, hollow shells.

A sovereign fell, bright and new, on the soft pile of the tablecloth.

– Three, Mr Deasy said, turning his little savingsbox about in his hand. These are handy things to have. See. This is for sovereigns. This is for shillings, sixpences, half-crowns. And here crowns. See. –

He shot from it two crowns and two shillings.

– Three twelve, he said. I think you'll find that's right.

– Thank you, sir, Stephen said, gathering the money together with shy haste and putting it all in a pocket of his trousers.

– No thanks at all, Mr Deasy said. You have earned it.

Stephen's hand, free again, went back to the hollow shells. Symbols too of beauty and of power. A lump in my pocket. Symbols soiled by greed and misery.

– Don't carry it like that, Mr Deasy said. You'll pull it out somewhere and lose it. You just buy one of these machines. You'll find them very handy.

Answer something.

– Mine would be often empty, Stephen said.

The same room and hour, the same wisdom: and I the same. Three times now. Three nooses round me here. Well. I can break them in this instant if I will.

– Because you don't save, Mr Deasy said, pointing his finger. You don't know yet what money is. Money is power, when you have lived as long as I have. I know, I know. If youth but knew. But what does Shakespeare say? *Put but money in thy purse.*

– Iago, Stephen murmured.

He lifted his gaze from the idle shells to the old man's stare.

– He knew what money was, Mr Deasy said. He made money. A poet but an Englishman too. Do you know what is the pride of the English? Do you know what is the proudest word you will ever hear from an English-man's mouth?

The seas' ruler. His seacold eyes looked on the empty bay: history is to blame: on me and on my words, unhating.

– That on his empire, Stephen said, the sun never sets.

– Ba! Mr Deasy cried. That's not English. A French Celt said that. He tapped his savingsbox against his thumbnail.

– I will tell you, he said solemnly, what is his proudest boast. *I paid my way*.

Good man, good man.

– *I paid my way. I never borrowed a shilling in my life.* Can you feel that? *I owe nothing*. Can you?

Mulligan, nine pounds, three pairs of socks, one pair brogues, ties. Curran, ten guineas. McCann, one guinea. Fred Ryan, two shillings. Temple, two lunches. Russell, one guinea, Cousins, ten shillings, Bob Reynolds, half a guinea, Köhler, three guineas, Mrs McKernan, five weeks' board. The lump I have is useless.

– For the moment, no, Stephen answered.

Mr Deasy laughed with rich delight, putting back his savingsbox.

– I knew you couldn't, he said joyously. But one day you must feel it. We are a generous people but we must also be just.

– I fear those big words, Stephen said, which make us so unhappy.

Mr Deasy stared sternly for some moments over the mantelpiece at the shapely bulk of a man in tartan fillibegs: Albert Edward, Prince of Wales.

– You think me an old fogey and an old tory, his thoughtful voice said. I saw three generations since O'Connell's time. I remember the famine. Do you know that the orange lodges agitated for repeal of the union twenty years before O'Connell did or before the prelates of your communion denounced him as a demagogue? You fenians forget some things.

Glorious, pious and immortal memory. The lodge of Diamond in Armagh the splendid behung with corpses of papishes. Hoarse, masked and armed, the planters' covenant. The black north and true blue bible. Croppies lie down.

Stephen sketched a brief gesture.

– I have rebel blood in me too, Mr Deasy said. On the spindle side. But I am descended from sir John Blackwood who voted for the union. We are all Irish, all kings' sons.

– Alas, Stephen said.

– *Per vias rectas*, Mr Deasy said firmly, was his motto. He voted for it and put on his topboots to ride to Dublin from the Ards of Down to do so.

> *Lal the ral the ra*
> *The rocky road to Dublin.*

A gruff squire on horseback with shiny topboots. Soft day, sir John. Soft day, your honour . . . Day . . . Day . . . Two topboots jog dangling on to Dublin. Lal the ral the ra, lal the ral the raddy.

– That reminds me, Mr Deasy said. You can do me a favour, Mr Dedalus, with some of your literary friends. I have a letter here for the press. Sit down a moment. I have just to copy the end.

He went to the desk near the window, pulled in his chair twice and read off some words from the sheet on the drum of his typewriter.

– Sit down. Excuse me, he said over his shoulder, *the dictates of common sense*. Just a moment.

He peered from under his shaggy brows at the manuscript by his elbow and, muttering, began to prod the stiff buttons of the keyboard slowly, some times blowing as he screwed up the drum to erase an error.

Stephen seated himself noiselessly before the princely presence. Framed around the walls images of vanished horses stood in homage, their meek heads poised in air: lord Hastings' Repulse, the duke of Westminster's Shotover, the duke of Beaufort's Ceylon, *prix de Paris*, 1866. Elfin riders sat them, watchful of a sign. He saw their speeds, backing king's colours, and shouted with the shouts of vanished crowds.

– Full stop, Mr Deasy bade his keys. But prompt ventilation of this important question . . .

Where Cranly led me to get rich quick, hunting his winners among the mudsplashed brakes, amid the bawls of bookies on their pitches and reek of the canteen, over the motley slush. Even money Fair Rebel: ten to one the field. Dicers and thimbleriggers we hurried by after the hoofs, the vying caps and jackets and past the meatfaced woman, a butcher's dame, nuzzling thirstily her clove of orange.

Shouts rang shrill from the boy's playfield and a whirring whistle.

Again: a goal. I am among them, among their battling bodies in a medley, the joust of life. You mean that knockkneed mother's darling who seems to be slightly crawsick? Jousts. Time shocked rebounds, shock by shock. Jousts, slush and uproar of battles, the frozen deathspew of the slain, a shout of spear spikes baited with men's bloodied guts.

– Now then, Mr Deasy said, rising.

He came to the table, pinning together his sheets. Stephen stood up.

– I have put the matter into a nutshell, Mr Deasy said. It's about the foot and mouth disease. Just look through it. There can be no two opinions on the matter.

May I trespass on your valuable space. That doctrine of *laissez faire* which so often in our history. Our cattle trade. The way of all our old industries. Liverpool ring which jockeyed the Galway harbour scheme. European conflagration. Grain supplies through the narrow waters of the channel. The pluterperfect imperturbability of the department of agriculture. Pardoned a classical allusion. Cassandra. By a woman who was no better than she should be. To come to the point at issue.

– I don't mince words, do I? Mr Deasy asked as Stephen read on.

Foot and mouth disease. Known as Koch's preparation. Serum and virus. Percentage of salted horses. Rinderpest. Emperor's horses at Mürzsteg, lower Austria. Veterinary surgeons. Mr Henry Blackwood Price. Courteous offer a fair trial. Dictates of common sense. Allimportant question. In every sense of the word take the bull by the horns. Thanking you for the hospitality of your columns.

– I want that to be printed and read, Mr Deasy said. You will see at the next outbreak they will put an embargo on Irish cattle. And it can be cured. It is cured. My cousin, Blackwood Price, writes to me it is regularly treated and cured in Austria by cattledoctors there. They offer to come over here. I am trying to work up influence with the department. Now I'm going to try publicity. I am surrounded by difficulties, by . . . intrigues, by . . . backstairs influence, by . . .

He raised his forefinger and beat the air oldly before his voice spoke.

– Mark my words, Mr Dedalus, he said. England is in the hands of the jews. In all the highest places: her finance, her press. And they are the signs of a nation's decay. Wherever they gather they eat up the nation's vital strength. I have seen it coming these years. As sure as we are standing here the jew merchants are already at their work of destruction. Old England is dying.

He stepped swiftly off, his eyes coming to blue life as they passed a broad sunbeam. He faced about and back again.

– Dying, he said, if not dead by now.

> *The harlot's cry from street to street*
> *Shall weave old England's winding sheet.*

His eyes open wide in vision stared sternly across the sunbeam in which he halted.

– A merchant, Stephen said, is one who buys cheap and sells dear, jew or gentile, is he not?

– They sinned against the light, Mr Deasy said gravely. And you can see the darkness in their eyes. And that is why they are wanderers on the earth to this day.

On the steps of the Paris Stock Exchange the goldskinned men quoting prices on their gemmed fingers. Gabbles of geese. They swarmed loud, uncouth about the temple, their heads thickplotting under maladroit silk hats. Not theirs: these clothes, this speech, these gestures. Their full slow eyes belied the words, the gestures eager and unoffending, but knew the rancours massed about them and knew their zeal was vain. Vain patience to heap and hoard. Time surely would scatter all. A hoard heaped by the roadside: plundered and passing on. Their eyes knew the years of wandering and, patient, knew the dishonours of their flesh.

– Who has not? Stephen said.

– What do you mean? Mr Deasy asked.

He came forward a pace and stood by the table. His underjaw fell sideways open uncertainly. Is this old wisdom? He waits to hear from me.

– History, Stephen said, is a nightmare from which I am trying to awake.

From the playfield the boys raised a shout. A whirring whistle: goal. What if that nightmare gave you a back kick?

– The ways of the Creator are not our ways, Mr Deasy said. All history moves towards one great goal, the manifestation of God.

Stephen jerked his thumb towards the window, saying:

– That is God.

Hooray! Ay! Whrrwhee!

– What? Mr Deasy asked.

– A shout in the street, Stephen answered, shrugging his shoulders.

Mr Deasy looked down and held for a while the wings of his nose tweaked between his fingers. Looking up again he set them free.

– I am happier than you are, he said. We have committed many errors and many sins. A woman brought sin into the world. For a woman who was no better than she should be, Helen, the runaway wife of Menelaus, ten years the Greeks made war on Troy. A faithless wife first brought the strangers to our shore here, MacMurrough's wife and her leman O'Rourke, prince of Breffni. A woman too brought Parnell low. Many errors, many failures but not the one sin. I am a struggler now at the end of my days. But I will fight for the right till the end.

> *For Ulster will fight*
> *And Ulster will be right.*

Stephen raised the sheets in his hand.

– Well, sir, he began.

– I foresee, Mr Deasy said, that you will not remain here very long at this work. You were not born to be a teacher, I think. Perhaps I am wrong.

– A learner rather, Stephen said.

And here what will you learn more?

Mr Deasy shook his head.

– Who knows? he said. To learn one must be humble. But life is the great teacher.

Stephen rustled the sheets again.

– As regards these, he began.

– Yes, Mr Deasy said. You have two copies there. If you can have them published at once.

Telegraph. Irish Homestead.

– I will try, Stephen said, and let you know tomorrow. I know two editors slightly.

– That will do, Mr Deasy said briskly. I wrote last night to Mr Field, M. P. There is a meeting of the cattletraders' association today at the City Arms Hotel. I asked him to lay my letter before the meeting. You see if you can get it into your two papers. What are they?

– *The Evening Telegraph* . . .

– That will do, Mr Deasy said. There is no time to lose. Now I have to answer that letter from my cousin.

– Good morning, sir, Stephen said, putting the sheets in his pocket. Thank you.

– Not at all, Mr Deasy said as he searched the papers on his desk. I like to break a lance with you, old as I am.

– Good morning, sir, Stephen said again, bowing to his bent back.

He went out by the open porch and down the gravel path under the trees, hearing the cries of voices and crack of sticks from the playfield. The lions couchant on the pillars as he passed out through the gate; toothless terrors. Still I will help him in his fight. Mulligan will dub me a new name: the bullockbefriending bard.

– Mr Dedalus!

Running after me. No more letters, I hope.

– Just one moment.

– Yes, sir, Stephen said, turning back at the gate.

Mr Deasy halted, breathing hard and swallowing his breath.

– I just wanted to say, he said. Ireland, they say, has the honour of being the only country which never persecuted the jews. Do you know that? No. And do you know why?

He frowned sternly on the bright air.

– Why, sir? Stephen asked, beginning to smile.

– Because she never let them in, Mr Deasy said solemnly.

A coughball of laughter leaped from his throat dragging after it a rattling chain of phlegm. He turned back quickly, coughing, laughing, his lifted arms waving to the air.

– She never let them in, he cried again through his laughter as he stamped on gaitered feet over the gravel of the path. That's why.

On his wise shoulders through the checkerwork of leaves the sun flung spangles, dancing coins.

* * * * *

◀ INELUCTABLE MODALITY OF THE VISIBLE: AT LEAST that if no more, thought through my eyes. Signatures of all things I am here to read, seaspawn and seawrack, the nearing tide, that rusty boot. Snotgreen, bluesilver, rust: coloured signs. Limits of the diaphane. But he adds: in bodies. Then he was aware of them bodies before of them coloured. How? By knocking his sconce against them, sure. Go easy. Bald he was and a millionaire, *maestro di color che sanno*. Limit of the diaphane in. Why in? Diaphane, adiaphane. If you can put your five fingers through it, it is a gate, if not a door. Shut your eyes and see.

Stephen closed his eyes to hear his boots crush crackling wrack and shells. You are walking through it howsomever. I am, a stride at a time. A very short space of time through very short times of space. Five, six: the *nacheinander*. Exactly: and that is the ineluctable modality of the audible. Open your eyes. No. Jesus! If I fell over a cliff that beetles o'er his base, fell through the *nebeneinander* ineluctably. I am getting on nicely in the dark. My ash sword hangs at my side. Tap with it: they do. My two feet in his boots are at the end of his legs, *nebeneinander*. Sounds solid: made by the mallet of *Los Demiurgos*. Am I walking into eternity along Sandymount strand? Crush, crack, crik, crick. Wild sea money. Dominie Deasy kens them a'.

> *Won't you come to Sandymount,*
> *Madeline the mare?*

Rhythm begins, you see. I hear. A catalectic tetrameter of iambs marching. No, agallop: *deline the mare*.

Open your eyes now. I will. One moment. Has all vanished since? If I open and am for ever in the black adiaphane. *Basta!* I will see if I can see.

See now. There all the time without you: and ever shall be, world without end.

They came down the steps from Leahy's terrace prudently, *Frauen-zimmer*: and down the shelving shore flabbily their splayed feet sinking in the silted sand. Like me, like Algy, coming down to our mighty mother. Number one swung lourdily her midwife's bag, the other's gamp poked in the beach. From the liberties, out for the day. Mrs Florence MacCabe, relict of the late Patk MacCabe, deeply lamented, of Bride Street. One of her sisterhood lugged me squealing into life. Creation from nothing. What has she in the bag? A misbirth with a trailing navelcord, hushed in ruddy wool. The cords of all link back, strandentwining cable of all flesh. That is why mystic monks. Will you be as gods? Gaze in your omphalos. Hello. Kinch here. Put me on to Edenville. Aleph, alpha: nought, nought, one.

Spouse and helpmate of Adam Kadmon: Heva, naked Eve. She had no navel. Gaze. Belly without blemish, bulging big, a buckler of taut vellum, no, whiteheaped corn, orient and immortal, standing from everlasting to everlasting. Womb of sin.

Wombed in sin darkness I was too, made not begotten. By them, the man with my voice and my eyes and a ghost-woman with ashes on her breath. They clasped and sundered, did the coupler's will. From before the ages He willed me and now may not will me away or ever. A *lex eterna* stays about Him. Is that then the divine substance wherein Father and Son are consubstantial? Where is poor dear Arius to try conclusions? Warring his life long on the contransmagnificandjewbangtantiality. Illstarred heresiarch. In a Greek watercloset he breathed his last: euthanasia. With beaded mitre and with crozier, stalled upon his throne, widower of a widowed see, with upstiffed omophorion, with clotted hinderparts.

Airs romped around him, nipping and eager airs. They are coming, waves. The whitemaned seahorses, champing, brightwindbridled, the steeds of Mananaan.

I mustn't forget his letter for the press. And after? The Ship, half twelve. By the way go easy with that money like a good young imbecile. Yes, I must.

His pace slackened. Here. Am I going to Aunt Sara's or not? My consubstantial father's voice. Did you see anything of your artist brother Stephen lately? No? Sure he's not down in Strasburg terrace with his aunt Sally? Couldn't he fly a bit higher than that, eh? And and and and tell us Stephen, how is uncle Si? O weeping God, the things I married into. De boys up in de hayloft. The drunken little costdrawer and his brother, the cornet player. Highly respectable gondoliers. And skeweyed Walter sirring his father, no less. Sir. Yes, sir. No, sir. Jesus wept: and no wonder, by Christ.

I pull the wheezy bell of their shuttered cottage: and wait. They take me for a dun, peer out from a coign of vantage.

– It's Stephen, sir.

– Let him in. Let Stephen in.

A bolt drawn back and Walter welcomes me.

– We thought you were someone else.

In his broad bed nuncle Richie, pillowed and blanketed, extends over the hillock of his knees a sturdy forearm. Cleanchested. He has washed the upper moiety.

– Morrow, nephew.

He lays aside the lapboard whereon he drafts his bills of costs for the eyes of Master Goff and Master Shapland Tandy, filing consents and common searches and a writ of *Duces Tecum*. A bogoak frame over his bald head: Wilde's *Requiescat*. The drone of his misleading whistle brings Walter back.

– Yes, sir?

– Malt for Richie and Stephen, tell mother. Where is she?

– Bathing Crissie, sir.

Papa's little bedpal. Lump of love.

– No, uncle Richie . . .

– Call me Richie. Damn your lithia water. It lowers. Whusky!

– Uncle Richie, really . . .

– Sit down or by the law Harry I'll knock you down. Walter squints vainly for a chair.

– He has nothing to sit down on, sir.

– He has nowhere to put it, you mug. Bring in our Chippendale chair. Would you like a bite of something? None of your damned lawdeedaw air here; the rich of a rasher fried with a herring? Sure? So much the better. We have nothing in the house but backache pills.

All'erta!

He drones bars of Ferrando's *aria di sortita*. The grandest number, Stephen, in the whole opera. Listen.

His tuneful whistle sounds again, finely shaded, with rushes of the air, his fists bigdrumming on his padded knees.

This wind is sweeter.

Houses of decay, mine, his and all. You told the Clongowes gentry you had an uncle a judge and an uncle a general in the army. Come out of them, Stephen. Beauty is not there. Nor in the stagnant bay of Marsh's library where you read the fading prophecies of Joachim Abbas. For whom? The hundredheaded rabble of the cathedral close. A hater of his kind ran from them to the wood of madness, his mane foaming in the moon, his eyeballs stars. Houyhnhnm, horsenostrilled. The oval equine faces, Temple, Buck Mulligan, Foxy Campbell. Lantern jaws. Abbas father, furious dean, what offence laid fire to their brains? Paff! *Descende, calve, ut ne nimium decalveris.* A garland of grey hair on his comminated head see him me clambering down to the footpace *(descende)*, clutching a monstrance, basiliskeyed. Get down, bald poll! A choir gives back menace and echo, assisting about the altar's horns, the snorted Latin of jack-priests moving burly in their albs, tonsured and oiled and gelded, fat with the fat of kidneys of wheat.

And at the same instant perhaps a priest round the corner is elevating it. Dringdring! And two streets off another locking it into a pyx. Dringadring! And in a ladychapel another taking housel all to his own cheek. Dringdring! Down, up, forward, back. Dan Occam thought of that, invincible doctor. A misty English morning the imp hypostasis tickled his brain. Bringing his host down and kneeling he heard twine with his second bell the first bell in the transept (he is lifting his) and, rising, heard (now I am lifting) their two bells (he is kneeling) twang in diphthong.

Cousin Stephen, you will never be a saint. Isle of saints. You were awfully holy, weren't you? You prayed to the Blessed Virgin that you might not have a red nose. You prayed to the devil in Serpentine avenue that the fubsy widow in front might lift her clothes still more from the wet street. *O si, certo!* Sell your soul for that, do, dyed rags pinned round a squaw. More tell me, more still! On the top of the Howth tram alone crying to the rain: *naked women!* What about that, eh?

What about what? What else were they invented for?

Reading two pages apiece of seven books every night, eh? I was young. You bowed to yourself in the mirror, stepping forward to applause earnestly, striking face. Hurray for the Goddamned idiot! Hray! No-one saw: tell no-one. Books you were going to write with letters for titles. Have you read his F? O yes, but I prefer Q. Yes, but W is wonderful. O yes, W. Remember your epiphanies on green oval leaves, deeply deep, copies to be sent if you died to all the great libraries of the world, including Alexandria? Someone was to read them there after a few thousand years, a mahamanvantara. Pico della Mirandola like. Ay, very like a whale. When one reads these strange pages of one long gone one feels that one is at one with one who once . . .

The grainy sand had gone from under his feet. His boots trod again a damp crackling mast, razorshells, squeaking pebbles, that on the un-numbered pebbles beats, wood sieved by the shipworm, lost Armada. Unwholesome sandflats waited to suck his treading soles, breathing upward sewage breath. He coasted them, walking warily. A porterbottle stood up, stogged to its waist, in the cakey sand dough. A sentinel: isle of dreadful thirst. Broken hoops on the shore; at the land a maze of dark cunning nets; farther away chalkscrawled backdoors and on the higher beach a drying-line with two crucified shirts. Ringsend: wigwams of brown steersmen and master mariners. Human shells.

He halted. I have passed the way to aunt Sara's. Am I not going there? Seems not. No-one about. He turned northeast and crossed the firmer sand towards the Pigeonhouse.

– *Qui vous a mis dans cette fichue position?*

– *C'est le pigeon, Joseph.*

Patrice, home on furlough, lapped warm milk with me in the bar MacMahon. Son of the wild goose, Kevin Egan of Paris. My father's a bird, he lapped the sweet *lait chaud* with pink young tongue, plump bunny's face. Lap, *lapin*. He hopes to win in the *gros lots*. About the nature of women he read in Michelet. But he must send me *La Vie de Jésus* by M. Léo Taxil. Lent it to his friend.

– *C'est tordant, vous savez. Moi je suis socialiste. Je ne crois pas en l'existence de Dieu. Faut pas le dire à mon père.*

– *Il croit?*

– *Mon père, oui.*

Schluss. He laps.

My Latin quarter hat. God, we simply must dress the character. I want puce gloves. You were a student, weren't you? Of what in the other devil's name? Paysayenn. P. C. N., you know: *physiques, chimiques et naturelles.* Aha. Eating your groatsworth of *mou en civet*, fleshpots of Egypt, elbowed by belching cabmen. Just say in the most natural tone: when I was in Paris, *boul' Mich'*, I used to. Yes, used to carry punched tickets to prove an alibi if they arrested you for murder somewhere. Justice. On the night of the seventeenth of February 1904 the prisoner was seen by two witnesses. Other fellow did it: other me. Hat, tie, overcoat, nose. *Lui, c'est moi.* You seem to have enjoyed yourself.

Proudly walking. Whom were you trying to walk like? Forget: a dispossessed. With mother's money order, eight shillings, the banging door of the post office slammed in your face by the usher. Hunger toothache. *Encore deux minutes.* Look clock. Must get. *Fermé.* Hired dog! Shoot him to bloody bits with a bang shotgun, bits man spattered walls all brass buttons. Bits all khrrrrklak in place clack back. Not hurt? O, that's all right. Shake hands. See what I meant, see? O, that's all right. Shake a shake. O, that's all only all right.

You were going to do wonders, what? Missionary to Europe after fiery Columbanus. Fiacre and Scotus on their creepystools in heaven spilt from their pintpots, loudlatinlaughing: *Euge! Euge!* Pretending to speak broken English as you dragged your valise, porter threepence, across the slimy pier at Newhaven. *Comment?* Rich booty you brought back; *Le Tutu*, five tattered numbers of *Pantalon Blanc et Culotte Rouge*, a blue French telegram, curiosity to show:

– Mother dying come home father.

The aunt thinks you killed your mother. That's why she won't.

> *Then here's a health to Mulligan's aunt*
> *And I'll tell you the reason why.*
> *She always kept things decent in*
> *The Hannigan famileye.*

His feet marched in sudden proud rhythm over the sand furrows, along by the boulders of the south wall. He stared at them proudly, piled stone mammoth skulls. Gold light on sea, on sand, on boulders. The sun is there, the slender trees, the lemon houses.

Paris rawly waking, crude sunlight on her lemon streets. Moist pith of farls of bread, the froggreen wormwood, her matin incense, court the air. Belluomo rises from the bed of his wife's lover's wife, the kerchiefed housewife is astir, a saucer of acetic acid in her hands. In Rodot's Yvonne and Madeleine newmake their tumbled beauties, shattering with gold teeth *chaussons* of pastry, their mouths yellowed with the *pus* of *flan breton*. Faces of Paris men go by, their wellpleased pleasers, curled conquistadores.

Noon slumbers. Kevin Egan rolls gunpowder cigarettes through fingers smeared with printer's ink, sipping his green fairy as Patrice his white. About us gobblers fork spiced beans down their gullets. *Un demi setier!* A jet of coffee steam from the burnished caldron. She serves me at his beck. *Il est irlandais. Hollandais? Non fromage. Deux irlandais, nous, Irlande, vous savez? Ah oui!* She thought you wanted a cheese *hollandais*. Your postprandial, do you know that word? Post-prandial. There was a fellow I knew once in Barcelona, queer fellow, used to call it his postprandial. Well: *slainte!* Around the slabbed tables the tangle of wined breaths and grumbling gorges. His breath hangs over our saucestained plates, the green fairy's fang thrusting between his lips. Of Ireland, the Dalcassians, of hopes, conspiracies, of Arthur Griffith now. To yoke me as his yokefellow, our crimes our common cause. You're your father's son. I know the voice. His fustian shirt, sanguineflowered, trembles its Spanish tassels at his secrets. M. Drumont, famous journalist, Drumont, know what he called queen Victoria? Old hag with the yellow teeth. *Vieille ogresse* with the *dents jaunes*. Maud Gonne, beautiful woman, *La Patrie*, M. Millevoye, Félix Faure, know how he died? Licentious men. The froeken, *bonne à tout faire*, who rubs male nakedness in the bath at Upsala. *Moi faire*, she said. *Tous les messieurs*. Not this *Monsieur*, I said. Most licentious custom. Bath a most private thing. I wouldn't let my brother, not even my own brother, most lascivious thing. Green eyes, I see you. Fang, I feel. Lascivious people.

The blue fuse burns deadly between hands and burns clear. Loose tobacco shreds catch fire: a flame and acrid smoke light our corner. Raw facebones under his peep of day boy's hat. How the head centre got away, authentic version. Got up as a young bride, man, veil, orangeblossoms, drove out the road to Malahide. Did, faith. Of lost leaders, the betrayed, wild escapes. Disguises, clutched at, gone, not here.

Spurned lover. I was a strapping young gossoon at that time, I tell you, I'll show you my likeness one day. I was, faith. Lover, for her love he prowled with colonel Richard Burke, tanist of his sept, under the walls of Clerkenwell and, crouching, saw a flame of vengeance hurl them upward in the fog. Shattered glass and toppling masonry. In gay Paree he hides, Egan of Paris, unsought by any save by me. Making his day's stations, the dingy printingcase, his three taverns, the Montmartre lair he sleeps short night in, rue de la Goutte-d'Or, damascened with flyblown faces of the gone. Loveless, landless, wifeless. She is quite nicey comfy without her outcast man, madame, in rue Gît-le-Cœur, canary and two buck lodgers. Peachy cheeks, a zebra skirt, frisky as a young thing's. Spurned and undespairing. Tell Pat you saw me, won't you? I wanted to get poor Pat a job one time. *Mon fils*, soldier of France. I taught him to sing. *The boys of Kilkenny are stout roaring blades*. Know that old lay? I taught Patrice that. Old Kilkenny: saint Canice, Strongbow's castle on the Nore. Goes like this. O, O. He takes me, Napper Tandy, by the hand.

> O, O the boys of
> Kilkenny . . .

Weak wasting hand on mine. They have forgotten Kevin Egan, not he them. Remembering thee, O Sion.

He had come nearer the edge of the sea and wet sand slapped his boots. The new air greeted him, harping in wild nerves, wind of wild air of seeds of brightness. Here, I am not walking out to the Kish lightship, am I? He stood suddenly, his feet beginning to sink slowly in the quaking soil. Turn back.

Turning, he scanned the shore south, his feet sinking again slowly in new sockets. The cold domed room of the tower waits. Through the barbicans the shafts of light are moving ever, slowly ever as my feet are sinking, creeping duskward over the dial floor. Blue dusk, nightfall, deep blue night. In the darkness of the dome they wait, their pushed-back chairs, my obelisk valise, around a board of abandoned platters. Who to clear it? He has the key. I will not sleep there when this night comes. A shut door of a silent tower entombing their blind bodies, the panthersahib and his pointer. Call: no answer. He lifted his feet up from the suck and turned back by the mole of boulders. Take all, keep all. My soul walks with me, form of forms. So in the moon's midwatches I pace the path above the rocks, in sable silvered, hearing Elsinore's tempting flood.

The flood is following me. I can watch it flow past from here. Get back then by the Poolbeg road to the strand there. He climbed over the sedge and eely oarweeds and sat on a stool of rock, resting his ashplant in a grike.

A bloated carcass of a dog lay lolled on bladderwrack. Before him the gunwale of a boat, sunk in sand. *Un coche ensablé*, Louis Veuillot called Gautier's prose. These heavy sands are language tide and wind have silted here. And there, the stoneheaps of dead builders, a warren of weasel rats. Hide gold there. Try it. You have some. Sands and stones. Heavy of the past. Sir Lout's toys. Mind you don't get one bang on the ear. I'm the bloody well gigant rolls all them bloody well boulders, bones for my stepping-stones. Feefawfum. I zmellz de bloodz oldz an Iridzman.

A point, live dog, grew into sight running across the sweep of sand. Lord, is he going to attack me? Respect his liberty. You will not be master of others or their slave. I have my stick. Sit tight. From farther away, walking shoreward across from the crested tide, figures, two. The two maries. They have tucked it safe among the bulrushes. Peekaboo. I see you. No, the dog. He is running back to them. Who?

Galleys of the Lochlanns ran here to beach, in quest of prey, their bloodbeaked prows riding low on a molten pewter surf. Dane vikings, torcs of tomahawks aglitter on their breasts when Malachi wore the collar of gold. A school of turlehide whales stranded in hot noon, spouting, hobbling in the shallows. Then from the starving cagework city a horde of jerkined dwarfs, my people, with flayers' knives, running, scaling, hacking in green blubbery whalemeat. Famine, plague and slaughters. Their blood is in me, their lusts my waves. I moved among them on the frozen Liffey, that I, a changeling, among the spluttering resin fires. I spoke to no-one: none to me.

The dog's bark ran towards him, stopped, ran back. Dog of my enemy. I just simply stood pale, silent, bayed about. *Terribilia meditans*. A primrose doublet, fortune's knave, smiled on my fear. For that are you pining, the bark of their applause? Pretenders: live their lives. The Bruce's brother, Thomas Fitzgerald, silken knight, Perkin Warbeck, York's false scion, in breeches of silk of whiterose ivory, wonder of a day, and Lambert Simnel, with a tail of nans and sutlers, a scullion crowned. All kings' sons. Paradise of pretenders then and now. He saved men from drowning and you shake at a cur's yelping. But the courtiers who mocked Guido in Or san Michele were in their own house. House of . . . We don't want any of your medieval abstrusiosities. Would you do what he did? A boat would be near, a lifebuoy. *Natürlich*, put there for you. Would you or would you not? The man that was drowned nine days ago off Maiden's rock. They are waiting for him now. The truth, spit it out. I would want to. I would try. I am not a strong swimmer. Water cold soft. When I put my face into it in the basin at Clongowes. Can't see! Who's behind me? Out quickly, quickly! Do you see the tide flowing quickly in on all sides, sheeting the lows of sands quickly, shellcocoacoloured? If I had land under my feet. I want his life still to be his, mine to be mine. A drowning man. His human eyes scream to me out of horror of his death. I . . . With him together down . . . I could not save her. Waters: bitter death: lost.

A woman and a man. I see her skirties. Pinned up, I bet.

Their dog ambled about a bank of dwindling sand, trotting, sniffing on all sides. Looking for something lost in a past life. Suddenly he made off like a bounding hare, ears flung back, chasing the shadow of a lowskimming gull. The man's shrieked whistle struck his limp ears. He turned, bounded back, came nearer, trotted on twinkling shanks. On a field tenney a buck, trippant, proper, unattired. At the lacefringe of the tide he halted with stiff forehoofs, seawardpointed ears. His snout lifted barked at the wavenoise, herds of seamorse. They serpented towards his feet, curling, unfurling many crests, every ninth, breaking, plashing, from far, from farther out, waves and waves.

Cocklepickers. They waded a little way in the water and, stooping, soused their bags, and, lifting them again, waded out. The dog yelped running to them, reared up and pawed them, dropping on all fours, again reared up at them with mute bearish fawning. Unheeded he kept by them as they came towards the drier sand, a rag of wolf's tongue red-panting from his jaws. His speckled body ambled ahead of them and then loped off at a calf's gallop. The carcass lay on his path. He stopped, sniffed, stalked round it, brother, nosing closer, went round it, sniffling rapidly like a dog all over the dead dog's bedraggled fell. Dogskull, dogsniff, eyes on the ground, moves to one great goal. Ah, poor dogsbody. Here lies poor dogsbody's body.

– Tatters! Out of that, you mongrel.

The cry brought him skulking back to his master and a blunt bootless kick sent him unscathed across a spit of sand, crouched in flight. He slunk back in a curve. Doesn't see me. Along by the edge of the mole he lolloped, dawdled, smelt a rock and from under a cocked hindleg pissed against it. He trotted forward and, lifting his hindleg, pissed quick short at an unsmelt rock. The simple pleasures of the poor. His hindpaws then scattered sand: then his forepaws dabbled and delved. Something he buried there, his grandmother. He rooted in the sand, dabbling, delving and stopped to listen to the air, scraped up the sand again with a fury of his claws, soon ceasing, a pard, a panther, got in spousebreach, vulturing the dead.

After he woke me up last night same dream or was it? Wait. Open hallway. Street of harlots. Remember. Haroun al Raschid. I am almosting it. That man led me, spoke. I was not afraid. The melon he had he held against my face. Smiled: creamfruit smell. That was the rule, said. In. Come. Red carpet spread. You will see who.

Shouldering their bags they trudged, the red Egyptians. His blued feet out of turnedup trousers slapped the clammy sand, a dull brick muffler strangling his unshaven neck. With woman steps she followed: the ruffian and his strolling mort. Spoils slung at her back. Loose sand and shellgrit crusted her bare feet. About her windraw face her hair trailed. Behind her lord his helpmate, bing awast, to Romeville. When night hides her body's flaws calling under her brown shawl from an archway where dogs have mired. Her fancyman is treating two Royal Dublins in O'Loughlin's of Blackpitts. Buss her, wap in rogue's rum lingo, for, O, my dimber wapping dell. A shefiend's whiteness under her rancid rags. Fumbally's lane that night: the tanyard smells.

> *White thy fambles, red thy gan*
> *And thy quarrons dainty is.*
> *Couch a hogshead with me then.*
> *In the darkmans clip and kiss.*

Morose delectation Aquinas tunbelly calls this, *frate porcospino*. Unfallen Adam rode and not rutted. Call away let him: *thy quarrons dainty is*. Language no whit worse than his. Monkwords, marybeads jabber on their girdles: rogue-words, tough nuggets patter in their pockets.

Passing now.

A side-eye at my Hamlet hat. If I were suddenly naked here as I sit? I am not. Across the sands of all the world, followed by the sun's flaming sword, to the west, trekking to evening lands. She trudges, schlepps, trains, drags, trascines her load. A tide westering, moondrawn, in her wake. Tides, myriadislanded, within her, blood not mine, *oinopa ponton*, a winedark sea. Behold the handmaid of the moon. In sleep the wet sign calls her hour, bids her rise. Bridebed, childbed, bed of death, ghostcandled. *Omnis caro ad te veniet.* He comes, pale vampire, through storm his eyes, his bat sails bloodying the sea, mouth to her mouth's kiss.

Here. Put a pin in that chap, will you? My tablets. Mouth to her kiss. No. Must be two of em. Glue 'em well. Mouth to her mouth's kiss.

His lips lipped and mouthed fleshless lips of air: mouth to her womb. Oomb, allwombing tomb. His mouth moulded issuing breath, unspeeched: ooeeehah: roar of cataractic planets, globed, blazing, roaring wayawayaway-awayawayaway. Paper. The banknotes, blast them. Old Deasy's letter. Here. Thanking you for hospitality tear the blank end off. Turning his back to the sun he bent over far to a table of rock and scribbled words. That's twice I forgot to take slips from the library counter.

His shadow lay over the rocks as he bent, ending. Why not endless till the farthest star? Darkly they are there behind this light, darkness shining in the brightness, delta of Cassiopeia, worlds. Me sits there with his augur's rod of ash, in borrowed sandals, by day beside a livid sea, unbeheld, in violet night walking beneath a reign of uncouth stars. I throw this ended shadow from me, manshape ineluctable, call it back. Endless, would it be mine, form of my form? Who watches me here? Who ever anywhere will read these written words? Signs on a white field. Somewhere to someone in your flutiest voice. The good bishop of Cloyne took the veil of the temple out of his shovel hat: veil of space with coloured emblems hatched on its field. Hold hard. Coloured on a flat: yes, that's right. Flat I see, then think distance, near, far, flat I see, east, back. Ah, see now. Falls back suddenly, frozen in stereoscope. Click does the trick. You find my words dark. Darkness is in our souls, do you not think? Flutier. Our souls, shamewounded by our sins, cling to us yet more, a woman to her lover clinging, the more the more.

She trusts me, her hand gentle, the longlashed eyes. Now where the blue hell am I bringing her beyond the veil? Into the ineluctable modality of the ineluctable visuality. She, she, she. What she? The virgin at Hodges Figgis' window on Monday looking in for one of the alphabet books you were going to write. Keen glance you gave her. Wrist through the braided jess of her sunshade. She lives in Leeson park, with a grief and kickshaws, a lady of letters. Talk that to some else, Stevie: a pickmeup. Bet she wears those curse of God stays suspenders and yellow stockings, darned with lumpy wool. Talk about apple dumplings, *piuttosto*. Where are your wits?

Touch me. Soft eyes. Soft soft soft hand. I am lonely here. O, touch me soon, now. What is that word known to all men? I am quiet here alone. Sad too. Touch, touch me.

He lay back at full stretch over the sharp rocks, cramming the scribbled note and pencil into a pocket, his hat tilted down on his eyes. That is Kevin Egan's movement I made nodding for his nap, sabbath sleep. *Et vidit Deus. Et erant valde bona.* Alo! *Bonjour,* welcome as the flowers in May. Under its leaf he watched through peacocktwittering lashes the southing sun. I am caught in this burning scene. Pan's hour, the faunal noon. Among gumheavy serpentplants, milkoozing fruits, where on the tawny waters leaves lie wide. Pain is far.

And no more turn aside and brood.

His gaze brooded on his broadtoed boots, a buck's castoffs *nebeneinander.* He counted the creases of rucked leather wherein another's foot had nested warm. The foot that beat the ground in tripudium, foot I dislove. But you were delighted when Esther Osvalt's shoe went on you: girl I knew in Paris. *Tiens, quel petit pied!* Staunch friend, a brother soul: Wilde's love that dare not speak its name. He now will leave me. And the blame? As I am. As I am. All or not at all.

In long lassoes from the Cock lake the water flowed full, covering green-goldenly lagoons of sand, rising, flowing. My ashplant will float away. I shall wait. No, they will pass on, passing chafing against the low rocks, swirling, passing. Better get this job over quick. Listen: a fourworded wave-speech: seesoo, hrss, rsseeiss, ooos. Vehement breath of waters amid sea-snakes, rearing horses, rocks. In cups of rocks it slops: flop, slop, slap: bounded in barrels. And, spent, its speech ceases. It flows purling, widely flowing, floating foampool, flower unfurling.

Under the upswelling tide he saw the writhing weeds lift languidly and sway reluctant arms, hising up their petticoats, in whispering water swaying and upturning coy silver fronds. Day by day: night by night: lifted, flooded and let fall. Lord, they are weary: and, whispered to, they sigh. Saint Ambrose heard it, sigh of leaves and waves, waiting, awaiting the fullness of their times, *diebus ac noctibus iniurias patiens ingemiscit.* To no end gathered: vainly then released, forth flowing, wending back: loom of the moon. Weary too in sight of lovers, lascivious men, a naked woman shining in her courts, she draws a toil of waters.

Five fathoms out there. Full fathom five thy father lies. At one he said. Found drowned. High water at Dublin bar. Driving before it a loose drift of rubble, fanshoals of fishes, silly shells. A corpse rising saltwhite from the undertow, bobbing landward, a pace a pace a porpoise. There he is. Hook it quick. Sunk though he be beneath the watery floor. We have him. Easy now.

Bag of corpsegas sopping in foul brine. A quiver of minnows, fat of a spongy titbit, flash through the slits of his buttoned trouserfly. God becomes man becomes fish becomes barnacle goose becomes featherbed mountain. Dead breaths I living breathe, tread dead dust, devour a urinous offal from all dead. Hauled stark over the gunwale he breathes upward the stench of his green grave, his leprous nosehole snoring to the sun.

A seachange this, brown eyes saltblue. Seadeath, mildest of all deaths known to man. Old Father Ocean. *Prix de Paris:* beware of imitations. Just you give it a fair trial. We enjoyed ourselves immensely.

Come. I thirst. Clouding over. No black clouds anywhere, are there? Thunderstorm. Allbright he falls, proud lightning of the intellect, *Lucifer, dico, qui nescit occasum.* No. My cockle hat and staff and his my sandal shoon. Where? To evening lands. Evening will find itself.

He took the hilt of his ashplant, lunging with it softly, dallying still. Yes, evening will find itself in me, without me. All days make their end. By the way next when is it? Tuesday will be the longest day. Of all the glad new year, mother, the rum tum tiddledy tum. Lawn Tennyson, gentleman poet. *Già.* For the old hag with the yellow teeth. And Monsieur Drumont, gentleman journalist. *Già.* My teeth are very bad. Why, I wonder? Feel. That one is going too. Shells. Ought I go to a dentist, I wonder, with that money? That one. Toothless Kinch, the superman. Why is that, I wonder, or does it mean something perhaps?

My handkerchief. He threw it. I remember. Did I not take it up?

His hand groped vainly in his pockets. No, I didn't. Better buy one.

He laid the dry snot picked from his nostril on a ledge of rock, carefully. For the rest let look who will.

Behind. Perhaps there is someone.

He turned his face over a shoulder, rere regardant. Moving through the air high spars of a threemaster, her sails brailed up on the crosstrees, homing, upstream, silently moving, a silent ship.

*   *   *   *   *

II

◀ MR LEOPOLD BLOOM ATE WITH RELISH THE INNER
organs of beasts and fowls. He liked thick giblet soup, nutty gizzards, a
stuffed roast heart, liver slices fried with crust-crumbs, fried hencod's roes.
Most of all he liked grilled mutton kidneys which gave to his palate a fine
tang of faintly scented urine.

Kidneys were in his mind as he moved about the kitchen softly, righting
her breakfast things on the humpy tray. Gelid light and air were in the
kitchen but out of doors gentle summer morning everywhere. Made him
feel a bit peckish.

The coals were reddening.

Another slice of bread and butter: three, four: right. She didn't like her
plate full. Right. He turned from the tray, lifted the kettle off the hob and
set it sideways on the fire. It sat there, dull and squat, its spout stuck out.
Cup of tea soon. Good. Mouth dry. The cat walked stiffly round a leg of
the table with tail on high.

– Mkgnao!

– O, there you are, Mr Bloom said, turning from the fire.

The cat mewed in answer and stalked again stiffly round a leg of the
table, mewing. Just how she stalks over my writingtable. Prr. Scratch my
head. Prr.

Mr Bloom watched curiously, kindly, the lithe black form. Clean to see:
the gloss of her sleek hide, the white button under the butt of her tail, the
green flashing eyes. He bent down to her, his hands on his knees.

– Milk for the pussens, he said.

– Mrkgnao! the cat cried.

They call them stupid. They understand what we say better than we
understand them. She understands all she wants to. Vindictive too. Wonder
what I look like to her. Height of a tower? No, she can jump me.

– Afraid of the chickens she is, he said mockingly. Afraid of the chook-
chooks. I never saw such a stupid pussens as the pussens.

Cruel. Her nature. Curious mice never squeal. Seem to like it.

– Mrkrgnao! the cat said loudly.

She blinked up out of her avid shameclosing eyes, mewing plaintively
and long, showing him her milkwhite teeth. He watched the dark eyeslits
narrowing with greed till her eyes were green stones. Then he went to the

dresser, took the jug Hanlon's milkman had just filled for him, poured warm-bubbled milk on a saucer and set it slowly on the floor.

– Gurrhr! she cried, running to lap.

He watched the bristles shining wirily in the weak light as she tipped three times and licked lightly. Wonder is it true if you clip them they can't mouse after. Why? They shine in the dark, perhaps, the tips. Or kind of feelers in the dark, perhaps.

He listened to her licking lap. Ham and eggs, no. No good eggs with this drouth. Want pure fresh water. Thursday: not a good day either for a mutton kidney at Buckley's. Fried with butter, a shake of pepper. Better a pork kidney at Dlugacz's. While the kettle is boiling. She lapped slower, then licking the saucer clean. Why are their tongues so rough? To lap better, all porous holes. Nothing she can eat? He glanced round him. No.

On quietly creaky boots he went up the staircase to the hall, paused by the bedroom door. She might like something tasty. Thin bread and butter she likes in the morning. Still perhaps: once in a way.

He said softly in the bare hall:

– I am going round the corner. Be back in a minute.

And when he had heard his voice say it he added:

– You don't want anything for breakfast?

A sleepy soft grunt answered:

– Mn.

No. She did not want anything. He heard then a warm heavy sigh, softer, as she turned over and the loose brass quoits of the bedstead jingled. Must get those settled really. Pity. All the way from Gibraltar. Forgotten any little Spanish she knew. Wonder what her father gave for it. Old style. Ah yes, of course. Bought it at the governor's auction. Got a short knock. Hard as nails at a bargain, old Tweedy. Yes, sir. At Plevna that was. I rose from the ranks, sir, and I'm proud of it. Still he had brains enough to make that corner in stamps. Now that was farseeing.

His hand took his hat from the peg over his initialled heavy overcoat, and his lost property office secondhand waterproof. Stamps: stickyback pictures. Daresay lots of officers are in the swim too. Course they do. The sweated legend in the crown of his hat told him mutely: Plasto's high grade ha. He peeped quickly inside the leather headband. White slip of paper. Quite safe.

On the doorstep he felt in his hip pocket for the latchkey. Not there. In the trousers I left off. Must get it. Potato I have. Creaky wardrobe. No use disturbing her. She turned over sleepily that time. He pulled the halldoor to after him very quietly, more, till the footleaf dropped gently over the threshold, a limp lid. Looked shut. All right till I come back anyhow.

He crossed to the bright side, avoiding the loose cellarflap of number seventyfive. The sun was nearing the steeple of George's church. Be a warm day I fancy. Specially in these black clothes feel it more. Black conducts, reflects (refracts is it?), the heat. But I couldn't go in that light suit. Make a picnic of it. His eyelids sank quietly often as he walked in happy warmth. Boland's breadvan delivering with trays our daily but she prefers yesterday's loaves turnovers crisp crowns hot. Makes you feel young. Somewhere in the east: early morning: set off at dawn, travel round in front of the sun, steal a day's march on him. Keep it up for ever never grow a day older technically. Walk along a strand, strange land, come to a city gate, sentry there, old ranker too, old Tweedy's big moustaches leaning on a long kind of a spear. Wander through awned streets. Turbaned faces going by. Dark caves of carpet shops, big man, Turko the terrible, seated cross-legged smoking a coiled pipe. Cries of sellers in the streets. Drink water scented with fennel, sherbet. Wander along all day. Might meet a robber or two. Well, meet him. Getting on to sundown. The shadows of the mosques along the pillars: priest with a scroll rolled up. A shiver of the trees, signal, the evening wind. I pass on. Fading gold sky. A mother watches from her doorway. She calls her children home in their dark language. High wall: beyond strings twanged. Night sky moon, violet, colour of Molly's new garters. Strings. Listen. A girl playing one of these instruments what do you call them: dulcimers. I pass.

Probably not a bit like it really. Kind of stuff you read: in the track of the sun. Sunburst on the titlepage. He smiled, pleasing himself. What Arthur Griffith said about the headpiece over the *Freeman* leader: a homerule sun rising up in the northwest from the laneway behind the bank of Ireland. He prolonged his pleased smile. Ikey touch that: homerule sun rising up in the northwest.

He approached Larry O'Rourke's. From the cellar grating floated up the flabby gush of porter. Through the open doorway the bar squirted out whiffs of ginger, teadust, biscuitmush. Good house, however: just the end of the city traffic. For instance M'Auley's down there: n. g. as position. Of course if they ran a tramline along the North Circular from the cattle market to the quays value would go up like a shot.

Bald head over the blind. Cute old codger. No use canvassing him for an ad. Still he knows his own business best. There he is, sure enough, my bold Larry, leaning against the sugarbin in his shirtsleeves watching the aproned curate swab up with mop and bucket. Simon Dedalus takes him off to a tee with his eyes screwed up. Do you know what I'm going to tell you? What's that, Mr O'Rourke? Do you know what? The Russians, they'd only be an eight o'clock breakfast for the Japanese.

Stop and say a word: about the funeral perhaps. Sad thing about poor Dignam, Mr O'Rourke.

Turning into Dorset street he said freshly in greeting through the doorway:

– Good day, Mr O'Rourke.

– Good day to you.

– Lovely weather, sir.

– 'Tis all that.

Where do they get the money? Coming up redheaded curates from the county Leitrim, rinsing empties and old man in the cellar. Then, lo and behold, they blossom out as Adam Findlaters or Dan Tallons. Then think of the competition. General thirst. Good puzzle would be cross Dublin without passing a pub. Save it they can't. Off the drunks perhaps. Put down three and carry five. What is that? A bob here and there, dribs and drabs. On the wholesale orders perhaps. Doing a double shuffle with the town travellers. Square it with the boss and we'll split the job, see?

How much would that tot to off the porter in the month? Say ten barrels of stuff. Say he got ten per cent off. O more. Ten. Fifteen. He passed Saint Joseph's, National school. Brats' clamour. Windows open. Fresh air helps memory. Or a lilt. Ahbeesee defeegee kelomen opeecue rustyouvee double you. Boys are they? Yes. Inishturk. Inishark. Inishboffin. At their joggerfry. Mine. Slieve Bloom.

He halted before Dlugacz's window, staring at the hanks of sausages, polonies, black and white. Fifty multiplied by. The figures whitened in his mind unsolved: displeased, he let them fade. The shiny links packed with forcemeat fed his gaze and he breathed in tranquilly the lukewarm breath of cooked spicy pig's blood.

A kidney oozed bloodgouts on the willowpatterned dish: the last. He stood by the nextdoor girl at the counter. Would she buy it too, calling the items from a slip in her hand. Chapped: washing soda. And a pound and a half of Denny's sausages. His eyes rested on her vigorous hips. Woods his name is. Wonder what he does. Wife is oldish. New blood. No followers allowed. Strong pair of arms. Whacking a carpet on the clothesline. She does whack it, by George. The way her crooked skirt swings at each whack.

The ferreteyed porkbutcher folded the sausages he had snipped off with blotchy fingers, sausagepink. Sound meat there like a stallfed heifer.

He took up a page from the pile of cut sheets. The model farm at

Kinnereth on the lakeshore of Tiberias. Can become ideal winter sana-
torium. Moses Montefiore. I thought he was. Farmhouse, wall round it,
blurred cattle cropping. He held the page from him: interesting: read it
nearer, the blurred cropping cattle, the page rustling. A young white heifer.
Those mornings in the cattlemarket the beasts lowing in their pens, branded
sheep, flop and fall of dung, the breeders in hobnailed boots trudging
through the litter, slapping a palm on a ripemeated hindquarter, there's a
prime one, unpeeled switches in their hands. He held the page aslant
patiently, bending his senses and his will, his soft subject gaze at rest. The
crooked skirt swinging whack by whack by whack.

The porkbutcher snapped two sheets from the pile, wrapped up her
prime sausages and made a red grimace.

– Now, my miss, he said.

She tendered a coin, smiling boldly, holding her thick wrist out.

– Thank you, my miss. And one shilling threepence change. For you,
please?

Mr Bloom pointed quickly. To catch up and walk behind her if she went
slowly, behind her moving hams. Pleasant to see first thing in the morning.
Hurry up, damn it. Make hay while the sun shines. She stood outside the
shop in sunlight and sauntered lazily to the right. He sighed down his nose:
they never understand. Sodachapped hands. Crusted toenails too. Brown
scapulars in tatters, defending her both ways. The sting of disregard glowed
to weak pleasure within his breast. For another: a constable off duty cuddled
her in Eccles Lane. They like them sizeable. Prime sausage. O please, Mr
Policeman, I'm lost in the wood.

– Threepence, please.

His hand accepted the moist tender gland and slid it into a sidepocket.
Then it fetched up three coins from his trousers' pocket and laid them on
the rubber prickles. They lay, were read quickly and quickly slid, disc by
disc, into the till.

– Thank you, sir. Another time.

A speck of eager fire from foxeyes thanked him. He withdrew his gaze
after an instant. No: better not: another time.

– Good morning, he said, moving away.

– Good morning, sir.

No sign. Gone. What matter?

He walked back along Dorset street, reading gravely. Agendath Netaim:
planter's company. To purchase vast sandy tracts from Turkish government
and plant with eucalyptus trees. Excellent for shade, fuel and construction.
Orangegroves and immense melonfields north of Jaffa. You pay eight marks

and they plant a dunam of land for you with olives, oranges, almonds or citrons. Olives cheaper: oranges need artificial irrigation. Every year you get a sending of the crop. Your name entered for life as owner in the book of the union. Can pay ten down and the balance in yearly instalments. Bleibtreustrasse 34, Berlin, W. 15.

Nothing doing. Still an idea behind it.

He looked at the cattle, blurred in silver heat. Silvered powdered olive-trees. Quiet long days: pruning ripening. Olives are packed in jars, eh? I have a few left from Andrews. Molly spitting them out. Knows the taste of them now. Oranges in tissue paper packed in crates. Citrons too. Wonder is poor Citron still alive in Saint Kevin's parade. And Mastiansky with the old cither. Pleasant evenings we had then. Molly in Citron's basketchair. Nice to hold, cool waxen fruit, hold in the hand, lift it to the nostrils and smell the perfume. Like that, heavy, sweet, wild perfume. Always the same, year after year. They fetched high prices too Moisel told me. Arbutus place: Pleasants street: pleasant old times. Must be without a flaw, he said. Coming all that way: Spain Gibraltar, Mediterranean, the Levant. Crates lined up on the quayside at Jaffa, chap ticking them off in a book, navvies handling them in soiled dungarees. There's whatdoyoucallhim out of. How do you? Doesn't see. Chap you know just to salute bit of a bore. His back is like that Norwegian captain's. Wonder if I'll meet him today. Watering cart. To provoke the rain. On earth as it is in heaven.

A cloud began to cover the sun wholly slowly wholly. Grey. Far.

No, not like that. A barren land, bare waste. Vulcanic lake, the dead sea: no fish, weedless, sunk deep in the earth. No wind would lift those waves, grey metal, poisonous foggy waters. Brimstone they called it raining down: the cities of the plain: Sodom, Gomorrah, Edom, All dead names. A dead sea in a dead land, grey and old. Old now. It bore the oldest, the first race. A bent hag crossed from Cassidy's clutching a naggin bottle by the neck. The oldest people. Wandered far away over all the earth, captivity to captivity, multiplying, dying, being born everywhere. It lay there now. Now it could bear no more. Dead: an old woman's: the grey sunken cunt of the world.

Desolation.

Grey horror seared his flesh. Folding the page into his pocket he turned into Eccles Street, hurrying homeward. Cold oils slid along his veins, chilling his blood: age crusting him with a salt cloak. Well, I am here now. Morning mouth bad images. Got up wrong side of the bed. Must begin again those Sandow's exercises. On the hands down. Blotchy brown brick houses. Number eighty still unlet. Why is that? Valuation is only twenty-eight. Towers, Battersby, North, MacArthur: parlour windows plastered with bills. Plasters on a sore eye. To smell the gentle smoke of tea, fume of the pan, sizzling butter. Be near her ample bedwarmed flesh. Yes, yes.

Quick warm sunlight came running from Berkeley Road, swiftly, in slim sandals, along the brightening footpath. Runs, she runs to meet me, a girl with gold hair on the wind.

Two letters and a card lay on the hallfloor. He stopped and gathered them. Mrs Marion Bloom. His quick heart slowed at once. Bold hand. Mrs Marion.

– Poldy!

Entering the bedroom he halfclosed his eyes and walked through warm yellow twilight towards her tousled head.

– Who are the letters for?

He looked at them. Mullingar. Milly.

– A letter for me from Milly, he said carefully, and a card to you. And a letter for you.

He laid her card and letter on the twill bedspread near the curve of her knees.

– Do you want the blind up?

Letting the blind up by gentle tugs halfway his backward eye saw her glance at the letter and tuck it under her pillow.

– That do? he asked, turning.

She was reading the card, propped on her elbow.

– She got the things, she said.

He waited till she had laid the card aside and curled herself back slowly with a snug sigh.

– Hurry up with that tea, she said. I'm parched.

– The kettle is boiling, he said.

But he delayed to clear the chair: her striped petticoat, tossed soiled linen: and lifted all in an armful on to the foot of the bed.

As he went down the kitchen stairs she called:

– Poldy!

– What?

– Scald the teapot.

On the boil sure enough: a plume of steam from the spout. He scalded and rinsed out the teapot and put in four full spoons of tea, tilting the kettle then to let water flow in. Having set it to draw, he took off the kettle and crushed the pan flat on the live coals and watched the lump of butter slide and melt. While he unwrapped the kidney the cat mewed hungrily against him. Give her too much meat she won't mouse. Say they won't eat pork. Kosher. Here. He let the bloodsmeared paper fall to her and dropped the kidney amid the sizzling butter sauce. Pepper. He sprinkled it through his fingers, ringwise, from the chipped eggcup.

Then he slit open his letter, glancing down the page and over. Thanks: new tam: Mr Coghlan: lough Owel picnic: young student: Blazes Boylan's seaside girls.

The tea was drawn. He filled his own moustachecup, sham crown Derby, smiling. Silly Milly's birthday gift. Only five she was then. No, wait: four. I gave her the amberoid necklace she broke. Putting pieces of folded brown paper in the letterbox for her. He smiled, pouring.

> O, Milly Bloom, you are my darling.
> You are my looking glass from night to morning.
> I'd rather have you without a farthing
> Than Katey Keogh with her ass and garden.

Poor old professor Goodwin. Dreadful old case. Still he was a courteous old chap. Oldfashioned way he used to bow Molly off the platform. And the little mirror in his silk hat. The night Milly brought it into the parlour. O, look what I found in professor Goodwin's hat! All we laughed. Sex breaking out even then. Pert little piece she was.

He prodded a fork into the kidney and slapped it over: then fitted the teapot on the tray. Its hump bumped as he took it up. Everything on it? Bread and butter, four, sugar, spoon, her cream. Yes. He carried it upstairs, his thumb hooked in the teapot handle.

Nudging the door open with his knee he carried the tray in and set it on the chair by the bedhead.

– What a time you were, she said.

She set the brasses jingling as she raised herself briskly, an elbow on the pillow. He looked calmly down on her bulk and between her large soft bubs, sloping within her nightdress like a shegoat's udder. The warmth of her couched body rose on the air, mingling with the fragrance of the tea she poured.

A strip of torn envelope peeped from under the dimpled pillow. In the act of going he stayed to straighten the bedspread.

– Who was the letter from? he asked.

Bold hand. Marion.

– O, Boylan, she said. He's bringing the programme.

– What are you singing?

– *Là ci darem* with J. C. Doyle, she said, and *Love's Old Sweet Song*.

Her full lips, drinking, smiled. Rather stale smell that incense leaves next day. Like foul flowerwater.

– Would you like the window open a little?

She doubled a slice of bread into her mouth, asking:

– What time is the funeral?

– Eleven, I think, he answered. I didn't see the paper.

Following the pointing of her finger he took up a leg of her soiled drawers from the bed. No? Then, a twisted grey garter looped round a stocking: rumpled, shiny sole.

– No: that book.

Other stocking. Her petticoat.

– It must have fell down, she said.

He felt here and there. *Voglio e non vorrei*. Wonder if she pronounces that right: *voglio*. Not in the bed. Must have slid down. He stooped and lifted the valance. The book, fallen, sprawled against the bulge of the orangekeyed chamberpot.

– Show here, she said. I put a mark in it. There's a word I wanted to ask you.

She swallowed a draught of tea from her cup held by nothandle and, having wiped her fingertips smartly on the blanket, began to search the text with the hairpin till she reached the word.

– Met him what? he asked.

– Here, she said. What does that mean?

He leaned downward and read near her polished thumbnail.

– Metempsychosis?

– Yes. Who's he when he's at home?

– Metempsychosis, he said, frowning. It's Greek: from the Greek. That means the transmigration of souls.

– O, rocks! she said. Tell us in plain words.

He smiled, glancing askance at her mocking eye. The same young eyes. The first night after the charades. Dolphin's Barn. He turned over the smudged pages. *Ruby: the Pride of the Ring*. Hello. Illustration. Fierce Italian with carriagewhip. Must be Ruby pride of the on the floor naked. Sheet kindly lent. *The monster Maffei desisted and flung his victim from him with an oath*. Cruelty behind it all. Doped animals. Trapeze at Hengler's. Had to look the other way. Mob gaping. Break your neck and we'll break our sides. Families of them. Bone them young so they metempsychosis. That we live after death. Our souls. That a man's soul after he dies. Dignam's soul . . .

– Did you finish it? he asked.

– Yes, she said. There's nothing smutty in it. Is she in love with the first fellow all the time?

– Never read it. Do you want another?

– Yes. Get another of Paul de Kock's. Nice name he has.

She poured more tea into her cup, watching its flow sideways.

Must get that Capel street library book renewed or they'll write to Kearney, my guarantor. Reincarnation: that's the word.

– Some people believe, he said, that we go on living in another body after death, that we lived before. They call it reincarnation. That we all lived before on the earth thousands of years ago or some other planet. They say we have forgotten it. Some say they remember their past lives.

The sluggish cream wound curdling spirals through her tea. Better remind her of the word: metempsychosis. An example would be better. An example.

The *Bath of the Nymph* over the bed. Given away with the Easter number of *Photo Bits*: Splendid masterpiece in art colours. Tea before you put milk in. Not unlike her with her hair down: slimmer. Three and six I gave for the frame. She said it would look nice over the bed. Naked nymphs: Greece: and for instance all the people that lived then.

He turned the pages back.

– Metempsychosis, he said, is what the ancient Greeks called it. They used to believe you could be changed into an animal or a tree, for instance. What they called nymphs, for example.

Her spoon ceased to stir up the sugar. She gazed straight before her, inhaling through her arched nostrils.

– There's a smell of burn, she said. Did you leave anything on the fire?

– The kidney! he cried suddenly.

He fitted the book roughly into his inner pocket and, stubbing his toes against the broken commode, hurried out towards the smell, stepping hastily down the stairs with a flurried stork's legs. Pungent smoke shot up in an angry jet from a side of the pan. By prodding a prong of the fork under the kidney he detached it and turned it turtle on its back. Only a little burned. He tossed it off the pan on to a plate and let the scanty brown gravy trickle over it.

Cup of tea now. He sat down, cut and buttered a slice of the loaf. He shore away the burnt flesh and flung it to the cat. Then he put a forkful into his mouth, chewing with discernment the toothsome pliant meat. Done to a turn. A mouthful of tea. Then he cut away dies of bread, sopped one in the gravy and put it in his mouth. What was that about some young student and a picnic? He creased out the letter at his side, reading it slowly as he chewed, sopping another die of bread in the gravy and raising it to his mouth.

Dearest Papli,

Thanks ever so much for the lovely birthday present. It suits me splendid. Everyone says I'm quite the belle in my new tam. I got mummy's lovely box of creams and am writing. They are lovely. I am getting on swimming in the photo business now. Mr Coghlan took one of me and Mrs will send when developed. We did great biz yesterday. Fair day and all the beef to the heels were in. We are going to lough Owel on Monday with a few friends to make a scrap picnic. Give my love to mummy and to yourself a big kiss and thanks. I hear them at the piano downstairs. There is to be a concert in the Greville Arms on Saturday. There is a young student comes here some evenings named Bannon his cousins or something are big swells he sings Boylan's (I was on the pop of writing Blazes Boylan's) song about those seaside girls. Tell him silly Milly sends my best respects. Must now close with fondest love.

    Your fond daughter,

                                                        MILLY.

P.S. Excuse bad writing, am in a hurry. Byby.

                                                        M.

Fifteen yesterday. Curious, fifteenth of the month too. Her first birthday away from home. Separation. Remember the summer morning she was born, running to knock up Mrs Thornton in Denzille street. Jolly old woman. Lots of babies she must have helped into the world. She knew from the first poor little Rudy wouldn't live. Well, God is good, sir. She knew at once. He would be eleven now if he had lived.

His vacant face stared pitying at the postscript. Excuse bad writing. Hurry. Piano downstairs. Coming out of her shell. Row with her in the XL Café about the bracelet. Wouldn't eat her cakes or speak or look. Saucebox. He sopped other dies of bread in the gravy and ate piece after piece of kidney. Twelve and six a week. Not much. Still, she might do worse. Music hall stage. Young student. He drank a draught of cooler tea to wash down his meal. Then he read the letter again: twice.

O well: she knows how to mind herself. But if not? No, nothing has happened. Of course it might. Wait in any case till it does. A wild piece of goods. Her slim legs running up the staircase. Destiny. Ripening now. Vain: very.

He smiled with troubled affection at the kitchen window. Day I caught her in the street pinching her cheeks to make them red. Anæmic a little. Was given milk too long. On the *Erin's King* that day round the Kish.

Damned old tub pitching about. Not a bit funky. Her pale blue scarf loose in the wind with her hair.

> *All dimpled cheeks and curls,*
> *Your head it simply swirls.*

Seaside girls. Torn envelope. Hands stuck in his trousers' pockets, jarvey off for the day, singing. Friend of the family. Swurls, he says. Pier with lamps, summer evening, band,

> *Those girls, those girls,*
> *Those lovely seaside girls.*

Milly too. Young kisses: the first. Far away now past. Mrs Marion. Reading lying back now, counting the strands of her hair, smiling, braiding.

A soft qualm regret, flowed down his backbone, increasing. Will happen, yes. Prevent. Useless: can't move. Girl's sweet light lips. Will happen too. He felt the flowing qualm spread over him. Useless to move now. Lips kissed, kissing kissed. Full gluey woman's lips.

Better where she is down there: away. Occupy her. Wanted a dog to pass the time. Might take a trip down there. August bank holiday, only two and six return. Six weeks off however. Might work a press pass. Or through M'Coy.

The cat, having cleaned all her fur, returned to the meatstained paper, nosed at it and stalked to the door. She looked back at him, mewing. Wants to go out. Wait before a door sometime it will open. Let her wait. Has the fidgets. Electric. Thunder in the air. Was washing at her ear with her back to the fire too.

He felt heavy, full: then a gentle loosening of his bowels. He stood up, undoing the waistband of his trousers. The cat mewed to him.

– Miaow! he said in answer. Wait till I'm ready.

Heaviness: hot day coming. Too much trouble to fag up the stairs to the landing.

A paper. He liked to read at stool. Hope no ape comes knocking just as I'm.

In the table drawer he found an old number of *Titbits*. He folded it under his armpit, went to the door and opened it. The cat went up in soft bounds. Ah, wanted to go upstairs, curl up in a ball on the bed.

Listening, he heard her voice:

– Come, come, pussy. Come.

He went out through the backdoor into the garden: stood to listen towards the next garden. No sound. Perhaps hanging clothes out to dry. The maid was in the garden. Fine morning.

He bent down to regard a lean file of spearmint growing by the wall.

Make a summerhouse here. Scarlet runners. Virginia creepers. Want to manure the whole place over, scabby soil. A coat of liver of sulphur. All soil like that without dung. Household slops. Loam, what is this that is? The hens in the next garden: their droppings are very good top dressing. Best of all though are the cattle, especially when they are fed on those oilcakes. Mulch of dung. Best thing to clean ladies' kid gloves. Dirty cleans. Ashes too. Reclaim the whole place. Grow peas in that corner there. Lettuce. Always have fresh greens then. Still gardens have their drawbacks. That bee or bluebottle here Whitmonday.

He walked on. Where is my hat, by the way? Must have put it back on the peg. Or hanging up on the floor. Funny, I don't remember that. Hallstand too full. Four umbrellas, her raincloak. Picking up the letters. Drago's shopbell ringing. Queer I was just thinking that moment. Brown brilliantined hair over his collar. Just had a wash and brushup. Wonder have I time for a bath this morning. Tara street. Chap in the paybox there got away James Stephens they say. O'Brien.

Deep voice that fellow Dlugacz has. Agenda what is it? Now, my miss. Enthusiast.

He kicked open the crazy door of the jakes. Better be careful not to get these trousers dirty for the funeral. He went in, bowing his head under the low lintel. Leaving the door ajar, amid the stench of mouldy limewash and stale cobwebs he undid his braces. Before sitting down he peered through a chink up at the nextdoor window. The king was in his countinghouse. Nobody.

Asquat on the cuckstool he folded out his paper turning its pages over on his bared knees. Something new and easy. No great hurry. Keep it a bit. Our prize titbit. *Matcham's Masterstroke*. Written by Mr Philip Beaufoy, Playgoers' club, London. Payment at the rate of one guinea a column has been made to the writer. Three and a half. Three pounds three. Three pounds thirteen and six.

Quietly he read, restraining himself, the first column and, yielding but resisting, began the second. Midway, his last resistance yielding, he allowed his bowels to ease themselves quietly as he read, reading still patiently that slight constipation of yesterday quite gone. Hope it's not too big bring on piles again. No, just right. So. Ah! Costive one tabloid of cascara sagrada. Life might be so. It did not move or touch him but it was something quick and neat. Print anything now. Silly season. He read on, seated calm above his own rising smell. Neat certainly. *Matcham often thinks of the masterstroke by which he won the laughing witch who now.* Begins and ends morally. *Hand in hand.* Smart. He glanced back through what he had read and, while feeling his water flow quietly, he envied kindly Mr Beaufoy who had written it and received payment of three pounds thirteen and six.

Might manage a sketch. By Mr and Mrs L. M. Bloom. Invent a story for some proverb which? Time I used to try jotting down on my cuff what she said dressing. Dislike dressing together. Nicked myself shaving. Biting her nether lip, hooking the placket of her skirt. Timing her. 9.15. Did Roberts pay you yet? 9.20. What had Gretta Conroy on? 9.23. What possessed me to buy this comb? 9.24. I'm swelled after that cabbage. A speck of dust on the patent leather of her boot.

Rubbing smartly in turn each welt against her stocking calf. Morning after the bazaar dance when May's band played Ponchielli's dance of the hours. Explain that morning hours, noon, then evening coming on, then night hours. Washing her teeth. That was the first night. Her head dancing. Her fansticks clicking. Is that Boylan well off? He has money. Why? I noticed he had a good smell off his breath dancing. No use humming then. Allude to it. Strange kind of music that last night. The mirror was in shadow. She rubbed her handglass briskly on her woollen vest against her full wagging bub. Peering into it. Lines in her eyes. It wouldn't pan out somehow.

Evening hours, girls in grey gauze. Night hours then black with daggers and eyemasks. Poetical idea pink, then golden, then grey, then black. Still true to life also. Day, then the night.

He tore away half the prize story sharply and wiped himself with it. Then he girded up his trousers, braced and buttoned himself. He pulled back the jerky shaky door of the jakes and came forth from the gloom into the air.

In the bright light, lightened and cooled in limb, he eyed carefully his black trousers, the ends, the knees, the houghs of the knees. What time is the funeral? Better find out in the paper.

A creak and a dark whirr in the air high up. The bells of George's church. They tolled the hour: loud dark iron.

> *Heigho! Heigho!*
> *Heigho! Heigho!*
> *Heigho! Heigho!*

Quarter to. There again: the overtone following through the air. A third. Poor Dignam!

*   *   *   *   *

◀ BY LORRIES ALONG SIR JOHN ROGERSON'S QUAY MR
Bloom walked soberly, past Windmill lane, Leask's the linseed crusher's,
the postal telegraph office. Could have given that address too. And past the
sailors' home. He turned from the morning noises of the quayside and
walked through Lime street. By Brady's cottages a boy for the skins lolled,
his bucket of offal linked, smoking a chewed fagbutt. A smaller girl with
scars of eczema on her forehead eyed him, listlessly holding her battered
caskhoop. Tell him if he smokes he won't grow. O let him! His life isn't
such a bed of roses! Waiting outside pubs to bring da home. Come home to
ma, da. Slack hour: won't be many there. He crossed Townsend street,
passed the frowning face of Bethel. El, yes: house of: Aleph, Beth. And past
Nichols' the undertaker's. At eleven it is. Time enough. Daresay Corny
Kelleher bagged that job for O'Neill's. Singing with his eyes shut. Corny.
Met her once in the park. In the dark. What a lark. Police tout. Her name
and address she then told with my tooraloom tooraloom tay. O, surely he
bagged it. Bury him cheap in a whatyoumaycall. With my tooraloom,
tooraloom, tooraloom, tooraloom.

In Westland row he halted before the window of the Belfast and Oriental
Tea Company and read the legends of leadpapered packets: choice blend,
finest quality, family tea. Rather warm. Tea. Must get some from Tom
Kernan. Couldn't ask him at a funeral, though. While his eyes still read
blandly he took off his hat quietly inhaling his hairoil and sent his right
hand with slow grace over his brow and hair. Very warm morning. Under
their dropped lids his eyes found the tiny bow of the leather headband
inside his high grade ha. Just there. His right hand came down into the
bowl of his hat. His fingers found quickly a card behind the headband and
transferred it to his waistcoat pocket.

So warm. His right hand once more more slowly went over again: choice
blend, made of the finest Ceylon brands. The far east. Lovely spot it must
be: the garden of the world, big lazy leaves to float about on, cactuses,
flowery meads, snaky lianas they call them. Wonder is it like that. Those
Cinghalese lobbing around in the sun, in *dolce far niente*. Not doing a hand's
turn all day. Sleep six months out of twelve. Too hot to quarrel. Influence
of the climate. Lethargy. Flowers of idleness. The air feeds most. Azotes.
Hothouse in Botanic gardens. Sensitive plants. Waterlilies. Petals too tired
to. Sleeping sickness in the air. Walk on roseleaves. Imagine trying to eat
tripe and cowheel. Where was the chap I saw in that picture somewhere?
Ah, in the dead sea, floating on his back, reading a book with a parasol
open. Couldn't sink if you tried: so thick with salt. Because the weight of

the water, no, the weight of the body in the water is equal to the weight of the. Or is it the volume is equal of the weight? It's a law something like that. Vance in High school cracking his fingerjoints, teaching. The college curriculum. Cracking curriculum. What is weight really when you say the weight? Thirtytwo feet per second, per second. Law of falling bodies: per second, per second. They all fall to the ground. The earth. It's the force of gravity of the earth is the weight.

He turned away and sauntered across the road. How did she walk with her sausages? Like that something. As he walked he took the folded *Freeman* from his sidepocket, unfolded it, rolled it lengthwise in a baton and tapped it at each sauntering step against his trouserleg. Careless air: just drop in to see. Per second, per second. Per second for every second it means. From the curbstone he darted a keen glance through the door of the postoffice. Too late box. Post here. No-one. In.

He handed the card through the brass grill.

– Are there any letters for me? he asked.

While the postmistress searched a pigeonhole he gazed at the recruiting poster with soldiers of all arms on parade: and held the tip of his baton against his nostrils, smelling freshprinted rag paper. No answer probably. Went too far last time.

The postmistress handed him back through the grill his card with a letter. He thanked and glanced rapidly at the typed envelope.

Henry Flower, Esq,

c/o P. O. Westland Row,

City.

Answered anyhow. He slipped card and letter into his sidepocket, reviewing again the soldiers on parade. Where's old Tweedy's regiment? Castoff soldier. There: bearskin cap and hackle plume. No, he's a grenadier. Pointed cuffs. There he is: royal Dublin fusiliers. Redcoats. Too showy. That must be why the women go after them. Uniform. Easier to enlist and drill. Maud Gonne's letter about taking them off O'Connell street at night: disgrace to our Irish capital. Griffith's paper is on the same tack now: an army rotten with venereal disease: overseas or halfseasover empire. Half baked they look: hypnotised like. Eyes front. Mark time. Table: able. Bed: ed. The King's own. Never see him dressed up as a fireman or a bobby. A mason, yes.

He strolled out of the postoffice and turned to the right. Talk: as if that would mend matters. His hand went into his pocket and a forefinger felt its

way under the flap of the envelope, ripping it open in jerks. Women will
pay a lot of heed, I don't think. His fingers drew forth the letter and
crumpled the envelope in his pocket. Something pinned on: photo perhaps.
Hair? No.

M'Coy. Get rid of him quickly. Take me out of my way. Hate company
when you.

– Hello, Bloom. Where are you off to?

– Hello, M'Coy. Nowhere in particular.

– How's the body?

– Fine. How are you?

– Just keeping alive, M'Coy said.

His eyes on the black tie and clothes he asked with low respect:

– Is there any . . . no trouble I hope? I see you're . . .

– O no, Mr Bloom said. Poor Dignam, you know. The funeral is today.

– To be sure, poor fellow. So it is. What time?

A photo it isn't. A badge maybe.

– E . . . eleven, Mr Bloom answered.

– I must try to get out there, M'Coy said. Eleven, is it? I only heard it last
night. Who was telling me? Holohan. You know Hoppy?

– I know.

Mr Bloom gazed across the road at the outsider drawn up before the
door of the Grosvenor. The porter hoisted the valise up on the well. She
stood still, waiting, while the man, husband, brother, like her, searched his
pockets for change. Stylish kind of coat with that roll collar, warm for a day
like this, looks like blanketcloth. Careless stand of her with her hands in
those patch pockets. Like that haughty creature at the polo match. Women
all for caste till you touch the spot. Handsome is and handsome does.
Reserved about to yield. The honourable Mrs and Brutus is an honourable
man. Possess her once take the starch out of her.

– I was with Bob Doran, he's on one of his periodical bends, and what do
you call him Bantam Lyons. Just down there in Conway's we were.

Doran, Lyons in Conway's. She raised a gloved hand to her hair. In
came Hoppy. Having a wet. Drawing back his head and gazing far from
beneath his veiled eyelids he saw the bright fawn skin shine in the glare, the
braided drums. Clearly I can see today. Moisture about gives long sight
perhaps. Talking of one thing or another. Lady's hand. Which side will she
get up?

– And he said: *Sad thing about our poor friend Paddy! What Paddy?* I said.
Poor little Paddy Dignam, he said.

Off to the country: Broadstone probably. High brown boots with laces dangling. Wellturned foot. What is he fostering over that change for? Sees me looking. Eye out for other fellow always. Good fallback. Two strings to her bow.

– *Why?* I said. *What's wrong with him?* I said.

Proud: rich: silk stockings.

– Yes, Mr Bloom said.

He moved a little to the side of M'Coy's talking head. Getting up in a minute.

– *What's wrong with him?* he said. *He's dead*, he said. And, faith, he filled up. *Is it Paddy Dignam?* I said. I couldn't believe it when I heard it. I was with him no later than Friday last or Thursday was it in the Arch. *Yes*, he said. *He's gone. He died on Monday, poor fellow.*

Watch! Watch! Silk flash rich stockings white. Watch!

A heavy tramcar honking its gong slewed between.

Lost it. Curse your noisy pugnose. Feels locked out of it. Paradise and the peri. Always happening like that. The very moment. Girl in Eustace street hallway Monday was it settling her garter. Her friend covering the display of. *Esprit de corps.* Well, what are you gaping at?

– Yes, yes, Mr Bloom said after a dull sigh. Another gone.

– One of the best, M'Coy said.

The tram passed. They drove off towards the Loop Line bridge, her rich gloved hand on the steel grip. Flicker, flicker: the laceflare of her hat in the sun: flicker, flick.

– Wife well, I suppose? M'Coy's changed voice said.

– O yes, Mr Bloom said. Tiptop, thanks.

He unrolled the newspaper baton idly and read idly:

> *What is home without*
> *Plumtree's Potted Meat?*
> *Incomplete.*
> *With it an abode of bliss.*

– My missus has just got an engagement. At least it's not settled yet.

Valise tack again. By the way no harm. I'm off that, thanks.

Mr Bloom turned his largelidded eyes with unhasty friendliness.

– My wife too, he said. She's going to sing at a swagger affair in the Ulster hall, Belfast, on the twentyfifth.

– That so? M'Coy said. Glad to hear that, old man. Who's getting it up?

Mrs Marion Bloom. Not up yet. Queen was in her bedroom eating bread and. No book. Blackened court cards laid along her thigh by sevens. Dark lady and fair man. Cat furry black ball. Torn strip of envelope.

Love's
Old
Sweet
Song
Comes lo-ve's old . . .

– It's a kind of a tour, don't you see? Mr Bloom said thoughtfully. *Sweet song*. There's a committee formed. Part shares and part profits.

M'Coy nodded, picking at his moustache stubble.

– O well, he said. That's good news.

He moved to go.

– Well, glad to see you looking fit, he said. Meet you knocking around.

– Yes, Mr Bloom said.

– Tell you what, M'Coy said. You might put down my name at the funeral, will you? I'd like to go but I mightn't be able, you see. There's a drowning case at Sandycove may turn up and then the coroner and myself would have to go down if the body is found. You just shove in my name if I'm not there, will you?

– I'll do that, Mr Bloom said, moving to get off. That'll be all right.

– Right, M'Coy said brightly. Thanks, old man. I'd go if I possibly could. Well, tolloll. Just C. P. M'Coy will do.

– That will be done, Mr Bloom answered firmly.

Didn't catch me napping that wheeze. The quick touch. Soft mark. I'd like my job. Valise I have a particular fancy for. Leather. Capped corners, riveted edges, double action lever lock. Bob Cowley lent him his for the Wicklow regatta concert last year and never heard tidings of it from that good day to this.

Mr Bloom, strolling towards Brunswick street, smiled. My missus has just got an. Reedy freckled soprano. Cheese-paring nose. Nice enough in its way: for a little ballad. No guts in it. You and me, don't you know? In the same boat. Softsoaping. Give you the needle that would. Can't he hear the difference? Think he's that way inclined a bit. Against my grain somehow. Thought that Belfast would fetch him. I hope that smallpox up there doesn't get worse. Suppose she wouldn't let herself be vaccinated again. Your wife and my wife.

Wonder is he pimping after me?

Mr Bloom stood at the corner, his eyes wandering over the multi-coloured hoardings. Cantrell and Cochrane's Ginger Ale (Aromatic). Clery's summer sale. No, he's going on straight. Hello. *Leah* tonight: Mrs Bandman Palmer. Like to see her in that again. *Hamlet* she played last night.

Male impersonator. Perhaps he was a woman. Why Ophelia committed suicide? Poor papa! How he used to talk about Kate Bateman in that! Outside the Adelphi in London waited all the afternoon to get in. Year before I was born that was: sixtyfive. And Ristori in Vienna. What is this the right name is? By Mosenthal it is. Rachel, is it? No. The scene he was always talking about where the old blind Abraham recognizes the voice and puts his fingers on his face.

– Nathan's voice! His son's voice! I hear the voice of Nathan who left his father to die of grief and misery in my arms, who left the house of his father and left the God of his father.

Every word is so deep, Leopold.

Poor papa! Poor man! I'm glad I didn't go into the room to look at his face. That day! O dear! O dear! Ffoo! Well, perhaps it was the best for him.

Mr Bloom went round the corner and passed the drooping nags of the hazard. No use thinking of it any more. Nosebag time. Wish I hadn't met that M'Coy fellow.

He came nearer and heard a crunching of gilded oats, the gently champing teeth. Their full buck eyes regarded him as he went by, amid the sweet oaten reek of horsepiss. Their Eldorado. Poor jugginses! Damn all they know or care about anything with their long noses stuck in nosebags. Too full for words. Still they get their feed all right and their doss. Gelded too: a stump of black guttapercha wagging limp between their haunches. Might be happy all the same that way. Good poor brutes they look. Still their neigh can be very irritating.

He drew the letter from his pocket and folded it into the newspaper he carried. Might just walk into her here. The lane is safer.

He passed the cabman's shelter. Curious the life of drifting cabbies, all weathers, all places, time or setdown, no will of their own. *Voglio e non.* Like to give them an odd cigarette. Sociable. Shout a few flying syllables as they pass. He hummed:

> *Là ci darem la mano*
> *La la lala la la.*

He turned into Cumberland street and, going on some paces, halted in the lee of the station wall. No-one. Meade's timberyard. Piled balks. Ruins and tenements. With careful tread he passed over a hopscotch court with its forgotten pickeystone. Not a sinner. Near the timberyard a squatted child at marbles, alone, shooting the taw with a cunnythumb. A wise tabby, a blinking sphinx, watched from her warm sill. Pity to disturb them. Mohammed cut a piece out of his mantle not to wake her. Open it. And once I played marbles when I went to that old dame's school. She liked mignonette. Mrs Ellis's. And Mr? He opened the letter within the newspaper.

A flower. I think it's a. A yellow flower with flattened petals. Not annoyed then? What does she say?

Dear Henry,

I got your last letter to me and thank you very much for it. I am sorry you did not like my last letter. Why did you enclose the stamps? I am awfully angry with you. I do wish I could punish you for that. I called you naughty boy because I do not like that other world. Please tell me what is the real meaning of that word. Are you not happy in your home you poor little naughty boy? I do wish I could do something for you. Please tell me what you think of poor me. I often think of the beautiful name you have. Dear Henry, when will we meet? I think of you so often you have no idea. I have never felt myself so much drawn to a man as you. I feel so bad about. Please write me a long letter and tell me more. Remember if you do not I will punish you. So now you know what I will do to you, you naughty boy, if you do not write. O how I long to meet you. Henry dear, do not deny my request before my patience are exhausted. Then I will tell you all. Goodbye now, naughty darling. I have such a bad headache today and write *by return* to your longing

MARTHA.

P. S. Do tell me what kind of perfume does your wife use. I want to know.

He tore the flower gravely from its pinhold smelt its almost no smell and placed it in his heart pocket. Language of flowers. They like it because no-one can hear. Or a poison bouquet to strike him down. Then, walking slowly forward, he read the letter again, murmuring here and there a word. Angry tulips with you darling manflower punish your cactus if you don't please poor forgetmenot how I long violets to dear roses when we soon anemone meet all naughty nightstalk wife Martha's perfume. Having read it all he took it from the newspaper and put it back in his sidepocket.

Weak joy opened his lips. Changed since the first letter. Wonder did she write it herself. Doing the indignant: a girl of good family like me, respectable character. Could meet one Sunday after the rosary. Thank you: not having any. Usual love scrimmage. Then running round corners. Bad as a row with Molly. Cigar has a cooling effect. Narcotic. Go further next time. Naughty boy: punish: afraid of words, of course. Brutal, why not? Try it anyhow. A bit at a time.

Fingering still the letter in his pocket he drew the pin out of it. Common pin, eh? He threw it on the road. Out of her clothes somewhere: pinned together. Queer the number of pins they always have. No roses without thorns.

Flat Dublin voices bawled in his head. Those two sluts that night in the Coombe, linked together in the rain.

> *O, Mairy lost the pin of her drawers.*
> *She didn't know what to do*
> *To keep it up*
> *To keep it up.*

It? Them. Such a bad headache. Has her roses probably. Or sitting all day typing. Eyefocus bad for stomach nerves. What perfume does your wife use? Now could you make out a thing like that?

To keep it up.

Martha, Mary. I saw that picture somewhere I forget now old master or faked for money. He is sitting in their house, talking. Mysterious. Also the two sluts in the Coombe would listen.

To keep it up.

Nice kind of evening feeling. No more wandering about. Just loll there: quiet dusk: let everything rip. Forget. Tell about places you have been, strange customs. The other one, jar on her head, was getting the supper: fruit, olives, lovely cool water out of the well stonecold like the hole in the wall at Ashtown. Must carry a paper goblet next time I go to the trotting-matches. She listens with big dark soft eyes. Tell her: more and more: all. Then a sigh: silence. Long long long rest.

Going under the railway arch he took out the envelope, tore it swiftly in shreds and scattered them towards the road. The shreds fluttered away, sank in the dank air: a white flutter then all sank.

Henry Flower. You could tear up a cheque for a hundred pounds in the same way. Simple bit of paper. Lord Iveagh once cashed a sevenfigure cheque for a million in the bank of Ireland. Shows you the money to be made out of porter. Still the other brother lord Ardilaun has to change his shirt four times a day, they say. Skin breeds lice or vermin. A million pounds, wait a moment. Twopence a pint, fourpence a quart, eightpence a gallon of porter, no, one and fourpence a gallon of porter. One and four into twenty: fifteen about. Yes, exactly. Fifteen millions of barrels of porter.

What am I saying barrels? Gallons. About a million barrels all the same.

An incoming train clanked heavily above his head, coach after coach. Barrels bumped in his head: dull porter slopped and churned inside. The bungholes sprang open and a huge dull flood leaked out, flowing together, winding through mudflats all over the level land, a lazy pooling swirl of liquor bearing along wideleaved flowers of its froth.

He had reached the open backdoor of All Hallows. Stepping into the porch he doffed his hat, took the card from his pocket and tucked it again behind the leather headband. Damn it. I might have tried to work M'Coy for a pass to Mullingar.

Same notice on the door. Sermon by the very reverend John Conmee S. J. on saint Peter Claver and the African mission. Save China's millions. Wonder how they explain it to the heathen Chinee. Prefer an ounce of opium. Celestials. Rank heresy for them. Prayers for the conversion of Gladstone they had too when he was almost unconscious. The protestants the same. Convert Dr. William J. Walsh. D. D. to the true religion. Buddha their god lying on his side in the museum. Taking it easy with hand under his cheek. Josssticks burning. Not like Ecce Homo. Crown of thorns and cross. Clever idea Saint Patrick the shamrock. Chopsticks? Conmee: Martin Cunningham knows him: distinguished looking. Sorry I didn't work him about getting Molly into the choir instead of that Father Farley who looked a fool but wasn't. They're taught that. He's not going out in bluey specs with the sweat rolling off him to baptise blacks, is he? The glasses would take their fancy, flashing. Like to see them sitting round in a ring with blub lips, entranced, listening. Still life. Lap it up like milk, I suppose.

The cold smell of sacred stone called him. He trod the worn steps, pushed the swingdoor and entered softly by the rere.

Something going on: some sodality. Pity so empty. Nice discreet place to be next some girl. Who is my neighbour? Jammed by the hour to slow music. That woman at midnight mass. Seventh heaven. Women knelt in the benches with crimson halters round their necks, heads bowed. A batch knelt at the altar rails. The priest went along by them, murmuring, holding the thing in his hands. He stopped at each, took out a communion, shook a drop or two (are they in water?) off it and put it neatly into her mouth. Her hat and head sank. Then the next one: a small old woman. The priest bent down to put it into her mouth, murmuring all the time. Latin. The next one. Shut your eyes and open your mouth. What? *Corpus*. Body. Corpse. Good idea the Latin. Stupefies them first. Hospice for the dying. They don't seem to chew it; only swallow it down. Rum idea: eating bits of a corpse why the cannibals cotton to it.

He stood aside watching their blind masks pass down the aisle, one by one, and seek their places. He approached a bench and seated himself in its corner, nursing his hat and newspaper. These pots we have to wear. We ought to have hats modelled on our heads. They were about him here and there, with heads still bowed in their crimson halters, waiting for it to melt in their stomachs. Something like those mazzoth: it's that sort of bread: unleavened shewbread. Look at them. Now I bet it makes them feel happy. Lollipop. It does. Yes, bread of angels it's called. There's a big idea behind it, kind of kingdom of God is within you feel. First communicants. Hoky-poky penny a lump. Then feel all like one family party, same in the theatre, all in the same swim. They do. I'm sure of that. Not so lonely. In our confraternity. Then come out a bit spreeish. Let off steam. Thing is if you really believe in it. Lourdes cure, waters of oblivion, and the Knock apparition, statues bleeding. Old fellow asleep near that confession box. Hence those snores. Blind faith. Safe in the arms of kingdom come. Lulls all pain. Wake this time next year.

He saw the priest stow the communion cup away, well in, and kneel an instant before it, showing a large grey bootsole from under the lace affair he had on. Suppose he lost the pin of his. He wouldn't know what to do to. Bald spot behind. Letters on his back I. N. R. I? No: I. H. S. Molly told me one time I asked her. I have sinned: or no: I have suffered, it is. And the other one? Iron nails ran in.

Meet one Sunday after the rosary. Do not deny my request. Turn up with a veil and black bag. Dusk and the light behind her. She might be here with a ribbon round her neck and do the other thing all the same on the sly. Their character. That fellow that turned queen's evidence on the invincibles he used to receive the, Carey was his name, the communion every morning. This very church. Peter Carey. No, Peter Claver I am thinking of. Denis Carey. And just imagine that. Wife and six children at home. And plotting that murder all the time. Those crawthumpers, now that's a good name for them, there's always something shiftylooking about them. They're not straight men of business either. O no she's not here: the flower: no, no. By the way did I tear up that envelope? Yes: under the bridge.

The priest was rinsing out the chalice: then he tossed off the dregs smartly. Wine. Makes it more aristocratic than for example if he drank what they are used to Guinness's porter or some temperance beverage Wheatley's Dublin hop bitters or Cantrell and Cochrane's ginger ale (aromatic). Doesn't give them any of it: shew wine: only the other. Cold comfort. Pious fraud but quite right: otherwise they'd have one old booser worse than another coming along, cadging for a drink. Queer the whole atmosphere of the. Quite right. Perfectly right that is.

Mr Bloom looked back towards the choir. Not going to be any music. Pity. Who has the organ here I wonder? Old Glynn he knew how to make that instrument talk, the *vibrato*: fifty pounds a year they say he had in Gardiner street. Molly was in fine voice that day, the *Stabat Mater* of Rossini. Father Bernard Vaughan's sermon first. Christ or Pilate? Christ, but don't keep us all night over it. Music they wanted. Footdrill stopped. Could hear a pin drop. I told her to pitch her voice against that corner. I could feel the thrill in the air, the full, the people looking up:

Quis est homo?

Some of that old sacred music is splendid. Mercadante: seven last words. Mozart's twelfth mass: the *Gloria* in that. Those old popes were keen on music, on art and statues and pictures of all kinds. Palestrina for example too. They had a gay old time while it lasted. Healthy too chanting, regular hours, then brew liqueurs. Benedictine. Green Chartreuse. Still, having eunuchs in their choir that was coming it a bit thick. What kind of voice is it? Must be curious to hear after their own strong basses. Connoisseurs. Suppose they wouldn't feel anything after. Kind of a placid. No worry. Fall into flesh don't they? Gluttons, tall, long legs. Who knows? Eunuch. One way out of it.

He saw the priest bend down and kiss the altar and then face about and bless all the people. All crossed themselves and stood up. Mr Bloom glanced about him and then stood up, looking over the risen hats. Stand up at the gospel of course. Then all settled down on their knees again and he sat back quietly in his bench. The priest came down from the altar, holding the thing out from him, and he and the massboy answered each other in Latin. Then the priest knelt down and began to read off a card:

– O God, our refuge and our strength . . .

Mr Bloom put his face forward to catch the words. English. Throw them the bone. I remember slightly. How long since your last mass? Gloria and immaculate virgin. Joseph her spouse. Peter and Paul. More interesting if you understood what it was all about. Wonderful organisation certainly, goes like clockwork. Confession. Everyone wants to. Then I will tell you all. Penance. Punish me, please. Great weapon in their hands. More than doctor or solicitor. Woman dying to. And I schsch- schschschsch. And did you chachachachacha? And why did you? Look down at her ring to find an excuse. Whispering gallery walls have ears. Husband learn to his surprise. God's little joke. Then out she comes. Repentance skindeep. Lovely shame. Pray at an altar. Hail Mary and Holy Mary. Flowers, incense, candles melting. Hide her blushes. Salvation army blatant imitation. Reformed prostitute will address the meeting. How I found the Lord. Squareheaded chaps those must be in Rome: they work the whole show. And don't they rake in the money too? Bequests also: to the P. P. for the time being in his absolute discretion. Masses for the repose of my soul to be said publicly with open doors. Monasteries and convents. The priest in the Fermanagh will case in the witness box. No browbeating him. He had his answer pat for everything. Liberty and exaltation of our holy mother the church. The doctors of the church: they mapped out the whole theology of it.

The priest prayed:

– Blessed Michael, archangel, defend us in the hour of conflict. Be our safeguard against the wickedness and snares of the devil (may God restrain him, we humbly pray): and do thou, O prince of the heavenly host, by the power of God thrust Satan down to hell and with him those other wicked spirits who wander through the world for the ruin of souls.

The priest and the massboy stood up and walked off. All over. The women remained behind: thanksgiving.

Better be shoving along. Brother Buzz. Come around with the plate perhaps. Pay your Easter duty.

He stood up. Hello. Were those two buttons of my waistcoat open all the time. Women enjoy it. Annoyed if you don't. Why didn't you tell me before. Never tell you. But we. Excuse, miss, there's a (whh!) just a (whh!) fluff. Or their skirt behind, placket unhooked. Glimpses of the moon. Still like you better untidy. Good job it wasn't farther south. He passed, discreetly buttoning, down the aisle and out through the main door into the light. He stood a moment unseeing by the cold black marble bowl while before him and behind two worshippers dipped furtive hands in the low tide of holy water. Trams: a car of Prescott's dyeworks: a widow in her weeds. Notice because I'm in mourning myself. He covered himself. How goes the time? Quarter past. Time enough yet. Better get that lotion made up. Where is this? Ah yes, the last time. Sweny's in Lincoln place. Chemists rarely move. Their green and gold beaconjars too heavy to stir. Hamilton Long's, founded in the year of the flood. Huguenot churchyard near there. Visit some day.

He walked southward along Westland row. But the recipe is in the other trousers. O, and I forgot that latchkey too. Bore this funeral affair. O well, poor fellow, it's not his fault. When was it I got it made up last? Wait. I changed a sovereign I remember. First of the month it must have been or the second. O he can look it up in the prescriptions book.

The chemist turned back page after page. Sandy shrivelled smell he seems to have. Shrunken skull. And old. Quest for the philosopher's stone. The alchemists. Drugs age you after mental excitement. Lethargy then. Why? Reaction. A lifetime in a night. Gradually changes your character.

Living all the day among herbs, ointments, disinfectants. All his alabaster lilypots. Mortar and pestle. Aq. Dist. Fol. Laur. Te Virid. Smell almost cure you like the dentist's doorbell. Doctor whack. He ought to physic himself a bit. Electuary or emulsion. The first fellow that picked an herb to cure himself had a bit of pluck. Simples. Want to be careful. Enough stuff here to chloroform you. Test: turns blue litmus paper red. Chloroform. Overdose of laudanum. Sleeping draughts. Lovephiltres. Paragoric poppy-syrup bad for cough. Clogs the pores or the phlegm. Poisons the only cures. Remedy where you least expect it. Clever of nature.

– About a fortnight ago, sir?

– Yes, Mr Bloom said.

He waited by the counter, inhaling the keen reek of drugs, the dusty dry smell of sponges and loofahs. Lot of time taken up telling your aches and pains.

– Sweet almond oil and tincture of benzoin, Mr Bloom said, and then orangeflower water. . .

It certainly did make her skin so delicate white like wax.

– And white wax also, he said.

Brings out the darkness of her eyes. Looking at me, the sheet up to her eyes, Spanish, smelling herself, when I was fixing the links in my cuffs. Those homely recipes are often the best: strawberries for the teeth: nettles and rainwater: oatmeal they say steeped in buttermilk. Skinfood. One of the old queen's sons, duke of Albany was it? had only one skin. Leopold yes. Three we have. Warts, bunions and pimples to make it worse. But you want a perfume too. What perfume does your? *Peau d'Espagne.* That orange-flower. Pure curd soap. Water is so fresh. Nice smell these soaps have. Time to get a bath round the corner. Hammam. Turkish. Massage. Dirt gets rolled up in your navel. Nicer if a nice girl did it. Also I think I. Yes I. Do it in the bath. Curious longing I. Water to water. Combine business with pleasure. Pity no time for massage. Feel fresh then all day. Funeral be rather glum.

– Yes, sir, the chemist said. That was two and nine. Have you brought a bottle?

– No, Mr Bloom said. Make it up, please. I'll call later in the day and I'll take one of those soaps. How much are they?

– Fourpence, sir.

Mr Bloom raised a cake to his nostrils. Sweet lemony wax.

– I'll take this one, he said. That makes three and a penny.

– Yes, sir, the chemist said. You can pay all together, sir, when you come back.

– Good, Mr Bloom said.

He strolled out of the shop, the newspaper baton under his armpit, the coolwrapped soap in his left hand.

At his armpit Bantam Lyons' voice and hand said:

– Hello, Bloom, what's the best news? Is that today's? Show us a minute.

Shaved off his moustache again, by Jove! Long cold upper lip. To look younger. He does look balmy. Younger than I am.

Bantam Lyons' yellow blacknailed fingers unrolled the baton. Wants a wash too. Take off the rough dirt. Good morning, have you used Pears' soap? Dandruff on his shoulders. Scalp wants oiling.

– I want to see about that French horse that's running today, Bantam Lyons said. Where the bugger is it?

He rustled the pleated pages, jerking his chin on his high collar. Barber's itch. Tight collar he'll lose his hair. Better leave him the paper and get shut of him.

– You can keep it, Mr Bloom said.

– Ascot. Gold cup. Wait, Bantam Lyons muttered. Half a mo. Maximum the second.

– I was just going to throw it away, Mr Bloom said.

Bantam Lyons raised his eyes suddenly and leered weakly.

– What's that? his sharp voice said.

– I say you can keep it, Mr Bloom answered. I was going to throw it away that moment.

Bantam Lyons doubted an instant, leering: then thrust the outspread sheets back on Mr Bloom's arms.

– I'll risk it, he said. Here, thanks.

He sped off towards Conway's corner. God speed scut.

Mr Bloom folded the sheets again to a neat square and lodged the soap in it, smiling. Silly lips of that chap. Betting. Regular hotbed of it lately. Messenger boys stealing to put on sixpence. Raffle for large tender turkey. Your Christmas dinner for threepence. Jack Fleming embezzling to gamble then smuggled off to America. Keeps a hotel now. They never come back. Fleshpots of Egypt.

He walked cheerfully towards the mosque of the baths. Remind you of a mosque redbaked bricks, the minarets. College sports today I see. He eyed the horseshoe poster over the gate of college park: cyclist doubled up like a cod in a pot. Damn bad ad. Now if they had made it round like a wheel. Then the spokes: sports, sports, sports: and the hub big: college. Something to catch the eye.

There's Hornblower standing at the porter's lodge. Keep him on hands:

might take a turn in there on the nod. How do you do, Mr Hornblower? How do you do, sir?

Heavenly weather really. If life was always like that. Cricket weather. Sit around under sunshades. Over after over. Out. They can't play it here. Duck for six wickets. Still Captain Buller broke a window in the Kildare street club with a slog to square leg. Donnybrook fair more in their line. And the skulls we were acracking when M'Carthy took the floor. Heatwave. Won't last. Always passing, the stream of life, which in the stream of life we trace is dearer than them all.

Enjoy a bath now: clean trough of water, cool enamel, the gentle tepid stream. This is my body.

He foresaw his pale body reclined in it at full, naked, in a womb of warmth, oiled by scented melting soap, softly laved. He saw his trunk and limbs riprippled over and sustained, buoyed lightly upward, lemonyellow: his navel, bud of flesh: and saw the dark tangled curls of his bush floating, floating hair of the stream around the limp father of thousands, a languid floating flower.

*   *   *   *   *

◀MARTIN CUNNINGHAM, FIRST, POKED HIS SILK-HATTED head into the creaking carriage and, entering deftly, seated himself. Mr Power stepped in after him, curving his height with care.

– Come on, Simon.

– After you, Mr Bloom said.

Mr Dedalus covered himself quickly and got in, saying:

– Yes, yes.

– Are we all here now? Martin Cunningham asked. Come along, Bloom.

Mr Bloom entered and sat in the vacant place. He pulled the door to after him and slammed it tight till it shut tight. He passed an arm through the armstrap and looked seriously from the open carriage window at the lowered blinds of the avenue. One dragged aside: an old woman peeping. Nose whiteflattened against the pane. Thanking her stars she was passed over. Extraordinary the interest they take in a corpse. Glad to see us go we give them such trouble coming. Job seems to suit them. Huggermugger in corners. Slop about in slipperslappers for fear he'd wake. Then getting it ready. Laying it out. Molly and Mrs Fleming making the bed. Pull it more to your side. Our windingsheet. Never know who will touch you dead. Wash and shampoo. I believe they clip the nails and the hair. Keep a bit in an envelope. Grow all the same after. Unclean job.

All waited. Nothing was said. Stowing in the wreaths probably. I am sitting on something hard. Ah, that soap in my hip pocket. Better shift it out of that. Wait for an opportunity.

All waited. Then wheels were heard from in front turning: then nearer: then horses' hoofs. A jolt. Their carriage began to move, creaking and swaying. Other hoofs and creaking wheels started behind. The blinds of the avenue passed and number nine with its craped knocker, door ajar. At walking pace.

They waited still, their knees jogging, till they had turned and were passing along the tramtracks. Tritonville road. Quicker. The wheels rattled rolling over the cobbled causeway and the crazy glasses shook rattling in the doorframes.

– What way is he taking us? Mr Power asked through both windows.

– Irishtown, Martin Cunningham said. Ringsend. Brunswick street.

Mr Dedalus nodded, looking out.

– That's a fine old custom, he said. I am glad to see it has not died out.

All watched awhile through their windows caps and hats lifted by passers. Respect. The carriage swerved from the tramtrack to the smoother road past Watery lane. Mr Bloom at gaze saw a lithe young man, clad in mourning, a wide hat.

– There's a friend of yours gone by, Dedalus, he said.

– Who is that?

– Your son and heir.

– Where is he? Mr Dedalus said, stretching over across.

The carriage, passing the open drains and mounds of rippedup roadway before the tenement houses, lurched round the corner and, swerving back to the tramtrack, rolled on noisily with chattering wheels. Mr Dedalus fell back, saying:

– Was that Mulligan cad with him? His *fidus Achates?*

– No, Mr Bloom said. He was alone.

– Down with his aunt Sally, I suppose, Mr Dedalus said, the Goulding faction, the drunken little costdrawer and Crissie, papa's little lump of dung, the wise child that knows her own father.

Mr Bloom smiled joylessly on Ringsend road. Wallace Bros the bottle-works. Dodder bridge.

Richie Goulding and the legal bag. Goulding, Collis and Ward he calls the firm. His jokes are getting a bit damp. Great card he was. Waltzing in Stamer street with Ignatius Gallaher on a Sunday morning, the landlady's two hats pinned on his head. Out on the rampage all night. Beginning to tell on him now: that backache of his, I fear. Wife ironing his back. Thinks he'll cure it with pills. All breadcrumbs they are. About six hundred per cent profit.

– He's in with a lowdown crowd, Mr Dedalus snarled. That Mulligan is a contaminated bloody doubledyed ruffian by all accounts. His name stinks all over Dublin. But with the help of God and His blessed mother I'll make it my business to write a letter one of those days to his mother or his aunt or whatever she is that will open her eye as wide as a gate. I'll tickle his catastrophe, believe you me.

He cried above the clatter of the wheels.

– I won't have her bastard of a nephew ruin my son. A counterjumper's son. Selling tapes in my cousin, Peter Paul M'Swiney's. Not likely.

He ceased. Mr Bloom glanced from his angry moustache to Mr Power's mild face and Martin Cunningham's eyes and beard, gravely shaking. Noisy selfwilled man. Full of his son. He is right. Something to hand on. If little Rudy had lived. See him grow up. Hear his voice in the house. Walking beside Molly in an Eton suit. My son. Me in his eyes. Strange feeling it would be. From me. Just a chance. Must have been that morning in Raymond terrace she was at the window, watching the two dogs at it by the wall of the cease to do evil. And the sergeant grinning up. She had that cream gown on with the rip she never stitched. Give us a touch, Poldy. God, I'm dying for it. How life begins.

Got big then. Had to refuse the Greystones concert. My son inside her. I could have helped him on in life. I could. Make him independent. Learn German too.

– Are we late? Mr Power asked.

– Ten minutes, Martin Cunningham said, looking at his watch.

Molly. Milly. Same thing watered down. Her tomboy oaths. O jumping Jupiter! Ye gods and little fishes! Still, she's a dear girl. Soon be a woman. Mullingar. Dearest Papli. Young student. Yes, yes: a woman too. Life. Life.

The carriage heeled over and back, their four trunks swaying.

– Corny might have given us a more commodious yoke, Mr Power said.

– He might, Mr Dedalus said, if he hadn't that squint troubling him. Do you follow me?

He closed his left eye. Martin Cunningham began to brush away crustcrumbs from under his thighs.

– What is this, he said, in the name of God? Crumbs?

– Someone seems to have been making a picnic party here lately, Mr Power said.

All raised their thighs, eyed with disfavour the mildewed buttonless leather of the seats. Mr Dedalus, twisting his nose, frowned downward and said:

– Unless I'm greatly mistaken. What do you think, Martin?

– It struck me too, Martin Cunningham said.

Mr Bloom set his thigh down. Glad I took that bath. Feel my feet quite clean. But I wish Mrs Fleming had darned these socks better.

Mr Dedalus sighed resignedly.

– After all, he said, it's the most natural thing in the world.

– Did Tom Kernan turn up? Martin Cunningham asked, twirling the peak of his beard gently.

– Yes, Mr Bloom answered. He's behind with Ned Lambert and Hynes.

– And Corny Kelleher himself? Mr Power asked.

– At the cemetery, Martin Cunningham said.

– I met M'Coy this morning, Mr Bloom said. He said he'd try to come.

The carriage halted short.

– What's wrong?

– We're stopped.

– Where are we?

Mr Bloom put his head out of the window.

– The grand canal, he said.

Gasworks. Whooping cough they say it cures. Good job Milly never got it. Poor children! Doubles them up black and blue in convulsions. Shame really. Got off lightly with illness compared. Only measles. Flaxseed tea. Scarlatina, influenza epidemics. Canvassing for death. Don't miss this chance. Dogs' home over there. Poor old Athos! Be good to Athos, Leopold, is my last wish. Thy will be done. We obey them in the grave. A dying scrawl. He took it to heart, pined away. Quiet brute. Old men's dogs usually are.

A raindrop spat on his hat. He drew back and saw an instant of shower spray dots over the grey flags. Apart. Curious. Like through a colander. I thought it would. My boots were creaking I remember now.

– The weather is changing, he said quietly.

– A pity it did not keep up fine, Martin Cunningham said.

– Wanted for the country, Mr Power said. There's the sun again coming out.

Mr Dedalus, peering through his glasses towards the veiled sun, hurled a mute curse at the sky.

– It's as uncertain as a child's bottom, he said.

– We're off again.

The carriage turned again its stiff wheels and their trunks swayed gently. Martin Cunningham twirled more quickly the peak of his beard.

– Tom Kernan was immense last night, he said. And Paddy Leonard taking him off to his face.

– O draw him out, Martin, Mr Power said eagerly. Wait till you hear him, Simon, on Ben Dollard's singing of *The Croppy Boy*.

– Immense, Martin Cunningham said pompously. *His singing of that simple ballad, Martin, is the most trenchant rendering I ever heard in the whole course of my experience.*

– Trenchant, Mr Power said laughing. He's dead nuts on that. And the retrospective arrangement.

– Did you read Dan Dawson's speech? Martin Cunningham asked.

– I did not then, Mr Dedalus said. Where is it?

– In the paper this morning.

Mr Bloom took the paper from his inside pocket. That book I must change for her.

– No, no, Mr Dedalus said quickly. Later on, please.

Mr Bloom's glance travelled down the edge of the paper, scanning the deaths. Callan, Coleman, Dignam, Fawcett, Lowry, Naumann, Peake, what Peake is that? is it the chap was in Crosbie and Alleyne's? no, Sexton, Urbright. Inked characters fast fading on the frayed breaking paper. Thanks to the Little Flower. Sadly missed. To the inexpressible grief of his. Aged 88 after a long and tedious illness. Month's mind Quinlan. On whose soul Sweet Jesus have mercy.

> It is now a month since dear Henry fled
> To his home up above in the sky
> While his family weeps and mourns his loss
> Hoping some day to meet him on high.

I tore up the envelope? Yes. Where did I put her letter after I read it in the bath? He patted his waistcoat pocket. There all right. Dear Henry fled. Before my patience are exhausted.

National school. Meade's yard. The hazard. Only two there now. Nodding. Full as a tick. Too much bone in their skulls. The other trotting round with a fare. An hour ago I was passing there. The jarvies raised their hats.

A pointsman's back straightened itself upright suddenly against a tramway standard by Mr Bloom's window. Couldn't they invent something automatic so that the wheel itself much handier? Well but that fellow would lose his job then? Well but then another fellow would get a job making the new invention?

Antient concert rooms. Nothing on there. A man in a buff suit with a crape armlet. Not much grief there. Quarter mourning. People in law, perhaps.

They went past the bleak pulpit of Saint Mark's, under the railway bridge, past the Queen's theatre: in silence. Hoardings. Eugene Stratton. Mrs Bandman Palmer. Could I go to see *Leah* tonight, I wonder. I said I. Or the *Lily of Killarney?* Elster Grimes Opera company. Big powerful change. Wet bright bills for next week. *Fun on the Bristol.* Martin Cunningham could work a pass for the Gaiety. Have to stand a drink or two. As broad as it's long.

He's coming in the afternoon. Her songs.

Plasto's. Sir Philip Crampton's memorial fountain bust. Who was he?

– How do you do? Martin Cunningham said, raising his palm to his brow in salute.

– He doesn't see us, Mr Power said. Yes, he does. How do you do?

– Who? Mr Dedalus asked.

– Blazes Boylan, Mr Power said. There he is airing his quiff.

Just that moment I was thinking.

Mr Dedalus bent across to salute. From the door of the Red Bank the white disc of a straw hat flashed reply: passed.

Mr Bloom reviewed the nails of his left hand, then those of his right hand. The nails, yes. Is there anything more in him that they she sees? Fascination. Worst man in Dublin. That keeps him alive. They sometimes feel what a person is. Instinct. But a type like that. My nails. I am just looking at them: well pared. And after: thinking alone. Body getting a bit softy. I would notice that from remembering. What causes that I suppose the skin can't contract quickly enough when the flesh falls off. But the shape is there. The shape is there still. Shoulders. Hips. Plump. Night of the dance dressing. Shift stuck between the cheeks behind.

He clasped his hands between his knees and, satisfied, sent his vacant glance over their faces.

Mr Power asked:

– How is the concert tour getting on, Bloom?

– O very well, Mr Bloom said. I hear great accounts of it. It's a good idea, you see . . .

– Are you going yourself?

– Well no, Mr Bloom said. In point of fact I have to go down to the county Clare on some private business. You see the idea is to tour the chief towns. What you lose on one you can make up on the other.

– Quite so, Martin Cunningham said. Mary Anderson is up there now.

– Have you good artists?

– Louis Werner is touring her, Mr Bloom said. O yes, we'll have all topnobbers. J. C. Doyle and John MacCormack I hope and. The best, in fact.

– And *Madame*, Mr Power said, smiling. Last but not least.

Mr Bloom unclasped his hands in a gesture of soft politeness and clasped them. Smith O'Brien. Someone has laid a bunch of flowers there. Woman. Must be his deathday. For many happy returns. The carriage wheeling by Farrell's statue united noiselessly their unresisting knees.

Oot: a dullgarbed old man from the curbstone tendered his wares, his mouth opening: oot.

– Four bootlaces for a penny.

Wonder why he was struck off the rolls. Had his office in Hume street. Same house as Molly's namesake. Tweedy, crown solicitor for Waterford. Has that silk hat ever since. Relics of old decency. Mourning too. Terrible comedown, poor wretch! Kicked about like snuff at a wake. O'Callaghan on his last legs.

And *Madame*. Twenty past eleven. Up. Mrs Fleming is in to clean. Doing her hair, humming: *voglio e non vorrei*. No: *vorrei e non*. Looking at the tips of her hairs to see if they are split. *Mi trema un poco il*. Beautiful on that *tre* her voice is: weeping tone. A thrush. A throstle. There is a word throstle that expressed that.

His eyes passed lightly over Mr Power's goodlooking face. Greyish over the ears. *Madame:* smiling. I smiled back. A smile goes a long way. Only politeness perhaps. Nice fellow. Who knows is that true about the woman he keeps? Not pleasant for the wife. Yet they say, who was it told me, there is no carnal. You would imagine that would get played out pretty quick. Yes, it was Crofton met him one evening bringing her a pound of rump-steak. What is this she was? Barmaid in Jury's. Or the Moira, was it?

They passed under the hugecloaked Liberator's form.

Martin Cunningham nudged Mr Power.

– Of the tribe of Reuben, he said.

A tall blackbearded figure, bent on a stick, stumping round the corner of Elvery's elephant house showed them a curved hand open on his spine.

– In all his pristine beauty, Mr Power said.

Mr Dedalus looked after the stumping figure and said mildly:

– The devil break the hasp of your back!

Mr Power, collapsing in laughter, shaded his face from the window as the carriage passed Gray's statue.

– We have all been there, Martin Cunningham said broadly.

His eyes met Mr Bloom's eyes. He caressed his beard, adding:

– Well, nearly all of us.

Mr Bloom began to speak with sudden eagerness to his companions' faces.

– That's an awfully good one that's going the rounds about Reuben J. and the son.

– About the boatman? Mr Power asked.

– Yes. Isn't it awfully good?

– What is that? Mr Dedalus asked. I didn't hear it.

– There was a girl in the case, Mr Bloom began, and he determined to send him to the isle of Man out of harm's way but when they were both . . .

– What? Mr Dedalus asked. That confirmed bloody hobbledehoy is it?

– Yes, Mr Bloom said. They were both on the way to the boat and he tried to drown . . . . .

– Drown Barabbas! Mr Dedalus cried. I wish to Christ he did!

Mr Power sent a long laugh down his shaded nostrils.

– No, Mr Bloom said, the son himself . . . . .

Martin Cunningham thwarted his speech rudely.

– Reuben J. and the son were piking it down the quay next the river on their way to the isle of Man boat and the young chiseller suddenly got loose and over the wall with him into the Liffey.

– For God's sake! Mr Dedalus exclaimed in fright. Is he dead?

– Dead! Martin Cunningham cried. Not he! A boatman got a pole and fished him out by the slack of the breeches and he was landed up to the father on the quay. More dead than alive. Half the town was there.

– Yes, Mr Bloom said. But the funny part is . . . . .

– And Reuben J., Martin Cunningham said, gave the boatman a florin for saving his son's life.

A stifled sigh came from under Mr Power's hand.

– O, he did, Martin Cunningham affirmed. Like a hero. A silver florin.

– Isn't it awfully good? Mr Bloom said eagerly.

– One and eightpence too much, Mr Dedalus said drily.

Mr Power's choked laugh burst quietly in the carriage.

Nelson's pillar.

– Eight plums a penny! Eight for a penny!

– We had better look a little serious, Martin Cunningham said.

Mr Dedalus sighed.

– And then indeed, he said, poor little Paddy wouldn't grudge us a laugh. Many a good one he told himself.

– The Lord forgive me! Mr Power said, wiping his wet eyes with his fingers. Poor Paddy! I little thought a week ago when I saw him last and he was in his usual health that I'd be driving after him like this. He's gone from us.

– As decent a little man as ever wore a hat, Mr Dedalus said. He went very suddenly.

– Breakdown, Martin Cunningham said. Heart.

He tapped his chest sadly.

Blazing face: redhot. Too much John Barleycorn. Cure for a red nose. Drink like the devil till it turns adelite. A lot of money he spent colouring it.

Mr Power gazed at the passing houses with rueful apprehension.

– He had a sudden death, poor fellow, he said.

– The best death, Mr Bloom said.

Their wide open eyes looked at him.

– No suffering, he said. A moment and all is over. Like dying in sleep.

No-one spoke.

Dead side of the street this. Dull business by day, land agents, temperance hotel, Falconer's railway guide, civil service college, Gill's, catholic club, the industrious blind. Why? Some reason. Sun or wind. At night too. Chummies and slaveys. Under the patronage of the late Father Mathew. Foundation stone for Parnell. Breakdown. Heart.

White horses with white frontlet plumes came round the Rotunda corner, galloping. A tiny coffin flashed by. In a hurry to bury. A mourning coach. Unmarried. Black for the married. Piebald for bachelors. Dun for a nun.

– Sad, Martin Cunningham said. A child.

A dwarf's face mauve and wrinkled like little Rudy's was. Dwarf's body, weak as putty, in a whitelined deal box. Burial friendly society pays. Penny a week for a sod of turf. Our. Little. Beggar. Baby. Meant nothing. Mistake of nature. If it's healthy it's from the mother. If not the man. Better luck next time.

– Poor little thing, Mr Dedalus said. It's well out of it.

The carriage climbed more slowly the hill of Rutland square. Rattle his bones. Over the stones. Only a pauper. Nobody owns.

– In the midst of life, Martin Cunningham said.

– But the worst of all, Mr Power said, is the man who takes his own life.

Martin Cunningham drew out his watch briskly, coughed and put it back.

– The greatest disgrace to have in the family, Mr Power added.

– Temporary insanity, of course, Martin Cunningham said decisively. We must take a charitable view of it.

– They say a man who does it is a coward, Mr Dedalus said.

– It is not for us to judge, Martin Cunningham said.

Mr Bloom, about to speak, closed his lips again. Martin Cunningham's large eyes. Looking away now. Sympathetic human man he is. Intelligent. Like Shakespeare's face. Always a good word to say. They have no mercy on that here or infanticide. Refuse christian burial. They used to drive a stake of wood through his heart in the grave. As if it wasn't broken already. Yet sometimes they repent too late. Found in the riverbed clutching rushes. He looked at me. And that awful drunkard of a wife of his. Setting up house for her time after time and then pawning the furniture on him every Saturday almost. Leading him the life of the damned. Wear the heart out of a stone, that. Monday morning start afresh. Shoulder to the wheel. Lord, she must have looked a sight that night, Dedalus told me he was in there. Drunk about the place and capering with Martin's umbrella:

> *And they call me the jewel of Asia,*
> *Of Asia,*
> *The geisha.*

He looked away from me. He knows. Rattle his bones.

That afternoon of the inquest. The redlabelled bottle on the table. The room in the hotel with hunting pictures. Stuffy it was. Sunlight through the slats of the Venetian blinds. The coroner's ears, big and hairy. Boots giving evidence. Thought he was asleep first. Then saw like yellow streaks on his face. Had slipped down to the foot of the bed. Verdict: overdose. Death by misadventure. The letter. For my son Leopold.

No more pain. Wake no more. Nobody owns.

The carriage rattled swiftly along Blessington street. Over the stones.

– We are going the pace, I think, Martin Cunningham said.

– God grant he doesn't upset us on the road, Mr Power said.

– I hope not, Martin Cunningham said. That will be a great race tomorrow in Germany. The Gordon Bennett.

– Yes, by Jove, Mr. Dedalus said. That will be worth seeing, faith.

As they turned into Berkeley street a streetorgan near the Basin sent over and after them a rollicking rattling song of the halls. Has anybody here seen Kelly? Kay ee double ell wy. Dead march from *Saul*. He's as bad as old Antonio. He left me on my ownio. Pirouette! The *Mater Misericordiæ*. Eccles street. My house down there. Big place. Ward for incurables there. Very encouraging. Our Lady's Hospice for the dying. Deadhouse handy underneath. Where old Mrs Riordan died. They look terrible the women. Her feeding cup and rubbing her mouth with the spoon. Then the screen round her bed for her to die. Nice young student that was dressed that bite the bee gave me. He's gone over to the lying-in hospital they told me. From one extreme to the other.

The carriage galloped round a corner: stopped.

– What's wrong now?

A divided drove of branded cattle passed the windows, lowing, slouching by on padded hoofs, whisking their tails slowly on their clotted bony croups. Outside them and through them ran raddled sheep bleating their fear.

– Emigrants, Mr Power said.

– Huuuh! the drover's voice cried, his switch sounding on their flanks. Huuuh! Out of that!

Thursday of course. Tomorrow is killing day. Springers. Cuffe sold them about twentyseven quid each. For Liverpool probably. Roast beef for old England. They buy up all the juicy ones. And then the fifth quarter is lost: all that raw stuff, hide, hair, horns. Comes to a big thing in a year. Dead meat trade. Byproducts of the slaughterhouses for tanneries, soap, margarine. Wonder if that dodge works now getting dicky meat off the train at Clonsilla.

The carriage moved on through the drove.

– I can't make out why the corporation doesn't run a tramline from the parkgate to the quays, Mr Bloom said. All those animals could be taken in trucks down to the boats.

– Instead of blocking up the thoroughfare, Martin Cunningham said. Quite right. They ought to.

– Yes, Mr Bloom said, and another thing I often thought is to have municipal funeral trams like they have in Milan, you know. Run the line out to the cemetery gates and have special trams, hearse and carriage and all. Don't you see what I mean?

– O that be damned for a story, Mr Dedalus said. Pullman car and saloon diningroom.

– A poor lookout for Corny, Mr Power added.

– Why? Mr Bloom asked, turning to Mr Dedalus. Wouldn't it be more decent than galloping two abreast?

– Well, there's something in that, Mr Dedalus granted.

– And, Martin Cunningham said, we wouldn't have scenes like that when the hearse capsized round Dunphy's and upset the coffin on to the road.

– That was terrible, Mr Power's shocked face said, and the corpse fell about the road. Terrible!

– First round Dunphy's, Mr Dedalus said, nodding. Gordon Bennett cup.

– Praises be to God! Martin Cunningham said piously.

Bom! Upset. A coffin bumped out on to the road. Burst open. Paddy Dignam shot out and rolling over stiff in the dust in a brown habit too large for him. Red face: grey now. Mouth fallen open. Asking what's up now. Quite right to close it. Looks horrid open. Then the insides decompose quickly. Much better to close up all the orifices. Yes, also. With wax. The sphincter loose. Seal up all.

– Dunphy's, Mr Power announced as the carriage turned right.

Dunphy's corner. Mourning coaches drawn up drowning their grief. A pause by the wayside. Tiptop position for a pub. Expect we'll pull up here on the way back to drink his health. Pass round the consolation. Elixir of life.

But suppose now it did happen. Would he bleed if a nail say cut him in the knocking about? He would and he wouldn't, I suppose. Depends on where. The circulation stops. Still some might ooze out of an artery. It would be better to bury them in red: a dark red.

In silence they drove along Phibsborough road. An empty hearse trotted by, coming from the cemetery: looks relieved.

Crossguns bridge: the royal canal.

Water rushed roaring through the sluices. A man stood on his dropping barge between clamps of turf. On the towpath by the lock a slacktethered horse. Aboard of the *Bugabu*.

Their eyes watched him. On the slow weedy waterway he had floated on his raft coastward over Ireland drawn by a haulage rope past beds of reeds, over slime, mudchoked bottles, carrion dogs. Athlone, Mullingar, Moyvalley, I could make a walking tour to see Milly by the canal. Or cycle down. Hire some old crock, safety. Wren had one the other day at the auction but a lady's. Developing waterways. James M'Cann's hobby to row me o'er the ferry. Cheaper transit. By easy stages. Houseboats. Camping out. Also hearses. To heaven by water. Perhaps I will without writing. Come as a surprise, Leixlip, Clonsilla. Dropping down, lock by lock to Dublin. With turf from the midland bogs. Salute. He lifted his brown straw hat, saluting Paddy Dignam.

They drove on past Brian Boroimhe house. Near it now.

– I wonder how is our friend Fogarty getting on, Mr Power said.

– Better ask Tom Kernan, Mr Dedalus said.

– How is that? Martin Cunningham said. Left him weeping I suppose.

– Though lost to sight, Mr Dedalus said, to memory dear.

The carriage steered left for Finglas road.

The stonecutter's yard on the right. Last lap. Crowded on the spit of land silent shapes appeared, white, sorrowful, holding out calm hands, knelt in grief, pointing. Fragments of shapes, hewn. In white silence: appealing. The best obtainable. Thos. H. Dennany, monumental builder and sculptor.

Passed.

On the curbstone before Jimmy Geary the sexton's an old tramp sat, grumbling, emptying the dirt and stones out of his huge dustbrown yawning boot. After life's journey.

Gloomy gardens then went by, one by one: gloomy houses.

Mr Power pointed.

– That is where Childs was murdered, he said. The last house.

– So it is, Mr Dedalus said. A gruesome case. Seymour Bushe got him off. Murdered his brother. Or so they said.

– The crown had no evidence, Mr Power said.

– Only circumstantial, Martin Cunningham said. That's the maxim of the law. Better for ninetynine guilty to escape than for one innocent person to be wrongfully condemned.

They looked. Murderer's ground. It passed darkly. Shuttered, tenantless, unweeded garden. Whole place gone to hell. Wrongfully condemned. Murder. The murderer's image in the eye of the murdered. They love reading about it. Man's head found in a garden. Her clothing consisted of. How she met her death. Recent outrage. The weapon used. Murderer is still at large. Clues. A shoelace. The body to be exhumed. Murder will out.

Cramped in this carriage. She mightn't like me to come that way without letting her know. Must be careful about women. Catch them once with their pants down. Never forgive you after. Fifteen.

The high railings of Prospects rippled past their gaze. Dark poplars, rare white forms. Forms more frequent, white shapes thronged amid the trees, white forms and fragments streaming by mutely, sustaining vain gestures on the air.

The felly harshed against the curbstone: stopped. Martin Cunningham put out his arm and, wrenching back the handle, shoved the door open with his knee. He stepped out. Mr Power and Mr Dedalus followed.

Change that soap now. Mr Bloom's hand unbuttoned his hip pocket swiftly and transferred the paperstuck soap to his inner handkerchief pocket. He stepped out of the carriage, replacing the newspaper his other hand still held.

Paltry funeral: coach and three carriages. It's all the same. Pallbearers, gold reins, requiem mass, firing a volley. Pomp of death. Beyond the hind carriage a hawker stood by his barrow of cakes and fruit. Simnel cakes those are, stuck together: cakes for the dead. Dogbiscuits. Who ate them? Mourners coming out.

He followed his companions. Mr Kernan and Ned Lambert followed, Hynes walking after them. Corny Kelleher stood by the opened hearse and took out the two wreaths. He handed one to the boy.

Where is that child's funeral disappeared to?

A team of horses passed from Finglas with toiling plodding read, dragging through the funereal silence a creaking waggon on which lay a granite block. The waggoner marching at their head saluted.

Coffin now. Got here before us, dead as he is. Horse looking round at it with his plume skeowways. Dull eye: collar tight on his neck, pressing on a bloodvessel or something. Do they know what they cart out here every day? Must be twenty or thirty funerals every day. Then Mount Jerome for the protestants. Funerals all over the world everywhere every minute. Shovelling them under by the cartload doublequick. Thousands every hour. Too many in the world.

Mourners came out through the gates: woman and a girl. Leanjawed harpy, hard woman at a bargain, her bonnet awry. Girl's face stained with dirt and tears, holding the woman's arm looking up at her for a sign to cry. Fish's face, bloodless and livid.

The mutes shouldered the coffin and bore it in through the gates. So much dead weight. Felt heavier myself stepping out of that bath. First the stiff: then the friends of the stiff. Corny Kelleher and the boy followed with their wreaths. Who is that beside them? Ah, the brother in-law.

All walked after.

Martin Cunningham whispered:

– I was in mortal agony with you talking of suicide before Bloom.

– What? Mr Power whispered. How so?

– His father poisoned himself, Martin Cunningham whispered. Had the Queen's hotel in Ennis. You heard him say he was going to Clare. Anniversary.

– O God! Mr Power whispered. First I heard of it. Poisoned himself!

He glanced behind him to where a face with dark thinking eyes followed towards the cardinal's mausoleum. Speaking.

– Was he insured? Mr Bloom asked.

– I believe so, Mr Kernan answered, but the policy was heavily mortgaged. Martin is trying to get the youngster into Artane.

– How many children did he leave?

– Five. Ned Lambert says he'll try to get one of the girls into Todd's.

– A sad case, Mr Bloom said gently. Five young children.

– A great blow to the poor wife, Mr Kernan added.

– Indeed yes, Mr Bloom agreed.

Has the laugh at him now.

He looked down at the boots he had blacked and polished. She had outlived him, lost her husband. More dead for her than for me. One must outlive the other. Wise men say. There are more women than men in the world. Condole with her. Your terrible loss. I hope you'll soon follow him. For Hindu widows only. She would marry another. Him? No. Yet who knows after? Widowhood not the thing since the old queen died. Drawn on a guncarriage. Victoria and Albert. Frogmore memorial mourning. But in the end she put a few violets in her bonnet. Vain in her heart of hearts. All for a shadow. Consort not even a king. Her son was the substance. Something new to hope for not like the past she wanted back, waiting. It never comes. One must go first: alone under the ground: and lie no more in her warm bed.

– How are you, Simon? Ned Lambert said softly, clasping hands. Haven't seen you for a month of Sundays.

– Never better. How are all in Cork's own town?

– I was down there for the Cork park races on Easter Monday, Ned Lambert said. Same old six and eightpence. Stopped with Dick Tivy.

– And how is Dick, the solid man?

– Nothing between himself and heaven, Ned Lambert answered.

– By the holy Paul! Mr Dedalus said in subdued wonder. Dick Tivy bald?

– Martin is going to get up a whip for the youngsters, Ned Lambert said, pointing ahead. A few bob a skull. Just to keep them going till the insurance is cleared up.

– Yes, yes, Mr Dedalus said dubiously. Is that the eldest boy in front?

– Yes, Ned Lambert said, with the wife's brother. John Henry Menton is behind. He put down his name for a quid.

– I'll engage he did, Mr Dedalus said. I often told poor Paddy he ought to mind that job. John Henry is not the worst in the world.

– How did he lose it? Ned Lambert asked. Liquor, what?

– Many a good man's fault, Mr Dedalus said with a sigh.

They halted about the door of the mortuary chapel. Mr Bloom stood behind the boy with the wreath, looking down at his sleek combed hair and the slender furrowed neck inside his brandnew collar. Poor boy! Was he there when the father? Both unconscious. Lighten up at the last moment and recognise for the last time. All he might have done. I owe three shillings to O'Grady. Would he understand? The mutes bore the coffin into the chapel. Which end is his head?

After a moment he followed the others in, blinking in the screened light. The coffin lay on its bier before the chancel, four tall yellow candles at its corners. Always in front of us. Corny Kelleher, laying a wreath at each fore corner, beckoned to the boy to kneel. The mourners knelt here and there in praying desks. Mr Bloom stood behind near the font and, when all had knelt dropped carefully his unfolded newspaper from his pocket and knelt his right knee upon it. He fitted his black hat gently on his left knee and, holding its brim, bent over piously.

A server, bearing a brass bucket with something in it, came out through a door. The whitesmocked priest came after him tidying his stole with one hand, balancing with the other a little book against his toad's belly. Who'll read the book? I, said the rook.

They halted by the bier and the priest began to read out of his book with a fluent croak.

Father Coffey. I knew his name was like a coffin. *Domine-namine*. Bully about the muzzle he looks. Bosses the show. Muscular christian. Woe betide anyone that looks crooked at him: priest. Thou art Peter. Burst sideways like a sheep in clover Dedalus says he will. With a belly on him like a poisoned pup. Most amusing expressions that man finds. Hhhn: burst sideways.

– *Non intres in judicium cum servo tuo, Domine.*

Makes them feel more important to be prayed over in Latin. Requiem mass. Crape weepers. Blackedged notepaper. Your name on the altarlist. Chilly place this. Want to feed well, sitting in there all the morning in the gloom kicking his heels waiting for the next please. Eyes of a toad too. What swells him up that way? Molly gets swelled after cabbage. Air of the place maybe. Looks full up of bad gas. Must be an infernal lot of bad gas round the place. Butchers for instance: they get like raw beefsteaks. Who was telling me? Mervyn Brown. Down in the vaults of saint Werburgh's lovely old organ hundred and fifty they have to bore a hole in the coffins sometimes to let out the bad gas and burn it. Out it rushes: blue. One whiff of that and you're a goner.

My kneecap is hurting me. Ow. That's better.

The priest took a stick with a knob at the end of it out of the boy's bucket and shook it over the coffin. Then he walked to the other end and shook it again. Then he came back and put it back in the bucket. As you were before you rested. It's all written down: he has to do it.

– *Et ne nos inducas in tentationem.*

The server piped the answers in the treble. I often thought it would be better to have boy servants. Up to fifteen or so. After that of course . . .

Holy water that was, I expect. Shaking sleep out of it. He must be fed up with that job, shaking that thing over all the corpses they trot up. What harm if he could see what he was shaking it over. Every mortal day a fresh batch: middleaged men, old women, children, women dead in childbirth,

men with beards, baldheaded business men, consumptive girls with little
sparrow's breasts. All the year round he prayed the same thing over them all
and shook water on top of them: sleep. On Dignam now.

– *In paradisum.*

Said he was going to paradise or is in paradise. Says that over everybody.
Tiresome kind of a job. But he has to say something.

The priest closed his book and went off, followed by the server. Corny
Kelleher opened the sidedoors and the grave-diggers came in, hoisted the
coffin again, carried it out and shoved it on their cart. Corny Kelleher gave
one wreath to the boy and one to the brother-in-law. All followed them out
of the sidedoors into the mild grey air. Mr Bloom came last, folding his
paper again into his pocket. He gazed gravely at the ground till the coffin-
cart wheeled off to the left. The metal wheels ground the gravel with a
sharp grating cry and the pack of blunt boots followed the barrow along a
lane of sepulchres.

The ree the ra the ree the ra the roo. Lord, I mustn't lilt here.

– The O'Connell circle, Mr Dedalus said about him.

Mr Power's soft eyes went up to the apex of the lofty cone.

– He's at rest, he said, in the middle of his people, old Dan O'. But his
heart is buried in Rome. How many broken hearts are buried here, Simon!

– Her grave is over there, Jack, Mr Dedalus said. I'll soon be stretched
beside her. Let Him take me whenever He likes.

Breaking down, he began to weep to himself quietly, stumbling a little in
his walk. Mr Power took his arm.

– She's better where she is, he said kindly.

– I suppose so, Mr Dedalus said with a weak gasp. I suppose she is in
heaven if there is a heaven.

Corny Kelleher stepped aside from his rank and allowed the mourners to
plod by.

– Sad occasions, Mr Kernan began politely.

Mr Bloom closed his eyes and sadly twice bowed his head.

– The others are putting on their hats, Mr Kernan said. I suppose we can
do so too. We are the last. This cemetery is a treacherous place.

They covered their heads.

– The reverend gentleman read the service too quickly, don't you think?
Mr Kernan said with reproof.

Mr Bloom nodded gravely, looking in the quick bloodshot eyes. Secret
eyes, secret searching eyes. Mason, I think: not sure. Beside him again. We
are the last. In the same boat. Hope he'll say something else.

Mr Kernan added:

– The service of the Irish church, used in Mount Jerome, is simpler, more impressive, I must say.

Mr Bloom gave prudent assent. The language of course was another thing.

Mr Kernan said with solemnity:

– *I am the resurrection and the life.* That touches a man's inmost heart.

– It does, Mr Bloom said.

Your heart perhaps but what price the fellow in the six feet by two with his toes to the daisies? No touching that. Seat of the affections. Broken heart. A pump after all, pumping thousands of gallons of blood every day. One fine day it gets bunged up and there you are. Lots of them lying around here: lungs, hearts, livers. Old rusty pumps: damn the thing else. The resurrection and the life. Once you are dead you are dead. That last day idea. Knocking them all up out of their graves. Come forth, Lazarus! And he came fifth and lost the job. Get up! Last day! Then every fellow mousing around for his liver and his lights and the rest of his traps. Find damn all of himself that morning. Pennyweight of powder in a skull. Twelve grammes one pennyweight. Troy measure.

Corny Kelleher fell into step at their side.

– Everything went off A 1, he said. What?

He looked on them from his drawling eye. Policeman's shoulders. With your tooraloom tooraloom.

– As it should be, Mr Kernan said.

– What? Eh? Corny Kelleher said.

Mr Kernan assured him.

– Who is that chap behind with Tom Kernan? John Henry Menton asked. I know his face.

Ned Lambert glanced back.

– Bloom, he said, Madam Marion Tweedy that was, is, I mean, the soprano. She's his wife.

– O, to be sure, John Henry Menton said. I haven't seen her for some time. She was a finelooking woman. I danced with her, wait, fifteen seventeen golden years ago, at Mat Dillon's, in Roundtown. And a good armful she was.

He looked behind through the others.

– What is he? he asked. What does he do? Wasn't he in the stationery line? I fell foul of him one evening, I remember, at bowls.

Ned Lambert smiled.

– Yes, he was, he said, in Wisdom Hely's. A traveller for blottingpaper.

– In God's name, John Henry Menton said, what did she marry a coon like that for? She had plenty of game in her then.

– Has still, Ned Lambert said. He does some canvassing for ads.

John Henry Menton's large eyes stared ahead.

The barrow turned into a side lane. A portly man, ambushed among the grasses, raised his hat in homage. The gravediggers touched their caps.

– John O'Connell, Mr Power said, pleased. He never forgets a friend.

Mr O'Connell shook all their hands in silence. Mr Dedalus said:

– I am come to pay you another visit.

– My dear Simon, the caretaker answered in a low voice. I don't want your custom at all.

Saluting Ned Lambert and John Henry Menton he walked on at Martin Cunningham's side, puzzling two keys at his back.

– Did you hear that one, he asked them, about Mulcahy from the Coombe?

– I did not, Martin Cunningham said.

They bent their silk hats in concert and Hynes inclined his ear. The caretaker hung his thumbs in the loops of his gold watch chain and spoke in a discreet tone to their vacant smiles.

– They tell the story, he said, that two drunks came out here one foggy evening to look for the grave of a friend of theirs. They asked for Mulcahy from the Coombe and were told where he was buried. After traipsing about in the fog they found the grave, sure enough. One of the drunks spelt out the name: Terence Mulcahy. The other drunk was blinding up at a statue of our Saviour the widow had got put up.

The caretaker blinked up at one of the sepulchres they passed. He resumed:

– And, after blinking up at the sacred figure, *Not a bloody bit like the man,* says he. *That's not Mulcahy,* says he, *whoever done it.*

Rewarded by smiles he fell back and spoke with Corny Kelleher, accepting the dockets given him, turning them over and scanning them as he walked.

– That's all done with a purpose, Martin Cunningham explained to Hynes.

– I know, Hynes said, I know that.

– To cheer a fellow up, Martin Cunningham said. It's pure good-heartedness: damn the thing else.

Mr Bloom admired the caretaker's prosperous bulk. All want to be on good terms with him. Decent fellow, John O'Connell, real good sort. Keys: like Keyes's ad: no fear of anyone getting out, no passout checks. *Habeat corpus.* I must see about that ad after the funeral. Did I write Ballsbridge on the envelope I took to cover when she disturbed me writing to Martha? Hope it's not chucked in the dead letter office. Be the better of a shave.

Grey sprouting beard. That's the first sign when the hairs come out grey and temper getting cross. Silver threads among the grey. Fancy being his wife. Wonder how he had the gumption to propose to any girl. Come out and live in the graveyard. Dangle that before her. It might thrill her first. Courting death . . . Shades of night hovering here with all the dead stretched about. The shadows of the tombs when churchyards yawn and Daniel O'Connell must be a descendant I suppose who is this used to say he was a queer breedy man great catholic all the same like a big giant in the dark. Will o' the wisp. Gas of graves. Want to keep her mind off it to conceive at all. Women especially are so touchy. Tell her a ghost story in bed to make her sleep. Have you ever seen a ghost? Well, I have. It was a pitchdark night. The clock was on the stroke of twelve. Still they'd kiss all right if properly keyed up. Whores in Turkish graveyards. Learn anything if taken young. You might pick up a young widow here. Men like that. Love among the tombstones. Romeo. Spice of pleasure. In the midst of death we are in life. Both ends meet. Tantalising for the poor dead. Smell of frilled beefsteaks to the starving gnawing their vitals. Desire to grig people. Molly wanting to do it at the window. Eight children he has anyway.

He has seen a fair share go under in his time, lying around him field after field. Holy fields. More room if they buried them standing. Sitting or kneeling you couldn't. Standing? His head might come up some day above ground in a landslip with his hand pointing. All honeycombed the ground must be: oblong cells. And very neat he keeps it too, trim grass and edgings. His garden Major Gamble calls Mount Jerome. Well so it is. Ought to be flowers of sleep. Chinese cemeteries with giant poppies growing produce the best opium Mastiansky told me. The Botanic Gardens are just over there. It's the blood sinking in the earth gives new life. Same idea those jews they said killed the christian boy. Every man his price. Well preserved fat corpse gentleman, epicure, invaluable for fruit garden. A bargain. By carcass of William Wilkinson, auditor and accountant, lately deceased, three pounds thirteen and six. With thanks.

I daresay the soil would be quite fat with corpse manure, bones, flesh, nails, charnelhouses. Dreadful. Turning green and pink, decomposing. Rot quick in damp earth. The lean old ones tougher. Then a kind of a tallowy kind of a cheesy. Then begin to get black, treacle oozing out of them. Then dried up. Deathmoths. Of course the cells or whatever they are go on living. Changing about. Live for ever practically. Nothing to feed on feed on themselves.

But they must breed a devil of a lot of maggots. Soil must be simply swirling with them. Your head it simply swurls. Those pretty little seaside gurls. He looks cheerful enough over it. Gives him a sense of power seeing all the others go under first. Wonder how he looks at life. Cracking his jokes too: warms the cockles of his heart. The one about the bulletin. Spurgeon went to heaven 4 a.m. this morning. 11 p.m. (closing time). Not arrived yet. Peter. The dead themselves the men anyhow would like to hear an odd joke or the women to know what's in fashion. A juicy pear or ladies' punch, hot, strong and sweet. Keep out the damp. You must laugh sometimes so better do it that way. Gravediggers in *Hamlet*. Shows the profound knowledge of the human heart. Daren't joke about the dead for two years at least. *De mortuis nil nisi prius*. Go out of mourning first. Hard to imagine his funeral. Seems a sort of a joke. Read your own obituary notice they say you live longer. Gives you second wind. New lease of life.

– How many have you for tomorrow? the caretaker asked.

– Two, Corny Kelleher said. Half ten and eleven.

The caretaker put the papers in his pocket. The barrow had ceased to trundle. The mourners split and moved to each side of the hole, stepping with care round the graves. The gravediggers bore the coffin and set its nose on the brink, looping the bands round it.

Burying him. We come to bury Cæsar. His ides of March or June. He doesn't know who is here nor care.

Now who is that lankylooking galoot over there in the macintosh? Now who is he I'd like to know? Now, I'd give a trifle to know who he is. Always someone turns up you never dreamt of. A fellow could live on his lonesome all his life. Yes, he could. Still he'd have to get someone to sod him after he died though he could dig his own grave. We all do. Only man buries. No ants too. First thing strikes anybody. Bury the dead. Say Robinson Crusoe was true to life. Well then Friday buried him. Every Friday buries a Thursday if you come to look at it.

> *O, poor Robinson Crusoe,*
> *How could you possibly do so?*

Poor Dignam! His last lie on the earth in his box. When you think of them all it does seem a waste of wood. All gnawed through. They could invent a handsome bier with a kind of panel sliding let it down that way. Ay but they might object to be buried out of another fellow's. They're so particular. Lay me in my native earth. Bit of clay from the holy land. Only a mother and deadborn child ever buried in the one coffin. I see what it means. I see. To protect him as long as possible even in the earth. The Irishman's house is his coffin. Embalming in catacombs, mummies, the same idea.

Mr Bloom stood far back, his hat in his hand, counting the bared heads. Twelve. I'm thirteen. No. The chap in the macintosh is thirteen. Death's number. Where the deuce did he pop out of? He wasn't in the chapel, that I'll swear. Silly superstition that about thirteen.

Nice soft tweed Ned Lambert has in that suit. Tinge of purple. I had one like that when we lived in Lombard street west. Dressy fellow he was once. Used to change three suits in the day. Must get that grey suit of mine turned by Mesias. Hello. It's dyed. His wife I forgot he's not married or his landlady ought to have picked out those threads for him.

The coffin dived out of sight, eased down by the men straddled on the gravetrestles. They struggled up and out: and all uncovered. Twenty.

Pause.

If we were all suddenly somebody else.

Far away a donkey brayed. Rain. No such ass. Never see a dead one, they say. Shame of death. They hide. Also poor papa went away.

Gentle sweet air blew round the bared heads in a whisper. Whisper. The boy by the gravehead held his wreath with both hands staring quietly in the black open space. Mr Bloom moved behind the portly kindly caretaker. Well cut frockcoat. Weighing them up perhaps to see which will go next. Well it is a long rest. Feel no more. It's the moment you feel. Must be damned unpleasant. Can't believe it at first. Mistake must be: someone else. Try the house opposite. Wait, I wanted to. I haven't yet. Then darkened deathchamber. Light they want. Whispering around you. Would you like to see a priest? Then rambling and wandering. Delirium all you hid all your life. The death struggle. His sleep is not natural. Press his lower eyelid. Watching is his nose pointed is his jaw sinking are the soles of his feet yellow. Pull the pillow away and finish it off on the floor since he's doomed. Devil in that picture of sinner's death showing him a woman. Dying to embrace her in his shirt. Last act of *Lucia. Shall I nevermore behold thee?* Bam! expires. Gone at last. People talk about you a bit: forget you. Don't forget to pray for him. Remember him in your prayers. Even Parnell. Ivy day dying out. Then they follow: dropping into a hole one after the other.

We are praying now for the repose of his soul. Hoping you're well and not in hell. Nice change of air. Out of the fryingpan of life into the fire of purgatory.

Does he ever think of the hole waiting for himself? They say you do when you shiver in the sun. Someone walking over it. Callboy's warning. Near you. Mine over there towards Finglas, the plot I bought. Mamma poor mamma, and little Rudy.

The gravediggers took up their spades and flung heavy clods of clay in on the coffin. Mr Bloom turned his face. And if he was alive all the time? Whew! By Jingo, that would be awful! No, no: he is dead, of course. Of course he is dead. Monday he died. They ought to have some law to pierce the heart and make sure or an electric clock or a telephone in the coffin and some kind of a canvas airhole. Flag of distress. Three days. Rather long to keep them in summer. Just as well to get shut of them as soon as you are sure there's no.

The clay fell softer. Begin to be forgotten. Out of sight, out of mind.

The caretaker moved away a few paces and put on his hat. Had enough of it. The mourners took heart of grace, one by one, covering themselves without show. Mr Bloom put on his hat and saw the portly figure make its way deftly through the maze of graves. Quietly, sure of his ground, he traversed the dismal fields.

Hynes jotting down something in his notebook. Ah, the names. But he knows them all. No: coming to me.

– I am just taking the names, Hynes said below his breath. What is your christian name? I'm not sure.

– L, Mr Bloom said. Leopold. And you might put down M'Coy's name too. He asked me to.

– Charley, Hynes said writing. I know. He was on the *Freeman* once.

So he was before he got the job in the morgue under Louis Byrne. Good idea a postmortem for doctors. Find out what they imagine they know. He died of a Tuesday. Got the run. Levanted with the cash of a few ads. Charley, you're my darling. That was why he asked me to. O well, does no harm. I saw to that, M'Coy. Thanks, old chap: much obliged. Leave him under an obligation: costs nothing.

– And tell us, Hynes said, do you know that fellow in the, fellow was over there in the . . .

He looked around.

– Macintosh. Yes, I saw him, Mr Bloom said. Where is he now?

– M'Intosh, Hynes said, scribbling. I don't know who he is. Is that his name?

He moved away, looking about him.

– No, Mr Bloom began, turning and stopping. I say, Hynes!

Didn't hear. What? Where has he disappeared to? Not a sign. Well of all the. Has anybody here seen? Kay ee double ell. Become invisible. Good Lord, what became of him?

A seventh gravedigger came beside Mr Bloom to take up an idle spade.

– O, excuse me!

He stepped aside nimbly.

Clay, brown, damp, began to be seen in the hole. It rose. Nearly over. A mound of damp clods rose more, rose, and the gravediggers rested their spades. All uncovered again for a few instants. The boy propped his wreath against a corner: the brother-in-law his on a lump. The gravediggers put on their caps and carried their earthy spades towards the barrow. Then knocked the blades lightly on the turf: clean. One bent to pluck from the haft a long tuft of grass. One, leaving his mates, walked slowly on with shouldered weapon, its blade blueglancing. Silently at the gravehead another coiled the coffinband. His navelcord. The brother-in-law, turning away, placed something in his free hand. Thanks in silence. Sorry, sir: trouble. Headshake. I know that. For yourselves just.

The mourners moved away slowly, without aim, by devious paths, staying awhile to read a name on a tomb.

– Let us go round by the chief's grave, Hynes said. We have time.

– Let us, Mr Power said.

They turned to the right, following their slow thoughts. With awe Mr Power's blank voice spoke:

– Some say he is not in that grave at all. That the coffin was filled with stones. That one day he will come again.

Hynes shook his head.

– Parnell will never come again, he said. He's there, all that was mortal of him. Peace to his ashes.

Mr Bloom walked unheeded along his grove by saddened angels, crosses, broken pillars, family vaults, stone hopes praying with upcast eyes, old Ireland's hearts and hands. More sensible to spend the money on some charity for the living. Pray for the repose of the soul of. Does anybody really? Plant him and have done with him. Like down a coalshoot. Then lump them together to save time. All souls' day. Twentyseventh I'll be at his grave. Ten shillings for the gardener. He keeps it free of weeds. Old man himself. Bent down double with his shears clipping. Near death's door. Who passed away. Who departed this life. As if they did it of their own accord. Got the shove, all of them. Who kicked the bucket. More interesting if they told you what they were. So and so, wheelwright. I travelled for cork lino. I paid five shillings in the pound. Or a woman's with her saucepan. I cooked good Irish stew. Eulogy in a country churchyard it ought to be that poem of whose is it Wordsworth or Thomas Campbell. Entered into rest the protestants put it. Old Dr Murren's. The great physician called him home. Well it's God's acre for them. Nice country residence. Newly plastered and painted. Ideal spot to have a quiet smoke and read the *Church Times*. Marriage ads they never try to beautify. Rusty wreaths hung on knobs, garlands of bronzefoil. Better value that for the money. Still, the flowers are more poetical. The other gets rather tiresome, never withering. Expresses nothing. Immortelles.

A bird sat tamely perched on a poplar branch. Like stuffed. Like the wedding present alderman Hooper gave us. Hu! Not a budge out of him. Knows there are no catapults to let fly at him. Dead animal even sadder. Silly-Milly burying the little dead bird in the kitchen matchbox, a daisychain and bits of broken chainies on the grave.

The Sacred Heart that is: showing it. Heart on his sleeve. Ought to be sideways and red it should be painted like a real heart. Ireland was dedicated to it or whatever that. Seems anything but pleased. Why this infliction? Would birds come then and peck like the boy with the basket of fruit but he said no because they ought to have been afraid of the boy. Apollo that was.

How many! All these here once walked round Dublin. Faithful departed. As you are now so once were we.

Besides how could you remember everybody? Eyes, walk, voice. Well, the voice, yes: gramophone. Have a gramophone in every grave or keep it in the house. After dinner on a Sunday. Put on poor old greatgrandfather Kraahraark! Hellohellohello amawfullyglad kraark awfullygladaseeragain hellohello amarawf kopthsth. Remind you of the voice like the photograph reminds you of the face. Otherwise you couldn't remember the face after fifteen years, say. For instance who? For instance some fellow that died when I was in Wisdom Hely's.

Rtststr! A rattle of pebbles. Wait. Stop.

He looked down intently into a stone crypt. Some animal. Wait. There he goes.

An obese grey rat toddled along the side of the crypt, moving the pebbles. An old stager: greatgrandfather: he knows the ropes. The grey alive crushed itself in under the plinth, wriggled itself in under it. Good hidingplace for treasure.

Who lives there? Are laid the remains of Robert Emery. Robert Emmet was buried here by torchlight, wasn't he? Making his rounds.

Tail gone now.

One of those chaps would make short work of a fellow. Pick the bones clean no matter who it was. Ordinary meat for them. A corpse is meat gone bad. Well and what's cheese? Corpse of milk. I read in that *Voyages in China* that the Chinese say a white man smells like a corpse. Cremation better. Priests dead against it. Devilling for the other firm. Wholesale burners and Dutch oven dealers. Time of the plague. Quicklime fever pits to eat them. Lethal chamber. Ashes to ashes. Or bury at sea. Where is that Parsee tower of silence? Eaten by birds. Earth, fire, water. Drowning they say is the pleasantest. See your whole life in a flash. But being brought back to life no. Can't bury in the air however. Out of a flying machine. Wonder does the news go about whenever a fresh one is let down. Underground communication. We learned that from them. Wouldn't be surprised. Regular square feed for them. Flies come before he's well dead. Got wind of Dignam. They wouldn't care about the smell of it. Saltwhite crumbling mush of corpse: smell, taste like raw white turnips.

The gates glimmered in front: still open. Back to the world again. Enough of this place. Brings you a bit nearer every time. Last time I was here was Mrs Sinico's funeral. Poor papa too. The love that kills. And even scraping up the earth at night with a lantern like that case I read of to get at fresh buried females or even putrefied with running gravesores. Give you the creeps after a bit. I will appear to you after death. You will see my ghost after death. My ghost will haunt you after death. There is another world after death named hell. I do not like that other world she wrote. No more do I. Plenty to see and hear and feel yet. Feel live warm beings near you. Let them sleep in their maggoty beds. They are not going to get me this innings. Warm beds: warm fullblooded life.

Martin Cunningham emerged from a sidepath, talking gravely.

Solicitor, I think. I know his face. Menton. John Henry, solicitor, commissioner for oaths and affidavits. Dignam used to be in his office. Mat Dillon's long ago. Jolly Mat convivial evenings. Cold fowl, cigars, the Tantalus glasses. Heart of gold really. Yes, Menton. Got his rag out that evening on the bowling green because I sailed inside him. Pure fluke of mine: the bias. Why he took such a rooted dislike to me. Hate at first sight. Molly and Floey Dillon linked under the lilactree, laughing. Fellow always like that, mortified if women are by.

Got a dinge in the side of his hat. Carriage probably.

– Excuse me, sir, Mr Bloom said beside them.

They stopped.

– Your hat is a little crushed, Mr Bloom said, pointing.

John Henry Menton stared at him for an instant without moving.

– There, Martin Cunningham helped, pointing also.

John Henry Menton took off his hat, bulged out the dinge and smoothed the nap with care on his coatsleeve. He clapped the hat on his head again.

– It's all right now, Martin Cunningham said.

John Henry Menton jerked his head down in acknowledgment.

– Thank you, he said shortly.

They walked on towards the gates. Mr Bloom, chapfallen, drew behind a few paces so as not to overhear. Martin laying down the law. Martin could wind a sappyhead like that round his little finger without his seeing it.

Oyster eyes. Never mind. Be sorry after perhaps when it dawns on him. Get the pull over him that way.

Thank you. How grand we are this morning.

*   *   *   *   *

IN THE HEART OF THE HIBERNIAN METROPOLIS

◀ BEFORE NELSON'S PILLAR TRAMS SLOWED, SHUNTED, changed trolley, started for Blackrock, Kingstown and Dalkey, Clonskea, Rathgar and Terenure, Palmerston park and upper Rathmines, Sandymount Green, Rathmines, Ringsend and Sandymount Tower, Harold's Cross. The hoarse Dublin United Tramway Company's timekeeper bawled them off:

– Rathgar and Terenure!

– Come on, Sandymount Green!

Right and left parallel clanging ringing a doubledecker and a singledeck moved from their railheads, swerved to the down line, glided parallel.

– Start, Palmerston park!

THE WEARER OF THE CROWN

Under the porch of the general post office shoeblacks called and polished. Parked in North Prince's street His Majesty's vermilion mailcars, bearing on their sides the royal initials, E. R., received loudly flung sacks of letters, postcards, lettercards, parcels, insured and paid, for local, provincial, British and overseas delivery.

GENTLEMEN OF THE PRESS

Grossbooted draymen rolled barrels dullthudding out of Prince's stores and bumped them up on the brewery float. On the brewery float bumped dullthudding barrels rolled by grossbooted draymen out of Prince's stores.

– There it is, Red Murray said. Alexander Keyes.

– Just cut it out, will you? Mr Bloom said, and I'll take it round to the *Telegraph* office.

The door of Ruttledge's office creaked again. Davy Stephens, minute in a large capecoat, a small felt hat crowning his ringlets, passed out with a roll of papers under his cape, a king's courier.

Red Murray's long shears sliced out the advertisement from the newspaper in four clean strokes. Scissors and paste.

– I'll go through the printing works, Mr Bloom said, taking the cut square.

– Of course, if he wants a par, Red Murray said earnestly, a pen behind his ear, we can do him one.

– Right, Mr Bloom said with a nod. I'll rub that in.

We.

WILLIAM BRAYDEN, ESQUIRE, OF OAKLANDS, SANDYMOUNT

Red Murray touched Mr Bloom's arm with the shears and whispered:

– Brayden.

Mr Bloom turned and saw the liveried porter raise his lettered cap as a stately figure entered between the newsboards of the *Weekly Freeman and National Press* and the *Freeman's Journal and National Press*. Dullthudding Guinness's barrels. It passed stately up the staircase steered by an umbrella, a solemn beardframed face. The broadcloth back ascended each step: back. All his brains are in the nape of his neck, Simon Dedalus says. Welts of flesh behind on him. Fat folds of neck, fat, neck, fat, neck.

– Don't you think his face is like Our Saviour? Red Murray whispered.

The door of Ruttledge's office whispered: ee: cree. They always build one door opposite another for the wind to. Way in. Way out.

Our Saviour: beardframed oval face: talking in the dusk Mary, Martha. Steered by an umbrella sword to the footlights: Mario the tenor.

– Or like Mario, Mr Bloom said.

– Yes, Red Murray agreed. But Mario was said to be the picture of Our Saviour.

Jesus Mario with rougy cheeks, doublet and spindle legs. Hand on his heart. In *Martha*.

> *Co-ome thou lost one,*
> *Co-ome thou dear one.*

THE CROZIER AND THE PEN

– His grace phoned down twice this morning, Red Murray said gravely.

They watched the knees, legs, boots vanish. Neck.

A telegram boy stepped in nimbly, threw an envelope on the counter and stepped off posthaste with a word.

– *Freeman!*

Mr Bloom said slowly:

– Well, he is one of our saviours also.

A meek smile accompanied him as he lifted the counterflap, as he passed in through the sidedoor and along the warm dark stairs and passage, along the now reverberating boards. But will he save the circulation? Thumping, thumping.

He pushed in the glass swingdoor and entered, stepping over strewn packing paper. Through a lane of clanking drums he made his way towards Nannetti's reading closet.

WITH UNFEIGNED REGRET IT IS WE ANNOUNCE THE DISSOLUTION OF A MOST RESPECTED DUBLIN BURGESS

Hynes here too: account of the funeral probably. Thumping thump. This morning the remains of the late Mr Patrick Dignam. Machines. Smash a man to atoms if they got him caught. Rule the world today. His machineries are pegging away too. Like these, got out of hand: fermenting. Working away, tearing away. And that old grey rat tearing to get in.

HOW A GREAT DAILY ORGAN IS TURNED OUT

Mr Bloom halted behind the foreman's spare body, admiring a glossy crown.

Strange he never saw his real country. Ireland my country. Member for College green. He boomed that workaday worker tack for all it was worth. It's the ads and side features sell a weekly not the stale news in the official gazette. Queen Anne is dead. Published by authority in the year one thousand and. Demesne situate in the townland of Rosenallis, barony of Tinnachinch. To all whom it may concern schedule pursuant to statute showing return of number of mules and jennets exported from Ballina. Nature notes. Cartoons. Phil Blake's weekly Pat and Bull story. Uncle Toby's page for tiny tots. Country bumpkin's queries. Dear Mr Editor, what is a good cure for flatulence? I'd like that part. Learn a lot teaching others. The personal note M. A. P. Mainly all pictures. Shapely bathers on golden strand. World's biggest balloon. Double marriage of sisters celebrated. Two bridegrooms laughing heartily at each other. Cuprani too, printer. More Irish than the Irish.

The machines clanked in threefour time. Thump, thump, thump. Now if he got paralysed there and no one knew how to stop them they'd clank on and on the same, print it over and over and up and back. Monkeydoodle the whole thing. Want a cool head.

– Well, get it into the evening edition, councillor, Hynes said.

Soon be calling him my lord mayor. Long John is backing him they say.

The foreman, without answering, scribbled press on a corner of the sheet and made a sign to a typesetter. He handed the sheet silently over the dirty glass screen.

– Right: thanks, Hynes said moving off.

Mr Bloom stood in his way.

– If you want to draw the cashier is just going to lunch, he said, pointing backward with his thumb.

– Did you? Hynes asked.

– Mm, Mr Bloom said. Look sharp and you'll catch him.

– Thanks, old man, Hynes said. I'll tap him too.

He hurried on eagerly towards the *Freeman's Journal*.

Three bob I lent him in Meagher's. Three weeks. Third hint.

WE SEE THE CANVASSER AT WORK

Mr Bloom laid his cutting on Mr Nannetti's desk.

– Excuse me, councillor, he said. This ad, you see. Keyes, you remember.

Mr Nannetti considered the cutting a while and nodded.

– He wants it in for July, Mr Bloom said.

He doesn't hear it. Nannan. Iron nerves.

The foreman moved his pencil towards it.

– But wait, Mr Bloom said. He wants it changed. Keyes, you see. He wants two keys at the top.

Hell of a racket they make. Maybe he understands what I.

The foreman turned round to hear patiently and, lifting an elbow began to scratch slowly in the armpit of his alpaca jacket.

– Like that, Mr Bloom said, crossing his forefingers at the top.

Let him take that in first.

Mr Bloom, glancing sideways up from the cross he had made, saw the foreman's sallow face, think he has a touch of jaundice, and beyond the obedient reels feeding in huge webs of paper. Clank it. Clank it. Miles of it unreeled. What becomes of it after? O, wrap up meat, parcels: various uses, thousand and one things.

Slipping his words deftly into the pauses of the clanking he drew swiftly on the scarred woodwork.

HOUSE OF KEY(E)S

– Like that, see. Two crossed keys here. A circle. Then here the name Alexander Keyes, tea, wine and spirit merchant. So on.

Better not teach him his own business.

– You know yourself, councillor, just what he wants. Then round the top in leaded: the house of keys. You see? Do you think that's a good idea?

The foreman moved his scratching hand to his lower ribs and scratched there quietly.

– The idea, Mr Bloom said, is the house of keys. You know, councillor, the Manx parliament. Innuendo of home rule. Tourists, you know, from the isle of Man. Catches the eye, you see. Can you do that?

I could ask him perhaps about how to pronounce that *voglio*. But then if he didn't know only make it awkward for him. Better not.

– We can do that, the foreman said. Have you the design?

– I can get it, Mr Bloom said. It was in a Kilkenny paper. He has a house there too. I'll just run out and ask him. Well, you can do that and just a little par calling attention. You know the usual. High class licensed premises. Longfelt want. So on.

The foreman thought for an instant.

– We can do that, he said. Let him give us a three months' renewal.

A typesetter brought him a limp galleypage. He began to check it silently. Mr Bloom stood by, hearing the loud throbs of cranks, watching the silent typesetters at their cases.

ORTHOGRAPHICAL

Want to be sure of his spelling. Proof fever. Martin Cunningham forgot to give us his spellingbee conundrum this morning. It is amusing to view the unpar one ar alleled embarra two ars is it? double ess ment of a harassed pedlar while gauging au the symmetry of a peeled pear under a cemetery wall. Silly, isn't it? Cemetery put in of course on account of the symmetry.

I could have said when he clapped on his topper. Thank you. I ought to have said something about an old hat or something. No, I could have said. Looks as good as new now. See his phiz then.

Sllt. The nethermost deck of the first machine jogged forward its flyboard with sllt the first batch of quirefolded papers. Sllt. Almost human the way it sllt to call attention. Doing its level best to speak. That door too sllt creaking, asking to be shut. Everything speaks in its own way. Sllt.

NOTED CHURCHMAN AN OCCASIONAL CONTRIBUTOR

The foreman handed back the galleypage suddenly, saying:

– Wait. Where's the archbishop's letter? It's to be repeated in the *Telegraph*. Where's what's his name?

He looked about him round his loud unanswering machines.

– Monks, sir? a voice asked from the castingbox.

– Ay. Where's Monks?

– Monks!

Mr Bloom took up his cutting. Time to get out.

– Then I'll get the design, Mr Nannetti, he said, and you'll give it a good place I know.

– Monks!

– Yes, sir.

Three months' renewal. Want to get some wind off my chest first. Try it anyhow. Rub in August: good idea: horseshow month. Ballsbridge. Tourists over for the show.

A DAYFATHER

He walked on through the caseroom, passing an old man, bowed, spectacled, aproned. Old Monks, the dayfather. Queer lot of stuff he must have put through his hands in his time: obituary notices, pub's ads, speeches, divorce suits, found drowned. Nearing the end of his tether now. Sober serious man with a bit in the savingsbank I'd say. Wife a good cook and washer. Daughter working the machine in the parlour. Plain Jane, no damn nonsense.

AND IT WAS THE FEAST OF THE PASSOVER

He stayed in his walk to watch a typesetter neatly distributing type. Reads it backwards first. Quickly he does it. Must require some practice that. mangiD. kcirtaP. Poor papa with his hagadah book, reading backwards with his finger to me. Pessach. Next year in Jerusalem. Dear, O dear! All that long business about that brought us out of the land of Egypt and into the house of bondage *alleluia. Shema Israel Adonai Elohenu.* No, that's the other. Then the twelve brothers, Jacob's sons. And then the lamb and the cat and the dog and the stick and the water and the butcher and then the angel of death kills the butcher and he kills the ox and the dog kills the cat. Sounds a bit silly till you come to look into it well. Justice it means but it's everybody eating everyone else. That's what life is after all. How quickly he does that job. Practice makes perfect. Seems to see with his fingers.

Mr Bloom passed on out of the clanking noises through the gallery on to the landing. Now am I going to tram it out all the way and then catch him out perhaps? Better phone him up first. Number? Same as Citron's house. Twentyeight. Twentyeight double four.

ONLY ONCE MORE THAT SOAP

He went down the house staircase. Who the deuce scrawled all over these walls with matches? Looks as if they did it for a bet. Heavy greasy smell there always is in those works. Lukewarm glue in Thom's next door when I was there.

He took out his handkerchief to dab his nose. Citronlemon? Ah, the soap I put there. Lose it out of that pocket. Putting back his handkerchief he took out the soap and stowed it away, buttoned, into the hip pocket of his trousers.

What perfume does your wife use? I could go home still: tram: something

I forgot. Just to see before dressing. No. Here. No.

A sudden screech of laughter came from the *Evening Telegraph* office. Know who that is. What's up? Pop in a minute to phone. Ned Lambert it is.

He entered softly.

ERIN, GREEN GEM OF THE SILVER SEA

– The ghost walks, professor MacHugh murmured softly, biscuitfully to the dusty windowpane.

Mr Dedalus, staring from the empty fireplace at Ned Lambert's quizzing face, asked of it sourly:

– Agonising Christ, wouldn't it give you a heartburn on your arse?

Ned Lambert, seated on the table, read on:

– *Or again, note the meanderings of some purling rill as it babbles on its way, fanned by gentlest zephyrs tho' quarrelling with the stony obstacles, to the tumbling waters of Neptune's blue domain, mid mossy banks, played on by the glorious sunlight or 'neath the shadows cast o'er its pensive bosom by the overarching leafage of the giants of the forest.* What about that, Simon? he asked over the fringe of his newspaper. How's that for high?

– Changing his drink, Mr Dedalus said.

Ned Lambert, laughing, struck the newspaper on his knees, repeating:

– *The pensive bosom and the overarsing leafage.* O boys! O boys!

– And Xenophon looked upon Marathon, Mr Dedalus said, looking again on the fireplace and to the window, and Marathon looked on the sea.

– That will do, professor MacHugh cried from the window. I don't want to hear any more of the stuff.

He ate off the crescent of water biscuit he had been nibbling and, hungered, made ready to nibble the biscuit in his other hand.

High falutin stuff. Bladderbags. Ned Lambert is taking a day off I see. Rather upsets a man's day a funeral does. He has influence they say. Old Chatterton, the vice-chancellor, is his granduncle or his greatgranduncle. Close on ninety they say. Subleader for his death written this long time perhaps. Living to spite them. Might go first himself. Johnny, make room for your uncle. The right honourable Hedges Eyre Chatterton. Daresay he writes him an odd shaky cheque or two on gale days. Windfall when he kicks out. Alleluia.

– Just another spasm, Ned Lambert said.

– What is it? Mr Bloom asked.

– A recently discovered fragment of Cicero's, professor MacHugh answered with pomp of tone. *Our lovely land.*

SHORT BUT TO THE POINT

– Whose land? Mr Bloom said simply.

– Most pertinent question, the professor said between his chews. With an accent on the whose.

– Dan Dawson's land, Mr Dedalus said.

– Is it his speech last night? Mr Bloom asked.

Ned Lambert nodded.

– But listen to this, he said.

The doorknob hit Mr Bloom in the small of the back as the door was pushed in.

– Excuse me, J. J. O'Molloy said, entering.

Mr Bloom moved nimbly aside.

– I beg yours, he said.

– Good day, Jack.

– Come in. Come in.

– Good day.

– How are you, Dedalus?

– Well. And yourself?

J. J. O'Molloy shook his head.

SAD

Cleverest fellow at the junior bar he used to be. Decline poor chap. That hectic flush spells finis for a man. Touch and go with him. What's in the wind, I wonder. Money worry.

– *Or again if we but climb the serried mountain peaks.*

– You're looking extra.

– Is the editor to be seen? J. J. O'Molloy asked, looking towards the inner door.

– Very much so, professor MacHugh said. To be seen and heard. He's in his sanctum with Lenehan.

J. J. O'Molloy strolled to the sloping desk and began to turn back the pink pages of the file.

Practice dwindling. A mighthavebeen. Losing heart. Gambling. Debts of honour. Reaping the whirlwind. Used to get good retainers from D. and T. Fitzgerald. Their wigs to show their grey matter. Brains on their sleeve like the statue in Glasnevin. Believe he does some literary work for the *Express* with Gabriel Conroy. Wellread fellow. Myles Crawford began on the *Independent.* Funny the way those newspaper men veer about when they get wind of a new opening. Weathercocks. Hot and cold in the same breath. Wouldn't know which to believe. One story good till you hear the next. Go for one another baldheaded in the papers and then all blows over. Hailfellow well met the next moment.

– Ah, listen to this for God' sake, Ned Lambert pleaded. *Or again if we but climb the serried mountain peaks . . .*

– Bombast! the professor broke in testily. Enough of the inflated windbag!

– *Peaks,* Ned Lambert went on, *towering high on high, to bathe our souls, as it were . . .*

– Bathe his lips, Mr Dedalus said. Blessed and eternal God! Yes? Is he taking anything for it?

– *As 'twere, in the peerless panorama of Ireland's portfolio, unmatched, despite their wellpraised prototypes in other vaunted prize regions, for very beauty, of bosky grove and undulating plain and luscious pastureland of vernal green, steeped in the transcendent translucent glow of our mild mysterious Irish twilight . . .*

HIS NATIVE DORIC

– The moon, professor MacHugh said. He forgot Hamlet.

– *That mantles the vista far and wide and wait till the glowing orb of the moon shines forth to irradiate her silver effulgence.*

– O! Mr Dedalus cried, giving vent to to a hopeless groan, shite and onions! That'll do, Ned. Life is too short.

He took off his silk hat and, blowing out impatiently his bushy moustache, welshcombed his hair with raking fingers.

Ned Lambert tossed the newspaper aside, chuckling with delight. An instant after a hoarse bark of laughter burst over professor MacHugh's unshaven blackspectacled face.

– Doughy Daw! he cried.

WHAT WETHERUP SAID

All very fine to jeer at it now in cold print but it goes down like hot cake that stuff. He was in the bakery line too wasn't he? Why they call him Doughy Daw. Feathered his nest well anyhow. Daughter engaged to that chap in the inland revenue office with the motor. Hooked that nicely. Entertainments open house. Big blow out. Wetherup always said that. Get a grip of them by the stomach.

The inner door was opened violently and a scarlet beaked face, crested by a comb of feathery hair, thrust itself in. The bold blue eyes stared about them and the harsh voice asked:

– What is it?

– And here comes the sham squire himself, professor MacHugh said grandly.

– Getououthat, you bloody old pedagogue! the editor said in recognition.

– Come, Ned, Mr Dedalus said, putting on his hat. I must get a drink after that.

– Drink! the editor cried. No drinks served before mass.

– Quite right too, Mr Dedalus said, going out. Come on, Ned.

Ned Lambert sidled down from the table. The editor's blue eyes roved towards Mr Bloom's face, shadowed by a smile.

– Will you join us, Myles? Ned Lambert asked.

Memorable battles recalled

– North Cork militia! the editor cried, striding to the mantelpiece. We won every time! North Cork and Spanish officers!

– Where was that, Myles? Ned Lambert asked with a reflective glance at his toecaps.

– In Ohio! the editor shouted.

– So it was, begad, Ned Lambert agreed.

Passing out, he whispered to J. J. O'Molloy:

– Incipient jigs. Sad case.

– Ohio! the editor crowed in high treble from his uplifted scarlet face. My Ohio!

– A perfect cretic! the professor said. Long, short and long.

O, HARP EOLIAN

He took a reel of dental floss from his waistcoat pocket and, breaking off a piece, twanged it smartly between two and two of his resonant unwashed teeth.

– Bingbang, bangbang.

Mr Bloom, seeing the coast clear, made for the inner door.

– Just a moment, Mr Crawford, he said. I just want to phone about an ad. He went in.

– What about that leader this evening? professor MacHugh asked, coming to the editor and laying a firm hand on his shoulder.

– That'll be all right, Myles Crawford said more calmly. Never you fret. Hello, Jack. That's all right.

– Good day, Myles, J. J. O'Molloy said, letting the pages he held slip limply back on the file. Is that Canada swindle case on today?

The telephone whirred inside.

– Twenty eight . . . No, twenty . . . Double four . . . Yes.

SPOT THE WINNER

Lenehan came out of the inner office with *Sports* tissues.

– Who wants a dead cert for the Gold cup? he asked. Sceptre with O. Madden up.

He tossed the tissues on to the table.

Screams of newsboys barefoot in the hall rushed near and the door was flung open.

– Hush, Lenehan said. I hear feetstoops.

Professor MacHugh strode across the room and seized the cringing urchin by the collar as the others scampered out of the hall and down the steps. The tissues rustled up in the draught, floated softly in the air blue scrawls and under the table came to earth.

– It wasn't me, sir. It was the big fellow shoved me, sir.

– Throw him out and shut the door, the editor said. There's a hurricane blowing.

Lenehan began to paw the tissues up from the floor, grunting as he stooped twice.

– Waiting for the racing special, sir, the newsboy said. It was Pat Farrell shoved me, sir.

He pointed to two faces peering in round the doorframe.

– Him, sir.

– Out of this with you, professor MacHugh said gruffly.

He hustled the boy out and banged the door to.

J. J. O'Molloy turned the files crackingly over, murmuring, seeking:

– Continued on page six, column four.

– Yes . . . *Evening Telegraph* here, Mr Bloom phoned from the inner office. Is the boss . . .? Yes, *Telegraph* . . . To where? . . . Aha! Which auction rooms? . . . Aha! I see . . . Right. I'll catch him.

A COLLISION ENSUES

The bell whirred again as he rang off. He came in quickly and bumped against Lenehan who was struggling up with the second tissue.

– *Pardon, monsieur*, Lenehan said, clutching him for an instant and making a grimace.

– My fault, Mr Bloom said, suffering his grip. Are you hurt? I'm in a hurry.

– Knee, Lenehan said.

He made a comic face and whined, rubbing his knee.

– The accumulation of the *anno Domini*.

– Sorry, Mr Bloom said.

He went to the door and, holding it ajar, paused. J. J. O'Molloy slapped the heavy pages over. The noise of two shrill voices, a mouthorgan, echoed in the bare hallway from the newsboys squatted on the doorsteps:

> We are the boys of Wexford
> Who fought with heart and hand.

EXIT BLOOM

– I'm just running round to Bachelor's walk, Mr Bloom said, about this ad of Keyes's. Want to fix it up. They tell me he's round there in Dillon's.

He looked indecisively for a moment at their faces. The editor who, leaning against the mantelshelf, had propped his head on his hand suddenly stretched forth an arm amply.

– Begone! he said. The world is before you.

– Back in no time, Mr Bloom said, hurrying out.

J. J. O'Molloy took the tissues from Lenehan's hand and read them, blowing them apart gently, without comment.

– He'll get that advertisement, the professor said, staring through his blackrimmed spectacles over the crossblind. Look at the young scamps after him.

– Show! Where? Lenehan cried, running to the window.

A STREET CORTÈGE

Both smiled over the crossblind at the file of capering newsboys in Mr Bloom's wake, the last zigzagging white on the breeze a mocking kite, a tail of white bowknots.

– Look at the young guttersnipe behind him hue and cry, Lenehan said, and you'll kick. O, my rib risible! Taking off his flat spaugs and the walk. Small nines. Steal upon larks.

He began to mazurka in swift caricature cross the floor on sliding feet past the fireplace to J. J. O'Molloy who placed the tissues in his receiving hands.

– What's that? Myles Crawford said with a start. Where are the other two gone?

– Who? the professor said, turning. They're gone round to the Oval for a drink. Paddy Hooper is there with Jack Hall. Came over last night.

– Come on then, Myles Crawford said. Where's my hat?

He walked jerkily into the office behind, parting the vent of his jacket, jingling his keys in his back pocket. They jingled then in the air and against the wood as he locked his desk drawer.

– He's pretty well on, professor MacHugh said in a low voice.

– Seems to be, J. J. O'Molloy said, taking out a cigarette case in murmuring meditation, but it is not always as it seems. Who has the most matches?

The calumet of peace

He offered a cigarette to the professor and took one himself. Lenehan promptly struck a match for them and lit their cigarettes in turn. J. J. O'Molloy opened his case again and offered it.

– *Thanky vous*, Lenehan said, helping himself.

The editor came from the inner office, a straw hat awry on his brow. He declaimed in song, pointing sternly at professor MacHugh:

> 'Twas rank and fame that tempted thee,
> 'Twas empire charmed thy heart.

The professor grinned, locking his long lips.

– Eh? You bloody old Roman empire? Myles Crawford said.

He took a cigarette from the open case. Lenehan, lighting it for him with quick grace, said:

– Silence for my brandnew riddle!

– *Imperium romanum*, J. J. O'Molloy said gently. It sounds nobler than British or Brixton. The word reminds one somehow of fat in the fire.

Myles Crawford blew his first puff violently towards the ceiling.

– That's it, he said. We are the fat. You and I are the fat in the fire. We haven't got the chance of a snowball in hell.

THE GRANDEUR THAT WAS ROME

– Wait a moment, professor MacHugh said, raising two quiet claws. We mustn't be led away by words, by sounds of words. We think of Rome, imperial, imperious, imperative.

He extended elocutionary arms from frayed stained shirt-cuffs, pausing:

– What was their civilization? Vast, I allow: but vile. Cloacæ: sewers. The Jews in the wilderness and on the mountaintop said: *It is meet to be here. Let us build an altar to Jehovah.* The Roman, like the Englishman who follows in his footsteps, brought to every new shore on which he set his foot (on our shore he never set it) only his cloacal obsession. He gazed about him in his toga and he said: *It is meet to be here. Let us construct a watercloset.*

– Which they accordingly did do, Lenehan said. Our old ancient ancestors, as we read in the first chapter of Guinness's, were partial to the running stream.

– They were nature's gentlemen, J. J. O'Molloy murmured. But we have also Roman law.

– And Pontius Pilate is its prophet, professor MacHugh responded.

– Do you know that story about chief Baron Palles? J. J. O'Molloy asked. It was at the royal university dinner. Everything was going swimmingly . . .

– First my riddle, Lenehan said. Are you ready?

Mr O'Madden Burke, tall in copious grey of Donegal tweed, came in from the hallway. Stephen Dedalus, behind him, uncovered as he entered.

– *Entrez, mes enfants!* Lenehan cried.

– I escort a suppliant, Mr O'Madden Burke said melodiously. Youth led by Experience visits Notoriety.

– How do you do? the editor said, holding out a hand. Come in. Your governor is just gone.

?   ?   ?

Lenehan said to all:

– Silence! What opera resembles a railway line? Reflect, ponder, excogitate, reply.

Stephen handed over the typed sheets, pointing to the title and signature.

– Who? the editor asked.

Bit torn off.

– Mr Garrett Deasy, Stephen said.

– That old pelters, the editor said. Who tore it? Was he short taken?

> *On swift sail flaming*
> *From storm and south*
> *He comes, pale vampire,*
> *Mouth to my mouth.*

– Good day, Stephen, the professor said, coming to peer over their shoulders. Foot and mouth? Are you turned . . . ?

Bullockbefriending bard.

SHINDY IN WELLKNOWN RESTAURANT

– Good day, sir, Stephen answered, blushing. The letter is not mine. Mr Garrett Deasy asked me to . . .

– O, I know him, Myles Crawford said, and knew his wife too. The bloodiest old tartar God ever made. By Jesus, she had the foot and mouth disease and no mistake! The night she threw the soup in the waiter's face in the Star and Garter. Oho!

A woman brought sin into the world. For Helen, the runaway wife of Menelaus, ten years the Greeks. O'Rourke, prince of Breffni.

– Is he a widower? Stephen asked.

– Ay, a grass one, Myles Crawford said, his eye running down the type-script. Emperor's horses. Habsburg. An Irishman saved his life on the ramparts of Vienna. Don't you forget! Maximilian Karl O'Donnell, graf von Tirconnel in Ireland. Sent his heir over to make the king an Austrian fieldmarshal now. Going to be trouble there one day. Wild geese. O yes, every time. Don't you forget that!

– The moot point is did he forget it? J. J. O'Molloy said quietly, turning a horseshoe paperweight. Saving princes is a thank you job.

Professor MacHugh turned on him.

– And if not? he said.

– I'll tell you how it was, Myles Crawford began. A Hungarian it was one day . . .

LOST CAUSES NOBLE MARQUESS MENTIONED

– We were always loyal to lost causes, the professor said. Success for us is the death of the intellect and of the imagination. We were never loyal to the successful. We serve them. I teach the blatant Latin language. I speak the tongue of a race the acme of whose mentality is the maxim: time is money. Material domination. *Dominus!* Lord! Where is the spirituality? Lord Jesus! Lord Salisbury. A sofa in a westend club. But the Greek!

KYRIE ELEISON!

A smile of light brightened his darkrimmed eyes, lengthened his long lips.

– The Greek! he said again. *Kyrios!* Shining word! The vowels the Semite and the Saxon know not. *Kyrie!* The radiance of the intellect. I ought to profess Greek, the language of the mind. *Kyrie eleison!* The closetmaker and the cloacamaker will never be lords of our spirit. We are liege subjects of the catholic chivalry of Europe that foundered at Trafalgar and of the empire of the spirit, not an *imperium*, that went under with the Athenian fleets at Ægospotami. Yes, yes. They went under. Pyrrhus, misled by an oracle, made a last attempt to retrieve the fortunes of Greece. Loyal to a lost cause.

He strode away from them towards the window.

– They went forth to battle, Mr O'Madden Burke said greyly, but they always fell.

– Boohoo! Lenehan wept with a little noise. Owing to a brick received in the latter half of the *matinée*. Poor, poor, poor Pyrrhus!

He whispered then near Stephen's ear:

LENEHAN'S LIMERICK

There's a ponderous pundit MacHugh
Who wears goggles of ebony hue.
As he mostly sees double
To wear them why trouble?
I can't see the Joe Miller. Can you?

In mourning for Sallust, Mulligan says. Whose mother is beastly dead.
Myles Crawford crammed the sheets into a sidepocket.

– That'll be all right, he said. I'll read the rest after. That'll be all right.

Lenehan extended his hands in protest.

– But my riddle! he said. What opera is like a railway line?

– Opera? Mr O'Madden Burke's sphinx face reriddled.

Lenehan announced gladly:

– *The Rose of Castille*. See the wheeze? Rows of cast steel. Gee!

He poked Mr O'Madden Burke mildly in the spleen. Mr O'Madden
Burke fell back with grace on his umbrella, feigning a gasp.

– Help! he sighed. I feel a strong weakness.

Lenehan, rising to tiptoe, fanned his face rapidly with the rustling tissues.

The professor, returning by way of the files, swept his hand across
Stephen's and Mr O'Madden Burke's loose ties.

– Paris, past and present, he said. You look like communards.

– Like fellows who had blown up the bastille, J. J. O'Molloy said in quiet
mockery. Or was it you shot the lord lieutenant of Finland between you?
You look as though you had done the deed. General Bobrikoff.

OMNIUM GATHERUM

– We were only thinking about it, Stephen said.

– All the talents, Myles Crawford said. Law, the classics . . .

– The turf, Lenehan put in.

– Literature, the press.

– If Bloom were here, the professor said. The gentle art of advertisement.

– And Madam Bloom, Mr O'Madden Burke added. The vocal muse.
Dublin's prime favourite.

Lenehan gave a loud cough.

– Ahem! he said very softly. O, for a fresh of breath air! I caught a cold in
the park. The gate was open.

YOU CAN DO IT!

The editor laid a nervous hand on Stephen's shoulder.

– I want you to write something for me, he said. Something with a bite in it. You can do it. I see it in your face. *In the lexicon of youth* . . .

See it in your face. See it in your eye. Lazy idle little schemer.

– Foot and mouth disease! the editor cried in scornful invective. Great nationalist meeting in Borris-in-Ossory. All balls! Bulldosing the public! Give them something with a bite in it. Put us all into it, damn its soul. Father Son and Holy Ghost and Jakes M'Carthy.

– We can all supply mental pabulum, Mr O'Madden Burke said.

Stephen raised his eyes to the bold unheeding stare.

– He wants you for the pressgang, J. J. O'Molloy said.

THE GREAT GALLAHER

– You can do it, Myles Crawford repeated, clenching his hand in emphasis. Wait a minute. We'll paralyse Europe as Ignatius Gallaher used to say when he was on the shaughraun, doing billiardmarking in the Clarence. Gallaher, that was a pressman for you. That was a pen. You know how he made his mark? I'll tell you. That was the smartest piece of journalism ever known. That was in eightyone, sixth of May, time of the invincibles, murder in the Phœnix park, before you were born, I suppose. I'll show you.

He pushed past them to the files.

– Look at here, he said, turning. The *New York World* cabled for a special. Remember that time?

Professor MacHugh nodded.

– *New York World*, the editor said, excitedly pushing back his straw hat. Where it took place. Tim Kelly, or Kavanagh I mean, Joe Brady and the rest of them. Where Skin-the-goat drove the car. Whole route, see?

– Skin-the-goat, Mr O'Madden Burke said. Fitzharris. He has that cabman's shelter, they say, down there at Butt bridge. Holohan told me. You know Holohan?

– Hop and carry one, is it? Myles Crawford said.

– And poor Gumley is down there too, so he told me, minding stones for the corporation. A night watchman.

Stephen turned in surprise.

– Gumley? he said. You don't say so? A friend of my father's, is he?

– Never mind Gumley, Myles Crawford cried angrily. Let Gumley mind the stones, see they don't run away. Look at here. What did Ignatius Gallaher do? I'll tell you. Inspiration of genius. Cabled right away. Have you *Weekly Freeman* of 17 March? Right. Have you got that?

He flung back pages of the files and stuck his finger on a point.

– Take page four, advertisement for Bransome's coffee let us say. Have you got that? Right.

The telephone whirred.

A DISTANT VOICE

– I'll answer it, the professor said going.

– B is parkgate. Good.

His finger leaped and struck point after point, vibrating.

– T is viceregal lodge. C is where murder took place. K is Knockmaroon gate.

The loose flesh of his neck shook like a cock's wattles. An illstarched dicky jutted up and with a rude gesture he thrust it back into his waistcoat.

– Hello? *Evening Telegraph* here ... Hello? ... Who's there? ... Yes ... Yes ... Yes ...

– F to P is the route Skin-the-goat drove the car for an alibi. Inchicore, Roundtown, Windy Arbour, Palmerston Park, Ranelagh. F. A. B. P. Got that? X is Davy's publichouse in upper Leeson street.

The professor came to the inner door.

– Bloom is at the telephone, he said.

– Tell him go to hell, the editor said promptly. X is Burke's publichouse, see?

CLEVER, VERY

– Clever, Lenehan said. Very.

– Gave it to them on a hot plate, Myles Crawford said, the whole bloody history.

Nightmare from which you will never awake.

– I saw it, the editor said proudly. I was present, Dick Adams, the besthearted bloody Corkman the Lord ever put the breath of life in, and myself.

Lenehan bowed to a shape of air, announcing:

– Madam, I'm Adam. And Able was I ere I saw Elba.

– History! Myles Crawford cried. The Old Woman of Prince's street was there first. There was weeping and gnashing of teeth over that. Out of an advertisement. Gregor Grey made the design for it. That gave him the leg up. Then Paddy Hooper worked Tay Pay who took him on to the *Star*. Now he's got in with Blumenfeld. That's press. That's talent. Pyatt! He was all their daddies.

– The father of scare journalism, Lenehan confirmed, and the brother-in-law of Chris Callinan.

– Hello? . . . Are you there? . . . Yes, he's here still. Come across yourself.

– Where do you find a pressman like that now, eh? the editor cried.

He flung the pages down.

– Clamn dever, Lenehan said to Mr O'Madden Burke.

– Very smart, Mr O'Madden Burke said.

Professor MacHugh came from the inner office.

– Talking about the invincibles, he said, did you see that some hawkers were up before the recorder . . .

– O yes, J. J. O'Molloy said eagerly. Lady Dudley was walking home through the park to see all the trees that were blown down by that cyclone last year and thought she'd buy a view of Dublin. And it turned out to be a commemoration postcard of Joe Brady or Number One or Skin-the-goat. Right outside the viceregal lodge, imagine!

– They're only in the hook and eye department, Myles Crawford said. Psha! Press and the bar! Where have you a man now at the bar like those fellows, like Whiteside, like Isaac Butt, like silvertongued O'Hagan? Eh? Ah, bloody nonsense! Only in the halfpenny place!

His mouth continued to twitch unspeaking in nervous curls of disdain.

Would anyone wish that mouth for her kiss? How do you know? Why did you write it then?

RHYMES AND REASONS

Mouth, south. Is the mouth south someway? Or the south a mouth? Must be some. South, pout, out, shout, drouth. Rhymes: two men dressed the same, looking the same, two by two.

> . . . . *la tua pace*
> . . . . *che parlar ti piace*
> . . . . *mentrechè il vento, come fa, si tace.*

He saw them three by three, approaching girls, in green, in rose, in russet, entwining, *per l'aer perso* in mauve, in purple, *quella pacifica oriafiamma*, in gold of oriflamme, *di rimirar fè più ardenti*. But I old men, penitent, leadenfooted, underdarkneath the night: mouth south: tomb womb.

– Speak up for yourself, Mr O'Madden Burke said.

SUFFICIENT FOR THE DAY . . .

J. J. O'Molloy, smiling palely, took up the gage.

– My dear Myles, he said, flinging his cigarette aside, you put a false construction on my words. I hold no brief, as at present advised, for the third profession *qua* profession but your Cork legs are running away with you. Why not bring in Henry Grattan and Flood and Demosthenes and Edmund Burke? Ignatius Gallaher we all know and his Chapelizod boss, Harmsworth of the farthing press, and his American cousin of the Bowery gutter sheet not to mention *Paddy Kelly's Budget, Pue's Occurrences* and our watchful friend *The Skibbereen Eagle*. Why bring in a master of forensic eloquence like Whiteside? Sufficient for the day is the newspaper thereof.

LINKS TH BYGONE DAYS OF YOREWI

– Grattan and Flood wrote for this very paper, the editor cried in his face. Irish volunteers. Where are you now? Established 1763. Dr Lucas. Who have you now like John Philpot Curran? Psha!

– Well, J. J. O'Molloy said, Bushe K. C., for example.

– Bushe? the editor said. Well, yes. Bushe, yes. He has a strain of it in his blood. Kendal Bushe or I mean Seymour Bushe.

– He would have been on the bench long ago, the professor said, only for . . . But no matter.

J. J. O'Molloy turned to Stephen and said quietly and slowly:

– One of the most polished periods I think I ever listened to in my life fell from the lips of Seymour Bushe. It was in that case of fratricide, the Childs murder case. Bushe defended him.

And in the porches of mine ear did pour.

By the way how did he find that out? He died in his sleep. Or the other story, beast with two backs?

– What was that? the professor asked.

ITALIA, MAGISTRA ARTIUM

– He spoke on the law of evidence, J. J. O'Molloy said, of Roman justice as contrasted with the earlier Mosaic code, the *lex talionis*. And he cited the Moses of Michelangelo in the Vatican.

– Ha.

– A few wellchosen words, Lenehan prefaced. Silence!

Pause. J. J. O'Molloy took out his cigarette case.

False lull. Something quite ordinary.

Messenger took out his matchbox thoughtfully and lit his cigar.

I have often thought since on looking back over that strange time that it was that small act, trivial in itself, that striking of that match, that determined the whole after-course of both our lives.

A POLISHED PERIOD

J. J. O'Molloy resumed, moulding his words:

– He said of it: *that stony effigy in frozen music, horned and terrible, of the human form divine, that eternal symbol of wisdom and prophecy which, if aught that the imagination or the hand of sculptor has wrought in marble of soul-transfigured and of soultransfiguring deserves to live, deserves to live.*

His slim hand with a wave graced echo and fall.

– Fine! Myles Crawford said at once.

– The divine afflatus, Mr O'Madden Burke said.

– You like it? J. J. O'Molloy asked Stephen.

Stephen, his blood wooed by grace of language and gesture, blushed. He took a cigarette from the case. J. J. O'Molloy offered his case to Myles Crawford. Lenehan lit their cigarettes as before and took his trophy, saying:

– Muchibus thankibus.

A MAN OF HIGH MORALE

– Professor Magennis was speaking to me about you, J. J. O'Molloy said to Stephen. What do you think really of that hermetic crowd, the opal hush poets: A. E. the master mystic? That Blavatsky woman started it. She was a nice old bag of tricks. A. E. has been telling some yankee interviewer that you came to him in the small hours of the morning to ask him about planes of consciousness. Magennis thinks you must have been pulling A. E.'s leg. He is a man of the very highest morale, Magennis.

Speaking about me. What did he say? What did he say? What did he say about me? Don't ask.

– No, thanks, professor MacHugh said, waving the cigarette case aside. Wait a moment. Let me say one thing. The finest display of oratory I ever heard was a speech made by John F. Taylor at the college historical society. Mr Justice Fitzgibbon, the present lord justice of appeal, had spoken and the paper under debate was an essay (new for those days), advocating the revival of the Irish tongue.

He turned towards Myles Crawford and said:

– You know Gerald Fitzgibbon. Then you can imagine the style of his discourse.

– He is sitting with Tim Healy, J. J. O'Molloy said, rumour has it, on the Trinity college estates commission.

– He is sitting with a sweet thing in a child's frock, Myles Crawford said. Go on. Well?

– It was the speech, mark you, the professor said, of a finished orator, full of courteous haughtiness and pouring in chastened diction, I will not say the vials of his wrath but pouring the proud man's contumely upon the new movement. It was then a new movement. We were weak, therefore worthless.

He closed his long thin lips an instant but, eager to be on, raised an outspanned hand to his spectacles and, with trembling thumb and ringfinger touching lightly the black rims, steadied them to a new focus.

IMPROMPTU

In ferial tone he addressed J. J. O'Molloy:

– Taylor had come there, you must know, from a sick bed. That he had prepared his speech I do not believe for there was not even one short-handwriter in the hall. His dark lean face had a growth of shaggy beard round it. He wore a loose neckcloth and altogether he looked (though he was not) a dying man.

His gaze turned at once but slowly from J. J. O'Molloy's towards Stephen's face and then bent at once to the ground, seeking. His unglazed linen collar appeared behind his bent head, soiled by his withering hair. Still seeking, he said:

– When Fitzgibbon's speech had ended John F. Taylor rose to reply. Briefly, as well as I can bring them to mind, his words were these.

He raised his head firmly. His eyes bethought themselves once more. Witless shellfish swam in the gross lenses to and fro, seeking outlet.

He began:

– *Mr chairman, ladies and gentlemen: Great was my admiration in listening to the remarks addressed to the youth of Ireland a moment since by my learned friend. It seemed to me that I had been transported into a country far away from this country, into an age remote from this age, that I stood in ancient Egypt and that I was listening to the speech of some highpriest of that land addressed to the youthful Moses.*

His listeners held their cigarettes poised to hear, their smokes ascending in frail stalks that flowered with his speech. *And let our crooked smokes.* Noble words coming. Look out. Could you try your hand at it yourself?

– *And it seemed to me that I heard the voice of that Egyptian highpriest raised in a tone of like haughtiness and like pride. I heard his words and their meaning was revealed to me.*

FROM THE FATHERS

It was revealed to me that those things are good which yet are corrupted which neither if they were supremely good nor unless they were good could be corrupted. Ah, curse you! That's saint Augustine.

– Why will you jews not accept our culture, our religion and our language? You are a tribe of nomad herdsmen; we are a mighty people. You have no cities nor no wealth: our cities are hives of humanity and our galleys, trireme and quadrireme, laden with all manner merchandise furrow the waters of the known globe. You have but emerged from primitive conditions: we have a literature, a priesthood, an agelong history and a polity.

Nile.

Child, man, effigy.

By the Nilebank the babemaries kneel, cradle of bulrushes: a man supple in combat: stonehorned, stonebearded, heart of stone.

– You pray to a local and obscure idol: our temples, majestic and mysterious, are the abodes of Isis and Osiris, of Horus and Ammon Ra. Yours serfdom, awe and humbleness: ours thunder and the seas. Israel is weak and few are her children: Egypt is an host and terrible are her arms. Vagrants and daylabourers are you called: the world trembles at our name.

A dumb belch of hunger cleft his speech. He lifted his voice above it boldly:

– But, ladies and gentlemen, had the youthful Moses listened to and accepted that view of life, had he bowed his head and bowed his will and bowed his spirit before that arrogant admonition he would never have brought the chosen people out of their house of bondage nor followed the pillar of the cloud by day. He would never have spoken with the Eternal amid lightnings on Sinai's mountaintop nor ever have come down with the light of inspiration shining in his countenance and bearing in his arms the tables of the law, graven in the language of the outlaw.

He ceased and looked at them, enjoying silence.

OMINOUS – FOR HIM!

J. J. O'Molloy said not without regret:

– And yet he died without having entered the land of promise.

– A sudden - at - the - moment - though - from - lingering - illness - often - previously - expectorated - demise, Lenehan said. And with a great future behind him.

The troop of bare feet was heard rushing along the hallway and pattering up the staircase.

– That is oratory, the professor said, uncontradicted.

Gone with the wind. Hosts at Mullaghmast and Tara of the kings. Miles of ears of porches. The tribune's words howled and scattered to the four winds. A people sheltered within his voice. Dead noise. Akasic records of all that ever anywhere wherever was. Love and laud him: me no more.

I have money.

– Gentlemen, Stephen said. As the next motion on the agenda paper may I suggest that the house do now adjourn?

– You take my breath away. It is not perchance a French compliment? Mr O'Madden Burke asked. 'Tis the hour, methinks, when the winejug, metaphorically speaking, is most grateful in Ye ancient hostelry.

– That it be and hereby is resolutely resolved. All who are in favour say ay, Lenehan announced. The contrary no. I declare it carried. To which particular boosing shed? . . . My casting vote is: Mooney's!

He led the way, admonishing:

– We will sternly refuse to partake of strong waters, will we not? Yes, we will not. By no manner of means.

Mr O'Madden Burke, following close, said with an ally's lunge of his umbrella:

– Lay on, Macduff!

– Chip of the old block! the editor cried, slapping Stephen on the shoulder. Let us go. Where are those blasted keys?

He fumbled in his pocket, pulling out the crushed typesheets.

– Foot and mouth. I know. That'll be all right. That'll go in. Where are they? That's all right.

He thrust the sheets back and went into the inner office.

LET US HOPE

J. J. O'Molloy, about to follow him in, said quietly to Stephen:

– I hope you will live to see it published. Myles, one moment.

He went into the inner office, closing the door behind him.

– Come along, Stephen, the professor said. That is fine, isn't it? It has the prophetic vision. *Fuit Ilium!* The sack of windy Troy. Kingdoms of this world. The masters of the Mediterranean are fellaheen today.

The first newsboy came pattering down the stairs at their heels and rushed out into the street, yelling:

– Racing special!

Dublin. I have much, much to learn.

They turned to the left along Abbey street.

– I have a vision too, Stephen said.

– Yes, the professor said, skipping to get into step. Crawford will follow.

Another newsboy shot past them, yelling as he ran:

– Racing special!

DEAR DIRTY DUBLIN

Dubliners.

– Two Dublin vestals, Stephen said, elderly and pious, have lived fifty and fiftythree years in Fumbally's lane.

– Where is that? the professor asked.

– Off Blackpitts.

Damp night reeking of hungry dough. Against the wall. Face glistening tallow under her fustian shawl. Frantic hearts. Akasic records. Quicker, darlint!

On now. Dare it. Let there be life.

– They want to see the views of Dublin from the top of Nelson's pillar. They save up three and tenpence in a red tin letterbox moneybox. They shake out the threepenny bits and a sixpence and coax out the pennies with the blade of a knife. Two and three in silver and one and seven in coppers. They put on their bonnets and best clothes and take their umbrellas for fear it may come on to rain.

– Wise virgins, professor MacHugh said.

LIFE ON THE RAW

– They buy one and fourpenceworth of brawn and four slices of panloaf at the north city dining rooms in Marlborough street from Miss Kate Collins, proprietress . . . They purchase four and twenty ripe plums from a girl at the foot of Nelson's pillar to take off the thirst of the brawn. They give two threepenny bits to the gentleman at the turnstile and begin to waddle slowly up the winding staircase, grunting, encouraging each other, afraid of the dark, panting, one asking the other have you the brawn, praising God and the Blessed Virgin, threatening to come down, peeping at the airslits. Glory be to God. They had no idea it was that high.

Their names are Anne Kearns and Florence MacCabe. Anne Kearns has the lumbago for which she rubs on Lourdes water given her by a lady who got a bottleful from a passionist father. Florence MacCabe takes a crubeen and a bottle of double X for supper every Saturday.

– Antithesis, the professor said, nodding twice. Vestal virgins. I can see them. What's keeping our friend?

He turned.

A bevy of scampering newsboys rushed down the steps, scampering in all directions, yelling, their white papers fluttering. Hard after them Myles Crawford appeared on the steps, his hat aureoling his scarlet face, talking with J. J. O'Molloy.

– Come along, the professor cried, waving his arm.

He set off again to walk by Stephen's side.

RETURN OF BLOOM

– Yes, he said. I see them.

Mr Bloom, breathless, caught in a whirl of wild newsboys near the offices of the *Irish Catholic* and *Dublin Penny Journal*, called:

– Mr Crawford! A moment!

– *Telegraph!* Racing special!

– What is it? Myles Crawford said, falling back a pace.

A newsboy cried in Mr Bloom's face:

– Terrible tragedy in Rathmines! A child bit by a bellows!

INTERVIEW WITH THE EDITOR

– Just this ad, Mr Bloom said, pushing through towards the steps, puffing, and taking the cutting from his pocket. I spoke with Mr Keyes just now. He'll give a renewal for two months, he says. After he'll see. But he wants a par to call attention in the *Telegraph* too, the Saturday pink. And he wants it if it's not too late I told councillor Nannetti from the *Kilkenny People*. I can have access to it in the national library. House of keys, don't you see? His name is Keyes. It's a play on the name. But he practically promised he'd give the renewal. But he wants just a little puff. What will I tell him, Mr Crawford?

K. M. A.

– Will you tell him he can kiss my arse? Myles Crawford said, throwing out his arm for emphasis. Tell him that straight from the stable.

A bit nervy. Look out for squalls. All off for a drink. Arm in arm. Lenehan's yachting cap on the cadge beyond. Usual blarney. Wonder is that young Dedalus the moving spirit. Has a good pair of boots on him today. Last time I saw him he had his heels on view. Been walking in muck somewhere. Careless chap. What was he doing in Irishtown?

– Well, Mr Bloom said, his eyes returning, if I can get the design I suppose it's worth a short par. He'd give the ad I think. I'll tell him . . .

K. M. R. I. A.

– He can kiss my royal Irish arse, Myles Crawford cried loudly over his shoulder. Any time he likes, tell him.

While Mr Bloom stood weighing the point and about to smile he strode on jerkily.

RAISING THE WIND

– *Nulla bona*, Jack, he said, raising his hand to his chin. I'm up to here. I've been through the hoop myself. I was looking for a fellow to back a bill for me no later than last week. You must take the will for the deed. Sorry, Jack. With a heart and a half if I could raise the wind anyhow.

J. J. O'Molloy pulled a long face and walked on silently. They caught up on the others and walked abreast.

– When they have eaten the brawn and the bread and wiped their twenty fingers in the paper the bread was wrapped in, they go nearer to the railings.

– Something for you, the professor explained to Myles Crawford. Two old Dublin women on the top of Nelson's pillar.

SOME COLUMN!–THAT'S WHAT WADDLER ONE SAID

– That's new, Myles Crawford said. That's copy. Out for the waxies' Dargle. Two old trickies, what?

– But they are afraid the pillar will fall, Stephen went on. They see the roofs and argue about where the different churches are: Rathmines' blue dome, Adam and Eve's, saint Laurence O'Toole's. But it makes them giddy to look so they pull up their skirts . . .

THOSE SLIGHTLY RAMBUNCTIOUS FEMALES

– Easy all, Myles Crawford said, no poetic licence. We're in the arch-diocese here.

– And settle down on their striped petticoats, peering up at the statue of the onehandled adulterer.

– Onehandled adulterer! the professor cried. I like that. I see the idea. I see what you mean.

DAMES DONATE DUBLIN'S CITS SPEEDPILLS
VELOCITOUS AEROLITHS, BELIEF

– It gives them a crick in their necks, Stephen said, and they are too tired to look up or down or to speak. They put the bag of plums between them and eat the plums out of it, one after another, wiping off with their hand-kerchiefs the plumjuice that dribbles out of their mouths and spitting the plumstones slowly out between the railings.

He gave a sudden loud young laugh as a close. Lenehan and Mr O'Madden Burke, hearing, turned, beckoned and led on across towards Mooney's.

– Finished? Myles Crawford said. So long as they do no worse.

SOPHIST WALLOPS HAUGHTY HELEN SQUARE ON PROBOSCIS.
SPARTANS GNASH MOLARS. ITHACANS VOW PEN IS CHAMP.

– You remind me of Antisthenes, the professor said, a disciple of Gorgias, the sophist. It is said of him that none could tell if he were bitterer against others or against himself. He was the son of a noble and a bondwoman.

And he wrote a book in which he took away the palm of beauty from Argive
Helen and handed it to poor Penelope.

Poor Penelope. Penelope Rich.

They made ready to cross O'Connell street.

HELLO THERE, CENTRAL!

At various points along the eight lines tramcars with motionless trolleys
stood in their tracks, bound for or from Rathmines, Rathfarnham, Blackrock, Kingstown and Dalkey, Sandymount Green, Ringsend and Sandymount Tower, Donnybrook, Palmerston Park and Upper Rathmines, all
still, becalmed in short circuit. Hackney cars, cabs, delivery waggons, mail-
vans, private broughams, aerated mineral water floats with rattling crates of
bottles, rattled, rolled, horsedrawn, rapidly.

WHAT? – AND LIKEWISE – WHERE?

– But what do you call it? Myles Crawford asked. Where did they get the
plums?

VIRGILIAN, SAYS PEDAGOGUE. SOPHOMORE PLUMPS
FOR OLD MAN MOSES

– Call it, wait, the professor said, opening his long lips wide to reflect.
Call it, let me see. Call it: *deus nobis hæc otia fecit.*

– No, Stephen said, I call it *A Pisgah Sight of Palestine or the Parable of the
Plums.*

– I see, the professor said.

He laughed richly.

– I see, he said again with new pleasure. Moses and the promised land.
We gave him that idea, he added to J. J. O'Molloy.

HORATIO IS CYNOSURE THIS FAIR JUNE DAY

J. J. O'Molloy sent a weary sidelong glance towards the statue and held
his peace.

– I see, the professor said.

He halted on sir John Gray's pavement island and peered aloft at Nelson
through the meshes of his wry smile.

DIMINISHED DIGITS PROVE TOO TITILLATING FOR FRISKY FRUMPS.
ANNE WIMBLES, FLO WANGLES – YET CAN YOU BLAME THEM?

– Onehandled adulterer, he said grimly. That tickles me I must say.

– Tickled the old ones too, Myles Crawford said, if the God Almighty's
truth was known.

*   *   *   *   *

◀ PINEAPPLE ROCK, LEMON PLATT, BUTTER SCOTCH. A sugarsticky girl shovelling scoopfuls of creams for a christian brother. Some school treat. Bad for their tummies. Lozenge and comfit manufacturer to His Majesty the King. God. Save. Our. Sitting on his throne, sucking red jujubes white.

A sombre Y. M. C. A. young man, watchful among the warm sweet fumes of Graham Lemon's, placed a throwaway in a hand of Mr Bloom.

Heart to heart talks.

Bloo . . . Me? No.

Blood of the Lamb.

His slow feet walked him riverward, reading. Are you saved? All are washed in the blood of the lamb. God wants blood victim. Birth, hymen, martyr, war, foundation of a building, sacrifice, kidney burntoffering, druid's altars. Elijah is coming. Dr John Alexander Dowie, restorer of the church in Zion, is coming.

Is coming! Is coming!! Is coming!!!
All heartily welcome.

Paying game. Torry and Alexander last year. Polygamy. His wife will put the stopper on that. Where was that ad some Birmingham firm the luminous crucifix? Our Saviour. Wake up in the dead of night and see him on the wall, hanging. Pepper's ghost idea. Iron nails ran in.

Phosphorus it must be done with. If you leave a bit of codfish for instance. I could see the bluey silver over it. Night I went down to the pantry in the kitchen. Don't like all the smells in it waiting to rush out. What was it she wanted? The Malaga raisins. Thinking of Spain. Before Rudy was born. The phosphorescence, that bluey greeny. Very good for the brain.

From Butler's monument house corner he glanced along Bachelor's walk. Dedalus' daughter there still outside Dillon's auctionrooms. Must be selling off some old furniture. Knew her eyes at once from the father. Lobbing about waiting for him. Home always breaks up when the mother goes. Fifteen children he had. Birth every year almost. That's in their theology or the priest won't give the poor woman the confession, the absolution. Increase and multiply. Did you ever hear such an idea? Eat you out of house and home. No families themselves to feed. Living on the fat of the land. Their butteries and larders. I'd like to see them do the black fast Yom Kippur. Crossbuns. One meal and a collation for fear he'd collapse on the altar. A housekeeper of one of those fellows if you could pick it out of her. Never pick it out of her. Like getting L. s. d. out of him. Does himself well.

No guests. All for number one. Watching his water. Bring your own bread and butter. His reverence. Mum's the word.

Good Lord, that poor child's dress is in flitters. Underfed she looks too. Potatoes and marge, marge and potatoes. It's after they feel it. Proof of the pudding. Undermines the constitution.

As he set foot on O'Connell bridge a puffball of smoke plumed up from the parapet. Brewery barge with export stout. England. Sea air sours it, I heard. Be interesting some day get a pass through Hancock to see the brewery. Regular world in itself. Vats of porter, wonderful. Rats get in too. Drink themselves bloated as big as a collie floating. Dead drunk on the porter. Drink till they puke again like christians. Imagine drinking that! Rats: vats. Well of course if we knew all the things.

Looking down he saw flapping strongly, wheeling between the gaunt quay walls, gulls. Rough weather outside. If I threw myself down? Reuben J's son must have swallowed a good bellyful of that sewage. One and eightpence too much. Hhhhm. It's the droll way he comes out with the things. Knows how to tell a story too.

They wheeled lower. Looking for grub. Wait.

He threw down among them a crumpled paper ball. Elijah thirtytwo feet per sec is com. Not a bit. The ball bobbed unheeded on the wake of swells, floated under by the bridge piers. Not such damn fools. Also the day I threw that stale cake out of the Erin's King picked it up in the wake fifty yards astern. Live by their wits. They wheeled, flapping.

> *The hungry famished gull*
> *Flaps o'er the waters dull.*

That is how poets write, the similar sounds. But then Shakespeare has no rhymes: blank verse. The flow of the language it is. The thoughts. Solemn.

> *Hamlet, I am thy father's spirit*
> *Doomed for a certain time to walk the earth.*

– Two apples a penny! Two for a penny!

His gaze passed over the glazed apples serried on her stand. Australians they must be this time of year. Shiny peels: polishes them up with a rag or a handkerchief.

Wait. Those poor birds.

He halted again and bought from the old applewoman two Banbury cakes for a penny and broke the brittle paste and threw its fragments down into the Liffey. See that? The gulls swooped silently two, then all, from their heights, pouncing on prey. Gone. Every morsel.

Aware of their greed and cunning he shook the powdery crumb from his hands. They never expected that. Manna. Live on fishy flesh they have to, all sea birds, gulls, seagoose. Swans from Anna Liffey swim down here sometimes to preen themselves. No accounting for tastes. Wonder what kind is swanmeat. Robinson Crusoe had to live on them.

They wheeled, flapping weakly. I'm not going to throw any more. Penny quite enough. Lot of thanks I get. Not even a caw. They spread foot and mouth disease too. If you cram a turkey, say, on chestnut meal it tastes like that. Eat pig like pig. But then why is it that saltwater fish are not salty? How is that?

His eyes sought answer from the river and saw a rowboat rock at anchor on the treacly swells lazily its plastered board.

Kino's

II/-

Trousers.

Good idea that. Wonder if he pays rent to the corporation. How can you own water really? It's always flowing in a stream, never the same, which in the stream of life we trace. Because life is a stream. All kinds of places are good for ads. That quack doctor for the clap used to be stuck up in all the greenhouses. Never see it now. Strictly confidential. Dr Hy Franks. Didn't cost him a red like Maginni the dancing master self advertisement. Got fellows to stick them up or stick them up himself for that matter on the q. t. running in to loosen a button. Fly by night. Just the place too. Post No Bills. Post iio Pills. Some chap with a dose burning him.

If he . . .

O!

Eh?

No . . . No.

No, no. I don't believe it. He wouldn't surely?

No, no.

Mr Bloom moved forward raising his troubled eyes. Think no more about that. After one. Timeball on the ballast office is down. Dunsink time. Fascinating little book that is of Sir Robert Ball's. Parallax. I never exactly understood. There's a priest. Could ask him. Par it's Greek: parallel, parallax. Met him pikehoses she called it till I told her about the transmigration. O rocks!

Mr Bloom smiled O rocks at two windows of the ballast office. She's right after all. Only big words for ordinary things on account of the sound. She's not exactly witty. Can be rude too. Blurt out what I was thinking. Still I don't know. She used to say Ben Dollard had a base barreltone voice. He has legs like barrels and you'd think he was singing into a barrel. Now, isn't that wit? They used to call him big Ben. Not half as witty as calling him base barreltone. Appetite like an albatross. Get outside of a baron of beef. Powerful man he was at storing away number one Bass. Barrel of Bass. See? It all works out.

A procession of whitesmocked men marched slowly towards him along the gutter, scarlet sashes across their boards. Bargains. Like that priest they are this morning: we have sinned: we have suffered. He read the scarlet letters on their five tall white hats: H. E. L. Y. S. Wisdom Hely's. Y lagging behind drew a chunk of bread from under his foreboard, crammed it into his mouth and munched as he walked. Our staple food. Three bob a day, walking along the gutters, street after street. Just keep skin and bone together, bread and skilly. They are not Boyl: no: M'Glade's men. Doesn't bring in any business either. I suggested to him about a transparent show cart with two smart girls sitting inside writing letters, copybooks, envelopes, blotting paper. I bet that would have caught on. Smart girls writing something catch the eye at once. Everyone dying to know what she's writing. Get twenty of them round you if you stare at nothing. Have a finger in the pie. Women too. Curiosity. Pillar of salt. Wouldn't have it of course because he didn't think of it himself first. Or the inkbottle I suggested with a false stain of black celluloid. His ideas for ads like Plumtree's potted under the obituaries, cold meat department. You can't lick 'em. What? Our envelopes. Hello! Jones, where are you going? Can't stop, Robinson, I am hastening to purchase the only reliable inkeraser *Kansell*, sold by Hely's Ltd, 85 Dame Street. Well out of that ruck I am. Devil of a job it was collecting accounts of those convents. Tranquilla convent. That was a nice nun there, really sweet face. Wimple suited her small head. Sister? Sister? I am sure she was crossed in love by her eyes. Very hard to bargain with that sort of woman. I disturbed her at her devotions that morning. But glad to communicate with the outside world. Our great day, she said. Feast of Our Lady of Mount Carmel. Sweet name too: caramel. She knew, I think she knew by the way she. If she had married she would have changed. I suppose they really were short of money. Fried everything in the best butter all the same. No lard for them. My heart's broke eating dripping. They like buttering themselves in and out. Molly tasting it, her veil up. Sister? Pat Claffey, the pawnbroker's daughter. It was a nun they say invented barbed wire.

He crossed Westmoreland street when apostrophe S had plodded by. Rover cycleshop. Those races are on today. How long ago is that? Year Phil Gilligan died. We were in Lombard street west. Wait, was in Thom's. Got the job in Wisdom Hely's year we married. Six years. Ten years ago:

ninetyfour he died, yes that's right, the big fire at Arnott's. Val Dillon was lord mayor. The Glencree dinner. Alderman Robert O'Reilly emptying the port into his soup before the flag fell, Bobbob lapping it for the inner alderman. Couldn't hear what the band played. For what we have already received may the Lord make us. Milly was a kiddy then. Molly had that elephantgrey dress with the braided frogs. Mantailored with selfcovered buttons. She didn't like it because I sprained my ankle first day she wore choir picnic at the Sugarloaf. As if that. Old Goodwin's tall hat done up with some sticky stuff. Flies' picnic too. Never put a dress on her back like it. Fitted her like a glove, shoulder and hips. Just beginning to plump it out well. Rabbit pie we had that day. People looking after her.

Happy. Happier then. Snug little room that was with the red wallpaper, Dockrell's, one and ninepence a dozen. Milly's tubbing night. American soap I bought: elderflower. Cosy smell of her bathwater. Funny she looked soaped all over. Shapely too. Now photography. Poor papa's daguerreotype atelier he told me of. Hereditary taste.

He walked along the curbstone.

Stream of life. What was the name of that priestylooking chap was always squinting in when he passed? Weak eyes, woman. Stopped in Citron's saint Kevin's parade. Pen something. Pendennis? My memory is getting. Pen . . .? of course it's years ago. Noise of the trams probably. Well, if he couldn't remember the dayfather's name that he sees every day.

Bartell d'Arcy was the tenor, just coming out then. Seeing her home after practice. Conceited fellow with his waxedup moustache. Gave her that song *Winds that blow from the south*.

Windy night that was I went to fetch her there was that lodge meeting on about those lottery tickets after Goodwin's concert in the supper room or oakroom of the mansion house. He and I behind. Sheet of her music blew out of my hand against the high school railings. Lucky it didn't. Thing like that spoils the effect of a night for her. Professor Goodwin linking her in front. Shaky on his pins, poor old sot. His farewell concerts. Positively last appearance on any stage. May be for months and may be for never. Remember her laughing at the wind, her blizzard collar up. Corner of Harcourt road remember that gust? Brrfoo! Blew up all her skirts and her boa nearly smothered old Goodwin. She did get flushed in the wind. Remember when we got home raking up the fire and frying up those pieces of lap of mutton for her supper with the Chutney sauce she liked. And the mulled rum. Could see her in the bedroom from the hearth unclamping the busk of her stays. White.

Swish and soft flop her stays made on the bed. Always warm from her.

Always liked to let herself out. Sitting there after till near two, taking out her hairpins. Milly tucked up in beddyhouse. Happy. Happy. That was the night . . .

– O, Mr Bloom, how do you do?

– O, how do you do, Mrs Breen?

– No use complaining. How is Molly those times? Haven't seen her for ages.

– In the pink, Mr Bloom said gaily, Milly has a position down in Mullingar, you know.

– Go away! Isn't that grand for her?

– Yes, in a photographer's there. Getting on like a house on fire. How are all your charges?

– All on the baker's list, Mrs Breen said.

How many has she? No other in sight.

– You're in black I see. You have no . . .

– No, Mr Bloom said. I have just come from a funeral.

Going to crop up all day, I foresee. Who's dead, when and what did he die of? Turn up like a bad penny.

– O dear me, Mrs Breen said, I hope it wasn't any near relation.

May as well get her sympathy.

– Dignam, Mr Bloom said. An old friend of mine. He died quite suddenly, poor fellow. Heart trouble, I believe. Funeral was this morning.

> *Your funeral's tomorrow*
> *While you're coming through the rye.*
> *Diddlediddle dumdum*
> *Diddlediddle . . .*

– Sad to lose the old friends, Mrs Breen's womaneyes said melancholily.

Now that's quite enough about that. Just quietly: husband.

– And your lord and master?

Mrs Breen turned up her two large eyes. Hasn't lost them anyhow.

– O, don't be talking, she said. He's a caution to rattlesnakes. He's in there now with his lawbooks finding out the law of libel. He has me heart-scalded. Wait till I show you.

Hot mockturtle vapour and steam of newbaked jampuffs rolypoly poured out from Harrison's. The heavy noonreek tickled the top of Mr Bloom's gullet. Want to make good pastry, butter, best flour, Demerara sugar, or they'd taste it with the hot tea. Or is it from her? A barefoot arab stood over the grating, breathing in the fumes. Deaden the gnaw of hunger that way. Pleasure or pain is it? Penny dinner. Knife and fork chained to the table.

Opening her handbag, chipped leather, hatpin: ought to have a guard on those things. Stick it in a chap's eye in the tram. Rummaging. Open. Money. Please take one. Devils if they lose sixpence. Raise Cain. Husband barging. Where's the ten shillings I gave you on Monday? Are you feeding your little brother's family? Soiled handkerchief: medicine-bottle. Pastille that was fell. What is she? . . .

– There must be a new moon out, she said. He's always bad then. Do you know what he did last night?

Her hand ceased to rummage. Her eyes fixed themselves on him, wide in alarm, yet smiling.

– What? Mr Bloom asked.

Let her speak. Look straight in her eyes. I believe you. Trust me.

– Woke me up in the night, she said. Dream he had, a nightmare.

Indiges.

– Said the ace of spades was walking up the stairs.

– The ace of spades! Mr Bloom said.

She took a folded postcard from her handbag.

– Read that, she said. He got it this morning.

– What is it? Mr Bloom asked, taking the card. U. P.?

– U. P.: up, she said. Someone taking a rise out of him. It's a great shame for them whoever he is.

– Indeed it is, Mr Bloom said.

She took back the card, sighing.

– And now he's going round to Mr Menton's office. He's going to take an action for ten thousand pounds, he says.

She folded the card into her untidy bag and snapped the catch.

Same blue serge dress she had two years ago, the nap bleaching. Seen its best days. Wispish hair over her ears. And that dowdy toque, three old grapes to take the harm out of it. Shabby genteel. She used to be a tasty dresser. Lines round her mouth. Only a year or so older than Molly.

See the eye that woman gave her, passing. Cruel. The unfair sex.

He looked still at her, holding back behind his look his discontent. Pungent mockturtle oxtail mulligatawny. I'm hungry too. Flakes of pastry on the gusset of her dress: daub of sugary flour stuck to her cheek. Rhubarb tart with liberal fillings, rich fruit interior. Josie Powell that was. In Luke Doyle's long ago, Dolphin's Barn, the charades. U. P.: up.

Change the subject.

– Do you ever see anything of Mrs Beaufoy, Mr Bloom asked.

– Mina Purefoy? she said.

Philip Beaufoy I was thinking. Playgoers' club. Matcham often thinks of the masterstroke. Did I pull the chain? Yes. The last act.

– Yes.

– I just called to ask on the way in is she over it. She's in the lying-in hospital in Holles street. Dr Horne got her in. She's three days bad now.

– O, Mr Bloom said. I'm sorry to hear that.

– Yes, Mrs Breen said. And a houseful of kids at home. It's a very stiff birth, the nurse told me.

– O, Mr Bloom said.

His heavy pitying gaze absorbed her news. His tongue clacked in compassion. Dth! Dth!

– I'm sorry to hear that, he said. Poor thing! Three days! That's terrible for her.

Mrs Breen nodded.

– She was taken bad on the Tuesday . . .

Mr Bloom touched her funnybone gently, warning her.

– Mind! Let this man pass.

A bony form strode along the curbstone from the river, staring with a rapt gaze into the sunlight through a heavy stringed glass. Tight as a skullpiece a tiny hat gripped his head. From his arm a folded dustcoat, a stick and an umbrella dangled to his stride.

– Watch him, Mr Bloom said. He always walks outside the lampposts. Watch!

– Who is he if it's a fair question, Mrs Breen asked. Is he dotty?

– His name is Cashel Boyle O'Connor Fitzmaurice Tisdall Farrell, Mr Bloom said, smiling. Watch!

– He has enough of them, she said. Denis will be like that one of these days.

She broke off suddenly.

– There he is, she said. I must go after him. Goodbye. Remember me to Molly, won't you?

– I will, Mr Bloom said.

He watched her dodge through passers towards the shopfronts. Denis Breen in skimpy frockcoat and blue canvas shoes shuffled out of Harrison's hugging two heavy tomes to his ribs. Blown in from the bay. Like old times. He suffered her to overtake him without surprise and thrust his dull grey beard towards her, his loose jaw wagging as he spoke earnestly.

Meshuggah. Off his chump.

Mr Bloom walked on again easily, seeing ahead of him in sunlight the tight skullpiece, the dangling stick, umbrella, dustcoat. Going the two days. Watch him! Out he goes again. One way of getting on in the world.

And that other old mosey lunatic in those duds. Hard time she must have with him.

U. P.: up. I'll take my oath that's Alf Bergan or Richie Goulding. Wrote it for a lark in the Scotch house, I bet anything. Round to Menton's office. His oyster eyes staring at the postcard. Be a feast for the gods.

He passed the *Irish Times*. There might be other answers lying there. Like to answer them all. Good system for criminals. Code. At their lunch now. Clerk with the glasses there doesn't know me. O, leave them there to simmer. Enough bother wading through fortyfour of them. Wanted smart lady typist to aid gentleman in literary work. I called you naughty darling because I do not like that other world. Please tell me what is the meaning. Please tell me what perfume does your wife. Tell me who made the world. The way they spring those questions on you. And the other one Lizzie Twigg. My literary efforts have had the good fortune to meet with the approval of the eminent poet A. E. (Mr Geo Russell). No time to do her hair drinking sloppy tea with a book of poetry.

Best paper by long chalks for a small ad. Got the provinces now. Cook and general, exc cuisine, housemaid kept. Wanted live man for spirit counter. Resp girl (R. C.) wishes to hear of post in fruit or pork shop. James Carlisle made that. Six and a half percent dividend. Made a big deal on Coates's shares. Ca'canny. Cunning old Scotch hunks. All the toady news. Our gracious and popular vicereine. Bought the *Irish Field* now. Lady Mountcashel has quite recovered after her confinement and rode out with the Ward Union stag-hounds at the enlargement yesterday at Rathoath. Uneatable fox. Pothunters too. Fear injects juices make it tender enough for them. Riding astride. Sit her horse like a man. Weightcarrying huntress. No sidesaddle or pillion for her, not for Joe. First to the meet and in at the death. Strong as a brood mare some of those horsey women. Swagger around livery stables. Toss off a glass of brandy neat while you'd say knife. That one at the Grosvenor this morning. Up with her on the car: wishwish. Stonewall or fivebarred gate put her mount to it. Think that pugnosed driver did it out of spite. Who is this she was like? O yes! Mrs Miriam Dandrade that sold me her old wraps and black underclothes in the Shelbourne hotel. Divorced Spanish American. Didn't take a feather out of her my handling them. As if I was her clotheshorse. Saw her in the viceregal party when Stubbs the park ranger got me in with Whelan of the *Express*. Scavenging what the quality left. High tea. Mayonnaise I poured on the plums thinking it was custard. Her ears ought to have tingled for a few weeks after. Want to be a bull for her. Born courtesan. No nursery work for her, thanks.

Poor Mrs Purefoy! Methodist husband. Method in his madness. Saffron bun and milk and soda lunch in the educational dairy. Eating with a stopwatch, thirtytwo chews to the minute. Still his muttonchop whiskers grew. Supposed to be well connected. Theodore's cousin in Dublin Castle. One tony relative in every family. Hardy annuals he presents her with. Saw him out at the Three Jolly Topers marching along bareheaded and his eldest boy carrying one in a marketnet. The squallers. Poor thing! Then having to give the breast year after year all hours of the night. Selfish those t.t's are. Dog in the manger. Only one lump of sugar in my tea, if you please.

He stood at Fleet street crossing. Luncheon interval a sixpenny at Rowe's? Must look up that ad in the national library. An eightpenny in the Burton. Better. On my way.

He walked on past Bolton's Westmoreland house. Tea. Tea. Tea. I forgot to tap Tom Kernan.

Sss. Dth, dth, dth! Three days imagine groaning on a bed with a vinegared handkerchief round her forehead, her belly swollen out! Phew! Dreadful simply! Child's head too big: forceps. Doubled up inside her trying to butt its way out blindly, groping for the way out. Kill me that would. Lucky Molly got over hers lightly. They ought to invent something to stop that. Life with hard labour. Twilightsleep idea: queen Victoria was given that. Nine she had. A good layer. Old woman that lived in a shoe she had so many children. Suppose he was consumptive. Time someone thought about it instead of gassing about the what was it the pensive bosom of the silver effulgence. Flapdoodle to feed fools on. They could easily have big establishments. Whole thing quite painless out of all the taxes give every child born five quid at compound interest up to twentyone, five per cent is a hundred shillings and five tiresome pounds, multiply by twenty decimal system, encourage people to put by money save hundred and ten and a bit twentyone years want to work it out on paper come to a tidy sum, more than you think.

Not stillborn of course. They are not even registered. Trouble for nothing.

Funny sight two of them together, their bellies out. Molly and Mrs Moisel. Mothers' meeting. Phthisis retires for the time being, then returns. How flat they look after all of a sudden! Peaceful eyes. Weight off their minds. Old Mrs Thornton was a jolly old soul. All my babies, she said. The spoon of pap in her mouth before she fed them. O, that's nyumyum. Got her hand crushed by old Tom Wall's son. His first bow to the public. Head like a prize pumpkin. Snuffy Dr Murren. People knocking them up at all hours. For God'sake doctor. Wife in her throes. Then keep them waiting months for their fee. To attendance on your wife. No gratitude in people. Humane doctors, most of them.

Before the huge high door of the Irish house of parliament a flock of pigeons flew. Their little frolic after meals. Who will we do it on? I pick the fellow in black. Here goes. Here's good luck. Must be thrilling from the air. Apjohn, myself and Owen Goldberg up in the trees near Goose green playing the monkeys. Mackerel they called me.

A squad of constables debouched from College street, marching in Indian file. Goose step. Foodheated faces, sweating helmets, patting their truncheons. After their feed with a good load of fat soup under their belts. Policeman's lot is oft a happy one. They split up into groups and scattered, saluting towards their beats. Let out to graze. Best moment to attack one in pudding time. A punch in his dinner. A squad of others, marching irregularly, rounded Trinity railings, making for the station. Bound for their troughs. Prepare to receive cavalry. Prepare to receive soup.

He crossed under Tommy Moore's roguish finger. They did right to put him up over a urinal: meeting of the waters. Ought to be places for women. Running into cakeshops. Settle my hat straight. *There is not in this wide world a vallee.* Great song of Julia Morkan's. Kept her voice up to the very last. Pupil of Michael Balfe's wasn't she?

He gazed after the last broad tunic. Nasty customers to tackle. Jack Power could a tale unfold: father a G man. If a fellow gave them trouble being lagged they let him have it hot and heavy in the bridewell. Can't blame them after all with the job they have especially the young hornies. That horse policeman the day Joe Chamberlain was given his degree in Trinity he got a run for his money. My word he did! His horse's hoofs clattering after us down Abbey street. Luck I had the presence of mind to dive into Manning's or I was souped. He did come a wallop, by George. Must have cracked his skull on the cobblestones. I oughtn't to have got myself swept along with those medicals. And the Trinity jibs in their mortarboards. Looking for trouble. Still I got to know that young Dixon who dressed that sting for me in the Mater and now he's in Holles street where Mrs Purefoy. Wheels within wheels. Police whistle in my ears still. All skedaddled. Why he fixed on me. Give me in charge. Right here it began.

– Up the Boers!

– Three cheers for De Wet!

– We'll hang Joe Chamberlain on a sourapple tree.

Silly billies: mob of young cubs yelling their guts out. Vinegar hill. The Butter exchange band. Few years time half of them magistrates and civil servants. War comes on: into the army helterskelter: same fellows used to whether on the scaffold high.

Never know who you're talking to. Corny Kelleher he has Harvey Duff in his eye. Like that Peter or Denis or James Carey that blew the gaff on the invincibles. Member of the corporation too. Egging raw youths on to get in the know. All the time drawing secret service pay from the castle. Drop him like a hot potato. Why those plain clothes men are always courting slaveys. Easily twig a man used to uniform. Square-pushing up against a backdoor. Maul her a bit. Then the next thing on the menu. And who is the gentleman does be visiting there? Was the young master saying anything? Peeping Tom through the keyhole. Decoy duck. Hotblooded young student fooling round her fat arms ironing.

– Are those yours, Mary?

– I don't wear such things . . . Stop or I'll tell the missus on you. Out half the night.

– There are great times coming, Mary. Wait till you see.

– Ah, get along with your great times coming.

Barmaids too. Tobacco shopgirls.

James Stephens' idea was the best. He knew them. Circles of ten so that a fellow couldn't round on more than his own ring. Sinn Fein. Back out you get the knife. Hidden hand. Stay in. The firing squad. Turnkey's daughter got him out of Richmond, off from Lusk. Putting up in the Buckingham Palace hotel under their very noses. Garibaldi.

You must have a certain fascination: Parnell. Arthur Griffith is a square-headed fellow but he has no go in him for the mob. Want to gas about our lovely land. Gammon and spinach. Dublin Bakery Company's tearoom. Debating societies. That republicanism is the best form of government. That the language question should take precedence of the economic question. Have your daughters inveigling them to your house. Stuff them up with meat and drink. Michaelmas goose. Here's a good lump of thyme seasoning under the apron for you. Have another quart of goosegrease before it gets too cold. Halffed enthusiasts. Penny roll and a walk with the band. No grace for the carver. The thought that the other chap pays best sauce in the world. Make themselves thoroughly at home. Shove us over those apricots, meaning peaches. The not far distant day. Home Rule sun rising up in the northwest.

His smile faded as he walked, a heavy cloud hiding the sun slowly, shadowing Trinity's surly front. Trams passed one another, ingoing, outgoing, clanging. Useless words. Things go on same; day after day: squads of police marching out, back: trams in, out. Those two loonies mooching about. Dignam carted off. Mina Purefoy swollen belly on a bed groaning to have a child tugged out of her. One born every second somewhere. Other dying every second. Since I fed the birds five minutes. Three hundred kicked the bucket. Other three hundred born, washing the blood off, all are washed in the blood of the lamb, bawling maaaaaa.

Cityful passing away, other cityful coming, passing away too: other coming on, passing on. Houses, lines of houses, streets, miles of pavements, piledup bricks, stones. Changing hands. This owner, that. Landlord never dies they say. Other steps into his shoes when he gets his notice to quit. They buy the place up with gold and still they have all the gold. Swindle in it somewhere. Piled up in cities, worn away age after age. Pyramids in sand. Built on bread and onions. Slaves Chinese wall. Babylon. Big stones left. Round towers. Rest rubble, sprawling suburbs, jerrybuilt, Kerwan's mushroom houses, built of breeze. Shelter for the night.

No one is anything.

This is the very worst hour of the day. Vitality. Dull, gloomy: hate this hour. Feel as if I had been eaten and spewed.

Provost's house. The reverend Dr Salmon: tinned salmon. Well tinned in there. Wouldn't live in it if they paid me. Hope they have liver and bacon today. Nature abhors a vacuum.

The sun freed itself slowly and lit glints of light among the silver ware in Walter Sexton's window opposite by which John Howard Parnell passed, unseeing.

There he is: the brother. Image of him. Haunting face. Now that's a coincidence. Course hundreds of times you think of a person and don't meet him. Like a man walking in his sleep. No-one knows him. Must be a corporation meeting today. They say he never put on the city marshal's uniform since he got the job. Charley Boulger used to come out on his high horse, cocked hat, puffed, powdered and shaved. Look at the woebegone walk of him. Eaten a bad egg. Poached eyes on ghost. I have a pain. Great man's brother: his brother's brother. He'd look nice on the city charger. Drop into the D. B. C. probably for his coffee, play chess there. His brother used men as pawns. Let them all go to pot. Afraid to pass a remark on him. Freeze them up with that eye of his. That's the fascination: the name. All a bit touched. Mad Fanny and his other sister Mrs Dickinson driving about with scarlet harness. Bolt upright like surgeon M'Ardle. Still David Sheehy beat him for south Meath. Apply for the Chiltern Hundreds and retire into public life. The patriot's banquet. Eating orangepeels in the park. Simon Dedalus said when they put him in parliament that Parnell would come back from the grave and lead him out of the House of Commons by the arm.

– Of the twoheaded octopus, one of whose heads is the head upon which
the ends of the world have forgotten to come while the other speaks with a
Scotch accent. The tentacles . . .

They passed from behind Mr Bloom along the curbstone. Beard and
bicycle. Young woman.

And there he is too. Now that's really a coincidence: secondtime. Coming
events cast their shadows before. With the approval of the eminent poet Mr
Geo Russell. That might be Lizzie Twigg with him. A. E.: what does that
mean? Initials perhaps. Albert Edward, Arthur Edmund, Alphonsus Eb Ed
El Esquire. What was he saying? The ends of the world with a Scotch
accent. Tentacles: octopus. Something occult: symbolism. Holding forth.
She's taking it all in. Not saying a word. To aid gentleman in literary work.

His eyes followed the high figure in homespun, beard and bicycle, a
listening woman at his side. Coming from the vegetarian. Only wegge-
bobbles and fruit. Don't eat a beefsteak. If you do the eyes of that cow will
pursue you through all eternity. They say it's healthier. Wind and watery
though. Tried it. Keep you on the run all day. Bad as a bloater. Dreams all
night. Why do they call that thing they gave me nutsteak? Nutarians.
Fruitarians. To give you the idea you are eating rumpsteak. Absurd. Salty
too. They cook in soda. Keep you sitting by the tap all night.

Her stockings are loose over her ankles. I detest that: so tasteless. Those
literary etherial people they are all. Dreamy, cloudy, symbolistic. Esthetes
they are. I wouldn't be surprised if it was that kind of food you see produces
the like waves of the brain the poetical. For example one of those policemen
sweating Irish stew into their shirts; you couldn't squeeze a line of poetry
out of him. Don't know what poetry is even. Must be in a certain mood.

> *The dreamy cloudy gull*
> *Waves o'er the waters dull.*

He crossed at Nassau street corner and stood before the window of
Yeates and Son, pricing the field glasses. Or will I drop into old Harris's
and have a chat with young Sinclair? Wellmannered fellow. Probably at his
lunch. Must get those old glasses of mine set right. Gœrz lenses, six guineas.
Germans making their way everywhere. Sell on easy terms to capture trade.
Undercutting. Might chance on a pair in the railway lost property office.
Astonishing the things people leave behind them in trains and cloak rooms.
What do they be thinking about? Women too. Incredible. Last year travelling
to Ennis had to pick up that farmer's daughter's bag and hand it to her at
Limerick junction. Unclaimed money too. There's a little watch up there
on the roof of the bank to test those glasses by.

His lids came down on the lower rims of his irides. Can't see it. If you imagine it's there you can almost see it. Can't see it.

He faced about and, standing between the awnings, held out his right hand at arm's length towards the sun. Wanted to try that often. Yes: completely. The tip of his little finger blotted out the sun's disk. Must be the focus where the rays cross. If I had black glasses. Interesting. There was a lot of talk about those sunspots when we were in Lombard street west. Terrific explosions they are. There will be a total eclipse this year: autumn some time.

Now that I come to think of it, that ball falls at Greenwich time. It's the clock is worked by an electric wire from Dunsink. Must go out there some first Saturday of the month. If I could get an introduction to professor Joly or learn up something about his family. That would do to: man always feels complimented. Flattery where least expected. Nobleman proud to be descended from some king's mistress. His foremother. Lay it on with a trowel. Cap in hand goes through the land. Not go in and blurt out what you know you're not to: what's parallax? Show this gentleman the door.

Ah.

His hand fell again to his side.

Never know anything about it. Waste of time. Gasballs spinning about, crossing each other, passing. Same old dingdong always. Gas, then solid, then world, then cold, then dead shell drifting around, frozen rock like that pineapple rock. The moon. Must be a new moon, she said. I believe there is.

He went on by la Maison Claire.

Wait. The full moon was the night we were Sunday fortnight exactly there is a new moon. Walking down by the Tolka. Not bad for a Fairview moon. She was humming: The young May moon she's beaming, love. He other side of her. Elbow, arm. He. Glowworm's la-amp is gleaming, love. Touch. Fingers. Asking. Answer. Yes.

Stop. Stop. If it was it was. Must.

Mr Bloom, quick breathing, slowlier walking, passed Adam court.

With a keep quiet relief, his eyes took note: this is street here middle of the day Bob Doran's bottle shoulders. On his annual bend, M'Coy said. They drink in order to say or do something or *cherchez la femme*. Up in the Coombe with chummies and streetwalkers and then the rest of the year as sober as a judge.

Yes. Thought so. Sloping into the Empire. Gone. Plain soda would do him good. Where Pat Kinsella had his Harp theatre before Whitbred ran the Queen's. Broth of a boy. Dion Boucicault business with his harvestmoon

face in a poky bonnet. Three Purty Maids from School. How time flies eh?
Showing long red pantaloons under his skirts. Drinkers, drinking, laughed
spluttering, their drink against their breath. More power, Pat. Coarse red:
fun for drunkards: guffaw and smoke. Take off that white hat. His parboiled
eyes. Where is he now? Beggar somewhere. The harp that once did starve
us all.

I was happier then. Or was that I? Or am I now I? Twentyeight I was.
She twentythree when we left Lombard street west something changed.
Could never like it again after Rudy. Can't bring back time. Like holding
water in your hand. Would you go back to then? Just beginning then.
Would you? Are you not happy in your home, you poor little naughty boy?
Wants to sew on buttons for me. I must answer. Write it in the library.

Grafton street gay with housed awnings lured his senses. Muslin prints,
silk, dames and dowagers, jingle of harnesses, hoofthuds lowringing in the
baking causeway. Thick feet that woman has in the white stockings. Hope
the rain mucks them up on her. Country bred chawbacon. All the beef to
the heels were in. Always gives a woman clumsy feet. Molly looks out of
plumb.

He passed, dallying, the windows of Brown Thomas, silk mercers.
Cascades of ribbons. Flimsy China silks. A tilted urn poured from its
mouth a flood of bloodhued poplin: lustrous blood. The huguenots brought
that here. *La causa è santa!* Tara tara. Great chorus that. Tara. Must be
washed in rainwater. Meyerbeer. Tara: bom bom bom.

Pincushions. I'm a long time threatening to buy one. Stick them all over
the place. Needles in window curtains.

He bared slightly his left forearm. Scrape: nearly gone. Not today anyhow. Must go back for that lotion. For her birthday perhaps. Junejuly
augseptember eighth. Nearly three months off. Then she mightn't like it.
Women won't pick up pins. Say it cuts lo.

Gleaming silks, petticoats on slim brass rails, rays of flat silk stockings.

Useless to go back. Had to be. Tell me all.

High voices. Sunwarm silk. Jingling harnesses. All for a woman, home
and houses, silk webs, silver, rich fruits, spicy from Jaffa. Agendath Netaim.
Wealth of the world.

A warm human plumpness settled down on his brain. His brain yielded.
Perfume of embraces all him assailed. With hungered flesh obscurely, he
mutely craved to adore.

Duke street. Here we are. Must eat. The Burton. Feel better then.

He turned Combridge's corner, still pursued. Jingling hoofthuds.
Perfumed bodies, warm, full. All kissed, yielded: in deep summer fields,

tangled pressed grass, in trickling hallways of tenements, along sofas, creaking beds.

– Jack, love!

– Darling!

– Kiss me, Reggy!

– My boy!

– Love!

His heart astir he pushed in the door of the Burton restaurant. Stink gripped his trembling breath: pungent meatjuice, slop of greens. See the animals feed.

Men, men, men.

Perched on high stools by the bar, hats shoved back, at the tables calling for more bread no charge, swilling, wolfing gobfuls of sloppy food, their eyes bulging, wiping wetted moustaches. A pallid suetfaced young man polished his tumbler knife fork and spoon with his napkin. New set of microbes. A man with an infant's saucestained napkin tucked round him shovelled gurgling soup down his gullet. A man spitting back on his plate: halfmasticated gristle: no teeth to chewchewchew it. Chump chop from the grill. Bolting to get it over. Sad booser's eyes. Bitten off more than he can chew. Am I like that? See ourselves as others see us. Hungry man is an angry man. Working tooth and jaw. Don't! O! A bone! That last pagan king of Ireland Cormac in the schoolpoem choked himself at Sletty southward of the Boyne. Wonder what he was eating. Something galoptious. Saint Patrick converted him to Christianity. Couldn't swallow it all however.

– Roast beef and cabbage.

– One stew.

Smells of men. His gorge rose. Spaton sawdust, sweetish warmish cigarette smoke, reek of plug, spilt beer, men's beery piss, the stale of ferment.

Couldn't eat a morsel here. Fellow sharpening knife and fork, to eat all before him, old chap picking his tootles. Slight spasm, full, chewing the cud. Before and after. Grace after meals. Look on this picture then on that. Scoffing up stew-gravy with sopping sippets of bread. Lick it off the plate, man! Get out of this.

He gazed round the stooled and tabled eaters, tightening the wings of his nose.

– Two stouts here.

– One corned and cabbage.

That fellow ramming a knifeful of cabbage down as if his life depended on it. Good stroke. Give me the fidgets to look. Safer to eat from his three hands. Tear it limb from limb. Second nature to him. Born with a silver knife in his mouth. That's witty, I think. Or no. Silver means born rich. Born with a knife. But then the allusion is lost.

An illgirt server gathered sticky clattering plates. Rock, the bailiff, standing at the bar blew the foamy crown from his tankard. Well up: it splashed yellow near his boot. A diner, knife and fork upright, elbows on table, ready for a second helping stared towards the foodlift across his stained square of newspaper. Other chap telling him something with his mouth full. Sympathetic listener. Table talk. I munched hum un thu Unchster Bunk un Munchday. Ha? Did you, faith?

Mr Bloom raised two fingers doubtfully to his lips. His eyes said.

– Not here. Don't see him.

Out. I hate dirty eaters.

He backed towards the door. Get a light snack in Davy Byrne's. Stopgap. Keep me going. Had a good breakfast.

– Roast and mashed here.

– Pint of stout.

Every fellow for his own, tooth and nail. Gulp. Grub. Gulp. Gobstuff.

He came out into clearer air and turned back towards Grafton street. Eat or be eaten. Kill! Kill!

Suppose that communal kitchen years to come perhaps. All trotting down with porringers and tommycans to be filled. Devour contents in the street. John Howard Parnell example the provost of Trinity every mother's son don't talk of your provosts and provost of Trinity women and children, cabmen, priests, parsons, fieldmarshals, archbishops. From Ailesbury road, Clyde road, artisans' dwellings north Dublin union, lord mayor in his gingerbread coach, old queen in a bathchair. My plate's empty. After you with our incorporated drinkingcup. Like sir Philip Crampton's fountain. Rub off the microbes with your handkerchief. Next chap rubs on a new batch with his. Father O'Flynn would make hares of them all. Have rows all the same. All for number one. Children fighting for the scrapings of the pot. Want a soup pot as big as the Phœnix Park. Harpooning flitches and hindquarters out of it. Hate people all round you. City Arms hotel *table d'hôte* she called it. Soup, joint and sweet. Never know whose thoughts you're chewing. Then who'd wash up all the plates and forks? Might be all feeding on tabloids that time. Teeth getting worse and worse.

After all there's a lot in that vegetarian fine flavour of things from the earth garlic, of course, it stinks Italian organ-grinders crisp of onions, mushrooms truffles. Pain to animal too. Pluck and draw fowl. Wretched brutes there at the cattlemarket waiting for the poleaxe to split their skulls open. Moo. Poor trembling calves. Meh. Staggering bob. Bubble and squeak. Butchers' buckets wobble lights. Give us that brisket off the hook. Plup. Rawhead and bloody bones. Flayed glasseyed sheep hung from their haunches, sheepsnouts bloodypapered snivelling nosejam on sawdust. Top and lashers going out. Don't maul them pieces, young one.

Hot fresh blood they prescribe for decline. Blood always needed. Insidious. Lick it up, smoking hot, thick sugary. Famished ghosts.

Ah, I'm hungry.

He entered Davy Byrne's. Moral pub. He doesn't chat. Stands a drink now and then. But in leapyear once in four. Cashed a cheque for me once.

What will I take now? He drew his watch. Let me see now. Shandygaff?

– Hello, Bloom! Nosey Flynn said from his nook.

– Hello, Flynn.

– How's things?

– Tiptop . . . Let me see. I'll take a glass of burgundy and . . . let me see.

Sardines on the shelves. Almost taste them by looking. Sandwich? Ham and his descendants mustered and bred there. Potted meats. What is home without Plumtree's potted meat? Incomplete. What a stupid ad! Under the obituary notices they stuck it. All up a plumtree. Dignam's potted meat. Cannibals would with lemon and rice. White missionary too salty. Like pickled pork. Expect the chief consumes the parts of honour. Ought to be tough from exercise. His wives in a row to watch the effect. *There was a right royal old nigger. Who ate or something the somethings of the reverend Mr MacTrigger.* With it an abode of bliss. Lord knows what concoction. Cauls mouldy tripes windpipes faked and minced up. Puzzle find the meat. Kosher. No meat and milk together. Hygiene that was what they call now. Yom kippur fast spring cleaning of inside. Peace and war depend on some fellow's digestion. Religions. Christmas turkeys and geese. Slaughter of innocents. Eat, drink and be merry. Then casual wards full after. Heads bandaged. Cheese digests all but itself. Mighty cheese.

– Have you a cheese sandwich?

– Yes, sir.

Like a few olives too if they had them. Italian I prefer. Good glass of burgundy; take away that. Lubricate. A nice salad, cool as a cucumber. Tom Kernan can dress. Puts gusto into it. Pure olive oil. Milly served me that cutlet with a sprig of parsley. Take one Spanish onion. God made food, the devil the cooks. Devilled crab.

– Wife well?

– Quite well, thanks . . . A cheese sandwich, then. Gorgonzola, have you?

– Yes, sir.

Nosey Flynn sipped his grog.

– Doing any singing those times?

Look at his mouth. Could whistle in his own ear. Flap ears to match. Music. Knows as much about it as my coachman. Still better tell him. Does no harm. Free ad.

– She's engaged for a big tour end of this month. You may have heard perhaps.

– No. O, that's the style. Who's getting it up?

The curate served.

– How much is that?

– Seven d., sir . . . Thank you, sir.

Mr Bloom cut his sandwich into slender strips. *Mr MacTrigger*. Easier than the dreamy creamy stuff. *His five hundred wives. Had the time of their lives.*

– Mustard, sir?

– Thank you.

He studded under each lifted strip yellow blobs. *Their lives.* I have it. *It grew bigger and bigger and bigger.*

– Getting it up? he said. Well, it's like a company idea, you see. Part shares and part profits.

– Ay, now I remember, Nosey Flynn said, putting his hand in his pocket to scratch his groin. Who is this was telling me? Isn't Blazes Boylan mixed up in it?

A warm shock of air heat of mustard hauched on Mr Bloom's heart. He raised his eyes and met the stare of a bilious clock. Two. Pub clock five minutes fast. Time going on. Hands moving. Two. Not yet.

His midriff yearned then upward, sank within him, yearned more longly, longingly.

Wine.

He smellsipped the cordial juice and, bidding his throat strongly to speed it, set his wineglass delicately down.

– Yes, he said. He's the organiser in point of fact.

No fear. No brains.

Nosey Flynn snuffled and scratched. Flea having a good square meal.

– He had a good slice of luck, Jack Mooney was telling me, over that boxing match Myler Keogh won again that soldier in the Portobello barracks. By God, he had the little kipper down in the county Carlow he was telling me . . .

Hope that dewdrop doesn't come down into his glass. No, snuffled it up.

– For near a month, man, before it came off. Sucking duck eggs by God till further orders. Keep him off the boose, see? O, by God, Blazes is a hairy chap.

Davy Byrne came forward from the hindbar in tuckstitched shirt sleeves, cleaning his lips with two wipes of his napkin. Herring's blush. Whose smile upon each feature plays with such and such replete. Too much fat on the parsnips.

– And here's himself and pepper on him, Nosey Flynn said. Can you give us a good one for the Gold cup?

– I'm off that, Mr Flynn, Davy Byrne answered. I never put anything on a horse.

– You're right there, Nosey Flynn said.

Mr Bloom ate his strips of sandwich, fresh clean bread, with relish of disgust, pungent mustard, the feety savour of green cheese. Sips of his wine soothed his palate. Not logwood that. Tastes fuller this weather with the chill off.

Nice quiet bar. Nice piece of wood in that counter. Nicely planed. Like the way it curves there.

– I wouldn't do anything at all in that line, Davy Byrne said. It ruined many a man the same horses.

Vintners' sweepstake. Licensed for the sale of beer, wine and spirits for consumption on the premises. Heads I win tails you lose.

– True for you, Nosey Flynn said. Unless you're in the know. There's no straight sport going now. Lenehan gets some good ones. He's giving Sceptre today. Zinfandel's the favourite, lord Howard de Walden's, won at Epsom. Morny Cannon is riding him. I could have got seven to one against Saint Amant a fortnight before.

– That so? Davy Byrne said . . .

He went towards the window and, taking up the petty cash book, scanned its pages.

– I could, faith, Nosey Flynn said snuffling. That was a rare bit of horseflesh. Saint Frusquin was her sire. She won in a thunderstorm, Rothschild's filly, with wadding in her ears. Blue jacket and yellow cap. Bad luck to big Ben Dollard and his John O'Gaunt. He put me off it. Ay.

He drank resignedly from his tumbler, running his fingers down the flutes.

– Ay, he said, sighing.

Mr Bloom, champing standing, looked upon his sigh. Nosey numskull. Will I tell him that horse Lenehan? He knows already. Better let him forget. Go and lose more. Fool and his money. Dewdrop coming down again. Cold nose he'd have kissing a woman. Still they might like. Prickly beards they like. Dog's cold noses. Old Mrs Riordan with the rumbling stomach's Skye terrier in the City Arms hotel. Molly fondling him in her lap. O the big doggybowwowsywowsy!

Wine soaked and softened rolled pith of bread mustard a moment mawkish cheese. Nice wine it is. Taste it better because I'm not thirsty. Bath of course does that. Just a bite or two. Then about six o'clock I can. Six, six. Time will be gone then. She . . .

Mild fire of wine kindled his veins. I wanted that badly. Felt so off colour. His eyes unhungrily saw shelves of tins, sardines, gaudy lobsters' claws. All the odd things people pick up for food. Out of shells, periwinkles with a pin, off trees, snails out of the ground the French eat, out of the sea with bait on a hook. Silly fish learn nothing in a thousand years. If you didn't know risky putting anything into your mouth. Poisonous berries. Johnny Magories. Roundness you think good. Gaudy colour warns you off. One fellow told another and so on. Try it on the dog first. Led on by the smell or the look. Tempting fruit. Ice cones. Cream. Instinct. Orangegroves for instance. Need artificial irrigation. Bleibtreustrasse. Yes but what about oysters? Unsightly like a clot of phlegm. Filthy shells. Devil to open them too. Who found them out? Garbage, sewage they feed on. Fizz and Red bank oysters. Effect on the sexual. Aphrodis. He was in the Red bank this morning. Was he oyster old fish at table. Perhaps he young flesh in bed. No. June has no ar no oysters. But there are people like tainted game. Jugged hare. First catch your hare. Chinese eating eggs fifty years old, blue and green again. Dinner of thirty courses. Each dish harmless might mix inside. Idea for a poison mystery. That archduke Leopold was it. No. Yes, or was it Otto one of those Habsburgs? Or who was it used to eat the scruff off his own head? Cheapest lunch in town. Of course, aristocrats. Then the others copy to be in the fashion. Milly too rock oil and flour. Raw pastry I like myself. Half the catch of oysters they throw back in the sea to keep up the price. Cheap. No one would buy. Caviare. Do the grand. Hock in green glasses. Swell blowout. Lady this. Powdered bosom pearls. The *élite. Crème de la crème.* They want special dishes to pretend they're. Hermit with a platter of pulse keep down the stings of the flesh. Know me come eat with me. Royal sturgeon. High sheriff, Coffey, the butcher, right to venisons of the forest from his ex. Send him back the half of a cow. Spread I saw down in the Master of the Rolls' kitchen area. Whitehatted *chef* like a rabbi. Combustible duck. Curly cabbage *à la duchesse de Parme.* Just as well to write it on the bill of fare so you can know what you've eaten too many drugs spoil the broth. I know it myself. Dosing it with Edwards' desiccated soup. Geese stuffed silly for them. Lobsters boiled alive. Do ptake some ptarmigan. Wouldn't mind being a waiter in a swell hotel. Tips, evening dress, halfnaked ladies. May I tempt you to a little more filleted lemon sole, miss Dubedat? Yes, do bedad. And she did bedad. Huguenot name I expect that. A miss Dubedat lived in Killiney I remember. *Du, de la*, French. Still it's the same fish, perhaps old Micky Hanlon of Moore street ripped the guts out of making money, hand over fist, finger in fishes' gills, can't write his name on a cheque, think he was painting the landscape with his mouth twisted. Moooikill A Aitcha Ha. Ignorant as a kish of brogues, worth fifty thousand pounds.

Stuck on the pane two flies buzzed, stuck.

Glowing wine on his palate lingered swallowed. Crushing in the wine-press grapes of Burgundy. Sun's heat it is. Seems to a secret touch telling me memory. Touched his sense moistened remembered. Hidden under wild ferns on Howth. Below us bay sleeping sky. No sound. The sky. The bay purple by the Lion's head. Green by Drumleck. Yellow-green towards Sutton. Fields of undersea, the lines faint brown in grass, buried cities. Pillowed on my coat she had her hair, earwigs in the heather scrub my hand under her nape, you'll toss me all. O wonder! Coolsoft with ointments her hand touched me, caressed: her eyes upon me did not turn away. Ravished over her I lay, full lips full open, kissed her mouth. Yum. Softly she gave me in my mouth the seedcake warm and chewed. Mawkish pulp her mouth had mumbled sweet and sour with spittle. Joy: I ate it: joy. Young life, her lips that gave me pouting. Soft, warm, sticky gumjelly lips. Flowers her eyes were, take me, willing eyes. Pebbles fell. She lay still. A goat. No-one. High on Ben Howth rhododendrons a nannygoat walking surefooted, dropping currants. Screened under ferns she laughed warmfolded. Wildly I lay on her, kissed her; eyes, her lips, her stretched neck, beating, woman's breasts full in her blouse of nun's veiling, fat nipples upright. Hot I tongued her. She kissed me. I was kissed. All yielding she tossed my hair. Kissed, she kissed me.

Me. And me now.

Stuck, the flies buzzed.

His downcast eyes followed the silent veining of the oaken slab. Beauty: it curves: curves are beauty. Shapely goddesses, Venus, Juno: curves the world admires. Can see them library museum standing in the round hall, naked goddesses. Aids to digestion. They don't care what man looks. All to see. Never speaking, I mean to say to fellows like Flynn. Suppose she did Pygmalion and Galatea what would she say first? Mortal! Put you in your proper place. Quaffing nectar at mess with gods, golden dishes, all ambrosial. Not like a tanner lunch we have, boiled mutton, carrots and turnips, bottle of Allsop. Nectar, imagine it drinking electricity: gods' food. Lovely forms of woman sculped Junonian. Immortal lovely. And we stuffing food in one hole and out behind: food, chyle, blood, dung, earth, food: have to feed it like stoking an engine. They have no. Never looked. I'll look today. Keeper won't see. Bend down let something fall see if she.

Dribbling a quiet message from his bladder came to go to do not to do there to do. A man and ready he drained his glass to the lees and walked, to men too they gave themselves, manly conscious, lay with men lovers, a youth enjoyed her, to the yard.

When the sound of his boots had ceased Davy Byrne said from his book:

– What is this he is? Isn't he in the insurance line?

– He's out of that long ago, Nosey Flynn said. He does canvassing for the *Freeman*.

– I know him well to see, Davy Byrne said. Is he in trouble?

– Trouble? Nosey Flynn said. Not that I heard of. Why?

– I noticed he was in mourning.

– Was he? Nosey Flynn said. So he was, faith. I asked him how was all at home. You're right, by God. So he was.

– I never broach the subject, Davy Byrne said humanely, if I see a gentleman is in trouble that way. It only brings it up fresh in their minds.

– It's not the wife anyhow, Nosey Flynn said. I met him the day before yesterday and he coming out of that Irish farm dairy John Wyse Nolan's wife has in Henry street with a jar of cream in his hand taking it home to his better half. She's well nourished, I tell you. Plovers on toast.

– And is he doing for the *Freeman?* Davy Byrne said.

Nosey Flynn pursed his lips.

– He doesn't buy cream on the ads he picks up. You can make bacon of that.

– How so? Davy Byrne asked, coming from his book.

Nosey Flynn made swift passes in the air with juggling fingers. He winked.

– He's in the craft, he said.

– Do you tell me so? Davy Byrne said.

– Very much so, Nosey Flynn said. Ancient free and accepted order. Light, life and love, by God. They give him a leg up. I was told that by a, well, I won't say who.

– Is that a fact?

– O, it's a fine order, Nosey Flynn said. They stick to you when you're down. I know a fellow was trying to get into it, but they're as close as damn it. By God they did right to keep the women out of it.

Davy Byrne smiledyawnednodded all in one:

– Iiiiiichaaaaaaach!

– There was one woman, Nosey Flynn said, hid herself in a clock to find out what they do be doing. But be damned but they smelt her out and swore her in on the spot a master mason. That was one of the Saint Legers of Doneraile.

Davy Byrne, sated after his yawn, said with tearwashed eyes:

– And is that a fact? Decent quiet man he is. I often saw him in here and I never once saw him, you know, over the line.

– God Almighty couldn't make him drunk, Nosey Flynn said firmly. Slips off when the fun gets too hot. Didn't you see him look at his watch? Ah, you weren't there. If you ask him to have a drink first thing he does he outs with the watch to see what he ought to imbibe. Declare to God he does.

– There are some like that, Davy Byrne said. He's a safe man, I'd say.

– He's not too bad, Nosey Flynn said, snuffling it up. He has been known to put his hand down too to help a fellow. Give the devil his due. O, Bloom has his good points. But there's one thing he'll never do.

His hand scrawled a dry pen signature beside his grog.

– I know, Davy Byrne said.

– Nothing in black and white, Nosey Flynn said.

Paddy Leonard and Bantam Lyons came in. Tom Rochford followed, a plaining hand on his claret waistcoat.

– Day, Mr Byrne.

– Day, gentlemen.

They paused at the counter.

– Who's standing? Paddy Leonard asked.

– I'm sitting anyhow, Nosey Flynn answered.

– Well, what'll it be? Paddy Leonard asked.

– I'll take a stone ginger, Bantam Lyons said.

– How much? Paddy Leonard cried. Since when, for God' sake? What's yours, Tom?

– How is the main drainage? Nosey Flynn asked, sipping.

For answer Tom Rochford pressed his hand to his breastbone and hiccupped.

– Would I trouble you for a glass of fresh water, Mr Byrne? he said.

– Certainly, sir.

Paddy Leonard eyed his alemates.

– Lord love a duck, he said, look at what I'm standing drinks to! Cold water and gingerpop! Two fellows that would suck whisky off a sore leg. He has some bloody horse up his sleeve for the Gold cup. A dead snip.

– Zinfandel is it? Nosey Flynn asked.

Tom Rochford spilt powder from a twisted paper into the water set before him.

– That cursed dyspepsia, he said before drinking.

– Breadsoda is very good, Davy Byrne said.

Tom Rochford nodded and drank.

– Is it Zinfandel?

– Say nothing, Bantam Lyons winked. I'm going to plunge five bob on my own.

– Tell us if you're worth your salt and be damned to you, Paddy Leonard said. Who gave it to you?

Mr Bloom on his way out raised three fingers in greeting.

– So long, Nosey Flynn said.

The others turned.

– That's the man now that gave it to me, Bantam Lyons whispered.

– Prrwht! Paddy Leonard said with scorn. Mr Byrne, sir, we'll take two of your small Jamesons after that and a . . .

– Stone ginger, Davy Byrne added civilly.

– Ay, Paddy Leonard said. A suckingbottle for the baby.

Mr Bloom walked towards Dawson street, his tongue brushing his teeth smooth. Something green it would have to be: spinach say. Then with those Röntgen rays searchlight you could.

At Duke lane a ravenous terrier choked up a sick knuckly cud on the cobble stones and lapped it with new zest. Surfeit. Returned with thanks having fully digested the contents. First sweet then savoury. Mr Bloom coasted warily. Ruminants. His second course. Their upper jaw they move. Wonder if Tom Rochford will do anything with that invention of his. Wasting time explaining it to Flynn's mouth. Lean people long mouths. Ought to be a hall or a place where inventors could go in and invent free. Course then you'd have all the cranks pestering.

He hummed, prolonging in solemn echo, the closes of the bars:

> *Don Giovanni, a cenar teco*
> *M'invitasti.*

Feel better. Burgundy. Good pick me up. Who distilled first? Some chap in the blues. Dutch courage. That *Kilkenny People* in the national library now I must.

Bare clean closestools, waiting, in the window of William Miller, plumber, turned back his thoughts. They could: and watch it all the way down, swallow a pin sometimes come out of the ribs years after, tour round the body, changing biliary duct, spleen squirting liver, gastric juice coils of intestines like pipes. But the poor buffer would have to stand all the time with his insides entrails on show. Science.

– *A cenar teco.*

What does that *teco* mean? Tonight perhaps.

> *Don Giovanni, thou hast me invited*
> *To come to supper tonight,*
> *The rum the rumdum.*

Doesn't go properly.

Keyes: two months if I get Nannetti to. That'll be two pounds ten, about two pounds eight. Three Hynes owes me. Two eleven. Presscott's ad. Two fifteen. Five guineas about. On the pig's back.

Could buy one of those silk petticoats for Molly, colour of her new garters.

Today. Today. Not think.

Tour the south then. What about English watering places? Brighton, Margate. Piers by moonlight. Her voice floating out. Those lovely seaside girls. Against John Long's a drowsing loafer lounged in heavy thought, gnawing a crusted knuckle. Handy man wants job. Small wages. Will eat anything.

Mr Bloom turned at Gray's confectioner's window of unbought tarts and passed the reverend Thomas Connellan's bookstore. *Why I left the church of Rome? Bird's Nest.* Women run him. They say they used to give pauper children soup to change to protestants in the time of the potato blight. Society over the way papa went to for the conversion of poor jews. Same bait. Why we left the church of Rome?

A blind stripling stood tapping the curbstone with his slender cane. No tram in sight. Wants to cross.

– Do you want to cross? Mr Bloom asked.

The blind stripling did not answer. His wall face frowned weakly. He moved his head uncertainly.

– You're in Dawson street, Mr Bloom said. Molesworth street is opposite. Do you want to cross? There's nothing in the way.

The cane moved out trembling to the left. Mr Bloom's eye followed its line and saw again the dyeworks' van drawn up before Drago's. Where I saw his brilliantined hair just when I was. Horse drooping. Driver in John Long's. Slaking his drouth.

– There's a van there, Mr Bloom said, but it's not moving. I'll see you across. Do you want to go to Molesworth street?

– Yes, the stripling answered. South Frederick street.

– Come, Mr Bloom said.

He touched the thin elbow gently: then took the limp seeing hand to guide it forward.

Say something to him. Better not do the condescending. They mistrust what you tell them. Pass a common remark.

– The rain kept off.

No answer.

Stains on his coat. Slobbers his food, I suppose. Tastes all different for him. Have to be spoonfed first. Like a child's hand his hand. Like Milly's was. Sensitive. Sizing me up I daresay from my hand. Wonder if he has a name. Van. Keep his cane clear of the horse's legs tired drudge get his doze. That's right. Clear. Behind a bull: in front of a horse.

– Thanks, sir.

Knows I'm a man. Voice.

– Right now? First turn to the left.

The blind stripling tapped the curbstone and went on his way, drawing his cane back, feeling again.

Mr Bloom walked behind the eyeless feet, a flatcut suit of herringbone tweed. Poor young fellow! How on earth did he know that van was there? Must have felt it. See things in their foreheads perhaps. Kind of sense of volume. Weight would he feel it if something was removed. Feel a gap. Queer idea of Dublin he must have, tapping his way round by the stones. Could he walk in a beeline if he hadn't that cane? Bloodless pious face like a fellow going in to be a priest.

Penrose! That was that chap's name.

Look at all the things they can learn to do. Read with their fingers. Tune pianos. Or we are surprised they have any brains. Why we think a deformed person or a hunchback clever if he says something we might say. Of course the other senses are more. Embroider. Plait baskets. People ought to help. Work basket I could buy Molly's birthday. Hates sewing. Might take an objection. Dark men they call them.

Sense of smell must be stronger too. Smells on all sides bunched together. Each person too. Then the spring, the summer: smells. Tastes. They say you can't taste wines with your eyes shut or a cold in the head. Also smoke in the dark they say get no pleasure.

And with a woman, for instance. More shameless not seeing. That girl passing the Stewart institution, head in the air. Look at me. I have them all on. Must be strange not to see her. Kind of a form in his mind's eye. The voice temperature when he touches her with fingers must almost see the lines, the curves. His hands on her hair, for instance. Say it was black for instance. Good. We call it black. Then passing over her white skin. Different feel perhaps. Feeling of white.

Postoffice. Must answer. Fag today. Send her a postal order two shillings half a crown. Accept my little present. Stationer's just here too. Wait. Think over it.

With a gentle finger he felt ever so slowly the hair combed back above his ears. Again. Fibres of fine fine straw. Then gently his finger felt the skin of his right cheek. Downy hair there too. Not smooth enough. The belly is the smoothest. No-one about. There he goes into Frederick street. Perhaps to Levenston's dancing academy piano. Might be settling my braces.

Walking by Doran's public house he slid his hand between waistcoat and trousers and, pulling aside his shirt gently, felt a slack fold of his belly. But I know it's whiteyellow. Want to try in the dark to see.

He withdrew his hand and pulled his dress to.

Poor fellow! Quite a boy. Terrible. Really terrible. What dreams would he have, not seeing? Life a dream for him. Where is the justice being born that way? All those women and children excursion beanfeast burned and drowned in New York. Holocaust. Karma they call that transmigration for sins you did in a past life the reincarnation met him pikehoses. Dear, dear, dear. Pity of course: but somehow you can't cotton on to them someway.

Sir Frederick Falkiner going into the freemasons' hall. Solemn as Troy. After his good lunch in Earlsfort terrace. Old legal cronies cracking a magnum. Tales of the bench and assizes and annals of the bluecoat school. I sentenced him to ten years. I suppose he'd turn up his nose at that stuff I drank. Vintage wine for them, the year marked on a dusty bottle. Has his own ideas of justice in the recorder's court. Wellmeaning old man. Police chargesheets crammed with cases get their percentage manufacturing crime. Sends them to the rightabout. The devil on moneylenders. Gave Reuben J. a great strawcalling. Now he's really what they call a dirty jew. Power those judges have. Crusty old topers in wigs. Bear with a sore paw. And may the Lord have mercy on your soul.

Hello, placard. Mirus bazaar. His excellency the lord lieutenant. Six-teenth today it is. In aid of funds for Mercer's hospital. *The Messiah* was first given for that. Yes. Handel. What about going out there. Ballsbridge. Drop in on Keyes. No use sticking to him like a leech. Wear out my welcome. Sure to know someone on the gate.

Mr Bloom came to Kildare Street. First I must. Library.

Straw hat in sunlight. Tan shoes. Turnedup trousers. It is. It is.

His heart quopped softly. To the right. Museum. Goddesses. He swerved to the right.

Is it? Almost certain. Won't look. Wine in my face. Why did I? Too heady. Yes, it is. The walk. Not see. Not see. Get on.

Making for the museum gate with long windy strides he lifted his eyes. Handsome building. Sir Thomas Deane designed. Not following me?

Didn't see me perhaps. Light in his eyes.

The flutter of his breath came forth in short sighs. Quick. Cold statues: quiet there. Safe in a minute.

No, didn't see me. After two. Just at the gate.

My heart!

His eyes beating looked steadfastly at cream curves of stone. Sir Thomas Deane was the Greek architecture.

Look for something I.

His hasty hand went quick into a pocket, took out, read unfolded Agendath Netaim. Where did I?

Busy looking for.

He thrust back quickly Agendath.

Afternoon she said.

I am looking for that. Yes, that. Try all pockets. Handker. *Freeman*. Where did I? Ah, yes. Trousers. Purse. Potato. Where did I?

Hurry. Walk quietly. Moment more. My heart.

His hand looking for the where did I put found in his hip pocket soap lotion have to call tepid paper stuck. Ah, soap there! Yes. Gate.

Safe!

* * * * *

◀ URBANE, TO COMFORT THEM, THE QUAKER LIBRARIAN purred:

– And we have, have we not, those priceless pages of *Wilhelm Meister?* A great poet on a great brother poet. A hesitating soul taking arms against a sea of troubles, torn by conflicting doubts, as one sees in real life.

He came a step a sinkapace forward on neatsleather creaking and a step backward a sinkapace on the solemn floor.

A noiseless attendant, setting open the door but slightly, made him a noiseless beck.

– Directly, said he, creaking to go, albeit lingering. The beautiful ineffectual dreamer who comes to grief against hard facts. One always feels that Goethe's judgments are so true. True in the larger analysis.

Twicreakingly analysis he corantoed off. Bald, most zealous by the door he gave his large ear all to the attendant's words: heard them: and was gone.

Two left.

– Monsieur de la Palisse, Stephen sneered, was alive fifteen minutes before his death.

– Have you found those six brave medicals, John Eglinton asked with elder's gall, to write *Paradise Lost* at your dictation? *The Sorrows of Satan* he calls it.

Smile. Smile Cranly's smile.

> *First he tickled her*
> *Then he patted her*
> *Then he passed the female catheter.*
> *For he was a medical*
> *Jolly old medi . . .*

– I feel you would need one more for *Hamlet*. Seven is dear to the mystic mind. The shining seven W. B. calls them.

Glittereyed, his rufous skull close to his greencapped desklamp sought the face, bearded amid darkgreener shadow, an ollav, holyeyed. He laughed low: a sizar's laugh of Trinity: unanswered.

> *Orchestral Satan, weeping many a rood*
> *Tears such as angels weep.*
> *Ed egli avea del cul fatto trombetta.*

He holds my follies hostage.

Cranly's eleven true Wicklowmen to free their sireland. Gaptoothed Kathleen, her four beautiful green fields, the stranger in her house. And one more to hail him: *ave, rabbi.* The Tinahely twelve. In the shadow of the glen he cooees for them. My soul's youth I gave him, night by night. Godspeed. Good hunting.

Mulligan has my telegram.

Folly. Persist.

– Our young Irish bards, John Eglinton censured, have yet to create a figure which the world will set beside Saxon Shakespeare's Hamlet though I admire him, as old Ben did, on this side idolatry.

– All these questions are purely academic, Russell oracled out of his shadow. I mean, whether Hamlet is Shakespeare or James I or Essex. Clergymen's discussions of the historicity of Jesus. Art has to reveal to us ideas, formless spiritual essences. The supreme question about a work of art is out of how deep a life does it spring. The painting of Gustave Moreau is the painting of ideas. The deepest poetry of Shelley, the words of Hamlet bring our mind into contact with the eternal wisdom, Plato's world of ideas. All the rest is the speculation of schoolboys for schoolboys.

A. E. has been telling some yankee interviewer. Wall, tarnation strike me!

– The schoolmen were schoolboys first, Stephen said superpolitely. Aristotle was once Plato's schoolboy.

– And has remained so, one should hope, John Eglinton sedately said. One can see him, a model schoolboy with his diploma under his arm.

He laughed again at the now smiling bearded face.

Formless spiritual. Father, Word and Holy Breath. Allfather, the heavenly man. Hiesos Kristos, magician of the beautiful, the Logos who suffers in us at every moment. This verily is that. I am the fire upon the altar. I am the sacrificial butter.

Dunlop, Judge, the noblest Roman of them all, A. E., Arval, the Name Ineffable, in heaven hight, K. H., their master, whose identity is no secret to adepts. Brothers of the great white lodge always watching to see if they can help. The Christ with the bridesister, moisture of light, born of an ensouled virgin, repentant sophia, departed to the plane of buddhi. The life esoteric is not for ordinary person. O. P. must work off bad karma first. Mrs Cooper Oakley once glimpsed our very illustrious sister H. P. B's elemental.

O, fie! Out on't! *Pfuiteufel!* You naughtn't to look, missus, so you naughtn't when a lady's ashowing of her elemental.

Mr Best entered, tall, young, mild, light. He bore in his hand with grace a notebook, new, large, clean, bright.

– That model schoolboy, Stephen said, would find Hamlet's musings about the afterlife of his princely soul, the improbable, insignificant and undramatic monologue, as shallow as Plato's.

John Eglinton, frowning, said, waxing wroth:

– Upon my word it makes my blood boil to hear anyone compare Aristotle with Plato.

– Which of the two, Stephen asked, would have banished me from his commonwealth?

Unsheathe your dagger definitions. Horseness is the whatness of all-horse. Streams of tendency and eons they worship. God: noise in the street: very peripatetic. Space: what you damn well have to see. Through spaces smaller than red globules of man's blood they creepycrawl after Blake's buttocks into eternity of which this vegetable world is but a shadow. Hold to the now, the here, through which all future plunges to the past.

Mr Best came forward, amiable, towards his colleague.

– Haines is gone, he said.

– Is he?

– I was showing him Jubainville's book. He's quite enthusiastic, don't you know, about Hyde's *Lovesongs of Connacht*. I couldn't bring him in to hear the discussion. He's gone to Gill's to buy it.

> *Bound thee forth, my booklet, quick*
> *To greet the callous public.*
> *Writ, I ween, 'twas not my wish*
> *In lean unlovely English.*

– The peatsmoke is going to his head, John Eglinton opined.

We feel in England. Penitent thief. Gone. I smoked his baccy. Green twinkling stone. An emerald set in the ring of the sea.

– People do not know how dangerous lovesongs can be, the auric egg of Russell warned occultly. The movements which work revolutions in the world are born out of the dreams and visions in a peasant's heart on the hillside. For them the earth is not an exploitable ground but the living mother. The rarefied air of the academy and the arena produce the six-shilling novel, the musichall song, France produces the finest flower of corruption in Mallarmé but the desirable life is revealed only to the poor of heart, the life of Homer's Phæacians.

From these words Mr Best turned an unoffending face to Stephen.

– Mallarmé, don't you know, he said, has written those wonderful prose poems Stephen MacKenna used to read to me in Paris. The one about *Hamlet*. He says: *il se promène, lisant au livre de lui-même*, don't you know, *reading the book of himself*. He describes *Hamlet* given in a French town, don't you know, a provincial town. They advertised it.

His free hand graciously wrote tiny signs in air.

HAMLET
ou
LE DISTRAIT
Pièce de Shakespeare

He repeated to John Eglinton's newgathered frown:

– *Pièce de Shakespeare*, don't you know. It's so French, the French point of view. *Hamlet ou* . . .

– The absentminded beggar, Stephen ended.

John Eglinton laughed.

– Yes, I suppose it would be, he said. Excellent people, no doubt, but distressingly shortsighted in some matters.

Sumptuous and stagnant exaggeration of murder.

– A deathsman of the soul Robert Greene called him, Stephen said. Not for nothing was he a butcher's son wielding the sledded poleaxe and spitting in his palm. Nine lives are taken off for his father's one, Our Father who art in purgatory. Khaki Hamlets don't hesitate to shoot. The bloodboltered shambles in act five is a forecast of the concentration camp sung by Mr Swinburne.

Cranly, I his mute orderly, following battles from afar.

> *Whelps and dams of murderous foes whom none*
> *But we had spared . . .*

Between the Saxon smile and yankee yawp. The devil and the deep sea.

– He will have it that *Hamlet* is a ghoststory, John Eglinton said for Mr Best's behoof. Like the fat boy in Pickwick he wants to make our flesh creep.

> *List! List! O list!*

My flesh hears him: creeping, hears.

> *If thou didst ever . . .*

– What is a ghost? Stephen said with tingling energy. One who has faded into impalpability through death, through absence, through change of manners. Elizabethan London lay as far from Stratford as corrupt Paris lies from virgin Dublin. Who is the ghost from *limbo patrum*, returning to the world that has forgotten him? Who is king Hamlet?

John Eglinton shifted his spare body, leaning back to judge.

Lifted.

– It is this hour of a day in mid June, Stephen said, begging with a swift glance their hearing. The flag is up on the playhouse by the bankside. The bear Sackerson growls in the pit near it, Paris garden. Canvasclimbers who sailed with Drake chew their sausages among the groundlings.

Local colour. Work in all you know. Make them accomplices.

– Shakespeare has left the huguenot's house in Silver street and walks by the swanmews along the riverbank. But he does not stay to feed the pen chivying her game of cygnets towards the rushes. The swan of Avon has other thoughts.

Composition of place. Ignatius Loyola, make haste to help me!

– The play begins. A player comes on under the shadow, made up in the castoff mail of a court buck, a wellset man with a bass voice. It is the ghost, the king, a king and no king, and the player is Shakespeare who has studied *Hamlet* all the years of his life which were not vanity in order to play the part of the spectre. He speaks the words to Burbage, the young player who stands before him beyond the rack of cerecloth, calling him by a name:

> *Hamlet, I am thy father's spirit*

bidding him list. To a son he speaks, the son of his soul, the prince, young Hamlet and to the son of his body, Hamnet Shakespeare, who has died in Stratford that his namesake may live for ever.

– Is it possible that that player Shakespeare, a ghost by absence, and in the vesture of buried Denmark, a ghost by death, speaking his own words to his own son's name (had Hamnet Shakespeare lived he would have been prince Hamlet's twin) is it possible, I want to know, or probable that he did not draw or foresee the logical conclusion of those premises: you are the dispossessed son: I am the murdered father: your mother is the guilty queen, Ann Shakespeare, born Hathaway?

– But this prying into the family life of a great man, Russell began impatiently.

Art thou there, truepenny?

– Interesting only to the parish clerk. I mean, we have the plays. I mean when we read the poetry of *King Lear* what is it to us how the poet lived? As for living, our servants can do that for us, Villiers de l'Isle has said. Peeping and prying into greenroom gossip of the day, the poet's drinking, the poet's debts. We have *King Lear*: and it is immortal.

Mr Best's face appealed to, agreed.

Flow over them with your waves and with your waters, Mananaan, Mananaan MacLir . . . . .

How now, sirrah, that pound he lent you when you were hungry?

Marry, I wanted it.

Take thou this noble.

Go to! You spent most of it in Georgina Johnson's bed, clergyman's daughter. Agenbite of inwit.

Do you intend to pay it back?

O, yes.

When? Now?

Well . . . no.

When, then?

I paid my way. I paid my way.

Steady on. He's from beyant Boyne water. The northeast corner. You owe it.

Wait. Five months. Molecules all change. I am other I now. Other I got pound.

Buzz. Buzz.

But I, entelechy, form of forms, am I by memory because under ever-changing forms.

I that sinned and prayed and fasted.

A child Conmee saved from pandies.

I, I and I. I.

A. E. I. O. U.

– Do you mean to fly in the face of the tradition of three centuries? John Eglinton's carping voice asked. Her ghost at least has been laid for ever. She died, for literature at least, before she was born.

– She died, Stephen retorted, sixtyseven years after she was born. She saw him into and out of the world. She took his first embraces. She bore his children and she laid pennies on his eyes to keep his eyelids closed when he lay on his deathbed.

Mother's deathbed. Candle. The sheeted mirror. Who brought me into this world lies there, bronzelidded, under few cheap flowers. *Liliata rutilantium.*

I wept alone.

John Eglinton looked in the tangled glowworm of his lamp.

– The world believes that Shakespeare made a mistake, he said, and got out of it as quickly and as best he could.

– Bosh! Stephen said rudely. A man of genius makes no mistakes. His errors are volitional and are the portals of discovery.

Portals of discovery opened to let in the quaker librarian, softcreak-footed, bald, eared and assiduous.

– A shrew, John Eglinton said shrewdly, is not a useful portal of discovery, one should imagine. What useful discovery did Socrates learn from Xanthippe?

– Dialectic, Stephen answered: and from his mother how to bring thoughts into the world. What he learnt from his other wife Myrto *(absit nomen!)* Socratididion's Epipsychidion, no man, not a woman, will ever know. But neither the midwife's lore nor the caudlectures saved him from the archons of Sinn Fein and their noggin of hemlock.

– But Ann Hathaway? Mr Best's quiet voice said forgetfully. Yes, we seem to be forgetting her as Shakespeare himself forgot her.

His look went from brooder's beard to carper's skull, to remind, to chide them not unkindly, then to the baldpink lollard costard, guiltless though maligned.

– He had a good groatsworth of wit, Stephen said, and no truant memory. He carried a memory in his wallet as he trudged to Romeville whistling *The girl I left behind me.* If the earthquake did not time it we should know where to place poor Wat, sitting in his form, the cry of hounds, the studded bridle and her blue windows. That memory, *Venus and Adonis,* lay in the bechamber of every light-of-love in London. Is Katharine the shrew ill-favoured? Hortensio calls her young and beautiful. Do you think the writer of *Antony and Cleopatra*, a passionate pilgrim, had his eyes in the back of his head that he chose the ugliest doxy in all Warwickshire to lie withal? Good: he left her and gained the world of men. But his boywomen are the women of a boy. Their life, thought, speech are lent them by males. He chose badly? He was chosen, it seems to me. If others have their will Ann hath a way. By cock, she was to blame. She put the comether on him, sweet and twentysix. The greyeyed goddess who bends over the boy Adonis, stooping to conquer, as prologue to the swelling act, is a boldfaced Stratford wench who tumbles in a cornfield a lover younger than herself.

And my turn? When?

Come!

– Ryefield, Mr Best said brightly, gladly, raising his new book, gladly brightly.

He murmured then with blond delight for all:

> *Between the acres of the rye*
> *These pretty countryfolk would lie.*

Paris: the wellpleased pleaser.

A tall figure in bearded homespun rose from shadow and unveiled its cooperative watch.

– I am afraid I am due at the *Homestead*.

Whither away? Exploitable ground.

– Are you going, John Eglinton's active eyebrows asked. Shall we see you at Moore's tonight? Piper is coming.

– Piper! Mr Best piped. Is Piper back?

Peter Piper pecked a peck of pick of peck of pickled pepper.

– I don't know if I can. Thursday. We have our meeting. If I can get away in time.

Yogibogeybox in Dawson chambers. *Isis Unveiled*. Their Pali book we tried to pawn. Crosslegged under an umbrel umbershoot he thrones an Aztec logos, functioning on astral levels, their oversoul, mahamahatma. The faithful hermetists await the light, ripe for chelaship, ringroundabout him. Louis H. Victory. T. Caulfield Irwin. Lotus ladies tend them i'the eyes, their pineal glands aglow. Filled with his god he thrones, Buddh under plantain. Gulfer of souls, engulfer. Hesouls, shesouls, shoals of souls. Engulfed with wailing creecries, whirled, whirling, they bewail.

In quintessential triviality
For years in this fleshcase a shesoul dwelt.

– They say we are to have a literary surprise, the quaker librarian said, friendly and earnest. Mr Russell, rumour has it, is gathering together a sheaf of our younger poets' verses. We are all looking forward anxiously.

Anxiously he glanced in the cone of lamplight where three faces, lighted, shone.

See this. Remember.

Stephen looked down on a wide headless caubeen, hung on his ashplant-handle over his knee. My casque and sword. Touch lightly with two index fingers. Aristotle's experiment. One or two? Necessity is that in virtue of which it is impossible that one can be otherwise. Argal, one hat is one hat.

Listen.

Young Colum and Starkey. George Roberts is doing the commercial part. Longworth will give it a good puff in the *Express*. O, will he? I liked Colum's *Drover*. Yes, I think he has that queer thing, genius. Do you think he has genius really? Yeats admired his line: *As in wild earth a Grecian vase*. Did he? I hope you'll be able to come tonight. Malachi Mulligan is coming too. Moore asked him to bring Haines. Did you hear Miss Mitchell's joke about Moore and Martyn? That Moore is Martyn's wild oats? Awfully clever, isn't it? They remind one of don Quixote and Sancho Panza. Our national epic has yet to be written, Dr Sigerson says. Moore is the man for it. A knight of the rueful countenance here in Dublin. With a saffron kilt? O'Neill Russell? O, yes, he must speak the grand old tongue. And his Dulcinea? James Stephens is doing some clever sketches. We are becoming important, it seems.

Cordelia. *Cordoglio*. Lir's loneliest daughter.

Nookshotten. Now your best French polish.

– Thank you very much, Mr Russell, Stephen said, rising. If you will be so kind as to give the letter to Mr Norman . . . . .

– O, yes. If he considers it important it will go in. We have so much correspondence.

– I understand, Stephen said. Thanks.

God ild you. The pigs' paper. Bullockbefriending.

– Synge has promised me an article for *Dana* too. Are we going to be read? I feel we are. The Gaelic league wants something in Irish. I hope you will come round tonight. Bring Starkey.

Stephen sat down.

The quaker librarian came from the leavetakers. Blushing his mask said:

– Mr Dedalus, your views are most illuminating.

He creaked to and fro, tiptoing up nearer heaven by the altitude of a chopine, and, covered by the noise of outgoing, said low:

– Is it your view, then, that she was not faithful to the poet?

Alarmed face asks me. Why did he come? Courtesy or an inward light?

– Where there is a reconciliation, Stephen said, there must have been first a sundering.

– Yes.

Christfox in leather trews, hiding, a runaway in blighted treeforks from hue and cry. Knowing no vixen, walking lonely in the chase. Women he won to him, tender people, a whore of Babylon, ladies of justices, bully tapsters' wives. Fox and geese. And in New place a slack dishonoured body that once was comely, once as sweet, as fresh as cinnamon, now her leaves falling, all, bare, frighted of the narrow grave and unforgiven.

– Yes. So you think . . .

The door closed behind the outgoer.

Rest suddenly possessed the discreet vaulted cell, rest of warm and brooding air.

A vestal's lamp.

Here he ponders things that were not: what Caesar would have lived to do had he believed the soothsayer: what might have been: possibilities of the possible as possible: things not known: what name Achilles bore when he lived among women.

Coffined thoughts around me, in mummycases, embalmed in spice of words. Thoth, god of libraries, a birdgod, moonycrowned. And I heard the voice of that Egyptian highpriest. *In painted chambers loaded with tilebooks.*

They are still. Once quick in the brains of men. Still: but an itch of death is in them, to tell me in my ear a maudlin tale, urge me to wreak their will.

– Certainly, John Eglinton mused, of all great men he is the most enigmatic. We know nothing but that he lived and suffered. Not even so much. Others abide our question. A shadow hangs over all the rest.

– But *Hamlet* is so personal, isn't it? Mr Best pleaded. I mean, a kind of private paper, don't you know, of his private life. I mean I don't care a button, don't you know, who is killed or who is guilty . . .

He rested an innocent book on the edge of the desk, smiling his defiance. His private papers in the original. *Ta an bad ar an tir. Taim imo shagart.* Put beurla on it, littlejohn.

Quoth littlejohn Eglinton:

– I was prepared for paradoxes from what Malachi Mulligan told us but I may as well warn you that if you want to shake my belief that Shakespeare is Hamlet you have a stern task before you.

Bear with me.

Stephen withstood the bane of miscreant eyes, glinting stern under wrinkled brows. A basilisk. *E quando vede l'uomo l'attosca.* Messer Brunetto, I thank thee for the word.

– As we, or mother Dana, weave and unweave our bodies, Stephen said, from day to day, their molecules shuttled to and fro, so does the artist weave and unweave his image. And as the mole on my right breast is where it was when I was born, though all my body has been woven of new stuff time after time, so through the ghost of the unquiet father the image of the unliving son looks forth. In the intense instant of imagination, when the mind, Shelley says, is a fading coal, that which I was is that which I am and that which in possibility I may come to be. So in the future, the sister of the past, I may see myself as I sit here now but by reflection from that which then I shall be.

Drummond of Hawthornden helped you at that stile.

– Yes, Mr Best said youngly, I feel Hamlet quite young, The bitterness might be from the father but the passages with Ophelia are surely from the son.

Has the wrong sow by the lug. He is in my father. I am in his son.

– That mole is the last to go, Stephen said, laughing.

John Eglinton made a nothing pleasing mow.

– If that were the birthmark of genius, he said, genius would be a drug in the market. The plays of Shakespeare's later years which Renan admired so much breathe another spirit.

– The spirit of reconciliation, the quaker librarian breathed.

– There can be no reconciliation, Stephen said, if there has not been a sundering.

Said that.

– If you want to know what are the events which cast their shadow over the hell of time of *King Lear, Othello, Hamlet, Troilus and Cressida,* look to see when and how the shadow lifts. What softens the heart of a man, shipwrecked in storms dire, Tried, like another Ulysses, Pericles, prince of Tyre?

Head, redconecapped, buffeted, brineblinded.

– A child, a girl placed in his arms, Marina.

– The leaning of sophists towards the bypaths of apocrypha is a constant quantity, John Eglinton detected. The highroads are dreary but they lead to the town.

Good Bacon: gone musty. Shakespeare Bacon's wild oats. Cypherjugglers going the highroads. Seekers on the great quest. What town, good masters? Mummed in names: A. E., eon: Magee, John Eglinton. East of the sun, west of the moon: *Tir na n-og*. Booted the twain and staved.

> *How many miles to Dublin?*
> *Three score and ten, sir.*
> *Will we be there by candlelight?*

– Mr Brandes accepts it, Stephen said, as the first play of the closing period.

– Does he? What does Mr Sidney Lee, or Mr Simon Lazarus, as some aver his name is, say of it?

– Marina, Stephen said, a child of storm, Miranda, a wonder, Perdita, that which was lost. What was lost is given back to him: his daughter's child. *My dearest wife*, Pericles says, *was like this maid*. Will any man love the daughter if he has not loved the mother?

– The art of being a grandfather, Mr Best gan murmur. *L'art d'être grand . . .*

– His own image to a man with that queer thing genius is the standard of all experience, material and moral. Such an appeal will touch him. The images of other males of his blood will repel him. He will see in them grotesque attempts of nature to foretell or repeat himself.

The benign forehead of the quaker librarian enkindled rosily with hope.

– I hope Mr Dedalus will work out his theory for the enlightenment of the public. And we ought to mention another Irish commentator, Mr George Bernard Shaw. Nor should we forget Mr Frank Harris. His articles on Shakespeare in the *Saturday Review* were surely brilliant. Oddly enough he too draws for us an unhappy relation with the dark lady of the sonnets. The favoured rival is William Herbert, earl of Pembroke. I own that if the poet must be rejected, such a rejection would seem more in harmony with– what shall I say?–our notions of what ought not to have been.

Felicitously he ceased and held a meek head among them, auk's egg, prize of their fray.

He thous and thees her with grave husbandwords. Dost love, Miriam? Dost love thy man?

– That may be too, Stephen said. There is a saying of Goethe's which Mr Magee likes to quote. Beware of what you wish for in youth because you will get it in middle life. Why does he send to one who is a *buonaroba*, a bay where all men ride, a maid of honour with a scandalous girlhood, a lordling to woo for him? He was himself a lord of language and had made himself a coistrel gentleman and had written *Romeo and Juliet*. Why? Belief in himself has been untimely killed. He was overborne in a cornfield first (ryefield, I should say) and he will never be a victor in his own eyes after nor play victoriously the game of laugh and lie down. Assumed dongiovannism will not save him. No later undoing will undo the first undoing. The tusk of the boar has wounded him there where love lies ableeding. If the shrew is worsted yet there remains to her woman's invisible weapon. There is, I feel in the words, some goad of the flesh driving him into a new passion, a darker shadow of the first, darkening even his own understanding of himself. A like fate awaits him and the two rages commingle in a whirlpool.

They list. And in the porches of their ears I pour.

– The soul has been before stricken mortally, a poison poured in the porch of a sleeping ear. But those who are done to death in sleep cannot know the manner of their quell unless their Creator endow their souls with that knowledge in the life to come. The poisoning and the beast with two backs that urged it king Hamlet's ghost could not know of were he not endowed with knowledge by his creator. That is why the speech (his lean unlovely English) is always turned elsewhere, backward. Ravisher and ravished, what he would but would not, go with him from Lucrece's bluecircled ivory globes to Imogen's breast, bare, with its mole cinquespotted. He goes back, weary of the creation he has piled up to hide him from himself, an old dog licking an old sore. But, because loss is his gain, he passes on towards eternity in undiminished personality, untaught by the wisdom he has written or by the laws he has revealed. His beaver is up. He is a ghost, a shadow now, the wind by Elsinore's rocks or what you will, the sea's voice, a voice heard only in the heart of him who is the substance of his shadow, the son consubstantial with the father.

– Amen! responded from the doorway.

Hast thou found me, O mine enemy?

Entr'acte.

A ribald face, sullen as a dean's, Buck Mulligan came forwards then blithe in motley, towards the greeting of their smiles. My telegram.

– You were speaking of the gaseous vertebrate, if I mistake not? he asked of Stephen.

Primrosevested he greeted gaily with his doffed Panama as with a bauble.

They make him welcome. *Was Du verlachst wirst Du noch dienen.*

Brood of mockers: Photius, pseudomalachi, Johann Most.

He Who Himself begot, middler the Holy Ghost, and Himself sent Himself, Agenbuyer, between Himself and others, Who, put upon by His fiends, stripped and whipped, was nailed like bat to barndoor, starved on crosstree, Who let Him bury, stood up, harrowed hell, fared into heaven and there these nineteen hundred years sitteth on the right hand of His Own Self but yet shall come in the latter day to doom the quick and dead when all the quick shall be dead already.

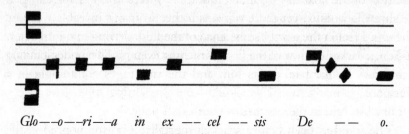

Glo——o——ri——a   in   ex —— cel —— sis   De   —— o.

He lifts hands. Veils fall. O, flowers! Bells with bells with bells aquiring.

– Yes, indeed, the quaker librarian said. A most instructive discussion. Mr Mulligan, I'll be bound, has his theory too of the play and of Shakespeare. All sides of life should be represented.

He smiled on all sides equally.

Buck Mulligan thought, puzzled:

– Shakespeare? he said. I seem to know the name.

A flying sunny smile rayed in his loose features.

– To be sure, he said, remembering brightly. The chap that writes like Synge.

Mr Best turned to him:

– Haines missed you, he said. Did you meet him? He'll see you after at the D. B. C. He's gone to Gill's to buy Hyde's *Lovesongs of Connacht*.

– I came through the museum, Buck Mulligan said. Was he here?

– The bard's fellowcountrymen, John Eglinton answered, are rather tired perhaps of our brilliancies of theorising. I hear that an actress played Hamlet for the fourhundredandeighth time last night in Dublin. Vining held that the prince was a woman. Has no-one made him out to be an Irishman? Judge Barton, I believe, is searching for some clues. He swears (His Highness not His Lordship) by saint Patrick.

– The most brilliant of all is that story of Wilde's, Mr Best said, lifting his brilliant notebook. That *Portrait of Mr W. H.* where he proves that the sonnets were written by a Willie Hughes, a man all hues.

– For Willie Hughes, is it not? the quaker librarian asked.

Or Hughie Wills. Mr William Himself. W. H.: who am I?

– I mean, for Willie Hughes, Mr Best said, amending his gloss easily. Of course it's all paradox, don't you know, Hughes and hews and hues the colour, but it's so typical the way he works it out. It's the very essence of Wilde, don't you know. The light touch.

His glance touched their faces lightly as he smiled, a blond ephebe. Tame essence of Wilde.

You're darned witty. Three drams of usquebaugh you drank with Dan Deasy's ducats.

How much did I spend? O, a few shillings.

For a plump of pressmen. Humour wet and dry.

Wit. You would give your five wits for youth's proud livery he pranks in. Lineaments of gratified desire.

There be many mo. Take her for me. In pairing time. Jove, a cool ruttime send them. Yea, turtledove her.

Eve. Naked wheatbellied sin. A snake coils her, fang in's kiss.

– Do you think it is only a paradox, the quaker librarian was asking. The mocker is never taken seriously when he is most serious.

They talked seriously of mocker's seriousness.

Buck Mulligan's again heavy face eyed Stephen awhile. Then, his head wagging, he came near, drew a folded telegram from his pocket. His mobile lips read, smiling with new delight.

– Telegram! he said. Wonderful inspiration! Telegram! A papal bull!

He sat on a corner of the unlit desk, reading aloud joyfully:

– *The sentimentalist is he who would enjoy without incurring the immense debtorship for a thing done.* Signed: Dedalus. Where did you launch it from? The kips? No. College Green. Have you drunk the four quid? The aunt is going to call on your unsubstantial father. Telegram! Malachi Mulligan, the Ship, lower Abbey street. O, you peerless mummer! O, you priestified kinchite!

Joyfully he thrust message and envelope into a pocket but keened in querulous brogue:

– It's what I'm telling you, mister honey, it's queer and sick we were, Haines and myself, the time himself brought it in. 'Twas murmur we did for a gallus potion would rouse a friar, I'm thinking, and he limp with leching. And we one hour and two hours and three hours in Connery's sitting civil waiting for pints apiece.

He wailed:

– And we to be there, mavrone, and you to be unbeknownst sending us your conglomerations the way we to have our tongues out a yard long like the drouthy clerics do be fainting for a pussful.

Stephen laughed.

Quickly, warningfully Buck Mulligan bent down:

– The tramper Synge is looking for you, he said, to murder you. He heard you pissed on his halldoor in Glasthule. He's out in pampooties to murder you.

– Me! Stephen exclaimed. That was your contribution to literature.

Buck Mulligan gleefully bent back, laughing to the dark eavesdropping ceiling.

– Murder you! he laughed.

Harsh gargoyle face that warred against me over our mess of hash of lights in rue Saint-André-des-Arts. In words of words for words, palabras. Oisin with Patrick. Faunman he met in Clamart woods, brandishing a winebottle. *C'est vendredi saint!* Murthering Irish. His image, wandering, he met. I mine. I met a fool i' the forest.

– Mr Lyster, an attendant said from the door ajar.

– . . . in which everyone can find his own. So Mr Justice Madden in his *Diary of Master William Silence* has found the hunting terms . . . Yes? What is it?

– There's a gentleman here, sir, the attendant said, coming forward and offering a card. From the *Freeman*. He wants to see the files of the *Kilkenny People* for last year.

– Certainly, certainly, certainly. Is the gentleman? . . .

He took the eager card, glanced, not saw, laid down, unglanced, looked, asked, creaked, asked:

– Is he? . . . O, there!

Brisk in a galliard he was off and out. In the daylit corridor he talked with voluble pains of zeal, in duty bound, most fair, most kind, most honest broadbrim.

– This gentleman? *Freeman's Journal? Kilkenny People?* To be sure. Good day, sir. *Kilkenny* . . . We have certainly . . .

A patient silhouette waited, listening.

– All the leading provincial . . . *Northern Whig, Cork Examiner, Enniscorthy Guardian,* 1903 . . . Will you please? . . . Evans, conduct this gentleman . . . If you just follow the atten . . . Or please allow me . . . This way . . . Please, sir . . .

Voluble, dutiful, he led the way to all the provincial papers, a bowing dark figure following his hasty heels.

The door closed.

– The sheeny! Buck Mulligan cried.

He jumped up and snatched the card.

– What's his name? Ikey Moses? Bloom.

He rattled on.

– Jehovah, collector of prepuces, is no more. I found him over in the museum when I went to hail the foamborn Aphrodite. The Greek mouth that has never been twisted in prayer. Every day we must do homage to her. *Life of life, thy lips enkindle.*

Suddenly he turned to Stephen:

– He knows you. He knows your old fellow. O, I fear me, he is Greeker than the Greeks. His pale Galilean eyes were upon her mesial groove. Venus Kallipyge. O, the thunder of those loins! *The god pursuing the maiden hid.*

– We want to hear more, John Eglinton decided with Mr Best's approval. We begin to be interested in Mrs S. Till now we had thought of her, if at all, as a patient Griselda, a Penelope stayathome.

– Antisthenes, pupil of Gorgias, Stephen said, took the palm of beauty from Kyrios Menelaus' brooddam, Argive Helen, the wooden mare of Troy in whom a score of heroes slept, and handed it to poor Penelope. Twenty years he lived in London and, during part of that time, he drew a salary equal to that of the lord chancellor of Ireland. His life was rich. His art, more than the art of feudalism, as Walt Whitman called it, is the art of surfeit. Hot herringpies, green mugs of sack, honeysauces, sugar of roses, marchpane, gooseberried pigeons, ringocandies. Sir Walter Raleigh, when they arrested him, had half a million francs on his back including a pair of fancy stays. The gombeen woman Eliza Tudor had underlinen enough to vie with her of Sheba. Twenty years he dallied there between conjugial love and its chaste delights and scortatory love and its foul pleasures. You know Manningham's story of the burgher's wife who bade Dick Burbage to her bed after she had seen him in *Richard III* and how Shakespeare, overhearing, without more ado about nothing, took the cow by the horns and, when Burbage came knocking at the gate, answered from the capon's blankets: *William the conqueror came before Richard III.* And the gay lakin, mistress Fitton, mount and cry O, and his dainty birdsnies, lady Penelope Rich, a clean quality woman is suited for a player, and the punks of the bankside, a penny a time.

Cours-la-Reine. *Encore vingt sous. Nous ferons de petites cochonneries. Minette? Tu veux?*

– The height of fine society. And sir William Davenant of Oxford's mother with her cup of canary for every cockcanary.

Buck Mulligan, his pious eyes upturned, prayed:

– Blessed Margaret Mary Anycock!

– And Harry of six wives' daughter and other lady friends from neighbour seats, as Lawn Tennyson, gentleman poet, sings. But all those twenty years what do you suppose poor Penelope in Stratford was doing behind the diamond panes?

Do and do. Thing done. In a rosery of Fetter Lane of Gerard, herbalist, he walks, greyedauburn. An azured harebell like her veins. Lids of Juno's eyes, violets. He walks. One life is all. One body. Do. But do. Afar, in a reek of lust and squalor, hands are laid on whiteness.

Buck Mulligan rapped John Eglinton's desk sharply.

– Whom do you suspect? he challenged.

– Say that he is the spurned lover in the sonnets. Once spurned twice spurned. But the court wanton spurned him for a lord, his dearmylove.

Love that dare not speak its name.

– As an Englishman, you mean, John sturdy Eglinton put in, he loved a lord.

Old wall where sudden lizards flash. At Charenton I watched them.

– It seems so, Stephen said, when he wants to do for him, and for all other and singular uneared wombs, the holy office an ostler does for the stallion. Maybe, like Socrates, he had a midwife to mother as he had a shrew to wife. But she, the giglot wanton, did not break a bedvow. Two deeds are rank in that ghost's mind: a broken vow and the dullbrained yokel on whom her favour has declined, deceased husband's brother. Sweet Ann I take it, was hot in the blood. Once a wooer twice a wooer.

Stephen turned boldly in his chair.

– The burden of proof is with you not with me, he said, frowning. If you deny that in the fifth scene of *Hamlet* he has branded her with infamy, tell me why there is no mention of her during the thirtyfour years between the day she married him and the day she buried him. All those women saw their men down and under: Mary, her goodman John, Ann, her poor dear Willun, when he went and died on her, raging that he was the first to go, Joan, her four brothers, Judith, her husband and all her sons, Susan, her husband too, while Susan's daughter, Elizabeth, to use granddaddy's words, wed her second, having killed her first.

O yes, mention there is. In the years when he was living richly in royal London to pay a debt she had to borrow forty shillings from her father's shepherd. Explain you then. Explain the swansong too wherein he has commended her to posterity.

He faced their silence.

To whom thus Eglinton:

You mean the will.

That has been explained, I believe, by jurists.

She was entitled to her widow's dower

At common law. His legal knowledge was great

Our judges tell us.
          Him Satan fleers,
Mocker:
          And therefore he left out her name
From the first draft but he did not leave out
The presents for his granddaughter, for his daughters,
For his sister, for his old cronies in Stratford
And in London. And therefore when he was urged,
As I believe, to name her
He left her his
Secondbest
Bed.
                    Punkt

Leftherhis
Secondbest
Bestabed
Secabest
Leftabed.

Woa!

– Pretty countryfolk had few chattels then, John Eglinton observed, as they have still if our peasant plays are true to type.

– He was a rich countrygentleman, Stephen said, with a coat of arms and landed estate at Stratford and a house in Ireland yard, a capitalist shareholder, a bill promoter, a tithefarmer. Why did he not leave her his best bed if he wished her to snore away the rest of her nights in peace?

– It is clear that there were two beds, a best and a secondbest, Mr Secondbest Best said finely.

– *Separatio a mensa et a thalamo*, bettered Buck Mulligan and was smiled on.

– Antiquity mentions famous beds, Second Eglinton puckered, bed-smiling. Let me think.

– Antiquity mentions that Stagyrite schoolurchin and bald heathen sage, Stephen said, who when dying in exile frees and endows his slaves, pays tribute to his elders, wills to be laid in earth near the bones of his dead wife and bids his friends be kind to an old mistress (don't forget Nell Gwynn Herpyllis) and let her live in his villa.

– Do you mean he died so? Mr Best asked with slight concern. I mean . . .

– He died dead drunk, Buck Mulligan capped. A quart of ale is a dish for a king. O, I must tell you what Dowden said!

– What? asked Besteglinton.

William Shakespeare and company, limited. The people's William. For terms apply: E. Dowden, Highfield house . . .

– Lovely! Buck Mulligan suspired amorously. I asked him what he thought of the charge of pederasty brought against the bard. He lifted his hands and said: *All we can say is that life ran very high in those days*. Lovely!

Catamite.

– The sense of beauty leads us astray, said beautifulinsadness Best to ugling Eglinton.

Steadfast John replied severe:

– The doctor can tell us what those words mean. You cannot eat your cake and have it.

Sayest thou so? Will they wrest from us, from me the palm of beauty?

– And the sense of property, Stephen said. He drew Shylock out of his own long pocket. The son of a maltjobber and moneylender he was himself a cornjobber and moneylender with ten tods of corn hoarded in the famine riots. His borrowers are no doubt those divers of worship mentioned by Chettle Falstaff who reported his uprightness of dealing. He sued a fellow-player for the price of a few bags of malt and exacted his pound of flesh in interest for every money lent. How else could Aubrey's ostler and callboy get rich quick? All events brought grist to his mill. Shylock chimes with the jewbaiting that followed the hanging and quartering of the queen's leech Lopez, his jew's heart being plucked forth while the sheeny was yet alive: *Hamlet* and *Macbeth* with the coming to the throne of a Scotch philoso-phaster with a turn for witchroasting. The lost armada is his jeer in *Love's Labour Lost*. His pageants, the histories, sail fullbellied on a tide of Mafeking enthusiasm. Warwickshire jesuits are tried and we have a porter's theory of equivocation. The *Sea Venture* comes home from Bermudas and the play Renan admired is written with Patsy Caliban, our American cousin. The sugared sonnets follow Sidney's. As for fay Elizabeth, otherwise carroty Bess, the gross virgin who inspired *The Merry Wives of Windsor*, let some meinherr from Almany grope his life long for deephid meanings in the depth of the buckbasket.

I think you're getting on very nicely. Just mix up a mixture of theolo-logicophilolological. *Mingo, minxi, mictum, mingere.*

– Prove that he was a jew, John Eglinton dared, expectantly. Your dean of studies holds he was a holy Roman.

Sufflaminandus sum.

– He was made in Germany, Stephen replied, as the champion French polisher of Italian scandals.

– A myriadminded man, Mr Best reminded. Coleridge called him myriadminded.

Amplius. In societate humana hoc est maxime necessarium ut sit amicitia inter multos.

– Saint Thomas, Stephen began . . .

– *Ora pro nobis*, Monk Mulligan groaned, sinking to a chair.

There he keened a wailing rune.

– *Pogue mahone! Acushla machree!* It's destroyed we are from this day! It's destroyed we are surely!

All smiled their smiles.

– Saint Thomas, Stephen, smiling, said, whose gorbellied works I enjoy reading in the original, writing of incest from a standpoint different from that of the new Viennese school Mr Magee spoke of, likens it in his wise and curious way to an avarice of the emotions. He means that the love so given to one near in blood is covetously withheld from some stranger who, it may be, hungers for it. Jews, whom christians tax with avarice, are of all races the most given to intermarriage. Accusations are made in anger. The christian laws which built up the hoards of the jews (for whom, as for the lollards, storm was shelter) bound their affections too with hoops of steel. Whether these be sins or virtues old Nobodaddy will tell us at doomsday leet. But a man who holds so tightly to what he calls his rights over what he calls his debts will hold tightly also to what he calls his rights over her whom he calls his wife. No sir smile neighbour shall covet his ox or his wife or his manservant or his maidservant or his jackass.

– Or his jennyass, Buck Mulligan antiphoned.

– Gentle Will is being roughly handled, gentle Mr Best said gently.

– Which Will? gagged sweetly Buck Mulligan. We are getting mixed.

– The will to live, John Eglinton philosophised, for poor Ann, Will's widow, is the will to die.

– *Requiescat!* Stephen prayed.

> *What of all the will to do?*
> *It has vanished long ago . . .*

– She lies laid out in stark stiffness in that secondbest bed, the mobled queen, even though you prove that a bed in those days was as rare as a motorcar is now and that its carvings were the wonder of seven parishes. In old age she takes up with gospellers (one stayed at New Place and drank a quart of sack the town paid for but in which bed he slept it skills not to ask) and heard she had a soul. She read or had read to her his chapbooks preferring them to the *Merry Wives* and, loosing her nightly waters on the jordan, she thought over *Hooks and Eyes for Believers' Breeches* and *The most Spiritual Snuffbox to Make the Most Devout Souls Sneeze*. Venus had twisted her lips in prayer. Agenbite of inwit: remorse of conscience. It is an age of exhausted whoredom groping for its god.

– History shows that to be true, *inquit Eglintonus Chronolologos*. The ages succeed one another. But we have it on high authority that a man's worst enemies shall be those of his own house and family. I feel that Russell is right. What do we care for his wife and father? I should say that only family poets have family lives. Falstaff was not a family man. I feel that the fat knight is his supreme creation.

Lean, he lay back. Shy, deny thy kindred, the unco guid. Shy supping with the godless, he sneaks the cup. A sire in Ultonian Antrim bade it him. Visits him here on quarter days. Mr Magee, sir, there's a gentleman to see you. Me? Says he's your father, sir. Give me my Wordsworth. Enter Magee Mor Matthew, a rugged rough rugheaded kern, in strossers with a buttoned codpiece, his nether stocks bemired with clauber of ten forests, a wand of wilding in his hand.

Your own? He knows your old fellow. The widower.

Hurrying to her squalid deathlair from gay Paris on the quayside I touched his hand. The voice, new warmth, speaking. Dr Bob Kenny is attending her. The eyes that wish me well. But do not know me.

– A father, Stephen said, battling against hopelessness, is a necessary evil. He wrote the play in the months that followed his father's death. If you hold that he, a greying man with two marriageable daughters, with thirtyfive years of life, *nel mezzo del cammin di nostra vita*, with fifty of experience, is the beardless undergraduate from Wittenberg then you must hold that his seventyyear old mother is the lustful queen. No. The corpse of John Shakespeare does not walk the night. From hour to hour it rots and rots. He rests, disarmed of fatherhood, having devised that mystical estate upon his son. Boccaccio's Calandrino was the first and last man who felt himself with child. Fatherhood, in the sense of conscious begetting, is unknown to man. It is a mystical estate, an apostolic succession, from only begetter to only begotten. On that mystery and not on the madonna which the cunning Italian intellect flung to the mob of Europe the church is founded and founded irremovably because founded, like the world, macro- and microcosm, upon the void. Upon incertitude, upon unlikelihood. *Amor matris*, subjective and objective genitive, may be the only true thing in life. Paternity may be a legal fiction. Who is the father of any son that any son should love him or he any son?

What the hell are you driving at?

I know. Shut up. Blast you! I have reasons.

Amplius. Adhuc. Iterum. Postea.

Are you condemned to do this?

– They are sundered by a bodily shame so steadfast that the criminal annals of the world, stained with all other incests and bestialities hardly record its breach. Sons with mothers, sires with daughters, lesbic sisters, loves that dare not speak their name, nephews with grandmothers, jailbirds with keyholes, queens with prize bulls. The son unborn mars beauty: born, he brings pain, divides affection, increases care. He is a male: his growth is his father's decline, his youth his father's envy, his friend his father's enemy.

In rue Monsieur-le-Prince I thought it.

– What links them in nature? An instant of blind rut.

Am I father? If I were?

Shrunken uncertain hand.

– Sabellius, the African, subtlest heresiarch of all the beasts of the field, held that the Father was Himself His Own Son. The bulldog of Aquin, with whom no word shall be impossible, refutes him. Well: if the father who has not a son be not a father can the son who has not a father be a son? When Rutlandbaconsouthamptonshakespeare or another poet of the same name in the comedy of errors wrote *Hamlet* he was not the father of his own son merely but, being no more a son, he was and felt himself the father of all his race, the father of his own grandfather, the father of his unborn grandson who, by the same token, never was born for nature, as Mr Magee understands her, abhors perfection.

Eglintoneyes, quick with pleasure, looked up shybrightly. Gladly glancing, a merry puritan, through the twisted eglantine.

Flatter. Rarely. But flatter.

– Himself his own father, Sonmulligan told himself. Wait. I am big with child. I have an unborn child in my brain. Pallas Athena! A play! The play's the thing! Let me parturiate!

He clasped his paunchbrow with both birthaiding hands.

– As for his family, Stephen said, his mother's name lives in the forest of Arden. Her death brought from him the scene with Volumnia in *Coriolanus*. His boyson's death is the deathscene of young Arthur in *King John*. Hamlet, the black prince, is Hamnet Shakespeare. Who the girls in *The Tempest*, in *Pericles*, in *Winter's Tale* are we know. Who Cleopatra, fleshpot of Egypt, and Cressid and Venus are we may guess. But there is another member of his family who is recorded.

– The plot thickens, John Eglinton said.

The quaker librarian, quaking, tiptoed in, quake, his mask, quake, with haste, quake, quack.

Door closed. Cell. Day.

They list. Three. They.

I you he they.

Come, mess.

STEPHEN

He had three brothers, Gilbert, Edmund, Richard. Gilbert in his old age told some cavaliers he got a pass for nowt from Maister Gatherer one time mass he did and he seen his brud Maister Wull the playwriter up in Lunnon in a wrastling play wud a man on's back. The playhouse sausage filled Gilbert's soul. He is nowhere: but an Edmund and a Richard are recorded in the works of sweet William.

MAGEEGLINJOHN

Names! What's in a name?

BEST

That is my name, Richard, don't you know. I hope you are going to say a good word for Richard, don't you know, for my sake.   (*Laughter.*)

BUCK MULLIGAN

(*Piano, diminuendo.*)
> Then outspoke medical Dick
> To his comrade medical Davy . . .

STEPHEN

In his trinity of black Wills, the villain shakebags, Iago, Richard Crookback, Edmund in *King Lear*, two bear the wicked uncles' names. Nay, that last play was written or being written while his brother Edmund lay dying in Southwark.

BEST

I hope Edmund is going to catch it. I don't want Richard, my name . . .
          (*Laughter.*)

QUAKERLYSTER

(*A tempo.*) But he that filches from me my good name . . .

STEPHEN

(*Stringendo.*) He has hidden his own name, a fair name, William, in the plays, a super here, a clown there, as a painter of old Italy set his face in a

dark corner of his canvas. He has revealed it in the sonnets where there is
Will in overplus. Like John O'Gaunt his name is dear to him, as dear as the
coat of arms he toadied for, on a bend sable a spear or steeled argent,
honorificabilitudinitatibus, dearer than his glory of greatest shakescene in
the country. What's in a name? That is what we ask ourselves in childhood
when we write the name that we are told is ours. A star, a daystar, a firedrake
rose at his birth. It shone by day in the heavens alone, brighter than Venus
in the night, and by night it shone over delta in Cassiopeia, the recumbent
constellation which is the signature of his initial among the stars. His eyes
watched it, lowlying on the horizon, eastward of the bear, as he walked by
the slumberous summer fields at midnight, returning from Shottery and
from her arms.

Both satisfied. I too.

Don't tell them he was nine years old when it was quenched.

And from her arms.

Wait to be wooed and won. Ay, meacock. Who will woo you?

Read the skies. *Autontimerumenos. Bous Stephanoumenos.* Where's your
configuration? Stephen, Stephen, cut the bread even. S. D: *sua donna. Già:
di lui. Gelindo risolve di non amar S. D.*

– What is that, Mr Dedalus? the quaker librarian asked. Was it a celestial
phenomenon?

– A star by night, Stephen said, a pillar of the cloud by day.

What more's to speak?

Stephen looked on his hat, his stick, his boots.

Stephanos, my crown. My sword. His boots are spoiling the shape of my
feet. Buy a pair. Holes in my socks. Handkerchief too.

– You make good use of the name, John Eglinton allowed. Your own
name is strange enough. I suppose it explains your fantastical humour.

Me, Magee and Mulligan.

Fabulous artificer, the hawklike man. You flew. Whereto? Newhaven-
Dieppe, steerage passenger. Paris and back. Lapwing. Icarus. *Pater, ait.*
Seabedabbled, fallen, weltering. Lapwing you are. Lapwing he.

Mr Best eagerquietly lifted his book to say:

– That's very interesting because that brother motive, don't you know,
we find also in the old Irish myths. Just what you say. The three brothers
Shakespeare. In Grimm too, don't you know, the fairytales. The third
brother that marries the sleeping beauty and wins the best prize.

Best of Best brothers. Good, better, best.

The quaker librarian springhalted near.

– I should like to know, he said, which brother you . . . I understand you to suggest there was misconduct with one of the brothers . . . But perhaps I am anticipating?

He caught himself in the act: looked at all: refrained.

An attendant from the doorway called:

– Mr Lyster! Father Dineen wants . . .

– O! Father Dineen! Directly.

Swiftly rectly creaking rectly rectly he was rectly gone.

John Eglinton touched the foil.

– Come, he said. Let us hear what you have to say of Richard and Edmund. You kept them for the last, didn't you?

– In asking you to remember those two noble kinsmen nuncle Richie and nuncle Edmund, Stephen answered, I feel I am asking too much perhaps. A brother is as easily forgotten as an umbrella.

Lapwing.

Where is your brother? Apothecaries' hall. My whetstone. Him, then Cranly, Mulligan: now these. Speech, speech. But act. Act speech. They mock to try you. Act. Be acted on.

Lapwing.

I am tired of my voice, the voice of Esau. My kingdom for a drink.

On.

– You will say those names were already in the chronicles from which he took the stuff of his plays. Why did he take them rather than others? Richard, a whoreson crookback, misbegotten, makes love to a widowed Ann (what's in a name?), woos and wins her, a whoreson merry widow. Richard the conqueror, third brother, came after William the conquered. The other four acts of that play hang limply from that first. Of all his kings Richard is the only king unshielded by Shakespeare's reverence, the angel of the world. Why is the underplot of *King Lear* in which Edmund figures lifted out of Sidney's *Arcadia* and spatchcocked on to a Celtic legend older than history?

– That was Will's way, John Eglinton defended. We should not now combine a Norse saga with an excerpt from a novel by George Meredith. *Que voulez-vous?* Moore would say. He puts Bohemia on the seacoast and makes Ulysses quote Aristotle.

– Why? Stephen answered himself. Because the theme of the false or the usurping or the adulterous brother or all three in one is to Shakespeare, what the poor is not, always with him. The note of banishment, banishment from the heart, banishment from home, sounds uninterruptedly from *The Two Gentlemen of Verona* onward till Prospero breaks his staff, buries it certain fathoms in the earth and drowns his book. It doubles itself in the middle of his life, reflects itself in another, repeats itself, protasis, epitasis, catastasis, catastrophe. It repeats itself again when he is near the grave, when his married daughter Susan, chip of the old block, is accused of adultery. But it was the original sin that darkened his understanding, weakened his will and left in him a strong inclination to evil. The words are those of my lords bishops of Maynooth: an original sin and, like original sin, committed by another in whose sin he too has sinned. It is between the lines of his last written words, it is petrified on his tombstone under which her four bones are not to be laid. Age has not withered it. Beauty and peace have not done it away. It is in infinite variety everywhere in the world he has created, in *Much Ado about Nothing*, twice in *As you like It*, in *The Tempest*, in *Hamlet*, in *Measure for Measure*, and in all the other plays which I have not read.

He laughed to free his mind from his mind's bondage.

Judge Eglinton summed up.

– The truth is midway, he affirmed. He is the ghost and the prince. He is all in all.

– He is, Stephen said. The boy of act one is the mature man of act five. All in all. In *Cymbeline*, in *Othello* he is bawd and cuckold. He acts and is acted on. Lover of an ideal or a perversion, like José he kills the real Carmen. His unremitting intellect is the hornmad Iago ceaselessly willing that the moor in him shall suffer.

– Cuckoo! Cuckoo! Cuck Mulligan clucked lewdly. O word of fear!

Dark dome received, reverbed.

– And what a character is Iago! undaunted John Eglinton exclaimed. When all is said Dumas *fils* (or is it Dumas *père?*) is right. After God Shakespeare has created most.

– Man delights him not nor woman neither, Stephen said. He returns after a life of absence to that spot of earth where he was born, where he has always been, man and boy, a silent witness and there, his journey of life ended, he plants his mulberrytree in the earth. Then dies. The motion is ended. Gravediggers bury Hamlet *père* and Hamlet *fils*. A king and a prince at last in death, with incidental music. And, what though murdered and betrayed, bewept by all frail tender hearts for, Dane or Dubliner, sorrow for the dead is the only husband from whom they refuse to be divorced. If you like the epilogue look long on it: prosperous Prospero, the good man rewarded, Lizzie, grandpa's lump of love, and nuncle Richie, the bad man taken off by poetic justice to the place where the bad niggers go. Strong curtain. He found in the world without as actual what was in his world within as possible. Maeterlinck says: *If Socrates leave his house today he will find the sage seated on his doorstep. If Judas go forth tonight it is to Judas his steps will tend.* Every life is many days, day after day. We walk through ourselves, meeting robbers, ghosts, giants, old men, young men, wives, widows, brothers-in-love. But always meeting ourselves. The playwright who wrote the folio of this world and wrote it badly (He gave us light first and the sun two days later), the lord of things as they are whom the most Roman of catholics call *dio boia*, hangman god, is doubtless all in all in all of us, ostler and butcher, and would be bawd and cuckold too but that in the economy of heaven, foretold by Hamlet, there are no more marriages, glorified man, an androgynous angel, being a wife unto himself.

– *Eureka!* Buck Mulligan cried. *Eureka!*

Suddenly happied he jumped up and reached in a stride John Eglinton's desk.

– May I? he said. The Lord has spoken to Malachi.

He began to scribble on a slip of paper.

Take some slips from the counter going out.

– Those who are married, Mr Best, douce herald, said, all save one, shall live. The rest shall keep as they are.

He laughed, unmarried, at Eglinton Johannes, of arts a bachelor.

Unwed, unfancied, ware of wiles, they fingerponder nightly each his variorum edition of *The Taming of the Shrew.*

– You are a delusion, said roundly John Eglinton to Stephen. You have brought us all this way to show us a French triangle. Do you believe your own theory?

– No, Stephen said promptly.

– Are you going to write it? Mr Best asked. You ought to make it a dialogue, don't you know, like the Platonic dialogues Wilde wrote.

John Eclecticon doubly smiled.

– Well, in that case, he said, I don't see why you should expect payment for it since you don't believe it yourself. Dowden believes there is some mystery in *Hamlet* but will say no more. Herr Bleibtreu, the man Piper met in Berlin, who is working up that Rutland theory, believes that the secret is hidden in the Stratford monument. He is going to visit the present duke, Piper says, and prove to him that his ancestor wrote the plays. It will come as a surprise to his grace. But he believes his theory.

I believe, O Lord, help my unbelief. That is, help me to believe or help me to unbelieve? Who helps to believe? *Egomen.* Who to unbelieve? Other chap.

– You are the only contributor to *Dana* who asks for pieces of silver. Then I don't know about the next number. Fred Ryan wants space for an article on economics.

Fraidrine. Two pieces of silver he lent me. Tide you over. Economics.

– For a guinea, Stephen said, you can publish this interview.

Buck Mulligan stood up from his laughing scribbling, laughing: and then gravely said, honeying malice:

– I called upon the bard Kinch at his summer residence in upper Mecklenburgh street and found him deep in the study of the *Summa contra Gentiles* in the company of two gonorrheal ladies, Fresh Nelly and Rosalie, the coalquay whore.

He broke away.

– Come, Kinch. Come, wandering Ængus of the birds.

Come, Kinch, you have eaten all we left. Ay. I will serve you your orts and offals.

Stephen rose.

Life is many days. This will end.

– We shall see you tonight, John Eglinton said. *Notre ami* Moore says Malachi Mulligan must be there.

Buck Mulligan flaunted his slip and panama.

– Monsieur Moore, he said, lecturer on French letters to the youth of Ireland. I'll be there. Come, Kinch, the bards must drink. Can you walk straight?

Laughing he . . .

Swill till eleven. Irish nights entertainment.

Lubber . . .

Stephen followed a lubber . . .

One day in the national library we had a discussion. Shakes. After his lub back I followed. I gall his kibe.

Stephen, greeting, then all amort, followed a lubber jester, a wellkempt head, newbarbered, out of the vaulted cell into a shattering daylight of no thoughts.

What have I learned? Of them? Of me?

Walk like Haines now.

The constant readers' room. In the readers' book Cashel Boyle O'Connor Fitzmaurice Tisdall Farrell parafes his polysyllables. Item: was Hamlet mad? The quaker's pate godlily with a priesteen in booktalk.

– O please do, sir . . . I shall be most pleased . . .

Amused Buck Mulligan mused in pleasant murmur with himself, self-nodding:

– A pleased bottom.

The turnstile.

Is that? . . . Blueribboned hat . . . Idly writing . . . What? Looked? . . .

The curving balustrade; smoothsliding Mincius.

Puck Mulligan, panamahelmeted, went step by step, iambing, trolling:

> *John Eglinton, my jo, John.*
> *Why won't you wed a wife?*

He sputtered to the air:

– O, the chinless Chinaman! Chin Chon Eg Lin Ton. We went over to their playbox, Haines and I, the plumbers' hall. Our players are creating a new art for Europe like the Greeks or M. Maeterlinck. Abbey theatre! I smell the public sweat of monks.

He spat blank.

Forgot: any more than he forgot the whipping lousy Lucy gave him. And left the *femme de trente ans*. And why no other children born? And his first child a girl?

Afterwit. Go back.

The dour recluse still there (he has his cake) and the douce youngling, minion of pleasure, Phedo's toyable fair hair.

Eh . . . I just eh . . . wanted . . . I forgot . . . he . . .

– Longworth and M'Curdy Atkinson were there . . .

Puck Mulligan footed featly, trilling:

> *I hardly hear the purlieu cry*
> *Or a Tommy talk as I pass one by*
> *Before my thoughts begin to run*
> *On F. M'Curdy Atkinson,*
> *The same that had the wooden leg*
> *And that filibustering fillibeg*
> *That never dared to slake his drouth,*
> *Magee that had the chinless mouth.*
> *Being afraid to marry on earth*
> *They masturbated for all they were worth.*

Jest on. Know thyself.

Halted below me, a quizzer looks at me. I halt.

– Mournful mummer, Buck Mulligan moaned. Synge has left off wearing black to be like nature. Only crows, priests and English coal are black.

A laugh tripped over his lips.

– Longworth is awfully sick, he said, after what you wrote about that old hake Gregory. O you inquisitional drunken jew jesuit! She gets you a job on the paper and then you go and slate her drivel to Jaysus. Couldn't you do the Yeats touch?

He went on and down, mopping, chanting with waving graceful arms:

– The most beautiful book that has come out of our country in my time. One thinks of Homer.

He stopped at the stairfoot.

– I have conceived a play for the mummers, he said solemnly.

The pillared Moorish hall, shadows entwined. Gone the nine men's morrice with caps of indices.

In sweetly varying voices Buck Mulligan read his tablet:

Everyman His Own Wife
or
A Honeymoon in the Hand
(a national immorality in three orgasms)
by
Ballocky Mulligan

He turned a happy patch's smirk to Stephen, saying:

– The disguise, I fear, is thin. But listen.

He read, *marcato*:

– Characters:

> Toby Tostoff (a ruined Pole).
> Crab (a bushranger).
> Medical Dick
>   and   } (two birds with one stone).
> Medical Davy
> Mother Grogan (a watercarrier).
> Fresh Nelly
>   and
> Rosalie (the coalquay whore).

He laughed, lolling a to and fro head, walking on, followed by Stephen: and mirthfully he told the shadows, souls of men:

– O, the night in the Camden hall when the daughters of Erin had to lift their skirts to step over you as you lay in your mulberrycoloured, multi-coloured, multitudinous vomit!

– The most innocent son of Erin, Stephen said, for whom they ever lifted them.

About to pass through the doorway, feeling one behind, he stood aside.

Part. The moment is now. Where then? If Socrates leave his house today, if Judas go forth tonight. Why? That lies in space which I in time must come to, ineluctably.

My will: his will that fronts me. Seas between.

A man passed out between them, bowing, greeting.

– Good day again, Buck Mulligan said.

The portico.

Here I watched the birds for augury. Ængus of the birds. They go, they come. Last night I flew. Easily flew. Men wondered. Street of harlots after. A creamfruit melon he held to me. In. You will see.

– The wandering jew, Buck Mulligan whispered with clown's awe. Did you see his eye? He looked upon you to lust after you. I fear thee, ancient mariner. O, Kinch, thou art in peril. Get thee a breechpad.

Manner of Oxenford.

Day. Wheelbarrow sun over arch of bridge.

A dark back went before them. Step of a pard, down, out by the gateway, under portcullis barbs.

They followed.

Offend me still. Speak on.

Kind air defined the coigns of houses in Kildare street. No birds. Frail from the housetops two plumes of smoke ascended, pluming, and in a flaw of softness softly were blown.

Cease to strive. Peace of the druid priests of Cymbeline, hierophantic: from wide earth an altar.

> *Laud we the gods*
> *And let our crooked smokes climb to their nostrils*
> *From our bless'd altars.*

*   *   *   *   *

◀ THE SUPERIOR, THE VERY REVEREND JOHN CONMEE S. J., Reset his smooth watch in his interior pocket as he came down the presbytery steps. Five to three. Just nice time to walk to Artane. What was that boy's name again? Dignam, yes. *Vere dignum et justum est.* Brother Swan was the person to see. Mr Cunningham's letter. Yes. Oblige him, if possible. Good practical catholic: useful at mission time.

A onelegged sailor, swinging himself onward by lazy jerks of his crutches, growled some notes. He jerked short before the convent of the sisters of charity and held out a peaked cap for alms towards the very reverend John Conmee S. J. Father Conmee blessed him in the sun for his purse held, he knew, one silver crown.

Father Conmee crossed to Mountjoy square. He thought, but not for long, of soldiers and sailors, whose legs had been shot off by cannonballs, ending their days in some pauper ward, and of cardinal Wolsey's words: *If I had served my God as I had served my king He would not have abandoned me in my old days*. He walked by the treeshade of sunnywinking leaves and towards him came the wife of Mr David Sheehy M. P.

– Very well, indeed, father. And you father?

Father Conmee was wonderfully well indeed. He would go to Buxton probably for the waters. And her boys, were they getting on well at Belvedere? Was that so? Father Conmee was very glad indeed to hear that. And Mr Sheehy himself? Still in London. The house was still sitting, to be sure it was. Beautiful weather it was, delightful indeed. Yes, it was very probable that Father Bernard Vaughan would come again to preach. O, yes: a very great success. A wonderful man really.

Father Conmee was very glad to see the wife of Mr David Sheehy M. P. looking so well and he begged to be remembered to Mr David Sheehy M. P. Yes, he would certainly call.

– Good afternoon, Mrs Sheehy.

Father Conmee doffed his silk hat, as he took leave, at the jet beads of her mantilla inkshining in the sun. And smiled yet again in going. He had cleaned his teeth, he knew, with arecanut paste.

Father Conmee walked and, walking, smiled for he thought on Father Bernard Vaughan's droll eyes and cockney voice.

– Pilate! Wy don't you old back that owlin mob?

A zealous man, however. Really he was. And really did great good in his way. Beyond a doubt. He loved Ireland, he said, and he loved the Irish. Of good family too would one think it? Welsh, were they not?

O, lest he forget. That letter to father provincial.

Father Conmee stopped three little schoolboys at the corner of Mountjoy square. Yes: they were from Belvedere. The little house: Aha. And were they good boys at school? O. That was very good now. And what was his name? Jack Sohan. And his name? Ger. Gallaher. And the other little man? His name was Brunny Lynam. O, that was a very nice name to have.

Father Conmee gave a letter from his breast to master Brunny Lynam and pointed to the red pillarbox at the corner of Fitzgibbon street.

– But mind you don't post yourself into the box, little man, he said.

The boys sixeyed Father Conmee and laughed.

– O, sir.

– Well, let me see if you can post a letter, Father Conmee said.

Master Brunny Lynam ran across the road and put Father Conmee's letter to father provincial into the mouth of the bright red letterbox, Father

Conmee smiled and nodded and smiled and walked along Mountjoy square east.

Mr Denis J. Maginni, professor of dancing, &c., in silk hat, slate frock coat with silk facings, white kerchief tie, tight lavender trousers, canary gloves and pointed patent boots, walking with grave deportment most respectfully took the curbstone as he passed lady Maxwell at the corner of Dignam's court.

Was that not Mrs M'Guinness?

Mrs M'Guinness, stately, silverhaired, bowed to Father Conmee from the farther footpath along which she sailed. And Father Conmee smiled and saluted. How did she do?

A fine carriage she had. Like Mary, queen of Scots, something. And to think that she was a pawnbroker. Well, now! Such a . . . what should he say? . . . such a queenly mien.

Father Conmee walked down Great Charles Street and glanced at the shutup free church on his left. The reverend T. R. Greene B. A. will (D. V.) speak. The incumbent they called him. He felt it incumbent on him to say a few words. But one should be charitable. Invincible ignorance. They acted according to their lights.

Father Conmee turned the corner and walked along the North Circular road. It was a wonder that there was not a tramline in such an important thoroughfare. Surely, there ought to be.

A band of satchelled schoolboys crossed from Richmond street. All raised untidy caps. Father Conmee greeted them more than once benignly. Christian brother boys.

Father Conmee smelled incense on his right hand as he walked. Saint Joseph's church, Portland row. For aged and virtuous females. Father Conmee raised his hat to the Blessed Sacrament. Virtuous: but occasionally they were also badtempered.

Near Aldborough house Father Conmee thought of that spendthrift nobleman. And now it was an office or something.

Father Conmee began to walk along the North Strand road and was saluted by Mr William Gallagher who stood in the doorway of his shop. Father Conmee saluted Mr William Gallagher and perceived the odours that came from baconflitches and ample cools of butter. He passed Grogan's the tobacconist against which newsboards leaned and told of a dreadful catastrophe in New York. In America those things were continually happening. Unfortunate people to die like that, unprepared. Still, an act of perfect contrition.

Father Conmee went by Daniel Bergin's publichouse against the window of which two unlabouring men lounged. They saluted him and were saluted.

Father Conmee passed H. J. O'Neill's funeral establishment where Corny Kelleher totted figures in the daybook while he chewed a blade of hay. A constable on his beat saluted Father Conmee and Father Conmee saluted the constable. In Youkstetter's, the porkbutcher's, Father Conmee observed pig's puddings, white and black and red, lying neatly curled in tubes.

Moored under the trees of Charleville Mall Father Conmee saw a turf-barge, a towhorse with pendent head, a bargeman with a hat of dirty straw seated amidships, smoking and staring at a branch of poplar above him. It was idyllic: and Father Conmee reflected on the providence of the Creator who had made turf to be in bogs where men might dig it out and bring it to town and hamlet to make fires in the houses of poor people.

On Newcomen bridge the very reverend John Conmee S. J. of saint Francis Xavier's church, upper Gardiner street, stepped on to an outward bound tram.

Off an inward bound tram stepped the reverend Nicholas Dudley C. C. of saint Agatha's church, north William street, on to Newcomen bridge.

At Newcomen bridge Father Conmee stepped into an outward bound tram for he disliked to traverse on foot the dingy way past Mud Island.

Father Conmee sat in a corner of the tramcar, a blue ticket tucked with care in the eye of one plump kid glove, while four shillings, a sixpence and five pennies chuted from his other plump glovepalm into his purse. Passing the ivy church he reflected that the ticket inspector usually made his visit when one had carelessly thrown away the ticket. The solemnity of the occupants of the car seemed to Father Conmee excessive for a journey so short and cheap. Father Conmee liked cheerful decorum.

It was a peaceful day. The gentleman with the glasses opposite Father Conmee had finished explaining and looked down. His wife, Father Conmee supposed. A tiny yawn opened the mouth of the wife of the gentleman with the glasses. She raised her small gloved fist, yawned ever so gently, tiptapping her small gloved fist on her opening mouth and smiled tinily, sweetly.

Father Conmee perceived her perfume in the car. He perceived also that the awkward man at the other side of her was sitting on the edge of the seat.

Father Conmee at the altarrails placed the host with difficulty in the mouth of the awkward old man who had the shaky head.

At Annesley bridge the tram halted and, when it was about to go, an old woman rose suddenly from her place to alight. The conductor pulled the bellstrap to stay the car for her. She passed out with her basket and a market net: and Father Conmee saw the conductor help her and net and basket down: and Father Conmee thought that, as she had nearly passed the end of the penny fare, she was one of those good souls who had always to be told twice *bless you, my child*, that they have been absolved, *pray for me*. But they had so many worries in life, so many cares, poor creatures.

From the hoardings Mr Eugene Stratton grinned with thick niggerlips at Father Conmee.

Father Conmee thought of the souls of black and brown and yellow men and of his sermon of saint Peter Claver S. J. and the African mission and of the propagation of the faith and of the millions of black and brown and yellow souls that had not received the baptism of water when their last hour came like a thief in the night. That book by the Belgian jesuit, *Le Nombre des Élus*, seemed to Father Conmee a reasonable plea. Those were millions of human souls created by God in His Own likeness to whom the faith had not (D. V.) been brought. But they were God's souls created by God. It seemed to Father Conmee a pity that they should all be lost, a waste, if one might say.

At the Howth road stop Father Conmee alighted, was saluted by the conductor and saluted in his turn.

The Malahide road was quiet. It pleased Father Conmee, road and name. The joybells were ringing in gay Malahide. Lord Talbot de Malahide, immediate hereditary lord admiral of Malahide and the seas adjoining. Then came the call to arms and she was maid, wife and widow in one day. Those were oldworldish days, loyal times in joyous town-lands, old times in the barony.

Father Conmee, walking, thought of his little book *Old Times in the Barony* and of the book that might be written about jesuit houses and of Mary Rochfort, daughter of lord Molesworth, first countess of Belvedere.

A listless lady, no more young, walked alone the shore of lough Ennel, Mary, first countess of Belvedere, listlessly walking in the evening, not startled when an otter plunged. Who could know the truth? Not the jealous lord Belvedere and not her confessor if she had not committed adultery fully, *eiaculatio seminis inter vas naturale mulieris*, with her husband's brother? She would half confess if she had not all sinned as women did. Only God knew and she and he, her husband's brother.

Father Conmee thought of that tyrannous incontinence, needed however for men's race on earth, and of the ways of God which were not our ways.

Don John Conmee walked and moved in times of yore. He was humane and honoured there. He bore in mind secrets confessed and he smiled at smiling noble faces in a beeswaxed drawingroom, ceiled with full fruit clusters. And the hands of a bride and of a bridegroom, noble to noble, were impalmed by don John Conmee.

It was a charming day.

The lychgate of a field showed Father Conmee breadths of cabbages, curtseying to him with ample underleaves. The sky showed him a flock of small white clouds going slowly down the wind. *Moutonner*, the French said. A homely and just word.

Father Conmee, reading his office, watched a flock of muttoning clouds over Rathcoffey. His thinsocked ankles were tickled by the stubble of Clongowes field. He walked there, reading in the evening and heard the cries of the boys' lines at their play, young cries in the quiet evening. He was their rector: his reign was mild.

Father Conmee drew off his gloves and took his rededged breviary out. An ivory bookmark told him the page.

Nones. He should have read that before lunch. But lady Maxwell had come.

Father Conmee read in secret *Pater* and *Ave* and crossed his breast. *Deus in adiutorium.*

He walked calmly and read mutely the nones, walking and reading till he came to *Res* in *Beati immaculati: Principium verborum tuorum veritas: in eternum omnia iudicia iustitiæ tuæ.*

A flushed young man came from a gap of a hedge and after him came a young woman with wild nodding daisies in her hand. The young man raised his cap abruptly: the young woman abruptly bent and with slow care detached from her light skirt a clinging twig.

Father Conmee blessed both gravely and turned a thin page of his breviary. *Sin: Principes persecuti sunt me gratis: et a verbis tuis formidavit cor meum.*

*

Corny Kelleher closed his long daybook and glanced with his drooping eye at a pine coffinlid sentried in a corner. He pulled himself erect, went to it and, spinning it on its axle, viewed its shape and brass furnishings. Chewing his blade of hay he laid the coffinlid by and came to the doorway. There he tilted his hatbrim to give shade to his eyes and leaned against the doorcase, looking idly out.

Father John Conmee stepped into the Dollymount tram on Newcomen bridge.

Corny Kelleher locked his largefooted boots and gazed, his hat downtilted, chewing his blade of hay.

Constable 57C, on his beat, stood to pass the time of day.

– That's a fine day, Mr Kelleher.

– Ay, Corny Kelleher said.

– It's very close, the constable said.

Corny Kelleher sped a silent jet of hayjuice arching from his mouth while a generous white arm from a window in Eccles street flung forth a coin.

– What's the best news? he asked.

– I seen that particular party last evening, the constable said with bated breath.

*

A onelegged sailor crutched himself round MacConnell's corner, skirting Rabaiotti's icecream car, and jerked himself up Eccles street. Towards Larry O'Rourke, in shirtsleeves in his doorway, he growled unamiably.

– *For England* . . .

He swung himself violently forward past Katey and Boody Dedalus, halted and growled:

– *home and beauty.*

J. J. O'Molloy's white careworn face was told that Mr Lambert was in the warehouse with a visitor.

A stout lady stopped, took a copper coin from her purse and dropped it into the cap held out to her. The sailor grumbled thanks and glanced sourly at the unheeding windows, sank his head and swung himself forward four strides.

He halted and growled angrily:

– *For England* . . .

Two barefoot urchins, sucking long liquorice laces, halted near him, gaping at his stump with their yellowslobbered mouths.

He swung himself forward in vigorous jerks, halted, lifted his head towards a window and bayed deeply:

– *home and beauty.*

The gay sweet chirping whistling within went on a bar or two, ceased. The blind of the window was drawn aside. A card *Unfurnished Apartments* slipped from the sash and fell. A plump bare generous arm shone, was seen, held forth from a white petticoatbodice and taut shiftstraps. A woman's hand flung forth a coin over the area railings. It fell on the path.

One of the urchins ran to it, picked it up and dropped it into the minstrel's cap, saying:

– There, sir.

*

Katey and Boody Dedalus shoved in the door of the close steaming kitchen.

– Did you put in the books? Boody asked.

Maggy at the range rammed down a greyish mass beneath bubbling suds twice with her potstick and wiped her brow.

– They wouldn't give anything on them, she said.

Father Conmee walked through Clongowes fields, his thinsocked ankles tickled by stubble.

– Where did you try? Boody asked.

– M'Guinness's.

Boody stamped her foot and threw her satchel on the table.

– Bad cess to her big face! she cried.

Katey went to the range and peered with squinting eyes.

– What's in the pot? she asked.

– Shirts, Maggy said.

Boody cried angrily:

– Crickey, is there nothing for us to eat?

Katey, lifting the kettlelid in a pad of her stained skirt, asked:

– And what's in this?

A heavy fume gushed in answer.

– Peasoup, Maggy said.

– Where did you get it? Katey asked.

– Sister Mary Patrick, Maggy said.

The lacquey rang his bell.

– Barang!

Boody sat down at the table and said hungrily:

– Give us it here!

Maggy poured yellow thick soup from the kettle into a bowl. Katey, sitting opposite Boody, said quietly, as her fingertip lifted to her mouth random crumbs.

– A good job we have that much. Where's Dilly?

– Gone to meet father, Maggy said.

Boody, breaking big chunks of bread into the yellow soup, added:

– Our father who art not in heaven.

Maggy, pouring yellow soup in Katey's bowl, exclaimed:

– Boody! For shame!

A skiff, a crumpled throwaway, Elijah is coming, rode lightly down the Liffey, under Loopline bridge, shooting the rapids where water chafed around the bridgepiers, sailing eastward past hulls and anchorchains, between the Customhouse old dock and George's quay.

*

The blond girl in Thornton's bedded the wicker basket with rustling fibre. Blazes Boylan handed her the bottle swathed in pink tissue paper and a small jar.

– Put these in first, will you? he said.

– Yes, sir, the blond girl said, and the fruit on top.

– That'll do, game ball, Blazes Boylan said.

She bestowed fat pears neatly, head by tail, and among them ripe shamefaced peaches.

Blazes Boylan walked here and there in new tan shoes about the fruit-smelling shop, lifting fruits, young juicy crinkled and plump red tomatoes, sniffing smells.

H. E. L. Y.'S. filed before him, tallwhitehatted, past Tangier lane, plodding towards their goal.

He turned suddenly from a chip of strawberries, drew a gold watch from his fob and held it at its chain's length.

– Can you send them by tram? Now?

A darkbacked figure under Merchants' arch scanned books on the hawker's car.

– Certainly, sir. Is it in the city?

– O, yes, Blazes Boylan said. Ten minutes.

The blond girl handed him a docket and pencil.

– Will you write the address, sir?

Blazes Boylan at the counter wrote and pushed the docket to her.

– Send it at once, will you? he said. It's for an invalid.

– Yes, sir. I will, sir.

Blazes Boylan rattled merry money in his trousers' pocket.

– What's the damage? he asked.

The blond girl's slim fingers reckoned the fruits.

Blazes Boylan looked into the cut of her blouse. A young pullet. He took a red carnation from the tall stemglass.

– This for me? he asked gallantly.

The blond girl glanced sideways at him, got up regardless, with his tie a bit crooked, blushing.

– Yes, sir, she said.

Bending archly she reckoned again fat pears and blushing peaches.

Blazes Boylan looked in her blouse with more favour, the stalk of the red flower between his smiling teeth.

– May I say a word to your telephone, missy? he asked roguishly.

*

– *Ma!* Almidano Artifoni said.

He gazed over Stephen's shoulder at Goldsmith's knobby poll.

Two carfuls of tourists passed slowly, their women sitting fore, gripping frankly the handrests. Pale faces. Men's arms frankly round their stunted forms. They looked from Trinity to the blind columned porch of the bank of Ireland where pigeons roocoocooed.

– *Anch'io ho avuto di queste idee*, Almidano Artifoni said, *quand' ero giovine come Lei. Eppoi mi sono convinto che il mondo è una bestia. È peccato. Perchè la sua voce . . . sarebbe un cespite di rendita, via. Invece, Lei si sacrifica.*

– *Sacrifizio incruento*, Stephen said smiling, swaying his ashplant in slow swingswong from its midpoint, lightly.

– *Speriamo*, the round mustachioed face said pleasantly. *Ma, dia retta a me. Ci rifletta.*

By the stern stone hand of Grattan, bidding halt, an Inchicore tram unloaded straggling Highland soldiers of a band.

– *Ci rifletterò*, Stephen said, glancing down the solid trouserleg.

– *Ma, sul serio, eh?* Almidano Artifoni said.

His heavy hand took Stephen's firmly. Human eyes. They gazed curiously an instant and turned quickly towards a Dalkey tram.

– *Eccolo*, Almidano Artifoni said in friendly haste. *Venga a trovarmi e ci pensi. Addio, caro.*

– *Arrivederla, maestro*, Stephen said, raising his hat when his hand was freed. *E grazie.*

– *Di che?* Almidano Artifoni said. *Scusi, eh? Tante belle cose!*

Almidano Artifoni, holding up a baton of rolled music as a signal, trotted on stout trousers after the Dalkey tram. In vain he trotted, signalling in vain among the rout of barekneed gillies smuggling implements of music through Trinity gates.

*

Miss Dunne hid the Capel street library copy of *The Woman in White* far back in her drawer and rolled a sheet of gaudy notepaper into her typewriter.

Too much mystery business in it. Is he in love with that one, Marion? Change it and get another by Mary Cecil Haye.

The disk shot down the groove, wobbled a while, ceased and ogled them: six.

Miss Dunne clicked on the keyboard:

– 16 June 1904.

Five tallwhitehatted sandwichmen between Monypeny's corner and the slab where Wolfe Tone's statue was not, eeled themselves turning H. E. L. Y.'S and plodded back as they had come.

Then she stared at the large poster of Marie Kendall, charming soubrette, and, listlessly lolling, scribbled on the jotter sixteens and capital esses. Mustard hair and dauby cheeks. She's not nicelooking, is she? The way she is holding up her bit of a skirt. Wonder will that fellow be at the band tonight. If I could get that dressmaker to make a concertina skirt like Susy Nagle's. They kick out grand. Shannon and all the boatclub swells never took his eyes off her. Hope to goodness he won't keep me here till seven.

The telephone rang rudely by her ear.

– Hello. Yes, sir. No, sir. Yes, sir. I'll ring them up after five. Only those two, sir, for Belfast and Liverpool. All right, sir. Then I can go after six if you're not back. A quarter after. Yes, sir. Twentyseven and six. I'll tell him. Yes: one, seven, six.

She scribbled three figures on an envelope.

– Mr Boylan! Hello! That gentleman from *Sport* was in looking for you. Mr Lenehan, yes. He said he'll be in the Ormond at four. No, sir. Yes, sir. I'll ring them up after five.

*

Two pink faces turned in the flare of the tiny torch.

– Who's that? Ned Lambert asked. Is that Crotty?

– Ringabella and Crosshaven, a voice replied, groping for foothold.

– Hello, Jack, is that yourself? Ned Lambert said, raising in salute his pliant lath among the flickering arches. Come on. Mind your steps there.

The vesta in the clergyman's uplifted hand consumed itself in a long soft flame and was let fall. At their feet its red speck died: and mouldy air closed round them.

– How interesting! a refined accent said in the gloom.

– Yes, sir, Ned Lambert said heartily. We are standing in the historic council chamber of saint Mary's abbey where silken Thomas proclaimed himself a rebel in 1534. This is the most historic spot in all Dublin. O'Madden Burke is going to write something about it one of these days. The old bank of Ireland was over the way till the time of the union and the original jews' temple was here too before they built their synagogue over in Adelaide road. You were never here before, Jack, were you?

– No, Ned.

– He rode down through Dame walk, the refined accent said, if my memory serves me. The mansion of the Kildares was in Thomas court.

– That's right, Ned Lambert said. That's quite right, sir.

– If you will be so kind then, the clergyman said, the next time to allow me perhaps . . .

– Certainly, Ned Lambert said. Bring the camera whenever you like. I'll get those bags cleared away from the windows. You can take it from here or from here.

In the still faint light he moved about, tapping with his lath the piled seedbags and points of vantage on the floor.

From a long face a beard and gaze hung on a chessboard.

– I'm deeply obliged, Mr Lambert, the clergyman said. I won't trespass on your valuable time . . .

– You're welcome, sir, Ned Lambert said. Drop in whenever you like. Next week, say. Can you see?

– Yes, yes. Good afternoon, Mr Lambert. Very pleased to have met you.

– Pleasure is mine, sir, Ned Lambert answered.

He followed his guest to the outlet and then whirled his lath away among the pillars. With J. J. O'Molloy he came forth slowly into Mary's abbey where draymen were loading floats with sacks of carob and palm nut meal, O'Connor, Wexford.

He stood to read the card in his hand.

– The reverend Hugh C. Love, Rathcoffey. Present address: Saint Michael's, Sallins. Nice young chap he is. He's writing a book about the Fitzgeralds he told me. He's well up in history, faith.

The young woman with slow care detached from her light skirt a clinging twig.

– I thought you were at a new gunpowder plot, J. J. O'Molloy said.

Ned Lambert cracked his fingers in the air.

– God, he cried. I forgot to tell him that one about the earl of Kildare after he set fire to Cashel cathedral. You know that one? *I'm bloody sorry I did it*, says he, *but I declare to God I thought the archbishop was inside.* He mightn't like it, though. What? God, I'll tell him anyhow. That was the great earl, the Fitzgerald Mor. Hot members they were all of them, the Geraldines.

The horses he passed started nervously under their slack harness. He slapped a piebald haunch quivering near him and cried:

– Woa, sonny!

He turned to J. J. O'Molloy and asked:

– Well, Jack. What is it? What's the trouble? Wait a while. Hold hard.

With gaping mouth and head far back he stood still and, after an instant, sneezed loudly.

– Chow! he said. Blast you!

– The dust from those sacks, J. J. O'Molloy said politely.

– No, Ned Lambert gasped, I caught a . . . cold night before . . . blast your soul . . . night before last . . . and there was a hell of a lot of draught . . .

He held his handkerchief ready for the coming . . .

– I was . . . this morning . . . poor little . . . what do you call him . . . Chow! . . . Mother of Moses!

*

Tom Rochford took the top disk from the pile he clasped against his claret waistcoat.

– See? he said. Say it's turn six. In here, see. Turn Now On.

He slid it into the left slot for them. It shot down the groove, wobbled a while, ceased, ogling them: six.

Lawyers of the past, haughty, pleading, beheld pass from the consolidated taxing office to Nisi Prius court Richie Goulding carrying the costbag of Goulding, Collis and Ward and heard rustling from the admiralty division of king's bench to the court of appeal an elderly female with false teeth smiling incredulously and a black silk skirt of great amplitude.

– See? he said. See now the last one I put in is over here. Turns Over. The impact. Leverage, see?

He showed them the rising column of disks on the right.

– Smart idea, Nosey Flynn said, snuffling. So a fellow coming in late can see what turn is on and what turns are over.

– See? Tom Rochford said.

He slid in a disk for himself: and watched it shoot, wobble, ogle, stop: four. Turn Now On.

– I'll see him now in the Ormond, Lenehan said, and sound him. One good turn deserves another.

– Do, Tom Rochford said. Tell him I'm Boylan with impatience.

– Goodnight, M'Coy said abruptly, when you two begin . . .

Nosey Flynn stooped towards the lever, snuffling at it.

– But how does it work here, Tommy? he asked.

– Tooraloo, Lenehan said, see you later.

He followed M'Coy out across the tiny square of Crampton court.

– He's a hero, he said simply.

– I know, M'Coy said. The drain, you mean.

– Drain? Lenehan said. It was down a manhole.

They passed Dan Lowry's musichall where Marie Kendall, charming soubrette, smiled on them from a poster a dauby smile.

Going down the path of Sycamore street beside the Empire musichall Lenehan showed M'Coy how the whole thing was. One of those manholes like a bloody gaspipe and there was the poor devil stuck down in it half choked with sewer gas. Down went Tom Rochford anyhow, booky's vest and all, with the rope round him. And be damned but he got the rope round the poor devil and the two were hauled up.

– The act of a hero, he said.

At the Dolphin they halted to allow the ambulance car to gallop past them for Jervis street.

– This way, he said, walking to the right. I want to pop into Lynam's to see Sceptre's starting price. What's the time by your gold watch and chain?

M'Coy peered into Marcus Tertius Moses' sombre office, then at O'Neill's clock.

– After three, he said. Who's riding her?

– O. Madden, Lenehan said. And a game filly she is.

While he waited in Temple bar M'Coy dodged a banana peel with gentle pushes of his toe from the path to the gutter. Fellow might damn easy get a nasty fall there coming along tight in the dark.

The gates of the drive opened wide to give egress to the viceregal cavalcade.

– Even money, Lenehan said returning. I knocked against Bantam Lyons in there going to back a bloody horse someone gave him that hasn't an earthly. Through here.

They went up the steps and under Merchants' arch. A darkbacked figure scanned books on the hawker's cart.

– There he is, Lenehan said.

– Wonder what he is buying, M'Coy said, glancing behind.

– *Leopoldo or the Bloom is on the Rye*, Lenehan said.

– He's dead nuts on sales, M'Coy said. I was with him one day and he bought a book from an old one in Liffey street for two bob. There were fine plates in it worth double the money, the stars and the moon and comets with long tails. Astronomy it was about.

Lenehan laughed.

– I'll tell you a damn good one about comets' tails, he said. Come over in the sun.

They crossed to the metal bridge and went along Wellington quay by the river wall.

Master Patrick Aloysius Dignam came out of Mangan's, late Fehrenbach's, carrying a pound and a half of porksteaks.

– There was a big spread out at Glencree reformatory, Lenehan said eagerly. The annual dinner you know. Boiled shirt affair. The lord mayor was there, Val Dillon it was, and sir Charles Cameron and Dan Dawson spoke and there was music. Bartell D'Arcy sang and Benjamin Dollard . . .

– I know, M'Coy broke in. My missus sang there once.

– Did she? Lenehan said.

A card *Unfurnished Apartments* reappeared on the windowsash of number 7 Eccles street.

He checked his tale a moment but broke out in a wheezy laugh.

– But wait till I tell you, he said. Delahunt of Camden street had the catering and yours truly was chief bottlewasher. Bloom and the wife were there. Lashings of stuff we put up: port wine and sherry and curaçao to which we did ample justice. Fast and furious it was. After liquids came solids. Cold joints galore and mince pies . . .

– I know, M'Coy said. The year the missus was there . . .

Lenehan linked his arm warmly.

– But wait till I tell you, he said. We had a midnight lunch too after all the jollification and when we sallied forth it was blue o'clock the morning after the night before. Coming home it was a gorgeous winter's night on the Featherbed Mountain. Bloom and Chris Callinan were on one side of the car and I was with the wife on the other. We started singing glees and duets: *Lo, the early beam of morning*. She was well primed with a good load of Delahunt's port under her bellyband. Every jolt the bloody car gave I had her bumping up against me. Hell's delights! She has a fine pair, God bless her. Like that.

He held his caved hands a cubit from him, frowning:

– I was tucking the rug under her and settling her boa all the time. Know what I mean?

His hands moulded ample curves of air. He shut his eyes tight in delight, his body shrinking, and blew a sweet chirp from his lips.

– The lad stood to attention anyhow, he said with a sigh. She's a gamey mare and no mistake. Bloom was pointing out all the stars and the comets in the heavens to Chris Callinan and the jarvey: the great bear and Hercules and the dragon and the whole jingbang lot. But, by God, I was lost, so to speak, in the milky way. He knows them all, faith. At last she spotted a weeny weeshy one miles away. *And what star is that, Poldy?* says she. By God, she had Bloom cornered. *That one, is it?* says Chris Callinan, *sure that's only what you might call a pinprick.* By God, he wasn't far wide of the mark.

Lenehan stopped and leaned on the riverwall, panting with soft laughter.

– I'm weak, he gasped.

M'Coy's white face smiled about it at instants and grew grave. Lenehan walked on again. He lifted his yachtingcap and scratched his hindhead rapidly. He glanced sideways in the sunlight at M'Coy.

– He's a cultured allroundman, Bloom is, he said seriously. He's not one of your common or garden . . . you know . . . There's a touch of the artist about old Bloom.

*

Mr Bloom turned over idly pages of *The Awful Disclosures of Maria Monk*, then of Aristotle's *Masterpiece*. Crooked botched print. Plates: infants cuddled in a ball in bloodred wombs like livers of slaughtered cows. Lots of them like that at this moment all over the world. All butting with their skulls to get out of it. Child born every minute somewhere. Mrs Purefoy.

He laid both books aside and glanced at the third: *Tales of the Ghetto* by Leopold von Sacher Masoch.

– That I had, he said, pushing it by.

The shopman let two volumes fall on the counter.

– Them are two good ones, he said.

Onions of his breath came across the counter out of his ruined mouth. He bent to make a bundle of the other books, hugged them against his unbuttoned waistcoat and bore them off behind the dingy curtain.

On O'Connell bridge many persons observed the grave deportment and gay apparel of Mr Denis J. Maginni, professor of dancing &c.

Mr Bloom, alone, looked at the titles. *Fair Tyrants* by James Lovebirch. Know the kind that is. Had it? Yes.

He opened it. Thought so.

A woman's voice behind the dingy curtain. Listen: The man.

No: she wouldn't like that much. Got her it once.

He read the other title: *Sweets of Sin*. More in her line. Let us see.

He read where his finger opened.

– *All the dollarbills her husband gave her were spent in the stores on wondrous gowns and costliest frillies. For him! For Raoul!*

Yes. This. Here. Try.

– *Her mouth glued on his in a luscious voluptuous kiss while his hands felt for the opulent curves inside her deshabillé.*

Yes. Take this. The end.

– *You are late, he spoke hoarsely, eyeing her with a suspicious glare. The beautiful woman threw off her sabletrimmed wrap, displaying her queenly shoulders and heaving embonpoint. An imperceptible smile played round her perfect lips as she turned to him calmly.*

Mr Bloom read again: *The beautiful woman.*

Warmth showered gently over him, cowing his flesh. Flesh yielded amid rumpled clothes. Whites of eyes swooning up. His nostrils arched themselves for prey. Melting breast ointments *(for him! For Raoul!)*. Armpits' oniony sweat. Fishgluey slime *(her heaving embonpoint!)*. Feel! Press! Crushed! Sulphur dung of lions!

Young! Young!

An elderly female, no more young, left the building of the courts of chancery, king's bench, exchequer and common pleas having heard in the lord chancellor's court the case in lunacy of Potterton, in the admiralty division the summons, exparte motion, of the owners of the Lady Cairns versus the owners of the barque Mona, in the court of appeal reservation of judgment in the case of Harvey versus the Ocean Accident and Guarantee Corporation.

Phlegmy coughs shook the air of the bookshop, bulging out the dingy curtains. The shopman's uncombed grey head came out and his unshaven reddened face, coughing. He raked his throat rudely, spat phlegm on the floor. He put his boot on what he had spat, wiping his sole along it and bent, showing a rawskinned crown, scantily haired.

Mr Bloom beheld it.

Mastering his troubled breath, he said:

– I'll take this one.

The shopman lifted eyes bleared with old rheum.

– *Sweets of Sin*, he said, tapping on it. That's a good one.

*

The lacquey by the door of Dillon's auctionrooms shook his handbell twice again and viewed himself in the chalked mirror of the cabinet.

Dilly Dedalus, listening by the curbstone, heard the beats of the bell, the cries of the auctioneer within. Four and nine. Those lovely curtains. Five shillings. Cosy curtains. Selling new at two guineas. Any advance on five shillings? Going for five shillings.

The lacquey lifted his handbell and shook it:

– Barang!

Bang of the lastlap bell spurred the halfmile wheelmen to their sprint. J. A. Jackson, W. E. Wylie, A. Munro and H. T. Gahan, their stretched necks wagging, negotiated the curve by the College Library.

Mr Dedalus, tugging a long moustache, came round from Williams's row. He halted near his daughter.

– It's time for you, she said.

– Stand up straight for the love of the Lord Jesus, Mr Dedalus said. Are you trying to imitate your uncle John the cornetplayer, head upon shoulders? Melancholy God!

Dilly shrugged her shoulders. Mr Dedalus placed his hands on them and held them back.

– Stand up straight, girl, he said. You'll get curvature of the spine. Do you know what you look like?

He let his head sink suddenly down and forward, hunching his shoulders and dropping his underjaw.

– Give it up, father, Dilly said. All the people are looking at you.

Mr Dedalus drew himself upright and tugged again at his moustache.

– Did you get any money? Dilly asked.

– Where would I get money? Mr Dedalus said. There is no-one in Dublin would lend me fourpence.

– You got some, Dilly said, looking in his eyes.

– How do you know that? Mr Dedalus asked, his tongue in his cheek.

Mr Kernan, pleased with the order he had booked, walked boldly along James's street.

– I know you did, Dilly answered. Were you in the Scotch house now?

– I was not then, Mr Dedalus said, smiling. Was it the little nuns taught you to be so saucy? Here.

He handed her a shilling.

– See if you can do anything with that, he said.

– I suppose you got five, Dilly said. Give me more than that.

– Wait awhile, Mr Dedalus said threateningly. You're like the rest of them, are you? An insolent pack of little bitches since your poor mother died. But wait awhile. You'll all get a short shrift and a long day from me. Low blackguardism! I'm going to get rid of you. Wouldn't care if I was stretched out stiff. He's dead. The man upstairs is dead.

He left her and walked on. Dilly followed quickly and pulled his coat.

– Well, what is it? he said, stopping.

The lacquey rang his bell behind their backs.

– Barang!

– Curse your bloody blatant soul, Mr Dedalus cried, turning on him.

The lacquey, aware of comment, shook the lolling clapper of his bell but feebly:

– Bang!

Mr Dedalus stared at him.

– Watch him, he said. It's instructive. I wonder will he allow us to talk.

– You got more than that, father, Dilly said.

– I'm going to show you a little trick, Mr Dedalus said. I'll leave you all where Jesus left the jews. Look, that's all I have. I got two shillings from Jack Power and I spent twopence for a shave for the funeral.

He drew forth a handful of copper coins nervously.

– Can't you look for some money somewhere? Dilly said.

Mr Dedalus thought and nodded.

– I will, he said gravely. I looked all along the gutter in O'Connell street. I'll try this one now.

– You're very funny, Dilly said, grinning.

– Here, Mr Dedalus said, handing her two pennies. Get a glass of milk for yourself and a bun or a something. I'll be home shortly.

He put the other coins in his pocket and started to walk on.

The viceregal cavalcade passed, greeted by obsequious policemen, out of Parkgate.

– I'm sure you have another shilling, Dilly said.

The lacquey banged loudly.

Mr Dedalus amid the din walked off, murmuring to himself with a pursing mincing mouth:

– The little nuns! Nice little things! O, sure they wouldn't do anything! O, sure they wouldn't really! Is it little sister Monica!

*

From the sundial towards James's Gate walked Mr Kernan pleased with the order he had booked for Pulbrook Robertson boldly along James's street, past Shackleton's offices. Got round him all right. How do you do, Mr Crimmins? First rate, sir. I was afraid you might be up in your other establishment in Pimlico. How are things going? Just keeping alive. Lovely weather we are having. Yes, indeed. Good for the country. Those farmers are always grumbling. I'll just take a thimbleful of your best gin, Mr Crimmins. A small gin, sir. Yes, sir. Terrible affair that General Slocum explosion. Terrible, terrible! A thousand casualties. And heartrending scenes. Men trampling down women and children. Most brutal thing. What do they say was the cause? Spontaneous combustion: most scandalous revelation. Not a single lifeboat would float and the firehose all burst. What I can't understand is how the inspectors ever allowed a boat like that . . . Now you are talking straight, Mr Crimmins. You know why? Palmoil. Is that a fact? Without a doubt. Well now, look at that. And America they say is the land of the free. I thought we were bad here.

I smiled at him. *America*, I said, quietly, just like that. *What is it? The sweepings of every country including our own. Isn't that true?* That's a fact.

Graft, my dear sir. Well, of course, where there's money going there's always someone to pick it up.

Saw him looking at my frockcoat. Dress does it. Nothing like a dressy appearance. Bowls them over.

– Hello, Simon, Father Cowley said. How are things?

– Hello, Bob, old man, Mr Dedalus answered stopping.

Mr Kernan halted and preened himself before the sloping mirror of Peter Kennedy, hairdresser. Stylish coat, beyond a doubt. Scott of Dawson street. Well worth the half sovereign I gave Neary for it. Never built under three guineas. Fits me down to the ground. Some Kildare street club toff had it probably. John Mulligan, the manager of the Hibernian bank, gave me a very sharp eye yesterday on Carlisle bridge as if he remembered me.

Aham! Must dress the character for those fellows. Knight of the road. Gentleman. And now, Mr Crimmins, may we have the honour of your custom again, sir. The cup that cheers but not inebriates, as the old saying has it.

North wall and sir John Rogerson's quay, with hulls and anchorchains, sailing westward, sailed by a skiff, a crumpled throwaway, rocked on the ferry-wash, Elijah is coming.

Mr Kernan glanced in farewell at his image. High colour, of course. Grizzled moustache. Returned Indian officer. Bravely he bore his stumpy body forward on spatted feet, squaring his shoulders. Is that Lambert's brother over the way, Sam? What? Yes. He's as like it as damn it. No. The windscreen of that motorcar in the sun there. Just a flash like that. Damn like him.

Aham! Hot spirit of juniper juice warmed his vitals and his breath. Good drop of gin, that was. His frocktails winked in bright sunshine to his fat strut.

Down there Emmet was hanged, drawn and quartered. Greasy black rope. Dogs licking the blood off the street when the lord lieutenant's wife drove by in her noddy.

Let me see. Is he buried in saint Michan's? Or no, there was a midnight burial in Glasnevin. Corpse brought in through a secret door in the wall. Dignam is there now. Went out in a puff. Well, well. Better turn down here. Make a detour.

Mr Kernan turned and walked down the slope of Watling street by the corner of Guinness's visitors' waitingroom. Outside the Dublin Distillers Company's stores an outside car without fare or jarvey stood, the reins knotted to the wheel. Damn dangerous thing. Some Tipperary bosthoon endangering the lives of the citizens. Runaway horse.

Denis Breen with his tomes, weary of having waited an hour in John Henry Menton's office, led his wife over O'Connell bridge, bound for the office of Messrs Collis and Ward.

Mr Kernan approached Island street.

Times of the troubles. Must ask Ned Lambert to lend me those reminiscences of sir Jonah Barrington. When you look back on it all now in a kind of retrospective arrangement. Gaming at Daly's. No cardsharping then. One of those fellows got his hand nailed to the table by a dagger. Somewhere here Lord Edward Fitzgerald escaped from major Sirr. Stables behind Moira house.

Damn good gin that was.

Fine dashing young nobleman. Good stock, of course. That ruffian, that sham squire, with his violet gloves, gave him away. Course they were on the wrong side. They rose in dark and evil days. Fine poem that is: Ingram. They were gentlemen. Ben Dollard does sing that ballad touchingly. Masterly rendition.

At the siege of Ross did my father fall.

A cavalcade in easy trot along Pembroke quay passed, outriders leaping, leaping in their, in their saddles. Frock-coats. Cream sunshades.

Mr Kernan hurried forward, blowing pursily.

His Excellency! Too bad! Just missed that by a hair. Damn it! What a pity!

*

Stephen Dedalus watched through the webbed window the lapidary's fingers prove a timedulled chain. Dust webbed the window and the showtrays. Dust darkened the toiling fingers with their vulture nails. Dust slept on dull coils of bronze and silver, lozenges of cinnabar, on rubies, leprous and winedark stones.

Born all in the dark wormy earth, cold specks of fire, evil lights shining in the darkness. Where fallen archangels flung the stars of their brows. Muddy swinesnouts, hands, root and root, gripe and wrest them.

She dances in a foul gloom where gum burns with garlic. A sailorman, rustbearded, sips from a beaker rum and eyes her. A long and seafed silent rut. She dances, capers, wagging her sowish haunches and her hips, on her gross belly flapping a ruby egg.

Old Russell with a smeared shammy rag burnished again his gem, turned it and held it at the point of his Moses' beard. Grandfather ape gloating on a stolen hoard.

And you who wrest old images from the burial earth! The brainsick words of sophists: Antisthenes. A lore of drugs. Orient and immortal wheat standing from everlasting to everlasting.

Two old women fresh from their whiff of the briny trudged through Irishtown along London bridge road, one with a sanded umbrella, one with a midwife's bag in which eleven cockles rolled.

The whirr of flapping leathern bands and hum of dynamos from the powerhouse urged Stephen to be on. Beingless beings. Stop! Throb always without you and the throb always within. Your heart you sing of. I between them. Where? Between two roaring worlds where they swirl, I. Shatter them, one and both. But stun myself too in the blow. Shatter me you who can. Bawd and butcher, were the words. I say! Not yet awhile. A look around.

Yes, quite true. Very large and wonderful and keeps famous time. You say right, sir. A Monday morning, 'twas so, indeed.

Stephen went down Bedford row, the handle of the ash clacking against his shoulderblade. In Clohissey's window a faded 1860 print of Heenan boxing Sayers held his eye. Staring backers with square hats stood round the roped prizering. The heavyweights in light loincloths proposed gently each to other his bulbous fists. And they are throbbing: heroes' hearts.

He turned and halted by the slanted bookcart.

– Twopence each, the huckster said. Four for sixpence.

Tattered pages. *The Irish Beekeeper. Life and Miracles of the Curé of Ars. Pocket Guide to Killarney.*

I might find here one of my pawned schoolprizes. *Stephano Dedalo, alumno optimo, palmam ferenti.*

Father Conmee, having read his little hours, walked through the hamlet of Donnycarney, murmuring vespers.

Binding too good probably, what is this? Eighth and ninth book of Moses. Secret of all secrets. Seal of King David. Thumbed pages: read and read. Who has passed here before me? How to soften chapped hands. Recipe for white wine vinegar. How to win a woman's love. For me this. Say the following talisman three times with hands folded:

– *Se el yilo nebrakada femininum! Amor me solo! Sanktus! Amen.*

Who wrote this? Charms and invocations of the most blessed abbot Peter Salanka to all true believers divulged. As good as any other abbot's charms, as mumbling Joachim's. Down, baldynoddle, or we'll wool your wool.

– What are you doing here, Stephen.

Dilly's high shoulders and shabby dress.

Shut the book quick. Don't let see.

– What are you doing? Stephen said.

A Stuart face of nonesuch Charles, lank locks falling at its sides. It glowed as she crouched feeding the fire with broken boots. I told her of Paris. Late lieabed under a quilt of old overcoats, fingering a pinchbeck bracelet, Dan Kelly's token. *Nebrakada femininum.*

– What have you there? Stephen asked.

– I bought it from the other cart for a penny, Dilly said, laughing nervously. Is it any good?

My eyes they say she has. Do others see me so? Quick, far and daring. Shadow of my mind.

He took the coverless book from her hand. Chardenal's French primer.

– What did you buy that for? he asked. To learn French?

She nodded, reddening and closing tight her lips.

Show no surprise. Quite natural.

– Here, Stephen said. It's all right. Mind Maggy doesn't pawn it on you. I suppose all my books are gone.

– Some, Dilly said. We had to.

She is drowning. Agenbite. Save her. Agenbite. All against us. She will drown me with her, eyes and hair. Lank coils of seaweed hair around me, my heart, my soul. Salt green death.

We.

Agenbite of inwit. Inwit's agenbite.

Misery! Misery!

*

– Hello, Simon, Father Cowley said. How are things?

– Hello, Bob, old man, Mr Dedalus answered, stopping.

They clasped hands loudly outside Reddy and Daughter's. Father Cowley brushed his moustache often downward with a scooping hand.

– What's the best news? Mr Dedalus said.

– Why then not much, Father Cowley said. I'm barricaded up, Simon, with two men prowling around the house trying to effect an entrance.

– Jolly, Mr Dedalus said. Who is it?

– O, Father Cowley said. A certain gombeen man of our acquaintance.

– With a broken back, is it? Mr Dedalus asked.

– The same, Simon, Father Cowley answered. Reuben of that ilk. I'm just waiting for Ben Dollard. He's going to say a word to Long John to get him to take those two men off. All I want is a little time.

He looked with vague hope up and down the quay, a big apple bulging in his neck.

– I know, Mr Dedalus said, nodding. Poor old bockedy Ben! He's always doing a good turn for someone. Hold hard!

He put on his glasses and gazed towards the metal bridge an instant.

– There he is, by God, he said, arse and pockets.

Ben Dollard's loose blue cutaway and square hat above large slops crossed the quay in full gait from the metal bridge. He came towards them at an amble, scratching actively behind his coattails.

As he came near Mr Dedalus greeted:

– Hold that fellow with the bad trousers.

– Hold him now, Ben Dollard said.

Mr Dedalus eyed with cold wandering scorn various points of Ben Dollard's figure. Then, turning to Father Cowley with a nod, he muttered sneeringly:

– That's a pretty garment, isn't it, for a summer's day?

– Why, God eternally curse your soul, Ben Dollard growled furiously, I threw out more clothes in my time than you ever saw.

He stood beside them beaming on them first and on his roomy clothes from points of which Mr Dedalus flicked fluff, saying:

– They were made for a man in his health, Ben, anyhow.

– Bad luck to the jewman that made them, Ben Dollard said. Thanks be to God he's not paid yet.

– And how is that *basso profondo*, Benjamin? Father Cowley asked.

Cashel Boyle O'Connor Fitzmaurice Tisdall Farrell, murmuring, glassy-eyed, strode past the Kildare street club.

Ben Dollard frowned and, making suddenly a chanter's mouth, gave forth a deep note.

– Aw! he said.

– That's the style, Mr Dedalus said, nodding to its drone.

– What about that? Ben Dollard said. Not too dusty? What?

He turned to both.

– That'll do, Father Cowley said, nodding also.

The reverend Hugh C. Love walked from the old Chapterhouse of saint Mary's abbey past James and Charles Kennedy's, rectifiers, attended by Geraldines tall and personable, towards the Tholsel beyond the Ford of Hurdles.

Ben Dollard with a heavy list towards the shopfronts led them forward, his joyful fingers in the air.

– Come along with me to the subsheriff's office, he said. I want to show you the new beauty Rock has for a bailiff. He's a cross between Lobengula and Lynchehaun. He's well worth seeing, mind you. Come along. I saw John Henry Menton casually in the Bodega just now and it will cost me a fall if I don't . . . wait awhile . . . We're on the right lay, Bob, believe you me.

– For a few days tell him, Father Cowley said anxiously.

Ben Dollard halted and stared, his loud orifice open, a dangling button of his coat wagging brightbacked from its thread as he wiped away the heavy shraums that clogged his eyes to hear aright.

– What few days? he boomed. Hasn't your landlord distrained for rent?

– He has, Father Cowley said.

– Then our friend's writ is not worth the paper it's printed on, Ben Dollard said. The landlord has the prior claim. I gave him all the particulars. 29 Windsor avenue. Love is the name?

– That's right, Father Cowley said. The reverend Mr Love. He's a minister in the country somewhere. But are you sure of that?

– You can tell Barabbas from me, Ben Dollard said, that he can put that writ where Jacko put the nuts.

He led Father Cowley boldly forward linked to his bulk.

– Filberts I believe they were, Mr Dedalus said, as he dropped his glasses on his coatfront, following them.

*

– The youngster will be all right, Martin Cunningham said, as they passed out of the Castleyard gate.

The policeman touched his forehead.

– God bless you, Martin Cunningham said, cheerily.

He signed to the waiting jarvey who chucked at the reins and set on towards Lord Edward street.

Bronze by gold, Miss Kennedy's head by Miss Douce's head, appeared above the crossblind of the Ormond hotel.

– Yes, Martin Cunningham said, fingering his beard. I wrote to Father Conmee and laid the whole case before him.

– You could try our friend, Mr Power suggested backward.

– Boyd? Martin Cunningham said shortly. Touch me not.

John Wyse Nolan, lagging behind, reading the list, came after them quickly down Cork hill.

On the steps of the City hall Councillor Nannetti, descending, hailed Alderman Cowley and Councillor Abraham Lyon ascending.

The castle car wheeled empty into upper Exchange street.

– Look here Martin, John Wyse Nolan said, overtaking them at the *Mail* office. I see Bloom put his name down for five shillings.

– Quite right, Martin Cunningham said, taking the list. And put down the five shillings too.

– Without a second word either, Mr Power said.

– Strange but true, Martin Cunningham added.

John Wyse Nolan opened wide eyes.

– I'll say there is much kindness in the jew, he quoted elegantly.

They went down Parliament street.

– There's Jimmy Henry, Mr Power said, just heading for Kavanagh's.

– Righto, Martin Cunningham said. Here goes.

Outside *la Maison Claire* Blazes Boylan waylaid Jack Mooney's brother-in-law, humpy, tight, making for the liberties.

John Wyse Nolan fell back with Mr Power, while Martin Cunningham took the elbow of a dapper little man in a shower of hail suit who walked uncertainly with hasty steps past Micky Anderson's watches.

– The assistant town clerk's corns are giving him some trouble, John Wyse Nolan told Mr Power.

They followed round the corner towards James Kavanagh's winerooms. The empty castle car fronted them at rest in Essex gate. Martin Cunningham, speaking always, showed often the list at which Jimmy Henry did not glance.

– And Long John Fanning is here too, John Wyse Nolan said, as large as life.

The tall form of Long John Fanning filled the doorway where he stood.

– Good day, Mr Subsheriff, Martin Cunningham said, as all halted and greeted.

Long John Fanning made no way for them. He removed his large Henry Clay decisively and his large fierce eyes scowled intelligently over all their faces.

– Are the conscript fathers pursuing their peaceful deliberations? he said, with rich acrid utterance to the assistant town clerk.

Hell open to christians they were having, Jimmy Henry said pettishly, about their damned Irish language. Where was the marshal, he wanted to know, to keep order in the council chamber. And old Barlow the macebearer laid up with asthma, no mace on the table, nothing in order, no quorum even and Hutchinson, the lord mayor, in Llandudno and little Lorcan Sherlock doing *locum tenens* for him. Damned Irish language, of our forefathers.

Long John Fanning blew a plume of smoke from his lips.

Martin Cunningham spoke by turns, twirling the peak of his beard, to the assistant town clerk and the subsheriff, while John Wyse Nolan held his peace.

– What Dignam was that? Long John Fanning asked.

Jimmy Henry made a grimace and lifted his left foot.

– O, my corns! he said plaintively. Come upstairs for goodness' sake till I sit down somewhere. Uff! Ooo! Mind!

Testily he made room for himself beside Long John Fanning's flank and passed in and up the stairs.

– Come on up, Martin Cunningham said to the sub-sheriff. I don't think you knew him or perhaps you did, though.

With John Wyse Nolan Mr Power followed them in.

– Decent little soul he was, Mr Power said to the stalwart back of Long John Fanning ascending towards Long John Fanning in the mirror.

– Rather lowsized, Dignam of Menton's office that was, Martin Cunningham said.

Long John Fanning could not remember him.

Clatter of horsehoofs sounded from the air.

– What's that? Martin Cunningham said.

All turned where they stood; John Wyse Nolan came down again. From the cool shadow of the doorway he saw the horses pass Parliament street, harness and glossy pasterns in sunlight shimmering. Gaily they went past before his cool unfriendly eyes, not quickly. In saddles of the leaders, leaping leaders, rode outriders.

– What was it? Martin Cunningham asked, as they went on up the staircase.

– The lord lieutenant general and general governor of Ireland, John Wyse Nolan answered from the stairfoot.

*

As they trod across the thick carpet Buck Mulligan whispered behind his panama to Haines.

– Parnell's brother. There in the corner.

They chose a small table near the window opposite a long-faced man whose beard and gaze hung intently down on a chessboard.

– Is that he? Haines asked, twisting round in his seat.

– Yes, Mulligan said. That's John Howard, his brother, our city marshal.

John Howard Parnell translated a white bishop quietly and his grey claw went up again to his forehead whereat it rested.

An instant after, under its screen, his eyes looked quickly, ghostbright, at his foe and fell once more upon a working corner.

– I'll take a *mélange*, Haines said to the waitress.

– Two *mélanges*, Buck Mulligan said. And bring us some scones and butter and some cakes as well.

When she had gone he said, laughing:

– We call it D. B. C. because they have damn bad cakes. O, but you missed Dedalus on *Hamlet*.

Haines opened his newbought book.

– I'm sorry, he said. Shakespeare is the happy hunting ground of all minds that have lost their balance.

The onelegged sailor growled at the area of 14 Nelson street:

– *England expects* . . .

Buck Mulligan's primrose waistcoat shook gaily to his laughter.

– You should see him, he said, when his body loses its balance. Wandering Ængus I call him.

– I am sure he has an *idée fixe*, Haines said, pinching his chin thoughtfully with thumb and forefinger. Now I am speculating what it would be likely to be. Such persons always have.

Buck Mulligan bent across the table gravely.

– They drove his wits astray, he said, by visions of hell. He will never capture the Attic note. The note of Swinburne, of all poets, the white death and the ruddy birth. That is his tragedy. He can never be a poet. The joy of creation . . .

– Eternal punishment, Haines said, nodding curtly. I see. I tackled him this morning on belief. There was something on his mind, I saw. It's rather interesting because Professor Pokorny of Vienna makes an interesting point out of that.

Buck Mulligan's watchful eyes saw the waitress come. He helped her to unload her tray.

– He can find no trace of hell in ancient Irish myth, Haines said, amid the cheerful cups. The moral idea seems lacking, the sense of destiny, of retribution. Rather strange he should have just that fixed idea. Does he write anything for your movement?

He sank two lumps of sugar deftly longwise through the whipped cream. Buck Mulligan slit a steaming scone in two and plastered butter over its smoking pith. He bit off a soft piece hungrily.

– Ten years, he said, chewing and laughing. He is going to write something in ten years.

– Seems a long way off, Haines said, thoughtfully lifting his spoon. Still, I shouldn't wonder if he did after all.

He tasted a spoonful from the creamy cone of his cup.

– This is real Irish cream I take it, he said with forbearance. I don't want to be imposed on.

Elijah, skiff, light crumpled throwaway, sailed eastward by flanks of ships and trawlers, amid an archipelago of corks, beyond new Wapping street past Benson's ferry, and by the threemasted schooner *Rosevean* from Bridgwater with bricks.

*

Almidano Artifoni walked past Holles street, past Sewell's yard. Behind him Cashel Boyle O'Connor Fitzmaurice Tisdall Farrell with stickumbrelladustcoat dangling, shunned the lamp before Mr Law Smith's house and, crossing, walked along Merrion square. Distantly behind him a blind stripling tapped his way by the wall of College Park.

Cashel Boyle O'Connor Fitzmaurice Tisdall Farrell walked as far as Mr Lewis Werner's cheerful windows, then turned and strode back along Merrion square, his stickumbrelladustcoat dangling.

At the corner of Wilde's he halted, frowned at Elijah's name announced on the Metropolitan Hall, frowned at the distant pleasance of duke's lawn. His eyeglass flashed frowning in the sun. With ratsteeth bared he muttered:

– *Coactus volui.*

He strode on for Clare street, grinding his fierce word.

As he strode past Mr Bloom's dental windows the sway of his dustcoat brushed rudely from its angle a slender tapping cane and swept onwards, having buffeted a thewless body. The blind stripling turned his sickly face after the striding form.

– God's curse on you, he said sourly, whoever you are! You're blinder nor I am, you bitch's bastard!

*

Opposite Ruggy O'Donohoe's Master Patrick Aloysius Dignam, pawing the pound and half of Mangan's, late Fehrenbach's, porksteaks he had been sent for, went along warm Wicklow street dawdling. It was too blooming dull sitting in the parlour with Mrs Stoer and Mrs Quigley and Mrs MacDowell and the blind down and they all at their sniffles and sipping sups of the superior tawny sherry uncle Barney brought from Tunney's. And they eating crumbs of the cottage fruit cake jawing the whole blooming time and sighing.

After Wicklow lane the window of Madame Doyle, court dress milliner, stopped him. He stood looking in at the two puckers stripped to their pelts and putting up their props. From the sidemirrors two mourning Masters Dignam gaped silently. Myler Keogh, Dublin's pet lamb, will meet sergeant-major Bennett, the Portobello bruiser, for a purse of fifty sovereigns, God, that'd be a good pucking match to see. Myler Keogh, that's the chap sparring out to him with the green sash. Two bar entrance, soldiers half price. I could easy do a bunk on ma. Master Dignam on his left turned as he turned. That's me in mourning. When is it? May the twentysecond. Sure, the blooming thing is all over. He turned to the right and on his right Master Dignam turned, his cap awry, his collar sticking up. Buttoning it down, his chin lifted, he saw the image of Marie Kendall, charming soubrette, beside the two puckers. One of them mots that do be in the packets of fags Stoer smokes that his old fellow welted hell out of him for one time he found out.

Master Dignam got his collar down and dawdled on. The best pucker going for strength was Fitzsimons. One puck in the wind from that fellow would knock you into the middle of next week, man. But the best pucker for science was Jem Corbet before Fitzsimons knocked the stuffings out of him, dodging and all.

In Grafton street Master Dignam saw a red flower in a toff's mouth and a swell pair of kicks on him and he listening to what the drunk was telling him and grinning all the time.

No Sandymount tram.

Master Dignam walked along Nassau street, shifted the porksteaks to his other hand. His collar sprang up again and he tugged it down. The blooming stud was too small for the buttonhole of the shirt, blooming end to it. He met schoolboys with stachels. I'm not going tomorrow either, stay away till Monday. He met other schoolboys. Do they notice I'm in mourning? Uncle Barney said he'd get it into the paper tonight. Then they'll all see it in the paper and read my name printed and pa's name.

His face got all grey instead of being red like it was and there was a fly walking over it up to his eye. The scrunch that was when they were screwing the screws into the coffin: and the bumps when they were bringing it downstairs.

Pa was inside it and ma crying in the parlour and uncle Barney telling the men how to get it round the bend. A big coffin it was, and high and heavylooking. How was that? The last night pa was boosed he was standing on the landing there bawling out for his boots to go out to Tunney's for to boose more and he looked butty and short in his shirt. Never see him again. Death, that is. Pa is dead. My father is dead. He told me to be a good son to ma. I couldn't hear the other things he said but I saw his tongue and his teeth trying to say it better. Poor pa. That was Mr Dignam, my father. I hope he is in purgatory now because he went to confession to father Conroy on Saturday night.

*

William Humble, earl of Dudley, and Lady Dudley, accompanied by lieutenantcolonel Hesseltine, drove out after luncheon from the viceregal lodge. In the following carriage were the honourable Mrs Paget, Miss de Courcy and the honourable Gerald Ward, A. D. C. in attendance.

The cavalcade passed out by the lower gate of Phœnix Park saluted by obsequious policemen and proceeded past Kingsbridge along the northern quays. The viceroy was most cordially greeted on his way through the metropolis. At Bloody bridge Mr Thomas Kernan beyond the river greeted him vainly from afar. Between Queen's and Whitworth bridges Lord Dudley's viceregal carriages passed and were unsaluted by Mr Dudley White, B. L., M. A., who stood on Arran Quay outside Mrs M. E. White's, the pawnbroker's, at the corner of Arran street west stroking his nose with his forefinger, undecided whether he should arrive at Phibsborough more quickly by a triple change of tram or by hailing a car or on foot through Smithfield, Constitution hill and Broadstone terminus. In the porch of Four Courts Richie Goulding with the costsbag of Goulding, Collis and Ward saw him with surprise. Past Richmond bridge at the doorstep of the office of Reuben J. Dodd, solicitor, agent for the Patriotic Insurance Company, an elderly female about to enter changed her plan and retracing her steps by King's windows smiled credulously on the representative of His Majesty. From its sluice in Wood quay wall under Tom Devan's office Poddle river hung out in fealty a tongue of liquid sewage. Above the crossblind of the Ormond Hotel, gold by bronze, Miss Kennedy's head by Miss Douce's head watched and admired. On Ormond quay Mr Simon Dedalus, steering his way from the greenhouse for the subsheriff's office, stood still in midstreet and brought his hat low. His Excellency graciously returned Mr Dedalus' greeting. From Cahill's corner the reverend Hugh C. Love, M. A., made obeisance unperceived, mindful of lords deputies whose hands benignant had held of yore rich advowsons. On Grattan bridge Lenehan and M'Coy, taking leave of each other, watched the carriages go by. Passing by Roger Greene's office and Dollard's big red printinghouse Gerty MacDowell, carrying the Catesby's cork lino letters for her father who was laid up, knew by the style it was the lord and lady lieutenant but she couldn't see what Her Excellency had on because the tram and Spring's big yellow furniture van had to stop in front of her on account of its being the lord lieutenant. Beyond Lundy Foot's from the shaded door of Kavanagh's winerooms John Wyse Nolan smiled with unseen coldness towards the lord lieutenantgeneral and general governor of Ireland. The Right Honourable William Humble, earl of Dudley, G. C. V. O., passed Micky Anderson's all times ticking watches and Henry and James's wax smartsuited freshcheeked models, the gentleman Henry, *dernier cri* James. Over against Dame gate Tom Rochford and Nosey Flynn watched the approach of the cavalcade. Tom Rochford, seeing the eyes of lady Dudley on him, took his thumbs quickly out of the pockets of his claret waistcoat and doffed his cap to her. A charming *soubrette*, great Marie Kendall, with dauby cheeks and lifted skirt, smiled daubily from her poster upon William Humble, earl of Dudley, and upon lieutenantcolonel H. G. Hesseltine and also upon the honourable Gerald Ward A. D. C. From the window of the D. B. C. Buck Mulligan gaily, and Haines gravely, gazed down on the viceregal equipage over the shoulders of eager guests, whose mass of forms darkened the chessboard whereon John Howard Parnell looked intently. In Fownes's street, Dilly Dedalus, straining her sight upward from Chardenal's first French primer, saw sunshades spanned and wheelspokes spinning in the glare. John Henry Menton, filling the doorway of Commercial Buildings, stared from winebig oyster eyes, holding a fat gold hunter watch not looked at in his fat left hand not feeling it. Where the foreleg of King Billy's horse pawed the air Mrs Breen plucked her hastening husband back from under the hoofs of the outriders. She shouted in his ear the tidings. Understanding, he shifted his tomes to his left breast and saluted the second carriage. The honourable Gerald Ward A. D. C., agreeably surprised, made haste to reply. At Ponsonby's corner a jaded white flagon H. halted and four tallhatted white flagons halted behind him, E. L. Y.' S., while outriders pranced past and carriages. Opposite Pigott's music warerooms Mr Denis J. Maginni professor of dancing & c, gaily apparelled, gravely walked, outpassed by a viceroy and unobserved. By the provost's wall came jauntily Blazes Boylan, stepping in tan shoes and socks with skyblue clocks to the refrain of *My girl's a Yorkshire girl.*

Blazes Boylan presented to the leaders' skyblue frontlets and high action a skyblue tie, a widebrimmed straw hat at a rakish angle and a suit of indigo serge. His hands in his jacket pockets forgot to salute but he offered to the three ladies the bold admiration of his eyes and the red flower between his lips. As they drove along Nassau street His Excellency drew the attention of his bowing consort to the programme of music which was being discoursed in College park. Unseen brazen highland laddies blared and drum-thumped after the *cortège*:

> But though she's a factory lass
> And wears no fancy clothes.
> Baraabum.
> Yet I've a sort of a
> Yorkshire relish for
> My little Yorkshire rose.
> Baraabum.

Thither of the wall the quartermile flat handicappers, M. C. Green, H. Thrift, T. M. Patey, C. Scaife, J. B. Jeffs, G. N. Morphy, F. Stevenson, C. Adderly, and W. C. Huggard started in pursuit. Striding past Finn's hotel, Cashel Boyle O'Connor Fitzmaurice Tisdall Farrell stared through a fierce eyeglass across the carriages at the head of Mr E. M. Solomons in the window of the Austro-Hungarian viceconsulate. Deep in Leinster street, by Trinity's postern, a loyal king's man, Hornblower, touched his tallyho cap. As the glossy horses pranced by Merrion square Master Patrick Aloysius Dignam, waiting, saw salutes being given to the gent with the topper and raised also his new black cap with fingers greased by porksteak paper. His collar too sprang up. The viceroy, on his way to inaugurate the Mirus bazaar in aid of funds for Mercer's hospital, drove with his following towards Lower Mount street. He passed a blind stripling opposite Broadbent's. In Lower Mount street a pedestrian in a brown macintosh, eating dry bread, passed swiftly and unscathed across the viceroy's path. At the Royal Canal bridge, from his hoarding, Mr Eugene Stratton, his blub lips agrin, bade all comers welcome to Pembroke township. At Haddington road corner two sanded women halted themselves, an umbrella and a bag in which eleven cockles rolled to view with wonder the lord mayor and lady mayoress without his golden chain. On Northumberland and Landsdowne roads His Excellency acknowledged punctually salutes from rare male walkers, the salute of two small schoolboys at the garden gate of the house said to have been admired by the late queen when visiting the Irish capital with her husband, the prince consort, in 1849, and the salute of Almidano Artifoni's sturdy trousers swallowed by a closing door.

*   *   *   *   *

◀ BRONZE BY GOLD HEARD THE HOOFIRONS, STEELY-RINGING

Imperthnthn thnthnthn.

Chips, picking chips off rocky thumbnail, chips.

Horrid! And gold flushed more.

A husky fifenote blew.

Blew. Blue bloom is on the

Gold pinnacled hair.

A jumping rose on satiny breasts of satin, rose of Castille.

Trilling, trilling: Idolores.

Peep! Who's in the . . . peepofgold?

Tink cried to bronze in pity.

And a call, pure, long and throbbing. Longindying call.

Decoy. Soft word. But look! The bright stars fade. O rose! Notes chirruping answer. Castille. The morn is breaking.

Jingle jingle jaunted jingling.

Coin rang. Clock clacked.

Avowal. *Sonnez.* I could. Rebound of garter. Not leave thee. Smack. *La cloche!* Thigh smack. Avowal. Warm. Sweetheart, goodbye!

Jingle. Bloo.

Boomed crashing chords. When love absorbs. War! War! The tympanum.

A sail! A veil awave upon the waves.

Lost. Throstle fluted. All is lost now.

Horn. Hawhorn.

When first he saw. Alas!

Full tup. Full throb.

Warbling. Ah, lure! Alluring.

Martha! Come!

Clapclop. Clipclap. Clappyclap.

Goodgod henev erheard inall.

Deaf bald Pat brought pad knife took up.

A moonlit nightcall: far: far.

I feel so sad. P. S. So lonely blooming.

Listen!

The spiked and winding cold seahorn. Have you the? Each and for other plash and silent roar.

Pearls: when she. Liszt's rhapsodies. Hissss.

You don't?

Did not: no, no: believe: Lidlyd. With a cock with a carra.

Black.

Deepsounding. Do, Ben, do.

Wait while you wait. Hee hee. Wait while you hee.

But wait!

Low in dark middle earth. Embedded ore.

Naminedamine. All gone. All fallen.

Tiny, her tremulous fernfoils of maidenhair.

Amen! He gnashed in fury.

Fro. To, fro. A baton cool protruding.

Bronzelydia by Minagold.

By bronze, by gold, in oceangreen of shadow. Bloom. Old Bloom.

One rapped, one tapped with a carra, with a cock.

Pray for him! Pray, good people!

His gouty fingers nakkering.

Big Benaben. Big Benben.

Last rose Castille of summer left bloom I feel so sad alone.

Pwee! Little wind piped wee.

True men. Lid Ker Cow De and Doll. Ay, ay. Like you men. Will lift your tschink with tschunk.

Fff! Oo!

Where bronze from anear? Where gold from afar? Where hoofs?

Rrrpr. Kraa. Kraandl.

Then, not till then. My eppripfftaph. Be pfrwritt.

Done.

Begin!

Bronze by gold, Miss Douce's head by Miss Kennedy's head, over the crossblind of the Ormond bar heard the viceregal hoofs go by, ringing steel.

– Is that her? asked Miss Kennedy.

Miss Douce said yes, sitting with his ex, pearl grey and *eau de Nil*.

– Exquisite contrast, Miss Kennedy said.

When all agog Miss Douce said eagerly:

– Look at the fellow in the tall silk.

– Who? Where? gold asked more eagerly.

– In the second carriage, Miss Douce's wet lips said, laughing in the sun. He's looking. Mind till I see.

She darted, bronze, to the backmost corner, flattening her face against the pane in a halo of hurried breath.

Her wet lips tittered:

– He's killed looking back.

She laughed:

– O wept! Aren't men frightful idiots?

With sadness.

Miss Kennedy sauntered sadly from bright light, twining a loose hair behind an ear. Sauntering sadly, gold no more, she twisted twined a hair. Sadly she twined in sauntering gold hair behind a curving ear.

– It's them has the fine times, sadly then she said.

A man.

Bloowho went by by Moulang's pipes, bearing in his breast the sweets of sin, by Wine's antiques in memory bearing sweet sinful words, by Carroll's dusky battered plate, for Raoul.

The boots to them, them in the bar, them barmaids came. For them unheeding him he banged on the counter his tray of chattering china. And

– There's your teas, he said.

Miss Kennedy with manners transposed the teatray down to an upturned lithia crate, safe from eyes, low.

– What is it? loud boots unmannerly asked.

– Find out, Miss Douce retorted, leaving her spyingpoint.

– Your *beau*, is it?

A haughty bronze replied:

– I'll complain to Mrs de Massey on you if I hear any more of your impertinent insolence.

– Imperthnthn thnthnthn, bootsnout sniffed rudely, as he retreated as she threatened as he had come.

Bloom.

On her flower frowning Miss Douce said:

– Most aggravating that young brat is. If he doesn't conduct himself I'll wring his ear for him a yard long.

Ladylike in exquisite contrast.

– Take no notice, Miss Kennedy rejoined.

She poured in a teacup tea, then back in the teapot tea. They cowered under their reef of counter, waiting on footstools, crates upturned, waiting for their teas to draw. They pawed their blouses, both of black satin, two and nine a yard, waiting for their teas to draw, and two and seven.

Yes, bronze from anear, by gold from afar, heard steel from anear, hoofs ring from afar, and heard steelhoofs ringhoof ringsteel.

– Am I awfully sunburnt?

Miss bronze unbloused her neck.

– No, said Miss Kennedy. It gets brown after. Did you try the borax with the cherry laurel water?

Miss Douce halfstood to see her skin askance in the barmirror gilded-lettered where hock and claret glasses shimmered and in their midst a shell.

– And leave it to my hands, she said.

– Try it with the glycerine, Miss Kennedy advised.

Bidding her neck and hands adieu Miss Douce

– Those things only bring out a rash, replied, reseated. I asked that old fogey in Boyd's for something for my skin.

Miss Kennedy, pouring now fulldrawn tea, grimaced and prayed:

– O, don't remind me of him for mercy'sake!

– But wait till I tell you, Miss Douce entreated.

Sweet tea Miss Kennedy having poured with milk plugged both two ears with little fingers.

– No, don't, she cried.

– I won't listen, she cried.

But Bloom?

Miss Douce grunted in snuffy fogey's tone:

– For your what? says he.

Miss Kennedy unplugged her ears to hear, to speak: but said, but prayed again:

– Don't let me think of him or I'll expire. The hideous old wretch! That night in the Antient Concert Rooms.

She sipped distastefully her brew, hot tea, a sip, sipped sweet tea.

– Here he was, Miss Douce said, cocking her bronze head three quarters, ruffling her nosewings. Hufa! Hufa!

Shrill shriek of laughter sprang from Miss Kennedy's throat. Miss Douce huffed and snorted down her nostrils that quivered imperthnthn like a shout in quest.

– O! shrieking, Miss Kennedy cried. Will you ever forget his goggle eye?

Miss Douce chimed in in deep bronze laughter, shouting:

– And your other eye!

Bloowhose dark eye read Aaron Figatner's name. Why do I always think Figather? Gathering figs I think. And Prosper Loré's huguenot name. By Bassi's blessed virgins Bloom's dark eyes went by. Bluerobed, white under, come to me. God they believe she is: or goddess. Those today. I could not see. That fellow spoke. A student. After with Dedalus' son. He might be Mulligan. All comely virgins. That brings those rakes of fellows in: her white.

By went his eyes. The sweets of sin. Sweet are the sweets.

Of sin.

In a giggling peal young goldbronze voices blended, Douce with Kennedy your other eye. They threw young heads back, bronze gigglegold, to let freely their laughter, screaming, your other, signals to each other, high piercing notes.

Ah, panting, sighing. Sighing, ah, fordone their mirth died down.

Miss Kennedy lipped her cup again, raised, drank a sip and gigglegiggled. Miss Douce, bending again over the teatray, ruffled again her nose and rolled droll fattened eyes. Again Kennygiggles, stooping her fair pinnacles of hair, stooping, her tortoise napecomb showed, spluttered out of her mouth her tea, choking in tea and laughter, coughing with choking, crying:

– O greasy eyes! Imagine being married to a man like that, she cried. With his bit of beard!

Douce gave full vent to a splendid yell, a full yell of full woman, delight, joy, indignation.

– Married to the greasy nose! she yelled.

Shrill, with deep laughter, after bronze in gold, they urged each each to peal after peal, ringing in changes, bronzegold goldbronze, shrilldeep, to laughter after laughter. And then laughed more. Greasy I knows. Exhausted, breathless their shaken heads they laid, braided and pinnacled by glossy-combed, against the counterledge. All flushed (O!), panting, sweating (O!), all breathless.

Married to Bloom, to greaseaseabloom.

– O saints above! Miss Douce said, sighed above her jumping rose. I wished I hadn't laughed so much. I feel all wet.

– O, Miss Douce! Miss Kennedy protested. You horrid thing!

And flushed yet more (you horrid!), more goldenly.

By Cantwell's offices roved Greaseabloom, by Ceppi's virgins, bright of their oils. Nannetti's father hawked those things about, wheedling at doors as I. Religion pays. Must see him about Keyes's par. Eat first. I want. Not yet. At four, she said. Time ever passing. Clockhands turning. On. Where eat? The Clarence, Dolphin. On. For Raoul. Eat. If I net five guineas with those ads. The violet silk petticoats. Not yet. The sweets of sin.

Flushed less, still less, goldenly paled.

Into their bar strolled Mr Dedalus. Chips, picking chips off one of his rocky thumbnails. Chips. He strolled.

– O welcome back, Miss Douce.

He held her hand. Enjoyed her holidays?

– Tiptop.

He hoped she had nice weather in Rostrevor.

– Gorgeous, she said. Look at the holy show I am. Lying out on the strand all day.

Bronze whiteness.

– That was exceedingly naughty of you, Mr Dedalus told her and pressed her hand indulgently. Tempting poor simple males.

Miss Douce of satin douced her arm away.

– O go away, she said. You're very simple, I don't think.

He was.

– Well now, I am, he mused. I looked so simple in the cradle they christened me simple Simon.

– You must have been a doaty, Miss Douce made answer. And what did the doctor order today?

– Well now, he mused, whatever you say yourself. I think I'll trouble you for some fresh water and a half glass of whisky.

Jingle.

– With the greatest alacrity, Miss Douce agreed.

With grace of alacrity towards the mirror gilt Cantrell and Cochrane's she turned herself. With grace she tapped a measure of gold whisky from her crystal keg. Forth from the skirt of his coat Mr Dedalus brought pouch and pipe. Alacrity she served. He blew through the flue two husky fifenotes.

– By Jove, he mused. I often wanted to see the Mourne mountains. Must be a great tonic in the air down there. But a long threatening comes at last, they say. Yes, yes.

Yes. He fingered shreds of hair, her maidenhair, her mermaid's, into the bowl. Chips. Shreds. Musing. Mute.

None not said nothing. Yes.

Gaily Miss Douce polished a tumbler, trilling:

– *O, Idolores, queen of the eastern seas!*

– Was Mr Lidwell in today?

In came Lenehan. Round him peered Lenehan. Mr Bloom reached Essex bridge. Yes, Mr Bloom crossed bridge of Yessex. To Martha I must write. Buy paper. Daly's. Girl there civil. Bloom. Old Bloom. Blue Bloom is on the rye.

– He was in at lunchtime, Miss Douce said.

Lenehan came forward.

– Was Mr Boylan looking for me?

He asked. She answered:

– Miss Kennedy, was Mr Boylan in while I was upstairs?

She asked. Miss voice of Kennedy answered, a second teacup poised, her gaze upon a page.

– No. He was not.

Miss gaze of Kennedy, heard not seen, read on. Lenehan round the sandwichbell wound his round body round.

– Peep! Who's in the corner?

No glance of Kennedy rewarding him he yet made overtures. To mind her stops. To read only the black ones: round o and crooked ess.

Jingle jaunty jingle.

Girlgold she read and did not glance. Take no notice. She took no notice while he read by rote a solfa fable for her, plappering flatly:

– Ah fox met ah stork. Said thee fox too thee stork: Will you put your bill down inn my troath and pull upp ah bone?

He droned in vain. Miss Douce turned to her tea aside.

He sighed, aside:

– Ah me! O my!

He greeted Mr Dedalus and got a nod.

– Greetings from the famous son of a famous father.

– Who may he be? Mr Dedalus asked.

Lenehan opened most genial arms. Who?

– Who may he be? he asked. Can you ask? Stephen, the youthful bard. Dry.

Mr Dedalus, famous father, laid by his dry filled pipe.

– I see, he said. I didn't recognize him for the moment. I hear he is keeping very select company. Have you seen him lately?

He had.

– I quaffed the nectarbowl with him this very day, said Lenehan. In Mooney's *en ville* and in Mooney's *sur mer*. He had received the rhino for the labour of his muse.

He smiled at bronze's teabathed lips, at listening lips and eyes.

– The *élite* of Erin hung upon his lips. The ponderous pundit, Hugh MacHugh, Dublin's most brilliant scribe and editor and that minstrel boy of the wild wet west who is known by the euphonious appellation of the O'Madden Burke.

After an interval Mr Dedalus raised his grog and

– That must have been highly diverting, said he. I see.

He see. He drank. With faraway mourning mountain eye. Set down his glass.

He looked towards the saloon door.

– I see you have moved the piano.

– The tuner was in today, Miss Douce replied, tuning it for the smoking concert and I never heard such an exquisite player.

– Is that a fact?

– Didn't he, Miss Kennedy? The real classical, you know. And blind too, poor fellow. Not twenty I'm sure he was.

– Is that a fact? Mr Dedalus said.

He drank and strayed away.

– So sad to look at his face, Miss Douce condoled.

God's curse on bitch's bastard.

Tink to her pity cried a diner's bell. To the door of the diningroom came bald Pat, came bothered Pat, came Pat, waiter of Ormond. Lager for diner. Lager without alacrity she served.

With patience Lenehan waited for Boylan with impatience, for jingle jaunty blazes boy.

Upholding the lid he (who?) gazed in the coffin (coffin?) at the oblique triple (piano!) wires. He pressed (the same who pressed indulgently her hand), soft pedalling a triple of keys to see the thicknesses of felt advancing, to hear the muffled hammerfall in action.

Two sheets cream vellum paper one reserve two envelopes when I was in Wisdom Hely's wise Bloom in Daly's Henry Flower bought. Are you not happy in your home? Flower to console me and a pin cuts lo. Means something, language of flow. Was it a daisy? Innocence that is. Respectable girl meet after mass. Tanks awfully muchly. Wise Bloom eyed on the door a poster, a swaying mermaid smoking mid nice waves. Smoke mermaids, coolest whiff of all. Hair streaming: lovelorn. For some man. For Raoul. He eyed and saw afar on Essex bridge a gay hat riding on a jauntingcar. It is. Third time. Coincidence.

Jingling on supple rubbers it jaunted from the bridge to Ormond quay. Follow. Risk it. Go quick. At four. Near now. Out.

– Twopence, sir, the shopgirl dared to say.

– Aha . . . I was forgetting . . . Excuse . . .

– And four.

At four she. Winsomely she on Bloohimwhom smiled. Bloo smi qui go. Ternoon. Think you're the only pebble on the beach? Does that to all. For men.

In drowsy silence gold bent on her page.

From the saloon a call came, long in dying. That was a tuningfork the tuner had that he forgot that he now struck. A call again. That he now poised that it now throbbed. You hear? It throbbed, pure, purer, softly and softlier, its buzzing prongs. Longer in dying call.

Pat paid for diner's popcorked bottle: and over tumbler tray and popcorked bottle ere he went he whispered, bald and bothered, with Miss Douce.

– *The bright stars fade . . .*

A voiceless song sang from within, singing:

– *. . . the morn is breaking.*

A duodene of birdnotes chirruped bright treble answer under sensitive hands. Brightly the keys, all twinkling, linked, all harpsichording, called to a voice to sing the strain of dewy morn, of youth, of love's leavetaking, life's, love's morn.

– *The dewdrops pearl . . .*

Lenehan's lips over the counter lisped a low whistle of decoy.

– But look this way, he said, rose of Castille.

Jingle jaunted by the curb and stopped.

She rose and closed her reading, rose of Castille. Fretted forlorn, dreamily rose.

– Did she fall or was she pushed? he asked her.

She answered, slighting:

– Ask no questions and you'll hear no lies.

Like lady, ladylike.

Blazes Boylan's smart tan shoes creaked on the barfloor where he strode. Yes, gold from anear by bronze from afar. Lenehan heard and knew and hailed him:

– See the conquering hero comes.

Between the car and window, warily walking, went Bloom, unconquered hero. See me he might. The seat he sat on: warm. Black wary hecat walked towards Richie Goulding's legal bag, lifted aloft saluting.

– *And I from thee* . . .

– I heard you were round, said Blazes Boylan.

He touched to fair Miss Kennedy a rim of his slanted straw. She smiled on him. But sister bronze outsmiled her, preening for him her richer hair, a bosom and a rose.

Boylan bespoke potions.

– What's your cry? Glass of bitter? Glass of bitter, please, and a sloegin for me. Wire in yet?

Not yet. At four he. All said four.

Cowley's red lugs and Adam's apple in the door of the sheriff's office. Avoid. Goulding a chance. What is he doing in the Ormond? Car waiting. Wait.

Hello. Where off to? Something to eat? I too was just. In here. What, Ormond? Best value in Dublin. Is that so? Diningroom. Sit tight there. See, not be seen. I think I'll join you. Come on. Richie led on. Bloom followed bag. Dinner fit for a prince.

Miss Douce reached high to take a flagon, stretching her satin arm, her bust, that all but burst, so high.

– O! O! jerked Lenehan, gasping at each stretch. O!

But easily she seized her prey and led it low in triumph.

– Why don't you grow? asked Blazes Boylan.

Shebronze, dealing from her jar thick syrupy liquor for his lips, looked as it flowed (flower in his coat: who gave him?), and syrupped with her voice:

– Fine goods in small parcels.

That is to say she. Neatly she poured slowsyrupy sloe.

– Here's fortune, Blazes said.

He pitched a broad coin down. Coin rang.

– Hold on, said Lenehan, till I . . .

– Fortune, he wished, lifting his bubbled ale.

– Sceptre will win in a canter, he said.

– I plunged a bit, said Boylan winking and drinking. Not on my own, you know. Fancy of a friend of mine.

Lenehan still drank and grinned at his tilted ale and at Miss Douce's lips that all but hummed, not shut, the oceansong her lips had trilled. Idolores. The eastern seas.

Clock whirred. Miss Kennnedy passed their way (flower, wonder who gave), bearing away teatray. Clock clacked.

Miss Douce took Boylan's coin, struck boldly the cash-register. It clanged. Clock clacked. Fair one of Egypt teased and sorted in the till and hummed and handed coins in change. Look to the west. A clack. For me.

– What time is that? asked Blazes Boylan. Four?

O'clock.

Lenehan, small eyes ahunger on her humming, bust ahumming, tugged Blazes Boylan's elbowsleeve.

– Let's hear the time, he said.

The bag of Goulding, Collis, Ward led Bloom by ryebloom flowered tables. Aimless he chose with agitated aim, bald Pat attending, a table near the door. Be near. At four. Has he forgotten? Perhaps a trick. Not come: whet appetite. I couldn't do. Wait, wait. Pat, waiter, waited.

Sparkling bronze azure eyed Blazure's skyblue bow and eyes.

– Go on, pressed Lenehan. There's no-one. He never heard.

– . . . *to Flora's lips did hie.*

High, a high note, pealed in the treble, clear.

Bronzedouce, communing with her rose that sank and rose, sought Blazes Boylan's flower and eyes.

– Please, please.

He pleaded over returning phrases of avowal.

– *I could not leave thee . . .*

– Afterwits, Miss Douce promised coyly.

– No, now, urged Lenehan. *Sonnez la cloche!* O do! There's no-one.

She looked. Quick. Miss Kenn out of earshot. Sudden bent. Two kindling faces watched her bend.

Quavering the chords strayed from the air, found it again, lost chord, and lost and found it faltering.

– Go on! Do! *Sonnez!*

Bending, she nipped a peak of skirt above her knee. Delayed. Taunted them still, bending, suspending, with wilful eyes.

– *Sonnez!*

Smack. She let free sudden in rebound her nipped elastic garter smack-warm against her smackable woman's warm-hosed thigh.

– *La cloche!* cried gleeful Lenehan. Trained by owner. No sawdust there.

She smilesmirked supercilious (wept! aren't men?), but, lightward gliding, mild she smiled on Boylan.

– You're the essence of vulgarity, she in gliding said.

Boylan, eyed, eyed. Tossed to fat lips his chalice, drankoff his tiny chalice, sucking the last fat violet syrupy drops. His spellbound eyes went after her gliding head as it went down the bar by mirrors, gilded arch for ginger ale, hock and claret glasses shimmering, a spiky shell, where it concerted, mirrored, bronze with sunnier bronze.

Yes, bronze from anearby.

– . . . *Sweetheart, goodbye!*

– I'm off, said Boylan with impatience.

He slid his chalice brisk away, grasped his change.

– Wait a shake, begged Lenehan, drinking quickly. I wanted to tell you. Tom Rochford . . .

– Come on to blazes, said Blazes Boylan, going.

Lenehan gulped to go.

– Got the horn or what? he said. Wait. I'm coming.

He followed the hasty creaking shoes but stood by nimbly by the threshold, saluting forms, a bulky with a slender.

– How do you do, Mr Dollard?

– Eh? How do? How do? Ben Dollard's vague bass answered, turning an instant from Father Cowley's woe. He won't give you any trouble, Bob. Alf Bergan will speak to the long fellow. We'll put a barleystraw in that Judas Iscariot's ear this time.

Sighing, Mr Dedalus came through the saloon, a finger soothing an eyelid.

– Hoho, we will, Ben Dollard yodled jollily. Come on, Simon, give us a ditty. We heard the piano.

Bald Pat, bothered waiter, waited for drink orders, Power for Richie. And Bloom? Let me see. Not make him walk twice. His corns. Four now. How warm this black is. Course nerves a bit. Refracts (is it?) heat. Let me see. Cider. Yes, bottle of cider.

– What's that? Mr Dedalus said. I was only vamping, man.

– Come on, come on, Ben Dollard called. Begone, dull care. Come, Bob.

He ambled Dollard, bulky slops, before them (hold that fellow with the: hold him now) into the saloon. He plumped him Dollard on the stool. His gouty paws plumped chords. Plumped stopped abrupt.

Bald Pat in the doorway met tealess gold returning. Bothered he wanted Power and cider. Bronze by the window watched, bronze from afar.

Jingle a tinkle jaunted.

Bloom heard a jing, a little sound. He's off. Light sob of breath Bloom sighed on the silent bluehued flowers. Jingling. He's gone. Jingle. Hear.

– Love and war, Ben, Mr Dedalus said. God be with old times.

Miss Douce's brave eyes, unregarded, turned from the crossblind, smitten by sunlight. Gone. Pensive (who knows?), smitten (the smiting light), she lowered the dropblind with a sliding cord. She drew down pensive (why did he go so quick when I?) about her bronze, over the bar where bald stood by sister gold, inexquisite contrast, contrast inexquisite nonexquisite, slow cool dim seagreen sliding depth of shadow, *eau de Nil.*

– Poor old Goodwin was the pianist that night, Father Cowley reminded them. There was a slight difference of opinion between himself and the Collard grand.

There was.

– A symposium all his own, Mr Dedalus said. The devil wouldn't stop him. He was a crotchety old fellow in the primary stage of drink.

– God, do you remember? Ben bulky Dollard said, turning from the punished keyboard. And by Japers I had no wedding garment.

They laughed all three. He had no wed. All trio laughed. No wedding garment.

– Our friend Bloom turned in handy that night, Mr Dedalus said. Where's my pipe by the way?

He wandered back to the bar to the lost chord pipe. Bald Pat carried two diners' drinks, Richie and Poldy. And Father Cowley laughed again.

– I saved the situation, Ben, I think.

– You did, averred Ben Dollard. I remember those tight trousers too. That was a brilliant idea, Bob.

Father Cowley blushed to his brilliant purply lobes. He saved the situa. Tight trou. Brilliant ide.

– I knew he was on the rocks, he said. The wife was playing the piano in the coffee palace on Saturdays for a very trifling consideration and who was it gave me the wheeze she was doing the other business? Do you remember? We had to search all Holles street to find them till the chap in Keogh's gave us the number. Remember?

Ben remembered, his broad visage wondering.

– By God she had some luxurious opera cloaks and things there.

Mr Dedalus wandered back, pipe in hand.

– Merrion square style. Balldresses, by God, and court dresses. He wouldn't take any money either. What? Any God's quantity of cocked hats and boleros and trunkhose. What?

– Ay, ay, Mr Dedalus nodded. Mrs Marion Bloom has left off clothes of all descriptions.

Jingle jaunted down the quays. Blazes sprawled on bounding tyres.

Liver and bacon. Steak and kidney pie. Right, sir. Right, Pat.

Mrs Marion met him pike hoses. Smell of burn of Paul de Kock. Nice name he.

– What's this her name was? A buxom lassy. Marion . . .

– Tweedy.

– Yes. Is she alive?

– And kicking.

– She was a daughter of . . .

– Daughter of the regiment.

– Yes, begad. I remember the old drummajor.

Mr Dedalus struck, whizzed, lit, puffed savoury puff after.

– Irish? I don't know, faith. Is she, Simon?

Puff after stiff, a puff, strong, savoury, crackling.

– Buccinator muscle is . . . What? . . . Bit rusty . . . O, she is . . . My Irish Molly, O.

He puffed a pungent plumy blast.

– From the rock of Gibraltar . . . all the way.

They pined in depth of ocean shadow, gold by the beerpull, bronze by maraschino, thoughtful all two, Mina Kennedy, 4 Lismore terrace, Drumcondra with Idolores, a queen, Dolores, silent.

Pat served uncovered dishes. Leopold cut liverslices. As said before he ate with relish the inner organs, nutty gizzards, fried cods'roes while Richie Goulding, Collis, Ward ate steak and kidney, steak then kidney, bite by bite of pie he ate Bloom ate they ate.

Bloom with Goulding, married in silence, ate. Dinners fit for princes.

By Bachelor's walk jogjaunty jingled Blazes Boylan, bachelor, in sun, in heat, mare's glossy rump atrot, with flick of whip, on bounding tyres: sprawled, warmseated, Boylan impatience, ardentbold. Horn. Have you the? Horn. Have you the? Haw haw horn.

Over their voices Dollard bassooned attack, booming over bombarding chords:

– *When love absorbs my ardent soul* . . .

Roll of Bensoulbenjamin rolled to the quivery loveshivery roofpanes.

– War! War! cried Father Cowley. You're the warrior.

– So I am, Ben Warrior laughed. I was thinking of your landlord. Love or money.

He stopped. He wagged huge beard, huge face over his blunder huge.

– Sure, you'd burst the tympanum of her ear, man, Mr Dedalus said through smoke aroma, with an organ like yours.

In bearded abundant laughter Dollard shook upon the keyboard. He would.

– Not to mention another membrane, Father Cowley added. Half time, Ben. *Amoroso ma non troppo*. Let me there.

Miss Kennedy served two gentlemen with tankards of cool stout. She passed a remark. It was indeed, first gentleman said, beautiful weather. They drank cool stout. Did she know where the lord lieutenant was going? And heard steelhoofs ringhoof ring. No, she couldn't say. But it would be in the paper. O, she needn't trouble. No trouble. She waved about her outspread *Independent*, searching, the lord lieutenant, her pinnacles of hair slowmoving, lord lieuten. Too much trouble, first gentleman said. O, not in the least. Way he looked that. Lord lieutenant. Gold by bronze heard iron steel.

– . . . . *my ardent soul*
    I care not foror the morrow.

In liver gravy Bloom mashed mashed potatoes. Love and war someone is. Ben Dollard's famous. Night he ran round to us to borrow a dress suit for that concert. Trousers tight as a drum on him. Musical porkers. Molly did laugh when he went out. Threw herself back across the bed, screaming, kicking. With all his belongings on show. O, saints above, I'm drenched! O, the women in the front row! O, I never laughed so many! Well, of course, that's what gives him the base barreltone. For instance eunuchs. Wonder who's playing. Nice touch. Must be Cowley. Musical. Knows whatever note you play. Bad breath he has, poor chap. Stopped.

Miss Douce, engaging, Lydia Douce, bowed to suave solicitor, George Lidwell, gentleman, entering. Good afternoon. She gave her moist, a lady's, hand to his firm clasp. Afternoon. Yes, she was back. To the old dingdong again.

– Your friends are inside, Mr Lidwell.

George Lidwell, suave, solicited, held a lydiahand.

Bloom ate liv as said before. Clean here at least. That chap in the Burton, gummy with gristle. No-one here: Goulding and I. Clean tables, flowers, mitres of napkins. Pat to and fro, bald Pat. Nothing to do. Best value in Dub.

Piano again. Cowley it is. Way he sits in to it, like one together, mutual understanding. Tiresome shapers scraping fiddles, eye on the bowend, sawing the 'cello, remind you of toothache. Her high long snore. Night we were in the box. Trombone under blowing like a grampus, between the acts, other brass chap unscrewing, emptying spittle. Conductor's legs too, bagstrousers, jiggedy jiggedy. Do right to hide them.

Jiggedy jingle jaunty jaunty.

Only the harp. Lovely gold glowering light. Girl touched it. Poop of a lovely. Gravy's rather good fit for a. Golden ship. Erin. The harp that once or twice. Cool hands. Ben Howth, the rhododendrons. We are their harps. I. He. Old. Young.

– Ah, I couldn't, man, Mr Dedalus said, shy, listless.

Strongly.

– Go on, blast you, Ben Dollard growled. Get it out in bits.

– *M'appari*, Simon, Father Cowley said.

Down stage he strode some paces, grave, tall in affliction, his long arms outheld. Hoarsely the apple of his throat hoarsed softly. Softly he sang to a dusty seascape there: *A Last Farewell*. A headland, a ship, a sail upon the billows. Farewell. A lovely girl, her veil awave upon the wind upon the headland, wind around her.

Cowley sang:

– *M'appari tutt'amor:*

Il mio sguardo l'incontr . . .

She waved, unhearing Cowley, her veil to one departing, dear one, to wind, love, speeding sail, return.

– Go on, Simon.

– Ah, sure my dancing days are done, Ben . . . Well . . .

Mr Dedalus laid his pipe to rest beside the tuningfork and, sitting touched the obedient keys.

– No, Simon, Father Cowley turned. Play it in the original. One flat.

The keys, obedient, rose higher, told, faltered, confessed, confused.

Up stage strode Father Cowley.

– Here, Simon. I'll accompany you, he said. Get up.

By Graham Lemon's pineapple rock, by Elvery's elephant jingle jogged. Steak, kidney, liver, mashed at meat fit for princes sat princes Bloom and Goulding. Princes at meat they raised and drank Power and cider.

Most beautiful tenor air ever written, Richie said: *Sonnambula*. He heard Joe Maas sing that one night. Ah, what M'Guckin! Yes. In his way. Choirboy style. Maas was the boy. Massboy. A lyrical tenor if you like. Never forget it. Never.

Tenderly Bloom over liverless bacon saw the tightened features strain. Backache he. Bright's bright eye. Next item on the programme. Paying the piper. Pills, pounded bread, worth a guinea a box. Stave it off awhile. Sings too: *Down among the dead men*. Appropriate. Kidney pie. Sweets to the.

Not making much hand of it. Best value in. Characteristic of him. Power. Particular about his drink. Flaw in the glass, fresh Vartry water. Fecking matches from counters to save. Then squander a sovereign in dribs and drabs. And when he's wanted not a farthing. Screwed refusing to pay his fare. Curious types.

Never would Richie forget that night. As long as he lived, never. In the gods of the old Royal with little Peake. And when the first note.

Speech paused on Richie's lips.

Coming out with a whopper now. Rhapsodies about damn all. Believes his own lies. Does really. Wonderful liar. But want a good memory.

– Which air is that? asked Leopold Bloom.

– *All is lost now.*

Richie cocked his lips apout. A low incipient note sweet banshee murmured all. A thrush. A throstle. His breath, birdsweet, good teeth he's proud of, fluted with plaintive woe. Is lost. Rich sound. Two notes in one there. Blackbird I heard in the hawthorn valley. Taking my motives he twined and turned them. All most too new call is lost in all. Echo. How sweet the answer. How is that done? All lost now. Mournful he whistled. Fall, surrender, lost.

Bloom bent leopold ear, turning a fringe of doyley down under the vase. Order. Yes, I remember. Lovely air. In sleep she went to him. Innocence in the moon. Still hold her back. Brave, don't know their danger. Call name. Touch water. Jingle jaunty. Too late. She longed to go. That's why. Woman. As easy stop the sea. Yes: all is lost.

– A beautiful air, said Bloom lost Leopold. I know it well.

Never in all his life had Richie Goulding.

He knows it well too. Or he feels. Still harping on his daughter. Wise child that knows her father, Dedalus said. Me?

Bloom askance over liverless saw. Face of the all is lost. Rollicking Richie once. Jokes old stale now. Wagging his ear. Napkinring in his eye. Now begging letters he sends his son with. Crosseyed Walter sir I did sir. Wouldn't trouble only I was expecting some money. Apologise.

Piano again. Sounds better than last time I heard. Tuned probably. Stopped again.

Dollard and Cowley still urged the lingering singer out with it.

– With it, Simon.

– It, Simon.

– Ladies and gentlemen, I am most deeply obliged by your kind solicitations.

– It, Simon.

– I have no money but if you will lend me your attention I shall endeavour to sing to you of a heart bowed down.

By the sandwichbell in screening shadow, Lydia her bronze and rose, a lady's grace, gave and withheld: as in cool glaucous *eau de Nil* Mina to tankards two her pinnacles of gold.

The harping chords of prelude closed. A chord longdrawn, expectant drew a voice away.

– *When first I saw that form endearing.*

Richie turned.

– Si Dedalus' voice, he said.

Braintipped, cheek touched with flame, they listened feeling that flow endearing flow over skin limbs human heart soul spine. Bloom signed to Pat, bald Pat is a waiter hard of hearing, to set ajar the door of the bar. The door of the bar. So. That will do. Pat, waiter, waited, waiting to hear, for he was hard of hear by the door.

– *Sorrow from me seemed to depart.*

Through the hush of air a voice sang to them, low, not rain, not leaves in murmur, like no voice of strings of reeds or whatdoyoucallthem dulcimers, touching their still ears with words, still hearts of their each his remembered lives. Good, good to hear: sorrow from them each seemed to from both depart when first they heard. When first they saw, lost Richie, Poldy, mercy of beauty, heard from a person wouldn't expect it in the least, her first merciful lovesoft oftloved word.

Love that is singing: love's old sweet song. Bloom unwound slowly the elastic band of his packet. Love's old sweet *sonnez la* gold. Bloom wound a skein round four forkfingers, stretched it, relaxed, and wound it round his troubled double, fourfold, in octave, gyved them fast.

– *Full of hope and all delighted . . .*

Tenors get women by the score. Increase their flow. Throw flower at his feet when will we meet? My head it simply. Jingle all delighted. He can't sing for tall hats. Your head it simply swurls. Perfumed for him. What perfume does your wife? I want to know. Jing. Stop. Knock. Last look at mirror always before she answers the door. The hall. There? How do you? I do well. There? What? Or? Phila of cachous, kissing comfits, in her satchel. Yes? Hands felt for the opulent.

Alas! The voice rose, sighing, changed: loud, full, shining, proud.

– *But alas, 'twas idle dreaming . . .*

Glorious tone he has still. Cork air softer also their brogue. Silly man! Could have made oceans of money. Singing wrong words. Wore out his wife: now sings. But hard to tell. Only the two themselves. If he doesn't break down. Keep a trot for the avenue. His hands and feet sing too. Drink. Nerves overstrung. Must be abstemious to sing. Jenny Lind soup: stock, sage, raw eggs, half pint of cream. For creamy dreamy.

Tenderness it welled: slow, swelling. Full it throbbed. That's the chat. Ha, give! Take! Throb, a throb, a pulsing proud erect.

Words? Music? No: it's what's behind.

Bloom looped, unlooped, noded, disnoded.

Bloom. Flood of warm jimjam lickitup secretness flowed to flow in music out, in desire, dark to lick flow, invading. Tipping her tepping her tapping her topping her. Tup. Pores to dilate dilating. Tup. The joy the feel the warm the. Tup. To pour o'er sluices pouring gushes. Flood, gush, flow, joygush, tupthrop. Now! Language of love.

– . . . *ray of hope* . . .

Beaming. Lydia for Lidwell squeak scarcely hear so ladylike the muse unsqueaked a ray of hope.

Martha it is. Coincidence. Just going to write. Lionel's song. Lovely name you have. Can't write. Accept my little pres. Play on her heartstrings pursestrings too. She's a. I called you naughty boy. Still the name: Martha. How strange! Today.

The voice of Lionel returned, weaker but unwearied. It sang again to Richie Poldy Lydia Lidwell also sang to Pat open mouth ear waiting, to wait. How first he saw that form endearing, how sorrow seemed to part, how look, form, word charmed him Gould Lidwell, won Pat Bloom's heart.

Wish I could see his face, though. Explain better. Why the barber in Drago's always looked my face when I spoke his face in the glass. Still hear it better here than in the bar though farther.

– *Each graceful look* . . .

First night when first I saw her at Mat Dillon's in Terenure. Yellow, black lace she wore. Musical chairs. We two the last. Fate. After her. Fate. Round and round slow. Quick round. We two. All looked. Halt. Down she sat. All ousted looked. Lips laughing. Yellow knees.

– *Charmed my eye* . . .

Singing. *Waiting* she sang. I turned her music. Full voice of perfume of what perfume does your lilactrees. Bosom I saw, both full, throat warbling. First I saw. She thanked me. Why did she me? Fate. Spanishy eyes. Under a peartree alone patio this hour in old Madrid one side in shadow Dolores shedolores. At me. Luring. Ah, alluring.

– *Martha! Ah, Martha!*

Quitting all languor Lionel cried in grief, in cry of passion dominant to love to return with deepening yet with rising chords of harmony. In cry of lionel loneliness that she should know, must Martha feel. For only her he waited. Where? Here there try there here all try where. Somewhere.

> – *Co-me, thou lost one!*
> *Co-me thou dear one!*

Alone. One love. One hope. One comfort me. Martha, chestnote, return.

– *Come!*

It soared, a bird, it held its flight, a swift pure cry, soar silver orb it leaped serene, speeding, sustained, to come, don't spin it out too long long breath he breath long life, soaring high, high resplendent, aflame, crowned, high in the effulgence symbolistic, high, of the etherial bosom, high, of the high vast irradiation everywhere all soaring all around about the all, the endlessnessnessness . . .

– *To me!*

Siopold!

Consumed.

Come. Well sung. All clapped. She ought to. Come. To me, to him, to her, you too, me, us.

– Bravo! Clapclap. Goodman, Simon. Clappyclapclap. Encore! Clap-clipclap. Sound as a bell. Bravo, Simon! Clapclopclap. Encore, enclap, said, cried, clapped all, Ben Dollard, Lydia Douce, George Lidwell, Pat, Mina, two gentlemen with two tankards, Cowley, first gent with tank and bronze Miss Douce and gold Miss Mina.

Blazes Boylan's smart tan shoes creaked on the barfloor, said before. Jingle by monuments of sir John Gray, Horatio onehandled Nelson, reverend father Theobald Matthew, jaunted as said before just now. Atrot, in heat, heatseated. *Cloche. Sonnez la. Cloche. Sonnez la.* Slower the mare went up the hill by the Rotunda, Rutland square. Too slow for Boylan, blazes Boylan, impatience Boylan, joggled the mare.

An afterclang of Cowley's chords closed, died on the air made richer.

And Richie Goulding drank his Power and Leopold Bloom his cider drank, Lidwell his Guinness, second gentleman said they would partake of two tankards if she did not mind. Miss Kennedy smirked, disserving, coral lips, at first, at second. She did not mind.

– Seven days in jail, Ben Dollard said, on bread and water. Then you'd sing, Simon, like a garden thrush.

Lionel Simon, singer, laughed. Father Bob Cowley played. Mina Kennedy served. Second gentleman paid. Tom Kernan strutted in; Lydia, admired, admired. But Bloom sang dumb.

Admiring.

Richie, admiring, descanted on that man's glorious voice. He remembered one night long ago. Never forget that night. Si sang *'Twas rank and fame:* in Ned Lambert's 'twas. Good God he never heard in all his life a note like that he never did *then false one we had better part* so clear so God he never heard *since love lives not* a clinking voice ask Lambert he can tell you too.

Goulding, a flush struggling in his pale, told Mr Bloom, face of the night, Si in Ned Lambert's, Dedalus' house, sang *'Twas rank and fame.*

He, Mr Bloom, listened while he, Richie Goulding, told him, Mr Bloom of the night he, Richie, heard him, Si Dedalus, sing *'Twas rank and fame* in his, Ned Lambert's house.

Brothers-in-law: relations. We never speak as we pass by. Rift in the lute I think. Treats him with scorn. See. He admires him all the more. The night Si sang. The human voice, two tiny silky cords. Wonderful, more than all the others.

That voice was a lamentation. Calmer now. It's in the silence you feel you hear. Vibrations. Now silent air.

Bloom ungyved his crisscrossed hands and with slack fingers plucked the slender catgut thong. He drew and plucked. It buzzed, it twanged. While Goulding talked of Barraclough's voice production, while Tom Kernan, harking back in a retrospective sort of arrangement, talked to listening Father Cowley who played a voluntary, who nodded as he played. While big Ben Dollard talked with Simon Dedalus lighting, who nodded as he smoked, who smoked.

Thou lost one. All songs on that theme. Yet more Bloom stretched his string. Cruel it seems. Let people get fond of each other: lure them on. Then tear asunder. Death. Explos. Knock on the head. Outtohelloutofthat. Humanlife. Dignam. Ugh, that rat's tail wriggling! Five bob I gave. *Corpus paradisum.* Corncrake croaker: belly like a poisoned pup. Gone. They sing. Forgotten. I too. And one day she with. Leave her: get tired. Suffer then. Snivel. Big Spanishy eyes goggling at nothing. Her wavyavyeavyheavyeavyevyevy hair un comb: 'd.

Yet too much happy bores. He stretched more, more. Are you not happy in your? Twang. It snapped.

Jingle into Dorset street.

Miss Douce withdrew her satiny arm, reproachful, pleased.

– Don't make half so free, said she, till we are better acquainted.

George Lidwell told her really and truly: but she did not believe.

First gentleman told Mina that was so. She asked him was that so. And second tankard told her so. That that was so.

Miss Douce, Miss Lydia, did not believe: Miss Kennedy, Mina, did not believe: George Lidwell, no: Miss Dou did not: the first, the first: gent with the tank: believe, no, no: did not, Miss Kenn: Lidlydiawell: the tank.

Better write it here. Quills in the postoffice chewed and twisted.

Bald Pat at a sign drew nigh. A pen and ink. He went. A pad. He went. A pad to blot. He heard, deaf Pat.

– Yes, Mr Bloom said, teasing the curling catgut fine. It certainly is. Few lines will do. My present. All that Italian florid music is. Who is this wrote? Know the name you know better. Take out sheet notepaper, envelope: unconcerned. It's so characteristic.

– Grandest number in the whole opera, Goulding said.

– It is, Bloom said.

Numbers it is. All music when you come to think. Two multiplied by two divided by half is twice one. Vibrations: chords those are. One plus two plus six is seven. Do anything you like with figures juggling. Always find out this equal to that, symmetry under a cemetery wall. He doesn't see my mourning. Callous: all for his own gut. Musemathematics. And you think you're listening to the etherial. But suppose you said it like: Martha, seven times nine minus x is thirtyfive thousand. Fall quite flat. It's on account of the sounds it is.

Instance he's playing now. Improvising. Might be what you like till you hear the words. Want to listen sharp. Hard. Begin all right: then hear chords a bit off: feel lost a bit. In and out of sacks over barrels, through wirefences, obstacle race. Time makes the tune. Question of mood you're in. Still always nice to hear. Except scales up and down, girls learning. Two together nextdoor neighbours. Ought to invent dummy pianos for that. *Blumenlied* I bought for her. The name. Playing it slow, a girl, night I came home, the girl. Door of the stables near Cecilia street. Milly no taste. Queer because we both I mean.

Bald deaf Pat brought quite flat pad ink. Pat set with ink pen quite flat pad. Pat took plate dish knife fork. Pat went.

It was the only language Mr Dedalus said to Ben. He heard them as a boy in Ringabella, Crosshaven, Ringabella, singing their barcaroles. Queenstown harbour full of Italian ships. Walking, you know, Ben, in the moonlight with those earthquake hats. Blending their voices. God, such music, Ben. Heard as a boy. Cross Ringabella haven mooncarole.

Sour pipe removed he held a shield of hand beside his lips that cooed a moonlight nightcall, clear from anear, a call from afar, replying.

Down the edge of his *Freeman* baton ranged Bloom's your other eye, scanning for where did I see that. Callan, Coleman, Dignam Patrick.

Heigho! Heigho! Fawcett. Aha! Just I was looking . . .

Hope he's not looking, cute as a rat. He held unfurled his *Freeman*. Can't see now. Remember write Greek ees. Bloom dipped, Bloo mur: dear sir. Dear Henry wrote: dear Mady. Got your lett and flow. Hell did I put? Some pock or oth. It is utterl imposs. Underline *imposs*. To write today.

Bore this. Bored Bloom tambourined gently with I am just reflecting fingers on flat pad Pat brought.

On. Know what I mean. No, change that ee. Accept my poor little pres enclos. Ask her no answ. Hold on. Five Dig. Two about here. Penny the gulls. Elijah is com. Seven Davy Byrne's. Is eight about. Say half a crown. My poor little pres: p. o. two and six. Write me a long. Do you despise? Jingle, have you the? So excited. Why do you call me naught? You naughty too? O, Mairy lost the pin of her. Bye for today. Yes, yes, will tell you. Want to. To keep it up. Call me that other. Other world she wrote. My patience are exhaust. To keep it up. You must believe. Believe. The tank. It. Is. True.

Folly am I writing? Husbands don't. That's marriage does, their wives. Because I'm away from. Suppose. But how? She must. Keep young. If she found out. Card in my high grade ha. No, not tell all. Useless pain. If they don't see. Woman. Sauce for the gander.

A hackney car, number three hundred and twentyfour, driver Barton James of number one Harmony avenue, Donnybrook, on which sat a fare, a young gentleman, stylishly dressed in an indigoblue serge suit made by George Robert Mesias, tailor and cutter, of number five Eden quay, and wearing a straw hat very dressy, bought of John Plasto of number one Great Brunswick street, hatter. Eh? This is the jingle that joggled and jingled. By Dlugacz' porkshop bright tubes of Agendath trotted a gallantbuttocked mare.

– Answering an ad? keen Richie's eyes asked Bloom.

– Yes, Mr Bloom said. Town traveller. Nothing doing, I expect.

Bloom mur: best references. But Henry wrote: it will excite me. You know now. In haste. Henry. Greek ee. Better add postcript. What is he playing now? Improvising intermezzo. P. S. The rum tum tum. How will you pun? You punish me? Crooked skirt swinging, whack by. Tell me I want to. Know. O. Course if I didn't I wouldn't ask. La la la ree. Trails off there sad in minor. Why minor sad? Sign H. They like sad tail at end. P. P. S. La la la ree. I feel so sad today. La ree. So lonely. Dee.

He blotted quick on pad of Pat. Envel. Address. Just copy out of paper. Murmured: Messrs Callan, Coleman and Co, limited. Henry wrote:

Miss Martha Clifford
c/o P. O.
Dolphin's barn lane
Dublin.

Blot over the other so he can't read. Right. Idea prize titbit. Something detective read off blottingpad. Payment at the rate of guinea per col. Matcham often thinks the laughing witch. Poor Mrs Purefoy. U. p.: up.

Too poetical that about the sad. Music did that. Music hath charms Shakespeare said. Quotations every day in the year. To be or not to be. Wisdom while you wait.

In Gerard's rosery of Fetter lane he walks, greyedauburn. One life is all. One body. Do. But do.

Done anyhow. Postal order stamp. Postoffice lower down. Walk now. Enough. Barney Kiernan's I promised to meet them. Dislike that job. House of mourning. Walk. Pat! Doesn't hear. Deaf beetle he is.

Car near there now. Talk. Talk. Pat! Doesn't. Settling those napkins. Lot of ground he must cover in the day. Paint face behind on him then he'd be two. Wish they'd sing more. Keep my mind off.

Bald Pat who is bothered mitred the napkins. Pat is a waiter hard of his hearing. Pat is a waiter who waits while you wait. Hee hee hee hee. He waits while you wait. Hee hee. A waiter is he. Hee hee hee hee. He waits while you wait. While you wait if you wait he will wait while you wait. Hee hee hee hee. Hoh. Wait while you wait.

Douce now. Douce Lydia. Bronze and rose.

She had a gorgeous, simply gorgeous, time. And look at the lovely shell she brought.

To the end of the bar to him she bore lightly the spiked and winding seahorn that he, George Lidwell, solicitor, might hear.

– Listen! she bade him.

Under Tom Kernan's ginhot words the accompanist wove music slow. Authentic fact. How Walter Bapty lost his voice. Well, sir, the husband took him by the throat. *Scoundrel*, said he. *You'll sing no more lovesongs.* He did, sir Tom. Bob Cowley wove. Tenors get wom. Cowley lay back.

Ah, now he heard, she holding it to his ear. Hear! He heard. Wonderful. She held it to her own and through the sifted light pale gold in contrast glided. To hear.

Tap.

Bloom through the bardoor saw a shell held at their ears. He heard more faintly that that they heard, each for herself alone, then each for other, hearing the plash of waves, loudly, a silent roar.

Bronze by a weary gold, anear, afar, they listened.

Her ear too is a shell, the peeping lobe there. Been to the seaside. Lovely seaside girls. Skin tanned raw. Should have put on coldcream first make it brown. Buttered toast. O and that lotion mustn't forget. Fever near her mouth. Your head it simply. Hair braided over: shell with seaweed. Why do they hide their ears with seaweed hair? And Turks their mouth, why? Her eyes over the sheet, a yashmak. Find the way in. A cave. No admittance except on business.

The sea they think they hear. Singing. A roar. The blood is it. Souse in the ear sometimes. Well, it's a sea. Corpuscle islands.

Wonderful really. So distinct. Again. George Lidwell held its murmur, hearing: then laid it by, gently.

– What are the wild waves saying? he asked her, smiled.

Charming, seasmiling and unanswering Lydia on Lidwell smiled.

Tap.

By Larry O'Rourke's, by Larry, bold Larry O', Boylan swayed and Boylan turned.

From the forsaken shell Miss Mina glided to her tankard waiting. No, she was not so lonely archly Miss Douce's head let Mr Lidwell know. Walks in the moonlight by the sea. No, not alone. With whom? She nobly answered: with a gentleman friend.

Bob Cowley's twinkling fingers in the treble played again. The landlord has the prior. A little time. Long John. Big Ben. Lightly he played a light bright tinkling measure for tripping ladies, arch and smiling, and for their gallants, gentlemen friends. One: one, one, one: two, one, three, four.

Sea, wind, leaves, thunder, waters, cows lowing, the cattle market, cocks, hens don't crow, snakes hissss. There's music everywhere. Ruttledge's door: ee creaking. No, that's noise. Minuet of *Don Giovanni* he's playing now. Court dresses of all descriptions in castle chambers dancing. Misery. Peasants outside. Green starving faces eating dockleaves. Nice that is. Look: look, look, look, look, look: you look at us.

That's joyful I can feel. Never have written it. Why? My joy is other joy. But both are joys. Yes, joy it must be. Mere fact of music shows you are. Often thought she was in the dumps till she began to lilt. Then know.

M'Coy valise. My wife and your wife. Squealing cat. Like tearing silk. When she talks like the clapper of a bellows. They can't manage men's intervals. Gap in their voices too. Fill me. I'm warm, dark, open. Molly in *quis est homo:* Mercadante. My ear against the wall to hear. Want a woman who can deliver the goods.

Jog jig jogged stopped. Dandy tan shoe of dandy Boylan socks skyblue clocks came light to earth.

O, look we are so! Chamber music. Could make a kind of pun on that. It is a kind of music I often thought when she. Acoustics that is. Tinkling. Empty vessels make most noise. Because the acoustics, the resonance changes according as the weight of the water is equal to the law of falling water. Like those rhapsodies of Liszt's, Hungarian, gipsyeyed. Pearls. Drops. Rain. Diddle iddle addle addle oodle oodle. Hiss. Now. Maybe now. Before.

One rapped on a door, one tapped with a knock, did he knock Paul de Kock, with a loud proud knocker, with a cock carracarracarra cock. Cockcock.

Tap.

– *Qui sdegno*, Ben, said Father Cowley.

– No, Ben, Tom Kernan interfered, *The Croppy Boy*. Our native Doric.

– Ay do, Ben, Mr Dedalus said. Good men and true.

– Do, do, they begged in one.

I'll go. Here, Pat, return. Come. He came, he came, he did not stay. To me. How much?

– What key? Six sharps?

– F sharp major, Ben Dollard said.

Bob Cowley's outstretched talons gripped the black deep-sounding chords.

Must go prince Bloom told Richie prince. No, Richie said. Yes, must. Got money somewhere. He's on for a razzle backache spree. Much? He seehears lipspeech. One and nine. Penny for yourself. Here. Give him twopence tip. Deaf, bothered. But perhaps he has wife and family waiting, waiting Patty come home. Hee hee hee hee. Deaf wait while they wait.

But wait. But hear. Chords dark. Lugugugubrious. Low. In a cave of the dark middle earth. Embedded ore. Lump-music.

The voice of dark age, of unlove, earth's fatigue made grave approach, and painful, come from afar, from hoary mountains, called on good men and true. The priest he sought, with him would he speak a word.

Tap.

Ben Dollard's voice barreltone. Doing his level best to say it. Croak of vast manless moonless womoonless marsh. Other comedown. Big ships' chandler's business he did once. Remember: rosiny ropes, ships' lanterns. Failed to the tune of ten thousand pounds. Now in the Iveagh home. Cubicle number so and so. Number one Bass did that for him.

The priest's at home. A false priest's servant bade him welcome. Step in. The holy father. Curlycues of chords.

Ruin them. Wreck their lives. Then build them cubicles to end their days in. Hushaby. Lullaby. Die, dog. Little dog, die.

The voice of warning, solemn warning, told them the youth had entered a lonely hall, told them how solemn fell his footstep there, told them the gloomy chamber, the vested priest sitting to shrive.

Decent soul. Bit addled now. Thinks he'll win in *Answers* poets' picture puzzle. We hand you crisp five pound note. Bird sitting hatching in a nest. Lay of the last minstrel he thought it was. See blank tee what domestic animal? Tee dash ar most courageous mariner. Good voice he has still. No eunuch yet with all his belongings.

Listen. Bloom listened. Richie Goulding listened. And by the door deaf Pat, bald Pat, tipped Pat, listened.

The chords harped slower.

The voice of penance and of grief came slow, embellished tremulous. Ben's contrite beard confessed: *in nomine Domini*, in God's name. He knelt. He beat his hand upon his breast, confessing: *mea culpa*.

Latin again. That holds them like birdlime. Priest with the communion corpus for those women. Chap in the mortuary, coffin or coffey, *corpus-nomine*. Wonder where that rat is by now. Scrape.

Tap.

They listened: tankards and Miss Kennedy, George Lidwell eyelid well expressive, fullbusted satin, Kernan, Si.

The sighing voice of sorrow sang. His sins. Since easter he had cursed three times. You bitch's bast. And once at masstime he had gone to play. Once by the churchyard he had passed and for his mother's rest he had not prayed. A boy. A croppy boy.

Bronze, listening by the beerpull, gazed far away. Soulfully. Doesn't half know I'm. Molly great dab at seeing anyone looking.

Bronze gazed far sideways. Mirror there. Is that best side of her face? They always know. Knock at the door. Last tip to titivate.

Cockcarracarra.

What do they think when they hear music? Way to catch rattlesnakes. Night Michael Gunn gave us the box. Tuning up. Shah of Persia liked that best. Remind him of home sweet home. Wiped his nose in curtain too. Custom his country perhaps. That's music too. Not as bad as it sounds. Tootling. Brasses braying asses through uptrunks. Double-basses, helpless, gashes in their sides. Woodwinds mooing cows. Semigrand open crocodile music hath jaws. Woodwind like Goodwin's name.

She looked fine. Her crocus dress she wore, lowcut, belongings on show. Clove her breath was always in theatre when she bent to ask a question. Told her what Spinoza says in that book of poor papa's. Hypnotised, listening. Eyes like that. She bent. Chap in dresscircle, staring down into her with his operaglass for all he was worth. Beauty of music you must hear twice. Nature woman half a look. God made the country man the tune. Met him pike hoses. Philosophy. O rocks!

All gone. All fallen. At the siege of Ross his father, at Gorey all his brothers fell. To Wexford, we are the boys of Wexford, he would. Last of his name and race.

I too, last my race. Milly young student. Well, my fault perhaps. No son. Rudy. Too late now. Or if not? If not? If still?

He bore no hate.

Hate. Love. Those are names. Rudy. Soon I am old.

Big Ben his voice unfolded. Great voice, Richie Goulding said, a flush struggling in his pale, to Bloom, soon old but when was young.

Ireland comes now. My country above the king. She listens. Who fears to speak of nineteen four? Time to be shoving. Looked enough.

– *Bless me, father*, Dollard the croppy cried. *Bless me and let me go.*

Tap.

Bloom looked, unblessed to go. Got up to kill: on eighteen bob a week. Fellows shell out the dibs. Want to keep your weathereye open. Those girls, those lovely. By the sad sea waves. Chorusgirl's romance. Letters read out for breach of promise. From Chickabiddy's own Mumpsypum. Laughter in court. Henry. I never signed it. The lovely name you.

Low sank the music, air and words. Then hastened. The false priest rustling soldier from his cassock. A yeoman captain. They know it all by heart. The thrill they itch for. Yeoman cap.

Tap. Tap.

Thrilled, she listened, bending in sympathy to hear.

Blank face. Virgin should say: or fingered only. Write something on it: page. If not what becomes of them? Decline, despair. Keeps them young. Even admire themselves. See. Play on her. Lip blow. Body of white woman, a flute alive. Blow gentle. Loud. Three holes all women. Goddess I didn't see. They want it: not too much polite. That's why he gets them. Gold in your pocket, brass in your face. With look to look: songs without words. Molly that hurdygurdy boy. She knew he meant the monkey was sick. Or because so like the Spanish. Understand animals too that way. Solomon did. Gift of nature.

Ventriloquise. My lips closed. Think in my stom. What?

Will? You? I. Want. You. To.

With hoarse rude fury the yeoman cursed. Swelling in apoplectic bitch's bastard. A good thought, boy, to come. One hour's your time to live, your last.

Tap. Tap.

Thrill now. Pity they feel. To wipe away a tear for martyrs. For all things dying, want to, dying to, die. For that all things born. Poor Mrs Purefoy. Hope she's over. Because their wombs.

A liquid of womb of woman eyeball gazed under a fence of lashes, calmly, hearing. See real beauty of the eye when she not speaks. On yonder river. At each slow satiny heaving bosom's wave (her heaving embon) red rose rose slowly, sank red rose. Heartbeats her breath: breath that is life. And all the tiny tiny fernfoils trembled of maidenhair.

But look. The bright stars fade. O rose! Castille. The morn. Ha. Lidwell. For him then not for. Infatuated. I like that? See her from here though. Popped corks, splashes of beerfroth, stacks of empties.

On the smooth jutting beerpull laid Lydia hand lightly, plumply, leave it to my hands. All lost in pity for croppy. Fro, to: to, fro: over the polished knob (she knows his eyes, my eyes, her eyes) her thumb and finger passed in pity: passed, repassed and, gently touching, then slid so smoothly, slowly down, a cool firm white enamel baton protruding through their sliding ring.

With a cock with a carra.

Tap. Tap. Tap.

I hold this house. Amen. He gnashed in fury. Traitors swing.

The chords consented. Very sad thing. But had to be.

Get out before the end. Thanks, that was heavenly. Where's my hat. Pass by her. Can leave that *Freeman*. Letter I have. Suppose she were the? No. Walk, walk, walk. Like Cashel Boylo Connoro Coylo Tisdall Maurice Tisntdall Farrell. Waaaaaaalk.

Well, I must be. Are you off? Yrfmstbyes. Blmstup. O'er ryehigh blue. Bloom stood up. Ow. Soap feeling rather sticky behind. Must have sweated: music. That lotion, remember. Well, so long. High grade. Card inside, yes.

By deaf Pat in the doorway, straining ear, Bloom passed.

At Geneva barrack that young man died. At Passage was his body laid. Dolor! O, he dolores! The voice of the mournful chanter called to dolorous prayer.

By rose, by satiny bosom, by the fondling hand, by slops, by empties, by popped corks, greeting in going, past eyes and maidenhair, bronze and faint gold in deepseashadow, went Bloom, soft Bloom, I feel so lonely Bloom.

Tap. Tap. Tap.

Pray for him, prayed the bass of Dollard. You who hear in peace. Breathe a prayer, drop a tear, good men, good people. He was the croppy boy.

Scaring eavesdropping boots croppy bootsboy Bloom in the Ormond hallway heard growls and roars of bravo, fat backslapping, their boots all treading, boots not the boots the boy. General chorus off for a swill to wash it down. Glad I avoided.

– Come on, Ben, Simon Dedalus said. By God, you're as good as ever you were.

– Better, said Tomgin Kernan. Most trenchant rendition of that ballad, upon my soul and honour it is.

– Lablache, said Father Cowley.

Ben Dollard bulkily cachuchad towards the bar, mightily praisefed and all big roseate, on heavyfooted feet, his gouty fingers nakkering castagnettes in the air.

Big Benaben Dollard. Big Benben. Big Benben.

Rrr.

And deepmoved all, Simon trumping compassion from foghorn nose, all laughing, they brought him forth, Ben Dollard, in right good cheer.

– You're looking rubicund, George Lidwell said.

Miss Douce composed her rose to wait.

– Ben machree, said Mr Dedalus, clapping Ben's fat back shoulderblade. Fit as a fiddle, only he has a lot of adipose tissue concealed about his person.

Rrrrrrsss.

– Fat of death, Simon, Ben Dollard growled.

Richie rift in the lute alone sat: Goulding, Collis, Ward. Uncertainly he waited. Unpaid Pat too.

Tap. Tap. Tap. Tap.

Miss Mina Kennedy brought near her lips to ear of tankard one.

– Mr Dollard, they murmured low.

– Dollard, murmured tankard.

Tank one believed: Miss Kenn when she: that doll he was: she doll: the tank.

He murmured that he knew the name. The name was familiar to him, that is to say. That was to say he had heard the name of Dollard, was it? Dollard, yes.

Yes, her lips said more loudly, Mr Dollard. He sang that song lovely, murmured Mina. And *The last rose of summer* was a lovely song. Mina loved that song. Tankard loved the song that Mina.

'Tis the last rose of summer dollard left Bloom felt wind wound round inside.

Gassy thing that cider: binding too. Wait. Postoffice near Reuben J's one and eightpence too. Get shut of it. Dodge round by Greek street. Wish I hadn't promised to meet. Freer in air. Music. Gets on your nerves. Beerpull. Her hand that rocks the cradle rules the. Ben Howth. That rules the world.

Far. Far. Far. Far.

Tap. Tap. Tap. Tap.

Up the quay went Lionelleopold, naughty Henry with letter for Mady, with sweets of sin with frillies for Raoul with met him pike hoses went Poldy on.

Tap blind walked tapping by the tap the curbstone tapping, tap by tap.

Cowley, he stuns himself with it; kind of drunkenness. Better give way only half way the way of a man with a maid. Instance enthusiasts. All ears. Not lose a demisemiquaver. Eyes shut. Head nodding in time. Dotty. You daren't budge. Thinking strictly prohibited. Always talking shop. Fiddle-faddle about notes.

All a kind of attempt to talk. Unpleasant when it stops because you never know exac. Organ in Gardiner street. Old Glynn fifty quid a year. Queer up there in the cockloft alone with stops and locks and keys. Seated all day at the organ. Maunder on for hours, talking to himself or the other fellow blowing the bellows. Growl angry, then shriek cursing (want to have wadding or something in his no don't she cried), then all of a soft sudden wee little wee little pippy wind.

Pwee! A wee little wind piped eeee. In Bloom's little wee.

– Was he? Mr Dedalus said, returning, with fetched pipe. I was with him this morning at poor little Paddy Dignam's . . .

– Ay, the Lord have mercy on him.

– By the by there's a tuningfork in there on the . . .

Tap. Tap. Tap. Tap.

– The wife has a fine voice. Or had. What? Lidwell asked.

– O, that must be the tuner, Lydia said to Simonlionel first I saw, forgot it when he was here.

Blind he was she told George Lidwell second I saw. And played so exquisitely, treat to hear. Exquisite contrast: bronzelid minagold.

– Shout! Ben Dollard shouted, pouring. Sing out!

– 'Ildo! cried Father Cowley.

Rrrrrr.

I feel I want . . .

Tap. Tap. Tap. Tap. Tap.

– Very, Mr Dedalus said, staring hard at a headless sardine.

Under the sandwichbell lay on a bier of bread one last, one lonely, last sardine of summer. Bloom alone.

– Very, he stared. The lower register, for choice.

Tap. Tap. Tap. Tap. Tap. Tap. Tap. Tap.

Bloom went by Barry's. Wish I could. Wait. That wonderworker if I had. Twentyfour solicitors in that one house. Litigation. Love one another. Piles of parchment. Messrs Pick and Pocket have power of attorney. Goulding, Collis, Ward.

But for example the chap that wallops the big drum. His vocation: Micky Rooney's band. Wonder how it first struck him. Sitting at home after pig's cheek and cabbage nursing it in the armchair. Rehearsing his band part. Pom. Pompedy. Jolly for the wife. Asses' skins. Welt them through life, then wallop after death. Pom. Wallop. Seems to be what you call yashmak or I mean kismet. Fate.

Tap. Tap. A stripling, blind, with a tapping cane, came taptaptapping by Daly's window where a mermaid, hair all streaming (but he couldn't see), blew whiffs of a mermaid (blind couldn't), mermaid coolest whiff of all.

Instruments. A blade of grass, shell of her hands, then blow. Even comb and tissuepaper you can knock a tune out of. Molly in her shift in Lombard street west, hair down. I suppose each kind of trade made its own, don't you see? Hunter with a horn. Haw. Have you the? *Cloche. Sonnez la!* Shepherd his pipe. Policeman a whistle. Locks and keys! Sweep! Four o'clock's all's well! Sleep! All is lost now. Drum? Pompedy. Wait, I know. Towncrier, bumbailiff. Long John. Waken the dead. Pom. Dignam. Poor little *nomine-domine*. Pom. It is music, I mean of course it's all pom pom pom very much what they call *da capo*. Still you can hear. As we march we march along, march along. Pom.

I must really. Fff. Now if I did that at a banquet. Just a question of custom shah of Persia. Breathe a prayer, drop a tear. All the same he must have been a bit of a natural not to see it was a yeoman cap. Muffled up. Wonder who was that chap at the grave in the brown mackin. O, the whore of the lane!

A frowsy whore with black straw sailor hat askew came glazily in the day along the quay towards Mr Bloom. When first he saw that form endearing. Yes, it is. I feel so lonely. Wet night in the lane. Horn. Who had the? Heehaw. Shesaw. Off her beat here. What is she? Hope she. Psst! Any chance of your wash. Knew Molly. Had me decked. Stout lady does be with you in the brown costume. Put you off your stroke. That appointment we made. Knowing we'd never, well hardly ever. Too dear too near to home sweet home. Sees me, does she? Looks a fright in the day. Face like dip. Damn her! O, well, she has to live like the rest. Look in here.

In Lionel Marks's antique saleshop window haughty Henry Lionel Leopold dear Henry Flower earnestly Mr Leopold Bloom envisaged candlestick melodeon oozing maggoty blowbags. Bargain: six bob. Might learn to play. Cheap. Let her pass. Course everything is dear if you don't want it. That's what good salesman is. Make you buy what he wants to sell. Chap sold me the Swedish razor he shaved me with. Wanted to charge me for the edge he gave it. She's passing now. Six bob.

Must be the cider or perhaps the burgund.

Near bronze from anear near gold from afar they chinked their clinking glasses all, brighteyed and gallant, before bronze Lydia's tempting last rose of summer, rose of Castille. First Lid, De, Cow, Ker, Doll, a fifth: Lidwell, Si Dedalus, Bob Cowley, Kernan and Big Ben Dollard.

Tap. A youth entered a lonely Ormond hall.

Bloom viewed a gallant pictured hero in Lionel Marks's window. Robert Emmet's last words. Seven last words. Of Meyerbeer that is.

– True men like you men.

– Ay, ay, Ben.

– Will lift your glass with us.

They lifted.

Tschink. Tschunk.

Tip. An unseeing stripling stood in the door. He saw not bronze. He saw not gold. Nor Ben nor Bob nor Tom nor Si nor George nor tanks nor Richie nor Pat. Hee hee hee hee. He did not see.

Seabloom, greaseabloom viewed last words. Softly. *When my country takes her place among.*

Prrprr.

Must be the bur.

Fff. Oo. Rrpr.

Nations of the earth. No-one behind. She's passed. *Then and not till then.* Tram. Kran, kran, kran. Good oppor. Coming. Krandlkrankran. I'm sure it's the burgund. Yes. One, two, *Let my epitaph be.* Karaaaaaaa. *Written. I have.*

Pprrpffrrppffff.

Done.

*   *   *   *   *

◀ I WAS JUST PASSING THE TIME OF DAY WITH OLD Troy of the D. M. P. at the corner of Arbour hill there and be damned but a bloody sweep came along and he near drove his gear into my eye. I turned around to let him have the weight of my tongue when who should I see dodging along Stony Batter only Joe Hynes.

– Lo, Joe, says I. How are you blowing? Did you see that bloody chimneysweep near shove my eye out with his brush?

– Soot's luck, says Joe. Who's the old ballocks you were talking to?

– Old Troy, says I, was in the force. I'm on two minds not to give that fellow in charge for obstructing the thoroughfare with his brooms and ladders.

– What are you doing round those parts? says Joe.

– Devil a much, says I. There is a bloody big foxy thief beyond by the garrison church at the corner of Chicken Lane – old Troy was just giving me a wrinkle about him – lifted any God's quantity of tea and sugar to pay three bob a week said he had a farm in the county Down off a hop of my thumb by the name of Moses Herzog over there near Heytesbury street.

– Circumcised! says Joe.

– Ay, says I. A bit off the top. An old plumber named Geraghty. I'm hanging on to his taw now for the past fortnight and I can't get a penny out of him.

– That the lay you're on now? says Joe.

– Ay, says I. How are the mighty fallen! Collector of bad and doubtful debts. But that's the most notorious bloody robber you'd meet in a day's walk and the face on him all pockmarks would hold a shower of rain. *Tell him*, says he, *I dare him*, says he, *and I doubledare him to send you round here again or if he does*, says he, *I'll have him summonsed up before the court, so will I, for trading without a licence.* And he after stuffing himself till he's fit to burst! Jesus, I had to laugh at the little jewy getting his shirt out. *He drink me my teas. He eat me my sugars. Because he no pay me my moneys?*

For nonperishable goods bought of Moses Herzog, of 13 Saint Kevin's parade, Wood quay ward, merchant, hereinafter called the vendor, and sold and delivered to Michael E. Geraghty, Esquire, of 29 Arbour Hill in the city of Dublin, Arran quay ward, gentleman, hereinafter called the purchaser, videlicet, five pounds avoirdupois of first choice tea at three shillings per pound avoirdupois and three stone avoirdupois of sugar, crushed crystal, at three pence per pound avoirdupois, the said purchaser debtor to the said vendor of one pound five shillings and six pence sterling for value received which amount shall be paid by said purchaser to said vendor in weekly instalments every seven calendar days of three shillings and no pence sterling: and the said nonperishable goods shall not be pawned or pledged or sold or otherwise alienated by the said purchaser but shall be and remain and be held to be the sole and exclusive property of the said vendor to be disposed of at his good will and pleasure until the said amount shall have been duly paid by the said purchaser to the said vendor in the manner herein set forth as this day hereby agreed between the said vendor his heirs, successors, trustees and assigns of the one part and the said purchaser, his heirs, successors, trustees and assigns of the other part.

– Are you a strict t. t.? says Joe.

– Not taking anything between drinks, says I.

– What about paying our respects to our friend? says Joe.

– Who? says I. Sure, he's in John of God's off his head, poor man.

– Drinking his own stuff? says Joe.

– Ay, says I. Whisky and water on the brain.

– Come around to Barney Kiernan's, says Joe. I want to see the citizen.

– Barney mavourneen's be it, says I. Anything strange or wonderful, Joe?

– Not a word, says Joe. I was up at that meeting in the City Arms.

– What was that, Joe? says I.

– Cattle traders, says Joe, about the foot and mouth disease. I want to give the citizen the hard word about it.

So we went around by the Linenhall barracks and the back of the courthouse talking of one thing or another. Decent fellow Joe when he has it but sure like that he never has it. Jesus, I couldn't get over that bloody foxy Geraghty, the daylight robber. For trading without a licence, says he.

In Inisfail the fair there lies a land, the land of holy Michan. There rises a watchtower beheld of men afar. There sleep the mighty dead as in life they slept, warriors and princes of high renown. A pleasant land it is in sooth of murmuring waters, fishful streams where sport the gunnard, the plaice, the roach, the halibut, the gibbed haddock, the grilse, the dab, the brill, the flounder, the mixed coarse fish generally and other denizens of the aqueous kingdom too numerous to be enumerated. In the mild breezes of the west and of the east the lofty trees wave in different directions their first class foliage, the wafty sycamore, the Lebanonian cedar, the exalted planetree, the eugenic eucalyptus and other ornaments of the arboreal world with which that region is thoroughly well supplied. Lovely maidens sit in close proximity to the roots of the lovely trees singing the most lovely songs while they play with all kinds of lovely objects as for example golden ingots, silvery fishes, crans of herrings, drafts of eels, codlings, creels of fingerlings, purple seagems and playful insects. And heroes voyage from afar to woo them, from Elbana to Slievemargy, the peerless princes of unfettered Munster and of Connacht the just and of smooth sleek Leinster and of Cruachan's land and of Armagh the splendid and of the noble district of Boyle, princes, the sons of kings.

And there rises a shining palace whose crystal glittering roof is seen by mariners who traverse the extensive sea in barks built expressly for that purpose and thither come all herds and fatlings and first fruits of that land for O'Connell Fitzsimon takes toll of them, a chieftain descended from chieftains. Thither the extremely large wains bring foison of the fields, flaskets of cauliflowers, floats of spinach, pineapple chunks, Rangoon beans, strikes of tomatoes, drums of figs, drills of Swedes, spherical potatoes and tallies of iridescent kale, York and Savoy, and trays of onions, pearls of the earth, and punnets of mushrooms and custard marrows and fat vetches and bere and rape and red green yellow brown russet sweet big bitter ripe pomellated apples and chips of strawberries and sieves of gooseberries, pulpy and pelurious, and strawberries fit for princes and raspberries from their canes.

I dare him, says he, and I doubledare him. Come out here, Geraghty, you notorious bloody hill and dale robber!

And by that way wend the herds innumerable of bellwethers and flushed ewes and shearling rams and lambs and stubble geese and medium steers and roaring mares and polled calves and longwools and storesheep and Cuffe's prime springers and culls and sowpigs and baconhogs and the various different varieties of highly distinguished swine and Angus heifers and polly bullocks of immaculate pedigree together with prime premiated milchcows and beeves: and there is ever heard a trampling, cackling, roaring, lowing, bleating, bellowing, rumbling, grunting, champing, chewing, of sheep and pigs and heavyhooved kine from pasturelands of Lush and Rush and Carrickmines and from the streamy vales of Thomond, from M'Gillicuddy's reeks the inaccessible and lordly Shannon the unfathomable, and from the gentle declivities of the place of the race of Kiar, their udders distended with superabundance of milk and butts of butter and rennets of cheese and farmer's firkins and targets of lamb and crannocks of corn and oblong eggs, in great hundreds, various in size, the agate with the dun.

So we turned into Barney Kiernan's and there sure enough was the citizen up in the corner having a great confab with himself and that bloody mangy mongrel, Garryowen, and he waiting for what the sky would drop in the way of drink.

– There he is, says I, in his gloryhole, with his cruiskeen lawn and his load of papers, working for the cause.

The bloody mongrel let a grouse out of him would give you the creeps. Be a corporal work of mercy if someone would take the life of that bloody dog. I'm told for a fact he ate a good part of the breeches off a constabulary man in Santry that came round one time with a blue paper about a licence.

– Stand and deliver, says he.

– That's all right, citizen, says Joe. Friends here.

– Pass, friends, says he.

Then he rubs his hand in his eye and says he:

– What's your opinion of the times?

Doing the rapparee and Rory of the hill. But, begob, Joe was equal to the occasion.

– I think the markets are on a rise, says he, sliding his hand down his fork.

So begob the citizen claps his paw on his knee and he says:

– Foreign wars is the cause of it.

And says Joe, sticking his thumb in his pocket:

– It's the Russians wish to tyrannise.

– Arrah, give over your bloody codding Joe, says I, I've a thirst on me I wouldn't sell for half a crown.

– Give it a name, citizen, says Joe.

– Wine of the country, says he.

– What's yours? says Joe.

– Ditto MacAnaspey, says I.

– Three pints, Terry, says Joe. And how's the old heart, citizen? says he.

– Never better, *a chara*, says he. What Garry? Are we going to win? Eh?

And with that he took the bloody old towser by the scruff of the neck and, by Jesus, he near throttled him.

The figure seated on a large boulder at the foot of a round tower was that of a broadshouldered deepchested stronglimbed frankeyed redhaired freely freckled shaggybearded widemouthed largenosed longheaded deepvoiced barekneed brawnyhanded hairylegged ruddyfaced, sinewyarmed hero. From shoulder to shoulder he measured several ells and his rocklike mountainous knees were covered, as was likewise the rest of his body wherever visible, with a strong growth of tawny prickly hair in hue and toughness similar to the mountain gorse (*Ulex Europeus*). The widewinged nostrils, from which bristles of the same tawny hue projected, were of such capaciousness that within their cavernous obscurity the fieldlark might easily have lodged her nest. The eyes in which a tear and a smile strove ever for the mastery were of the dimensions of a goodsized cauliflower. A powerful current of warm breath issued at regular intervals from the profound cavity of his mouth while in rhythmic resonance the loud strong hale reverberations of his formidable heart thundered rumblingly causing the ground, the summit of the lofty tower and the still loftier walls of the cave to vibrate and tremble.

He wore a long unsleeved garment of recently flayed oxhide reaching to the knees in a loose kilt and this was bound about his middle by a girdle of plaited straw and rushes. Beneath this he wore trews of deerskin, roughly stitched with gut. His nether extremities were encased in high Balbriggan buskins dyed in lichen purple, the feet being shod with brogues of salted cowhide laced with the windpipe of the same beast. From his girdle hung a row of seastones which dangled at every movement of his portentous frame and on these were graven with rude yet striking art the tribal images of many Irish heroes and heroines of antiquity, Cuchulin, Conn of hundred battles, Niall of nine hostages, Brian of Kincora, the Ardri Malachi, Art MacMurragh, Shane O'Neill, Father John Murphy, Owen Roe, Patrick Sarsfield, Red Hugh O'Donnell, Red Jim MacDermott, Soggarth Eoghan O'Growney, Michael Dwyer, Francy Higgins, Henry Joy M'Cracken, Goliath, Horace Wheatley, Thomas Conneff, Peg Woffington, the Village Blacksmith, Captain Moonlight, Captain Boycott, Dante Alighieri, Christopher Columbus, S. Fursa, S. Brendan, Marshal MacMahon, Charlemagne, Theobald Wolfe Tone, the Mother of the Maccabees, the Last of the Mohicans, the Rose of Castille, the Man for Galway, The Man that Broke the Bank at Monte Carlo, The Man in the Gap, The Woman Who Didn't, Benjamin Franklin, Napoleon Bonaparte, John L. Sullivan, Cleopatra, Savourneen Deelish, Julius Caesar, Paracelsus, sir Thomas Lipton, William Tell, Michelangelo, Hayes, Muhammad, the Bride of Lammermoor, Peter the Hermit, Peter the Packer, Dark Rosaleen, Patrick W. Shakespeare, Brian Confucius, Murtagh Gutenberg, Patricio Velasquez, Captain Nemo, Tristan and Isolde, the first Prince of Wales, Thomas Cook and Son, the Bold Soldier Boy, Arrah na Pogue, Dick Turpin, Ludwig Beethoven, the Colleen Bawn, Waddler Healy, Angus the Culdee, Dolly Mount, Sidney Parade, Ben Howth, Valentine Greatrakes, Adam and Eve, Arthur Wellesley, Boss Croker, Herodotus, Jack the Giantkiller, Gautama Buddha, Lady Godiva, The Lily of Killarney, Balor of the Evil Eye, the Queen of Sheba, Acky Nagle, Joe Nagle, Alessandro Volta, Jeremiah O'Donovan Rossa, Don Philip O'Sullivan Beare. A couched spear of acuminated granite rested by him while at his feet reposed a savage animal of the canine tribe whose stertorous gasps announced that he was sunk in uneasy slumber, a supposition confirmed by hoarse growls and spasmodic movements which his master repressed from time to time by tranquillising blows of a mighty cudgel rudely fashioned out of paleolithic stone.

So anyhow Terry brought the three pints Joe was standing and begob the sight nearly left my eyes when I saw him land out a quid. O, as true as I'm telling you. A goodlooking sovereign.

– And there's more where that came from, says he.

– Were you robbing the poorbox, Joe? says I.

– Sweat of my brow, says Joe. 'Twas the prudent member gave me the wheeze.

– I saw him before I met you, says I, sloping around by Pill lane and Greek street with his cod's eye counting up all the guts of the fish.

Who comes through Michan's land, bedight in sable armour? O'Bloom, the son of Rory: it is he. Impervious to fear is Rory's son: he of the prudent soul.

– For the old woman of Prince's street, says the citizen, the subsidised organ. The pledgebound party on the floor of the house. And look at this blasted rag, says he. Look at this, says he. *The Irish Independent*, if you please, founded by Parnell to be the workingman's friend. Listen to the births and deaths in the *Irish all for Ireland Independent* and I'll thank you and the marriages.

And he starts reading them out:

– Gordon, Barnfield Crescent, Exeter; Redmayne of Iffley, Saint Anne's on Sea, the wife of William T. Redmayne, of a son. How's that, eh? Wright and Flint, Vincent and Gillett to Rotha Marion daughter of Rosa and the late George Alfred Gillett, 179 Clapham Road, Stockwell, Playwood and Ridsdale at Saint Jude's Kensington by the very reverend Dr Forrest, Dean of Worcester, eh? Deaths. Bristow, at Whitehall lane, London: Carr, Stoke Newington, of gastritis and heart disease: Cockburn, at the Moat house, Chepstow . . .

– I know that fellow, says Joe, from bitter experience.

– Cockburn. Dimsey, wife of David Dimsey, late of the admiralty: Miller, Tottenham, aged eightyfive: Welsh, June 12, at 35 Canning Street, Liverpool, Isabella Helen. How's that for a national press, eh, my brown son? How's that for Martin Murphy, the Bantry jobber?

– Ah, well, says Joe, handing round the boose. Thanks be to God they had the start of us. Drink that, citizen.

– I will, says he, honourable person.

– Health, Joe, says I. And all down the form.

Ah! Ow! Don't be talking! I was blue mouldy for the want of that pint. Declare to God I could hear it hit the pit of my stomach with a click.

And lo, as they quaffed their cup of joy, a godlike messenger came swiftly in, radiant as the eye of heaven, a comely youth and behind him there passed an elder of noble gait and countenance, bearing the sacred scrolls of law and with him his lady wife, a dame of peerless lineage, fairest of her race.

Little Alf Bergan popped in round the door and hid behind Barney's snug, squeezed up with the laughing, and who was sitting up there in the corner that I hadn't seen snoring drunk, blind to the world, only Bob Doran. I didn't know what was up and Alf kept making signs out of the door. And begob what was it only that bloody old pantaloon Denis Breen in his bath slippers with two bloody big books tucked under his oxter and the wife hotfoot after him, unfortunate wretched woman trotting like a poodle. I thought Alf would split.

– Look at him, says he. Breen. He's traipsing all round Dublin with a postcard someone sent him with u. p.: up on it to take a li . . .

And he doubled up.

– Take a what? says I.

– Libel action, says he, for ten thousand pounds.

– O, hell! says I.

The bloody mongrel began to growl that'd put the fear of God in you seeing something was up but the citizen gave him a kick in the ribs.

– *Bi i dho husht*, says he.

– Who? says Joe.

– Breen, says Alf. He was in John Henry Menton's and then he went round to Collis and Ward's and then Tom Rochford met him and sent him round to the subsheriff's for a lark. O God, I've a pain laughing. U. p.: up. The long fellow gave him an eye as good as a process and now the bloody old lunatic is gone round to Green Street to look for a G. man.

– When is long John going to hang that fellow in Mountjoy? says Joe.

– Bergan, says Bob Doran, waking up. Is that Alf Bergan?

– Yes, says Alf. Hanging? Wait till I show you. Here, Terry, give us a pony. That bloody old fool! Ten thousand pounds. You should have seen long John's eye. U. p . . .

And he started laughing.

– Who are you laughing at? says Bob Doran. Is that Bergan?

– Hurry up, Terry boy, says Alf.

Terence O'Ryan heard him and straightway brought him a crystal cup full of the foaming ebon ale which the noble twin brothers Bungiveagh and Bungardilaun brew ever in their divine alevats, cunning as the sons of deathless Leda. For they garner the succulent berries of the hop and mass and sift and bruise and brew them and they mix therewith sour juices and bring the must to the sacred fire and cease not night or day from their toil, those cunning brothers, lords of the vat.

Then did you, chivalrous Terence, hand forth, as to the manner born, that nectarous beverage and you offered the crystal cup to him that thirsted, the soul of chivalry, in beauty akin to the immortals.

But he the young chief of the O'Bergan's, could ill brook to be outdone in generous deeds but gave therefor with gracious gesture a testoon of costliest bronze. Thereon embossed in excellent smithwork was seen the image of a queen of regal port, scion of the house of Brunswick, Victoria her name, Her Most Excellent Majesty, by grace of God of the United Kingdom of Great Britain and Ireland and of the British dominions beyond the sea, queen, defender of the faith, Empress of India, even she, who bore rule, a victress over many peoples, the wellbeloved, for they knew and loved her from the rising of the sun to the going down thereof, the pale, the dark, the ruddy and the ethiop.

– What's that bloody freemason doing, says the citizen, prowling up and down outside?

– What's that? says Joe,

– Here you are, says Alf, chucking out the rhino. Talking about hanging. I'll show you something you never saw. Hangmen's letters. Look at here.

So he took a bundle of wisps of letters and envelopes out of his pocket.

– Are you codding? say I.

– Honest injun, says Alf. Read them.

So Joe took up the letters.

– Who are you laughing at? says Bob Doran.

So I saw there was going to be bit of a dust. Bob's a queer chap when the porter's up in him so says I just to make talk:

– How's Willy Murray those times, Alf?

– I don't know, says Alf. I saw him just now in Capel Street with Paddy Dignam. Only I was running after that . . .

– You what? says Joe, throwing down the letters. With who?

– With Dignam, says Alf.

– Is it Paddy? says Joe.

– Yes, says Alf. Why?

– Don't you know he's dead? says Joe.

– Paddy Dignam dead? says Alf.

– Ay, says Joe.

– Sure I'm after seeing him not five minutes ago, says Alf, as plain as a pikestaff.

– Who's dead? says Bob Doran.

– You saw his ghost then, says Joe, God between us and harm.

– What? says Alf. Good Christ, only five . . . What? . . . and Willy Murray with him, the two of them there near whatdoyoucallhim's . . . What? Dignam dead?

– What about Dignam? says Bob Doran. Who's talking about . . .?

– Dead! says Alf. He is no more dead than you are.

– Maybe so, says Joe. They took the liberty of burying him this morning anyhow.

– Paddy? says Alf.

– Ay, says Joe. He paid the debt of nature, God be merciful to him.

– Good Christ! says Alf.

Begob he was what you might call flabbergasted.

In the darkness spirit hands were felt to flutter and when prayer by tantras had been directed to the proper quarter a faint but increasing luminosity of ruby light became gradually visible, the apparition of the etheric double being particularly lifelike owing to the discharge of jivic rays from the crown of the head and face. Communication was effected through the pituitary body and also by means of the orangefiery and scarlet rays emanating from the sacral region and solar plexus. Questioned by his earthname as to his whereabouts in the heavenworld he stated that he was now on the path of pralaya or return but was still submitted to trial at the hands of certain bloodthirsty entities on the lower astral levels. In reply to a question as to his first sensations in the great divide beyond he stated that previously he had seen as in a glass darkly but that those who had passed over had summit possibilities of atmic development opened up to them. Interrogated as to whether life there resembled our experience in the flesh he stated that he had heard from more favoured beings now in the spirit that their abodes were equipped with every modern home comfort such as talafana, alavatar, hatakalda, wataklasat and that the highest adepts were steeped in waves of volupcy of the very purest nature. Having requested a quart of buttermilk this was brought and evidently afforded relief. Asked if he had any message for the living he exhorted all who were still at the wrong side of Maya to acknowledge the true path for it was reported in devanic circles that Mars and Jupiter were out for mischief on the eastern angle where the ram has power. It was then queried whether there were any special desires on the part of the defunct and the reply was: *We greet you, friends of earth, who are still in the body. Mind C. K. doesn't pile it on.* It was ascertained that the reference was to Mr Cornelius Kelleher, manager of Messrs H. J. O'Neill's popular funeral establishment, a personal friend of the defunct, who had been responsible for the carrying out of the interment arrangements. Before departing he requested that it should be told to his dear son Patsy that the other boot which he had been looking for was at present under the commode in the return room and that the pair should be sent to Cullen's to be soled only as the heels were still good. He stated that this had greatly perturbed his peace of mind in the other region and earnestly requested that his desire should be made known.

Assurances were given that the matter would be attended to and it was intimated that this had given satisfaction.

He is gone from mortal haunts: O'Dignam, sun of our morning. Fleet was his foot on the bracken: Patrick of the beamy brow. Wail, Banba, with your wind: and wail, O ocean, with your whirlwind.

– There he is again, says the citizen, staring out.

– Who? says I.

– Bloom, says he. He's on point duty up and down there for the last ten minutes.

And, begob, I saw his physog do a peep in and then slidder off again.

Little Alf was knocked bawways. Faith, he was.

– Good Christ! says he. I could have sworn it was him.

And says Bob Doran, with the hat on the back of his poll, lowest blackguard in Dublin when he's under the influence:

– Who said Christ is good?

– I beg your parsnips, says Alf.

– Is that a good Christ, says Bob Doran, to take away poor little Willy Dignam?

– Ah, well, says Alf, trying to pass it off. He's over all his troubles.

But Bob Doran shouts out of him.

– He's a bloody ruffian I say, to take away poor little Willy Dignam.

Terry came down and tipped him the wink to keep quiet, that they didn't want that kind of talk in a respectable licensed premises. And Bob Doran starts doing the weeps about Paddy Dignam, true as you're there.

– The finest man, says he, snivelling, the finest purest character.

The tear is bloody near your eye. Talking through his bloody hat. Fitter for him to go home to the little sleepwalking bitch he married, Mooney, the bumbailiff's daughter. Mother kept a kip in Hardwicke street that used to be stravaging about the landings Bantam Lyons told me that was stopping there at two in the morning without a stitch on her, exposing her person, open to all comers, fair field and no favour.

– The noblest, the truest, says he. And he's gone, poor little Willy, poor little Paddy Dignam.

And mournful and with a heavy heart he bewept the extinction of that beam of heaven.

Old Garryowen started growling again at Bloom that was skeezing round the door.

– Come in, come on, he won't eat you, says the citizen.

So Bloom slopes in with his cod's eye on the dog and he asks Terry was Martin Cunningham there.

– O, Christ M'Keown, says Joe, reading one of the letters. Listen to this, will you?

And he starts reading out one.

7, *Hunter Street, Liverpool.*

To the High Sheriff of Dublin, Dublin.

Honoured sir i beg to offer my services in the abovementioned painful case i hanged Joe Gann in Bootle jail on the 12 of February 1900 and i hanged . . .

– Show us, Joe, says I.

– *. . . private Arthur Chace for fowl murder of Jessie Tilsit in Pentonville prison and i was assistant when . . .*

– Jesus, says I.

– *. . . Billington executed the awful murderer Toad Smith . . .*

The citizen made a grab at the letter.

– Hold hard, says Joe, *i have a special nack of putting the noose once in he can't get out hoping to be favoured i remain, honoured sir, my terms is five ginnese.*

H. Rumbold,
Master Barber.

– And a barbarous bloody barbarian he is too, says the citizen.

– And the dirty scrawl of the wretch, says Joe. Here, says he, take them to hell out of my sight, Alf. Hello, Bloom, says he, what will you have?

So they started arguing about the point, Bloom saying he wouldn't and couldn't and excuse him no offence and all to that and then he said well he'd just take a cigar. Gob, he's a prudent member and no mistake.

– Give us one of your prime stinkers, Terry, says Joe.

And Alf was telling us there was one chap sent in a mourning card with a black border round it.

– They're all barbers, says he, from the black country that would hang their own fathers for five quid down and travelling expenses.

And he was telling us there's two fellows waiting below to pull his heels down when he gets the drop and choke him properly and then they chop up the rope after and sell the bits for a few bob a skull.

In the dark land they bide, the vengeful knights of the razor. Their deadly coil they grasp: yea, and therein they lead to Erebus whatsoever wight hath done a deed of blood for I will on nowise suffer it even so saith the Lord.

So they started talking about capital punishment and of course Bloom comes out with the why and the wherefore and all the codology of the business and the old dog smelling him all the time I'm told those Jewies does have a sort of a queer odour coming off them for dogs about I don't know what all deterrent effect and so forth and so on.

– There's one thing it hasn't a deterrent effect on, says Alf.

– What's that? says Joe.

– The poor bugger's tool that's being hanged, says Alf.

– That so? says Joe.

– God's truth, says Alf. I heard that from the head warder that was in Kilmainham when they hanged Joe Brady, the invincible. He told me when they cut him down after the drop it was standing up in their faces like a poker.

– Ruling passion strong in death, says Joe, as someone said.

– That can be explained by science, says Bloom. It's only a natural phenomenon, don't you see, because on account of the . . .

And then he starts with his jawbreakers about phenomenon and science and this phenomenon and the other phenomenon.

The distinguished scientist Herr Professor Luitpold Blumenduft tendered medical evidence to the effect that the instantaneous fracture of the cervical vertebrae and consequent scission of the spinal cord would, according to the best approved traditions of medical science, be calculated to inevitably produce in the human subject a violent ganglionic stimulus of the nerve centres, causing the pores of the *corpora cavernosa* to rapidly dilate in such a way as to instantaneously facilitate the flow of blood to that part of the human anatomy known as the penis or male organ resulting in the phenomenon which has been denominated by the faculty a morbid upwards and outwards philoprogenitive erection *in articulo mortis per diminutionem capitis*.

So of course the citizen was only waiting for the wink of the word and he starts gassing out of him about the invincibles and the old guard and the men of sixtyseven and who fears to speak of ninetyeight and Joe with him about all the fellows that were hanged, drawn and transported for the cause by drumhead courtmartial and a new Ireland and new this, that and the other. Talking about new Ireland he ought to go and get a new dog so he ought. Mangy ravenous brute sniffling and sneezing all round the place and scratching his scabs and round he goes to Bob Doran that was standing Alf a half one sucking up for what he could get. So of couse Bob Doran starts doing the bloody fool with him:

– Give us the paw! Give the paw, doggy! Good old doggy. Give us the paw here! Give us the paw!

Arrah! bloody end to the paw he'd paw and Alf trying to keep him from tumbling off the bloody stool atop of the bloody old dog and he talking all kinds of drivel about training by kindness and thoroughbred dog and intelligent dog: give you the bloody pip. Then he starts scraping a few bits of old biscuit out of the bottom of a Jacob's tin he told Terry to bring. Gob, he golloped it down like old boots and his tongue hanging out of him a yard long for more. Near ate the tin and all, hungry bloody mongrel.

And the citizen and Bloom having an argument about the point, the brothers Sheares and Wolfe Tone beyond on Arbour Hill and Robert Emmet and die for your country, the Tommy Moore touch about Sara Curran and she's far from the land. And Bloom, of course, with his knockmedown cigar putting on swank with his lardy face. Phenomenon! The fat heap he married is a nice old phenomenon with a back on her like a ballalley. Time they were stopping up in the *City Arms* Pisser Burke told me there was an old one there with a cracked loodheramaun of a nephew and Bloom trying to get the soft side of her doing the mollycoddle playing bézique to come in for a bit of the wampum in her will and not eating meat of a Friday because the old one was always thumping her craw and taking the lout out for a walk. And one time he led him the rounds of Dublin and, by the holy farmer, he never cried crack till he brought him home as drunk as a boiled owl and he said he did it to teach him the evils of alcohol and by herrings if the three women didn't near roast him it's a queer story, the old one, Bloom's wife and Mrs O'Dowd that kept the hotel. Jesus, I had to laugh at Pisser Burke taking them off chewing the fat and Bloom with his *but don't you see?* and *but on the other hand.* And sure, more be token, the lout I'm told was in Power's after, the blender's, round in Cope street going home footless in a cab five times in the week after drinking his way through all the samples in the bloody establishment. Phenomenon!

– The memory of the dead, says the citizen taking up his pintglass and glaring at Bloom.

– Ay, ay, says Joe.

– You don't grasp my point, says Bloom. What I mean is . . .

– *Sinn Fein!* says the citizen. *Sinn fein amhain!* The friends we love are by our side and the foes we hate before us.

The last farewell was affecting in the extreme. From the belfries far and near the funereal deathbell tolled unceasingly while all around the gloomy precincts rolled the ominous warning of a hundred muffled drums punctuated by the hollow booming of pieces of ordnance. The deafening claps of thunder and the dazzling flashes of lightning which lit up the ghastly scene testified that the artillery of heaven had lent its supernatural pomp to the already gruesome spectacle. A torrential rain poured down from the floodgates of the angry heavens upon the bared heads of the assembled multitude which numbered at the lowest computation five hundred thousand persons. A posse of Dublin Metropolitan police superintended by the Chief Commissioner in person maintained order in the vast throng for whom the York Street brass and reed band whiled away the intervening time by admirably rendering on their blackdraped instruments the matchless melody endeared to us from the cradle by Speranza's plaintive muse. Special quick excursion trains and upholstered charabancs had been provided for the comfort of our country cousins of whom there were large contingents. Considerable amusement was caused by the favourite Dublin streetsingers L-n-h-n and M-ll-g-n who sang *The Night before Larry was stretched* in their usual mirthprovoking fashion. Our two inimitable drolls did a roaring trade with their broadsheets among lovers of the comedy element and nobody who has a corner in his heart for real Irish fun without vulgarity will grudge them their hardearned pennies. The children of the Male and Female Foundling Hospital who thronged the windows overlooking the scene were delighted with this unexpected addition to the day's entertainment and a word of praise is due to the Little Sisters of the Poor for their excellent idea of affording the poor fatherless and motherless children a genuinely instructive treat. The viceregal houseparty which included many wellknown ladies was chaperoned by Their Excellencies to the most favourable positions on the grand stand while the picturesque foreign delegation known as the Friends of the Emerald Isle was accommodated on a tribune directly opposite. The delegation, present in full force, consisted of Commendatore Bacibaci Beninobenone (the semiparalysed *doyen* of the party who had to be assisted to his seat by the aid of a powerful steam crane), Monsieur Pierrepaul Petitépatant, the Grandjoker Vladinmire Pokethankertscheff, the Archjoker Leopold Rudolph von Schwanzenbad-Hodenthaler, Countess Marha Virága Kisászony Putrápesthi, Hiram Y. Bomboost, Count Athanatos Karamelopulos, Ali Baba Backsheesh Rahat Lokum Effendi, Señor Hidalgo Caballero Don Pecadillo y Palabras y Paternoster de la Malora de la Malaria, Hokopoko Harakiri, Hi Hung Chang, Olaf Kobberkeddelsen, Mynheer Trik van Trumps, Pan Poleaxe Paddyrisky, Goosepond Prhklstr Kratchinabritchisitch, Herr Hurhausdirektorpräsident Hans Chuechli-Steuerli, Nationalgymnasiummuseumsanatoriumandsuspensoriums-ordinaryprivatdocentgeneralhistoryspecialprofessordoctor Kriegfried Ueberallgemein. All the delegates without exception expressed themselves in the strongest possible heterogeneous terms concerning the nameless barbarity which they had been called upon to witness. An animated altercation (in which all took part) ensued among the F. O. T. E. I. as to whether the eighth or the ninth of March was the correct date of the birth of Ireland's patron saint. In the course of the argument cannonballs, scimitars, boomerangs, blunderbusses, stinkpots, meatchoppers, umbrellas, catapults, knuckledusters, sandbags, lumps of pig iron were resorted to and blows were freely exchanged. The baby policeman, Constable MacFadden, summoned by special courier from Booterstown, quickly restored order and with lightning promptitude proposed the seventeenth of the month as a solution equally honourable for both contending parties. The readywitted ninefooter's suggestion at once appealed to all and was unanimously accepted. Constable MacFadden was heartily congratulated by all the F. O. T. E. I., several of whom were bleeding profusely. Commendatore Beninobenone having been extricated from underneath the presidential armchair, it was explained by his legal adviser Avvocato Pagamimi that the various articles secreted in his thirtytwo pockets had been abstracted by him during the affray from the pockets of his junior colleagues in the hope of bringing them to their senses. The objects (which included several hundred ladies' and gentlemen's gold and silver watches) were promptly restored to their rightful owners and general harmony reigned supreme.

Quietly, unassumingly, Rumbold, stepped on to the scaffold in faultless morning dress and wearing his favourite flower the *Gladiolus Cruentus*. He announced his presence by that gentle Rumboldian cough which so many have tried (unsuccessfully) to imitate – short, painstaking yet withal so characteristic of the man. The arrival of the world-renowned headsman was greeted by a roar of acclamation from the huge concourse, the viceregal ladies waving their handkerchiefs in their excitement while the even more excitable foreign delegates cheered vociferously in a medley of cries, *hoch*, *banzai, eljen, zivio, chinchin, polla kronia, hiphip, vive, Allah*, amid which the ringing *evviva* of the delegate of the land of song (a high double F recalling those piercingly lovely notes with which the eunuch Catalani beglamoured our greatgreatgrandmothers) was easily distinguishable. It was exactly seventeen o'clock. The signal for prayer was then promptly given by megaphone and in an instant all heads were bared, the commendatore's patriarchal sombrero, which has been in the possession of his family since the revolution of Rienzi, being removed by his medical adviser in attendance, Dr Pippi. The learned prelate who administered the last comforts of holy religion to the hero martyr when about to pay the death penalty knelt in a most christian spirit in a pool of rainwater, his cassock above his hoary head, and offered up to the throne of grace fervent prayers of supplication. Hard by the block stood the grim figure of the executioner, his visage being concealed in a tengallon pot with two circular perforated apertures through which his eyes glowered furiously. As he awaited the fatal signal he tested the edge of his horrible weapon by honing it upon his brawny forearm or decapitated in rapid succession a flock of sheep which had been provided by the admirers of his fell but necessary office. On a handsome mahogany table near him were neatly arranged the quartering knife, the various finely tempered disembowelling appliances (specially supplied by the worldfamous firm of cutlers, Messrs John Round and Sons, Sheffield), a terracotta saucepan for the reception of the duodenum, colon, blind intestine and appendix etc when successfully extracted and two commodious milkjugs destined to receive the most precious blood of the most precious victim. The housesteward of the amalgamated cats' and dogs' home was in attendance to convey these vessels when replenished to that beneficent institution. Quite an excellent repast consisting of rashers and eggs, fried steak and onions, done to a nicety, delicious hot breakfast rolls and invigorating tea had been considerately provided by the authorities for the consumption of the central figure of the tragedy who was in capital spirits when prepared for death and evinced the keenest interest in the proceedings from beginning to end but he, with an abnegation rare in these our times, rose nobly to the occasion and expressed the dying wish (immediately acceded to) that the meal should be divided in aliquot parts among the members of the sick and indigent roomkeepers' association as a token of his regard and esteem. The *nec* and *non plus ultra* of emotion were reached when the blushing bride elect burst her way through the serried ranks of the bystanders and flung herself upon the muscular bosom of him who was about to be launched into eternity for her sake. The hero folded her willowy form in a loving embrace murmuring fondly *Sheila, my own*. Encouraged by this use of her christian name she kissed passionately all the various suitable areas of his person which the decencies of prison garb permitted her ardour to reach. She swore to him as they mingled the salt streams of their tears that she would cherish his memory, that she would never forget her hero boy who went to his death with a song on his lips as if he were but going to a hurling match in Clonturk park. She brought back to his recollection the happy days of blissful childhood together on the banks of Anna Liffey when they had indulged in the innocent pastimes of the young and, oblivious of the dreadful present, they both laughed heartily, all the spectators, including the venerable pastor, joining in the general merriment. That monster audience simply rocked with delight. But anon they were overcome with grief and clasped their hands for the last time. A fresh torrent of tears burst from their lachrymal ducts and the vast concourse of people, touched to the inmost core, broke into heartrending sobs, not the least affected being the aged prebendary himself. Big strong men, officers of the peace and genial giants of the royal Irish constabulary, were making frank use of their hand-kerchiefs and it is safe to say that there was not a dry eye in that record assemblage. A most romantic incident occurred when a handsome young Oxford graduate, noted for his chivalry towards the fair sex, stepped forward and, presenting his visiting card, bankbook and genealogical tree solicited the hand of the hapless young lady, requesting her to name the day, and was accepted on the spot. Every lady in the audience was presented with a tasteful souvenir of the occasion in the shape of skull and crossbones brooch, a timely and generous act which evoked a fresh outburst of emotion: and when the gallant young Oxonian (the bearer, by the way, of one of the most time-honoured names in Albion's history) placed on the finger of his blushing *fiancée* an expensive engagement ring with emeralds set in the form of a fourleaved shamrock excitement knew no bounds. Nay, even the stern provostmarshal, lieutenant-colonel Tomkin-Maxwell ffrenchmullan Tomlinson, who presided on the sad occasion, he who had blown a con-siderable number of sepoys from the cannonmouth without flinching, could not now restrain his natural emotion. With his mailed gauntlet he brushed away a furtive tear and was overheard by those privileged burghers who happened to be in his immediate *entourage* to murmur to himself in a faltering undertone:

– God blimey if she aint a clinker, that there bleeding tart. Blimey it makes me kind of bleeding cry, straight, it does, when I sees her cause I thinks of my old mashtub what's waiting for me down Limehouse way.

So then the citizen begins talking about the Irish language and the corporation meeting and all to that and the shoneens that can't speak their own language and Joe chipping in because he stuck someone for a quid and Bloom putting in his old goo with his twopenny stump that he cadged off of Joe and talking about the Gaelic league and the antitreating league and drink, the curse of Ireland. Antitreating is about the size of it. Gob, he'd let you pour all manner of drink down his throat till the Lord would call him before you'd ever see the froth of his pint. And one night I went in with a fellow into one of their musical evenings, song and dance about she could get up on a truss of hay she could my Maureen Lay and there was a fellow with a Ballyhooly blue ribbon badge spiffing out of him in Irish and a lot of colleen bawns going about with temperance beverages and selling medals and oranges and lemonade and a few old dry buns, gob, flahoolagh entertainment, don't be talking. Ireland sober is Ireland free. And then an old fellow starts blowing into his bagpipes and all the gougers shuffling their feet to the tune the old cow died of. And one or two sky pilots having an eye around that there was no goings on with the females, hitting below the belt.

So howandever, as I was saying, the old dog seeing the tin was empty starts mousing around by Joe and me. I'd train him by kindness, so I would, if he was my dog. Give him a rousing fine kick now and again where it wouldn't blind him.

– Afraid he'll bite you? says the citizen, sneering.

– No, says I. But he might take my leg for a lamppost.

So he calls the old dog over.

– What's on you, Garry? says he.

Then he starts hauling and mauling and talking to him in Irish and the old towser growling, letting on to answer, like a duet in the opera. Such growling you never heard as they let off between them. Someone that has nothing better to do ought to write a letter *pro bono publico* to the papers about the muzzling order for a dog the like of that. Growling and grousing and his eye all bloodshot from the drouth is in it and the hydrophobia dropping out of his jaws.

All those who are interested in the spread of human culture among the lower animals (and their name is legion) should make a point of not missing the really marvellous exhibition of cynanthropy given by the famous old Irish red wolfdog setter formerly known by the *sobriquet* of Garryowen and recently rechristened by his large circle of friends and acquaintances Owen Garry. The exhibition, which is the result of years of training by kindness and a carefully thoughtout dietary system, comprises, among other achievements, the recitation of verse. Our greatest living phonetic expert (wild horses shall not drag it from us!) has left no stone unturned in his efforts to delucidate and compare the verse recited and has found it bears a *striking* resemblance (the italics are ours) to the ranns of ancient Celtic bards. We are not speaking so much of those delightful lovesongs with which the writer who conceals his identity under the graceful pseudonym of the Little Sweet Branch has familiarised the bookloving world but rather (as a contributor D. O. C. points out in an interesting communication published by an evening contemporary) of the harsher and more personal note which is found in the satirical effusions of the famous Raftery and of Donald MacConsidine to say nothing of a more modern lyrist at present very much in the public eye. We subjoin a specimen which has been rendered into English by an eminent scholar whose name for the moment we are not at liberty to disclose though we believe that our readers will find the topical allusion rather more than an indication. The metrical system of the canine original, which recalls the intricate alliterative and isosyllabic rules of the Welsh englyn, is infinitely more complicated but we believe our readers will agree that the spirit has been well caught. Perhaps it should be added that the effect is greatly increased if Owen's verse be spoken somewhat slowly and indistinctly in a tone suggestive of suppressed rancour.

> *The curse of my curses*
> *Seven days every day*
> *And seven dry Thursdays*
> *On you, Barney Kiernan,*
> *Has no sup of water*
> *To cool my courage,*
> *And my guts red roaring*
> *After Lowry's lights.*

So he told Terry to bring some water for the dog and, gob, you could hear him lapping it up a mile off. And Joe asked him would he have another.

– I will, says he, *a chara*, to show there's no ill feeling.

Gob, he's not as green as he's cabbagelooking. Arsing around from one pub to another, leaving it to your own honour, with old Giltrap's dog and getting fed up by the ratepayers and corporators. Entertainment for man and beast. And says Joe:

– Could you make a hole in another pint?

– Could a swim duck? says I.

– Same again, Terry, says Joe. Are you sure you won't have anything in the way of liquid refreshment? says he.

– Thank you, no, says Bloom. As a matter of fact I just wanted to meet Martin Cunningham, don't you see, about this insurance of poor Dignam's. Martin asked me to go to the house. You see, he, Dignam, I mean, didn't serve any notice of the assignment on the company at the time and nominally under the act the mortgagee can't recover on the policy.

– Holy Wars, says Joe laughing, that's a good one if old Shylock is landed. So the wife comes out top dog, what?

– Well, that's a point, says Bloom, for the wife's admirers.

– Whose admirers? says Joe.

– The wife's advisers, I mean, says Bloom.

Then he starts all confused mucking it up about the mortgagor under the act like the lord chancellor giving it out on the bench and for the benefit of the wife and that a trust is created but on the other hand that Dignam owed Bridgeman the money and if now the wife or the widow contested the mortgagee's right till he near had the head of me addled with his mortgagor under the act. He was bloody safe he wasn't run in himself under the act that time as a rogue and vagabond only he had a friend in court. Selling bazaar tickets or what do you call it royal Hungarian privileged lottery. True as you're there. O, commend me to an israelite! Royal and privileged Hungarian robbery.

So Bob Doran comes lurching around asking Bloom to tell Mrs Dignam he was sorry for her trouble and he was very sorry about the funeral and to tell her that he said and everyone who knew him said that there was never a truer, a finer than poor little Willy that's dead to tell her. Choking with bloody foolery. And shaking Bloom's hand doing the tragic to tell her that. Shake hands, brother. You're a rogue and I'm another.

– Let me, said he, so far presume upon our acquaintance which, however slight it may appear if judged by the standard of mere time, is founded, as I hope and believe, on a sentiment of mutual esteem, as to request of you this favour. But, should I have overstepped the limits of reserve let the sincerity of my feelings be the excuse for my boldness.

– No, rejoined the other, I appreciate to the full the motives which actuate your conduct and I shall discharge the office you entrust to me consoled by the reflection that, though the errand be one of sorrow, this proof of your confidence sweetens in some measure the bitterness of the cup.

– Then suffer me to take your hand, said he. The goodness of your heart, I feel sure, will dictate to you better than my inadequate words the expressions which are most suitable to convey an emotion whose poignancy, were I to give vent to my feelings, would deprive me even of speech.

And off with him and out trying to walk straight. Boosed at five o'clock. Night he was near being lagged only Paddy Leonard knew the bobby, 14 A. Blind to the world up in a shebeen in Bride street after closing time, fornicating with two shawls and a bully on guard, drinking porter out of teacups. And calling himself a Frenchy for the shawls, Joseph Manuo, and talking against the catholic religion and he serving mass in Adam and Eve's when he was young with his eyes shut who wrote the new testament and the old testament and hugging and smugging. And the two shawls killed with the laughing, picking his pockets the bloody fool and he spilling the porter all over the bed and the two shawls screeching laughing at one another. *How is your testament? Have you got an old testament?* Only Paddy was passing there, I tell you what. Then see him of a Sunday with his little

concubine of a wife, and she wagging her tail up the aisle of the chapel, with
her patent boots on her, no less, and her violets, nice as pie, doing the little
lady. Jack Mooney's sister. And the old prostitute of a mother procuring
rooms to street couples. Gob, Jack made him toe the line. Told him if he
didn't patch up the pot, Jesus, he'd kick the shite out of him.

So Terry brought the three pints.

– Here, says Joe, doing the honours. Here, citizen.

– *Slan leat*, says he.

– Fortune, Joe, says I. Good health, citizen.

Gob, he had his mouth half way down the tumbler already. Want a small
fortune to keep him in drinks.

– Who is the long fellow running for the mayoralty, Alf? says Joe.

– Friend of yours, says Alf.

– Nannan? says Joe. The mimber?

– I won't mention any names, says Alf.

– I thought so, says Joe. I saw him up at that meeting now with William
Field, M. P., the cattle traders.

– Hairy Iopas, says the citizen, that exploded volcano, the darling of all
countries and the idol of his own.

So Joe starts telling the citizen about the foot and mouth disease and the
cattle traders and taking action in the matter and the citizen sending them
all to the rightabout and Bloom coming out with his sheepdip for the scab
and a hoose drench for coughing calves and the guaranteed remedy for
timber tongue. Because he was up one time in a knacker's yard. Walking
about with his book and pencil here's my head and my heels are coming till
Joe Cuffe gave him the order of the boot for giving lip to a grazier. Mister
Knowall. Teach your grandmother how to milk ducks. Pisser Burke was
telling me in the hotel the wife used to be in rivers of tears sometimes with
Mrs O'Dowd crying her eyes out with her eight inches of fat all over her.
Couldn't loosen her farting strings but old cod's eye was waltzing around
her showing her how to do it. What's your programme today? Ay. Humane
methods. Because the poor animals suffer and experts say and the best
known remedy that doesn't cause pain to the animal and on the sore spot
administer gently. Gob, he'd have a soft hand under a hen.

Ga Ga Gara. Klook Klook Klook. Black Liz is our hen. She lays eggs for
us. When she lays her egg she is so glad. Gara. Klook Klook Klook. Then
comes good uncle Leo. He puts his hand under black Liz and takes her
fresh egg. Ga ga ga ga Gara. Klook Klook Klook.

– Anyhow, says Joe. Field and Nannetti are going over tonight to London
to ask about it on the floor of the House of Commons.

– Are you sure, says Bloom, the councillor is going. I wanted to see him, as it happens.

– Well, he's going off by the mailboat, says Joe, tonight.

– That's too bad, saysBloom. I wanted particularly. Perhaps only Mr Field is going. I couldn't phone. No. You're sure?

– Nannan's going too, says Joe. The league told him to ask a question tomorrow about the commissioner of police forbidding Irish games in the park. What do you think of that, citizen? *The Sluagh na h-Eireann.*

Mr Cowe Conacre (Multifarnham. Nat): Arising out of the question of my honourable friend, the member for Shillelagh, may I ask the right honourable gentleman whether the Government has issued orders that these animals shall be slaughtered though no medical evidence is forth-coming as to their pathological condition?

Mr Allfours (Tamoshant. Con): Honourable members are already in possession of the evidence produced before a committee of the whole house. I feel I cannot usefully add anything to that. The answer to the honourable member's question is in the affirmative.

Mr Orelli (Montenotte. Nat): Have similar orders been issued for the slaughter of human animals who dare to play Irish games in the Phœnix park?

Mr Allfours: The answer is in the negative.

Mr Cowe Conacre: Has the right honourable gentleman's famous Mitchelstown telegram inspired the policy of gentlemen on the treasury bench? (O! O!)

Mr Allfours: I must have notice of that question.

Mr Staylewit (Buncombe. Ind.): Don't hesitate to shoot.

(Ironical opposition cheers.)

The speaker: Order! Order!

(The house rises. Cheers.)

– There's the man, says Joe, that made the Gaelic sports revival. There he is sitting there. The man that got away James Stephens. The champion of all Ireland at putting the sixteen pound shot. What was your best throw, citizen?

– *Na bacleis,* says the citizen, letting on to be modest. There was a time I was as good as the next fellow anyhow.

– Put it there, citizen, says Joe. You were and a bloody sight better.

– Is that really a fact? says Alf.

– Yes, says Bloom. That's well known. Do you not know that?

So off they started about Irish sport and shoneen games the like of the lawn tennis and about hurley and putting the stone and racy of the soil and building up a nation once again and all of that. And of course Bloom had to have his say too about if a fellow had a rower's heart violent exercise was bad. I declare to my antimacassar if you took up a straw from the bloody floor and if you said to Bloom: *Look at, Bloom. Do you see that straw? That's a straw*. Declare to my aunt he'd talk about it for an hour so he would and talk steady.

A most interesting discussion took place in the ancient hall of *Brian O'Ciarnain's* in *Sraid na Bretaine Bheag*, under the auspices of *Sluagh na h-Eireann*, on the revival of ancient Gaelic sports and the importance of physical culture, as understood in ancient Greece and ancient Rome and ancient Ireland, for the development of the race. The venerable president of this noble order was in the chair and the attendance was of large dimensions. After an instructive discourse by the chairman, a magnificent oration eloquently and forcibly expressed, a most interesting and instructive discussion of the usual high standard of excellence ensued as to the desirability of the revivability of the ancient games and sports of our ancient panceltic forefathers. The wellknown and highly respected worker in the cause of our old tongue, Mr Joseph M'Carthy Hynes, made an eloquent appeal for the resuscitation of the ancient Gaelic sports and pastimes, practised morning and evening by Finn MacCool, as calculated to revive the best traditions of manly strength and power handed down to us from ancient ages. L. Bloom, who met with a mixed reception of applause and hisses, having espoused the negative the vocalist chairman brought the discussion to a close, in response to repeated requests and hearty plaudits from all parts of a bumper house, by a remarkably noteworthy rendering of the immortal Thomas Osborne Davis' evergreen verses (happily too familiar to need recalling here) *A nation once again* in the execution of which the veteran patriot champion may be said without fear of contradiction to have fairly excelled himself. The Irish Caruso-Garibaldi was in superlative form and his stentorian notes were heard to the greatest advantage in the timehonoured anthem sung as only our citizen can sing it. His superb highclass vocalism, which by its superquality greatly enhanced his already international reputation, was vociferously applauded by the large audience amongst which were to be noticed many prominent members of the clergy as well as representatives of the press and the bar and the other learned professions. The proceedings then terminated.

Amongst the clergy present were the very rev. William Delany, S. J., L. L. D.; the rt rev. Gerald Molloy, D. D.; the rev. P. J. Kavanagh, C. S. Sp.; the rev. T. Waters, C. C.; the rev. John M. Ivers, P. P.; the rev. P. J. Cleary, O. S. F.; the rev. L. J. Hickey, O. P.; the very rev. Fr. Nicholas, O. S. F. C.; the very rev. B. Gorman, O. D. C.; the rev. T. Maher, S. J.; the very rev.

James Murphy, S. J.; the rev. John Lavery, V. F.; the very rev. William Doherty, D. D.; the rev. Peter Fagan, O. M.; the rev. T. Brangan, O. S. A.; the rev. J. Flavin, C. C.; the rev. M. A. Hackett, C. C.; the rev. W. Hurley, C. C.; the rt rev. Mgr M'Manus, V. G.; the rev. B. R. Slattery, O. M. I.; the very rev. M. D. Scally, P. P.; the rev. F. T. Purcell, O. P.; the very rev. Timothy canon Gorman P. P.; the rev. J. Flanagan, C. C. The laity included P. Fay, T. Quirke, etc., etc.

– Talking about violent exercise, says Alf, were you at that Keogh-Bennett match?

– No, says Joe.

– I heard So and So made a cool hundred quid over it. says Alf.

– Who? Blazes? says Joe.

And says Bloom:

– What I meant about tennis, for example, is the agility and training of the eye.

– Ay, Blazes, says Alf. He let out that Myler was on the beer to run the odds and he swatting all the time.

– We know him, says the citizen. The traitor's son. We know what put English gold in his pocket.

– True for you, says Joe.

And Bloom cuts in again about lawn tennis and the circulation of the blood, asking Alf:

– Now don't you think, Bergan?

– Myler dusted the floor with him, says Alf. Heenan and Sayers was only a bloody fool to it. Handed him the father and mother of a beating. See the little kipper not up to his navel and the big fellow swiping. God, he gave him one last puck in the wind. Queensberry rules and all, made him puke what he never ate.

It was a historic and a hefty battle when Myler and Percy were scheduled to don the gloves for the purse of fifty sovereigns. Handicapped as he was by lack of poundage, Dublin's pet lamb made up for it by superlative skill in ringcraft. The final bout of fireworks was a gruelling for both champions. The welterweight sergeantmajor had tapped some lively claret in the previous mixup during which Keogh had been receivergeneral of rights and lefts, the artilleryman putting in some neat work on the pet's nose, and Myler came on looking groggy. The soldier got to business leading off with a powerful left jab to which the Irish gladiator retaliated by shooting out a stiff one flush to the point of Bennett's jaw. The redcoat ducked but the Dubliner lifted him with a left hook, the body punch being a fine one. The men came to handigrips. Myler quickly became busy and got his man under, the bout ending with the bulkier man on the ropes, Myler punishing him. The Englishman, whose right eye was nearly closed, took his corner where he was liberally drenched with water and, when the bell went, came on gamey and brimful of pluck, confident of knocking out the fistic Eblanite in jigtime. It was a fight to a finish and the best man for it. The two fought like tigers and excitement ran fever high. The referee twice cautioned Pucking Percy for holding but the pet was tricky and his footwork a treat to watch. After a brisk exchange of courtesies during which a smart upper cut of the military man brought blood freely from his opponent's mouth the lamb suddenly waded in all over his man and landed a terrific left to Battling Bennett's stomach, flooring him flat. It was a knockout clean and clever. Amid tense expectation the Portobello bruiser was being counted out when Bennett's second Ole Pfotts Wettstein threw in the towel and the Santry boy was declared victor to the frenzied cheers of the public who broke through the ringropes and fairly mobbed him with delight.

– He knows which side his bread is buttered, says Alf. I hear he's running a concert tour now up in the north.

– He is, says Joe. Isn't he?

– Who? says Bloom. Ah, yes, That's quite true. Yes, a kind of summer tour, you see. Just a holiday.

– Mrs B. is the bright particular star, isn't she? says Joe.

– My wife? says Bloom. She's singing, yes. I think it will be a success too. He's an excellent man to organise. Excellent.

Hoho begob, says I to myself, says I. That explains the milk in the cocoanut and absence of hair on the animal's chest. Blazes doing the tootle on the flute. Concert tour. Dirty Dan the dodger's son off Island bridge that sold the same horses twice over to the government to fight the Boers. Old Whatwhat. I called about the poor and water rate, Mr Boylan. You what? The water rate, Mr Boylan. You whatwhat? That's the bucko that'll organise her, take my tip. 'Twixt me and you Caddereesh.

Pride of Calpe's rocky mount, the ravenhaired daughter of Tweedy. There grew she to peerless beauty where loquat and almond scent the air. The gardens of Alameda knew her step: the garths of olives knew and bowed. The chaste spouse of Leopold is she: Marion of the bountiful bosoms.

And lo, there entered one of the clan of the O'Molloys, a comely hero of white face yet withal somewhat ruddy, his majesty's counsel learned in the law, and with him the prince and heir of the noble line of Lambert.

– Hello, Ned.

– Hello, Alf.

– Hello, Jack.

– Hello, Joe.

– God save you, says the citizen.

– Save you kindly, says J. J. What'll it be, Ned?

– Half one, says Ned.

So J. J. ordered the drinks.

– Were you round at the court? says Joe.

– Yes, says J. J. He'll square that, Ned, says he.

– Hope so, says Ned.

Now what were those two at? J. J. getting him off the grand jury list and the other give him a leg over the stile. With his name in Stubbs's. Playing cards, hobnobbing with flash toffs with a swank glass in their eye, drinking fizz and he half smothered in writs and garnishee orders. Pawning his gold watch in Cummins of Francis street where no-one would know him in the private office when I was there with Pisser releasing his boots out of the pop. What's your name, sir? Dunne, says he. Ay, and done, says I. Gob, he'll come home by weeping cross one of these days, I'm thinking.

– Did you see that bloody lunatic Breen round there, says Alf. U. p. up.

– Yes, says J. J. Looking for a private detective.

– Ay, says Ned, and he wanted right go wrong to address the court only Corny Kelleher got round him telling him to get the handwriting examined first.

– Ten thousand pounds, says Alf, laughing. God I'd give anything to hear him before a judge and jury.

– Was it you did it, Alf? says Joe. The truth, the whole truth and nothing but the truth, so help you Jimmy Johnson.

– Me? says Alf. Don't cast your nasturtiums on my character.

– Whatever statement you make, says Joe, will be taken down in evidence against you.

– Of course an action would lie, says J. J. It implies that he is not *compos mentis*. U. p. up.

– *Compos* your eye! says Alf, laughing. Do you know that he's balmy? Look at his head. Do you know that some mornings he has to get his hat on with a shoehorn?

– Yes, says J. J., but the truth of a libel is no defence to an indictment for publishing it in the eyes of the law.

– Ha, ha, Alf, says Joe.

– Still, says Bloom, on account of the poor woman, I mean his wife.

– Pity about her, says the citizen. Or any other woman marries a half and half.

– How half and half? says Bloom. Do you mean he . . .

– Half and half I mean, says the citizen. A fellow that's neither fish nor flesh.

– Nor good red herring, says Joe.

– That what's I mean, says the citizen. A pishogue, if you know what that is.

Begob I saw there was trouble coming. And Bloom explained he meant, on account of it being cruel for the wife having to go round after the old stuttering fool. Cruelty to animals so it is to let that bloody povertystricken Breen out on grass with his beard out tripping him, bringing down the rain. And she with her nose cockahoop after she married him because a cousin of his old fellow's was pew opener to the pope. Picture of him on the wall with his smashall sweeney's moustaches. The signor Brini from Summerhill, the eyetallyano, papal zouave to the Holy Father, has left the quay and gone to Moss street. And who was he, tell us? A nobody, two pair back and passages, at seven shillings a week, and he covered with all kinds of breastplates bidding defiance to the world.

– And moreover, says J. J., a postcard is publication. It was held to be sufficient evidence of malice in the testcase Sadgrove v. Hole. In my opinion an action might lie.

Six and eightpence, please. Who wants your opinion? Let us drink our pints in peace. Gob, we won't be let even do that much itself.

– Well, good health, Jack, says Ned.

– Good health, Ned, says J. J.

– There he is again, says Joe.

– Where? says Alf.

And begob there he was passing the door with his books under his oxter and the wife beside him and Corny Kelleher with his wall eye looking in as they went past, talking to him like a father, trying to sell him a secondhand coffin.

– How did that Canada swindle case go off? says Joe.

– Remanded, says J. J.

One of the bottlenosed fraternity it was went by the name of James Wought alias Saphiro alias Spark and Spiro, put an ad in the papers saying he'd give a passage to Canada for twenty bob. What? Do you see any green in the white of my eye? Course it was a bloody barney. What? Swindled them all, skivvies and badhachs from the county Meath, ay, and his own kidney too. J. J. was telling us there was an ancient Hebrew Zaretsky or something weeping in the witnessbox with his hat on him, swearing by the holy Moses he was stuck for two quid.

– Who tried the case? says Joe.

– Recorder, says Ned.

– Poor old sir Frederick, says Alf, you can cod him up to the two eyes.

– Heart as big as a lion, says Ned. Tell him a tale of woe about arrears of rent and a sick wife and a squad of kids and, faith, he'll dissolve in tears on the bench.

– Ay, says Alf. Reuben J. was bloody lucky he didn't clap him in the dock the other day for suing poor little Gumley that's minding stones for the corporation there near Butt bridge.

And he starts taking off the old recorder letting on to cry:

– A most scandalous thing! This poor hardworking man! How many children? Ten, did you say?

– Yes, your worship. And my wife has the typhoid!

– And a wife with typhoid fever! Scandalous! Leave the court immediately, sir. No, sir, I'll make no order for payment. How dare you, sir, come up before me and ask me to make an order! A poor hardworking industrious man! I dismiss the case.

And whereas on the sixteenth day of the month of the oxeyed goddess and in the third week after the feastday of the Holy and Undivided Trinity, the daughter of the skies, the virgin moon being then in her first quarter, it came to pass that those learned judges repaired them to the halls of law. There master Courtenay, sitting in his own chamber, gave his rede and master Justice Andrews sitting without a jury in the probate court, weighed well and pondered the claims of the first chargeant upon the property in the matter of the will propounded and final testamentary disposition *in re* the real and personal estate of the late lamented Jacob Halliday, vintner, deceased versus Livingstone, an infant, of unsound mind, and another. And to the solemn court of Green street there came sir Frederick the Falconer. And he sat him there about the hour of five o'clock to administer the law of the brehons at the commission for all that and those parts to be holden in and for the county of the city of Dublin. And there sat with him the high sinhedrim of the twelve tribes of Iar, for every tribe one man, of the tribe of Patrick and of the tribe of Hugh and of the tribe of Owen and of the tribe of Conn and of the tribe of Oscar and of the tribe of Fergus and of the tribe of Finn and of the tribe of Dermot and of the tribe of Cormac and of the tribe of Kevin and of the tribe of Caolte and of the tribe of Ossian, there being in all twelve good men and true. And he conjured them by Him who died on rood that they should well and truly try and true delivrance make in the issue joined between their sovereign lord the king and the prisoner at the bar and true verdict give according to the evidence so help them God and kiss the books. And they rose in their seats, those twelve of Iar, and they swore by the name of Him who is from everlasting that they would do His rightwiseness. And straightway the minions of the law led forth from their donjon keep one whom the sleuthhounds of justice had apprehended in consequence of information received. And they shackled him hand and foot and would take of him ne bail ne mainprise but preferred a charge against him for he was a malefactor.

– Those are nice things, says the citizen, coming over here to Ireland filling the country with bugs.

So Bloom lets on he heard nothing and he starts talking with Joe telling him he needn't trouble about that little matter till the first but if he would just say a word to Mr Crawford. And so Joe swore high and holy by this and by that he'd do the devil and all.

– Because you see, says Bloom, for an advertisement you must have repetition. That's the whole secret.

– Rely on me, says Joe.

– Swindling the peasants, says the citizen, and the poor of Ireland. We want no more strangers in our house.

– O I'm sure that will be all right, Hynes, says Bloom. It's just that Keyes you see.

– Consider that done, says Joe.

– Very kind of you, says Bloom.

– The strangers, says the citizen. Our own fault. We let them come in. We brought them. The adulteress and her paramour brought the Saxon robbers here.

– Decree *nisi*, says J. J.

And Bloom letting on to be awfully deeply interested in nothing, a spider's web in the corner behind the barrel, and the citizen scowling after him and the old dog at his feet looking up to know who to bite and when.

– A dishonoured wife, says the citizen, that's what's the cause of all our misfortunes.

– And here she is, says Alf, that was giggling over the *Police Gazette* with Terry on the counter, in all her warpaint.

– Give us a squint at her, says I.

And what was it only one of the smutty yankee pictures Terry borrows off of Corny Kelleher. Secrets for enlarging your private parts. Misconduct of society belle. Norman W. Tupper, wealthy Chicago contractor, finds pretty but faithless wife in lap of officer Taylor. Belle in her bloomers misconducting herself and her fancy man feeling for her tickles and Norman W. Tupper bouncing in with his peashooter just in time to be late after she doing the trick of the loop with officer Taylor.

– O jakers, Jenny, says Joe, how short your shirt is!

– There's hair, Joe, says I. Get a queer old tailend of corned beef off of that one, what?

So anyhow in came John Wyse Nolan and Lenehan with him with a face on him as long as a late breakfast.

– Well, says the citizen, what's the latest from the scene of action? What did those tinkers in the cityhall at their caucus meeting decide about the Irish language?

O'Nolan, clad in shining armour, row bending made obeisance to the puissant and high and mighty chief of all Erin and did him to wit of that which had befallen, how that the grave elders of the most obedient city, second of the realm, had met them in the tholsel, and there, after due prayers to the gods who dwell in ether supernal, had taken solemn counsel whereby they might, if so be it might be, bring once more into honour among mortal men the winged speech of the seadivided Gael.

– It's on the march, says the citizen. To hell with the bloody brutal Sassenachs and their *patois*.

So J. J. puts in a word doing the toff about one story was good till you heard another and blinking facts and the Nelson policy putting your blind eye to the telescope and drawing up a bill of attainder to impeach a nation and Bloom trying to back him up moderation and botheration and their colonies and their civilisation.

– Their syphilisation, you mean, says the citizen. To hell with them! The curse of a goodfornothing God light sideways on the bloody thicklugged sons of whores' gets! No music and no art and no literature worthy of the name. Any civilisation they have they stole from us. Tonguetied sons of bastards' ghosts.

– The European family, says J. J . . .

– They're not European, says the citizen. I was in Europe with Kevin Egan of Paris. You wouldn't see a trace of them or their language anywhere in Europe except in a *cabinet d'aisance*.

And says John Wyse:

– Full many a flower is born to blush unseen.

And says Lenehan that knows a bit of the lingo:

– *Conspuez les Anglais! Perfide Albion!*

He said and then lifted he in his rude great brawny strengthy hands the medher of dark strong foamy ale and, uttering his tribal slogan *Lamh Dearg Abu*, he drank to the undoing of his foes, a race of mighty valorous heroes, rulers of the waves, who sit on thrones of alabaster silent as the deathless gods.

– What's up with you, says I to Lenehan. You look like a fellow that had lost a bob and found a tanner.

– Gold cup, says he.

– Who won, Mr Lenehan? says Terry.

– *Throwaway*, says he, at twenty to one. A rank outsider. And the rest nowhere.

– And Bass's mare? says Terry.

– Still running, says he. We're all in a cart. Boylan plunged two quid on my tip *Sceptre* for himself and a lady friend.

– I had half a crown myself, says Terry, on *Zinfandel* that Mr Flynn gave me. Lord Howard de Walden's.

– Twenty to one, says Lenehan. Such is life in an outhouse. *Throwaway*, says he. Takes the biscuit and talking about bunions. Frailty, thy name is *Sceptre*.

So he went over to the biscuit tin Bob Doran left to see if there was anything he could lift on the nod, the old cur after him backing his luck with his mangy snout up. Old mother Hubbard went to the cupboard.

– Not there, my child, says he.

– Keep your pecker up, says Joe. She'd have won the money only for the other dog.

And J. J. and the citizen arguing about law and history with Bloom sticking in an odd word.

– Some people, says Bloom, can see the mote in others' eyes but they can't see the beam in their own.

– *Raimeis*, says the citizen. There's no-one as blind as the fellow that won't see, if you know what that means. Where are our missing twenty millions of Irish should be here today instead of four, our lost tribes? And our potteries and textiles, the finest in the whole world! And our wool that was sold in Rome in the time of Juvenal and our flax and our damask from the looms of Antrim and our Limerick lace, our tanneries and our white flint glass down there by Ballybough and our Huguenot poplin that we have since Jacquard de Lyon and our woven silk and our Foxford tweeds and ivory raised point from the Carmelite convent in New Ross, nothing like it in the whole wide world! Where are the Greek merchants that came through the pillars of Hercules, the Gibraltar now grabbed by the foe of mankind, with gold and Tyrian purple to sell in Wexford at the fair of

Carmen? Read Tacitus and Ptolemy, even Giraldus Cambrensis. Wine, peltries, Connemara marble, silver from Tipperary, second to none, our farfamed horses even today, the Irish hobbies, with king Philip of Spain offering to pay customs duties for the right to fish in our waters. What do the yellowjohns of Anglia owe us for our ruined trade and our ruined hearths? And the beds of the Barrow and Shannon they won't deepen with millions of acres of marsh and bog to make us all die of consumption.

– As treeless as Portugal we'll be soon, says John Wyse, or Heligoland with its one tree if something is not done to reafforest the land. Larches, firs, all the trees of the conifer family are going fast. I was reading a report of lord Castletown's . . .

– Save them, says the citizen, the giant ash of Galway and the chieftain elm of Kildare with a fortyfoot bole and an acre of foliage. Save the trees of Ireland for the future men of Ireland on the fair hills of Eire, O.

– Europe has its eyes on you, says Lenehan.

The fashionable international world attended *en masse* this afternoon at the wedding of the chevalier Jean Wyse de Neaulan, grand high chief ranger of the Irish National Foresters, with Miss Fir Conifer of Pine Valley. Lady Sylvester Elmshade, Mrs Barbara Lovebirch, Mrs Poll Ash, Mrs Holly Hazeleyes, Miss Daphne Bays, Miss Dorothy Canebrake, Mrs Clyde Twelve-trees, Mrs Rowan Greene, Mrs Helen Vinegadding, Miss Virginia Creeper, Miss Gladys Beech, Miss Olive Garth, Miss Blanche Maple, Mrs Maud Mahogany, Miss Myra Myrtle, Miss Priscilla Elderflower, Miss Bee Honey-suckle, Miss Grace Poplar, Miss O Mimosa San, Miss Rachel Cedarfrond, the Misses Lilian and Viola Lilac, Miss Timidity Aspenall, Mrs Kitty Dewey-Mosse, Miss May Hawthorne, Mrs Gloriana Palme, Mrs Liana Forrest, Mrs Arabella Blackwood and Mrs Norma Holyoake of Oakholme Regis graced the ceremony by their presence. The bride who was given away by her father, the M'Conifer of the Glands, looked exquisitely charming in a creation carried out in green mercerised silk, moulded on an underslip of gloaming grey, sashed with a yoke of broad emerald and finished with a triple flounce of darkerhued fringe, the scheme being relieved by bretelles and hip insertions of acorn bronze. The maids of honour, Miss Larch Conifer and Miss Spruce Conifer, sisters of the bride, wore very becoming costumes in the same tone, a dainty *motif* of plume rose being worked into the pleats in a pinstripe and repeated capriciously in the jadegreen toques in the form o heron feathers of paletinted coral. Senhor Enrique Flor presided at the organ with his wellknown ability and, in addition to the prescribed numbers of the nuptial mass, played a new and striking arrangement of *Woodman, spare that tree* at the conclusion of the

service. On leaving the church of Saint Fiacre *in Horto* after the papal
blessing the happy pair were subjected to a playful crossfire of hazelnuts,
beechmast, bayleaves, catkins of willow, ivytod, hollyberries, mistletoe sprigs
and quicken shoots. Mr and Mrs Wyse Conifer Neaulan will spend a quiet
honeymoon in the Black Forest.

– And our eyes are on Europe, says the citizen. We had our trade with
Spain and the French and with the Flemings before those mongrels were
pupped, Spanish ale in Galway, the winebark on the winedark waterway.

– And will again, says Joe.

– And with the help of the holy mother of God we will again, says the
citizen, clapping his thigh. Our harbours that are empty will be full again,
Queenstown, Kinsale, Galway, Blacksod Bay, Ventry in the kingdom of
Kerry, Killybegs, the third largest harbour in the wide world with a fleet of
masts of the Galway Lynches and the Cavan O'Reillys and the O'Kennedys
of Dublin when the earl of Desmond could make a treaty with the emperor
Charles the Fifth himself. And will again, says he, when the first Irish
battleship is seen breasting the waves with our own flag to the fore, none of
your Henry Tudor's harps, no, the oldest flag afloat, the flag of the province
of Desmond and Thomond, three crowns on a blue field, the three sons of
Milesius.

And he took the last swig out of the pint, Moya. All wind and piss like a
tanyard cat. Cows in Connacht have long horns. As much as his bloody life
is worth to go down and address his tall talk to the assembled multitude in
Shanagolden where he daren't show his nose with the Molly Maguires
looking for him to let daylight through him for grabbing the holding of an
evicted tenant.

– Hear, hear to that, says John Wyse. What will you have?

– An imperial yeomanry, says Lenehan, to celebrate the occasion.

– Half one, Terry, says John Wyse, and a hands up. Terry! Are you asleep?

– Yes, sir, says Terry. Small whisky and bottle of Allsop. Right, sir.

Hanging over the bloody paper with Alf looking for spicy bits instead of
attending to the general public. Picture of a butting match, trying to crack
their bloody skulls, one chap going for the other with his head down like a
bull at a gate. And another one: *Black Beast Burned in Omaha, Ga.* A lot of
Deadwood Dicks in slouch hats and they firing at a sambo strung up on a
tree with his tongue out and a bonfire under him. Gob, they ought to
drown him in the sea after and electrocute and crucify him to make sure of
their job.

– But what about the fighting navy, says Ned, that keeps our foes at bay?

– I'll tell you what about it, says the citizen. Hell upon earth it is. Read the revelations that's going on in the papers about flogging on the training ships at Portsmouth. A fellow writes that calls himself *Disgusted One*.

So he starts telling us about corporal punishment and about the crew of tars and officers and rearadmirals drawn up in cocked hats and the parson with his protestant bible to witness punishment and a young lad brought out, howling for his ma, and they tie him down on the buttend of a gun.

– A rump and dozen, says the citizen, was what that old ruffian sir John Beresford called it but the modern God's Englishman calls it caning on the breech.

And says John Wyse:

– 'Tis a custom more honoured in the breach than in the observance.

Then he was telling us the master at arms comes along with a long cane and he draws out and he flogs the bloody backside off of the poor lad till he yells meila murder.

– That's your glorious British navy, says the citizen, that bosses the earth. The fellows that never will be slaves, with the only hereditary chamber on the face of God's earth and their land in the hands of a dozen gamehogs and cottonball barons. That's the great empire they boast about of drudges and whipped serfs.

– On which the sun never rises, says Joe.

– And the tragedy of it is, says the citizen, they believe it. The unfortunate yahoos believe it.

They believe in rod, the scourger almighty, creator of hell upon earth and in Jacky Tar, the son of a gun, who was conceived of unholy boast, born of the fighting navy, suffered under rump and dozen, was scarified, flayed and curried, yelled like bloody hell, the third day he arose again from the bed, steered into haven, sitteth on his beamend till further orders whence he shall come to drudge for a living and be paid.

– But, says Bloom, isn't discipline the same everywhere? I mean wouldn't it be the same here if you put force against force?

Didn't I tell you? As true as I'm drinking this porter if he was at his last gasp he'd try to downface you that dying was living.

– We'll put force against force, says the citizen. We have our greater Ireland beyond the sea. They were driven out of house and home in the black 47. Their mudcabins and their shielings by the roadside were laid low by the batteringram and the *Times* rubbed its hands and told the white-livered Saxons there would soon be as few Irish in Ireland as redskins in America. Even the grand Turk sent us his piastres. But the Sassenach tried to starve the nation at home while the land was full of crops that the British hyenas bought and sold in Rio de Janeiro. Ay, they drove out the peasants in hordes. Twenty thousand of them died in the coffinships. But those that came to the land of the free remember the land of bondage. And they will come again and with a vengeance, no cravens, the sons of Granuaile, the champions of Kathleen ni Houlihan.

– Perfectly true, says Bloom. But my point was . . .

– We are a long time waiting for that day, citizen, says Ned. Since the poor old woman told us that the French were on the sea and landed at Killala.

– Ay, says John Wyse. We fought for the royal Stuarts that reneged us against the Williamites and they betrayed us. Remember Limerick and the broken treatystone. We gave our best blood to France and Spain, the wild geese. Fontenoy, eh? And Sarsfield and O'Donnell, duke of Tetuan in Spain, and Ulysses Browne of Camus that was fieldmarshal to Maria Teresa. But what did we ever get for it?

– The French! says the citizen. Set of dancing masters! Do you know what it is? They were never worth a roasted fart to Ireland. Aren't they trying to make an *Entente cordiale* now at Tay Pay's dinnerparty with perfidious Albion? Firebrands of Europe and they always were?

– *Conspuez les Français*, says Lenehan, nobbling his beer.

– And as for the Prooshians and the Hanoverians, says Joe, haven't we had enough of those sausageeating bastards on the throne from George the elector down to the German lad and the flatulent old bitch that's dead?

Jesus, I had to laugh at the way he came out with that about the old one with the winkers on her blind drunk in her royal palace every night of God, old Vic, with her jorum of mountain dew and her coachman carting her up body and bones to roll into bed and she pulling him by the whiskers and singing him old bits of songs about *Ehren on the Rhine* and come where the boose is cheaper.

– Well! says J. J. We have Edward the peacemaker now.

– Tell that to a fool, says the citizen. There's a bloody sight more pox than pax about that boyo. Edward Guelph-Wettin!

– And what do you think, says Joe, of the holy boys, the priests and bishops of Ireland doing up his room in Maynooth in his Satanic Majesty's racing colours and sticking up pictures of all the horses his jockeys rode. The earl of Dublin, no less.

– They ought to have stuck up all the women he rode himself, says little Alf.

And says J. J.:

– Considerations of space influenced their lordships' decision.

– Will you try another, citizen? says Joe.

– Yes, sir, says he, I will.

– You? says Joe.

– Beholden to you, Joe, says I. May your shadow never grow less.

– Repeat that dose, says Joe.

Bloom was talking and talking with John Wyse and he quite excited with his dunducketymudcoloured mug on him and his old plumeyes rolling about.

– Persecution, says he, all the history of the world is full of it. Perpetuating national hatred among nations.

– But do you know what a nation means? says John Wyse.

– Yes, says Bloom.

– What is it? says John Wyse.

– A nation? says Bloom. A nation is the same people living in the same place.

– By God, then, says Ned, laughing, if that's so I'm a nation for I'm living in the same place for the past five years.

So of course everyone had a laugh at Bloom and says he, trying to muck out of it:

– Or also living in different places.

– That covers my case, says Joe.

– What is your nation if I may ask, says the citizen.

– Ireland, says Bloom. I was born here. Ireland.

The citizen said nothing only cleared the spit out of his gullet and, gob, he spat a Red bank oyster out of him right in the corner.

– After you with the push, Joe, says he, taking out his handkerchief to swab himself dry.

– Here you are, citizen, says Joe. Take that in your right hand and repeat after me the following words.

The muchtreasured and intricately embroidered ancient Irish facecloth attributed to Solomon of Droma and Manus Tomaltach og MacDonogh, authors of the Book of Ballymote, was then carefully produced and called forth prolonged admiration. No need to dwell on the legendary beauty of the cornerpieces, the acme of art, wherein one can distinctly discern each of the four evangelists in turn presenting to each of the four masters his evangelical symbol a bogoak sceptre, a North American puma (a far nobler king of beasts than the British article, be it said in passing), a Kerry calf and a golden eagle from Carrantuohill. The scenes depicted on the emunctory field, showing our ancient duns and raths and cromlechs and grianauns and seats of learning and maledictive stones, are as wonderfully beautiful and the pigments as delicate as when the Sligo illuminators gave free rein to their artistic fantasy long long ago in the time of the Barmecides. Glendalough, the lovely lakes of Killarney, the ruins of Clonmacnois, Cong

Abbey, Glen Inagh and the Twelve Pins, Ireland's Eye, the Green Hills of Tallaght, Croagh Patrick, the brewery of Messrs Arthur Guinness, Son and Company (Limited), Lough Neagh's banks, the vale of Ovoca, Isolde's tower, the Mapas obelisk, Sir Patrick Dun's hospital, Cape Clear, the glen of Aherlow, Lynch's castle, the Scotch house, Rathdown Union Workhouse at Loughlinstown, Tullamore jail, Castleconnel rapids, Kilballymacshona-kill, the cross at Monasterboice, Jury's Hotel, S. Patrick's Purgatory, the Salmon Leap, Maynooth college refectory, Curley's hole, the three birth-places of the first duke of Wellington, the rock of Cashel, the bog of Allen, the Henry Street Warehouse, Fingal's Cave–all these moving scenes are still there for us today rendered more beautiful still by the waters of sorrow which have passed over them and by the rich incrustations of time.

– Shove us over the drink, says I. Which is which?

– That's mine, says Joe, as the devil said to the dead policeman.

– And I belong to a race too, says Bloom, that is hated and persecuted. Also now. This very moment. This very instant.

Gob, he near burnt his fingers with the butt of his old cigar.

– Robbed, says he. Plundered. Insulted. Persecuted. Taking what belongs to us by right. At this very moment, says he, putting up his fist, sold by auction off in Morocco like slaves or cattles.

– Are you talking about the new Jerusalem? says the citizen.

– I'm talking about injustice, says Bloom.

– Right, says John Wyse. Stand up to it then with force like men.

That's an almanac picture for you. Mark for a softnosed bullet. Old lardyface standing up to the business end of a gun. Gob, he'd adorn a sweepingbrush, so he would, if he only had a nurse's apron on him. And then he collapses all of a sudden, twisting around all the opposite, as limp as a wet rag.

– But it's no use, says he. Force, hatred, history, all that. That's not life for men and women, insult and hatred. And everybody knows that it's the very opposite of that that is really life.

– What? says Alf.

– Love, says Bloom. I mean the opposite of hatred. I must go now, says he to John Wyse. Just round to the court a moment to see if Martin is there. If he comes just say I'll be back in a second. Just a moment.

Who's hindering you? And off he pops like greased lightning.

– A new apostle to the gentiles, says the citizen. Universal love.

– Well, says John Wyse, isn't that what we're told? Love your neighbours.

– That chap? says the citizen. Beggar my neighbour is his motto. Love, Moya! He's a nice pattern of a Romeo and Juliet.

Love loves to love love. Nurse loves the new chemist. Constable 14 A loves Mary Kelly. Gerty MacDowell loves the boy that has the bicycle. M. B. loves a fair gentleman. Li Chi Han lovey up kissy Cha Pu Chow. Jumbo, the elephant, loves Alice, the elephant. Old Mr Verschoyle with the ear trumpet loves old Mrs Verschoyle with the turnedin eye. The man in the brown macintosh loves a lady who is dead. His Majesty the King loves Her Majesty the Queen. Mrs Norman W. Tupper loves officer Taylor. You love a certain person. And this person loves that other person because everybody loves somebody but God loves everybody.

– Well, Joe, says I, your very good health and song. More power, citizen.

– Hurrah, there, says Joe.

– The blessing of God and Mary and Patrick on you, says the citizen.

And he ups with his pint to wet his whistle.

– We know those canters, says he, preaching and picking your pocket. What about sanctimonious Cromwell and his ironsides that put the women and children of Drogheda to the sword with the bible text *God is love* pasted round the mouth of his cannon? The bible! Did you read that skit in the *United Irishman* today about that Zulu chief that's visiting England?

– What's that? says Joe.

So the citizen takes up one of his paraphernalia papers and he starts reading out:

– A delegation of the chief cotton magnates of Manchester was presented yesterday to His Majesty the Alaki of Abeakuta by Gold Stick in Waiting, Lord Walkup on Eggs, to tender to His Majesty the heartfelt thanks of British traders for the facilities afforded them in his dominions. The delegation partook of luncheon at the conclusion of which the dusky potentate, in the course of a happy speech, freely translated by the British chaplain, the reverend Ananias Praisegod Barebones, tendered his best thanks to Massa Walkup and emphasised the cordial relations existing between Abeakuta and the British Empire, stating that he treasured as one of his dearest possessions an illuminated bible, the volume of the word of God and the secret of England's greatness, graciously presented to him by the white chief woman, the great squaw Victoria, with a personal dedication from the august hand of the Royal Donor. The Alaki then drank a lovingcup of firstshot usquebaugh to the toast *Black and White* from the skull of his immediate predecessor in the dynasty Kakachakachak, surnamed Forty Warts, after which he visited the chief factory of Cottonopolis and signed his mark in the visitors' book, subsequently executing an old Abeakutic wardance, in the course of which he swallowed several knives and forks, amid hilarious applause from the girl hands.

– Widow woman, says Ned, I wouldn't doubt her. Wonder did he put that bible to the same use as I would.

– Same only more so, says Lenehan. And thereafter in that fruitful land the broadleaved mango flourished exceedingly.

– Is that by Griffith? says John Wyse.

– No, says the citizen. It's not signed Shanganagh. It's only initialled: P.

– And a very good initial too, says Joe.

– That's how it's worked, says the citizen. Trade follows the flag.

– Well, says J. J., if they're any worse than those Belgians in the Congo Free State they must be bad. Did you read that report by a man what's this his name is?

– Casement, says the citizen. He's an Irishman.

– Yes, that's the man, says J. J. Raping the women and girls and flogging the natives on the belly to squeeze all the red rubber they can out of them.

– I know where he's gone, says Lenehan, cracking his fingers.

– Who? says I.

– Bloom, says he, the courthouse is a blind. He had a few bob on *Throwaway* and he's gone to gather in the shekels.

– Is it that whiteeyed kaffir? says the citizen, that never backed a horse in anger in his life.

That's where he's gone, says Lenehan. I met Bantam Lyons going to back that horse only I put him off it and he told me Bloom gave him the tip. Bet you what you like he has a hundred shillings to five on. He's the only man in Dublin has it. A dark horse.

– He's a bloody dark horse himself, says Joe.

– Mind, Joe, says I. Show us the entrance out.

– There you are, says Terry.

Goodbye Ireland I'm going to Gort. So I just went round to the back of the yard to pumpship and begob (hundred shillings to five) while I was letting off my (*Throwaway* twenty to) letting off my load gob says I to myself I knew he was uneasy in his (two pints off of Joe and one in Slattery's off) in his mind to get off the mark to (hundred shillings is five quid) and when they were in the (dark horse) Pisser Burke was telling me card party and letting on the child was sick (gob, must have done about a gallon) flabbyarse of a wife speaking down the tube *she's better* or *she's* (ow!) all a plan so he could vamoose with the pool if he won or (Jesus, full up I was) trading without a licence (ow!) Ireland my nation says he (hoik! phthook!) never be up to those bloody (there's the last of it) Jerusalem (ah!) cuckoos.

So anyhow when I got back they were at it dingdong, John Wyse saying it was Bloom gave the idea for Sinn Fein to Griffith to put in his paper all kinds of jerrymandering, packed juries and swindling the taxes off of the Government and appointing consuls all over the world to walk about selling Irish industries. Robbing Peter to pay Paul. Gob, that puts the bloody kybosh on it if old sloppy eyes is mucking up the show. Give us a bloody chance. God save Ireland from the likes of that bloody mouseabout. Mr Bloom with his argol bargol. And his old fellow before him perpetrating frauds, old Methusalem Bloom, the robbing bagman, that poisoned himself with the prussic acid after he swamping the country with his baubles and his penny diamonds. Loans by post on easy terms. Any amount of money advanced on note of hand. Distance no object. No security. Gob he's like Lanty MacHale's goat that'd go a piece of the road with every one.

– Well, it's a fact, says John Wyse. And there's the man now that'll tell you about it, Martin Cunningham.

Sure enough the castle car drove up with Martin on it and Jack Power with him and a fellow named Crofter or Crofton, pensioner out of the collector general's, an orangeman Blackburn does have on the registration and he drawing his pay or Crawford gallivanting around the country at the king's expense.

Our travellers reached the rustic hostelry and alighted from their palfreys.

– Ho, varlet! cried he, who by his mien seemed the leader of the party. Saucy knave! To us!

So saying he knocked loudly with his swordhilt upon the open lattice.

Mine host came forth at the summons girding him with his tabard.

– Give you good den, my masters, said he with an obsequious bow.

– Bestir thyself, sirrah! cried he who had knocked. Look to our steeds. And for ourselves give us of your best for ifaith we need it.

– Lackaday, good masters, said the host, my poor house has but a bare larder. I know not what to offer your lordships.

– How now, fellow? cried the second of the party, a man of pleasant countenance, so servest thou the king's messengers, Master Taptun?

An instantaneous change overspread the landlord's visage.

– Cry you mercy, gentlemen, he said humbly. An you be the king's messengers (God shield His Majesty!) you shall not want for aught. The king's friends (God bless His Majesty!) shall not go afasting in my house I warrant me.

– Then about! cried the traveller who had not spoken, a lusty trencherman by his aspect. Hast aught to give us?

Mine host bowed again as he made answer:

– What say you, good masters, to a squab pigeon pasty, some collops of venison, a saddle of veal, widgeon with crisp hog's bacon, a boar's head with pistachios, a bason of jolly custard, a medlar tansy and a flagon of old Rhenish?

– Gadzooks! cried the last speaker. That likes me well. Pistachios!

– Aha! cried he of the pleasant countenance. A poor house and a bare larder, quotha! 'Tis a merry rogue.

So in comes Martin asking where was Bloom.

– Where is he? says Lenehan. Defrauding widows and orphans.

– Isn't that a fact, says John Wyse, what I was telling the citizen about Bloom and the Sinn Fein?

– That's so, says Martin. Or so they allege.

– Who made those allegations? says Alf.

– I, says Joe. I'm the alligator.

– And after all, says John Wyse, why can't a jew love his country like the next fellow?

– Why not? says J. J., when he's quite sure which country it is.

– Is he a jew or a gentile or a holy Roman or a swaddler or what the hell is he? says Ned. Or who is he? No offence, Crofton.

– We don't want him, says Crofter the Orangeman or presbyterian.

– Who is Junius? says J. J.

– He's a perverted jew, says Martin, from a place in Hungary and it was he drew up all the plans according to the Hungarian system. We know that in the castle.

– Isn't he a cousin of Bloom the dentist? says Jack Power.

– Not at all, says Martin. Only namesakes. His name was Virag. The father's name that poisoned himself. He changed it by deedpoll, the father did.

– That's the new Messiah for Ireland! says the citizen. Island of saints and sages!

– Well, they're still waiting for their redeemer, says Martin. For that matter so are we.

– Yes, says J. J., and every male that's born they think it may be their Messiah. And every jew is in a tall state of excitement, I believe, till he knows if he's a father or a mother.

– Expecting every moment will be his next, says Lenehan.

– O, by God, says Ned, you should have seen Bloom before that son of his that died was born. I met him one day in the south city markets buying a tin of Neave's food six weeks before the wife was delivered.

– *En ventre sa mère*, says J. J.

– Do you call that a man? says the citizen.

– I wonder did he ever put it out of sight, says Joe.

– Well, there were two children born anyhow, says Jack Power.

– And who does he suspect? says the citizen.

Gob, there's many a true word spoken in jest. One of those mixed middlings he is. Lying up in the hotel Pisser was telling me once a month with headache like a totty with her courses. Do you know what I'm telling you? It'd be an act of God to take a hold of a fellow the like of that and throw him in the bloody sea. Justifiable homicide, so it would. Then sloping off with his five quid without putting up a pint of stuff like a man. Give us your blessing. Not as much as would blind your eye.

– Charity to the neighbour, says Martin. But where is he? We can't wait.

– A wolf in sheep's clothing, says the citizen. That's what he is. Virag from Hungary! Ahasuerus I call him. Cursed by God.

– Have you time for a brief libation, Martin? says Ned.

– Only one, says Martin. We must be quick. J. J. and S.

– You, Jack? Crofton? Three half ones, Terry.

– Saint Patrick would want to land again at Ballykinlar and convert us, says the citizen, after allowing things like that to contaminate our shores.

– Well, says Martin, rapping for his glass. God bless all here is my prayer.

– Amen, says the citizen.

– And I'm sure he will, says Joe.

And at the sound of the sacring bell, headed by a crucifer with acolytes, thurifers, boatbearers, readers, ostiarii, deacons and subdeacons, the blessed company drew nigh of mitred abbots and priors and guardians and monks and friars: the monks of Benedict of Spoleto, Carthusians and Camaldolesi, Cistercians and Olivetans, Oratorians and Vallombrosans, and the friars of Augustine, Brigittines, Premonstratesians, Servi, Trinitarians, and the children of Peter Nolasco: and therewith from Carmel mount the children of Elijah prophet led by Albert bishop and by Teresa of Avila, calced and other: and friars brown and grey, sons of poor Francis, capuchins, cordeliers, minimes and observants and the daughters of Clara: and the sons of Dominic, the friars preachers, and the sons of Vincent: and the monks of S. Wolstan: and Ignatius his children: and the confraternity of the christian brothers led by the reverend brother Edmund Ignatius Rice. And after came all saints and martyrs, virgins and confessors: S. Cyr and S. Isidore Arator and S. James the Less and S. Phocas of Sinope and S. Julian Hospitator and S. Felix de Cantalice and S. Simon Stylites and S. Stephen Protomartyr and S. John of God and S. Ferreol and S. Leugarde and S. Theodotus and S. Vulmar and S. Richard and S. Vincent de Paul and S. Martin of Todi and S. Martin of Tours and S. Alfred and S. Joseph and S. Denis and S. Cornelius and S. Leopold and S. Bernard and S. Terence and S. Edward and S. Owen Caniculus and S. Anonymous and S. Eponymous and S. Pseudonymous and S. Homonymous and S. Paronymous and S. Synonymous and S. Laurence O' Toole and S. James of Dingle and Compostella and S. Columcille and S. Columba and S. Celestine and S. Colman and S. Kevin and S. Brendan and S. Frigidian and S. Senan and S. Fachtna and S. Columbanous and S. Gall and S. Fursey and S. Fintan and S. Fiacre and S. John Nepomuc and S. Thomas Aquinas and S. Ives of Brittany and S. Michan and S. Herman-Joseph and the three patrons of holy youth S. Aloysius Gonzaga and S. Stanislaus Kostka and S. John Berchmans and the saints Gervasius, Servasius and Bonifacius and S. Bride and S. Kieran and S. Canice of Kilkenny and S. Jarlath of Tuam and S. Finbarr and S. Pappin of Ballymun and Brother Aloysius Pacificus and Brother Louis Bellicosus and the saints Rose of Lima and of Viterbo and S. Martha of Bethany and S. Mary of Egypt and S. Lucy and S. Brigid and S. Attracta and S. Dympna and S. Ita and S. Marion Calpensis and the Blessed Sister Teresa of the Child Jesus and S. Barbara and S. Scholastica and S. Ursula with eleven thousand virgins. And all came with nimbi and aureoles and gloriae, bearing palms and harps and swords and olive crowns, in robes whereon were woven the blessed symbols of their efficacies, inkhorns, arrows, loaves, cruses, fetters, axes, trees, bridges, babes in a bathtub, shells, wallets, shears, keys, dragons, lilies, buckshot, beards, hogs, lamps, bellows, beehives, soupladles, stars, snakes, anvils, boxes of vaseline, bells, crutches, forceps, stags' horns, watertight boots, hawks, millstones, eyes on a dish, wax candles, aspergills, unicorns. And as they wended their way by Nelson's Pillar, Henry Street, Mary Street, Capel Street, Little Britain Street, chanting the introit in *Epiphania Domini* which beginneth *Surge, illuminare* and thereafter most sweetly the gradual *Omnes* which saith *de Saba venient* they did divers wonders such as casting out devils, raising the dead to life, multiplying fishes, healing the halt and the blind, discovering various articles which had been mislaid, interpreting and fulfilling the scriptures, blessing and prophesying. And last, beneath a canopy of cloth of gold came the reverend Father O'Flynn attended by Malachi and Patrick. And when the good fathers had reached the appointed place, the house of Bernard Kiernan and Co, limited, 8, 9 and 10 little Britain street, wholesale grocers, wine and brandy shippers, licensed for the sale of beer, wine and spirits for consumption on the premises, the celebrant blessed the house and censed the mullioned windows and the groynes and the vaults and the arrises and the capitals and the pediments and the cornices and the engrailed arches and the spires and the cupolas and sprinkled the lintels thereof with blessed water and prayed that God might bless that house as he had blessed the house of Abraham and Isaac and Jacob and make the angels of His light to inhabit therein. And entering he blessed the viands and the beverages and the company of all the blessed answered his prayers.

– *Adiutorium nostrum in nomine Domini.*

– *Qui fecit cœlum et terram.*

– *Dominus vobiscum.*

– *Et cum spiritu tuo.*

And he laid his hands upon the blessed and gave thanks and he prayed and they all with him prayed:

– *Deus, cuius verbo sanctificantur omnia, benedictionem tuam effunde super creaturas istas: et præsta ut quisquis eis secundum legem et voluntatem Tuam cum gratiarum actione usus fuerit per invocationem sanctissimi nominis Tui corporis sanitatem et animæ tutelam Te auctore percipiat per Christum Dominum nostrum.*

– And so say all of us, says Jack.

– Thousand a year, Lambert, says Crofton or Crawford.

– Right, says Ned, taking up his John Jameson. And butter for fish.

I was just looking round to see who the happy thought would strike when be damned but in he comes again letting on to be in a hell of a hurry.

– I was just round at the courthouse, says he, looking for you. I hope I'm not . . .

– No, says Martin, we're ready.

Courthouse my eye and your pockets hanging down with gold and silver. Mean bloody scut. Stand us a drink itself. Devil a sweet fear! There's a jew for you! All for number one. Cute as a shithouse rat. Hundred to five.

– Don't tell anyone, says the citizen.

– Beg your pardon, says he.

– Come on boys, says Martin, seeing it was looking blue. Come along now.

– Don't tell anyone, says the citizen, letting a bawl out of him. It's a secret.

And the bloody dog woke up and let a growl.

– Bye bye all, says Martin.

And he got them out as quick as he could, Jack Power and Crofton or whatever you call him and him in the middle of them letting on to be all at sea up with them on the bloody jaunting car.

– Off with you, says Martin to the jarvey.

The milkwhite dolphin tossed his mane and, rising in the golden poop, the helmsman spread the bellying sail upon the wind and stood off forward with all sail set, the spinnaker to larboard. A many comely nymphs drew nigh to starboard and to larboard and, clinging to the sides of the noble bark, they linked their shining forms as doth the cunning wheelwright when he fashions about the heart of his wheel the equidistant rays whereof each one is sister to another and he binds them all with an outer ring and giveth speed to the feet of men whenas they ride to a hosting or contend for the smile of ladies fair. Even so did they come and set them, those willing nymphs, the undying sisters. And they laughed, sporting in a circle of their foam: and the bark clave the waves.

But begob I was just lowering the heel of the pint when I saw the citizen getting up to waddle to the door, puffing and blowing with the dropsy and he cursing the curse of Cromwell on him, bell, book and candle in Irish, spitting and spatting out of him and Joe and little Alf round him like a leprechaun trying to peacify him.

– Let me alone, says he.

And begob he got as far as the door and they holding him and he bawls out of him:

– Three cheers for Israel!

Arrah, sit down on the parliamentary side of your arse for Christ' sake and don't be making a public exhibition of yourself. Jesus, there's always some bloody clown or other kicking up a bloody murder about bloody nothing. Gob, it'd turn the porter sour in your guts, so it would.

And all the ragamuffins and sluts of the nation round the door and Martin telling the jarvey to drive ahead and the citizen bawling and Alf and Joe at him to whisht and he on his high horse about the jews and the loafers calling for a speech and Jack Power trying to get him to sit down on the car and hold his bloody jaw and a loafer with a patch over his eye starts singing *If the man in the moon was a jew*, *jew*, *jew* and a slut shouts out of her:

– Eh, mister! Your fly is open, mister!

And says he:

– Mendelssohn was a jew and Karl Marx and Mercadante and Spinoza. And the Saviour was a jew and his father was a jew. Your God.

– He had no father, says Martin. That'll do now. Drive ahead.

– Whose God? says the citizen.

– Well, his uncle was a jew, says he. Your God was a jew. Christ was a jew like me.

Gob, the citizen made a plunge back into the shop.

– By Jesus, says he, I'll brain that bloody jewman for using the holy name. By Jesus, I'll crucify him so I will. Give us that biscuitbox here.

– Stop! Stop! says Joe.

A large and appreciative gathering of friends and acquaintances from the metropolis and greater Dublin assembled in their thousands to bid farewell to Nagyaságos uram Lipóti Virag, late of Messrs Alexander Thom's, printers to His Majesty, on the occasion of his departure for the distant clime of Százharminczbrojúgulyás-Dugulás (Meadow of Murmuring Waters). The ceremony which went off with great *éclat* was characterised by the most affecting cordiality. An illuminated scroll of ancient Irish vellum, the work of Irish artists, was presented to the distinguished phenomenologist on behalf of a large section of the community and was accompanied by the gift of a silver casket, tastefully executed in the style of ancient Celtic ornament, a work which reflects every credit on the makers, Messrs Jacob *agus* Jacob. The departing guest was the recipient of a hearty ovation, many of those who were present being visibly moved when the select orchestra of Irish pipes struck up the wellknown strains of *Come Back to Erin*, followed immediately by *Rakóczy's March*. Tarbarrels and bonfires were lighted along the coastline of the four seas on the summits of the Hill of Howth, Three Rock Mountain, Sugarloaf, Bray Head, the mountains of Mourne, the Galtees, the Ox and Donegal and Sperrin peaks, the Nagles and the Bograghs, the Connemara hills, the reeks of M'Gillicuddy, Slieve Aughty, Slieve Bernagh and Slieve Bloom. Amid cheers that rent the welkin, responded to by answering cheers from a big muster of henchmen on the distant Cambrian and Caledonian hills, the mastodontic pleasureship slowly moved away saluted by a final floral tribute from the representatives of the fair sex who were present in large numbers while, as it proceeded down the river, escorted by a flotilla of barges, the flags of the Ballast office and Custom House were dipped in salute as were also those of the electrical power station at the Pigeonhouse. *Visszontlátásra, kedvés barátom! Visszontlátásra!* Gone but not forgotten.

Gob, the devil wouldn't stop him till he got hold of the bloody tin anyhow and out with him and little Alf hanging on to his elbow and he shouting like a stuck pig, as good as any bloody play in the Queen's royal theatre.

– Where is he till I murder him?

And Ned and J. G. paralysed with the laughing.

– Bloody wars, says I, I'll be in for the last gospel.

But as luck would have it the jarvey got the nag's head round the other way and off with him.

– Hold on, citizen, says Joe. Stop.

Begob he drew his hand and made a swipe and let fly. Mercy of God the sun was in his eyes or he'd have left him for dead. Gob, he near sent it into the county Longford. The bloody nag took fright and the old mongrel after the car like bloody hell and all the populace shouting and laughing and the old tinbox clattering along the street.

The catastrophe was terrific and instantaneous in its effect. The observatory of Dunsink registered in all eleven shocks, all of the fifth grade of Mercalli's scale, and there is no record extant of a similar seismic disturbance in our island since the earthquake of 1534, the year of the rebellion of Silken Thomas. The epicentre appears to have been that part of the metropolis which constitutes the Inn's Quay ward and parish of Saint Michan covering a surface of fortyone acres, two roods and one square pole or perch. All the lordly residences in the vicinity of the palace of justice were demolished and that noble edifice itself, in which at the time of the catastrophe important legal debates were in progress, is literally a mass of ruins beneath which it is to be feared all the occupants have been buried alive. From the reports of eyewitnesses it transpires that the seismic waves were accompanied by a violent atmospheric perturbation of cyclonic character. An article of headgear since ascertained to belong to the much respected clerk of the crown and peace Mr George Fottrell and a silk umbrella with gold handle with the engraved initials, coat of arms and house number of the erudite and worshipful chairman of quarter sessions sir Frederick Falkiner, recorder of Dublin, have been discovered by search parties in remote parts of the island, respectively, the former on the third basaltic ridge of the giant's causeway, the latter embedded to the extent of one foot three inches in the sandy beach of Holeopen bay near the old head of Kinsale. Other eyewitnesses depose that they observed an incandescent object of enormous proportions hurtling through the atmosphere at a terrifying velocity in a trajectory directed south west by west. Messages of condolence and sympathy are being hourly received from all parts of the different continents and the sovereign pontiff has been graciously pleased to decree that a special *missa pro defunctis* shall be celebrated simultaneously by the ordinaries of each and every cathedral church of all the episcopal dioceses subject to the spiritual authority of the Holy See in suffrage of the souls of those faithful departed who have been so unexpectedly called away from our midst. The work of salvage, removal of *débris*, human remains etc has been entrusted to Messrs Michael Meade and Son, 159, Great Brunswick Street, and Messrs T. C. Martin, 77, 78, 79 and 80, North Wall, assisted by the men and officers of the Duke of Cornwall's light infantry under the general supervision of H. R. H., rear admiral the right honourable sir Hercules Hannibal Habeas Corpus

Anderson K. G., K. P., K. T., P. C., K. C. B., M. P., J. P., M. B., D. S. O.,
S. O. D., M. F. H., M. R. I. A., B. L., Mus. Doc., P. L. G., F. T. C. D., F. R.
U. I., F. R. C. P. I. and F. R. C. S. I.

You never saw the like of it in all your born puff. Gob, if he got that
lottery ticket on the side of his poll he'd remember the gold cup, he would
so, but begob the citizen would have been lagged for assault and battery and
Joe for aiding and abetting. The jarvey saved his life by furious driving as
sure as God made Moses. What? O, Jesus, he did. And he let a volley of
oaths after him.

– Did I kill him, says he, or what?

And he shouting to the bloody dog:

– After him, Garry! After him, boy!

And the last we saw was the bloody car rounding the corner and old
sheepsface on it gesticulating and the bloody mongrel after it with his lugs
back for all he was bloody well worth to tear him limb from limb. Hundred
to five! Jesus, he took the value of it out of him, I promise you.

When, lo, there came about them all a great brightness and they beheld
the chariot wherein He stood ascend to heaven. And they beheld Him in
the chariot, clothed upon in the glory of the brightness, having raiment as
of the sun, fair as the moon and terrible that for awe they durst not look
upon Him. And there came a voice out of heaven, calling: *Elijah! Elijah!*
And he answered with a main cry: *Abba! Adonai!* And they beheld Him even
Him, ben Bloom Elijah, amid clouds of angels ascend to the glory of the
brightness at an angle of fortyfive degrees over Donohoe's in Little Green
Street like a shot off a shovel.

*   *   *   *   *

◀ THE SUMMER EVENING HAD BEGUN TO FOLD THE world in its mysterious embrace. Far away in the west the sun was setting and the last glow of all too fleeting day lingered lovingly on sea and strand, on the proud promontory of dear old Howth guarding as ever the waters of the bay, on the weedgrown rocks along Sandymount shore and, last but not least, on the quiet church whence there streamed forth at times upon the stillness the voice of prayer to her who is in her pure radiance a beacon ever to the storm-tossed heart of man, Mary, star of the sea.

The three girl friends were seated on the rocks, enjoying the evening scene and the air which was fresh but not too chilly. Many a time and oft were they wont to come there to that favourite nook to have a cosy chat beside the sparkling waves and discuss matters feminine, Cissy Caffrey and Edy Boardman with the baby in the pushcar and Tommy and Jacky Caffrey, two little curlyheaded boys, dressed in sailor suits with caps to match and the name H. M. S. Belleisle printed on both. For Tommy and Jacky Caffrey were twins, scarce four years old and very noisy and spoiled twins sometimes but for all that darling little fellows with bright merry faces and endearing ways about them. They were dabbling in the sand with their spades and buckets, building castles as children do, or playing with their big coloured ball, happy as the day was long. And Edy Boardman was rocking the chubby baby to and fro in the pushcar while that young gentleman fairly chuckled with delight. He was but eleven months and nine days old and, though still a tiny toddler, was just beginning to lisp his first babyish words. Cissy Caffrey bent over him to tease his fat little plucks and the dainty dimple in his chin.

– Now, baby, Cissy Caffrey said. Say out big, big. I want a drink of water.

And baby prattled after her:

– A jink a jink a jawbo.

Cissy Caffrey cuddled the wee chap for she was awfully fond of children, so patient with little sufferers and Tommy Caffrey could never be got to take his castor oil unless it was Cissy Caffrey that held his nose and promised him the scatty heel of the loaf of brown bread with golden syrup on. What a persuasive power that girl had! But to be sure baby was as good as gold, a perfect little dote in his new fancy bib. None of your spoilt beauties, Flora MacFlimsy sort, was Cissy Caffrey. A truerhearted lass never drew the breath of life, always with a laugh in her gipsylike eyes and a frolicsome word on her cherryripe red lips, a girl lovable in the extreme. And Edy Boardman laughed too at the quaint language of little brother.

But just then there was a slight altercation between Master Tommy and

Master Jacky. Boys will be boys and our two twins were no exception to this golden rule. The apple of discord was a certain castle of sand which Master Jacky had built and Master Tommy would have it right go wrong that it was to be architecturally improved by a frontdoor like the Martello tower had. But if Master Tommy was headstrong Master Jacky was self-willed too and, true to the maxim that every little Irishman's house is his castle, he fell upon his hated rival and to such purpose that the wouldbe assailant came to grief and (alas to relate!) the coveted castle too. Needless to say the cries of discomfited Master Tommy drew the attention of the girl friends.

– Come here, Tommy, his sister called imperatively, at once! And you, Jacky, for shame to throw poor Tommy in the dirty sand. Wait till I catch you for that.

His eyes misty with unshed tears Master Tommy came at her call for their big sister's word was law with the twins. And in a sad plight he was after his misadventure. His little man-o'-war top and unmentionables were full of sand but Cissy was a past mistress in the art of smoothing over life's tiny troubles and and very quickly not one speck of sand was to be seen on his smart little suit. Still the blue eyes were glistening with hot tears that would well up so she kissed away the hurtness and shook her hand at Master Jacky the culprit and said if she was near him she wouldn't be far from him, her eyes dancing in admonition.

– Nasty bold Jacky! she cried.

She put an arm round the little mariner and coaxed winningly:

– What's your name? Butter and cream?

– Tell us who is your sweetheart, spoke Edy Boardman. Is Cissy your sweetheart?

– Nao, tearful Tommy said.

– Is Edy Boardman your sweetheart? Cissy queried.

– Nao, Tommy said.

– I know, Edy Boardman said none too amiably with an arch glance from her shortsighted eyes. I know who is Tommy's sweetheart, Gerty is Tommy's sweetheart.

– Nao, Tommy said on the verge of tears.

Cissy's quick motherwit guessed what was amiss and she whispered to Edy Boardman to take him there behind the pushcar where the gentlemen couldn't see and to mind he didn't wet his new tan shoes.

But who was Gerty?

Gerty MacDowell who was seated near her companions, lost in thought, gazing far away into the distance was in very truth as fair a specimen of winsome Irish girlhood as one could wish to see. She was pronounced beautiful by all who knew her though, as folks often said, she was more a Giltrap than a MacDowell. Her figure was slight and graceful, inclining even to fragility but those iron jelloids she had been taking of late had done her a world of good much better than the Widow Welch's female pills and she was much better of those discharges she used to get and that tired feeling. The waxen pallor of her face was almost spiritual in its ivorylike purity though her rosebud mouth was a genuine Cupid's bow, Greekly perfect. Her hands were of finely veined alabaster with tapering fingers and as white as lemon juice and queen of ointments could make them though it was not true that she used to wear kid gloves in bed or take a milk footbath either. Bertha Supple told that once to Edy Boardman, a deliberate lie, when she was black out at daggers drawn with Gerty (the girl chums had of course their little tiffs from time to time like the rest of mortals) and she told her not let on whatever she did that it was her that told her or she'd never speak to her again. No. Honour where honour is due. There was an innate refinement, a languid queenly *hauteur* about Gerty which was unmistakably evidenced in her delicate hands and higharched instep. Had kind fate but willed her to be born a gentlewoman of high degree in her own right and had she only received the benefit of a good education Gerty MacDowell might easily have held her own beside any lady in the land and have seen herself exquisitely gowned with jewels on her brow and patrician suitors at her feet vying with one another to pay their devoirs to her. Mayhap it was this, the love that might have been, that lent to her softly-featured face at whiles a look, tense with suppressed meaning, that imparted a strange yearning tendency to the beautiful eyes, a charm few could resist. Why have women such eyes of witchery? Gerty's were of the bluest Irish blue, set off by lustrous lashes and dark expressive brows. Time was when those brows were not so silkilyseductive. It was Madame Vera Verity, directress of the Woman Beautiful page of the Princess novelette, who had first advised her to try eyebrowleine which gave that haunting expression to the eyes, so becoming in leaders of fashion, and she had never regretted it. Then there was blushing scientifically cured and how to be tall increase your height and you have a beautiful face but your nose? That would suit Mrs Dignam because she had a button one. But Gerty's crowning glory was her wealth of wonderful hair. It was dark brown with a natural wave in it. She had cut it that very morning on account of the new moon and it nestled about her pretty head in a profusion of luxuriant clusters and pared her nails too, Thursday for wealth. And just now at Edy's words as a telltale flush, delicate as the faintest rosebloom, crept into her cheeks she looked so lovely in her sweet girlish shyness that of a surety God's fair land of Ireland did not hold her equal.

For an instant she was silent with rather sad downcast eyes. She was about to retort but something checked the words on her tongue. Inclination prompted her to speak out: dignity told her to be silent. The pretty lips pouted a while but then she glanced up and broke out into a joyous little laugh which had in it all the freshness of a young May morning. She knew right well, no-one better, what made squinty Edy say that because of him cooling in his attentions when it was simply a lovers' quarrel. As per usual somebody's nose was out of joint about the boy that had the bicycle always riding up and down in front of her window. Only now his father kept him in the evenings studying hard to get an exhibition in the intermediate that was on and he was going to Trinity college to study for a doctor when he left the high school like his brother W. E. Wylie who was racing in the bicycle races in Trinity college university. Little recked he perhaps for what she felt, that dull aching void in her heart sometimes, piercing to the core. Yet he was young and perchance he might learn to love her in time. They were protestants in his family and of course Gerty knew Who came first and after Him the blessed Virgin and then Saint Joseph. But he was undeniably handsome with an exquisite nose and he was what he looked, every inch a gentleman, the shape of his head too at the back without his cap on that she would know anywhere something off the common and the way he turned the bicycle at the lamp with his hands off the bars and also the nice perfume of those good cigarettes and besides they were both of a size and that was why Edy Boardman thought she was so frightfully clever because he didn't go and ride up and down in front of her bit of a garden.

Gerty was dressed simply but with the instinctive taste of a votary of Dame Fashion for she felt that there was just a might that he might be out. A neat blouse of electric blue, selftinted by dolly dyes (because it was expected in the *Lady's Pictorial* that electric blue would be worn), with a smart vee opening down to the division and kerchief pocket (in which she always kept a piece of cottonwool scented with her favourite perfume because the handkerchief spoiled the sit) and a navy threequarter skirt cut to the stride showed off her slim graceful figure to perfection. She wore a coquettish little love of a hat of wideleaved nigger straw contrast trimmed with an underbrim of eggblue chenille and at the side a butterfly bow to tone. All Tuesday week afternoon she was hunting to match that chenille but at last she found what she wanted at Clery's summer sales, the very it, slightly shopsoiled but you would never notice, seven fingers two and a penny. She did it up all by herself and what joy was hers when she tried it on then, smiling at the lovely reflection which the mirror gave back to her! And when she put it on the waterjug to keep the shape she knew that that would take the shine out of some people she knew. Her shoes were the newest thing in footwear (Edy Boardman prided herself that she was very *petite* but she never had a foot like Gerty MacDowell, a five, and never would ash, oak or elm) with patent toecaps and just one smart buckle at her higharched instep. Her wellturned ankle displayed its perfect proportions beneath her skirt and just the proper amount and no more of her shapely limbs encased in finespun hose with highspliced heels and wide garter tops. As for undies they were Gerty's chief care and who that knows the fluttering hopes and fears of sweet seventeen (though Gerty would never see seventeen again) can find it in his heart to blame her? She had four dinky sets, with awfully pretty stitchery, three garments and nighties extra, and each set slotted with different coloured ribbons, rosepink, pale blue, mauve and peagreen and she aired them herself and blued them when they came home from the wash and ironed them and she had a brickbat to keep the iron on because she wouldn't trust those washerwomen as far as she'd see them scorching the things. She was wearing the blue for luck, hoping against hope, her own colour and the lucky colour too for a bride to have a bit of blue somewhere on her because the green she wore that day week brought grief because his father brought him in to study for the intermediate exhibition and because she thought perhaps he might be out because when she was dressing that morning she nearly slipped up the old pair on her inside out and that was for luck and lovers' meetings if you put those things on inside out so long as it wasn't of a Friday.

And yet and yet! That strained look on her face! A gnawing sorrow is there all the time. Her very soul is in her eyes and she would give worlds to be in the privacy of her own familiar chamber where, giving way to tears, she could have a good cry and relieve her pentup feelings. Though not too much because she knew how to cry nicely before the mirror. You are lovely, Gerty, it said. The paly light of evening falls upon a face infinitely sad and wistful. Gerty MacDowell yearns in vain. Yes, she had known from the first that her daydream of a marriage has been arranged and the weddingbells ringing for Mrs Reggy Wylie T. C. D. (because the one who married the elder brother would be Mrs Wylie) and in the fashionable intelligence Mrs Gertrude Wylie was wearing a sumptuous confection of grey trimmed with expensive blue fox was not to be. He was too young to understand. He would not believe in love, a woman's birthright. The night of the party long ago in Stoers' (he was still in short trousers) when they were alone and he stole an arm round her waist she went white to the very lips. He called her little one in a strangely husky voice and snatched a half kiss (the first!) but it was only the end of her nose and then he hastened from the room with a remark about refreshments. Impetuous fellow! Strength of character had never been Reggy Wylie's strong point and he who would woo and win Gerty MacDowell must be a man among men. But waiting, always waiting to be asked and it was leap year too and would soon be over. No prince charming is her beau ideal to lay a rare and wondrous love at her feet but rather a manly man with a strong quiet face who had not found his ideal, perhaps his hair slightly flecked with grey, and who would understand, take her in his sheltering arms, strain her to him in all the strength of his deep passionate nature and comfort her with a long long kiss. It would be like heaven. For such a one she yearns this balmy summer eve. With all the heart of her she longs to be his only, his affianced bride for riches for poor, in sickness in health, till death us two part, from this to this day forward.

And while Edy Boardman was with little Tommy behind the pushcar she was just thinking would the day ever come when she could call herself his little wife to be. Then they could talk about her till they went blue in the face, Bertha Supple too, and Edy, the spitfire, because she would be twenty-two in November. She would care for him with creature comforts too for Gerty was womanly wise and knew that a mere man liked that feeling of hominess. Her griddlecakes done to a goldenbrown hue and queen Ann's pudding of delightful creaminess had won golden opinions from all because she had a lucky hand also for lighting a fire, dredge in the fine selfraising flour and always stir in the same direction then cream the milk and sugar and whisk well the white of eggs though she didn't like the eating part when there were any people that made her shy and often she wondered why you couldn't eat something poetical like violets or roses and they would have a beautifully appointed drawingroom with pictures and engravings and the photograph of grandpapa Giltrap's lovely dog Garryowen that almost talked, it was so human, and chintz covers for the chairs and that silver toastrack in Clery's summer jumble sales like they have in rich houses. He would be tall with broad shoulders (she had always admired tall men for a husband) with glistening white teeth under his carefully trimmed sweeping moustache and they would go on the continent for their honeymoon (three wonderful weeks!) and then, when they settled down in a nice snug and cosy little homely house, every morning they would both have brekky, simple but perfectly served, for their own two selves and before he went out to business he would give his dear little wifey a good hearty hug and gaze for a moment deep down into her eyes.

Edy Boardman asked Tommy Caffrey was he done and he said yes, so then she buttoned up his little knickerbockers for him and told him to run off and play with Jacky and to be good now and not to fight. But Tommy said he wanted the ball and Edy told him no that baby was playing with the ball and if he took it there'd be wigs on the green but Tommy said it was his ball and he wanted his ball and he pranced on the ground, if you please. The temper of him! O, he was a man already was little Tommy Caffrey since he was out of pinnies. Edy told him no, no and to be off now with him and she told Cissy Caffrey not to give in to him.

– You're not my sister, naughty Tommy said. It's my ball.

But Cissy Caffrey told baby Boardman to look up, look up high at her finger and she snatched the ball quickly and threw it along the sand and Tommy after it in full career, having won the day.

– Anything for a quiet life, laughed Ciss.

And she tickled tiny tot's two cheeks to make him forget and played here's the lord mayor, here's his two horses, here's his gingerbread carriage and here, he walks in, chinchopper, chinchopper, chinchopper chin. But Edy got as cross as two sticks about him getting his own way like that from everyone always petting him.

– I'd like to give him something, she said, so I would, where I won't say.

– On the beetoteetom, laughed Cissy merrily.

Gerty MacDowell bent down her head and crimsoned at the idea of Cissy saying an unladylike thing like that out loud she'd he ashamed of her life to say, flushing a deep rosy red, and Edy Boardman said she was sure the gentleman opposite heard what she said. But not a pin cared Ciss.

– Let him! she said with a pert toss of her head and a piquant tilt of her nose. Give it to him too on the same place as quick as I'd look at him.

Madcap Ciss with her golliwog curls. You had to laugh at her sometimes. For instance when she asked you would you have some more Chinese tea and jaspberry ram and when she drew the jugs too and the men's faces on her nails with red ink make you split your sides or when she wanted to go where you know she said she wanted to run and pay a visit to the Miss White. That was just like Cissycums. O, and will you ever forget the evening she dressed up in her father's suit and hat and the burned cork moustache and walked down Tritonville road, smoking a cigarette? There was none to come up to her for fun. But she was sincerity itself, one of the bravest and truest hearts heaven ever made, not one of your twofaced things, too sweet to be wholesome.

And then there came out upon the air the sound of voices and the pealing anthem of the organ. It was the men's temperance retreat conducted by the missioner, the reverend John Hughes S. J., rosary, sermon and benediction of the Most Blessed Sacrament. They were there gathered together without distinction of social class (and a most edifying spectacle it was to see) in that simple fane beside the waves, after the storms of this weary world, kneeling before the feet of the immaculate, reciting the litany of Our Lady of Loreto, beseeching her to intercede for them, the old familiar words, holy Mary, holy virgin of virgins. How sad to poor Gerty's ears! Had her father only avoided the clutches of the demon drink, by taking the pledge or those powders the drink habit cured in Pearson's Weekly, she might now be rolling in her carriage, second to none. Over and over had she told herself that as she mused by the dying embers in a brown study without the lamp because she hated two lights or oftentimes gazing out of the window dreamily by the hour at the rain falling on the rusty bucket, thinking. But that vile decoction which has ruined so many hearths and homes had cast its shadow over her childhood days. Nay, she had even witnessed in the home circle deeds of violence caused by intemperance and had seen her own father, a prey to the fumes of intoxication, forget himself completely for if there was one thing of all things that Gerty knew it was the man who lifts his hand to a woman save in the way of kindness deserves to be branded as the lowest of the low.

And still the voices sang in supplication to the Virgin most powerful, Virgin most merciful. And Gerty, wrapt in thought, scarce saw or heard her companions or the twins at their boyish gambols or the gentleman off Sandymount green that Cissy Caffrey called the man that was so like himself passing along the strand taking a short walk. You never saw him anyway screwed but still and for all that she would not like him for a father because he was too old or something or on account of his face (it was a palpable case of doctor Fell) or his carbuncly nose with the pimples on it and his sandy moustache a bit white under his nose. Poor father! With all his faults she loved him still when he sang *Tell me, Mary, how to woo thee* or *My love and cottage near Rochelle* and they had stewed cockles and lettuce with Lazenby's salad dressing for supper and when he sang *The moon hath raised* with Mr Dignam that died suddenly and was buried, God have mercy on him, from a stroke. Her mother's birthday that was and Charley was home on his holidays and Tom and Mr Dignam and Mrs and Patsy and Freddy Dignam and they were to have had a group taken. No-one would have thought the end was so near. Now he was laid to rest. And her mother said to him to let that be a warning to him for the rest of his days and he couldn't even go to the funeral on account of the gout and she had to go into town to bring him the letters and samples from his office about Catesby's cork lino, artistic standard designs, fit for a palace, gives tiptop wear and always bright and cheery in the home.

A sterling good daughter was Gerty just like a second mother in the house, a ministering angel too with a little heart worth its weight in gold. And when her mother had those raging splitting headaches who was it rubbed on the menthol cone on her forehead but Gerty though she didn't like her mother taking pinches of snuff and that was the only single thing they ever had words about, taking snuff. Everyone thought the world of her for her gentle ways. It was Gerty who turned off the gas at the main every night and it was Gerty who tacked up on the wall of that place where she never forgot every fortnight the chlorate of lime Mr Tunney the grocer's christmas almanac the picture of halcyon days where a young gentleman in the costume they used to wear then with a threecornered hat was offering a bunch of flowers to his ladylove with oldtime chivalry through her lattice window. You could see there was a story behind it. The colours were done something lovely. She was in a soft clinging white in a studied attitude and the gentleman was in chocolate and he looked a thorough aristocrat. She often looked at them dreamily when there for a certain purpose and felt her own arms that were white and soft just like hers with the sleeves back and thought about those times because she had found out in Walker's pronouncing dictionary that belonged to grandpapa Giltrap about the halcyon days what they meant.

The twins were now playing in the most approved brotherly fashion, till at last Master Jacky who was really as bold as brass there was no getting behind that deliberately kicked the ball as hard as ever he could down towards the seaweedy rocks. Needless to say poor Tommy was not slow to voice his dismay but luckily the gentleman in black who was sitting there by himself came gallantly to the rescue and intercepted the ball. Our two champions claimed their plaything with lusty cries and to avoid trouble Cissy Caffrey called to the gentleman to throw it to her please. The gentleman aimed the ball once or twice and then threw it up the strand towards Cissy Caffrey but it rolled down the slope and stopped right under Gerty's skirt near the little pool by the rock. The twins clamoured again for it and Cissy told her to kick it away and let them fight for it so Gerty drew back her foot but she wished their stupid ball hadn't come rolling down to her and she gave a kick but she missed and Edy and Cissy laughed.

– If you fail try again, Edy Boardman said.

Gerty smiled assent and bit her lip. A delicate pink crept into her pretty cheek but she was determined to let them see so she just lifted her skirt a little but just enough and took good aim and gave the ball a jolly good kick and it went ever so far and the two twins after it down towards the shingle. Pure jealousy of course it was nothing else to draw attention on account of the gentleman opposite looking. She felt the warm flush, a danger signal always with Gerty MacDowell, surging and flaming into her cheeks. Till then they had only exchanged glances of the most casual but now under the brim of her new hat she ventured a look at him and the face that met her gaze there in the twilight, wan and strangely drawn, seemed to her the saddest she had ever seen.

Through the open window of the church the fragrant incense was wafted and with it the fragrant names of her who was conceived without stain of original sin, spiritual vessel, pray for us, honourable vessel, pray for us, vessel of singular devotion, pray for us, mystical rose. And careworn hearts were there and toilers for their daily bread and many who had erred and wandered, their eyes wet with contrition but for all that bright with hope for the reverend father Hughes had told them what the great saint Bernard said in his famous prayer of Mary, the most pious Virgin's intercessory power that it was not recorded in any age that those who implored her powerful protection were ever abandoned by her.

The twins were now playing again right merrily for the troubles of childhood are but as fleeting summer showers. Cissy played with baby Boardman till he crowed with glee, clapping baby hands in air. Peep she cried behind the hood of the pushcar and Edy asked where was Cissy gone and then Cissy popped up her head and cried ah! and, my word, didn't the little chap enjoy that! And then she told him to say papa.

– Say papa, baby. Say pa pa pa pa pa pa pa.

And baby did his level best to say it for he was very intelligent for eleven months everyone said and big for his age and the picture of health, a perfect little bunch of love, and he would certainly turn out to be something great, they said.

– Haja ja ja haja.

Cissy wiped his little mouth with the dribbling bib and wanted him to sit up properly, and say pa pa pa but when she undid the strap she cried out, holy saint Denis, that he was possing wet and to double the half blanket the other way under him. Of course his infant majesty was most obstreperous at such toilet formalities and he let everyone know it:

– Habaa baaaahabaaa baaaa.

And two great big lovely big tears coursing down his cheeks. It was all no use soothering him with no, nono, baby, no and telling him about the geegee and where was the puffpuff but Ciss, always readywitted, gave him in his mouth the teat of the suckingbottle and the young heathen was quickly appeased.

Gerty wished to goodness they would take their squalling baby home out of that and not get on her nerves no hour to be out and the little brats of twins. She gazed out towards the distant sea. It was like the paintings that man used to do on the pavement with all the coloured chalks and such a pity too leaving them there to be all blotted out, the evening and the clouds coming out and the Bailey light on Howth and to hear the music like that and the perfume of those incense they burned in the church like a kind of waft. And while she gazed her heart went pitapat. Yes, it was her he was looking at and there was meaning in his look. His eyes burned into her as though they would search her through and through, read her very soul. Wonderful eyes they were, superbly expressive, but could you trust them? People were so queer. She could see at once by his dark eyes and his pale intellectual face that he was a foreigner, the image of the photo she had of Martin Harvey, the matinée idol, only for the moustache which she preferred because she wasn't stagestruck like Winny Rippingham that wanted they two to always dress the same on account of a play but she could not see whether he had an aquiline nose or a slightly *retroussé* from where he was sitting. He was in deep mourning, she could see that, and the story of a haunting sorrow was written on his face. She would have given worlds to know what it was. He was looking up so intently, so still and he saw her kick the ball and perhaps he could see the bright steel buckles of her shoes if she swung them like that thoughtfully with the toes down. She was glad that something told her to put on the transparent stockings thinking Reggy Wylie might be out but that was far away. Here was that of which she had so often dreamed. It was he who mattered and there was joy on her face because she wanted him because she felt instinctively that he was like no-one else. The very heart of the girlwoman went out to him, her dream-husband, because she knew on the instant it was him. If he had suffered, more sinned against than sinning, or even, even, if he had been himself a sinner, a wicked man, she cared not. Even if he was a protestant or methodist she could convert him easily if he truly loved her. There were wounds that wanted healing with heartbalm. She was a womanly woman not like other flighty girls, unfeminine, he had known, those cyclists showing off what they hadn't got and she just yearned to know all, to forgive all if she could make him fall in love with her, make him forget the memory of the past. Then mayhap he would embrace her gently, like a real man, crushing her soft body to him, and love her, his ownest girlie, for herself alone.

Refuge of sinners. Comfortress of the afflicted. *Ora pro nobis*. Well has it been said that whosoever prays to her with faith and constancy can never be lost or cast away: and fitly is she too a haven of refuge for the afflicted because of the seven dolours which transpierced her own heart. Gerty could picture the whole scene in the church, the stained glass windows lighted up, the candles, the flowers and the blue banners of the blessed Virgin's sodality and Father Conroy was helping Canon O'Hanlon at the altar, carrying things in and out with his eyes cast down. He looked almost a saint and his confessionbox was so quiet and clean and dark and his hands were just like white wax and if ever she became a Dominican nun in their white habit perhaps he might come to the convent for the novena of Saint Dominic. He told her that time when she told him about that in confession crimsoning up to the roots of her hair for fear he could see, not to be troubled because that was only the voice of nature and we were all subject to nature's laws, he said, in this life and that that was no sin because that came from the nature of woman instituted by God, he said, and that Our Blessed Lady herself said to the archangel Gabriel be it done unto me according to Thy Word. He was so kind and holy and often and often she thought and thought could she work a ruched teacosy with embroidered floral design for him as a present or a clock but they had a clock she noticed on the mantelpiece white and gold with a canary bird that came out of a little house to tell the time the day she went there about the flowers for the forty hours' adoration because it was hard to know what sort of a present to give or perhaps an album of illuminated views of Dublin or some place.

The exasperating little brats of twins began to quarrel again and Jacky threw the ball out towards the sea and they both ran after it. Little monkeys common as ditch-water. Someone ought to take them and give them a good hiding for themselves to keep them in their places, the both of them. And Cissy and Edy shouted after them to come back because they were afraid the tide might come in on them and be drowned.

– Jacky! Tommy!

Not they! What a great notion they had! So Cissy said it was the very last time she'd ever bring them out. She jumped up and called them and she ran down the slope past him, tossing her hair behind her which had a good enough colour if there had been more of it but with all the thingamerry she was always rubbing into it she couldn't get it to grow long because it wasn't natural so she could just go and throw her hat at it. She ran with long gandery strides it was a wonder she didn't rip up her skirt at the side that was too tight on her because there was a lot of the tomboy about Cissy Caffrey and she was a forward piece whenever she thought she had a good opportunity to show off and just because she was a good runner she ran like that so that he could see all the end of her petticoat running and her skinny shanks up as far as possible. It would have served her just right if she had

tripped up over something accidentally on purpose with her high crooked
French heels on her to make her look tall and got a fine tumble. *Tableau!*
That would have been a very charming exposé for a gentleman like that to
witness.

Queen of angels, queen of patriarchs, queen of prophets, of all saints,
they prayed, queen of the most holy rosary and then Father Conroy handed
the thurible to Canon O'Hanlon and he put in the incense and censed the
Blessed Sacrament and Cissy Caffrey caught the two twins and she was
itching to give then a ringing good clip on the ear but she didn't because
she thought he might be watching but she never made a bigger mistake in
all her life because Gerty could see without looking that he never took his
eyes off of her and then Canon O'Hanlon handed the thurible back to
Father Conroy and knelt down looking up at the Blessed Sacrament and
the choir began to sing *Tantum ergo* and she just swung her foot in and out
in time as the music rose and fell to the *Tantumer gosa cramen turn*. Three
and eleven she paid for those stockings in Sparrow's of George's street on
the Tuesday, no the Monday before Easter and there wasn't a brack on
them and that was what he was looking at, transparent, and not at her
insignificant ones that had neither shape nor form (the cheek of her!)
because he had eyes in his head to see the difference for himself.

Cissy came up along the strand with the two twins and their ball with her
hat anyhow on her to one side after her run and she did look a streel
tugging the two kids along with the flimsy blouse she bought only a fortnight before like a rag on her back and a bit of her petticoat hanging like a
caricature. Gerty just took off her hat for a moment to settle her hair and a
prettier, a daintier head of nutbrown tresses was never seen on a girl's
shoulders, a radiant little vision, in sooth, almost maddening in its sweetness.
You would have to travel many a long mile before you found a head of hair
the like of that. She could almost see the swift answering flush of admiration
in his eyes that set her tingling in every nerve. She put on her hat so that
she could see from underneath the brim and swung her buckled shoe faster
for her breath caught as she caught the expression in his eyes. He was eying
her as a snake eyes its prey. Her woman's instinct told her that she had
raised the devil in him and at the thought a burning scarlet swept from
throat to brow till the lovely colour of her face became a glorious rose.

Edy Boardman was noticing it too because she was squinting at Gerty,
half smiling, with her specs, like an old maid, pretending to nurse the baby.
Irritable little gnat she was and always would be and that was why no-one
could get on with her, poking her nose into what was no concern of hers.
And she said to Gerty:

– A penny for your thoughts.

– What? replied Gerty with a smile reinforced by the whitest of teeth. I was only wondering was it late.

Because she wished to goodness they'd take the snottynosed twins and their baby home to the mischief out of that so that was why she just gave a gentle hint about its being late. And when Cissy came up Edy asked her the time and Miss Cissy, as glib as you like, said it was half past kissing time, time to kiss again. But Edy wanted to know because they were told to be in early.

– Wait, said Cissy, I'll ask my uncle Peter over there what's the time by his conundrum.

So over she went and when he saw her coming she could see him take his hand out of his pocket, getting nervous, and beginning to play with his watchchain, looking at the church. Passionate nature though he was Gerty could see that he had enormous control over himself. One moment he had been there, fascinated by a loveliness that made him gaze and the next moment it was the quiet gravefaced gentleman, selfcontrol expressed in every line of his distinguishedlooking figure.

Cissy said to excuse her would he mind telling her what was the right time and Gerty could see him taking out his watch, listening to it and looking up and clearing his throat and he said he was very sorry his watch was stopped but he thought it must be after eight because the sun was set. His voice had a cultured ring in it and though he spoke in measured accents there was a suspicion of a quiver in the mellow tones. Cissy said thanks and came back with her tongue out and said uncle said his waterworks were out of order.

Then they sang the second verse of the *Tantum ergo* and Canon O'Hanlon got up again and censed the Blessed Sacrament and knelt down and he told Father Conroy that one of the candles was just going to set fire to the flowers and Father Conroy got up and settled it all right and she could see the gentleman winding his watch and listening to the works and she swung her leg more in and out in time. It was getting darker but he could see and he was looking all the time that he was winding the watch or whatever he was doing to it and then he put it back and put his hands back into his pockets. She felt a kind of a sensation rushing all over her and she knew by the feel of her scalp and that irritation against her stays that that thing must be coming on because the last time too was when she clipped her hair on account of the moon. His dark eyes fixed themselves on her again drinking in her every contour, literally worshipping at her shrine. If ever there was undisguised admiration in a man's passionate gaze it was there plain to be seen on that man's face. It is for you, Gertrude MacDowell, and you know it.

Edy began to get ready to go and it was high time for her and Gerty noticed that that little hint she gave had the desired effect because it was a long way along the strand to where there was the place to push up the pushcar and Cissy took off the twins' caps and tidied their hair to make herself attractive of course and Canon O'Hanlon stood up with his cope poking up at his neck and Father Conroy handed him the card to read off and he read out *Panem de cœlo præstitisti eis* and Edy and Cissy were talking about the time all the time and asking her but Gerty could pay them back in their own coin and she just answered with scathing politeness when Edy asked her was she heartbroken about her best boy throwing her over. Gerty winced sharply. A brief cold blaze shone from her eyes that spoke volumes of scorn immeasurable. It hurt. O yes, it cut deep because Edy had her own quiet way of saying things like that she knew would wound like the confounded little cat she was. Gerty's lips parted swiftly to frame the word but she fought back the sob that rose to her throat, so slim, so flawless, so beautifully moulded it seemed one an artist might have dreamed of. She had loved him better than he knew. Lighthearted deceiver and fickle like all his sex he would never understand what he had meant to her and for an instant there was in the blue eyes a quick stinging of tears. Their eyes were probing her mercilessly but with a brave effort she sparkled back in sympathy as she glanced at her new conquest for them to see.

– O, responded Gerty, quick as lightning, laughing, and the proud head flashed up, I can throw my cap at who I like because it's leap year.

Her words rang out crystalclear, more musical than the cooing of the ringdove but they cut the silence icily. There was that in her young voice that told that she was not a one to be lightly trifled with. As for Mr Reggy with his swank and his bit of money she could just chuck him aside as if he was so much filth and never again would she cast as much as a second thought on him and tear his silly postcard into a dozen pieces. And if ever after he dared to presume she could give him one look of measured scorn that would make him shrivel up on the spot. Miss puny little Edy's countenance fell to no slight extent and Gerty could see by her looking as black as thunder that she was simply in a towering rage though she hid it, the little kinnatt, because that shaft had struck home for her petty jealousy and they both knew that she was something aloof, apart in another sphere, that she was not of them and there was somebody else too that knew it and saw it so they could put that in their pipe and smoke it.

Edy straightened up baby Boardman to get ready to go and Cissy tucked in the ball and the spades and buckets and it was high time too because the sandman was on his way for Master Boardman junior and Cissy told him too that Billy Winks was coming and that baby was to go deedaw and baby looked just too ducky, laughing up out of his gleeful eyes, and Cissy poked him like that out of fun in his wee fat tummy and baby, without as much as by your leave, sent up his compliments on to his brandnew dribbling bib.

– O my! Puddeny pie! protested Ciss. He has his bib destroyed.

The slight *contretemps* claimed her attention but in two twos she set that little matter to rights.

Gerty stifled a smothered exclamation and gave a nervous cough and Edy asked what and she was just going to tell her to catch it while it was flying but she was ever ladylike in her deportment so she simply passed it off with consummate tact by saying that that was the benediction because just then the bell rang out from the steeple over the quiet seashore because Canon O'Hanlon was up on the altar with the veil that Father Conroy put round him round his shoulders giving the benediction with the blessed Sacrament in his hands.

How moving the scene there in the gathering twilight, the last glimpse of Erin, the touching chime of those evening bells and at the same time a bat flew forth from the ivied belfry through the dusk, hither, thither, with a tiny lost cry. And she could see far away the lights of the lighthouses so picturesque she would have loved to do with a box of paints because it was easier than to make a man and soon the lamplighter would be going his rounds past the presbyterian church grounds and along by shady Tritonville avenue where the couples walked and lighting the lamp near her window where Reggy Wylie used to turn his freewheel like she read in that book *The Lamplighter* by Miss Cummins, author of *Mabel Vaughan* and other tales. For Gerty had her dreams that no-one knew of. She loved to read poetry and when she got a keepsake from Bertha Supple of that lovely confession album with the coralpink cover to write her thoughts in she laid it in the drawer of her toilettable which, though it did not err on the side of luxury, was scrupulously neat and clean. It was there she kept her girlish treasures trove, the tortoiseshell combs, her child of Mary badge, the white-rose scent, the eyebrowleine, her alabaster pouncetbox and the ribbons to change when her things came home from the wash and there were some beautiful thoughts written in it in violet ink that she bought in Hely's of Dame Street for she felt that she too could write poetry if she could only express herself like that poem that appealed to her so deeply that she had copied out of the newspaper she found one evening round the potherbs. *Art thou real, my ideal?* it was called by Louis J. Walsh, Magherafelt, and after there was something about *twilight, wilt thou ever?* and ofttimes the beauty of poetry, so sad in its transient loveliness, had misted her eyes with silent tears that the years were slipping by for her, one by one, and but for that one shortcoming she knew she need fear no competition and that was an accident coming down Dalkey hill and she always tried to conceal it. But it must end she felt. If she saw that magic lure in his eyes there would be no holding back for her. Love laughs at locksmiths. She would make the great sacrifice. Her every effort would be to share his thoughts. Dearer than the whole world would she be to him and gild his days with happiness. There was the allimportant question and she was dying to know was he a married man or a widower who had lost his wife or some tragedy like the nobleman with the foreign name from the land of song had to have her put into a madhouse, cruel only to be kind. But even if – what then? Would it make a very great difference? From everything in the least indelicate her finebred nature instinctively recoiled. She loathed that sort of person, the fallen women off the accommodation walk beside the Dodder that went with the soldiers and coarse men, with no respect for a girl's honour, degrading the sex and being taken up to the police station. No, no: not that. They would be just good friends like a big brother and sister without all that other in spite of the conventions of Society with a big ess. Perhaps it was an old flame he was in mourning for from the days beyond recall. She thought she understood. She would try to understand him because men were so different. The old love was waiting, waiting with little white hands stretched out, with blue appealing eyes. Heart of mine! She would follow her dream of love, the dictates of her heart that told her he was her all in all, the only man in all the world for her for love was the master guide. Nothing else mattered. Come what might she would be wild, untrammelled, free.

Canon O'Hanlon put the Blessed Sacrament back into the tabernacle and the choir sang *Laudate Dominum omnes gentes* and then he locked the tabernacle door because the benediction was over and Father Conroy handed him his hat to put on and crosscat Edy asked wasn't she coming but Jacky Caffrey called out:

– O, look, Cissy!

And they all looked was it sheet lightning but Tommy saw it too over the trees beside the church, blue and then green and purple.

– It's fireworks, Cissy Caffrey said.

And they all ran down the strand to see over the houses and the church, helterskelter, Edy with the pushcar with baby Boardman in it and Cissy holding Tommy and Jacky by the hand so they wouldn't fall running.

– Come on, Gerty, Cissy, called. It's the bazaar fireworks.

But Gerty was adamant. She had no intention of being at their beck and call. If they could run like rossies she could sit so she said she could see from where she was. The eyes that were fastened upon her set her pulses tingling. She looked at him a moment, meeting his glance, and a light broke in upon her. Whitehot passion was in that face, passion silent as the grave and it had made her his. At last they were left alone without the others to pry and pass remarks and she knew he could be trusted to the death, steadfast, a sterling man, a man of inflexible honour to his fingertips. His hands and face were working and a tremor went over her. She leaned back far to look up where the fireworks were and she caught her knee in her hands so as not to fall back looking up and there was no-one to see only him and her when she revealed all her graceful beautifully shaped legs like that, supply soft and delicately rounded, and she seemed to hear the panting of his heart, his hoarse breathing, because she knew about the passion of men like that, hot-blooded, because Bertha Supple told her once in dead secret and made her swear she'd never about the gentleman lodger that was staying with them out of the Congested Districts Board that had pictures cut out of papers of those skirtdancers and highkickers and she said he used to do something not very nice that you could imagine sometimes in the bed. But this was altogether different from a thing like that because there was all the difference because she could almost feel him draw her face to his and the first quick hot touch of his handsome lips. Besides there was absolution so long as you didn't do the other thing before being married and there ought to be women priests that would understand without your telling out and Cissy Caffrey too sometimes had that dreamy kind of dreamy look in her eyes so that she too, my dear, and Winny Rippingham so mad about actors' photographs and besides it was on account of that other thing coming on the way it did.

And Jacky Caffrey shouted to look, there was another and she leaned back and the garters were blue to match on account of the transparent and they all saw it and shouted to look, look there it was and she leaned back ever so far to see the fireworks and something queer was flying about through the air, a soft thing to and fro, dark. And she saw a long Roman candle going up over the trees up, up, and, in the tense hush, they were all breathless with excitement as it went higher and higher and she had to lean back more and more to look up after it, high, high, almost out of sight, and her face was suffused with a divine, an entrancing blush from straining back and he could see her other things too, nainsook knickers, the fabric that caresses the skin, better than those other pettiwidth, the green, four and eleven, on account of being white and she let him and she saw that he saw and then it went so high it went out of sight a moment and she was trembling in every limb from being bent so far back he had a full view high up above her knee where no-one ever not even on the swing or wading and she wasn't ashamed and he wasn't either to look in that immodest way like that because he couldn't resist the sight of the wondrous revealment half offered like those skirtdancers behaving so immodest before gentlemen looking and he kept on looking, looking. She would fain have cried to him chokingly, held out her snowy slender arms to him to come, to feel his lips laid on her white brow the cry of a young girl's love, a little strangled cry, wrung from her, that cry that has rung through the ages. And then a rocket sprang and bang shot blind and O! then the Roman candle burst and it was like a sigh of O! and everyone cried O! O! in raptures and it gushed out of it a stream of rain gold hair threads and they shed and ah! they were all greeny dewy stars falling with golden, O so lovely! O so soft, sweet, soft!

Then all melted away dewily in the grey air: all was silent. Ah! She glanced at him as she bent forward quickly, a pathetic little glance of piteous protest, of shy reproach under which he coloured like a girl. He was leaning back against the rock behind. Leopold Bloom (for it is he) stands silent, with bowed bead before those young guileless eyes. What a brute he had been! At it again? A fair unsullied soul had called to him and, wretch that he was, how had he answered? An utter cad he had been. He of all men! But there was an infinite store of mercy in those eyes, for him too a word of pardon even though he had erred and sinned and wandered. Should a girl tell? No, a thousand times no. That was their secret, only theirs, alone in the hiding twilight and there was none to know or tell save the little bat that flew so softly through the evening to and fro and little bats don't tell.

Cissy Caffrey whistled, imitating the boys in the football field to show what a great person she was: and then she cried:

– Gerty! Gerty! We're going. Come on. We can see from farther up.

Gerty had an idea, one of love's little ruses. She slipped a hand into her kerchief pocket and took out the wadding and waved in reply of course without letting him and then slipped it back. Wonder if he's too far to. She rose. Was it goodbye? No. She had to go but they would meet again, there, and she would dream of that till then, tomorrow, of her dream of yester eve. She drew herself up to her full height. Their souls met in a last lingering glance and the eyes that reached her heart, full of a strange shining, hung enraptured on her sweet flowerlike face. She half smiled at him wanly, a sweet forgiving smile, a smile that verged on tears, and then they parted.

Slowly without looking back she went down the uneven strand to Cissy, to Edy, to Jacky and Tommy Caffrey, to little baby Boardman. It was darker now and there were stones and bits of wood on the strand and slippy seaweed. She walked with a certain quiet dignity characteristic of her but with care and very slowly because Gerty MacDowell was . . .

Tight boots? No. She's lame! O!

Mr Bloom watched her as she limped away. Poor girl! That's why she's left on the shelf and the others did a sprint. Thought something was wrong by the cut of her jib. Jilted beauty. A defect is ten times worse in a woman. But makes them polite. Glad I didn't know it when she was on show. Hot little devil all the same. Wouldn't mind. Curiosity like a nun or a negress or a girl with glasses. That squinty one is delicate. Near her monthlies, I expect, makes them feel ticklish. I have such a bad headache today. Where did I put the letter? Yes, all right. All kinds of crazy longings. Licking pennies. Girl in Tranquilla convent that nun told me liked to smell rock oil. Virgins go mad in the end I suppose. Sister? How many women in Dublin have it today? Martha, she. Something in the air. That's the moon. But then why don't all women menstruate at the same time with same moon, I mean? Depends on the time they were born, I suppose. Or all start scratch then get out of step. Sometimes Molly and Milly together. Anyhow I got the best of that. Damned glad I didn't do it in the bath this morning over her silly I will punish you letter. Made up for that tram-driver this morning. That gouger M'Coy stopping me to say nothing. And his wife engagement in the country valise, voice like a pickaxe. Thankful for small mercies. Cheap too. Yours for the asking. Because they want it themselves. Their natural craving. Shoals of them every evening poured out of offices. Reserve better. Don't want it they throw it at you. Catch em alive, O. Pity they can't see themselves. A dream of wellfilled hose. Where was that? Ah, yes. Mutoscope pictures in Capel street: for men only. Peeping Tom. Willy's hat and what the girls did with it. Do they snapshot those girls or is it all a fake? *Lingerie* does it. Felt for the curves inside her *deshabillé*. Excites them also when they're. I'm all clean come and dirty me. And they like dressing one another for the sacrifice. Milly delighted with Molly's new blouse. At first. Put them all on to take them all off. Molly. Why I bought her the violet garters. Us too: the tie he wore, his lovely socks and turnedup trousers. He wore a pair of gaiters the night that first we met. His lovely shirt was shining beneath his what? of jet. Say a woman loses a charm with every pin she takes out. Pinned together. O Mairy lost the pin of her. Dressed up to the nines for somebody. Fashion part of their charm. Just changes when you're on the track of the secret. Except the east: Mary, Martha: now as then. No reasonable offer refused. She wasn't in a hurry either. Always off to a fellow when they are. They never forget an appointment. Out on spec probably. They believe in chance because like themselves. And the others inclined to give her an odd dig. Girl friends at school, arms round each other's necks or with ten fingers locked, kissing and whispering secrets about nothing in the convent garden. Nuns with whitewashed faces, cool coif and their rosaries going up and down, vindictive too for what they can't get. Barbed wire. Be sure now and write to me. And I'll write to you. Now won't you? Molly and Josie Powell. Till Mr Right comes along then meet once in a blue moon. *Tableau!* O, look who it is for the love of God! How are you at all? What have you been doing with yourself? Kiss and delighted to, kiss, to see you. Picking holes in each other's appearance. You're looking splendid. Sister souls showing their teeth at one another. How many have you left? Wouldn't lend each other a pinch of salt.

Ah!

Devils they are when that's coming on them. Dark devilish appearance. Molly often told me feel things a ton weight. Scratch the sole of my foot. O that way! O, that's exquisite! Feel it myself too. Good to rest once in a way. Wonder if it's bad to go with them then. Safe in one way. Turns milk, makes fiddlestrings snap. Something about withering plants I read in a garden. Besides they say if the flower withers she wears she's a flirt. All are. Daresay she felt I. When you feel like that you often meet what you feel. Liked me or what? Dress they look at. Always know a fellow courting: collars and cuffs. Well cocks and lions do the same and stags. Same time might prefer a tie undone or something. Trousers? Suppose I when I was? No. Gently does it. Dislike rough and tumble. Kiss in the dark and never tell. Saw something in me. Wonder what. Sooner have me as I am than some poet chap with bearsgrease, plastery hair lovelock over his dexter optic. To aid gentleman in literary. Ought to attend to my appearance my age. Didn't let her see me in profile. Still, you never know. Pretty girls and ugly men marrying. Beauty and the beast. Besides I can't be so if Molly. Took off her hat to show her hair. Wide brim bought to hide her face, meeting someone might know her, bend down or carry a bunch of flowers to smell. Hair strong in rut. Ten bob I got for Molly's combings when we were on the rocks in Holles street. Why not? Suppose he gave her money. Why not? All a prejudice. She's worth ten, fifteen, more a pound. What? I think so. All that for nothing. Bold hand. Mrs Marion. Did I forget to write address on that letter like the postcard I sent to Flynn. And the day I went to Drimmie's without a necktie. Wrangle with Molly it was put me off. No, I remember. Richie Goulding. He's another. Weighs on his mind. Funny my watch stopped at half past four. Dust. Shark liver oil they use to clean could do it myself. Save. Was that just when he, she?

O, he did. Into her. She did. Done.

Ah!

Mr Bloom with careful hand recomposed his wet shirt. O Lord, that little limping devil. Begins to feel cold and clammy. Aftereffect not pleasant. Still you have to get rid of it someway. They don't care. Complimented perhaps. Go home to nicey bread and milky and say night prayers with the kiddies. Well, aren't they. See her as she is spoil all. Must have the stage setting, the rouge, costume, position, music. The name too. *Amours* of actresses. Nell Gwynn, Mrs Bracegirdle, Maud Branscombe. Curtain up. Moonlight silver effulgence. Maiden discovered with pensive bosom. Little sweetheart come and kiss me. Still I feel. The strength it gives a man. That's the secret of it. Good job I let off there behind coming out of Dignam's. Cider that was. Otherwise I couldn't have. Makes you want to sing after. *Lacaus esant taratara.* Suppose I spoke to her. What about? Bad plan however if you don't know how to end the conversation. Ask them a question they ask you another. Good idea if you're in a cart. Wonderful of course if you say: good evening, and you see she's on for it: good evening. O but the dark evening in the Appian way I nearly spoke to Mrs Clinch O thinking she was. Whew! Girl in Meath street that night. All the dirty things I made her say all wrong of course. My arks she called it. It's so hard to find one who. Aho! If you don't answer when they solicit must be horrible for them till they harden. And kissed my hand when I gave her the extra two shillings. Parrots. Press the button and the bird will squeak. Wish she hadn't called me sir. O, her mouth in the dark! And you a married man with a single girl! That's what they enjoy. Taking a man from another woman. Or even hear of it. Different with me. Glad to get away from other chap's wife. Eating off his cold plate. Chap in the Burton today spitting back gumchewed gristle. French letter still in my pocketbook. Cause of half the trouble. But might happen sometime, I don't think. Come in. All is prepared. I dreamt. What? Worst is beginning. How they change the venue when it's not what they like. Ask you do you like mushrooms because she once knew a gentleman who. Or ask you what someone was going to say when he changed his mind and stopped. Yet if I went the whole hog, say: I want to, something like that. Because I did. She too. Offend her. Then make it up. Pretend to want something awfully, then cry off for her sake. Flatters them. She must have been thinking of someone else all the time. What harm? Must since she came to the use of reason, he, he and he. First kiss does the trick. The propitious moment. Something inside them goes pop. Mushy like, tell by their eye, on the sly. First thoughts are best. Remember that till their dying day. Molly, lieutenant Mulvey that kissed her under the Moorish wall beside the gardens. Fifteen she told me. But her breasts were developed. Fell asleep then. After Glencree dinner that was when we drove home the featherbed mountain. Gnashing her teeth in sleep. Lord mayor had his eye on her too. Val Dillon. Apoplectic.

There she is with them down there for the fireworks. My fireworks. Up like a rocket, down like a stick. And the children, twins they must be, waiting for something to happen. Want to be grownups. Dressing in mother's clothes. Time enough, understand all the ways of the world. And the dark one with the mop head and the nigger mouth. I knew she could whistle. Mouth made for that. Like Molly. Why that high class whore in Jammet's wore her veil only to her nose. Would you mind, please, telling me the right time? I'll tell you the right time up a dark lane. Say prunes and prisms forty times every morning, cure for fat lips. Caressing the little boy too. Onlookers see most of the game. Of course they understand birds, animals, babies. In their line.

Didn't look back when she was going down the strand. Wouldn't give that satisfaction. Those girls, those girls, those lovely seaside girls. Fine eyes she had, clear. It's the white of the eye brings that out not so much the pupil. Did she know what I? Course. Like a cat sitting beyond a dog's jump. Women never meet one like that Wilkins in the high school drawing a picture of Venus with all his belongings on show. Call that innocence? Poor idiot! His wife has her work cut out for her. Never see them sit on a bench marked *Wet Paint*. Eyes all over them. Look under the bed for what's not there. Longing to get the fright of their lives. Sharp as needles they are. When I said to Molly the man at the corner of Cuffe street was goodlooking, thought she might like, twigged at once he had a false arm. Had too. Where do they get that? Typist going up Roger Greene's stairs two at a time to show her understandings. Handed down from father to mother to daughter, I mean. Bred in the bone. Milly for example drying her handkerchief on the mirror to save the ironing. Best place for an ad to catch a woman's eye on a mirror. And when I sent her for Molly's Paisley shawl to Presscott's, by the way that ad I must, carrying home the change in her stocking. Clever little minx! I never told her. Neat way she carries parcels too. Attract men, small thing like that. Holding up her hand, shaking it, to let the blood flow back when it was red. Who did you learn that from? Nobody. Something the nurse taught me. O, don't they know? Three years old she was in front of Molly's dressingtable just before we left Lombard street west. Me have a nice face. Mullingar. Who knows? Ways of the world. Young student.

Straight on her pins anyway not like the other. Still she was game. Lord, I am wet. Devil you are. Swell of her calf. Transparent stockings, stretched to breaking point. Not like that frump today. A. E. Rumpled stockings. Or the one in Grafton street. White. Wow! Beef to the heel.

A monkey puzzle rocket burst, spluttering in darting crackles. Zrads and zrads, zrads, zrads. And Cissy and Tommy ran out to see and Edy after with the pushcar and then Gerty beyond the curve of the rocks. Will she? Watch! Watch! See! Looked round. She smelt an onion. Darling, I saw your. I saw all.

Lord!

Did me good all the same. Off colour after Kiernan's, Dignam's. For this relief much thanks. In *Hamlet*, that is. Lord! It was all things combined. Excitement. When she leaned back felt an ache at the butt of my tongue. Your head it simply swirls. He's right. Might have made a worse fool of myself however. Instead of talking about nothing. Then I will tell you all. Still it was a kind of language between us. It couldn't be? No, Gerty they called her. Might be false name however like my and the address Dolphin's barn a blind.

Her maiden name was Jemima Brown
And she lived with her mother in Irishtown.

Place made me think of that I suppose. All tarred with the same brush. Wiping pens in their stockings. But the ball rolled down to her as if it understood. Every bullet has its billet. Course I never could throw anything straight at school. Crooked as a ram's horn. Sad however because it lasts only a few years till they settle down to potwalloping and papa's pants will soon fit Willy and fullers' earth for the baby when they hold him out to do ah ah. No soft job. Saves them. Keeps them out of harm's way. Nature. Washing child, washing corpse. Dignam. Children's hands always round them. Cocoanut skulls, monkeys, not even closed at first, sour milk in their swaddles and tainted curds. Oughtn't to have given that child an empty teat to suck. Fill it up with wind. Mrs Beaufoy, Purefoy. Must call to the hospital. Wonder is nurse Callan there still. She used to look over some nights when Molly was in the Coffee Palace. That young doctor O'Hare I noticed her brushing his coat. And Mrs Breen and Mrs Dignam once like that too, marriageable. Worst of all at night Mrs Duggan told me in the City Arms. Husband rolling in drunk, stink of pub off him like a polecat. Have that in your nose in the dark, whiff of stale boose. Then ask in the morning: was I drunk last night? Bad policy however to fault the husband. Chickens come home to roost. They stick by one another like glue. Maybe the women's fault also. That's where Molly can knock spots off them. It is the blood of the south. Moorish. Also the form, the figure. Hands felt for the opulent. Just compare for instance those others. Wife locked up at home, skeleton in the cupboard. Allow me to introduce my. Then they trot you out some kind of a nondescript, wouldn't know what to call her. Always see a fellow's weak point in his wife. Still there's destiny in it, falling in love. Have their own secrets between them. Chaps that would go to the dogs if some woman didn't take them in hand. Then little chits of girls, height of a shilling in coppers, with little hubbies. As God made them He matched them. Sometimes children turn out well enough. Twice nought makes one. Or old rich chap of seventy and blushing bride. Marry in May and repent in December. This wet is very unpleasant. Stuck. Well the foreskin is not back. Better detach.

Ow!

Other hand a sixfooter with a wifey up to his watchpocket. Long and the short of it. Big he and little she. Very strange about my watch. Wristwatches are always going wrong. Wonder is there any magnetic influence between the person because that was about the time he. Yes, I suppose at once. Cat's away the mice will play. I remember looking in Pill lane. Also that now is magnetism. Back of everything magnetism. Earth for instance pulling this and being pulled. That causes movement. And time? Well that's the time the movement takes. Then if one thing stopped the whole ghesabo would stop bit by bit. Because it's arranged. Magnetic needle tells you what's going on in the sun, the stars. Little piece of steel iron. When you hold out the fork. Come. Come. Tip. Woman and man that is. Fork and steel. Molly, he. Dress up and look and suggest and let you see and see more and defy you if you're a man to see that and, like a sneeze coming, legs, look, look and if you have any guts in you. Tip. Have to let fly.

Wonder how is she feeling in that region. Shame all put on before third person. More put out about a hole in her stocking. Molly, her underjaw stuck out head back, about the farmer in the ridingboots and spurs at the horse show. And when the painters were in Lombard street west. Fine voice that fellow had. How Giuglini began. Smell that I did, like flowers. It was too. Violets. Came from the turpentine probably in the paint. Make their own use of everything. Same time doing it scraped her slipper on the floor so they wouldn't hear. But lots of them can't kick the beam, I think. Keep that thing up for hours. Kind of a general all round over me and half down my back.

Wait. Hm. Hm. Yes. That's her perfume. Why she waved her hand. I leave you this to think of me when I'm far away on the pillow. What is it?

Heliotrope? No, Hyacinth? Hm. Roses, I think. She'd like scent of that kind. Sweet and cheap: soon sour. Why Molly likes opoponax. Suits her with a little jessamine mixed. Her high notes and her low notes. At the dance night she met him, dance of the hours. Heat brought it out. She was wearing her black and it had the perfume of the time before. Good conductor, is it? Or bad? Light too. Suppose there's some connection. For instance if you go into a cellar where it's dark. Mysterious thing too. Why did I smell it only now? Took its time in coming like herself, slow but sure. Suppose it's ever so many millions of tiny grains blown across. Yes, it is. Because those spice islands, Cinghalese this morning, smell them leagues off. Tell you what it is. It's like a fine veil or web they have all over the skin, fine like what do you call it gossamer and they're always spinning it out of them, fine as anything, rainbow colours without knowing it. Clings to everything she takes off. Vamp of her stockings. Warm shoe. Stays. Drawers: little kick, taking them off. Byby till next time. Also the cat likes to sniff in her shift on the bed. Know her smell in a thousand. Bathwater too. Reminds me of strawberries and cream. Wonder where it is really. There or the armpits or under the neck. Because you get it out of all holes and corners. Hyacinth perfume made of oil or ether or something. Muskrat. Bag under their tails one grain pour off odour for years. Dogs at each other behind. Good evening. Evening. How do you sniff? Hm. Hm. Very well, thank you. Animals go by that. Yes now, look at it that way. We're the same. Some women for instance warn you off when they have their period. Come near. Then get a hogo you could hang your hat on. Like what? Potted herrings gone stale or. Boof! Please keep off the grass.

Perhaps they get a man smell off us. What though? Cigary gloves Long John had on his desk the other. Breath? What you eat and drink gives that. No. Mansmell, I mean. Must be connected with that because priests that are supposed to be are different. Women buzz round it like flies round treacle. Railed off the altar get on to it at any cost. The tree of forbidden priest. O father, will you? Let me be the first to. That diffuses itself all through the body, permeates. Source of life and it's extremely curious the smell. Celery sauce. Let me.

Mr Bloom inserted his nose. Hm. Into the. Hm. Opening of his waistcoat. Almonds or. No. Lemons it is. Ah no, that's the soap.

O by the by that lotion. I knew there was something on my mind. Never went back and the soap not paid. Dislike carrying bottles like that hag this morning. Hynes might have paid me that three shillings. I could mention Meagher's just to remind him. Still if he works that paragraph. Two and nine. Bad opinion of me he'll have. Call tomorrow. How much do I owe you? Three and nine? Two and nine, sir. Ah. Might stop him giving credit another time. Lose your customers that way. Pubs do. Fellow run up a bill on the slate and then slinking around the back streets into somewhere else.

Here's this nobleman passed before, Blown in from the bay. Just went as far as turn back. Always at home at dinnertime. Looks mangled out: had a good tuck in. Enjoying nature now. Grace after meals. After supper walk a mile. Sure he has a small bank balance somewhere, government sit. Walk after him now make him awkward like those newsboys me today. Still you learn something. See ourselves as others see us. So long as women don't mock what matter? That's the way to find out. Ask yourself who is he now. *The Mystery Man on the Beach*, prize titbit story by Mr Leopold Bloom. Payment at the rate of one guinea per column. And that fellow today at the graveside in the brown macintosh. Corns on his kismet however. Healthy perhaps absorb all the. Whistle brings rain they say. Must be some somewhere. Salt in the Ormond damp. The body feels the atmosphere. Old Betty's joints are on the rack. Mother Shipton's prophecy that is about ships around they fly in the twinkling. No. Signs of rain it is. The royal reader. And distant hills seem coming nigh.

Howth. Bailey light. Two, four, six, eight, nine. See. Has to change or they might think it a house. Wreckers. Grace Darling. People afraid of the dark. Also glowworms, cyclists: lightingup time. Jewels diamonds flash better. Light is a kind of reassuring. Not going to hurt you. Better now of course than long ago. Country roads. Run you through the small guts for nothing. Still two types there are you bob against. Scowl or smile. Pardon! Not at all. Best time to spray plants too in the shade after the sun. Some light still. Red rays are longest. Roygbiv Vance taught us: red, orange, yellow, green, blue, indigo, violet. A star I see. Venus? Can't tell yet. Two, when three it's night. Were those nightclouds there all the time? Looks like a phantom ship. No. Wait. Trees are they? An optical illusion. Mirage. Land of the setting sun this. Homerule sun setting in the southeast. My native land, goodnight.

Dew falling. Bad for you, dear, to sit on that stone. Brings on white fluxions. Never have little baby then less he was big strong fight his way up through. Might get piles myself. Sticks too like a summer cold, sore on the mouth. Cut with grass or paper worst. Friction of the position. Like to be that rock she sat on. O sweet little, you don't know how nice you looked. I begin to like them at that age. Green apples. Grab at all that offer. Suppose it's the only time we cross legs, seated. Also the library today: those girl graduates. Happy chairs under them. But it's the evening influence. They feel all that. Open like flowers, know their hours, sunflowers, Jerusalem artichokes, in ballrooms, chandeliers, avenues under the lamps. Nightstock in Mat Dillon's garden where I kissed her shoulder. Wish I had a full length oilpainting of her then. June that was too I wooed. The year returns. History repeats itself. Ye crags and peaks I'm with you once again. Life, love, voyage round your own little world. And now? Sad about her lame of course but must be on your guard not to feel too much pity. They take advantage.

All quiet on Howth now. The distant hills seem. Where we. The rhododendrons. I am a fool perhaps. He gets the plums and I the plumstones. Where I come in. All that old hill has seen. Names change: that's all. Lovers: yum yum.

Tired I feel now. Will I get up? O wait. Drained all the manhood out of me, little wretch. She kissed me. My youth. Never again. Only once it comes. Or hers. Take the train there tomorrow. No. Returning not the same. Like kids your second visit to a house. The new I want. Nothing new under the sun. Care of P. O. Dolphin's barn. Are you not happy in your? Naughty darling. At Dolphin's barn charades in Luke Doyle's house. Mat Dillon and his bevy of daughters: Tiny, Atty, Floey, Maimy, Louy, Hetty. Molly too. Eightyseven that was. Year before we. And the old major partial to his drop of spirits. Curious she an only child, I an only child. So it returns. Think you're escaping and run into yourself. Longest way round is the shortest way home. And just when he and she. Circus horse walking in a ring. Rip van Winkle we played. Rip: tear in Henny Doyle's overcoat. Van: breadvan delivering. Winkle: cockles and periwinkles. Then I did Rip van Winkle coming back. She leaned on the sideboard watching. Moorish eyes. Twenty years asleep in Sleepy Hollow. All changed. Forgotten. The young are old. His gun rusty from the dew.

Ba. What is that flying about? Swallow? Bat probably. Thinks I'm a tree, so blind. Have birds no smell? Metempsychosis. They believed you could be changed into a tree from grief. Weeping willow. Ba. There he goes. Funny little beggar. Wonder where he lives. Belfry up there. Very likely. Hanging by his heels in the odour of sanctity. Bell scared him out, I suppose. Mass seems to be over. Could hear them all at it. Pray for us. And pray for us. And pray for us. Good idea the repetition. Same thing with ads. Buy from us. And buy from us. Yes, there's the light in the priest's house. Their frugal meal. Remember about the mistake in the valuation when I was in Thom's. Twentyeight it is. Two houses they have. Gabriel Conroy's brother is curate. Ba. Again. Wonder why they come out at night like mice. They're a mixed breed. Birds are like hopping mice. What frightens them, light or noise? Better sit still. All instinct like the bird in drouth got water out of the end of a jar by throwing in pebbles. Like a little man in a cloak he is with tiny hands. Weeny bones. Almost see them shimmering, kind of a bluey white. Colours depend on the light you see. Stare the sun for example like the eagle then look at a shoe see a blotch blob yellowish. Wants to stamp his trademark on everything. Instance, that cat this morning on the staircase. Colour of brown turf. Say you never see them with three colours. Not true. That half tabbywhite tortoiseshell in the *City Arms* with the letter em on her forehead. Body fifty different colours. Howth a while ago amethyst. Glass flashing. That's how that wise man what's his name with the burning glass. Then the heather goes on fire. It can't be tourists' matches. What? Perhaps the sticks dry rub together in the wind and light. Or broken bottles in the furze act as a burning glass in the sun. Archimedes. I have it! My memory's not so bad.

Ba. Who knows what they're always flying for. Insects? That bee last week got into the room playing with his shadow on the ceiling. Might be the one bit me, come back to see. Birds too never find out what they say. Like our small talk. And says she and says he. Nerve they have to fly over the ocean and back. Lot must be killed in storms, telegraph wires. Dreadful life sailors have too. Big brutes of oceangoing steamers floundering along in the dark, lowing out like seacows. *Faugh a ballagh*. Out of that, bloody curse to you. Others in vessels, bit of a handkerchief sail, pitched about like snuff at a wake when the stormy winds do blow. Married too. Sometimes away for years at the ends of the earth somewhere. No ends really because it's round. Wife in every port they say. She has a good job if she minds it till Johnny comes marching home again. If ever he does. Smelling the tail end of ports. How can they like the sea? Yet they do. The anchor's weighed. Off he sails with a scapular or a medal on him for luck. Well? And the tephilim no what's this they call it poor papa's father had on his door to touch. That brought us out of the land of Egypt and into the house of bondage. Something in all those superstitions because when you go out never know what dangers. Hanging on to a plank or astride of a beam for grim life, lifebelt round round him, gulping salt water, and that's the last of his nibs till the sharks catch hold of him. Do fish ever get seasick?

Then you have a beautiful calm without a cloud, smooth sea, placid, crew and cargo in smithereens, Davy Jones' locker. Moon looking down. Not my fault, old cockalorum.

A lost long candle wandered up the sky from Mirus bazaar in search of funds for Mercer's hospital and broke, drooping, and shed a cluster of violet but one white stars. They floated, fell: they faded. The shepherd's hour: the hour of holding: hour of tryst. From house to house, giving his everwelcome double knock, went the nine o'clock postman, the glowworm's lamp at his belt gleaming here and there through the laurel hedges. And among the five young trees a hoisted lintstock lit the lamp at Leahy's terrace. By screens of lighted windows, by equal gardens a shrill voice went crying, wailing: *Evening Telegraph, stop press edition! Result of the Gold Cup race!* and from the door of Dignam's house a boy ran out and called. Twittering the bat flew here, flew there. Far out over the sands the coming surf crept, grey. Howth settled for slumber tired of long days, of yumyum rhododendrons (he was old) and felt gladly the night breeze lift, ruffle his fell of ferns. He lay but opened a red eye unsleeping, deep and slowly breathing, slumberous but awake. And far on Kish bank the anchored lightship twinkled, winked at Mr Bloom.

Life those chaps out there must have, stuck in the same spot. Irish Lights board. Penance for their sins. Coastguards too. Rocket and breeches buoy and lifeboat. Day we went out for the pleasure cruise in the Erin's King, throwing them the sack of old papers. Bears in the zoo. Filthy trip. Drunkards out to shake up their livers. Puking overboard to feed the herrings. Nausea. And the women, fear of God in their faces. Milly, no sign of funk. Her blue scarf loose, laughing. Don't know what death is at that age. And then their stomachs clean. But being lost they fear. When we hid behind the tree at Crumlin. I didn't want to. Mamma! Mamma! Babes in the wood. Frightening them with masks too. Throwing them up in the air to catch them. I'll murder you. Is it only half fun? Or children playing battle. Whole earnest. How can people aim guns at each other? Sometimes they go off. Poor kids. Only troubles wildfire and nettlerash. Calomel purge I got her for that. After getting better asleep with Molly. Very same teeth she has. What do they love? Another themselves? But the morning she chased her with the umbrella. Perhaps so as not to hurt. I felt her pulse. Ticking. Little hand it was: now big. Dearest Papli. All that the hand says when you touch. Loved to count my waistcoat buttons. Her first stays I remember. Made me laugh to see. Little paps to begin with. Left one is more sensitive, I think. Mine too. Nearer the heart. Padding themselves out if fat is in fashion. Her growing pains at night, calling, wakening me. Frightened she was when her nature came on her first. Poor child! Strange moment for the mother too. Brings back her girlhood. Gibraltar. Looking from Buena Vista. O'Hara's tower. The seabirds screaming. Old Barbary ape that gobbled all his family. Sundown, gunfire for the men to cross the lines. Looking out over the sea she told me. Evening like this, but clear, no clouds. I always thought I'd marry a lord or a gentleman with a private yacht. *Buenas noches, señorita. El hombre ama la muchacha hermosa.* Why me? Because you were so foreign from the others.

Better not stick here all night like a limpet. This weather makes you dull.

Must be getting on for nine by the light. Go home. Too late for *Leah*, *Lily of Killarney*. No. Might be still up. Call to the hospital to see. Hope she's over. Long day I've had. Martha, the bath, funeral, house of keys, museum with those goddesses, Dedalus' song. Then that bawler in Barney Kiernan's. Got my own back there. Drunken ranters. What I said about his God made him wince. Mistake to hit back. Or? No. Ought to go home and laugh at themselves. Always want to be swilling in company. Afraid to be alone like a child of two. Suppose he hit me. Look at it other way round. Not so bad then. Perhaps not to hurt he meant. Three cheers for Israel. Three cheers for the sister-in-law he hawked about, three fangs in her mouth. Same style of beauty. Particularly nice old party for a cup of tea. The sister of the wife of the wild man of Borneo has just come to town. Imagine that in the early morning at close range. Everyone to his taste as Morris said when he kissed the cow. But Dignam's put the boots on it. Houses of mourning so depressing because you never know. Anyhow she wants the money. Must call to those Scottish widows as I promised. Strange name. Takes it for granted we're going to pop off first. That widow on Monday was it outside Cramer's that looked at me. Buried the poor husband but progressing favourably on the premium. Her widow's mite. Well? What do you expect her to do? Must wheedle her way along. Widower I hate to see. Looks so forlorn. Poor man O'Connor wife and five children poisoned by mussels here. The sewage. Hopeless. Some good matronly woman in a porkpie hat to mother him. Take him in tow, platter face and a large apron. Ladies' grey flannelette bloomers, three shillings a pair, astonishing bargain. Plain and loved, loved for ever, they say. Ugly: no woman thinks she is. Love, lie and be handsome for tomorrow we die. See him sometimes walking about trying to find out who played the trick. U. p.: up. Fate that is. He, not me. Also a shop often noticed. Curse seems to dog it. Dreamt last night? Wait. Something confused. She had red slippers on. Turkish. Wore the breeches. Suppose she does. Would I like her in pyjamas? Damned hard to answer. Nannetti's gone. Mail-boat. Near Holyhead by now. Must nail that ad of Keyes's. Work Hynes and Crawford. Petticoats for Molly. She has something to put in them. What's that? Might be money.

Mr Bloom stooped and turned over a piece of paper on the strand. He brought it near his eyes and peered. Letter? No. Can't read. Better go. Better. I'm tired to move. Page of an old copybook. All those holes and pebbles. Who could count them? Never know what you find. Bottle with story of a treasure in it thrown from a wreck. Parcels post. Children always want to throw things in the sea. Trust? Bread cast on the waters. What's this? Bit of stick.

O! Exhausted that female has me. Not so young now. Will she come here tomorrow? Wait for her somewhere for ever. Must come back. Murderers do. Will I?

Mr Bloom with his stick gently vexed the thick sand at his foot. Write a message for her. Might remain. What?

I.

Some flatfoot tramp on it in the morning. Useless. Washed away. Tide comes here a pool near her foot. Bend, see my face there, dark mirror, breathe on it, stirs. All these rocks with lines and scars and letters. O, those transparent! Besides they don't know. What is the meaning of that other world. I called you naughty boy because I do not like.

AM. A.

No room. Let it go.

Mr Bloom effaced the letters with his slow boot. Hopeless thing sand. Nothing grows in it. All fades. No fear of big vessels coming up here. Except Guinness's barges. Round the Kish in eighty days. Done half by design.

He flung his wooden pen away. The stick fell in silted sand, stuck. Now if you were trying to do that for a week on end you couldn't. Chance. We'll never meet again. But it was lovely. Goodbye, dear. Thanks. Made me feel so young.

Short snooze now if I had. Must be near nine. Liverpool boat long gone. Not even the smoke. And she can do the other. Did too. And Belfast. I won't go. Race there, race back to Ennis. Let him. Just close my eyes a moment. Won't sleep though. Half dream. It never comes the same. Bat again. No harm in him. Just a few.

O sweety all your little girlwhite up I saw dirty bracegirdle made me do love sticky we two naughty Grace darling she him half past the bed met him pike hoses frillies for Raoul to perfume your wife black hair heave under embon *señorita* young eyes Mulvey plump years dreams return tail end Agendath swoony lovey showed me her next year in drawers return next in her next her next.

A bat flew. Here. There. Here. Far in the grey a bell chimed. Mr Bloom with open mouth, his left boot sanded sideways, leaned, breathed. Just for a few.

Cuckoo.
Cuckoo.
Cuckoo.

The clock on the mantelpiece in the priest's house cooed where Canon

O'Hanlon and Father Conroy and the reverend John Hughes S. J. were taking tea and sodabread and butter and fried mutton chops with catsup and talking about

Cuckoo.

Cuckoo.

Cuckoo.

Because it was a little canarybird bird that came out of its little house to tell the time that Gerty MacDowell noticed the time she was there because she was as quick anything about a thing like that, was Gerty MacDowell, and she noticed at once that that foreign gentleman that was sitting on the rocks looking was

Cuckoo.

Cuckoo.

Cuckoo.

* * * * *

◀ DESHIL HOLLES EAMUS. DESHIL HOLLES EAMUS. Deshil Holles Eamus.

Send us, bright one, light one, Horhorn, quickening and wombfruit. Send us, bright one, light one, Horhorn, quickening and wombfruit. Send us bright one, light one, Horhorn, quickening and wombfruit.

Hoopsa, boyaboy, hoopsa! Hoopsa, boyaboy, hoopsa! Hoopsa, boyaboy, hoopsa.

Universally that person's acumen is esteemed very little perceptive concerning whatsoever matters are being held as most profitably by mortals with sapience endowed to be studied who is ignorant of that which the most in doctrine erudite and certainly by reason of that in them high mind's ornament deserving of veneration constantly maintain when by general consent they affirm that other circumstances being equal by no exterior splendour is the prosperity of a nation more efficaciously asserted than by the measure of how far forward may have progressed the tribute of its solicitude for that proliferent continuance which of evils the original if it be absent when fortunately present constitutes the certain sign of omnipollent nature's incorrupted benefaction. For who is there who anything of some significance has apprehended but is conscious that that exterior splendour may be the surface of a downwardtending lutulent reality or on the contrary anyone so is there inilluminated as not to perceive that as no nature's boon can contend against the bounty of increase so it behoves every most just citizen to become the exhortator and admonisher of his semblables and to tremble lest what had in the past been by the nation excellently commenced might be in the future not with similar excellence accomplished if an inverecund habit shall have gradually traduced the honourable by ancestors transmitted customs to that thither of profundity that that one was audacious excessively who would have the hardihood to rise affirming that no more odious offence can for anyone be than to oblivious neglect to consign that evangel simultaneously command and promise which on all mortals with prophecy of abundance or with diminution's menace that exalted of reiteratedly procreating function ever irrevocably enjoined?

It is not why therefore we shall wonder if, as the best historians relate, among the Celts who nothing that was not in its nature admirable admired, the art of medicine shall have been highly honoured. Not to speak of hostels, leperyards, sweating chambers, plaguegraves, their greatest doctors, the O'Shiels, the O'Hickeys, the O'Lees, have sedulously set down the divers methods by which the sick and the relapsed found again health whether the malady had been the trembling withering or loose boyconnell flux. Certainly in every public work which in it anything of gravity contains preparation should be with importance commensurate and therefore a plan was by them adopted (whether by having preconsidered or as the maturation of experience it is difficult in being said which the discrepant opinions of subsequent inquirers are not up to the present congrued to render manifest) whereby maternity was so far from all accident possibility removed that whatever care the patient in that allhardest of woman hour chiefly required and not solely for the copiously opulent but also for her who not being sufficiently moneyed scarcely and often not even scarcely could subsist valiantly and for an inconsiderable emolument was provided.

To her nothing already then and thenceforward was anyway able to be molestful for this chiefly felt all citizens except with proliferent mothers prosperity at all not to can be and as they had received eternity gods mortals generation to befit them her beholding, when the case was so having itself, parturient in vehicle thereward carrying desire immense among all one another was impelling on of her to be received into that domicile. O thing of prudent nation not merely in being seen but also even in being related worthy of being praised that they her by anticipation went seeing mother, that she by them suddenly to be about to be cherished had been begun she felt!

Before born babe bliss had. Within womb won he worship. Whatever in that one case done commodiously done was. A couch by midwives attended with wholesome food reposeful cleanest swaddles as though forthbringing were now done and by wise foresight set: but to this no less of what drugs there is need and surgical implements which are pertaining to her case not omitting aspect of all very distracting spectacles in various latitudes by our terrestrial orb offered together with images, divine and human, the cogitation of which by sejunct females is to tumescence conducive or eases issue in the high sunbright wellbuilt fair home of mothers when, ostensibly far gone and reproductitive, it is come by her thereto to lie in, her term up.

Some man that wayfaring was stood by housedoor at night's oncoming. Of Israel's folk was that man that on earth wandering far had fared. Stark ruth of man his errand that him lone led till that house.

Of that house A. Horne is lord. Seventy beds keeps he there teeming mothers are wont that they lie for to thole and bring forth bairns hale so God's angel to Mary quoth. Watchers twey there walk, white sisters in ward sleepless. Smarts they still sickness soothing: in twelve moons thrice an hundred. Truest bedthanes they twain are, for Horne holding wariest ward.

In ward wary the watcher hearing come that man mildhearted eft rising with swire ywimpled to him her gate wide undid. Lo, levin leaping lightens in eyeblink Ireland's westward welkin! Full she dread that God the Wreaker all mankind would fordo with water for his evil sins. Christ's rood made she on breastbone and him drew that he would rathe infare under her thatch. That man her will wotting worthful went in Horne's house.

Loth to irk in Horne's hall hat holding the seeker stood. On her stow he ere was living with dear wife and lovesome daughter that then over land and seafloor nine years had long outwandered. Once her in townhithe meeting he to her bow had not doffed. Her to forgive now he craved with good ground of her allowed that that of him swiftseen face, hers, so young then had looked. Light swift her eyes kindled, bloom of blushes his word winning.

As her eyes then ongot his weeds swart therefor sorrow she feared. Glad after she was that ere adread was. Her he asked if O'Hare Doctor tidings sent from far coast and she with grameful sigh him answered that O'Hare Doctor in heaven was. Sad was the man that word to hear that him so heavied in bowels ruthful. All she there told him, ruing death for friend so young, algate sore unwilling God's rightwiseness to withsay. She said that he had a fair sweet death through God His goodness with masspriest to be shriven, holy housel and sick men's oil to his limbs. The man then right earnest asked the nun of which death the dead man was died and the nun answered him and said that he was died in Mona island through bellycrab three year agone come Childermas and she prayed to God the Allruthful to have his dear soul in his undeathliness. He heard her sad words, in held hat sad staring. So stood they there both awhile in wanhope, sorrowing one with other.

Therefore, everyman, look to that last end that is thy death and the dust that gripeth on every man that is born of woman for as he came naked forth from his mother's womb so naked shall he wend him at the last for to go as he came.

The man that was come into the house then spoke to the nursingwoman and he asked her how it fared with the woman that lay there in childbed. The nursingwoman answered him and said that that woman was in throes now full three days and that it would be a hard birth unneth to bear but that now in a little it would be. She said thereto that she had seen many births of women but never was none so hard as was that woman's birth. Then she set it forth all to him that time was had lived nigh that house. The man hearkened to her words for he felt with wonder women's woe in the travail that they have of motherhood and he wondered to look on her face that was a young face for any man to see but yet was she left after long years a handmaid. Nine twelve bloodflows chiding her childless.

And whiles they spake the door of the castle was opened and there nighed them a mickle noise as of many that sat there at meat. And there came against the place as they stood a young learning knight yclept Dixon. And the traveller Leopold was couth to him sithen it had happed that they had had ado each with other in the house of misericord where this learning knight lay by cause the traveller Leopold came there to be healed for he was sore wounded in his breast by a spear wherewith a horrible and dreadful dragon was smitten him for which he did do make a salve of volatile salt and chrism as much as he might suffice. And he said now that he should go into that castle for to make merry with them that were there. And the traveller Leopold said that he should go otherwhither for he was a man of cautels and a subtle. Also the lady was of his avis and reproved the learning knight though she trowed well that the traveller had said thing that was false for his subtility. But the learning knight would not hear say nay nor do her mandement ne have him in aught contrarious to his list and he said how it was a marvellous castle. And the traveller Leopold went into the castle for to rest him for a space being sore of limb after many marches environing in divers lands and sometimes venery.

And in the castle was set a board that was of the birchwood of Finlandy and it was upheld by four dwarfmen of that country but they durst not move more for enchantment. And on this board were frightful swords and knives that are made in a great cavern by swinking demons out of white flames that they fix in the horns of buffalos and stags that there abound marvellously. And there were vessels that are wrought by magic of Mahound out of seasand and the air by a warlock with his breath that he blares into them like to bubbles. And full fair cheer and rich was on the board that no wight could devise a fuller ne richer. And there was a vat of silver that was moved by craft to open in the which lay strange fishes withouten heads though misbelieving men nie that this be possible thing without they see it natheless they are so. And these fishes lie in an oily water brought there from Portugal land because of the fatness that therein is like to the juices of the olive press. And also it was marvel to see in that castle how by magic they make a compost out of fecund wheat kidneys out of Chaldee that by aid of certain angry spirits that they do into it swells up wondrously like to a vast mountain. And they teach the serpents there to entwine themselves up on long sticks out of the ground and of the scales of these serpents they brew out a brewage like to mead.

And the learning knight let pour for childe Leopold a draught and halp thereto the while all they that were there drank every each. And childe Leopold did up his beaver for to pleasure him and took apertly somewhat in amity for he never drank no manner of mead which he then put by and anon full privily he voided the more part in his neighbour glass and his neighbour nist not of his wile. And he sat down in that castle with them for to rest him there awhile. Thanked be Almighty God.

This meanwhile this good sister stood by the door and begged them at the reverence of Jesu our alther liege lord to leave their wassailing for there was above one quick with child a gentle dame, whose time hied fast. Sir Leopold heard on the upfloor cry on high and he wondered what cry that it was whether of child or woman and I marvel, said he, that it be not come or now. Meseems it dureth overlong. And he was ware and saw a franklin that hight Lenehan on that side the table that was older than any of the tother and for that they both were knights virtuous in the one emprise and eke by cause that he was elder he spoke to him full gently. But, said he, or it be long too she will bring forth by God His bounty and have joy of her childing for she hath waited marvellous long. And the franklin that had drunken said, Expecting each moment to be her next. Also he took the cup that stood tofore him for him needed never none asking nor desiring of him to drink and, Now drink, said he, fully delectably, and he quaffed as far as he might to their both's health for he was a passing good man of his lustiness. And sir Leopold that was the goodliest guest that ever sat in scholars' hall and that was the meekest man and the kindest that ever laid

husbandly hand under hen and that was the very truest knight of the world
one that ever did minion service to lady gentle pledged him courtly in the
cup. Woman's woe with wonder pondering.

Now let us speak of that fellowship that was there to the intent to be
drunken an they might. There was a sort of scholars along either side the
board, that is to wit, Dixon yclept junior of saint Mary Merciable's with
other his fellows Lynch and Madden, scholars of medicine, and the franklin
that hight Lenehan and one from Alba Longa, one Crotthers, and young
Stephen that had mien of a frere that was at head of the board and Costello
that men clepen Punch Costello all long of a mastery of him erewhile
gested (and of all them, reserved young Stephen, he was the most drunken
that demanded still of more mead) and beside the meek sir Leopold. But on
young Malachi they waited for that he promised to have come and such as
intended to no goodness said how he had broke his avow. And sir Leopold
sat with them for he bore fast friendship to sir Simon and to this his son
young Stephen and for that his languor becalmed him there after longest
wanderings insomuch as they feasted him for that time in the honourablest
manner. Ruth red him, love led on with will to wander, loth to leave.

For they were right witty scholars. And he heard their aresouns each gen
other as touching birth and righteousness, young Madden maintaining that
put such case it were hard the wife to die (for so it had fallen out a matter of
some year agone with a woman of Eblana in Horne's house that now was
trespassed out of this world and the self night next before her death all
leeches and pothecaries had taken counsel of her case). And they said farther
she should live because in the beginning they said the woman should bring
forth in pain and wherefore they that were of this imagination affirmed
how young Madden had said truth for he had conscience to let her die. And
not few and of these was young Lynch were in doubt that the world was
now right evil governed as it was never other howbeit the mean people
believed it otherwise but the law nor his judges did provide no remedy. A
redress God grant. This was scant said but all cried with one acclaim nay,
by our Virgin Mother, the wife should live and the babe to die. In colour
whereof they waxed hot upon that head what with argument and what for
their drinking but the franklin Lenehan was prompt each when to pour
them ale so that at the least way mirth might not lack. Then young Madden
showed all the whole affair and when he said how that she was dead and
how for holy religion sake by rede of palmer and bedesman and for a vow
he had made to Saint Ultan of Arbraccan her goodman husband would not
let her death whereby they were all wondrous grieved. To whom young
Stephen had these words following, Murmur, sirs, is eke oft among lay folk.

Both babe and parent now glorify their Maker, the one in limbo gloom, the other in purge fire. But, gramercy, what of those Godpossibled souls that we nightly impossibilise, which is the sin against the Holy Ghost, Very God, Lord and Giver of Life? For, sirs, he said, our lust is brief. We are means to those small creatures within us and nature has other ends than we. Then said Dixon junior to Punch Costello wist he what ends. But he had overmuch drunken and the best word he could have of him was that he would ever dishonest a woman whoso she were or wife or maid or leman if it so fortuned him to be delivered of his spleen of lustihead. Whereat Crotthers of Alba Longa sang young Malachi's praise of that beast the unicorn how once in the millennium he cometh by his horn the other all this while pricked forward with their jibes wherewith they did malice him, witnessing all and several by saint Foutinus his engines that he was able to do any manner of thing that lay in man to do. Thereat laughed they all right jocundly only young Stephen and sir Leopold which never durst laugh too open by reason of a strange humour which he would not bewray and also for that he rued for her that bare whoso she might be or wheresoever. Then spoke young Stephen orgulous of mother Church that would cast him out of her bosom, of law of canons, of Lilith, patron of abortions, of bigness wrought by wind of seeds of brightness or by potency of vampires mouth to mouth or, as Virgilius saith, by the influence of the occident or by the reek of moonflower or an she lie with a woman which her man has but lain with, *effectu secuto*, or peradventure in her bath according to the opinions of Averroes and Moses Maimonides. He said also how at the end of the second month a human soul was infused and how in all our holy mother foldeth ever souls for God's greater glory whereas that earthly mother which was but a dam to bring forth beastly should die by canon for so saith he that holdeth the fisherman's seal, even that blessed Peter on which rock was holy church for all ages founded. All they bachelors then asked of sir Leopold would he in like case so jeopard her person as risk life to save life. A wariness of mind he would answer as fitted all and, laying hand to jaw, he said dissembling, as his wont was, that as it was informed him, who had ever loved the art of physic as might a layman, and agreeing also with his experience of so seldom seen an accident it was good for that Mother Church belike at one blow had birth and death pence and in such sort deliverly he scaped their questions. That is truth, pardy, said Dixon, and, or I err, a pregnant word. Which hearing young Stephen was a marvellous glad man and he averred that he who stealeth from the poor lendeth to the Lord for he was of a wild manner when he was drunken and that he was now in that taking it appeared eftsoons.

But sir Leopold was passing grave maugre his word by cause he still had pity of the terrorcausing shrieking of shrill women in their labour and as he was minded of his good lady Marion that had borne him an only manchild which on his eleventh day on live had died and no man of art could save so dark is destiny. And she was wondrous stricken of heart for that evil hap and for his burial did him on a fair corselet of lamb's wool, the flower of the flock, lest he might perish utterly and lie akeled (for it was then about the midst of the winter) and now sir Leopold that had of his body no manchild for an heir looked upon him his friend's son and was shut up in sorrow for his forepassed happiness and as sad as he was that him failed a son of such gentle courage (for all accounted him of real parts) so grieved he also in no less measure for young Stephen for that he lived riotously with those wastrels and murdered his goods with whores.

About that present time young Stephen filled all cups that stood empty so as there remained but little mo if the prudenter had not shadowed their approach from him that still plied it very busily who, praying for the intentions of the sovereign pontiff, he gave them for a pledge the vicar of Christ which also as he said is vicar of Bray. Now drink we, quod he, of this mazer and quaff ye this mead which is not indeed parcel of my body but my soul's bodiment. Leave ye fraction of bread to them that live by bread alone. Be not afeard neither for any want for this will comfort more than the other will dismay. See ye here. And he showed them glistering coins of the tribute and goldsmiths' notes the worth of two pound nineteen shilling that he had, he said, for a song which he writ. They all admired to see the foresaid riches in such dearth of money as was herebefore. His words were then these as followeth: Know all men, he said, time's ruins build eternity's mansions. What means this? Desire's wind blasts the thorntree but after it becomes from a bramblebush to be a rose upon the rood of time. Mark me now. In woman's womb word is made flesh but in the spirit of the maker all flesh that passes becomes the word that shall not pass away. This is the postcreation. *Omnis caro ad te veniet.* No question but her name is puissant who aventried the dear corse of our Agenbuyer, Healer and Herd, our mighty mother and mother most venerable and Bernardus saith aptly that she hath an *omnipotentiam deiparae supplicem*, that is to wit, an almightiness of petition because she is the second Eve and she won us, saith Augustine too, whereas that other, our grandam, which we are linked up with by successive anastomosis of navelcords sold us all, seed, breed and generation, for a penny pippin. But here is the matter now. Or she knew him, that second I say, and was but creature of her creature, *vergine madre figlia di tuo figlio* or she knew him not and then stands she in the one denial or ignorancy with Peter Piscator who lives in the house that Jack built and with Joseph the Joiner patron of the happy demise of all unhappy marriages *parce que M. Léo Taxil nous a dit que qui l'avait mise dans cette fichue position c'était le sacré pigeon, ventre de Dieu! Entweder* transsubstantiality *oder* consubstantiality but in no case subsubstantiality. And all cried out upon it for a very scurvy word. A pregnancy without joy, he said, a birth without pangs, a body without blemish, a belly without bigness. Let the lewd with faith and fervour worship. With will will we withstand, withsay.

Hereupon Punch Costello dinged with his fist upon the board and would sing a bawdy catch *Staboo Stabella* about a wench that was put in pod of a jolly swashbuckler in Almany which he did now attack: *The first three months she was not well, Staboo*, when here nurse Quigley from the door angerly bid them hist ye should shame you nor was it not meet as she remembered them being her mind was to have all orderly against lord Andrew came for because she was jealous that no gasteful turmoil might shorten the honour of her guard. It was an ancient and a sad matron of a sedate look and christian walking, in habit dun beseeming her megrims and wrinkled visage, nor did her hortative want of it effect for incontinently Punch Costello was of them all embraided and they reclaimed the churl with civil rudeness some and with menace of blandishments others whiles all chode with him, a murrain seize the dolt, what a devil he would be at, thou chuff, thou puny, thou got in the peasestraw, thou losel, thou chitterling, thou spawn of a rebel, thou dykedropt, thou abortion thou, to shut up his drunken drool out of that like a curse of God ape, the good sir Leopold that had for his cognisance the flower of quiet, margerain gentle, advising also the time's occasion as most sacred and most worthy to be most sacred. In Horne's house rest should reign.

To be short this passage was scarce by when Master Dixon of Mary in Eccles, goodly grinning, asked young Stephen what was the reason why he had not cided to take friar's vows and he answered him obedience in the womb, chastity in the tomb but involuntary poverty all his days. Master Lenehan at this made return that he had heard of those nefarious deeds and how, as he heard hereof counted, he had besmirched the lily virtue of a confiding female which was corruption of minors and they all intershowed it too, waxing merry and toasting to his fathership. But he said very entirely it was clean contrary to their suppose for he was the eternal son and ever virgin. Thereat mirth grew in them the more and they rehearsed to him his curious rite of wedlock for the disrobing and deflowering of spouses, as the priests use in Madagascar island, she to be in guise of white and saffron, her groom in white and grain, with burning of nard and tapers, on a bridebed while clerks sung kyries and the anthem *Ut novetur sexus omnis corporis mysterium* till she was there unmaided. He gave them then a much admirable hymen minim by those delicate poets Master John Fletcher and Master Francis Beaumont that is in their *Maid's Tragedy* that was writ for a like twining of lovers: *To bed, to bed*, was the burden of it to be played with accompanable concent upon the virginals. An exquisite dulcet epithalame of most mollificative suadency for juveniles amatory whom the odoriferous flambeaus of the paranymphs have escorted to the quadrupedal proscenium of connubial communion. Well met they were, said Master Dixon, joyed, but, harkee, young sir, better were they named Beau Mount and Lecher for, by my troth, of such a mingling much might come. Young Stephen said indeed to his best remembrance they had but the one doxy between them and she of the stews to make shift with in delights amorous for life ran very high in those days and the custom of the country approved with it. Greater love than this, he said, no man hath that a man lay down his wife for his friend. Go thou and do likewise. Thus, or words to that effect, saith Zarathustra, sometime regius professor of French letters to the university of Oxtail nor breathed there ever that man to whom mankind was more beholden. Bring a stranger within thy tower it will go hard but thou wilt have the secondbest bed. *Orate, fratres, pro memetipso.* And all the people shall say, Amen. Remember, Erin, thy generations and thy days of old, how thou settedst little by me and by my word and broughtest in a stranger to my gates to commit fornication in my sight and to wax fat and kick like Jeshurum. Therefore hast thou sinned against the light and hast made me, thy lord, to be the slave of servants. Return, return, Clan Milly: forget me not, O Milesian. Why hast thou done this abomination before me that thou didst spurn me for a merchant of jalaps and didst deny me to the Roman and the Indian of dark speech with whom thy daughters did lie luxuriously? Look forth now, my people, upon the land of behest, even from Horeb and from Nebo and from Pisgah and from the Horns of Hatten unto a land flowing with milk and money. But thou hast suckled me with a bitter milk: my moon and my sun thou hast quenched for ever. And thou hast left me alone for ever in the dark ways of my bitterness: and with a kiss of ashes hast thou kissed my mouth. This tenebrosity of the interior, he proceeded to say, hath not been illumined by the wit of the septuagint nor so much as mentioned for the Orient from on high which brake hell's gates visited a darkness that was foraneous. Assuefaction minorates atrocities (as Tully saith of his darling Stoics) and Hamlet his father showeth the prince no blister of combustion. The adiaphane in the noon of life is an Egypt's plague which in the nights of prenativity and postmortemity is their most proper *ubi* and *quomodo*. And as the ends and ultimates of all things accord in some mean and measure with their inceptions and originals, that same multiplicit concordance which leads forth growth from birth accomplishing by a retrogressive metamorphosis that minishing and ablation towards the final which is agreeable unto nature so is it with our subsolar being. The aged sisters draw us into life: we wail, batten, sport, clip, clasp, sunder, dwindle, die: over us dead they bend. First saved from water of old Nile, among bulrushes, a bed of fasciated wattles: at last the cavity of a mountain, an occulted sepulchre amid the conclamation of the hillcat and the ossifrage. And as no man knows the ubicity of his tumulus nor to what processes we shall thereby be ushered nor whether to Tophet or to Edenville in the like way is all hidden when we would backward see from what region of remoteness the whatness of our whoness hath fetched his whenceness.

Thereto Punch Costello roared out mainly *Étienne chanson* but he loudly bid them lo, wisdom hath built herself a house, this vast majestic long-stablished vault, the crystal palace of the Creator all in applepie order, a penny for him who finds the pea.

> Behold the mansion reared by dedal Jack,
> See the malt stored in many a refluent sack,
> In the proud cirque of Jackjohn's bivouac.

A black crack of noise in the street here, alack, bawled, back. Loud on left Thor thundered: in anger awful the hammerhurler. Came now the storm that hist his heart. And Master Lynch bade him have a care to flout and witwanton as the god self was angered for his hellprate and paganry. And he that had erst challenged to be so doughty waxed pale as they might all mark and shrank together and his pitch that was before so haught uplift was now of a sudden quite plucked down and his heart shook within the cage of his breast as he tasted the rumour of that storm. Then did some mock and some jeer and Punch Costello fell hard again to his yale which Master Lenehan vowed he would do after and he was indeed but a word and a blow on any the least colour. But the braggart boaster cried that an old Nobodaddy was in his cups it was muchwhat indifferent and he would not lag behind his lead. But this was only to dye his desperation as cowed he crouched in Horne's hall. He drank indeed at one draught to pluck up a heart of any grace for it thundered long rumblingly over all the heavens so that Master Madden, being godly certain whiles, knocked him on his ribs upon that crack of doom and Master Bloom, at the braggart' side spoke to him calming words to slumber his great fear, advertising how it was no other thing but a hubbub noise that he heard, the discharge of fluid from the thunderhead, look you, having taken place, and all of the order of a natural phenomenon.

But was young Boasthard's fear vanquished by Calmer's words? No, for he had in his bosom a spike named Bitterness which could not by words be done away. And was he then neither calm like the one nor godly like the other? He was neither as much as he would have liked to be either. But could he not have endeavoured to have found again as in his youth the bottle Holiness that then he lived withal? Indeed not for Grace was not there to find that bottle. Heard he then in that clap the voice of the god Bringforth or, what Calmer said, a hubbub of Phenomenon? Heard? Why, he could not but hear unless he had plugged up the tube Understanding (which he had not done). For through that tube he saw that he was in the land of Phenomenon where he must for a certain one day die as he was like the rest too a passing show. And would he not accept to die like the rest and pass away? By no means would he and make more shows according as men do with wives which Phenomenon has commanded them to do by the book Law. Then wotted he nought of that other land which is called Believe-on-Me, that is the land of promise which behoves to the king Delightful and shall be for ever where there is no death and no birth neither wiving nor mothering at which all shall come as many as believe on it? Yes, Pious had told him of that land and Chaste had pointed him to the way but the reason was that in the way he fell in with a certain whore of an eyepleasing exterior whose name, she said, is Bird-in-the-Hand and she beguiled him wrong-ways from the true path by her flatteries that she said to him as, Ho, you pretty man, turn aside hither and I will show you a brave place, and she lay at him so flatteringly that she had him in her grot which is named Two-in-the-Bush or, by some learned, Carnal Concupiscence.

This was it what all that company that sat there at commons in Manse of Mothers the most lusted after and if they met with this whore Bird-in-the-Hand (which was within all foul plagues, monsters and a wicked devil) they would strain the last but they would make at her and know her. For regarding Believe-on-Me they said it was nought else but notion and they could conceive no thought of it for, first, Two-in-the-Bush whither she ticed them was the very goodliest grot and in it were four pillows on which were four tickets with these words printed on them, Pickaback and Topsy-turvy and Shameface and Cheek by Jowl and, second, for that foul plague Allpox and the monsters they cared not for them, for Preservative had given them a stout shield of oxengut and, third, that they might take no hurt neither from Offspring that was that wicked devil by virtue of this same shield which was named Killchild. So were they all in their blind

fancy, Mr Cavil and Mr Sometimes Godly, Mr Ape Swillale, Mr False
Franklin, Mr Dainty Dixon, Young Boasthard and Mr Cautious Calmer.
Wherein, O wretched company, were ye all deceived for that was the voice
of the god that was in a very grievous rage that he would presently lift his
arm and spill their souls for their abuses and their spillings done by them
contrariwise to his word which forth to bring brenningly biddeth.

So Thursday sixteenth June Patk. Dignam laid in clay of an apoplexy and
after hard drought, please God, rained, a bargeman coming in by water a
fifty mile or thereabout with turf saying the seed won't sprout, fields athirst,
very sadcoloured and stunk mightily, the quags and tofts too. Hard to
breathe and all the young quicks clean consumed without sprinkle this long
while back as no man remembered to be without. The rosy buds all gone
brown and spread out blobs and on the hills nought but dry flag and faggots
that would catch at first fire. All the world saying, for aught they knew, the
big wind of last February a year that did havoc the land so pitifully a small
thing beside this barrenness. But by and by, as said, this evening after
sundown, the wind sitting in the west, biggish swollen clouds to be seen as
the night increased and the weatherwise poring up at them and some sheet
lightnings at first and after, past ten of the clock, one great stroke with a
long thunder and in a brace of shakes all scamper pellmell within door for
the smoking shower, the men making shelter for their straws with a clout or
kerchief, womenfolk skipping off with kirtles catched up soon as the pour
came. In Ely place, Baggot street, Duke's lawn, thence through Merrion
green up to Holles street, a swash of water running that was before bonedry
and not one chair or coach or fiacre seen about but no more crack after that
first. Over against the Rt. Hon. Mr Justice Fitzgibbon's door (that is to
sit with Mr Healy the lawyer upon the college lands) Mal. Mulligan a
gentleman's gentleman that had but come from Mr Moore's the writer's
(that was a papish but is now, folk say, a good Williamite) chanced against
Alec. Bannon in a cut bob (which are now in with dance cloaks of Kendal
green) that was new got to town from Mullingar with the stage where his
coz and Mal M's brother will stay a month yet till Saint Swithin and asks
what in the earth he does there, he bound home and he to Andrew Horne's
being stayed for to crush a cup of wine, so he said, but would tell him of a
skittish heifer, big of her age and beef to the heel and all this while poured
with rain and so both together on to Horne's. There Leop. Bloom of
Crawford's journal sitting snug with a covey of wags, likely brangling
fellows, Dixon jun., scholar of my lady of Mercy, Vin. Lynch, a Scots
fellow, Will. Madden, T. Lenehan, very sad for a racinghorse he fancied
and Stephen D. Leop. Bloom there for a languor he had but was now

better, he having dreamed tonight a strange fancy of his dame Mrs Moll with red slippers on in pair of Turkey trunks which is thought by those in ken to be for a change and Mistress Purefoy there, that got in through pleading her belly, and now on the stools, poor body, two days past her term, the midwives sore put to it and can't deliver, she queasy for a bowl of riceslop that is a shrewd drier up of the insides and her breath very heavy more than good and should be a bullyboy from the knocks they say, but God give her soon issue. 'Tis her ninth chick to live, I hear, and Lady day bit off her last chick's nails that was then a twelvemonth and with other three all breastfed that died written out in a fair hand in the king's bible. Her hub fifty odd and a methodist but takes the Sacrament and is to be seen any fair sabbath with a pair of his boys off Bullock harbour dapping on the sound with a heavybraked reel or in a punt he has trailing for flounder and pollock and catches a fine bag, I hear. In sum an infinite great fall of rain and all refreshed and will much increase the harvest yet those in ken say after wind and water fire shall come for a prognostication of Malachi's almanac (and I hear that Mr Russell has done a prophetical charm of the same gist out of the Hindustanish for his farmer's gazette) to have three things in all but this a mere fetch without bottom of reason for old crones and bairns yet sometimes they are found in the right guess with their queerities no telling how.

With this came up Lenehan to the feet of the table to say how the letter was in that night's gazette and he made a show to find it about him (for he swore with an oath that he had been at pains about it) but on Stephen's persuasion he gave over to search and was bidden to sit near by which he did mighty brisk. He was a kind of sport gentleman that went for a merryandrew or honest pickle and what belonged of women, horseflesh or hot scandal he had it pat. To tell the truth he was mean in fortunes and for the most part hankered about the coffeehouses and low taverns with crimps, ostlers, bookies, Paul's men, runners, flatcaps, waistcoateers, ladies of the bagnio and other rogues of the game or with a chanceable catchpole or a tipstaff often at nights till broad day of whom he picked up between his sackpossets much loose gossip. He took his ordinary at a boilingcook's and if he had but gotten into him a mess of broken victuals or a platter of tripes with a bare tester in his purse he could always bring himself off with his tongue, some randy quip he had from a punk or whatnot that every mother's son of them would burst their sides. The other, Costello, that is, hearing this talk asked was it poetry or a tale. Faith, no, he says, Frank (that was his name), 'tis all about Kerry cows that are to be butchered along of the plague. But they can go hang, says he with a wink, for me with their bully beef, a pox on it. There's as good fish in this tin as ever came out of it and very friendly he offered to take of some salty sprats that stood by which he had eyed wishly in the meantime and found the place which was indeed the chief design of his embassy as he was sharpset. *Mort aux vaches*, says Frank then in the French language that had been indentured to a brandy shipper that has a winelodge in Bordeaux and he spoke French like a gentleman too. From a child this Frank had been a donought that his father, a head-borough, who could ill keep him to school to learn his letters and the use of the globes, matriculated at the university to study the mechanics but he took the bit between his teeth like a raw colt and was more familiar with the justiciary and the parish beadle than with his volumes. One time he would be a playactor, then a sutler or a welsher, then nought would keep him from the bearpit and the cocking main, then he was for the ocean sea or to hoof it on the roads with the Romany folk, kidnapping a squire's heir by favour of moonlight or fecking maid's linen or choking chickens behind a hedge. He had been off as many times as a cat has lives and back again with naked pockets as many more to his father the headborough who shed a pint of tears as often as he saw him. What, says Mr Leopold with his hands across, that was earnest to know the drift of it, will they slaughter all? I protest I saw them but this day morning going to the Liverpool boats, says he. I can scarce believe 'tis so bad, says he. And he had experience of the like brood beasts and of springers, greasy hoggets and wether wools having been some years before actuary for Mr Joseph Cuffe, a worthy salesmaster that drove his trade for live stock and meadow auctions hard by Mr Gavin Low's yard in Prussia street. I question with you there, says he. More like 'tis the hoose of the timber tongue. Mr Stephen, a little moved but very handsomely, told him no such matter and that he had dispatches from the emperor's chief tailtickler thanking him for the hospitality, that was sending over Doctor Rinderpest, the bestquoted cowcatcher in all Muscovy with a bolus or two of physic to take the bull by the horns. Come, come, says Mr Vincent, plain dealing. He'll find himself on the horns of a dilemma if he meddles with a bull that's Irish, says he. Irish by name and irish by nature, says Mr Stephen, and he sent the ale purling about. An Irish bull in an English chinashop. I conceive you, says Mr Dixon. It is that same bull that was sent to our island by farmer Nicholas, the bravest cattle breeder of them all with an emerald ring in his nose. True for you, says Mr Vincent cross the table, and a bullseye into the bargain, says he, and a plumper and a portlier bull, says he, never shit on shamrock. He had horns galore, a coat of gold and a sweet smoky breath coming out of his nostrils so that the women of our island, leaving doughballs and rollingpins, followed after him hanging his bulliness in daisychains. What for that, says Mr Dixon, but before he came over farmer Nicholas that was a eunuch had him properly gelded by a college of doctors who were no better off than himself. So be off now, says he, and do all my cousin german the Lord Harry tells you and take a farmer's blessing, and with that he slapped his posteriors very soundly. But the slap and the blessing stood him friend, says Mr Vincent, for to make up he taught him a trick worth two of the other so that maid, wife, abbess and widow to this day affirm that they would rather any time of the month whisper in his ear in the dark of a cowhouse or get a lick on the nape from his long holy tongue than lie with the finest strapping young ravisher in the four fields of all Ireland. Another then put in his word: And they dressed him, says he, in a point shift and petticoat with a tippet and girdle and ruffles on his wrists and clipped his forelock and rubbed him all over with spermacetic oil and built stables for him at every turn of the road with a gold manager in each full of the best hay in the market so that he could doss and dung to his heart's content. By this time the father of the faithful (for so they called him) was grown so heavy that he could scarce walk to pasture. To remedy which our cozening dames and damsels brought him his fodder in their apronlaps and as soon as his belly was full he would rear up on his hind quarters to show their ladyships a mystery and roar and bellow out of him in bull's language and they all after him. Ay, says another, and so pampered was he that he would suffer nought to grow in all the land but green grass for himself (for that was the only colour to his mind) and there was a board put up on a hillock in the middle of the island with a printed notice, saying: By the lord Harry green is the grass that grows on the ground. And, says Mr Dixon, if ever he got scent of a cattleraider in Roscommon or the wilds of Connemara or a husbandman in Sligo that was sowing as much as a handful of mustard or a bag of rapeseed out he run amok over half the countryside rooting up with his horns whatever was planted and all by lord Harry's orders. There was bad blood between them at first, says Mr Vincent, and the lord Harry called farmer Nicholas all the old Nicks in the world and an old whoremaster that kept seven trulls in his house and I'll meddle in his matters, says he. I'll make that animal smell hell, says he, with the help of that good pizzle my father left me. But one evening, says Mr Dixon, when the lord Harry was cleaning his royal pelt to go to dinner after winning a boatrace (he had spade oars for himself but the first rule of the course was that the others were to row with pitchforks) he discovered in himself a wonderful likeness to a bull and on picking up a blackthumbed chapbook that he kept in the pantry he found sure enough that he was a lefthanded descendant of the famous champion bull of the Romans, *Bos*

Bovum, which is good bog Latin for boss of the show. After that, says Mr Vincent, the lord Harry put his head into a cow's drinking trough in the presence of all his courtiers and pulling it out again told them all his new name. Then, with the water running off him, he got into an old smock and skirt that had belonged to his grandmother and bought a grammar of the bull's language to study but he could never learn a word of it except the first personal pronoun which he copied out big and got off by heart and if ever he went out for a walk he filled his pockets with chalk to write it up on what took his fancy, the side of rock or a teahouse table or a bale of cotton or a corkfloat. In short he and the bull of Ireland were soon as fast friends as an arse and a shirt. They were, says Mr Stephen, and the end was that the men of the island, seeing no help was toward as the ungrate women were all of one mind, made a wherry raft, loaded themselves and their bundles of chattels on shipboard, set all masts erect, manned the yards, sprang their luff, heaved to, spread three sheets in the wind, put her head between wind and water, weighed anchor, ported her helm, ran up the jolly Roger, gave three times three, let the bullgine run, pushed off in their bumboat and put to sea to recover the main of America. Which was the occasion, says Mr Vincent, of the composing by a boatswain of that rollicking chanty:

> – *Pope Peter's but a pissabed.*
> *A man's a man for a' that.*

Our worthy acquaintance, Mr Malachi Mulligan, now appeared in the doorway as the students were finishing their apologue accompanied with a friend whom he had just rencountered, a young gentleman, his name Alec Bannon, who had late come to town, it being his intention to buy a colour or a cornetcy in the fencibles and list for the wars. Mr Mulligan was civil enough to express some relish of it all the more as it jumped with a project of his own for the cure of the very evil that had been touched on. Whereat he handed round to the company a set of pasteboard cards which he had had printed that day at Mr Quinnell's bearing a legend printed in fair italics: *Mr Malachi Mulligan, Fertiliser and Incubator, Lambay Island.* His project, as he went on to expound, was to withdraw from the round of idle pleasures such as form the chief business of sir Fopling Popinjay and sir Milksop Quidnunc in town and to devote himself to the noblest task for which our bodily organism has been framed. Well, let us hear of it, good my friend, said Mr Dixon. I make no doubt it smacks of wenching. Come, be seated, both. 'Tis as cheap sitting as standing. Mr Mulligan accepted of the invitation and, expatiating on his design, told his hearers that he had been led into this thought by a consideration of the causes of sterility, both the inhibitory and the prohibitory, whether the inhibition in its turn were due to conjugal vexations or to a parsimony of the balance as well as whether the prohibition proceeded from defects congenital or from proclivities acquired. It grieved him plaguily, he said, to see the nuptial couch defrauded of its dearest pledges: and to reflect upon so many agreeable females with rich jointures, a prey for the vilest bonzes, who hide their flambeau under a bushel in an uncongenial cloister or lose their womanly bloom in the embraces of some unaccountable muskin when they might multiply the inlets of happiness, sacrificing the inestimable jewel of their sex when a hundred pretty fellows were at hand to caress, this, he assured them, made his heart weep. To curb this inconvenient (which he concluded due to a suppression of latent heat), having advised with certain counsellors of worth and inspected into this matter, he had resolved to purchase in fee simple for ever the freehold of Lambay island from its holder, lord Talbot de Malahide, a Tory gentleman of not much in favour with our ascendancy party. He proposed to set up there a national fertilising farm to be named *Omphalos* with an obelisk hewn and erected after the fashion of Egypt and to offer his dutiful yeoman services for the fecundation of any female of what grade of life soever who should there direct to him with the desire of fulfilling the functions of her natural. Money was no object, he said, nor would he take a penny for his pains. The poorest kitchenwench no less than the opulent lady of fashion, if so be their constructions and their tempers were warm persuaders for their petitions, would find in him their man. For his nutriment he shewed how he would feed himself exclusively upon a diet of savoury tubercles and fish and coneys there, the flesh of these latter prolific rodents being highly recommended for his purpose, both broiled and stewed with a blade of mace and a pod or two of capsicum chillies. After this homily which he delivered with much warmth of asseveration Mr Mulligan in a trice put off from his hat a kerchief with which he had shielded it. They both, it seems, had been overtaken by the rain and for all their mending their pace had taken water, as might be observed by Mr Mulligan's smallclothes of a hodden grey which was now somewhat piebald. His project meanwhile was very favourably entertained by his auditors and won hearty eulogies from all though Mr Dixon of Mary's excepted to it, asking with a finicking air did he purpose also to carry coals to Newcastle. Mr Mulligan however made court to the scholarly by an apt quotation from the classics which as it dwelt upon his memory seemed to him a sound and tasteful support of his contention: *Talis ac tanta depravatio hujus seculi, O quirites, ut matres familiarum nostræ lascivas cujuslibet semiviri libici titillationes testibus ponderosis atque excelsis erectionibus centurionum Romanorum magnopere anteponunt* while for those of ruder wit he drove home his point by analogies of the animal kingdom more suitable to their stomach, the buck and doe of the forest glade, the farmyard drake and duck.

Valuing himself not a little upon his elegance, being indeed a proper man of his person, this talkative now applied himself to his dress with animadversions of some heat upon the sudden whimsy of the atmospherics while the company lavished their encomiums upon the project he had advanced. The young gentleman, his friend, overjoyed as he was at a passage that had befallen him, could not forbear to tell it his nearest neighbour. Mr Mulligan, now perceiving the table, asked for whom were those loaves and fishes and, seeing the stranger, he made him a civil bow and said, Pray, sir, was you in need of any professional assistance we could give? Who, upon his offer, thanked him very heartily, though preserving his proper distance, and replied that he was come there about a lady, now an inmate of Horne's house, that was in an interesting condition, poor lady, from woman's woe (and here he fetched a deep sigh) to know if her happiness had yet taken place. Mr Dixon, to turn the table, took on to ask Mr Mulligan himself whether his incipient ventripotence, upon which he rallied him, betokened an ovoblastic gestation in the prostatic utricle or male womb or was due as with the noted physician, Mr Austin Meldon, to a wolf in the stomach. For answer Mr Mulligan, in a gale of laughter at his smalls, smote himself bravely below the diaphragm, exclaiming with an admirable droll mimic of Mother Grogan (the most excellent creature of her sex though 'tis pity she's a trollop): There's a belly that never bore a bastard. This was so happy a conceit that it renewed the storms of mirth and threw the whole room into the most violent agitations of delight. The spry rattle had run on in the same vein of mimicry but for some larum in the antechamber.

Here the listener who was none other than the Scotch student, a little fume of a fellow, blond as tow, congratulated in the liveliest fashion with the young gentleman and, interrupting the narrative at a salient point, having desired his visavis with a polite beck to have the obligingness to pass him a flagon of cordial waters at the same time by a questioning poise of the head (a whole century of polite breeding had not achieved so nice a gesture) to which was united an equivalent but contrary balance of the head asked the narrator as plainly as was ever done in words if he might treat him with a cup of it. *Mais bien sûr*, noble stranger, said he cheerily, *et mille compliments.* That you may and very opportunely. There wanted nothing but this cup to crown my felicity. But, gracious heaven, was I left with but a crust in my wallet and a cupful of water from the well, my God, I would accept of them and find it in my heart to kneel down upon the ground and give thanks to the powers above for the happiness vouchsafed me by the Giver of good things. With these words he approached the goblet to his lips, took a complacent draught of the cordial, slicked his hair and, opening his bosom, out popped a locket that hung from a silk riband that very picture which he had cherished ever since her hand had wrote therein. Gazing upon those features with a world of tenderness, Ah, Monsieur, he said, had you but beheld her as I did with these eyes at that affecting instant with her dainty tucker and her new coquette cap (a gift for her feast day as she told me) in such an artless disorder, of so melting a tenderness, 'pon my conscience, even you, Monsieur, had been impelled by generous nature to deliver yourself wholly into the hands of such an enemy or to quit the field for ever. I declare, I was never so touched in all my life. God I thank thee as the Author of my days! Thrice happy will he be whom so amiable a creature will bless with her favours. A sigh of affection gave eloquence to these words and, having replaced the locket in his bosom, he wiped his eye and sighed again. Beneficent Disseminator of blessings to all Thy creatures, how great and universal must be that sweetest of Thy tyrannies which can hold in thrall the free and the bond, the simple swain and the polished coxcomb, the lover in the heyday of reckless passion and the husband of maturer years. But indeed, sir, I wander from the point. How mingled and imperfect are all our sublunary joys! Maledicity! Would to God that foresight had remembered me to take my cloak along! I could weep to think of it. Then, though it had poured seven showers we were neither of us a penny the worse. But beshrew me, he cried, clapping hand to his forehead, tomorrow will be a new day and, thousand thunders, I know of a *marchand de capotes*, Monsieur Poyntz, from whom I can have for a *livre* as snug a cloak of the French fashion as ever kept a lady from wetting. Tut, Tut! cries Le Fécondateur, tripping in, my friend Monsieur Moore, that most accomplished traveller (I have just cracked a half bottle *avec lui* in a circle of the best wits of the town), is my authority that in Cape Horn, *ventre biche*, they have a rain that will wet through any, even the stoutest cloak. A drenching of that violence, he tells me, *sans blague*, has sent more than one luckless fellow in good earnest posthaste to another world. Pooh! A *livre!* cries Monsieur Lynch. The clumsy things are dear at a sou. One umbrella, were it no bigger than a fairy mushroom, is worth ten such stopgaps. No woman of any wit would wear one. My dear Kitty told me today that she would dance in a deluge before ever she would starve in such an ark of salvation for, as she reminded me (blushing piquantly and whispering in my ear though there was none to snap her words but giddy butterflies), dame Nature, by the divine blessing, has implanted it in our heart and it has become a household word that *il y a deux choses* for which the innocence of our original garb, in other circumstances a breach of the proprieties, is the fittest, nay the only, garment. The first, said she (and here my pretty philosopher, as I handed her to her tilbury, to fix my attention, gently tipped with her tongue the outer chamber of my ear), the first is a bath . . . but at this point a bell tinkling in the hall cut short a discourse which promised so bravely for the enrichment of our store of knowledge.

Amid the general vacant hilarity of the assembly a bell rang and while all were conjecturing what might be the cause Miss Callan entered and, having spoken a few words in a low tone to young Mr Dixon, retired with a profound bow to the company. The presence even for a moment among a party of debauchees of a woman endued with every quality of modesty and not less severe than beautiful refrained the humourous sallies even of the most licentious but her departure was the signal for an outbreak of ribaldry. Strike me silly, said Costello, a low fellow who was fuddled. A monstrous fine bit of cowflesh! I'll be sworn she has rendezvoused you. What, you dog? Have you a way with them? Gad's bud. Immensely so, said Mr Lynch. The bedside manner it is that they use in the Mater hospice. Demme, does not Doctor O'Gargle chuck the nuns there under the chin. As I look to be saved I had it from my Kitty who has been wardmaid there any time these seven months. Lawksamercy, doctor, cried the young blood in the primrose vest, feigning a womanish simper and immodest squirmings of his body, how you do tease a body! Drat the man! Bless me, I'm all of a wibblywobbly. Why, you're as bad as dear little Father Cantekissem that you are! May this pot of four half choke me, cried Costello, if she ain't in the family way. I knows a lady what's got a white swelling quick as I claps eyes on her. The young surgeon, however, rose and begged the company to excuse his retreat as the nurse had just then informed him that he was needed in the ward. Merciful providence had been pleased to put a period to the sufferings of the lady who was *enceinte* which she had borne with a laudable fortitude and she had given birth to a bouncing boy. I want patience, said he, with those who without wit to enliven or learning to instruct, revile an ennobling profession which, saving the reverence due to the Deity, is the greatest power for happiness upon the earth. I am positive when I say that if need were I could produce a cloud of witnesses to the excellence of her noble exercitations which, so far from being a byword, should be a glorious incentive in the human breast. I cannot away with them. What? Malign such an one, the amiable Miss Callan, who is the lustre of her own sex and the astonishment of ours and at an instant the most momentous that can befall a puny child of clay? Perish the thought! I shudder to think of the

future of a race where the seeds of such malice have been sown and where
no right reverence is rendered to mother and maid in house of Horne.
Having delivered himself of this rebuke he saluted those present on the by
and repaired to the door. A murmur of approval arose from all and some
were for ejecting the low soaker without more ado, a design which would
have been effected nor would he have received more than his bare deserts
had he not abridged his transgression by affirming with a horrid imprecation
(for he swore a round hand) that he was as good a son of the true fold as
ever drew breath. Stap my vitals, said he, them was always the sentiments of
honest Frank Costello which I was bred up most particular to honour thy
father and thy mother that had the best hand to a rolypoly or a hasty
pudding as you ever see what I always looks back on with a loving heart.

To revert to Mr Bloom who, after his first entry, had been conscious of
some impudent mocks which he, however, had borne with being the fruits
of that age upon which it is commonly charged that it knows not pity. The
young sparks, it is true, were as full of extravagancies as overgrown children:
the words of their tumultuary discussions were difficulty understood
and not often nice: their testiness and outrageous *mots* were such that his
intellects resiled from: nor were they scrupulously sensible of the proprieties
though their fund of strong animal spirits spoke in their behalf. But the
word of Mr Costello was an unwelcome language for him for he nauseated
the wretch that seemed to him a cropeared creature of a misshapen gibbosity
born out of wedlock and thrust like a crookback teethed and feet first into
the world, which the dint of the surgeon's pliers in his skull lent indeed a
colour to, so as it put him in thought of that missing link of creation's chain
desiderated by the late ingenious Mr Darwin. It was now for more than the
middle span of our allotted years that he had passed through the thousand
vicissitudes of existence and, being of a wary ascendancy and self a man of a
rare forecast, he had enjoined his heart to repress all motions of a rising
choler and, by intercepting them with the readiest precaution, foster within
his breast that plenitude of sufferance which base minds jeer at, rash judgers
scorn and all find tolerable and but tolerable. To those who create themselves wits at the cost of feminine delicacy (a habit of mind which he never
did hold with) to them he would concede neither to bear the name nor to
herit the tradition of a proper breeding: while for such that, having lost
all forbearance, can lose no more, there remained the sharp antidote of
experience to cause their insolency to beat a precipitate and inglorious
retreat. Not but what he could feel with mettlesome youth which, caring
nought for the mows of dotards or the gruntlings of the severe, is ever (as
the chaste fancy of the Holy Writer express it) for eating of the tree forbid

it yet not so far forth as to pretermit humanity upon any condition soever towards a gentlewoman when she was about her lawful occasions. To conclude, while from the sister's words he had reckoned upon a speedy delivery he was, however, it must be owned, not a little alleviated by the intelligence that the issue so auspicated after an ordeal of such duress now testified once more to the mercy as well as to the bounty of the Supreme Being.

Accordingly he broke his mind to his neighbour, saying that, to express his notion of the thing, his opinion (who ought not perchance to express one) was that one must have a cold constitution and a frigid genius not to be rejoiced by this freshest news of the fruition of her confinement since she had been in such pain through no fault of hers. The dressy young blade said it was her husband's that put her in that expectation or at least it ought to be unless she were another Ephesian matron. I must acquaint you, said Mr Crotthers, clapping on the table so as to evoke a resonant comment of emphasis, old Glory Allelujerum was round again today, an elderly man with dundrearies, preferring through his nose a request to have word of Wilhelmina, my life, as he calls her. I bade him hold himself in readiness for that the event would burst anon. 'Slife, I'll be round with you. I cannot but extol the virile potency of the old bucko that could still knock another child out of her. All fell to praising of it, each after his own fashion, though the same young blade held with his former view that another than her conjugial had been the man in the gap, a clerk in orders, a linkboy (virtuous) or an itinerant vendor of articles needed in every household. Singular, communed the guest with himself, the wonderfully unequal faculty of metempsychosis possessed by them, that the puerperal dormitory and the dissecting theatre should be the seminaries of such frivolity, that the mere acquisition of academic titles should suffice to transform in a pinch of time these votaries of levity into exemplary practitioners of an art which most men anywise eminent have esteemed the noblest. But, he further added, it is mayhap to relieve the pentup feelings that in common oppress them for I have more than once observed that birds of a feather laugh together.

But with what fitness, let it be asked, of the noble lord, his patron, has this alien, whom the concession of a gracious prince has admitted to civil rights, constituted himself the lord paramount of our internal polity? Where is now that gratitude which loyalty should have counselled? During the recent war whenever the enemy had a temporary advantage with his granados did this traitor to his kind not seize that moment to discharge his piece against the empire of which he is a tenant at will while he trembled for the security of his four per cents? Has he forgotten this as he forgets all benefits received? Or is it that from being a deluder of others he has become at last his own dupe as he is, if report belie him not, his own and his only enjoyer? Far be it from candour to violate the bedchamber of a respectable lady, the daughter of a gallant major, or to cast the most distant reflections upon her virtue but if he challenges attention there (as it was indeed highly his interest not to have done) then be it so. Unhappy woman she has been too long and too persistently denied her legitimate prerogative to listen to his objurgations with any other feeling than the derision of the desperate. He says this, a censor of morals, a very pelican in his piety, who did not scruple, oblivious of the ties of nature, to attempt illicit intercourse with a female domestic drawn from the lowest strata of society. Nay, had the hussy's scouringbrush not been her tutelary angel it had gone with her as hard as with Hagar, the Egyptian! In the question of the grazing lands his peevish asperity is notorious and in Mr Cuffe's hearing brought upon him from an indignant rancher a scathing retort couched in terms as straight-forward as they were bucolic. It ill becomes him to preach that gospel. Has he not nearer home a seedfield that lies fallow for the want of a ploughshare? A habit reprehensible at puberty is second nature and an opprobium in middle life. If he must dispense his balm of Gilead in nostrums and apothegms of dubious taste to restore to health a generation of unfledged profligates let his practice consist better with the doctrines that now engross him. His marital breast is the repository of secrets which decorum is reluctant to adduce. The lewd suggestions of some faded beauty may console him for a consort neglected and debauched but this new exponent of morals and healer of ills is at his best an exotic tree which, when rooted in its native orient, throve and flourished and was abundant in balm but, transplanted to a clime more temperate, its roots have lost their quondam vigour while the stuff that comes away from it is stagnant, acid and inoperative.

The news was imparted with a circumspection recalling the ceremonial usages of the Sublime Porte by the second female infirmarian to the junior medical officer in residence, who in his turn announced to the delegation that an heir had been born. When he had betaken himself to the women's apartment to assist at the prescribed ceremony of the afterbirth in the presence of the secretary of state for domestic affairs and the members of the privy council, silent in unanimous exhaustion and approbation, the delegates, chafing under the length and solemnity of their vigil and hoping that the joyful occurrence would palliate a licence which the simultaneous absence of abigail and officer rendered the easier broke out at once into a strife of tongues. In vain the voice of Mr Canvasser Bloom was heard en-deavouring to urge, to mollify, to restrain. The moment was too propitious for the display of that discursiveness which seemed the only bond of union among tempers so divergent. Every phase of the situation was successively eviscerated: the prenatal repugnance of uterine brothers, the Caesarean section, posthumity with respect to the father and, that rarer form, with respect to the mother, the fratricidal case known as the Childs murder and rendered memorable by the impassioned plea of Mr Advocate Bushe which secured the acquittal of the wrongfully accused, the rights of primogeniture and king's bounty touching twins and triplets, miscarriages and infanticides, simulated and dissimulated, acardiac *foetus in foetu*, aprosopia due to a congestion, the agnatia of certain chinless Chinamen (cited by Mr Candidate Mulligan) in consequence of defective reunion of the maxillary knobs along the medial line so that (as he said) one ear could hear what the other spoke, the benefits of anesthesia or twilight sleep, the prolongation of labour pains in advanced gravidancy by reason of pressure on the vein, the premature relentment of the amniotic fluid (as exemplified in the actual case) with consequent peril of sepsis to the matrix, artificial insemination by means of syringes, involution of the womb consequent upon the menopause, the problem of the perpetuation of the species in the case of females impregnated by delinquent rape, that distressing manner of delivery called by the Brandenburghers *Sturzgeburt*, the recorded instances of multigeminal, twikindled and monstrous births conceived during the catamenic period or of consanguineous parents – in a word all the cases of human nativity which Aristotle has classified in his masterpiece with chromolithographic illustration. The gravest problems of obstetrics and forensic medicine were examined with as much animation as the most popular beliefs on the state of pregnancy such as the forbidding to a gravid woman to step over a country stile lest, by her movement, the navel-cord should strangle her creature and the injunction upon her in the event of a yearning, ardently and ineffectually entertained, to place her hand against that part of her person which long usage has consecrated as the seat of castigation. The abnormalities of harelip, breastmole, supernumerary digits, negro's inkle, strawberry mark and portwine stain were alleged by one as a *primafacie* and natural hypothetical explanation of swineheaded (the case of Madame Grissel Steevens was not forgotten) or doghaired infants occasionally born. The hypothesis of a plasmic memory, advanced by the Caledonian envoy and worthy of the metaphysical traditions of the land he stood for, envisaged in such cases an arrest of embryonic development at some stage antecedent to the human. An outlandish delegate sustained against both these views with such heat as almost carried conviction the theory of copulation between women and the males of brutes, his authority being his own avouchment in support of fables such as that of the Minotaur which the genius of the elegant Latin poet has handed down to us in the pages of his Metamorphoses. The impression made by his words was immediate but shortlived. It was effaced as easily as it had been evoked by an allocution from Mr Candidate Mulligan in that vein of pleasantry which none better than he knew how to affect, postulating as the supremest object of desire a nice clean old man. Contemporaneously, a heated argument having arisen between Mr Delegate Madden and Mr Candidate Lynch regarding the juridical and theological dilemma in the event of one Siamese twin predeceasing the other, the difficulty by mutual consent was referred to Mr Canvasser Bloom for instant submittal to Mr Coadjutor Deacon Dedalus. Hitherto silent, whether the better to show by preternatural gravity that curious dignity of the garb with which he was invested or in obedience to an inward voice, he delivered briefly, and as some thought perfunctorily, the ecclesiastical ordinance forbidding man to put asunder what God has joined.

But Malachias' tale began to freeze them with horror. He conjured up the scene before them. The secret panel beside the chimney slid back and in the recess appeared . . . Haines! Which of us did not feel his flesh creep? He had a portfolio full of Celtic literature in one hand, in the other a phial marked *Poison*. Surprise, horror, loathing were depicted on all faces while he eyed them with a ghastly grin. I anticipated some such reception, he began with an eldritch laugh, for which, it seems, history is to blame. Yes, it is true. I am the murderer of Samuel Childs. And how I am punished! The inferno has no terrors for me. This is the appearance is on me. Tare and ages, what way would I be resting at all, he muttered thickly, and I tramping Dublin this while back with my share of songs and himself after me the like of a soulth or a bullawurrus? My hell, and Ireland's, is in this life. It is what I tried to obliterate my crime. Distractions, rookshooting, the Erse language (he recited some), laudanum (he raised the phial to his lips), camping out. In vain! His spectre stalks me. Dope is my only hope . . . Ah! Destruction! The black panther! With a cry he suddenly vanished and the panel slid back. An instant later his head appeared in the door opposite and said: Meet me at Westland row station at ten past eleven. He was gone! Tears gushed from the eyes of the dissipated host. The seer raised his hand to heaven, murmuring: The vendetta of Mananaan! The sage repeated *Lex talionis*. The sentimentalist is he who would enjoy without incurring the immense debtorship for a thing done. Malachias, overcome by emotion, ceased. The mystery was unveiled. Haines was the third brother. His real name was Childs. The black panther was himself the ghost of his own father. He drank drugs to obliterate. For this relief much thanks. The lonely house by the graveyard is uninhabited. No soul will live there. The spider pitches her web in the solitude. The nocturnal rat peers from his hole. A curse is on it. It is haunted. Murderer's ground.

What is the age of the soul of man? As she hath the virtue of the chameleon to change her hue at every new approach, to be gay with the merry and mournful with the downcast, so too is her age changeable as her mood. No longer is Leopold, as he sits there, ruminating, chewing the cud of reminiscence, that staid agent of publicity and holder of a modest substance in the funds. He is young Leopold, as in a retrospective arrangement, a mirror within a mirror (hey, presto!), he beholdeth himself. That young figure of then is seen, precociously manly, walking on a nipping morning from the old house in Clambrassil street to the high school, his booksatchel on him bandolierwise, and in it a goodly hunk of wheaten loaf, a mother's thought. Or it is the same figure, a year or so gone over, in his first hard hat (ah, that was a day!), already on the road, a fullfledged traveller for the family firm, equipped with an orderbook, a scented handkerchief (not for show only), his case of bright trinketware (alas, a thing now of the past!), and a quiverful of compliant smiles for this or that halfwon housewife reckoning it out upon her fingertips or for a budding virgin shyly acknowledging (but the heart? tell me!) his studied baisemoins. The scent, the smile but more than these, the dark eyes and oleaginous address brought home at duskfall many a commission to the head of the firm seated with Jacob's pipe after like labours in the paternal ingle (a meal of noodles, you may be sure, is aheating), reading through round horned spectacles some paper from the Europe of a month before. But hey, presto, the mirror is breathed on and the young knighterrant recedes, shrivels, to a tiny speck within the mist. Now he is himself paternal and these about him might be his sons. Who can say? The wise father knows his own child. He thinks of a drizzling night in Hatch street, hard by the bonded stores there, the first. Together (she is a poor waif, a child of shame, yours and mine and of all for a bare shilling and her luckpenny), together they hear the heavy tread of the watch as two raincaped shadows pass the new royal university. Bridie! Bridie Kelly! He will never forget the name, ever remember the night, first night, the bridenight. They are entwined in nethermost darkness, the willer with the willed, and in an instant (*fiat!*) light shall flood the world. Did heart leap to heart? Nay, fair reader. In a breath 'twas done but – hold! Back! It must not be! In terror the poor girl flees away through the murk. She is the bride of darkness, a daughter of night. She dare not bear the sunnygolden babe of day. No,

Leopold! Name and memory solace thee not. That youthful illusion of thy strength was taken from thee and in vain. No son of thy loins is by thee. There is none now to be for Leopold, what Leopold was for Rudolph.

The voices blend and fuse in clouded silence: silence that is the infinite of space: and swiftly, silently the soul is wafted over regions of cycles of cycles of generations that have lived. A region where grey twilight ever descends, never falls on wide sagegreen pasturefields, shedding her dusk, scattering a perennial dew of stars. She follows her mother with ungainly steps, a mare leading her fillyfoal. Twilight phantoms are they yet moulded in prophetic grace of structure, slim shapely haunches, a supple tendonous neck, the meek apprehensive skull. They fade, sad phantoms: all is gone. Agendath is a waste land, a home of screechowls and the sandblind upupa. Netaim, the golden, is no more. And on the highway of the clouds they come, muttering thunder of rebellion, the ghosts of beasts. Huuh! Hark! Huuh! Parallax stalks behind and goads them, the lancinating lightnings of whose brow are scorpions. Elk and yak, the bulls of Bashan and of Babylon, mammoth and mastodon, they come trooping to the sunken sea, *Lacus Mortis*. Ominous, revengeful zodiacal host! They moan, passing upon the clouds, horned and capricorned, the trumpeted with the tusked, the lion-maned the giantantlered, snouter and crawler, rodent, ruminant and pachyderm, all their moving moaning multitude, murderers of the sun.

Onward to the dead sea they tramp to drink, unslaked and with horrible gulpings, the salt somnolent inexhaustible flood. And the equine portent grows again, magnified in the deserted heavens, nay to heaven's own magnitude till it looms, vast, over the house of Virgo. And, lo, wonder of metempsychosis, it is she, the everlasting bride, harbinger of the daystar, the bride, ever virgin. It is she, Martha, thou lost one, Millicent, the young, the dear, the radiant. How serene does she now arise, a queen among the Pleiades, in the penultimate antelucan hour, shod in sandals of bright gold, coifed with a veil of what do you call it gossamer! It floats, it flows about her starborn flesh and loose it streams emerald, sapphire, mauve and heliotrope, sustained on currents of cold interstellar wind, winding, coiling, simply swirling, writhing in the skies a mysterious writing till after a myriad metamorphoses of symbol, it blazes, Alpha, a ruby and triangled sign upon the forehead of Taurus.

Francis was reminding Stephen of years before when they had been at school together in Conmee's time. He asked about Glaucon, Alcibiades, Pisistratus. Where were they now? Neither knew. You have spoken of the past and its phantoms, Stephen said. Why think of them? If I call them into life across the waters of Lethe will not the poor ghosts troop to my call? Who supposes it? I, Bous Stephanoumenos, bullockbefriending bard, am lord and giver of their life. He encircled his gadding hair with a coronal of vineleaves, smiling at Vincent. That answer and those leaves, Vincent said to him, will adorn you more fitly when something more, and greatly more, than a capful of light odes can call your genius father. All who wish you well hope this for you. All desire to see you bring forth the work you meditate. I heartily wish you may not fail them. O no, Vincent, Lenehan said, laying a hand on the shoulder near him, have no fear. He could not leave his mother an orphan. The young man's face grew dark. All could see how hard it was for him to be reminded of his promise and of his recent loss. He would have withdrawn from the feast had not the noise of voices allayed the smart. Madden had lost five drachmas on Sceptre for a whim of the rider's name: Lenehan as much more. He told them of the race. The flag fell and, huuh, off, scamper, the mare ran out freshly with O. Madden up. She was leading the field: all hearts were beating. Even Phyllis could not contain herself. She waved her scarf and cried: Huzzah! Sceptre wins! But in the straight on the run home when all were in close order the dark horse Throwaway drew level, reached, outstripped her. All was lost now. Phyllis was silent: her eyes were sad anemones. Juno, she cried, I am undone. But her lover consoled her and brought her a bright casket of gold in which lay some oval sugar-plums which she partook. A tear fell: one only. A whacking fine whip, said Lenehan, is W. Lane. Four winners yesterday and three today. What rider is like him? Mount him on the camel or the boisterous buffalo the victory in a hack canter is still his. But let us bear it as was the ancient wont. Mercy on the luckless! Poor Sceptre! he said with a light sigh. She is not the filly that she was. Never, by this hand, shall we behold such another. By gad, sir, a queen of them. Do you remember her, Vincent? I wish you could have seen my queen today, Vincent said, how young she was and radiant (Lalage were scarce fair beside her) in her yellow shoes and frock of muslin, I do not know the right name of it. The chestnuts that shaded us were in bloom: the air drooped with their persuasive odour and with pollen floating by us. In the sunny patches one might easily have cooked on a stone a batch of those buns with Corinth fruit in them that Periplepomenos sells in his booth near the bridge. But she had nought for her teeth but the arm with which I held her and in that she nibbled mischievously when I pressed too close. A week ago she lay ill, four days on the couch, but today she was free, blithe, mocked at peril. She is more taking then. Her posies too! Mad romp that it is, she had pulled her fill as we reclined together. And in your ear, my friend, you will not think who met us as we left the field. Conmee himself!

He was walking by the hedge, reading, I think a brevier book with, I doubt not, a witty letter in it from Glycera or Chloe to keep the page. The sweet creature turned all colours in her confusion, feigning to reprove a slight disorder in her dress: a slip of underwood clung there for the very trees adore her. When Conmee had passed she glanced at her lovely echo in the little mirror she carries. But he had been kind. In going by he had blessed us. The gods too are ever kind, Lenehan said. If I had poor luck with Bass's mare perhaps this draught of his may serve me more propensely. He was laying his hand upon a winejar: Malachi saw it and withheld his act, pointing to the stranger and to the scarlet label. Warily, Malachi whispered, preserve a druid silence. His soul is far away. It is as painful perhaps to be awakened from a vision as to be born. Any object, intensely regarded, may be a gate of access to the incorruptible eon of the gods. Do you not think it, Stephen? Theosophos told me so, Stephen answered, whom in a previous existence Egyptian priests initiated into the mysteries of karmic law. The lords of the moon, Theosophos told me, an orangefiery shipload from planet Alpha of the lunar chain, would not assume the etheric doubles and these were therefore incarnated by the rubycoloured egos from the second constellation.

However, as a matter of fact though, the preposterous surmise about him being in some description of a doldrums or other or mesmerised which was entirely due to a misconception of the shallowest character, was not the case at all. The individual whose visual organs, while the above was going on, were at this juncture commencing to exhibit symptoms of animation, was as astute if not astuter than any man living and anybody that conjectured the contrary would have found themselves pretty speedily in the wrong shop. During the past four minutes or thereabouts he had been staring hard at a certain amount of number one Bass bottled by Messrs Bass and Co at Burton-on-Trent which happened to be situated amongst a lot of others right opposite to where he was and which was certainly calculated to attract anyone's remark on account of its scarlet appearance. He was simply and solely, as it subsequently transpired for reasons best known to himself, which put quite an altogether different complexion on the proceedings, after the moment before's observations about boyhood days and the turf, recollecting two or three private transactions of his own which the other two were as mutually innocent of as the babe unborn. Eventually, however, both their eyes met and, as soon as it began to dawn on him that the other was endeavouring to help himself to the thing, he involuntarily determined to help him himself and so he accordingly took hold of the mediumsized glass recipient which contained the fluid sought after and made a capacious hole in it by pouring a lot of it out with, also at the same time however, a considerable degree of attentiveness in order not to upset any of the beer that was in it about the place.

The debate which ensued was in its scope and progress an epitome of the course of life. Neither place nor council was lacking in dignity. The debaters were the keenest in the land, the theme they were engaged on the loftiest and most vital. The high hall of Horne's house had never beheld an assembly so representative and so varied nor had the old rafters of that establishment ever listened to a language so encyclopaedic. A gallant scene in truth it made. Crotthers was there at the foot of the table in his striking Highland garb, his face glowing from the briny airs of the Mull of Galloway. There too, opposite to him was Lynch, whose countenance bore already the stigmata of early depravity and premature wisdom. Next the Scotchman was the place assigned to Costello, the eccentric, while at his side was seated in stolid repose the squat form of Madden. The chair of the resident indeed stood vacant before the hearth but on either flank of it the figure of Bannon in explorer's kit of tweed shorts and salted cowhide brogues contrasted sharply with the primrose elegance and townbred manners of Malachi Roland St John Mulligan. Lastly at the head of the board was the young poet who found a refuge from his labours of pedagogy and metaphysical inquisition in the convivial atmosphere of Socratic discussion, while to right and left of him were accommodated the flippant prognosticator, fresh from the hippodrome, and that vigilant wanderer, soiled by the dust of travel and combat and stained by the mire of an indelible dishonour, but from whose steadfast and constant heart no lure or peril or threat or degradation could ever efface the image of that voluptuous loveliness which the inspired pencil of Lafayette has limned for ages yet to come.

It had better be stated here and now at the outset that the perverted transcendentalism to which Mr S. Dedalus' (Div. Scep.) contentions would appear to prove him pretty badly addicted runs directly counter to accepted scientific methods. Science, it cannot be too often repeated, deals with tangible phenomena. The man of science like the man in the street has to face hardheaded facts that cannot be blinked and explain them as best he can. There may be, it is true, some questions which science cannot answer – at present – such as the first problem submitted by Mr L. Bloom (Pubb. Canv.) regarding the future determination of sex. Must we accept the view of Empedocles of Trinacria that the right ovary (the postmenstrual period, assert others) is responsible for the birth of males or are the too long neglected spermatozoa or nemasperms the differentiating factors or is it, as most embryologists incline to opine, such as Culpepper, Spallanzani,

Blumenbach, Lusk, Hertwig, Leopold and Valenti, a mixture of both? This would be tantamount to a cooperation (one of nature's favourite devices) between the *nisus formativus* of the nemasperm on the one hand and on the other a happily chosen position, *succubitus felix*, of the passive element. The other problem raised by the same inquirer is scarcely less vital: infant mortality. It is interesting because, as he pertinently remarks, we are all born in the same way but we all die in different ways. Mr M. Mulligan (Hyg. et Eug. Doc.) blames the sanitary conditions in which our grey-lunged citizens contract adenoids, pulmonary complaints etc. by inhaling the bacteria which lurk in dust. These factors, he alleges, and the revolting spectacles offered by our streets, hideous publicity posters, religious ministers of all denominations, mutilated soldiers and sailors, exposed scorbutic cardrivers, the suspended carcases of dead animals, paranoic bachelors and unfructified duennas – these, he said, were accountable for any and every fallingoff in the calibre of the race. Kalipedia, he prophesied, would soon be generally adopted and all the graces of life, genuinely good music, agreeable literature, light philosophy, instructive pictures, plastercast reproductions of the classical statues such as Venus and Apollo, artistic coloured photographs of prize babies, all these little attentions would enable ladies who were in a particular condition to pass the intervening months in a most enjoyable manner. Mr J. Crotthers (Disc. Bacc.) attributes some of these demises to abdominal trauma in the case of women workers subjected to heavy labours in the workshop and to marital discipline in the home but by far the vast majority to neglect, private or official, culminating in the exposure of newborn infants, the practice of criminal abortion or in the atrocious crime of infanticide. Although the former (we are thinking of neglect) is undoubtedly only too true the case he cites of nurses forgetting to count the sponges in the peritoneal cavity is too rare to be normative. In fact when one comes to look into it the wonder is that so many pregnancies and deliveries go off so well as they do, all things considered and in spite of our human shortcomings which often balk nature in her intentions. An ingenious suggestion is that thrown out by Mr V. Lynch (Bacc. Arith.) that both natality and mortality, as well as all other phenomena of evolution, tidal movements, lunar phases, blood temperatures, diseases in general, everything, in fine, in nature's vast workshop from the extinction of some remote sun to the blossoming of one of the countless flowers which beautify our public parks, is subject to a law of numeration as yet unascertained. Still the plain straightforward question why a child of normally healthy parents and seemingly a healthy child and properly looked after succumbs unaccountably in early childhood (though other children of the same marriage do not) must certainly, in the poet's words, give us pause. Nature, we may rest assured, has her own good and cogent reasons for whatever she does and in all probability such deaths are due to some law of anticipation by which organisms in which morbous germs have taken up their residence (modern science has conclusively shown that only the plasmic substance can be said to be immortal) tend to disappear at an increasingly earlier stage of development, an arrangement, which, though productive of pain to some of our feelings (notably the maternal) is nevertheless, some of us think, in the long run beneficial to the race in general in securing thereby the survival of the fittest. Mr S. Dedalus' (Div. Scep.) remark (or should it be called an interruption?) that an omnivorous being which can masticate, deglute, digest and apparently pass through the ordinary channel with pluterperfect imperturbability such multifarious aliments as cancrenous females emaciated by parturition, corpulent professional gentlemen, not to speak of jaundiced politicians and chlorotic nuns might possibly find gastric relief in an innocent collation of staggering bob, reveals as nought else could and in a very unsavoury light the tendency above alluded to. For the enlightenment of those who are not so intimately acquainted with the minutiae of the municipal abattoir as this morbidminded esthete and embryo philosopher who for all his overweening bumptiousness in things scientific can scarcely distinguish an acid from an alkali prides himself on being, it should perhaps be stated that staggering bob in the vile parlance of our lower class licensed victuallers signifies the cookable and eatable flesh of a calf newly dropped from its mother. In a recent public controversy with Mr L. Bloom (Pubb. Canv.) which took place in the commons' hall of the National Maternity Hospital, 29, 30 and 31 Holles street, of which, as is well known, Dr A. Horne (Lic. in Midw., F. K. Q. C. P. I.) is the able and popular master, he is reported by eyewitnesses as having stated that once a woman has let the cat into the bag (an esthetic allusion, presumably, to one of the most complicated and marvellous of all nature's processes, the act of sexual congress) she must let it out again or give it life, as he phrased it, to save her own. At the risk of her own was the telling rejoinder of his interlocutor none the less effective for the moderate and measured tone in which it was delivered.

Meanwhile the skill and patience of the physician had brought about a happy *accouchement*. It had been a weary weary while both for patient and doctor. All that surgical skill could do was done and the brave woman had manfully helped. She had. She had fought the good fight and now she was very very happy. Those who have passed on, who have gone before, are happy too as they gaze down and smile upon the touching scene. Reverently look at her as she reclines there with the motherlight in her eyes, that longing hunger for baby fingers (a pretty sight it is to see), in the first bloom of her new motherhood, breathing a silent prayer of thanksgiving to One above, the Universal Husband. And as her loving eyes behold her babe she wishes only one blessing more, to have her dear Doady there with her to share her joy, to lay in his arms that mite of God's clay, the fruit of their lawful embraces. He is older now (you and I may whisper it) and a trifle stooped in the shoulders yet in the whirligig of years a grave dignity has come to the conscientious second accountant of the Ulster bank, College Green branch. O Doady, loved one of old, faithful lifemate now, it may never be again, that faroff time of the roses! With the old shake of her pretty head she recalls those days. God, how beautiful now across the mist of years! But their children are grouped in her imagination about the bedside, hers and his, Charley, Mary Alice, Frederick Albert (if he had lived), Mamy, Budgy (Victoria Frances), Tom, Violet Constance Louisa, darling little Bobsy (called after our famous hero of the South African war, lord Bobs of Waterford and Candahar) and now this last pledge of their union, a Purefoy if ever there was one, with the true Purefoy nose. Young hopeful will be christened Mortimer Edward after the influential third cousin of Mr Purefoy in the Treasury Remembrancer's office, Dublin Castle. And so time wags on: but father Cronion has dealt lightly here. No, let no sigh break from that bosom, dear gentle Mina. And Doady, knock the ashes from your pipe, the seasoned briar you still fancy when the curfew rings for you (may it be the distant day!) and dout the light whereby you read in the Sacred Book for the oil too has run low and so with a tranquil heart to bed, to rest. He knows and will call in His own good time. You too have fought the good fight and played loyally your man's part. Sir, to you my hand. Well done, thou good and faithful servant!

There are sins or (let us call them as the world calls them) evil memories which are hidden away by man in the darkest places of the heart but they abide there and wait. He may suffer their memory to grow dim, let them be as though they had not been and all but persuade himself that they were not or at least were otherwise. Yet a chance word will call them forth suddenly and they will rise up to confront him in the most various circumstances, a vision or a dream, or while timbrel and harp soothe his senses or amid the cool silver tranquillity of the evening or at the feast at midnight when he is now filled with wine. Not to insult over him will the vision come as over one that lies under her wrath, not for vengeance to cut him off from the living but shrouded in the piteous vesture of the past, silent, remote, reproachful.

The stranger still regarded on the face before him a slow recession of that false calm there, imposed, as it seemed, by habit or some studied trick, upon words so embittered as to accuse in their speaker an unhealthiness, a *flair*, for the cruder things of life. A scene disengages itself in the observer's memory, evoked, it would seem, by a word of so natural a homeliness as if those days were really present there (as some thought) with their immediate pleasures. A shaven space of lawn one soft May evening, the well-remembered grove of lilacs at Roundtown, purple and white, fragrant slender spectators of the game but with much real interest in the pellets as they run slowly forward over the sward or collide and stop, one by its fellow, with a brief alert shock. And yonder about that grey urn where the water moves at times in thoughtful irrigation you saw another as fragrant sisterhood, Floey, Atty, Tiny and their darker friend with I know not what of arresting in her pose then, Our Lady of the Cherries, a comely brace of them pendent from an ear, bringing out the foreign warmth of the skin so daintily against the cool ardent fruit. A lad of four or five in linseywoolsey (blossomtime but there will be cheer in the kindly hearth when ere long the bowls are gathered and hutched) is standing on the urn secured by that circle of girlish fond hands. He frowns a little just as this young man does now with a perhaps too conscious enjoyment of danger but must needs glance at whiles towards where his mother watches from the *piazzetta* giving upon the flowerclose with a faint shadow of remoteness or of reproach *(alles Vergängliche)* in her glad look.

Mark this farther and remember. The end comes suddenly. Enter that antechamber of birth where the studious are assembled and note their faces. Nothing, as it seems, there of rash or violent. Quietude of custody rather, befitting their station in that house, the vigilant watch of shepherds and of angels about a crib in Bethlehem of Juda long ago. But as before the lightning the serried stormclouds, heavy with preponderant excess of moisture, in swollen masses turgidly distended, compass earth and sky in one vast slumber, impending above parched field and drowsy oxen and blighted growth of shrub and verdure till in an instant a flash rives their centres and with the reverberation of the thunder the cloudburst pours its torrent, so and not otherwise was the transformation, violent and instantaneous, upon the utterance of the Word.

Burke's! Outflings my lord Stephen, giving the cry, and a tag and bobtail of all them after, cockerel, jackanapes, welsher, pilldoctor, punctual Bloom at heels with a universal grabbing at headgear, ashplants, bilbos, Panama hats and scabbards, Zermatt alpenstocks and what not. A dedale of lusty youth, noble every student there. Nurse Callan taken aback in the hallway cannot stay them nor smiling surgeon coming downstairs with news of placentation ended, a full pound if a milligramme. They hark him on. The door! It is open? Ha! They are out tumultuously, off for a minute's race, all bravely legging it, Burke's of Denzille and Holles their ulterior goal. Dixon follows, giving them sharp language but raps out an oath, he too, and on. Bloom stays with nurse a thought to send a kind word to happy mother and nurseling up there. Doctor Diet and Doctor Quiet. Looks she too not other now? Ward of watching in Horne's house has told its tale in that washedout pallor. Them all being gone, a glance of motherwit helping he whispers close in going: Madam, when comes the storkbird for thee?

The air without is impregnated with raindew moisture, life essence celestial, glistering on Dublin stone there under starshiny *coelum*. God's air, the Allfather's air, scintillant circumambient cessile air. Breathe it deep into thee. By heaven, Theodore Purefoy, thou hast done a doughty deed and no botch! Thou art, I vow, the remarkablest progenitor barring none in this chaffering allincluding most farraginous chronicle. Astounding! In her lay a Godframed Godgiven preformed possibility which thou hast fructified with thy modicum of man's work. Cleave to her! Serve! Toil on, labour like a very bandog and let scholarment and all Malthusiasts go hang. Thou art all their daddies, Theodore. Art drooping under thy load, bemoiled with butcher's bills at home and ingots (not thine!) in the countinghouse? Head up! For every newbegotten thou shalt gather thy homer of ripe wheat. See, thy fleece is drenched. Dost envy Darby Dullman there with his Joan? A canting jay and a rheumeyed curdog is all their progeny. Pshaw, I tell thee! He is a mule, a dead gasteropod, without vim or stamina, not worth a cracked kreutzer. Copulation without population! No, say I! Herod's slaughter of the innocents were the truer name. Vegetables, forsooth, and sterile cohabitation! Give her beefsteaks, red, raw, bleeding! She is a hoary pandemonium of ills, enlarged glands, mumps, quinsy, bunions, hayfever, bedsores, ringworm, floating kidney, Derbyshire neck, warts, bilious attacks, gallstones, cold feet, varicose veins. A truce to threnes and trentals and jeremies and all such congenital defunctive music. Twenty years of it, regret them not. With thee it was not as with many that will and would and wait and never do. Thou sawest thy America, thy lifetask, and didst charge to cover like the transpontine bison. How saith Zarathusthra? *Deine Kuh Trübsal melkest Du. Nun trinkst Du die süsse Milch des Euters.* See! It displodes for thee in abundance. Drink, man, an udderful! Mother's milk, Purefoy, the milk of human kin, milk too of those burgeoning stars overhead, rutilant in thin rainvapour, punch milk, such as those rioters will quaff in their guzzlingden, milk of madness, the honeymilk of Canaan's land. Thy cow's dug was tough, what? Ay, but her milk is hot and sweet and fattening. No dollop this but thick rich bonnyclaber. To her, old patriarch! Pap! *Per deam Partulam et Pertundam nunc est bibendum!*

All off for a buster, armstrong, hollering down the street. Bonafides. Where you slep las nigh? Timothy of the battered naggin. Like ole Billyo. Any brollies or gumboots in the fambly? Where the Henry Nevil's sawbones and ole clo? Sorra one o me knows. Hurrah there, Dix! Forward the ribbon counter. Where's Punch? All serene. Jay, look at the drunken minister coming out of the maternity hospal! *Benedicat vos omnipotens Deus, Pater et Filius.* A make, mister. The Denzille lane boys. Hell, blast ye! Scoot. Righto, Isaacs, shove em out of the bleeding limelight. Yous join uz, dear sir? No hentrusion in life. Lou heap good man. Allee samee this bunch. *En avant, mes enfants!* Fire away number one on the gun. Burke's! Thence they advanced five parasangs. Slattery's mounted foot where's that bleeding awfur? Parson Steve, apostates' creed! No, no. Mulligan! Abaft there! Shove ahead. Keep a watch on the clock. Chuckingout time. Mullee! What's on you? *Ma mère m'a mariée.* British Beatitudes! *Ratamplan Digidi Boum Boum.* Ayes have it. To be printed and bound at the Druiddrum press by two designing females. Calf covers of pissedon green. Last word in art shades. Most beautiful book come out of Ireland my time. *Silentium!* Get a spurt on. Tention. Proceed to nearest canteen and there annex liquor stores. March! Tramp, tramp, tramp the boys are (atitudes!) parching. Beer, beef, business, bibles, bulldogs, battleships, buggery and bishops. Whether on the scaffold high. Beerbeef trample the bibles. When for Irelandear. Trample the trampellers. Thunderation! Keep the durned millingtary step. We fall. Bishops' boosebox. Halt! Heave to. Rugger. Scrum in. No touch kicking. Wow, my tootsies! You hurt? Most amazingly sorry!

Query. Who's astanding this here do? Proud possessor of damnall. Declare misery. Bet to the ropes. Me nantee saltee. Not a red at me this week gone. Yours? Mead of our fathers for the *Übermensch.* Dittoh. Five number ones. You, sir? Ginger cordial. Chase me, the cabby's caudle. Stimulate the caloric. Winding of his ticker. Stopped short never to go again when the old. Absinthe for me, savvy? *Caramba!* Have an eggnog or a prairie oyster. Enemy? Avuncular's got my timepiece. Ten to. Obligated awful. Don't mention it. Got a pectoral trauma, eh, Dix? Pos fact. Got bet be a boomblebee whenever he was settin sleepin in hes bit garten. Digs up near the Mater. Buckled he is. Know his dona? Yup, sartin, I do. Full of a dure. See her in her dishybilly. Peels off a credit. Lovey lovekin. None of your lean kine, not much. Pull down the blind, love. Two Ardilauns. Same here. Look slippery. If you fall don't wait to get up. Five, seven, nine. Fine! Got a prime pair of mincepies, no kid. And her take me to rests and her anker of rum. Must be seen to be believed. Your starving eyes and allbeplastered neck you stole my heart, O gluepot. Sir? Spud again the rheumatiz? All poppycock, you'll scuse me saying. For the hoi polloi. I vear thee beest a gert vool. Well, doc? Back fro Lapland? Your corporosity sagaciating O K? How's the squaws and papooses? Womanbody after going on the straw? Stand and deliver. Password. There's hair. Ours the white death and the ruddy birth. Hi! Spit in your own eye, boss. Mummer's wire. Cribbed out of Meredith. Jesified orchidised polycimical jesuit! Aunty mine's writing Pa Kinch. Baddybad Stephen lead astray goodygood Malachi.

Hurroo! Collar the leather, youngun. Roun wi the nappy. Here, Jock braw Hielentman's your barleybree. Lang may your lum reek and your kailpot boil! My tipple. *Merci*. Here's to us. How's that? Leg before wicket. Don't stain my brandnew sitinems. Give's a shake of pepper, you there. Catch aholt. Caraway seed to carry away. Twig? Shrieks of silence. Every cove to his gentry mort. Venus Pandemos. *Les petites femmes*. Bold bad girl from the town of Mullingar. Tell her I was axing at her. Hauding Sara by the wame. On the road to Malahide. Me? If she who seduced me had left but the name. What do you want for ninepence. Machree, Macruiskeen. Smutty Moll for a mattress jig. And a pull alltogether. *Ex!*

Waiting, guvnor? Most deciduously. Bet your boots on. Stunned like seeing as how no shiners is acoming, Underconstumble? He've got the chink *ad lib*. Seed near free poun on un a spell ago a said war hisn. Us come right in on your invite, see? Up to you, matey. Out with the oof. Two bar and a wing. You larn that go off of they there Frenchy bilks? Won't wash here for nuts nohow. Lil chile velly solly. Ise de cutest colour coon down our side. Gawds teruth, Chawley. We are nae fou. We're nae tha fou. Au reservoir, Mossoo. Tanks you.

'Tis, sure. What say? In the speakeasy. Tight. I shee you, shir. Bantam, two days teetee. Bowsing nowt but claretwine. Garn! Have a glint, do. Gum, I'm jiggered. And been to barber he have. Too full for words. With a railway bloke. How come you so? Opera he'd like? Rose of Castille. Rows of cast. Police! Some H_2O for a gent fainted. Look at Bantam's flowers. Gemini, he's going to holler. The colleen bawn, my colleen bawn. O, cheese it! Shut his blurry Dutch oven with a firm hand. Had the winner today till I tipped him a dead cert. The ruffin cly the nab of Stephen. Hand as give me the jady coppaleen. He strike a telegramboy paddock wire big bug Bass to the depot. Shove him a joey and grahamise. Mare on form hot order. Guinea to a goosegog. Tell a cram, that. Gospeltrue. Criminal diversion? I think that yes. Sure thing. Land him in chokeechokee if the harman beck copped the game. Madden back Madden's a maddening back. O, lust, our refuge and our strength. Decamping. Must you go? Off to mammy. Stand by. Hide my blushes someone. All in if he spots me. Comeahome, our Bantam. Horryvar, mong vioo. Dinna forget the cowslips for hersel. Cornfide. Wha gev ye thon colt? Pal to pal. Jannock. Of John Thomas, her spouse. No fake, old man Leo. S'elp me, honest injun. Shiver my timbers if I had. There's a great big holy friar. Vyfor you no me tell? Vel, I ses, if that aint a sheeny nachez, vel, I vil get misha mishinnah. Through yerd our lord, Amen.

You move a motion? Steve boy, you're going it some. More bluggy drunkables? Will immensely splendiferous stander permit one stooder of most extreme poverty and one largesize grandacious thirst to terminate one expensive inaugurated libation? Give's a breather. Landlord, landlord, have you good wine, staboo? Hoots, mon, wee drap to pree. Cut and come again. Right Boniface! Absinthe the lot. *Nos omnes biberimus viridum toxicum diabolus capiat posteriora nostra.* Closingtime, gents. Eh? Rome boose for the Bloom toff. I hear you say onions? Bloo? Cadges ads? Photo's papli, by all that's gorgeous, Play low, pardner. Slide. *Bonsoir la compagnie.* And snares of the poxfiend. Where's the buck and Namby Amby? Skunked? Leg bail. Aweel, ye maun e'en gang yer gates. Checkmate. King to tower. Kind Kristyann will yu help, yung man hoose frend tuk bungalo kee to find plais whear to lay crown off his hed 2 night. Crickey, I'm about sprung. Tarnally dog gone my shins if this beent the bestest puttiest longbreakyet. Item, curate, couple of cookies for this child. Cot's plood and prandypalls, none! Not a pite of sheeses? Thrust syphilis down to hell and with him those other licensed spirits. Time. Who wander through the world. Health all. *A la vôtre!*

Golly, whatten tunket's yon guy in the mackintosh? Dusty Rhodes. Peep at his wearables. By mighty! What's he got? Jubilee mutton. Bovril, by James. Wants it real bad. D'ye ken bare socks? Seedy cuss in the Richmond? Rawthere! Thought he had a deposit of lead in his penis. Trumpery insanity. Bartle the Bread we calls him. That, sir, was once a prosperous cit. Man all tattered and torn that married a maiden all forlorn. Slung her hook, she did. Here see lost love. Walking Mackintosh of lonely canyon. Tuck and turn in. Schedule time. Nix for the hornies. Pardon? See him today at a runefal? Chum o yourn passed in his checks? Ludamassy! Pore picanninies! Thou'll no be telling me thot, Pold veg! Did ums blubble bigsplash crytears cos frien Padney was took off in black bag? Of all de darkies Massa Pat was verra best. I never see the like since I was born. *Tiens, tiens,* but it is well sad, that my faith, yes. O get, rev on a gradient one in nine. Live axle drives are souped. Lay you two to one Jenatzy licks him ruddy well hollow. Jappies?

High angle fire, inyah! Sunk by war specials. Be worse for him, says he, nor any Rooshian. Time all. There's eleven of them. Get ye gone. Forward, woozy wobblers! Night. Night. May Allah, the Excellent One, your soul this night ever tremendously conserve.

Your attention! We're nae tha fou. The Leith police dismisseth us. The least tholice. Ware hawks for the chap puking. Unwell in his abominable regions. Yooka. Night. Mona, my thrue love. Yook. Mona, my own love. Ook.

Hark! Shut your obstropolos. Pflaap! Pflaap! Blaze on. There she goes. Brigade! Bout ship. Mount street way. Cut up. Pflaap! Tally ho. You not come? Run, skelter, race. Pflaaaap!

Lynch! Hey? Sign on long o me. Denzille lane this way. Change here for Bawdyhouse. We two, she said, will seek the kips where shady Mary is. Righto, any old time. *Laetabuntur in cubilibus suis*. You coming long? Whisper, who the sooty hell's the johnny in the black duds? Hush! Sinned against the light and even now that day is at hand when he shall come to judge the world by fire. Pflaap! *Ut implerentur scripturae*. Strike up a ballad. Then outspake medical Dick to his comrade medical Davy. Christicle, who's this excrement yellow gospeller on the Merrion hall? Elijah is coming. Washed in the Blood of the Lamb. Come on, you winefizzling ginsizzling booseguzzling existences! Come on, you dog-gone, bullnecked, beetlebrowed, hogjowled, peanutbrained, weaseleyed fourflushers, false alarms and excess baggage! Come on, you triple extract of infamy! Alexander J. Christ Dowie, that's yanked to glory most half this planet from 'Frisco Beach to Vladivostok. The Deity aint no nickel dime bumshow. I put it to you that he's on the square and a corking fine business proposition. He's the grandest thing yet and don't you forget it. Shout salvation in king Jesus. You'll need to rise precious early, you sinner there, if you want to diddle the Almighty God. Pflaaaap! Not half. He's got a coughmixture with a punch in it for you, my friend, in his backpocket. Just you try it on.

*   *   *   *   *

◀ (*THE MABBOT STREET ENTRANCE OF NIGHTTOWN, before which stretches an uncobbled tramsiding set with skeleton tracks, red and green will-o'-the-wisps and danger signals. Rows of flimsy houses with gaping doors. Rare lamps with faint rainbow fans. Round Rabaiotti's halted ice gondola stunted men and women squabble. They grab wafers between which are wedged lumps of coal and copper snow. Sucking, they scatter slowly. Children. The swancomb of the gondola, highreared, forges on through the murk, white and blue under a lighthouse. Whistles call and answer.*)

THE CALLS

Wait, my love, and I'll be with you.

THE ANSWERS

Round behind the stable.

(A deafmute idiot with goggle eyes, his shapeless mouth dribbling, jerks past, shaken in Saint Vitus' dance. A chain of children's hands imprisons him.)

THE CHILDREN

Kithogue! Salute.

THE IDIOT

(Lifts a palsied left arm and gurgles.) Grhahute!

THE CHILDREN

Where's the great light?

THE IDIOT

(Gobbing.) Ghaghahest.

(They release him. He jerks on. A pigmy woman swings on a rope slung between the railings, counting. A form sprawled against a dustbin and muffled by its arm and hat moves, groans, grinding growling teeth, and snores again. On a step a gnome totting among a rubbishtip crouches to shoulder a sack of rags and bones. A crone standing by with a smoky oil lamp rams the last bottle in the maw of his sack. He heaves his booty, tugs askew his peaked cap and hobbles off mutely. The crone makes back for her lair swaying her lamp. A bandy child, asquat on the doorstep with a papershuttlecock, crawls sidling after her in spurts, clutches her skirt, scrambles up. A drunken navvy grips with both hands the railings of an area, lurching heavily. At a corner two night watch in shoulder capes, their hands upon their staffholsters, loom tall. A plate crashes; a woman screams; a child wails. Oaths of a man roar, mutter, cease. Figures wander, lurk, peer from warrens. In a room lit by a candle stuck in a bottleneck a slut combs out the tatts from the hair of a scrofulous child. Cissy Caffrey's voice, still young, sings shrill from a lane.)

CISSY CAFFREY

I gave it to Molly
Because she was jolly,
The leg of the duck
The leg of the duck.

(Private Carr and Private Compton, swaggersticks tight in their oxters, as they march unsteadily rightaboutface and burst together from their mouths a volleyed fart. Laughter of men from the lane. A hoarse virago retorts.)

THE VIRAGO

Signs on you, hairy arse. More power the Cavan girl.

CISSY CAFFREY

More luck to me. Cavan, Cootehill and Belturbet. *(She sings.)*

> I gave it to Nelly
> To stick in her belly
> The leg of the duck
> The leg of the duck.

(Private Carr and Private Compton turn and counterretort, their tunics bloodbright in a lampglow, black sockets of caps on their blond copper polls. Stephen Dedalus and Lynch pass through the crowd close to the redcoats.)

PRIVATE COMPTON

(Jerks his finger.) Way for the parson.

PRIVATE CARR

(Turns and calls.) What ho, parson!

CISSY CAFFREY

(Her voice soaring higher.)

> She has it, she got it,
> Wherever she put it
> The leg of the duck.

(Stephen, flourishing the ashplant in his left hand, chants with joy the introit for paschal time. Lynch, his jockey cap low on his brow, attends him, a sneer of discontent wrinkling his face.)

STEPHEN

Vidi aquam egredientem de templo a latere dextro. Alleluia.
   (The famished snaggletusks of an elderly bawd protrude from a doorway.)

THE BAWD

(Her voice whispering huskily.) Sst! Come here till I tell you. Maidenhead inside. Sst.

STEPHEN

(Altius aliquantulum.) Et omnes ad quos pervenit aqua ista.

THE BAWD

(Spits in their trail her jet of venom.) Trinity medicals. Fallopian tube. All prick and no pence.

   (Edy Boardman, sniffling, crouched with Bertha Supple, draws her shawl across her nostrils.)

EDY BOARDMAN

(Bickering.) And says the one: I seen you up Faithful place with your square-

pusher, the greaser off the railway, in his cometobed hat. Did you, says I. That's not for you to say, says I. You never seen me in the mantrap with a married highlander, says I. The likes of her! Stag that one is. Stubborn as a mule! And her walking with two fellows the one time, Kildbride the enginedriver, and lancecorporal Oliphant.

STEPHEN

(*Triumphaliter.*) *Salvi facti i sunt.*

(*He flourishes his ashplant shivering the lamp image, shattering light over the world. A liver and white spaniel on the prowl slinks after him, growling. Lynch scares it with a kick.*)

LYNCH

So that?

STEPHEN

(*Looks behind.*) So that gesture, not music, not odours, would be a universal language, the gift of tongues rendering visible not the lay sense but the first entelechy, the structural rhythm.

LYNCH

Pornosophical philotheology. Metaphysics in Mecklenburg street!

STEPHEN

We have shrewridden Shakespeare and henpecked Socrates. Even the allwisest stagyrite was bitted, bridled and mounted by a light of love.

LYNCH

Ba!

STEPHEN

Anyway, who wants two gestures to illustrate a loaf and a jug? This movement illustrates the loaf and jug of bread and wine in Omar. Hold my stick.

LYNCH

Damn your yellow stick. Where are we going?

STEPHEN

Lecherous lynx, to *la belle dame sans merci*, Georgina Johnson, *ad deam qui laetificat juventutem meam.*

(*Stephen thrusts the ashplant on him and slowly holds out his hands, his head going back till both hands are a span from his breast, down turned in planes intersecting, the fingers about to part, the left being higher.*)

LYNCH

Which is the jug of bread? It skills not. That or the customhouse. Illustrate thou. Here take your crutch and walk.

(*They pass. Tommy Caffrey scrambles to a gaslamp and, clasping, climbs in spasms. From the top spur he slides down. Jacky Caffrey clasps to climb. The navvy lurches against the lamp. The twins scuttle off in the dark. The navvy, swaying, presses a forefinger against a wing of his nose and ejects from the farther nostril a long liquid jet of snot. Shouldering the lamp he staggers away through the crowd with his flaring cresset.*

Snakes of river fog creep slowly. From drains, clefts, cesspools, middens arise on all sides stagnant fumes. A glow leaps in the south beyond the seaward reaches of the river. The navvy staggering forward cleaves the crowd and lurches towards the tramsiding. On the farther side under the railway bridge Bloom appears flushed, panting, cramming bread and chocolate into a side pocket. From Gillen's hairdresser's window a composite portrait shows him gallant Nelson's image. A concave mirror at the side presents to him lovelorn longlost lugubru Booloohoom. Grave Gladstone sees him level, Bloom for Bloom. He passes, struck by the stare of truculent Wellington but in the convex mirror grin unstruck the bonham eyes and fatchuck cheekchops of Jollypoldy the rixdix doldy.

At Antonio Rabaiotti's door Bloom halts, sweated under the bright arclamps. He disappears. In a moment he reappears and hurries on.)

BLOOM

Fish and taters. N. g. Ah!

(He disappears into Olhousen's, the pork butcher's, under the downcoming rollshutter. A few moments later he emerges from under the shutter, puffing Poldy, blowing Bloohoom. In each hand he holds a parcel, one containing a lukewarm pig's crubeen, the other a cold sheep's trotter, sprinkled with whole-pepper. He gasps, standing upright. Then bending to one side he presses a parcel against his rib and groans.)

BLOOM

Stitch in my side. Why did I run?

(He takes breath with care and goes forward slowly towards the lampset siding. The glow leaps again.)

BLOOM

What is that? A flasher? Searchlight.

(He stands at Cormack's corner, watching.)

BLOOM

Aurora borealis or a steel foundry? Ah, the brigade, of course. South side anyhow. Big blaze. Might be his house. Beggar's bush. We're safe. *(He hums cheerfully.)* London's burning, London's burning! On fire, on fire! *(He catches sight of the navvy lurching through the crowd at the farther side of Talbot street.)* I'll miss him. Run. Quick. Better cross here.

(He darts to cross the road. Urchins shout.)

THE URCHINS

Mind out, mister!

(Two cyclists, with lighted paper lanterns aswing, swim by him, grazing him, their bells rattling.)

THE BELLS

Haltyaltyaltyall.

BLOOM

(Halts erect stung by a spasm.) Ow.

(He looks round, darts forward suddenly. Through rising fog a dragon sand-strewer, travelling at cautiomn, slews heavily down upon him, its huge red head-light winking, its trolley hissing on the wire. The motorman bangs his footgong.)

THE GONG

Bang Bang Bla Bak Blud Bugg Bloo.

(The brake cracks violently. Bloom, raising a policeman's whitegloved hand, blunders stifflegged, out of the track. The motorman thrown forward, pugnosed, on the guidewheel, yells as he slides past over chains and keys.)

THE MOTORMAN

Hey, shitbreeches, are you doing the hattrick?

BLOOM

(Bloom trickleaps to the curbstone and halts again. He brushes a mudflake from his cheek with a parcelled hand.)

No thoroughfare. Close shave that but cured the stitch. Must take up Sandow's exerciser again. On the hands down. Insure against street accident too. The Providential. *(He feels his trouser pocket.)* Poor mamma's panacea. Heel easily catch in tracks or bootlace in a cog. Day the wheel of the black Maria peeled off my shoe at Leonard's corner. Third time is the charm. Shoe trick. Insolent driver. I ought to report him. Tension makes them nervous. Might be the fellow balked me this morning with that horsey woman. Same style of beauty. Quick of him all the same. The stiff walk. True word spoken in jest. That awful cramp in Lad lane. Something poisonous I ate. Emblem of luck. Why? Probably lost cattle. Mark of the beast. *(He closes his eyes an instant.)* Bit light in the head. Monthly or effect of the other. Brainfogfag. That tired feeling. Too much for me now. Ow!

(A sinister figure leans on plaited legs against O'Beirne's wall, a visage unknown, injected with dark mercury. From under a wideleaved sombrero the figure regards him with evil eye.)

BLOOM

Buenas noches, señorita Blanca, que calle es esta?

THE FIGURE

(Impassive, raises a signal arm.) Password. *Sraid Mabbot.*

BLOOM

Haha. *Merci.* Esperanto. *Slan leath. (He mutters.)* Gaelic league spy, sent by that fireeater.

(He steps forward. A sackshouldered ragman bars his path. He steps left, ragsackman left.)

BLOOM

I beg.

(He swerves, sidles, stepsaside, slips past and on.)

BLOOM

Keep to the right, right, right. If there is a fingerpost planted by the Touring Club at Stepaside who procured that public boon? I who lost my way and contributed to the columns of the *Irish Cyclist* the letter headed, *In darkest Stepaside.* Keep, keep, keep to the right. Rags and bones, at midnight. A fence more likely. First place murderer makes for. Wash off his sins of the world.

(Jacky Caffrey, hunted by Tommy Caffrey, runs full tilt against Bloom.)

BLOOM

O.

(Shocked, on weak hams, he halts. Tommy and Jacky vanish there, there. Bloom pats with parcelled hands watch, fobpocket, bookpocket, pursepocket, sweets of sin, potato soap.)

BLOOM

Beware of pickpockets. Old thieves' dodge. Collide. Then snatch your purse.

(The retriever approaches sniffling, nose to the ground. A sprawled form sneezes. A stooped bearded figure appears garbed in the long caftan of an elder in Zion and a smoking cap with magenta tassels. Horned spectacles hang down at the wings of the nose. Yellow poison streaks are on the drawn face.)

RUDOLPH

Second halfcrown waste money today. I told you not go with drunken goy ever. So. You catch no money.

BLOOM

(Hides the crubeen and trotter behind his back and, crestfallen, feels warm and cold feetmeat.) Ja, ich weiss, papachi.

RUDOLPH

What you making down this place? Have you no soul? *(With feeble vulture talons he feels the silent face of Bloom.)* Are you not my son Leopold, the grandson of Leopold? Are you not my dear son Leopold who left the house of his father and left the god of his fathers Abraham and Jacob?

BLOOM

(With precaution.) I suppose so, father. Mosenthal. All that's left of him.

RUDOLPH

(Severely.) One night they bring you home drunk as dog after spend your good money. What you call them running chaps?

BLOOM

(In youth's smart blue Oxford suit with white vestslips, narrow-shouldered, in brown Alpine hat, wearing gent's sterling silver waterbury keyless watch and double curb Albert with seal attached, one side of him coated with stiffening mud.) Harriers, father. Only that once.

RUDOLPH

Once! Mud head to foot. Cut your hand open. Lockjaw. They make you kaput, Leopoldleben. You watch them chaps.

BLOOM

(Weakly.) They challenged me to a sprint. It was muddy. I slipped.

RUDOLPH

(With contempt.) Goim nachez. Nice spectacles for your poor mother!

BLOOM

Mamma!

ELLEN BLOOM

(In pantomime dame's stringed mobcap, crinoline and bustle, widow Twankey's blouse with muttonleg sleeves buttoned behind, grey mittens and cameo brooch, her hair plaited in a crispine net, appears over the staircase banisters, a slanted candlestick in her hand and cries out in shrill alarm.) O blessed Redeemer, what have they done to him! My smelling salts! *(She hauls up a reef of skirt and ransacks the pouch of her striped blay petticoat. A phial, an Agnus Dei, a shrivelled potato and a celluloid doll fall out.)* Sacred Heart of Mary, where were you at all, at all?

(Bloom, mumbling, his eyes downcast, begins to bestow his parcels in his filled pockets but desists, muttering.)

A VOICE

(Sharply.) Poldy!

BLOOM

Who? *(He ducks and wards off a blow clumsily.)* At your service.

(He looks up. Beside her mirage of datepalms a handsome woman in Turkish costume stands before him. Opulent curves fill out her scarlet trousers and jacket

slashed with gold. A wide yellow cummerbund girdles her. A white yashmak violet in the night, covers her face, leaving free only her large dark eyes and raven hair.)

BLOOM

Molly!

MARION

Welly? Mrs Marion from this out, my dear man, when you speak to me. *(Satirically.)* Has poor little hubby cold feet waiting so long?

BLOOM

(Shifts from foot to foot.) No, no. Not the least little bit.

(He breathes in deep agitation, swallowing gulps of air, questions, hopes, crubeens for her supper, things to tell her, excuses, desire, spellbound. A coin gleams on her forehead. On her feet are jewelled toerings. Her ankles are linked by a slender fetterchain. Beside her a camel, hooded with a turreting turban, waits. A silk ladder of innumerable rungs climbs to his bobbing howdah. He ambles near with disgruntled hindquarters. Fiercely she slaps his haunch, her goldcurb wristbangles angriling, scolding him in Moorish.)

MARION

Nebrakada! Feminimum.

(The camel, lifting a foreleg, plucks from a tree a large mango fruit, offers it to his mistress, blinking, in his cloven hoof, then droops his head and, grunting, with uplifted neck, fumbles to kneel. Bloom stoops his back for leapfrog.)

BLOOM

I can give you . . . I mean as your business menagerer . . . Mrs Marion . . . if you . . .

MARION

So you notice some change? *(Her hands passing slowly over her trinketed stomacher. A slow friendly mockery in her eyes.)* O Poldy, Poldy, you are a poor old stick in the mud! Go and see life. See the wide world.

BLOOM

I was just going back for that lotion whitewax, orangeflower water. Shop closes early on Thursday. But the first thing in the morning. *(He pats divers pockets.)* This moving kidney. Ah!

(He points to the south, then to the east. A cake of new clean lemon soap arises, diffusing light and perfume.)

THE SOAP

We're a capital couple are Bloom and I;
He brightens the earth, I polish the sky.

(The freckled face of Sweny, the druggist, appears in the disc of the soapsun.)

SWENY

Three and a penny, please.

BLOOM

Yes. For my wife, Mrs Marion. Special recipe.

MARION

(Softly.) Poldy!

BLOOM

Yes, ma'am?

MARION

Ti trema un poco il cuore?
(In disdain she saunters away, plump as a pampered pouter pigeon, humming the duet from Don Giovanni.*)*

BLOOM

Are you sure about that *Voglio?* I mean the pronunciati . . .
(He follows, followed by the sniffing terrier. The elderly bawd seizes his sleeve, the bristles of her chinmole glittering.)

THE BAWD

Ten shillings a maidenhead. Fresh thing was never touched. Fifteen. There's no-one in it only her old father that's dead drunk.
(She points. In the gap of her dark den furtive, rain-bedraggled, Bridie Kelly stands.)

BRIDIE

Hatch street. Any good in your mind?
(With a squeak she flaps her bat shawl and runs. A burly rough pursues with booted strides. He stumbles on the steps, recovers, plunges into gloom. Weak squeaks of laughter are heard, weaker.)

THE BAWD

(Her wolfeyes shining.) He's getting his pleasure. You won't get a virgin in the flash houses. Ten shillings. Don't be all night before the polis in plain clothes sees us. Sixtyseven is a bitch.
(Leering, Gerty MacDowell limps forward. She draws from behind, ogling, and shows coyly her bloodied clout.)

GERTY

With all my worldly goods I thee and thou. *(She murmurs.)* You did that. I hate you.

BLOOM

I? When? You're dreaming. I never saw you.

THE BAWD

Leave the gentleman alone, you cheat, Writing the gentleman false letters. Streetwalking and soliciting. Better for your mother take the strap to you at the bedpost, hussy like you.

GERTY

(To Bloom.) When you saw all the secrets of my bottom drawer. *(She paws his sleeve, slobbering.)* Dirty married man! I love you for doing that to me.

(She slides away crookedly. Mrs Breen in man's frieze overcoat with loose bellows pockets, stands in the causeway, her roguish eyes wideopen, smiling in all her herbivorous buckteeth.)

MRS BREEN

Mr . . .

BLOOM

(Coughs gravely.) Madam, when we last had this pleasure by letter dated the sixteenth instant . . .

MRS BREEN

Mr Bloom! You down here in the haunts of sin! I caught you nicely! Scamp!

BLOOM

(Hurriedly.) Not so loud my name. Whatever do you think me? Don't give me away. Walls have hears. How do you do? It's ages since I. You're looking splendid. Absolutely it. Seasonable weather we are having this time of year. Black refracts heat. Short cut home here. Interesting quarter. Rescue of fallen women Magdalen asylum. I am the secretary . . .

MRS BREEN

(Holds up a finger.) Now don't tell a big fib! I know somebody won't like that. O just wait till I see Molly! *(Slily.)* Account for yourself this very minute or woe betide you!

BLOOM

(Looks behind.) She often said she'd like to visit. Slumming. The exotic, you see. Negro servants too in livery if she had money. Othello black brute. Eugene Stratton. Even the bones and cornerman at the Livermore christies. Bohee brothers. Sweep for that matter.

(Tom and Sam Bohee, coloured coons in white duck suits, scarlet socks, upstarched Sambo chokers and large scarlet asters in their buttonholes leap out. Each has his banjo slung. Their paler smaller negroid hands jingle the twingtwang wires. Flashing white Kaffir eyes and tusks they rattle through a breakdown in clumsy clogs, twinging, singing, back to back, toe heel, heel toe, with smackfatclacking nigger lips.)

There's someone in the house with Dina
There's someone in the house, I know,
There's someone in the house with Dina
Playing on the old banjo.

(They whisk black masks from raw babby faces: then, chuckling, chortling, trumming, twanging they diddle diddle cakewalk dance away.)

BLOOM

(With a sour tenderish smile.) A little frivol, shall we, if you are so inclined? Would you like me perhaps to embrace you just for a fraction of a second?

MRS BREEN

(Screams gaily.) O, you ruck! You ought to see yourself!

BLOOM

For old sake'sake. I only meant a square party, a mixed marriage mingling of our different little conjugials. You know I had a soft corner for you. *(Gloomily.)* 'Twas I sent you that valentine of the dear gazelle.

MRS BREEN

Glory Alice, you do look a holy show! Killing simply. *(She puts out her hand inquisitively.)* What are you hiding behind your back? Tell us, there's a dear.

BLOOM

(Seizes her wrist with his free hand.) Josie Powell that was, prettiest deb in Dublin. How time flies by! Do you remember, harking back in a retrospective arrangement, Old Christmas night Georgina Simpson's housewarming while they were playing the Irving Bishop game, finding the pin blindfold and thoughtreading? Subject, what is in this snuff box?

MRS BREEN

You were the lion of the night with your seriocomic recitation and you looked the part. You were always a favourite with the ladies.

BLOOM

(Squire of dames, in dinner jacket with wateredsilk facings, blue masonic badge in his buttonhole, black bow and mother-of-pearl studs, a prismatic champagne glass tilted in his hand.) Ladies and gentlemen, I give you Ireland, home and beauty.

MRS BREEN

The dear dead days beyond recall. Love's old sweet song.

BLOOM

(Meaningfully dropping his voice.) I confess I'm teapot with curiosity to find out whether some person's something is a little teapot at present.

MRS BREEN

(Gushingly.) Tremendously teapot! London's teapot and I'm simply teapot all over me. (She rubs sides with him.) After the parlour mystery games and the crackers from the tree we sat on the staircase ottoman. Under the mistletoe. Two is company.

BLOOM

(Wearing a purple Napoleon hat with an amber halfmoon, his fingers and thumbs passing slowly down to her soft moist meaty palm which she surrenders gently.) The witching hour of night. I took the splinter out of this hand, carefully, slowly. (Tenderly, as he slips on her finger a ruby ring.) Là ci darem la mano.

MRS BREEN

(In a onepiece evening frock executed in moonlight blue, a tinsel sylph's diadem on her brow with her dancecard fallen beside her moonblue satin slipper, curves her palm softly, breathing quickly.) Voglio e non. You're hot! You're scalding! The left hand nearest the heart.

BLOOM

When you made your present choice they said it was beauty and the beast. I can never forgive you for that. (His clenched fist at his brow.) Think what it means. All you meant to me then. (Hoarsely.) Woman, it's breaking me!
   (Denis Breen, whitetallhatted, with Wisdom Hely's sandwichboard, shuffles past them in carpet slippers, his dull beard thrust out, muttering to right and left. Little Alf Bergan, cloaked in the pall of the ace of spades dogs him to left and right, doubled in laughter.)

ALF BERGAN

(Points jeering at the sandwich boards.) U. p.: Up.

MRS BREEN

(To Bloom.) High jinks below stairs. (She gives him the glad eye.) Why didn't you kiss the spot to make it well? You wanted to.

BLOOM

(Shocked.) Molly's best friend! Could you?

MRS BREEN

(Her pulpy tongue between her lips, offers a pigeon kiss.) Hnhn. The answer is a lemon. Have you a little present for me there?

BLOOM

(Offhandedly.) Kosher. A snack for supper. The home without potted meat is incomplete. I was at Leah. Mrs Bandman Palmer. Trenchant exponent of Shakespeare. Unfortunately threw away the programme. Rattling good place round there for pig's feet. Feel.

(Richie Goulding, three ladies' hats pinned on his head, appears weighted to one side by the black legal bag of Collis and Ward on which a skull and crossbones are painted in white limewash. He opens it and shows it full of polonies, kippered herrings, Findon haddies and tightpacked pills.)

RICHIE

Best value in Dub.

(Bald Pat, bothered beetle, stands on the curbstone, folding his napkin, waiting to wait.)

PAT

(Advances with a tilted dish of spillspilling gravy.) Steak and kidney. Bottle of lager. Hee hee hee. Wait till I wait.

RICHIE

Goodgod. Inev erate inall . . .

(With hanging head he marches doggedly forward. The navvy, lurching by, gores him with his flaming pronghorn.)

RICHIE

(With a cry of pain, his hand to his back.) Ah! Bright's! Lights!

BLOOM

(Points to the navvy.) A spy. Don't attract attention. I hate stupid crowds. I am not on pleasure bent. I am in a grave predicament.

MRS BREEN

Humbugging and deluthering as per usual with your cock and bull story.

BLOOM

I want to tell you a little secret about how I came to be here. But you must never tell. Not even Molly. I have a most particular reason.

MRS BREEN

(All agog.) O, not for worlds.

BLOOM

Let's walk on. Shall us?

MRS BREEN

Let's.

(The bawd makes an unheeded sign. Bloom walks on with Mrs Breen. The terrier follows, whining piteously, wagging his tail.)

THE BAWD

Jewman's melt!

BLOOM

(In an oatmeal sporting suit, a sprig of woodbine in the lapel, tony buff shirt,

shepherd's plaid Saint Andrew's cross scarftie, white spats, fawn dustcoat on his arm, tawny red brogues, fieldglasses in bandolier and a grey billycock hat.) Do you remember a long long time, years and years ago, just after Milly, Marionette we called her, was weaned when we all went together to Fairyhouse races, was it?

MRS BREEN

(In smart Saxe tailormade, white velours hat and spider veil.) Leopardstown.

BLOOM

I mean, Leopardstown. And Molly won seven shillings on a three year old named Nevertell and coming home along by Foxrock in that old fiveseater shanderadan of a waggonette you were in your heyday then and you had on that new hat of white velours with a surround of molefur that Mrs Hayes advised you to buy because it was marked down to nineteen and eleven, a bit of wire and an old rag of velveteen, and I'll lay you what you like she did it on purpose . . .

MRS BREEN

She did, of course, the cat! Don't tell me! Nice adviser!

BLOOM

Because it didn't suit you one quarter as well as the other ducky little tammy toque with the bird of paradise wing in it that I admired on you and you honestly looked just too fetching in it though it was a pity to kill it, you cruel creature, little mite of a thing with a heart the size of a fullstop.

MRS BREEN

(Squeezes his arm, simpers.) Naughty cruel I was.

BLOOM

(Low, secretly, ever more rapidly.) And Molly was eating a sandwich of spiced beef out of Mrs Joe Gallaher's lunch basket. Frankly, though she had her advisers or admirers, I never cared much for her style. She was . . .

MRS BREEN

Too . . .

BLOOM

Yes. And Molly was laughing because Rogers and Maggot O'Reilly were mimicking a cock as we passed a farmhouse and Marcus Tertius Moses, the tea merchant, drove past us in a gig with his daughter, Dancer Moses was her name, and the poodle in her lap bridled up and you asked me if I ever heard or read or knew or came across . . .

MRS BREEN

(Eagerly.) Yes, yes, yes, yes, yes, yes, yes.

(She fades from his side. Followed by the whining dog he walks on towards hellsgates. In an archway a standing woman, bent forward, her feet apart, pisses cowily. Outside a shuttered pub a bunch of loiterers listen to a tale which their broken snouted gaffer rasps out with raucous humour. An armless pair of them flop wrestling, growling, in maimed sodden playfight.)

THE GAFFER

(Crouches, his voice twisted in his snout.) And when Cairns came down from the scaffolding in Beaver Street what was he after doing it into only into the bucket of porter that was there waiting on the shavings for Derwan's plasterers.

THE LOITERERS

(Guffaw with cleft palates.) O jays!

(Their paintspeckled hats wag. Spattered with size and lime of their lodges they frisk limblessly about him.)

BLOOM

Coincidence too. They think it funny. Anything but that. Broad daylight. Trying to walk. Lucky no woman.

THE LOITERERS

Jays, that's a good one. Glauber salts. O jays, into the men's porter.

(Bloom passes. Cheap whores, singly, coupled, shawled, dishevelled, call from lanes, doors, corners.)

THE WHORES

Are you going far, queer fellow?

How's your middle leg?

Got a match on you?

Eh, come here till I stiffen it for you.

(He plodges through their sump towards the lighted street beyond. From a bulge of window curtains a gramophone rears a battered brazen trunk. In the shadow a shebeenkeeper haggles with the navvy and the two redcoats.)

THE NAVVY

(Belching.) Where's the bloody house?

THE SHEBEENKEEPER

Purdon street. Shilling a bottle of stout. Respectable woman.

THE NAVVY

(Gripping the two redcoats, staggers forward with them.) Come on, you British army!

PRIVATE CARR

(Behind his back.) He aint half balmy.

PRIVATE COMPTON

(Laughs.) What ho!

PRIVATE CARR

(To the navvy.) Portobello barracks canteen. You ask for Carr. Just Carr.

THE NAVVY

(Shouts.)   We are the boys. Of Wexford.

PRIVATE COMPTON

Say! What price the sergeantmajor?

PRIVATE CARR

Bennett? He's my pal. I love old Bennett.

THE NAVVY

(Shouts.)

The galling chain.

And free our native land.

(He staggers forward, dragging them with him. Bloom stops, at fault. The dog approaches, his tongue outlolling, panting.)

BLOOM

Wildgoose chase this. Disorderly houses. Lord knows where they are gone. Drunks cover distance double quick. Nice mixup. Scene at Westland row. Then jump in first class with third ticket. Then too far. Train with engine behind. Might have taken me to Malahide or a siding for the night or collision. Second drink does it. Once is a dose. What am I following him for? Still, he's the best of that lot. If I hadn't heard about Mrs Beaufoy Purefoy I wouldn't have gone and wouldn't have met. Kismet. He'll lose that cash. Relieving office here. Good biz for cheapjacks, organs. What do ye lack? Soon got, soon gone. Might have lost my life too with that mangongwheeltracktrolleyglarejuggernaut only for presence of mind. Can't always save you, though. If I had passed Truelock's window that day two minutes later would have been shot. Absence of body. Still if bullet only went through my coat get damages for shock, five hundred pounds. What was he? Kildare street club toff. God help his gamekeeper.

(He gazes ahead reading on the wall a scrawled chalk legend Wet Dream *and a phallic design.)*

Odd! Molly drawing on the frosted carriagepane at Kingstown. What's that like? *(Gaudy dollwomen loll in the lighted doorways, in window embrasures, smoking birdseye cigarettes. The odour of the sicksweet weed floats towards him in slow round ovalling wreaths.)*

THE WREATHS

Sweet are the sweets. Sweets of sin.

BLOOM

My spine's a bit limp. Go or turn? And this food? Eat it and get all pigsticky. Absurd I am. Waste of money. One and eight pence too much. *(The retriever drives a cold snivelling muzzle against his hand, wagging his tail.)* Strange how they take to me. Even that brute today. Better speak to him first. Like women they like *rencontres*. Stinks like a polecat. *Chacun son goût.* He might be mad. Fido. Uncertain in his movements. Good fellow! Garryowen! *(The wolfdog sprawls on his back, wriggling obscenely with begging paws, his long black tongue lolling out.)* Influence of his surroundings. Give and have done with it. Provided nobody. *(Calling encouraging words he shambles back with a furtive poacher's tread, dogged by the setter into a dark stalestunk corner. He unrolls one parcel and goes to dump the crubeen softly but holds back and feels the trotter.)* Sizeable for threepence. But then I have it in my left hand. Calls for more effort. Why? Smaller from want of use. O, let it slide. Two and six.

(With regret he lets unrolled crubeen and trotter slide. The mastiff mauls the bundle clumsily and gluts himself with growling greed, crunching the bones. Two raincaped watch approach, silent, vigilant. They murmur together.)

THE WATCH

Bloom. Of Bloom. For Bloom. Bloom.

(Each lays hand on Bloom's shoulder.)

FIRST WATCH

Caught in the act. Commit no nuisance.

BLOOM

(Stammers.) I am doing good to others.

(A covey of gulls, storm petrels, rises hungrily from Liffey slime with Banbury cakes in their beaks.)

THE GULLS

Kaw kave kankury kake.

BLOOM

The friend of man. Trained by kindness.

(He points. Bob Doran, toppling from a high barstool, sways over the munching spaniel.)

BOB DORAN

Towser. Give us the paw. Give the paw.

(The bulldog growls, his scruff standing, a gobbet of pig's knuckle between his molars through which rabid scumspittle dribbles. Bob Doran falls silently into an area.)

SECOND WATCH

Prevention of cruelty to animals.

BLOOM

(Enthusiastically.) A noble work! I scolded that tramdriver on Harold's cross bridge for illusing the poor horse with his harness scab. Bad French I got for my pains. Of course it was frosty and the last tram. All tales of circus life are highly demoralising.

(Signor Maffei, passion pale, in liontamer's costume with diamond studs in his shirtfront steps forward, holding a circus paper hoop, a curling carriagewhip and a revolver with which he covers the gorging boarhound.)

SIGNOR MAFFEI

(With a sinister smile.) Ladies and gentlemen, my educated greyhound. It was I broke in the bucking broncho Ajax with my patent spiked saddle for carnivores. Lash under the belly with a knotted thong. Block tackle and a strangling pully will bring your lion to heel, no matter how fractious, even *Leo ferox* there, the Libyan maneater. A redhot crowbar and some liniment rubbing on the burning part produced Fritz of Amsterdam, the thinking hyena. *(He glares.)* I possess the Indian sign. The glint of my eye does it with these breastsparklers. *(With a bewitching smile.)* I now introduce Mademoiselle Ruby, the pride of the ring.

FIRST WATCH

Come. Name and address.

BLOOM

I have forgotten for the moment. Ah, yes! *(He takes off his high grade hat, saluting.)* Dr Bloom, Leopold, dental surgeon. You have heard of von Bloom Pasha. Umpteen millions. *Donnerwetter!* Owns half Austria. Egypt. Cousin.

FIRST WATCH

Proof.

(A card falls from inside the leather headband of Bloom's hat.)

BLOOM

(In red fez, cadi's dress coat with broad green sash, wearing a false badge of the Legion of Honour, picks up the card hastily and offers it.) Allow me. My club is the Junior Army and Navy. Solicitors: Messrs John Henry Menton, 27 Bachelor's Walk.

FIRST WATCH

(Reads.) Henry Flower. No fixed abode. Unlawfully watching and besetting.

SECOND WATCH

An alibi. You are cautioned.

BLOOM

(Produces from his heartpocket a crumpled yellow flower.) This is the flower in question. It was given me by a man I don't know his name. *(Plausibly.)* You

know that old joke, rose of Castille. Bloom. The change of name Virag. *(He murmurs privately and confidentially.)* We are engaged you see, sergeant. Lady in the case. Love entanglement. *(He shoulders the second watch gently.)* Dash it all. It's a way we gallants have in the navy. Uniform that does it. *(He turns gravely to the first watch.)* Still, of course, you do get your Waterloo sometimes. Drop in some evening and have a glass of old Burgundy. *(To the second watch gaily.)* I'll introduce you, inspector. She's game. Do it in shake of a lamb's tail.

(A dark mercurialised face appears, leading a veiled figure.)

THE DARK MERCURY

The Castle is looking for him. He was drummed out of the army.

MARTHA   •

(Thickveiled, a crimson halter round her neck, a copy of the Irish Times *in her hand, in tone of reproach, pointing.)* Henry! Leopold! Leopold! Lionel, thou lost one! Clear my name.

FIRST WATCH

(Sternly.) Come to the station.

BLOOM

(Scared, hats himself, steps back then, plucking at his heart and lifting his right forearm on the square, he gives the sign and dueguard of fellowcraft.) No, no, worshipful master, light of love. Mistaken identity. The Lyons mail. Lesurques and Dubosc. You remember the Childs fratricide case. We medical men. By striking him dead with a hatchet. I am wrongfully accused. Better one guilty escape than ninetynine wrongfully condemned.

MARTHA

(Sobbing behind her veil.) Breach of promise. My real name is Peggy Griffin. He wrote to me that he was miserable. I'll tell my brother, the Bective rugger fullback, on you, heartless flirt.

BLOOM

(Behind his hand.) She's drunk. The woman is inebriated. *(He murmurs vaguely the past of Ephraim.)* Shitbroleeth.

SECOND WATCH

(Tears in his eyes, to Bloom.) You ought to be thoroughly well ashamed of yourself.

BLOOM

Gentlemen of the jury, let me explain. A pure mare's nest. I am a man misunderstood. I am being made a scapegoat of. I am a respectable married man, without a stain on my character. I live in Eccles street. My wife, I am the daughter of a most distinguished commander, a gallant upstanding gentleman, what do you call him, Majorgeneral Brian Tweedy, one of Britain's fighting men who helped to win our battles. Got his majority for the heroic defence of Rorke's Drift.

FIRST WATCH

Regiment.

BLOOM

(Turns to the gallery.) The royal Dublins, boys, the salt of the earth, known the world over. I think I see some old comrades in arms up there among you. The R. D. F. With our own Metropolitan police, guardians of our homes, the pluckiest lads and the finest body of men, as physique, in the service of our sovereign.

A VOICE

Turncoat! Up the Boers! Who booed Joe Chamberlain?

BLOOM

(His hand on the shoulder of the first watch.) My old dad too was a J. P. I'm as staunch a Britisher as you are, sir. I fought with the colours for king and country in the absentminded war under general Gough in the park and was disabled at Spion Kop and Bloemfontein, was mentioned in dispatches. I did all a white man could. *(With quiet feeling.)* Jim Bludso. Hold her nozzle again the bank.

FIRST WATCH

Profession or trade.

BLOOM

Well, I follow a literary occupation. Author-journalist. In fact we are just bringing out a collection of prize stories of which I am the inventor, something that is an entirely new departure. I am connected with the British and Irish press. If you ring up . . .

(Myles Crawford strides out jerkily, a quill between his teeth. His scarlet beak blazes within the aureole of his straw hat. He dangles a hank of Spanish onions in one hand and holds with the other hand a telephone receiver nozzle to his ear.)

MYLES CRAWFORD

(His cock's wattles wagging.) Hello, seventyseven eightfour. Hello. *Free-man's Urinal* and *Weekly Arsewiper* here. Paralyse Europe. You which? Bluebags? Who writes? Is it Bloom?

(Mr Philip Beaufoy, palefaced, stands in the witnessbox, in accurate morning dress, outbreast pocket with peak of handkerchief showing, creased lavender trousers and patent boots. He carries a large portfolio labelled Matcham's Masterstrokes.)

BEAUFOY

(*Drawls.*) No, you aren't, not by a long shot if I know it. I don't see it, that's all. No born gentleman, no one with the most rudimentary promptings of a gentleman would stoop to such particularly loathsome conduct. One, of those, my lord. A plagiarist. A soapy sneak masquerading as a literateur. It's perfectly obvious that with the most inherent baseness he has cribbed some of my bestselling books, really gorgeous stuff, a perfect gem, the love passages in which are beneath suspicion. The Beaufoy books of love and great possessions with which your lordship is doubtless familiar, are a household word throughout the kingdom.

BLOOM

(*Murmurs with hangdog meekness.*) That bit about the laughing witch hand in hand I take exception to, if I may . . .

BEAUFOY

(*His lip upcurled, smiles superciliously on the court.*) You funny ass, you! You're too beastly awfully weird for words! I don't think you need over excessively disincommodate yourself in that regard. My literary agent Mr J. B. Pinker is in attendance. I presume, my lord, we shall receive the usual witnesses' fees, shan't we? We are considerably out of pocket over this bally pressman johnny, this jackdaw of Rheims, who has not even been to a university.

BLOOM

(*Indistinctly.*) University of life. Bad art.

BEAUFOY

(*Shouts.*) It's a damnably foul lie showing the moral rottenness of the man! (*He extends his portfolio.*) We have here damning evidence, the *corpus delicti*, my lord, a specimen of my maturer work disfigured by the hallmark of the beast.

A VOICE FROM THE GALLERY

Moses, Moses, king of the jews,
Wiped his arse in the Daily News.

BLOOM

(*Bravely.*) Overdrawn.

BEAUFOY

You low cad! You ought to be ducked in the horsepond, you rotter! (*To the court.*) Why, look at the man's private life! Leading a quadruple existence! Street angel and house devil. Not fit to be mentioned in mixed society. The arch conspirator of the age.

BLOOM

(*To the court.*) And he, a bachelor, how . . .

FIRST WATCH

The King versus Bloom. Call the woman Driscoll.

THE CRIER

Mary Driscoll, scullerymaid!

(*Mary Driscoll, a slipshod servant girl approaches. She has a bucket on the crook of her arm and a scouringbrush in her hand.*)

SECOND WATCH

Another! Are you of the unfortunate class?

MARY DRISCOLL

(*Indignantly.*) I'm not a bad one. I bear a respectable character and was four months in my last place. I was in a situation, six pounds a year and my chances with Fridays out, and I had to leave owing to his carryings on.

FIRST WATCH

What do you tax him with?

MARY DRISCOLL

He made a certain suggestion but I thought more of myself as poor as I am.

BLOOM

(*In housejacket of ripplecloth, flannel trousers, heelless slippers, unshaven, his hair rumpled softly.*) I treated you white. I gave you mementos, smart emerald garters far above your station. Incautiously I took your part when you were accused of pilfering. There's a medium in all things. Play cricket.

MARY DRISCOLL

(*Excitedly.*) As God is looking down on me this night if ever I laid a hand to them oysters!

FIRST WATCH

The offence complained of? Did something happen?

MARY DRISCOLL

He surprised me in the rere of the premises, your honour, when the missus was out shopping one morning with a request for a safety pin. He held me and I was discoloured in four places as a result. And he interfered twict with my clothing.

BLOOM

She counterassaulted.

MARY DRISCOLL

(*Scornfully.*) I had more respect for the scouringbrush, so I had. I remonstrated with him, your lord, and he remarked: Keep it quiet!
(*General laughter.*)

GEORGES FOTTRELL

(Clerk of the crown and peace, resonantly.) Order in court! The accused will now make a bogus statement.

(Bloom, pleading not guilty and holding a fullblown waterlily, begins a long unintelligible speech. They would hear what counsel had to say in his stirring address to the grandjury. He was down and out but, though branded as a black sheep, if he might say so, he meant to reform, to retrieve the memory of the past in a purely sisterly way and return to nature as a purely domestic animal. A seven months' child, he had been carefully brought up and nurtured by an aged bedridden parent. There might have been lapses of an erring father but he wanted to turn over a new leaf and now, when at long last in sight of the whipping post, to lead a homely life in the evening of his days, permeated by the affectionate surroundings of the heaving bosom of the family. An acclimatised Britisher, he had seen that summer eve from the footplate of an engine cab of the Loop line railway company while the rain refrained from falling glimpses, as it were, through the windows of loveful households in Dublin city and urban district of scenes truly rural of happiness of the better land with Dockrell's wallpaper at one and ninepence a dozen, innocent Britishborn bairns lisping prayers to the Sacred Infant, youthful scholars grappling with their pensums, model young ladies playing on the pianoforte or anon all with fervour reciting the family rosary round the crackling Yulelog while in the boreens and green lanes the colleens with their swains strolled what times the strains of the organtoned melodeon Britannia metalbound with four acting stops and twelvefold bellows, a sacrifice, greatest bargain ever . . .)

(Renewed laughter. He mumbles incoherently. Reporters complain that they cannot hear.)

LONGHAND AND SHORTHAND

(Without looking up from their notebooks.) Loosen his boots.

PROFESSOR MACHUGH

(From the presstable, coughs and calls.)

Cough it up, man. Get it out in bits.

(The crossexamination proceeds re Bloom and the bucket. A large bucket. Bloom himself. Bowel trouble. In Beaver street. Gripe, yes. Quite bad. A plasterer's bucket. By walking stifflegged. Suffered untold misery. Deadly agony. About noon. Love or burgundy. Yes, some spinach. Crucial moment. He did not look in the bucket. Nobody. Rather a mess. Not completely. A Titbits back number.)

(Uproar and cat calls. Bloom in a torn frockcoat stained with whitewash dinged silk hat sideways on his head, a strip of stickingplaster across his nose, talks inaudibly.)

J. J. O'MOLLOY

(*In barrister's grey wig and stuffgown, speaking with a voice of pained protest.*) This is no place for indecent levity at the expense of an erring mortal disguised in liquor. We are not in a beargarden nor at an Oxford rag nor is this a travesty of justice. My client is an infant, a poor foreign immigrant who started scratch as a stowaway and is now trying to turn an honest penny. The trumped up misdemeanour was due to a momentary aberration of heredity, brought on by hallucination, such familiarities as the alleged guilty occurrence being quite permitted in my client's native place, the land of the Pharaoh. *Prima facie*, I put it to you that there was no attempt at carnally knowing. Intimacy did not occur and the offence complained of by Driscoll, that her virtue was solicited, was not repeated. I would deal in especial with atavism. There have been cases of shipwreck and somnambulism in my client's family. If the accused could speak he could a tale unfold one of the strangest that have ever been narrated between the covers of a book. He himself, my lord, is a physical wreck from cobbler's weak chest. His submission is that he is of Mongolian extraction and irresponsible for his actions. Not all there, in fact.

BLOOM

(*Barefoot, pigeonbreasted, in lascar's vest and trousers, apologetic toes turned in, opens his tiny mole's eyes and looks about him dazedly, passing a slow hand across his forehead. Then he hitches his belt sailor fashion and with a shrug of oriental obeisance salutes the court, pointing one thumb heavenward.*) Him makee velly muchee fine night. (*He begins to lilt simply.*)

> Li li poo lil chile,
> Blingee pigfoot evly night.
> Payee two shilly . . .

(*He is howled down.*)

J. J. O'MOLLOY

(*Hotly to the populace.*) This is a lonehand fight. By Hades, I will not have any client of mine gagged and badgered in this fashion by a pack of curs and laughing hyenas. The Mosaic code has superseded the law of the jungle. I say it and I say it emphatically without wishing for one moment to defeat the ends of justice, accused was not accessory before the act and prosecutrix has not been tampered with. The young person was treated by defendant as if she were his very own daughter. (*Bloom takes J. J. O'Molloy's hand and raises it to his lips.*) I shall call rebutting evidence to prove up to the hilt that the hidden hand is again at its old game. When in doubt persecute Bloom.

My client, an innately bashful man, would be the last man in the world to do anything ungentlemanly which injured modesty could object to or cast a stone at a girl who took the wrong turning when some dastard, responsible for her condition, had worked his own sweet will on her. He wants to go straight. I regard him as the whitest man I know. He is down on his luck at present owing to the mortgaging of his extensive property at Agendath Netaim in faraway Asia Minor, slides of which will now be shown. *(To Bloom.)* I suggest that you will do the handsome thing.

BLOOM

A penny in the pound.

(The mirage of the lake of Kinnereth with blurred cattle cropping in silver haze is projected on the wall. Moses Dlugacz, ferreteyed albino, in blue dungarees, stands up in the gallery, holding in each hand an orange citron and a pork kidney.)

DLUGACZ

(Hoarsely.) Bleibtreustrasse, Berlin, W. 13.

(J. J. O'Molloy steps on to a low plinth and holds the lapel of his coat with solemnity. His face lengthens, grows pale and bearded, with sunken eyes, the blotches of phthisis and hectic cheekbones of John F. Taylor. He applies his handkerchief to his mouth and scrutinises the galloping tide of rosepink blood.)

J. J. O'MOLLOY

(Almost voicelessly.) Excuse me, I am suffering from a severe chill, have recently come from a sickbed. A few wellchosen words. *(He assumes the avine head, foxy moustache and proboscidal eloquence of Seymour Bushe.)* When the angel's book comes to be opened if aught that the pensive bosom has inaugurated of soultransfigured and of soultransfiguring deserves to live I say accord the prisoner at the bar the sacred benefit of the doubt. *(A paper with something written on it is handed into court.)*

BLOOM

(In court dress.) Can give best references. Messrs Callan, Coleman. Mr Wisdom Hely J. P. My old chief Joe Cuffe. Mr V. B. Dillon, ex-lord mayor of Dublin. I have moved in the charmed circle of the highest . . . Queens of Dublin Society. *(Carelessly.)* I was just chatting this afternoon at the viceregal lodge to my old pals, sir Robert and lady Ball, astronomer royal, at the levee. Sir Bob, I said . . .

MRS YELVERTON BARRY

(In lowcorsaged opal balldress and elbowlength ivory gloves, wearing a sabletrimmed brick quilted dolman, a comb of brilliants and panache of osprey in her hair.) Arrest him, constable. He wrote me an anonymous letter in prentice backhand when my husband was in the North Riding of Tipperary on the

Munster circuit, signed James Lovebirch. He said that he had seen from the gods my peerless globes as I sat in a box of the *Theatre Royal* at a command performance of *La Cigale*. I deeply inflamed him, he said. He made improper overtures to me to misconduct myself at half past four p. m. on the following Thursday, Dunsink time. He offered to send me through the post a work of fiction by Monsieur Paul de Kock, entitled *The Girl with the Three Pairs of Stays*.

MRS BELLINGHAM

(In cap and seal coney mantle, wrapped up to the nose, steps out of her brougham and scans through tortoiseshell quizzing-glasses which she takes from inside her huge opossum muff.) Also to me. Yes, I believe it is the same objectionable person. Because he closed my carriage door outside sir Thornley Stoker's one sleety day during the cold snap of February ninetythree when even the grid of the wastepipe and ballstop in my bath cistern were frozen. Subsequently he enclosed a bloom of edelweiss culled on the heights, as he said, in my honour. I had it examined by a botanical expert and elicited the information that it was a blossom of the homegrown potato plant purloined from a forcingcase of the model farm.

MRS YELVERTON BARRY

Shame on him!

(A crowd of sluts and ragamuffins surges forward.)

THE SLUTS AND RAGAMUFFINS

(Screaming.) Stop thief! Hurrah there, Bluebeard! Three cheers for Ikey Mo!

SECOND WATCH

(Produces handcuffs.) Here are the darbies.

MRS BELLINGHAM

He addressed me in several handwritings with fulsome compliments as a Venus in furs and alleged profound pity for my frostbound coachman Balmer while in the same breath he expressed himself as envious of his earflaps and fleecy sheepskins and of his fortunate proximity to my person, when standing behind my chair wearing my livery and the armorial bearings of the Bellingham escutcheon garnished sable, a buck's head couped or. He lauded almost extravagantly my nether extremities, my swelling calves in silk hose drawn up to the limit and eulogised glowingly my other hidden treasures in priceless lace which, he said, he could conjure up. He urged me, stating that he felt it his mission in life to urge me, to defile the marriage bed, to commit adultery at the earliest possible opportunity.

THE HONOURABLE MRS MERVYN TALBOYS

(In amazon costume, hard hat, jackboots cockspurred, vermilion waistcoat, fawn musketeer gauntlets with braided drums, long train held up and hunting crop with which she strikes her welt constantly.) Also me. Because he saw me on the polo ground of the Phœnix park at the match All Ireland versus the Rest of Ireland. My eyes, I know, shone divinely as I watched Captain Slogger Dennehy of the Inniskillings win the final chukkar on his darling cob *Centaur.* This plebeian Don Juan observed me from behind a hackney car and sent me in double envelopes an obscene photograph, such as are sold after dark on Paris boulevards, insulting to any lady. I have it still. It represents a partially nude señorita, frail and lovely (his wife as he solemnly assured me, taken by him from nature), practising illicit intercourse with a muscular torero, evidently a blackguard. He urged me to do likewise, to misbehave, to sin with officers of the garrison. He implored me to soil his letter in an unspeakable manner, to chastise him as he richly deserves, to bestride and ride him, to give him a most vicious horsewhipping.

MRS BELLINGHAM

Me too.

MRS YELVERTON BARRY

Me too.

(Several highly respectable Dublin ladies hold up improper letters received from Bloom.)

THE HONOURABLE MRS MERVYN TALBOYS

(Stamps her jingling spurs in a sudden paroxysm of sudden fury.) I will, by the God above me. I'll scourge the pigeonlivered cur as long as I can stand over him. I'll flay him alive.

BLOOM

(His eyes closing, quails expectantly.) Here? *(He squirms.)* Again! *(He pants cringing.)* I love the danger.

THE HONOURABLE MRS MERVYN TALBOYS

Very much so! I'll make it hot for you. I'll make you dance Jack Latten for that.

MRS BELLINGHAM

Tan his breech well, the upstart! Write the stars and stripes on it!

MRS YELVERTON BARRY

Disgraceful! There's no excuse for him! A married man!

BLOOM

All these people. I meant only the spanking idea. A warm tingling glow without effusion. Refined birching to stimulate the circulation.

THE HONOURABLE MRS MERVYN TALBOYS

(*Laughs derisively.*) O, did you, my fine fellow? Well, by the living God, you'll get the surprise of your life now, believe me, the most unmerciful hiding a man ever bargained for. You have lashed the dormant tigress in my nature into fury.

MRS BELLINGHAM

(*Shakes her muff and quizzing-glasses vindictively.*) Make him smart, Hanna dear. Give him ginger. Thrash the mongrel within an inch of his life. The cat-o'-nine-tails. Geld him. Vivisect him.

BLOOM

(*Shuddering, shrinking, joins his hands with hangdog mien.*) O cold! O shivery! It was your ambrosial beauty. Forget, forgive. Kismet. Let me off this once. (*He offers the other cheek.*)

MRS YELVERTON BARRY

(*Severely.*) Don't do so on any account, Mrs Talboys! He should be soundly trounced!

THE HONOURABLE MRS MERVYN TALBOYS

(*Unbuttoning her gauntlet violently.*) I'll do no such thing. Pig dog and always was ever since he was pupped! To dare address me! I'll flog him black and blue in the public streets. I'll dig my spurs in him up to the rowel. He is a wellknown cuckold. (*She swishes her huntingcrop savagely in the air.*) Take down his trousers without loss of time. Come here, sir! Quick! Ready?

BLOOM

(*Trembling, beginning to obey.*) The weather has been so warm.
   (*Davy Stephens, ringleted, passes with a bevy of barefoot newsboys.*)

DAVY STEPHENS

Messenger of the Sacred Heart and *Evening Telegraph* with Saint Patrick's Day Supplement. Containing the new addresses of all the cuckolds in Dublin.
   (*The very reverend Canon O'Hanlon in cloth of gold cope elevates and exposes a marble timepiece. Before him Father Conroy and the reverend John Hughes S. J. bend low.*)

THE TIMEPIECE

(*Unportalling.*)

Cuckoo.

Cuckoo.

Cuckoo.

(*The brass quoits of a bed are heard to jingle.*)

THE QUOITS

Jigjag, Jigajiga. Jigjag.

(*A panel of fog rolls back rapidly, revealing rapidly in the jurybox the faces of Martin Cunningham, foreman silkhatted, Jack Power, Simon Dedalus, Tom Kernan, Ned Lambert, John Henry Menton, Myles Crawford, Lenehan, Paddy Leonard, Nosey Flynn, M'Coy and the featureless face of a Nameless One.*)

THE NAMELESS ONE

Bareback riding. Weight for age. Gob, he organised her.

THE JURORS

(*All their heads turned to his voice.*) Really?

THE NAMELESS ONE

(*Snarls.*) Arse over tip. Hundred shillings to five.

THE JURORS

(*All their heads lowered in assent.*) Most of us thought as much.

FIRST WATCH

He is a marked man. Another girl's plait cut. Wanted: Jack the Ripper. A thousand pounds reward.

SECOND WATCH

(*Awed, whispers.*) And in black. A mormon. Anarchist.

THE CRIER

(*Loudly.*) Whereas Leopold Bloom of no fixed abode is a wellknown dynamitard, forger, bigamist, bawd and cuckold and a public nuisance to the citizens of Dublin and whereas at this commission of assizes the most honourable . . .

(*His Honour, sir Frederick Falkiner, recorder of Dublin, in judicial garb of grey stone rises from the bench, stonebearded. He bears in his arms an umbrella sceptre. From his forehead arise starkly the Mosaic ramshorns.*)

THE RECORDER

I will put an end to this white slave traffic and rid Dublin of this odious pest. Scandalous! (*He dons the black cap.*) Let him be taken, Mr Subsheriff, from the dock where he now stands and detained in custody in Mountjoy prison during His Majesty's pleasure and there be hanged by the neck until he is dead and therein fail not at your peril or may the Lord have mercy on your soul. Remove him. (*A black skullcap descends upon his head.*)

(*The subsheriff Long John Fanning appears, smoking a pungent Henry Clay.*)

LONG JOHN FANNING

(*Scowls and calls with rich rolling utterance.*) Who'll hang Judas Iscariot?

(*H. Rumbold, master barber, in a bloodcoloured jerkin and tanner's apron, a rope coiled over his shoulder, mounts the block. A life preserver and a nailstudded bludgeon are stuck in his belt. He rubs grimly his grappling hands, knobbed with knuckledusters.)*

RUMBOLD

(To the recorder with sinister familiarity.) Hanging Harry, your Majesty, the Mersey terror. Five guineas a jugular. Neck or nothing.
(The bells of George's church toll slowly, loud dark iron.)

THE BELLS

Heigho! Heigho!

BLOOM

(Desperately.) Wait. Stop. Gulls. Good heart. I saw. Innocence. Girl in the monkeyhouse. Zoo. Lewd chimpanzees. *(Breathlessly.)* Pelvic basin. Her artless blush unmanned me. *(Overcome with emotion.)* I left the precincts. *(He turns to a figure in the crowd, appealing.)* Hynes, may I speak to you? You know me. That three shillings you can keep. If you want a little more . . .

HYNES

(Coldly.) You are a perfect stranger.

SECOND WATCH

(Points to the corner.) The bomb is here.

FIRST WATCH

Infernal machine with a time fuse.

BLOOM

No, no. Pig's feet. I was at a funeral.

FIRST WATCH

(Draws his truncheon.) Liar!
(The beagle lifts his snout, showing the grey scorbutic face of Paddy Dignam. He has gnawed all. He exhales a putrid carcasefed breath. He grows to human size and shape. His dachshund coat becomes a brown mortuary habit. His green eye flashes bloodshot. Half of one ear, all the nose and both thumbs are ghouleaten.)

PADDY DIGNAM

(In a hollow voice.) It is true. It was my funeral. Doctor Finucane pronounced life extinct when I succumbed to the disease from natural causes.
(He lifts his mutilated ashen face moonwards and bays lugubriously.)

BLOOM

(In triumph.) You hear?

PADDY DIGNAM

Bloom, I am Paddy Dignam's spirit. List, list, O list!

BLOOM

The voice is the voice of Esau.

SECOND WATCH

(*Blesses himself.*) How is that possible?

FIRST WATCH

It is not in the penny catechism.

PADDY DIGNAM

By metempsychosis. Spooks.

A VOICE

O rocks.

PADDY DIGNAM

(*Earnestly.*) Once I was in the employ of Mr J. H. Menton solicitor, commissioner for oaths and affidavits, of 27 Bachelor's Walk. Now I am defunct, the wall of the heart hypertrophied. Hard lines. The poor wife was awfully cut up. How is she bearing it? Keep her off that bottle of sherry. (*He looks round him.*) A lamp. I must satisfy an animal need. That buttermilk didn't agree with me.

(*The portly figure of John O'Connell, caretaker, stands forth, holding a bunch of keys tied with crape. Beside him stands Father Coffey, chaplain, toadbellied, wrynecked, in a surplice and bandanna nightcap, holding sleepily a staff of twisted poppies.*)

FATHER COFFEY

(*Yawns, then chants with a hoarse croak.*) Namine. Jacobs Vobiscuits. Amen.

JOHN O'CONNELL

(*Foghorns stormily through his megaphone.*) Dignam, Patrick T., deceased.

PADDY DIGNAM

(*With pricked up ears, winces.*) Overtones. (*He wriggles forward, places an ear to the ground.*) My master's voice!

JOHN O'CONNELL

Burial docket letter number U. P. Eightyfive thousand. Field seventeen. House of Keys. Plot, one hundred and one.

(*Paddy Dignam listens with visible effort, thinking, his tail stiffpointed, his ears cocked.*)

PADDY DIGNAM

Pray for the repose of his soul.

(*He worms down through a coalhole, his brown habit trailing its tether over rattling pebbles. After him toddles an obese grandfather rat on fungus turtle paws under a grey carapace. Dignam's voice, muffled, is heard baying under*) *ground:* Dignam's dead and gone below. *Tom Rochford, robinredbreasted, in cap and breeches, jumps from his twocolumned machine.)*

TOM ROCHFORD

(A hand to his breastbone, bows.) Reuben J. A florin I find him. *(He fixes the manhole with a resolute stare.)* My turn now on. Follow me up to Carlow.

(He executes a daredevil salmon leap in the air and is engulfed in the coalhole. Two discs on the columns wobble eyes of nought. All recedes. Bloom plodges forward again. He stands before a lighted house, listening. The kisses, winging from their bowers fly about him, twittering, warbling, cooing.)

THE KISSES

(Warbling.) Leo! *(Twittering.)* Icky licky micky sticky for Leo! *(Cooing.)* Coo coocoo! Yummyumm Womwom! *(Warbling.)* Big comebig! Pirou-ette! Leopopold! *(Twittering).* Leeolee! *(Warbling.)* O Leo!

(They rustle, flutter upon his garments, alight, bright giddy flecks, silvery sequins.)

BLOOM

A man's touch. Sad music. Church music. Perhaps here.

(Zoe Higgins, a young whore in a sapphire slip, closed with three bronze buckles, a slim black velvet fillet round her throat, nods, trips down the steps and accosts him.)

ZOE

Are you looking for someone? He's inside with his friend.

BLOOM

Is this Mrs Mack's?

ZOE

No, eightyone. Mrs Cohen's. You might go farther and fare worse. Mother Slipperslapper. *(Familiarly.)* She's on the job herself tonight with the vet, her tipster, that gives her all the winners and pays for her son in Oxford. Working overtime but her luck's turned today. *(Suspiciously.)* You're not his father, are you?

BLOOM

Not I!

ZOE

You both in black. Has little mousey any tickles tonight?

(His skin, alert, feels her fingertips approach. A hand slides over his left thigh.)

ZOE

How's the nuts?

BLOOM

Off side. Curiously they are on the right. Heavier I suppose. One in a million my tailor, Mesias, says.

ZOE

(*In sudden alarm.*) You've a hard chancre.

BLOOM

Not likely.

ZOE

I feel it.

(*Her hand slides into his left trouser pocket and brings out a hard black shrivelled potato. She regards it and Bloom with dumb moist lips.*)

BLOOM

A talisman. Heirloom.

ZOE

For Zoe? For keeps? For being so nice, eh?

(*She puts the potato greedily into a pocket, then links his arm, cuddling him with supple warmth. He smiles uneasily. Slowly, note by note, oriental music is played. He gazes in the tawny crystal of her eyes, ringed with kohol. His smile softens.*)

ZOE

You'll know me the next time.

BLOOM

(*Forlornly.*) I never loved a dear gazelle but it was sure to . . .

(*Gazelles are leaping, feeding on the mountains. Near are lakes. Round their shores file shadows black of cedargroves. Aroma rises, a strong hairgrowth of resin. It burns, the orient, a sky of sapphire, cleft by the bronze flight of eagles. Under it lies the womancity, nude, white, still, cool, in luxury. A fountain murmurs among damask roses. Mammoth roses murmur of scarlet winegrapes. A wine of shame, lust, blood exudes, strangely murmuring.*)

ZOE

(*Murmuring singsong with the music, her odalisk lips lusciously smeared with salve of swinefat and rosewater.*)

Schorach ani wenowach, benoith Hierushaloim.

BLOOM

(*Fascinated.*) I thought you were of good stock by your accent.

ZOE

And you know what thought did?

(*She bites his ear gently with little goldstopped teeth sending on him a cloying breath of stale garlic. The roses draw apart, disclose a sepulchre of the gold of kings and their mouldering bones.*)

BLOOM

(Draws back, mechanically caressing her right bub with a flat awkward hand.)
Are you a Dublin girl?

ZOE

(Catches a stray hair deftly and twists it to her coil.) No bloody fear. I'm English.
Have you a swaggerroot?

BLOOM

(As before.) Rarely smoke, dear. Cigar now and then. Childish device.
(Lewdly.) The mouth can be better engaged than with a cylinder of rank
weed.

ZOE

Go on. Make a stump speech out of it.

BLOOM

(In workman's corduroy overalls, black gansy with red floating tie and apache cap.)
Mankind is incorrigible. Sir Walter Raleigh brought from the new world
that potato and that weed, the one a killer of pestilence by absorption, the
other a poisoner of the ear, eye, heart, memory, will, understanding, all.
That is to say, he brought the poison a hundred years before another person
whose name I forget brought the food. Suicide. Lies. All our habits. Why,
look at our public life!
(Midnight chimes from distant steeples.)

THE CHIMES

Turn again, Leopold! Lord mayor of Dublin!

BLOOM

(In alderman's gown and chain.) Electors of Arran Quay, Inns Quay, Rotunda,
Mountjoy and North Dock, better run a tramline, I say, from the
cattlemarket to the river. That's the music of the future. That's my
programme. *Cui bono?* But our buccaneering Vanderdeckens in their
phantom ship of finance . . .

AN ELECTOR

Three times three for our future chief magistrate!
(The aurora borealis of the torchlight procession leaps.)

THE TORCHBEARERS

Hooray!
*(Several wellknown burgesses, city magnates and freemen of the city shake hands
with Bloom and congratulate him. Timothy Harrington, late thrice Lord Mayor
of Dublin, imposing in mayoral scarlet, gold chain and white silk tie, confers with
councillor Lorcan Sherlock, locum tenens. They nod vigorously in agreement.)*

LATE LORD MAYOR HARRINGTON

(In scarlet robe with mace, gold mayoral chain and large white silk scarf.) That alderman sir Leo Bloom's speech be printed at the expense of the ratepayers. That the house in which he was born be ornamented with a commemorative tablet and that the thoroughfare hitherto known as Cow Parlour off Cork street be henceforth designated Boulevard Bloom.

COUNCILLOR LORCAN SHERLOCK

Carried unanimously.

BLOOM

(Impassionedly.) These flying Dutchmen or lying Dutchmen as they recline in their upholstered poop, casting dice, what reck they? Machines is their cry, their chimera, their panacea. Laboursaving apparatuses, supplanters, bugbears, manufactured monsters for mutual murder, hideous hobgoblins produced by a horde of capitalistic lusts upon our prostituted labour. The poor man starves while they are grassing their royal mountain stags or shooting peasants and phartridges in their purblind pomp of pelf and power. But their reign is rover for rever and ever and ev . . .

(Prolonged applause. Venetian masts, maypoles and festal arches spring up. A streamer bearing the legends Cead Mile Failte *and* Mah Ttob Melek Israel *spans the street. All the windows are thronged with sightseers, chiefly ladies. Along the route the regiments of the royal Dublin fusiliers, the King's own Scottish borderers, the Cameron Highlanders and the Welsh Fusiliers, standing to attention keep back the crowd. Boys from High school are perched on the lampposts, telegraph poles, windowsills, cornices, gutters, chimneypots, railings, rainspouts, whistling and cheering. The pillar of the cloud appears. A fife and drum band is heard in the distance playing the Kol Nidre. The beaters approach with imperial eagles hoisted, trailing banners and waving oriental palms. The chryselephantine papal standard rises high, surrounded by pennons of the civic flag. The van of the procession appears headed by John Howard Parnell, city marshal, in a chessboard tabard, the Athlone Poursuivant and Ulster King of Arms. They are followed by the Right Honourable Joseph Hutchinson, lord mayor of Dublin, the lord mayor of Cork, their worships the mayors of Limerick, Galway, Sligo and Waterford, twentyeight Irish representative peers, sirdars, grandees and maharajahs bearing the cloth of estate, the Dublin Metropolitan Fire Brigade, the chapter of the saints of finance in their plutocratic order of precedence, the bishop of Down and Connor, His Eminence Michael cardinal Logue archbishop of Armagh, primate of all Ireland, His Grace, the most reverend Dr William Alexander, archbishop of Armagh, primate of all Ireland, the chief rabbi, the presbyterian moderator, the heads of the baptist, anabaptist, methodist and Moravian chapels and the honorary secretary of the society of*

friends. After them march the guilds and trades and trainbands with flying colours: coopers, bird fanciers, millwrights, newspaper canvassers, law scriveners, masseurs, vintners, trussmakers, chimney sweeps, lard refiners, tabinet and poplin weavers, farriers, Italian warehousemen, church decorators, bootjack manufacturers, undertakers, silk mercers, lapidaries, salesmasters, corkcutters, assessors of fire losses, dyers and cleaners, export bottlers, fellmongers, ticket-writers, heraldic seal engravers, horse repository hands, bullion brokers, cricket and archery outfitters, riddlemakers, egg and potato factors, hosiers and glovers, plumbing contractors. After them march gentlemen of the bed chamber, Black Rod, Deputy Garter, Gold Stick, the master of horse, the lord great chamberlain, the earl marshal, the high constable carrying the sword of state, saint Stephen's iron crown, the chalice and bible. Four buglers on foot blow a sennet. Beefeaters reply, winding clarions of welcome. Under an arch of triumph Bloom appears bareheaded, in a crimson velvet mantle trimmed with ermine, bearing Saint Edward's staff, the orb and sceptre with the dove, the curtana. He is seated on a milkwhite horse with long flowing crimson tail, richly caparisoned, with golden headstall. Wild excitement. The ladies from their balconies throw down rose-petals. The air is perfumed with essences. The men cheer. Bloom's boys run amid the bystanders with branches of hawthorn and wrenbushes.)

BLOOM'S BOYS

The wren, the wren,
The king of all birds,
Saint Stephen's his day,
Was caught in the furze.

A BLACKSMITH

(Murmurs.) For the Honour of God! And is that Bloom? He scarcely looks thirtyone.

A PAVIOR AND FLAGGER

That's the famous Bloom now, the world's greatest reformer. Hats off!
(All uncover their heads. Women whisper eagerly.)

A MILLIONAIRESS

(Richly.) Isn't he simply wonderful?

A NOBLEWOMAN

(Nobly.) All that man has seen!

A FEMINIST

(Masculinely.) And done!

A BELLHANGER

A classic face! He has the forehead of a thinker.
(Bloom's weather. A sunburst appears in the northwest.)

THE BISHOP OF DOWN AND CONNOR

I here present your undoubted emperor president and king chairman, the most serene and potent and very puissant ruler of this realm. God save Leopold the First!

ALL

God save Leopold the First!

BLOOM

(In dalmatic and purple mantle, to the bishop of Down and Connor, with dignity.) Thanks, somewhat eminent sir.

WILLIAM, ARCHBISHOP OF ARMAGH

(In purple stock and shovel hat.) Will you to your power cause law and mercy to be executed in all your judgments in Ireland and territories thereunto belonging?

BLOOM

(Placing his right hand on his testicles, swears.) So may the Creator deal with me. All this I promise to do.

MICHAEL, ARCHBISHOP OF ARMAGH

(Pours a cruse of hairoil over Bloom's head.) Gaudium magnum annuntio vobis. Habemus carneficem. Leopold, Patrick, Andrew, David, George, be thou anointed!

(Bloom assumes a mantle of cloth of gold and puts on a ruby ring. He ascends and stands on the stone of destiny. The representative peers put on at the same time their twentyeight crowns. Joybells ring in Christ church, Saint Patrick's, George's and gay Malahide. Mirus bazaar fireworks go up from all sides with symbolical phallopyrotechnic designs. The peers do homage, one by one, approaching and genuflecting.)

THE PEERS

I do become your liege man of life and limb to earthly worship.

(Bloom holds up his right hand on which sparkles the Koh-i-Noor diamond. His palfrey neighs. Immediate silence. Wireless intercontinental and interplanetary transmitters are set for reception of message.)

BLOOM

My subjects! We hereby nominate our faithful charger Copula Felix hereditary Grand Vizier and announce that we have this day repudiated our former spouse and have bestowed our royal hand upon the princess Selene, the splendour of night.

(The former morganatic spouse of Bloom is hastily removed in the Black Maria. The princess Selene, in moonblue robes, a silver crescent on her head, descends from a Sedan chair, borne by two giants. An outburst of cheering.)

JOHN HOWARD PARNELL

(*Raises the royal standard.*) Illustrious Bloom! Successor to my famous brother!

BLOOM

(*Embraces John Howard Parnell.*) We thank you from our heart, John, for this right royal welcome to green Erin, the promised land of our common ancestors.

(*The freedom of the city is presented to him embodied in a charter. The keys of Dublin, crossed on a crimson cushion, are given to him. He shows all that he is wearing green socks.*)

TOM KERNAN

You deserve it, your honour.

BLOOM

On this day twenty years ago we overcame the hereditary enemy at Ladysmith. Our howitzers and camel swivel guns played on his lines with telling effect. Half a league onward! They charge! All is lost now! Do we yield? No! We drive them headlong! Lo! We charge! Deploying to the left our light horse swept across the heights of Plevna and, uttering their warcry, *Bonafide Sabaoth*, sabred the Saracen gunners to a man.

THE CHAPEL OF FREEMAN TYPESETTERS

Hear! Hear!

JOHN WYSE NOLAN

There's the man that got away James Stephens.

A BLUECOAT SCHOOLBOY

Bravo!

AN OLD RESIDENT

You're a credit to your country, sir, that's what you are.

AN APPLEWOMAN

He's a man like Ireland wants.

BLOOM

My beloved subjects, a new era is about to dawn. I, Bloom, tell you verily it is even now at hand. Yea, on the word of a Bloom, ye shall ere long enter into the golden city which is to be, the new Bloomusalem in the Nova Hibernia of the future.

(*Thirtytwo workmen wearing rosettes, from all the counties of Ireland, under the guidance of Derwan the builder, construct the new Bloomusalem. It is a colossal edifice, with crystal roof, built in the shape of a huge pork kidney, containing forty thousand rooms. In the course of its extension several buildings and monuments, are demolished. Government offices are temporarily transferred*) *to railway sheds. Numerous houses are razed to the ground. The inhabitants are lodged in barrels and boxes, all marked in red with the letters: L. B. Several paupers fall from a ladder. A part of the walls of Dublin, crowded with loyal sightseers, collapses.)*

THE SIGHTSEERS

(Dying.) Morituri te salutant. (They die.)

(A man in a brown macintosh springs up through a trapdoor. He points an elongated figure at Bloom.)

THE MAN IN THE MACINTOSH

Don't you believe a word he says. That man is Leopold M'Intosh, the notorious fireraiser. His real name is Higgins.

BLOOM

Shoot him! Dog of a christian! So much for M'Intosh!

(A cannonshot. The man in the macintosh disappears. Bloom with his sceptre strikes down poppies. The instantaneous deaths of many powerful enemies, graziers, members of parliament, members of standing committees, are reported. Bloom's bodyguard distribute Maundy money, commemoration medals, loaves and fishes, temperance badges, expensive Henry Clay cigars, free cowbones for soup, rubber preservatives, in sealed envelopes tied with gold thread, butter scotch, pineapple rock, billets doux *in the form of cocked hats, readymade suits, porringers of toad in the hole, bottles of Jeyes' Fluid, purchase stamps, 40 days' indulgences, spurious coins, dairyfed pork sausages, theatre passes, season tickets available for all tram lines, coupons of the royal and privileged Hungarian lottery, penny dinner counters, cheap reprints of the World's Twelve Worst Books: Froggy and Fritz (politic), Care of the Baby (infantilic), 50 Meals for 7/ 6 (culinic), Was Jesus a Sun Myth? (historic), Expel that Pain (medic), Infant's Compendium of the Universe (cosmic), Let's All Chortle (hilaric), Canvasser's Vade Mecum (journalic), Loveletters of Mother Assistant (erotic), Who's Who in Space (astric), Songs that Reached Our Heart (melodic), Pennywise's Way to Wealth (parsimonic). A general rush and scramble. Women press forward to touch the hem of Bloom's robe. The lady Gwendolen Dubedat bursts through the throng, leaps on his horse and kisses him on both cheeks amid great acclamation. A magnesium flashlight photograph is taken. Babes and sucklings are held up.)*

THE WOMEN

Little father! Little father!

THE BABES AND SUCKLINGS

Clap clap hands till Poldy comes home,
Cakes in his pocket for Leo alone.

(Bloom, bending down, pokes Baby Boardman gently in the stomach.)

BABY BOARDMAN

(Hiccups, curdled milk flowing from his mouth.) Hajajaja.

BLOOM

(Shaking hands with a blind stripling.) My more than Brother! *(Placing his arms round the shoulders of an old couple.)* Dear old friends! *(He plays pussy fourcorners with ragged boys and girls.)* Peep! Bopeep! *(He wheels twins in a perambulator.)* Ticktacktwo wouldyousetashoe? *(He performs juggler's tricks, draws red, orange, yellow, green, blue, indigo and violet silk handkerchiefs from his mouth.)* Roygbiv. 32 feet per second. *(He consoles a widow.)* Absence makes the heart grow younger. *(He dances the Highland fling with grotesque antics.)* Leg it, ye devils! *(He kisses the bedsores of a palsied veteran.)* Honourable wounds! *(He trips up a fat policeman.)* U. p.: up. U. p.: up. *(He whispers in the ear of a blushing waitress and laughs kindly.)* Ah, naughty, naughty! *(He eats a raw turnip offered him by Maurice Butterly, farmer.)* Fine! Splendid! *(He refuses to accept three shillings offered him by Joseph Hynes, journalist.)* My dear fellow, not at all! *(He gives his coat to a beggar.)* Please accept. *(He takes part in a stomach race with elderly male and female cripples.)* Come on, boys! Wriggle it, girls!

THE CITIZEN

(Choked with emotion, brushes aside a tear in his emerald muffler.) May the good God bless him!

(The rams' horns sound for silence. The standard of Zion is hoisted.)

BLOOM

(Uncloaks impressively, revealing obesity, unrolls a paper and reads solemnly.) Aleph Beth Ghimel Daleth Hagadah Tephilim Kosher Yom Kippur Hanukah Roschaschana Beni Brith Bar Mitzvah Mazzoth Askenazim Meshuggah Talith.

(An official translation is read by Jimmy Henry, assistant town clerk.)

JIMMY HENRY

The Court of Conscience is now open. His Most Catholic Majesty will now administer open air justice. Free medical and legal advice, solution of doubles and other problems. All cordially invited. Given at this our loyal city of Dublin in the year 1 of the Paradisiacal Era.

PADDY LEONARD

What am I to do about my rates and taxes?

BLOOM

Pay them, my friend.

PADDY LEONARD

Thank you.

NOSEY FLYNN

Can I raise a mortgage on my fire insurance?

BLOOM

(*Obdurately.*) Sirs, take notice that by the law of torts you are bound over in your own recognisances for six months in the sum of five pounds.

J. J. O'MOLLOY

A Daniel did I say? Nay! A Peter O'Brien!

NOSEY FLYNN

Where do I draw the five pounds?

PISSER BURKE

For bladder trouble?

BLOOM

Acid. nit. hydrochlor dil., 20 minims,
Tinct. mix. vom., 4 minims.
Extr. taraxel. lig., 30 minims.
Aq. dis. ter in die.

CHRIS CALLINAN

What is the parallax of the subsolar ecliptic of Aldebaran?

BLOOM

Pleased to hear from you, Chris. K. 11.

JOE HYNES

Why aren't you in uniform?

BLOOM

When my progenitor of sainted memory wore the uniform of the Austrian despot in a dank prison where was yours?

BEN DOLLARD

Pansies?

BLOOM

Embellish (beautify) suburban gardens.

BEN DOLLARD

When twins arrive?

BLOOM

Father (pater, dad) starts thinking.

LARRY O'ROURKE

An eight day licence for my new premises. You remember me, sir Leo, when you were in number seven. I'm sending around a dozen of stout for the missus.

BLOOM

(Coldly.) You have the advantage of me. Lady Bloom accepts no presents.

CROFTON

This is indeed a festivity.

BLOOM

(Solemnly.) You call it a festivity. I call it a sacrament.

ALEXANDER KEYES

When will we have our own house of keys?

BLOOM

I stand for the reform of municipal morals and the plain ten commandments. New worlds for old. Union of all, jew, moslem and gentile. Three acres and a cow for all children of nature. Saloon motor hearses. Compulsory manual labour for all. All parks open to the public day and night. Electric dishscrubbers. Tuberculosis, lunacy, war and mendicancy must now cease. General amnesty, weekly carnival, with masked licence, bonuses for all, esperanto the universal brotherhood. No more patriotism of barspongers and dropsical impostors. Free money, free love and a free lay church in a free lay state.

O'MADDEN BURKE

Free fox in a free henroost.

DAVY BYRNE

(Yawning.) Iiiiiiiiaaaaaaach!

BLOOM

Mixed races and mixed marriage.

LENEHAN

What about mixed bathing?

(Bloom explains to those near him his schemes for social regeneration. All agree with him. The keeper of the Kildare Street museum appears, dragging a lorry on which are the shaking statues of several naked goddesses, Venus Callipyge, Venus Pandemos, Venus Metempsychosis, and plaster figures, also naked, representing the new nine muses, Commerce, Operatic Music, Amor, Publicity, Manufacture, Liberty of Speech, Plural Voting, Gastronomy, Private Hygiene, Seaside Concert Entertainments, Painless Obstetrics and Astronomy for the People.)

FATHER FARLEY

He is an episcopalian, an agnostic, an anythingarian seeking to overthrow our holy faith.

MRS RIORDAN

(Tears up her will.) I'm disappointed in you! You bad man!

MOTHER GROGAN

(Removes her boot to throw it at Bloom.) You beast! You abominable person!

NOSEY FLYNN

Give us a tune, Bloom. One of the old sweet songs.

BLOOM

(With rollicking humour.)

I vowed that I never would leave her,
She turned out a cruel deceiver.
With my tooraloom tooraloom tooraloom tooraloom.

HOPPY HOLOHAN

Good old Bloom! There's nobody like him after all.

PADDY LEONARD

Stage Irishman!

BLOOM

What railway opera is like a tramline in Gibraltar? The Rows of Casteele.
(Laughter.)

LENEHAN

Plagiarist! Down with Bloom!

THE VEILED SIBYL

(Enthusiastically.) I'm a Bloomite and I glory in it. I believe in him in spite of
all. I'd give my life for him, the funniest man on earth.

BLOOM

(Winks at the bystanders.) I bet she's a bonny lassie.

THEODORE PUREFOY

(In fishingcap and oilskin jacket.) He employs a mechanical device to frustrate
the sacred ends of nature.

THE VEILED SIBYL

(Stabs herself.) My hero god! *(She dies.)*
    *(Many most attractive and enthusiastic women also commit suicide by stabbing,
    drowning, drinking prussic acid, aconite, arsenic, opening their veins, refusing
    food, casting themselves under steamrollers, from the top of Nelson's Pillar, into
    the great vat of Guinness's brewery, asphyxiating themselves by placing their
    heads in gas ovens, hanging themselves in stylish garters, leaping from windows
    of different storeys.)*

ALEXANDER J. DOWIE

(Violently.) Fellowchristians and antiBloomites, the man called Bloom is
from the roots of hell, a disgrace to christian men. A fiendish libertine from

his earliest years this stinking goat of Mendes gave precocious signs of infantile debauchery recalling the cities of the plain, with a dissolute granddam. This vile hypocrite, bronzed with infamy, is the white bull mentioned in the Apocalypse. A worshipper of the Scarlet Woman, intrigue is the very breath of his nostrils. The stake faggots and the caldron of boiling oil are for him. Caliban!

THE MOB

Lynch him! Roast him! He's as bad as Parnell was. Mr Fox!

(*Mother Grogan throws her boot at Bloom. Several shopkeepers from upper and lower Dorset street throw objects of little or no commercial value, hambones, condensed milk tins, unsaleable cabbage, stale bread, sheeps' tails, odd pieces of fat.*)

BLOOM

(*Excitedly.*) This is midsummer madness, some ghastly joke again. By heaven, I am guiltless as the unsunned snow! It was my brother Henry. He is my double. He lives in number 2 Dolphin's Barn. Slander, the viper, has wrongfully accused me. Fellowcountrymen, *sgenl inn ban bata coisde gan capall*. I call on my old friend, Dr Malachi Mulligan, sex specialist, to give medical testimony on my behalf.

DR MULLIGAN

(*In motor jerkin, green motorgoggles on his brow.*) Dr Bloom is bisexually abnormal. He has recently escaped from Dr Eustace's private asylum for demented gentlemen. Born out of bedlock hereditary epilepsy is present, the consequence of unbridled lust. Traces of elephantiasis have been discovered among his ascendants. There are marked symptoms of chronic exhibitionism. Ambidexterity is also latent. He is prematurely bald from selfabuse, perversely idealistic in consequence, a reformed rake, and has metal teeth. In consequence of a family complex he has temporarily lost his memory and I believe him to be more sinned against than sinning. I have made a pervaginal examination and, after application of the acid test to 5427 anal, axillary, pectoral and pubic hairs, I declare him to be *virgo intacta*.

(*Bloom holds his high grade hat over his genital organs.*)

DR MADDEN

Hypsospadia is also marked. In the interest of coming generations I suggest that the parts affected should be preserved in spirits of wine in the national teratological museum.

DR CROTTHERS

I have examined the patient's urine. It is albuminoid. Salivation is insufficient, the patellar reflex intermittent.

DR PUNCH COSTELLO

The *fetor judaicus* is most perceptible.

DR DIXON

(Reads a bill of health.) Professor Bloom is a finished example of the new womanly man. His moral nature is simple and lovable. Many have found him a dear man, a dear person. He is a rather quaint fellow on the whole, coy though not feebleminded in the medical sense. He has written a really beautiful letter, a poem in itself, to the court missionary of the Reformed Priests' Protection Society which clears up everything. He is practically a total abstainer and I can affirm that he sleeps on a straw litter and eats the most Spartan food, cold dried grocer's peas. He wears a hairshirt winter and summer and scourges himself every Saturday. He was, I understand, at one time a firstclass misdemeanant in Glencree reformatory. Another report states that he was a very posthumous child. I appeal for clemency in the name of the most sacred word our vocal organs have ever been called upon to speak. He is about to have a baby.

(General commotion and compassion. Women faint. A wealthy American makes a street collection for Bloom. Gold and silver coins, blank cheques, banknotes, jewels, treasury bonds, maturing bills of exchange, I. O. U's, wedding rings, watchchains, lockets, necklaces and bracelets are rapidly collected.)

BLOOM

O, I so want to be a mother.

MRS THORNTON

(In nursetender's gown.) Embrace me tight, dear. You'll be soon over it. Tight, dear.

(Bloom embraces her tightly and bears eight male yellow and white children. They appear on a redcarpeted staircase adorned with expensive plants. All are handsome, with valuable metallic faces, wellmade, respectably dressed and wellconducted, speaking five modern languages fluently and interested in various arts and sciences. Each has his name printed in legible letters on his shirtfront: Nasodoro, Goldfinger, Chrysostomos, Maindorée, Silversmile, Silberselber, Vifargent, Panargyros. They are immediately appointed to positions of high public trust in several different countries as managing directors of banks, traffic managers of railways, chairmen of limited liability companies, vice chairmen of hotel syndicates.)

A VOICE

Bloom, are you the Messiah ben Joseph or ben David?

BLOOM

(Darkly.) You have said it.

BROTHER BUZZ

Then perform a miracle.

BANTAM LYONS

Prophesy who will win the Saint Leger.

(Bloom walks on a net, covers his left eye with his left ear, passes through several walls, climbs Nelson's Pillar, hangs from the top ledge by his eyelids, eats twelve dozen oysters (shells included), heals several sufferers from king's evil, contracts his face so as to resemble many historical personages, Lord Beaconsfield, Lord Byron, Wat Tyler, Moses of Egypt, Moses Maimonides, Moses Mendelssohn, Henry Irving, Rip van Winkle, Kossuth, Jean Jacques Rousseau, Baron Leopold Rothschild, Robinson Crusoe, Sherlock Holmes, Pasteur, turns each foot simultaneously in different directions, bids the tide turn back, eclipses the sun by extending his little finger.)

BRINI, PAPAL NUNCIO

(In papal zouave's uniform, steel cuirasses as breastplate, armplates, thighplates, legplates, large profane moustaches and brown paper mitre.)

Leopoldi autem generatio. Moses begat Noah and Noah begat Eunuch and Eunuch begat O'Halloran and O'Halloran begat Guggenheim and Guggenheim begat Agendath and Agendath begat Netaim and Netaim begat Le Hirsch and Le Hirsch begat Jesurum and Jesurum begat MacKay and MacKay begat Ostrolopsky and Ostrolopsky begat Smerdoz and Smerdoz begat Weiss and Weiss begat Schwarz and Schwarz begat Adrianopoli and Adrianopoli begat Aranjuez and Aranjuez begat Lewy Lawson and Lewy Lawson begat Ichabudonosor and Ichabudonosor begat O'Donnell Magnus and O'Donnell Magnus begat Christbaum and Christbaum begat Ben Maimun and Ben Maimun begat Dusty Rhodes and Dusty Rhodes begat Benamor and Benamor begat Jones-Smith and Jones-Smith begat Savorgnanovich and Savorgnanovich begat Jasperstone and Jasperstone begat Vingtetunieme and Vingtetunieme begat Szombathely and Szombathely begat Virag and Virag begat Bloom *et vocabitur nomen eius Emmanuel.*

A DEADHAND

(Writes on the wall.) Bloom is a cod.

A CRAB

(In bushranger's kit.) What did you do in the cattlecreep behind Kilbarrack?

A FEMALE INFANT

(Shakes a rattle.) And under Ballybough bridge?

A HOLLYBUSH

And in the devil's glen?

BLOOM

(Blushes furiously all over from front to nates, three tears falling from his left eye.)
Spare my past.

THE IRISH EVICTED TENANTS

(In bodycoats, kneebreeches, with Donnybrook fair shillelaghs.) Sjambok him!
　(Bloom with asses' ears seats himself in the pillory with crossed arms, his feet protruding. He whistles Don Giovanni, a cenar teco. *Artane orphans, joining hands, caper round him. Girls of the Prison Gate Mission, joining hands, caper round in the opposite direction.)*

THE ARTANE ORPHANS

You hig, you hog, you dirty dog!
You think the ladies love you!

THE PRISON GATE GIRLS

If you see kay
Tell him he may
See you in tea
Tell him from me.

HORNBLOWER

(In ephod and huntingcap, announces.) And he shall carry the sins of the people to Azazel, the spirit which is in the wilderness, and to Lilith, the nighthag. And they shall stone him and defile him, yea, all from Agendath Netaim and from Mizraim, the land of Ham.
　(All the people cast soft pantomime stones at Bloom. Many bonafide travellers and ownerless dogs come near him and defile him. Mastiansky and Citron approach in gaberdines, wearing long earlocks. They wag their beards at Bloom.)

MASTIANSKY AND CITRON

Belial! Laemlein of Istria! the false Messiah! Abulafia!
　(George S. Mesias, Bloom's tailor, appears, a tailor's goose under his arm, presenting a bill.)

MESIAS

To alteration one pair trousers eleven shillings.

BLOOM

(Rubs his hands cheerfully.) Just like old times. Poor Bloom!
　(Reuben J. Dodd, blackbearded Iscariot, bad shepherd, bearing on his shoulders the drowned corpse of his son, approaches the pillory.)

REUBEN J.

(Whispers hoarsely.) The squeak is out. A split is gone for the flatties. Nip the first rattler.

THE FIRE BRIGADE

Pflaap!

BROTHER BUZZ

(Invests Bloom in a yellow habit with embroidery of painted flames and high pointed hat. He places a bag of gunpowder round his neck and hands him over to the civil power, saying.) Forgive him his trespasses.

(Lieutenant Myers of the Dublin Fire Brigade by general request sets fire to Bloom. Lamentations.)

THE CITIZEN

Thank heaven!

BLOOM

(In a seamless garment marked I. H. S. stands upright amid phœnix flames.) Weep not for me, O daughters of Erin.

(He exhibits to Dublin reporters traces of burning. The daughters of Erin, in black garments with large prayerbooks and long lighted candles in their hands, kneel down and pray.)

THE DAUGHTERS OF ERIN

Kidney of Bloom, pray for us.
Flower of the Bath, pray for us.
Mentor of Menton, pray for us.
Canvasser for the Freeman, pray for us.
Charitable Mason, pray for us.
Wandering Soap, pray for us.
Sweets of Sin, pray for us.
Music without Words, pray for us.
Reprover of the Citizen, pray for us.
Friend of all Frillies, pray for us.
Midwife Most Merciful, pray for us.
Potato Preservative against Plague and Pestilence, pray for us.

(A choir of six hundred voices, conducted by Mr Vincent O'Brien, sings the Alleluia chorus, accompanied on the organ by Joseph Glynn. Bloom becomes mute, shrunken, carbonised.)

ZOE

Talk away till you're black in the face.

BLOOM

(In caubeen with clay pipe stuck in the band, dusty brogues, an emigrant's red handkerchief bundle in his hand, leading a black bogoak pig by a sugaun, with a smile in his eye.) Let me be going now, woman of the house, for by all the goats in Connemara I'm after having the father and mother of a bating.

(With a tear in his eye.) All insanity. Patriotism, sorrow for the dead, music, future of the race. To be or not to be. Life's dream is o'er. End it peacefully. They can live on. *(He gazes far away mournfully.)* I am ruined. A few pastilles of aconite. The blinds drawn. A letter. Then lie back to rest. *(He breathes softly.)* No more. I have lived. Fare. Farewell.

ZOE

(Stiffly, her finger in her neckfillet.) Honest? Till the next time. *(She sneers.)* Suppose you got up the wrong side of the bed or came too quick with your best girl. O, I can read your thoughts.

BLOOM

(Bitterly.) Man and woman, love, what is it? A cork and bottle.

ZOE

(In sudden sulks.) I hate a rotter that's insincere. Give a bleeding whore a chance.

BLOOM

(Repentantly.) I am very disagreeable. You are a necessary evil. Where are you from? London?

ZOE

(Glibly.) Hog's Norton where the pigs plays the organs. I'm Yorkshire born. *(She holds his hand which is feeling for her nipple.)* I say, Tommy Tittlemouse. Stop that and begin worse. Have you cash for a short time? Ten shillings?

BLOOM

(Smiles, nods slowly.) More, houri, more.

ZOE

And more's mother? *(She pats him offhandedly with velvet paws.)* Are you coming into the musicroom to see our new pianola? Come and I'll peel off.

BLOOM

(Feeling his occiput dubiously with the unparalleled embarrassment of a harassed pedlar gauging the symmetry of her peeled pears.) Somebody would be dreadfully jealous if she knew. The greeneyed monster. *(Earnestly.)* You know how difficult it is. I needn't tell you.

ZOE

(Flattered.) What the eye can't see the heart can't grieve for. *(She pats him.)* Come.

BLOOM

Laughing witch! The hand that rocks the cradle.

ZOE

Babby!

BLOOM

(In babylinen and pelisse, bigheaded, with a caul of dark hair, fixes big eyes on her fluid slip and counts its bronze buckles with a chubby finger, his moist tongue lolling and lisping.) One two tlee: tlee tlwo tlone.

THE BUCKLES

Love me. Love me not. Love me.

ZOE

Silent means consent. *(With little parted talons she captures his hand, her forefinger giving to his palm the passtouch of secret monitor, luring him to doom.)* Hot hands cold gizzard.

(He hesitates amid scents, music, temptations. She leads him towards the steps, drawing him by the odour of her armpits, the vice of her painted eyes, the rustle of her slip in whose sinuous folds lurks the lion reek of all the male brutes that have possessed her.)

THE MALE BRUTES

(Exhaling sulphur of rut and dung and ramping in their loosebox, faintly roaring, their drugged heads swaying to and fro.) Good!

(Zoe and Bloom reach the doorway where two sister whores are seated. They examine him curiously from under their pencilled brows and smile to his hasty bow. He trips awkwardly.)

ZOE

(Her lucky hand instantly saving him.) Hoopsa! Don't fall upstairs.

BLOOM

The just man falls seven times. *(He stands aside at the threshold.)* After you is good manners.

ZOE

Ladies first, gentlemen after.

(She crosses the threshold. He hesitates. She turns and, holding out her hands, draws him over. He hops. On the antlered rack of the hall hang a man's hat and waterproof. Bloom uncovers himself but, seeing them, frowns, then smiles, preoccupied. A door on the return landing is thrown open. A man in purple shirt and grey trousers, brownsocked, passes with an ape's gait, his bald head and goatee beard upheld, hugging a full waterjugjar, his twotailed black braces dangling at heels. Averting his face quickly Bloom bends to examine on the halltable the spaniel eyes of a running fox: then, his lifted head sniffing, follows Zoe into the musicroom. A shade of mauve tissuepaper dims the light of the chandelier. Round and round a moth flies, colliding, escaping. The floor is covered with an oilcloth mosaic of jade and azure and cinnabar rhomboids. Footmarks are stamped over it in all senses, heel to heel, heel to hollow, toe to toe, feet locked,

a morris of shuffling feet without body phantoms, all in a scrimmage higgledypiggledy. The walls are tapestried with a paper of yewfronds and clear glades. In the grate is spread a screen of peacock feathers. Lynch squats crosslegged on the hearthrug of matted hair, his cap back to the front. With a wand he beats time slowly. Kitty Ricketts, a bony pallid whore in navy costume, doeskin gloves rolled back from a coral wristlet, a chain purse in her hand, sits perched on the edge of the table swinging her leg and glancing at herself in the gilt mirror over the mantelpiece. A tag of her corset lace hangs slightly below her jacket. Lynch indicates mockingly the couple at the piano.)

KITTY

(Coughs behind her hand.) She's a bit imbecillic. *(She signs with a waggling forefinger.)* Blemblem. *(Lynch lifts up her skirt and white petticoat with the wand. She settles them down quickly.)* Respect yourself. *(She hiccups, then bends quickly her sailor hat under which her hair glows, red with henna.)* O, excuse!

ZOE

More limelight, Charley. *(She goes to the chandelier and turns the gas full cock.)*

KITTY

(Peers at the gasjet.) What ails it tonight?

LYNCH

(Deeply.) Enter a ghost and hobgoblins.

ZOE

Clap on the back for Zoe.

(The wand in Lynch's hand flashes: a brass poker. Stephen stands at the pianola on which sprawl his hat and ashplant. With two fingers he repeats once more the series of empty fifths. Florry Talbot, a blond feeble goosefat whore in a tatterdemalion gown of mildewed strawberry lolls spreadeagle in the sofa corner, her limp forearm pendent over the bolster, listening. A heavy stye droops over her sleepy eyelid.)

KITTY

(Hiccups again with a kick of her horsed foot.) O, excuse!

ZOE

(Promptly.) Your boy's thinking of you. Tie a knot on your shift.

(Kitty Ricketts bends her head. Her boa uncoils, slides, glides over her shoulder, back, arm, chair to the ground. Lynch lifts the curled caterpillar on his wand. She snakes her neck, nestling. Stephen glances behind at the squatted figure with its cap back to the front.)

STEPHEN

As a matter of fact it is of no importance whether Benedetto Marcello found it or made it. The rite is the poet's rest. It may be an old hymn to

Demeter or also illustrate *Cæla enarrant gloriam Domini*. It is susceptible of nodes or modes as far apart as hyperphrygian and mixolydian and of texts so divergent as priests haihooping round David's that is Circe's or what am I saying Ceres' altar and David's tip from the stable to his chief bassoonist about his almightiness. *Mais, nom de nom,* that is another pair of trousers. *Jetez la gourme. Faut que jeunesse se passe. (He stops, points at Lynch's cap, smiles, laughs.)* Which side is your knowledge bump?

THE CAP

(With saturnine spleen.) Bah! It is because it is. Woman's reason. Jewgreek is greekjew. Extremes meet. Death is the highest form of life. Bah!

STEPHEN

You remember fairly accurately all my errors, boasts, mistakes. How long shall I continue to close my eyes to disloyalty? Whetstone!

THE CAP

Bah!

STEPHEN

Here's another for you. *(He frowns.)* The reason is because the fundamental and the dominant are separated by the greatest possible interval which . . .

THE CAP

Which? Finish. You can't.

STEPHEN

(With an effort.) Interval which. Is the greatest possible ellipse. Consistent with. The ultimate return. The octave. Which.

THE CAP

Which?

(Outside the gramophone begins to blare The Holy City.*)*

STEPHEN

(Abruptly.) What went forth to the ends of the world to traverse not itself. God, the sun, Shakespeare, a commercial traveller, having itself traversed in reality itself, becomes that self. Wait a moment. Wait a second. Damn that fellow's noise in the street. Self which it itself was ineluctably preconditioned to become. *Ecco!*

LYNCH

(With a mocking whinny of laughter grins at Bloom and Zoe Higgins.) What a learned speech, eh?

ZOE

(Briskly.) God help your head, he knows more than you have forgotten.
(With obese stupidity Florry Talbot regards Stephen.)

FLORRY

They say the last day is coming this summer.

KITTY

No!

ZOE

(*Explodes in laughter.*) Great unjust God!

FLORRY

(*Offended.*) Well, it was in the papers about Antichrist. O, my foot's tickling.

(*Ragged barefoot newsboys jogging a wagtail kite, patter past, yelling.*)

THE NEWSBOYS

Stop press edition. Result of the rockinghorse races. Sea serpent in the royal canal. Safe arrival of Antichrist.

(*Stephen turns and sees Bloom.*)

STEPHEN

A time, times and half a time.

(*Reuben J. Antichrist, wandering jew, a clutching hand open on his spine, stumps forward. Across his loins is slung a pilgrim's wallet from which protrude promissory notes and dishonoured bills. Aloft over his shoulder he bears a long boatpole from the hook of which the sodden huddled mass of his only son, saved from Liffey waters, hangs from the slack of its breeches. A hobgoblin in the image of Punch Costello, hipshot, crookbacked, hydrocephalic, prognathic with receding forehead and Ally Sloper nose tumbles in somersaults through the gathering darkness.*)

ALL

What?

THE HOBGOBLIN

(*His jaws chattering, capers to and fro, goggling his eyes, squeaking, kangaroohopping, with outstretched clutching arms, then all at once thrusts his lipless face through the fork of his thighs.*) Il vient! C'est moi! L'homme qui rit! L'homme primigène! (*He whirls round and round with dervish howls.*) Sieurs et dames, faites vos jeux! (*He crouches juggling. Tiny roulette planets fly from his hands.*) Les jeux sont faits! (*The planets rush together, uttering crepitant cracks.*) Rien n'va plus. (*The planets, buoyant balloons, sail swollen up and away. He springs off into vacuum.*)

FLORRY

(*Sinking into torpor, crosses herself secretly.*) The end of the world!

(*A female tepid effluvium leaks out from her. Nebulous obscurity occupies space. Through the drifting fog without the gramophone blares over coughs and feetshuffling.*)

THE GRAMOPHONE

Jerusalem!

Open your gates and sing

Hosanna . . .

(A rocket rushes up the sky and bursts. A white star falls from it, proclaiming the consummation of all things and second coming of Elijah. Along an infinite invisible tightrope taut from zenith to nadir the End of the World, a twoheaded octopus in gillie's kilts, busby and tartan filibegs, whirls through the murk, head over heels, in the form of the Three Legs of Man.)

THE END OF THE WORLD

(With a Scotch accent.) Wha'll dance the keel row, the keel row, the keel row?

(Over the passing drift and choking breathcoughs, Elijah's voice, harsh as a corncrake's, jars on high. Perspiring in a loose lawn surplice with funnel sleeves he is seen, vergerfaced, above a rostrum about which the banner of old glory is draped. He thumps the parapet.)

ELIJAH

No yapping, if you please, in this booth. Jake Crane, Creole Sue, Dave Campbell, Abe Kirschner, do your coughing with your mouths shut. Say, I am operating all this trunk line. Boys, do it now. God's time is 12.25. Tell mother you'll be there. Rush your order and you play a slick ace. Join on right here! Book through to eternity junction, the nonstop run. Just one word more. Are you a god or a doggone clod? If the second advent came to Coney Island are we ready? Florry Christ, Stephen Christ, Zoe Christ, Bloom Christ, Kitty Christ, Lynch Christ, it's up to you to sense that cosmic force. Have we cold feet about the cosmos? No. Be on the side of the angels. Be a prism. You have that something within, the higher self. You can rub shoulders with a Jesus, a Gautama, an Ingersoll. Are you all in this vibration? I say you are. You once nobble that, congregation, and a buck joy ride to heaven becomes a back number. You got me? It's a life-brightener, sure. The hottest stuff ever was. It's the whole pie with jam in. It's just the cutest snappiest line out. It is immense, supersumptuous. It restores. It vibrates. I know and I am some vibrator. Joking apart and getting down to bedrock, A. J. Christ Dowie and the harmonial philosophy, have you got that? O. K. Seventyseven west sixtyninth street. Got me? That's it. You call me up by sunphone any old time. Bumboosers, save your stamps. *(He shouts.)* Now then our glory song. All join heartily in the singing. Encore! *(He sings.)* Jeru . . .

THE GRAMOPHONE

(Drowning his voice.)

Whorusalaminyourhighhohhhh ... *(The disc rasps gratingly against the needle.)*

THE THREE WHORES

(Covering their ears, squawk.) Ahhkkk!

ELIJAH

(In rolledup shirtsleeves, black in the face, shouts at the top of his voice, his arms uplifted.) Big Brother up there, Mr President, you hear what I done just been saying to you. Certainly, I sort of believe strong in you, Mr President. I certainly am thinking now Miss Higgins and Miss Ricketts got religion way inside them. Certainly seems to me I don't never see no wusser scared female than the way you been, Miss Florry, just now as I done seed you. Mr President, you come long and help me save our sisters dear. *(He winks at his audience.)* Our Mr President, he twig the whole lot and he ain't saying nothing.

KITTY-KATE

I forgot myself. In a weak moment I erred and did what I did on Constitution hill. I was confirmed by the bishop. My mother's sister married a Montmorency. It was a working plumber was my ruination when I was pure.

ZOE-FANNY

I let him larrup it into me for the fun of it.

FLORRY-TERESA

It was in consequence of a portwine beverage on top of Hennessy's three stars. I was guilty with Whelan when he slipped into the bed.

STEPHEN

In the beginning was the word, in the end the world without end. Blessed be the eight beatitudes.

(The beatitudes, Dixon, Madden, Crotthers, Costello, Lenehan, Bannon, Mulligan and Lynch in white surgical students' gowns, four abreast, goosestepping, tramp fast past in noisy marching.)

THE BEATITUDES

(Incoherently.) Beer beef battledog buybull businum barnum buggerum bishop.

LYSTER

(In quakergrey kneebreeches and broadbrimmed hat, says discreetly.) He is our friend. I need not mention names. Seek thou the light.

(He corantos by. Best enters in hairdresser attire, shinily laundered, his locks in curlpapers. He leads John Eglinton who wears a mandarin's kimono of Nankeen yellow, lizard-lettered, and a high pagoda hat.)

BEST

(Smiling, lifts the hat and displays a shaven poll from the crown of which bristles a pigtail toupee tied with an orange topknot.) I was just beautifying him, don't you know. A thing of beauty, don't you know, Yeats says, or I mean, Keats says.

JOHN EGLINTON

(Produces a greencapped dark lantern and flashes it towards a corner; with carping accent.) Esthetics and cosmetics are for the boudoir. I am out for truth. Plain truth for a plain man. Tanderagee wants the facts and means to get them.

(In the cone of the searchlight behind the coalscuttle, ollave, holyeyed, the bearded figure of Mananaan MacLir broods, chin on knees. He rises slowly. A cold seawind blows from his druid mantle. About his head writhe eels and elvers. He is encrusted with weeds and shells. His right hand holds a bicycle pump. His left hand grasps a huge crayfish by its two talons.)

MANANAAN MACLIR

(With a voice of waves.) Aum! Hek! Wal! Ak! Lub! Mor! Ma! White yoghin of the Gods. Occult pimander of Hermes Trismegistos. *(With a voice of whistling seawind.)* Punarjanam patsypunjaub! I won't have my leg pulled. It has been said by one: beware the left, the cult of Shakti. *(With a cry of stormbirds.)* Shakti, Shiva! Dark hidden Father! *(He smites with his bicycle pump the crayfish in his left hand. On its cooperative dial glow the twelve signs of the zodiac. He wails with the vehemence of the ocean.)* Aum! Baum! Pyjaum! I am the light of the homestead, I am the dreamery creamery butter.

(A skeleton judashand strangles the light. The green light wanes to mauve. The gasjet wails whistling.)

THE GASJET

Pooah! Pfuiiiiii!

(Zoe runs to the chandelier and, crooking her leg, adjusts the mantle.)

ZOE

Who has a fag as I'm here?

LYNCH

(Tossing a cigarette on to the table.) Here.

ZOE

(Her head perched aside in mock pride.) Is that the way to hand the *pot* to a lady? *(She stretches up to light the cigarette over the flame, twirling it slowly, showing the brown tufts of her armpits. Lynch with his poker lifts boldly a side of her slip. Bare from her garters up her flesh appears under the sapphire a nixie's green. She puffs calmly at her cigarette.)* Can you see the beauty spot of my behind?

LYNCH

I'm not looking.

ZOE

(Makes sheep's eyes.) No? You wouldn't do a less thing. Would you suck a lemon?

(Squinting in mock shame she glances with sidelong meaning at Bloom then twists round towards him, pulling her slip free of the poker. Blue fluid again flows over her flesh. Bloom stands, smiling desirously, twirling his thumbs. Kitty Ricketts licks her middle finger with her spittle and gazing in the mirror, smooths both eyebrows. Lipoti Virag, basilicogrammate, chutes rapidly down through the chimneyflue and struts two steps to the left on gawky pink stilts. He is sausaged into several overcoats and wears a brown macintosh under which he holds a roll of parchment. In his left eye flashes the monocle of Cashel Boyle O'Connor Fitzmaurice Tisdall Farrell. On his head is perched an Egyptian pshent. Two quills project over his ears.)

VIRAG

(Heels together, bows.) My name is Virag Lipoti, of Szombathely. *(He coughs thoughtfully, drily.)* Promiscuous nakedness is much in evidence hereabouts, eh? Inadvertently her backview revealed the fact that she is not wearing those rather intimate garments of which you are a particular devotee. The injection mark on the thigh I hope you perceived? Good.

BLOOM

Granpapachi. But . . .

VIRAG

Number two on the other hand, she of the cherry rouge and coiffeuse white, whose hair owes not a little to our tribal elixir of gopherwood is in walking costume and tightly staysed by her sit, I should opine. Backbone in front, so to say. Correct me but I always understood that the act so performed by skittish humans with glimpses of lingerie appealed to you in virtue of its exhibitionististicicity. In a word. Hippogriff. Am I right?

BLOOM

She is rather lean.

VIRAG

(Not unpleasantly.) Absolutely! Well observed and those pannier pockets of the skirt and slightly pegtop effect are devised to suggest bunchiness of hip. A new purchase at some monster sale for which a gull has been mulcted. Meretricious finery to deceive the eye. Observe the attention to details of dustspecks. Never put on you tomorrow what you can wear today. Parallax! *(With a nervous twitch of his head.)* Did you hear my brain go snap? Pollysyllabax!

BLOOM

(An elbow resting in a hand, a forefinger against his cheek.) She seems sad.

VIRAG

(Cynically, his weasel teeth bared yellow, draws down his left eye with a finger and barks hoarsely.) Hoax! Beware of the flapper and bogus mournful. Lily of the alley. All possess bachelor's button discovered by Rualdus Colombus. Tumble her. Columble her. Chameleon. *(More genially).* Well then, permit me to draw your attention to item number three. There is plenty of her visible to the naked eye. Observe the mass of oxygenated vegetable matter on her skull. What ho, she bumps! The ugly duckling of the party, longcasted and deep in keel.

BLOOM

(Regretfully.) When you come out without your gun.

VIRAG

We can do you all brands mild, medium and strong. Pay your money, take your choice. How happy could you be with either . . .

BLOOM

With? . . .

VIRAG

(His tongue upcurling.) Lyum! Look. Her beam is broad. She is coated with quite a considerable layer of fat. Obviously mammal in weight of bosom you remark that she has in front well to the fore two protuberances of very respectable dimensions, inclined to fall in the noonday soupplate, while on her rere lower down are two additional protuberances, suggestive of potent rectum and tumescent for palpation which leave nothing to be desired save compactness. Such fleshy parts are the product of careful nurture. When coopfattened their livers reach an elephantine size. Pellets of new bread with fennygreek and gumbenjamin swamped down by potions of green tea endow them during their brief existence with natural pincushions of quite colossal blubber. That suits your book, eh? Fleshhotpots of Egypt to hanker after. Wallow in it. Lycopodium. *(His throat twitches.)* Slapbang! There he goes again.

BLOOM

The stye I dislike.

VIRAG

(Arches his eyebrows.) Contact with a goldring, they say. *Argumentum ad feminam,* as we said in old Rome and ancient Greece in the consulship of Diplodocus and Ichthyosaurus. For the rest Eve's sovereign remedy. Not for sale. Hire only. Huguenot. *(He twitches.)* It is a funny sound. *(He coughs*

encouragingly.) But possibly it is only a wart. I presume you shall have remembered what I will have taught you on that head? Wheatenmeal with honey and nutmeg.

BLOOM

(Reflecting.) Wheatenmeal with lycopodium and syllabax. This searching ordeal. It has been an unusually fatiguing day, a chapter of accidents. Wait. I mean, wartsblood spreads warts, you said . . .

VIRAG

(Severely, his nose hardhumped, his side eye winking.) Stop twirling your thumbs and have a good old thunk. See, you have forgotten. Exercise your mnemotechnic. *La causa è santa.* Tara. Tara. *(Aside.)* He will surely remember.

BLOOM

Rosemary also did I understand you to say or willpower over parasitic tissues. Then nay no I have an inkling. The touch of a deadhand cures. Mnemo?

VIRAG

(Excitedly.) I say so. I say so. E'en so. Technic. *(He taps his parchmentroll energetically.)* This book tells you how to act with all descriptive particulars. Consult index for agitated fear of aconite, melancholy of muriatic, priapic pulsatilla. Virag is going to talk about amputation. Our old friend caustic. They must be starved. Snip off with horsehair under the denned neck. But, to change the venue to the Bulgar and the Basque, have you made up your mind whether you like or dislike women in male habiliments? *(With a dry snigger.)* You intended to devote an entire year to the study of the religious problem and the summer months of 1882 to square the circle and win that million. Pomegranate! From the sublime to the ridiculous is but a step. Pyjamas, let us say? Or stockingette gusseted knickers, closed? Or, put we the case, those complicated combinations, camiknickers? *(He crows derisively.)* Keekeereekee!

> *(Bloom surveys uncertainly the three whores, then gazes at the veiled mauve light, hearing the everflying moth.)*

BLOOM

I wanted then to have now concluded. Nightdress was never. Hence this. But tomorrow is a new day will be. Past was is today. What now is will then tomorrow as now was be past yester.

VIRAG

(Prompts into his ear in a pig's whisper.) Insects of the day spend their brief existence in reiterated coition, lured by the smell of the inferiorly

pulchritudinous female possessing extendified pudendal verve in dorsal region. Pretty Poll! *(His yellow parrotbeak gabbles nasally.)* They had a proverb in the Carpathians in or about the year five thousand five hundred and fifty of our era. One tablespoonful of honey will attract friend Bruin more than half a dozen barrels of first choice malt vinegar. Bear's buzz bothers bees. But of this apart. At another time we may resume. We were very pleased, we others. *(He coughs and, bending his brow, rubs his nose thoughtfully with a scooping hand.)* You shall find that these night insects follow the light. An illusion for remember their complex unadjustable eye. For all these knotty points see the seventeenth book of my Fundamentals of Sexology or the Love Passion which Doctor L. B. says is the book sensation of the year. Some, to example, there are again whose movements are automatic. Perceive. That is his appropriate sun. Nightbird nightsun nighttown. Chase me, Charley! Buzz!

BLOOM

Bee or bluebottle too other day butting shadow on wall dazed self then me wandered dazed down shirt good job I . . .

VIRAG

(His face impassive, laughs in a rich feminine key.) Splendid! Spanish fly in his fly or mustard plaster on his dibble. *(He gabbles gluttonously with turkey wattles.)* Bubbly jock! Bubbly jock! Where are we? Open Sesame! Cometh forth! *(He unrolls his parchment rapidly and reads, his glowworm's nose running backwards over the letters which he claws.)* Stay, good friend. I bring thee thy answer. Redbank oysters wil shortly be upon us. I'm the best o'cook. Those succulent bivalves may help us and the truffles of Perigord, tubers dislodged through mister omnivorous porker, were unsurpassed in cases of nervous debility or viragitis. Though they stink yet they sting. *(He wags his head with cackling raillery.)* Jocular. With my eyeglass in my ocular.

BLOOM

(Absently.) Ocularly woman's bivalve case is worse. Always open sesame. The cloven sex. Why they fear vermin, creeping things. Yet Eve and the serpent contradict. Not a historical fact. Obvious analogy to my idea. Serpents too are gluttons for woman's milk. Wind their way through miles of omnivorous forest to sucksucculent her breast dry. Like those bubblyjocular Roman matrons one reads of in Elephantuliasis.

VIRAG

(His mouth projected in hard wrinkles, eyes stonily forlornly closed, psalms in outlandish monotone.) That the cows with their those distended udders that they have been the known . . .

BLOOM

I am going to scream. I beg your pardon. Ah? So. *(He repeats.)* Spontaneously to seek out the saurian's lair in order to entrust their teats to his avid suction. Ant milks aphis. *(Profoundly.)* Instinct rules the world. In life. In death.

VIRAG

(Head askew, arches his back and hunched wingshoulders, peers at the moth out of blear bulged eyes, points a horning claw and cries.) Who's Ger Ger? Who's dear Gerald? O, I much fear he shall be most badly burned. Will some pleashe pershon not now impediment so catastrophics mit agitation of firstclass tablenumpkin? *(He mews.)* Luss puss puss puss! *(He sighs, draws back and stares sideways down with dropping underjaw.)* Well, well. He doth rest anon.

> I'm a tiny tiny thing
> Ever flying in the spring
> Round and round a ringaring.
> Long ago I was a king,
> Now I do this kind of thing
> On the wing, on the wing!
> Bing!

(He rushes against the mauve shade flapping noisily.) Pretty pretty pretty pretty pretty pretty petticoats.

(From left upper entrance with two sliding steps Henry Flower comes forward to left front centre. He wears a dark mantle and drooping plumed sombrero. He carries a silver-stringed inlaid dulcimer and a longstemmed bamboo Jacob's pipe, its clay bowl fashioned as a female head. He wears dark velvet hose and silverbuckled pumps. He has the romantic Saviour's face with flowing locks, thin beard and moustache. His spindlelegs and sparrow feet are those of the tenor Mario, prince of Candia. He settles down his goffered ruffs and moistens his lips with a passage of his amorous tongue.)

HENRY

(In a low dulcet voice, touching the strings of his guitar.) There is a flower that bloometh.

(Virag truculent, his jowl set, stares at the lamp. Grave Bloom regards Zoe's neck. Henry gallant turns with pendent dewlap to the piano.)

STEPHEN

(To himself.) Play with your eyes shut. Imitate pa. Filling my belly with husks of swine. Too much of this. I will arise and go to my. Expect this is the. Steve, thou art in a parlous way. Must visit old Deasy or telegraph. Our

interview of this morning has left on me a deep impression. Though our ages. Will write fully tomorrow. I'm partially drunk, by the way. *(He touches the keys again.)* Minor chord comes now. Yes. Not much however.

(Almidano Artifoni holds out a batonroll of music with vigorous moustache-work.)

ARTIFONT

Ci rifletta. Lei rovina tutto.

FLORRY

Sing us something. Love's old sweet song.

STEPHEN

No voice. I am a most finished artist. Lynch, did I show you the letter about the lute?

FLORRY

(Smirking.) The bird that can sing and won't sing.

(The Siamese twins, Philip Drunk and Philip Sober, two Oxford dons with lawnmowers, appear in the window embrasure. Both are masked with Matthew Arnold's face.)

PHILIP SOBER

Take a fool's advice. All is not well. Work it out with the buttend of a pencil, like a good young idiot. Three pounds twelve you got, two notes, one sovereign, two crowns, if youth but knew. Mooney's en ville, Mooney's sur mer, the Moira, Larchet's, Holles street hospital, Burke's. Eh? I am watching you.

PHILIP DRUNK

(Impatiently.) Ah, bosh, man. Go to hell! I paid my way. If I could only find out about octaves. Reduplication of personality. Who was it told me his name? *(His lawnmower begins to purr.)* Aha, yes. *Zoè mou sas agapo.* Have a notion I was here before. When was it not Atkinson his card I have somewhere. Mac somebody. Unmack I have it. He told me about, hold on, Swinburne, was it, no?

FLORRY

And the song?

STEPHEN

Spirit is willing but the flesh is weak.

FLORRY

Are you out of Maynooth? You're like someone I knew once.

STEPHEN

Out of it now. *(To himself.)* Clever.

PHILIP DRUNK AND PHILIP SOBER

(Their lawnmowers purring with a rigadoon of grasshalms.) Clever ever. Out of it. Out of it. By the by have you the book, the thing, the ashplant? Yes, there it, yes. Cleverever outofitnow. Keep in condition. Do like us.

ZOE

There was a priest down here two nights ago to do his bit of business with his coat buttoned up. You needn't try to hide, I says to him. I know you've a Roman collar.

VIRAG

Perfectly logical from his standpoint. Fall of man. *(Harshly, his pupils waxing.)* To hell with the pope! Nothing new under the sun. I am the Virag who disclosed the sex secrets of monks and maidens. Why I left the Church of Rome. Read the Priest, the Woman and the Confessional. Penrose. Flipperty Jippert. *(He wriggles.)* Woman, undoing with sweet pudor her belt of rushrope, offers her allmoist yoni to man's lingam. Short time after man presents woman with pieces of jungle meat. Woman shows joy and covers herself with featherskins. Man loves her yoni fiercely with big lingam, the stiff one. *(He cries.)* Coactus volui. Then giddy woman will run about. Strong man grasps woman's wrist. Woman squeals, bites, spucks. Man, now fierce angry, strikes woman's fat yadgana. *(He chases his tail.)* Piffpaff! Popo! *(He stops, sneezes.)* Pchp! *(He worries his butt.)* Prrrrrht!

LYNCH

I hope you gave the good father a penance. Nine glorias for shooting a bishop.

ZOE

(Spouts walrus smoke through her nostrils.) He couldn't get a connection. Only, you know, sensation. A dry rush.

BLOOM

Poor man!

ZOE

(Lightly.) Only for what happened him.

BLOOM

How?

VIRAG

(A diabolic rictus of black luminosity contracting his visage, cranes his scraggy neck forward. He lifts a mooncalf nozzle and howls.) Verfluchte Goim! He had a father, forty fathers. He never existed. Pig God! He had two left feet. He was Judas Iacchias, a Libyan eunuch, the pope's bastard. *(He leans out on tortured forepaws, elbows bent rigid, his eye agonising in his flat skullneck and yelps over the mute world.)* A son of a whore. Apocalypse.

KITTY

And Mary Shortall that was in the lock with the pox she got from Jimmy Pidgeon in the blue caps had a child off him that couldn't swallow and was smothered with the convulsions in the mattress and we all subscribed for the funeral.

PHILIP DRUNK

(Gravely.) Qui vous a mis dans cette fichue position, Philippe?

PHILIP SOBER

(Gaily.) C'était le sacré pigeon, Philippe.

(Kitty unpins her hat and sets it down calmly, patting her henna hair. And a prettier, a daintier head of winsome curls was never seen on a whore's shoulders. Lynch puts on her hat. She whips it off.)

LYNCH

(Laughs.) And to such delights has Metchnikoff inoculated anthropoid apes.

FLORRY

(Nods.) Locomotor ataxy.

ZOE

(Gaily.) O, my dictionary.

LYNCH

Three wise virgins.

VIRAG

(Agueshaken, profuse yellow spawn foaming over his bony epileptic lips.) She sold lovephiltres, whitewax, orange flower. Panther, the Roman centurion, polluted her with his genitories. *(He sticks out a flickering phosphorescent scorpion tongue, his hand on his fork.)* Messiah! He burst her tympanum. *(With gibbering baboon's cries he jerks his hips in the cynical spasm.)* Hik! Hek! Hak! Hok! Huk! Kok! Kuk!

(Ben Jumbo Dollard, rubicund, musclebound, hairynostrilled, hugebearded, cabbageeared, shaggychested, shockmaned, fatpapped, stands forth, his loins and genitals tightened into a pair of black bathing bagslops.)

BEN DOLLARD

(Nakkering castanet bones in his huge padded paws, yodels jovially in base barreltone.) When love absorbs my ardent soul.

(The virgins, Nurse Callan and Nurse Quigley, burst through the ringkeepers and the ropes and mob him with open arms.)

THE VIRGINS

(Gushingly.) Big Ben! Ben MacChree!

A VOICE

Hold that fellow with the bad breeches.

BEN DOLLARD

(Smites his thigh in abundant laughter.) Hold him now.

HENRY

(Caressing on his breast a severed female head, murmurs.) Thine heart, mine love. *(He plucks his lutestrings.)* When first I saw . . .

VIRAG

(Sloughing his skins, his multitudinous plumage moulting.) Rats! *(He yawns, showing a coalblack throat and closes his jaws by an upward push of his parchment roll.)* After having said which I took my departure. Farewell. Fare thee well. Dreck!

(Henry Flower combs his moustache and beard rapidly with a pocketcomb and gives a cow's lick to his hair. Steered by his rapier, he glides to the door, his wild harp slung behind him. Virag reaches the door in two ungainly stilthops, his tail cocked, and deftly claps sideways on the wall a pusyellow flybill, butting it with his head.)

THE FLYBILL

K. 11. post no bills. Strictly confidential. Dr Hy Franks.

HENRY

All is lost now.

(Virag unscrews his head in a trice and holds it under his arm.)

VIRAG'S HEAD

Quack!

(Exeunt severally.)

STEPHEN

(Over his shoulder to Zoe.) You would have preferred the fighting parson who founded the protestant error. But beware Antisthenes, the dog sage, and the last end of Arius Heresiarchus. The agony in the closet.

LYNCH

All one and the same God to her.

STEPHEN

(Devoutly.) And Sovereign Lord of all things.

FLORRY

(To Stephen.) I'm sure you are a spoiled priest. Or a monk.

LYNCH

He is. A cardinal's son.

STEPHEN

Cardinal sin. Monks of the screw.

(*His Eminence, Simon Stephen Cardinal Dedalus, Primate of all Ireland, appears in the doorway, dressed in red soutane, sandals and socks. Seven dwarf simian acolytes, also in red, cardinal sins, uphold his train, peeping under it. He wears a battered silk hat sideways on his head. His thumbs are stuck in his armpits and his palms outspread. Round his neck hangs a rosary of corks ending on his breast in a corkscrew cross. Releasing his thumbs, he invokes grace from on high with large wave gestures and proclaims with bloated pomp.*)

THE CARDINAL

Conservio lies captured.
He lies in the lowest dungeon
With manacles and chains around his limbs
Weighing upwards of three tons.

(*He looks at all for a moment, his right eye closed tight, his left cheek puffed out. Then, unable to repress his merriment, he rocks to and fro, arms akimbo, and sings with broad rollicking humour.*)

O, the poor little fellow
Hi-hi-hi-hi-his legs they were yellow
He was plump, fat and heavy and brisk as a snake
But some bloody savage
To graize his white cabbage
He murdered Nell Flaherty's duckloving drake.

(*A multitude of midges swarms over his robe. He scratches himself with crossed arms at his ribs, grimacing, and exclaims.*)

I'm suffering the agony of the damned. By the hoky fiddle, thanks be to Jesus those funny little chaps are not unanimous. If they were they'd walk me off the face of the bloody globe.

(*His head aslant, he blesses curtly with fore and middle fingers, imparts the Easter kiss and doubleshuffles off comically, swaying his hat from side to side, shrinking quickly to the size of his trainbearers. The dwarf acolytes, giggling, peeping, nudging, ogling, Easterkissing, zigzag behind him. His voice is heard mellow from afar, merciful, male, melodious.*)

Shall carry my heart to thee,
Shall carry my heart to thee,
And the breath of the balmy night
Shall carry my heart to thee.

(*The trick doorhandle turns.*)

THE DOORHANDLE

Theeee.

ZOE

The devil is in that door.

(*A male form passes down the creaking staircase and is heard taking the water-proof and hat from the rack. Bloom starts forward involuntarily and, half closing the door as he passes, takes the chocolate from his pocket and offers it nervously to Zoe.*)

ZOE

(*Sniffs his hair briskly.*) Hum. Thank your mother for the rabbits. I'm very fond of what I like.

BLOOM

(*Hearing a male voice in talk with the whores on the doorstep, pricks his ears.*) If it were he? After? Or because not? Or the double event?

ZOE

(*Tears open the silverfoil.*) Fingers was made before forks. (*She breaks off and nibbles a piece, gives a piece to Kitty Ricketts and then turns kittenishly to Lynch.*) No objection to French lozenges? (*He nods. She taunts him.*) Have it now or wait till you get it? (*He opens his mouth, his head cocked. She whirls the prize in left circle. His head follows. She whirls it back in right circle. He eyes her.*) Catch.

(*She tosses a piece. With an adroit snap he catches it and bites it through with a crack.*)

KITTY

(*Chewing.*) The engineer I was with at the bazaar does have lovely ones. Full of the best liqueurs. And the viceroy was there with his lady. The gas we had on the Toft's hobbyhorses. I'm giddy still.

BLOOM

(*In Svengali's fur overcoat, with folded arms and Napoleonic forelock, frowns in ventriloquial exorcism with piercing eagle glance towards the door. Then, rigid, with left foot advanced, he makes a swift pass with impelling fingers and gives the sign of past master, drawing his right arm downwards from his left shoulder.*) Go, go, go, I conjure you, whoever you are.

(*A male cough & tread are heard passing through the mist outside. Bloom's features relax. He places a hand in his waistcoat, posing calmly. Zoe offers him chocolate.*)

BLOOM

(*Solemnly.*) Thanks.

ZOE

Do as you're bid. Here.

(*A firm heelclacking is heard on Cthe stairs.*)

BLOOM

(Takes the chocolate.) Aphrodisiac? But I thought it. Vanilla calms or? Mnemo. Confused light confuses memory. Red influences lupus. Colours affect women's characters, any they have. This black makes me sad. Eat and be merry for tomorrow. *(He eats.)* Influence taste too, mauve. But it is so long since I. Seems new. Aphro. That priest. Must come. Better late than never. Try truffles at Andrews.

(The door opens. Bella Cohen, a massive whoremistress enters. She is dressed in a threequarter ivory gown, fringed round the hem with tasselled selvedge and cools herself, flirting a black horn fan like Minnie Hauck in Carmen. *On her left hand are wedding and keeper rings. Her eyes are deeply carboned. She has a sprouting moustache. Her olive face is heavy, slightly sweated and fullnosed, with orangetainted nostrils. She has large pendant beryl eardrops.)*

BELLA

My word! I'm all of a mucksweat.

(She glances around her at the couples. Then her eyes rest on Bloom with hard insistence. Her large fan winnows wind towards her heated face, neck and embonpoint. Her falcon eyes glitter.)

THE FAN

(Flirting quickly, then slowly.) Married, I see.

BLOOM

Yes . . . Partly, I have mislaid . . .

THE FAN

(Half opening, then closing.) And the missus is master. Petticoat government.

BLOOM

(Looks down with a sheepish grin.) That is so.

THE FAN

(Folding together, rests against her eardrop.) Have you forgotten me?

BLOOM

Nes. Yo.

THE FAN

(Folded akimbo against her waist.) Is me her was you dreamed before? Was then she him you us since knew? Am all them and the same now we?

(Bella approaches, gently tapping with the fan.)

BLOOM

(Wincing.) Powerful being. In my eyes read that slumber which women love.

THE FAN

(Tapping.) We have met. You are mine. It is fate.

BLOOM

(*Cowed.*) Exuberant female. Enormously I desiderate your domination. I am exhausted, abandoned, no more young. I stand, so to speak, with an unposted letter bearing the extra regulation fee before the too late box of the general postoffice of human life. The door and window open at a right angle cause a draught of thirtytwo feet per second according to the law of falling bodies. I have felt this instant a twinge of sciatica in my left glutear muscle. It runs in our family. Poor dear papa, a widower, was a regular barometer from it. He believed in animal heat. A skin of tabby lined his winter waistcoat. Near the end, remembering king David and the Sunamite, he shared his bed with Athos, faithful after death. A dog's spittle, as you probably . . . (*He winces.*) Ah!

RICHIE GOULDING

(*Bagweighted, passes the door.*) Mocking is catch. Best value in Dub. Fit for a prince's liver and kidney.

THE FAN

(*Tapping.*) All things end. Be mine. Now.

BLOOM

(*Undecided.*) All now? I should not have parted with my talisman. Rain, exposure at dewfall on the sea rocks, a peccadillo at my time of life. Every phenomenon has a natural cause.

THE FAN

(*Points downwards slowly.*) You may.

BLOOM

(*Looks downwards and perceives her unfastened bootlace.*) We are observed.

THE FAN

(*Points downwards quickly.*) You must.

BLOOM

(*With desire, with reluctance.*) I can make a true black knot. Learned when I served my time and worked the mail order line for Kellet's. Experienced hand. Every knot says a lot. Let me. In courtesy. I knelt once before today. Ah!

(*Bella raises her gown slightly and, steadying her pose, lifts to the edge of a chair a plump buskined hoof and a full pastern, silksocked. Bloom, stifflegged, ageing, bends over her hoof and with gentle fingers draws out and in her laces.*)

BLOOM

(*Murmurs lovingly.*) To be a shoefitter in Mansfield's was my love's young dream, the darling joys of sweet buttonhooking, to lace up crisscrossed to kneelength the dressy kid footwear satinlined, so incredibly small, of Clyde Road ladies. Even their wax model Raymonde I visited daily to admire her cobweb hose and stick of rhubarb toe, as worn in Paris.

THE HOOF

Smell my hot goathide. Feel my royal weight.

BLOOM

(Crosslacing.) Too tight?

THE HOOF

If you bungle, Handy Andy, I'll kick your football for you.

BLOOM

Not to lace the wrong eyelet as I did the night of the bazaar dance. Bad luck. Nook in wrong tache of her . . . person you mentioned. That night she met . . . Now!

(He knots the lace. Bella places her foot on the floor. Bloom raises his head. Her heavy face, her eyes strike him in midbrow. His eyes grow dull, darker and pouched, his nose thickens.)

BLOOM

(Mumbles.) Awaiting your further orders, we remain, gentlemen . . .

BELLO

(With a hard basilisk stare, in a baritone voice.) Hound of dishonour!

BLOOM

(Infatuated.) Empress!

BELLO

(His heavy cheekchops sagging.) Adorer of the adulterous rump!

BLOOM

(Plaintively.) Hugeness!

BELLO

Dungdevourer!

BLOOM

(With sinews semiflexed.) Magnificence.

BELLO

Down! *(He taps her on the shoulder with his fan.)* Incline feet forward! Slide left foot one pace back. You will fall. You are falling. On the hands down!

BLOOM

(Her eyes upturned in the sign of admiration, closing.) Truffles!

(With a piercing epileptic cry she sinks on all fours, grunting, snuffling, rooting at his feet, then lies, shamming dead with eyes shut tight, trembling eyelids, bowed upon the ground in the attitude of most excellent master.)

BELLO

(With bobbed hair, purple gills, fat moustache rings round his shaven mouth, in mountaineer's puttees, green silverbuttoned coat, sport skirt and alpine hat with moorcock's feather, his hands stuck deep in his breeches pockets, places his heel on her neck and grinds it in.) Feel my entire weight. Bow, bondslave, before the throne of your despot's glorious heels, so glistening in their proud erectness.

BLOOM

(Enthralled, bleats.) I promise never to disobey.

BELLO

(Laughs loudly.) Holy smoke! You little know what's in store for you. I'm the tartar to settle your little lot and break you in! I'll bet Kentucky cocktails all round I shame it out of you, old son. Cheek me, I dare you. If you do tremble in anticipation of heel discipline to be inflicted in gym costume.

(Bloom creeps under the sofa and peers out through the fringe.)

ZOE

(Widening her slip to screen her.) She's not here.

BLOOM

(Closing her eyes.) She's not here.

FLORRY

(Hiding her with her gown.) She didn't mean it, Mr Bello. She'll be good, sir.

KITTY

Don't be too hard on her, Mr Bello. Sure you won't, ma'amsir.

BELLO

(Coaxingly.) Come, ducky dear. I want a word with you, darling, just to administer correction. Just a little heart to heart talk, sweety. *(Bloom puts out her timid head.)* There's a good girly now. *(Bello grabs her hair violently and drags her forward.)* I only want to correct you for your own good on a soft safe spot. How's that tender behind? O, ever so gently, pet. Begin to get ready.

BLOOM

(Fainting.) Don't tear my . . .

BELLO

(Savagely.) The nosering, the pliers, the bastinado, the hanging hook, the knout I'll make you kiss while the flutes play like the Nubian slave of old. You're in for it this time. I'll make you remember me for the balance of your natural life. *(His forehead veins swollen, his face congested.)* I shall sit on your ottomansaddleback every morning after my thumping good breakfast of Matterson's fat ham rashers and a bottle of Guinness's porter. *(He belches.)* And suck my thumping good Stock Exchange cigar while I read the *Licensed*

Victualler's Gazette. Very possibly I shall have you slaughtered and skewered in my stables and enjoy a slice of you with crisp crackling from the baking tin basted and baked like sucking pig with rice and lemon or currant sauce. It will hurt you.

(*He twists her arm. Bloom squeaks, turning turtle.*)

BLOOM

Don't be cruel, nurse! Don't!

BELLO

(*Twisting.*) Another!

BLOOM

(*Screams.*) O, it's hell itself! Every nerve in my body aches like mad!

BELLO

(*Shouts.*) Good, by the rumping jumping general! That's the best bit of news I heard these six weeks. Here, don't keep me waiting, damn you. (*He slaps her face.*)

BLOOM

(*Whimpers.*) You're after hitting me. I'll tell . . .

BELLO

Hold him down, girls, till I squat on him.

ZOE

Yes. Walk on him! I will.

FLORRY

I will. Don't be greedy.

KITTY

No, me. Lend him to me.

(*The brothel cook, Mrs Keogh, wrinkled, greybearded, in a greasy bib, men's grey and green socks and brogues, flour-smeared, a rollingpin stuck with raw pastry in her bare red arm and hand, appears at the door.*)

MRS KEOGH

(*Ferociously.*) Can I help? (*They hold and pinion Bloom.*)

BELLO

(*Squats, with a grunt, on Bloom's upturned face, puffing cigarsmoke, nursing a fat leg.*) I see Keating Clay is elected chairman of the Richmond Asylum and bytheby Guinness's preference shares are at sixteen three quarters. Curse me for a fool that I didn't buy that lot Craig and Gardner told me about. Just my infernal luck, curse it. And that Goddamned outsider *Throwaway* at twenty to one. (*He quenches his cigar angrily on Bloom's ear.*) Where's that Goddamned cursed ashtray?

BLOOM

(Goaded, buttocksmothered.) O! O! Monsters! Cruel one!

BELLO

Ask for that every ten minutes. Beg, pray for it as you never prayed before. *(He thrusts out a figged fist and foul cigar.)* Here, kiss that. Both. Kiss. *(He throws a leg astride and, pressing with horseman's knees, calls in a hard voice.)* Gee up! A cockhorse to Banbury cross. I'll ride him for the Eclipse stakes. *(He bends sideways and squeezes his mount's testicles roughly, shouting.)* Ho! off we pop! I'll nurse you in proper fashion. *(He horserides cockhorse, leaping in the saddle.)* The lady goes a pace a pace and the coachman goes a trot a trot and the gentleman goes a gallop a gallop a gallop a gallop.

FLORRY

(Pulls at Bello.) Let me on him now. You had enough. I asked before you.

ZOE

(Pulling at Florry.) Me. Me. Are you not finished with him yet, suckeress?

BLOOM

(Stifling.) Can't.

BELLO

Well, I'm not. Wait. *(He holds in his breath.)* Curse it. Here. This bung's about burst. *(He uncorks himself behind: then, contorting his features, farts loudly.)* Take that! *(He recorks himself.)* Yes, by Jingo, sixteen three quarters.

BLOOM

(A sweat breaking out over him.) Not man. *(He sniffs.)* Woman.

BELLO

(Stands up.) No more blow hot and cold. What you longed for has come to pass. Henceforth you are unmanned and mine in earnest, a thing under the yoke. Now for your punishment frock. You will shed your male garments, you understand, Ruby Cohen? and don the shot silk luxuriously rustling over head and shoulders and quickly too.

BLOOM

(Shrinks.) Silk, mistress said! O crinkly! scrapy! Must I tiptouch it with my nails?

BELLO

(Points to his whores.) As they are now, so will you be, wigged, singed, perfumesprayed, ricepowdered, with smoothshaven armpits. Tape measurements will be taken next your skin. You will be laced with cruel force into vicelike corsets of soft dove coutille, with whalebone busk, to the diamond trimmed pelvis, the absolute outside edge, while your figure,

plumper than when at large, will be restrained in nettight frocks, pretty two ounce petticoats and fringes and things stamped, of course, with my house-flag, creations of lovely lingerie for Alice and nice scent for Alice. Alice will feel the pullpull. Martha and Mary will be a little chilly at first in such delicate thighcasing but the frilly flimsiness of lace round your bare knees will remind you . . .

BLOOM

(*A charming soubrette with dauby cheeks, mustard hair and large male hands and nose, leering mouth.*) I tried her things on only once, a small prank, in Holles street. When we were hardup I washed them to save the laundry bill. My own shirts I turned. It was the purest thrift.

BELLO

(*Jeers.*) Little jobs that make mother pleased, eh! and showed off coquett-ishly in your domino at the mirror behind closedrawn blinds your unskirted thighs and hegoat's udders, in various poses of surrender, eh? Ho! Ho! I have to laugh! That secondhand black operatop shift and short trunk leg naughties all split up the stitches at her last rape that Mrs Miriam Dandrade sold you from the Shelbourne Hotel, eh?

BLOOM

Miriam. Black. Demimondaine.

BELLO

(*Guffaws.*) Christ Almighty, it's too tickling, this! You were a nicelooking Miriam when you clipped off your backgate hairs and lay swooning in the thing across the bed as Mrs Dandrade, about to be violated by Lieutenant Smythe-Smythe, Mr Philip Augustus Blockwell, M. P., Signor Laci Daremo, the robust tenor, blueeyed Bert, the liftboy, Henry Fleury of Gordon Bennett fame, Sheridan, the quadroon Crœsus, the varsity wetbob eight from old Trinity, Ponto, her splendid Newfoundland and Bobs, dowager duchess of Manorhamilton. (*He guffaws again.*) Christ, wouldn't it make a Siamese cat laugh?

BLOOM

(*Her hands and features working.*) It was Gerald converted me to be a true corsetlover when I was female impersonator in the High School play *Vice Versa*. It was dear Gerald. He got that kink, fascinated by sister's stays. Now dearest Gerald uses pinky greasepaint and gilds his eyelids. Cult of the beautiful.

BELLO

(*With wicked glee.*) Beautiful! Give us a breather! When you took your seat with womanish care, lifting your billowy flounces, on the smoothworn throne.

BLOOM

Science. To compare the various joys we each enjoy, *(Earnestly.)* And really it's better the position . . . because often I used to wet . . .

BELLO

(Sternly.) No insubordination. The sawdust is there in the corner for you. I gave you strict instructions, didn't I? Do it standing, sir! I'll teach you to behave like a jinkleman! If I catch a trace on your swaddles. Aha! By the ass of the Dorans you'll find I'm a martinet. The sins of your past are rising against you. Many. Hundreds.

THE SINS OF THE PAST

(In a medley of voices.) He went through a form of clandestine marriage with at least one woman in the shadow of the Black Church. Unspeakable messages he telephoned mentally to Miss Dunn at an address in d'Olier Street while he presented himself indecently to the instrument in the callbox. By word and deed he encouraged a nocturnal strumpet to deposit fecal and other matter in an unsanitary outhouse attached to empty premises. In five public conveniences he wrote pencilled messages offering his nuptial partner to all strongmembered males. And by the offensively smelling vitriol works did he not pass night after night by loving courting couples to see if and what and how much he could see? Did he not lie in bed, the gross boar, gloating over a nauseous fragment of wellused toilet paper presented to him by a nasty harlot, stimulated by gingerbread and a postal order?

BELLO

(Whistles loudly.) Say! What was the most revolting piece of obscenity in all your career of crime? Go the whole hog. Puke it out. Be candid for once.

(Mute inhuman faces throng forward, leering, vanishing, gibbering, Booloohoom. Poldy Kock, Bootlaces a penny, Cassidy's hag, blind stripling, Larry Rhinoceros, the girl, the woman, the whore, the other, the . . .)

BLOOM

Don't ask me: Our mutual faith. Pleasants street. I only thought the half of the . . . I swear on my sacred oath . . .

BELLO

(Peremptorily.) Answer. Repugnant wretch! I insist on knowing. Tell me something to amuse me, smut or a bloody good ghoststory or a line of poetry, quick, quick, quick! Where? How? What time? With how many? I give you just three seconds. One! Two! Thr . . . !

BLOOM

(Docile, gurgles.) I rererepugnosed in rerererepugnant . . .

BELLO

(Imperiously.) O get out, you skunk! Hold your tongue! Speak when you're spoken to.

BLOOM

(Bows.) Master! Mistress! Mantamer!
          (He lifts his arms. His bangle bracelets fall.)

BELLO

(Satirically.) By day you will souse and bat our smelling underclothes, also when we ladies are unwell, and swab out our latrines with dress pinned up and a dishclout tied to your tail. Won't that be nice? *(He places a ruby ring on her finger.)* And there now! With this ring I thee own. Say, thank you, mistress.

BLOOM

Thank you, mistress.

BELLO

You will make the beds, get my tub ready, empty the pisspots in the different rooms, including old Mrs Keogh's the cook's, a sandy one. Ay, and rinse the seven of them well, mind, or lap it up like champagne. Drink me piping hot. Hop! you will dance attendance or I'll lecture you on your misdeeds, Miss Ruby, and spank your bare bot right well, miss, with the hairbrush. You'll be taught the error of your ways. At night your wellcreamed braceleted hands will wear fortythreebutton gloves newpowdered with talc and having delicately scented fingertips. For such favours knights of old laid down their lives. *(He chuckles.)* My boys will be no end charmed to see you so ladylike, the colonel, above all. When they come here the night before the wedding to fondle my new attraction in gilded heels. First, I'll have a go at you myself. A man I know on the turf named Charles Alberta Marsh (I was in bed with him just now and another gentleman out of the Hanaper and Petty Bag office) is on the lookout for a maid of all work at a short knock. Swell the bust. Smile. Droop shoulders. What offers? *(He points.)* For that lot trained by owner to fetch and carry, basket in mouth. *(He bares his arm and plunges it elbowdeep in Bloom's vulva.)* There's fine depth for you! What, boys? That give you a hardon? *(He shoves his arm in a bidder's face.)* Here, wet the deck and wipe it round!

A BIDDER

A florin!
     (Dillon's lacquey rings his handbell.)

A VOICE

One and eightpence too much.

THE LACQUEY

Barang!

CHARLES ALBERTA MARSH

Must be virgin. Good breath. Clean.

BELLO

(*Gives a rap with his gavel.*) Two bar. Rockbottom figure and cheap at the price. Fourteen hands high. Touch and examine his points. Handle him. This downy skin, these soft muscles, this tender flesh. If I had only my gold piercer here! And quite easy to milk. Three newlaid gallons a day. A pure stockgetter, due to lay within the hour. His sire's milk record was a thousand gallons of whole milk in forty weeks. Whoa, my jewel! Beg up! Whoa! (*He brands his initial C on Bloom's croup.*) So! Warranted Cohen! What advance on two bob, gentlemen?

A DARKVISAGED MAN

(*In disguised accent.*) Hoondert punt sterlink.

VOICES

(*Subdued.*) For the Caliph Haroun Al Raschid.

BELLO

(*Gaily.*) Right. Let them all come. The scanty, daringly short skirt, riding up at the knee to show a peep of white pantelette, is a potent weapon and transparent stockings, emeraldgartered, with the long straight seam trailing up beyond the knee, appeal to the better instincts of the *blasé* man about town. Learn the smooth mincing walk on four inch Louis XV heels, the Grecian bend with provoking croup, the thighs fluescent, knees modestly kissing. Bring all your power of fascination to bear on them. Pander to their Gomorrahan vices.

BLOOM

(*Bends his blushing face into his armpit and simpers with forefinger in mouth.*) O, I know what you're hinting at now.

BELLO

What else are you good for, an impotent thing like you? (*He stoops and, peering, pokes with his fan rudely under the fat suet folds of Bloom's haunches.*) Up! Up! Manx cat! What have we here? Where's your curly teapot gone to or who docked it on you, cockyolly? Sing, birdy, sing. It's as limp as a boy of six's doing his pooly behind a cart. Buy a bucket or sell your pump. (*Loudly.*) Can you do a man's job?

BLOOM

Eccles Street . . .

BELLO

(*Sarcastically.*) I wouldn't hurt your feelings for the world but there's a man of brawn in possession there. The tables are turned, my gay young fellow! He is something like a fullgrown outdoor man. Well for you, you muff, if you had that weapon with knobs and lumbs and warts all over it. He shot his bolt, I can tell you! Foot to foot, knee to knee, belly to belly, bubs to breast! He's no eunuch. A shock of red hair he has sticking out of him behind like a furzebush! Wait for nine months, my lad! Holy ginger, it's kicking and coughing up and down in her guts already! That makes you wild, don't it? Touches the spot? (*He spits in contempt.*) Spittoon!

BLOOM

I was indecently treated, I . . . inform the police. Hundred pounds. Unmentionable. I . . .

BELLO

Would if you could, lame duck. A downpour we want, not your drizzle.

BLOOM

To drive me mad! Moll! I forgot! Forgive! Moll! . . . We . . . Still . . .

BELLO

(*Ruhtlessly.*) No, Leopold Bloom, all is changed by woman's will since you slept horizontal in Sleepy Hollow your night of twenty years. Return and see.
    (*Old Sleepy Hollow calls over the wold.*)

SLEEPY HOLLOW

Rip Van Winkle! Rip Van Winkle!

BLOOM

(*In tattered moccasins with a rusty fowlingpiece, tiptoeing, finger-tipping, his haggard bony bearded face peering through the diamond panes, cries out.*) I see her! It's she! The first night at Mat Dillon's! But that dress, the green! And her hair is dyed gold and he . . .

BELLO

(*Laughs mockingly.*) That's your daughter, you owl, with a Mullingar student.
    (*Milly Bloom, fairhaired, greenvested, slimsandalled, her blue scarf in the seawind simply swirling, breaks from the arms of her lover and calls, her young eyes wonderwide.*)

MILLY

My! It's Papli! But. O Papli, how old you've grown!

BELLO

Changed, eh? Our whatnot, our writing table where we never wrote, Aunt Hegarty's armchair, our classic reprints of old masters. A man and his menfriends are living there in clover. The *Cuckoos' Rest!* Why not? How many women had you, say? Following them up dark streets, flatfoot, exciting them by your smothered grunts. What, you male prostitute? Blameless dames with parcels of groceries. Turn about. Sauce for the goose, my gander, O.

BLOOM

They . . . I . . .

BELLO

(Cuttingly.) Their heelmarks will stamp the Brusselette carpet you bought at Wren's auction. In their horseplay with Moll the romp to find the buck flea in her breeches they will deface the little statue you carried home in the rain for art for art's sake. They will violate the secrets of your bottom drawer. Pages will be torn from your handbook of astronomy to make them pipespills. And they will spit in your ten shilling brass fender from Hampton Leedom's.

BLOOM

Ten and six. The act of low scoundrels. Let me go. I will return. I will prove . . .

A VOICE

Swear!
    (Bloom clenches his fists and crawls forward, a bowie knife between his teeth.)

BELLO

As a paying guest or a kept man? Too late. You have made your secondbest bed and others must lie in it. Your epitaph is written. You are down and out and don't you forget it, old bean.

BLOOM

Justice! All Ireland versus one! Has nobody . . .?
    (He bites his thumb.)

BELLO

Die and be damned to you if you have any sense of decency or grace about you. I can give you a rare old wine that'll send you skipping to hell and back. Sign a will and leave us any coin you have. If you have none see you damn well get it, steal it, rob it! We'll bury you in our shrubbery jakes where you'll be dead and dirty with old Cuck Cohen, my stepnephew I married, the bloody old gouty procurator and sodomite with a crick in his neck, and my other ten or eleven husbands, whatever the buggers' names were, suffocated in the one cesspool. *(He explodes in a loud phlegmy laugh.)* We'll manure you, Mr Flower! *(He pipes scoffingly.)* Byby, Poldy! Byby, Papli!

BLOOM

(Clasps his head.) My will power! Memory! I have sinned! I have suff . . .
(He weeps tearlessly.)

BELLO

(Sneers.) Crybaby! Crocodile tears!

(Bloom, broken, closely veiled for the sacrifice, sobs, his face to the earth. The passing bell is heard. Darkshawled figures of the circumcised, in sackcloth and ashes, stand by the wailing wall. M. Shulomowitz, Joseph Goldwater, Moses Herzog, Harris Rosenberg, M. Moisel, J. Citron, Minnie Watchman, O. Mastiansky, the Reverend Leopold Abramovitz, Chazen. With swaying arms they wail in pneuma over the recreant Bloom.)

THE CIRCUMCISED

(In a dark guttural chant as they cast dead sea fruit upon him, no flowers.) Shema Israel Adonai Elohenu Adonai Echad.

VOICES

(Sighing.) So he's gone. Ah yes. Yes, indeed. Bloom? Never heard of him. No? Queer kind of chap. There's the widow. That so? Ah, yes.

(From the suttee pyre the flame of gum camphire ascends. The pall of incense smoke screens and disperses. Out of her oak frame a nymph with hair unbound, lightly clad in teabrown art colours, descends from her grotto and passing under interlacing yews, stands over Bloom.)

THE YEWS

(Their leaves whispering.) Sister. Our sister. Ssh.

THE NYMPH

(Softly.) Mortal! *(Kindly.)* Nay, dost not weepest!

BLOOM

(Crawls jellily forward under the boughs, streaked by sunlight, with dignity.) This position. I felt it was expected of me. Force of habit.

THE NYMPH

Mortal! You found me in evil company, highkickers, coster picnic makers, pugilists, popular generals, immoral panto boys in flesh tights and the nifty shimmy dancers, La Aurora and Karini, musical act, the hit of the century. I was hidden in cheap pink paper that smelt of rock oil. I was surrounded by the stale smut of clubmen, stories to disturb callow youth, ads for transparencies, truedup dice and bustpads, proprietary articles and why wear a truss with testimonial from ruptured gentleman. Useful hints to the married.

BLOOM

(Lifts a turtle head towards her lap.) We have met before. On another star.

THE NYMPH

(Sadly.) Rubber goods. Neverrip. Brand as supplied to the aristocracy. Corsets for men. I cure fits or money refunded. Unsolicited testimonials for Professor Waldmann's wonderful chest exuber. My bust developed four inches in three weeks, reports Mrs Gus Rublin with photo.

BLOOM

You mean *Photo Bits?*

THE NYMPH

I do. You bore me away, framed me in oak and tinsel, set me above your marriage couch. Unseen, one summer eve, you kissed me in four places. And with loving pencil you shaded my eyes, my bosom and my shame.

BLOOM

(Humbly kisses her long hair.) Your classic curves, beautiful immortal. I was glad to look on you, to praise you, a thing of beauty, almost to pray.

THE NYMPH

During dark nights I heard your praise.

BLOOM

(Quickly.) Yes, yes. You mean that I . . . Sleep reveals the worst side of everyone, children perhaps excepted. I know I fell out of my bed or rather was pushed. Steel wine is said to cure snoring. For the rest there is that English invention, pamphlet of which I received some days ago, incorrectly addressed. It claims to afford a noiseless inoffensive vent. *(He sighs.)* 'Twas ever thus. Frailty, thy name is marriage.

THE NYMPH

(Her fingers in her ears.) And words. They are not in my dictionary.

BLOOM

You understood them?

THE YEWS

Ssh.

THE NYMPH

(Covers her face with her hand.) What have I not seen in that chamber? What must my eyes look down on?

BLOOM

(Apologetically.) I know. Soiled personal linen, wrong side up with care. The quoits are loose. From Gibraltar by long sea, long ago.

THE NYMPH

(Bends her head.) Worse! Worse!

BLOOM

(Reflects precautiously.) That antiquated commode. It wasn't her weight. She scaled just eleven stone nine. She put on nine pounds after weaning. It was a crack and want of glue. Eh? And that absurd orangekeyed utensil which has only one handle.

(The sound of a waterfall is heard in bright cascade.)

THE WATERFALL

Poulaphouca Poulaphouca
Poulaphouca Poulaphouca.

THE YEWS

(Mingling their boughs.) Listen. Whisper. She is right, our sister. We grew by Poulaphouca waterfall. We gave shade on languorous summer days.

JOHN WYSE NOLAN

(In the background, in Irish National Forester's uniform, doffs his plumed hat.) Prosper! Give shade on languorous days, trees of Ireland!

THE YEWS

(Murmuring.) Who came to Poulaphouca with the high school excursion? Who left his nutquesting classmates to seek our shade?

BLOOM

(Pigeonbreasted, bottleshouldered, padded, in nondescript juvenile grey and black striped suit, too small for him, white tennis shoes, bordered stockings with turnover tops, and a red school cap with badge.) I was in my teens, a growing boy. A little then sufficed, a jolting car, the mingling odours of the ladies' cloakroom and lavatory, the throng penned tight on the old Royal stairs, for they love crushes, instincts of the herd, and the dark sexsmelling theatre unbridles vice. Even a pricelist of their hosiery. And then the heat. There were sunspots that summer. End of school. And tipsycake. Halcyon days.

(Halcyon Days, high school boys in blue and white football jerseys and shorts, Master Donald Turnbull, Master Abraham Chatterton, Master Owen Goldberg, Master Jack Meredith, Master Percy Apjohn, stand in a clearing of the trees and shout to Master Leopold Bloom.)

THE HALCYON DAYS

Mackerel! Live us again. Hurray! *(They cheer.)*

BLOOM

(Hobbledehoy, warmgloved, mammamufflered, stunned with spent snowballs, struggles to rise.) Again! I feel sixteen! What a lark! Let's ring all the bells in Montague Street. *(He cheers feebly.)* Hurray for the High School!

THE ECHO

Fool!

THE YEWS

(Rustling.) She is right, our sister. Whisper. *(Whispered kisses are heard in all the wood. Faces of hamadryads peep out from the boles and among the leaves and break blossoming into bloom.)* Who profaned our silent shade?

THE NYMPH

(Coyly through parting fingers.) There! In the open air?

THE YEWS

(Sweeping downward.) Sister, yes. And on our virgin sward.

THE WATERFALL

Poulaphouca Poulaphouca
Phoucaphouca Phoucaphouca.

THE NYMPH

(With wide fingers.) O! Infamy!

BLOOM

I was precocious. Youth. The fauns. I sacrificed to the god of the forest. The flowers that bloom in the spring. It was pairing time. Capillary attraction is a natural phenomenon. Lotty Clarke, flaxenhaired, I saw at her night toilette through illclosed curtains, with poor papa's operaglasses. The wanton ate grass wildly. She rolled downhill at Rialto Bridge to tempt me with her flow of animal spirits. She climbed their crooked tree and I . . . A saint couldn't resist it. The demon possessed me. Besides, who saw?

(Staggering Bob, a whitepolled calf, thrusts a ruminating head with humid nostrils through the foliage.)

STAGGERING BOB

Me. Me see.

BLOOM

Simply satisfying a need. *(With pathos.)* No girl would when I went girling. Too ugly. They wouldn't play . . .

(High on Ben Howth through rhododendrons a nannygoat passes, plumpuddered, buttytailed, dropping currants.)

THE NANNYGOAT

(Bleats.) Megegaggegg! Nannannanny!

BLOOM

(Hatless, flushed, covered with burrs of thistledown and gorsepine.) Regularly engaged. Circumstances alter cases. *(He gazes intently downwards on the water.)* Thirtytwo head over heels per second. Press nightmare. Giddy

Elijah. Fall from cliff. Sad end of government printer's clerk. *(Through silversilent summer air the dummy of Bloom, rolled in a mummy, rolls rotatingly from the Lion's Head cliff into the purple waiting waters.)*

THE DUMMYMUMMY

Bbbbblllllbbblblodschbg?

(Far out in the bay between Bailey and Kish lights the Erin's King *sails, sending a broadening plume of coalsmoke from her funnel towards the land.)*

COUNCILLOR NANNETTI

(Alone on deck, in dark alpaca, yellow kitefaced, his hand in his waistcoat opening, declaims.) When my country takes her place among the nations of the earth, then, and not till then, let my epitaph be written. I have . . .

BLOOM

Done. Prff.

THE NYMPH

(Loftily.) We immortals, as you saw today have not such a place and no hair there either. We are stonecold and pure. We eat electric light. *(She arches her body in lascivious crispation, placing her forefinger in her mouth.)* Spoke to me. Heard from behind. How then could you . . .?

BLOOM

(Pacing the heather abjectly.) O, I have been a perfect pig. Enemas too, I have administered. One third of a pint of quassia, to which add a tablespoonful of rocksalt. Up the fundament. With Hamilton Long's syringe, the ladies' friend.

THE NYMPH

In my presence. The powderpuff. *(She blushes and makes a knee.)* And the rest.

BLOOM

(Dejected.) Yes. *Peccavi!* I have paid homage on that living altar where the back changes name. *(With sudden fervour.)* For why should the dainty scented jewelled hand, the hand that rules . . . ?

(Figures wind serpenting in slow woodland pattern around the treestems, cooeeing.)

THE VOICE OF KITTY

(In the thicket.) Show us one of them cushions.

THE VOICE OF FLORRY

Here.

(A grouse wings clumsily through the underwood.)

THE VOICE OF LYNCH

(In the thicket.) Whew! Piping hot!

THE VOICE OF ZOE

(From the thicket.) Came from a hot place.

THE VOICE OF VIRAG

(A birdchief, bluestreaked and feathered in war panoply with his assegai, striding through a crackling canebrake over beechmast and acorns.) Hot! Hot! Ware Sitting Bull!

BLOOM

It overpowers me. The warm impress of her warm form. Even to sit where a woman has sat, especially with divaricated thighs, as though to grant the last favours, most especially with previously well uplifted white sateen coatpans. So womanly full. It fills me full.

THE WATERFALL

Phillaphulla Poulaphouca
Poulaphouca Poulaphouca.

THE YEWS

Ssh! Sister, speak!

THE NYMPH

(Eyeless, in nun's white habit, coif and huge winged wimple, softly, with remote eyes.) Tranquilla convent. Sister Agatha. Mount Carmel, the apparitions of Knock and Lourdes. No more desire. *(She reclines her head, sighing.)* Only the ethereal. Where dreamy creamy gull waves o'er the waters dull.

(Bloom half rises. His back trousers' button snaps.)

THE BUTTON

Bip!

(Two sluts of the Coombe dance rainily by, shawled, yelling flatly.)

THE SLUTS

O Leopold lost the pin of his drawers
He didn't know what to do,
To keep it up,
To keep it up.

BLOOM

(Coldly.) You have broken the spell. The last straw. If there were only ethereal where would you all be, postulants and novices? Shy but willing, like an ass pissing.

THE YEWS

(Their silverfoil of leaves precipitating, their skinny arms ageing and swaying.) Deciduously!

THE NYMPH

Sacrilege! To attempt my virtue! (*A large moist stain appears on her robe.*) Sully my innocence! You are not fit to touch the garment of a pure woman. (*She clutches in her robe.*) Wait, Satan. You'll sing no more lovesongs. Amen. Amen. Amen. Amen. (*She draws a poniard and, clad in the sheathmail of an elected knight of nine, strikes at his loins.*) Nekum!

BLOOM

(*Starts up, seizes her hand.*) Hoy! Nebrakada! Cat of nine lives! Fair play, madam. No pruning knife. The fox and the grapes, is it? What do we lack with your barbed wire? Crucifix not thick enough? (*He clutches her veil.*) A holy abbot you want or Brophy, the lame gardener, or the spoutless statue of the watercarrier or good Mother Alphonsus, eh Reynard?

THE NYMPH

(*With a cry, flees from him unveiled, her plaster cast cracking, a cloud of stench escaping from the cracks.*) Poli . . . !

BLOOM

(*Calls after her.*) As if you didn't get it on the double yourselves. No jerks and multiple mucosities all over you. I tried it. Your strength our weakness. What's our studfee? What will you pay on the nail? You fee men dancers on the Riviera, I read. (*The fleeing nymph raises a keen.*) Eh! I have sixteen years of black slave labour behind me. And would a jury give me five shillings alimony to morrow, eh? Fool someone else, not me. (*He sniffs.*) But. Onions. Stale. Sulphur. Grease.

(*The figure of Bella Cohen stands before him.*)

BELLA

You'll know me the next time.

BLOOM

(*Composed, regards her.*) Passée. Mutton dressed as lamb. Long in the tooth and superfluous hairs. A raw onion the last thing at night would benefit your complexion. And take some double chin drill. Your eyes are as vapid as the glass eyes of your stuffed fox. They have the dimensions of your other features, that's all. I'm not a triple screw propeller.

BELLA

(*Contemptuously.*) You're not game, in fact. (*Her sowcunt barks.*) Fohracht!

BLOOM

(*Contemptuously.*) Clean your nailless middle finger first, the cold spunk of your bully is dripping from your cockscomb. Take a handful of hay and wipe yourself.

BELLA

I know you, canvasser! Dead cod!

BLOOM

I saw him, kipkeeper! Pox and gleet vendor!

BELLA

(Turns to the piano.) Which of you was playing the dead march from *Saul?*

ZOE

Me. Mind your cornflowers. *(She darts to the piano and bangs chords on it with crossed arms.)* The cat's ramble through the slag. *(She glances back.)* Eh? Who's making love to my sweeties? *(She darts back to the table.)* What's yours is mine and what's mine is my own.

(Kitty disconcerted coats her teeth with the silver paper. Bloom approaches Zoe.)

BLOOM

(Gently.) Give me back that potato, will you?

ZOE

Forfeits, a fine thing and a superfine thing.

BLOOM

(With feeling.) It is nothing, but still a relic of poor mamma.

ZOE

Give a thing and take it back
God'll ask you where is that
You'll say you don't know
God'll send you down below.

BLOOM

There is a memory attached to it. I should like to have it.

STEPHEN

To have or not to have, that is the question.

ZOE

Here. *(She hauls up a reef of her slip, revealing her bare thigh and unrolls the potato from the top of her stocking.)* Those that hides knows where to find.

BELLA

(Frowns.) Here. This isn't a musical peepshow. And don't you smash that piano. Who's paying here?

(She goes to the pianola. Stephen fumbles in his pocket and, taking out a banknote by its corner, hands it to her.)

STEPHEN

(With exaggerated politeness.) This silken purse I made out of the sow's ear of

the public. Madam, excuse me. If you allow me. *(He indicates vaguely Lynch and Bloom.)* We are all in the same sweepstake, Kinch and Lynch. *Dans ce bordel où tenons nostre état.*

LYNCH

(Calls from the hearth.) Dedalus! Give her your blessing for me.

STEPHEN

(Hands Bella a coin.) Gold. She has it.

BELLA

(Looks at the money, then at Zoe, Florrie and Kitty.) Do you want three girls? It's ten shillings here.

STEPHEN

(Delightedly.) A hundred thousand apologies. *(He fumbles again and takes out and hands her two crowns.)* Permit, *brevi manu*, my sight is somewhat troubled.
    (Bella goes to the table to count the money while Stephen talks to himself in monosyllables. Zoe bounds over to the table. Kitty leans over Zoe's neck. Lynch gets up, rights his cap and, clasping Kitty's waist, adds his head to the group.)

FLORRY

(Strives heavily to rise.) Ow! My foot's asleep. *(She limps over to the table. Bloom approaches.)*

BELLA, ZOE, KITTY, LYNCH, BLOOM

(Chattering and squabbling.) The gentleman . . . ten shillings . . . paying for the three . . . allow me a moment . . . this gentleman pays separate . . . who's touching it? . . . ow . . . mind who you're pinching . . . are you staying the night or a short time? . . . who did? . . . you're a liar, excuse me . . . the gentleman paid down like a gentleman . . . drink . . . it's long after eleven.

STEPHEN

(At the pianola, making a gesture of abhorrence.) No bottles! What, eleven? A riddle.

ZOE

(Lifting up her pettigown and folding a half sovereign into the top of her stocking.) Hard earned on the flat of my back.

LYNCH

(Lifting Kitty from the table.) Come!

KITTY

Wait. *(She clutches the two crowns.)*

FLORRY

And me?

LYNCH

Hoopla! *(He lifts her, carries her and bumps her down on the sofa.)*

STEPHEN

The fox crew, the cocks flew,
The bells in heaven
Were striking eleven.
'Tis time for her poor soul
To get out of heaven.

BLOOM

(Quietly lays a half sovereign on the table between Bella and Florry.) So. Allow me. *(He takes up the poundnote.)* Three times ten. We're square.

BELLA

(Admiringly.) You're such a slyboots, old cocky. I could kiss you.

ZOE

(Points.) Hum? Deep as a drawwell. *(Lynch bends Kitty back over the sofa and kisses her. Bloom goes with the poundnote to Stephen.)*

BLOOM

This is yours.

STEPHEN

How is that? *Le distrait* or absentminded beggar. *(He fumbles again in his pocket and draws out a handful of coins. An object falls.)* That fell.

BLOOM

(Stooping, picks up and hands a box of matches.) This.

STEPHEN

Lucifer. Thanks.

BLOOM

(Quietly.) You had better hand over that cash to me to take care of. Why pay more?

STEPHEN

(Hands him all his coins.) Be just before you are generous.

BLOOM

I will but is it wise? *(He counts.)* One, seven, eleven, and five. Six. Eleven. I don't answer for what you may have lost.

STEPHEN

Why striking eleven? Proparoxyton. Moment before the next Lessing says. Thirsty fox. *(He laughs loudly.)* Burying his grandmother. Probably he killed her.

BLOOM

That is one pound six and eleven. One pound seven, say.

STEPHEN

Doesn't matter a rambling damn.

BLOOM

No, but . . .

STEPHEN

(Comes to the table.) Cigarette, please. *(Lynch tosses a cigarette from the sofa to the table.)* And so Georgina Johnson is dead and married. *(A cigarette appears on the table. Stephen looks at it.)* Wonder. Parlour magic. Married. Hm. *(He strikes a match and proceeds to light the cigarette with enigmatic melancholy.)*

LYNCH

(Watching him.) You would have a better chance of lighting it if you held the match nearer.

STEPHEN

(Brings the match nearer his eye.) Lynx eye. Must get glasses. Broke them yesterday. Sixteen years ago. Distance. The eye sees all flat. *(He draws the match away. It goes out.)* Brain thinks. Near: far. Ineluctable modality of the visible. *(He frowns mysteriously.)* Hm. Sphinx. The beast that has two backs at midnight. Married.

ZOE

It was a commercial traveller married her and took her away with him.

FLORRY

(Nods.) Mr Lambe from London.

STEPHEN

Lamb of London, who takest away the sins of our world.

LYNCH

(Embracing Kitty on the sofa, chants deeply.) Dona nobis pacem.
  (The cigarette slips from Stephen's fingers. Bloom picks it up and throws it into the grate.)

BLOOM

Don't smoke. You ought to eat. Cursed dog I met. *(To Zoe.)* You have nothing?

ZOE

Is he hungry?

STEPHEN

(Extends his hand to her smiling and chants to the air of the bloodoath in the Dusk of the Gods.)

Hangende Hunger,
Fragende Frau,
Macht uns alle kaput.

ZOE

(Tragically.) Hamlet, I am thy father's gimlet! *(She takes his hand.)* Blue eye'd beauty, I'll read your hand. *(She points to his forehead.)* No wit, no wrinkles. *(She counts.)* Two, three, Mars, that's courage. *(Stephen shakes his head.)* No kid.

LYNCH

Sheet lightning courage. The youth who could not shiver and shake. *(To Zoe.)* Who taught you palmistry?

ZOE

(Turns.) Ask my ballocks that I haven't got. *(To Stephen.)* I see it in your face. The eye, like that. *(She frowns with lowered head.)*

LYNCH

(Laughing, slaps Kitty behind twice.) Like that. Pandy bat.
    (Twice loudly a pandybat cracks, the coffin of the pianola flies open, the bald little round jack-in-the-box head of Father Dolan springs up.)

FATHER DOLAN

Any boy want flogging? Broke his glasses? Lazy idle little schemer. See it in your eye.
    (Mild, benign, rectorial, reproving, the head of Don John Conmee rises from the pianola coffin.)

DON JOHN CONMEE

Now, Father Dolan! Now. I'm sure that Stephen is a very good little boy.

ZOE

(Examining Stephen's palm.) Woman's hand.

STEPHEN

(Murmurs.) Continue. Lie. Hold me. Caress. I never could read His hand-writing except His criminal thumbprint on the haddock.

ZOE

What day were you born?

STEPHEN

Thursday. Today.

ZOE

Thursday's child has far to go. *(She traces lines on his hand.)* Line of fate. Influential friends.

FLORRY

(Pointing.) Imagination.

ZOE

Mount of the moon. You'll meet with a . . . *(She peers at his hands abruptly.)* I won't tell you what's not good for you. Or do you want to know?

BLOOM

(Detaches her fingers and offers his palm.) More harm than good. Here. Read mine.

BELLA

Show. *(She turns up Bloom's hand.)* I thought so. Knobby knuckles, for the women.

ZOE

(Peering at Bloom's palm.) Gridiron. Travels beyond the sea and marry money.

BLOOM

Wrong.

ZOE

(Quickly.) O, I see. Short little finger. Henpecked husband. That wrong?
   (Black Liz, a huge rooster hatching in a chalked circle, rises, stretches her wings and clucks.)

BLACK LIZ

Gara. Klook. Klook. Klook.
          (She sidles from her newlaid egg and waddles off.)

BLOOM

(Points to his hand.) That weal there is an accident. Fell and cut it twentytwo years ago. I was sixteen.

ZOE

I see, says the blind man. Tell us news.

STEPHEN

See? Moves to one great goal. I am twentytwo too. Sixteen years ago I twentytwo tumbled, twentytwo years ago he sixteen fell off his hobbyhorse. *(He winces.)* Hurt my hand somewhere. Must see a dentist. Money?
   (Zoe whispers to Florry. They giggle. Bloom releases his hand and writes idly on the table in backhand, pencilling slow curves.)

FLORRY

What?
   (A hackneycar, number three hundred and twentyfour, with a gallantbuttocked mare, driven by James Barton, Harmony Avenue, Donnybrook, trots past.

Blazes Boylan and Lenehan sprawl swaying on the sideseats. The Ormond boots crouches behind on the axle. Sadly over the crossblind Lydia Douce and Mina Kennedy gaze.)

THE BOOTS

(Jogging, mocks them with thumb and wriggling wormfingers.) Haw, haw, have you the horn?

(Bronze by gold they whisper.)

ZOE

(To Florry.) Whisper.

(They whisper again.)

(Over the well of the car Blazes Boylan leans, his boater straw set sideways, a red flower in his mouth. Lenehan, in a yachtsman's cap and white shoes, officiously detaches a long hair from Blazes Boylan's shoulder.)

LENEHAN

Ho! What do I here behold? Were you brushing the cobwebs off a few quims?

BOYLAN

(Seated, smiles.) Plucking a turkey.

LENEHAN

A good night's work.

BOYLAN

(Holding up four thick bluntungulated fingers, winks.) Blazes Kate! Up to sample or your money back. *(He holds out a forefinger.)* Smell that.

LENEHAN

(Smells gleefully.) Ah! Lobster and mayonnaise. Ah!

ZOE AND FLORRY

(Laugh together.) Ha ha ha ha.

BOYLAN

(Jumps surely from the car and calls loudly for all to hear.) Hello, Bloom! Mrs Bloom up yet?

BLOOM

(In a flunkey's plum plush coat and kneebreeches, buff stockings and powdered wig.) I'm afraid not, sir, the last articles . . .

BOYLAN

(Tosses him sixpence.) Here, to buy yourself a gin and splash. *(He hangs his hat smartly on a peg of Bloom's antlered head.)* Show me in. I have a little private business with your wife. You understand?

BLOOM

Thank you, sir. Yes, sir, Madam Tweedy is in her bath, sir.

MARION

He ought to feel himself highly honoured. *(She plops splashing out of the water.)* Raoul, darling, come and dry me. I'm in my pelt. Only my new hat and a carriage sponge.

BOYLAN

(A merry twinkle in his eye.) Topping!

BELLA

What? What is it?

(Zoe whispers to her.)

MARION

Let him look, the pishogue! Pimp! And scourge himself! I'll write to a powerful prostitute or Bartholomona, the bearded woman, to raise weals out on him an inch thick and make him bring me back a signed and stamped receipt.

BELLA

(Laughing.) Ho ho ho ho.

BOYLAN

(To Bloom, over his shoulder.) You can apply your eye to the keyhole and play with yourself while I just go through her a few times.

BLOOM

Thank you, sir. I will, sir. May I bring two men chums to witness the deed and take a snapshot? *(He holds an ointment jar.)* Vaseline, sir? Orange-flower? . . . Lukewarm water? . . .

KITTY

(From the sofa.) Tell us, Florry. Tell us. What.

(Florry whispers to her. Whispering lovewords murmur liplapping loudly, poppysmic plopslop.)

MINA KENNEDY

(Her eyes upturned.) O, it must be like the scent of geraniums and lovely peaches! O, he simply idolises every bit of her! Stuck together! Covered with kisses!

LYDIA DOUCE

(Her mouth opening.) Yumyum. O, he's carrying her round the room doing it! Ride a cock horse. You could hear them in Paris and New York. Like mouthfuls of strawberries and cream.

KITTY

(Laughing.) Hee hee hee.

BOYLAN'S VOICE

(Sweetly, hoarsely, in the pit of his stomach.) Ah! Gooblazeqruk brukarchkrasht!

MARION'S VOICE

(Hoarsely, sweetly rising to her throat.) O! Weeshwashtkissimapooisthnapoo-huck!

BLOOM

(His eyes wildly dilated, clasps himself.) Show! Hide! Show! Plough her! More! Shoot!

BELLA, ZOE, FLORRY, KITTY

Ho ho! Ha ha! Hee hee!

LYNCH

(Points.) The mirror up to nature. *(He laughs.)* Hu hu hu hu hu hu.

(Stephen and Bloom gaze in the mirror. The face of William Shakespeare, beardless, appears there, rigid in facial paralysis, crowned by the reflection of the reindeer antlered hatrack in the hall.)

SHAKESPEARE

(In dignified ventriloquy.) 'Tis the loud laugh bespeaks the vacant mind. *(To Bloom.)* Thou thoughtest as how thou wastest invisible. Gaze. *(He crows with a black capon's laugh.)* Iagogo! How my Oldfellow chokit his Thursday-momun. Iagogogo!

BLOOM

(Smiles yellowly at the whores.) When will I hear the joke?

ZOE

Before you're twice married and once a widower.

BLOOM

Lapses are condoned. Even the great Napoleon, when measurements were taken near the skin after his death . . .

(Mrs Dignam, widow woman, her snubnose and cheeks flushed with deathtalk, tears and Tunny's tawny sherry, hurries by in her weeds, her bonnet awry, rouging and powdering her cheeks, lips and nose, a pen chivvying her brood of cygnets. Beneath her skirt appear her late husband's everyday trousers and turnedup boots, large eights. She holds a Scottish widow's insurance policy and large marqueeumbrella under which her brood runs with her, Patsy hopping on one short foot, his collar loose, a hank of porksteaks dangling, Freddy whimpering, Susy with a crying cod's mouth, Alice struggling with the baby. She cuffs them on, her streamers flaunting aloft.)

FREDDY

Ah, ma, you're dragging me along!

SUSY

Mamma, the beeftea is fizzing over!

SHAKESPEARE

(With paralytic rage.) Weda seca whokilla farst.

(The face of Martin Cunningham, bearded, refeatures Shakespeare's beardless face. The marqueeumbrella sways drunkenly, the children run aside. Under the umbrella appears Mrs Cunningham in Merry Widow hat and kimono gown. She glides sidling and bowing, twisting japanesily.)

MRS CUNNINGHAM

(Sings.)

And they call me the jewel of Asia.

MARTIN CUNNINGHAM

(Gazes on her impassive.) Immense! Most bloody awful demirep!

STEPHEN

Et exaltabuntur cornua iusti. Queens lay with prize bulls. Remember Pasiphae for whose lust my grandoldgrossfather made the first confessionbox. Forget not Madam Grissel Steevens nor the suine scions of the house of Lambert. And Noah was drunk with wine. And his ark was open.

BELLA

None of that here. Come to the wrong shop.

LYNCH

Let him alone. He's back from Paris.

ZOE

(Runs to Stephen and links him.) O go on! Give us some parleyvoo.

(Stephen claps hat on head and leaps over to the fireplace, where he stands with shrugged shoulders, finny hands outspread, a painted smile on his face.)

LYNCH

(Pommelling on the sofa.) Rmm Rmm Rmm Rrrrrrmmmmm.

STEPHEN

(Gabbles, with marionette jerks.) Thousand places of entertainment to expenses your evenings with lovely ladies saling gloves and other things perhaps her heart beerchops perfect fashionable house very eccentric where lots cocottes beautiful dressed much about princesses like are dancing cancan and walking there parisian clowneries extra foolish for bachelors foreigns the same if talking a poor english how much smart they are on things love and sensations

voluptuous. Misters very selects for is pleasure must to visit heaven and hell
show with mortuary candles and they tears silver which occur every night.
Perfectly shocking terrific of religion's things mockery seen in universal
world. All chic womans which arrive full of modesty then disrobe and
squeal loud to see vampire man debauch nun very fresh young with *dessous
troublants. (He clacks his tongue loudly.) Ho, la la! Ce pif qu'il a!*

LYNCH

Vive le vampire!

THE WHORES

Bravo! Parleyvoo!

STEPHEN

(Grimacing with head back, laughs loudly, clapping himself.) Great success of
laughing. Angels much prostitutes like and holy apostles big damn ruffians.
Demimondaines nicely handsome sparkling of diamonds very amiable
costumed. Or do you are fond better what belongs they moderns pleasure
turpitude of old mans? *(He points about him with grotesque gestures which
Lynch and the whores reply to.)* Caoutchouc statue woman reversible or
lifesize tompeeptoms virgins nudities very lesbic the kiss five ten times.
Enter gentlemen to see in mirrors every positions trapezes all that machine
there besides also if desire act awfully bestial butcher's boy pollutes in
warm veal liver or omlette on the belly *pièce de Shakespeare.*

BELLA

(Clapping her belly, sinks back on the sofa with a shout of laughter.) An omelette
on the . . . Ho! ho! ho! ho! . . . Omelette on the . . .

STEPHEN

(Mincingly.) I love you, Sir darling. Speak you englishman tongue for *double
entente cordiale.* O yes, *mon loup.* How much cost? Waterloo. Watercloset.
(He ceases suddenly and holds up a forefinger.)

BELLA

(Laughing.) Omelette . . .

THE WHORES

(Laughing.) Encore! Encore!

STEPHEN

Mark me. I dreamt of a watermelon.

ZOE

Go abroad and love a foreign lady.

LYNCH

Across the world for a wife.

FLORRY

Dreams go by contraries.

STEPHEN

(*Extending his arms.*) It was here. Street of harlots. In Serpentine Avenue Beelzebub showed me her, a fubsy widow. Where's the red carpet spread?

BLOOM

(*Approaching Stephen.*) Look . . .

STEPHEN

No, I flew. My foes beneath me. And ever shall be. World without end. (*He cries.*) Pater! Free!

BLOOM

I say, look . . .

STEPHEN

Break my spirit, will he? *O merde alors!* (*He cries, his vulture talons sharpened.*) Hola! Hillyho!

(*Simon Dedalus' voice hilloes in answer, somewhat sleepy but ready.*)

SIMON

That's all right. (*He swoops uncertainly through the air, wheeling, uttering cries of heartening, on strong ponderous buzzard wings.*) Ho, boy! Are you going to win? Hoop! Pschatt! Stable with those halfcastes. Wouldn't let them within the bawl of an ass. Head up! Keep our flag flying! An eagle gules volant in a field argent displayed. Ulster king at arms! hai hoop! (*He makes the beagle's call giving tongue.*) Bulbul! Burblblbrurblbl! Hai, boy!

(*The fronds and spaces of the wallpaper file rapidly across country. A stout fox drawn from covert, brush pointed, having buried his grandmother, runs swift for the open, brighteyed, seeking badger earth, under the leaves. The pack of staghounds follows, nose to the ground, sniffing their quarry, beaglebaying, burblbrbling to be blooded. Ward Union huntsmen and huntswomen live with them, hot for a kill. From Six Mile Point, Flathouse, Nine Mile Stone follow the footpeople with knotty sticks, salmongaffs, lassos, flockmasters with stockwhips, bearbaiters with tomtoms, toreadors with bullswords, grey negroes waving torches. The crowd bawls of dicers, crown and anchor players, thimbleriggers, broadsmen. Crows and touts, hoarse bookies in high wizard hats clamour deafeningly.*)

THE CROWD

Card of the races. Racing card!

Ten to one the field!

Tommy on the clay here! Tommy on the clay!

Ten to one bar one. Ten to one bar one.

Try your luck on spinning Jenny!

Ten to one bar one!
Sell the monkey, boys! Sell the monkey!
I'll give ten to one!
Ten to one bar one!

(A dark horse riderless, bolts like a phantom past the winning-post, his mane moonfoaming, his eyeballs stars. The field follows, a bunch of bucking mounts. Skeleton horses: Sceptre, Maximum the Second, Zinfandel, the Duke of Westminster's Shotover, Repulse, the Duke of Beaufort's Ceylon, prix de Paris. Dwarfs ride them, rusty armoured, leaping, leaping in their saddles. Last in a drizzle of rain, on a broken-winded isabelle nag, Cock of the North, the favourite, honey cap, green jacket, orange sleeves, Garrett Deasy up, gripping the reins, a hockey stick at the ready. His nag, stumbling on whitegaitered feet, jogs along the rocky road.)

THE ORANGE LODGES

(Jeering.) Get down and push, mister. Last lap! You'll be home the night!

GARRETT DEASY

(Bolt upright, his nailscraped face plastered with postage stamps, brandishes his hockeystick, his blue eyes flashing in the prism of the chandelier as his mount lopes by at schooling gallop.)

Per vias rectas!

(A yoke of buckets leopards all over him and his rearing nag, a torrent of mutton broth with dancing coins of carrots, barley, onions, turnips, potatoes.)

THE GREEN LODGES

Soft day, sir John! Soft day, your honour!

(Private Carr, Private Compton and Cissy Caffrey pass beneath the windows, singing in discord.)

STEPHEN

Hark! Our friend, noise in the street!

ZOE

(Holds up her hand.) Stop!

PRIVATE CARR, PRIVATE COMPTON AND CISSY CAFFREY

Yet I've a sort a
Yorkshire relish for . . .

ZOE

That's me. *(She claps her hands.)* Dance! Dance! *(She runs to the pianola.)* Who has twopence?

BLOOM

Who'll? . . .

LYNCH

(Handing her coins.) Here.

STEPHEN

(Cracking his fingers impatiently.) Quick! Quick! Where's my augur's rod?
(He runs to the piano and takes his ashplant, beating his foot in tripudium.)

ZOE

(Turns the drumhandle.) There.

(She drops two pennies in the slot. Gold pink and violet lights start forth. The drum turns purring in low hesitation waltz. Professor Goodwin, in a bowknotted periwig, in court dress, wearing a stained inverness cape, bent in two from incredible age, totters across the room, his hands fluttering. He sits tinily on the piano stool and lifts and beats handless sticks of arms on the keyboard, nodding with damsel's grace, his bowknot bobbing.)

ZOE

(Twirls around herself, heeltapping.) Dance. Anybody here for there? Who'll dance?

(The pianola, with changing lights plays in waltz time the prelude of My Girl's a Yorkshire Girl. *Stephen throws his ashplant on the table and seizes Zoe around the waist. Florry and Bella push the table towards the fireplace. Stephen, arming Zoe with exaggerated grace, begins to waltz her around the room. Her sleeve, falling from gracing arms, reveals a white fleshflower of vaccination. Bloom stands aside. Between the curtains, Professor Maginni inserts a leg on the toepoint of which spins a silk hat. With a deft kick, he sends it spinning to his crown and jauntyhatted skates in. He wears a slate frockcoat with claret silk lapels, a gorget of cream tulle, a green lowcut waistcoat, stock collar with white kerchief, tight lavender trousers, patent pumps and canary gloves. In his buttonhole is a dahlia. He twirls in reversed directions a clouded cane, then wedges it tight in his oxter. He places a hand limply on his breastbone, bows and fondles his flower and buttons.)*

MAGINNI

The poetry of motion, art of callisthenics. No connection with Madam Legget Byrne's or Levinstone's. Fancy dress balls arranged. Deportment. The Katty Lanner steps. So. Watch me! My terpsichorean abilities. *(He minuets forward three paces on tripping bee's feet.)* Tout le monde en avant! Révérence! Tout le monde en place!

(The prelude ceases. Professor Goodwin, beating vague arms, shrivels, shrinks, his live cape falling about the stool. The air, in firmer waltz time, pounds. Stephen and Zoe circle freely. The lights change, glow, fade, gold, rose, violet.)

THE PIANOLA

Two young fellows were talking about their girls, girls, girls,
Sweethearts they'd left behind . . .

*(From a corner the morning hours run out, goldhaired, slim, in girlish blue,
waspwaisted, with innocent hands. Nimbly they dance, twirling their skipping
ropes. The hours of noon follow in amber gold. Laughing linked, high haircombs
flashing, they catch the sun in mocking mirrors, lifting their arms.)*

MAGINNI

(Clipclaps glovesilent hands.) Carré! Avant deux! Breathe evenly! *Balance!*
*(The morning and noon hours waltz in their places, turning, advancing to
each other, shaping their curves, bowing vis à vis. Cavaliers behind them arch
and suspend their arms, with hands descending to, touching, rising from their
shoulders.)*

HOURS

You may touch my . . .

CAVALIERS

May I touch your?

HOURS

O, but lightly!

CAVALIERS

O, so lightly!

THE PIANOLA

My little shy little lass has a waist,

*(Zoe and Stephen turn boldly with looser swing. The twilight hours advance,
from long landshadows, dispersed, lagging, languideyed, their cheeks delicate
with cipria and false faint bloom. They are in grey gauze with dark bat sleeves
that flutter in the land breeze.)*

MAGINNI

Avant huit! Traversé! Salut! Cours de mains! Croisé!
*(The night hours steal to the last place. Morning, noon and twilight hours
retreat before them. They are masked, with daggered hair and bracelets of dull
bells. Weary, they curchycurchy under veils.)*

THE BRACELETS

Heigho! Heigho!

ZOE

(Twisting, her hand to her brow.) O!

MAGINNI

Les tiroirs! Chaîne de dames! La corbeille! Dos à dos!

(Arabesquing wearily, they weave a pattern on the floor, weaving, unweaving, curtseying, twisting, simply swirling.)

ZOE

I'm giddy.

(She frees herself, droops on a chair, Stephen seizes Florry and turns with her.)

MAGINNI

Boulangère! Les ronds! Les ponts! Chevaux de bois! Escargots!

(Twining, receding, with interchanging hands, the night hours link, each with arching arms, in a mosaic of movements. Stephen and Florry turn cumbrously.)

MAGINNI

Dansez avec vos dames! Changez de dames! Donnez le petit bouquet à votre dame! Remerciez!

THE PIANOLA

Best, best of all,
Baraabum!

KITTY

(Jumps up.) O, they played that on the hobbyhorses at the Mirus bazaar!

(She runs to Stephen. He leaves Florry brusquely and seizes Kitty. A screaming bittern's harsh high whistle shrieks. Groangrousegurgling Toft's cumbersome whirligig turns slowly the room right roundabout the room.)

THE PIANOLA

My girl's a Yorkshire girl.

ZOE

Yorkshire through and through.

Come on all!

(She seizes Florry and waltzes her.)

STEPHEN

Pas seul!

(He wheels Kitty into Lynch's arms, snatches up his ashplant from the table and takes the floor. All wheel, whirl, waltz, twirl. Bloombella, Kittylynch, Florryzoe, jujuby women. Stephen with hat ashplant frogsplits in middle highkicks with skykicking mouth shut hand clasp part under thigh, with clang tinkle boom-hammer tallyho hornblower blue green yellow flashes. Toft's cumbersome turns with hobbyhorse riders from gilded snakes dangled, bowels fandango leaping spurn soil foot and fall again.)

THE PIANOLA

Though she's a factory lass
And wears no fancy clothes.

(*Closeclutched swift swifter with glareblareflare scudding they scotlootshoot lumbering by. Baraabum!*)

TUTTI

Encore! Bis! Bravo! Encore!

SIMON

Think of your mother's people!

STEPHEN

Dance of death.

(*Bang fresh barang bang of lacquey's bell, horse, nag, steer, piglings, Conmee on Christass lame crutch and leg sailor in cockboat armfolded ropepulling hitching stamp hornpipe through and through, Baraabum! On nags, hogs, bellhorses, Gadarene swine, Corny in coffin. Steel shark stone onehandled Nelson, two trickies Frauenzimmer plumstained from pram falling bawling. Gum, he's a champion. Fuseblue peer from barrel rev. evensong Love on hackney jaunt Blazes blind coddoubled bicyclers Dilly with snowcake no fancy clothes. Then in last wiswitchback lumbering up and down bump mashtub sort of viceroy and reine relish for tublumber bumpshire rose. Baraabum!*)

(*The couples fall aside. Stephen whirls giddily. Room whirls back. Eyes closed, he totters. Red rails fly spacewards. Stars all around suns turn roundabout. Bright midges dance on wall. He stops dead.*)

STEPHEN

Ho!

(*Stephen's mother, emaciated, rises stark through the floor in leper grey with a wreath of faded orange blossoms and a torn bridal veil, her face worn and noseless, green with grave mould. Her hair is scant and lank. She fixes her bluecircled hollow eyesockets on Stephen and opens her toothless mouth uttering a silent word. A choir of virgins and confessors sing voicelessly.*)

THE CHOIR

Liliata rutilantium te confessorum . . .
Iubilantium te virginum . . .

(*From the top of a tower Buck Mulligan, in particoloured jester's dress of puce and yellow and clown's cap with curling bell, stands gaping at her, a smoking buttered split scone in his hand.*)

BUCK MULLIGAN

She's beastly dead. The pity of it! Mulligan meets the afflicted mother. *(He upturns his eyes.)* Mercurial Malachi.

THE MOTHER

(With the subtle smile of death's madness.) I was once the beautiful May Goulding. I am dead.

STEPHEN

(Horrorstruck.) Lemur, who are you? What bogeyman's trick is this?

BUCK MULLIGAN

(Shakes his curling capbell.) The mockery of it! Kinch killed her dogsbody bitchbody. She kicked the bucket. *(Tears of molten butter fall from his eyes into the scone.)* Our great sweet mother! *Epi oinopa ponton.*

THE MOTHER

(Comes nearer, breathing upon him softly her breath of wetted ashes.) All must go through it, Stephen. More women than men in the world. You too. Time will come.

STEPHEN

(Choking with fright, remorse and horror.) They said I killed you, mother. He offended your memory. Cancer did it, not I. Destiny.

THE MOTHER

(A green rill of bile trickling from a side of her mouth.) You sang that song to me. *Love's bitter mystery.*

STEPHEN

(Eagerly.) Tell me the word, mother, if you know now. The word known to all men.

THE MOTHER

Who saved you the night you jumped into the train at Dalkey with Paddy Lee? Who had pity for you when you were sad among the strangers? Prayer is all powerful. Prayer for the suffering souls in the Ursuline manual, and forty days' indulgence. Repent, Stephen.

STEPHEN

The ghoul! Hyena!

THE MOTHER

I pray for you in my other world. Get Dilly to make you that boiled rice every night after your brain work. Years and years I loved you, O my son, my firstborn, when you lay in my womb.

ZOE

(Fanning herself with the grate fan.) I'm melting!

FLORRY

(Points to Stephen.) Look! He's white.

BLOOM

(Goes to the window to open it more.) Giddy.

THE MOTHER

(With smouldering eyes.) Repent! O, the fire of hell!

STEPHEN

(Panting.) The corpsechewer! Raw head and bloody bones!

THE MOTHER

(Her face drawing near and nearer, sending out an ashen breath.) Beware! *(She raises her blackened, withered right arm slowly towards Stephen's breast with outstretched fingers.)* Beware! God's hand! *(A green crab with malignant red eyes sticks deep its grinning claws in Stephen's heart.)*

STEPHEN

(Strangled with rage.) Shite! *(His features grow drawn and grey and old.)*

BLOOM

(At the window.) What?

STEPHEN

Ah non, par exemple! The intellectual imagination! With me all or not at all. *Non serviam!*

FLORRY

Give him some cold water. Wait. *(She rushes out.)*

THE MOTHER

(Wrings her hands slowly, moaning desperately.) O Sacred Heart of Jesus, have mercy on him! Save him from hell, O divine Sacred Heart!

STEPHEN

No! No! No! Break my spirit all of you if you can! I'll bring you all to heel!

THE MOTHER

(In the agony of her deathrattle.) Have mercy on Stephen, Lord, for my sake! Inexpressible was my anguish when expiring with love, grief and agony on Mount Calvary.

STEPHEN

Nothung!

(He lifts his ashplant high with both hands and smashes the chandelier. Time's livid final flame leaps and, in the following darkness, ruin of all space, shattered glass and toppling masonry.)

THE GASJET

Pwfungg!

BLOOM

Stop!

LYNCH

(Rushes forward and seizes Stephen's hand.) Here! Hold on! Don't run amok!

BELLA

Police!

(Stephen, abandoning his ashplant, his head and arms thrown back stark, beats the ground and flees from the room past the whores at the door.)

BELLA

(Screams.) After him!

(The two whores rush to the halldoors. Lynch and Kitty and Zoe stampede from the room. They talk excitedly. Bloom follows, returns.)

THE WHORES

(Jammed in the doorway, pointing.) Down there.

ZOE

(Pointing.) There. There's something up.

BELLA

Who pays for the lamp? *(She seizes Bloom's coattail.)* There. You were with him. The lamp's broken.

BLOOM

(Rushes to the hall, rushes back.) What lamp, woman?

A WHORE

He tore his coat.

BELLA

(Her eyes hard with anger and cupidity, points.) Who's to pay for that? Ten shillings. You're a witness.

BLOOM

(Snatches up Stephen's ashplant.) Me? Ten shillings? Haven't you lifted enough off him? Didn't he . . .!

BELLA

(Loudly.) Here, none of your tall talk. This isn't a brothel. A ten shilling house.

BLOOM

(His hand under the lamp, pulls the chain. Pulling, the gasjet lights up a crushed mauve purple shade. He raises the ashplant.) Only the chimney's broken. Here is all he . . .

BELLA

(Shrinks back and screams.) Jesus! Don't!

BLOOM

(Warding off a blow.) To show you how he hit the paper. There's not a sixpenceworth of damage done. Ten shillings!

FLORRY

(With a glass of water, enters.) Where is he?

BELLA

Do you want me to call the police?

BLOOM

O, I know. Bulldog on the premises. But he's a Trinity student. Patrons of your establishment. Gentlemen that pay the rent. *(He makes a masonic sign.)* Know what I mean? Nephew of the vicechancellor. You don't want a scandal.

BELLA

(Angrily.) Trinity! Coming down here ragging after the boat races and paying nothing. Are you my commander here? Where is he? I'll charge him. Disgrace him, I will. *(She shouts.)* Zoe! Zoe!

BLOOM

(Urgently.) And if it were your own son in Oxford! *(Warningly.)* I know.

BELLA

(Almost speechless.) Who are you incog?

ZOE

(In the doorway.) There's a row on.

BLOOM

What? Where? *(He throws a shilling on the table and shouts.)* That's for the chimney. Where? I need mountain air.

(He hurries out through the hall. The whores point. Florry follows, spilling water from her tilted tumbler. On the doorstep all the whores clustered talk volubly, pointing to the right where the fog has cleared off. From the left arrives a jingling hackney car. It slows to in front of the house. Bloom at the halldoor perceives Corny Kelleher who is about to dismount from the car with two silent lechers. He averts his face. Bella from within the hall urges on her whores. They blow ickylickysticky yumyum kisses. Corny Kelleher replies with a ghostly lewd smile. The silent lechers turn to pay the jarvey. Zoe and Kitty still point right. Bloom, parting them swiftly, draws his caliph's hood and poncho and hurries down the steps with sideways face. Incog Haroun al Raschid, he flits behind the silent lechers and hastens on by the railings with fleet step of a pard strewing the

drag behind him, torn envelopes drenched in aniseed. The ashplant marks his stride. A pack of bloodhounds led by Hornblower of Trinity brandishing a dogwhip in tallyho cap, and an old pair of grey trousers, follows from far, picking up the scent, nearer, baying, panting, at fault, breaking away, throwing their tongues, biting his heels, leaping at his tail. He walks, runs, zigzags, gallops, lugs laid back. He is pelted with gravel, cabbagestumps, biscuitboxes, eggs, potatoes, dead codfish, woman's slipperslappers. After him, freshfound, the hue and cry zigzag gallops in hot pursuit of follow my leader: 65 C 66 C night watch, John Henry Menton, Wisdom Hely, V. B. Dillon, Councillor Nannetti, Alexander Keyes, Larry O'Rourke, Joe Cuffe, Mrs O'Dowd, Pisser Burke, The Nameless One, Mrs Riordan, The Citizen, Garryowen, Whatdoyoucallhim, Strangeface, Fellowthatslike, Sawhimbefore, Chapwith, Chris Callinan, sir Charles Cameron, Benjamin Dollard, Lenehan, Bartell d'Arcy, Joe Hynes, red Murray, editor Brayden, T. M. Healy, Mr Justice Fitzgibbon, John Howard Parnell, the reverend Tinned Salmon, Professor Joly, Mrs Breen, Denis Breen, Theodore Purefoy, Mina Purefoy, the Westland Row postmistress, C. P. M'Coy, friend of Lyons, Hoppy Holohan, man in the street, other man in the street, Footballboots, pugnosed driver, rich protestant lady, Davy Byrne, Mrs Ellen M'Guinness, Mrs Joe Gallaher, George Lidwell, Jimmy Henry on corns, Super-intendent Laracy, Father Cowley, Crofton out of the Collector General's, Dan Dawson, dental surgeon Bloom with tweezers, Mrs Bob Doran, Mrs Kennefick, Mrs Wyse Nolan, John Wyse Nolan, handsomemarriedwomanrubbedagainst-widebehindinClonskeatram, the bookseller of Sweets of Sin, Miss Dubedat-andshedidbedad, Mesdames Gerald and Stanislaus Moran of Roebuck, the managing clerk of Drimmie's, colonel Hayes, Mastiansky, Citron, Penrose, Aaron Figatner, Moses Herzog, Michael E. Geraghty, Inspector Troy, Mrs Galbraith, the constable off Eccles Street corner, old doctor Brady with stethoscope, the mystery man on the beach, a retriever, Mrs Miriam Dandrade and all her lovers.)

THE HUE AND CRY

(Helterskelterpelterwelter.) He's Bloom! Stop Bloom! Stopabloom! Stopper-robber! Hi! Hi! Stop him on the corner!

(At the corner of Beaver Street beneath the scaffolding Bloom panting stops on the fringe of the noisy quarrelling knot, a lot not knowing a jot what hi! hi! row and wrangle round the whowhat brawlaltogether.)

STEPHEN

(With elaborate gestures, breathing deeply and slowly.) You are my guests. The uninvited. By virtue of the fifth of George and seventh of Edward. History to blame. Fabled by mothers of memory.

PRIVATE CARR

(To Cissy Caffrey.) Was he insulting you?

STEPHEN

Addressed her in vocative feminine. Probably neuter. Ungenitive.

VOICES

No, he didn't. The girl's telling lies. He was in Mrs Cohen's. What's up?
Soldiers and civilians.

CISSY CAFFREY

I was in company with the soldiers and they left me to do – you know and
the young man ran up behind me. But I'm faithful to the man that's treating
me though I'm only a shilling whore.

STEPHEN

(Catches sight of Kitty's and Lynch's heads.) Hail, Sisyphus. *(He points to himself
and the others.)* Poetic. Neopoetic.

VOICES

She's faithfultheman.

CISSY CAFFREY

Yes, to go with him. And me with a soldier friend.

PRIVATE COMPTON

He doesn't half want a thick ear, the blighter. Biff him one, Harry.

PRIVATE CARR

(To Cissy.) Was he insulting you while me and him was having a piss?

LORD TENNYSON

(In Union Jack blazer and cricket flannels, bareheaded, flowing-bearded.) Their's
not to reason why.

PRIVATE COMPTON

Biff him, Harry.

STEPHEN

(To Private Compton.) I don't know your name but you are quite right.
Doctor Swift says one man in armour will beat ten men in their shirts. Shirt
is synechdoche. Part for the whole.

CISSY CAFFREY

(To the crowd.) No, I was with the private.

STEPHEN

(Amiably.) Why not? The bold soldier boy. In my opinion every lady for
example . . .

PRIVATE CARR

(His cap awry, advancing to Stephen.) Say, how would it be, governor, if I was to bash in your jaw?

STEPHEN

(Looks up in the sky.) How? Very unpleasant. Noble art of selfpretence. Personally, I detest action. *(He waves his hand.)* Hand hurts me slightly. *Enfin, ce sont vos oignons. (To Cissy Caffrey.)* Some trouble is on here. What is it, precisely?

DOLLY GRAY

(From her balcony waves her handkerchief, giving the sign of the heroine of Jericho.) Rahab. Cook's son, goodbye. Safe home to Dolly. Dream of the girl you left behind and she will dream of you.

(The soldiers turn their swimming eyes.)

BLOOM

(Elbowing through the crowd, plucks Stephen's sleeve vigorously.) Come now, professor, that carman is waiting.

STEPHEN

(Turns.) Eh? *(He disengages himself.)* Why should I not speak to him or to any human being who walks upright upon this oblate orange? *(He points his finger.)* I'm not afraid of what I can talk to if I see his eye. Retaining the perpendicular.

(He staggers a pace back.)

BLOOM

(Propping him.) Retain your own.

STEPHEN

(Laughs emptily.) My centre of gravity is displaced. I have forgotten the trick. Let us sit down somewhere and discuss. Struggle for life is the law of existence but modern philirenists, notably the tsar and the king of England, have invented arbitration. *(He taps his brow.)* But in here it is I must kill the priest and the king.

BIDDY THE CLAP

Did you hear what the professor said? He's a professor out of the college.

CUNTY KATE

I did. I heard that.

BIDDY THE CLAP

He expresses himself with much marked refinement of phraseology.

CUNTY KATE

Indeed, yes. And at the same time with such apposite trenchancy.

PRIVATE CARR

(Pulls himself free and comes forward.) What's that you're saying about my king?

(Edward the Seventh appears in an archway. He wears a white jersey on which an image of the Sacred Heart is stitched, with the insignia of Garter and Thistle, Golden Fleece, Elephant of Denmark, Skinner's and Probyn's horse, Lincoln's Inn bencher and ancient and honourable artillery company of Massachusetts. He sucks a red jujube. He is robed as a grand elect perfect and sublime mason with trowel and apron, marked made in Germany. In his left hand he holds a plasterer's bucket on which is printed: Défense d'uriner. *A roar of welcome greets him.)*

EDWARD THE SEVENTH

(Slowly, solemnly but indistinctly.) Peace, perfect peace. For identification bucket in my hand. Cheerio, boys. *(He turns to his subjects.)* We have come here to witness a clean straight fight and we heartily wish both men the best of good luck. Mahak makar a back.

(He shakes hands with Private Carr, Private Compton, Stephen, Bloom and Lynch. General applause. Edward the Seventh lifts the bucket graciously in acknowledgement.)

PRIVATE CARR

(To Stephen.) Say it again.

STEPHEN

(Nervous, friendly, pulls himself up.) I understand your point of view, though I have no king myself for the moment. This is the age of patent medicine. A discussion is difficult down here. But this is the point. You die for your country, suppose. *(He places his arm on Private Carr's sleeve.)* Not that I wish it for you. But I say: Let my country die for me. Up to the present it has done so. I don't want it to die. Damn death. Long live life!

EDWARD THE SEVENTH

(Levitates over heaps of slain in the garb and with the halo of Joking Jesus, a white jujube in his phosphorescent face.)

My methods are new and are causing surprise.
To make the blind see I throw dust in their eyes.

STEPHEN

Kings and unicorns! *(He falls back a pace.)* Come somewhere and we'll . . . What was that girl saying? . . .

PRIVATE COMPTON

Eh, Harry, give him a kick in the knackers. Stick one into Jerry.

BLOOM

(To the privates, softly.) He doesn't know what he's saying. Taking a little more than is good for him. Absinthe, the greeneyed monster. I know him. He's a gentleman, a poet. It's all right.

STEPHEN

(Nods, smiling and laughing.) Gentleman, patriot, scholar and judge of impostors.

PRIVATE CARR

I don't give a bugger who he is.

PRIVATE COMPTON

We don't give a bugger who he is.

STEPHEN

I seem to annoy them. Green rag to a bull.
    (Kevin Egan of Paris in black Spanish tasselled shirt and peep-o'-day boy's hat signs to Stephen.)

KEVIN EGAN

H'lo! *Bonjour!* The *vieille ogresse* with the *dents jaunes.*
    (Patrice Egan peeps from behind, his rabbit face nibbling a quince leaf.)

PATRICE

Socialiste!

DON EMILE PATRIZIO FRANZ RUPERT POPE HENNESSY

(In medieval hauberk, two wild geese valant on his helm, with noble indignation points a mailed hand against the privates.) Werf those eykes to footboden, big grand porcos of johnyellows todos covered of gravy!

BLOOM

(To Stephen.) Come home. You'll get into trouble.

STEPHEN

(Swaying.) I don't avoid it. He provokes my intelligence.

BIDDY THE CLAP

One immediately observes that he is of patrician lineage.

THE VIRAGO

Green above the red, says he. Wolfe Tone.

THE BAWD

The red's as good as the green, and better. Up the soldiers! Up King Edward!

A ROUGH

(Laughs.) Ay! Hands up to De Wet.

THE CITIZEN

(With a huge emerald muffler and shillelagh, calls.)

May the God above
Send down a cove
With teeth as sharp as razors
To slit the throat
Of the English dogs
That hanged our Irish leaders.

THE CROPPY BOY

(The rope noose round his neck, gripes in his issuing bowels with both hands.)

I bear no hate to a living thing,
But love my country beyond the king.

RUMBOLD, DEMON BARBER

(Accompanied by two blackmasked assistants, advances with a gladstone bag which he opens.) Ladies and gents, cleaver purchased by Mrs Pearcy to slay Mogg. Knife with which Voisin dismembered the wife of a compatriot and hid remains in a sheet in the cellar, the unfortunate female's throat being cut from ear to ear. Phial containing arsenic retrieved from the body of Miss Barrow which sent Seddon to the gallows.

(He jerks the rope, the assistants leap at the victim's legs and drag him downward, grunting: the croppy boy's tongue protrudes violently.)

THE CROPPY BOY

Horhot ho hray ho rhother's hest.

(He gives up the ghost. A violent erection of the hanged sends gouts of sperm spouting through his death clothes on to the cobblestones. Mrs Bellingham, Mrs Yelverton Barry and the Honourable Mrs Mervyn Talboys rush forward with their handkerchiefs to sop it up.)

RUMBOLD

I'm near it myself. *(He undoes the noose.)* Rope which hanged the awful rebel. Ten shillings a time as applied to His Royal Highness. *(He plunges his head into the gaping belly of the hanged and draws out his head again clotted with coiled and smoking entrails.)* My painful duty has now been done. God save the king!

EDWARD THE SEVENTH

(Dances slowly, solemnly, rattling his bucket and sings with soft contentment.)

On coronation day, on coronation day,
O, won't we have a merry time,
Drinking whisky, beer and wine!

PRIVATE CARR

Here. What are you saying about my king?

STEPHEN

(Throws up his hands.) O, this is too monotonous! Nothing. He wants my money and my life, though want must be his master, for some brutish empire of his. Money I haven't. *(He searches his pockets vaguely.)* Gave it to someone.

PRIVATE CARR

Who wants your bleeding money?

STEPHEN

(Tries to move off.) Will some one tell me where I am least likely to meet these necessary evils? *Ça se voit aussi à Paris.* Not that I . . . But by Saint Patrick! . . .

(The women's heads coalesce. Old Gummy Granny in sugarloaf hat appears seated on a toadstool, the deathflower of the potato blight on her breast.)

STEPHEN

Aha! I know you, grammer! Hamlet, revenge! The old sow that eats her farrow!

OLD GUMMY GRANNY

(Rocking to and fro.) Ireland's sweetheart, the king of Spain's daughter, alanna. Strangers in my house, bad manners to them! *(She keens with banshee woe.)* Ochone! Ochone! Silk of the kine! *(She wails.)* You met with poor old Ireland and how does she stand?

STEPHEN

How do I stand you? The hat trick! Where's the third person of the Blessed Trinity? Soggarth Aroon? The reverend Carrion Crow.

CISSY CAFFREY

(Shrill.) Stop them from fighting!

A ROUGH

Our men retreated.

PRIVATE CARR

(Tugging at his belt.) I'll wring the neck of any bugger says a word against my fucking king.

BLOOM

(Terrified.) He said nothing. Not a word. A pure misunderstanding.

THE CITIZEN

Erin go bragh!

(Major Tweedy and the Citizen exhibit to each other medals, decorations, trophies of war, wounds. Both salute with fierce hostility.)

PRIVATE COMPTON

Go it, Harry. Do him one in the eye. He's a proboer.

STEPHEN

Did I? When?

BLOOM

(To the redcoats.) We fought for you in South Africa, Irish missile troops. Isn't that history? Royal Dublin Fusiliers. Honoured by our monarch.

THE NAVVY

(Staggering past.) O, yes. O, God, yes! O, make the kwawr a krowawr! O! Bo! (Casqued halberdiers in armour thrust forward a pentice of gutted spear points. Major Tweedy, moustached like Turko the terrible, in bearskin cap with hackle plume and accoutrements, with epaulette, gilt chevrons and sabretache, his breast bright with medals, toes the line. He gives the pilgrim warrior's sign of the knights templars.)

MAJOR TWEEDY

(Growls gruffly.) Rorke's Drift! Up, guards, and at them! Mahal shalal hashbaz.

PRIVATE CARR

I'll do him in.

PRIVATE COMPTON

(Waves the crowd back.) Fair play, here. Make a bleeding butcher's shop of the bugger.
(Massed bands blare Garryowen and God save the king.)

CISSY CAFFREY

They're going to fight. For me!

CUNTY KATE

The brave and the fair.

BIDDY THE CLAP

Methinks you sable knight will joust it with the best.

CUNTY KATE

(Blushing deeply.) Nay, Madam. The gules doublet and merry Saint George for me!

STEPHEN

The harlot's cry from street to street
Shall weave old Ireland's windingsheet.

PRIVATE CARR

(Loosening his belt, shouts.) I'll wring the neck of any fucking bastard says a word against my bleeding fucking king.

BLOOM

(Shakes Cissy Caffrey's shoulders.) Speak, you! Are you struck dumb? You are the link between nations and generations. Speak, woman, sacred lifegiver.

CISSY CAFFREY

(Alarmed, seizes Private Carr's sleeve.) Amn't I with you? Amn't I your girl? Cissy's your girl. (She cries.) Police!

STEPHEN

(Ecstatically, to Cissy Caffrey.)

> White thy fambles, red thy gan
> And thy quarrons dainty is.

VOICES

Police!

DISTANT VOICES

Dublin's burning! Dublin's burning! On fire, on fire!

(Brimstone fires spring up. Dense clouds roll past. Heavy Gatling guns boom. Pandemonium. Troops deploy. Gallop of hoofs. Artillery. Hoarse commands. Bells clang. Backers shout. Drunkards bawl. Whores screech. Foghorns hoot. Cries of valour. Shrieks of dying. Pikes clash on cuirasses. Thieves rob the slain. Birds of prey, winging from the sea, rising from marshlands, swooping from eyries, hover screaming, gannets, cormorants, vultures, goshawks, climbing woodcocks, peregrines, merlins, blackgrouse, sea eagles, gulls, albatrosses, barnacle geese. The midnight sun is darkened. The earth trembles. The dead of Dublin from Prospect and Mount Jerome in white sheepskin overcoats and black goatfell cloaks arise and appear to many. A chasm opens with a noiseless yawn. Tom Rochford, winner in athlete's singlet and breeches, arrives at the head of the national hurdle handicap and leaps into the void. He is followed by a race of runners and leapers. In wild attitudes they spring from the brink. Their bodies plunge. Factory lasses with fancy clothes toss redhot Yorkshire baraabombs. Society ladies lift their skirts above their heads to protect themselves. Laughing witches in red cutty sarks ride through the air on broomsticks. Quakerlyster plasters blisters. It rains dragon's teeth. Armed heroes spring up from furrows. They exchange in amity the pass of knights of the red cross and fight duels with cavalry sabres: Wolfe Tone against Henry Grattan, Smith O'Brien against Daniel O'Connell, Michael Davitt against Isaac Butt, Justin M'Carthy against Parnell, Arthur Griffith against John Redmond, John O'Leary against Lear O'Johnny, Lord Edward Fitzgerald against Lord Gerald Fitzedward, The O'Donoghue of the Glens against The Glens of The Donoghue. On an eminence, the centre of the earth, rises the field altar of Saint Barbara. Black candles rise from its gospel and epistle horns. From the high barbicans of the tower two shafts

*of light fall on the smokepalled altarstone. On the altarstone Mrs Mina Purefoy,
goddess of unreason, lies naked, fettered, a chalice resting on her swollen belly.
Father Malachi O'Flynn, in a long petticoat and reversed chasuble, his two left
feet back to the front, celebrates camp mass. The Reverend Mr Hugh C. Haines
Love M. A. in a plain cassock and mortar board, his head and collar back to the
front, holds over the celebrant's head an open umbrella.)*

FATHER MALACHI O'FLYNN

Introibo ad altare diaboli.

THE REVEREND MR HAINES LOVE

To the devil which hath made glad my young days.

FATHER MALACHI O'FLYNN

(Takes from the chalice and elevates a blooddripping host.) Corpus Meum.

THE REVEREND MR HAINES LOVE

*(Raises high behind the celebrant's petticoats, revealing his grey bare hairy
buttocks between which a carrot is stuck.)* My body.

THE VOICE OF ALL THE DAMNED

Htengier Tnetopinmo Dog Drol eht rof, Aiulella!
(From on high the voice of Adonai calls.)

ADONAI

Dooooooooooog!

THE VOICE OF ALL THE BLESSED

Alleluia, for the Lord God Omnipotent reigneth!
(From on high the voice of Adonai calls.)

ADONAI

Goooooooooood!
(In strident discord peasants and townsmen of Orange and Green factions sing
Kick the Pope *and* Daily, daily sing to Mary.)

PRIVATE CARR

(With ferocious articulation.) I'll do him in, so help me fucking Christ! I'll
wring the bastard fucker's bleeding blasted fucking windpipe!

OLD GUMMY GRANNY

(Thrusts a dagger towards Stephen's hand.) Remove him, acushla. At 8.35 a.m.
you will be in heaven and Ireland will be free. *(She prays.)* O good God,
take him!

BLOOM

(Runs to Lynch.) Can't you get him away?

LYNCH

He likes dialectic, the universal language. Kitty! *(To Bloom.)*
Get him away, you. He won't listen to me.

(He drags Kitty away.)

STEPHEN

(Points.) Exit Judas. *Et laqueo se suspendit.*

BLOOM

(Runs to Stephen.) Come along with me now before worse happens. Here's
your stick.

STEPHEN

Stick, no. Reason. This feast of pure reason.

CISSY CAFFREY

(Pulling Private Carr.) Come on, you're boosed. He insulted me but I forgive
him. *(Shouting in his ear.)* I forgive him for insulting me.

BLOOM

(Over Stephen's shoulder.) Yes, go. You see he's incapable.

PRIVATE CARR

(Breaks loose.) I'll insult him.

*(He rushes towards Stephen, fists outstretched, and strikes him in the face.
Stephen totters, collapses, falls stunned. He lies prone, his face to the sky, his hat
rolling to the wall. Bloom follows and picks it up.)*

MAJOR TWEEDY

(Loudly.) Carbine in bucket! Cease fire! Salute!

THE RETRIEVER

(Barking furiously.) Ute ute ute ute ute ute ute ute.

THE CROWD

Let him up! Don't strike him when he's down! Air! Who? The soldier hit
him. He's a professor. Is he hurted? Don't manhandle him! He's fainted!

(The retriever, nosing on the fringe of the crowd, barks noisily.)

A HAG

What call had the redcoat to strike the gentleman and he under the influence.
Let them go and fight the Boers!

THE BAWD

Listen to who's talking! Hasn't the soldier a right to go with his girl? He
gave him the coward's blow.

(They grab at each other's hair, claw at each other and spit.)

THE RETRIEVER

(Barking.) Wow wow wow.

BLOOM

(Shoves them back, loudly.) Get back, stand back!

PRIVATE COMPTON

(Tugging his comrade.) Here bugger off, Harry. There's the cops! (Two raincaped watch, tall, stand in the group.)

FIRST WATCH

What's wrong here?

PRIVATE COMPTON

We were with this lady and he insulted us and assaulted my chum. (The retriever barks.) Who owns the bleeding tyke?

CISSY CAFFREY

(With expectation.) Is he bleeding?

A MAN

(Rising from his knees.) No. Gone off. He'll come to all right.

BLOOM

(Glances sharply at the man.) Leave him to me. I can easily . . .

SECOND WATCH

Who are you? Do you know him?

PRIVATE CARR

(Lurches towards the watch.) He insulted my lady friend.

BLOOM

(Angrily.) You hit him without provocation. I'm a witness. Constable, take his regimental number.

SECOND WATCH

I don't want your instructions in the discharge of my duty.

PRIVATE COMPTON

(Pulling his comrade.) Here, bugger off, Harry. Or Bennett'll have you in the lockup.

PRIVATE CARR

(Staggering as he is pulled away.) God fuck old Bennett! He's a whitearsed bugger. I don't give a shit for him.

FIRST WATCH

(Taking out his notebook.) What's his name?

BLOOM

(Peering over the crowd.) I just see a car there. If you give me a hand a second, sergeant . . .

FIRST WATCH

Name and address.

(Corny Kelleher, weepers round his hat, a death wreath in his hand, appears among the bystanders.)

BLOOM

(Quickly.) O, the very man! *(He whispers.)* Simon Dedalus' son. A bit sprung. Get those policemen to move those loafers back.

SECOND WATCH

Night, Mr Kelleher.

CORNY KELLEHER

(To the watch, with drawling eye.) That's all right. I know him. Won a bit on the races. Gold cup. Throwaway. *(He laughs.)* Twenty to one. Do you follow me?

FIRST WATCH

(Turns to the crowd.) Here, what are you all gaping at? Move on out of that.
(The crowd disperses slowly, muttering, down the lane.)

CORNY KELLEHER

Leave it to me, sergeant. That'll be all right. *(He laughs, shaking his head.)* We were often as bad ourselves, ay or worse. What? Eh, what?

FIRST WATCH

(Laughs.) I suppose so.

CORNY KELLEHER

(Nudges the second watch.) Come and wipe your name off the slate. *(He lilts, wagging his head.)* With my tooraloom tooraloom tooraloom tooraloom. What, eh, do you follow me?

SECOND WATCH

(Genially.) Ah, sure we were too.

CORNY KELLEHER

(Winking.) Boys will be boys. I've a car round there.

SECOND WATCH

All right, Mr Kelleher. Good night.

CORNY KELLEHER

I'll see to that.

BLOOM

(Shakes hands with both of the watch in turn.) Thank you very much, gentlemen, thank you. *(He mumbles confidentially.)* We don't want any scandal, you understand. Father is a well known, highly respected citizen. Just a little wild oats, you understand.

FIRST WATCH

O, I understand, sir.

SECOND WATCH

That's all right, sir.

FIRST WATCH

It was only in case of corporal injuries I'd have to report it at the station.

BLOOM

(*Nods rapidly.*) Naturally. Quite right. Only your bounden duty.

SECOND WATCH

It's our duty.

CORNY KELLEHER

Good night, men.

THE WATCH

(*Saluting together.*) Night, gentlemen. (*They move off with slow heavy tread.*)

BLOOM

(*Blows.*) Providential you came on the scene. You have a car? . . .

CORNY KELLEHER

(*Laughs, pointing his thumb over his right shoulder to the car brought up against the scaffolding.*) Two commercials that were standing fizz in Jammet's. Like princes, faith. One of them lost two quid on the race. Drowning his grief and were on for a go with the jolly girls. So I landed them up on Behan's car and down to nighttown.

BLOOM

I was just going home by Gardiner street when I happened to . . .

CORNY KELLEHER

(*Laughs.*) Sure they wanted me to join in with the mots. No, by God, says I. Not for old stagers like myself and yourself. (*He laughs again and leers with lacklustre eye.*) Thanks be to God we have it in the house what, eh, do you follow me? Hah! hah! hah!

BLOOM

(*Tries to laugh.*) He, he, he! Yes. Matter of fact I was just visiting an old friend of mine there, Virag, you don't know him (poor fellow he's laid up for the past week) and we had a liquor together and I was just making my way home . . .

(*The horse neighs.*)

THE HORSE

Hohohohohohoh! Hohohohome!

CORNY KELLEHER

Sure it was Behan, our jarvey there, that told me after we left the two commercials in Mrs Cohen's and I told him to pull up and got off to see. *(He laughs.)* Sober hearsedrivers a specialty. Will I give him a lift home? Where does he hang out? Somewhere in Cabra, what?

BLOOM

No, in Sandycove, I believe, from what he let drop.

(Stephen, prone, breathes to the stars. Corny Kelleher, asquint, drawls at the horse. Bloom in gloom, looms down.)

CORNY KELLEHER

(Scratches his nape.) Sandycove! *(He bends down and calls to Stephen.)* Eh! *(He calls again.)* Eh! He's covered with shavings anyhow. Take care they didn't lift anything off him.

BLOOM

No, no, no. I have his money and his hat here and stick.

CORNY KELLEHER

Ah well he'll get over it. No bones broken. Well, I'll shove along. *(He laughs.)* I've a rendezvous in the morning. Burying the dead. Safe home!

THE HORSE

(Neighs.) Hohohohohome.

BLOOM

Good night. I'll just wait and take him along in a few . . .

(Corny Kelleher returns to the outside car and mounts it. The horse harness jingles.)

CORNY KELLEHER

(From the car, standing.) Night.

BLOOM

Night.

(The jarvey chucks the reins and raises his whip encouragingly. The car and horse back slowly, awkwardly and turn. Corny Kelleher on the sideseat sways his head to and fro in sign of mirth at Bloom's plight. The jarvey joins in the mute pantomimic merriment nodding from the farther seat. Bloom shakes his head in mute mirthful reply. With thumb and palm Corny Kelleher reassures that the two bobbies will allow the sleep to continue for what else is to be done. With a slow nod Bloom conveys his gratitude as that is exactly what Stephen needs. The car jingles tooraloom round the corner of the tooraloom lane. Corny Kelleher again reassuralooms with his hand. Bloom with his hand assuralooms

Corny Kelleher that he is reassuraloomtay. The tinkling hoofs and jingling harness grow fainter with their tooraloolooolooloo lay. Bloom, holding in his hand Stephen's hat festooned with shavings and ashplant, stands irresolute. Then he bends to him and shakes him by the shoulder.)

BLOOM

Eh! Ho! *(There is no answer; he bends again.)* Mr Dedalus! *(There is no answer.)* The name if you call. Somnambulist. *(He bends again and, hesitating, brings his mouth near the face of the prostrate form.)* Stephen! *(There is no answer. He calls again.)* Stephen!

STEPHEN

(Groans.) Who? Black panther vampire. *(He sighs and stretches himself, then murmurs thickly with prolonged vowels.)*

Who ... drive ... Fergus now.
And pierce ... wood's woven shade? ...

(He turns on his left side, sighing, doubling himself together.)

BLOOM

Poetry. Well educated. Pity. *(He bends again and undoes the buttons of Stephen's waistcoat.)* To breathe. *(He brushes the wood shavings from Stephen's clothes with light hands and fingers.)* One pound seven. Not hurt anyhow. *(He listens.)* What!

STEPHEN

(Murmurs.)

... shadows ... the woods.
... white breast ... dim ...

(He stretches out his arms, sighs again and curls his body. Bloom holding his hat and ashplant stands erect. A dog barks in the distance. Bloom tightens and loosens his grip on the ashplant. He looks down on Stephen's face and form.)

BLOOM

(Communes with the night.) Face reminds me of his poor mother. In the shady wood. The deep white breast. Ferguson, I think I caught. A girl. Some girl. Best thing could happen him ... *(He murmurs.)* ... swear that I will always hail, ever conceal, never reveal, any part or parts, art or arts ... *(He murmurs.)* in the rough sands of the sea ... a cabletow's length from the shore ... where the tide ebbs ... and flows ...

(Silent, thoughtful, alert, he stands on guard, his fingers at his lips in the attitude of secret master. Against the dark wall a figure appears slowly, a fairy

boy of eleven, a changeling, kidnapped, dressed in an Eton suit with glass shoes and a little bronze helmet, holding a book in his hand. He reads from right to left inaudibly, smiling, kissing the page.)

BLOOM

(Wonderstruck, calls inaudibly.) Rudy!

RUDY

(Gazes unseeing into Bloom's eyes and goes on reading, kissing, smiling. He has a delicate mauve face. On his suit he has diamond and ruby buttons. In his free left hand he holds a slim ivory cane with a violet bowknot. A white lambkin peeps out of his waistcoat pocket.)

III

◀ PREPARATORY TO ANYTHING ELSE MR BLOOM
brushed off the greater bulk of the shavings and handed Stephen the hat
and ashplant and bucked him up generally in orthodox Samaritan fashion,
which he very badly needed. His (Stephen's) mind was not exactly what
you would call wandering but a bit unsteady and on his expressed desire
for some beverage to drink Mr Bloom, in view of the hour it was and there
being no pumps of Vartry water available for their ablutions, let alone
drinking purposes, hit upon an expedient by suggesting, off the reel, the
propriety of the cabman's shelter, as it was called, hardly a stonesthrow
away near Butt Bridge, where they might hit upon some drinkables in the
shape of a milk and soda or a mineral. But how to get there was the rub.
For the nonce he was rather nonplussed but inasmuch as the duty plainly
devolved upon him to take some measures on the subject he pondered
suitable ways and means during which Stephen repeatedly yawned. So far
as he could see he was rather pale in the face so that it occurred to him as
highly advisable to get a conveyance of some description which would
answer in their then condition, both of them being e. d. ed, particularly
Stephen, always assuming that there was such a thing to be found.
Accordingly, after a few such preliminaries, as, in spite of his having
forgotten to take up his rather soapsuddy handkerchief after it had done
yeoman service in the shaving line, brushing, they both walked together
along Beaver street, or, more properly, lane, as far as the farrier's and the
distinctly fetid atmosphere of the livery stables at the corner of Montgomery street where they made tracks to the left from thence debouching
into Amiens Street round by the corner of Dan Bergin's. But, as he
confidently anticipated, there was not a sign of a Jehu plying for hire
anywhere to be seen except a fourwheeler, probably engaged by some
fellows inside on the spree, outside the North Star Hotel and there was no
symptom of its budging a quarter of an inch when Mr Bloom, who was
anything but a professional whistler, endeavoured to hail it by emitting a
kind of a whistle, holding his arms arched over his head, twice.
This was a quandary but, bringing commonsense to bear on it, evidently
there was nothing for it but put a good face on the matter and foot it which
they accordingly did. So, bevelling around by Mullet's and the Signal
House, which they shortly reached, they proceeded perforce in the direction

of Amiens street railway terminus, Mr Bloom being handicapped by the circumstance that one of the back buttons of his trousers had, to vary the timehonoured adage, gone the way of all buttons, though, entering thoroughly into the spirit of the thing, he heroically made light of the mischance. So, as neither of them were particularly pressed for time, as it happened, and the temperature refreshing since it cleared up after the recent visitation of Jupiter Pluvius, they dandered along past by where the empty vehicle was waiting without a fare or a jarvey. As it so happened a Dublin United Tramways Company's sandstrewer happening to be returning the elder man recounted to his companion *à propos* of the incident his own truly miraculous escape of some little while back. They passed the main entrance of the Great Northern railway station, the starting point for Belfast, where of course all traffic was suspended at that late hour, and, passing the back door of the morgue (a not very enticing locality, not to say gruesome to a degree, more especially at night), ultimately gained the Dock Tavern and in due course turned into Store street, famous for its C division police station. Between this point and the high, at present unlit, warehouses of Beresford Place Stephen thought to think of Ibsen, associated with Baird's, the stone-cutter's in his mind somehow in Talbot Place, first turning on the right, while the other, who was acting as his *fidus Achates*, inhaled with infernal satisfaction the smell of James Rourke's city bakery, situated quite close to where they were, the very palatable odour indeed of our daily bread, of all commodities of the public the primary and most indispensable. Bread, the staff of life, earn your bread, O tell me where is fancy bread? At Rourke's the baker's, it is said.

En route, to his taciturn, and, not to put too fine a point on it, not yet perfectly sober companion, Mr Bloom, who at all events, was in complete possession of his faculties, never more so, in fact disgustingly sober, spoke a word of caution *re* the dangers of nighttown, women of ill fame and swell mobsmen, which, barely permissible once in a while, though not as a habitual practice, was of the nature of a regular deathtrap for young fellows of his age particularly if they had acquired drinking habits under the influence of liquor unless you knew a little juijitsu for every contingency as even a fellow on the broad of his back could administer a nasty kick if you didn't look out. Highly providential was the appearance on the scene of Corny Kelleher when Stephen was blissfully unconscious that, but for that man in the gap turning up at the eleventh hour, the finis might have been that he might have been a candidate for the accident ward, or, failing that, the Bridewell and an appearance in the court next day before Mr Tobias, or, he being the solicitor, rather old Wall, he meant to say, or Malony which simply spelt ruin for a chap when it got bruited about. The reason he mentioned the fact was that a lot of those policemen, whom he cordially disliked, were admittedly unscrupulous in the service of the Crown and, as Mr Bloom put it, recalling a case or two in the A Division in Clanbrassil street, prepared to swear a hole through a ten gallon pot. Never on the spot when wanted but in quiet parts of the city, Pembroke Road, for example, the guardians of the law were well in evidence, the obvious reason being they were paid to protect the upper classes. Another thing he commented on was equipping soldiers with fire-arms or sidearms of any description, liable to go off at any time, which was tantamount to inciting them against civilians should by any chance they fall out over anything. You frittered away your time, he very sensibly maintained, and health and also character besides which the squandermania of the thing, fast women of the *demimonde* ran away with a lot of £. s. d. into the bargain and the greatest danger of all was who you got drunk with though, touching the much vexed question of stimulants he relished a glass of choice old wine in season as both nourishing and blood-making and possessing aperient virtues (notably a good burgundy which he was a staunch believer in) still never beyond a certain point where he invariably drew the line as it simply led to trouble all round to say nothing of your being at the tender mercy of others practically. Most of all he commented adversely on the desertion of Stephen by all his pubhunting *confrères* but one, a most glaring piece of ratting on the part of his brother medicos under all the circs.

– And that one was Judas, said Stephen, who up to then had said nothing whatsoever of any kind.

Discussing these and kindred topics they made a beeline across the back of the Customhouse and passed under the Loop Line bridge when a brazier of coke burning in front of a sentrybox, or something like one, attracted their rather lagging footsteps. Stephen of his own accord stopped for no special reason to look at the heap of barren cobblestones and by the light emanating from the brazier he could just make out the darker figure of the corporation watchman inside the gloom of the sentrybox. He began to remember that this had happened, or had been mentioned as having happened, before but it cost him no small effort before he remembered that he recognised in the sentry a quondam friend of his father's, Gumley. To avoid a meeting he drew nearer to the pillars of the railway bridge.

– Someone saluted you, Mr Bloom said.

A figure of middle height on the prowl, evidently, under the arches saluted again, calling: *Night!* Stephen, of course, started rather dizzily and stopped to return the compliment. Mr Bloom, actuated by motives of inherent delicacy, inasmuch as he always believed in minding his own business, moved off but nevertheless remained on the *qui vive* with just a shade of anxiety though not funkyish in the least. Although unusual in the Dublin area, he knew that it was not by any means unknown for desperadoes who had next to nothing to live on to be about waylaying and generally terrorising peaceable pedestrians by placing a pistol at their head in some secluded spot outside the city proper, famished loiterers of the Thames embankment category they might be hanging about there or simply marauders ready to decamp with whatever boodle they could in one fell swoop at a moment's notice, your money or your life, leaving you there to point a moral, gagged and garrotted.

Stephen, that is when the accosting figure came to close quarters, though he was not in any over sober state himself, recognised Corley's breath redolent of rotten cornjuice. Lord John Corley, some called him, and his genealogy came about in this wise. He was the eldest son of Inspector Corley of the G Division, lately deceased, who had married a certain Katherine Brophy, the daughter of a Louth farmer. His grandfather, Patrick Michael Corley, of New Ross, had married the widow of a publican there whose maiden name had been Katherine (also) Talbot. Rumour had it, though not proved, that she descended from the house of the Lords Talbot de Malahide in whose mansion, really an unquestionably fine residence of its kind and well worth seeing, his mother or aunt or some relative had enjoyed the distinction of being in service in the washkitchen. This, there-fore, was the reason why the still comparatively young though dissolute man who now addressed Stephen was spoken of by some with facetious proclivities as Lord John Corley.

Taking Stephen on one side he had the customary doleful ditty to tell. Not as much as a farthing to purchase a night's lodgings. His friends had all deserted him. Furthermore, he had a row with Lenehan and called him to Stephen a mean bloody swab with a sprinkling of other uncalledfor expressions. He was out of a job and implored of Stephen to tell him where on God's earth he could get something, anything at all to do. No, it was the daughter of the mother in the washkitchen that was fostersister to the heir of the house or else they were connected through the mother in some way, both occurrences happening at the same time of the whole thing wasn't a complete fabrication from start to finish. Anyhow, he was all in.

– I wouldn't ask you, only, pursued he, on my solemn oath and God knows I'm on the rocks.

– There'll be a job to morrow or the next day, Stephen told him, in a boys' school at Dalkey for a gentleman usher. Mr Garrett Deasy. Try it. You may mention my name.

– Ah, God, Corley replied, sure I couldn't teach in a school, man. I was never one of your bright ones, he added with a half laugh. Got stuck twice in the junior at the Christian Brothers.

– I have no place to sleep myself, Stephen informed him.

Corley, at the first go-off, was inclined to suspect it was something to do with Stephen being fired out of his digs for bringing in a bloody tart off the street. There was a dosshouse in Marlborough street, Mrs Maloney's, but it was only a tanner touch and full of undesirables but M'Conachie told him you got a decent enough do in the Brazen Head over in Winetavern street (which was distantly suggestive to the person addressed of friar Bacon) for a bob. He was starving too though he hadn't said a word about it.

Though this sort of thing went on every other night or very near it still Stephen's feelings got the better of him in a sense though he knew that Corley's brandnew rigmarole, on a par with the others, was hardly deserving of much credence. However, *haud ignarus malorum miseris succurrere disco*, etcetera, as the Latin poet remarks, especially as luck would have it he got paid his screw after every middle of the month on the sixteenth which was the date of the month as a matter of fact though a good bit of the wherewithal was demolished. But the cream of the joke was nothing would get it out of Corley's head that he was living in affluence and hadn't a thing to do but hand out the needful–whereas. He put his hand in a pocket anyhow, not with the idea of finding any food there, but thinking he might lend him anything up to a bob or so in lieu so that he might endeavour at all events and get sufficient to eat. But the result was in the negative for, to his chagrin, he found his cash missing. A few broken biscuits were all the result of his investigation. He tried his hardest to recollect for the moment whether he had lost, as well he might have, or left, because in that con-tingency it was not a pleasant lookout, very much the reverse, in fact. He was altogether too fagged out to institute a thorough search though he tried to recollect about biscuits he dimly remembered. Who now exactly gave them, or where was, or did he buy? However, in another pocket he came across what he surmised in the dark were pennies, erroneously, however, as it turned out.

– Those are halfcrowns, man, Corley corrected him.

And so in point of fact they turned out to be. Stephen lent him one of them.

– Thanks, Corley answered. You're a gentleman. I'll pay you back some time. Who's that with you? I saw him a few times in the Bleeding Horse in Camden street with Boylan the billsticker. You might put in a good word for us to get me taken on there. I'd carry a sandwichboard only the girl in the office told me they're full up for the next three weeks, man. God, you've to book ahead, man, you'd think it was for the Carl Rosa. I don't give a shite anyway so long as I get a job even as a crossing sweeper.

Subsequently, being not quite so down in the mouth after the two-and-six he got, he informed Stephen about a fellow by the name of Bags Comisky that he said Stephen knew well out of Fullam's, the shipchandler's bookkeeper there, that used to be often round in Nagle's back with O'Mara and a little chap with a stutter the name of Tighe. Anyhow, he was lagged the night before last and fined ten bob for a drunk and disorderly and refusing to go with the constable.

Mr Bloom in the meanwhile kept dodging about in the vicinity of the cobblestones near the brazier of coke in front of the corporation watchman's sentrybox, who, evidently a glutton for work, it struck him, was having a quiet forty winks for all intents and purposes on his own private account while Dublin slept. He threw an odd eye at the same time now and then at Stephen's anything but immaculately attired interlocutor as if he had seen that nobleman somewhere or other though where he was not in a position to truthfully state nor had he the remotest idea when. Being a levelheaded individual who could give points to not a few in point of shrewd observation, he also remarked on his very dilapidated hat and slouchy wearing apparel generally, testifying to a chronic impecuniosity. Probably he was one of his hangerson but for the matter of that it was merely a question of one preying on his nextdoor neighbour all round, in every deep, so to put it, a deeper depth and for the matter of that if the man in the street chanced to be in the dock himself penal servitude, with or without the option of a fine, would be a very *rara avis* altogether. In any case he had a consummate amount of cool assurance intercepting people at that hour of the night or morning. Pretty thick that was certainly.

The pair parted company and Stephen rejoined Mr Bloom, who with his practised eye, was not without perceiving that he had succumbed to the blandiloquence of the other parasite. Alluding to the encounter he said, laughingly, Stephen, that is:

– He's down on his luck. He asked me to ask you to ask somebody named Boylan, a billsticker, to give him a job as a sandwichman.

At this intelligence, in which he seemingly evinced little interest, Mr Bloom gazed abstractedly for the space of a half a second or so in the direction of a bucket dredger, rejoicing in the farfamed name of Eblana, moored alongside Customhouse Quay and quite possibly out of repair, whereupon he observed evasively:

– Everybody gets their own ration of luck, they say. Now you mention it his face was familiar to me. But leaving that for the moment, how much did you part with, he queried, if I am not too inquisitive?

– Half-a-crown, Stephen responded. I daresay he needs it to sleep some-where.

– Needs, Mr Bloom ejaculated, professing not the least surprise at the intelligence, I can quite credit the assertion and I guarantee he invariably does. Everyone according to his needs and everyone according to his deeds. But talking about things in general, where, added he with a smile, will you sleep yourself? Walking to Sandycove is out of the question and, even supposing you did, you won't get in after what occurred at Westland Row station. Simply fag out there for nothing. I don't mean to presume to dictate to you in the slightest degree but why did you leave your father's house?

– To seek misfortune, was Stephen's answer.

– I met your respected father on a recent occasion, Mr Bloom diplo-matically returned. Today, in fact, or, to be strictly accurate, on yesterday. Where does he live at present? I gathered in the course of conversation that he had moved.

– I believe he is in Dublin somewhere, Stephen answered unconcernedly. Why?

– A gifted man, Mr Bloom said of Mr Dedalus senior, in more respects than one and a born *raconteur* if ever there was one. He takes great pride, quite legitimately, out of you. Yout could go back, perhaps, he hazarded, still thinking of the very unpleasant scene at Westland Row terminus when it was perfectly evident that the other two, Mulligan, that is, and that English tourist friend of his, who eventually euchred their third companion, were patently trying, as if the whole bally station belonged to them, to give Stephen the slip in the confusion.

There was no response forthcoming to the suggestion, however, such as it was, Stephen's mind's eye being too busily engaged in repicturing his family hearth the last time he saw it, with his sister, Dilly, sitting by the ingle, her hair hanging down, waiting for some weak Trinidad shell cocoa that was in the sootcoated kettle to be done so that she and he could drink it with the oatmeal water for milk after the Friday herrings they had eaten at two a penny, with an egg apiece for Maggy, Boody and Katey, the cat meanwhile under the mangle devouring a mess of eggshells and charred fish heads and bones on a square of brown paper in accordance with the third precept of the church to fast and abstain on the days commanded, it being quarter tense or, if not, ember days or something like that.

– No, Mr Bloom repeated again, I wouldn't personally repose much trust in that boon companion of yours who contributes the humorous element, Dr Mulligan, as a guide, philosopher, and friend, if I were in your shoes. He knows which side his bread is buttered on though in all probability he never realised what it is to be without regular meals. Of course you didn't notice as much as I did but it wouldn't occasion me the least surprise to learn that a pinch of tobacco or some narcotic was put in your drink for some ulterior object.

He understood, however, from all he heard, that Dr Mulligan was a versatile allround man, by no means confined to medicine only, who was rapidly coming to the fore in his line and, if the report was verified, bade fair to enjoy a flourishing practice in the not too distant future as a tony medical practitioner drawing a handsome fee for his services in addition to which professional status his rescue of that man from certain drowning by artificial respiration and what they call first aid at Skerries, or Malahide was it? was, he was bound to admit, an exceedingly plucky deed which he could not too highly praise, so that frankly he was utterly at a loss to fathom what earthly reason could be at the back of it except he put it down to sheer cussedness or jealousy, pure and simple.

– Except it simply amounts to one thing and he is what they call picking your brains, he ventured to throw out.

The guarded glance of half solicitude, half curiosity, augmented by friendliness which he gave at Stephen's at present morose expression of features did not throw a flood of light, none at all in fact, on the problem as to whether he had let himself be badly bamboozled, to judge by two or three lowspirited remarks he let drop, or, the other way about, saw through the affair, and, for some reason or other best known to himself, allowed matters to more or less . . . Grinding poverty did have that effect and he more than conjectured that, high educational abilities though he possessed, he experienced no little difficulty in making both ends meet.

Adjacent to the men's public urinal he perceived an icecream car round which a group of presumably Italians in heated altercation were getting rid of voluble expressions in their vivacious language in a particularly animated way, there being some little differences between the parties.

– *Putana madonna, che ci dia i quattrini! Ho ragione? Culo rotto!*

– *Intendiamoci. Mezzo sovrano più . . .*

– *Dice lui, però.*

– *Farabutto! Mortacci sui!*

Mr Bloom and Stephen entered the cabman's shelter, an unpretentious wooden structure, where, prior to then, he had rarely, if ever, been before; the former having previously whispered to the latter a few hints anent the keeper of it, said to be the once famous Skin-the-Goat, Fitzharris, the invincible, though he wouldn't vouch for the actual facts, which quite possibly there was not one vestige of truth in. A few moments later saw our two noctambules safely seated in a discreet corner, only to be greeted by stares from the decidedly miscellaneous collection of waifs and strays and other nondescript specimens of the genus *homo*, already there engaged in eating and drinking, diversified by conversation, for whom they seemingly formed an object of marked curiosity.

– Now touching a cup of coffee, Mr Bloom ventured to plausibly suggest to break the ice, it occurs to me you ought to sample something in the shape of solid food, say a roll of some description.

Accordingly his first act was with characteristic *sangfroid* to order these commodities quietly. The *hoi polloi* of jarvies or stevedores, or whatever they were, after a cursory examination, turned their eyes, apparently dissatisfied, away, though one redbearded bibulous individual, a portion of whose hair was greyish, a sailor, probably, still stared for some appreciable time before transferring his rapt attention to the floor.

Mr Bloom, availing himself of the right of free speech, he having just a bowing acquaintance with the language in dispute though, to be sure, rather in a quandary over *voglio*, remarked to his *protégé* in an audible tone of voice, *apropos* of the battle royal in the street which was still raging fast and furious:

– A beautiful language. I mean for singing purposes. Why do you not write your poetry in that language? *Bella Poetria!* it is so melodious and full. *Belladonna voglio.*

Stephen, who was trying his dead best to yawn, if he could, suffering from dead lassitude generally, replied:

– To fill the ear of a cow elephant. They were haggling over money.

– Is that so? Mr Bloom asked. Of course, he subjoined pensively, at the inward reflection of there being more languages to start with than were absolutely necessary, it may be only the southern glamour that surrounds it.

The keeper of the shelter in the middle of this *tête-à-tête* put a boiling swimming cup of a choice concoction labelled coffee on the table and a rather antediluvian specimen of a bun, or so it seemed, after which he beat a retreat to his counter. Mr Bloom determining to have a good square look at him later on so as not to appear to . . . for which reason he encouraged Stephen to proceed with his eyes while he did the honours by surreptitiously pushing the cup of what was temporarily supposed to be called coffee gradually nearer him.

– Sounds are impostures, Stephen said after a pause of some little time.

Like names, Cicero, Podmore, Napoleon, Mr Goodbody, Jesus, Mr Doyle. Shakespeares were as common as Murphies. What's in a name?

– Yes, to be sure, Mr Bloom unaffectedly concurred. Of course. Our name was changed too, he added, pushing the socalled roll across.

The redbearded sailor, who had his weather eye on the newcomers, boarded Stephen, whom he had singled out for attention in particular, squarely by asking:

– And what might your name be?

Just in the nick of time Mr Bloom touched his companion's boot but Stephen, apparently disregarding the warm pressure, from an unexpected quarter, answered:

– Dedalus.

The sailor stared at him heavily from a pair of drowsy baggy eyes, rather bunged up from excessive use of boose, preferably good old Hollands and water.

– You know Simon Dedalus? he asked at length.

– I've heard of him, Stephen said.

Mr Bloom was all at sea for a moment, seeing the others evidently eavesdropping too.

– He's Irish, the seaman bold affirmed, staring still in much the same way and nodding. All Irish.

– All too Irish, Stephen rejoined.

As for Mr Bloom he could neither make head or tail of the whole business and he was just asking himself what possible connection when the sailor, of his own accord, turned to the other occupants of the shelter with the remark:

– I seen him shoot two eggs off two bottles at fifty yards over his shoulder. The left hand dead shot.

Though he was slightly hampered by an occasional stammer and his gestures being also clumsy as it was still he did his best to explain.

– Bottle out there, say. Fifty yards measured. Eggs on the bottles. Cocks his gun over his shoulder. Aims.

He turned his body half round, shut up his right eye completely, then he screwed his features up some way sideways and glared out into the night with an unprepossessing cast of countenance.

– Pom, he then shouted once.

The entire audience waited, anticipating an additional detonation, there being still a further egg.

– Pom, he shouted twice.

Egg two evidently demolished, he nodded and winked, adding blood-thirstily:

– Buffalo Bill shoots to kill,
Never missed nor he never will.

A silence ensued till Mr Bloom for agreeableness' sake just felt like asking him whether it was for a marksmanship competition like the Bisley.

– Beg pardon, the sailor said.

– Long ago? Mr Bloom pursued without flinching a hairsbreadth.

– Why, the sailor replied, relaxing to a certain extent under the magic influence of diamond cut diamond, it might be a matter of ten years. He toured the wide world with Hengler's Royal Circus. I seen him do that in Stockholm.

– Curious coincidence, Mr Bloom confided to Stephen unobtrusively.

– Murphy's my name, the sailor continued, W. B. Murphy, of Carrigaloe. Know where that is?

– Queenstown Harbour, Stephen replied.

– That's right, the sailor said. Fort Camden and Fort Carlisle. That's where I hails from. My little woman's down there. She's waiting for me, I know. *For England, home and beauty.* She's my own true wife I haven't seen for seven years now, sailing about.

Mr Bloom could easily picture his advent on this scene–the homecoming to the mariner's roadside shieling after having diddled Davy Jones – a rainy night with a blind moon. Across the world for a wife. Quite a number of stories there were on that particular Alice Ben Bolt topic, Enoch Arden and Rip van Winkle and does anybody hereabouts remember Caoc O'Leary, a favourite and most trying declamation piece, by the way, of poor John Casey and a bit of perfect poetry in its own small way. Never about the runaway wife coming back, however much devoted to the absentee. The face at the window! Judge of his astonishment when he finally did breast the tape and the awful truth dawned upon him anent his better half, wrecked in his affections. You little expected me but I've come to stay and make a fresh start. There she sits, a grass widow, at the selfsame fireside. Believes me dead. Rocked in the cradle of the deep. And there sits uncle Chubb or Tomkin, as the case might be, the publican of the Crown and Anchor, in shirtsleeves, eating rumpsteak and onions. No chair for father. Boo! The wind! Her brandnew arrival is on her knee, *post mortem* child. With a high ro! and a randy ro! and my galloping tearing tandy O! Bow to the inevitable. Grin and bear it. I remain with much love your brokenhearted husband, W. B. Murphy.

The sailor, who scarcely seemed to be a Dublin resident, turned to one of the jarvies with the request:

– You don't happen to have such a thing as a spare chaw about you, do you?

The jarvey addressed, as it happened, had not but the keeper took a die of plug from his good jacket hanging on a nail and the desired object was passed from hand to hand.

– Thank you, the sailor said.

He deposited the quid in his gob and, chewing, and with some slow stammers, proceeded:

– We come up this morning eleven o'clock. The threemaster *Rosevean* from Bridgwater with bricks. I shipped to get over. Paid off this afternoon. There's my discharge. See? W. B. Murphy, A. B. S.

In confirmation of which statement he extricated from an inside pocket and handed to his neighbours a not very cleanlooking folded document.

– You must have seen a fair share of the world, the keeper remarked, leaning on the counter.

– Why, the sailor answered, upon reflection upon it, I've circumnavigated a bit since I first joined on. I was in the Red Sea. I was in China and North America and South America. I seen icebergs plenty, growlers. I was in Stockholm and the Black Sea, the Dardanelles, under Captain Dalton the best bloody man that ever scuttled a ship. I seen Russia. *Gospodi pomilooy.* That's how the Russians prays.

– You seen queer sights, don't be talking, put in a jarvey.

– Why, the sailor said, shifting his partially chewed plug, I seen queer things too, ups and downs. I seen a crocodile bite the fluke of an anchor same as I chew that quid.

He took out of his mouth the pulpy quid and, lodging it between his teeth, bit ferociously.

– Khaan! Like that. And I seen maneaters in Peru that eats corpses and the livers of horses. Look here. Here they are. A friend of mine sent me.

He fumbled out a picture postcard from his inside pocket, which seemed to be in its way a species of repository, and pushed it along the table. The printed matter on it stated: *Choza de Indios. Beni, Bolivia.*

All focused their attention on the scene exhibited, at a group of savage women in striped loincloths, squatted, blinking, suckling, frowning, sleeping, amid a swarm of infants (there must have been quite a score of them) outside some primitive shanties of osier.

– Chews coca all day long, the communicative tarpaulin added. Stomachs like breadgraters. Cuts off their diddies when they can't bear no more children. See them there stark ballocknaked eating a dead horse's liver raw.

His postcard proved a centre of attraction for Messrs the greenhorns for several minutes, if not more.

– Know how to keep them off? he inquired genially.

Nobody volunteering a statement, he winked, saying:

– Glass. That boggles 'em. Glass.

Mr Bloom, without evincing surprise, unostentatiously turned over the card to peruse the partially obliterated address and postmark. It ran as follows: *Tarjeta Postal. Señor A. Boudin, Galeria Becche, Santiago, Chile*. There was no message evidently, as he took particular notice. Though not an implicit believer in the lurid story narrated (or the eggsniping transaction for that matter despite William Tell and the Lazarillo-Don Cesar de Bazan incident depicted in *Maritana* on which occasion the former's ball passed through the latter's hat), having detected a discrepancy between his name (assuming he was the person he represented himself to be and not sailing under false colours after having boxed the compass on the strict q.t. some-where) and the fictitious addressee of the missive which made him nourish some suspicions of our friend's *bona fides* nevertheless it reminded him in a way of a longcherished plan he meant to one day realise some Wednesday or Saturday of travelling to London *via* long sea not to say that he had ever travelled extensively to any great extent but he was at heart a born adventurer though by a trick of fate he had consistently remained a land-lubber except you call going to Holyhead which was his longest. Martin Cunningham frequently said he would work a pass through Egan but some deuced hitch or other eternally cropped up with the net result that the scheme fell through. But even suppose it did come to planking down the needful and breaking Boyd's heart it was not so dear, purse permitting, a few guineas at the outside, considering the fare to Mullingar where he figured on going was five and six there and back. The trip would benefit health on account of the bracing ozone and be in every way thoroughly pleasurable, especially for a chap whose liver was out of order, seeing the different places along the route, Plymouth, Falmouth, Southampton and so on, culminating in an instructive tour of the sights of the great metro-polis, the spectacle of our modern Babylon where doubtless he would see the greatest improvement tower, abbey, wealth of Park Lane to renew acquaintance with. Another thing just struck him as a by no means bad notion was he might have a gaze around on the spot to see about trying to make arrangements about a concert tour of summer music embracing the most prominent pleasure resorts, Margate with mixed bathing and firstrate hydros and spas, Eastbourne, Scarborough, Margate and so on, beautiful Bournemouth, the Channel islands and similar bijou spots, which might prove highly remunerative. Not, of course, with a hole and corner scratch company or local ladies on the job, witness Mrs C. P. M'Coy type–lend me your valise and I'll post you the ticket. No, something top notch, an all star Irish caste, the Tweedy-Flower grand opera company with his own legal consort as leading lady as a sort of counterblast to the Elster Grimes and Moody-Manners, perfectly simple matter and he was quite sanguine of success, providing puffs in the local papers could be managed by some fellow with a bit of bounce who could pull the indispensable wires and thus combine business with pleasure. But who? That was the rub.

Also, without being actually positive, it struck him a great field was to be opened up in the line of opening up new routes to keep pace with the times *apropos* of the Fishguard-Rosslare route which, it was mooted, was once more on the *tapis* in the circumlocution departments with the usual quantity of red tape and dillydallying of effete fogeydom and dunderheads generally. A great opportunity there certainly was for push and enterprise to meet the travelling needs of the public at large, the average man, i.e. Brown, Robinson and Co.

It was a subject of regret and absurd as well on the face of it and no small blame to our vaunted society that the man in the street, when the system really needed toning up, for a matter of a couple of paltry pounds, was debarred from seeing more of the world they lived in instead of being always cooped up since my old stick-in-the-mud took me for a wife. After all, hang it, they had their eleven and more humdrum months of it and merited a radical change of *venue* after the grind of city life in the summertime, for choice, when Dame Nature is at her spectacular best, constituting nothing short of a new lease of life. There were equally excellent opportunities for vacationists in the home island, delightful sylvan spots for rejuvenation, offering a plethora of attractions as well as a bracing tonic for the system in and around Dublin and its picturesque environs, even, Poulaphouca, to which there was a steam tram, but also farther away from the madding crowd, in Wicklow, rightly termed the garden of Ireland, an ideal neighbourhood for elderly wheelmen, so long as it didn't come down, and in the wilds of Donegal where, if report spoke true, the *coup d'œil* was exceedingly grand, though the lastnamed locality was not easily getatable so that the influx of visitors was not as yet all that it might be considering the signal benefits to be derived from it, while Howth with its historic associations and otherwise, Silken Thomas, Grace O'Malley, George IV, rhododendrons several hundred feet above sealevel was a favourite haunt with all sorts and conditions of men, especially in the spring when young men's fancy, though it had its own toll of deaths by falling off the cliffs by design or accidentally, usually, by the way, on their left leg, it being only about three quarters of an hour's run from the pillar. Because of course uptodate tourist travelling was as yet merely in its infancy, so to speak, and the accommodation left much to be desired. Interesting to fathom, it seemed to him, from a motive of curiosity pure and simple, was whether it was the traffic that created the route or vice-versa or the two sides in fact. He turned back the other side of the card picture and passed it along to Stephen.

– I seen a Chinese one time, related the doughty narrator, that had little pills like putty and he put them in the water and they opened, and every pill was something different. One was a ship, another was a house, another was a flower. Cooks rats in your soup, he appetisingly added, the Chinese does.

Possibly perceiving an expression of dubiosity on their faces, the globe-trotter went on adhering to his adventures.

– And I seen a man killed in Trieste by an Italian chap. Knife in his back. Knife like that.

Whilst speaking he produced a dangerous looking clasp-knife, quite in keeping with his character, and held it in the striking position.

– In a knockingshop it was count of a tryon between two smugglers. Fellow hid behind a door, come up behind him. Like that. *Prepare to meet your God*, says he. Chuck! It went into his back up to the butt.

His heavy glance, drowsily roaming about, kind of defied their further questions even should they by any chance want to. That's a good bit of steel, repeated he, examining his formidable *stiletto*.

After which harrowing *dénouement* sufficient to appal the stoutest he snapped the blade to and stowed the weapon in question away as before in his chamber of horrors, otherwise pocket.

– They're great for the cold steel, somebody who was evidently quite in the dark said for the benefit of them all. That was why they thought the park murders of the invincibles was done by foreigners on account of them using knives.

At this remark, passed obviously in the spirit of *where ignorance is bliss*, Mr Bloom and Stephen, each in his own particular way, both instinctively exchanged meaning glances, in a religious silence of the strictly *entre nous* variety however, towards where Skin-the-Goat, *alias* the keeper, was drawing spurts of liquid from his boiler affair. His inscrutable face, which was really a work of art, a perfect study in itself, beggaring description, conveyed the impression that he didn't understand one jot of what was going on. Funny very.

There ensued a somewhat lengthy pause. One man was reading by fits and starts a stained by coffee evening journal; another, the card with the natives *choza de*; another, the seaman's discharge. Mr Bloom, so far as he was personally concerned, was just pondering in pensive mood. He vividly recollected when the occurrence alluded to took place as well as yesterday, some score of years previously, in the days of the land troubles when it took the civilised world by storm, figuratively speaking, early in the eighties, eightyone to be correct, when he was just turned fifteen.

– Ay, boss, the sailor broke in. Give us back them papers.

The request being complied with, he clawed them up with a scrape.

– Have you seen the Rock of Gibraltar? Mr Bloom inquired.

The sailor grimaced, chewing, in a way that might be read as yes, ay, or no.

– Ah, you've touched there too, Mr Bloom said, Europa point, thinking he had, in the hope that the rover might possibly by some reminiscences but he failed to do so, simply letting spurt a jet of spew into the sawdust, and shook his head with a sort of lazy scorn.

– What year would that be about? Mr Bloom interpolated. Can you recall the boats?

Our *soi-disant* sailor munched heavily awhile, hungrily, before answering.

– I'm tired of all them rocks in the sea, he said, and boats and ships. Salt junk all the time.

Tired, seemingly, he ceased. His questioner, perceiving that he was not likely to get a great deal of change out of such a wily old customer, fell to woolgathering on the enormous dimensions of the water about the globe. Suffice it to say that, as a casual glance at the map revealed, it covered fully three fourths of it and he fully realised accordingly what it meant, to rule the waves. On more than one occasion – a dozen at the lowest – near the North Bull at Dollymount he had remarked a superannuated old salt, evidently derelict, seated habitually near the not particularly redolent sea on the wall, staring quite obviously at it and it at him, dreaming of fresh woods and pastures new as someone somewhere sings. And it left him wondering why. Possibly he had tried to find out the secret for himself, floundering up and down the antipodes and all that sort of thing and over and under – well, not exactly under – tempting the fates. And the odds were twenty to nil there was really no secret about it at all. Nevertheless, without going into the *minutiae* of the business, the eloquent fact remained that the sea was there in all its glory and in the natural course of things somebody or other had to sail on it and fly in the face of providence though it merely went to show how people usually contrived to load that sort of onus on to the other fellow like the hell idea and the lottery and insurance, which were run on identically the same lines so that for that very reason, if no other, lifeboat Sunday was a very laudable institution to which the public at large, no matter where living, inland or seaside, as the case might be, having it brought home to them like that, should extend its gratitude also to the harbourmasters and coastguard service who had to man the rigging and push off and out amid the elements, whatever the season, when duty called *Ireland expects that every man* and so on, and sometimes had a terrible time of it in the wintertime not forgetting the Irish lights, Kish and others, liable to capsize at any moment rounding which he once with his daughter had experienced some remarkably choppy, not to say stormy, weather.

– There was a fellow sailed with me in the *Rover*, the old seadog, himself a rover, proceeded. Went ashore and took up a soft job as gentleman's valet at six quid a month. Them are his trousers I've on me and he gave me an oilskin and that jackknife. I'm game for that job, shaving and brushup. I hate roaming about. There's my son now, Danny, run off to sea and his mother got him took in a draper's in Cork where he could be drawing easy money.

– What age is he? queried one hearer who, by the way, seen from the side, bore a distant resemblance to Henry Campbell, the townclerk, away from the carking cares of office, unwashed, of course, and in a seedy getup and a strong suspicion of nosepaint about the nasal appendage.

– Why, the sailor answered with a slow puzzled utterance. My son Danny? He'd be about eighteen now, way I figure it.

The Skibbereen father hereupon tore open his grey or unclean anyhow shirt with his two hands and scratched away at his chest on which was to be seen an image tattooed in blue Chinese ink, intended to represent an anchor.

– There was lice in that bunk in Bridgwater, he remarked. Sure as nuts. I must get a wash tomorrow or next day. It's them black lads I objects to. I hate those buggers. Sucks your blood dry, they does.

Seeing they were all looking at his chest, he accommodatingly dragged his shirt more open so that, on top of the timehonoured symbol of the mariner's hope and rest, they had a full view of the figure 16 and a young man's sideface looking frowningly rather.

– Tattoo, the exhibitor explained. That was done when we were lying becalmed off Odessa in the Black Sea under Captain Dalton. Fellow the name of Antonio done that. There he is himself, a Greek.

– Did it hurt much doing it? one asked the sailor.

That worthy, however, was busily engaged in collecting round the someway in his. Squeezing or . . .

– See here, he said, showing Antonio. There he is, cursing the mate. And there he is now, he added. The same fellow, pulling the skin with his fingers, some special knack evidently, and he laughing at a yarn.

And in point of fact the young man named Antonio's livid face did actually look like forced smiling and the curious effect excited the unreserved admiration of everybody, including Skin-the-Goat who this time stretched over.

– Ay, ay, sighed the sailor, looking down on his manly chest. He's gone too. Ate by sharks after. Ay, ay.

He let go of the skin so that the profile resumed the normal expression of before.

– Neat bit of work, longshoreman one said.

– And what's the number for? loafer number two queried.

– Eaten alive? a third asked the sailor.

– Ay, ay, sighed again the latter personage, more cheerily this time, with some sort of a half smile, for a brief duration only, in the direction of the questioner about the number. A Greek he was.

And then he added, with rather gallowsbird humour, considering his alleged end:

> – *As bad as old Antonio.*
> *For he left me on my ownio.*

The face of a streetwalker, glazed and haggard under a black straw hat, peered askew round the door of the shelter, palpably reconnoitring on her own with the object of bringing more grist to her mill. Mr Bloom, scarcely knowing which way to look, turned away on the moment, flusterfied but outwardly calm, and picking up from the table the pink sheet of the Abbey street organ which the jarvey, if such he was, had laid aside, he picked it up and looked at the pink of the paper though why pink? His reason for so doing was he recognised on the moment round the door the same face he had caught a fleeting glimpse of that afternoon on Ormond Quay, the partially idiotic female, namely, of the lane, who knew the lady in the brown costume does be with you (Mrs B.), and begged the chance of his washing. Also why washing, which seemed rather vague than not?

Your washing. Still, candour compelled him to admit that he had washed his wife's undergarments when soiled in Holles Street and women would and did too a man's similar garments initialled with Bewley and Draper's marking ink (hers were, that is) if they really loved him, that is to say. Love me, love my dirty shirt. Still, just then, being on tenterhooks, he desired the female's room more than her company so it came as a genuine relief when the keeper made her a rude sign to take herself off. Round the side of the

Evening Telegraph he just caught a fleeting glimpse of her face round the side of the door with a kind of demented glassy grin showing that she was not exactly all there, viewing with evident amusement the group of gazers round Skipper Murphy's nautical chest and then there was no more of her.

– The gunboat, the keeper said.

– It beats me, Mr Bloom confided to Stephen, medically I am speaking, how a wretched creature like that from the Lock Hospital, reeking with disease, can be barefaced enough to solicit or how any man in his sober senses, if he values his health in the least. Unfortunate creature! Of course, I suppose some man is ultimately responsible for her condition. Still no matter what the cause is from . . .

Stephen had not noticed her and shrugged his shoulders, merely remarking:

– In this country people sell much more than she ever had and do a roaring trade. Fear not them that sell the body but have not power to buy the soul. She is a bad merchant. She buys dear and sells cheap.

The elder man, though not by any manner of means an old maid or a prude, said that it was nothing short of a crying scandal that ought to be put a stop to *instanter* to say that women of that stamp (quite apart from any oldmaidish squeamishness on the subject), a necessary evil, were not licensed and medically inspected by the proper authorities, a thing he could truthfully state he, as a *paterfamilias*, was a stalwart advocate of from the very first start. Whoever embarked on a policy of the sort, he said, and ventilated the matter thoroughly would confer a lasting boon on everybody concerned.

– You, as a good catholic, he observed, talking of body and soul, believe in the soul. Or do you mean the intelligence, the brainpower as such, as distinct from any outside object, the table, let us say, that cup? I believe in that myself because it has been explained by competent men as the convolutions of the grey matter. Otherwise we would never have such inventions as X rays, for instance. Do you?

Thus cornered, Stephen had to make a superhuman effort of memory to try and concentrate and remember before he could say:

– They tell me on the best authority it is a simple substance and therefore incorruptible. It would be immortal, I understand, but for the possibility of its annihilation by its First Cause, Who, from all I can hear, is quite capable of adding that to the number of His other practical jokes, *corruptio per se* and *corruptio per accidens* both being excluded by court etiquette.

Mr Bloom thoroughly acquiesced in the general gist of this though the mystical finesse involved was a bit out of his sublunary depth still he felt bound to enter a demurrer on the head of simple, promptly rejoining:

– Simple? I shouldn't think that is the proper word. Of course, I grant you, to concede a point, you do knock across a simple soul once in a blue moon. But what I am anxious to arrive at is it is one thing for instance to invent those rays Röntgen did, or the telescope like Edison, though I believe it was before his time, Galileo was the man I mean. The same applies to the laws, for example, of a farreaching natural phenomenon such as electricity but it's a horse of quite another colour to say you believe in the existence of a supernatural God.

– O, that, Stephen expostulated, has been proved conclusively by several of the best known passages in Holy Writ, apart from circumstantial evidence.

On this knotty point, however, the views of the pair, poles apart as they were, both in schooling and everything else, with the marked difference in their respective ages, clashed.

– Has been? the more experienced of the two objected, sticking to his original point. I'm not so sure about that. That's a matter of every man's opinion and, without dragging in the sectarian side of the business, I beg to differ with you *in toto* there. My belief is, to tell you the candid truth, that those bits were genuine forgeries all of them put in by monks most probably or it's the big question of our national poet over again, who precisely wrote them, like *Hamlet* and Bacon, as you who know your Shakespeare infinitely better than I, of course I needn't tell you. Can't you drink that coffee, by the way? Let me stir it and take a piece of that bun. It's like one of our skipper's bricks disguised. Still, no one can give what he hasn't got. Try a bit.

– Couldn't, Stephen contrived to get out, his mental organs for the moment refusing to dictate further.

Faultfinding being a proverbially bad hat, Mr Bloom thought well to stir, or try to, the clotted sugar from the bottom and reflected with something approaching acrimony on the Coffee Palace and its temperance (and lucrative) work. To be sure it was a legitimate object and beyond yea or nay did a world of good. Shelters such as the present one they were in run on teetotal lines for vagrants at night, concerts, dramatic evenings, and useful lectures (admittance free) by qualified men for the lower orders. On the other hand, he had a distinct and painful recollection they paid his wife, Madam Marion Tweedy who had been prominently associated with it at one time, a very modest remuneration indeed for her pianoplaying. The idea, he was strongly inclined to believe, was to do good and net a profit, there being no competition to speak of. Sulphate of copper poison, SO_4 or something in some dried peas he remembered reading of in a cheap eatinghouse somewhere but he couldn't remember when it was or where. Anyhow, inspection, medical inspection, of all eatables, seemed to him more than ever necessary which possibly accounted for the vogue of Dr Tibble's Vi-Cocoa on account of the medical analysis involved.

– Have a shot at it now, he ventured to say of the coffee after being stirred.

Thus prevailed on to at any rate taste it, Stephen lifted the heavy mug from the brown puddle – it clopped out of it when taken up – by the handle and took a sip of the offending beverage.

– Still, it's solid food, his good genius urged, I'm a stickler for solid food, his one and only reason being not gormandising in the least but regular meals as the *sine qua non* for any kind of proper work, mental or manual. You ought to eat more solid food. You would feel a different man.

– Liquids I can eat, Stephen said. But oblige me by taking away that knife. I can't look at the point of it. It reminds me of Roman history.

Mr Bloom promptly did as suggested and removed the incriminated article, a blunt hornhandled ordinary knife with nothing particularly Roman or antique about it to the lay eye, observing that the point was the least conspicuous point about it.

– Our mutual friend's stories are like himself, Mr Bloom, *apropos* of knives, remarked to his *confidante sotto voce*. Do you think they are genuine? He could spin those yarns for hours on end all night long and lie like old boots. Look at him.

Yet still, though his eyes were thick with sleep and sea air, life was full of a host of things and coincidences of a terrible nature and it was quite within the bounds of possibility that it was not an entire fabrication though at first blush there was not much inherent probability in all the spoof he got off his chest being strictly accurate gospel.

He had been meantime taking stock of the individual in front of him and Sherlockholmesing him up, ever since he clapped eyes on him. Though a wellpreserved man of no little stamina, if a trifle prone to baldness, there was something spurious in the cut of his jib that suggested a jail delivery and it required no violent stretch of imagination to associate such a weird-looking specimen with the oakum and treadmill fraternity. He might even have done for his man, supposing it was his own case he told, as people often did about others, namely, that he killed him himself and had served his four or five goodlooking years in durance vile to say nothing of the Antonio personage (no relation to the dramatic personage of identical name who sprang from the pen of our national poet) who expiated his crimes in the melodramatic manner above described. On the other hand he might be only bluffing, a pardonable weakness, because meeting unmistakable mugs, Dublin residents, like those jarvies waiting news from abroad, would tempt any ancient mariner who sailed the ocean seas to draw the long bow about the schooner *Hesperus* and etcetera. And when all was said and done, the lies a fellow told about himself couldn't probably hold a proverbial candle to the wholesale whoppers other fellows coined about him.

– Mind you, I'm not saying that it's all a pure invention, he resumed. Analogous scenes are occasionally, if not often, met with. Giants, though, that is rather a far cry you see once in a way. Marcella, the midget queen. In those waxworks in Henry street I myself saw some Aztecs, as they are called, sitting bowlegged. They couldn't straighten their legs if you paid them because the muscles here, you see, he proceeded, indicating on his companion the brief outline, the sinews, or whatever you like to call them, behind the right knee, were utterly powerless from sitting that way so long cramped up, being adored as gods. There's an example again of simple souls.

However, reverting to friend Sinbad and his horrifying adventures (who reminded him a bit of Ludwig, *alias* Ledwidge, when he occupied the boards of the Gaiety when Michael Gunn was identified with the management in the *Flying Dutchman*, a stupendous success, and his host of admirers came in large numbers, everyone simply flocking to hear him though ships of any sort, phantom or the reverse, on the stage usually fell a bit flat as also did trains), there was nothing intrinsically incompatible about it, he conceded. On the contrary, that stab in the back touch was quite in keeping with those Italianos, though candidly he was none the less free to admit those ice creamers and friers in the fish way, not to mention the chip potato variety and so forth, over in little Italy there, near the Coombe, were sober thrifty hardworking fellows except perhaps a bit too given to pothunting the harmless necessary animal of the feline persuasion of others at night so as to have a good old succulent tuck in with garlic *de rigueur* off him or her next day on the quiet and, he added, on the cheap.

– Spaniards, for instance, he continued, passionate temperaments like that, impetuous as Old Nick, are given to taking the law into their own hands and give you your quietus double quick with those poignards they carry in the abdomen. It comes from the great heat, climate generally. My wife is, so to speak, Spanish, half, that is. Point of fact she could actually claim Spanish nationality if she wanted, having been born in (technically) Spain, i. e. Gibraltar. She has the Spanish type. Quite dark, regular brunette, black. I, for one, certainly believe climate accounts for character. That's why I asked you if you wrote your poetry in Italian.

– The temperaments at the door, Stephen interposed with, were very passionate about ten shillings. *Roberto ruba roba sua.*

– Quite so, Mr Bloom dittoed.

– Then, Stephen said, staring and rambling on to himself or some unknown listener somewhere, we have the impetuosity of Dante and the isosceles triangle, Miss Portinari, he fell in love with and Leonardo and san Tommaso Mastino.

– It's in the blood, Mr Bloom acceded at once. All are washed in the blood of the sun. Coincidence, I just happened to be in the Kildare street Museum today, shortly prior to our meeting, if I can so call it, and I was just looking at those antique statues there. The splendid proportions of hips, bosom. You simply don't knock against those kind of women here. An exception here and there. Handsome, yes, pretty in a way you find, but what I'm talking about is the female form. Besides, they have so little taste in dress, most of them, which greatly enhances a woman's natural beauty, no matter what you say. Rumpled stockings – it may be, possibly is, a foible of mine, but still it's a thing I simply hate to see.

Interest, however, was starting to flag somewhat all round and the others got on to talking about accidents at sea, ships lost in a fog, collisions with icebergs, all that sort of thing. Shipahoy, of course, had his own say to say. He had doubled the Cape a few odd times and weathered a monsoon, a kind of wind, in the China seas and through all those perils of the deep there was one thing, he declared, stood to him, or words to that effect, a pious medal he had that saved him.

So then after that they drifted on to the wreck of Daunt's rock, wreck of that illfated Norwegian barque – nobody could think of her name for the moment till the jarvey who had really quite a look of Henry Campbell remembered it, *Palme*, on Booterstown Strand, that was the talk of the town that year (Albert William Quill wrote a fine piece of original verse of distinctive merit on the topic for the Irish *Times*) breakers running over her and crowds and crowds on the shore in commotion petrified with horror. Then someone said something about the case of the s. s. *Lady Cairns* of Swansea, run into by the *Mona*, which was on an opposite tack, in rather muggyish weather and lost with all hands on deck. No aid was given. Her master, the *Mona's*, said he was afraid his collision bulkhead would give way. She had no water, it appears, in her hold.

At this stage an incident happened. It having become necessary for him to unfurl a reef, the sailor vacated his seat.

– Let me cross your bows, mate, he said to his neighbour, who was just gently dropping off into a peaceful doze.

He made tracks heavily, slowly, with a dumpy sort of a gait to the door, stepped heavily down the one step there was out of the shelter and bore due left. While he was in the act of getting his bearings, Mr Bloom, who noticed when he stood up that he had two flasks of presumably ship's rum sticking one out of each pocket for the private consumption of his burning interior, saw him produce a bottle and uncork it, or unscrew, and, applying its nozzle to his lips, take a good old delectable swig out of it with a gurgling noise. The irrepressible Bloom, who also had a shrewd suspicion that the old stager went out on a manœuvre after the counterattraction in the shape of a female, who, however, had disappeared to all intents and purposes, could, by straining, just perceive him, when duly refreshed by his rum puncheon exploit, gazing up at the piers and girders of the Loop Line, rather out of his depth, as of course it was all radically altered since his last visit and greatly improved. Some person or persons invisible directed him to the male urinal erected by the cleansing committee all over the place for the purpose but, after a brief space of time during which silence reigned supreme, the sailor, evidently giving it a wide berth, eased himself close at hand, the noise of his bilgewater some little time subsequently splashing on the ground where it apparently woke a horse of the cabrank.

A hoof scooped anyway for new foothold after sleep and harness jingled. Slightly disturbed in his sentrybox by the brazier of live coke, the watcher of the corporation, who, though now broken down and fast breaking up, was none other in stern reality than the Gumley aforesaid, now practically on the parish rates, given the temporary job by Pat Tobin in all human probability, from dictates of humanity, knowing him before – shifted about and shuffled in his box before composing his limbs again in the arms of Morpheus. A truly amazing piece of hard times in its most virulent form on a fellow most respectably connected and familiarised with decent home comforts all his life who came in for a cool £100 a year at one time which of course the doublebarrelled ass proceeded to make general ducks and drakes of. And there he was at the end of his tether after having often painted the town tolerably pink, without a beggarly stiver. He drank, needless to be told, and it pointed only once more a moral when he might quite easily be in a large way of business if – a big if, however – he had contrived to cure himself of his particular partiality.

All, meantime, were loudly lamenting the falling off in Irish shipping, coastwise and foreign as well, which was all part and parcel of the same thing. A Palgrave Murphy boat was put off the ways at Alexandra Basin, the only launch that year. Right enough the harbours were there only no ships ever called.

There were wrecks and wrecks, the keeper said, who was evidently *au fait*.

What he wanted to ascertain was why that ship ran bang against the only rock in Galway Bay when the Galway Harbour scheme was mooted by a Mr Worthington or some name like that, eh? Ask her captain, he advised them, how much palmoil the British Government gave him for that day's work. Captain John Lever of the Lever line.

– Am I right, skipper? he queried of the sailor now returning after his private potation and the rest of his exertions.

That worthy, picking up the scent of the fagend of the song or words, growled in wouldbe music, but with great vim, some kind of chanty or other in seconds or thirds. Mr Bloom's sharp ears heard him then expectorate the plug probably (which it was), so that he must have lodged it for the time being in his fist while he did the drinking and making water jobs and found it a bit sour after the liquid fire in question. Anyhow in he rolled after his successful libation – *cum* – potation, introducing an atmosphere of drink into the *soirée*, boisterously trolling, like a veritable son of a seacook:

> – *The biscuits was as hard as brass,*
>   *And the beef as salt as Lot's wife's arse.*
> *O Johnny Lever!*
> *Johnny Lever, O!*

After which effusion the redoubtable specimen duly arrived on the scene and, regaining his seat, he sank rather than sat heavily on the form provided.

Skin-the-Goat, assuming he was he, evidently with an axe to grind, was airing his grievances in a forcible-feeble philippic anent the natural resources of Ireland, or something of that sort, which he described in his lengthy dissertation as the richest country bar none on the face of God's earth, far and away superior to England, with coal in large quantities, six million pounds' worth of pork exported every year, ten millions between butter and eggs, and all the riches drained out of it by England levying taxes on the poor people that paid through the nose always, and gobbling up the best meat in the market, and a lot more surplus steam in the same vein. Their conversation accordingly became general and all agreed that that was a fact. You could grow any mortal thing in Irish soil, he stated, and there was Colonel Everard down there in Cavan growing tobacco. Where would you find anywhere the like of Irish bacon? But a day of reckoning, he stated *crescendo* with no uncertain voice – thoroughly monopolising all the conversation – was in store for mighty England, despite her power of pelf on account of her crimes. There would be a fall and the greatest fall in history.

The Germans and the Japs were going to have their little lookin, he affirmed. The Boers were the beginning of the end. Brummagem England was toppling already and her downfall would be Ireland, her Achilles heel, which he explained to them about the vulnerable point of Achilles, the Greek hero – a point his auditors at once seized as he completely gripped their attention by showing the tendon referred to on his boot. His advice to every Irishman was: stay in the land of your birth and work for Ireland and live for Ireland. Ireland, Parnell said, could not spare a single one of her sons.

Silence all round marked the termination of his *finale*. The impervious navigator heard these lurid tidings undismayed.

– Take a bit of doing, boss, retaliated that rough diamond palpably a bit peeved in response to the foregoing truism.

To which cold douche, referring to downfall and so on, the keeper concurred but nevertheless held to his main view.

– Who's the best troops in the army? the grizzled old veteran irately interrogated. And the best jumpers and racers? And the best admirals and generals we've got? Tell me that.

– The Irish for choice, retorted the cabby like Campbell, facial blemishes apart.

– That's right, the old tarpaulin corroborated. The Irish catholic peasant. He's the backbone of our empire. You know Jem Mullins?

While allowing him his individual opinions, as every man, the keeper added he cared nothing for any empire, ours or his, and considered no Irishman worthy of his salt that served it. Then they began to have a few irascible words, when it waxed hotter, both, needless to say, appealing to the listeners who followed the passage of arms with interest so long as they didn't indulge in recriminations and come to blows.

From inside information extending over a series of years Mr Bloom was rather inclined to poohpooh the suggestion as egregious balderdash for, pending that consummation devoutly to be or not to be wished for, he was fully cognisant of the fact that their neighbours across the channel, unless they were much bigger fools than he took them for, rather concealed their strength than the opposite. It was quite on a par with the quixotic idea in certain quarters that in a hundred million years the coal seam of the sister island would be played out and if, as time went on, that turned out to be how the cat jumped all he could personally say on the matter was that as a host of contingencies, equally relevant to the issue, might occur ere then it was highly advisable in the interim to try to make the most of both countries, even though poles apart. Another little interesting point, the amours of whores and chummies, to put it in common parlance, reminded him Irish soldiers had as often fought for England as against her, more so, in fact. And now, why? So the scene between the pair of them, the licensee of the place, rumoured to be or have been Fitzharris, the famous invincible, and the other, obviously bogus, reminded him forcibly as being on all fours with the confidence trick, supposing, that is, it was prearranged, as the lookeron, a student of the human soul, if anything, the others seeing least of the game. And as for the lessee or keeper, who probably wasn't the other person at all, he (Bloom) couldn't help feeling, and most properly, it was better to give people like that the goby unless you were a blithering idiot altogether and refuse to have anything to do with them as a golden rule in private life and their felonsetting, there always being the offchance of a Dannyman coming forward and turning queen's evidence – or king's now – like Denis or Peter Carey, an idea he utterly repudiated. Quite apart from that, he disliked those careers of wrongdoing and crime on principle. Yet, though such criminal propensities had never been an inmate of his bosom in any shape or form, he certainly did feel, and no denying it (while inwardly remaining what he was), a certain kind of admiration for a man who had actually brandished a knife, cold steel, with the courage of his political convictions though, personally, he would never be a party to any such thing, off the same bat as those love vendettas of the south – have her or swing for her – when the husband frequently, after some words passed between the two concerning her relations with the other lucky mortal (the man having had the pair watched), inflicted fatal injuries on his adored one as a result of an alternative postnuptial *liaison* by plunging his knife into her until it just struck him that Fitz, nicknamed Skin-the-Goat, merely drove the car for the actual perpetrators of the outrage and so was not, if he was reliably informed, actually party to the ambush which, in point of fact, was the plea some legal luminary saved his skin on. In any case that was very ancient history by now and as for our friend, the pseudo Skin-the-etcetera, he had transparently outlived his welcome. He ought to have either died naturally or on the scaffold high. Like actresses, always farewell – positively last performance then come up smiling again. Generous to a fault, of course, temperamental, no economising or any idea of the sort, always snapping at the bone for the shadow. So similarly he had a very shrewd suspicion that Mr Johnny Lever got rid of some £. s. d. in the course of his perambulations round the docks in the congenial atmosphere of the *Old Ireland* tavern, come back to Erin and so on. Then as for the others, he had heard not so long before the same identical lingo, as he told Stephen how he simply but effectually silenced the offender.

– He took umbrage at something or other, that muchinjured but on the whole eventempered person declared, I let slip. He called me a jew, and in a heated fashion, offensively. So I, without deviating from plain facts in the least, told him his God, I mean Christ, was a jew too, and all his family, like me, though in reality I'm not. That was one for him. A soft answer turns away wrath. He hadn't a word to say for himself as everyone saw. Am I not right?

He turned a long you are wrong gaze on Stephen of timorous dark pride at the soft impeachment, with a glance also of entreaty for he seemed to glean in a kind of a way that it wasn't all exactly . . .

– *Ex quibus*, Stephen mumbled in a noncommittal accent, their two or four eyes conversing, *Christus* or Bloom his name is, or, after all, any other, *secundum carnem*.

– Of course, Mr Bloom proceeded to stipulate, you must look at both sides of the question. It is hard to lay down any hard and fast rules as to right and wrong but room for improvement all round there certainly is though every country, they say, our own distressful included, has the government it deserves. But with a little goodwill all round. It's all very fine to boast of mutual superiority but what about mutual equality? I resent violence or intolerance in any shape or form. It never reaches anything or stops anything. A revolution must come on the due instalments plan. It's a patent absurdity on the face of it to hate people because they live round the corner and speak another vernacular, so to speak.

– Memorable bloody bridge battle and seven minutes' war, Stephen assented, between Skinner's alley and Ormond market.

Yes, Mr Bloom thoroughly agreed, entirely endorsing the remark, that was overwhelmingly right and the whole world was overwhelmingly full of that sort of thing.

– You just took the words out of my mouth, he said. A hocuspocus of conflicting evidence that candidly you couldn't remotely . . .

All those wretched quarrels, in his humble opinion, stirring up bad blood – bump of combativeness or gland of some kind, erroneously supposed to be about a punctilio of honour and a flag – were very largely a question of the money question which was at the back of everything, greed and jealousy, people never knowing when to stop.

– They accuse – remarked he audibly. He turned away from the others, who probably . . . and spoke nearer to, so as the others . . . in case they . . .

– Jews, he softly imparted in an aside in Stephen's ear, are accused of ruining. Not a vestige of truth in it, I can safely say. History – would you be surprised to learn? – proves up to the hilt Spain decayed when the

Inquisition hounded the jews out and England prospered when Cromwell, an uncommonly able ruffian, who, in other respects, has much to answer for, imported them. Why? Because they are practical and are proved to be so. I don't want to indulge in any . . . because you know the standard works on the subject, and then, orthodox as you are . . . But in the economic, not touching religion, domain, the priest spells poverty. Spain again, you saw in the war, compared with goahead America. Turks, it's in the dogma. Because if they didn't believe they'd go straight to heaven when they die they'd try to live better – at least, so I think. That's the juggle on which the p.p.'s raise the wind on false pretences. I'm, he resumed, with dramatic force, as good an Irishman as that rude person I told you about at the outset and I want to see everyone, concluded he, all creeds and classes *pro rata* having a comfortable tidysized income, in no niggard fashion either, something in the neighbourhood of £300 per annum. That's the vital issue at stake and it's feasible and would be provocative of friendlier intercourse between man and man. At least that's my idea for what it's worth. I call that patriotism. *Ubi patria*, as we learned a small smattering of in our classical day in *Alma Mater, vita bene*. Where you can live well, the sense is, if you work.

Over his untasteable apology for a cup of coffee, listening to this synopsis of things in general, Stephen stared at nothing in particular. He could hear, of course, all kinds of words changing colour like those crabs about Ringsend in the morning, burrowing quickly into all colours of different sorts of the same sand where they had a home somewhere beneath or seemed to. Then he looked up and saw the eyes that said or didn't say the words the voice he heard said – if you work.

– Count me out, he managed to remark, meaning to work.

The eyes were surprised at this observation, because as he, the person who owned them pro. tem. observed, or rather, his voice speaking did: All must work, have to, together.

– I mean, of course, the other hastened to affirm, work in the widest possible sense. Also literary labour, not merely for the kudos of the thing. Writing for the newspapers which is the readiest channel nowadays. That's work too. Important work. After all, from the little I know of you, after all the money expended on your education, you are entitled to recoup yourself and command your price. You have every bit as much right to live by your pen in pursuit of your philosophy as the peasant has. What? You both belong to Ireland, the brain and the brawn. Each is equally important.

– You suspect, Stephen retorted with a sort of a half laugh, that I may be important because I belong to the *faubourg Saint-Patrice* called Ireland for short.

– I would go a step farther, Mr Bloom insinuated.

– But I suspect, Stephen interrupted, that Ireland must be important because it belongs to me.

– What belongs? queried Mr Bloom, bending, fancying he was perhaps under some misapprehension. Excuse me. Unfortunately I didn't catch the latter portion. What was it you? . . .

Stephen, patently crosstempered, repeated and shoved aside his mug of coffee, or whatever you like to call it, none too politely, adding:

– We can't change the country. Let us change the subject.

At this pertinent suggestion, Mr Bloom, to change the subject, looked down, but in a quandary, as he couldn't tell exactly what construction to put on belongs to which sounded rather a far cry. The rebuke of some kind was clearer than the other part. Needless to say, the fumes of his recent orgy spoke then with some asperity in a curious bitter way, foreign to his sober state. Probably the home life, to which Mr Bloom attached the utmost importance, had not been all that was needful or he hadn't been familiarised with the the right sort of people. With a touch of fear for the young man beside him, whom he furtively scrutinised with an air of some consternation remembering he had just come back from Paris, the eyes more especially reminding him forcibly of father and sister, failing to throw much light on the subject, however, he brought to mind instances of cultured fellows that promised so brilliantly, nipped in the bud of premature decay, and nobody to blame but themselves. For instance, there was the case of O'Callaghan, for one, the half crazy faddist, respectably connected, though of inadequate means, with his mad vagaries, among whose other gay doings when rotto and making himself a nuisance to everybody all round he was in the habit of ostentatiously sporting in public a suit of brown paper (a fact). And then the usual *dénouement* after the fun had gone on fast and furious he got landed into hot water and had to be spirited away by a few friends, after a strong hint to a blind horse from John Mallon of Lower Castle Yard, so as not to be made amenable under section two of the Criminal Law Amendment Act, certain names of those subpœnaed being handed in but not divulged, for reasons which will occur to anyone with a pick of brains. Briefly, putting two and two together, six sixteen, which he pointedly turned a deaf ear to, Antonio and so forth, jockeys and esthetes and the tattoo which was all the go in the seventies or thereabouts, even in the House of Lords, because early in life the occupant of the throne, then heir apparent, the other members of the upper ten and other high personages simply following in the footsteps of the head of the state, he reflected about the errors of notorieties and crowned heads running counter to morality such as the

Cornwall case a number of years before under their veneer in a way scarcely intended by nature, a thing good Mrs Grundy as the law stands was terribly down on, though not for the reason they thought they were probably, whatever it was, except women chiefly, who were always fiddling more or less at one another, it being largely a matter of dress and all the rest of it. Ladies who like distinctive underclothing should, and every welltailored man must, trying to make the gap wider between them by innuendo and give more of a genuine fillip to acts of impropriety between the two, she unbuttoned his and then he untied her, mind the pin, whereas savages in the cannibal islands, say, at ninety degrees in the shade not caring a continental. However, reverting to the original, there were on the other hand others who had forced their way to the top from the lowest rung by the aid of their bootstraps. Sheer force of natural genius, that. With brains, sir.

For which and further reasons he felt it was interest and duty even to wait on and profit by the unlookedfor occasion, though why, he could not exactly tell, being, as it was, already several shillings to the bad, having, in fact, let himself in for it. Still, to cultivate the acquaintance of someone of no uncommon calibre who could provide food for reflection would amply repay any small . . . Intellectual stimulation as such was, he felt, from time to time a firstrate tonic for the mind. Added to which was the coincidence of meeting, discussion, dance, row, old salt, of the here today and gone tomorrow type, night loafers, the whole galaxy of events, all went to make up a miniature cameo of the world we live in, especially as the lives of the submerged tenth, viz., coalminers, divers, scavengers etc., were very much under the microscope lately. To improve the shining hour he wondered whether he might meet with anything approaching the same luck as Mr Philip Beaufoy if taken down in writing. Suppose he were to pen something out of the common groove (as he fully intended doing) at the rate of one guinea per column, *My Experiences*, let us say, *in a Cabman's Shelter*.

The pink edition, extra sporting, of the *Telegraph*, tell a graphic lie, lay, as luck would have it, beside his elbow and as he was just puzzling again, far from satisfied, over a country belonging to him and the preceding rebus the vessel came from Bridgwater and the postcard was addressed to A. Boudin, find the captain's age, his eyes went aimlessly over the respective captions which came under his special province, the allembracing give us this day our daily press. First he got a bit of a start but it turned out to be only something about somebody named H. du Boyes, agent for typewriters or something like that. Great battle Tokio. Lovemaking in Irish £200 damages. Gordon Bennett. Emigration swindle. Letter from His Grace William †. Ascot *Throwaway* recalls Derby of '92 when Captain Marshall's dark horse,

Sir Hugo, captured the blue riband at long odds. New York disaster, thousand lives lost. Foot and Mouth. Funeral of the late Mr Patrick Dignam.

So to change the subject he read about Dignam, R. I. P., which, he reflected, was anything but a gay sendoff.

– *This morning* (Hynes put it in, of course), *the remains of the late Mr Patrick Dignam were removed from his residence, n° 9 Newbridge Avenue, Sandymount, for interment in Glasnevin. The deceased gentleman was a most popular and genial personality in city life and his demise, after a brief illness, came as great shock to citizens of all classes by whom he is deeply regretted. The obsequies, at which many friends of the deceased were present, were carried out* (certainly Hynes wrote it with a nudge from Corny) *by Messrs. H. J. O'Neill & Son, 164 North Strand road. The mourners included: Patk. Dignam (son), Bernard Corrigan (brother-in-law), John Henry Menton, solr., Martin Cunningham, John Power eatondph 1/8 ador dorador douradora* (must be where he called Monks the dayfather about Keyes's ad), *Thomas Kernan, Simon Dedalus, Stephen Dedalus, B. A., Edward J. Lambert, Cornelius Kelleher, Joseph M'C. Hynes, L. Boom, C. P. M'Coy, – M'Intosh, and several others.*

Nettled not a little by *L. Boom* (as it incorrectly stated) and the line of bitched type, but tickled to death simultaneously by C. P. M'Coy and Stephen Dedalus, B. A., who were conspicuous, needless to say, by their total absence (to say nothing of M'Intosh), L. Boom pointed it out to his companion B. A., engaged in stifling another yawn, half nervousness, not forgetting the usual crop of nonsensical howlers of misprints.

– Is that first epistle to the Hebrews, he asked, as soon as his bottom jaw would let him, in? Text: open thy mouth and put thy foot in it.

– It is, really, Mr Bloom said (though first he fancied he alluded to the archbishop till he added about foot and mouth with which there could be no possible connection) overjoyed to set his mind at rest and a bit flabbergasted at Myles Crawford's after all managing the thing, there.

While the other was reading it on page two Boom (to give him for the nonce his new misnomer) whiled away a few odd leisure moments in fits and starts with the account of the third event at Ascot on page three, his sidevalue 1,000 sovs., with 3,000 sovs. in specie added for entire colts and fillies, Mr F. Alexander's *Throwaway,* b. h. by *Rightaway,* 5 yrs, 9 st 4 lbs, Thrale (W. Lane) 1. Lord Howard de Walden's *Zinfandel* (M. Cannon) 2. Mr W. Bass's *Sceptre,* 3. Betting 5 to 4 on *Zinfandel,* 20 to 1 *Throwaway* (off). *Throwaway* and *Zinfandel* stood close order. It was anybody's race then the rank outsider drew to the fore got long lead, beating lord Howard de Walden's chestnut colt and Mr W. Bass's bay filly Sceptre on a 2½ mile course. Winner trained by Braine so that Lenehan's version of the business was all pure buncombe. Secured the verdict cleverly by a length. 1,000 sovs, with 3000 in specie. Also ran J. de Bremond's (French horse Bantam Lyons was anxiously inquiring after not in yet but expected any minute) *Maximum II*. Different ways of bringing off a coup. Lovemaking damages. Though that half baked Lyons ran off at a tangent in his impetuosity to get left. Of course, gambling eminently lent itself to that sort of thing though, as the event turned out, the poor fool hadn't much reason to congratulate himself on his pick, the forlorn hope. Guesswork it reduced itself to eventually.

– There was every indication they would arrive at that, Mr Bloom said.

– Who? the other, whose hand by the way was hurt, said.

One morning you would open the paper, the cabman affirmed, and read, *Return of Parnell*. He bet them what they liked. A Dublin fusilier was in that shelter one night and said he saw him in South Africa. Pride it was killed him. He ought to have done away with himself or lain low for a time after Committee Room No. 15 until he was his old self again with no-one to point a finger at him. Then they would all to a man have gone down on their marrowbones to him to come back when he had recovered his senses. Dead he wasn't. Simply absconded somewhere. The coffin they brought over was full of stones. He changed his name to De Wet, the Boer general. He made a mistake to fight the priests. And so forth and so on.

All the same Bloom (properly so dubbed) was rather surprised at their memories for in nine cases out of ten it was a case of tarbarrels, and not singly but in their thousands, and then complete oblivion because it was twenty odd years. Highly unlikely, of course, there was even a shadow of truth in the stories and, even supposing, he thought a return highly in-advisable, all things considered. Something evidently riled them in his death. Either he petered out too tamely of acute pneumonia just when his various different political arrangements were nearing completion or whether it transpired he owed his death to his having neglected to change his boots and clothes after a wetting when a cold resulted and failing to consult a specialist he being confined to his room till he eventually died of it amid widespread regret before a fortnight was at an end or quite possibly they were distressed to find the job was taken out of their hands. Of course nobody being acquainted with his movements even before, there was absolutely no clue as to his whereabouts which were decidedly of the *Alice, where art thou* order even prior to his starting to go under several aliases such as Fox and Stewart, so the remark which emanated from friend cabby might be within the bounds of possibility. Naturally then, it would prey on his mind as a born leader of men, which undoubtedly he was, and a commanding figure, a sixfooter or at any rate five feet ten or eleven in his stockinged feet, whereas

Messrs So-and-So who, though they weren't even a patch on the former man, ruled the roost after their redeeming features were very few and far between. It certainly pointed a moral, the idol with feet of clay. And then seventytwo of his trusty henchmen rounding on him with mutual mudslinging. And the identical same with murderers. You had to come back – that haunting sense kind of drew you – to show the understudy in the title *rôle* how to. He saw him once on the auspicious occasion when they broke up the type in the *Insuppressible* or was it *United Ireland*, a privilege he keenly appreciated, and, in point of fact, handed him his silk hat when it was knocked off and he said *Thank you*, excited as he undoubtedly was under his frigid expression notwithstanding the little misadventure mentioned between the cup and the lip – what's bred in the bone. Still, as regards return, you were a lucky dog if they didn't set the terrier at you directly you got back. Then a lot of shillyshally usually followed. Tom for and Dick and Harry against. And then, number one, you came up against the man in possession and had to produce your credentials, like the claimant in the Tichborne case, Roger Charles Tichborne, *Bella* was the boat's name to the best of his recollection he, the heir, went down in, as the evidence went to show, and there was a tattoo mark too in Indian ink, Lord Bellew, was it? As he might very easily have picked up the details from some pal on board ship and then, when got up to tally with the description given, introduce himself with, *Excuse me, my name is So-and-So* or some such commonplace remark. A more prudent course, Mr Bloom said to the not over effusive, in fact like the distinguished personage under discussion beside him, would have been to sound the lie of the land first.

– That bitch, that English whore, did for him, the shebeen proprietor commented. She put the first nail in his coffin.

– Fine lump of a woman, all the same, the *soi-disant* townclerk, Henry Campbell remarked, and plenty of her. I seen her picture in a barber's. Her husband was a captain or an officer.

– Ay, Skin-the-Goat amusingly added. He was, and a cottonball one.

This gratuitous contribution of a humorous character occasioned a fair amount of laughter among his *entourage*. As regards Bloom, he, without the faintest suspicion of a smile, merely gazed in the direction of the door and reflected upon the historic story which had aroused extraordinary interest at the time when the facts, to make matters worse, were made public with the usual affectionate letters that passed between them, full of sweet nothings. First, it was strictly platonic till nature intervened and an attachment sprang up between them, till bit by bit matters came to a climax and the matter became the talk of the town till the staggering blow came as a welcome intelligence to not a few evildisposed however, who were resolved upon encouraging his downfall though the thing was public property all along though not to anything like the sensational extent that it subsequently blossomed into. Since their names were coupled, though, since he was her declared favourite, where was the particular necessity to proclaim it to the rank and file from the housetops, the fact namely, that he had shared her bedroom, which came out in the witnessbox on oath when a thrill went through the packed court literally electrifying everybody in the shape of witnesses swearing to having witnessed him on such and such a particular date in the act of scrambling out of an upstairs apartment with the assistance of a ladder in night apparel, having gained admittance in the same fashion, a fact that the weeklies, addicted to the lubric a little, simply coined shoals of money out of. Whereas the simple fact of the case was it was simply a case of the husband not being up to the scratch with nothing in common between them beyond the name and then a real man arriving on the scene, strong to the verge of weakness, falling a victim to her siren charms and forgetting home ties. The usual sequel, to bask in the loved one's smiles. The eternal question of the life connubial, needless to say, cropped up. Can real love, supposing there happens to be another chap in the case, exist between married folk? Though it was no concern of theirs absolutely if he regarded her with affection carried away by a wave of folly. A magnificent specimen of manhood he was truly, augmented obviously by gifts of a high order as compared with the other military supernumerary, that is (who was just the usual everyday *farewell, my gallant captain* kind of an individual in the light dragoons, the 18th hussars to be accurate), and inflammable doubtless (the fallen leader, that is, not the other) in his own peculiar way which she of course, woman, quickly perceived as highly likely to carve his way to fame, which he almost bid fair to do till the priests and ministers of the gospel as a whole, his erstwhile staunch adherents and his beloved evicted tenants for whom he had done yeoman service in the rural parts of the country by taking up the cudgels on their behalf in a way that exceeded their most sanguine expectations, very effectually cooked his matrimonial goose, thereby heaping coals of fire on his head, much in the same way as the fabled ass's kick. Looking back now in a retrospective kind of arrangement, all seemed a kind of dream. And the coming back was the worst thing you ever did because it went without saying you would feel out of place as things always moved with the times. Why, as he reflected, Irishtown Strand, a locality he had not been in for quite a number of years, looked different somehow since, as it happened, he went to reside on the north side. North or south however, it was just the wellknown case of hot passion, pure and simple, upsetting the applecart with a vengeance and just bore out the very thing he was saying, as she also was Spanish or half so, types that wouldn't do things by halves, passionate abandon of the south, casting every shred of decency to the winds.

– Just bears out what I was saying, he with glowing bosom said to Stephen. And, if I don't greatly mistake, she was Spanish too.

– The king of Spain's daughter, Stephen answered, adding something or other rather muddled about farewell and adieu to you Spanish onions and the first land called the Deadman and from Ramhead to Scilly was so and so many . . .

– Was she? Bloom ejaculated surprised, though not astonished by any means. I never heard that rumour before. Possible, especially there it was, as she lived there. So, Spain.

Carefully avoiding a book in his pocket *Sweets of*, which reminded him by the by of that Capel street library book out of date, he took out his pocket-book and, turning over the various contents rapidly, finally he . . .

– Do you consider, by the by, he said, thoughtfully selecting a faded photo which he laid on the table, that a Spanish type?

Stephen, obviously addressed, looked down on the photo showing a large sized lady, with her fleshy charms on evidence in an open fashion, as she was in the full bloom of womanhood, in evening dress cut ostentatiously low for the occasion to give a liberal display of bosom, with more than vision of breasts, her full lips parted, and some perfect teeth, standing near, ostensibly with gravity, a piano, on the rest of which was *In old Madrid*, a ballad, pretty in its way, which was then all the vogue. Her (the lady's) eyes, dark, large, looked at Stephen, about to smile about something to be admired, Lafayette of Westmoreland street, Dublin's premier photographic artist, being responsible for the esthetic execution.

– Mrs Bloom, my wife the *prima donna*, Madam Marion Tweedy, Bloom indicated. Taken a few years since. In or about '96. Very like her then.

Beside the young man he looked also at the photo of the lady now his legal wife who, he intimated, was the accomplished daughter of Major Brian Tweedy and displayed at an early age remarkable proficiency as a singer having even made her bow to the public when her years numbered barely sweet sixteen. As for the face, it was a speaking likeness in expression but it did not do justice to her figure, which came in for a lot of notice usually and which did not come out to the best advantage in that getup. She could without difficulty, he said, have posed for the ensemble, not to dwell on certain opulent curves of the . . . He dwelt, being a bit of an artist in his spare time, on the female form in general developmentally because, as it so happened, no later than that afternoon, he had seen those Grecian statues, perfectly developed as works of art, in the National Museum. Marble could give the original, shoulders, back, all the symmetry. All the rest, yes, Puritanism. It does though, St Joseph's sovereign . . . whereas no photo could, because it simply wasn't art, in a word.

The spirit moving him, he would much have liked to follow Jack Tar's good example and leave the likeness there for a very few minutes to speak for itself on the plea he . . . so that the other could drink in the beauty for himself, her stage presence being, frankly, a treat in itself which the camera could not at all do justice to. But it was scarcely professional etiquette so, though it was a warm pleasant sort of a night now yet wonderfully cool for the season considering, for sunshine after storm . . . And he did feel a kind of need there and then to follow suit like a kind of inward voice and satisfy a possible need by moving a motion. Nevertheless, he sat tight, just viewing the slightly soiled photo creased by opulent curves, none the worse for wear, however, and looked away thoughtfully with the intention of not further increasing the other's possible embarrassment while gauging her symmetry of heaving *embonpoint*. In fact, the slight soiling was only an added charm, like the case of linen slightly soiled, good as new, much better, in fact, with the starch out Suppose she was gone when he? . . . I looked for the lamp which she told me came into his mind but merely as a passing fancy of his because he then recollected the morning littered bed etcetera and the book about Ruby with met him pike hoses (*sic*) in it which must have fell down sufficiently appropriately beside the domestic chamber-pot with apologies to Lindley Murray.

The vicinity of the young man he certainly relished, educated, *distingué*, and impulsive into the bargain, far and away the pick of the bunch, though you wouldn't think he had it in him . . . yet you would. Besides he said the picture was handsome which, say what you like, it was, though at the moment she was distinctly stouter. And why not? An awful lot of make-believe went on about that sort of thing involving a lifelong slur with the usual splash page of letterpress about the same old matrimonial tangle alleging misconduct with professional golfer or the newest stage favourite instead of being honest and aboveboard about the whole business. How they were fated to meet and an attachment sprang up between the two so that their names were coupled in the public eye was told in court with letters containing the habitual mushy and compromising expressions, leaving no loophole, to show that they openly cohabited two or three times a week at some wellknown seaside hotel and relations, when the thing ran its normal course, became in due course intimate. Then the decree *nisi* and the King's

Proctor to show cause why and, he failing to quash it, *nisi* was made absolute. But as for that, the two misdemeanants, wrapped up as they largely were in one another, could safely afford to ignore it as they very largely did till the matter was put in the hands of a solicitor, who filed a petition for the party wronged in due course. He, Bloom, enjoyed the distinction of being close to Erin's uncrowned king in the flesh when the thing occurred on the historic *fracas* when the fallen leader's – who notoriously stuck to his guns to the last drop even when clothed in the mantle of adultery – (leader's) trusty henchmen to the number of ten or a dozen or possibly even more than that penetrated into the printing works of the *Insuppressible* or no it was *United Ireland* (a by no means, by the by, appropriate appellative) and broke up the typecases with hammers or something like that all on account of some scurrilous effusions from the facile pens of the O'Brienite scribes at the usual mudslinging occupation, reflecting on the erstwhile tribune's private morals. Though palpably a radically altered man, he was still a commanding figure, though carelessly garbed as usual, with that look of settled purpose which went a long way with the shillyshallyers till they discovered to their vast discomfiture that their idol had feet of clay, after placing him upon a pedestal, which she, however, was the first to perceive. As those were particularly hot times in the general hullaballoo Bloom sustained a minor injury from a nasty prod of some chap's elbow in the crowd that of course congregated lodging some place about the pit of the stomach, fortunately not of a grave character. His hat (Parnell's) was inadvertently knocked off and, as a matter of strict history, Bloom was the man who picked it up in the crush after witnessing the occurrence meaning to return it to him (and return it to him he did with the utmost celerity) who, panting and hatless and whose thoughts were miles away from his hat at the time, being a gentleman born with a stake in the country, he, as a matter of fact, having gone into it more for the kudos of the thing than anything else, what's bred in the bone, instilled into him in infancy at his mother's knee in the shape of knowing what good form was came out at once because he turned round to the donor and thanked him with perfect *aplomb*, saying: *Thank you, sir* though in a very different tone of voice from the ornament of the legal profession whose headgear Bloom also set to rights earlier in the course of the day, history repeating itself with a difference; after the burial of a mutual friend when they had left him alone in his glory after the grim task of having committed his remains to the grave.

On the other hand what incensed him more inwardly was the blatant jokes of the cabmen and so on, who passed it all off as a jest, laughing immoderately, pretending to understand everything, the why and the wherefore, and in reality not knowing their own minds, it being a case for the two parties themselves unless it ensued that the legitimate husband happened to be a party to it owing to some anonymous letter from the usual boy Jones, who happened to come across them at the crucial moment in a loving position locked in one another's arms drawing attention to their illicit proceedings and leading up to a domestic rumpus and the erring fair one begging forgiveness of her lord and master upon her knees and promising to sever the connection and not receive his visits any more if only the aggrieved husband would overlook the matter and let bygones be bygones, with tears in her eyes, though possibly with her tongue in her fair cheek at the same time, as quite possibly there were several others. He personally, being of a sceptical bias, believed, and didn't make the smallest bones about saying so either, that man, or men in the plural, were always hanging around on the waiting list about a lady, even supposing she was the best wife in the world and they got on fairly well together for the sake of argument, when, neglecting her duties, she chose to be tired of wedded life, and was on for a little flutter in polite debauchery to press their attentions on her with improper intent, the upshot being that her affections centred on another, the cause of many *liaisons* between still attractive married women getting on for fair and forty and younger men, no doubt as several famous cases of feminine infatuation proved up to the hilt.

It was a thousand pities a young fellow blessed with an allowance of brains, as his neighbour obviously was, should waste his valuable time with profligate women, who might present him with a nice dose to last him his lifetime. In the nature of single blessedness he would one day take unto himself a wife when Miss Right came on the scene but in the interim ladies' society was a *conditio sine qua non* though he had the gravest possible doubts, not that he wanted in the smallest to pump Stephen about Miss Ferguson (who was very possibly the particular lodestar who brought him down to Irishtown so early in the morning), as to whether he would find much satisfaction basking in the boy and girl courtship idea and the company of smirking misses without a penny to their names bi- or tri-weekly with the orthodox preliminary canter of complimentpaying and walking out leading up to fond lovers' ways and flowers and chocs. To think of him house and homeless, rooked by some landladly worse than any stepmother, was really too bad at his age. The queer suddenly things he popped out with attracted the elder man who was several years the other's senior or like his father. But something substantial he certainly ought to eat, were it only an eggflip made on unadulterated maternal nutriment or, failing that, the homely Humpty Dumpty boiled.

– At what o'clock did you dine? he questioned of the slim form and tired though unwrinkled face.

– Some time yesterday, Stephen said.

– Yesterday, exclaimed Bloom till he remembered it was already tomorrow, Friday. Ah, you mean it's after twelve!

– The day before yesterday, Stephen said, improving on himself.

Literally astounded at this piece of intelligence, Bloom reflected. Though they didn't see eye to eye in everything, a certain analogy there somehow was, as if both their minds were travelling, so to speak, in the one train of thought. At his age when dabbling in politics roughly some score of years previously when he had been a *quasi* aspirant to parliamentary honours in the Buckshot Foster days he too recollected in retrospect (which was a source of keen satisfaction in itself) he had a sneaking regard for those same ultra ideas. For instance, when the evicted tenants' question, then at its first inception, bulked largely in people's minds though, it goes without saying, not contributing a copper or pinning his faith absolutely to its dictums, some of which wouldn't exactly hold water, he at the outset in principle, at all events, was in thorough sympathy with peasant possession, as voicing the trend of modern opinion, a partiality, however, which, realising his mistake, he was subsequently partially cured of, and even was twitted with going a step further than Michael Davitt in the striking views he at one time inculcated as a backtothelander, which was one reason he strongly resented the innuendo put upon him in so barefaced a fashion at the gathering of the clans in Barney Kiernan's so that he, though often considerably misunderstood and the least pugnacious of mortals, be it repeated, departed from his customary habit to give him (metaphorically) one in the gizzard though so far as politics themselves were concerned, he was only too conscious of the casualties invariably resulting from propaganda and displays of mutual animosity and the misery and suffering it entailed as a foregone conclusion on fine young fellows, chiefly, destruction of the fittest, in a word.

Anyhow, upon weighing the pros and cons, getting on for one as it was, it was high time to be retiring for the night. The crux was it was a bit risky to bring him home as eventualities might possibly ensue (somebody having a temper of her own sometimes) and spoil the hash altogether as on the night he misguidedly brought home a dog (breed unknown) with a lame paw, not that the cases were either identical or the reverse, though he had hurt his hand too, to Ontario Terrace, as he very distinctly remembered, having been there, so to speak. On the other hand it was altogether far and away too late for the Sandymount or Sandycove suggestion so that he was in some perplexity as to which of the two alternatives . . . Everything pointed to the fact that it behoved him to avail himself to the full of the opportunity, all things considered. His initial impression was that he was a bit standoffish or not over effusive but it grew on him someway. For one thing he mightn't what you call jump at the idea, if approached, and what mostly worried him was he didn't know how to lead up to it or word it exactly, supposing he did entertain the proposal, as it would afford him very great personal pleasure if he would allow him to help to put coin in his way or some wardrobe, if found suitable. At all events he wound up by concluding, eschewing for the nonce hidebound precedent, a cup of Epps's cocoa and a shakedown for the night plus the use of a rug or two and overcoat doubled into a pillow. At least he would be in safe hands and as warm as a toast on a trivet. He failed to perceive any very vast amount of harm in that always with the proviso no rumpus of any sort was kicked up. A move had to be made because that merry old soul, the grasswidower in question who appeared to be glued to the spot, didn't appear in any particular hurry to wend his way home to his dearly beloved Queenstown and it was highly likely some sponger's bawdy-house of retired beauties off Sheriff street lower would be the best clue to that equivocal character's whereabouts for a few days to come, alternately racking their feelings (the mermaids') with sixchamber revolver anecdotes verging on the tropical calculated to freeze the marrow of anybody's bones and mauling their largesized charms betweenwhiles with rough and tumble gusto to the accompaniment of large potations of potheen and the usual blarney about himself for as to who he in reality was let XX equal my right name and address, as Mr Algebra remarks *passim*. At the same time he inwardly chuckled over his repartee to the blood and ouns champion about his God being a jew. People could put up with being bitten by a wolf but what properly riled them was a bite from a sheep. The most vulnerable point too of tender Achilles, your God was a jew, because mostly they appeared to imagine he came from Carrick-on-Shannon or somewhere about in the county Sligo.

– I propose, our hero eventually suggested, after mature reflection while prudently pocketing her photo, as it's rather stuffy here, you just come with me and talk things over. My diggings are quite close in the vicinity. You can't drink that stuff. Wait, I'll just pay this lot.

The best plan clearly being to clear out, the remainder being plain sailing, he beckoned, while prudently pocketing the photo, to the keeper of the shanty, who didn't seem to . . .

– Yes, that's the best, he assured Stephen, to whom for the matter of that Brazen Head or him or anywhere else was all more or less . . .

All kinds of Utopian plans were flashing through his (Bloom's) busy brain. Education (the genuine article), literature, journalism, prize titbits, up to date billing, hydros and concert tours in English watering resorts packed with theatres, turning money away, duets in Italian with the accent perfectly true to nature and a quantity of other things, no necessity of course to tell the world and his wife from the housetops about it and a slice of luck. An opening was all was wanted. Because he more than suspected he had his father's voice to bank his hopes on which it was quite on the cards he had so it would be just as well, by the way no harm, to trail the conversation in the direction of that particular red herring just to . . .

The cabby read out of the paper he had got hold of that the former viceroy, earl Cadogan, had presided at the cabdrivers' association dinner in London somewhere. Silence with a yawn or two accompanied this thrilling announcement. Then the old specimen in the corner who appeared to have some spark of vitality left read out that sir Anthony MacDonnell had left Euston for the chief secretary's lodge or words to that effect. To which absorbing piece of intelligence echo answered why.

– Give us a squint at that literature, grandfather, the ancient mariner put in, manifesting some natural impatience.

– And welcome, answered the elderly party thus addressed.

The sailor lugged out from a case he had a pair of greenish goggles which he very slowly hooked over his nose and both ears.

– Are you bad in the eyes? the sympathetic personage like the town clerk queried.

– Why, answered the seafarer with the tartan beard, who seemingly was a bit of a literary cove in his own small way, staring out of seagreen portholes as you might well describe them as, I uses goggles reading. Sand in the Red Sea done that. One time I could read a book in the dark, manner of speaking. *The Arabian Nights Entertainment* was my favourite and *Red as a Rose is She*.

Thereupon he pawed the journal open and pored upon Lord only knows what, found drowned or the exploits of King Willow, Iremonger having made a hundred and something second wicket not out for Notts, during which time (completely regardless of Ire) the keeper was intensely occupied loosening an apparently new or secondhand boot which manifestly pinched him, as he muttered against whoever it was sold it, all of them who were sufficiently awake enough to be picked out by their facial expressions, that is to say, either simply looking on glumly or passing a trivial remark.

To cut a long story short Bloom, grasping the situation, was the first to rise to his feet so as not to outstay their welcome having first and foremost, being as good as his word that he would foot the bill for the occasion, taken the wise precaution to unobtrusively motion to mine host as a parting shot a scarcely perceptible sign when the others were not looking to the effect that the amount due was forthcoming, making a grand total of fourpence (the amount he deposited unobtrusively in four coppers, literally the last of the Mohicans) he having previously spotted on the printed pricelist for all who ran to read opposite to him in unmistakable figures, coffee 2d., confectionery do., and honestly well worth twice the money once in a way, as Wetherup used to remark.

– Come, he counselled, to close the *séance*.

Seeing that the ruse worked and the coast was clear, they left the shelter or shanty together and the *élite* society of oilskin and company whom nothing short of an earthquake would move out of their *dolce far niente*. Stephen, who confessed to still feeling poorly and fagged out, paused at the, for a moment . . . the door to . . .

– One thing I never understood, he said, to be original on the spur of the moment, why they put tables upside down at night, I mean chairs upside down on the tables in cafés.

To which impromptu the neverfailing Bloom replied without a moment's hesitation, saying straight off:

– To sweep the floor in the morning.

So saying he skipped around nimbly, considering frankly, at the same time apologetic, to get on his companion's right, a habit of his, by the by, the right side being, in classical idiom, his tender Achilles. The night air was certainly now a treat to breathe though Stephen was a bit weak on his pins.

– It will (the air) do you good, Bloom said, meaning also the walk, in a moment. The only thing is to walk then you'll feel a different man. It's not far. Lean on me.

Accordingly he passed his left arm in Stephen's right and led him on accordingly.

– Yes, Stephen said uncertainly, because he thought he felt a strange kind of flesh of a different man approach him, sinewless and wobbly and all that.

Anyhow, they passed the sentrybox with stones, brazier, etc. where the municipal supernumerary, ex-Gumley, was still to all intents and purposes wrapped in the arms of Murphy, as the adage has it, dreaming of fresh fields and pastures new. And *apropos* of coffin of stones, the analogy was not at all bad, as it was in fact a stoning to death on the part of seventytwo out of eighty odd constituencies that ratted at the time of the split and chiefly the belauded peasant class, probably the selfsame evicted tenants he had put in their holdings.

So they passed on to chatting about music, a form of art for which Bloom, as a pure amateur, possessed the greatest love, as they made tracks arm-in-arm across Beresford place. Wagnerian music, though confessedly grand in its way, was a bit too heavy for Bloom and hard to follow at the first go-off but the music of Mercadante's *Huguenots*, Meyerbeer's *Seven Last Words on the Cross*, and Mozart's *Twelfth Mass*, he simply revelled in, the *Gloria* in that being to his mind the acme of first class music as such, literally knocking everything else into a cocked hat. He infinitely preferred the sacred music of the catholic church to anything the opposite shop could offer in that line such as those Moody and Sankey hymns or *Bid me to live and I will live thy protestant to be*. He also yielded to none in his admiration of Rossini's *Stabat Mater*, a work simply abounding in immortal numbers, in which his wife, Madam Marion Tweedy, made a hit, a veritable sensation, he might safely say greatly adding to her other laurels and putting the others totally in the shade in the jesuit fathers' church in Upper Gardiner street, the sacred edifice being thronged to the doors to hear her with virtuosos, or *virtuosi* rather. There was the unanimous opinion that there was none to come up to her and, suffice it to say in a place of worship for music of a sacred character, there was a generally voiced desire for an encore. On the whole, though favouring preferably light opera of the *Don Giovanni* description, and *Martha*, a gem in its line, he had a *penchant*, though with only a surface knowledge, for the severe classical school such as Mendelssohn. And talking of that, taking it for granted he knew all about the old favourites, he mentioned *par excellence* Lionel's air in *Martha*, *M'appari*, which, curiously enough, he heard, or overheard, to be more accurate, on yesterday, a privilege he keenly appreciated, from the lips of Stephen's respected father, sung to perfection, a study of the number, in fact, which made all the others take a back seat. Stephen, in reply to a politely put query, said he didn't but launched out into praises of Shakespeare's songs, at least of in or about that period, the lutenist Dowland who lived in Fetter Lane near Gerard the herbalist, who *anno ludendo hausi, Doulandus*, an instrument he was contemplating purchasing from Mr Arnold Dolmetsch, whom Bloom did not quite recall, though the name certainly sounded familiar, for sixtyfive guineas and Farnaby and son with their *dux* and *comes* conceits and Byrd (William), who played the virginals, he said, in the Queen's Chapel or anywhere else he found them and one Tomkins who made toys or airs and John Bull.

On the roadway which they were approaching whilst still speaking beyond the swing chain, a horse, dragging a sweeper, paced on the paven ground, brushing a long swathe of mire up so that with the noise Bloom was not perfectly certain whether he had caught aright the allusion to sixtyfive guineas and John Bull. He inquired if it was John Bull the political celebrity of that ilk, as it struck him, the two identical names, as a striking coincidence.

By the chains, the horse slowly swerved to turn, which perceiving, Bloom, who was keeping a sharp lookout as usual plucked the other's sleeve gently, jocosely remarking:

– Our lives are in peril to night. Beware of the steamroller.

They thereupon stopped. Bloom looked at the head of a horse not worth anything like sixtyfive guineas, suddenly in evidence in the dark quite near, so that it seemed new, a different grouping of bones and even flesh, because palpably it was a fourwalker, a hipshaker, a blackbuttocker, a taildangler, a headhanger, putting his hind foot foremost the while the lord of his creation sat on the perch, busy with his thoughts. But such a good poor brute, he was sorry he hadn't a lump of sugar but, as he wisely reflected, you could scarcely be prepared for every emergency that might crop up. He was just a big foolish nervous noodly kind of a horse, without a second care in the world. But even a dog, he reflected, take that mongrel in Barney Kiernan's, of the same size, would be a holy horror to face. But it was no animal's fault in particular if he was built that way like the camel, ship of the desert, distilling grapes into potheen in his hump. Nine tenths of them all could be caged or trained, nothing beyond the art of man barring the bees; whale with a harpoon hairpin, alligator, tickle the small of his back and he sees the joke; chalk a circle for a rooster; tiger, my eagle eye. These timely reflections anent the brutes of the field occupied his mind, somewhat distracted from Stephen's words, while the ship of the street was manœuvring and Stephen went on about the highly interesting old . . .

– What's this I was saying? Ah, yes! My wife, he intimated, plunging *in medias res*, would have the greatest of pleasure in making your acquaintance as she is passionately attached to music of any kind.

He looked sideways in a friendly fashion at the sideface of Stephen, image of his mother, which was not quite the same as the usual blackguard type they unquestionably had an indubitable hankering after as he was perhaps not that way built.

Still, supposing he had his father's gift, as he more than suspected, it opened up new vistas in his mind, such as Lady Fingall's Irish industries concert on the preceding Monday, and aristocracy in general.

Exquisite variations he was now describing on an air *Youth here has End* by Jans Pieter Sweelinck, a Dutchman of Amsterdam where the frows come from. Even more he liked an old German song of *Johannes Jeep* about the clear sea and the voices of sirens, sweet murderers of men, which boggled Bloom a bit:

Von der Sirenen Listigkeit
Tun die Poeten dichten.

These opening bars he sang and translated *extempore*. Bloom, nodding, said he perfectly understood and begged him to go on by all means, which he did.

A phenomenally beautiful tenor voice like that, the rarest of boons, which Bloom appreciated at the very first note he got out, could easily, if properly handled by some recognised authority on voice production such as Barraclough and being able to read music into the bargain, command its own price where baritones were ten a penny and procure for its fortunate possessor in the near future an *entrée* into fashionable houses in the best residential quarters, of financial magnates in a large way of business and titled people where, with his university degree of B. A. (a huge ad in its way) and gentlemanly bearing to all the more influence the good impression he would infallibly score a distinct success, being blessed with brains which also could be utilised for the purpose and other requisites, if his clothes were properly attended to, so as to the better worm his way into their good graces as he, a youthful tyro in society's sartorial niceties, hardly understood how a little thing like that could militate against you. It was in fact only a matter of months and he could easily foresee him participating in their musical and artistic *conversaziones* during the festivities of the Christmas season, for choice, causing a slight flutter in the dovecotes of the fair sex and being made a lot of by ladies out for sensation, cases of which, as he happened to know, were on record, in fact, without giving the show away, he himself once upon a time, if he cared to, could easily have . . . Added to which of course, would be the pecuniary emolument by no means to be sneezed at, going hand in hand with his tuition fees. Not, he parenthesised, that for the sake of filthy lucre he need necessarily embrace the lyric platform as a walk in life for any lengthy space of time but a step in the required direction it was, beyond yea or nay, and both monetarily and mentally it contained no reflection on his dignity in the smallest and it often turned in uncommonly handy to be handed a cheque at a muchneeded moment when every little helped. Besides, though taste latterly had deteriorated to a degree, original music like that, different from the conventional rut, would rapidly have a great vogue, as it would be a decided novelty for Dublin's musical world after the usual hackneyed run of catchy tenor solos foisted on a confiding public by Ivan St Austell and Hilton St Just and their *genus omne*. Yes, beyond a shadow of a doubt, he could, with all the cards in his hand and he had a capital opening to make a name for himself and win a high place in the city's esteem where he could command a stiff figure and, booking ahead, give a grand concert for the patrons of the King street house, given a backerup, if one were forthcoming to kick him upstairs, so to speak – a big *if*, however – with some impetus of the goahead sort to obviate the inevitable procrastination which often tripped up a too much fêted prince of good fellows and it need not detract from the other by one iota as, being his own master, he would have heaps of time to practise literature in his spare moments when desirous of so doing without its clashing with his vocal career or containing anything derogatory whatsoever as it was a matter for himself alone. In fact, he had the ball at his feet and that was the very reason why the other, possessed of a remarkably sharp nose for smelling a rat of any sort, hung on to him at all.

The horse was just then . . . and later on, at a propitious opportunity he purposed (Bloom did), without anyway prying into his private affairs on the *fools step in where angels* principle advising him to sever his connection with a certain budding practitioner, who, he noticed, was prone to disparage, and even, to a slight extent, with some hilarious pretext, when not present, deprecate him, or whatever you like to call it, which, in Bloom's humble opinion, threw a nasty sidelight on that side of a person's character – no pun intended.

The horse, having reached the end of his tether, so to speak, halted, and, rearing high a proud feathering tail, added his quota by letting fall on the floor, which the brush would soon brush up and polish, three smoking globes of turds. Slowly, three times, one after another, from a full crupper, he mired. And humanely his driver waited till he (or she) had ended, patient in his scythed car.

Side by side Bloom, profiting by the *contretemps*, with Stephen passed through the gap of the chains, divided by the upright, and, stepping over a strand of mire, went across towards Gardiner street lower, Stephen singing more boldly, but not loudly, the end of the ballad:

Und alle Schiffe brücken.

The driver never said a word, good, bad or indifferent. He merely watched the two figures, as he sat on his lowbacked car, both black – one full, one lean – walk towards the railway bridge, *to be married by Father Maher*. As they walked, they at times stopped and walked again, continuing their *tête-à-tête* (which of course he was utterly out of), about sirens, enemies of man's reason, mingled with a number of other topics of the same category, usurpers, historical cases of the kind while the man in the sweeper car or you might as well call it in the sleeper car who in any case couldn't possibly hear because they were too far simply sat in his seat near the end of lower Gardiner street *and looked after their lowbacked car.*

*   *   *   *   *

◀ WHAT PARALLEL COURSES DID BLOOM AND STEPHEN follow returning?

Starting united both at normal walking pace from Beresford place they followed in the order named Lower and Middle Gardiner streets and Mountjoy square, west: then, at reduced pace, each bearing left, Gardiner's place by an inadvertence as far as the farther corner of Temple street, north: then at reduced pace with interruptions of halt, bearing right, Temple street, north, as far as Hardwicke place. Approaching, disparate, at relaxed walking pace they crossed both the circus before George's church diametrically, the chord in any circle being less than the arc which it subtends.

Of what did the duumvirate deliberate during their itinerary?

Music, literature, Ireland, Dublin, Paris, friendship, woman, prostitution, diet, the influence of gaslight or the light of arc and glowlamps on the growth of adjoining paraheliotropic trees, exposed corporation emergency dustbuckets, the Roman catholic church, ecclesiastical celibacy, the Irish nation, jesuit education, careers, the study of medicine, the past day, the maleficent influence of the presabbath, Stephen's collapse.

Did Bloom discover common factors of similarity between their respective like and unlike reactions to experience?

Both were sensitive to artistic impressions musical in preference to plastic or pictorial. Both preferred a continental to an insular manner of life, a cisatlantic to a transatlantic place of residence. Both indurated by early domestic training and an inherited tenacity of heterodox resistance professed their disbelief in many orthodox religious, national, social and ethical doctrines. Both admitted the alternately stimulatng and obtunding influence of heterosexual magnetism.

Were their views on some points divergent?

Stephen dissented openly from Bloom's views on the importance of dietary and civic selfhelp while Bloom dissented tacitly from Stephen's views on the eternal affirmation of the spirit of man in literature. Bloom assented covertly to Stephen's rectification of the anachronism involved in assigning the date of the conversion of the Irish nation to christianity from druidism by Patrick son of Calpornus, son of Potitus, son of Odyssus, sent by pope Celestine I in the year 432 in the reign of Leary to the year 260 or thereabouts in the reign of Cormac MacArt († 266 A.D.) suffocated by imperfect deglutition of aliment at Sletty and interred at Rossnaree. The collapse which Bloom ascribed to gastric inanition and certain chemical compounds of varying degrees of adulteration and alcoholic strength, accelerated by mental exertion and the velocity of rapid circular motion in a relaxing atmosphere, Stephen attributed to the reapparition of a matutinal cloud (perceived by both from two different points of observation, Sandycove and Dublin) at first no bigger than a woman's hand.

Was there one point on which their views were equal and negative?

The influence of gaslight or electric light on the growth of adjoining paraheliotropic trees.

Had Bloom discussed similar subjects during nocturnal perambulations in the past?

In 1884 with Owen Goldberg and Cecil Turnbull at night on public thoroughfares between Longwood avenue and Leonard's corner and Leonard's corner and Synge street and Synge street and Bloomfield avenue. In 1885 with Percy Apjohn in the evenings, reclined against the wall between Gibraltar villa and Bloomfield house in Crumlin, barony of Uppercross. In 1886 occasionally with casual acquaintances and prospective purchasers on doorsteps, in front parlours, in third class railway carriages of suburban lines. In 1888 frequently with major Brian Tweedy and his daughter Miss Marion Tweedy, together and separately on the lounge in Matthew Dillon's house in Roundtown. Once in 1892 and once in 1893 with Julius Mastiansky, on both occasions in the parlour of his (Bloom's) house in Lombard street, west.

What reflection concerning the irregular sequence of dates 1884, 1885, 1886, 1888, 1892, 1893, 1904 did Bloom make before their arrival at their destination?

He reflected that the progressive extension of the field of individual development and experience was regressively accompanied by a restriction of the converse domain of interindividual relations.

As in what ways?

From inexistence to existence he came to many and was as one received: existence with existence he was with any as any with any: from existence to nonexistence gone he would be by all as none perceived.

What action did Bloom make on their arrival at their destination?

At the housesteps of the 4th of the equidifferent uneven numbers, number 7 Eccles street, he inserted his hand mechanically into the back pocket of his trousers to obtain his latchkey.

Was it there?

It was in the corresponding pocket of the trousers which he had worn on the day but one preceding.

Why was he doubly irritated?

Because he had forgotten and because he remembered that he had reminded himself twice not to forget.

What were then the alternatives before the, premeditatedly (respectively) and inadvertently, keyless couple?

To enter or not to enter. To knock or not to knock.

Bloom's decision?

A stratagem. Resting his feet on the dwarf wall, he climbed over the area railings, compressed his hat on his head, grasped two points at the lower union of rails and stiles, lowered his body gradually by its length of five feet nine inches and a half to within two feet ten inches of the area pavement, and allowed his body to move freely in space by separating himself from the railings and crouching in preparation for the impact of the fall.

Did he fall?

By his body's known weight of eleven stone and four pounds in avoirdupois measure, as certified by the graduated machine for periodical self-weighing in the premises of Francis Frœdman, pharmaceutical chemist of 19 Frederick street, north, on the last feast of the Ascension, to wit, the twelfth day of May of the bissextile year one thousand nine hundred and four of the christian era (jewish era five thousand six hundred and sixtyfour, mohammedan era one thousand three hundred and twentytwo), golden number 5, epact 13, solar cycle 9, dominical letters C B, Roman indication 2, Julian period 6617, MXMIV.

Did he rise uninjured by concussion?

Regaining new stable equilibrium he rose uninjured though concussed by the impact, raised the latch of the area door by the exertion of force at its freely moving flange and by leverage of the first kind applied at its fulcrum gained retarded access to the kitchen through the subadjacent scullery, ignited a lucifer match by friction, set free inflammable coal gas by turning on the ventcock, lit a high flame which, by regulating, he reduced to quiescent candescence and lit finally a portable candle.

What discrete succession of images did Stephen meanwhile perceive?

Reclined against the area railings he perceived through the transparent kitchen panes a man regulating a gasflame of 14 C P, a man lighting a candle, a man removing in turn each of his two boots, a man leaving the kitchen holding a candle of 1 C P.

Did the man reappear elsewhere?

After a lapse of four minutes the glimmer of his candle was discernible through the semitransparent semicircular glass fanlight over the halldoor. The halldoor turned gradually on its hinges. In the open space of the doorway the man reappeared without his hat, with his candle.

Did Stephen obey his sign?

Yes, entering softly, he helped to close and chain the door and followed softly along the hallway the man's back and listed feet and lighted candle past a lighted crevice of doorway on the left and carefully down a turning staircase of more than five steps into the kitchen of Bloom's house.

What did Bloom do?

He extinguished the candle by a sharp expiration of breath upon its flame, drew two spoonseat deal chairs to the hearthstone, one for Stephen with its back to the area window, the other for himself when necessary, knelt on one knee, composed in the grate a pyre of crosslaid resintipped sticks and various coloured papers and irregular polygons of best Abram coal at twentyone shillings a ton from the yard of Messrs Flower and M'Donald of 14 D'Olier street, kindled it at three projecting points of paper with one ignited lucifer match, thereby releasing the potential energy contained in the fuel by allowing its carbon and hydrogen elements to enter into free union with the oxygen of the air.

Of what similar apparitions did Stephen think?

Of others elsewhere in other times who, kneeling on one knee or on two, had kindled fires for him, of Brother Michael in the infirmary of the college of the Society of Jesus at Clongowes Wood, Sallins, in the county of Kildare: of his father, Simon Dedalus, in an unfurnished room of his first residence in Dublin, number thirteen Fitzgibbon street: of his godmother Miss Kate Morkan in the house of her dying sister Miss Julia Morkan at 15 Usher's Island: of his mother Mary, wife of Simon Dedalus, in the kitchen of number twelve North Richmond street on the morning of the feast of Saint Francis-Xavier 1898: of the dean of studies, Father Butt, in the physics' theatre of university College, 16 Stephen's green, north: of his sister Dilly (Delia) in his father's house in Cabra.

What did Stephen see on raising his gaze to the height of a yard from the fire towards the opposite wall?

Under a row of five coiled spring housebells a curvilinear rope, stretched between two holdfasts athwart across the recess beside the chimney pier, from which hung four small-sized square handkerchiefs folded unattached consecutively in adjacent rectangles and one pair of ladies' grey hose with lisle suspender tops and feet in their habitual position clamped by three erect wooden pegs two at their outer extremities and the third at their point of junction.

What did Bloom see on the range?

On the right (smaller) hob a blue enamelled saucepan: on the left (larger) hob a black iron kettle.

What did Bloom do at the range?

He removed the saucepan to the left hob, rose and carried the iron kettle to the sink in order to tap the current by turning the faucet to let it flow.

Did it flow?

Yes. From Roundwood reservoir in county Wicklow of a cubic capacity of 2,400 million gallons, percolating through a subterranean aqueduct of filter mains of single and double pipeage constructed at an initial plant cost of £5 per linear yard by way of the Dargle, Rathdown, Glen of the Downs and Callowhill to the 26 acre reservoir at Stillorgan, a distance of 22 statute miles, and thence, through a system of relieving tanks, by a gradient of 250 feet to the city boundary at Eustace bridge, upper Leeson street, though from prolonged summer drouth and daily supply of 12 1/2 million gallons the water had fallen below the sill of the overflow weir for which reason the borough surveyor and waterworks engineer, Mr Spencer Harty, C. E., on the instructions of the waterworks committee, had prohibited the use of municipal water for purposes other than those of consumption (envisaging the possibility of recourse being had to the impotable water of the Grand and Royal canals as in 1893) particularly as the South Dublin Guardians, notwithstanding their ration of 15 gallons per day per pauper supplied through a 6 inch meter, had been convicted of a wastage of 20,000 gallons per night by a reading of their meter on the affirmation of the law agent of the corporation, Mr Ignatius Rice, solicitor, thereby acting to the detriment of another section of the public, selfsupporting taxpayers, solvent, sound.

What in water did Bloom, waterlover, drawer of water, watercarrier returning to the range, admire?

Its universality: its democratic equality and constancy to its nature in seeking its own level: its vastness in the ocean of Mercator's projection: its unplumbed profundity in the Sundam trench of the Pacific exceeding 8,000 fathoms: the restlessness of its waves and surface particles visiting in turn all points of its seaboard: the independence of its units: the variability of states of sea: its hydrostatic quiescence in calm: its hydrokinetic turgidity in neap and spring tides: its subsidence after devastation: its sterility in the circumpolar icecaps, arctic and antarctic: its climatic and commercial significance: its preponderance of 3 to 1 over the dry land of the globe: its indisputable hegemony extending in square leagues over all the region below the subequatorial tropic of Capricorn: the multisecular stability of its primeval basin: its luteofulvous bed: its capacity to dissolve and hold in solution all soluble substances including millions of tons of the most precious metals: its slow erosions of peninsulas and downwardtending promontories: its alluvial deposits: its weight and volume and density: its imperturbability in lagoons and highland tarns: its gradation of colours in the torrid and temperate and frigid zones: its vehicular ramifications in continental lake-contained streams and confluent oceanflowing rivers with their tributaries and transoceanic currents: gulfstream, north and south equatorial courses: its violence in seaquakes, waterspouts, artesian wells, eruptions, torrents, eddies, freshets, spates, groundswells, watersheds, waterpartings, geysers, cataracts, whirlpools, maelstroms, inundations, deluges, cloudbursts: its vast circumterrestrial ahorizontal curve: its secrecy in springs, and latent humidity, revealed by rhabdomantic or hygrometric instruments and exemplified by the hole in the wall at Ashtown gate, saturation of air, distillation of dew: the simplicity of its composition, two constituent parts of hydrogen with one constituent part of oxygen: its healing virtues: its buoyancy in the waters of the Dead Sea: its persevering penetrativeness in runnels, gullies, inadequate dams, leaks on shipboard: its properties for cleansing, quenching thirst and fire, nourishing vegetation: its infallibility as paradigm and paragon: its metamorphoses as vapour, mist, cloud, rain, sleet, snow, hail: its strength in rigid hydrants: its variety of forms in loughs and bays and gulfs and bights and guts and lagoons and atolls and archipelagos and sounds and fjords and minches and tidal estuaries and arms of sea: its solidity in glaciers, icebergs, icefloes: its docility in working hydraulic millwheels, turbines, dynamos, electric power stations, bleach-works, tanneries, scutchmills: its utility in canals, rivers, if navigable, floating and graving docks: its potentiality derivable from harnessed tides or water-courses falling from level to level: its submarine fauna and flora (anacoustic, photophobe) numerically, if not literally, the inhabitants of the globe: its ubiquity as constituting 90% of the human body: the noxiousness of its effluvia in lacustrine marshes, pestilential fens, faded flower-water, stagnant pools in the waning moon.

Having set the halffilled kettle on the now burning coals, why did he return to the stillflowing tap?

To wash his soiled hands with a partially consumed tablet of Barrington's lemonflavoured soap, to which paper still adhered (bought thirteen hours previously for fourpence and still unpaid for), in fresh cold neverchanging everchanging water and dry them, face and hands, in a long redbordered holland cloth passed over a wooden revolving roller.

What reason did Stephen give for declining Bloom's offer?

That he was hydrophobe, hating partial contact by immersion or total by submersion in cold water (his last bath having taken place in the month of October of the preceding year), disliking the aqueous substances of glass and crystal, distrusting aquacities of thought and language.

What impeded Bloom from giving Stephen counsels of hygiene and prophylactic to which should be added suggestions concerning a preliminary wetting of the head and contraction of the muscles with rapid splashing of the face and neck and thoracic and epigastric region in case of sea or river bathing, the parts of the human anatomy most sensitive to cold being the nape, stomach and thenar or sole of foot?

The incompatibility of aquacity with the erratic originality of genius.

What additional didactic counsels did he similarly repress?

Dietary: concerning the respective percentage of protein and caloric energy in bacon, salt ling and butter, the absence of the former in the lastnamed and the abundance of the latter in the firstnamed.

Which seemed to the host to be the predominant qualities of his guest?
Confidence in himself, an equal and opposite power of abandonment and recuperation.

What concomitant phenomenon took place in the vessel of liquid by the agency of fire?
The phenomenon of ebullition. Fanned by a constant updraught of ventilation between the kitchen and the chimneyflue, ignition was communicated from the faggots of precombustible fuel to polyhedral masses of bituminous coal, containing in compressed mineral from the foliated fossilised decidua of primeval forests which had in turn derived their vegetative existence from the sun, primal source of heat (radiant), transmitted through omnipresent luminiferous diathermanous ether. Heat (convected), a mode of motion developed by such combustion, was constantly and increasingly conveyed from the source of calorification to the liquid contained in the vessel, being radiated through the uneven unpolished dark surface of the metal iron, in part reflected, in part absorbed, in part transmitted, gradually raising the temperature of the water from normal to boiling point, a rise in temperature expressible as the result of an expenditure of 72 thermal units needed to raise 1 pound of water from 50° to 212° Fahrenheit.

What announced the accomplishment of this rise in temperature?
A double falciform ejection of water vapour from under the kettlelid at both sides simultaneously.

For what personal purpose could Bloom have applied the water so boiled?
To shave himself.

What advantages attended shaving by night?
A softer beard: a softer brush if intentionally allowed to remain from shave to shave in its agglutinated lather: a softer skin if unexpectedly encountering female acquaintances in remote places at incustomary hours: quiet reflections upon the course of the day: a cleaner sensation when awaking after a fresher sleep since matutinal noises, premonitions and perturbations, a clattered milkcan, a postman's double knock, a paper read,

reread while lathering, relathering the same spot, a shock, a shoot, with thought of aught he sought though fraught with nought might cause a faster rate of shaving and a nick on which incision plaster with precision cut and humected and applied adhered which was to be done.

Why did absence of light disturb him less than presence of noise?

Because of the surety of the sense of touch in his firm full masculine feminine passive active hand.

What quality did it (his hand) possess but with what counteracting influence?

The operative surgical quality but that he was reluctant to shed human blood even when the end justified the means, preferring, in their natural order, heliotherapy, psychophysicotherapeutics, osteopathic surgery.

What lay under exposure on the lower middle and upper shelves of the kitchen dresser opened by Bloom?

On the lower shelf five vertical breakfast plates, six horizontal breakfast saucers on which rested inverted breakfast cups, a moustachecup, uninverted, and saucer of Crown Derby, four white goldrimmed eggcups, and open shammy purse displaying coins, mostly copper, and a phial of aromatic violet comfits. On the middle shelf a chipped eggcup containing pepper, a drum of table salt, four conglomerated black olives in oleaginous paper, an empty pot of Plumtree's potted meat, an oval wicker basket bedded with fibre and containing one Jersey pear, a halfempty bottle of William Gilbey and Co's white invalid port, half disrobed of its swathe of coralpink tissue paper, a packet of Epps's soluble cocoa, five ounces of Anne Lynch's choice tea at 2/- per lb. in a crinkled leadpaper bag, a cylindrical canister containing the best crystallised lump sugar, two onions, one the larger, Spanish, entire, the other, smaller, Irish, bisected with augmented surface and more redolent, a jar of Irish Model Dairy's cream, a jug of brown crockery containing a noggin and a quarter of soured adulterated milk, converted by heat into water, acidulous serum and semisolidified curds, which added to the quantity subtracted for Mr Bloom's and Mrs Fleming's breakfasts made one imperial pint, the total quantity originally delivered, two cloves, a halfpenny and a small dish containing a slice of fresh ribsteak. On the upper shelf a battery of jamjars of various sizes and proveniences.

What attracted his attention lying on the apron of the dresser?

Four polygonal fragments of two lacerated scarlet betting tickets, numbered 8 87, 8 86.

What reminiscences temporarily corrugated his brow?

Reminiscences of coincidences, truth stranger than fiction, preindicative of the result of the Gold Cup flat handicap, the official and definitive result of which he had read in the *Evening Telegraph*, late pink edition, in the cabman's shelter, at Butt bridge.

Where had previous intimations of the result, effected or projected, been received by him?

In Bernard Kiernan's licensed premises 8, 9 and 10 Little Britain street: in David Byrne's licensed premises, 14 Duke street: in O'Connell street lower, outside Graham Lemon's when a dark man had placed in his hand a throwaway (subsequently thrown away), advertising Elijah, restorer of the church in Zion: in Lincoln place outside the premises of F. W. Sweny and Co (Limited) dispensing chemists, when, when Frederick M. (Bantam) Lyons had rapidly and successively requested, perused and restituted the copy of the current issue of the *Freeman's Journal* and *National Press* which he had been about to throw away (subsequently thrown away), he had proceeded towards the oriental edifice of the Turkish and Warm Baths, 11 Leinster street, with the light of inspiration shining in his countenance and bearing in his arms the secret of the race, graven in the language of prediction.

What qualifying considerations allayed his perturbations?

The difficulties of interpretation since the significance of any event followed its occurrence as variably as the acoustic report followed the electrical discharge and of counterestimating against an actual loss by failure to interpret the total sum of possible losses proceeding originally from a successful interpretation.

His mood?

He had not risked, he did not expect, he had not been disappointed, he was satisfied.

What satisfied him?

To have sustained no positive loss. To have brought a positive gain to others. Light to the gentiles.

How did Bloom prepare a collation for a gentile?

He poured into two teacups two level spoonfuls, four in all, of Epps's soluble cocoa and proceeded according to the directions for use printed on the label, to each adding after sufficient time for infusion the prescribed ingredients for diffusion in the manner and in the quantity prescribed.

What supererogatory marks of special hospitality did the host show his guest?

Relinquishing his symposiarchal right to the moustache cup of imitation Crown Derby presented to him by his only daughter, Millicent (Milly), he substituted a cup identical with that of his guest and served extraordinarily to his guest and, in reduced measure, to himself, the viscous cream ordinarily reserved for the breakfast of his wife Marion (Molly).

Was the guest conscious of and did he acknowledge these marks of hospitality?

His attention was directed to them by his host jocosely and he accepted them seriously as they drank in jocoserious silence Epps's massproduct, the creature cocoa.

Were there marks of hospitality which he contemplated but suppressed, reserving them for another and for himself on future occasions to complete the act begun?

The reparation of a fissure of the length of $1^1/_2$ inches in the right side of his guest's jacket. A gift to his guest of one of the four lady's handkerchiefs, if and when ascertained to be in a presentable condition.

Who drank more quickly?

Bloom, having the advantage of ten seconds at the initiation and taking, from the concave surface of a spoon along the handle of which a steady flow of heat was conducted, three sips to his opponents's one, six to two, nine to three.

What cerebration accompanied his frequentative act?

Concluding by inspection but erroneously that his silent companion was engaged in mental composition be reflected on the pleasures derived from literature of instruction rather than of amusement as he himself had applied to the works of William Shakespeare more than once for the solution of difficult problems in imaginary or real life.

Had he found their solution?

In spite of careful and repeated reading of certain classical passages, aided by a glossary, he had derived imperfect conviction from the text, the answers not bearing on all points.

What lines concluded his first piece of original verse written by him, potential poet, at the age of 11 in 1877 on the occasion of the offering of three prizes of 10/-, 5/- and 2/6 respectively by the *Shamrock*, a weekly newspaper?

> *An ambition to squint*
> *At my verses in print*
> *Makes me hope that for these you'll find room.*
> *If you so condescend*
> *Then please place at the end*
> *The name of yours truly, L. Bloom.*

Did he find four separating forces between his temporary guest and him? Name, age, race, creed.

What anagrams had he made on his name in youth?
Leopold Bloom
Ellpodbomool
Molldopeloob.
Bollopedoom
Old Ollebo, M. P.

What acrostic upon the abbreviation of his first name had he (kinetic poet) sent to Miss Marion Tweedy on the 14 February 1888?

> *Poets oft have sung in rhyme*
> *Of music sweet their praise divine.*
> *Let them hymn it nine times nine.*
> *Dearer far than song or wine,*
> *You are mine. The world is mine.*

What had prevented him from completing a topical song (music by R. G. Johnston) on the events of the past, or fixtures for the actual years, entitled *If Brian Boru could but come back and see old Dublin now*, commissioned by Michael Gunn, lessee of the Gaiety Theatre, 46, 47, 48, 49 South King street, and to be introduced into the sixth scene, the valley of diamonds, of the second edition (30 January 1893) of the grand annual Christmas pantomime *Sinbad the Sailor* (written by Greenleaf Whittier, scenery by George A. Jackson and Cecil Hicks, costumes by Mrs and Miss Whelan, produced by R. Shelton 26 December 1892 under the personal supervision of Mrs Michael Gunn, ballets by Jessie Noir, harlequinade by Thomas Otto) and sung by Nelly Bouverist, principal girl?

Firstly, oscillation between events of imperial and of local interest, the anticipated diamond jubilee of Queen Victoria (born 1820, acceded 1837) and the posticipated opening of the new municipal fish market: secondly, apprehension of opposition from extreme circles on the questions of the respective visits of Their Royal Highnesses, the duke and duchess of York (real), and of His Majesty King Brian Boru (imaginary); thirdly, a conflict between professional etiquette and professional emulation concerning the recent erections of the Grand Lyric Hall on Burgh Quay and the Theatre Royal in Hawkins street: fourthly, distraction resultant from compassion for Nelly Bouverist's non-intellectual, non-political, non-topical expression of countenance and concupiscence caused by Nelly Bouverist's revelations of white articles of non-intellectual, non-political, non-topical under-clothing while she (Nelly Bouverist) was in the articles: fifthly, the difficulties of the selection of appropriate music and humorous allusions from *Everybody's Book of Jokes* (1000 pages and a laugh in every one): sixthly, the rhymes homophonous and cacophonous, associated with the names of the new lord mayor, Daniel Tallon, the new high sheriff, Thomas Pile and the new solicitorgeneral, Dunbar Plunket Barton.

What relation existed between their ages?

16 years before in 1888 when Bloom was of Stephen's present age Stephen was 6. 16 years after in 1920 when Stephen would be of Bloom's present age Bloom would be 54. In 1936 when Bloom would be 70 and Stephen 54 their ages initially in the ratio of 16 to 0 would be as $17^{1/2}$ to $13^{1/2}$, the proportion increasing and the disparity diminishing according as arbitrary future years were added, for if the proportion existing in 1883 had continued immutable, conceiving that to be possible, till then 1904 when Stephen was 22 Bloom would be 374 and in 1920 when Stephen would be 38, as Bloom then was, Bloom would be 646 while in 1952 when Stephen would have attained the maximum postdiluvian age of 70 Bloom, being 1190 years alive having been born in the year 714, would have surpassed by 221 years the maximum antediluvian age, that of Methusalah, 969 years, while, if Stephen would continue to live until he would attain that age in the year 3072 A. D., Bloom would have been obliged to have been alive 83,300 years, having been obliged to have been born in the year 81,396 B. C.

What events might nullify these calculations?

The cessation of existence of both or either, the inauguration of a new era or calendar, the annihilation of the world and consequent extermination of the human species, inevitable but impredictable.

How many previous encounters proved their preexisting acquaintance?

Two. The first in the lilacgarden of Matthew Dillon's house, Medina Villa, Kimmage road, Roundtown, in 1887, in the company of Stephen's mother, Stephen being then of the age of 5 and reluctant to give his hand in salutation. The second in the coffeeroom of Breslin's hotel on a rainy Sunday in the January of 1892, in the company of Stephen's father and Stephen's granduncle, Stephen being then 5 years older.

Did Bloom accept the invitation to dinner given then by the son and afterwards seconded by the father?

Very gratefully, with grateful appreciation, with sincere appreciative gratitude, in appreciatively grateful sincerity of regret, he declined.

Did their conversation on the subject of these reminiscences reveal a third connecting link between them?

Mrs Riordan, a widow of independent means, had resided in the house of Stephen's parents from 1 September 1888 to 29 December 1891 and had also resided during the years 1892, 1893 and 1894 in the City Arms Hotel owned by Elizabeth O'Dowd of 54 Prussia street where during parts of the years 1893 and 1894 she had been a constant informant of Bloom who resided also in the same hotel, being at that time a clerk in the employment of Joseph Cuffe of 5 Smithfield for the superintendence of sales in the adjacent Dublin Cattle market on the North Circular road.

Had he performed any special corporal work of mercy for her?

He had sometimes propelled her on warm summer evenings, an infirm widow of independent, if limited means, in her convalescent bathchair with slow revolutions of its wheels as far as the corner of the North Circular road opposite Mr Gavin Low's place of business where she had remained for a certain time scanning through his onelensed binocular fieldglasses unrecognisable citizens on tramcars, roadster bicycles, equipped with inflated pneumatic tyres, hackney carriages, tandems, private and hired landaus, dogcarts, ponytraps and brakes passing from the city to the Phœnix Park and *vice versa*.

Why could he then support that his vigil with the greater equanimity?

Because in middle youth he had often sat observing through a rondel of bossed glass of a multicoloured pane the spectacle offered with continual changes of the thoroughfare without, pedestrians, quadrupeds, velocipedes, vehicles, passing slowly, quickly, evenly, round and round and round the rim of a round precipitous globe.

What distinct different memories had each of her now eight years deceased?

The older, her bezique cards and counters, her Skye terrier, her suppositious wealth, her lapses of responsiveness and incipient catarrhal deafness: the younger, her lamp of colza oil before the statue of the Immaculate Conception, her green and maroon brushes for Charles Stewart Parnell and for Michael Davitt, her tissue papers.

Were there no means still remaining to him to achieve the rejuvenation which these reminiscences divulged to a younger companion rendered the more desirable?

The indoor exercises, formerly intermittently practised, subsequently abandoned, prescribed in Eugen Sandow's *Physical Strength and How To Obtain It* which, designed particularly for commercial men engaged in sedentary occupations, were to be made with mental concentration in front of a mirror so as to bring into play the various families of muscles and produce successively a pleasant relaxation and the most pleasant repristination of juvenile agility.

Had any special agility been his in earlier youth?

Though ringweight lifting had been beyond his strength and the full circle gyration beyond his courage yet as a High School scholar he had excelled in his stable and protracted execution of the half lever movement on the parallel bars in consequence of his abnormally developed abdominal muscles.

Did either openly allude to their racial difference?
Neither.

What, reduced to their simplest reciprocal form, were Bloom's thoughts about Stephen's thoughts about Bloom and Bloom's thoughts about Stephen's thoughts about Bloom's thoughts about Stephen?

He thought that he thought that he was a jew whereas he knew that he knew that he knew that he was not.

What, the enclosures of reticence removed, were their respective parentages?

Bloom, only born male transubstantial heir of Rudolf Virag (subsequently Rudolf Bloom) of Szombathely, Vienna, Budapest, Milan, London and Dublin and of Ellen Higgins, second daughter of Julius Higgins (born

Karoly) and Fanny Higgins (born Hegarty); Stephen, eldest surviving male consubstantial heir of Simon Dedalus of Cork and Dublin and of Mary, daughter of Richard and Christina Goulding (born Grier).

Had Bloom and Stephen been baptised, and where and by whom, cleric or layman?

Bloom (three times) by the reverend Mr Gilmer Johnston M. A. alone in the protestant church of Saint Nicolas Without, Coombe; by James O'Connor, Philip Gilligan and James Fitzpatrick, together, under a pump in the village of Swords; and by the reverend Charles Malone C. C., in the church of the Three Patrons, Rathgar. Stephen (once) by the reverend Charles Malone, C. C., alone, in the church of the Three Patrons, Rathgar.

Did they find their educational careers similar?

Substituting Stephen for Bloom Stoom would have passed successively through a dame's school and the high school. Substituting Bloom for Stephen Blephen would have passed successively through the preparatory, junior, middle and senior grades of the intermediate and through the matriculation, first arts second arts and arts degree courses of the royal university.

Why did Bloom refrain from stating that he had frequented the university of life?

Because of his fluctuating incertitude as to whether this observation had or had not been already made by him to Stephen or by Stephen to him.

What two temperaments did they individually represent?

The scientific. The artistic.

What proofs did Bloom adduce to prove that his tendency was towards applied, rather than towards pure, science?

Certain possible inventions of which he had cogitated when reclining in a state of supine repletion to aid digestion, stimulated by his appreciation of the importance of inventions now common but once revolutionary for example, the aeronautic parachute, the reflecting telescope, the spiral cork-screw, the safety pin, the mineral water siphon, the canal lock with winch and sluice, the suction pump.

Were these inventions principally intended for an improved scheme of kindergarten?

Yes, rendering obsolete popguns, elastic airbladders, games of hazard, catapults. They comprised astronomical kaleidoscopes exhibiting the twelve constellations of the zodiac from Aries to Pisces, miniature mechanical orreries, arithmetical gelatine lozenges, geometrical to correspond with zoological biscuits, globemap playing balls, historically costumed dolls.

What also stimulated him in his cogitations?

The financial success achieved by Ephraim Marks and Charles A. James, the former by his 1d. bazaar at 42 George's street, South, the latter at his 6 1/2 d. shop and world's fancy fair and waxwork exhibition at 30 Henry street, admission 2d., children 1d.; and the infinite possibilities hitherto unexploited of the modern art of advertisement if condensed in triliteral monoideal symbols, vertically of maximum visibility (divined), horizontally of maximum legibility (deciphered) and of magnetising efficacy to arrest involuntary attention, to interest, to convince, to decide.

Such as?

K. 11. Kino's 11/- Trousers.

House of Keys. Alexander J. Keyes.

Such as not?

Look at this long candle. Calculate when it burns out and you receive gratis 1 pair of our special non-compo boots, guaranteed 1 candle power. Address: Barclay and Cook, 18 Talbot Street.

Bacilikil (Insect Powder).

Veribest (Boot Blacking).

Uwantit (Combined pocket twoblade penknife with corkscrew, nailfile and pipecleaner).

Such as never?

What is home without Plumtree's Potted Meat?

Incomplete.

With it an abode of bliss.

Manufactured by George Plumtree, 23 Merchants' quay, Dublin, put up in 4 oz. pots, and inserted by Councillor Joseph P. Nannetti, M. P., Rotunda Ward, 19 Hardwicke street, under the obituary notices and anniversaries of deceases. The name on the label is Plumtree. A plumtree in a meatpot, registered trade mark. Beware of imitations. Peatmot. Trumplee. Montpat. Plamtroo.

Which example did he adduce to induce Stephen to deduce that originality, though producing its own reward, does not invariably conduce to success?

His own ideated and rejected project of an illuminated showcart, drawn by a beast of burden, in which two smartly dressed girls were to be seated engaged in writing.

What suggested scene was then constructed by Stephen?

Solitary hotel in mountain pass. Autumn. Twilight. Fire lit. In dark corner young man seated. Young woman enters. Restless. Solitary. She sits. She goes to window. She stands. She sits. Twilight. She thinks. On solitary hotel paper she writes. She thinks. She writes. She sighs. Wheels and hoofs. She hurries out. He comes from his dark corner. He seizes solitary paper. He holds it towards fire. Twilight. He reads. Solitary.

What?

In sloping, upright and backhands: Queen's hotel, Queen's hotel, Queen's Ho . . .

What suggested scene was then reconstructed by Bloom?

The Queen's Hotel, Ennis, County Clare, where Rudolph Bloom (Rudolf Virag) died on the evening of the 27 June 1886, at some hour unstated, in consequence of an overdose of monkshood (aconite) self-administered in the form of a neuralgic liniment, composed of 2 parts of aconite liniment to 1 of chloroform liniment (purchased by him at 10.20 a.m. on the morning of 27 June 1886 at the medical hall of Francis Dennehy, 17 Church street, Ennis) after having, though not in consequence of having, purchased at 3.15 p.m. on the afternoon of 27 June 1886 a new boater straw hat, extra smart (after having, though not in consequence of having, purchased at the hour and in the place aforesaid, the toxin aforesaid), at the general drapery store of James Cullen, 4 Main street, Ennis.

Did he attribute this homonymity to information or coincidence or intuition?

Coincidence.

Did he depict the scene verbally for his guest to see?

He preferred himself to see another's face and listen to another's words by which potential narration was realised and kinetic temperament relieved.

Did he see only a second coincidence in the second scene narrated to him, described by the narrator as *A Pisgah Sight of Palestine* or *The Parable of the Plums?*

It, with the preceding scene and with others unnarrated but existent by implication, to which add essays on various subjects or moral apothegms (e.g. *My Favourite Hero* or *Procrastination is the Thief of Time*) composed during school-years, seemed to him to contain in itself and in conjunction with the personal equation certain possibilities of financial, social, personal and sexual success, whether specially collected and selected as model peda-gogic themes (of cent per cent merit) for the use of preparatory and junior grade students or contributed in printed form, following the precedent of Philip Beaufoy or Doctor Dick or Heblon's *Studies in Blue*, to a publication of certified circulation and solvency or employed verbally as intellectual stimulation for sympathetic auditors, tacitly appreciative of successful narrative and confidently augurative of successful achievement, during the increasingly longer nights gradually following the summer solstice on the day but three following, videlicet, Tuesday, 21 June (S. Aloysius Gonzaga), sunrise 3.33 a.m., sunset 8.29 p.m.

Which domestic problem as much as, if not more than, any other frequently engaged his mind?

What to do with our wives.

What had been his hypothetical singular solutions?

Parlour games (dominos, halma, tiddledywinks, spillikins, cup and ball, nap, spoil five, bezique, twentyfive, beggar my neighbour, draughts, chess or backgammon): embroidery, darning or knitting for the policeaided clothing society: musical duets, mandoline and guitar, piano and flute, guitar and piano: legal scrivenery or envelope addressing: biweekly visits to variety entertainments: commercial activity as pleasantly commanding and pleasingly obeyed mistress proprietress in a cool dairy shop or warm cigar divan: the clandestine satisfaction of erotic irritation in masculine brothels, state inspected and medically controlled: social visits, at regular infrequent prevented intervals and with regular frequent preventive superintendence, to and from female acquaintances of recognised respectability in the vicinity: courses of evening instruction specially designed to render liberal instruction agreeable.

What instances of deficient mental development in his wife inclined him in favour of the lastmentioned (ninth) solution?

In disoccupied moments she had more than once covered a sheet of paper with signs and hieroglyphics which she stated were Greek and Irish and Hebrew characters. She had interrogated constantly at varying intervals as to the correct method of writing the capital initial of the name of a city in Canada, Quebec. She understood little of political complications, internal, or balance of power, external. In calculating the addenda of bills she frequently had recourse to digital aid. After completion of laconic epistolary compositions she abandoned the implement of calligraphy in the encaustic pigment exposed to the corrosive action of copperas, green vitriol and nutgall. Unusual polysyllables of foreign origin she interpreted phonetically or by false analogy or by both: metempsychosis (met him pike hoses), *alias* (a mendacious person mentioned in sacred Scripture).

What compensated in the false balance of her intelligence for these and such deficiencies of judgment regarding persons, places and things?

The false apparent parallelism of all perpendicular arms of all balances, proved true by construction. The counterbalance of her proficiency of judgment regarding one person, proved true by experiment.

How had he attempted to remedy this state of comparative ignorance?

Variously. By leaving in a conspicuous place a certain book open at a certain page: by assuming in her, when alluding explanatorily, latent knowledge: by open ridicule in her presence of some absent other's ignorant lapse.

With what success had he attempted direct instruction?

She followed not all, a part of the whole, gave attention with interest, comprehended with surprise, with care repeated, with greater difficulty remembered, forgot with ease, with misgiving reremembered, rerepeated with error.

What system had proved more effective?

Indirect suggestion implicating self-interest.

Example?

She disliked umbrella with rain, he liked woman with umbrella, she disliked new hat with rain, he liked woman with new hat, he bought new hat with rain, she carried umbrella with new hat.

Accepting the analogy implied in his guest's parable which examples of postexilic eminence did he adduce?

Three seekers of the pure truth, Moses of Egypt, Moses Maimonides, author of *More Nebukim* (Guide of the Perplexed) and Moses Mendelssohn of such eminence that from Moses (of Egypt) to Moses (Mendelssohn) there arose none like Moses (Maimonides).

What statement was made, under correction, by Bloom concerning a fourth seeker of pure truth, by name Aristotle, mentioned, with permission, by Stephen?

That the seeker mentioned had been a pupil of a rabbinical philosopher, name uncertain.

Were other anapocryphal illustrious sons of the law and children of a selected or rejected race mentioned?

Felix Bartholdy Mendelssohn (composer), Baruch Spinoza (philosopher), Mendoza (pugilist), Ferdinand Lassalle (reformer, duellist).

What fragments of verse from the ancient Hebrew and ancient Irish languages were cited with modulations of voice and translation of texts by guest to host and by host to guest?

By Stephen: *suil, suil, suil arun, suil go siocair agus, suil go cuin* (walk, walk, walk your way, walk in safety, walk with care).

By Bloom: *Kifeloch, harimon rakatejch m'baad l'zamatejch* (thy temple amid thy hair is as a slice of pomegranate).

How was a glyphic comparison of the phonic symbols of both languages made in substantiation of the oral comparison?

On the penultimate blank page of a book of inferior literary style, entitled *Sweets of Sin* (produced by Bloom and so manipulated that its front cover came in contact with the surface of the table) with a pencil (supplied by Stephen) Stephen wrote the Irish characters for gee, eh, dee, em, simple and modified, and Bloom in turn wrote the Hebrew characters ghimel, aleph, daleth and (in the absence of mem) a substituted goph, explaining their arithmetical values as ordinal and cardinal numbers, videlicet 3, 1, 4 and 100.

Was the knowledge possessed by both of each of these languages, the extinct and the revived, theoretical or practical?

Theoretical, being confined to certain grammatical rules of accidence and syntax and practically excluding vocabulary.

What points of contact existed between these languages and between the peoples who spoke them?

The presence of guttural sounds, diacritic aspirations, epenthetic and servile letters in both languages: their antiquity, both having been taught on the plain of Shinar 242 years after the deluge in the seminary instituted by Fenius Farsaigh, descendant of Noah, progenitor of Israel, and ascendant of Heber and Heremon, progenitors of Ireland: their archeological, genealogical, hagiographical, exegetical, homilectic, toponomastic, historical and religious literatures comprising the works of rabbis and culdees, Torah, Talmud (Mischna and Ghemara) Massor, Pentateuch, Book of the Dun Cow, Book of Ballymote, Garland of Howth, Book of Kells: their dispersal, persecution, survival and revival: the isolation of their synagogical and ecclesiastical rites in ghetto (S. Mary's Abbey) and masshouse (Adam and Eve's tavern): the proscription of their national costumes in penal laws and jewish dress acts: the restoration in Chanan David of Zion and the possibility of Irish political autonomy or devolution.

What anthem did Bloom chant partially in anticipation of that multiple, ethnically irreductible consummation?

Kolod balejwaw pnimah
Nefesch, jehudi, homijah.

Why was the chant arrested at the conclusion of this first distich?
In consequence of defective mnemotechnic.

How did the chanter compensate for this deficiency?
By a periphrastic version of the general text.

In what common study did their mutual reflections merge?
The increasing simplification traceable from the Egyptian epigraphic hieroglyphs to the Greek and Roman alphabets and the anticipation of modern stenography and telegraphic code in the cuneiform inscriptions (Semitic) and the virgular quinquecostate ogham writing (Celtic).

Did the guest comply with his host's request?
Doubly, by appending his signature in Irish and Roman characters.

What was Stephen's auditive sensation?
He heard in a profound ancient male unfamiliar melody the accumulation of the past.

What was Bloom's visual sensation?

He saw in a quick young male familiar form the predestination of a future.

What were Stephen's and Bloom's quasisimultaneous volitional quasi-sensations of concealed identities?

Visually, Stephen's: The traditional figure of hypostasis, depicted by Johannes Damascenus, Lentulus Romanus and Epiphanius Monachus as leucodermic, sesquipedalian with winedark hair.

Auditively, Bloom's: The traditional accent of the ecstasy of catastrophe.

What future careers had been possible for Bloom in the past and with what exemplars?

In the church, Roman, Anglican, or Nonconformist: exemplars, the very reverend John Conmee S. J., the reverend T. Salmon, D. D., provost of Trinity college, Dr Alexander J. Dowie. At the bar, English or Irish: exemplars, Seymour Bushe, K. C., Rufus Isaacs, K. C. On the stage, modern or Shakespearean exemplars, Charles Wyndham, high comedian, Osmond Tearle († 1901), exponent of Shakespeare.

Did the host encourage his guest to chant in a modulated voice a strange legend on an allied theme?

Reassuringly, their place where none could hear them talk being secluded, reassured, the decocted beverages, allowing for subsolid residual sediment of a mechanical mixture, water plus sugar plus cream plus cocoa, having been consumed.

Recite the first (major) part of this chanted legend?

> *Little Harry Hughes and his schoolfellows all*
> *Went out for to play ball.*
> *And the very first ball little Harry Hughes played*
> *He drove it o'er the jew's garden wall.*
> *And the very second ball little Harry Hughes played*
> *He broke the jew's windows all.*

How did the son of Rudolph receive this first part?

With unmixed feeling. Smiling, a jew, he heard with pleasure and saw the unbroken kitchen window.

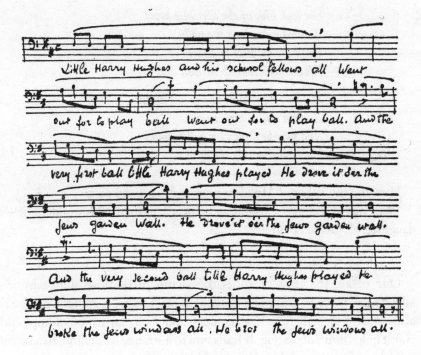

Recite the second part (minor) of the legend.

> *Then out came the jew's daughter*
> *And she all dressed in green.*
> *«Come back, come back, you pretty little boy,*
> *And play your ball again.»*
>
> *«I can't come back and I won't come back*
> *Without my schoolfellows all,*
> *For if my master he did hear*
> *He'd make it a sorry ball.»*

She took him by the lilywhite hand
And led him along the hall
Until she led him to a room
Where none could hear him call.

She took a penknife out of her pocket
And cut off his little head,
And now he'll play his ball no more
For he lies among the dead.

How did the father of Millicent receive this second part?

With mixed feelings. Unsmiling, he heard and saw with wonder a jew's daughter, all dressed in green.

Condense Stephen's commentary.

One of all, the least of all, is the victim predestined. Once by inadvertence, twice by design he challenges his destiny. It comes when he is abandoned and challenges him reluctant and, as an apparition of hope and youth holds him unresisting. It leads him to a strange habitation, to a secret infidel apartment, and there, implacable, immolates him, consenting.

Why was the host (victim predestined) sad?

He wished that a tale of a deed should be told of a deed not by him should by him not be told.

Why was the host (reluctant, unresisting) still?

In accordance with the law of the conservation of energy.

Why was the host (secret infidel) silent?

He weighed the possible evidences for and against ritual murder: the incitation of the hierarchy, the superstition of the populace, the propagation of rumour in continued fraction of veridicity, the envy of opulence, the influence of retaliation, the sporadic reappearance of atavistic delinquency, the mitigating circumstances of fanaticism, hypnotic suggestion and somnambulism.

From which (if any) of these mental or physical disorders was he not totally immune?

From hypnotic suggestion: once, waking, he had not recognised his sleeping apartment: more than once, waking, he had been for an indefinite time incapable of moving or uttering sounds. From somnambulism: once, sleeping, his body had risen, crouched and crawled in the direction of a heatless fire and, having attained its destination, there, curled, unheated, in night attire had lain, sleeping.

Had this latter or any cognate phenomenon declared itself in any member of his family?

Twice, in Holles street and in Ontario terrace, his daughter Millicent (Milly) at the ages of 6 and 8 years had uttered in sleep an exclamation of terror and had replied to the interrogations of two figures in night attire with a vacant mute expression.

What other infantile memories had he of her?

15 june 1889. A querulous newborn female infant crying to cause and lessen congestion. A child renamed Padney Socks she shook with shocks her moneybox: counted his three free moneypenny buttons one, tloo, tlee: a doll, a boy, a sailor she cast away: blond, born of two dark, she had blond ancestry, remote, a violation, Herr Hauptmann Hainau, Austrian army, proximate, a hallucination, lieutenant Mulvey, British navy.

What endemic characteristics were present?

Conversely the nasal and frontal formation was derived in a direct line of lineage which, though interrupted, would continue at distant intervals to its most distant intervals.

What memories had he of her adolescence?

She relegated her hoop and skippingrope to a recess. On the duke's lawn entreated by an English visitor, she declined to permit him to make and take away her photographic image (objection not stated). On the South Circular road in the company of Elsa Potter, followed by an individual of sinister aspect, she went half way down Stamer street and turned abruptly back (reason of change not stated). On the vigil of the 15th anniversary of her birth she wrote a letter from Mullingar, county Westmeath, making a brief allusion to a local student (faculty and year not stated).

Did that first division, portending a second division, afflict him?

Less than he had imagined, more than he had hoped.

What second departure was contemporaneously perceived by him similarly if differently?

A temporary departure of his cat.

Why similarly, why differently?

Similarly, because actuated by a secret purpose the quest of a new male (Mullingar student) or of a healing herb (valerian). Differently, because of different possible returns to the inhabitants or to the habitation.

In other respects were their differences similar?

In passivity, in economy, in the instinct of tradition, in unexpectedness.

As?

Inasmuch as leaning she sustained her blond hair for him to ribbon it for her (cf. neckarching cat). Moreover, on the free surface of the lake in Stephen's green amid inverted reflections of trees her uncommented spit, describing concentric circles of waterrings, indicated by the constancy of its permanence the locus of a somnolent prostrate fish (cf. mousewatching cat). Again, in order to remember the date, combatants, issue and consequences of a famous military engagement she pulled a plait of her hair (cf. earwashing cat). Furthermore, silly Milly, she dreamed of having had an unspoken unremembered conversation with a horse whose name had been Joseph to whom (which) she had offered a tumblerful of lemonade which it (he) had appeared to have accepted (cf. hearthdreaming cat). Hence in passivity, in economy, in the instinct of tradition, in unexpectedness, their differences were similar.

In what way had he utilised gifts 1) an owl, 2) a clock, given as matrimonial auguries, to interest and to instruct her?

As object lessons to explain: 1) the nature and habits of oviparous animals, the possibility of aerial flight, certain abnormalities of vision, the secular process of imbalsamation: 2) the principle of the pendulum, exemplified in bob, wheelgear and regulator, the translation in terms of human or social regulation of the various positions clockwise of movable indicators on an unmoving dial, the exactitude of the recurrence per hour of an instant in each hour, when the longer and the shorter indicator were at the same angle of inclination, *videlicet*, 5 5/11 minutes past each hour per hour in arithmetical progression.

In what manners did she reciprocate?

She remembered: on the 27th anniversary of his birth she presented to him a breakfast moustachecup of imitation crown Derby porcelain ware. She provided: at quarter day or thereabouts if or when purchases had been made by him not for her she showed herself attentive to his necessities, anticipating his desires. She admired: a natural phenomenon having been explained by him not for her she expressed the immediate desire to possess without gradual acquisition a fraction of his science, the moiety, the quarter, a thousandth part.

What proposal did Bloom, diambulist, father of Milly, somnambulist, make to Stephen, noctambulist?

To pass in repose the hours intervening between Thursday (proper) and Friday (normal) on an extemporised cubicle in the apartment immediately above the kitchen and immediately adjacent to the sleeping apartment of his host and hostess.

What various advantages would or might have resulted from a prolongation of such extemporisation?

For the guest: security of domicile and seclusion of study. For the host: rejuvenation of intelligence, vicarious satisfaction. For the hostess: disintegration of obsession, acquisition of correct Italian pronunciation.

Why might these several provisional contingencies between a guest and a hostess not necessarily preclude or be precluded by a permanent eventuality of reconciliatory union between a schoolfellow and a jew's daughter?

Because the way to daughter led through mother, the way to mother through daughter.

To what inconsequent polysyllabic question of his host did the guest return a monosyllabic negative answer?

If he had known the late Mrs Emily Sinico, accidentally killed at Sydney Parade railway station, 14 October 1903.

What inchoate corollary statement was consequently suppressed by the host?

A statement explanatory of his absence on the occasion of the interment of Mrs Mary Dedalus, born Goulding, 26 June 1903, vigil of the anniversary of the decease of Rudolph Bloom (born Virag).

Was the proposal of asylum accepted?

Promptly, inexplicably, with amicability, gratefully it was declined.

What exchange of money took place between host and guest?

The former returned to the latter, without interest, a sum of money (£1. 7s. 0.), one pound seven shillings, advanced by the latter to the former.

What counterproposals were alternately advanced, accepted, modified, declined, restated in other terms, reaccepted, ratified, reconfirmed?

To inaugurate a prearranged course of Italian instruction, place the residence of the instructed. To inaugurate a course of vocal instruction, place the residence of the instructress. To inaugurate a series of static, semistatic and peripatetic intellectual dialogues, places the residence of both speakers (if both speakers were resident in the same place), the Ship hotel and tavern, 6 Lower Abbey street (W. and E. Connery, proprietors), the National Library of Ireland, 10 Kildare street, the National Maternity Hospital, 29, 30 and 31 Holles street, a public garden, the vicinity of a place of worship, a conjunction of two or more public thoroughfares, the point of bisection of a right line drawn between their residences (if both speakers were resident in different places).

What rendered problematic for Bloom the realisation of these mutually selfexcluding propositions?

The irreparability of the past: once at a performance of Albert Hengler's circus in the Rotunda, Rutland square, Dublin, an intuitive particoloured clown in quest of paternity had penetrated from the ring to a place in the auditorium where Bloom, solitary, was seated and had publicly declared to an exhilarated audience that he (Bloom) was his (the clown's) papa. The imprevidibility of the future: once in the summer of 1898 he (Bloom) had marked a florin (2s.) with three notches on the milled edge and tendered it in payment of an account due to and received by J. and T. Davy, family grocers, 1 Charlemont Mall, Grand Canal, for circulation on the waters of civic finance, for possible, circuitous or direct, return.

Was the clown Bloom's son?
No.

Had Bloom's coin returned?
Never.

Why would a recurrent frustration the more depress him?
Because at the critical turningpoint of human existence he desired to amend many social conditions, the product of inequality and avarice and international animosity.

He believed then that human life was infinitely perfectible, eliminating these conditions?

There remained the generic conditions imposed by natural, as distinct from human law, as integral parts of the human whole: the necessity of destruction to procure alimentary sustenance: the painful character of the ultimate functions of separate existence, the agonies of birth and death: the monotonous menstruation of simian and (particularly) human females extending from the age of puberty to the menopause: inevitable accidents at sea, in mines and factories: certain very painful maladies and their resultant surgical operations, innate lunacy and congenital criminality, decimating epidemics: catastrophic cataclysms which make terror the basis of human mentality: seismic upheavals the epicentres of which are located in densely populated regions: the fact of vital growth, through convulsions of metamorphosis, from infancy through maturity to decay.

Why did he desist from speculation?

Because it was a task for a superior intelligence to substitute other more acceptable phenomena in place of the less acceptable phenomena to be removed.

Did Stephen participate in his dejection?

He affirmed his significance as a conscious rational animal proceeding syllogistically from the known to the unknown and a conscious rational reagent between a micro and a macrocosm ineluctably constructed upon the incertitude of the void.

Was this affirmation apprehended by Bloom?
Not verbally. Substantially.

What comforted his misapprehension?

That as a competent keyless citizen he had proceeded energetically from the unknown to the known through the incertitude of the void.

In what order of precedence, with what attendant ceremony was the exodus from the house of bondage to the wilderness of inhabitation effected?

Lighted Candle in Stick borne by
BLOOM.
Diaconal Hat on Ashplant borne by
STEPHEN.

With what intonation *secreto* of what commemorative psalm?

The 113th, *modus peregrinus: In exitu Israël de Egypto: domus Jacob de populo barbaro.*

What did each do at the door of egress?

Bloom set the candlestick on the floor. Stephen put the hat on his head.

For what creature was the door of egress a door of ingress?

For a cat.

What spectacle confronted them when they, first the host, then the guest, emerged silently, doubly dark, from obscurity by a passage from the rere of the house into the penumbra of the garden?

The heaventree of stars hung with humid nightblue fruit.

With what meditations did Bloom accompany his demonstration to his companion of various constellations?

Meditations of evolution increasingly vaster: of the moon invisible in incipient lunation, approaching perigee: of the infinite lattiginous scintillating uncondensed milky way, discernible by daylight by an observer placed at the lower end of a cylindrical vertical shaft 5000 ft deep sunk from the surface towards the centre of the earth: of Sirius (alpha in Canis Major) 10 lightyears (57,000, 000, 000, 000 miles) distant and in volume 900 times the dimension of our planet: of Arcturus: of the precession of equinoxes: of Orion with belt and sextuple sun theta and nebula in which 100 of our solar systems could be contained: of moribund and of nascent new stars such as Nova in 1901: of our system plunging towards the constellation of Hercules: of the parallax or parallactic drift of socalled fixed stars, in reality evermoving from immeasurably remote eons to infinitely remote futures in comparison with which the years, threescore and ten, of allotted human life formed a parenthesis of infinitesimal brevity.

Were there obverse meditations of involution increasingly less vast?

Of the eons of geological periods recorded in the stratifications of the earth: of the myriad minute entomological organic existences concealed in cavities of the earth, beneath removable stones, in hives and mounds, of microbes, germs, bacteria, bacilli, spermatozoa: of the incalculable trillions of billions of millions of imperceptible molecules contained by cohesion of molecular affinity in a single pinhead: of the universe of human serum constellated with red and white bodies, themselves universes of void space constellated with other bodies, each, in continuity, its universe of divisible component bodies of which each was again divisible in divisions of redivisible component bodies, dividends and divisors ever diminishing without actual division till, if the progress were carried far enough, nought nowhere was never reached.

Why did he not elaborate these calculations to a more precise result?

Because some years previously in 1886 when occupied with the problem of the quadrature of the circle he had learned of the existence of a number computed to a relative degree of accuracy to be of such magnitude and of so many places, e.g., the 9th power of the 9th power of 9, that, the result having been obtained, 33 closely printed volumes of 1000 pages each of innumerable quires and reams of India paper would have to be requisitioned in order to contain the complete tale of its printed integers of units, tens, hundreds, thousands, tens of thousands, hundreds of thousands, millions, tens of millions, hundreds of millions, billions, the nucleus of the nebula of every digit of every series containing succinctly the potentiality of being raised to the utmost kinetic elaboration of any power of any of its powers.

Did he find the problem of the inhabitability of the planets and their satellites by a race, given in species, and of the possible social and moral redemption of said race by a redeemer, easier of solution?

Of a different order of difficulty. Conscious that the human organism, normally capable of sustaining an atmospheric pressure of 19 tons, when elevated to a considerable altitude in the terrestrial atmosphere suffered with arithmetical progression of intensity, according as the line of demarcation between troposphere and statosphere was approximated, from nasal hemorrhage, impeded respiration and vertigo, when proposing this problem for solution he had conjectured as a working hypothesis which could not be proved impossible that a more adaptable and differently anatomically constructed race of beings might subsist otherwise under Martian, Mercurial, Veneral, Jovian, Saturnian, Neptunian or Uranian sufficient and equivalent conditions, though an apogean humanity of beings created in varying forms with finite differences resulting similar to the whole and to one another would probably there as here remain inalterably and inalienably attached to vanities, to vanities of vanities and all that is vanity.

And the problem of possible redemption?
The minor was proved by the major.

Which various features of the constellations were in turn considered?

The various colours significant of various degrees of vitality (white, yellow, crimson, vermilion, cinnabar): their degrees of brilliancy: their magnitudes revealed up to and including the 7th: their positions: the waggoner's star: Walsingham way: the chariot of David: the annular cinctures of Saturn: the condensation of spiral nebulae into suns: the interdependent gyrations of double suns: the independent synchronous discoveries of Galileo, Simon Marius, Piazzi, Le Verrier, Herschel, Galle: the systematisations attempted by Bode and Kepler of cubes of distances and squares of times of revolution: the almost infinite compressibility of hirsute comets and their vast elliptical egressive and reentrant orbits from perihelion to aphelion: the sidereal origin of meteoric stones: the Libyan floods on Mars about the period of the birth of the younger astroscopist: the annual recurrence of meteoric showers about the period of the feast of S. Lawrence (martyr, 10 August): the monthly recurrence known as the new moon with the old moon in her arms: the posited influence of celestial on human bodies: the appearance of a star (1st magnitude) of exceeding brilliancy dominating by night and day (a new luminous sun generated by the collision and amalgamation in incandescence of two nonluminous exsuns) about the period of the birth of William Shakespeare over delta in the recumbent neversetting constellation of Cassiopeia and of a star (2nd magnitude) of similar origin but lesser brilliancy which had appeared in and disappeared from the constellation of the Corona Septentrionalis about the period of the birth of Leopold Bloom and of other stars of (presumably) similar origin which had (effectively or presumably) appeared in and disappeared from the constellation of Andromeda about the period of the birth of Stephen Dedalus, and in and from the constellation of Auriga some years after the birth and death of Rudolph Bloom, junior, and in and from other constellations some years before or after the birth or death of other persons: the attendant phenomena of eclipses, solar and lunar, from immersion to emersion, abatement of wind, transit of shadow, taciturnity of winged creatures, emergence of nocturnal or crepuscular animals, persistence of infernal light, obscurity of terrestrial waters, pallor of human beings.

His (Bloom's) logical conclusion, having weighed the matter and allowing for possible error?

That it was not a heaventree, not a heavengrot, not a heavenbeast, not a heavenman. That it was a Utopia, there being no known method from the known to the unknown: an infinity, renderable equally finite by the supposititious probable apposition of one or more bodies equally of the same and of different magnitudes: a mobility of illusory forms immobilised in space, remobilised in air: a past which possibly had ceased to exist as a present before its future spectators had entered actual present existence.

Was he more convinced of the esthetic value of the spectacle?

Indubitably in consequence of the reiterated examples of poets in the delirium of the frenzy of attachment or in the abasement of rejection invoking ardent sympathetic constellations or the frigidity of the satellite of their planet.

Did he then accept as an article of belief the theory of astrological influences upon sublunary disasters?

It seemed to him as possible of proof as of confutation and the nomenclature employed in its selenographical charts as attributable to verifiable intuition as to fallacious analogy: the lake of dreams, the sea of rains, the gulf of dews, the ocean of fecundity.

What special affinities appeared to him to exist between the moon and woman?

Her antiquity in preceding and surviving successive tellurian generations: her nocturnal predominance: her satellitic dependence: her luminary reflection: her constancy under all her phases, rising, and setting by her appointed times, waxing and waning: the forced invariability of her aspect: her indeterminate response to inaffirmative interrogation: her potency over effluent and refluent waters: her power to enamour, to mortify, to invest with beauty, to render insane, to incite to and aid delinquency: the tranquil inscrutability of her visage: the terribility of her isolated dominant implacable resplendent propinquity: her omens of tempest and of calm: the stimulation of her light, her motion and her presence: the admonition of her craters, her arid seas, her silence: her splendour, when visible: her attraction, when invisible.

What visible luminous sign attracted Bloom's, who attracted Stephen's gaze?

In the second storey (rere) of his (Bloom's) house the light of a paraffin oil lamp with oblique shade projected on a screen of roller blind supplied by Frank O'Hara, window blind, curtain pole and revolving shutter manufacturer, 16 Aungier street.

How did he elucidate the mystery of an invisible person, his wife Marion (Molly) Bloom, denoted by a visible splendid sign, a lamp?

With indirect and direct verbal allusions or affirmations: with subdued affection and admiration: with description: with impediment: with suggestion.

Both then were silent?

Silent, each contemplating the other in both mirrors of the reciprocal flesh of theirhisnothis fellowfaces.

Were they indefinitely inactive?

At Stephen's suggestion, at Bloom's instigation both, first Stephen, then Bloom, in penumbra urinated, their sides contiguous, their organs of micturition reciprocally rendered invisible by manual circumposition, their gazes, first Bloom's, then Stephen's, elevated to the projected luminous and semiluminous shadow.

Similarly?

The trajectories of their, first sequent, the simultaneous, urinations were dissimilar: Bloom's longer, less irruent, in the incomplete form of the bifurcated penultimate alphabetical letter who in his ultimate year at High School (1880) had been capable of attaining the point of greatest altitude against the whole concurrent strength of the institution, 210 scholars: Stephen's higher, more sibilant, who in the ultimate hours of the previous day had augmented by diuretic consumption an insistent vesical pressure.

What different problems presented themselves to each concerning the invisible audible collateral organ of the other?

To Bloom: the problems of irritability, tumescence, rigidity, reactivity, dimension, sanitariness, pelosity. To Stephen: the problem of the sacerdotal integrity of Jesus circumcised (1st January, holiday of obligation to hear mass and abstain from unnecessary servile work) and the problem as to whether the divine prepuce, the carnal bridal ring of the holy Roman catholic apostolic church, conserved in Calcata, were deserving of simple hyperduly or of the fourth degree of latria accorded to the abscission of such divine excrescences as hair and toenails.

What celestial sign was by both simultaneously observed?

A star precipitated with great apparent velocity across the firmament from Vega in the Lyre above the zenith beyond the stargroup of the Tress of Berenice towards the zodiacal sign of Leo.

How did the centripetal remainer afford egress to the centrifugal departer?

By inserting the barrel of an arruginated male key in the hole of an unstable female lock, obtaining a purchase on the bow of the key and turning its wards from right to left, withdrawing a bolt from its staple, pulling inward spasmodically an obsolescent unhinged door and revealing an aperture for free egress and free ingress.

How did they take leave, one of the other, in separation?

Standing perpendicular at the same door and on different sides of its base, the lines of their valedictory arms, meeting at any point and forming any angle less than the sum of two right angles.

What sound accompanied the union of their tangent, the disunion of their (respectively) centrifugal and centripetal hands?

The sound of the peal of the hour of the night by the chime of the bells in the church of Saint George.

What echoes of that sound were by both and each heard?

By Stephen:

> *Liliata rutilantium. Turma circumdet.*
> *Iubilantium te virginum. Chorus excipiat.*

By Bloom:

> *Heigho, heigho,*
> *Heigho, heigho.*

Where were the several members of the company which with Bloom that day at the bidding of that peal had travelled from Sandymount in the south to Glasnevin in the north?

Martin Cunningham (in bed), Jack Power (in bed), Simon Dedalus (in bed), Tom Kernan (in bed), Ned Lambert (in bed), Joe Hynes (in bed), John Henry Menton (in bed), Bernard Corrigan (in bed), Patsy Dignam (in bed), Paddy Dignam (in the grave).

Alone, what did Bloom hear?

The double reverberation of retreating feet on the heavenborn earth, the double vibration of a jew's harp in the resonant lane.

Alone, what did Bloom feel?

The cold of intersteller space, thousands of degrees below freezing point or the absolute zero of Fahrenheit, Centigrade or Réaumur: the incipient intimations of proximate dawn.

Of what did bellchime and handtouch and footstep and lonechill remind him?

Of companions now in various manners in different places defunct: Percy Apjohn (killed in action, Modder River), Philip Gilligan (phthisis, Jervis Street hospital), Matthew F. Kane (accidental drowning, Dublin Bay), Philip Moisel (pyemia, Heytesbury street), Michael Hart (phthisis, Mater Misericordiæ hospital), Patrick Dignam (apoplexy, Sandymount).

What prospect of what phenomena inclined him to remain?

The disparition of three final stars, the diffusion of daybreak, the apparition of a new solar disk.

Had he ever been a spectator of those phenomena?

Once, in 1887 after a protracted performance of charades in the house of Luke Doyle, Kimmage, he had awaited with patience the apparition of the diurnal phenomenon, seated on a wall, his gaze turned in the direction of Mizrach, the east.

He remembered the initial paraphenomena?

More active air, a matutinal distant cock, ecclesiastical clocks at various points, avine music, the isolated tread of an early wayfarer, the visible diffusion of the light of an invisible luminous body, the first golden limb of the resurgent sun perceptible low on the horizon.

Did he remain?

With deep inspiration he returned, retraversing the garden, reentering the passage, reclosing the door. With brief suspiration he reassumed the candle, reascended the stairs, reapproached the door of the front room, hallfloor, and reentered.

What suddenly arrested his ingress?

The right temporal lobe of the hollow sphere of his cranium came into contact with a solid timber angle where, an infinitesimal but sensible fraction of a second later, a painful sensation was located in consequence of antecedent sensations transmitted and registered.

Describe the alterations effected in the disposition of the articles of furnitures?

A sofa upholstered in prune plush had been translocated from opposite the door to the ingleside near the compactly furled Union Jack (an alteration which he had frequently intended to execute): the blue and white checker inlaid majolicatopped table had been placed opposite the door in the place vacated by the prune plush sofa: the walnut sideboard (a projecting angle of which had momentarily arrested his ingress) had been moved from its position beside the door to a more advantageous but more perilous position in front of the door: two chairs had been moved from right and left of the ingleside to the position originally occupied by the blue and white checker inlaid majolicatopped table.

Describe them.

One: a squat stuffed easychair with stout arms extended and back slanted to the rere, which, repelled in recoil, had then upturned an irregular fringe of a rectangular rug and now displayed on its amply upholstered seat a centralised diffusing and diminishing discolouration. The other: a slender splayfoot chair of glossy cane curves, placed directly opposite the former, its frame from top to seat and from seat to base being varnished dark brown, its seat being a bright circle of white plaited rush.

What significances attached to these two chairs?

Significances of similitude, of posture, of symbolism, of circumstantial evidence, of testimonial supermanence.

What occupied the position originally occupied by the sideboard?

A vertical piano (Cadby) with exposed keyboard, its closed coffin supporting a pair of long yellow ladies' gloves and an emerald ashtray containing four consumed matches, a partly consumed cigarette and two discoloured ends of cigarettes, its musicrest supporting the music in the key of G natural for voice and piano of *Love's Old Sweet Song* (words by G. Clifton Bingham, composed by J. L. Molloy, sung by Madam Antoinette Sterling) open at the last page with the final indications *ad libitum*, *forte*, pedal, *animato*, sustained, pedal, *ritirando*, close.

With what sensations did Bloom contemplate in rotation these objects?

With strain, elevating a candlestick: with pain, feeling on his right temple a contused tumescence: with attention, focusing his gaze on a large dull passive and slender bright active: with solicitation, bending and downturning the upturned rugfringe: with amusement, remembering Dr Malachi Mulligan's scheme of colour containing the gradation of green: with pleasure, repeating the words and antecedent act and perceiving through various channels of internal sensibility the consequent and concomitant tepid pleasant diffusion of gradual discolouration.

His next proceeding?

From an open box on the majolicatopped table he extracted a black diminutive cone, one inch in height, placed it on its circular base on a small tin plate, placed his candlestick in the right corner of the mantelpiece, produced from his waistcoat a folded page of prospectus (illustrated) entitled Agendath Netaim, unfolded the same, examined it superficially, rolled it into a thin cylinder, ignited it in the candleflame, applied it when ignited to the apex of the cone till the latter reached the stage of rutilance, placed the cylinder in the basin of the candlestick disposing its unconsumed part in such a manner as to facilitate total combustion.

What followed this operation?

That truncated conical crater summit of the diminutive volcano emitted a vertical and serpentine fume redolent of aromatic oriental incense.

What homothetic objects, other than the candlestick, stood on the mantelpiece?

A timepiece of striated Connemara marble, stopped at the hour of 4.46 a. m. on the 21 March 1896, matrimonial gift of Matthew Dillon: a dwarf tree of glacial arborescence under a transparent bellshade, matrimonial gift of Luke and Caroline Doyle: an embalmed owl, matrimonial gift of Alderman John Hooper.

What interchanges of looks took place between these three objects and Bloom?

In the mirror of the giltbordered pierglass the undecorated back of the dwarf tree regarded the upright back of the embalmed owl. Before the mirror the matrimonial gift of Alderman John Hooper with a clear melancholy wise bright motionless compassionate gaze regarded Bloom while Bloom with obscure tranquil profound motionless compassionated gaze regarded the matrimonial gift of Luke and Caroline Doyle.

What composite asymmetrical image in the mirror then attracted his attention?

The image of a solitary (ipsorelative) mutable (aliorelative) man.

Why solitary (ipsorelative)?

> *Brothers and sisters had he none,*
> *Yet that man's father was his grandfather's son.*

Why mutable (aliorelative)?

From infancy to maturity he had resembled his maternal procreatrix. From maturity to senility he would increasingly resemble his paternal creator.

What final visual impression was communicated to him by the mirror?

The optical reflection of several inverted volumes improperly arranged and not in the order of their common letters with scintillating titles on the two bookshelves opposite.

Catalogue these books.

Thom's Dublin Post Office Directory, 1886.

Denis Florence M'Carthy's *Poetical Works* (copper beechleaf bookmark at p. 5).

Shakespeare's *Works* (dark crimson morocco, goldtooled).

The Useful Ready Reckoner (brown cloth).

The Secret History of the Court of Charles II (red cloth, tooled binding).

The Child's Guide (blue cloth).

When We Were Boys by William O'Brien M. P. (green cloth, slightly faded, envelope bookmark at p. 217).

Thoughts from Spinoza (maroon leather).

The Story of the Heavens by Sir Robert Ball (blue cloth).

Ellis's *Three Trips to Madagascar* (brown cloth, title obliterated).

The Stark-Munro Letters by A. Conan Doyle, property of the City of Dublin Public Library, 106 Capel Street, lent 21 May (Whitsun Eve) 1904, due 4 June 1904, 13 days overdue (black cloth binding, bearing white letternumber ticket).

Voyages in China by 'Viator' (recovered with brown paper, red ink title).

Philosophy of the Talmud (sewn pamphlet).

Lockhart's *Life of Napoleon* (cover wanting, marginal annotations, minimising victories, aggrandising defeats of the protagonist).

Soll und Haben by Gustav Freytag (black boards, Gothic characters, cigarette coupon bookmark at p. 24).

Hozier's *History of the Russo-Turkish War* (brown cloth, 2 volumes, with gummed label, Garrison Library, Governor's Parade, Gibraltar, on verso of cover).

Laurence Bloomfield in Ireland by William Allingham (second edition, green cloth, gilt trefoil design, previous owner's name on recto of flyleaf erased).

A Handbook of Astronomy (cover, brown leather, detached, 5 plates, antique letterpress long primer, author's footnotes nonpareil, marginal clues brevier, captions small pica).

The Hidden Life of Christ (black boards).

In the Track of the Sun (yellow cloth, titlepage missing, recurrent title intestation).

Physical Strength and How to Obtain It by Eugen Sandow (red cloth).

Short but yet Plain Elements of Geometry written in French by F. Ignat. Pardies and rendered into Englifh by John Harris D. D. London, printed for R. Knaplock at the Bifhop's Head MDCCXI, with dedicatory epiftle to his worthy friend Charles Cox, efquire, Member of Parliament for the burgh of Southwark and having ink calligraphed statement on the flyleaf certifying that the book was the property of Michael Gallagher, dated this 10th day of May 1822 and requefting the perfon who should find it, if the book should be loft or go aftray, to reftore it to Michal Gallagher, carpenter, Dufery Gate, Ennifcorthy, county Wicklow, the fineft place in the world.

What reflections occupied his mind during the process of reversion of the inverted volumes?

The necessity of order, a place for everything and everything in its place: the deficient appreciation of literature possessed by females: the incongruity of an apple incuneated in a tumbler and of an umbrella inclined in a closestool: the insecurity of hiding any secret document behind, beneath or between the pages of a book.

Which volume was the largest in bulk?

Hozier's *History of the Russo-Turkish War*.

What among other data did the second volume of the work in question contain?

The name of a decisive battle (forgotten), frequently remembered by a decisive officer, major Brian Cooper Tweedy (remembered).

Why, firstly and secondly, did he not consult the work in question?

Firstly, in order to exercise mnemotechnic: secondly, because after an interval of amnesia, when seated at the central table, about to consult the work in question, he remembered by mnemotechnic the name of the military engagement, Plevna.

What caused him consolation in his sitting posture?

The candour, nudity, pose, tranquillity, youth, grace, sex, counsel of a statue erect in the centre of the table, an image of Narcissus purchased by auction from P. A. Wren, 9 Bachelor's Walk.

What caused him irritation in his sitting posture?

Inhibitory pressure of collar (size 17) and waistcoat (5 buttons), two articles of clothing superfluous in the costume of mature males and inelastic to alterations of mass by expansion.

How was the irritation allayed?

He removed his collar, with contained black necktie and collapsible stud, from his neck to a position on the left of the table. He unbuttoned successively in reversed direction waistcoat, trousers, shirt and vest along the medial line of irregular incrispated black hairs extending in triangular convergence from the pelvic basin over the circumference of the abdomen and umbilicular fossicle along the medial line of nodes to the intersection of the sixth pectoral vertebræ, thence produced both ways at right angles and terminating in circles described about two equidistant points, right and left, on the summits of the mammary prominences. He unbraced successively each of six minus one braced trouser buttons, arranged in pairs, of which one incomplete.

What involuntary actions followed?

He compressed between 2 fingers the flesh circumjacent to a cicatrice in the left infracostal region below the diaphragm resulting from a sting inflicted 2 weeks and 3 days previously (23 May 1904) by a bee. He scratched imprecisely with his right hand, though insensible of prurition, various points and surfaces of his partly exposed, wholly abluted skin. He inserted his left hand into the left lower pocket of his waistcoat and extracted and replaced a silver coin (1 shilling), placed there (presumably) on the occasion (17 October 1903) of the interment of Mrs Emily Sinico, Sydney Parade.

Compile the budget for 16 June 1904.

Debit	£. s. d.	Credit	£. s. d.
1 Pork kidney	0. 0. 3	Cash in hand	0. 4. 9
1 Copy *Freeman's Journal*	0. 0. 1	Commission recd. *Freeman's Journal*	
1 Bath and gratification	0. 1. 6		1. 7. 6
Tramfare	0. 0. 1	Loan (Stephen Dedalus)	1. 7. 0
1 In Memoriam Patrick Dignam			£. 2. 19. 3
	0. 5. 0		
2 Banbury cakes	0. 0. 1		
1 Lunch	0. 0. 7		
1 Renewal fee for book	0. 1. 0		
1 Packet notepaper and envelopes			
	0. 0. 2		
1 Dinner and gratification	0. 2. 0		
1 Postal order and stamp	0. 2. 8		
Tramfare	0. 0. 1		
1 Pig's Foot	0. 0. 4		
1 Sheep's Trotter	0. 0. 3		
1 Cake Fry's plain chocolate	0. 0. 1		
1 Square soda bread	0. 0. 4		
1 Coffee and bun	0. 0. 4		
Loan (Stephen Dedalus) refunded			
	1. 7. 0		
BALANCE	0. 17. 5		
	£. 2. 19. 3		

Did the process of divestiture continue?

Sensible of a benignant persistent ache in his footsoles he extended his foot to one side and observed the creases, protuberances and salient points caused by foot pressure in the course of walking repeatedly in several different directions, then, inclined, he disnoded the laceknots, unhooked and loosened the laces, took off each of his two boots for the second time, detached the partially moistened right sock through the fore part of which the nail of his great toe had again effracted, raised his right foot and, having unhooked a purple elastic sock suspender, took off his right sock, placed his unclothed right foot on the margin of the seat of his chair, picked at and gently lacerated the protruding part of the great toenail, raised the part lacerated to his nostrils and inhaled the odour of the quick, then with satisfaction threw away the lacerated unguical fragment.

Why with satisfaction?

Because the odour inhaled corresponded to other odours inhaled of other unguical fragments, picked and lacerated by Master Bloom, pupil of Mrs Ellis's juvenile school, patiently each night in the act of brief genuflection and nocturnal prayer and ambitious meditation.

In what ultimate ambition had all concurrent and consecutive ambitions now coalesced?

Not to inherit by right of primogeniture, gavelkind or borough English, or possess in perpetuity an extensive demesne of a sufficient number of acres, roods and perches, statute land measure (valuation £42), of grazing turbary surrounding a baronial hall with gatelodge and carriage drive nor, on the other hand, a terracehouse or semidetached villa, described as *Rus in Urbe* or *Qui si Sana*, but to purchase by private treaty in fee simple a thatched bungalowshaped 2 storey dwellinghouse of southerly aspect, surmounted by vane and lightning conductor, connected with the earth, with porch covered by parasitic plants (ivy or Virginia creeper), halldoor, olive green, with smart carriage finish and neat doorbrasses, stucco front with gilt tracery at eaves and gable, rising, if possible, upon a gentle eminence with agreeable prospect from balcony with stone pillar parapet over unoccupied and unoccupyable interjacent pastures and standing in 5 or 6 acres of its own ground, at such a distance from the nearest public thoroughfare as to render its houselights visible at night above and through a quickset hornbeam hedge of topiary cutting, situate at a given point not less than 1 statute mile from the periphery of the metropolis, within a time limit of not more than 5 minutes from tram or train line (e. g., Dundrum, south, or Sutton, north, both localities equally reported by trial to resemble the terrestrial poles in being favourable climates for phthisical subjects), the premises to be held under feefarmgrant, lease 999 years, the messuage to consist of 1 drawingroom with baywindow (2 lancets), thermometer affixed, 1 sittingroom, 4 bedrooms, 2 servant's rooms, tiled kitchen with close range and scullery, lounge hall fitted with linen wallpresses, fumed oak sectional bookcase containing the Encyclopaedia Britannica and New Century Dictionary, transverse obsolete medieval and oriental weapons, dinner gong, alabaster lamp, bowl pendant, vulcanite automatic telephone receiver with adjacent directory, handtufted Axminster carpet with cream ground and trellis border, loo table with pillar and claw legs, hearth with massive firebrasses and ormolu mantel chronometer clock, guaranteed timekeeper with cathedral chime, barometer with hygrographic chart, comfortable lounge settees and corner fitments, upholstered in ruby plush with good springing and sunk centre, three banner Japanese screen and cuspidors (club style, rich winecoloured leather, gloss renewable with a minimum of labour by use of linseed oil and vinegar) and pyramidically prismatic central chandelier lustre, bentwood perch with a fingertame parrot (expurgated language), embossed mural paper at 10/- per dozen with transverse swags of carmine floral design and top crown frieze, staircase, three continuous flights at successive right angles, of varnished clear-grained oak, treads and risers, newel, balusters and handrail, with steppedup panel dado, dressed with camphorated wax, bathroom, hot and cold supply, reclining and shower: water closet on mezzanine provided with opaque singlepane oblong window, tipup seat, bracket lamp, brass tierod brace, armrests, footstool and artistic oleograph on inner face of door: ditto, plain: servant's apartments with separate sanitary and hygienic necessaries for cook, general and betweenmaid (salary, rising by biennial unearned increments of £2, with comprehensive fidelity insurance annual bonus (£1) and retiring allowance (based on the 65 system) after 30 years' service', pantry, buttery, larder, refrigerator, outoffices, coal and wood cellarage with winebin (still and sparkling vintages) for distinguished guests, if entertained to dinner (evening dress), carbon monoxide gas supply throughout.

What additional attractions might the grounds contain?

As addenda, a tennis and fives court, a shrubbery, a glass summerhouse with tropical palms, equipped in the best botanical manner, a rockery with waterspray, a beehive arranged on humane principles, oval flowerbeds in rectangular grassplots set with eccentric ellipses of scarlet and chrome tulips, blue scillas, crocuses, polyanthus, sweet William, sweet pea, lily of the valley, (bulbs obtainable from sir James W. Mackey (Limited) [wholesale and retail] seed and bulb merchant and nurseryman, agent for chemical manures, 23 Sackville street, upper), an orchard, kitchen garden and vinery, protected against illegal trespassers by glasstopped mural enclosures, a lumbershed with padlock for various inventoried implements.

As?

Eeltraps, lobsterpots, fishingrods, hatchet, steelyard, grindstone, clodcrusher, swatheturner, carriagesack, telescope ladder, 10 tooth rake, washing clogs, haytedder, tumbling rake, billhook, paintpot, brush, hoe and so on.

What improvements might be subsequently introduced?

A rabbitry and fowlrun, a dovecote, a botanical conservatory, 2 hammocks (lady's and gentleman's), a sundial shaded and sheltered by laburnum or lilac trees, an exotically harmonically accorded Japanese tinkle gatebell affixed to left lateral gatepost, a capacious waterbutt, a lawnmower with side delivery and grassbox, a lawnsprinkler with hydraulic hose.

What facilities of transit were desirable?

When citybound frequent connection by train or tram from their respective intermediate station or terminal. When countrybound velocipedes, a chainless freewheel roadster cycle with side basketcar attached, or draught conveyance, a donkey with wicker trap or smart phaeton with good working solidungular cob (roan gelding, 14h).

What might be the name of this erigible or erected residence?
Bloom Cottage. Saint Leopold's. Flowerville.

Could Bloom of 7 Eccles street foresee Bloom of Flowerville?

In loose allwool garments with Harris tweed cap, price 8/6, and useful garden boots with elastic gussets and wateringcan, planting aligned young firtrees, syringing, pruning, staking, sowing hayseed, trundling a weedladen wheelbarrow without excessive fatigue at sunset amid the scent of newmown hay, ameliorating the soil, multiplying wisdom, achieving longevity.

What syllabus of intellectual pursuits was simultaneously possible?

Snapshot photography, comparative study of religions, folklore relative to various amatory and superstitious practices, contemplation of the celestial constellations.

What lighter recreations?

Outdoor: garden and fieldwork, cycling on level macadamised causeways, ascents of moderately high hills, natation in secluded fresh water and unmolested river boating in secure wherry or light curricle with kedge anchor on reaches free from weirs and rapids (period of estivation), vespertinal perambulation or equestrian circumprocession with inspection of sterile landscape and contrastingly agreeable cottager's fires of smoking peat turves (period of hibernation). Indoor discussion in tepid security of unsolved historical and criminal problems: lecture of unexpurgated exotic erotic masterpieces: house carpentry with toolbox containing hammer, awl, nails, screws, tintacks, gimlet, tweezers, bullnose plane and turnscrew.

Might he become a gentleman farmer of field produce and live stock?

Not impossibly, with 1 or 2 stripper cows, 1 pike of upland hay and requisite farming implements, e. g., an end-to-end churn, a turnip pulper etc.

What would be his civic functions and social status among the county families and landed gentry?

Arranged successively in ascending powers of hierarchical order, that of gardener, groundsman, cultivator, breeder, and at the zenith of his career, resident magistrate or justice of the peace with a family crest and coat of arms and appropriate classical motto *(Semper paratus)*, duly recorded in the court directory (Bloom, Leopold P., M. P., P. C., K. P., L. L. D. *honoris causa*, Bloomville, Dundrum) and mentioned in court and fashionable intelligence (Mr and Mrs Leopold Bloom have left Kingstown for England).

What course of action did he outline for himself in such capacity?

A course that lay between undue clemency and excessive rigour: the dispensation in a heterogeneous society of arbitrary classes, incessantly rearranged in terms of greater and lesser social inequality, of unbiassed homogeneous indisputable justice, tempered with mitigants of the widest possible latitude but exactable to the uttermost farthing with confiscation of estate, real and personal, to the crown. Loyal to the highest constituted power in the land, actuated by an innate love of rectitude his aims would be the strict maintenance of public order, the repression of many abuses though not of all simultaneously (every measure of reform or retrenchment being a preliminary solution to be contained by fluxion in the final solution), the upholding of the letter of the law (common, statute and law merchant) against all traversers in covin and trespassers acting in contravention of bylaws and regulations, all resuscitators (by trespass and petty larceny of kindlings) of venville rights, obsolete by desuetude, all orotund instigators of international persecution, all perpetuators of international animosities, all menial molestors of domestic conviviality, all recalcitrant violators of domestic connubiality.

Prove that he had loved rectitude from his earliest youth.

To master Percy Apjohn at High School in 1880 he had divulged his disbelief in the tenets of the Irish (protestant) church (to which his father Rudolf Virag, later Rudolph Bloom, had been converted from the Israelitic faith and communion in 1865 by the Society for promoting Christianity among the jews) subsequently abjured by him in favour of Roman catholicism at the epoch of and with a view to his matrimony in 1888. To Daniel Magrane and Francis Wade in 1882 during a juvenile friendship (terminated by the premature emigration of the former) he had advocated during nocturnal perambulations the political theory of colonial (e. g. Canadian) expansion and the evolutionary theories of Charles Darwin, expounded in

The Descent of Man and *The Origin of Species.* In 1885 he had publicly expressed his adherence to the collective and national economic programme advocated by James Fintan Lalor, John Fisher Murray, John Mitchel, J. F. X. O'Brien and others, the agrarian policy of Michael Davitt, the constitutional agitation of Charles Stewart Parnell (M. P. for Cork City), the programme of peace, retrenchment and reform of William Ewart Gladstone (M. P. for Midlothian, N. B.) and, in support of his political convictions, had climbed up into a secure position amid the ramifications of a tree on Northumberland road to see the entrance (2 February 1888) into the capital of a demonstrative torchlight procession of 20,000, divided into 120 trade corporations, bearing 2,000 torches in escort of the marquess of Ripon and John Morley.

How much and how did he propose to pay for this country residence?

As per prospectus of the Industrious Foreign Acclimatised Nationalised Friendly Stateaided Building Society (incorporated 1874), a maximum of £60 per annum, being 1/6th of an assured income, derived from giltedged securities, representing at 5% simple interest on capital of £1,200 (estimate of price at 20 years purchase) of which 1/3rd to be paid on acquisition and the balance in the form of annual rent, viz. £800 plus 2½% interest on the same, repayable quarterly in equal annual instalments until extinction by amorti ation of loan advanced for purchase within a period of 20 years, amounting to an annual rental of £64, headrent included, the titledeeds to remain in possession of the lender or lenders with a saving clause envisaging forced sale, foreclosure and mutual compensation in the event of protracted failure to pay the terms assigned, otherwise the messuage to become the absolute property of the tenant occupier upon expiry of the period of years stipulated.

What rapid but insecure means to opulence might facilitate immediate purchase?

A private wireless telegraph which would transmit by dot and dash system the result of a national equine handicap (flat or steeplechase) of 1 or more miles and furlongs won by an outsider at odds of 50 to 1 at 3 hr. 8 m. p. m. at Ascot (Greenwich time) the message being received and available for betting purposes in Dublin at 2. 59 p. m. (Dunsink time). The unexpected discovery of an object of great monetary value: precious stone, valuable adhesive or unpressed postage stamps (7-shilling, mauve, imperforate, Hamburg, 1866: 4 pence, rose, blue, paper perforate, Great Britain, 1855: 1 franc, stone, official, rouletted, diagonal surcharge, Luxembourg, 1878), antique dynastical ring, unique relic in unusual repositories or by unusual means: from the air (dropped by an eagle in flight), by fire amid the carbonised remains of an incendiated edifice), in the sea (amid flotsam, jetsam, lagan and derelict), on earth (in the gizzard of a comestible fowl). A Spanish prisoner's donation of a distant treasure of valuables or specie or bullion lodged with a solvent banking corporation 100 years previously at 5% compound interest of the collective worth of £5,000,000 stg (five million pounds sterling). A contract with an inconsiderate contractee for the delivery of 32 consignments of some given commodity in consideration of cash payment on delivery at the initial rate of 1/4d. to be increased constantly in the geometrical progression of 2 (1/4d., 1/2d., 1d., 2d., 4d., 8d., 1s. 4d., 2s. 8d. to 32 terms). A prepared scheme based on a study of the laws of probability to break the bank at Monte Carlo. A solution of the secular problem of the quadrature of the circle, government premium £1,000,000 sterling.

Was vast wealth acquirable through industrial channels?

The reclamation of dunams of waste arenary soil, proposed in the prospectus of Agendath Netaim, Bleibtreustrasse, Berlin, W.15, by the cultivation of orange plantations and melonfields and reafforestation. The utilisation of waste paper, fells of sewer rodents, human excrement possessing chemical properties, in view of the vast production of the first, vast number of the second and immense quantity of the third, every normal human being of average vitality and appetite producing annually, cancelling byproducts of water, a sum total of 80 lbs. (mixed animal and vegetable diet), to be multiplied by 4,386,035 the total population of Ireland according to the census returns of 1901.

Were there schemes of wider scope?

A scheme to be formulated and submitted for approval to the harbour commissioners for the exploitation of white coal (hydraulic power), obtained by hydroelectric plant at peak of tide at Dublin bar or at head of water at Poulaphouca or Powerscourt or catchment basins of main streams for the economic production of 500,000 W. H. P. of electricity. A scheme to enclose the peninsular delta of the North Bull at Dollymount and erect on the space of the foreland, used for golf links and rifle ranges, an asphalted esplanade with casinos, booths, shooting galleries, hotels, boardinghouses, readingrooms, establishments for mixed bathing. A scheme for the use of dogvans and goatvans for the delivery of early morning milk. A scheme for the development of Irish tourist traffic in and around Dublin by means of petrolpropelled riverboats, plying in the fluvial fairway between Island bridge and Ringsend, charabancs, narrow gauge local railways, and pleasure steamers for coastwise navigation [10/- per person per day, guide (trilingual) included]. A scheme for the repristination of passenger and goods traffics over Irish waterways, when freed from weedbeds. A scheme to connect by tramline the Cattle Market (North Circular road and Prussia street) with the quays (Sheriff street, lower, and East Wall), parallel with the Link line railway laid (in conjunction with the Great Southern and Western railway line) between the cattle park, Liffey junction, and terminus of Midland Great Western railway 43 to 45 North Wall, in proximity to the terminal stations or Dublin branches of Great Central Railway, Midland Railway of England, City of Dublin Steam Packet Company, Lancashire Yorkshire Railway Company, Dublin and Glasgow Steam Packet Company, Glasgow Dublin and Londonderry Steam Packet Company (Laird line), British and Irish Steam Packet Company, Dublin and Morecambe Steamers, London and North Western Railway Company, Dublin Port and Docks Board Landing Sheds and transit sheds of Palgrave, Murphy and Company, steamship owners, agents for steamers from Mediterranean, Spain, Portugal, France, Belgium and Holland and for animal transport and of additional mileage operated by the Dublin United Tramways Company, limited, to be covered by graziers' fees.

Positing what protasis would the contraction for such several schemes become a natural and necessary apodosis?

Given a guarantee equal to the sum sought, the support, by deed of gift and transfer vouchers during donor's lifetime or by bequest after donor's painless extinction, of eminent financiers (Blum Pasha, Rothschild, Guggenheim, Hirsch, Montefiore, Morgan, Rockefeller) possessing fortunes in 6 figures, amassed during a successful life, and joining capital with opportunity the thing required was done.

What eventually would render him independent of such wealth?
The independent discovery of a goldseam of inexhaustible ore.

For what reason did he meditate on schemes so difficult of realisation?
It was one of his axioms that similar meditations or the automatic relation to himself of a narrative concerning himself or tranquil recollection of the past when practised habitually before retiring for the night alleviated fatigue and produced as a result sound repose and renovated vitality.

His justifications?

As a physicist he had learned that of the 70 years of complete human life at least 2/7ths, viz., 20 years passed in sleep. As a philosopher he knew that at the termination of any allotted life only an infinitesimal part of any person's desires has been realised. As a physiologist he believed in the artificial placation of malignant agencies chiefly operative during somnolence.

What did he fear?

The committal of homicide or suicide during sleep by an aberration of the light of reason, the incommensurable categorical intelligence situated in the cerebral convolutions.

What were habitually his final meditations?

Of some one sole unique advertisement to cause passers to stop in wonder, a poster novelty, with all extraneous accretions excluded, reduced to its simplest and most efficient terms not exceeding the span of casual vision and congruous with the velocity of modern life.

What did the first drawer unlocked contain?

A Vere Foster's handwriting copybook, property of Milly (Millicent) Bloom, certain pages of which bore diagram drawings marked *Papli*, which showed a large globular head with 5 hairs erect, 2 eyes in profile, the trunk full front with 3 large buttons, 1 triangular foot: 2 fading photographs of queen Alexandra of England and of Maud Branscombe, actress and professional beauty: a Yuletide card, bearing on it a pictorial representation of a parasitic plant, the legend *Mizpah*, the date Xmas 1892, the name of the senders, from Mr and Mrs M. Comerford, the versicle: *May this Yuletide bring to thee, Joy and peace and welcome glee:* a butt of red partly liquefied sealing wax, obtained from the stores department of Messrs Hely's, Ltd., 89, 90 and 91 Dame street: a box containing the remainder of a gross of gilt 'J' pennibs, obtained from same department of same firm: an old sandglass which rolled containing sand which rolled: a sealed prophecy (never unsealed) written by Leopold Bloom in 1886 concerning the consequences of the passing into law of William Ewart Gladstone's Home Rule bill of 1886 (never passed into law): a bazaar ticket N° 2004, of S. Kevin's Charity Fair, price 6d. 100 prizes: an infantile epistle, dated, small em monday, reading: capital pee Papli comma capital aitch How are you note of interrogation capital eye I am very well full stop new paragraph signature with flourishes capital em Milly no stop: a cameo brooch, property of Ellen Bloom (born Higgins), deceased: 3 typewritten letters, addressee, Henry Flower, c/o P.

O. Westland Row, addresser, Martha Clifford, c/o P. O. Dolphin's Barn: the transliterated name and address of the addresser of the 3 letters in reserved alphabetic boustrophedontic punctated quadrilinear cryptogram (vowels suppressed) N. IGS. /WI. UU. OX/W. OKS. MH/Y. IM: a press cutting from an English weekly periodical *Modern Society*, subject corporal chastisement in girls' schools: a pink ribbon which had festooned an Easter egg in the year 1899: two partly uncoiled rubber preservatives with reserve pockets, purchased by post from Box 32, P. O., Charing Cross, London, W. C.: 1 pack of 1 dozen creamlaid envelopes and faintruled notepaper, watermarked, now reduced by 3: some assorted Austrian-Hungarian coins: 2 coupons of the Royal and Privileged Hungarian Lottery: a lowpower magnifying glass: 2 erotic photocards showing: a) buccal coition between nude señorita (rere presentation, superior position) and nude torero (fore presentation, inferior position): b) anal violation by male religious (fully clothed, eyes abject) of female religious (partly clothed, eyes direct), purchased by post from Box 32, P. O., Charing Cross, London, W. C.,: a press cutting of recipe for renovation of old tan boots: a 1d. adhesive stamp, lavender, of the reign of Queen Victoria: a chart of measurements of Leopold Bloom compiled before, during and after 2 months of consecutive use of Sandow-Whiteley's pulley exerciser (men's 15/-, athlete's 20/-) viz., chest 28 in. and 29 ½ in., biceps 9 in., and 10 in., forearm 8 ½ and 9 in., thigh 10 in. and 12 in., calf 11 in. and 12 in.: 1 prospectus of the Wonderworker, the world's greatest remedy for rectal complaints direct from Wonderworker, Coventry House, South Place, London E. C., addressed to Mrs L. Bloom with brief accompanying note commencing: Dear Madam.

Quote the textual terms in which the prospectus claimed advantages for this thaumaturgic remedy.

It heals and soothes while you sleep, in case of trouble in breaking wind, assists nature in the most formidable way, insuring instant relief in discharge of gases, keeping parts clean and free natural action, an initial outlay of 7/6 making a new man of you and life worth living. Ladies find Wonderworker especially useful, a pleasant surprise when they note delightful result like a cool drink of fresh spring water on a sultry summer's day. Recommend it to your lady and gentlemen friends, lasts a lifetime. Insert long round end. Wonderworker.

Were there testimonials?

Numerous. From clergyman, British naval officer, wellknown author, city man, hospital nurse, lady, mother of five, absentminded beggar.

How did absentminded beggar's concluding testimonial conclude?

What a pity the government did not supply our men with wonderworkers during the South African campaign! What a relief it would have been!

What object did Bloom add to this collection of objects?

A 4th typewritten letter received by Henry Flower (let H. F. be L. B.) from Martha Clifford (find M. C.).

What pleasant reflection accompanied this action?

The reflection that, apart from the letter in question, his magnetic face, form and address had been favourably received during the course of the preceding day by a wife (Mrs Josephine Breen, born Josie Powell); a nurse, Miss Callan (Christian name unknown), a maid, Gertrude (Gerty, family name unknown).

What possibility suggested itself?

The possibility of exercising virile power of fascination in the most immediate future after an expensive repast in a private apartment in the company of an elegant courtesan, of corporal beauty, moderately mercenary, variously instructed, a lady by origin.

What did the 2nd drawer contain?

Documents: the birth certificate of Leopold Paula Bloom: an endowment assurance policy of £500 in the Scottish Widows' Assurance Society intestated Millicent (Milly) Bloom, coming into force at 25 years as with profit policy of £430, £462-10-0 and £500 at 60 years or death, 65 years or death and death, respectively, or with profit policy (paidup) of £299-10-0 together with cash payment of £133-10-0, at option: a bank passbook issued by the Ulster Bank, College Green branch showing statement of a/c for half year ending 31 December 1903, balance in depositor's favour: £18-14-6 (eighteen pounds, fourteen shillings and sixpence, sterling), net personalty: certificate of possession of £900 Canadian 4% (inscribed) government stock (free of stamp duty): dockets of the Catholic Cemeteries' (Glasnevin) Committee, relative to a graveplot purchased: a local press cutting concerning change of name by deedpoll.

Quote the textual terms of this notice.

I, Rudolph Virag, now resident at n° 52 Clanbrassil street, Dublin, formerly of Szombathely in the kingdom of Hungary, hereby give notice that I have assumed and intend henceforth upon all occasions and at all times to be known by the name of Rudolph Bloom.

What other objects relative to Rudolph Bloom (born Virag) were in the 2nd drawer?

An indistinct daguerreotype of Rudolph Virag and his father Leopold Virag executed in the year 1852 in the portrait atelier of their (respectively) 1st and 2nd cousin, Stefan Virag of Szesfehervar, Hungary. An ancient hagadah book in which a pair of hornrimmed convex spectacles inserted marked the passage of thanksgiving in the ritual prayers for Pessach (Passover): a photocard of the Queen's Hotel, Ennis, proprietor, Rudolph Bloom: an envelope addressed *To my Dear Son Leopold.*

What fractions of phrases did the lecture of those five whole words evoke?

Tomorrow will be a week that I received . . . it is no use Leopold to be . . . with your dear mother . . . that is not more to stand . . . to her . . . all for me is out . . . be kind to Athos, Leopold . . . my dear son . . . always . . . of me . . . *das Herz* . . . *Gott* . . . *dein* . . .

What reminiscences of a human subject suffering from progressive melancholia did these objects evoke in Bloom?

An old man widower, unkempt hair, in bed, with head covered, sighing: an infirm dog, Athos: aconite, resorted to by increasing doses of grains and scruples as a palliative of recrudescent neuralgia: the face in death of a septuagenarian suicide by poison.

Why did Bloom experience a sentiment of remorse?

Because in immature impatience he had treated with disrespect certain beliefs and practices.

As?

The prohibition of the use of fleshmeat and milk at one meal, the hebdomadary symposium of incoordinately abstract, perfervidly concrete mercantile coexreligionist excompatriots: the circumcision of male infants: the supernatural character of Judaic scripture: the ineffability of the tetragrammaron: the sanctity of the sabbath.

How did these beliefs and practices now appear to him?

Not more rational than they had then appeared, not less rational than other beliefs and practices now appeared.

What first reminiscence had he of Rudolph Bloom (deceased)?

Rudolph Bloom (deceased) narrated to his son Leopold Bloom (aged 6) a retrospective arrangement of migrations and settlements in and between Dublin, London, Florence, Milan, Vienna, Budapest, Szombathely, with statements of satisfaction (his grandfather having seen Maria Theresa, empress of Austria, queen of Hungary), with commercial advice (having taken care of pence, the pounds having taken care of themselves). Leopold Bloom (aged 6) had accompanied these narrations by constant consultation of a geographical map of Europe (political) and by suggestions for the establishment of affiliated business premises in the various centres mentioned.

Had time equally but differently obliterated the memory of these migrations in narrator and listener?

In narrator by the access of years and in consequence of the use of narcotic toxin: in listener by the access of years and in consequence of the action of distraction upon vicarious experiences.

What idiosyncrasies of the narrator were concomitant products of amnesia?

Occasionally he ate without having previously removed his hat. Occasionally he drank voraciously the juice of gooseberry fool from an inclined plate. Occasionally he removed from his lips the traces of food by means of a lacerated envelope or other accessible fragment of paper.

What two phenomena of senescence were more frequent?

The myopic digital calculation of coins, eructation consequent upon repletion.

What object offered partial consolation for these reminiscences?

The endowment policy, the bank passbook, the certificate of the possession of scrip.

Reduce Bloom by cross multiplication of reverses of fortune, from which these supports protected him, and by elimination of all positive values to a negligible negative irrational unreal quantity.

Successively, in descending helotic order: Poverty: that of the outdoor hawker of imitation jewellery, the dun for the recovery of bad and doubtful debts, the poor rate and deputy cess collector. Mendicancy: that of the fraudulent bankrupt with negligible assets paying 1s. 4d. in the £, sandwich-man, distributor of throwaways, nocturnal vagrant, insinuating sycophant, maimed sailor, blind stripling, superannuated bailiff's man, marfeast, lickplate, spoilsport, pickthank, eccentric public laughingstock seated on bench of public park under discarded perforated umbrella. Destitution: the inmate of Old Man's House (Royal Hospital), Kilmainham, the inmate of Simpson's Hospital for reduced but respectable men permanently disabled by gout or want of sight. Nadir of misery: the aged impotent disfranchised ratesupported moribund lunatic pauper.

With which attendant indignities?

The unsympathetic indifference of previously amiable females, the contempt of muscular males, the acceptance of fragments of bread, the simulated ignorance of casual acquaintances, the latration of illegitimate unlicensed vagabond dogs, the infantile discharge of decomposed vegetable missiles, worth little or nothing or less than nothing.

By what could such a situation be precluded?
By decease (change of state), by departure (change of place).

Which preferably?
The latter, by the line of least resistance.

What considerations rendered it not entirely undesirable?
Constant cohabitation impeding mutual toleration of personal defects. The habit of independent purchase increasingly cultivated. The necessity to counteract by impermanent sojourn the permanence of arrest.

What considerations rendered it not irrational?
The parties concerned, uniting, had increased and multiplied, which being done, offspring produced and educed to maturity, the parties, if now disunited were obliged to reunite for increase and multiplication, which was absurd, to form by reunion the original couple of uniting parties, which was impossible.

What considerations rendered it desirable?
The attractive character of certain localities in Ireland and abroad, as represented in general geographical maps of polychrome design or in special ordnance survey charts by employment of scale numerals and hachures.

In Ireland?
The cliffs of Moher, the windy wilds of Connemara, lough Neagh with submerged petrified city, the Giant's Causeway, Fort Camden and Fort Carlisle, the Golden Vale of Tipperary, the islands of Aran, the pastures of

royal Meath, Brigid's elm in Kildare, the Queen's Island shipyard in Belfast, the Salmon Leap, the lakes of Killarney.

Abroad?

Ceylon (with spicegardens supplying tea to Thomas Kernan, agent for Pulbrook, Robertson and Co, 2 Mincing lane, London, E.C., 5 Dame street, Dublin), Jerusalem, the holy city (with mosque of Omar and gate of Damascus, goal of aspiration), the straits of Gibraltar (the unique birthplace of Marion Tweedy), the Parthenon (containing statues, nude Grecian divinities), the Wall street money market (which controlled international finance), the Plaza de Toros at La Linea, Spain (where O'Hara of the Camerons had slain the bull), Niagara (over which no human being had passed with impunity), the land of the Eskimos (eaters of soap), the forbidden country of Thibet (from which no traveller returns), the bay of Naples (to see which was to die), the Dead Sea.

Under what guidance, following what signs?

At sea, septentrional, by night the polestar, located at the point of intersection of the right line from beta to alpha in Ursa Major produced and divided externally at omega and the hypotenuse of the rightangled triangle formed by the line alpha omega so produced and the line alpha delta of Ursa Major. On land, meridional, a bispherical moon, revealed in imperfect varying phases of lunation through the posterior interstice of the imperfectly occluded skirt of a carnose negligent perambulating female, a pillar of the cloud by day.

What public advertisement would divulge the occultation of the departed?

£5 reward lost, stolen or strayed from his residence 7 Eccles street, missing gent about 40, answering to the name of Bloom, Leopold (Poldy), height 5 ft 9 1/2 inches, full build, olive complexion, may have since grown a beard, when last seen was wearing a black suit. Above sum will be paid for information leading to his discovery.

What universal binomial denominations would be his as entity and nonentity?

Assumed by any or known to none. Everyman or Noman.

What tributes his?

Honour and gifts of strangers, the friends of Everyman. A nymph immortal, beauty, the bride of Noman.

Would the departed never nowhere nohow reappear?

Ever he would wander, selfcompelled, to the extreme limit of his cometary orbit, beyond the fixed stars and variable suns and telescopic planets, astronomical waifs and strays, to the extreme boundary of space, passing from land to land, among peoples, amid events. Somewhere imperceptibly he would hear and somehow reluctantly, suncompelled, obey the summons of recall. Whence, disappearing from the constellation of the Northern Crown he would somehow reappear reborn above delta in the constellation of Cassiopeia and after incalculable eons of peregrination return an estranged avenger, a wreaker of justice on malefactors, a dark crusader, a sleeper awakened, with financial resources (by supposition) surpassing those of Rothschild or of the silver king.

What would render such return irrational?

An unsatisfactory equation between an exodus and return in time through reversible space and an exodus and return in space through irreversible time.

What play of forces, inducing inertia, rendered departure undesirable?

The lateness of the hour, rendering procrastinatory: the obscurity of the night, rendering invisible: the uncertainty of thoroughfares, rendering perilous: the necessity for repose, obviating movement: the proximity of an occupied bed, obviating research: the anticipation of warmth (human) tempered with coolness (linen), obviating desire and rendering desirable: the statue of Narcissus, sound without echo, desired desire.

What advantages were possessed by an occupied, as distinct from an unoccupied bed?

The removal of nocturnal solitude, the superior quality of human (mature female) to inhuman (hotwaterjar) calefaction, the stimulation of matutinal contact, the economy of mangling done on the premises in the case of trousers accurately folded and placed lengthwise between the spring mattress (striped) and the woollen mattress (biscuit section).

What past consecutive causes, before rising preapprehended, of accumulated fatigue did Bloom, before rising, silently recapitulate?

The preparation of breakfast (burnt offering): intestinal congestion and premeditative defecation (holy of holies): the bath (rite of John): the funeral (rite of Samuel): the advertisement of Alexander Keyes (Urim and Thummin): the unsubstantial lunch (rite of Melchizedek): the visit to museum and national library (holy place): the bookhunt along Bedford row, Merchants' Arch, Wellington Quay (Simchath Torah): the music in the Ormond Hotel (Shira Shirim): the altercation with a truculent troglodyte in Bernard Kiernan's premises (holocaust): a blank period of time including a cardrive, a visit to a house of mourning, a leavetaking (wilderness): the eroticism produced by feminine exhibitionism (rite of Onan): the prolonged delivery of Mrs Mina Purefoy (heave offering): the visit to the disorderly house of Mrs Bella Cohen, 82 Tyrone street, lower, and subsequent brawl and chance medley in Beaver street (Armageddon): nocturnal perambulation to and from the cabman's shelter, Butt Bridge (atonement).

What selfimposed enigma did Bloom about to rise in order to go so as to conclude lest he should not conclude involuntarily apprehend?

The cause of a brief sharp unforeseen heard loud lone crack emitted by the insentient material of a strainveined timber table.

What selfinvolved enigma did Bloom risen, going, gathering multicoloured multiform multitudinous garments, voluntarily apprehending, not comprehend?

Who was M'Intosh?

What selfevident enigma pondered with desultory constancy during 30 years did Bloom now, having effected natural obscurity by the extinction of artificial light, silently suddenly comprehend?

Where was Moses when the candle went out?

What imperfections in a perfect day did Bloom, walking, silently, successively, enumerate?

A provisional failure to obtain renewal of an advertisement, to obtain a certain quantity of tea from Thomas Kernan (agent for Pulbrook, Robertson and C°, 5 Dame street, Dublin, and 2 Mincing lane, London, E.C.), to certify the presence or absence of posterior rectal orifice in the case of Hellenic female divinities, to obtain admission (gratuitous or paid) to the performance of *Leah* by Mrs Bandman Palmer at the Gaiety Theatre, 46, 47, 48, 49, South King street.

What impression of an absent face did Bloom, arrested, silently recall?

The face of her father, the late Major Brian Cooper Tweedy, Royal Dublin Fusiliers, of Gibraltar and Rehoboth, Dolphin's Barn.

What recurrent impressions of the same were possible by the hypothesis?

Retreating, at the terminus of the Great Northern Railway, Amiens street, with constant uniform acceleration, along parallel lines meeting at infinity, if produced: along parallel lines, reproduced from infinity, with constant uniform retardation, at the terminus of the Great Northern Railway, Amiens street, returning.

What miscellaneous effects of female personal wearing apparel were perceived by him?

A pair of new inodorous halfsilk black ladies' hose, a pair of new violet garters, a pair of outsize ladies' drawers of India mull, cut on generous lines, redolent of opoponax, jessamine and Muratti's Turkish cigarettes and containing a long bright steel safety pin, folded curvilinear, a camisole of batiste with thin lace border, an accordion underskirt of blue silk moirette, all these objects being disposed irregularly on the top of a rectangular trunk, quadruple battened, having capped corners, with multicoloured labels, initialled on its fore side in white lettering B. C. T. (Brian Cooper Tweedy).

What impersonal objects were perceived?

A commode, one leg fractured, totally covered by square cretonne cutting, apple design, on which rested a lady's black straw hat. Orange-keyed ware, bought of Henry Price, basket, fancy goods, chinaware and ironmongery manufacturer, 21, 22, 23 Moore street, disposed irregularly on the washstand and floor, and consisting of basin, soapdish and brushtray (on the washstand, together), pitcher and night article (on the floor, separate).

Bloom's acts?

He deposited the articles of clothing on a chair, removed his remaining articles of clothing, took from beneath the bolster at the head of the bed a folded long white nightshirt, inserted his head and arms into the proper apertures of the nightshirt, removed a pillow from the head to the foot of the bed, prepared the bedlinen accordingly and entered the bed.

How?

With circumspection, as invariably when entering an abode (his own or not his own): with solicitude, the snake-spiral springs of the mattress being old, the brass quoits and pendent viper radii loose and tremulous under stress and strain: prudently, as entering a lair or ambush of lust or adder: lightly, the less to disturb: reverently, the bed of conception and of birth, of consummation of marriage and of breach of marriage, of sleep and of death.

What did his limbs, when gradually extended, encounter?

New clean bedlinen, additional odours, the presence of a human form, female, hers, the imprint of a human form, male, not his, some crumbs, some flakes of potted meat, recooked, which he removed.

If he had smiled why would he have smiled?

To reflect that each one who enters imagines himself to be the first to enter whereas he is always the last term of a preceding series even if the first term of a succeeding one, each imagining himself to be first, last, only and alone, whereas he is neither first nor last nor only nor alone in a series originating in and repeated to infinity.

What preceding series?

Assuming Mulvey to be the first term of his series, Penrose, Bartell d'Arcy, professor Goodwin, Julius Mastiansky, John Henry Menton, Father Bernard Corrigan, a farmer at the Royal Dublin Society's Horse Show, Maggot O'Reilly, Matthew Dillon, Valentine Blake Dillon (Lord Mayor of Dublin), Christopher Callinan, Lenehan, an Italian organ-grinder, an unknown gentleman in the Gaiety Theatre, Benjamin Dollard, Simon Dedalus, Andrew (Pisser) Burke, Joseph Cuffe, Wisdom Hely, Alderman John Hooper, Dr Francis Brady, Father Sebastian of Mount Argus, a bootblack at the General Post Office, Hugh E. (Blazes) Boylan and so each and so on to no last term.

What were his reflections concerning the last member of this series and late occupant of the bed?

Reflections on his vigour (a bounder), corporal proportion (a billsticker), commercial ability (a bester), impressionability (a boaster).

Why for the observer impressionability in addition to vigour, corporal proportion and commercial ability?

Because he had observed with augmenting frequency in the preceding members of the same series the same concupiscence, inflammably trans-mitted first with alarm, then with understanding, then with desire, finally with fatigue, with alternating symptoms of epicene comprehension and apprehension.

With what antagonistic sentiments were his subsequent reflections affected?

Envy, jealousy, abnegation, equanimity.

Envy?

Of a bodily and mental male organism specially adapted for the super-incumbent posture of energetic human copulation and energetic piston and cylinder movement necessary for the complete satisfaction of a constant but not acute concupiscence resident in a bodily and mental female organism, passive but not obtuse.

Jealousy?

Because a nature full and volatile in its free state, was alternately the agent and reagent of attraction. Because action between agents and reagents at all instants varied, with inverse proportion of increase and decrease, with incessant circular extension and radial reentrance. Because the controlled contemplation of the fluctuation of attraction produced, if desired, a fluctuation of pleasure.

Abnegation?

In virtue of a) acquaintance initiated in September 1903 in the establish-ment of George Mesias, merchant tailor and outfitter, 5 Eden Quay, b) hospitality extended and received in kind, reciprocated and reappropriated in person, c) comparative youth subject to impulses of ambition and mag-nanimity, colleagual altruism and amorous egoism, d) extraracial attraction, intraracial inhibition, supraracial prerogative, e) an imminent provincial musical tour, common current expenses, net proceeds divided.

Equanimity?

As natural as any and every natural act of a nature expressed or under-stood executed in natured nature by natural creatures in accordance with his, her and their natured natures, of dissimilar similarity. As not as calamitous as a cataclysmic annihilation of the planet in consequence of collision with a dark sun. As less reprehensible than theft, highway robbery, cruelty to children and animals, obtaining money under false pretences, forgery, embezzlement, misappropriation of public money, betrayal of public trust, malingering, mayhem, corruption of minors, criminal libel, blackmail, contempt of court, arson, treason, felony, mutiny on the high seas, trespass, burglary, jailbreaking, practice of unnatural vice, desertion from armed forces in the field, perjury, poaching, usury, intelligence with the king's enemies, impersonation, criminal assault, manslaughter, wilful and premeditated murder. As not more abnormal than all other altered processes of adaptation to altered conditions of existence, resulting in a reciprocal equilibrium between the bodily organism and its attendant circumstances, foods, beverages, acquired habits, indulged inclinations, significant disease. As more than inevitable, irreparable.

Why more abnegation than jealousy, less envy than equanimity?

From outrage (matrimony) to outrage (adultery) there arose nought but outrage (copulation) yet the matrimonial violator of the matrimonially violated had not been outraged by the adulterous violator of the adulterously violated.

What retribution, if any?

Assassination, never, as two wrongs did not make one right. Duel by combat, no. Divorce, not now. Exposure by mechanical artifice (automatic bed) or individual testimony (concealed ocular witness), not yet. Suit for damages by legal influence or simulation of assault with evidence of injuries sustained (selfinflicted), not impossibly. If any, positively, connivance, introduction of emulation (material, a prosperous rival agency of publicity: moral, a successful rival agent of intimacy), depreciation, alienation, humiliation, separation protecting the one separated from the other, protecting separator from both.

By what reflections did he, a conscious reactor against the void incertitude, justify to himself his sentiments?

The preordained frangibility of the hymen, the presupposed intangibility of the thing in itself: the incongruity and disproportion between the selfprolonging tension of the thing proposed to be done and the selfabbreviating relaxation of the thing done: the fallaciously inferred debility of the female, the muscularity of the male: the variations of ethical codes: the natural grammatical transition by inversion involving no alteration of sense of an aorist preterite proposition (parsed as masculine subject, monosyllabic onomatopœic transitive verb with direct feminine object) from the active voice into its correlative aorist preterite proposition (parsed as feminine subject, auxiliary verb and quasimonosyllabic onomatopœic past participle with complementary masculine agent) in the passive voice: the continued product of seminators by generation: the continual production of semen by distillation: the futility of triumph or protest or vindication: the inanity of extolled virtue: the lethargy of nescient matter: the apathy of the stars.

In what final satisfaction did these antagonistic sentiments and reflections reduced to their simplest forms, converge?

Satisfaction at the ubiquity in eastern and western terrestrial hemispheres, in all habitable lands and islands explored or unexplored (the land of the midnight sun, the islands of the blessed, the isles of Greece, the land of promise) of adipose posterior female hemispheres, redolent of milk and honey and of excretory sanguine and seminal warmth, reminiscent of secular families of curves of amplitude, insusceptible of moods of impression or of contrarieties of expression, expressive of mute immutable mature animality.

The visible signs of antesatisfaction?
An approximate erection: a solicitous adversion: a gradual elevation: a tentative revelation; a silent contemplation.

Then?
He kissed the plump mellow yellow smellow melons of her rump, on each plump melonous hemisphere, in their mellow yellow furrow, with obscure prolonged provocative melonsmellonous osculation.

The visible signs of postsatisfaction?
A silent contemplation: a tentative velation: a gradual abasement: a solicitous aversion: a proximate erection.

What followed this silent action?
Somnolent invocation, less somnolent recognition, incipient excitation, catechetical interrogation.

With what modifications did the narrator reply to this interrogation?
Negative: he omitted to mention the clandestine correspondence between Martha Clifford and Henry Flower, the public altercation at, in and in the vicinity of the licensed premises of Bernard Kiernan and Co, Limited, 8, 9 and 10 Little Britain street, the erotic provocation and response thereto caused by the exhibitionism of Gertrude (Gerty), surname unknown. Positive: he included mention of a performance by Mrs Bandman Palmer of *Leah* at the Gaiety Theatre, 46, 47, 48, 49 South King street, an invitation to supper at Wynn's (Murphy's) Hotel 35, 36, and 37 Lower Abbey street, a volume of peccaminous pornographical tendency entitled *Sweets of Sin*, anonymous, author a gentleman of fashion, a temporary concussion caused by a falsely calculated movement in the course of a postcenal gymnastic display, the victim (since completely recovered) being Stephen Dedalus, professor and author, eldest surviving son of Simon Dedalus, of no fixed occupation, an aeronautical feat executed by him (narrator) in the presence of a witness, the professor and author aforesaid, with promptitude of decision and gymnastic flexibility.

Was the narration otherwise unaltered by modifications?
Absolutely.

Which event or person emerged as the salient point of his narration?
Stephen Dedalus, professor and author.

What limitations of activity and inhibitions of conjugal rights were perceived by listener and narrator concerning themselves during the course of this intermittent and increasingly more laconic narration?

By the listener a limitation of fertility inasmuch as marriage had been celebrated 1 calendar month after the 18th anniversary of her birth (8 September 1870), viz. 8 October, and consummated on the same date with female issue born 15 June 1889, having been anticipatorily consummated on the 10 September of the same year and complete carnal intercourse, with ejaculation of semen within the natural female organ, having last taken place 5 weeks previous, viz. 27 November 1893, to the birth on 29 December 1893 of second (and only male) issue, deceased 9 January 1894, aged 11 days, there remained a period of 10 years, 5 months and 18 days during which carnal intercourse had been incomplete, without ejaculation of semen within the natural female organ. By the narrator a limitation of activity, mental and corporal, inasmuch as complete mental intercourse between himself and the listener had not taken place since the consummation of puberty, indicated by catamenic hemorrhage, of the female issue of narrator and listener, 15 September 1903, there remained a period of 9 months and 1 day during which in consequence of a preestablished natural comprehension in incomprehension between the consummated females (listener and issue), complete corporal liberty of action had been circumscribed.

How?
By various reiterated feminine interrogation concerning the masculine destination whither, the place where, the time at which, the duration for which, the object with which in the case of temporary absences, projected or effected.

What moved visibly above the listener's and the narrator's invisible thoughts?
The upcast reflection of a lamp and shade, an inconstant series of concentric circles of varying gradations of light and shadow.

In what directions did listener and narrator lie?

Listener, S. E. by E.: Narrator, N. W. by W.: on the 53rd parallel of latitude, N. and 6th meridian of longitude, W.: at an angle of 45° to the terrestrial equator.

In what state of rest or motion?

At rest relatively to themselves and to each other. In motion being each and both carried westward, forward and rereward respectively, by the proper perpetual motion of the earth through everchanging tracks of never-changing space.

In what posture?

Listener: reclined semilaterally, left, left hand under head, right leg extended in a straight line and resting on left leg, flexed, in the attitude of Gea-Tellus, fulfilled, recumbent, big with seed. Narrator: reclined laterally, left, with right and left legs flexed, the indexfinger and thumb of the right hand resting on the bridge of the nose, in the attitude depicted on a snapshot photograph made by Percy Apjohn, the childman weary, the manchild in the womb.

Womb? Weary?

He rests. He has travelled.

With?

Sinbad the Sailor and Tinbad the Tailor and Jinbad the Jailer and Whinbad the Whaler and Ninbad the Nailer and Finbad the Failer and Binbad the Bailer and Pinbad the Pailer and Minbad the Mailer and Hinbad the Hailer and Rinbad the Railer and Dinbad the Kailer and Vinbad the Quailer and Linbad the Yailer and Xinbad the Phthailer.

When?

Going to dark bed there was a square round Sinbad the Sailor roc's auk's egg in the night of the bed of all the auks of the rocs of Darkinbad the Brightdayler.

Where?

●

*   *   *   *   *

◀ YES BECAUSE HE NEVER DID A THING LIKE THAT before as ask to get his breakfast in bed with a couple of eggs since the *City Arms* hotel when he used to be pretending to be laid up with a sick voice doing his highness to make himself interesting to that old faggot Mrs Riordan that he thought he had a great leg of and she never left us a farthing all for masses for herself and her soul greatest miser ever was actually afraid to lay out 4d for her methylated spirit telling me all her ailments she had too much old chat in her about politics and earthquakes and the end of the world let us have a bit of fun first God help the world if all the women were her sort down on bathingsuits and lownecks of course nobody wanted her to wear I suppose she was pious because no man would look at her twice I hope Ill never be like her a wonder she didnt want us to cover our faces but she was a welleducated woman certainly and her gabby talk about Mr Riordan here and Mr Riordan there I suppose he was glad to get shut of her and her dog smelling my fur and always edging to get up under my petticoats especially then still I like that in him polite to old women like that and waiters and beggars too hes not proud out of nothing but not always if ever he got anything really serious the matter with him its much better for them go into a hospital where everything is clean but I suppose Id have to dring it into him for a month yes and then wed have a hospital nurse next thing on the carpet have him staying there till they throw him out or a nun maybe like the smutty photo he has shes as much a nun as Im not yes because theyre so weak and puling when theyre sick they want a woman to get well if his nose bleeds youd think it was O tragic and that dyinglooking one off the south circular when he sprained his foot at the choir party at the sugarloaf Mountain the day I wore that dress Miss Stack bringing him flowers the worst old ones she could find at the bottom of the basket anything at all to get into a mans bedroom with her old maids voice trying to imagine he was dying on account of her to never see thy face again though he looked more like a man with his beard a bit grown in the bed father was the same besides I hate bandaging and dosing when he cut his toe with the razor paring his corns afraid hed get blood poisoning but if it was a thing I was sick then wed see what attention only of course the woman hides it not to give all the trouble they do yes he came somewhere Im sure by his appetite anyway love its not or hed be off his feed thinking of her so either it was one of those night women if it was down there he was really and the hotel story he made up a pack of lies to hide it planning it Hynes kept me who did I meet ah yes I met do you remember Menton and who else who let me see that big babbyface I saw him and he not long married flirting with a young girl at Pooles Myriorama and turned my back on him when he slinked out looking quite conscious what harm but he had the impudence to make up to me one time well done to him mouth almighty and his boiled eyes of all the big stupoes I ever met and thats called a solicitor only for I hate having a long wrangle in bed or else if its not that its some little bitch or other he got in with somewhere or picked up on the sly if they only knew him as well as I do yes because the day before yesterday he was scribbling something a letter when I came into the front room for the matches to show him Dignams death in the paper as if something told me and he covered it up with the blottingpaper pretending to be thinking about business so very probably that was it to somebody who thinks she has a softy in him because all men get a bit like that at his age especially getting on to forty he is now so as to wheedle any money she can out of him no fool like an old fool and then the usual kissing my bottom was to hide it not that I care two straws who he does it with or knew before that way though Id like to find out so long as I dont have the two of them under my nose all the time like that slut that Mary we had in Ontario terrace padding out her false bottom to excite him bad enough to get the smell of those painted women off him once or twice I had a suspicion by getting him to come near me when I found the long hair on his coat without that one when I went into the kitchen pretending he was drinking water 1 woman is not enough for them it was all his fault of course ruining servants then proposing that she could eat at our table on Christmas if you please O no thank you not in my house stealing my potatoes and the oysters 2/6 per doz going out to see her aunt if you please common robbery so it was but I was sure he had something on with that one it takes me to find out a thing like that he said you have no proof it was her proof O yes her aunt was very fond of oysters but I told her what I thought of her suggesting me to go out to be alone with her I wouldnt lower myself to spy on them the garters I found in her room the Friday she was out that was enough for me a little bit too much I saw too that her face swelled up on her with temper when I gave her her weeks notice better do without them altogether do out the rooms myself quicker only for the damn cooking and throwing out the dirt I gave it to him anyhow either she or me leaves the house I couldnt even touch him if I thought he was with a dirty barefaced liar and sloven like that one denying it up to my face and singing about the place in the W C too because she knew she was too well off yes because he couldnt possibly do without it that long so he must do it somewhere and the last time he came on my bottom when was it the night Boylan gave my hand a great squeeze going along by the Tolka in my hand there steals another I just pressed the back of his like

that with my thumb to squeeze back singing the young May Moon shes
beaming love because he has an idea about him and me hes not such a fool
he said Im dining out and going to the Gaiety though Im not going to give
him the satisfaction in any case God knows hes change in a way not to be
always and ever wearing the same old hat unless I paid some nicelooking
boy to do it since I cant do it myself a young boy would like me Id confuse
him a little alone with him if we were Id let him see my garters the new
ones and make him turn red looking at him seduce him I know what boys
feel with that down on their cheek doing that frigging drawing out the
thing by the hour question and answer would you do this that and the other
with the coalman yes with a bishop yes I would because I told him about
some Dean or Bishop was sitting beside me in the jews Temples gardens
when I was knitting that woollen thing a stranger to Dublin what place
was it and so on about the monuments and he tired me out with statues
encouraging him making him worse than he is who is in your mind now tell
me who are you thinking of who is it tell me his name who tell me who the
German Emperor is it yes imagine Im him think of him can you feel him
trying to make a whore of me what he never will he ought to give it up now
at this age of his life simply ruination for any woman and no satisfaction in
it pretending to like it till he comes and then finish it off myself anyway and
it makes your lips pale anyhow its done now once and for all with all the
talk of the world about it people make its only the first time after that its
just the ordinary do it and think no more about it why cant you kiss a man
without going and marrying him first you sometimes love to wildly when
you feel that way so nice all over you you cant help yourself I wish some
man or other would take me sometime when hes there and kiss me in his
arms theres nothing like a kiss long and hot down to your soul almost
paralyses you then I hate that confession when I used to go to Father
Corrigan he touched me father and what harm if he did where and I said on
the canal bank like a fool but whereabouts on your person my child on the
leg behind high up was it yes rather high up was it where you sit down yes
O Lord couldnt he say bottom right out and have done with it what has
that got to do with it and did you whatever way he put it I forget no father
and I always think of the real father what did he want to know for when I
already confessed it to God he had a nice fat hand the palm moist always I
wouldnt mind feeling it neither would he Id say by the bullneck in his
horsecollar I wonder did he know me in the box I could see his face he
couldnt see mine of course hed never turn or let on still his eyes were red
when his father died theyre lost for a woman of course must be terrible
when a man cries let alone them Id like to be embraced by one in his

vestments and the smell of incense off him like the pope besides theres no
danger with a priest if youre married hes too careful about himself then
give something to H H the pope for a penance I wonder was he satisfied
with me one thing I didnt like his slapping me behind going away so
familiarly in the hall though I laughed Im not a horse or an ass am I I
suppose he was thinking of his father I wonder is he awake thinking of me
or dreaming am I in it who gave him that flower he said he bought he smelt
of some kind of a drink not whisky or stout or perhaps the sweety kind of
paste they stick their bills up with some liquor Id like to sip those rich-
looking green and yellow expensive drinks those stagedoor johnnies drink
with the opera hats I tasted one with my finger dipped out of that American
that had the squirrel talking stamps with father he had all he could do to
keep himself from falling asleep after the last time we took the port and
potted meat it had a fine salty taste yes because I felt lovely and tired myself
and fell asleep as sound as a top the moment I popped straight into bed till
that thunder woke me up as if the world was coming to an end God be
merciful to us I thought the heavens were coming down about us to punish
when I blessed myself and said a Hail Mary like those awful thunderbolts in
Gibraltar and they come and tell you theres no God what could you do if it
was running and rushing about nothing only make an act of contrition the
candle I lit that evening in Whitefriars street chapel for the month of May
see it brought its luck though hed scoff if he heard because he never goes to
church mass or meeting he says your soul you have no soul inside only grey
matter because he doesnt know what it is to have one yes when I lit the
lamp yes because he must have come 3 or 4 times with that tremendous big
red brute of a thing he has I thought the vein or whatever the dickens they
call it was going to burst though his nose is not so big after I took off all my
things with the blinds down after my hours dressing and perfuming and
combing it like iron or some kind of a thick crowbar standing all the time
he must have eaten oysters I think a few dozen he was in great singing voice
no I never in all my life felt anyone had one the size of that to make you feel
full up he must have eaten a whole sheep after whats the idea making us like
that with a big hole in the middle of us like a Stallion driving it up into you
because thats all they want out of you with that determined vicious look in
his eye I had to halfshut my eyes still he hasnt such a tremendous amount of
spunk in him when I made him pull it out and do it on me considering how
big it is so much the better in case any of it wasnt washed out properly the
last time I let him finish it in me nice invention they made for women for
him to get all the pleasure but if someone gave them a touch of it themselves
theyd know what I went through with Milly nobody would believe cutting

her teeth too and Mina Purefoys husband give us a swing out of your
whiskers filling her up with a child or twins once a year as regular as the
clock always with a smell of children off her the one they called budgers or
something like a nigger with a shock of hair on it Jesusjack the child is a
black the last time I was there a squad of them falling over one another and
bawling you couldnt hear your ears supposed to be healthy not satisfied till
they have us swollen out like elephants or I dont know what supposing I
risked having another not off him though still if he was married Im sure hed
have a fine strong child but I dont know Poldy has more spunk in him yes
thatd be awfully jolly I suppose it was meeting Josie Powell and the funeral
and thinking about me and Boylan set him off well he can think what he
likes now if thatll do him any good I know they were spooning a bit when I
came on the scene he was dancing and sitting out with her the night of
Georgina Simpsons housewarming and then he wanted to ram it down my
neck on account of not liking to see her a wallflower that was why we had
the standup row over politics he began it not me when he said about Our
Lord being a carpenter at last he made me cry of course a woman is so
sensitive about every thing I was fuming with myself after for giving in only
for I knew he was gone on me and the first socialist he said He was he
annoyed me so much I couldnt put him into a temper still he knows a lot of
mixed up things especially about the body and the insides I often wanted to
study up that myself what we have inside us in that family physician I could
always hear his voice talking when the room was crowded and watch him
after that I pretended I had on a coolness with her over him because he
used to be a bit on the jealous side whenever he asked who are you going to
and I said over to Floey and he made me the present of lord Byrons poems
and the three pairs of gloves so that finished that I could quite easily get
him to make it up any time I know how Id even supposing he got in with
her again and was going out to see her somewhere Id know if he refused to
eat the onions I know plenty of ways ask him to tuck down the collar of my
blouse or touch him with my veil and gloves on going out 1 kiss then would
send them all spinning however alright well see then let him go to her she
of course would only be too delighted to pretend shes mad in love with him
that I wouldnt so much mind Id just go to her and ask her do you love him
and look her square in the eyes she couldnt fool me but he might imagine
he was and make a declaration with his plabbery kind of a manner to her
like he did to me though I had the devils own job to get it out of him
though I liked him for that it showed he could hold in and wasnt to be got
for the asking he was on the pop of asking me too the night in the kitchen I
was rolling the potato cake theres something I want to say to you only for I

put him off letting on I was in a temper with my hands and arms full of
pasty flour in any case I let out too much the night before talking of dreams
so I didnt want to let him know more than was good for him she used to be
always embracing me Josie whenever he was there meaning him of course
glauming me over and when I said I washed up and down as far as possible
asking me did you wash possible the women are always egging on to that
putting it on thick when hes there they know by his sly eye blinking a bit
putting on the indifferent when they come out with something the kind he
is what spoils him I dont wonder in the least because he was very handsome
at that time trying to look like lord Byron I said I liked though he was too
beautiful for a man and he was a little before we got engaged afterwards
though she didnt like it so much the day I was in fits of laughing with the
giggles I couldnt stop about all my hairpins falling one after another with
the mass of hair I had youre always in great humour she said yes because it
grigged her because she knew what it meant because I used to tell her a
good bit of what went on between us not all but just enough to make her
mouth water but that wasnt my fault she didnt darken the door much after
we were married I wonder what shes got like now after living with that
dotty husband of hers she had her face beginning to look drawn and run
down the last time I saw her she must have been just after a row with him
because I saw on the moment she was edging to draw down a conversation
about husbands and talk about him to run him down what was it she told
me O yes that sometimes he used to go to bed with his muddy boots on
when the maggot takes him just imagine having to get into bed with a thing
like that that might murder you any moment what a man well its not the
one way everyone goes mad Poldy anyway whatever he does always wipes
his feet on the mat when he comes in wet or shine and always blacks his
own boots too and he always takes off his hat when he comes up in the
street like that and now hes going about in his slippers to look for £10000
for a postcard up up O Sweetheart May wouldnt a thing like that simply
bore you stiff to extinction actually too stupid even to take his boots off now
what could you make of a man like that Id rather die 20 times over than
marry another of their sex of course hed never find another woman like me
to put up with him the way I do know me come sleep with me yes and he
knows that too at the bottom of his heart take that Mrs Maybrick that
poisoned her husband for what I wonder in love with some other man yes it
was found out on her wasnt she the downright villain to go and do a thing
like that of course some men can be dreadfully aggravating drive you mad
and always the worst word in the world what do they ask us to marry them
for if were so bad as all that comes to yes because they cant get on without

us white Arsenic she put in his tea off flypaper wasnt it I wonder why they call it that if I asked him hed say its from the Greek leave us as wise as we were before she must have been madly in love with the other fellow to run the chance of being hanged O she didnt care if that was her nature what could she do besides theyre not brutes enough to go and hang a woman surely are they

theyre all so different Boylan talking about the shape of my foot he noticed at once even before he was introduced when I was in the D B C with Poldy laughing and trying to listen I was waggling my foot we both ordered 2 teas and plain bread and butter I saw him looking with his two old maids of sisters when I stood up and asked the girl where it was what do I care with it dropping out of me and that black closed breeches he made me buy takes you half an hour to let them down wetting all myself always with some brandnew fad every other week such a long one I did I forgot my suede gloves on the seat behind that I never got after some robber of a woman and he wanted me to put it in the Irish Times lost in the ladies lavatory D B C Dame street finder return to Mrs Marion Bloom and I saw his eyes on my feet going out through the turning door he was looking when I looked back and I went there for tea 2 days after in the hope but he wasnt now how did that excite him because I was crossing them when we were in the other room first he meant the shoes that are too tight to walk in my hand is nice like that if I only had a ring with the stone for my month a nice aquamarine Ill stick him for one and a gold bracelet I dont like my foot so much still I made him spend once with my foot the night after Goodwins botchup of a concert so cold and windy it was well we had that rum in the house to mull and the fire wasnt black out when he asked to take off my stockings lying on the hearthrug in Lombard street well and another time it was my muddy boots hed like me to walk in all the horses dung I could find but of course hes not natural like the rest of the world that I what did he say I could give 9 points in 10 to Katty Lanner and beat her what does that mean I asked him I forget what he said because the stoppress edition just passed and the man with the curly hair in the Lucan dairy thats so polite I think I saw his face before somewhere I noticed him when I was tasting the butter so I took my time Bartell dArcy too that he used to make fun of when he commenced kissing me on the choir stairs after I sang Gounods *Ave Maria* what are we waiting for O my heart kiss me straight on the brow and part which is my brown part he was pretty hot for all his tinny voice too my low notes he was always raving about if you can believe him I liked the way he used his mouth singing then he said wasnt it terrible to do that there in a place like that I dont see anything so terrible about it Ill tell him about that some day not now and surprise him ay and Ill take him there and show him the very place too we did it so now there you are like it or lump it he thinks nothing can happen without him knowing he hadnt an idea about my mother till we were engaged otherwise hed never have got me so cheap as he did he was 10 times worse himself anyhow begging me to give him a tiny bit cut off my drawers that was the evening coming along Kenilworth square he kissed me in the eye of my glove and I had to take it off asking me questions is it permitted to inquire the shape of my bedroom so I let him keep it as if I forgot it to think of me when I saw him slip it into his pocket of course hes mad on the subject of drawers thats plain to be seen always skeezing at those brazenfaced things on the bicycles with their skirts blowing up to their navels even when Milly and I were out with him at the open air fete that one in the cream muslin standing right against the sun so he could see every atom she had on when he saw me from behind following in the rain I saw him before he saw me however standing at the corner of the Harolds cross road with a new raincoat on him with the muffler in the Zingari colours to show off his complexion and the brown hat looking slyboots as usual what was he doing there where hed no business they can go and get whatever they like from anything at all with a skirt on it and were not to ask any questions but they want to know where were you where are you going I could feel him coming along skulking after me his eyes on my neck he had been keeping away from the house he felt it was getting too warm for him so I half turned and stopped then he pestered me to say yes till I took off my glove slowly watching him he said my openwork sleeves were too cold for the rain anything for an excuse to put his hand anear me drawers drawers the whole blessed time till I promised to give him the pair off my doll to carry about in his waistcoat pocket *O Maria Santissima* he did look a big fool dreeping in the rain splendid set of teeth he had made me hungry to look at them and beseeched of me to lift the orange petticoat I had on with sunray pleats that there was nobody he said hed kneel down in the wet if I didnt so persevering he would too and ruin his new raincoat you never know what freak theyd take alone with you theyre so savage for it if anyone was passing so I lifted them a bit and touched his trousers outside the way I used to Gardner after with my ring hand to keep him from doing worse where it was too public I was dying to find out was he circumcised he was shaking like a jelly all over they want to do everything too quick take all the pleasure out of it and father waiting all the time for his dinner he told me to say I left my purse in the butchers and had to go back for it what a Deceiver then he wrote me that letter with all those words in it how could he have the face to any woman after his company manners making it so

awkward after when we met asking me have I offended you with my eyelids
down of course he saw I wasnt he had a few brains not like that other fool
Henny Doyle he was always breaking or tearing something in the charades
I hate an unlucky man and if I knew what it meant of course I had to say no
for form sake dont understand you I said and wasnt it natural so it is of
course it used to be written up with a picture of a womans on that wall in
Gibraltar with that word I couldnt find anywhere only for children seeing it
too young then writing a letter every morning sometimes twice a day I liked
the way he made love then he knew the way to take a woman when he sent
me the 8 big poppies because mine was the 8th then I wrote the night he
kissed my heart at Dolphins barn I couldnt describe it simply it makes you
feel like nothing on earth but he never knew how to embrace well like
Gardner I hope hell come on Monday as he said at the same time four I
hate people who come at all hours answer the door you think its the
vegetables then its somebody and you all undressed or the door of the filthy
sloppy kitchen blows open the day old frostyface Goodwin called about the
concert in Lombard street and I just after dinner all flushed and tossed with
boiling old stew dont look at me professor I had to say Im a fright yes but
he was a real old gent in his way it was impossible to be more respectful
nobody to say youre out you have to peep out through the blind like the
messengerboy today I thought it was a putoff first him sending the port and
the peaches first and I was just beginning to yawn with nerves thinking he
was trying to make a fool of me when I knew his tattarrattat at the door he
must have been a bit late because it was 1/4 after 3 when I saw the 2
Dedalus girls coming from school I never know the time even that watch he
gave me never seems to go properly Id want to get it looked after when I
threw the penny to that lame sailor for England home and beauty when
I was whistling there is a charming girl I love and I hadnt even put on my
clean shift or powdered myself or a thing then this day week were to go to
Belfast just as well he has to go to Ennis his fathers anniversary the 27th it
wouldnt be pleasant if he did suppose our rooms at the hotel were beside
each other and any fooling went on in the new bed I couldnt tell him to
stop and not bother me with him in the next room or perhaps some
protestant clergyman with a cough knocking on the wall then he wouldnt
believe next day we didnt do something its all very well a husband but you
cant fool a lover after me telling him we never did anything of course he
didnt believe me no its better hes going where he is besides something
always happens with him the time going to the Mallow Concert at Maryborough ordering boiling soup for the two of us then the bell rang out he
walks down the platform with the soup splashing about taking spoonfuls of

it hadnt he the nerve and the waiter after him making a holy show of us
screeching and confusion for the engine to start but he wouldnt pay till he
finished it the two gentlemen in the 3rd class carriage said he was quite
right so he was too hes so pigheaded sometimes when he gets a thing into
his head a good job he was able to open the carriage door with his knife or
theyd have taken us on to Cork I suppose that was done out of revenge on
him O I love jaunting in a train or a car with lovely soft cushions I wonder
will he take a 1st class for me he might want to do it in the train by tipping
the guard well O I suppose therell be the usual idiots of men gaping at us
with their eyes as stupid as ever they can possibly be that was an exceptional
man that common workman that left us alone in the carriage that day going
to Howth Id like to find out something about him 1 or 2 tunnels perhaps
then you have to look out of the window all the nicer then coming back
suppose I never came back what would they say eloped with him that gets
you on on the stage the last concert I sang at where its over a year ago when
was it St Teresas hall Clarendon St little chits of missies they have now
singing Kathleen Kearney and her like on account of father being in the
army and my singing the absentminded beggar and wearing a brooch for
lord Roberts when I had the map of it all and Poldy not Irish enough was it
him managed it this time I wouldnt put it past him like he got me on to sing
in the *Stabat Mater* by going around saying he was putting Lead Kindly
Light to music I put him up to that till the jesuits found out he was a
freemason thumping the piano lead Thou me on copied from some old
opera yes and he was going about with some of them Sinner Fein lately or
whatever they call themselves talking his usual trash and nonsense he says
that little man he showed me without the neck is very intelligent the coming
man Griffith is he well he doesnt look it thats all I can say still it must have
been him he knew there was a boycott I hate the mention of politics after
the war that Pretoria and Ladysmith and Bloemfontein where Gardner
Lieut Stanley G 8th Bn 2nd East Lancs Rgt of enteric fever he was a lovely
fellow in khaki and just the right height over me Im sure he was brave too
he said I was lovely the evening we kissed goodbye at the canal lock my
Irish beauty he was pale with excitement about going away or wed be seen
from the road he couldnt stand properly and I so hot as I never felt they
could have made their peace in the beginning or old oom Paul and the rest
of the old Krugers go and fight it out between them instead of dragging on
for years killing any finelooking men there were with their fever if he was
even decently shot it wouldnt have been so bad I love to see a regiment pass
in review the first time I saw the Spanish cavalry at La Roque it was lovely
after looking across the bay from Algeciras all the lights of the rock like

fireflies or those sham battles on the 15 acres the Black Watch with their kilts in time at the march past the 10th hussars the prince of Wales own or the lancers O the lancers theyre grand or the Dublins that won Tugela his father made his money over selling the horses for the cavalry well he could buy me a nice present up in Belfast after what I gave theyve lovely linen up there or one of those nice kimono things I must buy a mothball like I had before to keep in the drawer with them it would be exciting going around with him shopping buying those things in a new city better leave this ring behind want to keep turning and turning to get it over the knuckle there or they might bell it round the town in their papers or tell the police on me but theyd think were married O let them all go and smother themselves for the fat lot I care he has plenty of money and hes not a marrying man so somebody better get it out of him if I could find out whether he likes me I looked a bit washy of course when I looked close in the handglass powdering a mirror never gives you the expression besides scrooching down on me like that all the time with his big hipbones hes heavy too with his hairy chest for this heat always having to lie down for them better for him put it into me from behind the way Mrs Mastiansky told me her husband made her like the dogs do it and stick out her tongue as far as ever she could and he so quiet and mild with his tingating cither can you ever be up to men the way it takes them lovely stuff in that blue suit he had on and stylish tie and socks with the skyblue silk things on them hes certainly welloff I know by the cut his clothes have and his heavy watch but he was like a perfect devil for a few minutes after he came back with the stop press tearing up the tickets and swearing blazes because he lost 20 quid he said he lost over that outsider that won and half he put on for me on account of Lenehans tip cursing him to the lowest pits that sponger he was making free with me after the Glencree dinner coming back that long joult over the featherbed mountain after the lord Mayor looking at me with his dirty eyes Val Dillon that big heathen I first noticed him at dessert when I was cracking the nuts with my teeth I wished I could have picked every morsel of that chicken out of my fingers it was so tasty and browned and as tender as anything only for I didnt want to eat everything on my plate those forks and fishslicers were hallmarked silver too I wish I had some I could easily have slipped a couple into my muff when I was playing with them then always hanging out of them for money in a restaurant for the bit you put down your throat we have to be thankful for our mangy cup of tea itself as a great compliment to be noticed the way the world is divided in any case if its going to go on I want at least two other good chemises for one thing and but I dont know what kind of drawers he likes none at all I think didnt he say yes and half the girls in Gibraltar never wore them either naked as God made them that Andalusian singing her Manola she didnt make much secret of what she hadnt yes and the second pair of silkette stockings is laddered after one days wear I could have brought them back to Lewers this morning and kick up a row and made that one change them only not to upset myself and run the risk of walking into him and ruining the whole thing and one of those kidfitting corsets Id want advertised cheap in the Gentlewoman with elastic gores on the hips he saved the one I have but thats no good what did they say they give a delightful figure line 11/6 obviating that unsightly broad appearance across the lower back to reduce flesh my belly is a bit too big Ill have to knock off the stout at dinner or am I getting too fond of it the last they sent from ORourkes was as flat as a pancake he makes his money easy Larry they call him the old mangy parcel he sent at Xmas a cottage cake and a bottle of hogwash he tried to palm off as claret that he couldnt get anyone to drink God spare his spit for fear hed die of the drouth or I must do a few breathing exercises I wonder is that antifat any good might overdo it thin ones are not so much the fashion now garters that much I have the violet pair I wore today thats all he bought me out of the cheque he got on the first O no there was the face lotion I finished the last of yesterday that made my skin like new I told him over and over again get that made up in the same place and dont forget it God only knows whether he did after all I said to him Ill know by the bottle anyway if not I suppose Ill only have to wash in my piss like beeftea or chickensoup with some of that opoponax and violet I thought it was beginning to look coarse or old a bit the skin underneath is much finer where it peeled off there on my finger after the burn its a pity it isnt all like that and the four paltry handkerchiefs about 6/ - in all sure you cant get on in this world without style all going in food and rent when I get it Ill lash it around I tell you in fine style I always want to throw a handful of tea into the pot measuring and mincing if I buy a pair of old brogues itself do you like those new shoes yes how much were they Ive no clothes at all the brown costume and the skirt and jacket and the one at the cleaners 3 whats that for any woman cutting up this old hat and patching up the other the men wont look at you and women try to walk on you because they know youve no man then with all the things getting dearer every day for the 4 years more I have of life up to 35 no Im what am I at all Ill be 33 in September will I what O well look at that Mrs Galbraith shes much older than me I saw her when I was out last week her beautys on the wane she was a lovely woman magnificent head of hair on her down to her waist tossing it back like that like Kitty OShea in Grantham street 1st thing I did every morning to look across see her combing it as if she loved it and

was full of it pity I only got to know her the day before we left and that Mrs
Langtry the Jersey Lily the prince of Wales was in love with I suppose hes
like the first man going the roads only for the name of a king theyre all
made the one way only a black mans Id like to try a beauty up to what was
she 45 there was some funny story about the jealous old husband what was
it all and an oyster knife he went no he made her wear a kind of a tin thing
around her and the prince of Wales yes he had the oyster knife cant be true
a thing like that like some of those books he brings me the works of Master
Francois somebody supposed to be a priest about a child born out of her ear
because her bumgut fell out a nice word for any priest to write and her a – e
as if any fool wouldnt know what that meant I hate that pretending of all
things with the old blackguards face on him anybody can see its not true
and that Ruby and Fair Tyrants he brought me that twice I remember
when I came to page 50 the part about where she hangs him up out of a
hook with a cord flagellate sure theres nothing for a woman in that all
invention made up about he drinking the champagne out of her slipper
after the ball was over like the infant Jesus in the crib at Inchicore in the
Blessed Virgins arms sure no woman could have a child that big taken out
of her and I thought first it came out of her side because how could she go
to the chamber when she wanted to and she a rich lady of course she felt
honoured H. R. H. he was in Gibraltar the year I was born I bet he found
lilies there too where he planted the tree he planted more than that in his
time he might have planted me too if hed come a bit sooner then I wouldnt
be here as I am he ought to chuck that Freeman with the paltry few shillings
he knocks out of it and go into an office or something where hed get
regular pay or a bank where they could put him up on a throne to count the
money all the day of course he prefers plottering about the house so you
cant stir with him any side whats your programme today I wish hed even
smoke a pipe like father to get the smell of a man or pretending to be
mooching about for advertisements when he could have been in Mr Cuffes
still only for what he did then sending me to try and patch it up I could have
got him promoted there to be the manager he gave me a great mirada once
or twice first he was as stiff as the mischief really and truly Mrs Bloom only
I felt rotten simply with the old rubbishy dress that I lost the leads out of
the tails with no cut in it but theyre coming into fashion again I bought it
simply to please him I knew it was no good by the finish pity I changed my
mind of going to Todd and Burns as I said and not Lees it was just like the
shop itself rummage sale a lot of trash I hate those rich shops get on your
nerves nothing kills me altogether only he thinks he knows a great lot about
a womans dress and cooking mathering everything he can scour off the

shelves into it if I went by his advices every blessed hat I put on does that
suit me yes take that thats alright the one like a wedding cake standing up
miles off my head he said suited me or the dishcover one coming down on
my backside on pins and needles about the shop girl in that place in Grafton
street I had the misfortune to bring him into and she as insolent as ever she
could be with her smirk saying Im afraid were giving you too much trouble
whats she there for but I stared it out of her yes he was awfully stiff and no
wonder but he changed the second time he looked Poldy pigheaded as
usual like the soup but I could see him looking very hard at my chest when
he stood up to open the door for me it was nice of him to show me out in
any case Im extremely sorry Mrs Bloom believe me without making it too
marked the first time after him being insulted and me being supposed to be
his wife I just half smiled I know my chest was out that way at the door
when he said Im extremely sorry and Im sure you were

   yes I think he made them a bit firmer sucking them like that so long he
made me thirsty titties he calls them I had to laugh yes this one anyhow stiff
the nipple gets for the least thing Ill get him to keep that up and Ill take
those eggs beaten up with marsala fatten them out for him what are all
those veins and things curious the way its made 2 the same in case of twins
theyre supposed to represent beauty placed up there like those statues in
the museum one of them pretending to hide it with her hand are they so
beautiful of course compared with what a man looks like with his two bags
full and his other thing hanging down out of him or sticking up at you like
a hatrack no wonder they hide it with a cabbageleaf the woman is beauty of
course thats admitted when he said I could pose for a picture naked to some
rich fellow in Holles street when he lost the job in Helys and I was selling
the clothes and strumming in the coffee palace would I be like that bath of
the nymph with my hair down yes only shes younger or Im a little like that
dirty bitch in that Spanish photo he has the nymphs used they go about like
that I asked him that disgusting Cameron highlander behind the meat
market or that other wretch with the red head behind the tree where the
statue of the fish used to be when I was passing pretending he was pissing
standing out for me to see it with his babyclothes up to one side the Queens
own they were a nice lot its well the Surreys relieved them theyre always
trying to show it to you every time nearly I passed outside the mens green-
house near the Harcourt street station just to try some fellow or other
trying to catch my eye or if it was 1 of the 7 wonders of the world O and the
stink of those rotten places the night coming home with Poldy after the
Comerfords party oranges and lemonade to make you feel nice and watery
I went into 1 of them it was so biting cold I couldnt keep it when was that

93 the canal was frozen yes it was a few months after a pity a couple of the
Camerons werent there to see me squatting in the mens place meadero I
tried to draw a picture of it before I tore it up like a sausage or something I
wonder theyre not afraid going about of getting a kick or a bang or something there and that word met something with hoses in it and he came out
with some jawbreakers about the incarnation he never can explain a thing
simply the way a body can understand then he goes and burns the bottom
out of the pan all for his Kidney this one not so much theres the mark of his
teeth still where he tried to bite the nipple I had to scream out arent they
fearful trying to hurt you I had a great breast of milk with Milly enough for
two what was the reason of that he said I could have got a pound a week as
a wet nurse all swelled out the morning that delicate looking student that
stopped in No 28 with the Citrons Penrose nearly caught me washing
through the window only for I snapped up the towel to my face that was his
studenting hurt me they used to weaning her till he got doctor Brady to
give me the Belladonna prescription I had to get him to suck them they
were so hard he said it was sweeter and thicker than cows then he wanted to
milk me into the tea well hes beyond everything I declare somebody ought
to put him in the budget if I only could remember the one half of the things
and write a book out of it the works of Master Poldy yes and its so much
smoother the skin much an hour he was at them Im sure by the clock like
some kind of a big infant I had at me they want everything in their mouth
all the pleasure those men get out of a woman I can feel his mouth O Lord
I must stretch myself I wished he was here or somebody to let myself go
with and come again like that I feel all fire inside me or if I could dream it
when he made me spend the 2nd time tickling me behind with his finger I
was coming for about 5 minutes with my legs round him I had to hug him
after O Lord I wanted to shout out all sorts of things fuck or shit or anything
at all only not to look ugly or those lines from the strain who knows the way
hed take it you want to feel your way with a man theyre not all like him
thank God some of them want you to be so nice about it I noticed the
contrast he does it and doesnt talk I gave my eyes that look with my hair a
bit loose from the tumbling and my tongue between my lips up to him the
savage brute Thursday Friday one Saturday two Sunday three O Lord I
cant wait till Monday

 frseeeeeeeefronnnng train somewhere whistling the strength those
engines have in them like big giants and the water rolling all over and out
of them all sides like the end of Loves old sweet sonnnng the poor men that
have to be out all the night from their wives and families in those roasting
engines stifling it was today Im glad I burned the half of those old Freemans

and Photo bits leaving things like that lying around hes getting very careless and threw the rest of them up in the W C Ill get him to cut them tomorrow for me instead of having them there for the next year to get a few pence for them have him asking wheres last Januarys paper and all those old overcoats I bundled out of the hall making the place hotter than it is the rain was lovely just after my beauty sleep I thought it was going to get like Gibraltar my goodness the heat there before the levanter came on black as night and the glare of the rock standing up in it like a big giant compared with their 3 Rock mountain they think is so great with the red sentries here and there the poplars and they all whitehot and the mosquito nets and the smell of the rainwater in those tanks watching the sun all the time weltering down on you faded all that lovely frock fathers friend Mrs Stanhope sent me from the B Marche Paris what a shame my dearest Doggerina she wrote on what she was very nice whats this her other name was just a P C to tell you I sent the little present have just had a jolly warm bath and feel a very clean dog now enjoyed it wogger she called him wogger wd give anything to be back in Gib and hear you sing in old Madrid or Waiting Concone is the name of those exercises he bought me one of those new some word I couldnt make out shawls amusing things but tear for the least thing still theyre lovely I think dont you will always think of the lovely teas we had together scrumptious currant scones and raspberry wafers I adore well now dearest Doggerina be sure and write soon kind she left out regards to your father also Captain Grove with love yrs affly x x x x x she didnt look a bit married just like a girl he was years older than her wogger he was awfully fond of me when he held down the wire with his foot for me to step over at the bullfight at La Linea when that matador Gomez was given the bulls ear clothes we have to wear whoever invented them expecting you to walk up Killiney hill then for example at that picnic all staysed up you cant do a blessed thing in them in a crowd run or jump out of the way thats why I was afraid when that other ferocious old Bull began to charge the banderillos with the sashes and the 2 things in their hats and the brutes of men shouting bravo toro sure the women were as bad in their nice white mantillas ripping all the whole insides out of those poor horses I never heard of such a thing in all my life yes he used to break his heart at me taking off the dog barking in bell lane poor brute and it sick what became of them ever I suppose theyre dead long ago the 2 of them its like all through a mist makes you feel so old I made the scones of course I had everything all to myself then a girl Hester we used to compare our hair mine was thicker than hers she showed me how to settle it at the back when I put it up and whats this else how to make a knot on a thread with the one hand we were like cousins what age was I then the night of the storm I slept in her bed she had her arms round me then we were fighting in the morning with the pillow what fun he was watching me whenever he got an opportunity at the band on the Alameda esplanade when I was with father and Captain Grove I looked up at the church first and then at the windows then down and our eyes met I felt something go through me like all needles my eyes were dancing I remember after when I looked at myself in the glass hardly recognised myself the change I had a splendid skin from the sun and the excitement like a rose I didnt get a wink of sleep it wouldnt have been nice on account of her but I could have stopped it in time she gave me the Moonstone to read that was the first I read of Wilkie Collins East Lynne I read and the shadow of Ashlydyat Mrs Henry Wood Henry Dunbar by that other woman I lent him afterwards with Mulveys photo in it so as he see I wasnt without and Lord Lytton Eugene Aram Molly bawn she gave me by Mrs Hungerford on account of the name I dont like books with a Molly in them like that one he brought me about the one from Flanders a whore always shoplifting anything she could cloth and stuff and yards of it this blanket is too heavy on me thats better I havent even one decent nightdress this thing gets all rolled up under me besides him and his fooling thats better I used to be weltering then in the heat my shift drenched with the sweat stuck in the cheeks of my bottom on the chair when I stood up they were so fattish and firm when I got up on the sofa cushions to see with my clothes up and the bugs tons of them at night and the mosquito nets I couldnt read a line Lord how long ago it seems centuries of course they never come back and she didnt put her address right on it either she may have noticed her wogger people were always going away and we never I remember that day with the waves and the boats with their high heads rocking and the swell of the ship those Officers uniforms on shore leave made me seasick he didnt say anything he was very serious I had the high buttoned boots on and my skirt was blowing she kissed me six or seven times didnt I cry yes I believe I did or near it my lips were taittering when I said goodbye she had a Gorgeous wrap of some special kind of blue colour on her for the voyage made very peculiarly to one side like and it was extremely pretty it got as dull as the devil after they went I was almost planning to run away mad out of it somewhere were never easy where we are father or aunt or marriage waiting always waiting to guiiiide him toooo me waiting nor speeeed his flying feet their damn guns bursting and booming all over the shop especially the Queens birthday and throwing everything down in all directions if you didnt open the windows when general Ulysses Grant whoever he was or did supposed to be some great fellow landed off the ship and old Sprague

the consul that was there from before the flood dressed up poor man and he
in mourning for the son then the same old reveille in the morning and
drums rolling and the unfortunate poor devils of soldiers walking about
with messtins smelling the place more than the old longbearded jews in
their jellibees and levites assembly and sound clear and gunfire for the men
to cross the lines and the warden marching with his keys to lock the gates
and the bagpipes and only Captain Groves and father talking about Rorkes
drift and Plevna and sir Garnet Wolseley and Gordon at Khartoum lighting
their pipes for them everytime they went out drunken old devil with his
grog on the windowsill catch him leaving any of it picking his nose trying to
think of some other dirty story to tell up in a corner but he never forgot
himself when I was there sending me out of the room on some blind excuse
paying his compliments the Bushmills whisky talking of course but hed do
the same to the next woman that came along I supposed he died of galloping
drink ages ago the days like years not a letter from a living soul except the
odd few I posted to myself with bits of paper in them so bored sometimes I
could fight with my nails listening to that old Arab with the one eye and his
heass of an instrument singing his heah heah aheah all my compriments on
your hotchapotch of your heass as bad as now with the hands hanging off
me looking out of the window if there was a nice fellow even in the opposite
house that medical in Holles street the nurse was after when I put on my
gloves and hat at the window to show I was going out not a notion what I
meant arent they thick never understand what you say even youd want to
print it up on a big poster for them not even if you shake hands twice with
the left he didnt recognise me either when I half frowned at him outside
Westland row chapel where does their great intelligence come in Id like to
know grey matter they have it all in their tail if you ask me those country
gougers up in the City Arms intelligence they had a damn sight less than
the bulls and cows they were selling the meat and the coalmans bell that
noisy bugger trying to swindle me with the wrong bill he took out of his hat
what a pair of paws and pots and pans and kettles to mend any broken
bottles for a poor man today and no visitors or post ever except his cheques
or some advertisement like that wonderworker they sent him addressed
dear Madam only his letter and the card from Milly this morning see she
wrote a letter to him who did I get the last letter from O Mrs Dwenn now
whatever possessed her to write after so many years to know the recipe I
had for pisto madrileno Floey Dillon since she wrote to say she was married
to a very rich architect if Im to believe all I hear with a villa and eight rooms
her father was an awfully nice man he was near seventy always good humour
well now Miss Tweedy or Miss Gillespie theres the pyannyer that was a

solid silver coffee service he had too on the mahogany sideboard then dying
so far away I hate people that have always their poor story to tell everybody
has their own troubles that poor Nancy Blake died a month ago of acute
pneumonia well I didnt know her so well as all that she was Floeys friend
more than mine its a bother having to answer he always tells me the wrong
things and no stops to say like making a speech your sad bereavement
symphathy I always make that mistake and newphew with 2 double yous in
I hope hell write me a longer letter the next time if its a thing he really likes
me O thanks be to the great God I got somebody to give me what I badly
wanted to put some heart up into me youve no chances at all in this place
like you used long ago I wish somebody would write me a loveletter his
wasnt much and I told him he could write what he liked yours ever Hugh
Boylan in Old Madrid silly women believe love is sighing I am dying still if
he wrote it I suppose thered be some truth in it true or no it fills up your
whole day and life always something to think about every moment and see
it all around you like a new world I could write the answer in bed to let him
imagine me short just a few words not those long crossed letters Atty Dillon
used to write to the fellow that was something in the four courts that jilted
her after out of the ladies letterwriter when I told her to say a few simple
words he could twist how he liked not acting with precipit precipitancy
with equal candour the greatest earthly happiness answer to a gentlemans
proposal affirmatively my goodness theres nothing else its all very fine for
them but as for being a woman as soon as youre old they might as well
throw you out in the bottom of the ashpit.

Mulveys was the first when I was in bed that morning and Mrs Rubio
brought it in with the coffee she stood there standing when I asked her to
hand me and I pointing at them I couldnt think of the word a hairpin to
open it with ah horquilla disobliging old thing and it staring her in the face
with her switch of false hair on her and vain about her appearance ugly as
she was near 80 or a 100 her face a mass of wrinkles with all her religion
domineering because she never could get over the Atlantic fleet coming in
half the ships of the world and the Union Jack flying with all her carabineros
because 4 drunken English sailors took all the rock from them and because
I didnt run into mass often enough in Santa Maria to please her with her
shawl up on her except when there was a marriage on with all her miracles
of the saints and her black blessed virgin with the silver dress and the sun
dancing 3 times on Easter Sunday morning and when the priest was going
by with the bell bringing the vatican to the dying blessing herself for his
Majestad an admirer he signed it I near jumped out of my skin I wanted to
pick him up when I saw him following me along the Calle Real in the shop

window then he tipped me just in passing I never thought hed write making an appointment I had it inside my petticoat bodice all day reading it up in every hole and corner while father was up at the drill instructing to find out by the handwriting or the language of stamps singing I remember shall I wear a white rose and I wanted to put on the old stupid clock to near the time he was the first man kissed me under the Moorish wall my sweetheart when a boy it never entered my head what kissing meant till he put his tongue in my mouth his mouth was sweetlike young I put my knee up to him a few times to learn the way what did I tell him I was engaged for fun to the son of a Spanish nobleman named Don Miguel de la Flora and he believed that I was to be married to him in 3 years time theres many a true word spoken in jest there is a flower that bloometh a few things I told him true about myself just for him to be imagining the Spanish girls he didnt like I suppose one of them wouldnt have him I got him excited he crushed all the flowers on my bosom he brought me he couldnt count the pesetas and the perragordas till I taught him Cappoquin he came from he said on the Blackwater but it was too short then the day before he left May yes it was May when the infant king of Spain was born Im always like that in the spring Id like a new fellow every year up on the tiptop under the rockgun near OHaras tower I told him it was struck by lightning and all about the old Barbary apes they sent to Clapham without a tail careering all over the show on each others back Mrs Rubio said she was a regular old rock scorpion robbing the chickens out of Inces farm and throw stones at you if you went anear he was looking at me I had that white blouse on open at the front to encourage him as much as I could without too openly they were just beginning to be plump I said I was tired we lay over the firtree cove a wild place I suppose it must be the highest rock in existence the galleries and casemates and those frightful rocks and Saint Michaels cave with the icicles or whatever they call them hanging down and ladders all the mud plotching my boots Im sure thats the way down the monkeys go under the sea to Africa when they die the ships out far like chips that was the Malta boat passing yes the sea and the sky you could do what you liked lie there for ever he caressed them outside they love doing that its the roundness there I was leaning over him with my white ricestraw hat to take the newness out of it the left side of my face the best my blouse open for his last day transparent kind of shirt he had I could see his chest pink he wanted to touch mine with his for a moment but I wouldnt let him he was awfully put out first for fear you never know consumption or leave me with a child embarazada that old servant Ines told me that one drop even if it got into you at all after I tried with the Banana but I was afraid it might break and get lost up in me somewhere yes because they once took something down out of a woman that was up there for years covered with limesalts theyre all mad to get in there where they come out of youd think they could never get far enough up and then theyre done with you in a way till the next time yes because theres a wonderful feeling there all the time so tender how did we finish it off yes O yes I pulled him off into my handkerchief pretending not to be excited but I opened my legs I wouldnt let him touch me inside my petticoat I had a skirt opening up the side I tortured the life out of him first tickling him I loved rousing that dog in the hotel rrrsssst awokwokawok his eyes shut and a bird flying below us he was shy all the same I liked him like that morning I made him blush a little when I got over him that way when I unbuttoned him and took his out and drew back the skin it had a kind of eye in it theyre all Buttons men down the middle on the wrong side of them Molly darling he called me what was his name Jack Joe Harry Mulvey was it yes I think a lieutenant he was rather fair he had a laughing kind of a voice so I went around to the whatyoucallit everything was whatyoucallit moustache had he he said hed come back Lord its just like yesterday to me and if I was married hed do it to me and I promised him yes faithfully Id let him block me now flying perhaps hes dead or killed or a Captain or admiral its nearly 20 years if I said firtree cove he would if he came up behind me and put his hands over my eyes to guess who I might recognise him hes young still about 40 perhaps hes married some girl on the black water and is quite changed they all do they havent half the character a woman has she little knows what I did with her beloved husband before he ever dreamt of her in broad daylight too in the sight of the whole world you might say they could have put an article about it in the Chronicle I was a bit wild after when I blew out the old bag the biscuits were in from Benady Bros and exploded it Lord what a bang all the woodcocks and pigeons screaming coming back the same way that we went over middle hill round by the old guardhouse and the jews burial place pretending to read out the Hebrew on them I wanted to fire his pistol he said he hadnt one he didnt know what to make of me with his peaked cap on that he always wore crooked as often as I settled it straight H M S Calypso swinging my hat that old Bishop that spoke off the altar his long preach about womans higher functions about girls now riding the bicycle and wearing peak caps and the new woman bloomers God send him sense and me more money I suppose theyre called after him I never thought that would be my name Bloom when I used to write it in print to see how it looked on a visiting card or practising for the butcher and oblige M Bloom youre looking blooming Josie used to say after I married him well its better than Breen or Briggs does brig or those awful names with bottom in them Mrs Ramsbottom or some other kind of a bottom Mulvey I wouldnt go mad about either or suppose I divorced him Mrs Boylan my mother whoever she was might have given me a nicer name the Lord knows after the lovely one she had Lunita Laredo the fun we had running along Willis road to Europa point twisting in and out all round the other side of Jersey they were shaking and dancing about in my blouse like Millys little ones now when she runs up the stairs I loved looking down at them I was jumping up at the pepper trees and the white poplars pulling the leaves off and throwing them at him he went to India he was to write the voyages those men have to make to the ends of the world and back its the least they might get a squeeze or two at a woman while they can going out to be drowned or blown up somewhere I went up windmill hill to the flats that Sunday morning with Captain Rubios that was dead spyglass like the sentry had he said hed have one or two from on board I wore that frock from the B Marche Paris and the coral necklace the straits shining I could see over to Morocco almost the bay of Tangier white and the Atlas mountain with snow on it and the straits like a river so clear Harry Molly Darling I was thinking of him on the sea all the time after at mass when my petticoat began to slip down at the elevation weeks and weeks I kept the handkerchief under my pillow for the smell of him there was no decent perfume to be got in that Gibraltar only that cheap peau despagne that faded and left a stink on you more than anything else I wanted to give him a memento he gave me that clumsy Claddagh ring for luck that I gave Gardner going to South Africa where those Boers killed him with their war and fever but they were well beaten all the same as if it brought its bad luck with it like an opal or pearl must have been pure 16 carat gold because it was very heavy I can see his face clean shaven Frseeeeeeeeeeeeeeeeeeeeeeeefrong that train again weeping tone once in the dear deaead days beyond recall close my eyes breath my lips forward kiss sad look eyes open piano ere oer the world the mists began I hate that istsbeg comes loves sweet ssooooooong Ill let that out full when I get in front of the footlights again Kathleen Kearney and her lot of squealers Miss This Miss That Miss Theother lot of sparrowfarts skitting around talking about politics they know as much about as my backside anything in the world to make themselves someway interesting Irish homemade beauties soldiers daughter am I ay and whose are you bootmakers and publicans I beg your pardon coach I thought you were a wheelbarrow theyd die down dead off their feet if ever they got a chance of walking down the Alameda on an officers arm like me on the bandnight my eyes flash my bust that they havent passion God help their poor head I knew more about men and life when I was 15 than theyll all know at 50 they dont know how to sing a song like that Gardner said no man could look at my mouth and teeth smiling like that and not think of it I was afraid he mightnt like my accent first he so English all father left me in spite of his stamps Ive my mothers eyes and figure anyhow he always said theyre so snotty about themselves some of those cads he wasnt a bit like that he was dead gone on my lips let them get a husband first thats fit to be looked at and a daughter like mine or see if they can excite a swell with money that can pick and choose whoever he wants like Boylan to do it 4 or 5 times locked in each others arms or the voice either I could have been a prima donna only I married him comes looooves old deep down chin back not too much make it double My Ladys Bower is too long for an encore about the moated grange at twilight and vaulted rooms yes Ill sing Winds that blow from the south that he gave after the choirstairs performance Ill change that lace on my black dress to show off my bubs and Ill yes by God Ill get that big fan mended make them burst with envy my hole is itching me always when I think of him I feel I want to I feel some wind in me better go easy not wake him have him at it again slobbering after washing every bit of myself back belly and sides if we had even a bath itself or my own room anyway I wish hed sleep in some bed by himself with his cold feet on me give us room even to let a fart God or do the least thing better yes hold them like that a bit on my side piano quietly sweeeee theres that train far away pianissimo eeeeeeee one more song

that was a relief wherever you be let your wind go free who knows if that pork chop I took with my cup of tea after was quite good with the heat I couldnt smell anything off it Im sure that queerlooking man in the porkbutchers is a great rogue I hope that lamp is not smoking fill my nose up with smuts better than having him leaving the gas on all night I couldnt rest easy in my bed in Gibraltar even getting up to see why am I so damned nervous about that though I like it in the winter its more company O Lord it was rotten cold too that winter when I was only about ten was I yes I had the big doll with all the funny clothes dressing her up and undressing that icy wind skeeting across from those mountains the something Nevada sierra nevada standing at the fire with the little bit of a short shift I had up to heat myself I loved dancing about in it then make a race back into bed Im sure that fellow opposite used to be there the whole time watching with the lights out in the summer and I in my skin hopping around I used to love myself then stripped at the washstand dabbing and creaming only when it came to the chamber performance I put out the light too so then there were 2 of us Goodbye to my sleep for this night anyhow I hope hes not going to get in with those medicals leading him astray to imagine hes young again coming in at 4 in the morning it must be if not more still he had the manners not to wake me what do they find to gabber about all night squandering money and getting drunker and drunker couldnt they drink water then he starts giving us his orders for eggs and tea Findon haddy and hot buttered toast I suppose well have him sitting up like the king of the country pumping the wrong end of the spoon up and down in his egg wherever he learned that from and I love to hear him falling up the stairs of a morning with the cups rattling on the tray and then play with the cat she rubs up against you for her own sake I wonder has she fleas shes as bad as a woman always licking and lecking but I hate their claws I wonder do they see anything that we cant staring like that when she sits at the top of the stairs so long and listening as I wait always what a robber too that lovely fresh plaice I bought I think Ill get a bit of fish tomorrow or today is it Friday yes I will with some blancmange with black currant jam like long ago not those 2 lb pots of mixed plum and apple from the London and Newcastle Williams and Woods goes twice as far only for the bones I hate those eels cod yes Ill get a nice piece of cod Im always getting enough for 3 forgetting anyway Im sick of that everlasting butchers meat from Buckleys loin chops and leg beef and rib steak and scrag of mutton and calfs pluck the very name is enough or a picnic suppose we all gave 5/- each and or let him pay and invite some other woman for him who Mrs Fleming and drive out to the furry glen or the strawberry beds wed have him examining all the horses toenails first like he does with the letters no not with Boylan there yes with some cold veal and ham mixed sandwiches there are little houses down at the bottom of the banks there on purpose but its as hot as blazes he says not a bank holiday anyhow I hate those ruck of Mary Ann coalboxes out for the day Whit Monday is a cursed day too no wonder that bee bit him better the seaside but Id never again in this life get into a boat with him after him at Bray telling the boatmen he knew how to row if anyone asked could he ride the steeplechase for the gold cup hed say yes then it came on to get rough the old thing crookeding about and the weight all down my side telling me to pull the right reins now pull the left and the tide all swamping in floods in through through the bottom and his oar slipping out of the stirrup its a mercy we werent all drowned he can swim of course me no theres no danger whatsoever keep yourself calm in his flannel trousers Id like to have tattered them down off him before all the people and give him what that one calls flagellate till he was black and blue do him all the good in the world only for that longnosed chap I dont know who he is with that other beauty Burke out of the City Arms hotel was there spying around as usual on the slip always where he wasnt wanted if there was a row on you vomit a better face there was no love lost between us thats 1 consolation I wonder what kind is that book he brought me Sweets of Sin by a gentleman of fashion some other Mr de Kock I suppose the people gave him that nickname going about with his tube from one woman to another I couldnt even change my new white shoes all ruined with the saltwater and the hat I had with that feather all blowy and tossed on me how annoying and provoking because the smell of the sea excited me of course the sardines and the bream in Catalan bay round the back of the rock they were fine all silver in the fishermens baskets old Luigi near a hundred they said came from Genoa and the tall old chap with the earrings I dont like a man you have to climb up to go get at I suppose theyre all dead and rotten long ago besides I dont like being alone in this big barracks of a place at night I suppose Ill have to put up with it I never brought a bit of salt in even when we moved in the confusion musical academy he was going to make on the first floor drawingroom with a brassplate or Blooms private hotel he suggested go and ruin himself altogether the way his father did down in Ennis like all the things he told father he was going to do and me but I saw through him telling me all the lovely places we could go for the honeymoon Venice by moonlight with the gondolas and the lake of Como he had a picture cut out of some paper of and mandolines and lanterns O how nice I said whatever I liked he was going to do immediately if not sooner will you be my man will you carry my can he ought to get a leather medal with a putty rim for all the plans he invents then leaving us here all day you never know what old beggar at the door for a crust with his long story might be a tramp and put his foot in the way to prevent me shutting it like that picture of that hardened criminal he was called in Lloyds Weekly News 20 years in jail then he comes out and murders an old woman for her money imagine his poor wife or mother or whoever she is such a face youd run miles away from I couldn't rest easy till I bolted all the doors and windows to make sure but its worse again being locked up like in a prison or a madhouse they ought to be all shot or the cat of nine tails a big brute like that that would attack a poor old woman to murder her in her bed Id cut them off so I would not that hed be much use still better than nothing the night I was sure I heard burglars in the kitchen and he went down in his shirt with a candle and a poker as if he was looking for a mouse as white as a sheet frightened out of his wits making as much noise as he possibly could for the burglars benefit there isnt much to steal indeed the Lord knows still its the feeling especially now with Milly away such an idea for him to send the girl down there to learn to take photographs on account of his grandfather instead of sending her to Skerrys academy where shed have to learn not like

me getting all at school only hed do a thing like that all the same on account
of me and Boylan thats why he did it Im certain the way he plots and plans
everything out I couldnt turn round with her in the place lately unless I
bolted the door first gave me the fidgets coming in without knocking first
when I put the chair against the door just as I was washing myself there
below with the glove g t on your nerves then doing the loglady all day put
her in a glasscase with two at a time to look at her if he knew she broke off
the hand off that little gimcrack statue with her roughness and carelessness
before she left that I got that little Italian boy to mend so that you cant see
the join for 2 shillings wouldnt even teem the potatoes for you of course
shes right not to ruin her hands I noticed he was always talking to her lately
at the table explaining things in the paper and she pretending to understand
sly of course that comes from his side of the house and helping her into her
coat but if there was anything wrong with her its me shed tell not him he
cant say I pretend things can he Im too honest as a matter of fact I suppose
he thinks Im finished out and laid on the shelf well Im not no nor anything
like it well see well see now shes well on for flirting too with Tom Devans
two sons imitating me whistling with those romps of Murray girls calling
for her can Milly come out please shes in great demand to pick what they
can out of her round in Nelson street riding Harry Devans bicycle at night
its as well he sent her where she is she was just getting out of bounds
wanting to go on the skatingrink and smoking their cigarettes through their
nose I smelt if off her dress when I was biting off the thread of the button I
sewed on to the bottom of her jacket she couldnt hide much from me I tell
you only I oughtnt to have stitched it and it on her it brings a parting and
the last plumpudding too split in 2 halves see it comes out no matter what
they say her tongue is a bit too long for my taste your blouse is open too
low she says to me the pan calling the kettle blackbottom and I had to tell
her not to cock her legs up like that on show on the windowsill before all
the people passing they all look at her like me when I was her age of course
any old rag looks well on you then a great touchmenot too in her own way
at the Only Way in the Theatre royal take your foot away out of that I hate
people touching me afraid of her life Id crush her skirt with the pleats a lot
of that touching must go on in theatres in the crush in the dark theyre
always trying to wiggle up to you that fellow in the pit at the pit at the
Gaiety for Beerbohm Tree in Trilby the last time Ill ever go there to be
squashed like that for any Trilby or her barebum every two minutes tipping
me there and looking away hes a bit daft I think I saw him after trying to get
near two stylish dressed ladies outside Switzers window at the same little
game I recognised him on the moment the face and everything but he didnt

remember me and she didnt even want me to kiss her at the Broadstone going away well I hope shell get someone to dance attendance on her the way I did when she was down with the mumps her glands swollen wheres this and wheres that of course she cant feel anything deep yet I never came properly till I was what 22 or so it went into the wrong place always only the usual girls nonsense and giggling that Conny Connolly writing to her in white ink on black paper sealed with sealingwax though she clapped when the curtain came down because he looked so handsome then we had Martin Harvey for breakfast dinner and supper I thought to myself afterwards it must be real love if a man gives up his life for her that way for nothing I suppose there are few men like that left its hard to believe in it though unless it really happened to me the majority of them with not a particle of love in their natures to find two people like that nowadays full up of each other that would feel the same way as you do theyre usually a bit foolish in the head his father must have been a bit queer to go and poison himself after her still poor old man I suppose he felt lost always making love to my things too the few old rags I have wanting to put her hair up at 15 my powder too only ruin her skin on her shes time enough for that all her life after of course shes restless knowing shes pretty with her lips so red a pity they wont stay that way I was too but theres no use going to the fair with the thing answering me like a fishwoman when I asked to go for a half a stone of potatoes the day we met Mrs Joe Gallaher at the trottingmatches and she pretended not to see us in her trap with Friery the solicitor we werent grand enough till I gave her 2 damn fine cracks across the ear for herself take that now for answering me like that and that for your impudence she had me that exasperated of course contradicting I was badtempered too because how was it there was a weed in the tea or I didnt sleep the night before cheese I ate was it and I told her over and over again not to leave knives crossed like that because she has nobody to command her as she said herself well if he doesnt correct her faith I will that was the last time she turned on the teartap I was just like that myself they darent order me about the place its his fault of course having the two of us slaving here instead of getting in a woman long ago am I ever going to have a proper servant again of course then shed see him coming Id have to let her know or shed revenge it arent they a nuisance that old Mrs Flemming you have to be walking round after her putting the things into her hands sneezing and farting into the pots well of course shes old she cant help it a good job I found that rotten old smelly dishcloth that got lost behind the dresser I knew there was something and opened the window to let out the smell bringing in his friends to entertain them like the night he walked home with a dog if you

please that might have been mad especially Simon Dedalus son his father
such a criticiser with his glasses up with his tall hat on him at the cricket
match and a great big hole in his sock one thing laughing at the other and
his son that got all those prizes for whatever he won them in the intermediate imagine climbing over the railings if anybody saw him that knew
us wonder he didnt tear a big hole in his grand funeral trousers as if the one
nature gave wasnt enough for anybody hawking him down into the dirty
old kitchen now is he right in his head I ask pity it wasnt washing day my
old pair of drawers might have been hanging up too on the line on
exhibition for all hed ever care with the ironmould mark the stupid old
bundle burned on them he might think was something else and she never
even rendered down the fat I told her and now shes going such as she was
on account of her paralysed husband getting worse theres always something
wrong with them disease or they have to go under an operation or if its not
that its drink and he beats her Ill have to hunt around again for someone
every day I get up theres some new thing on sweet God sweet God well
when Im stretched out dead in my grave I suppose Ill have some peace I
want to get up a minute if Im let wait O Jesus wait yes that thing has come
on me yes now wouldnt that afflict you of course all the poking and rooting
and ploughing he had up in me now what am I to do Friday Saturday
Sunday wouldnt that pester the soul out of a body unless he likes it some
men do God knows theres always something wrong with us 5 days every 3
or 4 weeks usual monthly auction isnt it simply sickening that night it came
on me like that the one and only time we were in a box that Michael Gunn
gave him to see Mrs Kendal and her husband at the Gaiety something he
did about insurance for him Drimmies I was fit to be tied though I wouldnt
give in with that gentleman of fashion staring down at me with his glasses
and him the other side of me talking about Spinoza and his soul thats dead
I suppose millions of years ago I smiled the best I could all in a swamp
leaning forward as if I was interested having to sit it out then to the last tag
I wont forget that wife of Scarli in a hurry supposed to be a fast play about
adultery that idiot in the gallery hissing the woman adulteress he shouted I
suppose he went and had a woman in the next lane running round all the
back ways after to make up for it I wish he had what I had then hed boo I
bet the cat itself is better off than us have we too much blood up in us or
what O patience above its pouring out of me like the sea anyhow he didnt
make me pregnant as big as he is I dont want to ruin the clean sheets the
clean linen I wore brought it on too damn it damn it and they always want
to see a stain on the bed to know youre a virgin for them all thats troubling
them theyre such fools too you could be a widow or divorced 40 times over

a daub of red ink would do or blackberry juice no thats too purply O Jamesy
let me up out of this pooh sweets of sin whoever suggested that business for
women what between clothes and cooking and children this damned old
bed too jingling like the dickens I suppose they could hear us away over the
other side of the park till I suggested to put the quilt on the floor with the
pillow under my bottom I wonder is it nicer in the day I think it is easy I
think Ill cut all this hair off me there scalding me I might look like a young
girl wouldnt he get the great suckin the next time he turned up my clothes
on me Id give anything to see his face wheres the chamber gone easy Ive a
holy horror of its breaking under me after that old commode I wonder was
I too heavy sitting on his knee I made him sit on the easychair purposely
when I took off only my blouse and skirt first in the other room he was so
busy where he oughtnt to be he never felt me I hope my breath was sweet
after those kissing comfits easy God I remember one time I could scout it
out straight whistling like a man almost easy O Lord how noisy I hope
theyre bubbles on it for a wad of money from some fellow Ill have to
perfume it in the morning dont forget I bet he never saw a better pair of
thighs than that look how white they are the smoothest place is right there
between this bit here how soft like a peach easy God I wouldnt mind being
a man and get up on a lovely woman O Lord what a row youre making like
the jersey lily easy O how the waters come down at Lahore

who knows is there anything the matter with my insides or have I something growing in me getting that thing like that every week when was it last
I Whit Monday yes its only about 3 weeks I ought to go to the doctor only
it would be like before I married him when I had that white thing coming
from me and Floey made me go to that dry old stick Dr Collins for womens
diseases on Pembroke road your vagina he called it I suppose thats how he
got all the gilt mirrors and carpets getting round those rich ones off
Stephens green running up to him for every little fiddlefaddle her vagina
and her cochinchina theyve money of course so theyre all right I wouldnt
marry him not if he was the last man in the world besides theres something
queer about their children always smelling around those filthy bitches all
sides asking me if what I did had an offensive odour what did he want me to
do but the one thing gold maybe what a question if I smathered it all over
his wrinkly old face for him with all my compriment I suppose hed know
then and could you pass it easily pass what I thought he was talking about
the rock of Gibraltar the way he put it thats a very nice invention too by the
way only I like letting myself down after in the hole as far as I can squeeze
and pull the chain then to flush it nice cool pins and needles still theres
something in it I suppose I always used to know by Millys when she was a

child whether she had worms or not still all the same paying him for that
how much is that doctor one guinea please and asking me had I frequent
omissions where do those old fellows get all the words they have omissions
with his short-sighted eyes on me cocked sideways I wouldnt trust him too
far to give me chloroform or God knows what else still I liked him when he
sat down to write the thing out frowning so severe his nose intelligent like
that you be damned you lying strap O anything no matter who except an
idiot he was clever enough to spot that of course that was all thinking of
him and his mad crazy letters my Precious one everything connected with
your glorious Body everything underlined that comes from it is a thing of
beauty and of joy for ever something he got out of some nonsensical book
that he had me always at myself 4 or 5 times a day sometimes and I said I
hadnt are you sure O yes I said I am quite sure in a way that shut him up I
knew what was coming next only natural weakness it was he excited me I
dont know how the first night ever we met when I was living in Rehoboth
terrace we stood staring at one another for about 10 minutes as if we met
somewhere I suppose on account of my being jewess looking after my
mother he used to amuse me the things he said with the half sloothering
smile on him and all the Doyles said he was going to stand for a member of
Parliament O wasnt I the born fool to believe all his blather about home
rule and the land league sending me that long strool of a song out of the
Huguenots to sing in French to be more classy O beau pays de la Touraine
that I never even sang once explaining and rigmaroling about religion and
persecution he wont let you enjoy anything naturally then might he as a
great favour the very 1st opportunity he got a chance in Brighton square
running into my bedroom pretending the ink got on his hands to wash it
off with the Albion milk and sulphur soap I used to use and the gelatine still
round it O I laughed myself sick at him that day Id better not make an all
night sitting on this affair they ought to make chambers a natural size so
that a woman could sit on it properly he kneels down to do it I suppose
there isnt in all creation another man with the habits he has look at the way
hes sleeping at the foot of the bed how can he without a hard bolster its well
he doesnt kick or he might knock out all my teeth breathing with his hand
on his nose like that Indian god he took me to show one wet Sunday in the
museum in Kildare street all yellow in a pinafore lying on his side on his
hand with his ten toes sticking out that he said was a bigger religion than
the jews and Our Lords both put together all over Asia imitating him as hes
always imitating everybody I suppose he used to sleep at the foot of the bed
too with his big square feet up in his wifes mouth damn this stinking thing
anyway wheres this those napkins are ah yes I know I hope the old press

doesnt creak ah I knew it would hes sleeping hard had a good time somewhere still she must have given him great value for his money of course he
has to pay for it from her O this nuisance of a thing I hope theyll have
something better for us in the other world tying ourselves up God help us
thats all right for tonight now the lumpy old jingly bed always reminds me
of old Cohen I suppose he scratched himself in it often enough and he
thinks father bought it from Lord Napier that I used to admire when I was
a little girl because I told him easy piano O I like my bed God here we are
as bad as ever after 16 years how many houses were we in at all Raymond
terrace and Ontario terrace and Lombard street and Holles street and he
goes about whistling every time were on the run again his huguenots or the
frogs march pretending to help the men with our 4 sticks of furniture and
then the City Arms hotel worse and worse says Warden Daly that charming
place on the landing always somebody inside praying then leaving all their
stinks after them always know who was in there last every time were just
getting on right something happens or he puts his big foot in it Thoms and
Helys and Mr Cuffes and Drimmies either hes going to be run into prison
over his old lottery tickets that was to be all our salvations or he goes and
gives impudence well have him coming home with the sack soon out of the
Freeman too like the rest on account of those Sinner Fein or the freemasons
then well see if the little man he showed me dribbling along in the wet all
by himself round by Coadys lane will give him much consolation that he
says is so capable and sincerely Irish he is indeed judging by the sincerity of
the trousers I saw on him wait theres Georges church bells wait 3 quarters
the hour wait 2 oclock well thats a nice hour of the night for him to be
coming home at to anybody climbing down into the area if anybody saw
him Ill knock him off that little habit tomorrow first Ill look at his shirt to
see or Ill see if he has that French letter still in his pocketbook I suppose he
thinks I dont know deceitful men all their 20 pockets arent enough for their
lies then why should we tell them even if its the truth they dont believe you
then tucked up in bed like those babies in the Aristocrats Masterpiece he
brought me another time as if we hadnt enough of that in real life without
some old Aristocrat or whatever his name is disgusting you more with those
rotten pictures children with two heads and no legs thats the kind of villainy
theyre always dreaming about with not another thing in their empty heads
they ought to get slow poison the half of them then tea and toast for him
buttered on both sides and newlaid eggs I suppose Im nothing any more
when I wouldnt let him lick me in Holles street one night man man tyrant
as ever for the one thing he slept on the floor half the night naked the way
the jews used when somebody dies belonged to them and wouldnt eat any

breakfast or speak a word wanting to be petted so I thought I stood out enough for one time and let him he does it all wrong too thinking only of his own pleasure his tongue is too flat or I dont know what he forgets that we then I dont Ill make him do it again if he doesnt mind himself and lock him down to sleep in the coalcellar with the blackbeetles I wonder was it her Josie off her head with my castoffs hes such a born liar too no hed never have the courage with a married woman thats why he wants me and Boylan though as for her Denis as she calls him that forlornlooking spectacle you couldnt call him a husband yes its some little bitch hes got in with even when I was with him with Milly at the College races that Hornblower with the childs bonnet on the top of his nob let us into by the back way he was throwing his sheeps eyes at those two doing skirt duty up and down I tried to wink at him first no use of course and thats the way his money goes this is the fruits of Mr Paddy Dignam yes they were all in great style at the grand funeral in the paper Boylan brought in if they saw a real officers funeral thatd be something reversed arms muffled drums the poor horse walking behind in black L Boom and Tom Kernan that drunken little barrelly man that bit his tongue off falling down the mens W C drunk in some place or other and Martin Cunningham and the two Dedaluses and Fanny MCoys husband white head of cabbage skinny thing with a turn in her eye trying to sing my songs shed want to be born all over again and her old green dress with the lowneck as she cant attract them any other way like dabbling on a rainy day I see it all now plainly and they call that friendship killing and then burying one another and they all with their wives and families at home more especially Jack Power keeping that barmaid he does of course his wife is always sick or going to be sick or just getting better of it and hes a goodlooking man still though hes getting a bit grey over the ears theyre a nice lot all of them well theyre not going to get my husband again into their clutches if I can help it making fun of him then behind his back I know well when he goes on with his idiotics because he has sense enough not to squander every penny piece he earns down their gullets and looks after his wife and family goodfornothings poor Paddy Dignam all the same Im sorry in a way for him what are his wife and 5 children going to do unless he was insured comical little teetotum always stuck up in some pub corner and her or her son waiting Bill Bailey wont you please come home her widows weeds wont improve her appearance theyre awfully becoming though if youre goodlooking what men wasnt he yes he was at the Glencree dinner and Ben Dollard base barreltone the night he borrowed the swallow-tail to sing out of in Holles street squeezed and squashed into them and grinning all over his big Dolly face like a wellwhipped childs botty didnt he look a balmy ballocks sure enough that must have been a spectacle on the stage imagine paying 5/- in the preserved seats for that to see him and Simon Dedalus too he was always turning up half screwed singing the second verse first the old love is the new was one of his so sweetly sang the maiden on the hawthorn bough he was always on for flirtyfying too when I sang Maritana with him at Freddy Mayers private opera he had a delicious glorious voice Phœbe dearest goodbye *sweet*heart he always sang it not like Bartell dArcy sweet *tart* goodbye of course he had the gift of the voice so there was no art in it all over you like a warm showerbath O Maritana wildwood flower we sang splendidly though it was a bit too high for my register even transposed and he was married at the time to May Goulding but then hed say or do something to knock the good out of it hes a widower now I wonder what sort is his son he says hes an author and going to be a university professor of Italian and Im to take lessons what is the driving at now showing him my photo its not good of me I ought to have got it taken in drapery that never looks out of fashion still I look young in it I wonder he didnt make him a present of it altogether and me too after all why not I saw him driving down to the Kingsbridge station with his father and mother I was in mourning thats 11 years ago now yes hed be 11 though what was the good in going into mourning for what was neither one thing nor the other of course he insisted hed go into mourning for the cat I suppose hes a man now by this time he was an innocent boy then and a darling little fellow in his lord Fauntleroy suit and curly hair like a prince on the stage when I saw him at Mat Dillons he liked me too I remember they all do wait by God yes wait yes hold on he was on the cards this morning when I laid out the deck union with a young stranger neither dark nor fair you met before I thought it meant him but hes no chicken nor a stranger either besides my face was turned the other way what was the 7th card after that the 10 of spades for a Journey by land then there was a letter on its way and scandals too the 3 queens and the 8 of diamonds for a rise in society yes wait it all came out and 2 red 8s for new garments look at that and didnt I dream something too yes there was something about poetry in it I hope he hasnt long greasy hair hanging into his eyes or standing up like a red Indian what do they go about like that for only getting themselves and their poetry laughed at I always liked poetry when I was a girl first I thought he was a poet like Byron and not an ounce of it in his composition I thought he was quite different I wonder is he too young hes about wait 88 I was married 88 Milly is 15 yesterday 89 what age was he then at Dillons 5 or 6 about 88 I suppose hes 20 or more Im not too old for him if hes 23 or 24 I hope hes not that stuck up university student sort no otherwise he wouldnt go sitting down in the

old kitchen with him taking Eppss cocoa and talking of course he pretended
to understand it all probably he told him he was out of Trinity college hes
very young to be a professor I hope hes not a professor like Goodwin was
he was a patent professor of John Jameson they all write about some woman
in their poetry well I suppose he wont find many like me where softly sighs
of love the light guitar where poetry is in the air the blue sea and the moon
shining so beautifully coming back on the nightboat from Tarifa the lighthouse at Europa point the guitar that fellow played was so expressive will I
never go back there again all new faces two glancing eyes a lattice hid Ill
sing that for him theyre my eyes if hes anything of a poet two eyes as darkly
bright as loves own star arent those beautiful words as loves young star itll
be a change the Lord knows to have an intelligent person to talk to about
yourself not always listening to him and Billy Prescotts ad and Keyess ad
and Tom the Devils ad then if anything goes wrong in their business we
have to suffer Im sure hes very distinguished Id like to meet a man like that
God not those other ruck besides hes young those fine young men I could
see down in Margate strand bathing place from the side of the rock standing
up in the sun naked like a God or something and then plunging into the sea
with them why arent all men like that thered be some consolation for a
woman like that lovely little statue he bought I could look at him all day
long curly head and his shoulders his finger up for you to listen theres real
beauty and poetry for you I often felt I wanted to kiss him all over also his
lovely young cock there so simple I wouldnt mind taking him in my mouth
if nobody was looking as if it was asking you to suck it so clean and white he
looked with his boyish face I would too in 1/2 a minute even if some of it
went down what its only like gruel or the dew theres no danger besides hed
be so clean compared with those pigs of men I suppose never dream of
washing it from 1 years end to the other the most of them only thats what
gives the women the moustaches Im sure itll be grand if I can only get in
with a handsome young poet at my age Ill throw them the 1st thing in the
morning till I see if the wishcard comes out or Ill try pairing the lady herself
and see if he comes out Ill read and study all I can find or learn a bit off by
heart if I knew who he likes so he wont think me stupid if he thinks all
women are the same and I can teach him the other part Ill make him feel all
over him till he half faints under me then hell write about me lover and
mistress publicly too with our 2 photographs in all the papers when he
becomes famous O but then what am I going to do about him though

no thats no way for him has he no manners nor no refinement nor no
nothing in his nature slapping us behind like that on my bottom because I
didnt call him Hugh the ignoramus that doesnt know poetry from a cabbage

thats what you get for not keeping them in their proper place pulling off his shoes and trousers there on the chair before me so barefaced without even asking permission and standing out that vulgar way in the half of a shirt they wear to be admired like a priest or a butcher or those old hypocrites in the time of Julius Caesar of course hes right enough in his way to pass the time as a joke sure you might as well be in bed with what with a lion God Im sure hed have something better to say for himself an old Lion would O well I suppose its because they were so plump and tempting in my short petticoat he couldnt resist they excite myself sometimes its well for men all the amount of pleasure they get off a womans body were so round and white for them always I wished I was one myself for a change just to try with that thing they have swelling upon you so hard and at the same time so soft when you touch it my uncle John has a thing long I heard those cornerboys saying passing the corner of Marrowbone lane my aunt Mary has a thing hairy because it was dark and they knew a girl was passing it didnt make me blush why should it either its only nature and he puts his thing long into my aunt Marys hairy etcetera and turns out to be you put the handle in a sweepingbrush men again all over they can pick and choose what they please a married woman or a fast widow or a girl for their different tastes like those houses round behind Irish street no but were to be always chained up theyre not going to be chaining me up no damn fear once I start I tell you for stupid husbands jealousy why cant we all remain friends over it instead of quarrelling her husband found it out what they did together well naturally and if he did can he undo it hes coronado anyway whatever he does and then he going to the other mad extreme about the wife in Fair Tyrants of course the man never even casts a 2nd thought on the husband or wife either its the woman he wants and he gets her what else were we given all those desires for Id like to know I cant help it if Im young still can I its a wonder Im not an old shrivelled hag before my time living with him so cold never embracing me except sometimes when hes asleep the wrong end of me not knowing I suppose who he has any man thatd kiss a womans bottom Id throw my hat at him after that hed kiss anything unnatural where we havent 1 atom of any kind of expression in us all of us the same 2 lumps of lard before ever I do that to a man pfooh the dirty brutes the mere thought is enough I kiss the feet of you señorita theres some sense in that didnt he kiss our halldoor yes he did what a madman nobody understands his cracked ideas but me still of course a woman wants to be embraced 20 times a day almost to make her look young no matter by who so long as to be in love or loved by somebody if the fellow you want isnt there sometimes by the Lord God I was thinking would I go around by the quays there some dark evening where nobodyd

know me and pick up a sailor off the sea thatd be hot on for it and not care a
pin whose I was only to do it off up in a gate somewhere or one of those
wildlooking gipsies in Rathfarnham had their camp pitched near the
Bloomfield laundry to try and steal our things if they could I only sent mine
there a few times for the name model laundry sending me back over and
over some old ones old stockings that blackguardlooking fellow with the
fine eyes peeling a switch attack me in the dark and ride me up against the
wall without a word or a murderer anybody what they do themselves the
fine gentlemen in their silk hats that K C lives up somewhere this way
coming out of Hardwicke lane the night he gave us the fish supper on
account of winning over the boxing match of course it was for me he gave it
I knew him by his gaiters and the walk and when I turned round a minute
after just to see there was a woman after coming out of it too some filthy
prostitute then he goes home to his wife after that only I suppose the half of
those sailors are rotten again with disease O move over your big carcass out
of that for the love of Mike listen to him the winds that waft my sighs to thee
so well he may sleep and sigh the great Suggester Don Poldo de la Flora if
he knew how he came out on the cards this morning hed have something to
sigh for a dark man in some perplexity between 2 7s too in prison for Lord
knows what he does that I dont know and Im to be slooching around down
in the kitchen to get his lordship his breakfast while hes rolled up like a
mummy will I indeed did you ever see me running Id just like to see myself
at it show them attention and they treat you like dirt I dont care what
anybody says itd be much better for the world to be governed by the women
in it you wouldnt see women going and killing one another and slaughtering
when do you ever see women rolling around drunk like they do or gambling
every penny they have and losing it on horses yes because a woman whatever
she does she knows where to stop sure they wouldnt be in the world at all
only for us they dont know what it is to be a woman and a mother how could
they where would they all of them be if they hadnt all a mother to look after
them what I never had thats why I suppose hes running wild now out at
night away from his books and studies and not living at home on account of
the usual rowy house I suppose well its a poor case that those that have a fine
son like that theyre not satisfied and I none was he not able to make one it
wasnt my fault we came together when I was watching the two dogs up in
her behind in the middle of the naked street that disheartened me altogether
I suppose I oughtnt to have buried him in that little woolly jacket I knitted
crying as I was but give it to some poor child but I knew well Id never have
another our 1st death too it was we were never the same since O Im not
going to think myself into the glooms about that any more I wonder why he

wouldnt stay the night I felt all the time it was somebody strange he brought
in instead of roving around the city meeting God knows who nightwalkers
and pickpockets his poor mother wouldnt like that if she was alive ruining
himself for life perhaps still its a lovely hour so silent I used to love coming
home after dances the air of the night they have friends they can talk to weve
none either he wants what he wont get or its some woman ready to stick her
knife in you I hate that in women no wonder they treat us the way they do
we are a dreadful lot of bitches I suppose its all the troubles we have makes
us so snappy Im not like that he could easy have slept in there on the sofa in
the other room I suppose he was as shy as a boy he being so young hardly 20
of me in the next room hed have heard me on the chamber arrah what harm
Dedalus I wonder its like those names in Gibraltar Delapaz Delagracia they
had the devils queer names there father Vial plana of Santa Maria that gave
me the rosary Rosales y OReilly in the Calle las Siete Revueltas and Pisimbo
and Mrs Opisso in Governor street O what a name Id go and drown myself
in the first river if I had a name like her O my and all the bits of streets
Paradise ramp and Bedlam ramp and Rodgers ramp and Crutchetts ramp
and the devils gap steps well small blame to me if I am a harumscarum I
know I am a bit I declare to God I dont feel a day older than then I wonder
could I get my tongue round any of the Spanish como esta usted muy bien
gracias y usted see I havent forgotten it all I thought I had only for the
grammar a noun is the name of any person place or thing pity I never tried
to read that novel cantankerous Mrs Rubio lent me by Valera with the
questions in it all upside down the two ways I always knew wed go away in
the end I can tell him the Spanish and he tell me the Italian then hell see Im
not so ignorant what a pity he didnt stay Im sure the poor fellow was dead
tired and wanted a good sleep badly I could have brought him in his breakfast
in bed with a bit of toast so long as I didnt do it on the knife for bad luck or
if the woman was going her rounds with the watercress and something nice
and tasty there are a few olives in the kitchen he might like I never could
bear the look of them in Abrines I could do the criada the room looks all
right since I changed it the other way you see something was telling me all
the time Id have to introduce myself not knowing me from Adam very
funny wouldnt it Im his wife or pretend we were in Spain with him half
awake without a Gods notion where he is dos huevos estrellados señor Lord
the cracked things come into my head sometimes itd be great fun supposing
he stayed with us why not theres the room upstairs empty and Millys bed in
the back room he could do his writing and studies at the table in there for all
the scribbling he does at it and if he wants to read in bed in the morning like
me as hes making the breakfast for 1 he can make it for 2 Im sure Im not

going to take in lodgers off the street for him if he takes a gesabo of a house like this Id love to have a long talk with an intelligent welleducated person Id have to get a nice pair of red slippers like those Turks with the fez used to sell or yellow and a nice semitransparent morning gown that I badly want or a peachblossom dressing jacket like the one long ago in Walpoles only 8/6 or 18/6 Ill just give him one more chance Ill get up early in the morning Im sick of Cohens old bed in any case I might go over to the markets to see all the vegetables and cabbages and tomatoes and carrots and all kinds of splendid fruits all coming in lovely and fresh who knows whod be the 1st man Id meet theyre out looking for it in the morning Mamy Dillon used to say they are and the night too that was her massgoing Id love a big juicy pear now to melt in your mouth like when I used to be in the longing way then Ill throw him up his eggs and tea in the moustachecup she gave him to make his mouth bigger I suppose hed like my nice cream too I know what Ill do Ill go about rather gay not too much singing a bit now and then mi fa pietà Masetto then Ill start dressing myself to go out presto non son più forte Ill put on my best shift and drawers let him have a good eyeful out of that to make his micky stand for him Ill let him know if thats what he wanted that his wife is fucked yes and damn well fucked too up to my neck nearly not by him 5 or 6 times handrunning theres the mark of his spunk on the clean sheet I wouldnt bother to even iron it out that ought to satisfy him if you dont believe me feel my belly unless I made him stand there and put him into me Ive a mind to tell him every scrap and make him do it in front of me serve him right its all his own fault if I am an adulteress as the thing in the gallery said O much about it if thats all the harm ever we did in this vale of tears God knows its not much doesnt everybody only they hide it I suppose thats what a woman is supposed to be there for or He wouldn't have made us the way He did so attractive to men then if he wants to kiss my bottom Ill drag open my drawers and bulge it right out in his face as large as life he can stick his tongue 7 miles up my hole as hes there my brown part then Ill tell him I want £1 or perhaps 30/ Ill tell him I want to buy underclothes then if he gives me that well he wont be too bad I dont want to soak it all out of him like other women do I could often have written out a fine cheque for myself and write his name on it for a couple of pounds a few times he forgot to lock it up besides he wont spend it Ill let him do it off on me behind provided he doesnt smear all my good drawers O I suppose that cant be helped Ill do the indifferent 1 or 2 questions Ill know by the answers when hes like that he cant keep a thing back I know every turn in him Ill tighten my bottom well and let out a few smutty words smellrump or lick my shit or the first mad thing comes into my head then Ill suggest about yes O wait now sonny my turn is coming Ill be quite gay and friendly over it O but I was forgetting this bloody pest of a thing pfooh you wouldnt know which to laugh or cry were such a mixture of plum and apple no Ill have to wear the old things so much the better itll be more pointed hell never know whether he did it nor not there thats good enough for you any old thing at all then Ill wipe him off me just like a business his omission then Ill go out Ill have him eying up at the ceiling where is she gone now make him want me thats the only way a quarter after what an unearthly hour I suppose theyre just getting up in China now combing out their pigtails for the day well soon have the nuns ringing the angelus theyve nobody coming in to spoil their sleep except an odd priest or two for his night office the alarmclock next door at cockshout clattering the brains out of itself let me see if I can doze off 1 2 3 4 5 what kind of flowers are those they invented like the stars the wallpaper in Lombard street was much nicer the apron he gave me was like that something only I only wore it twice better lower this lamp and try again so as I can get up early Ill go to Lambes there beside Findlaters and get them so send us some flowers to put about the place in case he brings him home tomorrow today I mean no no Fridays an unlucky day first I want to do the place up someway the dust grows in it I think while Im asleep then we can have music and cigarettes I can accompany him first I must clean the keys of the piano with milk whatll I wear shall I wear a white rose or those fairy cakes in Liptons I love the smell of a rich big shop at 7 1/2d a lb or the other ones with the cherries in them and the pinky sugar 11d a couple of lbs of course a nice plant for the middle of the table Id get that cheaper in wait wheres this I saw them not long ago I love flowers Id love to have the whole place swimming in roses God of heaven theres nothing like nature the wild mountains then the sea and the waves rushing then the beautiful country with fields of oats and wheat and all kinds of things and all the fine cattle going about that would do your heart good to see rivers and lakes and flowers all sorts of shapes and smells and colours springing up even out of the ditches primroses and violets nature it is as for them saying theres no God I wouldnt give a snap of my two fingers for all their learning why dont they go and create something I often asked him atheists or whatever they call themselves go and wash the cobbles off themselves first then they go howling for the priest and they dying and why why because theyre afraid of hell on account of their bad conscience ah yes I know them well who was the first person in the universe before there was anybody that made it all who ah that they dont know neither do I so there you are they might as well try to stop the sun from rising tomorrow the sun shines for you he said the day we were lying among the rhododendrons on Howth head in the grey tweed suit and his straw hat the day I got him to propose to me yes first I gave him the bit of seedcake out of my mouth and it was leapyear like now yes 16 years ago my God after that long kiss I near lost my breath yes he said I was a flower of the mountain yes so we are flowers all a womans body yes that was one true thing he said in his life and the sun shines for you today yes that was why I liked him because I saw he understood or felt what a woman is and I knew I could always get round him and I gave him all the pleasure I could leading him on till he asked me to say yes and I wouldnt answer first only looked out over the sea and the sky I was thinking of so many things he didnt know of Mulvey and Mr Stanhope and Hester and father and old captain Groves and the sailors playing all birds fly and I say stoop and washing up dishes they called it on the pier and the sentry in front of the governors house with the thing round his white helmet poor devil half roasted and the Spanish girls laughing in their shawls and their tall combs and the auctions in the morning the Greeks and the jews and the Arabs and the devil knows who else from all the ends of Europe and Duke street and the fowl market all clucking outside Larby Sharons and the poor donkeys slipping half asleep and the vague fellows in the cloaks asleep in the shade on the steps and the bigs wheels of the carts of the bulls and the old castle thousands of years old yes and those handsome Moors all in white and turbans like kings asking you to sit down in their little bit of a shop and Ronda with the old windows of the posadas glancing eyes a lattice hid for her lover to kiss the iron and the wineshops half open at night and the castanets and the night we missed the boat at Algeciras the watchman going about serene with his lamp and O that awful deepdown torrent O and the sea the sea crimson sometimes like fire and the glorious sunsets and the figtrees in the Alameda gardens yes and all the queer little streets and pink and blue and yellow houses and the rosegardens and the jessamine and geraniums and cactuses and Gibraltar as a girl where I was a Flower of the mountain yes when I put the rose in my hair like the Andalusian girls used or shall I wear a red yes and how he kissed me under the Moorish wall and I thought well as well him as another and then I asked him with my eyes to ask again yes and then he asked me would I yes to say yes my mountain flower and first I put my arms around him yes and drew him down to me so he could feel my breasts all perfume yes and his heart was going like mad and yes I said yes I will Yes.

Trieste-Zürich-Paris, 1914–1921.

THE END

FINNEGANS WAKE

PUBLISHER'S NOTE

Finnegans Wake is a work which takes allusion to new and still unsurpassed extremes, but it is the text of the *Wake* itself, rather than the referencing of its allusiveness, that is the first fascination of Joyce's last great work, and it is the text alone that is presented here in *The Complete Novels of James Joyce*. The reader who wishes to access the wealth of annotative literature relating to the *Wake* must turn to an edition of the text in its traditional format. The Wordsworth edition (*Finnegans Wake*, Wordsworth Classics, Ware, 2012), which uniquely gives line numbers, book and episode numbers on each page, is perhaps the most convenient edition of the *Wake* to use in tandem with the referencing system employed in the critical and annotative literature. This latter includes such classics as James S. Atherton, *The Books at the 'Wake': A Study of Literary Allusions in James Joyce's 'Finnegans Wake'* (1959); Louis O. Mink, *A 'Finnegans Wake' Gazetteer* (1978); Adaline Glasheen, *Third Census of 'Finnegans Wake': An Index of the Characters and Their Roles* (third edition, 1977); and *A 'Wake' Newslitter*, the journal which ran from 1962 to 1984. The standard synthesis of these extraordinary efforts to unpick the *Wake* is Roland McHugh's *Annotations to 'Finnegans Wake'* (revised edition, 1991).

BOOK I

RIVERRUN, PAST EVE AND ADAM'S, FROM SWERVE OF
shore to bend of bay, brings us by a commodius vicus of recirculation back
to Howth Castle and Environs.

Sir Tristram, violer d'amores, fr'over the short sea, had passencore
rearrived from North Armorica on this side the scraggy isthmus of Europe
Minor to wielderfight his penisolate war: nor
had topsawyer's rocks by the stream Oconee exaggerated themselse to
Laurens County's gorgios while they went doublin their mumper all the
time: nor avoice from afire bellowsed mishe mishe to tauftauf thuartpeatrick
not yet, though venissoon after, had a kidscad buttended a bland old isaac:
not yet, though all's fair in vanessy, were sosie sesthers wroth with twone
nathandjoe. Rot a peck of pa's malt had Jhem or Shen brewed by arclight
and rory end to the regginbrow was to be seen ringsome on the aquaface.

The fall (bababadalgharaghtakamminarronnkonnbronntonner ronntuonnthunntrovarrhounawnskawntoohoohoordenenthurnuk!) of a once wallstrait oldparr is retaled early in bed and later on life down through all
christian minstrelsy. The great fall of the offwall entailed at such short
notice the pftjschute of Finnegan, erse solid man, that the humptyhillhead
of humself prumptly sends an unquiring one well to the west in quest of his
tumptytumtoes: and their upturnpikepointandplace is at the knock out in
the park where oranges have been laid to rust upon the green since devlinsfirst loved livvy.

What clashes here of wills gen wonts, oystrygods gaggin fishygods!
Brékkek Kékkek Kékkek Kékkek! Kóax Kóax Kóax! Ualu Ualu Ualu!
Quaouauh! Where the Baddelaries partisans are still out to mathmaster
Malachus Micgranes and the Verdons catapelting the camibalistics out of
the Whoyteboyce of Hoodie Head. Assiegates and boomeringstroms. Sod's
brood, be me fear! Sanglorians, save! Arms apeal with larms, appalling.
Killykillkilly: a toll, a toll. What chance cuddleys, what cashels aired and
ventilated! What bidimetoloves sinduced by what tegotetabsolvers! What
true feeling for their's hayair with what strawng voice of false jiccup! O here
here how hoth sprowled met the duskt the father of fornicationists but, (O
my shining stars and body!) how hath fanespanned most high heaven the
skysign of soft advertisement! But was iz? Iseut? Ere were sewers? The oaks

of ald now they lie in peat yet elms leap where askes lay. Phall if you but will, rise you must: and none so soon either shall the pharce for the nunce come to a setdown secular phoenish.

Bygmester Finnegan, of the Stuttering Hand, freemen's maurer, lived in the broadest way immarginable in his rushlit toofarback for messuages before joshuan judges had given us numbers or Helviticus committed deuteronomy (one yeastyday he sternly struxk his tete in a tub for to watsch the future of his fates but ere he swiftly stook it out again, by the might of moses, the very water was eviparated and all the guennesses had met their exodus so that ought to show you what a pentschanjeuchy chap he was!) and during mighty odd years this man of hod, cement and edifices in Toper's Thorp piled buildung supra buildung pon the banks for the livers by the Soangso. He addle liddle phifie Annie ugged the little craythur. Wither hayre in honds tuck up your part inher. Oftwhile balbulous, mithre ahead, with goodly trowel in grasp and ivoroiled overalls which he habitacularly fondseed, like Haroun Childeric Eggeberth he would caligulate by multiplicables the alltitude and malltitude until he seesaw by neatlight of the liquor wheretwin 'twas born, his roundhead staple of other days to rise in undress maisonry upstanded (joygrantit!), a waalworth of a skyerscape of most eyeful hoyth entowerly, erigenating from next to nothing and celescalating the himals and all, hierarchitectitiptitoploftical, with a burning bush abob off its baubletop and with larrons o'toolers clittering up and tombles a'buckets clottering down.

Of the first was he to bare arms and a name: Wassaily Booslaeugh of Riesengeborg. His crest of huroldry, in vert with ancillars, troublant, argent, a hegoak, poursuivant, horrid, horned. His scutschum fessed, with archers strung, helio, of the second. Hootch is for husbandman handling his hoe. Hohohoho, Mister Finn, you're going to be Mister Finnagain! Comeday morm and, O, you're vine! Sendday's eve and, ah, you're vinegar! Hahahaha, Mister Funn, you're going to be fined again!

What then agentlike brought about that tragoady thundersday this municipal sin business? Our cubehouse still rocks as earwitness to the thunder of his arafatas but we hear also through successive ages that shebby choruysh of unkalified muzzlenimiissilehims that would blackguardise the whitestone ever hurtleturtled out of heaven. Stay us wherefore in our search for tighteousness, O Sustainer, what time we rise and when we take up to toothmick and before we lump down upown our leatherbed and in the night and at the fading of the stars! For a nod to the nabir is better than wink to the wabsanti. Otherways wesways like that provost scoffing bedoueen the jebel and the jpysian sea. Cropherb the crunchbracken shall

decide. Then we'll know if the feast is a flyday. She has a gift of seek on site
and she allcasually ansars helpers, the dreamydeary. Heed! Heed! It may
half been a missfired brick, as some say, or it mought have been due to a
collupsus of his back promises, as others looked at it. (There extand by now
one thousand and one stories, all told, of the same.) But so sore did abe
ite ivvy's holired abbles, (what with the wallhall's horrors of rollsrights,
carhacks, stonengens, kisstvanes, tramtrees, fargobawlers, autokinotons,
hippohobbilies, streetfleets, tournintaxes, megaphoggs, circuses and wards-
moats and basilikerks and aeropagods and the hoyse and the jollybrool and
the peeler in the coat and the mecklenburk bitch bite at his ear and the
merlinburrow burrocks and his fore old porecourts, the bore the more, and
his blightblack workingstacks at twelvepins a dozen and the noobibusses
sleighding along Safetyfirst Street and the derryjellybies snooping around
Tell-No-Tailors' Corner and the fumes and the hopes and the strupithump
of his ville's indigenous romekeepers, homesweepers, domecreepers, thurum
and thurum in fancymud murumd and all the uproor from all the aufroofs,
a roof for may and a reef for hugh butt under his bridge suits tony) wan
warning Phill filt tippling full. His howd feeled heavy, his hoddit did shake.
(There was a wall of course in erection) Dimb! He stottered from the latter.
Damb! he was dud. Dumb! Mastabatoom, mastabadtomm, when a mon
merries his lute is all long. For whole the world to see.

Shize? I should shee! Macool, Macool, orra whyi deed ye diie? of a trying
thirstay mournin? Sobs they sighdid at Fillagain's chrissormiss wake, all
the hoolivans of the nation, prostrated in their consternation and their
duodisimally profusive plethora of ululation. There was plumbs and grumes
and cheriffs and citherers and raiders and cinemen too. And the all gianed in
with the shoutmost shoviality. Agog and magog and the round of them
agrog. To the continuation of that celebration until Hanandhunigan's
extermination! Some in kinkin corass, more, kankan keening. Belling him
up and filling him down. He's stiff but he's steady is Priam Olim! 'Twas he
was the dacent gaylabouring youth. Sharpen his pillowscone, tap up his
bier! E'erawhere in this whorl would ye hear sich a din again? With their
deepbrow fundigs and the dusty fidelios. They laid him brawdawn alanglast
bed. With a bockalips of finisky fore his feet. And a barrowload of guenesis
hoer his head. Tee the tootal of the fluid hang the twoddle of the fuddled, O!

Hurrah, thereis but young gleve for the owl globe wheels in view which
is tautaulogically the same thing. Well, Him a being so on the flounder of
his bulk like an overgrown babeling, let wee peep, see, at Hom, well, see
peegee ought he ought, platterplate.⌐ Hum! From Shopalist to Bailywick
or from ashtun to baronoath or from Buythebanks to Roundthehead or

from the foot of the bill to ireglint's eye he calmly extensolies. And all the way (a horn!) from fiord to fjell his baywinds' oboboes shall wail him rockbound (hoahoahoah!) in swimswamswum and all the livvylong night, the delldale dalppling night, the night of bluerybells, her flittaflute in tricky trochees (O carina! O carina!) wake him. With her issavan essavans and her patterjackmartins about all them inns and ouses. Tilling a teel of a tum, telling a toll of a teary turty Taubling. Grace before Glutton. For what we are, gifs a gross if we are, about to believe. So pool the begg and pass the kish for crawsake. Omen. So sigh us. Grampupus is fallen down but grinny sprids the boord. Whase on the joint of a desh? Finfoefom the Fush. Whase be his baken head? A loaf of Singpantry's Kennedy bread. And whase hitched to the hop in his tayle? A glass of Danu U'Dunnell's foamous olde Dobbelin ayle. But, lo, as you would quaffoff his fraudstuff and sink teeth through that pyth of a flowerwhite bodey behold of him as behemoth for he is noewhemoe. Finiche! Only a fadograph of a yestern scene. Almost rubicund Salmosalar, ancient fromout the ages of the Agapemonides, he is smolten in our mist, woebecanned and packt away. So that meal's dead off for summan, schlook, schlice and goodridhirring.

Yet may we not see still the brontoichthyan form outlined aslumbered, even in our own nighttime by the sedge of the troutling stream that Bronto loved and Brunto has a lean on. *Hic cubat edilis. Apud libertinam parvulam.* Whatif she be in flags or flitters, reekierags or sundyechosies, with a mint of mines or beggar a pinnyweight. Arrah, sure, we all love little Anny Ruiny, or, we mean to say, lovelittle Anna Rayiny, when unda her brella, mid piddle med puddle, she ninnygoes nannygoes nancing by. Yoh! Brontolone slaaps, yoh snoores. Upon Benn Heather, in Seeple Isout too. The cranic head on him, caster of his reasons, peer yuthner in yondmist. Whooth? His clay feet, swarded in verdigrass, stick up starck where he last fellonem, by the mund of the magazine wall, where our maggy seen all, with her sisterin shawl. While over against this belles' alliance beyind Ill Sixty, ollollowed ill! bagsides of the fort, bom, tarabom, tarabom, lurk the ombushes, the site of the lyffing-in-wait of the upjock and hockums. Hence when the clouds roll by, jamey, a proudseye view is enjoyable of our mounding's mass, now Wallinstone national museum, with, in some greenish distance, the charmful waterloose country and the two quitewhite villagettes who hear show of themselves so gigglesomes minxt the follyages, the prettilees! Penetrators are permitted into the museomound free. Welsh and the Paddy Patkinses, one shelenk! Redismembers invalids of old guard find poussepousse pousseypram to sate the sort of their butt. For her passkey supply to the janitrix, the mistress Kathe. Tip.

This the way to the museyroom. Mind your hats goan in! Now yiz are in the Willingdone Museyroom. This is a Prooshious gunn. This is a ffrinch. Tip. This is the flag of the Prooshious, the Cap and Soracer. This is the bullet that byng the flag of the Prooshious. This is the ffrinch that fire on the Bull that bang the flag of the Prooshious. Saloos the Crossgunn! Up with your pike and fork! Tip. (Bullsfoot! Fine!) This is the triplewon hat of Lipoleum. Tip. Lipoleumhat. This is the Willingdone on his same white harse, the Cokenhape. This is the big Sraughter Willingdone, grand and magentic in his goldtin spurs and his ironed dux and his quarterbrass woodyshoes and his magnate's gharters and his bangkok's best and goliar's goloshes and his pulluponeasyan wartrews. This is his big wide harse. Tip. This is the three lipoleum boyne grouching down in the living detch. This is an inimyskilling inglis, this is a scotcher grey, this is a davy, stooping. This is the bog lipoleum mordering the lipoleum beg. A Gallawghurs argaumunt. This is the petty lipoleum boy that was nayther bag nor bug. Assaye, assaye! Touchole Fitz Tuomush. Dirty MacDyke. And Hairy O'Hurry. All of them arminus-varminus. This is Delian alps. This is Mont Tivel, this is Mont Tipsey, this is the Grand Mons Injun. This is the crimealine of the alps hooping to sheltershock the three lipoleums. This is the jinnies with their legahorns feinting to read in their handmade's book of stralegy while making their war undisides the Willingdone. The jinnies is a cooin her hand and the jinnies is a ravin her hair and the Willingdone git the band up. This is big Willingdone mormorial tallowscoop Wounderworker obscides on the flanks of the jinnies. Sexcaliber hrosspower. Tip. This is me Belchum sneaking his phillippy out of his most Awful Grimmest Sunshat Cromwelly. Looted. This is the jinnies' hastings dispatch for to irrigate the Willingdone. Dispatch in thin red lines cross the shortfront of me Belchum. Yaw, yaw, yaw! Leaper Orthor. Fear siecken! Fieldgaze thy tiny frow. Hugacting. Nap. That was the tictacs of the jinnies for to fontannoy the Willingdone. Shee, shee, shee! The jinnies is jillous agincourting all the lipoleums. And the lipoleums is gonn boycottoncrezy onto the one Willingdone. And the Willingdone git the band up. This is bode Belchum, bonnet to busby, breaking his secred word with a ball up his ear to the Willingdone. This is the Willingdone's hurold dispitchback. Dispitch desployed on the regions rare of me Belchum. Salamangra! Ayi, ayi, ayi! Cherry jinnies. Figtreeyou! Damn fairy ann, Voutre. Willingdone. That was the first joke of Willingdone, tic for tac. Hee, hee, hee! This is me Belchum in his twelvemile cowchooks, weet, tweet and stampforth foremost, footing the camp for the jinnies. Drink a sip, drankasup, for he's as sooner buy a guinness than he'd stale store stout. This is Rooshious balls. This is a ttrinch. This is mistletropes. This is Canon Futter with the popynose. After his hundred days' indulgence. This is the blessed. Tarra's widdars! This is jinnies in the bonny bawn blooches. This is lipoleums in the rowdy howses. This is the Willingdone, by the splinters of Cork, order fire. Tonnerre! (Bullsear! Play!) This is camelry, this is floodens, this is the solphereens in action, this is their mobbily, this is panickburns. Almeidagad! Arthiz too loose! This is Willingdone cry. Brum! Brum! Cumbrum! This is jinnies cry. Underwetter! Goat strip Finnlambs! This is jinnies rinning away to their onsterlists dowan a bunkersheels. With a nip nippy nip and a trip trippy trip so airy. For their heart's right there. Tip. This is me Belchum's tinkyou tankyou silvoor plate for citchin the crapes in the cool of his canister. Poor the pay! This is the bissmark of the marathon merry of the jinnies they left behind them. This is the Willingdone branlish his same marmorial tallowscoop Sophy-Key-Po for his royal divorsion on the rinnaway jinnies. Gambariste della porca! Dalaveras fimmieras! This is the pettiest of the lipoleums, Toffeethief, that spy on the Willingdone from his big white harse, the Capeinhope. Stonewall Willingdone is an old maxy montrumeny. Lipoleums is nice hung bushellors. This is hiena hinnessy laughing alout at the Willingdone. This is lipsyg dooley krieging the funk from the hinnessy. This is the hinndoo Shimar Shin between the dooley boy and the hinnessy. Tip. This is the wixy old Willingdone picket up the half of the threefoiled hat of lipoleums fromoud of the bluddle filth. This is the hinndoo waxing ranjymad for a bombshoob. This is the Willingdone hanking the half of the hat of lipoleums up the tail on the buckside of his big white harse. Tip. That was the last joke of Willingdone. Hit, hit, hit! This is the same white harse of the Willingdone, Culpenhelp, waggling his tailoscrupp with the half of a hat of lipoleums to insoult on the hinndoo seeboy. Hney, hney, hney! (Bullsrag! Foul!) This is the seeboy, madrashattaras, upjump and pumpim, cry to the Willingdone: Ap Pukkaru! Pukka Yurap! This is the Willingdone, bornstable ghentleman, tinders his maxbotch to the cursigan Shimar Shin. Basucker youstead! This is the dooforhim seeboy blow the whole of the half of the hat of lipoleums off of the top of the tail on the back of his big wide harse. Tip (Bullseye! Game!) How Copenhagen ended. This way the museyroom. Mind your boots goan out.

   Phew!

What a warm time we were in there but how keling is here the airabouts! We nowhere she lives but you mussna tell annaone for the lamp of Jig-a-Lanthern! It's a candlelittle houthse of a month and one windies. Downadown, High Downadown. And nummered quaintlymine. And such reasonable weather too! The wagrant wind's awalt'zaround the piltdowns and on every blasted knollyrock (if you can spot fifty I spy four more) there's that gnarlybird ygathering, a runalittle, doalittle, preealittle, pouralittle, wipe-alittle, kicksalittle, severalittle, eatalittle, whinealittle, kenalittle, helfalittle, pelfalittle gnarlybird. A verytableland of bleakbardfields! Under his seven wrothschields lies one, Lumproar. His glav toside him. Skud ontorsed. Our pigeons pair are flewn for northcliffs. The three of crows have flapped it southenly, kraaking of de baccle to the kvarters of that sky whence triboos answer; Wail, 'tis well! She niver comes out when Thon's on shower or when Thon's flash with his Nixy girls or when Thon's blowing toomcracks down the gaels of Thon. No nubo no! Neblas on you liv! Her would be too moochy afreet. Of Burymeleg and Bindmerollingeyes and all the deed in the woe. Fe fo fom! She jist does hopes till byes will be byes. Here, and it goes on to appear now, she comes, a peacefugle, a parody's bird, a peri potmother, a pringlpik in the ilandiskippy, with peewee and powwows in beggybaggy on her bickybacky and a flick flask fleckflinging its pixylighting pacts' huemeramybows, picking here, pecking there, pussypussy plunder-pussy. But it's the armitides toonigh, militopucos, and toomourn we wish for a muddy kissmans to the minutia workers and there's to be a gorgeups truce for happinest childher everwere. Come nebo me and suso sing the day we sallybright. She's burrowed the coacher's headlight the better to pry (who goes cute goes siocur and shoos aroun) and all spoiled goods go into her nabsack: curtrages and rattlin buttins, nappy spattees and flasks of all nations, clavicures and scampulars, maps, keys and woodpiles of haypennies and moonled brooches with bloodstaned breeks in em, boaston nightgarters and masses of shoesets and nickelly nacks and foder allmicheal and a lugly parson of cates and howitzer muchears and midgers and maggets, ills and ells with loffs of toffs and pleures of bells and the last sigh that come fro the hart (bucklied!) and the fairest sin the sunsaw (that's cearc!). With Kiss. Kiss Criss. Cross Criss. Kiss Cross. Undo lives 'end. Slain.

How bootifull and how truetowife of her, when strengly forebidden, to steal our historic presents from the past postpropheticals so as to will make us all lordy heirs and ladymaidesses of a pretty nice kettle of fruit. She is livving in our midst of debt and laffing through all plores for us (her birth is uncontrollable), with a naperon for her mask and her sabboes kickin arias (so sair! so solly!) if yous ask me and I saack you. Hou! Hou! Gricks may rise and Troysirs fall (there being two sights for ever a picture) for in the byways of high improvidence that's what makes lifework leaving and the world's a cell for citters to cit in. Let young wimman run away with the story and let young min talk smooth behind the butteler's back. She knows her knight's duty while Luntum sleeps. Did ye save any tin? says he. Did I what? with a grin says she. And we all like a marriedann because she is mercenary. Though the length of the land lies under liquidation (floote!) and there's nare a hairbrow nor an eyebush on this glaubrous phace of Herrschuft Whatarwelter she'll loan a vesta and hire some peat and sarch the shores her cockles to heat and she'll do all a turfwoman can to piff the business on. Paff. To puff the blaziness on. Poffpoff. And even if Humpty shell fall frumpty times as awkward again in the beardsboosoloom of all our grand remonstrancers there'll be iggs for the brekkers come to mournhim, sunny side up with care. So true is it that therewhere's a turnover the tay is wet too and when you think you ketch sight of a hind make sure but you're cocked by a hin.

Then as she is on her behaviourite job of quainance bandy, fruting for firstlings and taking her tithe, we may take our review of the two mounds to see nothing of the himples here as at elsewhere, by sixes and sevens, like so many heegills and collines, sitton aroont, scentbreeched ant somepotreek, in their swishawish satins and their taffetaffe tights, playing Wharton's Folly, at a treepurty on the planko in the purk. Stand up, mickos! Make strake for minnas! By order, Nicholas Proud. We may see and hear nothing if we choose of the shortlegged bergins off Corkhill or the bergamoors of Arbourhill or the bergagambols of Summerhill or the bergincellies of Miseryhill or the countrybossed bergones of Constitutionhill though every crowd has its several tones and every trade has its clever mechanics and each harmonical has a point of its own, Olaf's on the rise and Ivor's on the lift and Sitric's place's between them. But all they are all there scraping along to sneeze out a likelihood that will solve and salve life's robulous rebus, hopping round his middle like kippers on a griddle, O, as he lays dormont from the macroborg of Holdhard to the microbirg of Pied de Poudre. Behove this sound of Irish sense. Really? Here English might be seen. Royally? One sovereign punned to petery pence. Regally? The silence speaks the scene. Fake!

So This Is Dyoublong?

Hush! Caution! Echoland!

How charmingly exquisite! It reminds you of the outwashed engravure that we used to be blurring on the blotchwall of his innkempt house. Used they? (I am sure that tiring chabelshoveller with the mujikal chocolat box, Miry Mitchel, is listening) I say, the remains of the outworn gravemure where used to be blurried the Ptollmens of the Incabus. Used we? (He is only pretendant to be stugging at the jubalee harp from a second existed lishener, Fiery Farrelly.) It is well known. Lokk for himself and see the old butte new. Dbln. W. K. O. O. Hear? By the mausolime wall. Fimfim fimfim. With a grand funferall. Fumfum fumfum. 'Tis optophone which ontophanes. List! Wheatstone's magic lyer. They will be tuggling foriver. They will be lichening for allof. They will be pretumbling forover. The harpsdischord shall be theirs for ollaves.

Four things therefore, saith our herodotary Mammon Lujius in his grand old historiorum, wrote near Boriorum, bluest book in baile's annals, f.t. in Dyffinarsky ne'er sall fail til heathersmoke and cloudweed Eire's ile sall pall. And here now they are, the fear of um. T. Totities! *Unum.* (Adar.) A bulbenboss surmounted upon an alderman. Ay, ay! *Duum.* (Nizam.) A shoe on a puir old wobban. Ah, ho! *Triom.* (Tamuz.) An auburn mayde, o'brine a'bride, to be desarted. Adear, adear! *Quodlibus.* (Marchessvan.) A penn no weightier nor a polepost. And so. And all. (Succoth.)

So, how idlers' wind turning pages on pages, as innocens with anaclete play popeye antipop, the leaves of the living in the boke of the deeds, annals of themselves timing the cycles of events grand and national, bring fassilwise to pass how.

1132 A.D. Men like to ants or emmets wondern upon a groot hwide Whallfisk which lay in a Runnel. Blubby wares upat Ublanium.

566 A.D. On Baalfire's night of this year after deluge a crone that hadde a wickered Kish for to hale dead tunes from the bog lookit under the blay of her Kish as she ran for to sothisfeige her cowrieosity and be me sawl but she found hersell sackvulle of swart goody quickenshoon ant small illigant brogues, so rich in sweat. Blurry works at Hurdlesford.

(Silent.)

566 A.D. At this time it fell out that a brazenlockt damsel grieved (*sobralasolas!*) because that Puppette her minion was ravisht of her by the ogre Puropeus Pious. Bloody wars in Ballyaughacleeaghbally.

1132 A.D. Two sons at an hour were born until a goodman and his hag. These sons called themselves Caddy and Primas. Primas was a santryman and drilled all decent people. Caddy went to Winehouse and wrote o peace a farce. Blotty words for Dublin.

Somewhere, parently, in the ginnandgo gap between antediluvious and annadominant the copyist must have fled with his scroll. The billy flood rose or an elk charged him or the sultrup worldwright from the excelsissimost empyrean (bolt, in sum) earthspake or the Dannamen gallous banged pan the bliddy duran. A scribicide then and there is led off under old's code with some fine covered by six marks or ninepins in metalmen for the sake of his labour's dross while it will be only now and again in our rear of o'er era, as an upshoot of military and civil engagements, that a gynecure was let on to the scuffold for taking that same fine sum covertly by meddlement with the drawers of his neighbour's safe.

Now after all that farfatch'd and peragrine or dingnant or clere lift we our ears, eyes of the darkness, from the tome of *Liber Lividus* and, (toh!), how paisibly eirenical, all dimmering dunes and gloamering glades, self-stretches afore us our fredeland's plain! Lean neath stone pine the pastor lies with his crook; young pricket by pricket's sister nibbleth on returned viridities; amaid her rocking grasses the herb trinity shams lowliness; skyup is of evergrey. Thus, too, for donkey's years. Since the bouts of Hebear and Hairyman the cornflowers have been staying at Ballymun, the duskrose has choosed out Goatstown's hedges, twolips have pressed togatherthem by sweet Rush, townland of twinedlights, the whitethorn and the redthorn have fairygeyed the mayvalleys of Knockmaroon, and, though for rings round them, during a chiliad of perihelygangs, the Formoreans have brittled the tooath of the Danes and the Oxman has been pestered by the Firebugs and the Joynts have thrown up jerrybuilding to the Kevanses and Little on the Green is childsfather to the City (Year! Year! And laughtears!), these paxsealing buttonholes have quadrilled across the centuries and whiff now whafft to us, fresh and made-of-all-smiles as, on the eve of Killallwho.

The babbelers with their thangas vain have been (confusium hold them!) they were and went; thigging thugs were and houhnhymn songtoms were and comely norgels were and pollyfool fiansees. Menn have thawed, clerks have surssurhummed, the blond has sought of the brune: Elsekiss thou may, mean Kerry piggy?: and the duncledames have countered with the hellish fellows: Who ails tongue coddeau, aspace of dumbillsilly? And they fell upong one another: and themselves they have fallen. And still nowanights and by nights of yore do all bold floras of the field to their shyfaun lovers say only: Cull me ere I wilt to thee!: and, but a little later: Pluck me whilst I blush! Well may they wilt, marry, and profusedly blush, be troth! For that saying is as old as the howitts. Lave a whale a while in a whillbarrow (isn't it the truath I'm tallin ye?) to have fins and flippers that shimmy and shake. Tim Timmycan timped hir, tampting Tam. Fleppety! Flippety! Fleapow!

Hop!

In the name of Anem this carl on the kopje in pelted thongs a parth a lone who the joebiggar be he? Forshapen his pigmaid hoagshead, shroonk his plodsfoot. He hath locktoes, this shortshins, and, Obeold that's pectoral, his mammamuscles most mousterious. It is slaking nuncheon out of some thing's brain pan. Me seemeth a dragon man. He is almonthst on the kiep fief by here, is Comestipple Sacksoun, be it junipery or febrewery, marracks or alebrill or the ramping riots of pouriose and froriose. What a quhare soort of a mahan. It is evident the michindaddy. Lets we overstep his fire defences and these kraals of slitsucked marrogbones. (Cave!) He can

prapsposterus the pillory way to Hirculos pillar. Come on, fool porterfull,
hosiered women blown monk sewer? Scuse us, chorley guy! You tollerday
donsk? N. You tolkatiff scowegian? Nn. You spigotty anglease? Nnn. You
phonio saxo? Nnnn. Clear all so! 'Tis a Jute. Let us swop hats and excheck
a few strong verbs weak oach eather yapyazzard abast the blooty creeks.

Jute. — Yutah!

Mutt. — Mukk's pleasurad.

Jute. — Are you jeff?

Mutt. — Somehards.

Jute. — But you are not jeffmute?

Mutt. — Noho. Only an utterer.

Jute. — Whoa? Whoat is the mutter with you?

Mutt. — I became a stun a stummer.

Jute. — What a hauhauhauhaudibble thing, to be cause! How, Mutt?

Mutt. — Aput the buttle, surd.

Jute. — Whose poddle? Wherein?

Mutt. — The Inns of Dungtarf where Used awe to be he.

Jute. — You that side your voise are almost inedible to me. Become a
bitskin more wiseable, as if I were you.

Mutt. — Has? Has at? Hasatency? Urp, Boohooru! Booru Usurp! I
trumple from rath in mine mines when I rimimirim!

Jute. — One eyegonblack. Bisons is bisons. Let me fore all your hasitancy
cross your qualm with trink gilt. Here have sylvan coyne, a piece
of oak. Ghinees hies good for you.

Mutt. — Louee, louee! How wooden I not know it, the intellible greyt-
cloak of Cedric Silkyshag! Cead mealy faulty rices for one
dabblin bar. Old grilsy growlsy! He was poached on in that
eggtentical spot. Here where the liveries, Monomark. There
where the missers moony, Minnikin passe.

Jute. — Simply because as Taciturn pretells, our wrongstoryshortener,
he dumptied the wholeborrow of rubbages on to soil here.

Mutt. — Just how a puddinstone inat the brookcells by a riverpool.

Jute. — Load Allmarshy! Wid wad for a norse like?

Mutt. — Somular with a bull on a clompturf. Rooks roarum rex roome! I
could snore to him of the spumy horn, with his woolseley side
in, by the neck I am sutton on, did Brian d' of Linn.

Jute. — Boildoyle and rawhoney on me when I can beuraly forsstand a
weird from sturk to finnic in such a patwhat as your rutter-
damrotter. Onheard of and um&scene! Gut aftermeal! See you
doomed.

Mutt. — Quite agreem. Bussave a sec. Walk a dun blink roundward this
albutisle and you skull see how olde ye plaine of my Elters,
hunfree and ours, where wone to wail whimbrel to peewee o'er
the saltings, where wilby citie by law of isthmon, where by a
droit of signory, icefloe was from his Inn the Byggning to whose
Finishthere Punct. Let erehim ruhmuhrmuhr. Mearmerge
two races, swete and brack. Morthering rue. Hither, craching
eastuards, they are in surgence: hence, cool at ebb, they
requiesce. Countlessness of livestories have netherfallen by this
plage, flick as flowflakes, litters from aloft, like a waast wizzard
all of whirlworlds. Now are all tombed to the mound, isges to
isges, erde from erde. Pride, O pride, thy prize!

Jute. — 'Stench!

Mutt. — Fiatfuit! Hereinunder lyethey. Llarge by the smal an' everynight life olso th'estrange, babylone the greatgrandhotelled with
tit tit tittlehouse, alp on earwig, drukn on ild, likeas equal to
anequal in this sound seemetery which iz leebez luv.

Jute. — 'Zmorde!

Mutt. — Meldundleize! By the fearse wave behoughted. Despond's sung.
And thanacestross mound have swollup them all. This ourth of
years is not save brickdust and being humus the same roturns.
He who runes may rede it on all fours. O'c'stle, n'wc'stle, tr'c'stle,
crumbling! Sell me sooth the fare for Humblin! Humblady Fair.
But speak it allsosiftly, moulder! Be in your whisht!

Jute. —Whysht?

Mutt. —The gyant Forficules with Amni the fay.

Jute. —Howe?

Mutt. —Here is viceking's graab.

Jute. —Hwaad!

Mutt. —Ore you astoneaged, jute you?

Jute. —Oye am thonthorstrok, thing mud.

(Stoop) if you are abcedminded, to this claybook, what curios of signs
(please stoop), in this allaphbed! Can you rede (since We and Thou had it
out already) its world? It is the same told of all. Many. Miscegenations on
miscegenations. Tieckle. They lived und laughed ant loved end left. Forsin.
Thy thingdome is given to the Meades and Porsons. The meandertale,
aloss and again, of our old Heidenburgh in the days when Head-in-Clouds
walked the earth. In the ignorance that implies impression that knits knowledge that finds the nameform that whets the wits that convey contacts that
sweeten sensation that drives desire that adheres to attachment that dogs

death that bitches birth that entails the ensuance of existentiality. But with a rush out of his navel reaching the reredos of Ramasbatham. A terricolous vivelyonview this; queer and it continues to be quaky. A hatch, a celt, an earshare the pourquose of which was to cassay the earthcrust at all of hours, furrowards, bagawards, like yoxen at the turnpaht. Here say figurines billy-coose arming and mounting. Mounting and arming bellicose figurines see here. Futhorc, this liffle effingee is for a firefing called a flintforfall. Face at the eased! O I fay! Face at the waist! Ho, you fie! Upwap and dump em, ᚛ ace to ᚜ ace! When a part so ptee does duty for the holos we soon grow to use of an allforabit. Here (please to stoop) are selveran cued peteet peas of quite a pecuniar interest inaslittle as they are the pellets that make the tomtummy's pay roll. Right rank ragnar rocks and with these rox orangotangos rangled rough and rightgorong. Wisha, wisha, whydidtha? Thik is for thorn that's thuck in its thoil like thumfool's thraitor thrust for vengeance. What a mnice old mness it all mnakes! A middenhide hoard of objects! Olives, beets, kimmells, dollies, alfrids, beatties, cormacks and daltons. Owlets' eegs (O stoop to please!) are here, creakish from age and all now quite epsilene, and oldwolldy wobblewers, haudworth a wipe o grass. Sss! See the snake wurrums everyside! Our durlbin is sworming in sneaks. They came to our island from triangular Toucheaterre beyond the wet prairie rared up in the midst of the cargon of prohibitive pomefructs but along landed Paddy Wippingham and the his garbagecans cotched the creeps of them pricker than our whosethere outofman could quick up her whatsthats. Somedivide and sumthelot but the tally turns round the same balifuson. Racketeers and bottloggers.

Axe on thwacks on thracks, axenwise. One by one place one be three dittoh and one before. Two nursus one make a plausible free and idim behind. Starting off with a big boaboa and threelegged calvers and ivargraine jadesses with a message in their mouths. And a hundreadfilled unleaven-weight of liberorumqueue to con an we can till allhorrors eve. What a meanderthalltale to unfurl and with what an end in view of squattor and anntisquattor and postproneauntisquattor! To say too us to be every tim, nick and larry of us, sons of the sod, sons, littlesons, yea and lealittlesons, when usses not to be, every sue, siss and sally of us, dugters of Nan! Accusative ahnsire! Damadam to infinities!

True there was in nillohs dieybos as yet no lumpend papeer in the waste, and mightmountain Penn still groaned for the micies to let flee. All was of ancientry. You gave me a boot (signs on it!) and I ate the wind. I quizzed you a quid (with for what?) and you went to the quod. But the world, mind, is, was and will be writing its own wrunes for ever, man, on all matters that fall under the ban of our infrarational senses fore the last milch-camel, the heartvein throbbing between his eyebrowns, has still to moor before the tomb of his cousin charmian where his date is tethered by the palm that's hers. But the horn, the drinking, the day of dread are not now. A bone, a pebble, a ramskin; chip them, chap them, cut them up allways; leave them to terracook in the muttheringpot: and Gutenmorg with his cromagnom charter, tintingfast and great primer must once for omniboss step rubrick-redd out of the wordpress else is there no virtue more in alcohoran. For that (the rapt one warns) is what papyr is meed of, made of, hides and hints and misses in prints. Till ye finally (though not yet endlike) meet with the acquaintance of Mister Typus, Mistress Tope and all the little typtopies. Fillstup. So you need hardly spell me how every word will be bound over to carry three score and ten toptypsical readings throughout the book of Doublends Jined (may his forehead be darkened with mud who would sunder!) till Daleth, mahomahouma, who oped it closeth thereof the. Dor.

Cry not yet! There's many a smile to Nondum, with sytty maids per man, sir, and the park's so dark by kindlelight. But look what you have in your handself! The movibles are scrawling in motions, marching, all of them ago, in pitpat and zingzang for every busy eerie whig's a bit of a torytale to tell. One's upon a thyme and two's behind their lettice leap and three's among the strubbely beds. And the chicks picked their teeths and the dombkey he begay began. You can ask your ass if he believes it. And so cuddy me only wallops have heels. That one of a wife with folty barnets. For then was the age when hoops ran high. Of a noarch and a chopwife; of a pomme full grave and a fammy of levity; or of golden youths that wanted gelding; or of what the mischievmiss made a man do. Malmarriedad he was reversogassed by the frisque of her frasques and her prytty pyrrhique. Maye faye, she's la gaye this snaky woman! From that trippiery toe expectung-pelick! Veil, volantine, valentine eyes. She's the very besch Winnie blows Nay on good. Flou inn, flow ann. Hohore! So it's sure it was her not we! But lay it easy, gentle mien, we are in rearing of a norewhig. So weenybeeny-veenyteeny. Comsy see! Het wis if ee newt. Lissom! lissom! I am doing it. Hark, the corne entreats! And the larpnotes prittle.

It was of a night, late, lang time agone, in an auldstane eld, when Adam was delvin and his madameen spinning watersilts, when mulk mountynotty man was everybully and the first leal ribberrobber that ever had her ainway everybuddy to his lovesaking eyes and everybilly lived alove with everybiddy else, and Jarl van Hoother had his burnt head high up in his lamphouse, laying cold hands on himself. And his two little jiminies, cousins of ourn, Tristopher and Hilary, were kickaheeling their dummy on the oil cloth

flure of his homerigh, castle and earthenhouse. And, be dermot, who come
to the keep of his inn only the niece-of-his-in-law, the prankquean. And the
prankquean pulled a rosy one and made her wit foreninst the dour. And she
lit up and fireland was ablaze. And spoke she to the dour in her petty
perusienne: Mark the Wans, why do I am alook alike a poss of porterpease?
And that was how the skirtmisshes began. But the dour handworded her
grace in dootch nossow: Shut! So her grace o'malice kidsnapped up the
jiminy Tristopher and into the shandy westerness she rain, rain, rain. And
Jarl van Hoother warlessed after her with soft dovesgall: Stop deef stop
come back to my earin stop. But she swaradid to him: Unlikelihud. And
there was a brannewail that same sabboath night of falling angles somewhere
in Erio. And the prankquean went for her forty years' walk in Tourlemonde
and she washed the blessings of the lovespots off the jiminy with soap
sulliver suddles and she had her four owlers masters for to tauch him his
tickles and she converted him to the onesure allgood and he became a
luderman. So then she started to rain and to rain and, be redtom, she was
back again at Jarl van Hoother's in a brace of samers and the jiminy with her
in her pinafrond, lace at night, at another time. And where did she come but
to the bar of his bristolry. And Jarl von Hoother had his baretholobruised
heels drowned in his cellarmalt, shaking warm hands with himself and the
jimminy hilary and the dummy in their first infancy were below on the
tearsheet, wringing and coughing, like brodar and histher. And the prankquean nipped a paly one and lit up again and redcocks flew flackering from
the hillcombs. And she made her witter before the wicked, saying: Mark the
Twy, why do I am alook alike two poss of porterpease? And: Shut! says the
wicked, handwording her madesty. So her madesty 'a forethought' set down
a jiminy and took up a jiminy and all the lilipath ways to Woeman's Land
she rain, rain, rain. And Jarl von Hoother bleethered atter her with a loud
finegale: Stop domb stop come back with my earring stop. But the prankquean swaradid: Am liking it. And there was a wild old grannewwail that
laurency night of starshootings somewhere in Erio. And the prankquean
went for her forty years' walk in Turnlemeem and she punched the curses
of cromcruwell with the nail of a top into the jiminy and she had her four
larksical monitrix to touch him his tears and she provorted him to the
onecertain allsecure and he became a tristian. So then she started raining,
raining, and in a pair of changers, be dom ter, she was back again at Jarl von
Hoother's and the Larryhill with her under her abromette. And why would
she halt at all if not by the ward of his mansionhome of another nice lace for
the third charm? And Jarl von Hoother had his hurricane hips up to his
pantrybox, ruminating in his holdfour stomachs (Dare! O dare!), ant the

jiminy Toughertrees and the dummy were belove on the watercloth, kissing and spitting, and roguing and poghuing, like knavepaltry and naivebride and in their second infancy. And the prankquean picked a blank and lit out and the valleys lay twinkling. And she made her wittest in front of the arkway of trihump, asking: Mark the Tris, why do I am alook alike three poss of porter pease? But that was how the skirtmishes endupped. For like the campbells acoming with a fork lance of lightning, Jarl von Hoother Boanerges himself, the old terror of the dames, came hip hop handihap out through the pikeopened arkway of his three shuttoned castles, in his broad-ginger hat and his civic chollar and his allabuff hemmed and his bullbraggin soxangloves and his ladbroke breeks and his cattegut bandolair and his furframed panuncular cumbottes like a rudd yellan gruebleen orangeman in his violet indignonation, to the whole longth of the strongth of his bowman's bill. And he clopped his rude hand to his eacy hitch and he ordurd and his thick spch spck for her to shut up shop, dappy. And the duppy shot the shutter clup (Perkodhuskurunbarggruauyagokgorlayorgromgremmit-ghundhurthrumathunaradidillifaititillibumullunukkunun!) And they all drank free. For one man in his armour was a fat match always for any girls under shurts. And that was the first peace of illiterative porthery in all the flamend floody flatuous world. How kirssy the tiler made a sweet unclose to the Narwhealian captol. Saw fore shalt thou sea. Betoun ye and be. The prankquean was to hold her dummyship and the jimminies was to keep the peacewave and van Hoother was to git the wind up. Thus the hearsomeness of the burger felicitates the whole of the polis.

O foenix culprit! Ex nickylow malo comes mickelmassed bonum. Hill, rill, ones in company, billeted, less be proud of. Breast high and bestride! Only for that these will not breathe upon Norronesen or Irenean the secrest of their soorcelossness. Quarry silex, Homfrie Noanswa! Undy gentian festyknees, Livia Noanswa? Wolkencap is on him, frowned; audiurient, he would evesdrip, were it mous at hand, were it dinn of bottles in the far ear. Murk, his vales are darkling. With lipth she lithpeth to him all to time of thuch on thuch and thow on thow. She he she ho she ha to la. Hairfluke, if he could bad twig her! Impalpabunt, he abhears. The soundwaves are his buffeteers; they trompe him with their trompes; the wave of roary and the wave of hooshed and the wave of hawhawhawrd and the wave of neverheed-themhorseluggarsandlisteltomine. Landloughed by his neaghboormistress and perpetrified in his offsprung, sabes and suckers, the moaning pipers could tell him to his faceback, the louthly one whose loab we are devorers of, how butt for his hold halibutt, or her to her pudor puff, the lipalip one whose libe we drink at, how biff for her tiddywink of a windfall, our breed and washer givers, there would not be a holey spier on the town nor a vestal flouting in the dock, nay to make plein avowels, nor a yew nor an eye to play cash cash in Novo Nilbud by swamplight nor a' toole o' tall o' toll and noddy hint to the convaynience.

He dug in and dug out by the skill of his tilth for himself and all belonging to him and he sweated his crew beneath his auspice for the living and he urned his dread, that dragon volant, and he made louse for us and delivered us to boll weevils amain, that mighty liberator, Unfru-Chikda-Uru-Wukru and begad he did, our ancestor most worshipful, till he thought of a better one in his windower's house with that blushmantle upon him from earsend to earsend. And would again could whispring grassies wake him and may again when the fiery bird disembers. And will again if so be sooth by elder to his youngers shall be said. Have you whines for my wedding, did you bring bride and bedding, will you whoop for my deading is a? Wake? *Usqueadbaugham!*

Anam muck an dhoul! Did ye drink me doornail?

Now be aisy, good Mr Finnimore, sir. And take your laysure like a god on pension and don't be walking abroad. Sure you'd only lose yourself in Healiopolis now the way your roads in Kapelavaster are that winding there after the calvary, the North Umbrian and the Fivs Barrow and Waddlings Raid and the Bower Moore and wet your feet maybe with the foggy dew's abroad. Meeting some sick old bankrupt or the Cottericks' donkey with his shoe hanging, clankatachankata, or a slut snoring with an impure infant on a bench. 'Twould turn you against life, so 'twould. And the weather's that mean too. To part from Devlin is hard as Nugent knew, to leave the clean tanglesome one lushier than its neighbour enfranchisable fields but let your ghost have no grievance. You're better off, sir, where you are, primesigned in the full of your dress, bloodeagle waistcoat and all, remembering your shapes and sizes on the pillow of your babycurls under your sycamore by the keld water where the Tory's clay will scare the varmints and have all you want, pouch, gloves, flask, bricket, kerchief, ring and amberulla, the whole treasure of the pyre, in the land of souls with Homin and Broin Baroke and pole ole Lonan and Nobucketnozzler and the Guinnghis Khan. And we'll be coming here, the ombre players, to rake your gravel and bringing you presents, won't we, fenians? And it isn't our spittle we'll stint you of, is it, druids? Not shabbty little imagettes, pennydirts and dodgemyeyes you buy in the soottee stores. But offerings of the field. Mieliodories, that Doctor Faherty, the madison man, taught to gooden you. Poppypap's a passport out. And honey is the holiest thing ever was, hive, comb and earwax, the food for glory, (mind you keep the pot or your nectar cup may yield too

light!) and some goat's milk, sir, like the maid used to bring you. Your fame
is spreading like Basilico's ointment since the Fintan Lalors piped you
overborder and there's whole households beyond the Bothnians and they
calling names after you. The menhere's always talking of you sitting around
on the pig's cheeks under the sacred rooftree, over the bowls of memory
where every hollow holds a hallow, with a pledge till the drengs, in the
Salmon House. And admiring to our supershillelagh where the palmsweat
on high is the mark of your manument. All the toethpicks ever Eirenesians
chewed on are chips chepped from that battery block. If you were bowed
and soild and letdown itself from the oner of the load it was that paddy-
planters might pack up plenty and when you were undone in every point
fore the laps of goddesses you showed our labourlasses how to free was easy.
The game old Gunne, they do be saying, (skull!) that was a planter for you,
a spicer of them all. Begog but he was, the G.O.G! He's duddandgunne
now and we're apter finding the sores of his sedeq but peace to his great
limbs, the buddhoch, with the last league long rest of him, while the
millioncandled eye of Tuskar sweeps the Moylean Main! There was never a
warlord in Great Erinnes and Brettland, no, nor in all Pike County like you,
they say. No, nor a king nor an ardking, bung king, sung king or hung king.
That you could fell an elmstree twelve urchins couldn't ring round and
hoist high the stone that Liam failed. Who but a Maccullaghmore the reise
of our fortunes and the faunayman at the funeral to compass our cause? If
you was hogglebully itself and most frifty like you was taken waters still
what all where was your like to lay the cable or who was the batter could
better Your Grace? Mick Mac Magnus MacCawley can take you off to the
pure perfection and Leatherbags Reynolds tries your shuffle and cut. But as
Hopkins and Hopkins puts it, you were the pale eggynaggy and a kis to tilly
up. We calls him the journeyall Buggaloffs since he went Jerusalemfaring in
Arssia Manor. You had a gamier cock than Pete, Jake or Martin and your
archgoose of geese stubbled for All Angels' Day. So may the priest of seven
worms and scalding tayboil, Papa Vestray, come never anear you as your
hair grows wheater beside the Liffey that's in Heaven! Hep, hep, hurrah
there! Hero! Seven times thereto we salute you! The whole bag of kits,
falconplumes and jackboots incloted, is where you flung them that time.
Your heart is in the system of the Shewolf and your crested head is in the
tropic of Copricapron. Your feet are in the cloister of Virgo. Your olala is in
the region of sahuls. And that's ashore as you were born. Your shuck tick's
swell. And that there texas is tow linen. The loamsome roam to Laffayette is
ended. Drop in your tracks, babe! Be not unrested! The headboddylwatcher
of the chempel of Isid, Totumcalmum, saith: I know thee, metherjar, I

know thee, salvation boat. For we have performed upon thee, thou abraman-ation, who comest ever without being invoked, whose coming is unknown, all the things which the company of the precentors and of the grammarians of Christpatrick's ordered concerning thee in the matter of the work of thy tombing. Howe of the shipmen, steep wall!

Everything's going on the same or so it appeals to all of us, in the old holmsted here. Coughings all over the sanctuary, bad scrant to me aunt Florenza. The horn for breakfast, one o'gong for lunch and dinnerchime. As popular as when Belly the First was keng and his members met in the Diet of Man. The same shop slop in the window. Jacob's lettercrackers and Dr Tipple's Vi-Cocoa and the Eswuards' desippated soup beside Mother Seagull's syrup. Meat took a drop when Reilly-Parsons failed. Coal's short but we've plenty of bog in the yard. And barley's up again, begrained to it. The lads is attending school nessans regular, sir, spelling beesknees with hathatansy and turning out tables by mudapplication. Allfor the books and never pegging smashers after Tom Bowe Glassarse or Timmy the Tosser. 'Tisraely the truth! No isn't it, roman pathoricks? You were the double-joynted janitor the morning they were delivered and you'll be a grandfer yet entirely when the ritehand seizes what the lovearm knows. Kevin's just a doat with his cherub cheek, chalking oghres on walls, and his little lamp and schoolbelt and bag of knicks, playing postman's knock round the diggings and if the seep were milk you could lieve his olde by his ide but, laus sake, the devil does be in that knirps of a Jerry sometimes, the tarandtan plaidboy, making encostive inkum out of the last of his lavings and writing a blue streak over his bourseday shirt. Hetty Jane's a child of Mary. She'll be coming (for they're sure to choose her) in her white of gold with a tourch of ivy to rekindle the flame on Felix Day. But Essie Shanahan has let down her skirts. You remember Essie in our Luna's Convent? They called her Holly Merry her lips were so ruddyberry and Pia de Purebelle when the redminers riots was on about her. Were I a clerk designate to the Williamswoods-menufactors I'd poster those pouters on every jamb in the town. She's making her rep at Lanner's twicenightly. With the tabarine tamtammers of the whirligigmagees. Beats that cachucha flat. 'Twould dilate your heart to go.

Aisy now, you decent man, with your knees and lie quiet and repose your honour's lordship! Hold him here, Ezekiel Irons, and may God strengthen you! It's our warm spirits, boys, he's spooring. Dimitrius O'Flagonan, cork that cure for the Clancartys! You swamped enough since Portobello to float the Pomeroy. Fetch neahere, Pat Koy! And fetch nouyou, Pam Yates! Be nayther angst of Wramawitch! Here's lumbos. Where misties swaddlum, where misches lodge none, where mystries pour kind on, O sleepy! So be yet!

I've an eye on queer Behan and old Kate and the butter, trust me. She'll do no jugglywuggly with her war souvenir postcards to help to build me murial, tippers! I'll trip your traps! Assure a sure there! And we put on your clock again, sir, for you. Did or didn't we, sharestutterers? So you won't be up a stump entirely. Nor shed your remnants. The sternwheel's crawling strong. I seen your missus in the hall. Like the queenoveire. Arrah, it's herself that's fine, too, don't be talking! Shirksends? You storyan Harry chap longa me Harry chap storyan grass woman plethy good trout. Shakeshands. Dibble a hayfork's wrong with her only her lex's salig. Boald Tib does be yawning and smirking cat's hours on the Pollockses' woolly round tabouretcushion watching her sewing a dream together, the tailor's daughter, stitch to her last. Or while waiting for winter to fire the enchantement, decoying more nesters to fall down the flue. It's an allavalonche that blows nopussy food. If you only were there to explain the meaning, best of men, and talk to her nice of guldenselver. The lips would moisten once again. As when you drove with her to Findrinny Fair. What with reins here and ribbons there all your hands were employed so she never knew was she on land or at sea or swooped through the blue like Airwinger's bride. She was flirtsome then and she's fluttersome yet. She can second a song and adores a scandal when the last post's gone by. Fond of a concertina and pairs passing when she's had her forty winks for supper after kanekannan and abbely dimpling and is in her merlin chair assotted, reading her Evening World. To see is it smarts, full lengths or swaggers. News, news, all the news. Death, a leopard, kills fellah in Fez. Angry scenes at Stormount. Stilla Star with her lucky in goingaways. Opportunity fair with the China floods and we hear these rosy rumours. Ding Tams he noise about all same Harry chap. She's seeking her way, a chickle a chuckle, in and out of their serial story, *Les Loves of Selskar et Pervenche*, freely adapted to *The Novvergin's Viv*. There'll be bluebells blowing in salty sepulchres the night she signs her final tear. Zee End. But that's a world of ways away. Till track laws time. No silver ash or switches for that one! While flattering candles flare. Anna Stacey's how are you! Worther waist in the noblest, says Adams and Sons, the wouldpay actionneers. Her hair's as brown as ever it was. And wivvy and wavy. Repose you now! Finn no more!

For, be that samesake sibsubstitute of a hooky salmon, there's already a big rody ram lad at random on the premises of his haunt of the hungred bordles, as it is told me. Shop Illicit, flourishing like a lord-major or a buaboabaybohm, litting flop a deadlop (aloose!) to lee but lifting a bennbranch a yardalong (Ivoeh!) the breezy side (for showm!), the height of Brewster's chimpney and as broad below as Phineas Barnum; humphing his share of the showthers is senken on him he's such a grandfallar, with a pocked wife in pickle that's a flyfire and three lice nittle clinkers, two twilling bugs and one midgit pucelle. And aither he cursed and recursed and was everseen doing what your fourfootlers saw or he was never done seeing what you coolpigeons know, weep the clouds aboon for smiledown witnesses, and that'll do now about the fairyhees and the frailyshees. Though Eset fibble it to the zephiroth and Artsa zoom it round her heavens for ever. Creator he has created for his creatured ones a creation. White monothoid? Red theatrocrat? And all the pinkprophets cohalething? Very much so! But however 'twas 'tis sure for one thing, what sherif Toragh voucherfors and Mapqiq makes put out, that the man, Humme the Cheapner, Esc, overseen as we thought him, yet a worthy of the naym, came at this timecoloured place where we live in our paroqial fermament one tide on another, with a bumrush in a hull of a wherry, the twin turbane dhow, *The Bey for Dybbling*, this archipelago's first visiting schooner, with a wicklowpattern waxenwench at her prow for a figurehead, the deadsea dugong updipdripping from his depths, and has been repreaching himself like a fishmummer these siktyten years ever since, his shebi by his shide, adi and aid, growing hoarish under his turban and changing cane sugar into sethulose starch (Tuttut's cess to him!) as also that, batin the bulkihood he bloats about when innebbiated, our old offender was humile, commune and ensectuous from his nature, which you may gauge after the bynames was put under him, in lashons of languages, (honnein suit and praisers be!) and, totalising him, even hamissim of himashim that he, sober serious, he is ee and no counter he who will be ultimendly respunchable for the hubbub caused in Edenborough.

[2]

NOW (TO FOREBARE FOR EVER SOLITTLE OF IRIS TREES and Lili O'Rangans), concerning the genesis of Harold or Humphrey Chimpden's occupational agnomen (we are back in the presurnames prodromarith period, of course just when enos chalked halltraps) and discarding once for all those theories from older sources which would link him back with such pivotal ancestors as the Glues, the Gravys, the Northeasts, the Ankers and the Earwickers of Sidlesham in the Hundred of Manhood or proclaim him offsprout of vikings who had founded wapentake and seddled hem in Herrick or Eric, the best authenticated version, the Dumlat, read the Reading of Hofed-ben-Edar, has it that it was this way. We are told how in the beginning it came to pass that like cabbaging Cincinnatus the grand old gardener was saving daylight under his redwoodtree one sultry sabbath afternoon, Hag Chivychas Eve, in prefall paradise peace by following his plough for rootles in the rere garden of mobhouse, ye olde marine hotel, when royalty was announced by runner to have been pleased to have halted itself on the highroad along which a leisureloving dogfox had cast followed, also at walking pace, by a lady pack of cocker spaniels. Forgetful of all save his vassal's plain fealty to the ethnarch Humphrey or Harold stayed not to yoke or saddle but stumbled out hotface as he was (his sweatful bandanna loose from his pocketcoat) hasting to the forecourts of his public in topee, surcingle, solascarf and plaid, plus fours, puttees and bulldog boots ruddled cinnabar with flagrant marl, jingling his turnpike keys and bearing aloft amid the fixed pikes of the hunting party a high perch atop of which a flowerpot was fixed earthside hoist with care. On his majesty, who was, or often feigned to be, noticeably longsighted from green youth and had been meaning to inquire what, in effect, had caused yon causeway to be thus potholed, asking substitutionally to be put wise as to whether paternoster and silver doctors were not now more fancied bait for lobstertrapping honest blunt Haromphreyld answered in no uncertain tones very similarly with a fearless forehead: Naw, yer maggers, aw war jist a cotchin on thon bluggy earwuggers. Our sailor king, who was draining a gugglet of obvious adamale, gift both and gorban, upon this, ceasing to swallow, smiled most heartily beneath his walrus moustaches and indulging that none too genial humour which William the Conk on the spindle side had inherited with the hereditary whitelock and some shortfingeredness from his greataunt Sophy, turned towards two of his retinue of gallowglasses, Michael, etheling lord of Leix and Offaly and the jubilee mayor of Drogheda, Elcock, (the two scatterguns being Michael M. Manning, protosyndic of Waterford and an Italian excellency named Giubilei according to a later version cited by the learned scholarch Canavan of Canmakenoise), in either case a triptychal religious family symbolising puritas of doctrina, business per usuals and the purchypatch of hamlock where the paddish preties grow and remarked dilsydulsily: Holybones of Saint Hubert how our red brother of Pourin-grainia would audibly fume did he know that we have for surtrusty bailiwick a turnpiker who is by turns a pikebailer no seldomer than an earwigger For he kinned Jom Pill with his court so gray and his haunts in his house in the mourning. (One still hears that pebble crusted laughta, japijap cheerycherrily, among the roadside tree the lady Holmpatrick planted and still one feels the amossive silence of the cladstone allegibelling: Ive mies outs ide Bourn.) Comes the question are these the facts of his nominigentilisation as recorded and accolated in both or either of the collateral andrewpaul-murphyc narratives. Are those their fata which we read in sibylline between the *fas* and its *nefas*? No dung on the road? And shall Nohomiah be our place like? Yea, Mulachy our kingable khan? We shall perhaps not so soon see. Pinck poncks that bail for seeks alicence where cumsceptres with scentaurs stay. Bear in mind, son of Hokmah, if so be you have metheg in your midness, this man is mountain and unto changeth doth one ascend. Heave we aside the fallacy, as punical as finikin, that it was not the king kingself but his inseparable sisters, uncontrollable nighttalkers, Skertsiraizde with Donyahzade, who afterwards, when the robberers shot up the socialights, came down into the world as amusers and were staged by Madame Sudlow as Rosa and Lily Miskinguette in the pantalime that two pitts paythronosed, Miliodorus and Galathee. The great fact emerges that after that historic date all holographs so far exhumed initialled by Haromphrey bear the sigla H.C.E. and while he was only and long and always good Dook Umphrey for the hungerlean spalpeens of Lucalizod and Chimbers to his cronies it was equally certainly a pleasant turn of the populace which gave him as sense of those normative letters the nickname Here Comes Everybody. An imposing everybody he always indeed looked, constantly the same as and equal to himself and magnificently well worthy of any and all such universalisation, every time he continually surveyed, amid vociferatings from in front of *Accept these few nutties!* and *Take off that white hat!*, relieved with *Stop his Grog* and *Put It in the Log* and *Loots in his* (bassvoco) *Boots*, from good start to happy finish the truly catholic assemblage gathered together in that king's treat house of satin alustrelike above floats and footlights from their assbawlveldts and oxgangs unanimously to clapplaud (the inspiration of his lifetime and the hits of their careers) Mr Wallenstein Washington Semperkelly's immergreen tourers in a command performance by special request with the courteous permission for pious purposes the homedromed and enliventh performance of problem passion play of the millentury, running strong since creation, *A Royal Divorce*, then near the approach towards the summit of its climax, with ambitious interval band selections from *The Bo' Girl* and *The Lily* on all horserie show command nights from his viceregal booth (his bossaloner is ceilinged there a cuckoospit less eminent than the redritualhoods of Maccabe and Cullen) where, a veritable Napoleon the Nth, our worldstage's practical jokepiece and retired cecelti-cocommediant in his own wise, this folksforefather all of the time sat, having the entirety of his house about him, with the invariable broad-stretched kerchief cooling his whole neck, nape and shoulderblades and in a wardrobe panelled tuxedo completely thrown back from a shirt well entitled a swallowall, on every point far outstarching the laundered clawhammers and marbletopped highboys of the pit stalls and early amphitheatre. The piece was this: look at the lamps. The cast was thus: see under the clock. Ladies circle: cloaks may be left. Pit, prommer and parterre, standing room only. Habituels conspicuously emergent.

A baser meaning has been read into these characters the literal sense of which decency can safely scarcely hint. It has been blurtingly bruited by certain wisecrackers (the stinks of Mohorat are in the nightplots of the morning), that he suffered from a vile disease. Athma, unmanner them! To such a suggestion the one selfrespecting answer is to affirm that there are certain statements which ought not to be, and one should like to hope to be able to add, ought not to be allowed to be made. Nor have his detractors, who, an imperfectly warmblooded race, apparently conceive him as a great white caterpillar capable of any and every enormity in the calendar recorded to the discredit of the Juke and Kellikek families, mended their case by insinuating that, alternately, he lay at one time under the ludicrous imputation of annoying Welsh fusiliers in the people's park. Hay, hay, hay! Hoq, hoq, hoq! Faun and Flora on the lea love that little old joq. To anyone who knew and loved the christlikeness of the big cleanminded giant H. C. Earwicker throughout his excellency long vicefreegal existence the mere suggestion of him as a lustsleuth nosing for trouble in a boobytrap rings particularly preposterous. Truth, beard on prophet, compels one to add that there is said to have been quondam (pfuit! pfuit!) some case of the kind implicating, it is interdum believed, a quidam (if he did not exist it would be necessary quoniam to invent him) abhout that time stambuling haround Dumbaling in leaky sneakers with his tarrk record who has remained topantically anonymos but (let us hue him Abdullah Gamellaxarksky) was, it is stated, posted at Mallon's at the instance of watch warriors of the vigilance committee and years afterwards, cries one even greater, Ibid, a commender of the frightful, seemingly, unto such as were sulhan sated, tropped head (pfiat! pfiat!) waiting his first of the month froods turn for thatt chopp pah kabbakks alicubi on the old house for the chargehard, Roche Haddocks off Hawkins Street. Lowe, you blondy liar, Gob scene you in the narked place and she what's edith ar home defileth these boyles! There's a cabful of bash indeed in the homeur of that meal. Slander, let it lie its flattest, has never been able to convict our good and great and no ordinary Southron Ear-wicker, that homogenius man, as a pious author called him, of any graver impropriety than that, advanced by some woodwards or regarders, who did not dare deny, the shomers, that they had, chin Ted, chin Tam, chinchin Taffyd, that day consumed their soul of the corn, of having behaved with ongentilmensky immodus opposite a pair of dainty maidservants in the swoolth of the rushy hollow whither, or so the two gown and pinners pleaded, dame nature in all innocency had spontaneously and about the same hour of the eventide sent them both but whose published combinations of silkinlaine testimonies are, where not dubiously pure, visibly divergent, as wapt from wept, on minor points touching the intimate nature of this, a first offence in vert or venison which was admittedly an incautious but, at its wildest, a partial exposure with such attenuating circumstances (garthen gaddeth green hwere sokeman brideth girling) as an abnormal Saint Swithin's summer and, (Jesses Rosasharon!) a ripe occasion to provoke it.

We can't do without them. Wives, rush to the restyours! Ofman will toman while led is the lol. Zessid's our kadem, villapleach, vollapluck. Fikup, for flesh nelly, el mundo nov, zole flen! If she's a lilyth, pull early! Pauline, allow! And malers abushed, keep black, keep black! Guiltless of much laid to him he was clearly for once at least he clearly expressed himself as being with still a trace of his erstwhile burr sod hence it has been received of us that it is true. They tell the story (an amalgam as absorbing as calzium chloereydes and hydrophobe sponges could make it) how one happygogusty Ides-of-April morning (the anniversary, as it fell out, of his first assumption of his mirthday suit and rights in appurtenance to the confusioning of human races) ages and ages after the alleged misdemeanour when the tried friend of all creation, tigerwood roadstaff to his stay, was billowing across the wide expanse of our greatest park in his caoutchouc kepi and great belt and hideinsacks and his blaufunx fustian and ironsides jackboots and Bhagafat gaiters and his rubberised inverness, he met a cad with a pipe. The latter, the luciferant not the oriuolate (who, the odds are, is still berting dagabout in the same straw bamer, carryin his overgoat under his schulder, sheepside out, so as to look more like a coumfry gentleman and signing the pledge as gaily as you please) hardily accosted him with: Guinness thaw tool in jew me dinner ouzel fin? (a nice how-do-you-do in Poolblack at the time as some of our olddaisers may still tremblingly recall) to ask could he tell him how much a clock it was that the clock struck had he any idea by cock's luck as his watch was bradys. Hesitency was clearly to be evitated. Execration as cleverly to be honnisoid. The Earwicker of that spurring instant, realising on fundamental liberal principles the supreme importance, nexally and noxally, of physical life (the nearest help relay being pingping K. O. Sempatrick's Day and the fenian rising) and unwishful as he felt of being hurled into eternity right then, plugged by a softnosed bullet from the sap, halted, quick on the draw, and replyin that he was feelin tipstaff, cue, prodooced from his gunpocket his Jurgensen's shrapnel waterbury, ours by communionism, his by usucapture, but, on the same stroke, hearing above the skirling of harsh Mother East old Fox Goodman, the bellmaster, over the wastes to south, at work upon the ten ton tonuant thunderous tenor toller in the speckled church (Couhounin's call!) told the inquiring kidder, by Jehova, it was twelve of em sidereal and tankard time, adding, buttall, as he bended deeply with smoked sardinish breath to give more pondus to the copperstick he presented (though this seems in some cumfusium with the chapstuck ginger which, as being of sours, acids, salts, sweets and bitters compompounded, we know him to have used as chaw-chaw for bone, muscle, blood, flesh and vimvital,) that whereas the hakusay accusation againstm had been made, what was known in high quarters as was stood stated in Morganspost, by a creature in youman form who was quite beneath parr and several degrees lower than yore triplehydrad snake. In greater support of his word (it, quaint 'anticipation of a famous phrase, has been reconstricted out of oral style into the verbal for all time with ritual rhythmics, in quiritary quietude, and toosammen-stucked from successive accounts by Noah Webster in the redaction known as the Sayings Attributive of H. C. Earwicker, prize on schillings, postlots free), the flaxen Gygas tapped his chronometrum drumdrum and, now standing full erect, above the ambijacent floodplain, scene of its happening, with one Berlin gauntlet chopstuck in the hough of his ellboge (by ancientest signlore his gesture meaning: ⅎ!) pointed at an angle of thirty-two degrees towards his *duc de Fer*'s overgrown milestone as fellow to his gage and after a rendypresent pause averred with solemn emotion's fire: Shsh shake, co-comeraid! Me only, them five ones, he is equal combat. I have won straight. Hence my nonation wide hotel and creamery establishments which for the honours of our mewmew mutual daughters, credit me, I am woo-woo willing to take my stand, sir, upon the monument, that sign of our ruru redemption, any hygienic day to this hour and to make my hoath to my sinnfinners, even if I get life for it, upon the Open Bible and before the Great Taskmaster's (I lift my hat!) and in the presence of the Deity Itself andwell of Bishop and Mrs Michan of High Church of England as of all such of said my immediate withdwellers and of every living sohole in every corner wheresoever of this globe in general which useth of my British to my backbone tongue and commutative justice that there is not one tittle of truth, allow me to tell you, in that purest of fibfib fabrications.

Gaping Gill, swift to mate errthors, stern to checkself, (diagnosing

through eustacetube that it was to make with a markedly postpuberal
hypertituitary type of Heidelberg mannleich cavern ethics) lufted his
slopingforward, bad Sweatagore good murrough and dublnotch on to it as
he was greedly obliged, and like a sensible ham, with infinite tact in the
delicate situation seen the touchy nature of its perilous theme, thanked um
for guilders received and time of day (not a little token abock all the same
that that was owl the God's clock it was) and, upon humble duty to greet his
Tyskminister and he shall gildthegap Gaper and thee his a mouldy voids,
went about his business, whoever it was, saluting corpses, as a metter of
corse (one could hound him out had one hart to for the monticules of scalp
and dandruff droppings blaze his trail) accompanied by his trusty snorler
and his permanent reflection, verbigracious; I have met with you, bird, too
late, or if not, too worm and early: and with tag for ildiot repeated in his
secondmouth language as many of the bigtimer's verbaten words which he
could balbly call to memory that same kveldeve, ere the hour of the
twattering of bards in the twitterlitter between Druidia and the Deepsleep
Sea, when suppertide and souvenir to Charlatan Mall jointly kem gently
and along the quiet darkenings of Grand and Royal, ff, flitmansfluh, and,
kk, 't crept i' hedge whenas to many a softongue's pawkytalk mude unswer u
sufter poghyogh, Arvanda always aquiassent, while, studying castelles in the
blowne and studding cowshots over the noran, he spat in careful converted-
ness a musaic dispensation about his *hearthstone*, if you please, (Irish saliva,
mawshe dho hole, but would a respectable prominently connected fellow of
Iro-European ascendances with welldressed ideas who knew the correct
thing such as Mr Shallwesigh or Mr Shallwelaugh expectorate after such a
callous fashion, no thank yous! when he had his belcher *spuckertuck* in his
pucket, pthuck?) musefed with his thockits after having supped of the dish
sot and pottage which he snobbishly dabbed Peach Bombay (it is rawly only
Lukanpukan pilzenpie which she knows which senaffed and pibered him), a
supreme of excelling peas, balled under minnshogue's milk into whitemalt
winesour, a proviant the littlebilker hoarsely relished, chaff it, in the snevel
season, being as fain o't as your rat wi'fennel; and on this celebrating
occasion of the happy escape, for a crowning of pot valiance, this regional
platter, benjamin of bouillis, with a spolish olive to middlepoint its zaynith,
was marrying itself (porkograso!) erebusqued very deluxiously with a bottle
of Phenice-Bruerie '98, followed for second nuptials by a Piessporter, Grand
Cur, of both of which cherished tablelights (though humble the bounquet
'tis a leaman's farewell) he obdurately sniffed the cobwebcrusted corks.

    Our cad's bit of strife (knee Bareniece Maxwelton) with a quick ear for
spittoons (as the aftertale hath it) glaned up as usual with dumbestic

husbandry (no persicks and armelians for thee, Pomeranzia!) but, slipping the clav in her claw, broke of the matter among a hundred and eleven others in her usual curtsey (how faint these first vhespers womanly are, a secret pispigliando, amad the lavurdy den of their manfolker!) the next night nudge one as was Hegesippus over a hup a 'chee, her eys dry and small and speech thicklish because he appeared a funny colour like he couldn't stood they old hens no longer, to her particular reverend, the director, whom she had been meaning in her mind primarily to speak with (hosch, intra! jist a timblespoon!) trusting, between cuppled lips and annie lawrie promises (mighshe never have Esnekerry pudden come Hunanov for her pecklapitschens!) that the gossiple so delivered in his epistolear, buried teatoastally in their Irish stew would go no further than his jesuit's cloth, yet (in vinars venitas! volatiles valetotum!) it was this overspoiled priest Mr Browne, disguised as a vincentian, who, when seized of the facts, was overheard, in his secondary personality as a Nolan and underreared, poul soul, by accident—if, that is, the incident it was an accident for here the ruah of Ecclectiastes of Hippo outpuffs the writress of Havvah-ban-Annah—to pianissime a slightly varied version of Crookedribs confidentials, (what Mère Aloyse said but for Jesuphine's sake!) hands between hahands, in fealty sworn (my bravor best! my fraur!) and, to the strains of *The Secret of Her Birth*, hushly pierce the rubiend aurellum of one Philly Thurnston, a layteacher of rural science and orthophonethics of a nearstout figure and about the middle of his forties during a priestly flutter for safe and sane bets at the hippic runfields of breezy Baldoyle on a date (W. W. goes through the card) easily capable of rememberance by all pickers-up of events national and Dublin details, the doubles of Perkin and Paullock, peer and prole, when the classic Encourage Hackney Plate was captured by two noses in a stablecloth finish, ek and nek, some and none, evelo nevelo, from the cream colt Bold Boy Cromwell after a clever getaway by Captain Chaplain Blount's roe hinny Saint Dalough, Drummer Coxon, nondepict third, at breakneck odds, thanks to you great little, bonny little, portey little, Winny Widger! you're all their nappies! who in his neverrip mud and purpular cap was surely leagues unlike any other phantomweight that ever toppitt our timber maggies.

'Twas two pisononse Timcoves (the wetter is pest, the renns are overt and come and the voax of the turfur is hurled on our lande) of the name of Treacle Tom as was just out of pop following the theft of a leg of Kehoe, Donnelly and Packenham's Finnish pork and his own blood and milk brother Frisky Shorty, (he was, to be exquisitely punctilious about them, both shorty and frisky) a tipster, come off the hulks, both of them awful poor, what was out on the bumaround for an oofbird game for a jimmy o'goblin or a small thick un as chanced, while the Seaforths was making the colleenbawl, to ear the passon in the motor clobber make use of his law language (Edzo, Edzo on), touchin the case of Mr Adams what was in all the sundays about it which he was rubbing noses with and having a gurgle off his own along of the butty bloke in the specs.

This Treacle Tom to whom reference has been made had been absent from his usual wild and woolly haunts in the land of counties capalleens for some time previous to that (he was, in fact, in the habit of frequenting common lodginghouses where he slept in a nude state, hailfellow with meth, in strange men's cots) but on racenight, blotto after divers tots of hell fire, red biddy, bull dog, blue ruin and creeping jenny, Eglandine's choicest herbage, supplied by the Duck and Doggies, the Galopping Primrose, Brigid Brewster's, the Cock, the Postboy's Horn, the Little Old Man's and All Swell That Aimswell, the Cup and the Stirrup, he sought his wellwarmed leababobed in a housingroom Abide With Oneanother at Block W.W., (why didn't he back it?) Pump Court, The Liberties, and, what with molta-puke on voltapuke, resnored alcoh alcoho alcoherently to the burden of *I come, my horse delayed*, nom num, the substance of the tale of the evangelical bussybozzy and the rusinurbean (the 'girls' he would keep calling them for the collarette and skirt, the sunbonnet and carnation) in parts (it seemed he was before the eyots of martas or otherwales the thirds of fossilyears, he having beham with katya when lavinias had her mens lease to sea in a psumpship doodly show whereat he was looking for fight niggers with whilde roarses) oft in the chilly night (the metagonistic! the epickthala-morous!) during uneasy slumber in their hearings of a small and stonybroke cashdraper's executive, Peter Cloran (discharged), O'Mara, an exprivate secretary of no fixed abode (locally known as Mildew Lisa), who had passed several nights, funnish enough, in a doorway under the blankets of homelessness on the bunk of iceland, pillowed upon the stone of destiny colder than man's knee or woman's breast, and Hosty, (no slouch of a name), an illstarred beachbusker, who, sans rootie and sans scrapie, suspicioning as how he was setting on a twoodstool on the verge of selfabyss, most starved, with melancholia over everything in general, (night birman, you served him with natigal's nano!) had been towhead tossing on his shakedown, devising ways and manners of means, of what he loved to ifidalicence somehow or other in the nation getting a hold of some chap's parabellum in the hope of taking a wing sociable and lighting upon a sidewheel dive somewhere off the Dullkey Downlairy and Bleakrooky tram-aline where he could throw true and go and blow the sibicidal napper off

himself for two bits to boldywell baltitude in the peace and quitybus of a one
sure shot bottle, he after having being trying all he knew with the lady's help
of Madam Gristle for upwards of eighteen calanders to get out of Sir
Patrick Dun's, through Sir Humphrey Jervis's and into the Saint Kevin's
bed in the Adelaide's hosspittles (from these incurable welleslays among
those uncarable wellasdays through Sant Iago by his cocklehat, goot Lazar,
deliver us!) without after having been able to jerrywangle it anysides. Lisa
O'Deavis and Roche Mongan (who had so much incommon, epipsychid-
ically; if the phrase be permitted *hostis et odor insuper petroperfractus*) as an
understood thing slept their sleep of the swimborne in the one sweet
undulant mother of tumblerbunks with Hosty just how the shavers in the
shaw the yokels in the yoats or, well, the wasters in the wilde, and the
bustling tweeny-dawn-of-all-works (meed of anthems here we pant!) had
not been many jiffies furbishing potlids, doorbrasses, scholars' applecheeks
and linkboy's metals when, ashhopperminded like no fella he go make
bakenbeggfuss longa white man, the rejuvenated busker (for after a good-
night's rave and rumble and a shinkhams topmorning with his coexes he
was not the same man) and his broadawake bedroom suite (our boys, as our
Byron called them) were up and ashuffle from the hogshome they lovenaned
The Barrel, cross Ebblinn's chilled hamlet (thrie routes and restings on
their then superficies curiously correspondant with those linea and puncta
where our tubenny habenny metro maniplumbs below the oberflake under-
rails and stations at this time of riding) to the thrummings of a crewth fiddle
which, cremoaning and cronauning, levey grevey, witty and wevey, appy,
leppy and playable, caressed the ears of the subjects of King Saint Finnerty
the Festive who, in brick homes of their own and in their flavory fraiseberry
beds, heeding hardly cry of honeyman, soed lavender or foyneboyne salmon
alive, with their priggish mouths all open for the larger appraisiation of this
longawaited Messiagh of roaratorios, were only halfpast atsweeeep and after
a brisk pause at a pawnbroking establishment for the prothetic purpose of
redeeming the songster's truly admirable false teeth and a prolonged visit to
a house of call at Cujas Place, fizz, the Old Sots' Hole in the parish of Saint
Cecily within the liberty of Ceolmore not a thousand or one national
leagues, that was, by Griffith's valuation, from the site of the statue of
Primewer Glasstone setting a match to the march of a maker (last of the
stewards peut-être), where, the tale rambles along, the trio of whackfol-
thediddlers was joined by a further—intentions—apply—tomorrow casual
and a decent sort of the hadbeen variety who had just been touching the
weekly insult, phewit, and all figblabbers (who saith of noun?) had stimulants
in the shape of gee and gees stood by the damn decent sort after which stag

luncheon and a few ones more just to celebrate yesterday, flushed with their firestufffortered friendship, the rascals came out of the licensed premises, (Browne's first, the small p.s. ex-ex-executive capahand in their sad rear like a lady's postscript: I want money. Pleasend), wiping their laughleaking lipes on their sleeves, how the bouckaleens shout their roscan generally (seinn fion, seinn fion's araun.) and the rhymers' world was with reason the richer for a wouldbe ballad, to the balledder of which the world of cumannity singing owes a tribute for having placed on the planet's melomap his lay of the vilest bogeyer but most attractionable avatar the world has ever had to explain for.

This, more krectly lubeen or fellow—me—lieder was first poured forth where Riau Liviau riots and col de Houdo humps, under the shadow of the monument of the shouldhavebeen legislator (Eleutheriodendron! Spare, woodmann, spare!) to an overflow meeting of all the nations in Lenster fullyfilling the visional area and, as a singleminded supercrowd, easily representative, what with masks, whet with faces, of all sections and cross sections (wineshop and cocoahouse poured out to brim up the broaching) of our liffeyside people (to omit to mention of the mainland minority and such as had wayfared *via* Watling, Ernin, Icknild and Stane, in chief a halted cockney car with its quotal of Hardmuth's hacks, a northern tory, a southern whig, an eastanglian chronicler and a landwester guardian) ranging from slips of young dublinos from Cutpurse Row having nothing better to do than walk about with their hands in their kneepants, sucking airwhackers, weedulicet, jumbobricks, side by side with truant officers, three woollen balls and poplin in search of a croust of pawn to busy professional gentle-men, a brace of palesmen with dundrearies, nooning toward Daly's, fresh from snipehitting and mallardmissing on Rutland heath, exchanging cold sneers, massgoing ladies from Hume Street in their chairs, the bearers baited, some wandering hamalags out of the adjacent cloverfields of Mosse's Gardens, an oblate father from Skinner's Alley, bricklayers, a fleming, in tabinet fumant, with spouse and dog, an aged hammersmith who had some chisellers by the hand, a bout of cudgel players, not a few sheep with the braxy, two bluecoat scholars, four broke gents out of Simpson's on the Rocks, a portly and a pert still tassing Turkey Coffee and orange shrub in tickeyes door, Peter Pim and Paul Fry and then Elliot and, O, Atkinson, suffering hell's delights from the blains of their annuitants' acorns not forgetting a deuce of dianas ridy for the hunt, a particularist prebendary pondering on the roman easter, the tonsure question and greek uniates, plunk em, a lace lappet head or two or three or four from a window, and so on down to a few good old souls, who, as they were juiced after taking their pledge over at the uncle's place, were evidently under the spell of liquor, from the wake of Tarry the Tailor a fair girl, a jolly postboy thinking off three flagons and one, a plumodrole, a half sir from the weaver's almshouse who clings and clings and chatchatchat clings to her, a wholedam's cloud-hued pittycoat, as child, as curiolater, as Caoch O'Leary. The wararrow went round, so it did, (a nation wants a gaze) and the ballad, in the felibrine trancoped metre affectioned by Taiocebo in his *Casudas de Poulichinello Artahut*, stumpstampaded on to a slip of blancovide and headed by an excessively rough and red woodcut, privately printed at the rimepress of Delville, soon fluttered its secret on white highway and brown byway to the rose of the winds and the blew of the gaels, from archway to lattice and from black hand to pink ear, village crying to village, through the five pussyfours green of the united states of Scotia Picta—and he who denays it, may his hairs be rubbed in dirt! To the added strains (so peacifold) of his majesty the flute, that onecrooned king of inscrewments, Piggott's purest, *ciello alsoliuto*, which Mr Delaney (Mr Delacey?), horn, anticipating a perfect downpour of plaudits among the rapsods, piped out of his decentsoort hat, looking still more like his purseyful namesake as men of Gaul noted, but before of to sputabout, the snowycrested curl amoist the leader's wild and moulting hair, 'Ductor' Hitchcock hoisted his fezzy fuzz at bludgeon's height signum to his companions of the chalice for the Loud Fellow, boys' and *silentium in curia!* (our maypole once more where he rose of old) and the canto was chantied there chorussed and christened where by the old tollgate, Saint Annona's Street and Church.

And around the lawn the rann it rann and this is the rann that Hosty made. Spoken. Boyles and Cahills, Skerretts and Pritchards, viersified and piersified may the treeth we tale of live in stoney. Here line the refrains of. Some vote him Vike, some mote him Mike, some dub him Llyn and Phin while others hail him Lug Bug Dan Lop, Lex, Lax, Gunne or Guinn. Some apt him Arth, some bapt him Barth, Coll, Noll, Soll, Will, Weel, Wall but I parse him Persse O'Reilly else he's called no name at all. Together. Arrah, leave it to Hosty, frosty Hosty, leave it to Hosty for he's the mann to rhyme the rann, the rann, the rann, the king of all ranns. Have you here? (Some ha) Have we where? (Some hant) Have you hered? (Others do) Have we whered? (Others dont) It's cumming, it's brumming! The clip, the clop! (All cla) Glass crash. The (klikkaklakkaklaskaklopatzklatschabattacreppycrotty-graddaghsemmihsammihnouithappluddyappladdypkonpkot!).

{ *Ardite, arditi!*
{ Music cue

THE BALLAD OF PERSSE O'REILLY

Have you heard of one Humpty Dumpty
How he fell with a roll and a rumble
And curled up like Lord Olofa Crumple
By the butt of the Magazine Wall,
    (Chorus) Of the Magazine Wall,
        Hump, helmet and all?

He was one time our King of the Castle
Now he's kicked about like a rotten old parsnip.
And from Green street he'll be sent by order of His Worship
To the penal jail of Mountjoy
    (Chorus) To the jail of Mountjoy!
        Jail him and joy.

He was fafafather of all schemes for to bother us
Slow coaches and immaculate contraceptives for the populace,
Mare's milk for the sick, seven dry Sundays a week,
Openair love and religion's reform,
    (Chorus) And religious reform,
        Hideous in form.

Arrah, why, says you, couldn't he manage it?
I'll go bail, my fine dairyman darling,
Like the bumping bull of the Cassidys
All your butter is in your horns.
    (Chorus) His butter is in his horns.
        Butter his horns!

(Repeat) Hurrah there, Hosty, frosty Hosty, change that shirt on ye,
Rhyme the rann, the king of all ranns!

Balbaccio, balbuccio!
We had chaw chaw chops, chairs, chewing gum, the chickenpox
and china chambers
Universally provided by this soffsoaping salesman.
Small wonder He'll Cheat E'erawan our local lads nicknamed him
When Chimpden first took the floor
(Chorus) With his bucketshop store
Down Bargainweg, Lower.

So snug he was in his hotel premises sumptuous
But soon we'll bonfire all his trash, tricks and trumpery
And 'tis short till sheriff Clancy'll be winding up his unlimited company
With the bailiff's bom at the door,
(Chorus) Bimbam at the door.
Then he'll bum no more.

Sweet bad luck on the waves washed to our island
The hooker of that hammerfast viking
And Gall's curse on the day when Eblana bay
Saw his black and tan man-o'-war.
(Chorus) Saw his man-o'-war.
On the harbour bar.

Where from? roars Poolbeg. Cookingha'pence, he bawls
Donnez-moi scampitle, wick an wipin'fampiny
Fingal Mac Oscar Onesine Bargearse Boniface
Thok's min gammelhole Norveegickers moniker
Og as ay are at gammelhore Norveegickers cod.
(Chorus) A Norwegian camel old cod.
He is, begod.

Lift it, Hosty, lift it, ye devil ye! up with the rann, the rhyming rann!
It was during some fresh water garden pumping
Or, according to the *Nursing Mirror*, while admiring the monkeys
That our heavyweight heathen Humpharey
Made bold a maid to woo
(Chorus) Woohoo, what'll she doo!
The general lost her maidenloo!

He ought to blush for himself, the old hayheaded philosopher,
For to go and shove himself that way on top of her.
Begob, he's the crux of the catalogue
Of our antediluvial zoo,
  (Chorus) Messrs. Billing and Coo.
   Noah's larks, good as noo.

He was joulting by Wellinton's monument
Our rotorious hippopopotamuns
When some bugger let down the backtrap of the omnibus
And he caught his death of fusiliers,
  (Chorus) With his rent in his rears.
   Give him six years.

'Tis sore pity for his innocent poor children
But look out for his missus legitimate!
When that frew gets a grip of old Earwicker
Won't there be earwigs on the green?
  (Chorus) Big earwigs on the green,
   The largest ever you seen.

  Suffoclose! Shikespower! Seudodanto! Anonymoses!

Then we'll have a free trade Gaels' band and mass meeting
For to sod the brave son of Scandiknavery.
And we'll bury him down in Oxmanstown
Along with the devil and Danes,
  (Chorus) With the deaf and dumb Danes,
   And all their remains.

And not all the king's men nor his horses
Will resurrect his corpus
For there's no true spell in Connacht or hell
  (bis) That's able to raise a Cain.

CHEST CEE! 'SDENSE! CORPO DI BARRAGIO! YOU SPOOF of visibility in a freakfog, of mixed sex cases among goats hill cat and plain mousey, Bigamy Bob and his old Shanvocht! The Blackfriars treacle plaster outrage be liddled! Therewith was released in that kingsrick of Humidia a poisoning volume of cloud barrage indeed. Yet all they who heard or redelivered are now with that family of bards and Vergobretas himself and the crowd of Caraculacticors as much no more as be they not yet now or had they then notever been. Canbe in some future we shall presently here amid those zouave players of Inkermann the mime mumming the mick and his nick miming their maggies, Hilton St Just (Mr Frank Smith), Ivanne Ste Austelle (Mr J. F. Jones), Coleman of Lucan taking four parts, a choir of the O'Daley O'Doyles doublesixing the chorus in *Fenn Mac Call and the Serven Feeries of Loch Neach, Galloper Troppler and Hurleyquinn* the zitherer of the past with his merrymen all, zimzim, zimzim. Of the persins sin this Eyrawyggla saga (which, thorough readable to int from and, is from tubb to buttom all falsetissues, antilibellous and nonactionable and this applies to its whole wholume) of poor Osti-Fosti, described as quite a musical genius in a small way and the owner of an exceedingly niced ear, with tenorist voice to match, not alone, but a very major poet of the poorly meritary order (he began Tuonisonian but worked his passage up as far as the we-all-hang-together Animandovites) no one end is known. If they whistled him before he had curtains up they are whistling him still after his curtain's doom's doom. *Ei fu.* His husband, poor old A'Hara (Okaroff?) crestfallen by things and down at heels at the time, they squeak, accepted the (Zassnoch!) ardree's shilling at the conclusion of the Crimean war and, having flown his wild geese, alohned in crowds to warnder on like Shuley Luney, enlisted in Tyrone's horse, the Irish whites, and soldiered a bit with Wolsey under the assumed name of Blanco Fusilovna Bucklovitch (spurious) after which the cawer and the marble halls of Pump Court Columbarium, the home of the old seakings, looked upon each other and queth their haven evermore for it transpires that on the other side of the water it came about that on the field of Vasileff's Cornix inauspiciously with his unit he perished, suying, this papal leafless to old chap give, rawl chawclates for mouther-in-louth. *Booil.* Poor old dear Paul Horan, to satisfy his literary as well as his criminal aspirations, at the suggestion thrown out by the doomster in loquacity lunacy, so says the Dublin Intelligence, was thrown into a Ridley's for inmates in the northern counties. Under the name of Orani he may have been the utility man of the troupe capable of sustaining long parts at short notice. He was. Sordid Sam, a dour decent deblancer, the unwashed, haunted always by his ham, the unwished, at a word from Israfel the Summoner, passed away painlessly after life's upsomdowns one hallowe'en night, ebbrous and in the state of nature, propelled from Behind into the great Beyond by footblows coulinclouted upon his oyster and atlas on behanged and behooved and behicked and behulked of his last fishandblood bedscrappers, a Northwegian and his mate of the Sheawolving class. Though the last straw glimt his baring this stage thunkhard is said (the pitfallen gagged him as 'Promptboxer') to have solemnly said—as had the brief thot but fell in till his head like a bass dropt neck fust in till a bung crate (cogged!): Me drames, O'Loughlins, has come through! Now let the centuple celves of my egourge as Micholas de Cusack calls them,—of all of whose I in my hereinafter of course by recourse demission me—by the coincidance of their contraries reamalgamerge in that indentity of undiscernibles where the Baxters and the Fleshmans may they cease to bidivil uns and (but at this poingt though the iron thrust of his cockspurt start might have prepared us we are wellnigh stinkpotthered by the mustardpunge in the tailend) this outandin brown candlestock melt Nolan's into peese! *Han var*. Disliken as he was to druriodrama, her wife Langley, the prophet, and the decentest dozendest short of a frusker whoever stuck his spickle through his spoke, disappeared, (in which toodooing he has taken all the French leaves unveilable out of Calomnequiller's Pravities) from the sourface of this earth, that austral plain he had transmaried himself to, so entirely spoorlessly (the mother of the book with a dustwhisk tabularasing his obliteration done upon her involucrum) as to tickle the speculative to all but opine (since the Levey who might have been Langley may have really been a redivivus of paganinism or a volunteer Vousden) that the hobo (who possessed a large amount of the humoresque) had transtuled his funster's latitat to its finsterest interrimost. *Bhi she*. Again, if Father San Browne, tea and toaster to that quaintesttest of yarnspinners is Padre Don Bruno, treu and troster to the queen of Iar-Spain, was the reverend, the sodality director, that eupeptic viceflayer, a barefaced carmelite, to whose palpitating pulpit (which of us but remembers the rarevalent and hornerable Fratomistor Nawlanmore and Brawne.) sinning society sirens (see the [Roman Catholic] presspassim) fortunately became so enthusiastically attached and was an objectionable ass who very occasionally cockaded a raffles ticket on his hat which he wore all to one side like the hangle of his pan (if Her Elegance saw him she'd have the canary!) and was semiprivately convicted of malpractices with his hotwashed tableknife (glossing over the cark in his pocket) that same snob of the dunhill, fully several yearschaums riper, encountered by the General on that redletter morning or maynoon jovesday and were they? *Fuitfuit.*

When Phishlin Phil wants throws his lip 'tis pholly to be fortune flonting and whoever's gone to mix Hotel by the salt say water there's nix to nothing we can do for he's never again to sea. It is nebuless an autodidact fact of the commonest that the shape of the average human cloudyphiz, whereas sallow has long daze faded, frequently altered its ego with the possing of the showers (Not original!). Whence it is a slopperish matter, given the wet and low visibility (since in this scherzarade of one's thousand one nightinesses that sword of certainty which would indentifide the body never falls) to idendifine the individuone in scratch wig, squarecuts, stock lavaleer, regattable oxeter, baggy pants and shufflers (he is often alluded to as Slypatrick, the llad in the llane) with already an incipience (lust!) in the direction of area baldness (one is continually firstmeeting with odd sorts of others at all sorts of ages!) who was asked by free boardschool shirkers in drenched coats overawall, Will, Conn and Otto, to tell them overagait, Vol, Pov and Dev, that fishabed ghoatstory of the haardly creditable edventyres of the Haberdasher, the two Curchies and the three Enkelchums in their Bearskin ghoats! Girles and jongers, but he has changed alok syne Thorkill's time! Ya, da, tra, gathery, pimp, shesses, shossafat, okodeboko, nine! Those many warts, those slummy patches, halfsinster wrinkles, (what has come over the face on wholebroader E?), and (shrine of Mount Mu save us!) the large fungopark he has grown! Drink!

Sport's a common thing. It was the Lord's own day for damp (to wait for a postponed regatta's eventualising is not of Battlecock Shettledore—Juxta—Mare only) and the request for a fully armed explanation was put (in Loo of Pat) to the porty (a native of the sisterisle—Meathman or Meccan?—by his brogue, exrace eyes, lokil calour and lucal odour which are said to have been average clownturkish (though the capelist's voiced nasal liquids and the way he sneezed at zees haul us back to the craogs and bryns of the Silurian Ordovices) who, the lesser pilgrimage accomplished, had made, pats' and pigs' older inselt, the south-east bluffs of the stranger stepshore, a *regifugium persecutorum*, hence hindquarters) as he paused at evenchime for some or so minutes (hit the pipe dannyboy! Time to won, barmon. I'll take ten to win.) amid the devil's one duldrum (Apple by her blossom window and Charlotte at her toss panomancy his sole admirers, his only tearts in store) for a fragrend culubosh during his weekend pastime of executing with

Anny Oakley deadliness (the consummatory pairs of provocatives, of which remained provokingly but two, the ones he fell for, Lili and Tutu, cork em!) empties which had not very long before contained Reid's family (you ruad that before, soaky, but all the bottles in sodemd histry will not soften your bloodathirst!) stout. Having reprimed his repeater and resiteroomed his timespiece His Revenances, with still a life or two to spare for the space of his occupancy of a world at a time, rose to his feet and there, far from Tolkaheim, in a quiet English garden (commonplace!), since known as Whiddington Wild, his simple intensive curolent vocality, my dearbraithers, my most dearbrathairs, as he, so is a supper as is a sipper, spake of the One and told of the Compassionate, called up before the triad of precoxious scaremakers (scoretaking: Spegulo ne helpas al malbellulo, Mi Kredas ke vi estas prava, Via dote la vizago rispondas fraulino) the now to ushere mythical habiliments of Our Farfar and Arthor of our doyne.

Television kills telephony in brothers' broil. Our eyes demand their turn. Let them be seen! And wolfbone balefires blaze the trailmost if only that Mary Nothing may burst her bibby buckshee. When they set fire then she's got to glow so we may stand some chances of warming to what every soorkabatcha, tum or hum, would like to know. The first Humphrey's latitudinous baver with puggaree behind, (calaboose belong bigboss belong Kang the Toll) his fourinhand bow, his elbaroom surtout, the refaced unmansionables of gingerine hue, the state slate umbrella, his gruff woolsely-wellesly with the finndrinn knopfs and the gauntlet upon the hand which in an hour not for him solely evil had struck down the might he mighthavebeen d'Esterre of whom his nation seemed almost already to be about to have need. Then, stealing his thunder, but in the befitting legomena of the smaller country, (probable words, possibly said, of field family gleaming) a bit duskish and flavoured with a smile, seein as ow his thoughts consisted chiefly of the cheerio, he aptly sketched for our soontobe second parents (sukand see whybe!) the touching seene. The solence of that stilling! Here one might a fin fell. Boomster rombombonant! It scenes like a landescape from Wildu Picturescu or some seem on some dimb Arras, dumb as Mum's mutyness, this mimage of the seventyseventh kusin of kristansen is odable to os across the wineless Ere no œdor nor mere eerie nor liss potent of suggestion than in the tales of the tingmount. (Prigged!)

And there oftafter, jauntyjogging, on an Irish visavis, insteadily with shoulder to shoulder Jehu will tell to Christianier, saint to sage, the humphriad of that fall and rise while daisy winks at her pinker sister among the tussocks and the copoll between the shafts mocks the couple on the car. And as your who may look like how on the owther side of his big

belttry your tyrs and cloes your noes and paradigm maymay rererise in eren.
Follow we up his whip vindicative. Thurston's! Lo bebold! *La arboro, lo
petrusu.* The augustan peacebetothem oaks, the monolith rising stark from
the moonlit pinebarren. In all fortitudinous ajaxious rowdinoisy tenuacity.
The angelus hour with ditchers bent upon their farm usetensiles, the soft
belling of the fallow deers (*doerehmoose genuane!*) advertising their milky
approach as midnight was striking the hours (*letate!*), and how brightly the
great tribune outed the sharkskin smokewallet (imitation!) from his frock,
kippers, and by Joshua, he tips un a topping swank cheroot, none of your
swellish soide, quoit the reverse, and how manfally he says, pluk to pluk and
lekan for lukan, he was to just pluggy well suck that brown boyo, my son,
and spend a whole half hour in Havana. Sorer of the kreeksmen, would not
thore be old high gothsprogue! Wherefore he met Master, he mean to say,
he do, sire, bester of redpublicans, at Eagle Cock Hostel on Lorenzo Tooley
street and how he wished his Honour the bannocks of Gort and Morya
and Bri Head and Puddyrick, yore Loudship, and a starchboxsitting in the
pit of his St Tomach's,——a strange wish for you, my friend, and it would
poleaxe your sonson's grandson utterly though your own old sweatand-
swear floruerunts heaved it hoch many as the times, when they were
turrified by the hitz.

Chee chee cheers for Upkingbilly and crow cru cramwells Downaboo!
Hup, boys, and hat him! See! Oilbeam they're lost we've fount rerem-
brandtsers, their hours to date link these heirs to here but wowhere are
those yours of Yestersdays? Farseeingetherich and Poolaulwoman Charach-
thercuss and his Ann van Vogt. D.e.e.d! Edned, ended or sleeping sound-
lessly? Favour with your tongues! *Intendite!*

Any dog's life you list you may still hear them at it, like sixes and seventies
as eversure as Halley's comet, ulemamen, sobranjewomen, storthingboys
and dumagirls, as they pass its bleak and bronze portal of your Casacon-
cordia: Huru more Nee, minny frickans? Hwoorledes har Dee det? Losdoor
onleft mladies, cue. Millecientotrigintadue scudi. Tippoty, kyrie, tippoty.
Cha kai rotty kai makkar, sahib? Despenseme Usted, senhor, en son succo,
sabez. O thaw bron orm, A'Cothraige, thinkinthou gaily? Lick-Pa-flai-hai-
pa-Pa-li-si-lang-lang. Epi alo, ecou, Batiste, tuvavnr dans Lptit boing going.
Ismeme de bumbac e meias de portocallie. O.O. Os pipos mios es demasiada
gruarso por O piccolo pocchino. Wee fee? Ung duro. Kocshis, szabad?
Mercy, and you? Gomagh, thak.

And, Cod, says he with mugger's tears: Would you care to know the prise
of a liard? Maggis, nick your nightynovel! Mass Tavener's at the mike
again! And that bag belly is the buck to goat it! Meggeg, m'gay chapjappy

fellow, I call our univalse to witness, as sicker as moyliffey eggs is known by our good househalters from yorehunderts of mamooth to be which they commercially are in ahoy high British quarters (conventional!) my guest-house and cowhaendel credits will immediately stand ohoh open as straight as that neighbouring monument's fabrication before the hygienic gllll (this was where the reverent sabboth and bottlebreaker with firbalk forthstretched touched upon his tricoloured boater, which he uplifted by its pickledhoopy (he gave Stetson one and a penny for it) whileas oleaginosity of ancestral-olosis sgocciolated down the both pendencies of his mutsohito liptails (Sencapetulo, a more modestuous conciliabulite never curled a torn pocket-mouth), cordially inwiting the adullescence who he was wising up to do in like manner what all did so as he was able to add) lobe before the Great Schoolmaster's. (I tell you no story.) Smile!

The house of Atreox is fallen indeedust (Ilyam, Ilyum! Maeromor Mournomates!) averging on blight like the mundibanks of Fennyana, but deeds bounds going arise again. Life, he himself said once, (his biografiend, in fact, kills him verysoon, if yet not, after) is a wake, livit or krikit, and on the bunk of our breadwinning lies the cropse of our seedfather, a phrase which the establisher of the world by law might pretinately write across the chestfront of all manorwombanborn. The scene, refreshed, reroused, was never to be forgotten, the hen and crusader everintermutuomergent, for later in the century one of that puisne band of factferreters, (then an excivily (out of the custom huts) (retired), (hurt), under the sixtyfives act) in a dressy black modern style and wewere shiny tan burlingtons, (tam, homd and dicky, quopriquos and peajagd) rehearsed it, pippa pointing, with a dignified (copied) bow to a namecousin of the late archdeacon F. X. Preserved Coppinger (a hot fellow in his night, may the mouther of guard have mastic on him!) in a pullwoman of our first transhibernian with one still sadder circumstance which is a dirkandurk heartskewerer if ever to bring bouncing brimmers from marbled eyes. Cycloptically through the windowdisks and with eddying awes the round eyes of the rundreisers, back to back, buck to bucker, on their airish chaunting car, beheld with intouristing anterestedness the clad pursue the bare, the bare the green, the green the frore, the frore the cladagain, as their convoy wheeled encirculingly abound the gigantig's lifetree, our fireleaved loverlucky blomsterbohm, phoenix in our woodless-ness, haughty, cacuminal, erubescent (repetition!) whose roots they be asches with lustres of peins. For as often as the Archicadenus, pleacing aside his *Irish Field* and craving their auriculars to recepticle particulars before they got the bump at Castlebar (mat and far!) spoke of it by request all, hearing in this new reading of the part whereby, because of Dyas in his machina, the new garrickson's grimacing grimaldism hypostasised by substintuation the axiomatic orerotundity of that once grand old elrington bawl, the copycus's description of that fellowcommuter's play upon countenants, could simply imagine themselves in their bosom's inmost core, as *pro tem locums*, time-sported acorss the yawning (abyss), as once they were seasiders, listening to the cockshyshooter's evensong evocation of the doomed but always ventriloquent Agitator, (nonot more plangorpound the billows o'er Thouna-wahallya Reef!) silkhouatted, a whallrhosmightiadd, aginsst the dusk of skumring, (would that fane be Saint Muezzin's calling—holy places!—and this fez brimless as brow of faithful toucher of the ground, did wish it were—blessed be the bones!—the ghazi, power of his sword.) his manslayer's gunwielder protended towards that overgrown leadpencil which was soon, monumentally at least, to rise as Molyvdokondylon to, to be, to be his mausoleum (O'dan stod tillsteyne at meisies aye skould show pon) while olover his exculpatory features, as Roland rung, a wee dropeen of grief about to sillonise his jouejous, the ghost of resignation diffused a spectral appealingness, as a young man's drown o'er the fate of his waters may gloat, similar in origin and akkurat in effective to a beam of sunshine upon a coffin plate.

Not olderwise Inn the days of the Bygning would our Traveller remote, unfriended, from van Demon's Land, some lazy skald or maundering pote, lift wearywilly his slowcut snobsic eyes to the semisigns of his zooteac and lengthily lingering along flaskneck, cracket cup, downtrodden brogue, turfsod, wildbroom, cabbageblad, stockfisch, longingly learn that there at the Angel were herberged for him poteen and tea and praties and baccy and wine width woman wordth warbling: and informally quasi-begin to presquesm'ile to queasithin' (Nonsense! There was not very much windy Nous blowing at the given moment through the hat of Mr Melancholy Slow!)

But in the pragma what formal cause made a smile of *that* tothink? Who was he to whom? (O'Breen's not his name nor the brown one his maid.) Whose are the placewheres? Kiwasti, kisker, kither, kitnabudja? Tal the tem of the tumulum. Giv the gav of the grube. Be it cudgelplayers' country, orfishfellows' town or leeklickers' land or panbpanungopovengreskey. What regnans raised the rains have levelled but we hear the pointers and can gauge their compass for the melos yields the mode and the mode the manners plicyman, plansiman, plousiman, plab. Tsin tsin tsin tsin! The forefarther folkers for a prize of two peaches with Ming, Ching and Shunny on the lie low lea. We'll sit down on the hope of the ghouly ghost for the titheman troubleth but his hantitat hies not here. They answer from their

Zoans; Hear the four of them! Hark torroar of them! I, says Armagh, and a'm proud o'it. I, says Clonakilty, God help us! I, says Deansgrange, and say nothing. I, says Barna, and whatabout it? Hee haw! Before he fell hill he filled heaven: a stream, alplapping streamlet, coyly coiled um, cool of her curls: We were but thermites then, wee, wee. Our antheap we sensed as a Hill of Allen, the Barrow for an People, one Jotnursfjaell: and it was a grummelung amung the porktroop that wonderstruck us as a thunder, yunder.

Thus the unfacts, did we possess them, are too imprecisely few to warrant our certitude, the evidencegivers by legpoll too untrustworthily irreperible where his adjugers are semmingly freak threes but his judicandees plainly minus twos. Nevertheless Madam's Toshowus waxes largely more lifeliked (entrance, one kudos; exits, free) and our notional gullery is now completely complacent, an exegious monument, aerily perennious. Oblige with your blackthorns; gamps, degrace! And there many have paused before that exposure of him by old Tom Quad, a flashback in which he sits sated, gowndabout, in clericalease habit, watching bland sol slithe dodgsomely into the nethermore, a globule of maugdleness about to corrugitate his mild dewed cheek and the tata of a tiny victorienne, Alys, pressed by his limper looser.

Yet certes one is. Eher the following winter had overed the pages of nature's book and till Ceadurbar-atta-Cleath became Dablena Tertia, the shadow of the huge outlander, maladik, multvult, magnoperous, had bulked at the bar of a rota of tribunals in manor hall as in thieves' kitchen, mid pillow talk and chithouse chat, on Marlborough Green as through Moles-worth Fields, here sentenced pro tried with Jedburgh justice, there acquitted con testimony with benefit of clergy. His Thing Mod have undone him: and his madthing has done him man. His beneficiaries are legion in the part he created: they number up his years. Greatwheel Dunlop was the name was on him: behung, all we are his bisaacles. As hollyday in his house so was he priest and king to that: ulvy came, envy saw, ivy conquered. Lou! Lou! They have waved his green boughs o'er him as they have torn him limb from lamb. For his muertification and uxpiration and dumnation and annuhulation. With schreis and grida, deprofound souspirs. Steady, sullivans! Mannequins pause! Longtong's breach is fallen down but Graunya's spreed's abroad. Ahdostay, feedailyones, and feel the Flucher's bawls for the total of your flouts is not fit to fan his fettle, O! Have a ring and sing wohl! Chin, chin! Chin, chin! And of course all chimed din width the eatmost boviality. Swiping rums and beaunes and sherries and ciders and negus and citron-nades too. The strongers. Oho, oho, Mester Begge, you're about to be bagged in the bog again. Bugge. But softsies seufsighed: Eheu, for gassies! But, lo! lo! by the threnning gods, human, erring and condonable, what the statues of our kuo, who is the messchef be our kuang, ashu ashure there, the unforgettable treeshade looms up behind the jostling judgements of those, as all should owe, malrecapturable days.

Tap and pat and tapatagain, (fire firstshot, Missiers the Refuseleers! Peingpeong! For saxonlootie!) three tommix, soldiers free, cockaleak and cappapee, of the Coldstream. Guards were walking, in (*pardonnez-leur, je vous en prie, eh?*) Montgomery Street. One voiced an opinion in which on either wide (*pardonnez!*), nodding, all the Finner Camps concurred (*je vous en prie, eh?*). It was the first woman, they said, souped him, that fatal wellesday, Lili Coninghams, by suggesting him they go in a field. Wroth mod eldfar, ruth redd stilstand, wrath wrackt wroth, confessed private Pat Marchison *retro*. (Terse!) Thus contenters with santoys play. One of our coming Vauxhall ontheboards who is resting for the moment (she has been callit by a noted stagey elecutioner a wastepacket Sittons) was interfeud in a waistend pewty parlour. Looking perhaps even more pewtyflushed in her cherryderry padouasoys, girdle and braces by the halfmoon and Seven Stars, russets from the Blackamoor's Head, amongst the climbing boys at his Eagle and Child and over the corn and hay emptors at their Black and All Black, Mrs F . . . A . . . saidaside, half in stage of whisper to her confidante glass, while recoopering her cartwheel chapot (ahat!—and we now know what thimbles a baquets on lallance a talls mean), she hoped Sid Arthar would git a Chrissman's portrout of orange and lemonsized orchids with hollegs and ether, from the feeatre of the Innocident, as the worryld had been uncained. Then, while it is odrous comparisoning to the sprangflowers of his burstday which was a viridable goddinpotty for the reinworms and the charlattinas and all branches of climatitis, it has been such a wanderful noyth untirely, added she, with many regards to Maha's pranjapansies. (Tart!) Prehistoric, obitered to his dictaphone an entychologist: his pro-penomen is a properismenon. A dustman nocknamed Sevenchurches in the employ of Messrs Achburn, Soulpetre and Ashreborn, prairmakers, Glintalook, was asked by the sisterhood the vexed question during his midday collation of leaver and buckrom alternatively with stenk and kitteney phie in a hashhoush and, thankeaven, responsed impulsively: We have just been propogandering his nullity suit and what they took out of his ear among my own crush. All our fellows at O'Dea's sages with Aratar Calaman he is a cemented brick, buck it all! A more nor usually sober cardriver, who was jauntingly hosing his runabout, Ginger Jane, took a strong view. Lorry hosed her as he talked and this is what he told rewritemen: Irewaker is just a plain pink joint reformee in private life but folks all have it by brehemons laws he has parliamentary honours. Eiskaffier said (Louigi's, you know that man's, brillant Savourain): *Mon foie*, you wish to ave some homelette, yes, lady! Good, mein leber! Your hegg he must break himself See, I crack, so, he sit in the poele, umbedimbt! A perspirer (over sixty) who was keeping up his tennises panted he kne ho har twa to clect infamatios but a diffpair flannels climb wall and trespassing on doorbell. After fullblown Braddon hear this fresky troterella! A railways barmaid's view (they call her Spilltears Rue) was thus expressed: to sympathisers of the Dole Line, Death Avenue, anent those objects of her pityprompted ministrance, to wet, man and his syphon. Ehim! It is ever too late to whissle when Phyllis floods her stable. It would be skarlot shame to jailahim in lockup, as was proposed to him by the Seddoms creature what matter what merrytricks went off with his revulverher in connections with ehim being a norphan and enjoining such wicked illth, ehim! Well done, Drumcollakill! Kitty Tyrrel is proud of you, was the reply of a B.O.T. official (O blame gnot the board!) while the Daughters Benkletter murmured in uniswoon: Golforgilhisjurylegs! Brian Lynsky, the cub curser, was questioned at his shouting box, Bawlonabraggat, and gave a snappy comeback, when saying: Paw! Once more I'll hellbowl! I am for caveman chase and sahara sex, burk you! Them two bitches ought to be leashed, canem! Up hog and hoar hunt! Paw! A wouldbe martyr, who is attending on sanit Asitas where he is being taught to wear bracelets, when grilled on the point, revealed the undoubted fact that the consequence would be that so long as Sankya Moondy played his mango tricks under the mysttetry, with shady apsaras sheltering in his leaves' licence and his shadowers torrifried by the potent bolts of indradiction, there would be fights all over Cuxhaven. (Tosh!) Missioner Ida Wombwell, the seventeen-yearold revivalist, said concerning the coincident of interfizzing with grenadines and other respectable and disgusted peersons using the park: That perpendicular person is a brut! But a magnificent brut! 'Caligula' (Mr Danl Magrath, bookmaker, wellknown to Eastrailian poorusers of the Sydney Parade Ballotin) was, as usual, antipodal with his: striving todie, hopening tomellow, Ware Splash. Cobbler. We have meat two hourly, sang out El Caplan Buycout, with the famous padre's turridur's capecast, meet too ourly, matadear! Dan Meiklejohn, precentor, of S.S. Smack and Olley's was probiverbal with his upsiduxit: *mutatus mutandus*. Dauran's lord ('Sniffpox') and Moirgan's lady ('Flatterfun') took sides and crossed and bowed to each other's views and recrossed themselves. The dirty dubs upin their flies, went too free, echoed the dainly drabs downin their scenities, una mona. Sylvia Silence, the girl detective (*Meminerva*, but by now one hears turtlings all over Doveland!) when supplied with informations as to the several facets of the case in her cozydozy bachelure's flat, quite overlooking John a'Dream's mews, leaned back in her really truly easy chair to query restfully through her vowelthreaded syllabelles: Have you evew thought, wepowtew, that sheew gweatness was his twadgedy? Nevewtheless accowding to my considewed attitudes fow this act he should pay the full penalty, pending puwsuance, as pew Subsec. 32, section II, of the C. L. A. act 1885, anything in this act to the contwawy notwithstanding. Jarley Jilke began to silke for he couldn't get home to Jelsey but ended with: He's got the sack that helped him moult instench of his gladsome rags. Meagher, a naval rating, seated on one of the granite cromlech setts of our new fishshambles for the usual aireating after the ever popular act, with whom were Questa and Puella, piquante and quoite, (this had a cold in her brain while that felt a sink in her summock, wit's wat, wot's wet) was encouraged, although nearvanashed himself, by one of his co-affianced to get your breath, Walt, and gobbit and when ther chidden by her fastra sastra to saddle up your pance, Naville, thus cor replied to her other's thankskissing: I lay my two fingerbuttons, fiancee Meagher, (he speaks!) he was to blame about your two velvetthighs up Horniman's Hill—as hook and eye blame him or any other piscman?—but I also think, Puellywally, by the siege of his trousers there was someone else behind it—you bet your boughtem blarneys—about their three drummers down Keysars Lane. (Trite!).

Be these meer marchant taylor's fablings of a race referend with oddman rex? Is now all seenheard then forgotten? Can it was, one is fain in this leaden age of letters now to wit, that so diversified outrages (they have still to come!) were planned and partly carried out against so staunch a covenanter if it be true than any of those recorded ever took place for many, we trow, beyessed to and denayed of, are given to us by some who use the truth but sparingly and we, on this side ought to sorrow for their pricking pens on that account. The seventh city, Urovivla, his citadear of refuge, whither (would we believe the laimen and their counts), beyond the outraved gales of Atreeatic, changing clues with a baggermalster, the hejirite had fled, silentioussuemeant under night's altosonority, shipalone, a raven of the wave, (be mercy, Mara! A he whence Rahoulas!) from the ostmen's dirtby on the old vic, to forget in expiating manslaughter and, reberthing in remarriment out of dead seekness to devine previdence, (if you are looking for the bilder deep your ear on the movietone!) to league his lot, palm and patte, with a papishee. For mine qvinne I thee giftake and bind my hosenband I thee halter. The wastobe land, a lottuse land, a luctuous land, Emeraldilluim, the peasant pastured, in which by the fourth commandment with promise his days apostolic were to be long by the abundant mercy of Him Which Thundereth From On High, murmured, would rise against him with all which in them were, franchisables and inhabitands, astea as agora, helotsphilots, do him hurt, poor jink, ghostly following bodily, as were he made a curse for them, the corruptible lay quick, all saints of incorruption of an holy nation, the common or ere-in-garden castaway, in red resurrection to condemn so they might convince him, first pharoah, Humpheres Cheops Exarchas, of their proper sins. Business bred to speak with a stiff upper lip to all men and most occasions the Man we wot of took little short of fighting chances but for all that he or his or his care were subjected to the horrors of the premier terror of Errorland. (perorhaps!)

We seem to us (the real Us!) to be reading our Amenti in the sixth sealed chapter of the going forth by black. It was after the show at Wednesbury that one tall man, humping a suspicious parcel, when returning late amid a dense particular on his home way from the second house of the Boore and Burgess Christy Menestrels by the old spot, Roy's Corner, had a barkiss revolver placed to his faced with the words: you're shot, major: by an unknowable assailant (masked) against whom he had been jealous over, Lotta Crabtree or Pomona Evlyn. More than that Whenn the Waylayer (not a Lucalizod diocesan or even of the Glendalough see, but hailing fro' the prow of Little Britain), mentioning in a byteway that he, the crawsopper, had, in edition to Reade's cutless centiblade, a loaded Hobson's which left only twin alternatives as, viceversa, either he would surely shoot her, the aunt, by pistol, (she could be okaysure of that!) or, failing of such, bash in Patch's blank face beyond recognition, pointedly asked with gaeilish gall wodkar blizzard's business Thornton had with that Kane's fender only to be answered by the aggravated assaulted that that that was the snaps for him, Midweeks, to sultry well go and find out if he was showery well able. But how transparingly nontrue, gentlewriter! His feet one is not a tall man, not at all, man. No such parson. No such fender. No such lumber. No such race. Was it supposedly in connection with a girls, Myramy Huey or Colores Archer, under Flaggy Bridge (for ann there is but one liv and hir newbridge is her old) or to explode his twelvechamber and force a shrievalty entrance that the heavybuilt Abelbody in a butcherblue blouse from One Life One Suit (a men's wear store), with a most decisive bottle of single in his possession, seized after dark by the town guard at Haveyoucaught-emerod's temperance gateway was there in a gate's way.

Fifthly, how parasoliloquisingly truetoned on his first time of hearing the wretch's statement that, muttering Irish, he had had had o'gloriously a'lot too much hanguest or hoshoe fine to drink in the House of Blazes, the

Parrot in Hell, the Orange Tree, the Glibt, the Sun, the Holy Lamb and, lapse not leashed, in Ramitdown's ship hotel since the morning moment he could dixtinguish a white thread from a black till the engine of the laws declosed unto Murray and was only falling fillthefluthered up against the gatestone pier which, with the cow's bonnet a'top o'it, he falsetook for a cattlepillar with purest peaceablest intentions. Yet how lamely hobbles the hoy of his then pseudojocax axplanation how, according to his own story, he vas a process server and was merely trying to open zozimus a bottlop stoub by mortially hammering his *magnum bonum* (the curter the club the sorer the savage) against the bludgey gate for the boots about the swan, Maurice Behan, who hastily into his shoes with nothing his hald barra tinnteack and came down with homp, shtemp and jumphet to the tiltyard from the wastes a'sleep in his obi ohny overclothes or choker, attracted by the norse of guns playing Delandy is cartager on the raglar rock to Dulyn, said war' prised safe in bed as he dreamed that he'd wealthes in mormon halls when wokenp by a fourth loud snore out of his land of byelo while hickstrey's maws was grazing in the moonlight by hearing hammering on the pandywhank scale emanating from the blind pig and anything like it (oonagh! oonagh!) in the whole history of the Mullingcan Inn he never. This battering babel allower the door and sideposts, he always said, was not in the very remotest like the belzey babble of a bottle of boose which would not rouse him out o' slumber deep but reminded him loads more of the martiallawsey marses of foreign musikants' instrumongs or the overthrewer to the third last days of Pompery, if anything. And that after this most nooningless knockturn the young reine came down desperate and the old liffopotamus started ploring all over the plains, as mud as she cud be, ruinating all the bouchers' schurts and the backers' wischandtugs so that be the chandeleure of the Rejaneyjailey they were all night wasching the walters of, the weltering walters off. Whyte.

Just one moment. A pinch in time of the ideal, musketeers! Alphos, Burkos and Caramis, leave Astrelea for the astrollajerries and for the love of the saunces and the honour of Keavens pike puddywhackback to Pamintul. And roll away the reel world, the reel world, the reel world! And call all your smokeblushes, Snowwhite and Rosered, if you will have the real cream! Now for a strawberry frolic! Filons, filoosh! *Cherchons la flamme!* Fammfamm! Fammfamm!

Come on, ordinary man with that large big nonobli head, and that blanko berbecked fischial ekksprezzion Machinsky Scapolopolos, Duzinascu or other. Your machelar's mutton leg's getting musclebound from being too pulled. Noah Beery weighed stone thousand one when Hazel was a hen. Now her fat's falling fast. Therefore, chatbags, why not yours? There are 29

sweet reasons why blossomtime's the best. Elders fall for green almonds
when they're raised on bruised stone root ginger though it winters on their
heads as if auctumned round their waistbands. If you'd had pains in your
hairs you wouldn't look so orgibald. You'd have Colley Macaires on your
lump of lead. Now listen, Mr Leer! And stow that sweatyfunnyadams
Simper! Take an old geeser who calls on his skirt. Note his sleek hair, so
elegant, *tableau vivant*. He vows her to be his own honeylamb, swears they
will be papa pals, by Sam, and share good times way down west in a
guaranteed happy lovenest when May moon she shines and they twit twinkle
all the night, combing the comet's tail up right and shooting popguns at the
stars. Creampuffs all to dime! Every nice, missymackenzies! For dear old
grumpapar, he's gone on the razzledar, through gazing and crazing and
blazing at the stars. Compree! She wants her wardrobe to hear from above
by return with cash so as she can buy her Peter Robinson trousseau and cut
a dash with Arty, Bert or possibly Charley Chance (who knows?) so tolloll
Mr Hunker you're too dada for me to dance (so off she goes!) and that's
how half the gels in town has got their bottom drars while grumpapar he's
trying to hitch his braces on to his trars. But old grum he's not so clean
dippy between sweet you and yum (not on your life, boy! not in those
trousers! not by a large jugful!) for someplace on the sly, where Furphy he
isn't by, old grum has his gel number two (bravevow, our Grum!) and he
would like to canoodle her too some part of the time for he is downright
fond of his number one but O he's fair mashed on peaches number two so
that if he could only canoodle the two, chivee chivoo, all three would feel
genuinely happy, it's as simple as A. B. C., the two mixers, we mean, with
their cherrybum chappy (for he is simply shamming dippy) if they all were
afloat in a dreamlifeboat, hugging two by two in his zoo-doo-you-doo, a
tofftoff for thee, missymissy for me and howcameyou-e'enso for Farber, in
his tippy, upindown dippy, tiptoptippy canoodle, can you? Finny.

Ack, ack, ack. With which clap, trap and soddenment, three to a loaf, our
mutual friends the fender and the bottle at the gate seem to be implicitly in
the same bateau, so to singen, bearing also several of the earmarks of
design, for there is in fact no use in putting a tooth in a snipery of that sort
and the amount of all those sort of things which has been going on onceaday
in and twiceaday out every other nachtistag among all kinds of promiscious
individuals at all ages in private homes and reeboos publikiss and allover all
and elsewhere throughout secular sequence the country over and overabroad
has been particularly stupendous. To be continued. Federals' Uniteds'
Transports' Unions' for Exultations' of Triumphants' Ecstasies.

But resuming inquiries. Will it ever be next morning the postal unionist's (officially called carrier's, Letters Scotch, Limited) strange fate (Fierce-endgiddyex he's hight, d.e., the losel that hucks around missivemaids' gummibacks) to hand in a huge chain envelope, written in seven divers stages of ink, from blanchessance to lavandaiette, every pothook and pancrook bespaking the wisherwife, superscribed and subpencilled by yours A Laughable Party, with afterwite, S.A.G., to Hyde and Cheek, Edenberry, Dubblenn, WC? Will whatever will be written in lappish language with inbursts of Maggyer always seem semposed, black looking white and white guarding black, in that siamixed twoatalk used twist stern swift and jolly roger? Will it bright upon us, nightle, and we plunging to our plight? Well, it might now, mircle, so it light. Always and ever till Cox's wife, twice Mrs Hahn, pokes her beak into the matter with Owen K. after her, to see whawa smutter after, will this kiribis pouch filled with litterish fragments lurk dormant in the paunch of that halpbrother of a herm, a pillarbox? The coffin, a triumph of the illusionist's art, at first blench naturally taken for a handharp (it is handwarp to tristinguish jubabe from jabule or either from tubote when all three have just been invened) had been removed from the hardware premises of Oetzmann and Nephew, a noted house of the gone-most west, which in the natural course of all things continues to supply funeral requisites of every needed description. Why needed, though? Indeed needed (wouldn't you feel like rattanfowl if you hadn't the oscar!) because the flash brides or bride in their lily boleros one games with at the Nivy-nubies' finery ball and your upright grooms that always come right up with you (and by jingo when they do!) what else in this mortal world, now ours, when meet there night, mid their nackt, me there naket, made their nought the hour strikes, would bring them rightcame back in the flesh, thumbs down, to their orses and their hashes.

To proceed. We might leave that nitrience of oxagiants to take its free of the air and just analectralyse that very chymerical combination, the gasbag where the warderworks. And try to pour somour heiterscene up thealmost-fere. In the bottled heliose case continuing, Long Lally Tobkids, the special, sporting a fine breast of medals, and a conscientious scripturereader to boot in the brick and tin choorch round the coroner, swore like a Norewheezian tailliur on the stand before the proper functionary that he was up against a right querrshnorrt of a mand in the butcher of the blues who, he guntinued, on last epening after delivering some carcasses mattonchepps and meatjutes on behalf of Messrs Otto Sands and Eastman, Limericked, Victuallers, went and, with his unmitigated astonissment, hickicked at the dun and dorass against all the runes and, when challenged about the pretended hick (it was kickup and down with him) on his solemn by the imputant imputed, said simply: I appop pie oath, Phillyps Captain. You did, as I sostressed before. You are deepknee in error, sir, Madam Tomkins, let me then tell you, replied with a gentlewomanly salaam MackPartland, (the meatman's family, and the oldest in the world except nick, name.) And Phelps was flayful with his peeler. But his phizz fell.

Now to the obverse. From velveteens to dimities is barely a fivefinger span and hence these camelback excesses are thought to have been instigated by one or either of the causing causes of all, those rushy hollow heroines in their skirtsleeves, be she magretta be she the posque. Oh! Oh! Because it is a horrible thing to have to say to say to day but one dilalah, Lupita Lorette, shortly after in a fit of the unexpectednesses drank carbolic with all her dear placid life before her and paled off while the other soiled dove that's her sister-in-love, Luperca Latouche, finding one day while dodging chores that she stripped teasily for binocular man and that her jambs were jimpjoyed to see each other, the nautchy girly soon found her fruitful hat too small for her and rapidly taking time, look, she rapidly took to necking, partying and selling her spare favours in the haymow or in lumber closets or in the greenawn *ad huck* (there are certain intimacies in all ladies' lavastories we just lease to imagination) or in the sweet churchyard close itself for a bit of soft coal or an array of thin trunks, serving whom in fine that same hot coney *a la Zingara* which our own little Graunya of the chilired cheeks dished up to the greatsire of Oscar, that son of a Coole. Houri of the coast of emerald, arrah of the lacessive poghue, Aslim-all-Muslim, the resigned to her surrender, did not she, come leinster's even, true dotter of a dearmud, (her pitch was Forty Steps and his perch old Cromwell's Quarters) with so valkirry a licence as sent many a poor pucker packing to perdition, again and again, ay, and again sfidare him, tease fido, eh tease fido, eh eh tease fido, toos topples topple, stop, dug of a dog of a dgiaour, ye! Angealousmei! And did not he, like Arcoforty, farfar off Bissavolo, missbrand her behaveyous with iridescent huecry of down right mean false sop lap sick dope? Tawfulsdreck! A reine of the shee, a shebeen quean, a queen of pranks. A kingly man, of royal mien, regally robed, exalted be his glory! So gave so take: Now not, not now! He would just a min. Suffering trumpet! He thought he want. Whath? Hear, O hear, living of the land! Hungreb, dead era, hark! He hea, eyes ravenous on her lippling lills. He hear her voi of day gon by. He hears! Zay, zay, zay! But, by the beer of his profit, he cannot answer. Upterputty till rise and shine! Nor needs none shaft ne stele from Phenicia or Little Asia to obelise on the spout, neither pobalclock neither folksstone, nor sunkenness in Tomar's Wood to bewray how erpressgangs score off the rued. The mouth that tells not will ever attract the unthinking tongue and so long as the obseen draws theirs which hear not so long till allearth's dumbnation shall the blind lead the deaf. Tatcho, tawney yeeklings! The column of lumps lends the pattrin of the leaves behind us. If violence to life, limb and chattels, often as not, has been the expression, direct or through an agent male, of womanhid offended, (ah! ah!), has not levy of black mail from the times the fairies were in it, and fain for wilde erthe blothoms followed an impressive private reputation for whispered sins?

Now by memory inspired, turn wheel again to the whole of the wall. Where Gyant Blyant fronts Peannlueamoore There was once upon a wall and a hooghoog wall a was and such a wallhole did exist. Ere ore or ire in Aaarlund. Or you Dair's Hair or you Diggin Mosses or your horde of orts and oriorts to garble a garthen of Odin and the lost paladays when all the eddams ended with aves. Armen? The doun is theirs and still to see for menags if he strikes a lousaforitch and we'll come to those baregazed shoeshines if you just shoodov a second. And let oggs be good old gaggles and Isther Estarr play Yesther Asterr. In the drema of Sorestost Areas, Diseased. A stonehinged gate then was for another thing while the suroptimist had bought and enlarged that shack under fair rental of one yearlyng sheep, (prime) value of sixpence, and one small yearlyng goat (cadet) value of eightpence, to grow old and happy (hogg it and kidd him) for the reminants of his years; and when everything was got up for the purpose he put an applegate on the place by no means as some pretext a bedstead in loo thereof to keep out donkeys (the pigdirt hanging from the jags to this hour makes that clear) and just thenabouts the iron gape, by old custom left open to prevent the cats from getting at the gout, was triplepatlockt on him on purpose by his faithful poorters to keep him inside probably and possibly enaunter he felt like sticking out his chest too far and tempting gracious providence by a stroll on the peoplade's eggday, unused as he was yet to being freely clodded.

O, by the by, lets wee brag of praties, it ought to be always remembered in connection with what has gone before that there was a northroomer, Herr Betreffender, out for his zimmer holedigs, digging in number 32 at the Rum and Puncheon (Branch of Dirty Dick's free house) in Laxlip (where the Sockeye Sammons were stopping at the time orange fasting) prior to that, a Kommerzial (Gorbotipacco, he was wreaking like Zentral Oylrubber) from Osterich, the U.S.E. paying (Gaul save the mark!) 11/- in the week (Gosh, these wholly romads!) of conscience money in the first deal of Yuly wheil he was, swishing beesnest with blessure, and swobbing broguen eeriesh myth brockendootsch, making his reporterage on Der Fall Adams for the Frankofurto Siding, a Fastland payrodicule, and er, consstated that one had on him the Lynn O'Brien, a meltoned lammswolle, disturbed, and wider he might the same zurichschicken other he would, with tosend and obertosend tonnowatters, one monkey's damages become. Now you must know, franksman, to make a heart of glass, that the game of gaze and bandstand butchery was merely a Patsy O'Strap tissue of threats and obuses such as roebucks raugh at pinnacle's peak and after this sort. Humphrey's unsolicited visitor, Davy or Titus, on a burgley's clan march from the middle west, a hikely excellent crude man about road who knew his Bullfoost Mountains like a starling bierd, after doing a long dance untidled to Cloudy Green, deposend his bockstump on the waityoumaywantme, after having blew some quaker's (for you! Oates!) in through the houseking's keyhole to attract attention, bleated through the gale outside which the tairor of his clothes was hogcallering, first, be the hirsuiter, that he would break his bulsheywigger's head for him, next, be the heeltapper, that he would break the gage over his lankyduckling head the same way he would crack a nut with a monkeywrench and, last of all, be the stirabouter, that he would give him his (or theumperom's or anybloody else's) thickerthanwater to drink and his bleday steppebrodhar's into the bucket. He demanded more wood alcohol to pitch in with, alleging that his granfather's was all taxis and that it was only after ten o'connell, and this his isbar was a public oven for the sake of irsk irskusky, and then, not easily discouraged, opened the wrathfloods of his atillarery and went on at a wicked rate, weathering against him in mooxed metaphores from eleven thirty to two in the afternoon without even a luncheonette interval for House, son of Clod, to come out, you jewbeggar, to be Executed Amen. Earwicker, that patternmind, that paradigmatic ear, receptoretentive as his of Dionysius, longsuffering although whitening under restraint in the sititout corner of his conservatory, behind faminebuilt walls, his thermos flask and ripidian flabel by his side and a walrus whisker-bristle for a tuskpick, compiled, while he mourned the flight of his wild guineese, a long list (now feared in part lost) to be kept on file of all abusive names he was called (we have been compelled for the rejoicement of foinne loidies ind the humours of Milltown etcetera by Josephine Brewster in the collision known as Contrastations with Inkermann and so on and son-onward, lacies in loo water, flee, celestials, one clean turv): *Firstnighter, Informer, Old Fruit, Yellow Whigger, Wheatears, Goldy Geit, Bogside Beauty, Yass We've Had His Badannas, York's Porker, Funnyface, At Baggotty's Bend He Bumped, Grease with the Butter, Opendoor Ospices, Cainandabler, Ireland's Eighth Wonderful Wonder, Beat My Price, Godsoilman, Moonface the Murderer, Hoary Hairy Hoax, Midnight Sunburst, Remove that Bible, Hebdromadary Publocation, Tummer the Lame the Tyrannous, Blau Clay, Tight before Teatime, Real Your*

Pantojoke, Acoustic Disturbance, Thinks He's Gobblasst the Good Dook of Ourguile,
W.D.'s Grace, Gibbering Bayamouth of Dublin, His Farther was a Mundzucker
and She had him in a Growler, Burnham and Bailey, Artist, Unworthy of the
Homely Protestant Religion, Terry Cotter, You're Welcome to Waterfood, signed
the Ribbonmen, Lobsterpot Lardling, All for Arthur of this Town, Hooshed the Cat
from the Bacon, Leathertogs Donald, The Ace and Deuce of Paupering, O'Reilly's
Delights to Kiss the Man behind the Borrel, Magogagog, Swad Puddlefoot, Gouty
Ghibeline, Loose Luther, Hatches Cocks' Eggs, Muddle the Plan, Luck before
Wedlock, I Divorce Thee Husband, Tanner and a Make, Go to Hellena or Come to
Connies, Piobald Puffpuff His Bride, Purged out of Burke's, He's None of Me
Causin, Barebearean, Peculiar Person, Grunt Owl's Facktotem, Twelve Months
Aristocrat, Lycanthrope, Flunkey Beadle Vamps the Tune Letting on He's Loney,
Thunder and Turf Married into Clandorf, Left Boot Sent on Approval, Cumberer
of Lord's Holy Ground, Stodge Arschmann, Awnt Yuke, Tommy Furlong's Pet
Plagues, Archdukon Cabbanger, Last Past the Post, Kennealey Won't Tell Thee off
Nancy's Gown, Scuttle to Cover, Salary Grab, Andy Mac Noon in Annie's Room,
Awl Out, Twitchbratschballs, Bombard Street Bester, Sublime Porter, A Ban for
Le King of the Burgaans and a Bom for Ye Sur of all the Ruttledges, O'Phelim's
Cutprice, And at Number Wan Wan Wan, What He Done to Castlecostello,
Sleeps with Feathers end Ropes, It is Known who Sold Horace the Rattler, Enclosed
find the Sons of Fingal, Swayed in his Falling, Wants a Wife and Forty of Them,
Let Him Do the Fair, Apeegeequanee Chimmuck, Plowp Goes his Whastle, Ruin
of the Small Trader, He— — Milkinghoneybeaverbrooker, Vee was a Vindner,
Sower Rapes, Armenian Atrocity, Sickfish Bellyup, Edomite,—'Man Devoyd of
the Commoner Characteristics of an Irish Nature, Bad Humborg, Hraabhraab,
Coocoohandler, Dirt, Miching Daddy, Born Burst Feet Foremost, Woolworth's
Worst, Easyathic Phallusaphist, Guilteypig's Bastard, Fast in the Barrel, Boose in
the Bed, Mister Fatmate, In Custody of the Polis, Boawwll's Alocutionist, Deposed,
but anarchistically respectsful of the liberties of the noninvasive individual,
did not respond a solitary wedgeword beyond such sedentarity, though it
was as easy as kissanywhere for the passive resistant in the booth he was in to
reach for the hello gripes and ring up Kimmage Outer 17.67, because, as
the fundamentalist explained, when at last shocked into speech, touchin his
woundid feelins in the fuchsiar the dominican mission for the sowsealist
potty was on at the time and he thought the rowmish devowtion known as
the howly rowsary might reeform ihm, Gonn. That more than considerably
unpleasant bullocky before he rang off drunkishly pegged a few glatt stones,
all of a size, by way of final mocks for his grapes, at the wicket in support of
his words that he was not guilphy but, after he had so slaunga vollayed,
reconnoitring through his semisubconscious the seriousness of what he

might have done had he really polished off his terrible intentions finally caused him to change the bawling and leave downg the whole grumus of brookpebbles pangpung and, having sobered up a bit, paces his groundould diablen lionndub, the flay the flegm, the floedy fleshener, (purse, purse, pursyfurse, I'll splish the splume of them all!) this backblocks boor bruskly put out his langwedge and quite quit the paleologic scene, telling how by his selfdenying ordnance he had left Hyland on the dissenting table, after exhorting Earwicker or, in slightly modified phraseology, Messrs or Missrs Earwicker, Seir, his feminisible name of multitude, to cocoa come outside to Mockerloo out of that for the honour of Crumlin, with his broody old flishguds, Gog's curse to thim, so as he could brianslog and burst him all dizzy, you go bail, like Potts Fracture did with Keddle Flatnose and nobodyatall with Wholyphamous and build rocks over him, or if he didn't, for two and thirty straws, be Cacao Campbell, he didn't know what he wouldn't do for him nor nobody else nomore nor him after which, batell martell, a brisha a milla a stroka a boola, so the rage of Malbruk, playing on the least change of his manjester's voice, the first heroic couplet from the fuguall tropical, Opus Elf, Thortytoe: *My schemes into obeyance for This time has had to fall:* they bit goodbyte to their thumb and, his bandol eer his solgier, dripdropdrap on pool or poldier, wishing the loff a falladelfian in the morning, proceeded with a Hubbleforth slouch in his slips backwords (*Et Cur Heli!*) in the directions of the duff and demb institutions about ten or eleven hundred years lurch away in the moonshiny gorge of Patself on the Bach. Adyoe!

And thus, with this rochelly exetur of Bully Acre, came to close that last stage in the siegings round our archicitadel which we would like to recall, if old Nestor Alexis would wink the worth for us, as Bar-le-Duc and Dog-an-Doras and Bangen-op-Zoom.

Yed he med leave to many a door beside of Oxmanswold for so witness his chambered cairns a cloudletlitter silent that are at browse up hill and down coombe and on eolithostroton, at Howth or at Coolock or even at Enniskerry, a theory none too rectiline of the evoluation of human society and a testament of the rocks from all the dead unto some the living. Olivers lambs we do call them, skatterlings of a stone, and they shall be gathered unto him, their herd and paladin, as nubilettes to cumule, in that day hwen, same the lightning lancer of Azava Arthurhonoured (some Finn, some Finn avant!), he skall wake from earthsleep, haught crested elmer, in his valle of briers of Greenman's Rise O, (lost leaders live! the heroes return!) and o'er dun and dale the Wulverulverlord (protect us!) his mighty horn skall roll, orland, roll.

For in those deyes his Deyus shall ask of Allprohome and call to himm: Allprohome! And he make answer: Add some. Nor wink nor wunk. *Anima-diabolum, mene credidisti mortuum?* Silence was in thy faustive halls, O Truiga, when thy green woods went dry but there will be sounds of manymirth on the night's ear ringing when our pantriarch of Comestowntonobble gets the pullover on his boots.

Liverpoor? Sot a bit of it! His braynes coolt parritch, his pelt nassy, his heart's adrone, his bluidstreams acrawl, his puff but a piff, his extremeties extremely so: Fengless, Pawmbroke, Chilblaimend and Baldowl. Humph is in his doge. Words weigh no no more to him than raindrips to Rethfernhim. Which we all like. Rain. When we sleep. Drops. But wait until our sleeping. Drain. Sdops.

[4]

AS THE LION IN OUR TEARGARTEN REMEMBERS THE nenuphars of his Nile (shall Ariuz forget Arioun or Boghas the baregams of the Marmarazalles from Marmeniere?) it may be, tots wearsense full a naggin in twentyg have sigilposted what in our brievingbust, the besieged bedreamt him stil and solely of those lililiths undeveiled which hat undone him, gone for age, and knew not the watchful treachers at his wake, and theirs to stay. Fooi, fooi, chamermissies! Zeepyzoepy, larcenlads! Zijnzijn Zijnzijn! It may be, we moest ons hasten selves te declareer it, that he reglimmed? presaw? the fields of heat and yields of wheat where corngold Ysit? shamed and shone. It may be, we habben to upseek a bitty door our good township's courants want we knew't, that with his deepseeing insight (had not wishing oftebeen but good time wasted), within his patriarchal shamanah, broadsteyne 'bove citie (Twillby! Twillby!) he conscious of enemies, a kingbilly whitehorsed in a Finglas mill, prayed, as he sat on anxious seat, (kunt ye neat gift mey toe bout a peer saft eyballds!) during that three and a hellof hours' agony of silence, *ex profundis malorum*, and bred with unfeigned charity that his wordwounder (an engles to the teeth who, nomened Nash of Girahash, would go anyold where in the weeping world on his mottled belly (the rab, the kreeponskneed!) for milk, music or married missusses) might, mercy to providential benevolence's who hates prudencies' astuteness, unfold into the first of a distinguished dynasty of his posteriors, blackfaced connemaras not of the fold but elder children of his household, his most besetting of ideas (*pace* his twelve predamanant passions) being the formation, as in more favoured climes, where the Meadow of Honey is guestfriendly and the Mountain of Joy receives, of a truly criminal stratum, Ham's cribcracking yeggs, thereby at last eliminating from all classes and masses with directly derivative decasualisation: *sigarius* (sic!) *vindicat urbes terrorum* (sicker!): and so, to mark a bank taal she arter, the obedience of the citizens elp the ealth of the ole.

Now gode. Let us leave theories there and return to here's here. Now hear. 'Tis gode again. The teak coffin, Pughglasspanelfitted, feets to the east, was to turn in later, and pitly patly near the porpus, materially effecting the cause. And this, liever, is the thinghowe. Any number of conservative public bodies, through a number of select and other committees having power to add to their number, before voting themselves and himself, town, port and garrison, by a fit and proper resolution, following a koorts order of the groundwet, once for all out of plotty existence, as a forescut, so you maateskippey might to you cuttinrunner on a neuw pack of klerds, made him, while his body still persisted, their present of a protem grave in Moyelta of the best Lough Neagh pattern, then as much in demand among misonesans as the Isle of Man today among limniphobes. Wacht even! It was in a fairly fishy kettlekerry, after the Fianna's foreman had taken his handful, enriched with ancient woods and dear dutchy deeplinns mid which were an old knoll and a troutbeck, vainyvain of her osiery and a chatty sally with any Wilt or Walt who would ongle her as Izaak did to the tickle of his rod and watch her waters of her sillying waters of and there now brown peater arripple (may their quilt gild lightly over his somnolulutent form!) Whoforyou lies his last, by the wrath of Bog, like the erst curst Hun in the bed of his treubleu Donawhu.

Best. This wastohavebeen underground heaven, or mole's paradise which was probably also an inversion of a phallopharos, intended to foster wheat crops and to ginger up tourist trade (its architecht, Mgr Peurelachasse, having been obcaecated lest he should petrifake suchanevver while the contractors Messrs T. A. Birkett and L. O. Tuohalls were made invulnerably venerable) first in the west, our misterbilder, Castlevillainous, openly damned and blasted by means of a hydromine, system, Sowan and Belting, exploded from a reinvented T.N.T. bombingpost up ahoy of eleven and thirty wingrests (*circiter*) to sternbooard out of his aerial thorpeto, Auton Dynamon, contacted with the expectant minefield by tins of improved ammonia lashed to her shieldplated gunwale, and fused into tripupcables, slipping through tholse and playing down from the conning tower into the ground battery fuseboxes, all differing as clocks from keys since nobody appeared to have the same time of beard, some saying by their Oorlog it was

Sygstryggs to nine, more holding with the Ryan vogt it was Dane to pfife. He afterwards whaanever his blaetther began to fail off him and his rough bark was wholly husky and, stoop by stoop, he neared it (wouldmanspare!) carefully lined the ferroconcrete result with rotproof bricks and mortar, fassed to fossed, and retired beneath the heptarchy of his towerettes, the beauchamp, byward, bull and lion, the white, the wardrobe and bloodied, so encouraging (insteppen, alls als hats beliefd!) additional useful councils public with hoofd offdealings which were welholden of ladykants te huur out such as the Breeders' Union, the Guild of Merchants of the Staple *et*, a.u.c. to present unto him with funebral pomp, over and above that, a stone slab with the usual Mac Pelah address of velediction, a very fairworded instance of falsemeaning adamelegy: We have done ours gohellt with you, Heer Herewhippit, overgiven it, skidoo!

But t'house and allaboardshoops! Show coffins, winding sheets, good-buy bierchepes, cinerary urns, liealoud blasses, snuffchests, poteentubbs, lacrimal vases, hoodendoses, reekwaterbeckers, breakmiddles, zootzaks for eatlust, including upyourhealthing rookworst and meathewersoftened forkenpootsies and for that matter, javel also, any kind of inhumationary bric au brac for the adornment of his glasstone honophreum, would, met these trein of konditiens, naturally follow, halas, in the ordinary course, enabling that roundtheworlder wandelingswight, did suches pass him, to live all safeathomely the presenile days of his life of opulence, ancient ere decrepitude, late lents last lenience, till stuffering stage, whaling away the whole of the while (*hypnos chilia eonion!*) lethelulled between explosion and reexplosion (Donnaurwatteur! Hunderthunder!) from grosskopp to megapod, embalmed, of grand age, rich in death anticipated.

But abide Zeit's sumonserving, rise afterfall. Blueblitzbolted from there, knowing the hingeworms of the hallmirks of habitationlesness, buried burrowing in Gehinnon, to proliferate through all his Unterwealth, seam by seam, sheol om sheol, and revisit our Uppercrust Sideria of Utilitarios, the divine one, the hoarder hidden propaguting his plutorpopular pro-geniem of pots and pans and pokers and puns from biddenland to boughten-land, the spearway fore the spoorway.

The other spring offensive on the heights of Abraham may have come about all quite by accidence, Foughtarundser (for Breedabrooda had at length presuaded him to have himself to be as septuply buried as the murdered Cian in Finntown), had not been three monads in his watery grave (what vigilantes and ridings then and spuitwyne pledges with aardappel frittling!) when portrifaction, dreyfussed as ever, began to ramp, ramp, ramp, the boys are parching. A hoodenwinkle gave the signal and a blessing paper freed the flood. Why did the patrizien make him scares with his gruntens? Because the druiven were muskating at the door. From both Celtiberian camps (granting at the onset for the sake of argument that men on the two sides in New South Ireland and Vetera Uladh, bluemin and pillfaces, during the ferment With the Pope or On the Pope, had, moors or letts, grant ideas, grunted) all conditions, poor cons and dives mor, each, of course, on the purely doffensive since the eternals were owlwise on their side every time, were drawn toowards their Bellona's Black Bottom, once Woolwhite's Waltz (Ohiboh, how becrimed, becursekissed and be- dumbtoit!) some for want of proper feeding in youth, others already caught in the honourable act of slicing careers for family and carvers in con- junction; and, if emaciated nough, the person garrotted may have suggested to whomever he took the ham of, the plain being involved in darkness, low cirque waggery, nay, even the first old wugger of himself in the flesh, whiggissimus incarnadined, when falsesighted by the ifsuchhewas bully on the hill for there had circulated freely fairly among his opposition the feeling that in so hibernating Massa Ewacka, who, previous to that demi- detached life, had been known of barmicidal days, cook said, between soups and savours, to get outside his own length of rainbow trout and taerts atta tarn as no man of woman born, nay could, like the great crested brebe, devour his threescoreten of roach per lifeday, ay, and as many minnow a minute (the big mix, may Gibbet choke him!) was, like the salmon of his ladderleap all this time of totality secretly and by suckage feeding on his own misplaced fat.

Ladies did not disdain those pagan ironed times of the firs; city (called after the ugliest Danadune) when a frond was a friend inneed to carry, as earwigs do their dead, their soil to the earthball where indeeth we shall calm decline, our legacy unknown. Venuses were gigglibly temptatrix, vulcans guffawably eruptious and the whole wives' world frockful of fickles. Fact, any human inyon you liked any erenoon or efter would take her bare godkin out, or an even pair of hem, (lugod! lugodoo!) and prettily pray with him (or with em even) everyhe to her taste, long for luck, tapette and tape petter and take pettest of all. (Tip!) Wells she'd woo and wills she's win but how the deer knowed where she'd marry! Arbour, bucketroom, caravan, ditch? Coach, carriage, wheelbarrow, dungcart?

Kate Strong, a widow (Tiptip!)—she pulls a lane picture for us, in a dreariodreama setting, glowing and very vidual, of old dumplan as she nosed it, a homelike cottage of elvanstone with droppings of biddies, stinkend pusshies, moggies' duggies, rotten witchawubbles, festering rubbages and beggars' bullets, if not worse, sending salmofarious germs in gleefully through the smithereen panes—Widow Strong, then, as her weaker had turned him to the wall (Tiptiptip!), did most all the scavenging from good King Hamlaugh's gulden dayne though her lean besom cleaned but sparingly and her bare statement reads that, there being no mac-adamised sidetracks on those old nekropolitan nights in, barring a foot-batter, Bryant's Causeway, bordered with speedwell, white clover and sorrel a wood knows, which left off, being beaten, where the plaintiff was struck, she left down, as scavengers, who will be scavengers must, her filthdump near the Serpentine in Phornix Park (at her time called Fine-well's Keepsacre but later tautaubapptossed Pat's Purge), that dangerfield circling butcherswood where fireworker oh flaherty engaged a nutter of castlemallards and ah for archer stunned's turk, all over which fossil foot-prints, bootmarks, fingersigns, elbowdints, breechbowls, a. s. o. were all successively traced of a most envolving description. What subtler timeplace of the weald than such wolfsbelly castrament to will hide a leabhar from Thursmen's brandihands or a loveletter, lostfully hers, that would be lust on Ma, than then when ructions ended, than here where race began: and by four hands of forethought the first babe of reconcilement is laid in its last cradle of hume sweet hume. Give over it! And no more of it! So pass the pick for child sake! O men!

For hear Allhighest sprack for krischnians as for propagana fidies and his nuptial eagles sharped their beaks of prey: and every morphyl man of us, pome by pome, falls back into this terrine: as it was let it be, says he! And it is as though where Agni araflammed and Mithra monished and Shiva slew as mayamutras the obluvial waters of our noarchic memory withdrew, windingly goharksome, to some hastyswasty timberman torchpriest, flamen-fan, the ward of the wind that lightened the fire that lay in the wood that Jove bolt, at his rude word. Posidonius O'Fluctuary! Lave that bloody stone as it is! What are you doing your dirty minx and his big treeblock way up your path? Slip around, you, by the rare of the ministers'! And, you, take that barrel back where you got it, Mac Shane's, and go the way your old one went, Hatchettsbury Road! And gish! how they gushed away, the pennyfares, a whole school for scamper, with their sashes flying sish behind them, all the little pirlypettes! Issy-la-Chapelle! Any lucans, please?

Yes, the viability of vicinals if invisible is invincible. And we are not trespassing on his corns either. Look at all the plotsch! Fluminian! If this was Hannibal's walk it was Hercules' work. And a hungried thousand of the unemancipated slaved the way. The mausoleum lies behind us (O Adgigasta, *multipopulipater!*) and there are milestones in their cheadmilias faultering along the tramestrack by Brahm and Anton Hermes! Per omnibus secular

seekalarum. Amain. But the past has made us this present of a rhedarhoad.
So more boher O'Connell! Though rainyhidden, you're rhinohide. And if
he's not a Romeo you may scallop your hat. Wereupunder in the fane of
Saint Fiacre! Halte!

It was hard by the howe's there, plainly on this disoluded and a buchan
cold spot, rupestric then, resurfaced that now is, that Luttrell sold if Lautrill
bought, in the saddle of the Brennan's (now Malpasplace?) pass, versts and
versts from true civilisation, not where his dreams top their traums halt
(Beneathere! Benathere!) but where livland yontide meared with the wilde,
saltlea with flood, that the attackler, a cropatkin, though under medium and
between colours with truly native pluck, engaged the Adversary who had
more in his eye than was less to his leg but whom for plunder sake, he
mistook in the heavy rain to be Oglethorpe or some other ginkus, Parr
aparrently, to whom the headandheelless chickenestegg bore some Michel-
angiolesque resemblance, making use of sacrilegious languages to the defect
that he would challenge their hemosphores to exterminate them but he
would cannonise the b—y b—r's life out of him and lay him out contritely
as smart as the b—r had his b—y nightprayers said, three patrecknocksters
and a couplet of hellmuirries (*tout est sacré pour un sacreur, femme à barbe ou
homme-nourrice*) at the same time, so as to plugg well let the blubbywail
ghoats out of him, catching holst of an oblong bar he had and with which he
usually broke furnitures he rose the stick at him. The boarder incident
prerepeated itself. The pair (whethertheywere Nippoluono engaging Wei-
Ling-Taou or de Razzkias trying to reconnoistre the general Boukeleff,
man may not say), struggled apairently for some considerable time, (the
cradle rocking equally to one and oppositely from the other on its law of
capture and recapture), under the All In rules around the booksafe, fighting
like purple top and tipperuhry Swede, (Secremented Servious of the Divine
Zeal!) and in the course of their tussle the toller man, who had opened his
bully bowl to beg, said to the miner who was carrying the worm (a handy
term for the portable distillery which consisted of three vats, two jars and
several bottles though we purposely say nothing of the stiff, both parties
having an interest in the spirits): Let me go, Pautheen! I hardly knew ye.
Later on, after the solstitial pause for refleshmeant, the same man (or a
different and younger him of the same ham) asked in the vermicular with a
very oggly chew-chin-grin: Was six victolios fifteen pigeon takee offa you,
tell he me, stlongfella, by picky-pocky ten to foul months behindaside?
There were some further collidabanter and severe tries to convert for the
best part of an hour and now a woden affair in the shape of a webley (we at
once recognise our old friend Ned of so many illortemporate letters) fell

from the intruser who, as stuck as that cat to that mouse in that tube of that
christchurch organ, (did the imnage of Girl Cloud Pensive flout above them
light young charm, in ribbons and pigtail?) whereupon became friendly
and, saying not his shirt to tear, to know wanted, joking and knobkerries, all
aside laying, if his change companion who stuck still to the invention of his
strongbox, with a tenacity corrobberating their mutual tenitorial rights,
happened to have the loots change of a tenpound crickler about him at the
moment, addling that hap so, he would pay him back the six vics odd, do
you see, out of that for what was taken on the man of samples last Yuni
or Yuly, do you follow me, Capn? To this the other, Billi with the Boule,
who had mummed and mauled up to that (for he was hesitency carried to
excelcism) rather amusedly replied: Woowoo would you be grossly surprised,
Hill, to learn that, as it so happens, I honestly have not such a thing as the
loo, as the least chance of a tinpanned crackler anywhere about me at the
present mohomoment but I believe I can see my way, as you suggest, it
being Yuletide or Yuddanfest and as it's mad nuts, son, for you when it's
hatter's hares, mon, for me, to advance you something like four and seven-
pence between hopping and trapping which you might just as well have, boy
baches, to buy J. J. and S. with. There was a minute silence before memory's
fire's rekindling and then. Heart alive! Which at very first wind of gay gay
and whiskwigs wick's ears pricked up, the starving gunman, strike him pink,
became strangely calm and forthright sware by all his lards porsenal that
the thorntree of sheol might ramify up his Sheofon to the lux apointlex but
he would go good to him suntime marx my word fort, for a chip off the
old Flint, (in the Nichtian glossery which purveys aprioric roots for
aposteriorious tongues this is nat language at any sinse of the world and one
might as fairly go and kish his sprogues as fail to certify whether the
wartrophy eluded at some lives earlier was that somethink like a jug, to
what, a coctable) and remarxing in languidoily, seemingly much more highly
pleased than tongue could tell at this opening of a lifetime and the foretaste
of the Dun Bank pearlmothers and the boy to wash down which he would
feed to himself in the Ruadh Cow at Tallaght and then into the Good
Woman at Ringsend and after her inat Conway's Inn at Blackrock and, first
to fall, cursed be all, where appetite would keenest be, atte, funeral fare or
fun fain real, Adam and Eve's in Quantity Street by the grace of gamy queen
Tailte, her will and testament: You stunning little southdowner! I'd know
you anywhere, Declaney, let me truthfully tell you in or out of the lexinction
of life and who the hell else, be your blanche patch on the boney part!
Goalball I've struck this daylit dielate night of nights, by golly! My hat, you
have some bully German grit, sundowner! He spud in his faust (axin); he

toped the raw best (pardun); he poked his pick (a tip is a tap): and he tucked his friend's leave. And, with French hen or the portlifowlium of hastes and leisures, about to continue that, the queer mixture exchanged the pax in embrace or poghue puxy as practised between brothers of the same breast, hillelulia, killelulia, allenalaw, and, having ratified before the god of the day their torgantruce which belittlers have schmallkalled the treatyng to cognac, turning his fez menialstrait in the direction of Moscas, he first got rid of a few mitsmillers and hurooshoos and levanted off with tubular jurbulance at a bull's run over the assback bridge, spitting his teeths on rooths, with the seven and four in danegeld and their humoral hurlbat or other uncertain weapon of *lignum vitae*, but so evermore rhumanasant of a toboggan poop, picked up to keep some crowplucking appointment with some rival rialtos anywheres between Pearidge and the Littlehorn while this poor delaney, who they left along with the confederate fender behind and who albeit ballsbluffed, bore up wonderfully wunder all of it with a whole number of plumsized contusiums, plus alasalah bruised coccyx, all over him, reported the occurance in the best way he could, to the flabbergaze of the whole lab, giving the Paddybanners the military salute as for his exilicy's the O'Daffy, in justifiable hope that, in nobiloroman review of the hugely sitisfactuary conclusium of their negotiations and the jugglemonkysh agripment deinderivative, some lotion or fomentation of poppyheads would be jennerously exhibited to the parts, at the nearest watchhouse in Vicar Lane, the white ground of his face all covered with digonally redcrossed nonfatal mammalian blood as proofpositive of the seriousness of his character and that he was bleeding in self defience (stanch it!) from the nostrils, lips, pavilion and palate, while some of his hitter's hairs had been pulled off his knut's head by Colt though otherwise his allround health appeared to be middling along as it proved most fortunate that not one of the two hundred and six bones and five hundred and one muscles in his corso was a whit the whorse for her whacking. Herwho?

Nowthen, leaving clashing ash, brawn and muscle and brassmade to oust earthernborn and rockcrystal to wreck isinglass but wurming along gradually for our savings backtowards motherwaters so many miles from bank and Dublin stone (olympiading even till the eleventh dynasty to reach that thuddysickend Hamlaugh) and to the question of boney's unlawfully obtaining a pierced paraflamme and claptrap fireguard there crops out the still more salient point of the politish leanings and town pursuits of our forebeer, El Don De Dunelli, (may his ship thicked stick in the bottol of the river and all his crewsers stock locked in the burral of the seas!) who, when within the black of your toenail, sir, of being mistakenly ambushed by one of the uddahveddahs, and as close as made no matter, mam, to being kayoed offhard when the hyougono heckler with the Peter the Painter wanted to hole him, was consistently practising the first of the primary and imprescriptible liberties of the pacific subject by circulating (be British, boys to your bellybone and chuck a chum a chance!) alongst one of our umphrohibited semitary thrufahrts, open to buggy and bike, to walk, Wellington Park road, with the curb or quaker's quacknostrum under his auxter and his alpenstuck in his redhand, a highly commendable exercise, or, number two of our *acta legitima plebeia*, on the brink (beware to baulk a man at his will!) of taking place upon a public seat, to what, bare by Butt's, most easterly (but all goes west!) of blackpool bridges, as a public protest and naturlikevice, without intent to annoy either, being praisegood thankfully for the wrathbereaved ringdove and the fearstung boaconstrictor and all the more right jollywell pleased, which he was, at having other people's weather.

But to return to the atlantic and Phenitia Proper. As if that were not to be enough for anyone but little headway, if any, was made in solving the wasnottobe crime cunundrum when a child of Maam, Festy King, of a family long and honourably associated with the tar and feather industries, who gave an address in old plomansch Mayo of the Saxons in the heart of a foulfamed potheen district, was subsequently haled up at the Old Bailey on the calends of Mars, under an incompatibly framed indictment of both the counts (from each equinoxious points of view, the one fellow's fetch being the other follow's person) that is to see, flying cushats out of his ouveralls and making fesses immodst his forces on the field. Oyeh! Oyeh! When the prisoner, soaked in methylated, appeared in dry dock, appatently ambrosiaurealised, like Kersse's Korduroy Karikature, wearing, besides stains, rents and patches, his fight shirt, straw braces, souwester and a policeman's corkscrew trowswers, all out of the true (as he had purposely torn up all his cymtrymanx bespokes in the mamertime), deposing for his exution with all the fluors of sparse in the royal Irish vocabulary how the whole padderjagmartin tripiezite suet and all the sulfeit of copperas had fallen off him quatz unaccountably like the chrystalisations of Alum on Even while he was trying for to stick fire to himcell, (in feacht he was dripping as he found upon stripping for a pipkin ofmalt as he feared the coold raine) it was attempted by the crown (P.C. Robort) to show that King, *elois* Crowbar, once known as Meleky, impersonating a climbing boy, rubbed some pixes of any luvial peatsmoor o'er his face, plucks and pussas, with a clanetourf as the best means of disguising himself and was to the middlewhite fair in Mudford of a Thoorsday, feishts of Peeler and

Pole, under the illassumed names of Tykingfest and Rabworc picked by
him and Anthony out of a tellafun book, ellegedly with a pedigree pig
(unlicensed) and a hyacinth. They were on that sea by the plain of Ir nine
hundred and ninetynine years and they never cried crack or ceased from
regular paddlewicking till that they landed their two and a trifling selves,
amadst camel and ass, greybeard and suckling, priest and pauper, matr-
matron and merrymeg, into the meddle of the mudstorm. The gathering,
convened by the Irish Angricultural and Prepostoral Ouraganisations, to
help the Irish muck to look his brother dane in the face and attended
thanks to Larry by large numbers, of christies and jew's totems, tospite of
the deluge, was distinctly of a scattery kind when the ballybricken he could
get no good of, after cockofthewalking through a few fancyfought mains
ate some of the doorweg, the pikey later selling the gentleman ratepayer
because she, Francie's sister, that is to say, ate a whole side of his (the
animal's) sty, on a struggle Street, *Qui Sta Troia*, in order to pay off, hiss or
lick, six doubloons fifteen arrears of his, the villain's not the rumbler's rent.

Remarkable evidence was given, anon, by an eye, ear, nose and throat
witness, whom Wesleyan chapelgoers suspected of being a plain clothes
priest W.P., situate at Nullnull, Medical Square, who, upon letting down
his rice and peacegreen coverdisk and having been sullenly cautioned against
yawning while being grilled, smiled (he had had a onebumper at parting
from Mrs Molroe in the morning) and stated to his eliciter under his morse
mustaccents (gobbless!) that he slept with a bonafides and that he would be
there to remember the filth of November, hatinaring, rowdy O, which, with
the jiboulees of Juno and the dates of ould lanxiety, was going, please the
Rainmaker, to decembs within the ephemerides of profane history, all
one with Tournay, Yetstoslay and Temorah, and one thing which would
pigstickularly strike a person of such sorely tried observational powers as
Sam, him and Moffat, though theirs not to reason why, the striking thing
about it was that he was patrified to see, hear, taste and smell, as his time of
night, how Hyacinth O'Donnell, B.A., described in the calendar as a mixer
and wordpainter, with part of a sivispacem (Gaeltact for dungfork) on the
fair green at the hour of twenty-four o'clock sought (the bullycassidy of the
friedhoffer!) to sack, sock, stab and slaughter singlehanded another two of
the old kings, Gush Mac Gale and Roaring O'Crian, Jr., both changelings,
unlucalised, of no address and in noncommunicables, between him and
whom, ever since wallops before the Mise of Lewes, bad blood existed on
the ground of the boer's trespass on the bull or because he firstparted
his polarbeeber hair in twoways, or because they were creepfoxed andt
grousuppers over a nippy in a noveletta, or because they could not say

meace, (mute and daft) meathe. The litigants, he said, local congsmen and donalds, kings of the arans and the dalkeys, kings of mud and tory, even the goat king of Killorglin, were egged on by their supporters in the shape of betterwomen with bowstrung hair of Carrothagenuine ruddiness, waving crimson petties and screaming from Isod's towertop. There were cries from the thicksets in court and from the macdublins on the bohernabreen of: Mind the bank from Banagher, Mick, sir! Prodooce O'Donner. Ay! Exhibit his relics! Bu! Use the tongue mor! Give lip less! But it oozed out in Deadman's Dark Scenery Court through crossexanimation of the case-hardened testis that when and where that knife of knifes the treepartied ambush was laid (roughly spouting around half hours 'twixt dusk in dawn, by Waterhose's Meddle Europeic Time, near Stop and Think, high chief evervirens and only abfalltree in auld the land) there was not as much light from the widowed moon as would dim a child's altar. The mixer, accordingly, was bluntly broached, and in the best basel to boot, as to whether he was one of those lucky cocks for whom the audible-visible-gnosible-edible world existed. That he was only too cognitively conatively cogitabundantly sure of it because, living, loving, breathing and sleeping morphomelosophopancreates, as he most significantly did, whenever he thought he heard he saw he felt he made a bell clipperclipperclipperclipper. Whether he was practically sure too of his lugs and truies names in this king and blouseman business? That he was pediculously so. Certified? As cad could be. Be lying! Be the lonee I will. It was Morbus O' Somebody? A'Quite. Szerday's Son? A satyr in weddens. And how did the greeneyed mister arrive at the B.A.? That it was like his poll. A crossgrained trapper with murty odd oogs, awflorated ares, inquiline nase and a twithcherous mouph? He would be. Who could bit you att to a tenyerdfuul when aastalled? Ballera jobbera. Some majar bore too? Iguines. And with tumblerous legs, redipnominated Helmingham Erchenwyne Rutter Egbert Crumwall Odin Maximus Esme Saxon Esa Vercingetorix Ethelwulf Rupprecht Ydwalla Bentley Osmund Dysart Yggdrasselmann? Holy Saint Eiffel, the very phoenix! It was Chudley Magnall once more between the deffodates and the dumb scene? The two childspies waapreesing him auza de Vologue but the renting of his rock was from the three wicked Vun-couverers Forests bent down awhits, arthou sure? Yubeti, Cumbilum comes! One of the oxmen's thingabossers, hvad? And had he been refresqued by the founts of bounty playing there—is—a—pain—aleland in Long's gourgling barral? A loss of Lordedward and a lack of sirphilip a surgeonet showeradown could suck more gargling bubbles out of the five lamps in Portterand's praise. Wirrgeling and maries? As whose wouldn't, laving his leaftime in Blackpool. But, of course, he could call himself Tem, too, if he had time to? You butt he could anytom. When he pleased? Win and place. A stoker temptated by evesdripping aginst the driver who was a witness as well? Sacred avatar, how the devil did they guess it! Two dreamyums in one dromium? Yes and no error. And both as like as a duel of lentils? Peacisely. So he was pelted out of the coram populo, was he? Be the powers that be he was. The prince in principel should not expose his person? Macchevuole! Rooskayman kamerad? Sooner Gallwegian he would say. Not unintoxicated, fair witness? Drunk as a fishup. Askt to whether she minded whither he smuked? Not if he barkst into phlegms. Anent his ajaciulations to his Crosscann Lorne, cossa? It was corso in cursu on coarser again. The gracious miss was we not doubt sensible how yellowatty on the forx was altered? That she esually was, O'Dowd me not! As to his religion, if any? It was the see-you-Sunday sort. Exactly what he meant by a pederast prig? Bejacob's, just a gent who prayed his lent. And if middleclassed portavorous was a usual beast? Bynight as useful as a vomit to a shorn man. If he had rognarised dtheir gcourts marsheyls? Dthat nday in ndays he had. Lindendelly, coke or skilllies spell me gart without a gate? Harlyadrope. The grazing rights (Mrs Magistra Martinetta) expired with the expiry of the goat's sire, if they were not mistaken? That he exactly could not tell the worshipfuls but his motherinwaders had the recipis for the price of the coffin and that he was there to tell them that herself was the velocipede that could tell them kitcat. A maundarin tongue in a pounderin jowl? Father ourder about the mathers of prenanciation. Distributary endings? And we recommends. *Quare hircum?* No answer. *Unde gentium fe . . . ?* No ah. Are you not danzzling on the age of a vulcano? Siar, I am deed. And how olld of him? He was intendant to study pulu. Which was meant in a shirt of two shifts macoghamade or up Finn, threehatted ladder? That a head in thighs under a bush at the sunface would bait a serpent to a millrace through the heather. Arm bird colour defdum ethnic fort perharps? Sure and glomsk handy jotalpheson as well. Hokey jasons, then, in a pigeegeeses? On a pontiff's order as ture as there's an ital on atac. As a gololy bit to joss? Leally and tululy. But, why this hankowchaff and whence this second tone, son-yet-sun? He had the cowtaw in his buxers flay of face. So this that Solasistras, setting odds evens at defiance, took the laud from Labouriter? What displaced Tob, Dilke and Halley, not been greatly in love with the game. And, changing the venders, from the king's head to the republican's arms, as to the pugnaxities evinxed from flagfall to antepost during the effrays round fatherthyme's beckside and the regents in the plantsown raining, with the skiddystars and the morkernwindup, how they appealed to him then? That it was wildfires night on all the bettygallaghers. Mickmichael's soords shrieking shrecks through the wilkinses and neckanicholas' toastingforks pricking prongs up the tunnybladders. Let there be fight? And there was. Foght. On the site of the Angel's, you said? Guinney's Gap, he said, between what they said and the pussykitties. In the middle of the garth, then? That they mushn't toucht it. The devoted couple was or were only two disappainted solicitresses on the job of the unfortunate class on Saturn's mountain fort? That was about it, jah! And Camellus then said to Gemellus: I should know you? Parfaitly. And Gemellus then said to Camellus: Yes, your brother? Obsolutely. And if it was all about that, egregious sir? About that and the other. If he was not alluding to the whole in the wall? That he was when he was not eluding from the whole of the woman. Briefly, how such beginall finally struck him now? Like the crack that bruck the bank in Multifarnham. Whether he fell in with what they meant? Cursed that he suppoxed he did. Thos Thoris, Thomar's Thom? The rudacist rotter in Roebuckdom. Surtopical? And subhuman. If it was, in yappanoise language, ach bad clap? Oo! Ah! Augs and ohrs with Rhian O'kehley to put it tertianly, we wrong? Shocking! Such as turly pearced our really's that he might, that he might never, that he might never that night? Treely and rurally. Bladyughfoulmoecklenburg-whurawhorascortastrumpapornanennykocksapastippatappatupperstrip-puckputtanach, eh? You have it alright.

Meirdreach an Oincuish! But a new complexion was put upon the matter when to the perplexedly uncondemnatory bench (whereon punic judgeship strove with penal law) the senior king of all, Pegger Festy, as soon as the outer layer of stucckomuck had been removed at the request of a few live jurors, declared in a loudburst of poesy, through his Brythonic interpreter on his oath, mhuith peisth mhuise as fearra bheura muirre hriosmas, whereas take notice be the relics of the bones of the story bouchal that was ate be Cliopatrick (the sow) princess of parked porkers, afore God and all their honours and king's commons that, what he would swear to the Tierney of Dundalgan or any other Tierney, yif live thurkells folloged him about sure that was no steal and that, nevertheless, what was deposited from that eyebold earbig noseknaving gutthroat, he did not fire a stone either before or after he was born down and up to that time. And, incidentalising that they might talk about Markarthy or they might walk to Baalastartey or they might join the nabour party and come on to Porterfeud this the sockdologer had the neck to endorse with the head bowed on him over his outturned noreaster by protesting to his lipreaders with a justbeencleaned barefaced-ness, abeam of moonlight's hope, in the same trelawney what he would impart, pleas bench, to the Llwyd Josus and the gentlemen in Jury's and the four of Masterers who had been all those yarns yearning for that good one about why he left Dublin, that, amreeta beaker coddling doom, as an Inishman was as good as any cantonnatal, if he was to parish by the market steak before the dorming of the mawn, he skuld never ask to see sight or light of this world or the other world or any either world, of Tyrenan-Og, as true as he was there in that jackabox that minute, or wield or wind (no thanks t'yous!) the inexousthausthible wassailhorn tot of iskybaush the hailth up the wailth of the endknown abgod of the fire of the moving way of the hawks with his heroes in Warhorror if ever in all his exchequered career he up or lave a chancery hand to take or throw the sign of a mortal stick or stone at man, yoelamb or salvation army either before or after being puptised down to that most holy and every blessed hour. Here, upon the halfkneed castleknocker's attempting kithoguishly to lilt his holymess the paws and make the sign of the Roman Godhelic faix, (Xaroshie, zdrst!—in his excitement the laddo had broken exthro Castilian into which the whole audience perseguired and pursuited him *olla podrida*) outbroke much yellachters from owners in the heall (Ha!) in which, under the mollification of methaglin, the testifighter reluctingly, but with ever so ladylike indecorum, joined. (Ha! Ha!)

The hilariohoot of Pegger's Windup cumjustled as neatly with the tristitone of the Wet Pinter's as were they *isce et ille* equals of opposites, evolved by a onesame power of nature or of spirit, *iste*, as the sole condition and means of its himundher manifestation and polarised for reunion by the symphysis of their antipathies. Distinctly different were their duasdestinies. Whereas the maidies of the bar, (a pairless trentene, a lunarised score) when the eranthus myrrmyrred: Show'm the Posed: fluttered and flattered around the willingly pressed, nominating him for the swiney prize, complimenting him, the captivating youth, on his having all his senses about him, stincking thyacinths through his curls (O feen! O deur!) and bringing busses to his cheeks, their masculine Oirisher Rose (his neece cleur!), and legando round his nice new neck for him and pizzicagnoling his woolywags, with their dindy dandy sugar de candy mechree me postheen flowns courier to belive them of all his untiring young dames and send treats in their times. Ymen. But it was not unobserved of those presents, their worships, how, of one among all, her deputised to defeme him by the Lunar Sisters' Celibacy Club, a lovelooking leapgirl, all all alonely, Gentia Gemma of the Make-giddyculling Reeks, he, wan and pale in his unmixed admiration, seemed blindly, mutely, tastelessly, tactlessly, innamorate with heruponhim in shining aminglement, the shaym of his hisu shifting into the shimmering of her hers, (youthsy, beautsy, hee's her chap and shey'll tell memmas when she gays whom) till the wild wishwish of her sheeshea melted most musically mid the dark deepdeep of his shayshaun.

And whereas distracted (for was not just this in effect which had just caused that the effect of that which it had caused to occur?) the four justicers laid their wigs together, Untius, Muncius, Punchus and Pylax but could do no worse than promulgate their standing verdict of Nolans Brumans whereoneafter King, having murdered all the English he knew, picked out his pockets and left the tribunal scotfree, trailing his Tommeylommey's tunic in his hurry, thereinunder proudly showing off the blink patch to his britgits to prove himself (an't plase yous!) a rael genteel. To the Switz bobbyguard's curial but courtlike: Commodore valley O hairy, Arthre jennyrosy?: the firewaterloover returted with such a vinesmelling fortytudor ages rawdownhams tanyouhide as would the latten stomach even of a tumass equinous (we were prepared for the chap's clap cap, the accent, but, took us as, by surprise and now we're geshing it like gush gash from a burner!) so that all the twofromthirty advocatesses within echo, pulling up their briefs at the krigkry: Shun the Punman!: safely and soundly soccered that fenemine Parish Poser, (how dare he!) umprumptu rightoway hames, much to his thanks, gratiasagam, to all the wrong donatrices, biss Drinkbattle's Dingy Dwellings where (for like your true venuson Esau he was dovetimid as the dears at Bottome) he shat in (zoo), like the muddy goalbind who he was (dun), the chassetitties belles conclaiming: You and your gift of your gaft of your garbage abaht our Farvver! and gaingridando: Hon! Verg! Nau! Putor! Skam! Schams! Shames!

And so it all ended. Artha kama dharma moksa. Ask Kavya for the kay. And so everybody heard their plaint and all listened to their plause. The letter! The litter! And the soother the bitther! Of eyebrow pencilled, by lipstipple penned. Borrowing a word and begging the question and stealing tinder and slipping like soap. From dark Rasa Lane a sigh and a weep, from Lesbia Looshe the beam in her eye, from lone Coogan Barry his arrow of song, from Sean Kelly's anagrim a blush at the name, from I am the Sullivan that trumpeting tramp, from Suffering Dufferin the Sit of her Style, from Kathleen May Vernon her Mebbe fair efforts, from Fillthepot Curran his scotchlove machreether, from hymn Op. 2 Phil Adolphos the weary O, the leery, O, from Samyouwill Leaver or Damyouwell Lover thatjolly old molly bit or that bored saunter by, from Timm Finn again's weak tribes, loss of strenghth to his sowheel, from the wedding on the greene, agirlies, the gretnass of joyboys, from Pat Mullen, Tom Mallon, Dan Meldon, Don Maldon a slickstick picnic made in Moate by Muldoons. The solid man saved by his sillied woman. Crackajolking away like a hearse on fire. The elm that whimpers at the top told the stone that moans when stricken. Wind broke it. Wave bore it. Reed wrote of it. Syce ran with it. Hand tore it and wild went war. Hen trieved it and plight pledged peace. It was folded with cunning, sealed with crime, uptied by a harlot, undone by a child. It was life but was it fair? It was free but was it art? The old hunks on the hill read it to perlection. It made ma make merry and sissy so shy and rubbed some shine off Shem and put some shame into Shaun. Yet Una and Ita spill famine with drought and Agrippa, the propastored, spells tripulations in his threne. Ah, furchte fruchte, timid Danaides! Ena milo melomon, frai is frau and swee is too, swee is two when swoo is free, ana mala woe is we! A pair of sycopanties with amygdaleine eyes, one old obster lumpky pumpkin and three meddlars on their slies. And that was how framm Sin fromm Son, acity arose, finfin funfun, a sitting arrows. Now tell me, tell me, tell me then!

    What was it?

    A . . . . !

    ? . . . . O!

So there you are now there they were, when all was over again, the four with them, setting around upin their judges' chambers, in the muniment room, of their marshalsea, under the suspices of Lally, around their old traditional tables of the law like Somany Solans to talk it over rallthe-sameagain. Well and druly dry. Suffering law the dring. Accourting to king's evelyns. So help her goat and kiss the bouc. Festives and highajinks and jintyaun and her beetyrossy bettydoaty and not to forget now a'duna o'darnel. The four of them and thank court now there were no more of them. So pass the push for port sake. Be it soon. Ah ho! And do you remember, Singabob, the badfather, the same, the great Howdoyoucallem, and his old nickname, Dirty Daddy Pantaloons, in his monopoleums, behind the war of the two roses, with Michael Victory, the sheemen's preester, before he caught his paper dispillsation from the poke, old Minace and Minster York? Do I mind? I mind the gush off the mon like Ballybock manure works on a tradewinds day. And the O'Moyly gracies and the O'Briny rossies chaffing him bluchface and playing him pranks. How do you do, todo, North Mister? Get into my way! Ah dearome forsailoshe! Gone over the bays! When ginabawdy meadabawdy! Yerra, why would he heed that old gasometer with his hooping coppin and his dyinboosycough and all the birds of the southside after her, Minxy Cunningham, their dear divorcee darling, jimmies and jonnies to be her jo? Hold hard. There's three other corners to our isle's cork float. Sure, 'tis well I can telesmell him H_2CE_3 that would take a township's breath away! Gob and I nose him too well as I do meself, heaving up the Kay Wall by the 32 to 11 with his limelooking horsebags full of sesameseed, the Whiteside Kaffir, and his sayman's effluvium and his scentpainted voice, puffing out his thundering big brown cabbage! Pa! Thawt I'm glad a gull for his pawsdeen fiunn! Goborro, sez he, Lankyshied! Gobugga ye, sez I! O breezes! I sniffed that lad long before anyone. It was when I was in my farfather out at the west and she and myself, the redheaded girl, firstnighting down Sycomore Lane. Fine feelplay we had of it mid the kissabetts frisking in the kool kurkle dusk of the lushiness. My perfume of the pampas, says she (meaning me) putting out her netherlights, and I'd sooner one precious sip at your pure mountain dew than enrich my acquaintance with that big brewer's belch.

And so they went on, the fourbottle men, the analists, unguam and nunguam and lunguam again, their anschluss about her whosebefore and his whereafters and how she was lost away away in the fern and how he was founded deap on deep in anear, and the rustlings and the twitterings and the raspings and the snappings and the sighings and the paintings and the ukukuings and the (hist!) the springapartings and the (hast!) the byby-scuttlings and all the scandalmunkers and the pure craigs that used to be (up) that time living and lying and rating and riding round Nunsbelly Square. And all the buds in the bush. And the laughing jackass. Harik! Harik! Harik! The rose is white in the darik! And Sunfella's nose has got rhinoceritis from haunting the roes in the parik! So all rogues lean to rhyme. And contradrinking themselves about Lillytrilly law pon hilly and Mrs Niall of the Nine Corsages and the old markiss their besterfar, and, arrah, sure there was never a marcus at all at all among the manlies and dear Sir Armoury, queer Sir Rumoury, and the old house by the churpelizod, and all the goings on so very wrong long before when they were going on retreat, in the old gammeldags, the four of them, in Milton's Park under lovely Father Whisperer and making her love with his stuffstuff in the languish of flowers and feeling to find was she mushymushy, and wasn't that vely both of them, the saucicissters, *a drahereen o machree!*, and (peep!) meeting waters most improper (peepette!) ballround the garden, trickle trickle trickle triss, please, miman, may I go flirting? farmers gone with a groom and how they used her, mused her, licksed her and cuddled. I differ with ye! Are you sure of yourself now? You're a liar, excuse me! I will not and you're another! And Lully holding their breach of the peace for them. Pool loll Lolly! To give and to take! And to forego the pasht! And all will be forgotten! Ah ho! It was too too bad to be falling out about her kindness pet and the shape of O O O O O O O O O Ourang's time. Well, all right, Lelly. And shakeahand. And schenkusmore. For Craig sake. Be it suck.

Well?

Well, even should not the framing up of such figments in the evidential order bring the true truth to light as fortuitously as a dim seer's setting of a starchart might (heaven helping it!) uncover the nakedness of an unknown body in the fields of blue or as forehearingly as the sibspeeches of all mankind have foliated (earth seizing them!) from the root of some funner's stotter all the soundest sense to be found immense our special mentalists now holds (*securus iudicat orbis terrarum*) that by such playing possum our hagious curious encestor bestly saved his brush with his posterity, you, charming coparcenors, us, heirs of his tailsie. Gundogs of all breeds were beagling with renounced urbiandorbic bugles, hot to run him, given law, on a scent breasthigh, keen for the worry. View! From his holt outratted across the Juletide's genial corsslands of Humfries Chase from Mullinahob and Peacockstown, then bearing right upon Tankardstown, the outlier, a white noelan which Mr Lœwensteil Fitz Urse's basset beaters had first misbadgered for a bruin of some swart, led bayers the run, then through Raystown and Horlockstown and, louping the loup, to Tankardstown again. Ear canny hare for doubling through Cheeverstown they raced him, through Loughlinstown and Nutstown to wind him by the Boolies. But from the good turn when he last was lost, check, upon Ye Hill of Rut in full winter coat with ticker pads, pointing for his rooming house his old nordest in his rolltoproyal hessians a deaf fuchser's volponism hid him close in covert, miraculously ravenfed and buoyed up, in rumer, reticule, onasum and abomasum, upon (may Allbrewham have his mead!) the creamclotted sherriness of cinnamon syllabub, Mikkelraved, Nikkelsaved. Hence hounds hied home. Preservative perseverance in the reeducation of his intestines was the rebuttal by whilk he sort of git the big bulge on the whole bunch of spasoakers, dieting against glues and gravies, in that sometime prestreet protown. Vainly violence, virulence and vituperation sought wellnigh utterly to attax and abridge, to derail and depontify, to enrate and inroad, to ongoad and unhume the great shipping mogul and underlinen overlord.

But the spoil of hesitants, the spell of hesitency. His atake is it ashe, tittery taw tatterytail, hasitense humponadimply, heyheyheyhey a winceywencky.

Assembly men murmured. Reynard is slow!

One feared for his days. Did there yawn? 'Twas his stommick. Eruct? The libber. A gush? From his visuals. Pung? Delivver him, orelode! He had laid violent hands on himself, it was brought in Fugger's Newsletter, lain down, all in, fagged out, with equally melancholy death. For the triduum of

Saturnalia his goatservant had paraded hiz willingsons in the Forum while the jenny infanted the lass to be greeted raucously (the Yardstated) with houx and epheus and measured with missiles too from a hundred of manhood and a wimmering of weibes. Big went the bang: then wildewide was quiet: a report: silence: last Fama put it under ether. The noase or the loal had dreven him blem, blem, stun blem. Sparks flew. He had fled again (open shunshema!) this country of exile, sloughed off, sidleshomed via the subterranean shored with bedboards, stowed away and ankered in a dutch bottom tank, the Arsa, *hod* S.S. Finlandia, and was even now occupying, under an islamitic newhame in his seventh generation, a physical body Cornelius Magrath's (badoldkarakter, commonorrong canbung) in Asia Major, where as Turk of the theater (first house all flatty: the king, eleven sharps) he had bepiastered the buikdanseuses from the opulence of his omnibox while as arab at the streetdoor he bepestered the bumbashaws for the alms of a para's pence. Wires hummed. Peacefully general astonishment assisted by regrettitude had put a term till his existence: he saw the family saggarth, resigned, put off his remainders, was recalled and scrapheaped by the Maker. Chirpings crossed. An infamous private ailment (vulgovario-veneral) had claimed endright, closed his vicious circle, snap. Jams jarred. He had walked towards the middle of an ornamental lilypond when innebriated up to the point where braced shirts meet knickerbockers, as wangfish daring the buoyant waters, when rodmen's firstaiding hands had rescued un from very possibly several feel of demifrish water. Mush spread. On Umbrella Street where he did drinks from a pumps a kind workman, Mr Whitlock, gave him a piece of wood. What words of power were made fas between them, ekenames and auchnomes, *acnomina ecnumina?* That, O that, did Hansard tell us, would gar ganz Dub's ear wag in every pub of all the citta! Batty believes a baton while Hogan hears a hod yet Heer prefers a punsil shapner and Cope and Bull go cup and ball. And the Cassidy— Craddock rome and reme round e'er a wiege ne'er a waage is still immer and immor awagering over it, a cradle with a care in it or a casket with a kick behind. Toties testies quoties questies. The war is in words and the wood is the world. Maply me, willowy we, hickory he and yew yourselves. Howforhim chirrupeth evereachbird! From golddawn glory to glowworm gleam. We were lowquacks did we not tacit turn. Elsewere there here no concern of the Guinnesses. But only the ruining of the rain has heard. *Estout pourporteral!* Cracklings cricked. A human pest cycling (pist!) and recycling (past!) about the sledgy streets, here he was (pust!) again! Morse nuisance noised. He was loose at large and (Oh baby!) might be anywhere when a disguised exnun, of huge standbuild and masculine manners in her fairly fat forties, Carpulenta Gygasta, hattracted hattention by harbitrary conduct with a homnibus. Aerials buzzed to coastal listeners of an oertax bror collector's budget, fullybigs, sporran, tie, tuft, tabard and bloody antichill cloak, its tailor's (Baernfather's) tab reading V.P.H., found nigh Scald-brothar's Hole, and divers shivered to think what kaind of beast, wolves, croppis's or fourpenny friars, had devoured him. C. W. cast wide. Hvidfinns lyk, drohneth svertgleam, Valkir lockt. On his pinksir's postern, the boys had it, at Whitweekend had been nailed an inkedup name and title, inscribed in the national cursives, accelerated, regressive, filiform, turreted and envenomoloped in piggotry: Move up. Mumpty! Mike room for Rumpty! By order, Nickekellous Plugg; and this go, no pentecostal jest about it, how gregarious his race soever or skilful learned wise cunning knowledgable clear profound his saying fortitudo fraught or prudentiaproven, were he chief, count, general, fieldmarshal, prince, king or Myles the Slasher in his person, with a moliamordhar mansion in the Breffnian empire and a place of inauguration on the hill of Tullymongan, there had been real murder, of the rayheallach royghal raxacraxian variety, the MacMahon chaps, it was, that had done him in. On the fidd of Verdor the rampart combatants had left him lion with his dexter handcoup wresterected in a pureede paumee bloody proper. Indeed not a few thick and thin wellwishers, mostly of the clontarfminded class, (Colonel John Bawle O'Roarke, fervxamplus), even ventured so far as to loan or beg copies of D. Blayncy's trilingual triweekly, Scatterbrains' Aftening Posht, so as to make certain sure onetime and be satisfied of their quasicontribusodalitarian's having become genuinely quite beetly dead whether by land whither by water. Transocean atalaclamoured him; The latter! The latter! Shall their hope then be silent or Macfarlane lack of lamentation? He lay under leagues of it in deep Bartholoman's Deep.

Achdung! Pozor! Attenshune! Vikeroy Besights Smucky Yung Pige-schoolies. Tri Paisdinernes Eventyr Med Lochlanner Fathach I Fioun-nisgehaven. Bannalanna Bangs Ballyhooly Out Of Her Buddaree Of A Bullavogue.

But, their bright little contemporaries notwithstanding, on the morrowing morn of the suicidal murder of the unrescued expatriate, aslike as asnake comes sliduant down that oaktree onto the duke of beavers, (you may have seen some liquidamber exude exotic from a balsam poplar at Parteen-a-lax Limestone. Road and cried Abies Magnifica! not, noble fir?) a quarter of nine, imploring his resipiency, saw the infallible spike of smoke's jutstiff punctual from the seventh gable of our Quintus Centimachus' porphyroid buttertower and then thirsty p.m. with oaths upon his lastingness (*En caecos harauspices! Annos longos patimur!*) the lamps of maintenance, beaconsfarafield innerhalf the zuggurat, all brevetnamed, the wasting wyvern, the tawny of his mane, the swinglowswaying bluepaw, the outstanding man, the lolllike lady, being litten for the long (O land, how long!) lifesnight, with suffusion of fineglass transom and leadlight panes.

Wherefore let it hardly by any being thinking be said either or thought that the prisoner of that sacred edifice, were he an Ivor the Boneless or an Olaf the Hide, was at his best a onestone parable, a rude breathing on the void of to be, a venter hearing his own bauchspeech in backwords, or, more strictly, but tristurned initials, the cluekey to a worldroom beyond the roomwhorld, for scarce one, or pathetically few of his dode canal sammenlivers cared seriously or for long to doubt with Kurt Iuld van Dijke (the gravitational pull perceived by certain fixed residents and the capture of uncertain comets chancedrifting through our system suggesting an authenticitatem of his aliquitudinis) the canonicity of his existence as a tesseract. Be still, O quick! Speak him dumb! Hush ye fronds of Ulma!

Dispersal women wondered. Was she fast?

Do tell us all about. As we want to hear allabout. So tellus tellas allabouter. The why or whether she looked alottylike like ussies and whether he had his wimdop like themses shut? Notes and queries, tipbids and answers, the laugh and the shout, the ards and downs. Now listed to one aneither and liss them down and smoothen out your leaves of rose. The war is o'er. Wimwim wimwim! Was it Unity Moore or Estella Swifte or Varina Fay or Quarta Quaedam? Toemaas, mark oom for yor ounckel! Pigeys, hold op med yer leg! Who, but who (for second time of asking) was then the scourge of the parts about folkrich Lucalizod it was wont to be asked, as, in ages behind of the Homo Capite Erectus, what price Peabody's money, or, to put it bluntly, whence is the herringtons' white cravat, as, in epochs more cainozoic, who struck Buckley though nowadays as thentimes every schoolfilly of sevenscore moons or more who know her intimologies and every colleen bawl aroof and every redflammelwaving warwife and widow-peace upon Dublin Wall for ever knows as yayas is yayas how it was Buckleyself (we need no blooding paper to tell it neither) who struck and the Russian generals, da! da!, instead of Buckley who was caddishly struck by him when be herselves. What fullpried paulpoison in the spy of three castles or which hatefilled smileyseller? And that such a vetriol of venom, that queen's head affranchisant, a quiet stinkingplaster zeal could cover, prepostered or postpaid! The loungelizards of the pumproom had their nine days' jeer, and pratschkats at their platschpails too and holenpolendom beside, Szpaszpas Szpissmas, the zhanyzhonies, when, still believing in her

owenglass, when izarres were twinklins, that the upper reaches of her
mouthless face and her impermanent waves were the better half of her, one
nearer him, dearer than all, first warming creature of his early morn,
bondwoman of the man of the house, and murrmurr of all the mackavicks,
she who had given his eye for her bed and a tooth for a child till one one
and one ten and one hundred again, O me and O ye! cadet and prim, the
hungray and anngreen (and if she is older now than her teeth she has hair
that is younger than thighne, my dear!) she who shuttered him after his fall
and waked him widowt sparing and gave him keen and made him able and
held adazillahs to each arche of his noes, she who will not rast her from her
running to seek him till, with the help of the okeamic, some such time that
she shall have been after hiding the crumbends of his enormousness in the
areyou lookingfor Pearlfar sea, (ur, uri, uria!) stood forth, burnzburn the
gorggony old danworld, in gogor's name, for gagar's sake, dragging
the countryside in her train, finickin here and funickin there, with her
louisequean's brogues and her culunder buzzle and her litde bolero boa and
all and two times twenty curlicornies for her headdress, specks on her
eyeux, and spudds on horeilles and a circusfix riding her Parisienne's
cockneze, a vaunt her straddle from Equerry Egon, when Tinktink in the
churchclose clinked Steploajazzyma Sunday, *Sola*, with pawns, prelates and
pookas pelotting in her piecebag, for Handiman the Chomp, Esquoro,
biskbask, to crush the slander's head.

Wery weeny wight, plead for Morandmor! *Notre Dame de la Ville*, mercy
of thy balmheartzyheat! Ogrowdnyk's beyond herbata tay, wort of the
drogist. Bulk him no bulkis. And let him rest, thou wayfarre, and take no
gravespoil from him! Neither mar his mound! The bane of Tut is on it.
Ware! But there's a little lady waiting and her name is A.L.P. And you'll
agree. She must be she. For her holden heirheaps hanging down her
back. He spenth his strenth amok haremscarems. Poppy Narancy, Giallia,
Chlora, Marinka, Anileen, Parme. And ilk a those dames had her rainbow
huemoures yet for whilko her whims but he coined a cure. Tifftiff today,
kissykissy tonay and agelong pine tomauranna. Then who but Crippled-
with-Children would speak up for Dropping-with-Sweat?

> *Sold him her lease of ninenineninetee,*
> *Tresses undresses so dyedyedaintee,*
> *Goo, the groot gudgeon, gulped it all.*
> *Hoo was the C. O. D.?*
>   Bum!

At Island Bridge she met her tide.
Attabom, attabom, attabombomboom!
The Fin had a flux and his Ebba a ride.
Attabom, attabom, attabombomboom!
We're all up to the years in hues and cribies.
That's what she's done for wee!
Woe!

Nomad may roam with Nabuch but let naaman laugh at Jordan! For we, we have taken our sheet upon her stones where we have hanged our hearts in her trees; and we list, as she bibs us, by the waters of babalong.

[5]

IN THE NAME OF ANNAH THE ALLMAZIFUL, THE EVER-living, the Bringer of Plurabilities, haloed be her eve, her singtime sung, her rill be run, unhemmed as it is uneven!

Her untitled mamafesta memorialising the Mosthighest has gone by many names at disjointed times. Thus we hear of, *The Augusta Angustissimost for Old Seabeastius' Salvation, Rockabill Booby in the Wave Trough, Here's to the Relicts of All Decencies, Anna Stessa's Rise to Notice, Knickle Down Duddy Gunne and Arishe Sir Cannon, My Golden One and My Selver Wedding, Amoury Treestam and Icy Siseule, Saith a Sawyer til a Strame, Ik dik dopedope et tu mihimihi, Buy Birthplate for a Bite, Which of your Hesterdays Mean Ye to Morra? Hoebegunne the Hebrewer Hit Waterman the Brayned, Arcs in His Ceiling Flee Chinx on the Flur, Rebus de Hibernicis, The Crazier Letters, Groans of a Britoness, Peter Peopler Picked a Plot to Pitch his Poppolin, An Apology for a Big* (some such nonoun as *Husband* or *husboat* or *hosebound* is probably understood for we have also the plutherplethoric *My Hoonsbood Hansbaad's a Journey to Porthergill gone and He Never Has the Hour*), *Ought We To Visit Him? For Ark see Zoo, Cleopater's Nedlework Ficturing Aldborougham on the Sahara with the Coombing of the Cammmels and the Parlourmaids of Aegypt, Cock in the Pot for Father, Placeat Vestrae, A New Cure for an Old Clap, Where Portentos they'd Grow Gonder how I'd Wish I Woose a Geese; Gettle Nettie, Thrust him not, When the Myrtles of Venice Played to Bloccus's Line, To Plenge Me High He Waives Chiltern on Friends, Oremunds Queue Visits Amen Mart, E'en Tho' I Granny a-be He would Fain Me Cuddle, Twenty of Chambers, Weighty Ten Beds and a Wan Ceteroom, I Led the Life, Through the Boxer Coxer Rising in the House with the Golden Stairs, The Following Fork, He's my*

O'Jerusalem and I'm his Po, The Best in the West, By the Stream of Zemzem under Zigzag Hill, The Man That Made His Mother in the Marlborry Train, Try Our Taal on a Taub, The Log of Anny to the Base All, Nopper Tipped a Nappiwenk to his Notylytl Dantsigirls, Prszss Orel Orel the King of Orlbrdsz, Intimier Minnelisp of an Extorreor Monolothe, Drink to Him, My Juckey, and Dhoult Bemine Thy Winnowing Sheet, I Ask You to Believe I was his Mistress, He Can Explain, From Victrolia Nuancee to Allbart Noahnsy, Da's a Daisy so Guimea your Handsel too, What Barbaras Done to a Barrel Organ Before the Rank, Tank and Bonnbtail, Huskvy Admortal, What Jumbo made to Jalice and what Anisette to Him, Ophelia's Culpreints, Hear Hubty Hublin, My Old Dansh, I am Older northe Rogues among Whisht I Slips and He Calls Me his Dual of Ayessha, Suppotes a Ventriliquorst Merries a Corpse, Lapps for Finns This Funnycoon's Week, How the Buckling Shut at Rush in January, Look to the Lady, From the Rise of the Dudge Pupublick to the Fall of the Potstille, Of the Two Ways of Opening the Mouth, I have not Stopped Water Where It Should Flow and I Know the Twentynine Names of Attraente, The Tortor of Tory Island Traits Galasia like his Milchcow, From Abbeygate to Crowalley Through a Lift in the Lude, Smocks for Their Graces and Me Aunt for Them Clodshoppers, How to Pull a Good Horuscoup even when Oldsire is Dead to the World, Inn the Gleam of Waherlow, Fathe He's Sukceded to My Esperations, Thee Steps Forward, Two Stops Back, My Skin Appeals to Three Senses and My Curly Lips Demand Columbkisses, Gage Street on a Crany's Savings, Them Lads made a Trion of Battlewatschers and They Totties a Doeit of Deers, In My Lord's Bed by One Whore Went Through It, Mum It is All Over, Cowpoyride by Twelve Acre Terriss in the Unique Estates of Amessican, He Gave me a Thou so I serve Him with Thee, Of all the Wide Torsos in all the Wild Glen, O'Donogh, White Donogh, He's Hue to Me Cry, I'm the Stitch in his Baskside You'd be Nought Without Mom, To Keep the Huskies off the Hustings and Picture Pets from Lifting Shops, Norsker Torsker Find the Poddle, He Perssed Me Here with the Ardour of a Tonnoburkes, A Boob Was Weeping This Mower was Reaping, O'Loughlin, Up from the Pit of my Stomach I Swish you the White of the Mourning, Inglo-Andeen Medoleys from Tommany Moohr, The Great Polynesional Entertrainer Exhibits Ballantine Brautchers with the Link of Natures, The Mimic of Meg Neg end the Mackeys, Entered as the Lastest Pigtarial and My Pooridiocal at Stitchioner's Hall, Siegfield Follies and or a Gentlehomme's Faut Pas, See the First Book of Jealesies Pessim, The Suspended Sentence, A Pretty Brick Story for Childsize Heroes, As Lo Our Sleep, I Knew I'd Got it in Me so Thit settles That, Thonderbalt Captain Smeth and La Belle Sauvage Pocahonteuse, Way for Wet Week Welikin's Douchka Marianne, The Last of the Fingallians, It Was Me Egged Him on to the Stork Exchange and Lent my Dutiful Face to His Customs, Chee Chee Cheels on their China Miction,

Pickedmeup Peters, Lumptytumtumpty had a Big Fall, Pimpimp Pimpimp, Measly Ventures of Two Lice and the Fall of Fruit, The Fokes Family Interior, If my Spreadeagles Wasn't so Tight I'd Loosen my Cursits on that Bunch of Maggiestraps, Allolosha Popofetts and Howke Cotchme Eye, Seen Aples and Thin Dyed, i big U to Beleaves from Love and Mother, Fine's Fault was no Felon, Exat Delvin Renter Life, The Flash that Flies from Vuggy's Eyes has Set Me Hair On Fire, His is the House that Malt Made, Divine Views from Back to the Front, Abe to Sare Stood Icyk Neuter till Brahm Taulked Him Common Sex, A Nibble at Eve Will That Bowal Relieve, Allfor Guineas, Sounds and Compliments Libidous, Seven Wives Awake Aweek, Airy Ann and Berber Blut, Amy Licks Porter While Huffy Chops Eads, Abbrace of Umbellas or a Tripple of Caines, Buttbutterbust, From the Manorlord Hoved to the Misses O'Mollies and from the Dames to their Sames, Manyfestoons for the Colleagues on the Green, An Outstanding Back and an Excellent Halfcentre if Called on, As Tree is Quick and Stone is White So ts My Washing Done by Night, First and Last Only True Account au about the Honorary Mirsu Earwicker, L.S.D., and the Snake (Nuggets!) by a Woman of the World who only can Tell Naked Truths about a Dear Man and all his Conspirators how they all Tried to Fall him Putting it all around Lucalizod about Privates Earwicker and a Pair of Sloppy Sluts plainly Showing all the Unmentionability falsely Accusing about the Raincoats.

The proteiform graph itself is a polyhedron of scripture. There was a time when naif alphabetters would have written it down the tracing of a purely deliquescent recidivist, possibly ambidextrous, snubnosed probably and presenting a strangely profound rainbowl in his (or her) occiput. To the hardily curiosing entomophilust then it has shown a very sexmosaic of nymphosis in which the eternal chimerahunter Oriolopos, now frond of sugars, then lief of saults, the sensory crowd in his belly coupled with an eye for the goods trooth bewilderblissed by their night effluvia with guns like drums and fondlers like forceps persequestellates his vanessas from flore to flore. Somehows this sounds like the purest kidooleyoon wherein our madernacerution of lour lore is rich. All's so herou from us him in a kitchernott darkness, by hasard and worn rolls arered, we must grope on till Zerogh hour like pou owl giaours as we are would we salve aught of moments for our aysore today. Amousin though not but. Closer inspection of the *bordereau* would reveal a multiplicity of personalities inflicted on the documents or document and some prevision of virtual crime or crimes might be made by anyone unwary enough before any suitable occasion for it or them had so far managed to happen along. In fact, under the closed eyes of the inspectors the traits featuring the *chiaroscuro* coalesce, their contrarieties eliminated, in one stable somebody similarly as by the providential warring of heartshaker with housebreaker and of dramdrinker against freethinker our social something bowls along bumpily, experiencing a jolting series of prearranged disappointments, down the long lane of (it's as semper as oxhousehumper) generations, more generations and still more generations.

Say, baroun lousadoor, who in hallhagal wrote the durn thing anyhow? Erect, beseated, mountback, against a partywall, below freezigrade, by the use of quill or style, with turbid or pellucid mind, accompanied or the reverse by mastication, interrupted by visit of seer to scribe or of scribe to site, atwixt two showers or atosst of a trike, rained upon or blown around, by a rightdown regular racer from the soil or by a too pained whittlewit laden with the loot of learning?

Now, patience; and remember patience is the great thing, and above all things else we must avoid anything like being or becoming out of patience. A good plan used by worried business folk who may not have had many momentums to master Kung's doctrine of the meang or the propriety codestruces of Carprimustimus is just to think of all the sinking fund of patience possessed in their conjoint names by both brothers Bruce with whom are incorporated their Scotch spider and Elberfeld's Calculating Horses. If after years upon years of delving in ditches dark one tubthumper more than others, Kinihoun or Kahanan, giardarner or mear measen-manonger, has got up for the darnall same purpose of reassuring us with all the barbar of the Carrageehouse that our great ascendant was properly speaking three syllables less than his own surname (yes, yes, less!), that the ear of Fionn Earwicker aforetime was the trademark of a broadcaster with wicker local jargon for an ace's patent (Hear! Calls! Everywhair!) then as to this radiooscillating epiepistle to which, cotton, silk or samite, kohol, gall or brickdust, we must ceaselessly return, whereabouts exactly at present in Siam, Hell or Tophet under that glorisol which plays touraloup with us in this Aludin's Cove of our cagacity is that bright soandsuch to slip us the dinkum oil?

Naysayers we know. To conclude purely negatively from the positive absence of political odia and monetary requests that its page cannot ever have been a penproduct of a man or woman of that period or those parts is only one more unlookedfor conclusion leaped at, being tantamount to inferring from the nonpresence of inverted commas (sometimes called quotation marks) on any page that its author was always constitutionally incapable of misappropriating the spoken words of others.

Luckily there is another cant to the questy. Has any fellow, of the dime a dozen type, it might with some profit some dull evening quietly be hinted—

has any usual sort of ornery josser, flatchested fortyish, faintly flatulent and given to ratiocination by syncopation in the elucidation of complications, of his greatest Fung Yang dynasdescendanced, only another the son of, in fact, ever looked sufficiently longly at a quite everydaylooking stamped addressed envelope? Admittedly it is an outer husk: its face, in all its featureful perfection of imperfection, is its fortune: it exhibits only the civil or military clothing of whatever passionpallid nudity or plaguepurple nakedness may happen to tuck itself under its flap. Yet to concentrate solely on the literal sense or even the psychological content of any document to the sore neglect of the enveloping facts themselves circumstantiating it is just as hurtful to sound sense (and let it be added to the truest taste) as were some fellow in the act of perhaps getting an intro from another fellow turning out to be a friend in need of his, say, to a lady of the latter's acquaintance, engaged in performing the elaborative antecistral ceremony of upstheres, straightaway to run off and vision her plump and plain in her natural altogether, preferring to close his blinkhard's eyes to the ethiquethical fact that she was, after all, wearing for the space of the time being some definite articles of evolutionary clothing, inharmonious creations, a captious critic might describe them as, or not strictly necessary or a trifle irritating here and there, but for all that suddenly full of local colour and personal perfume and suggestive, too, of so very much more and capable of being stretched, filled out, if need or wish were, of having their surprisingly like coincidental parts separated don't they now, for better survey by the deft hand of an expert, don't you know? Who in his heart doubts either that the facts of feminine clothiering are there all the time or that the feminine fiction, stranger than the facts, is there also at the same time, only a little to the rere? Or that one may be separated from the other? Or that both may then be contemplated simultaneously? Or that each may be taken up and considered in turn apart from the other?

Here let a few artifacts fend in their own favour. The river felt she wanted salt. That was just where Brien came in. The country asked for bearspaw for dindin! And boundin aboundin it got it surly. We who live under heaven, we of the clovery kingdom, we middlesins people have often watched the sky overreaching the land. We suddenly have. Our isle is Sainge. The place. That stern chuckler Mayhappy Mayhapnot, once said to repeation in that lutran conservatory way of his that Isitachapel-Asitalukin was the one place, *ult aut nult*, in this madh vaal of tares (whose verdhure's yellowed therever Phaiton parks his car while its tamelised tay is the drame of Drainophilias) where the possible was the improbable and the improbable the inevitable. If the proverbial bishop of our holy and undivided with this me ken or no me ken Zot is the Quiztune havvermashed had his twoe nails on the head we are in for a sequentiality of improbable possibles though possibly nobody after having grubbed up a lock of cwold cworn aboove his subject probably in Harrystotalies or the vivle will go out of his way to applaud him on the onboiassed back of his remark for utterly impossible as are all these events they are probably as like those which may have taken place as any others which never took person at all are ever likely to be. Ahahn!

About that original hen. Midwinter (fruur or kuur?) was in the offing and Premver a promise of a pril when, as kischabrigies sang life's old sahatsong, an iceclad shiverer, merest of bantlings observed a cold fowl behaviourising strangely on that fatal midden or chip factory or comicalbottomed copsjute (dump for short) afterwards changed into the orangery when in the course of deeper demolition unexpectedly one bushman's holiday its limon threw up a few spontaneous fragments of orangepeel, the last remains of an outdoor meal by some unknown sunseeker or placehider *illico* way back in his mistridden past. What child of a strandlooper but keepy little Kevin in the despondful surrounding of such sneezing cold would ever have trouved up on a strate that was called strete a motive for future saintity by euchring the finding of the Ardagh chalice by another heily innocent and beachwalker whilst trying with pious clamour to wheedle Tipperaw raw raw reeraw puteters out of Now Sealand in spignt of the patchpurple of the massacre, a dual a duel to die to day, goddam and biggod, sticks and stanks, of most of the Jacobiters.

The bird in the case was Belinda of the Dorans, a more than quinque-gintarian (Terziis prize with Serni medal, Cheepalizzy's Hane Exposition) and what she was scratching at the hour of klokking twelve looked for all this zogzag world like a goodishsized sheet of letterpaper originating by transhipt from Boston (Mass.) of the last of the first to Dear whom it proceded to mention Maggy well & allathome's health well only the hate turned the mild on *the van* Houtens and the general's elections with a *lovely* face of some born gentleman with a beautiful present of wedding cakes for dear thankyou Chriesty and with grand funferall of poor Father Michael don't forget unto life's & Muggy well how are you Maggy & hopes soon to hear well & must now close it with fondest to the twoinns with four crosskisses for holy paul holey comer holipoli whollyisland pee ess from (locust may eat all but this sign shall they never) affectionate largelooking tache of tch. The stain, and that a teastain (the overcautelousness of the masterbilker here, as usual, signing the page away), marked it off on the spout of the moment as a genuine relique of ancient Irish pleasant pottery of that lydialike languishing class known as a hurry-me-o'er-the-hazy.

Why then how?

Well, almost any photoist worth his chemicots will tip anyone asking him the teaser that if a negative of a horse happens to melt enough while drying, well, what you do get is, well, a positively grotesquely distorted macromass of all sorts of horsehappy values and masses of meltwhile horse. Tip. Well, this freely is what must have occurred to our missive (there's a sod of a turb for you! please wisp off the grass!) unfilthed from the boucher by the sagacity of a lookmelittle likemelong hen. Heated residence in the heart of the orangeflavoured mudmound had partly obliterated the negative to start with, causing some features palpably nearer your pecker to be swollen up most grossly while the farther back we manage to wiggle the more we need the loan of a lens to see as much as the hen saw. Tip.

You is feeling like you was lost in the bush, boy? You says: It is a puling sample jungle of woods. You most shouts out: Bethicket me for a stump of a beech if I have the poultriest notions what the farest he all means. Gee up, girly! The quad gospellers may own the targum but any of the Zingari shoolerim may pick a peck of kindlings yet from the sack of auld hensyne.

Lead, kindly fowl! They always did: ask the ages. What bird has done yesterday man may do next year, be it fly, be it moult, be it hatch, be it agreement in the nest. For her socioscientific sense is sound as a bell, sir, her volucrine automutativeness right on normalcy: she knows, she just feels she was kind of born to lay and love eggs (trust her to propagate the species and hoosh her fluffballs safe through din and danger!); lastly but mostly, in her genesic field it is all game and no gammon; she is ladylike in everything she does and plays the gentleman's part every time. Let us auspice it! Yes, before all this has time to end the golden age must return with its vengeance. Man will become dirigible, Ague will be rejuvenated, woman with her ridiculous white burden will reach by one step sublime incubation, the manewanting human lioness with her dishorned discipular manram will lie down together publicly flank upon fleece. No, assuredly, they are not justified, those gloompourers who grouse that letters have never been quite their old selves again since that weird weekday in bleak Janiveer (yet how palmy date in a waste's oasis!) when to the shock of both, Biddy Doran looked at literature.

And. She may be a mere marcella, this midget madgetcy, Misthress of Arths. But. It is not a hear or say of some anomorous letter, signed Toga Girilis, (teasy dear). We have a cop of her fist right against our nosibos. We note the paper with her jotty young watermark: *Notre Dame du Bon Marché*. And she has a heart of Arin! What lumililts as she fols with her fallimineers and her nadianods. As a strow will shaw she does the wind blague, recting to show the rudess of a robur curling and shewing the fansaties of a *frizette*. But how many of her readers realise that she is not out to dizzledazzle with a graith uncouthrement of postmantuam glasseries from the lapins and the grigs. Nuttings on her wilelife! Grabar gooden grandy for old almeanium adamologists like Dariaumaurius and Zovotrimaserovmeravmerouvian; (dmzn!); she feel plain plate one flat fact thing and if, lastways firdstwise, a man alones sine anyon anyons utharas has no rates to done a kik at with anyon anakars about tutus milking fores and the rereres on the outerrand asikin the tutus to be forrarder. Thingcrooklyexineverypasturesixdixlikence-himaroundhersthemaggerbykinkinkankanwithdownmindlookingated. Mesdaims, Marmouselles, Mescerfs! Silvapais! All schwants (schwrites) ischt tell the cock's trootabout him. Kapak kapuk. No minzies matter. He had to see life foully the plak and the smut, (schwrites). There were three men in him (schwrites). Dancings (schwrites) was his only ttoo feebles. With apple harlottes. And a little mollvogels. Spissially (schwrites) when they peaches. Honeys wore camelia paints. Yours very truthful. Add dapple inn. Yet is it but an old story, the tale of a Treestone with one Ysold, of a Mons held by tentpegs and his pal whatholoosed on the run, what Cadman could but Badman wouldn't, any Genoaman against any Venis, and why Kate takes charge of the waxworks.

Let us now, weather, health, dangers, public orders and other circumstances permitting, of perfectly convenient, if you police, after you, policepolice, pardoning mein, ich beam so fresch, bey? drop this jiggerypokery and talk straight turkey meet to mate, for while the ear, be we mikealls or nicholists, may sometimes be inclined to believe others the eye, whether browned or nolensed, find it devilish hard now and again even to believe itself. *Habes aures et num videbis? Habes oculos ac mannepalpabuat?* Tip! Drawing nearer to take our slant at it (since after all it has met with misfortune while all underground), let us see all there may remain to be seen.

I am a worker, a tombstone mason, anxious to pleace averyburies and jully glad when Christmas comes his once ayear. You are a poorjoist, unctuous to polise nopebobbies and tunnibelly soully when 'tis thime took o'er home, gin. We cannot say aye to aye. We cannot smile noes from noes. Still. One cannot help noticing that rather more than half of the lines run north-south in the Nemzes and Bukarahast directions while the others go west-east in search from Maliziies with Bulgarad for, tiny tot though it looks when schtschupnistling alongside other incunabula, it has its cardinal points for all that. These ruled barriers along which the traced words, run, march, halt, walk, stumble at doubtful points, stumble up again in comparative safety seem to have been drawn first of all in a pretty checker with lampblack and blackthorn. Such crossing is antechristian of course, but the use of the homeborn shillelagh as an aid to calligraphy shows a distinct advance from savagery to barbarism. It is seriously believed by some that the intention may have been geodetic, or, in the view of the cannier, domestic economical. But by writing thithaways end to end and turning, turning and end to end hithaways writing and with lines of litters slittering up and louds of latters slettering down, the old semetomyplace and jupetbackagain from tham Let Rise till Hum Lit. Sleep, where in the waste is the wisdom?

Another point, in addition to the original sand, pounce powder, drunkard paper or soft rag used (any vet or inhanger in ous sot's social can see the seen for seemself, a wee ftofty od room, the cheery spluttered on the one karrig, a darka disheen of voos from Dalbania, any gotsquantity of racky, a portogal and some buk setting out on the sofer, you remember the sort of softball sucker motru used to tell us when we were all biribiyas or nippies and messas) it has acquired accretions of terricious matter whilst loitering in the past. The teatimestained terminal (say not the tag, mummer, or our show's a failure!) is a cosy little brown study all to oneself and, whether it be thumbprint, mademark or just a poor trait of the artless, its importance in establishing the identities in the writer complexus (for if the hand was one, the minds of active and agitated were more than so) will be best appreciated by never forgetting that both before and after the battle of the Boyne it was a habit not to sign letters always. Tip. And it is surely a lesser ignorance to write a word with every consonant too few than to add all too many. The end? Say it with missiles then and thus arabesque the page. You have your cup of scalding Souchong, your taper's waxen drop, your cat's paw, the clove or coffinnail you chewed or champed as you worded it, your lark in clear air. So why, pray, sign anything as long as every word, letter, penstroke, paperspace is a perfect signature of its own? A true friend is known much more easily, and better into the bargain, by his personal touch, habits of full or undress, movements, response to appeals for charity than by his footwear, say. And, speaking anent Tiberias and other incestuish salacities among gerontophils, a word of warning about the tenderloined passion hinted at. Some softnosed peruser might mayhem take it up erogenously as the usual case of spoons, *prostituta in herba* plus dinky pinks deliberatively summer-saulting off her bisexycle, at the main entrance of curate's perpetual soutane suit with her one to see and awoh! who picks her up as gingerly as any balmbearer would to feel whereupon the virgin was most hurt and nicely asking: whyre have you been so grace a mauling and where were you chaste me child? Be who, farther potential? and so wider but we grisly old Sykos who have done our unsmiling bit on 'alices, when they were yung and easily freudened, in the penumbra of the procuring room and what oracular comepression we have had apply to them! could (did we care to sell our feebought silence *in camera*) tell our very moistnostrilled one that *father* in such virgated contexts is not always that undemonstrative relative (often held up to our contumacy) who settles our hashbill for us and what an innocent allabroad's adverb such as Michaelly looks like can be suggestive of under the pudendascope and, finally, what a neurasthene nympholept, endocrine-pineal typus, of inverted parentage with a prepossessing drauma present in her past and a priapic urge for congress with agnates before cognates fundamentally is feeling for under her lubricitous meiosis when she refers with liking to some feeler she fancie's face. And Mm. We could. Yet what need to say? 'Tis as human a little story as paper could well carry, in affect, as singsing so Salaman susuing to swittvitles while as unbluffingly blurtubruskblunt as an Esra, the cat, the cat's meeter, the meeter's cat's wife, the meeter's cat's wife's half better, the meeter's cat's wife's half better's meeter, and so back to our horses, for we also know, what we have perused from the pages of *I Was A Gemral*, that Showting up of Bulsklivism by 'Schottenboum', that Father Michael about this red time of the white terror equals the old regime and Margaret is the social revolution while cakes mean the party funds and dear thank you signifies national gratitude. In fine, we have heard, as it happened, of Spartacus intercellular. We are not corknered yet, dead hand! We can recall, with voluntears, the froggy jew, and sweeter far 'twere now westhinks in Dumbil's fair city ere one more year is o'er. We tourned our coasts to the good gay tunes. When from down swords the sea merged the oldowth guns and answer made the bold O' Dwyer. But. *Est modest in verbos.* Let a prostitute be whoso stands before a door and winks or parks herself in the fornix near a makeussin wall (sinsin! sinsin!) and the curate one who brings strong waters (gingin! gingin!), but also, and dinna forget, that there is many asleeps between someathome's first and moreinausland's last and that the beautiful presence of waiting kates will until life's (!) be more than enough to make any milkmike in the language of sweet tarts punch hell's hate into his twin nicky and that Maggy's tea, or your majesty, if heard as a boost from a born gentleman is (?). For if the lingo gasped between kicksheets, however basically English, were to be preached from the mouths of wickerchurchwardens and metaphysicians in the row and advokaatoes, allvoyous, demivoyelles, languoaths, lesbiels, dentelles, gutterhowls and furtz, where would their practice be or where the human race itself were the Pythagorean sesquipedalia of the panepistemion, however apically Volapucky, grunted and gromwelled, ichabod, habakuk, opanoff, uggamyg, hapaxle, gomenon, ppppfff, over country stiles, behind slated dwellinghouses, down blind lanes, or, when all fruit fails, under some sacking left on a coarse cart?

So hath been, love: tis tis: and will be: till wears and tears and ages. Thief us the night, steal we the air, shawl thiner liefest, mine! Here, Ohere, insult the fair! Traitor, bad hearer, brave! The lightning look, the birding cry, awe from the grave, ever-flowing on the times. Feueragusaria iordenwater; now godsun shine on menday's daughter; a good clap, a fore marriage, a bad wake, tell hell's well; such is manowife's lot of lose and win again, like he's gruen quhiskers on who's chin again, she plucketed them out but they grown in again. So what are you going to do about it? O dear!

If juness she saved! Ah ho! And if yulone he pouved! The olold stoliolum! From quiqui quinet to michemiche chelet and a jambebatiste to a brulobrulo! It is told in sounds in utter that, in signs so adds to, in universal, in polygluttural, in each auxiliary neutral idiom, sordomutics, florilingua, sheltafocal, flayflutter, a con's cubane, a pro's tutute, strassarab, ereperse and anythongue athall. Since nozzy Nanette tripped palmyways with Highho Harry there's a spurtfire turf a'kind o'kindling when oft as the souffsouff blows her peaties up and a claypot wet for thee, my Sitys, and talkatalka tell Tibbs has eve: and whathough (revilous life proving aye the death of ronaldses when winpower wine has bucked the kick on poor won man) billiousness has been billiousness during milliums of millenions and our mixed racings have been giving two hoots or three jeers for the grape, vine and brew and Pieter's in Nieuw Amsteldam and Paoli's where the poules go and rum smelt his end for him and he dined off sooth american (it would give one the frier even were one a normal Kettlelicker) this oldworld epistola of their weatherings and their marryings and their buryings and their natural selections has combled tumbled down to us fersch and made-at-all-hours like an ould cup on tay. As I was hottin me souser. Haha! And as you was caldin your dutchy hovel. Hoho! She tole the tail or her toon. Huhu!

Now, kapnimancy and infusionism may both fit as tight as two trivets but while we in our wee free state, holding to that prestatute in our charter, may have our irremovable doubts as to the whole sense of the lot, the interpretation of any phrase in the whole, the meaning of every word of a phrase so far deciphered out of it, however unfettered our Irish daily independence, we must vaunt no idle dubiosity as to its genuine authorship and holusbolus authoritativeness. And let us bringtheecease to beakerings on that clink, olmond bottler! On the face of it, to volt back to our desultory horses, and for your roughshod mind, bafflelost bull, the affair is a thing once for all done and there you are somewhere and finished in a certain time, be it a day

or a year or even supposing, it should eventually turn out to be a serial
number of goodness gracious alone knows how many days or years. Anyhow,
somehow and somewhere, before the bookflood or after her ebb, somebody
mentioned by name in his telephone directory, Coccolanius or Gallotaurus,
wrote it, wrote it all, wrote it all down, and there you are, full stop. O,
undoubtedly yes, and very potably so, but one who deeper thinks will always
bear in the baccbuccus of his mind that this downright there you are and
there it is is only all in his eye. Why?

Because, Soferim Bebel, if it goes to that, (and dormerwindow gossip will
cry it from the housetops no surelier than the writing on the wall will hue it
to the mod of men that mote in the main street) every person, place and
thing in the chaosmos of Alle anyway connected with the gobblydumped
turkery was moving and changing every part of the time: the travelling
inkhorn (possibly pot), the hare and turtle pen and paper, the continually
more and less intermisunderstanding minds of the anticollaborators, the as
time went on as it will variously inflected, differently pronounced, otherwise
spelled, changeably meaning vocable scriptsigns. No, so help me Petault, it
is not a miseffectual whyacinthinous riot of blots and blurs and bars and
balls and hoops and wriggles and juxtaposed jottings linked by spurts of
speed: it only looks as like it as damn it; and, sure, we ought really to rest
thankful that at this deleteful hour of dungflies dawning we have even a
written on with dried ink scrap of paper at all to show for ourselves, tare it
or leaf it, (and we are lufted to ourselves as the soulfisher when he led the cat
out of the bout) after all that we lost and plundered of it even to the hidmost
coignings of the earth and all it has gone through and by all means, after a
good ground kiss to Terracussa and for wars luck our lefftoff's flung over
our home homoplate, cling to it as with drowning hands, hoping against
hope all the while that, by the light of philophosy, (and may she never
folsage us!) things will begin to clear up a bit one way or another within the
next quarrel of an hour and be hanged to them as ten to one they will too,
please the pigs, as they ought to categorically, as, stricly between ourselves,
there is a limit to all things so this will never do.

For, with that farmfrow's foul flair for that flayfell foxfetor, (the calamite's
columitas calling for calamitous calamitance) who that scrutinising marvels
at those indignant whiplooplashes; those so prudently bolted or blocked
rounds; the touching reminiscence of an incompletet trail or dropped final;
a round thousand whirligig glorioles, prefaced by (alas!) now illegible airy
plumeflights, all tiberiously ambiembellishing the initials majuscule of Earwicker: the meant to be baffling chrismon trilithon sign ᚋ, finally called after
some his hes hecitency Hec, which, moved contrawatchwise, represents his

title in sigla as the smaller Δ, fontly called following a certain change of state
of grace of nature alp or delta, when single, stands for or tautologically
stands beside the consort: (though for that matter, since we have heard from
Cathay cyrcles how the hen is not mirely a tick or two after the first fifth
fourth of the second eighth twelfth—siangchang hongkong sansheneul—
but yirely the other and thirtieth of the ninth from the twentieth, our own
vulgar 432 and 1132 irrespectively, why not take the former for a village
inn, the latter for an upsidown bridge, a multiplication marking for crossroads ahead, which you like pothook for the family gibbet, their old four-
wheedler for the bucker's field, a tea anyway for a tryst someday, and his
onesidemissing for an allblind alley leading to an Irish plot in the Champ de
Mors, not?) the steady monologuy of the interiors; the pardonable confusion
for which some blame the cudgel and more blame the soot but unthanks to
which the pees with their caps awry are quite as often as not taken for kews
with their tails in their or are quite as often as not taken for pews with their
tails in their mouths, thence your pristopher polombos, hence our Kat
Kresbyterians; the curt witty wotty dashes never quite just right at the trim
trite truth letter; the sudden spluttered petulance of some capjtaljsed mIddle;
a word as cunningly hidden in its maze of confused drapery as a fieldmouse
in a nest of coloured ribbons: that absurdly bullsfooted bee declaring with
an even plainer dummpshow than does the mute commoner with us how
hard a thing it is to mpe mporn a gentlerman: and look at this prepronominal
funferal, engraved and retouched and edgewiped and puddenpadded, very
like a whale's egg farced with pemmican, as were it sentenced to be nuzzled
over a full trillion times for ever and a night till his noddle sink or swim by
that ideal reader suffering from an ideal insomnia: all those red raddled
obeli cayennepeppercast over the text, calling unnecessary attention to
errors, omissions, repetitions and misalignments: that (probably local or
personal) variant *maggers* for the more generally accepted *majesty* which is
but a trifle and yet may quietly amuse: those superciliouslooking crisscrossed
Greek ees awkwardlike perched there and here out of date like sick owls
hawked back to Athens: and the geegees too, jesuistically formed at first but
afterwards genuflected aggrily toewards the occident: the Ostrogothic kako-
graphy affected for certain phrases of Etruscan stabletalk and, in short, the
learning betrayed at almost every line's end: the headstrength (at least eleven
men of thirtytwo palfrycraft) revealed by a constant labour to make a ghimel
pass through the eye of an iota: this, for instance, utterly unexpected sinist-
rogyric return to one peculiar sore point in the past; those throne open
doubleyous (of an early muddy terranean origin whether man chooses to
damn them agglutinatively loo—too—blue—face—ache or illvoodawpeehole

or, kants koorts, topplefouls) seated with such floprightdown determination
and reminding uus ineluctably of nature at her naturalest while that fretful
fidget eff, the hornful digamma of your bornabarbar, rarely heard now save
when falling from the unfashionable lipsus of some hetarosexual (used always
in two boldfaced print types—one of them as wrongheaded as his Claudian
brother, is it worth while interrupting to say?—throughout the papyrus as
the revise mark) stalks all over the page broods sensationseeking an idea,
amid the verbiage, gaunt, stands dejectedly in the diapered window margin,
with its basque of bayleaves all aflutter about its forksfrogs, paces with a
frown, jerking to and fro, flinging phrases here, there, or returns inhibited,
with some half-halted suggestion, Ŀ, dragging its shoestring; the curious
warning sign before our protoparent's *ipsissima verba* (a very pure nondescript, by the way, sometimes a palmtailed otter, more often the arbutus
fruitflowerleaf of the cainapple) which paleographers call *a leak in the thatch*
or *the Aranman ingperwhis through the hole of his hat*, indicating that the
words which follow may be taken in any order desired, hole of Aran man
the hat through the whispering his ho (here keen again and begin again to
make soundsense and sensesound kin again); those haughtypitched disdotted
aiches easily of the rariest inasdroll as most of the jaywalking eyes we do
plough into halve, unconnected, principial, medial or final, always jims in
the jam, sahib, as pipless as threadworms: the innocent exhibitionism of
those frank yet capricious underlinings: that strange exotic serpentine, since
so properly banished from our scripture, about as freakwing a wetterhand
now as to see a rightheaded ladywhite don a corkhorse, which, in its
invincible insolence ever longer more and of more morosity, seems to
uncoil spirally and swell lacertinelazily before our eyes under pressure of
the writer's hand; the ungainly musicianlessness so painted in sculpting
selfsounder ah ha as blackartful as a *podatus* and dumbfounder oh ho
oaproariose as ten canons in skelterfugue: the studious omission of year
number and era name from the date, the one and only time when our
copyist seems at least to have grasped the beauty of restraint; the lubricitous
conjugation of the last with the first: the gipsy mating of a grand stylish
gravedigging with secondbest buns (an interpolation: these munchables
occur only in the Bootherbrowth family of MSS., Bb—Cod IV, Pap II, Brek
XI, Lun III, Dinn XVII, Sup XXX, Fullup M D C X C: the scholiast has
hungrily misheard a deadman's toller as a muffinbell): the four shortened
ampersands under which we can glypse at and feel for ourselves across all
those rushyears the warm soft short pants of the quickscribbler: the vocative
lapse from which it begins and the accusative hole in which it ends itself; the
aphasia of that heroic agony of recalling a once loved number leading slip

by slipper to a general amnesia of misnomering one's own: next those ars, rrrr! those ars all bellical, the highpriest's hieroglyph of kettletom and oddsbones, wrasted redhandedly from our hallowed rubric prayer for truce with booty, *O'Remus pro Romulo*, and rudely from the fane's pinnacle tossed down by porter to within an aim's ace of their quatrain of rubyjets among Those Who arse without the Temple nor since Roe's Distillery burn'd have quaff'd Night's firefill'd Cup But jig jog jug as Day the Dicebox Throws, whang, loyal six I lead, out wi'yer heart's bluid, blast ye, and there she's for you, sir, whang her, the fine ooman, rouge to her lobster locks, the rossy, whang, God and O'Mara has it with his ruddy old Villain Rufus, wait, whang, God and you're another he hasn't for there's my spoil five of spuds's trumps, whang, whack on his pigsking's Kisser for him, K. M. O'Mara where are you?; then (coming over to the left aisle corner down) the cruciform postscript from which three *basia* or shorter and smaller *oscula* have been overcarefully scraped away, plainly inspiring the tenebrous *Tunc* page of the Book of Kells (and then it need not be lost sight of that there are exactly three squads of candidates for the crucian rose awaiting their turn in the marginal panels of Columkiller, chugged in their three ballotboxes, then set apart for such hanging committees, where two was enough for anyone, starting with old Matthew himself, as he with great distinction said then just as since then people speaking have fallen into the custom, when speaking to a person, of saying two is company when the third person is the person darkly spoken of, and then that last labiolingual *basium* might be read as a *suavium* if whoever the embracer then was wrote with a tongue in his (or perhaps her) cheek as the case may have been then) and the fatal droopadwindle slope of the blamed scrawl, a sure sign of imperfectible moral blindness; the toomuchness, the fartoomanyness of all those four-legged ems: and why spell dear god with a big thick dhee (why, O why, O why?): the cut and dry aks and wise form of the semifinal; and, eighteenthly or twentyfourthly, but at least, thank Maurice, lastly when all is zed and done, the penelopean patience of its last paraphe, a colophon of no fewer than seven hundred and thirtytwo strokes tailed by a leaping lasso—who thus at all this marvelling but will press on hotly to see the vaulting feminine libido of those interbranching ogham sex upandinsweeps sternly controlled and easily repersuaded by the uniform matteroffactness of a meandering male fist?

Duff-Muggli, who now may be quoted by very kind arrangement (his dectroscophonious photosensition under suprasonic light control may be logged for by our none too distant futures as soon astone values can be turned out from Chromophilomos, Limited at a millicentime the microamp), first called this kind of paddygoeasy partnership the ulykkhean or tetrachiric or quadrumane or ducks and drakes or debts and dishes perplex (v. *Some Forestallings over that Studium of Sexophonologistic Schizophrenesis*, vol. xxiv, pp. 2–555) after the wellinformed observation, made miles apart from the Master by Tung-Toyd (cf. *Later Frustrations amengst the Neomugglian Teachings abaft the Semiunconscience, passim*) that in the case of the littleknown periplic bestteller popularly associated with the names of the wretched mariner (trianforan deffwedoff our plumsucked pattern shapekeeper) a Punic admiralty report, *From MacPerson's Oshean Round By the Tides of Jason's Cruise*, had been cleverly capsized and saucily republished as a dodecanesian baedeker of the every-tale-a-treat-initself variety which could hope satisfactorily to tickle me gander as game as your goose.

The unmistaken identity of the persons in the Tiberiast duplex came to light in the most devious of ways. The original document was in what is known as Hanno O'Nonhanno's unbrookable script, that is to say, it showed no signs of punctuation of any sort. Yet on holding the verso against a lit rush this new book of Morses responded most remarkably to the silent query of our world's oldest light and its recto let out the piquant fact that it was but pierced butnot punctured (in the university sense of the term) by numerous stabs and foliated gashes made by a pronged instrument. These paper wounds, four in type, were gradually and correctly understood to mean stop, please stop, do please stop, and O do please stop respectively, and following up their one true clue, the circumflexuous wall of a single-minded men's asylum, accentuated by bi tso fb rok engl a ssan dspl itch ina,—Yard inquiries pointed out → that they ad bîn "provoked" ay Λ fork, of à grave Brofèsor; àth é's Brèak—fast—table; acùtely profèššionally *piquéd*, to = introdùce a notion of time [ùpon à plane (?) sù ' ' fàç'e'] by pùnct! ingh oles (sic) in iSpace?! Deeply religious by nature and position, and warmly attached to Thee, and smearbread and better and Him and newlaidills, it was rightly suspected that such ire could not have been visited by him Brotfressor Prenderguest even underwittingly, upon the ancestral pneuma of one whom, with rheuma, he venerated shamelessly at least once a week at Cockspur Common as his apple in his eye and her first boys' best friend and, though plain English for a married lady misled heaps by the way, yet when some peerer or peeress detected that the fourleaved shamrock or quadrifoil jab was more recurrent wherever the script was clear and the term terse and that these two were the selfsame spots naturally selected for her perforations by Dame Partlet on her dungheap, thinkers all put grown in waterungspillfull Pratiland only and a playful fowl and musical me and not you in any case, two and two together, and, with a swarm of bisses honeyhunting after, a sigh for shyme (O, the pettybonny rouge!) separated modest mouths. So be it. And it was. The lettermaking of the explots of Fjorgn Camhelsson when he was in the Kvinnes country with Soldru's men. With acknowledgment of our fervour of the first instant he remains years most fainfully. For postscrapt see spoils. Though not yet had the sailor sipped that sup nor the humphar foamed to the fill. And fox and geese still kept the peace around *L'Auberge du Père Adam.*

Small need after that, old Jeromesolem, old Huffsnuff, old Andycox, old Olecasandrum, for quizzing your weekenders come to the R.Q. with: shoots off in a hiss, muddles up in a mussmass and his whole's a dismantled noondrunkard's son. Howbeit we heard not a son of sons to leave by him to oceanic society in his old man without a thing in his ignorance, Tulko MacHooley. And it was thus he was at every time, that son, and the other time, the day was in it and after the morrow Diremood is the name is on the writing chap of the psalter, the juxtajunctor of a dearmate and he passing out of one desire into its fellow. The daughters are after going and loojing for him, Torba's nicelookers of the fair neck. Wanted for millinary servance to olderly's person by the Totty Askinses. Formelly confounded with amother. Maybe growing a moustache, did you say, with an adorable look of amuzement? And uses noclass billiardhalls with an upandown ladder? Not Hans the Curier though had he had have only had some little laughings and some less of cheeks and were he not so warried by his bulb of persecussion he could have, ay, and would have, as true as Essex bridge. And not Gopheph go gossip, I declare to man! Noe! To all's much relief one's half hypothesis of that jabberjaw ape amok the showering jestnuts of Bruisanose was hotly dropped and his room taken up by that odious and still today insufficiently malestimated notesnatcher (kak, pfooi, bosh and fiety, much earny, Gus, poteen? Sez you!) Shem the Penman.

[6]

SO?

Who do you no tonigh, lazy and gentleman?

The echo is where in the back of the wodes; callhim forth!

(Shaun Mac Irewick, briefdragger, for the concern of Messrs Jhon Jhamieson and Song, rated one hundrick and thin per storehundred on this nightly quisquiquock of the twelve apostrophes, set by Jockit Mic Ereweak. He misunderstruck and aim for am ollo of number three of them and left his free natural ripostes to four of them in their own fine artful disorder.)

I. What secondtonone myther rector and maximost bridgesmaker was
the first to rise taller through his beanstale than the bluegum buaboababbaun
or the giganteous Wellingtonia Sequoia; went nudiboots with trouters into
a liffeyette when she was barely in her tricklies; was well known to claud a
conciliation cap onto the esker of his hooth; sports a chainganger's albert
solemenly over his hullender's epulence; thought he weighed a new ton
when there felled his first lapapple; gave the heinousness of choice to
everyknight betwixt yesterdicks and twomaries; had sevenal successive-
coloured serebanmaids on the same big white drawringroam horthrug; is a
Willbeforce to this hour at house as he was in heather; pumped the catholick
wartrey and shocked the prodestung boyne; killed his own hungery self in
anger as a young man; found fodder for five when allmarken rose goflooded;
with Hirish tutores Cornish made easy; voucher of rotables, toll of the road;
bred manyheaded stepsons for one leapyourown taughter; is too funny for
a fish and has too much outside for an insect; like a heptagon crystal
emprisoms trues and fauss for us; is infinite swell in unfitting induments;
once was he shovelled and once was he arsoned and once was he inundered
and she hung him out billbailey; has a quadrant in his tile to tell Toler cad
a'clog it is; offers chances to Long on but stands up to Legge before; found
coal at the end of his harrow and mossroses behind the seams; made a fort
out of his postern and wrote F.E.R.T. on his buckler; is escapemaster-in-
chief from all sorts of houdingplaces; if he outharrods against barkers, to the
shoolbred he acts whiteley; was evacuated at the mere appearance of
three germhuns and twice besieged by a sweep; from zoomorphology to
omnianimalism he is brooched by the spin of a coin; towers, an eddistoon
amid the lampless, casting swannbeams on the deep; threatens thunder
upon malefactors and sends whispers up fraufrau's froufrous; when Dook
Hookbackcrook upsits his ass booseworthies jeer and junket but they boos
him oos and baas his aas when he lukes like Hunkett Plunkett; by sosannsos
and search a party on a lady of this city; business, reading newspaper,
smoking cigar, arranging tumblers on table, eating meals, pleasure, etcetera,
etcetera, pleasure, eating meals, arranging tum-blers on table, smoking cigar,
reading newspaper, business; minerals, wash and brush up, local views, juju
toffee, comic and birthdays cards; those were the days and he was their
hero; pink sunset shower, red clay cloud, sorrow of Sahara, oxhide on Iren;
arraigned and attainted, listed and lited, pleaded and proved; catches his
check at banck of Indgangd and endurses his doom at chapel exit; brain of
the franks, hand of the christian, tongue of the north; commands to dinner
and calls the bluff; has a block at Morgen's and a hatache all the afternunch;
plays gehamerat when he's ernst but misses mausey when he's lustyg; walked

as far as the Head where he sat in state as the Rump; shows Early English tracemarks and a marigold window with manigilt lights, a myrioscope, two remarkable piscines and three wellworthseeing ambries; arches all portcullised and his nave dates from dots; is a horologe unstoppable and the Benn of all bells; fuit, isst and herit and though he's mildewstaned he's mouldystoned; is a quercuss in the forest but plane member for Megalopolis; mountunmighty, faunonfleetfoot; plank in our platform, blank in our scouturn; hidal, in carucates he is enumerated, hold as an earl, he counts; shipshaped phrase of buglooking words with a form like the easing moments of a graminivorous; to our dooms brought he law, our manoirs he made his vill of; was an overgrind to the underground and acqueduced for fierythroats; sends boys in socks acoughawhooping when he lets farth his carbonoxside and silk stockings show her shapings when he looses hose on hers; stocks dry puder for the Ill people and pinkun's pellets for all the Pale; gave his mundyfoot to Miserius, her pinch to Anna Livia, that superfine pigtail to Cerisia Cerosia and quid rides to Titius, Caius and Sempronius; made the man who had no notion of shopkeepers feel he'd rather play the duke than play the gentleman; shot two queans and shook three caskles when he won his game of dwarfs; fumes inwards like a strombolist till he smokes at both ends; manmote, befier of him, womankind, pietad!; shows one white drift of snow among the gorsegrowth of his crown and a chaperon of repentance on that which shed gore; pause and quies, triple bill; went by metro for the polis and then hoved by; to the finders, hail! woa, you that seek!; whom fillth had plenished, dearth devoured; hock is leading, cocoa comes next, emery tries for the flag; can dance the O'Bruin's polerpasse at Noolahn to his own orchistruss accompaniment; took place before the internatural convention of catholic midwives and found stead before the congress for the study of endonational calamities; makes a delictuous *entrée* and finishes off the course between sweets and savouries; flouts for forecasts, flairs for finds and the fun of the fray on the fairground; cleared out three hundred sixty five idles to set up one all khalassal for henwives hoping to have males; the flawhoolagh, the grasping one, the kindler of paschal fire; forbids us our trespassers as we forgate him; the phoenix be his pyre, the cineres his sire!; piles big pelium on little ossas like the pilluls of hirculeads; has an eatupus complex and a drinkthedregs kink; wurstmeats for chumps and cowcarlows for scullions; when he plies for our favour is very trolly ours; two psychic espousals and three desertions; may be matter of fact now but was futter of magd then; Cattermole Hill, exmountain of flesh was reared up by stress and sank under strain; tank it up, dank it up, tells the tailor to his tout; entoutcas for a man, but bit a thimble for a maid; blimp, blump; a dud letter,

a sing a song a sylble; a byword, a sentence with surcease; while stands his
canyouseehim frails shall fall; was hatched at Cellbridge but ejoculated
abrood; as it gan in the biguinnengs so wound up in a battle of Boss;
Roderick, Roderick, Roderick, O, you've gone the way of the Danes;
variously catalogued, regularly regrouped; a bushboys holoday, a quacker's
mating, a wenches' sandbath; the same homoheatherous checkinlossegg as
when sollyeye airly blew ye; real detonation but false report; spa mad but
inn sane; half emillian via bogus census but a no street hausmann when
allphannd; is the handiest of all andies and a most alleghant spot to dump
your hump; hands his secession to the new patricius but plumps pleb-
matically for the bloody old centuries; eats with doors open and ruts with
gates closed; some dub him Rotshield and more limn him Rockyfellow;
shows he's fly to both demisfairs but thries to cover up his tracers;
seven dovecotes cooclaim to have been pigeonheim to this homer, Smer-
rnion, Rhoebok, Kolonsreagh, Seapoint, Quayhowth, Ashtown, Ratheny;
independent of the lordship of chamberlain, acknowledging the rule of
Rome; we saw thy farm at Useful Prine, Domhnall, Domhnall; reeks like
Illbelpaese and looks like Iceland's ear; lodged at quot places, lived through
tot reigns; takes a szumbath for his weekend and a wassarnap for his
refreskment; after a good bout at stoolball enjoys Giroflee Giroflaa; what
Nevermore missed and Colombo found; believes in everyman his own
goaldkeeper and in Africa for the fullblacks; the arc of his drive was forty
full and his stumps were pulled at eighty; boasts him to the thick-in-thews
the oldest creater in Aryania and looks down on the Suiss family Collesons
whom he calls *les nouvelles roches*; though his heart, soul and spirit turn to
pharaoph times, his love, faith and hope stick to futuerism; light leglifters
cense him souriantes from afore while boor browbenders curse him grom-
melants to his hindmost; between youlasses and yeladst glimpse of Even; the
Lug his peak has, the Luk his pile; drinks tharr and wodhar for his asama
and eats the unparishable sow to styve off reglar rack; the beggars cloak
them reclined about his paddystool, the whores winken him as they walk
their side; on Christienmas at Advent Lodge, New Yealand, after a lenty
illness the roeverand Mr Easterling of pentecostitis, no followers by
bequest, fanfare all private; Gone Where Glory Waits Him (Ball, bulletist)
but Not Here Yet (Maxwell, clark); comminxed under articles but phoenished
a borgiess; from the vat on the bier through the burre in the dark to the
buttle of the bawn; is A1 an the highest but Roh re his root; filled fanned of
hackleberries whenas all was tuck and toss up for him as a yangster to fall
fou of hockinbechers wherein he had gauged the use of raisin; ads aliments,
das doles, raps rustics, tams turmoil; sas seed enough for a semination but

sues skivvies on the sly; learned to speak from hand to mouth till he could talk earish with his eyes shut; hacked his way through hickheckhocks but hanged hishelp from there hereafters; rialtos, annesleyg, binn and balls to say nothing atolk of New Comyn; the gleam of the glow of the shine of the sun through the dearth of the dirth on the blush of the brick of the viled ville of Barnehulme has dust turned to brown; these dyed to tartan him, rueroot, dulse, bracken, teasel, fuller's ash, sundew and cress; long gunn but not for cotton; stood his sharp assault of famine but grew girther, girther and girther; he has twenty four or so cousins germinating in the United States of America and a namesake with an initial difference in the once kingdom of Poland; his first's a young rose and his second's French-Egyptian and his whole means a slump at Christie's; forth of his pierced part came the woman of his dreams, blood thicker then water last trade overseas; buyshop of Glintylook, eorl of Hoed; you and I are in him surrented by brwn bldns; Elin's flee polt pelhaps but Hwang Chang evelytime; he one was your of highbigpipey boys but fancy him as smoking fags his at time of life; Mount of Mish, Mell of Moy; had two cardinal ventures and three capitol sinks; has a peep in his pocketbook and a packetboat in his keep; B.V.H., B.L.G., P.P.M., T.D.S., V.B.D., T.C.H., L.O.N.; is Breakfates, Lunger, Diener and Souper; as the streets were paved with cold he felt his topperairy; taught himself skating and learned how to fall; distinctly dirty but rather a dear; hoveth chieftains evrywehr, with morder; Ostman Effendi, Serge Paddishaw; baases two mmany, outpriams al' his parisites; first of the fenians, *roi des fainéants*; his Tiara of scones was held unfillable till one Liam Fail felled him in Westmunster; was struck out of his sittem when he rowed saulely to demask us and to our appauling predicament brought as plagues from Buddapest; put a matchhead on an aspenstalk and set the living a fire; speared the rod and spoiled the lightning; married with cakes and repunked with pleasure; till he was buried howhappy was he and he made the welkins ring with *Up Micawber!*; god at the top of the staircase, carrion on the mat of straw; the false hood of a spindler web chokes the cavemouth of his unsightliness but the nestlings that liven his leafscreen sing him a lover of arbuties; we strike hands over his bloodied warsheet but we are pledged entirely to his green mantle; our friend vikelegal, our swaran foi; under the four stones by his streams who vanished the wassailbowl at the joy of shells; Mora and Lora had a hill of a high time looking down on his confusion till firm look in readiness, forward spear and the windfoot of curach strewed the lakemist of Lego over the last of his fields; we darkened for you, faulterer, in the year of mourning but we'll fidhil to the dimtwinklers when the streamy morvenlight calls up the sunbeam; his striped pantaloons, his rather strange walk; *hereditatis columna erecta, hagion chiton eraphon*; nods a nap for the nonce but crows cheerio when they get ecunemical; is a simultaneous equator of elimbinated integras when three upon one is by inspection improper; has the most conical hodpiece of confusianist heronim and that chuchuffuous chinchin of his is like a footsey kungoloo around Taishanty-land; he's as globeful as a gasometer of lithium and luridity and he was thrice ten anular years before he wallowed round Raggiant Circos; the cabalstone at the coping of his cavin is a canine constant but only an amirican could apparoxemete the apeupresiosity of his atlast's alongement; sticklered rights and lefts at Baddersdown in his hunt for the boar trwth but made his end with the modareds that came at him in Camlenstrete; a hunnibal in exhaustive conflict, an otho to return; burning body to aiger air on melting mountain in wooing wave; we go into him sleepy children, we come out of him strucklers for life; he divested to save from the Mrs Drownings their rival queens while Grimshaw, Bragshaw and Renshaw made off with his storen clothes; taxed and rated, licensed and ranted; his threefaced stonehead was found on a whitehorse hill and the print of his costellous feet is seen in the goat's grasscircle; pull the blind, toll the deaf and call dumb, lame and halty; Miraculone, Monstrucceleen; led the upplaws at the Creation and hissed a snake charmer off her stays; hounded become haunter, hunter become fox; harrier, marrier, terrier, tav; Olaph the Oxman, Thorker the Tourable; you feel he is Vespasian yet you think of him as Aurelius; whuga-more, tradertory, socianist, commoniser; made a summer assault on our shores and begiddy got his sands full; first he shot down Raglan Road and then he tore up Marlborough Place; Cromlechheight and Crommalhill were his farfamed feetrests when our lurch as lout let free into the Lubar heloved; mareschalled his wardmotes and delimited the main; netted before nibbling, can scarce turn a scale but, grossed after meals, weighs a town in himself; Banba prayed for his conversion, Beurla missed that grand old voice; a Colossus among cabbages, the Melarancitrone of fruits; larger than life, doughtier than death; Gran Turco, orege forment; lachsembulger, leperlean; the sparkle of his genial fancy, the depth of his calm sagacity, the clearness of his spotless honour, the flow of his boundless benevolence; our family furbear, our tribal tarnpike; quary was he invincibled and cur was he burked; partitioned Irskaholm, united Irishmen; he took a svig at his own methyr but she tested a bit gorky and as for the salmon he was coming up in him all life long; comm, eilerdich hecklebury and sawyer thee, warden; silent as the bee in honey, stark as the breath on hauwck, Costello, Kinsella, Mahony, Moran, though you rope Amrique your home ruler is Dan; figure right, he is hoisted by the scurve of his shaggy neck, figure left, he is rationed in isobaric patties among the crew; one asks was he poisoned, one thinks how much did he leave; ex-gardener (Riesengebirger), fitted up with planturous existencies would make Roseoogreedy (mite's) little hose; taut sheets and scuppers awash but the oil silk mack Liebsterpet micks his aquascutum; the enjoyment he took in kay women, the employment he gave to gee men; sponsor to a squad of piercers, ally to a host of rawlies; against lightning, explosion, fire, earthquake, flood, whirlwind, burglary, third party, rot, loss of cash, loss of credit, impact of vehicles; can rant as grave as oxtail soup and chat as gay as a porto flippant; is unhesitent in his unionism and yet a pigotted nationalist; Sylviacola is shy of him, Matrosenhosens nose the joke; shows the sinews of peace in his chest-o-wars; fiefeofhome, ninehundred and thirtunine years of copyhold; is aldays open for polemypolity's sake when he's not suntimes closed for the love of Janus; sucks life's eleaxir from the pettipickles of the Jewess and ruoulls in sulks if any popeling runs down the Huguenots; Boomaport, Walleslee, Ubermeerschall Blowcher and Supercharger, Monsieur Ducrow, Mister Mudson, master gardiner; to one he's just paunch and judex, to another full of beans and brehons; hallucination, cauchman, ectoplasm; passed for baabaa blacksheep till he grew white woo woo woolly; was drummatoysed by Mac Milligan's daughter and put to music by one shoebard; all fitzpatricks in his emirate remember him, the boys of wetford hail him babu; indanified himself with boro tribute and was schenkt publicly to brigstoll; was given the light in drey orchafts and entumuled in threeplexes; his likeness is in Terrecuite and he giveth rest to the rainbowed; lebriety, frothearnity and quality; his reverse makes a virtue of necessity while his obverse mars a mother by invention; beskilk his gunwale and he's the second imperial, untie points, unhook tenters and he's lath and plaster; calls upon Allthing when he fails to appeal to Eachovos; basidens, ardree, kongsemma, rex-regulorum; stood into Dee mouth, then backed broadside on Baulacleeva; either eldorado or ultimate thole; a kraal of fou feud fires, a crawl of five pubs; laid out lashings of laveries to hunt down his family ancestors and then pled double trouble or quick quits to hush the buckers up; threw pebblets for luck over one sodden shoulder and dragooned peoplades armed to their teeth; pept as Gaudio Gambrinus, grim as Potter the Grave; ace of arts, deuce of damimonds, trouble of clubs, fear of spates; cumbrum, cumbrum, twiniceynurseys fore a drum but tre to uno tips the scale; reeled the titleroll opposite a brace of girdles in Silver on the Screen but was sequenced from the set as Crookback by the even more titulars, Rick, Dave and Barry; he can get on as early as the twentysecond of Mars but occasionally he doesn't come off before Virgintiquinque Germinal; his Indian name is

Hapapoosiesobjibway and his number in arithmosophy is the stars of the plough; took weapon in the province of the pike and let fling his line on Eelwick; moves in vicous cicles yet remews the same; the drain rats bless his offals while the park birds curse his floodlights; Portobello, Equadocta, Therecocta, Percorello; he pours into the softclad shellborn the hard cash earned in Watling Street; his birth proved accidental shows his death its grave mistake; brought us giant ivy from the land of younkers and be-witthered Apostolopolos with the gale of his gall; while satisfied that soft youthful bright matchless girls should bosom into fine silkclad joyous blooming young women is not so pleased that heavy swearsome strong-smelling irregularshaped men should blottout active handsome wellformed frankeyed boys; herald hairyfair, alloaf the wheat; husband your aunt and endow your nepos; hearken but hush it, screen him and see; time is, an archbishopric, time was, a tradesmen's entrance; beckburn brooked with wath, scale scarred by scow; his rainfall is a couple of kneehighs while his meanst grass temperature marked three in the shade; is the meltingpoint of snow and the bubblingplace of alcohol; has a tussle with the trulls and then does himself justice; hinted at in the eschatological chapters of Humphrey's *Justesse of the Jaypees* and hunted for by Theban recensors who sniff there's something behind the *Bug of the Deaf*; the king was in his cornerwall melking mark so murry, the queen was steep in armbour feeling fain and furry, the mayds was midst the hawthorns shoeing up their hose, out pimps the back guards (pomp!) and pump gun they goes; to all his foretellers he reared a stone and for all his comethers he planted a tree; forty acres, sixty miles, white stripe, red stripe, washes his fleet in annacrwatter; whou missed a porter so whot shall he do for he wanted to sit for Pimploco but they've caught him to stand for Sue?; Dutchlord, Dutchlord, overawes us; Head-mound, king and martyr, dunstung in the Yeast, Pitre-le-Pore-in Petrin, Barth-the-Grete-by-the-Exchange; he hestens towards dames troth and wedding hand like the prince of Orange and Nassau while he has trinity left behind him like Bowlbeggar Bill-the-Bustonly; brow of a hazelwood, pool in the dark; changes blowicks into bullocks and a well of Artesia into a bird of Arabia; the handwriting on his facewall, the cryptoconchoidsiphon-ostomata in his exprussians; his birthspot lies beyond the herospont and his burialplot in the pleasant little field; is the yldist kiosk on the pleninsula and the unguest hostel in Saint Scholarland; walked many hundreds and many score miles of streets and lit thousands in one nightlights in hectares of windows; his great wide cloak lies on fifteen acres and his little white horse decks by dozens our doors; O sorrow the sail and woe the rudder that were set for Mairie Quai!; his suns the huns, his dartars the tartars, are plenty here today; who repulsed from his burst the bombolts of Ostenton and falchioned each flash downsaduck in the deep; apersonal problem, a locative enigma; upright one, vehicule of arcanisation in the field, lying chap, flood-supplier of celiculation through ebblanes; a part of the whole as a port for a whale; Dear Hewitt Castello, Equerry, were daylighted with our outing and are looking backwards to unearly summers, from Rhoda Dundrums; is above the seedfruit level and outside the leguminiferous zone; when older links lock older hearts then he'll resemble she; can be built with glue and clippings, scrawled or voided on a buttress; the night express sings his story, the song of sparrownotes on his stave of wires; he crawls with lice, he swarms with saggarts; is as quiet as a mursque but can be as noisy as a sonogog; was Dilmun when his date was palmy and Mudlin when his nut was cracked; suck up the sease, lep laud at ease, one lip on his lap and one cushlin his crease; his porter has a mighty grasp and his baxters the boon of broadwhite; as far as wind dries and rain eats and sun turns and water bounds he is exalted and depressed, assembled and asundered; go away, we are deluded, come back, we are disghosted; bored the Ostrov, leapt the Inferus, swam the Mabbul and flure the Moyle; like fat, like fatlike tallow, of greasefulness, yea of dripping greasefulness; did not say to the old, old, did not say to the scorbutic, scorbutic; he has founded a house, Uru, a house he has founded to which he has assigned its fate; bears a raaven geulant on a fjeld duiv; ruz the halo offhis varlet when he appeared to his shecook as Haycock, Emmet, Boaro, Toaro, Osterich, Mangy and Skunk; pressed the beer of aled age out of the nettles of rashness; put a roof on the lodge for Hymn and a coq in his pot pro homo; was dapifer then pancircensor then hortifex magnus; the topes that tippled on him, the types that toppled off him; still starts our hares yet gates our goat; pocketbook packetboat, gapman gunrun; the light of other days, dire dreary darkness; our awful dad, Timour of Tortur; puzzling, startling, shocking, nay, perturbing; went puffing from king's brugh to new customs, doffing the gibbous off him to every breach of all size; with Pa's new heft and Papa's new helve he's Papapa's old cutlass Papapapa left us; when youngheaded oldshouldered and middlishneck aged about; caller herring everydaily, turgid tarpon overnight; see Loryon the comaleon that changed endocrine history by loeven his loaf with forty bannucks; she drove him dafe till he driv her blind up; the pigeons doves be perchin all over him one day on Baslesbridge and the ravens duv be pitchin their dark nets after him the next night behind Koenigstein's Arbour; tronf of the rep, comf of the priv, prosp of the pub; his headwood it's ideal if his feet are bally clay; he crashed in the hollow of the park, trees down, as he soared in the vaguum of the phoenix, stones up; looks like a moultain boultter and sounds like a rude word; the mountain view, some lumin pale round a lamp of succar in boinyn water; three shots a puddy at up blup saddle; made up to Miss MacCormack Ni Lacarthy who made off with Darly Dermod, swank and swarthy; once diamond cut garnet now dammat cuts groany; you might find him at the Florence but watch our for him in Wynn's Hotel; theer's his bow and wheer's his leaker and heer lays his bequiet hearse, deep; Swed Albiony, likeliest villain of the place; Hennery Canterel—Cockran, eggotisters, limitated; we take our tays and frees our fleas round sadurn's mounted foot; built the Lund's kirk and destroyed the church's land; who guesse his title grabs his deeds; fletch and prities, fash and chaps; artful Juke of Wilysly; Hugglebelly's Funniral; Kukkuk Kallikak; heard in camera and excruciated; boon when with benches billeted, bann if buckshotbackshattered; heavengendered, chaosfoedted, earthborn; his father presumptively ploughed it deep on overtime and his mother as all evince must have travailled her fair share; a footprinse on the Megacene, hetman unwhorsed by Searingsand; honorary captain of the extemporised fire brigade, reported to be friendly with the police; the door is still open; the old stock collar is coming back; not forgetting the time you laughed at Elder Charterhouse's duckwhite pants and the way you said the whole township can see his hairy legs; by stealth of a kersse her aulburntress abaft his nape she hung; when his kettle became a hearthsculdus our thorstyites set their lymphyamphyre; his yearletter concocted by masterhands of assays, his hallmark imposed by the standard of wrought plate; a pair of pectorals and a triplescreen to get a wind up; lights his pipe with a rosin tree and hires a towhorse to haul his shoes; cures slavey's scurvy, breaks barons boils; called to sell polosh and was found later in a bedroom; has his seat of justice, his house of mercy, his com o'copious and his stacks a'rye; prospector, he had a rooksacht, retrospector, he holds the holpenstake; won the freedom of new yoke for the minds of jugoslaves; acts active, peddles in passivism and is a gorgon of selfridgeousness; pours a laughsworth of his illformation over a larmsworth of salt; half heard the single maiden speech La Belle spun to her Grand Mount and wholed a lifetime by his ain fireside, wondering was it hebrew set to himmeltones or the quicksilversong of qwaternions; his troubles may be over but his doubles have still to come; the lobster pot that crabbed our keel, the garden pet that spoiled our squeezed peas; he stands in a lovely park, sea is not far, importunate towns of X, Y and Z are easily over reached; is an excrescence to civilised humanity and but a wart on Europe; wanamade singsigns to soundsense an yit he wanna git all his flesch nuemaid motts truly prural and plusible; has excisively large rings and is uncustomarily perfumed; lusteth ath he listeth the cleah whithpeh of a themise; is a prince of the fingallian in a hiberniad of hoolies; has a hodge to wherry him and a frenchy to curry him and a brabanson for his beeter and a fritz at his switch; was waylaid of a parker and beschotten by a buckeley; kicks lintils when he's cuppy and casts Jacob's arroroots, dime after dime, to poor waifstrays on the perish; reads the charms of H. C. Endersen all the weaks of his evenin and the crimes of Ivaun the Taurrible every strongday morn; soaps you soft to your face and slaps himself when he's badend; owns the bulgiest bungbarrel that ever was tiptapped in the privace of the Mullingar Inn; was bom with a nuasilver tongue in his mouth and went round the coast of Iron with his lift hand to the scene; raised but two fingers and yet smelt it would day; for whom it is easier to found a see in Ebblannah than for I or you to find a dubbeltye in Dampsterdamp; to live with whom is a lifemayor and to know whom a liberal education; was dipped in Hoily Olives and chrysmed in Scent Otooles; hears cricket on the earth but annoys the life out of predikants; still turns the durc's ear of Darius to the now thoroughly infurioted one of God; made Man with juts that jerk and minted money mong maney; likes a six acup pudding when he's come whome sweetwhome; has come through all the eras of livsadventure from moonshine and shampaying down to clouts and pottled porter; woollem the farsed, hahnreich the althe, charge the sackend, writchad the thord; if a mandrake shricked to convultures at last surviving his birth the weibduck will wail bitternly over the rotter's resurrection; loses weight in the moon night but gird girder by the sundawn; with one touch of nature set a veiled world agrin and went within a sheet of tissuepaper of the option of three gaols; who could see at one blick a saumon taken with a lance, hunters pursuing a doe, a swallowship in full sail, a whyterobe lifting a host; faced flappery like old King Cnut and turned his back like Cincinnatus; is a farfar and morefar and a hoar father Nakedbucker in villas old as new; squats aquart and cracks aquaint when it's flaggin in town and on haven; blows whiskery around his summit but stehts stout upon his footles; stutters fore he falls and goes mad entirely when he's waked; is Timb to the pearly mom and Tomb to the mourning night; and an he had the best bunbaked bricks in bould Babylon for his pitching plays he'd be lost for the want of his wan wubblin wall?

Answer: Finn MacCool!

2. Does your mutter know your mike?

Answer: When I tum meoptics, from suchurban prospects, 'tis my filial's bosom, doth behold with pride, that pontificator, and circumvallator, with his dam night garrulous, slipt by his side. Ann alive, the lisp of her, 'twould grig mountains whisper her, and the bergs of Iceland melt in waves of fire,

and her spoon-me-spondees, and her dirckle-me-ondenees, make the
Rageous Ossean, kneel and quaff a lyre! If Dann's dane, Ann's dirty, if he's
plane she's purty, if he's fane, she's flirty, with her auburnt streams, and
her coy cajoleries, and her dabblin drolleries, for to rouse his rudderup, or
to drench his dreams. If hot Hammurabi, or cowld Clesiastes, could espy
her pranklings, they'd burst bounds agin, and renounce their ruings, and
denounce their doings, for river and iver, and a night. Amin!

3. Which title is the true-to-type motto-in-lieu for that Tick for Teac
thatchment painted witt wheth one darkness, where asnake is under clover
and birds aprowl are in the rookeries and a magda went to monkishouse and
a riverpaard was spotted, which is not Whichcroft Whorort not Ousterholm
Dreyschluss not Haraldsby, grocer, not Vatandcan, vintner, not Houseboat
and Hive not Knox-atta-Belle not O'Faynix Coalprince not Wohn Squarr
Roomyeck not Ebblawn Downes not Le Decer Le Mieux not Benjamin's
Lea not Tholomew's Whaddingtun gnot Antwarp gnat Musca not Corry's
not Weir's not the Arch not The Smug not The Dotch House not The
Uval nothing Grand nothing Splendid (Grahot or Spletel) nayther *Erat Est
Erit* noor *Non michi sed luciphro?*

Answer: Thine obesity, O civilian, hits the felicitude of our orb!

4. What Irish capitol city (a dea o dea!) of two syllables and six letters,
with a deltic origin and a ruinous end, (ah dust oh dust!) can boost of having
a) the most extensive public park in the world, *b*) the most expensive brewing
industry in the world, *c*) the most expansive peopling thoroughfare in the
world, *d*) the most phillohippuc theobibbous paùpulation in the world: and
harmonise your abecedeed responses?

Answer: *a*) Delfas. And when ye'll hear the gould hommers of my heart,
my floxy loss, bingbanging again the ribs of yer resistance and the tender-
bolts of my rivets working to your destraction ye'll be sheverin wi' all yer
dinful sobs when *we'll* go riding acope-acurly, you with yer orange garland
and me with my conny cordial, down the greaseways of rollicking into the
waters of wetted life. *b*) Dorhqk. And sure where can you have such good
old chimes anywhere, and *leave* you, as on the Mash and how'tis I would be
engaging you with my plovery soft accents and descanting upover the scene
beunder me of your loose vines in their hairafall with them two loving loofs
braceleting the slims of your ankles and your mouth's flower rose and
sinking ofter the soapstone of silvry speech. *c*) Nublid. Isha, why wouldn't
we be happy, avourneen, on the mills'money he'll soon be leaving you as
soon as I've my own owned brooklined Georgian mansion's lawn to recruit
upon by Doctor Cheek's special orders and my copper's panful of soybeans
and Irish in my east hand and a James's Gate in my west, after all the errears

and erroriboose of combarative embottled history, and your goodself
churning over the newleaved butter (*more* power to you), the choicest and
the cheapest from Atlanta to Oconee, while I'll be drowsing in the gaarden.
d) Dalway. I hooked my thoroughgoing trotty the first down Spanish
Place, Mayo I make, Tuam I take, Sligo's sleek but Galway's grace. Holy
eel and Sainted Salmon, chucking chub and ducking dace, Rodiron's not
your aequal! says she, leppin half the lane. *abcd*) A bell a bell on Shalldoll
Steepbell, ond be'll go massplon pristmoss speople, Shand praise gon ness
our fayst moan *neople*, our prame *Shandeepen*, pay name muy *feepence*, moy
nay non *Aequallllllll!*

5. Whad slags of a loughladd would retten smuttyflesks, emptout old
mans, melk vitious geit, scareoff jackinjills fra tiddle anding, smoothpick
waste papish pastures, insides man outsiders angell, sprink dirted water
around village, newses, tobaggon and sweeds, plain general kept, louden on
the kirkpeal, foottreats given to malafides, outshriek hyelp hyelf nor his hair
efter buggelawrs, might underhold three barnets, putzpolish crotty bottes,
nightcoover all fireglims, serve's time till baass, grindstone his kniveses,
fullest boarded, lewd man of the method of godliness, perchance he nieows
and thans sits in the spoorwaggen, X.W.C.A. on Z.W.C.U., Doorsteps,
Limited, or Baywindaws Bros swobber preferred. Walther Clausetter's and
Sons with the H. E. Chimneys' Company to not skreve, will, on advices, be
bacon or stable hand, must begripe fullstandingly irers' langurge, jublander
or northquain bigger prefurred, all duties, kine rights, family fewd, outings
fived, may get earnst, no get combitsch, profusional drinklords to please
obstain, he is fatherlow soundigged inmoodmined pershoon but aleconner-
man, nay, *that* must he isn't?

Answer: Pore ole Joe!

6. What means the saloon slogan Summon In The Housesweep Dinah?

Answer: Tok. Galory bit of the sales of Cloth nowand I have to beeswax
the bringing in all the claub of the porks to us how I thawght I knew his
stain on the flower if me ask and can could speak and he called by me
midden name Tik. I am your honey honeysugger phwhtphwht tha Bay and
who bruk the dandleass and who seen the blackcullen jam for Tomorrha's
big pickneck I hope it'll pour prais the Climate of all Ireland I heard the
grackles and I skimming the crock on all your sangwidges fippence per leg
per drake. Tuk. And who eight the last of the goosebellies that was mowlding
from measlest years and who leff that there and who put that here and who
let the kilkenny stale the chump. Tek. And whowasit youwasit propped the
pot in the yard and whatinthe nameofsen lukeareyou rubbinthe sideofthe
flureofthe lobbywith. *Shite*! will you have a plateful? Tak.

7. Who are those component partners of our societate, the doorboy, the cleaner, the sojer, the crook, the squeezer, the lounger, the curman, the tourabout, the mussroomsniffer, the bleakablue tramp, the funpowther-plother, the christymansboxer, from their prés salés and Donnybrook prater and Roebuck's campos and the Ager Arountown and Crumglen's grassy but Kimmage's champ and Ashtown fields and Cabra fields and Finglas fields and Santry fields and the feels of Raheny and their fails and Baldoygle to them who are latecomers all the year's round by anticipation, are the porters of the passions in virtue of retroratiocination, and, con-tributting their conflingent controversies of differentiation, unify their voxes in a vote of vaticination, who crunch the crusts of comfort due to depredation, drain the mead for misery to incur intoxication, condone every evil by practical justification and condam any good to its own gratification, who are ruled, roped, duped and driven by those numen daimons, the feekeepers at their laws, nightly consternation, fortnightly fornication, monthly miserecordation and omniannual recreation, doyles when they deliberate but sullivans when they are swordsed, Matey, Teddy, Simon, Jorn, Pedher, Andy, Barty, Philly, Jamesy Mor and Tom, Matt and Jakes Mac Carty?

Answer: The Morphios!

8. And how war yore maggies?

Answer: They war loving, they love laughing, they laugh weeping, they weep smelling, they smell smiling, they smile hating, they hate thinking, they think feeling, they feel tempting, they tempt daring, they dare waiting, they wait taking, they take thanking, they thank seeking, as born for lorn in lore of love to live and wive by wile and rile by rule of ruse 'reathed rose and hose hol'd home, yeth cometh elope year, coach and four, Sweet Peck-at-my-Heart picks one man more.

9. Now, to be on anew and basking again in the panaroma of all flores of speech, if a human being duly fatigued by his dayety in the sooty, having plenxty off time on his gouty hands and vacants of space at his sleepish feet and as hapless behind the dreams of accuracy as any camelot prince of dinmurk, were at this auctual futule preteriting unstant, in the states of suspensive exanimation, accorded, throughout the eye of a noodle, with an earsighted view of old hopeinhaven with all the ingredient and egregiunt whights and ways to which in the curse of his persistence the course of his tory will had been having recourses, the reverberration of knotcracking awes, the reconjungation of nodebinding ayes, the redissolusingness of mindmouldered ease and the thereby hang of the Hoel of it, could such a none, whiles even led comesilencers to comeliewithhers and till

intempestuous Nox should catch the gallicry and spot lucan's dawn, byhold
at ones what is main and why tis twain, how one once meet melts in tother
wants poignings, the sap rising, the foles falling, the nimb now nihilant
round the girlyhead so becoming, the wrestless in the womb, all the rivals to
allsea, shakeagain, O disaster! shakealose, Ah how starring! but Heng's got a
bit of Horsa's nose and Jeff's got the signs of Ham round his mouth and the
beau that spun beautiful pales as it palls, what roserude and oragious grows
gelb and greem, blue out the ind of it! Violet's dyed! then *what* would that
fargazer seem to seemself to seem seeming of, dimm it all?

Answer: A collideorscape!

10. What bitter's love but yurning, what' sour lovemutch but a bref
burning till shee that drawes dothe smoake retourne?

Answer: I know, pepette, of course, dear, but listen, precious! Thanks,
pette, those are lovely, pitounette, delicious! But mind the wind, sweet!
What exquisite hands you have, you angiol, if you didn't gnaw your nails,
isn't it a wonder you're not achamed of me, you pig, you perfect little
pigaleen! I'll nudge you in a minute! I bet you use her best Perisian smear
off her vanity table to make them look so rosetop glowstop nostop. I know
her. Slight me, would she? For every got I care! Three creamings a day, the
first during her shower and wipe off with tissue. Then after cleanup and
of course before retiring. Beme shawl, when I think of that espos of a
Clancarbry, the foodbrawler, of the sociationist party with hiss blackleaded
chest, hello, Prendregast! that you, Innkipper, and all his fourteen other
fullback maulers or hurling stars or whatever the dagos they are, baiting at
my Lord Ornery's, just becups they won the egg and spoon there so ovally
provencial at Balldole. My Eilish assent he seed makes his admiracion. He is
seeking an opening and means to be first with me as his belle alliance.
Andoo musnoo play zeloso! Soso do todas. Such is Spanish. Stoop alittle
closer, fealse! Delightsome simply! Like Jolio and Romeune. I haven't fell
so turkish for ages and ages! Mine's me of squisious, the chocolate with a
soul. Extraordinary! Why, what are they all, the mucky lot of them only?
Sht! I wouldn't pay three hairpins for them. Peppt! That's rights, hold it
steady! Leg me pull. Pu! Come big to Iran. Poo! What are you nudging
for? No, I just thought you were. Listen, loviest! Of course it was *too* kind
of you, miser, to remember my sighs in shockings, my often expressed
wish when you were wandering about my trousseaurs and before I forget it
don't forget, in your extensions to my personality, when knotting my
remembrancetie, shoeweek will be trotting back with red heels at the end of
the moon but look what the fool bought cabbage head and, as I shall answer
to gracious heaven, I'll always in always remind of snappy new girters, me

being always the one for charms with my very best in proud and gloving even if he was to be vermillion miles my youth to live on, the rubberend Mr Polkingtone, the quonian fleshmonger who Mother Browne solicited me for unlawful converse with, with her mug of October (a pots on it!), creaking around on his old shanksaxle like a crosty old cornquake. Airman, waterwag, terrier, blazer! I'm fine, thanks ever! Ha! O mind you poo tickly. Sall I puhim in momou. Mummum. Funny spot to have a fingey! I'm terribly sorry, I swear to you I am! May you never see me in my birthday pelts seenso tutu and that her blanches mainges may rot leprous off her whatever winking maggis I'll bet by your cut you go fleurting after with all the glass on her and the jumps in her stomewhere! Haha! I suspected she was! Sink her! May they fire her for a barren ewe! So she says: Tay for thee? Well, I saith: Angst so mush: and desired she might not take it amiss if I esteemed her but an odd. If I did ate toughturf I'm not a mishymissy. Of course I know, pettest, you're so learningful and considerate in yourself, so friend of vegetables, you long cold cat you! Please by acquiester to meek my acquointance! Codling, snakelet, iciclist! My diaper has more life to it! Who drowned you in drears, man, or are you pillale with ink? Did a weep get past the gates of your pride? My tread on the clover, sweetness? Yes, the buttercups told me, hug me, damn it all, and I'll kiss you back to life, my peachest. I mean to make you suffer, meddlar, and I don't care this fig for contempt of courting. That I chid you, sweet sir? You know I'm tender by my eye. Can't you read by dazzling ones through me true? Bite my laughters, drink my tears. Pore into me, volumes, spell me stark and spill me swooning. I just don't care what my thwarters think. Transname me loveliness, now and here me for all times! I'd risk a policeman passing by, Magrath or even that beggar of a boots at the Post. The flame? O, pardone! That was what? Ah, did you speak, stuffstuff? More poestries from Chickspeer's with glee-choreal music or a jaculation from the garden of the soul. Of I be leib in the immoralities? O, you mean the strangle for love and the sowiveall of the prettiest? Yep, we open hap coseries in the home. And once upon a week I improve on myself I'm so keen on that New Free Woman with novel inside. I'm always as tickled as can be over Man in a Surplus by the Lady who Pays the Rates. But I'm as pie as is possible. Let's root out Brimstoker and give him the thrall of our lives. It's Dracula's nightout. For creepsake don't make a flush! Draw the shades, curfe you, and I'll beat any sonnamonk to love. Holy bug, how my highness would jump to make you flame your halve a bannan in two when I'd run my burning torchlight through (to adore me there and then cease to be? Whatever for, blossoms?) Your hairmejig if you had one. If I am laughing with you? No, lovingest, I'm not so dying to take my rise out of you, adored. Not in the very least. True as God made my Mamaw hiplength modesty coatmawther! It's only because the rison is I'm only any girl, you lovely fellow of my dreams, and because old somebooby is not a roundabout, my trysting of the tulipies, like that puff pape bucking Daveran assoiling us behinds. What a nerve! He thinks that's what the vesprey's for. How vain's that hope in cleric's heart Who still pursues th'adult' rous art, Cocksure that rusty gown of his Will make fair Sue forget his phiz! Tame Schwipps. Blessed Marguerite bosses, I hope they threw away the mould or else we'll have Ballshossers and Sourdamapplers with their medical assassiations all over the place. But hold hard till I've got my latchkey vote and I'll teach him when to wear what woman callours. On account of the gloss of the gleison Hasaboobrawbees isabeaubel. And because, you pluckless lankaloot, I hate the very thought of the thought of you and because, dearling, of course, adorest, I was always meant for an engindear from the French college, to be musband, *nomme d'engien*, when we do and contract with encho tencho solver when you are married to reading and writing which pleasebusiness now won't be long for he's so loopy on me and I'm so leapy like since the day he carried me from the boat, my saviored of eroes, to the beach and I left on his shoulder one fair hair to guide hand and mind to its softness. Ever so sorry! I beg your pardon, I was listening to every treasuried word I said fell from my dear mot's tongue otherwise how could I see what you were thinking of our granny? Only I wondered if I threw out my shaving water. Anyway, here's my arm, pulletneck. Gracefully yours. Move your mouth towards minth, more, preciousest, more on more! To please me, treasure. Don't be a, I'm not going to! Sh! nothing! A cricri somewhere! Buybuy! I'm fly! Hear, pippy, under the limes. You know bigtree are all against gravstone. They hisshistenency. Garnd ond mand! So chip chirp chirrup, cigolo, for the lug of Migo! The little passdoor, I go you before, so, and you're at my apron stage. Shy is him, dovey? Musforget there's an audience. I have been lost, angel. Cuddle, ye divil ye! It's our toot-a-toot. Hearhere! Sensation! Let them, their whole four courtships! Let them, Bigbawl and his boosers' eleven makes twelve territorials. The Old Sot's Hole that wants wide streets to commission their noisense in, at the Mitchells v. Nicholls. *Aves Selvae Acquae Valles!* And my waiting twenty classbirds, sitting on their stiles! Let me finger their eurhythmytic. And you'll see if I'm selfthought. They're all of them out to please. Wait! In the name of. And all the holly. And some the mistle and it Saint Yves. Hoost! Ahem! There's Ada, Bett, Celia, Delia, Ena, Fretta, Gilda, Hilda, Ita, Jess, Katty, Lou, (they make me cough as sure as I read them) Mina, Nippa, Opsy, Poll, Queeniee, Ruth, Saucy, Trix,

Una, Vela, Wanda, Xenia, Yva, Zulma, Phoebe, Thelma. And Mee! The reformatory boys is goaling in for the church so we've all comefeast like the groupsuppers and caught lipsolution from Anty Pravidance under penancies for myrtle sins. When their bride was married all my belles began ti ting. A ring a ring a rosaring! Then everyone will hear of it. Whoses wishes is the farther to my thoughts. But I'll plant them a poser for their nomanclatter. When they're out with the daynurse doing Chaperon Mall. Bright pigeons all over the whirrld will fly with my mistletoe message round their love-ribboned necks and d crumb of my cake for each chasta dieva. We keeps all and sundry papers. In th' amourlight, O my darling! No, I swear to you by Fibsburrow churchdome and Sainte Andrée's Undershift, by all I hold secret from my world and in my underworld of nighties and naughties and all the other wonderwearlds! Close your, notmust look! Now open, pet, your lips, pepette, like I used my sweet parted lipsabuss with Dan Holohan of facetious memory taught me after the flannel dance, with the proof of love, up Smock Alley the first night he smelled pouder and I coloured beneath my fan, *pipetta mia*, when you learned me the linguo to melt. Whowham would have ears like ours, the blackhaired! Do you like that, *silenzioso?* Are you enjoying, this same little me, my life, my love? Why do you like my whisping? Is it not divinely deluscious? But in't it bafforyou? *Misi misi!* Tell me till my thrillme comes! I will not break the seal. I am enjoying it still, I swear I am! Why do you prefer its in these dark nets, if why may ask, my sweetykins? Sh sh! Longears is flying. No, sweetissest, why would that ennoy me? But don't! You want to be slap well slapped for that. Your delighted lips, love, be careful! Mind my duvetyne dress above all! It's golded silvy, the newest sextones with princess effect. For Rutland blue's got out of passion. So, so, my precious! O, I can see the cost, chare! Don't tell me! Why, the boy in sheeps' lane knows that. If I sell whose, dears? Was I sold here' tears? You mean those conversation lozenges? How awful! The bold shame of me! I wouldn't, chickens, not for all the juliettes in the twinkly way! I could snap them when I see them winking at me in bed. I didn't did so, my intended, or was going to or thinking of. Shshsh! Don't start like that, you wretch! I thought ye knew all and more, ye aucthor, to explique to ones the significat of their exsystems with your nieu nivulon lead. It's only another queer fish or other in Brinbrou's damned old trouchorous river again, Gothewishegoths bless us and spare her! And gibos rest from the bosso! Excuse me for swearing, love, I swear to the sorrasims on their trons of Uian I didn't mean to by this alpin armlet! Did you really never in all our cantalang lives speak clothse to a girl's before? No! Not even to the charmermaid? How marfellows! Of course I believe you, my own dear doting liest, when you tell me. As I'd live to, O, I'd love to! Liss, liss! I muss whiss! Never that ever or I can remember dearstreaming faces, you may go through me! Never in all my whole white life of my matchless and pair. Or ever for bitter be the frucht of this hour! With my whiteness I thee woo and bind my silk breasths I thee bound! Always, Amory, amor andmore! Till always, thou lovest! Shshshsh! So long as the lucksmith. Laughs!

11. If you met on the binge a poor acheseyeld from Ailing, when the tune of his tremble shook shimmy on shin, while his countrary raged in the weak of his wailing, like a rugilant pugilant Lyon O'Lynn; if he maundered in misliness, plaining his plight or, played fox and lice, pricking and dropping hips teeth, or wringing his handcuffs for peace, the blind blighter, praying Dieuf and Domb Nostrums foh thomethinks to eath; if he weapt while he leapt and guffalled quith a quhimper, made cold blood a blue mundy and no bones without flech, taking kiss, kake or kick with a suck, sigh or simper, a diffle to larn and a dibble to lech; if the fain shinner pegged you to shave his immartial, wee skillmustered shoul with his ooh, hoodoodoo! broking wind that to wiles, woemaid sin he was partial, we don't think, Jones, we'd care to this evening, would you?

Answer: No, blank ye! So you think I have impulsivism? Did they tell you I am one of the fortysixths? And I suppose you heard I had a wag on my ears? And I suppose they told you too that my roll of life is not natural? But before proceeding to conclusively confute this begging question it would be far fitter for you, if you dare! to hasitate to consult with and consequentially attempt at my disposale of the same dime-cash problem elsewhere naturalistically of course, from the blinkpoint of so eminent a spatialist. From it you will here notice, Schott, upon my for the first remarking you that the sophology of Bitchson while driven as under by a purely dime-dime urge is not without his cashcash charackterricksticks, borrowed for its nonce ends from the fiery goodmother Miss Fortune (who the lost time we had the pleasure we have had our little *recherché* brush with, what, Schott?) and as I further could have told you as brisk as your D.B.C. behaviouristically *pailleté* with a coat of homoid icing which is in reality only a done by chance ridiculisation of the whoo-whoo and where's hairs theorics of Winestain. To put it all the more plumbsily. The speechform is a mere sorrogate. Whilst the quality and tality (I shall explex what you ought to mean by this with its proper when and where and why and how in the subsequent sentence) are alternativomentally harrogate and arrogate, as the gates may be.

Talis is a word often abused by many passims (I am working out a

quantum theory about it for it is really most tantumising state of affairs). A
pessim may frequent you to say: Have you been seeing much of Talis and
Talis those times? optimately meaning: Will you put up at hree of irish? Or
a ladyeater may perhaps have casualised as you temptoed her *à la sourdine:*
Of your plates? Is Talis de Talis, the swordswallower, who is on at the
Craterium the same Talis von Talis, the penscrusher, no funk you! who
runs his duly mile? Or this is a perhaps cleaner example. At a recent
postvortex piece infustigation of a determinised case of chronic spinosis an
extension lecturer on The Ague who out of matter of form was trying his
seesers, Dr's Het Ubeleeft, borrowed the question: Why's which Suchman's
talis qualis? to whom, as a fatter of macht, Dr Gedankje of Stoutgirth, who
was wiping his whistle, toarsely retoarted: While thou beast' one zoom of a
whorl! (Talis and Talis originally mean the same thing, hit it's: Qualis.)

Professor Loewy-Brueller (though as I shall promptly prove his whole
account of the Sennacherib as distinct from the Shalmanesir sanitational
reforms and of the Mr Skekels and Dr Hydes problem in the same connection differs *toto coelo* from the fruit of my own investigations—though
the reason I went to Jericho must remain for certain reasons a political
secret—especially as I shall shortly be wanted in Cavantry, I congratulate
myself, for the same and other reasons—as being again hopelessly vitiated
by what I have now resolved to call the dime and cash diamond fallacy) in
his talked off confession which recently met with such a leonine uproar on
its escape after its confinement *Why am I not born like a Gentleman and why
am I now so speakable about my own eatables* (Feigenbaumblatt and Father,
Judapest, 5688, A.M.) whole-heartedly takes off his gabbercoat and wig,
honest draughty fellow, in his public interest, to make us see how though, as
he says: 'by Allswill' the inception and the descent and the endswell of Man
is *temporarily* wrapped in obscenity, looking through at these accidents with
the faroscope of television, (this nightlife instrument needs still some sub-
tractional betterment in the readjustment of the more refrangible angles to
the squeals of his hypothesis on the outer tin sides), I can easily believe
heartily in my own most spacious immensity as my ownhouse and microbe-
most cosm when I am reassured by ratio that the cube of my volumes is to
the surfaces of their subjects as the sphericity of these globes (I am very
pressing for a parliamentary motion this term which, under my guidance,
would establish the deleteriousness of decorousness in the morbidisation
of the modern mandaboutwoman type) is to the feracity of Fairynelly's
vacuum. I need not anthrapologise for any obintentional (I must here correct
all that school of neoitalian or paleoparisien schola of tinkers and spanglers
who say I'm wrong *parcequeue* out of revolscian from romanitis I want to be)

downtrodding on my foes. Professor Levi-Brullo, F.D. of Sexe-Weiman-Eitelnaky finds, from experiments made by hinn with his Nuremberg eggs in the one hands and the watches cunldron apan the oven, though it is astensably a case of Ket's rebollions cooling the Popes back, because the number of squeer faiths in weekly circulation will not be appreciably augmented by the notherslogging of my cupolar clods. What the romantic in rags pines after like all tomtompions haunting crevices for a deadbeat escupement and what het importunes our *Mitleid* for in accornish with the Mortadarthella taradition is the poorest commononguardiant waste of time. *His* everpresent toes are always in retaliessian out throuth his overpast boots. Hear him squak! Teek heet to that looswallawer how he bolo the bat! Tyro a toray! *When* Mullocky won the couple of colds, *when* we were stripping in number three, I would like the neat drop that would malt in my mouth but I fail to see *when* (I am purposely refraining from expounding the obvious fallacy as to the specific gravitates of the two deglutables implied nor to the lapses lequou asousiated with the royal gorge through students of mixed hydrostatics and pneumodipsics will after some difficulties grapple away with my meinungs). Myrrdin aloer! as old Marsellas Cambriannus puts his. But, on Professor Llewellys ap Bryllars, F.D., Ph. Dr's showings, the plea, if he pleads, is all posh and robbage on a melodeontic scale since his man's *when* is no otherman's *quandour* (Mine, dank you?) while, for aught I care for the contrary, the all is *where* in love as war and the plane where me arts soar you'd aisy rouse a thunder from and where I cling true'tis there I climb tree and where Innocent looks best (pick!) there's holly in his ives.

As my explanations here are probably above your understandings, lattlebrattons, though as augmentatively uncomparisoned as Cadwan, Cadwallon and Cadwalloner, I shall revert to a more expletive method which I frequently use when I have to sermo with muddlecrass pupils. Imagine for my purpose that you are a squad of urchins, snifflynosed, goslingnecked, clothyheaded, tangled in your lacings, tingled in your pants, etsitaraw etcicero. And you, Bruno Nowlan, take your tongue out of your inkpot! As none of you knows javanese I will give all my easyfree translation of the old fabulist's parable. Allaboy Minor, take your head out of your satchel! *Audi*, Joe Peters! *Exaudi* facts!

The Mookse and The Gripes.

Gentes and laitymen, fullstoppers and semicolonials, hybreds and lubberds!

Eins within a space and a wearywide space it wast ere wohned a Mookse. The onesomeness wast alltolonely, archunsitslike, broady oval, and a Mookse he would a walking go (My hood! cries Antony Romeo), so one grandsumer evening, after a great morning and his good supper of gammon and spittish, having flabelled his eyes, pilleoled his nostrils, vacticanated his ears and palliumed his throats, he put on his impermeable, seized his impugnable, harped on his crown and stepped out of his immobile *De Rure Albo* (socolled becauld it was chalkfull of masterplasters and had borgeously letout gardens strown with cascadas, pintacostecas, horthoducts and currycombs) and set off from Ludstown a spasso to see how badness was badness in the weirdest of all pensible ways.

As he set off with his father's sword, his *lancia spezzata*, he was girded on, and with that between his legs and his tarkeels, our once in only Bragspear, he clanked, to my clinking, from veetoes to threetop, every inch of an immortal.

He had not walked over a pentiadpair of parsecs from his azylium when at the turning of the Shinshone Lanteran near Saint Bowery's-without-his-Walls he came (secunding to the one one oneth of the propecies, *Amnis Limina Permanent*) upon the most unconsciously boggylooking stream he ever locked his eyes with. Out of the colliens it took a rise by daubing itself Ninon. It looked little and it smelt of brown and it thought in narrows and it talked showshallow. And as it rinn it dribbled like any lively purliteasy: *My, my, my! Me and me! Little down dream don't I love thee!*

And, I declare, what was there on the yonder bank of the stream that would be a river, parched on a limb of the olum, bolt downright, but the Gripes? And no doubt he was fit to be dried for why had he not been having the juice of his times?

His pips had been neatly all drowned on him; his polps were charging odours every older minute; he was quickly for getting the dresser's desdaign on the flyleaf of his frons; and he was quietly for giving the bailiff's distrain on to the bulkside of his *cul de Pompe*. In all his specious heavings, as be lived by Optimus Maximus, the Mookse had never seen his Dubville brooder-on-low so nigh to a pickle.

Adrian (that was the Mookse now's assumptinome) stuccstill phiz-à-phiz to the Gripes in an accessit of aurignacian. But Allmookse must to Moodend much as Allrouts, austereways or wastersways, in roaming run through Room. Hic sor a stone, singularly illud, and on hoc stone Seter satt huc sate which it filled quite poposterously and by acclammitation to its fullest justotoryum and whereopum with his unfallable encyclicling upom his alloilable, diupetriark of the wouest, and the athemystsprinkled pederect he always walked with, *Deusdedit*, cheek by jowel with his frisherman's blague? *Bellua Triumphanes*, his everyway addedto wallat's collectium, for yea longer he lieved yea broader he betaught of it, the fetter, the summe and the haul it cost, he looked the first and last micahlike laicness of Quartus the Fifth and Quintus the Sixth and Sixtus the Seventh giving allnight sitting to Lio the Faultyfindth.

— Good appetite us, sir Mookse! How do you do it? cheeped the Gripes in a wherry whiggy maudelenian woice and the jackasses all within bawl laughed and brayed for his intentions for they knew their sly toad lowry now. I am rarumominum blessed to see you, my dear mouster. Will you not perhopes tell me everything if you are pleased, sanity? All about aulne and lithial and allsall allinall about awn and liseias? Ney?

Think of it! O miserendissimest retempter! A Gripes!

— Rats! bullowed the Mookse most telesphorously, the concionator, and the sissymusses and the zozzymusses in their robenhauses quailed to hear his tardeynois at all for you cannot wake a silken nouse out of a hoarse oar. Blast yourself and your anathomy infairioriboos! No, hang you for an animal rurale! I am superbly in my supremest poncif! Abase you, baldyqueens! Gather behind me, satraps! Rots!

— I am till infinity obliged with you, bowed the Gripes, his whine having gone to his palpruy head. I am still always having a wish on all my extremities. By the watch, what is the time, pace?

Figure it! The pining peever! To a Mookse!

— Ask my index, mund my achilles, swell my obolum, woshup my nase serene, answered the Mookse, rapidly by turning clement, urban, eugenious and celestian in the formose of good grogory humours. Quote awhore? That is quite about what I came on *my* missions with *my* intentions *laudibiliter* to settle with *you*, barbarousse. Let thor be orlog. Let Pauline be Irene. Let you be Beeton. And let me be Los Angeles. Now measure your length. Now estimate my capacity. Well, sour? Is this space of our couple of hours too dimensional for you, temporiser? Will you give you up? *Como? Fuert it?*

Sancta Patientia! You should have heard the voice that answered him! *Culla vosellina.*

— I was just thinkling upon that, swees Mooksey, but, for all the rime on my raisins, if I connow make my submission, I cannos give you up, the Gripes whimpered from nethermost of his wanhope. Ishallassobound-bewilsothoutoosezit. My tumble, loudy bullocker, is my own. My velicity is too fit in one stockend. And my spetial inexshellsis the belowing things ab ove. But I will never be abler to tell Your Honoriousness (here he near lost his limb) though my corked father was bott a pseudowaiter, whose o'cloak you ware.

Incredible! Well, hear the inevitable.

— Your temple, *sus in cribro!* Semperexcommunicambiambisumers. Tugurios-in-Newrobe or Tukurias-in-Ashies. Novarome, my creature, blievend bleives. My building space in lyonine city is always to let to leonlike Men, the Mookse in a most consistorous allocution pompifically with immediate jurisdiction constantinently concludded (what a crammer for the shapewrucked Gripes!). And I regret to proclaim that it is out of my temporal to help you from being killed by inchies, (what a thrust!), as we first met each other newwhere so airly. (Poor little sowsieved subsquashed Gripes! I begin to feel contemption for him!). My side, thank decretals, is as safe as motherour's houses, he continued, and I can seen from my holeydome what it is to be wholly sane. Unionjok and be joined to yok! Parysis, *tu sais*, crucycrooks, belongs to him who parises himself. And there I must leave you subject for the pressing. I can prove that against you, weight a momentum, mein goot enemy! or Cospol's not our star. I bet you this dozen odd. This foluminous dozen odd. *Quas primas*—but 'tis bitter to compote my knowledge's fructos of. Tomes.

Elevating, to give peint to his blick, his jewelled pederect to the allmysty cielung, he luckystruck blueild out of a few shouldbe santillants, a cloister of starabouts over Maples, a lucciolys in Teresa street and a stopsign before Sophy Barratt's, he gaddered togodder the odds docence of his vellumes, gresk, letton and russicruxian, onto the lapse of his prolegs, into umfullth onescuppered, and sat about his widerproof He proved it well whoonearth dry and drysick times, and *vremiament, tu cesses*, to the extinction of Niklaus altogether (Niklaus Alopysius having been the once Gripes's popwilled nimbum) by Neuclidius and Inexagoras and Mumfsen and Thumpsem, by Orasmus and by Amenius, by Anacletus the Jew and by Malachy the Augurer and by the Cappon's collection and after that, with Cheekee's gelatine and Alldaybrandy's formolon, he reproved it ehrltogether when not in that order sundering in some different order, alter three thirty and a hundred times by the binomial dioram and the penic walls and the ind, the Inklespill legends and the rure, the rule of the hoop and the blessons of expedience and the jus, the jugicants of Pontius Pilax and all the mummyscrips in Sick Bokes' Juncroom and the Chapters for the Cunning of the Chapters of the Conning Fox by Tail.

While that Mooksius with preprocession and with proprecession, duplicitly and diplussedly, was promulgating ipsofacts and sadcontras this raskolly Gripos he had allbust seceded in monophysicking his illsobordunates. But asawfulas he had caught his base semenoyous sarchnaktiers to combuccinate upon the silipses of his aspillouts and the acheporeoozers of his haggyown pneumax to synerethetise with the breadchestviousness of his sweeatovular ducose sofarfully the loggerthuds of his sakellaries were fond at variance with the synodals of his somepooliom and his babskissed nepogreasymost got the hoof from his philioquus.

— Efter thousand yaws, O Gripes con my sheepskins, yow will be belined to the world, enscayed Mookse the pius.

— Ofter thousand yores, amsered Gripes the gregary, be the goat of MacHammud's, yours may be still, O Mookse, more botheared.

— Us shall be chosen as the first of the last by the electress of Vale Hollow, obselved the Mookse nobily, for par the unicum of Elelijiacks, Us am in Our stabulary and that is what Ruby and Roby fall for, blissim.

The Pills, the Nasal Wash (Yardly's), the Army Man Cut, as british as bondstrict and as straightcut as when that brokenarched traveller from Nuzuland . . .

— Wee, cumfused the Gripes limply, shall not even be the last of the first, wee hope, when oust are visitated by the Veiled Horror. And, he added: Mee are relying entirely, see the fortethurd of Elissabed, on the weightiness of mear's breath. Puffut!

Unsightbared embouscher, relentless foe to social and business succes! (Hourihaleine) It might have been a happy evening but . . .

And they viterberated each other, *canis et coluber* with the wildest ever wielded since Tarriestinus lashed Pissasphaltium.

— Unuchorn!

— Ungulant!

— Uvuloid!

— Uskybeak!

And bullfolly answered volleyball.

Nuvoletta in her lightdress, spunn of sixteen shimmers, was looking down on them, leaning over the bannistars and listening all she childishly could. How she was brightened when Shouldrups in his glaubering hochskied his welkinstuck and how she was overclused when Kneesknobs on his zwivvel was makeacting such a paulse of himshelp! She was alone. All her nubied companions were asleeping with the squirrels. Their mivver, Mrs Moonan, was off in the Fuerst quarter scrubbing the backsteps of Number 28. Fuvver, that Skand, he was up in Norwood's sokaparlour, eating oceans of Voking's Blemish. Nuvoletta listened as she reflected herself, though the heavenly one with his constellatria and his emanations stood between, and she tried all she tried to make the Mookse look up at her (but *he* was fore too adiaptotously farseeing) and to make the Gripes hear how coy she could be (though he was much too schystimatically auricular about *his ens* to heed her) but it was all mild's vapour moist. Not even her feignt reflection,

Nuvoluccia, could they toke their gnoses off for their minds with intrepi-
fide fate and bungless curiasity, were conclaved with Heliogobbleus and
Commodus and Enobarbarus and whatever the coordinal dickens they did
as their damprauch of papyrs and buchstubs said. As if that was their
spiration! As if theirs could duiparate her queendim! As if she would be
third perty to search on search proceedings! She tried all the winsome
wonsome ways her four winds had taught her. She tossed her sfuma-
stelliacinous hair like *le princesse de la Petite Bretagne* and she rounded her
mignons arms like Mrs Cornwallis-West and she smiled over herself like
the beauty of the image of the pose of the daughter of the queen of the
Emperour of Irelande and she sighed after herself as were she born to
bride with Tristis Tristior Tristissimus. But, sweet madonine, she might
fair as well have carried her daisy's worth to Florida. For the Mookse,
a dogmad Accanite, were not amoosed and the Gripes, a dubliboused
Catalick, wis pinefully obliviscent.

I see, she sighed. There are menner.

The siss of the whisp of the sigh of the softzing at the stir of the ver grose
O arundo of a long one in midias reeds: and shades began to glidder along
the banks, greepsing, greepsing, duusk unto duusk, and it was as glooming
as gloaming could be in the waste of all peacable worlds. Metamnisia was
allsoonome coloroform brune; citherior spiane an eaulande, innemorous
and unnumerose. The Mookse had a sound eyes right but he could not all
hear. The Gripes had light ears left yet he could but ill see. He ceased. And
he ceased, tung and trit, and it was neversoever so dusk of both of them. But
still Moo thought on the deeps of the undths he would profoundth come
the morrokse and still Gri feeled of the scripes he would escipe if by grice he
had luck enoupes.

Oh, how it was duusk! From Vallee Maraia to Grasyaplaina, dormimust
echo! Ah dew! Ah dew! It was so duusk that the tears of night began to fall,
first by ones and twos, then by threes and fours, at last by fives and sixes of
sevens, for the tired ones were wecking, as we weep now with them. *O! O!
O! Par la pluie!*

Then there came down to the thither bank a woman of no appearance (I
believe she was a Black with chills at her feet) and she gathered up his
hoariness the Mookse motamourfully where he was spread and carried him
away to her invisible dwelling, thats hights, *Aquila Rapax*, for he was the
holy sacred solem and poshup spit of her boshop's apron. So you see the
Mookse he had reason as I knew and you knew and he knew all along. And
there came down to the hither bank a woman to all important (though they
say that she was comely, spite the cold in her heed) and, for he was as like it

as blow it to a hawker's hank, she plucked down the Gripes, torn panicky autotone, in angeu from his limb and cariad away its beotitubes with her to her unseen shieling, it is, *De Rore Coeli*. And so the poor Gripes got wrong; for that is always how a Gripes is, always was and always will.be. And it was never so thoughtful of either of them. And there were left now an only elmtree and but a stone. Polled with pietrous, Sierre but saule. O! Yes! And Nuvoletta, a lass.

Then Nuvoletta reflected for the last time in her little long life and she made up all her myriads of drifting minds in one. She cancelled all her engauzements. She climbed over the bannistars; she gave a childy cloudy cry: *Nuée! Nuée!* A lightdress fluttered. She was gone. And into the river that had been a stream (for a thousand of tears had gone eon her and come on her and she was stout and struck on dancing and her muddied name was Missisliffi) there fell a tear, a singult tear, the loveliest of all tears (I mean for those crylove fables fans who are 'keen' on the prettypretty commonface sort of thing you meet by hopeharrods) for it was a leaptear. But the river tripped on her by and by, lapping as though her heart was brook: *Why, why, why! Weh, O weh I'se so silly to be flowing but I no canna stay!*

No applause, please! Bast! The romescot nattleshaker will go round your circulation in *diu dursus*.

Allaboy, Major, I'll take your reactions in another place after themes. Nolan Browne, you may now leave the classroom. Joe, Peters, Fox.

As I have now successfully explained to you my own naturalborn rations which are even in excise of my vaultybrain insure me that I am a mouth's more deserving case by genius. I feel in symbathos for my ever devoted friend and halfaloafonwashed, Gnaccus Gnoccovitch. Darling gem! Darling smallfox! Horoseshoew! I could love that man like my own ambo for being so baileycliaver though he's a nawful curillass and I must slav to methodiousness. I want him to go and live like a theabild in charge of the night brigade on Tristan da Cunha, isle of manoverboard, where he'll make Number 106 and be near Inaccessible. (The meeting of mahoganies, be the waves, rementious me that this exposed sight though it pines for an umbrella of its own and needs a shelter belt of the true service sort to keep its boles clean,—the weeping beeches, Picea and Tillia, are in a wild state about it— ought to be classified, as Cricketbutt Willowm and his two nurserymen advisers suggested, under genus Inexhaustible when we refloat upon all the butternat, sweet gum and manna ash redcedara which is so purvulent there as if there was howthorns in Curraghchasa which ought to look as plane as a lodgepole to anybody until we are introduced to that pinetacotta of Verney Rubeus where the deodarty is pinctured for us in a pure stand, which we do not doubt ha has a habitat of doing, but without those selfsownseedlings which are a species of proof that the largest individual *can* occur at or in an olivetion such as East Conna Hillock where it mixes with foolth accacians and common sallies and is tender) *Vux Populus*, as we say in hickoryhockery and I wish we had some more glasses of *arbor vitae*. Why roat by the roadside or awn over alum pot? Alderman Whitebeaver is dakyo. He ought to go away for a change of ideas and he'd have a world of things to look back on. Do, sweet Daniel! If I weren't a jones in myself I'd elect myself to be his dolphin in the wildsbillow because he is such a barefooted rubber with my supersocks pulled over his face which I publicked in my bestback garden for the laetification of siderodromites and to the irony of the stars. You will say it is most unenglish and I shall hope to hear that you will not be wrong about it. But I further, feeling a bit husky in my truths.

Will you please come over and let us mooremoore murgessly to each's other down below our vices. I am underheerd by old billfaust. Wilsh is full of curks. The coolskittle is philip deblinite. Mr Wist is thereover beyeind the wantnot. Wilsh and wist are as thick of thins udder as faust on the deblinite. Sgunoshooto estas preter la tapizo malgranda. Lilegas al si en sia chambro. Kelkefoje funcktas, kelkefoje srumpas Shultroj. Houdian Kiel vi fartas, mia nigra sinjoro? And from the poignt of fun where I am crying to arrive you at they are on allfore as foibleminded as you can feel they are fablebodied.

My heeders will recoil with a great leisure how at the outbreak before trespassing on the space question where even michelangelines have fooled to dread I proved to mindself as to your sotisfiction how his abject all through (the *quickquid* of Professor Ciondolone's too frequently hypothecated *Bettlermensch*) is nothing so much more than a mere cashdime however genteel he may want ours, if we please (I am speaking to us in the second person), for to this graded intellecktuals dime is cash and the cash system (you must not be allowed to forget that this is all contained, I mean the system, in the dogmarks of origen on spurios) means that I cannot now have or nothave a piece of cheeps in your pocket at the same time and with the same manners as you can now nothalf or half the cheek apiece I've in mind unless Burrus and Caseous have not or not have seemaultaneously sysentangled themselves, selldear to soldthere, once in the dairy days of buy and buy.

Burrus, let us like to imagine, is a genuine prime, the real choice, full of natural greace, the mildest of milkstoffs yet unbeaten as a risicide and, of course, obsoletely unadulterous whereat Caseous is obversely the revise of him and in fact not an ideal choose by any meals, though the betterman of the two is meltingly addicted to the more casual side of the arrivaliste case and, let me say it at once, as zealous over him as is passably he. The seemsame home and histry seeks and hidepence which we used to be reading for our prepurgatory, hot, Schott? till Duddy shut the shopper op and Mutti, poor Mutti! brought us our poor suppy, (ah who! eh how!) in Acetius and Oleosus and Sellius Volatilis and Petrus Papricus! Our Old Party quite united round the Slatbowel at Commons: Pfarrer Salamoss himself and that sprog of a Pedersill and his Sprig of Thyme and a dozen of the Murphybuds and a score and more of the hot young Capels and Lettucia in her green-sleeves and you too and me three, twinsome bibs but hansome ates, like shakespill and eggs! But there's many a split pretext bowl and jowl; and (snob screwing that cork, Schott!) to understand this as well as you can, feeling how backward you are in your down-to-the-ground benches, I have completed the following arrangement for the coarse use of stools and if I don't make away with you I'm beyond Caesar outnulused.

The older sisars (Tyrants, regicide is too good for you!) become un-beurrable from age, (the compositor of the farce of dustiny however makes a thunpledrum mistake by letting off this pienofarte effect as his furst act as that is where the juke comes in) having been sort-of-nineknived and chewly removed (this soldier-author-batman for all his commontoryism is just another of those souftsiezed bubbles who never quite got the sandhurst out of his eyes so that the champaign he draws for us is as flop as a plankrieg) the twinfreer types are billed to make their reupprearance as the knew kneck and knife knickknots on the deserted *champ de bouteilles*. (A most cursery reading into the Persic-Uraliens hostery shows us how Fonnumag—ula picked up that propper numen out of a coll:ction of prifixes though to the permienting cannasure the Coucousien oafsprung of this sun of a kuk is as sattin as there's a tub in Tobolosk) *Ostiak della Vogul Marina!* But that I dannoy the fact of wanton to weste point I could paint you to that butter (cheese it!) if you had some wash. Mordvealive! Oh me none onsens! Why the case is as inessive and impossive as kezom hands! Their interlocative is conprovocative just as every hazzy hates to having a hazbane in her noze. Caseous may bethink himself a thought of a caviller but Burrus has the reachly roundered head that goes best with thofthinking defensive fideism. He has the lac of wisdom under every dent in his lofter while the other follow's onni vesy milky indeedmymy. Laughing over the linnuts and weeping off the uniun. He hisn't the hey og he lisn't the lug, poohoo. And each night sim misses mand he winks he had the semagen. It was aptly and corrigidly stated (and, it is royally needless for one *ex ungue Leonem* to say by whom) that his seeingscraft was that clarety as were the wholeborough of

Poutresbourg to be averlaunched over him pitchbatch he could still make out with his augstritch the green moat in Ireland's Eye. Let me sell you the fulltroth of Burrus when he wore a younker. Here it is, and chorming too, in six by sevens! A cleanly line, by the gods! A king off duty and a jaw for ever! And what a cheery ripe outlook, good help me Deus v Deus! If I were to speak my ohole mouthful to arinam about it you should call me the ormuzd aliment in your midst of faime. Eat ye up, heat ye up! sings the somun in the salm. *Butyrum et mel comedet ut sciat reprobare malum et eligere bonum.* This, of course, also explains why we were taught to play in the childhood: *Der Haensli ist ern Butterbrot, mein Butterbrot! Und Koebi iss dein Schtinkenkot! Ja! Ja! Ja!*

This in fact, just to show you, is Caseous, the brutherscutch or puir tyron: a hole or two, the highstinks aforefelt and anygo prigging wurms. Cheesugh! you complain. And Hi Hi High must say you are not Hoa Hoa Hoally in the wrong!

Thus we cannot escape our likes and mislikes, exiles or ambusheers, beggar and neighbour and—this is where the dimeshow advertisers advance the temporal relief plea—let us be tolerant of antipathies. *Nex quovis burro num fit mercaseus?* I am not hereby giving my final endorsement to the learned ignorants of the Cusanus philosophism in which old Nicholas pegs it down that the smarter the spin of the top the sounder the span of the buttom (what the worthy old auberginiste ought to have meant was: the more stolidly immobile *in space* appears to me the bottom which is presented to use in time by the top primomobilisk &c.). And I shall be misunderstord if understood to give an unconditional sinequam to the heroicised furibouts of the Nolanus theory, or, at any rate, of that substrate of apart from hissheory where the Theophil swoors that on principial he was the pointing start of his odiose by comparison and that whiles eggs will fall cheapened all over the walled the Bure will be dear on the Brie.

Now, while I am not out now to be taken up as unintentionally recommending the Silkebjorg tyrondynamon machine for the more economical helixtrolysis of these amboadipates until I can find space to look into it myself a little more closely first I shall go on with my decisions after having shown to you in good time how both products of our social stomach (the excellent Dr Burroman, I noticed by the way from his emended food theory, has been carefully digesting the very wholesome criticism I helped him to in my princeps edition which is all so munch to the cud) are mutuearly polarised the incompatabilily of any delusional acting as ambivalent to the fixation of his pivotism. Positing, as above, too males pooles, the one the pictor of the other and the omber the *Skotia* of the one, and looking wantingly around our undistributed middle between males we feel we must waistfully woent a female to focus and on this stage there pleasantly appears the cowrymaid M. whom we shall often meet below who introduces herself upon us at some precise hour which we shall again agree to call absolute zero or the babbling pumpt of platinism. And so like that former son of a kish who went up and out to found his farmer's ashes we come down home gently on our own turnedabout asses to meet Margareen.

We now romp through a period of pure lyricism of shamebred music (technologically, let me say, the appetising entry of this subject on a fool chest of vialds is plumply pudding the carp before doevre hors) evidenced by such words in distress as *I cream for thee, Sweet Margareen*, and the more hopeful *O Margareena! O Margareena! Still in the bowl is left a lump of gold!* (Correspondents, by the way, will keep on asking me what is the correct garnish to serve drisheens with. Tansy Sauce. Enough.) The pawnbreaking pathos of the first of these shoddy pieces reveals it as a Caseous effort. Burrus's bit is often used for a toast. Criniculture can tell us very precisely indeed how and why this particular streak of yellow silver first appeared on (not in) the bowel, that is to see, the human head, bald, black, bronze, brown, brindled, betteraved or blanchemanged where it might be usefully compared with an earwig on a fullbottom. I am offering this to Signorina Cuticura and I intend to take it up and bring it under the nosetice of Herr Harlene by way of diverting his attentions. Of course the unskilled singer continues to pervert our wiser ears by subordinating the space-element, that is to sing, the *aria*, to the time-factor, which ought to be killed, *ill tempor*. I should advise any unborn singer who may still be among my heeders to forget her temporal diaphragm at home (the best thing that could happen to it!) and attack the roulade with a swift *colpo di glottide* to the lug (though Maace I will insist was reclined from overdoing this, his recovery often being slow) and then, O! on the third dead beat, O! to cluse her eyes and aiopen her oath and see what spice I may send her. How? Cease thee, cantatrickee! I fain would be solo. Arouse thee, my valour! And save for e'er my true Bdur!

I shall have a word to say in a few yards about the acoustic and orchidectural management of the tonehall but, as ours is a vivarious where one plant's breaf is a lunger planner's byscent and you may not care for argon, it will be very convenient for me for the emolument to pursue Burrus and Caseous for a rung or two up their isocelating biangle. Every admirer has seen my goulache of Marge (she is so like the sister, you don't know, and they both dress A L I K E!) which I titled *The Very Picture of a Needlesswoman* which in the presence ornates our national cruetstand. This genre of portraiture of changes of mind in order to be truly torse should evoke the bush soul of females so I am leaving it to the experienced victim to complete the general suggestion by the mental addition of a wallopy bound or, should the zulugical zealot prefer it, a congorool teal. The hatboxes which composed Rhomba, lady Trabezond (Marge in her *excelsis*), also comprised the climactogram up which B and C may fondly be imagined ascending and are suggestive of gentlemen's spring modes, these modes carrying us back to the superimposed claylayers of eocene and pleastoseen formation and the gradual morphological changes in our body politic which Professor Ebahi-Ahuri of Philadespoinis (Ill)—whose bluebutterbust I have just given his coupe de grass to—neatly names a *boîte à surprises*. The boxes, if I may break the subject gently, are worth about fourpence pourbox but I am inventing a more patent process, foolproof and pryperfect (I should like to ask that Shedlock Homes person who is out for removing the roofs of our criminal classics by what *deductio ad domunum* he hopes *de tacto* to detect anything unless he happens of himself, *movibile tectu*, to have a slade off) after which they can be reduced to a fragment of their true crust by even the youngest of Margees if she will take plase to be seated and smile if I please.

Now there can be no question about it either that I having done as much, have quite got the size of that demilitery young female (we will continue to call her Marge) whose types may be met with in any public garden, wearing a very "dressy" affair, known as an "ethel" of instep length and with a real fur, reduced to 3/9, and muffin cap to tone (they are "angelskin" this fall), ostentatiously hemming apologetically over the shirtness of some "sweet" garment, when she is not sitting on all the free benches avidously reading about "it" but ovidently on the look out for "him" or so "thrilled" about the best dressed dolly pram and beautiful elbow competition or at the movies swallowing sobs and blowing bixed mixcuits over "childe" chaplain's "latest" or on the verge of the gutter with some bobbedhair brieffrocked babyma's toddler (the Smythe-Smythes now keep TWO domestics and aspire to THREE male ones, a shover, a butlegger and a sectary) held hostage at armslength, teaching His Infant Majesty how to make waters worse.

(I am closely watching Master Pules, as I have regions to suspect from my post that her "litde man" is a secondary schoolteacher under the boards of education, a voted disciple of Infantulus who is being utilised thus publicly by the *seducente infanta* to conceal her own more mascular personality by flaunting frivolish finery over men's inside clothes, for the femininny of that totamulier will always lack the musculink of a verumvirum. My solotions for the proper parturience of matres and the education of micturious mites must stand over from the moment till I tackle this tickler hussy for occupying my uttentions.)

Margareena she's very fond of Burrus but, alick and alack! she velly fond of chee. (The important influence exercised on everything by this eastasian import has not been till now fully flavoured though we can comfortably taste it in this case. I shall come back for a little more say farther on.) A cleopatrician in her own right she at once complicates the position while Burrus and Caseous are contending for her misstery by implicating herself with an elusive Antonius, a wop who would appear to hug a personal interest in refined chees of all chades at the same time as he wags an antomine art of being rude like the boor. This Antonius-Burrus-Caseous grouptriad may be said to equate the *qualis* equivalent with the older socalled *talis* on *talis* one just as quantly as in the hyperchemical economantarchy the tantum ergons irruminate the quantum urge so that eggs is to whey as whay is to zeed like your golfchild's abe boob caddy. And this is why any simple philadolphus of a fool you like to dress, an athemisthued lowtownian, exlegged phatrisight, may be awfully green to one side of him and fruitfully blue on the other which will not screen him however from appealing to my gropesarching eyes, through the strongholes of my acropoll, as a boosted blasted bleating blatant bloaten blasphorus blesphorous idiot who kennot tail a bomb from a painapple when he steals one and wannot psing his psalmen with the cong in our gregational pompoms with the canting crew.

No! Topsman to your Tarpeia! This thing, Mister Abby, is nefand. (And, taking off soutstuffs and alkalike matters, I hope we can kill time to reach the salt because there's some forceglass neutric assets bittering in the sold-pewter for you to plump your pottage in). The thundering legion has stormed Olymp that it end. Twelve tabular times till now have I edicted it. Merus Genius to Careous Caseous! *Moriture, te salutat!* My phemous themis race is run, so let Demoncracy take the highmost! (Abraham Tripier. Those old diligences are quite out of date. Read next answer). I'll beat you so lon. (Bigtempered. Why not take direct action. See previous reply.) My unchanging Word is sacred. The word is my Wife, to exponse and expound, to vend and to velnerate, and may the curlews crown our nuptias! Till Breath us depart! Wamen. Beware would you change with my years. Be as young as your grandmother! The ring man in the rong shop but the rite words by the rote order! *Ubi lingua nuncupassit, ibi fas! Adversus hostem semper sac!* She that will not feel my fulmoon let her peel to thee as the hoyden and the impudent! That mon that hoth no moses in his sole nor is not awed by conquists of word's law, who never with humself was fed and leaves his soil to lave his head, when his hope's in his highlows from whisking his woe, if he came to my preach, a proud pursebroken ranger, when the heavens were welling the spite of their spout, to beg for a bite in our bark *Noisdanger,*

would meself and Mac Jeffet, four-in-hand, foot him out?—ay!—were he
my own breastbrother, my doubled withd love and my singlebiassed hate,
were we bread by the same fire and signed with the same salt, had we tapped
from the same master and robbed the same till, were we tucked in the one
bed and bit by the one flea, homogallant and hemycapnoise, bum and
dingo, jack by churl, though it broke my heart to pray it, still I'd fear I'd hate
to say!

  12. *Sacer esto?*

  Answer: *Semus sumus!*

[7]

SHEM IS AS SHORT FOR SHEMUS AS JEM IS JOKY FOR
Jacob. A few toughnecks are still getatable who pretend that aboriginally he
was of respectable stemming (he was an outlex between the lines of Ragonar
Blaubarb ant Horrild Hairwire and an inlaw to Capt. the Hon. and Rev. Mr
Bbyrdwood de Trop Blogg was among his most distant connections) but
every honest to goodness man in the land of the space of today knows that
his back life will not stand being written about in black and white. Putting
truth and untruth together a shot may be made at what this hybrid actually
was like to look at.

  Shem's bodily getup, it seems, included an adze of a skull, an eight of a
larkseye, the whoel of a nose, one numb arm up a sleeve, fortytwo hairs off
his uncrown, eighteen to his mock lip, a trio of barbels from his megageg
chin (sowman's son), the wrong shoulder higher than the right, all ears, an
artificial tongue with a natural curl, not a foot to stand on, a handful of
thumbs, a blind stomach, a deaf heart, a loose liver, two fifths of two
buttocks, one gleetsteen avoirdupoider for him, a manroot of all evil, a
salmonkelt's thinskin, eelsblood in his cold toes, a bladder tristended, so
much so that young Master Shemmy on his very first debouch at the very
dawn of protohistory seeing himself such and such, when playing with
thistlewords in their garden nursery, Griefotrofio, at Phig Streat III, Shuvlin,
Old Hoeland, (would we go back there now for sounds, pillings and sense?
would we now for annas and annas? would we for fullscore eight and a
liretta? for twelve blocks one bob? for four testers one groat? not for a
dinar! not for jo!) dictited to of all his little brothron and sweestureens the
first riddle of the universe: asking, when is a man not a man?: telling them
take their time, yungfries, and wait till the tide stops (for from the first his

day was a fortnight) and offering the prize of a bittersweet crab, a little present from the past, for their copper age was yet unminted, to the winner. One said when the heavens are quakers, a second said when Bohemeand lips, a third said when he, no, when hold hard a jiffy, when he is a gnawstick and detarmined to, the next one said when the angel of death kicks the bucket of life, still another said when the wine's at witsends, and still another when lovely wooman stoops to conk him, one of the littliest said me, me, Sem, when pappa papared the harbour, one of the wittiest said, when he yeat ye abblokooken and he zmear hezelf zo zhooken, still one said when you are old I'm grey fall full wi sleep, and still another when wee deader walkner, and another when he is just only after having being semisized, another when yea, he hath no mananas, and one when dose pigs they begin now that they will flies up intil the looft. All were wrong, so Shem himself, the doctator, took the cake, the correct solution being—all give it up?—; when he is a—yours till the rending of the rocks,—Sham.

Shem was a sham and a low sham and his lowness creeped out first via foodstuffs. So low was he that he preferred Gibsen's teatime salmon tinned, as inexpensive as pleasing, to the plumpest roeheavy lax or the friskiest parr or smolt troutlet that ever was gaffed between Leixlip and Island Bridge and many was the time he repeated in his botulism that no junglegrown pineapple ever smacked like the whoppers you shook out of Ananias' cans, Findlater and Gladstone's, Corner House, Englend. None of your inchthick blueblooded Balaclava fried-at-belief-stakes or juicejelly legs of the Grex's molten mutton or greasilygristly grunters' goupons or slice upon slab of luscious goosebosom with lump after load of plumpudding stuffing all aswim in a swamp of bogoakgravy for that greekenhearted yude! Rosbif of Old Zealand! he could not attouch it. See what happens when your somatophage merman takes his fancy to our virgitarian swan? He even ran away with hunself and became a farsoonerite, saying he would far sooner muddle through the hash of lentils in Europe than meddle with Irrland's split little pea. Once when among those rebels in a state of hopelessly helpless intoxication the piscivore strove to lift a czitround peel to either nostril, hiccupping, apparently impromptued by the hibat he had with his glottal stop, that he kukkakould flowrish for ever by the smell, as the czitr, as the kcedron, like a scedar, of the founts, on mountains, with limon on, of Lebanon. O! the lowness of him was beneath all up to that sunk to! No likedbylike firewater or firstserved firstshot or gulletburn gin or honest brewbarrett beer either. O dear no! Instead the tragic jester sobbed himself wheywhingingly sick of life on some sort of a rhubarbarous maundarin yellagreen funkleblue windigut diodying applejack squeezed from sour

grapefruice and, to hear him twixt his sedimental cupslips when he had
gulfed down mmmmuch too mmmmany gourds of it retching off to almost
as low withswillers, who always knew notwithstanding when they had had
enough and were rightly indignant at the wretch's hospitality when they
found to their horror they could not carry another drop, it came straight
from the noble white fat, jo, openwide sat, jo, jo, her why hide that, jo jo jo,
the winevat, of the most serene magyansty az archdiochesse, if she is a duck,
she's a douches, and when she has a feherbour snot her fault, now is it?
artstouchups, funny you're grinning at, fancy you're in her yet, Fanny
Urinia.

Aint that swell, hey? Peamengro! Talk about lowness! Any dog's quantity
of it visibly oozed out thickly from this dirty little blacking beetle for the
very fourth snap the Tulloch-Turnbull girl with her coldblood kodak
shotted the as yet unremuneranded national apostate, who was cowardly
gun and camera shy, taking what he fondly thought was a short cut to Caer
Fere, Soak Amerigas, vias the shipsteam *Pridewin*, after having buried a
hatchet not so long before, by the wrong goods exeunt, nummer desh to
tren, into Patatapapaveri's, fruiterers and musical florists, with his *Ciaho,
chavi! Sat shin, shillipen?* she knew the vice out of bridewell was a bad fast
man by his walk on the spot.

[Johns is a different butcher's. Next place you are up town pay him a visit.
Or better still, come tobuy. You will enjoy cattlemen's spring meat. Johns is
now quite divorced from baking. Fattens, kills, flays, hangs, draws, quarters
and pieces. Feel his lambs! Ex! Feel how sheap! Exex! His liver too is great
value, a spatiality! Exexex! COMMUNICATED.]

Around that time, moravar, one generally, for luvvomony hoped or at
any rate suspected among morticians that he would early tum out badly,
develop hereditary pulmonary T.B., and do for himself one dandy time,
nay, of a pelting night blanketed creditors, hearing a coarse song and splash
off Eden Quay sighed and rolled over, sure all was up, but, though he fell
heavily and locally into debit, not even then could such an antinomian be
true to type. He would not put fire to his cerebrum; he would not throw
himself in Liffey; he would not explaud himself with pneumantics; he refused
to saffrocake himself with a sod. With the foreign devil's leave the fraid bom
fraud diddled even death. *Anzi,* cabled (but shaking the worth out of his
maulth: Guardacosta leporello? Szasas Kraicz!) from his Nearapoblican
asylum to his jonathan for a brother: Here tokay, gone tomory, we're
spluched, do something, Fireless. And had answer: Inconvenient, David.

You see, chaps, it will trickle out, freaksily of course, but the tom and the
shorty of it is: he was in his bardic memory low. All the time he kept on

treasuring with condign satisfaction each and every crumb of trektalk, covetous of his neighbour's word, and if ever, during a Munda conversazione commoted in the nation's interest, delicate tippits were thrown out to him touching his evil courses by some wellwishers, vainly pleading by scriptural arguments with the opprobrious papist about trying to brace up for the kidos of the thing, Scally wag, and be a men instead of a dem scrounger, dish it all, such as: Pray, what is the meaning, sousy, of that continental expression, if you ever came acrux it, we think it is a word transpiciously like *canaille?*: or: Did you anywhere, kennel, on your gullible's travels or during your rural troubadouring, happen to stumble upon a certain gay young nobleman whimpering to the name of Low Swine who always addresses women out of the one comer of his mouth, lives on loans and is furtivefree yours of age? without one sigh of haste like the supreme prig he was, and not a bit sorry, he would pull a vacant landlubber's face, root with earwaker's pensile in the outer of his lauscher and then, lisping, the prattlepate parnella, to kill time, and swatting his deadbest to think what under the canopies of Jansens Chrest would any decent son of an Albiogenselman who had bin to an university think, let a lent hit a hint and begin to tell all the intelligentsia admitted to that tamileasy samtalaisy conclamazzione (since, still and before physicians, lawyers merchant, belfry pollitians, agricolous manufraudurers, sacrestanes of the Pure River Society, philanthropicks lodging on as many boards round the panesthetic at the same time as possible) the whole lifelong swrine story of his entire low cornaille existence, abusing his deceased ancestors wherever the sods were and one moment tarabooming great blunderguns (poh!) about his farfamed fine Poppamore, Mr Humhum, whom history, climate and entertainment made the first of his sept and always up to debt, though Eavens ears ow many fines he faces, and another moment visanvrerssas, cruaching three jeers (pah!) for his rotten little ghost of a Peppybeg, Mr Himmyshimmy, a blighty, a reeky, a lighty, a scrapy, a babbly, a ninny, dirty seventh among thieves and always bottom sawyer, till nowan knowed how howmely howme could be, giving unsolicited testimony on behalf of the absent, as glib as eaveswater to those present (who meanwhile, with increasing lack of interest in his semantics, allowed various subconscious smickers to drivel slowly across their fichers), unconsciously explaining, for inkstands, with a meticulosity bordering on the insane, the various meanings of all the different foreign parts of speech he misused and cuttlefishing every lie unshrinkable about all the other people in the story, leaving out, of course, foreconsciously, the simple worf and plague and poison they had cornered him about until there was not a snoozer among them but was utterly undeceived in the heel of the reel by the recital of the rigmarole.

He went without saying that the cull disliked anything anyway approaching a plain straightforward standup or knockdown row and, as often as he was called in to umpire any octagonal argument among slangwhangers, the accomplished washout always used to rub shoulders with the last speaker and clasp shakers (the handtouch which is speech without words) and agree to every word as soon as half uttered, command me!, your servant, good, I revere you, how, my seer? be drinking that! quite truth, gratias, I'm yoush, see wha'm hearing?, also goods, please it, me sure?, be filling this!, quiso, you said it, apasafello, muchas grassyass, is there firing-on-me?, is their girlic-on-you?, to your good self, your sulphur, and then at once focuss his whole unbalanced attention upon the next octagonist who managed to catch a listener's eye, asking and imploring him out of his piteous onewinker, (*hemoptysia diadumenos*) whether there was anything in the world he could do to please him and to overflow his tumbletantaliser for him yet once more.

One hailcannon night (for his departure was attended by a heavy downpour) as very recently as some thousand rains ago he was therefore treated with what closely resembled parsonal violence, being soggert all unsuspectingly through the deserted village of Tumblin-on-the-Leafy from Mr Vanhomrigh's house at 81 bis Mabbot's Mall as far as Green Patch beyond the brickfields of Salmon Pool by rival teams of slowspiers counter quicklimers who finally, as rahilly they had been deteened out rawther laetich, thought, busnis hits busnis, they had better be streaking for home after their Auborne-to-Auborne, with thanks for the pleasant evening, one and all disgustedly, instead of ruggering him back, and awake, reconciled (though they were as jealous as could be cullions about all the truffles they had brought on him) to a friendship, fast and furious, which merely arose out of the noxious pervert's perfect lowness. Again there was a hope that people, looking on him with the contemp of the contempibles, after first gaving him a roll in the dirt, might pity and forgive him, if properly deloused, but the pleb was born a Quicklow and sank alowing till he stank out of sight.

All Saints beat Belial! Mickil Goals to Nichil! Notpossible! Already?
In Nowhere has yet the Whole World taken part of himself for his Wife;
By Nowhere have Poorparents been sentenced to Worms, Blood and Thunder
for Life
Not yet has the Emp from Corpsica forced the Arth out of Engleterre;
Not yet have the Sachsen and Judder on the Mound of a Word made Warre;
Not yet Witchywithcy of Wench struck Fire of his Heath from on Hoath;
Not yet his Arcobaleine forespoken Peacepeace upon Oath;

Cleftfoot from Hempal must tumpel, Blamefool Gardener's bound to fall;
Broken Eggs will poursuive bitten Apples for where theirs is Will there's his Wall;
But the Mountstill frowns on the Millstream while their Madsons leap his Bier
And her Rillstrill liffs to His Murkesty all her daft Daughters laff in her Ear.
Till the four Shores of deff Tory Island let the douze dumm Eirewhiggs raille!
Hirp! Hirp! for their Missed Understandings! chirps the Ballat of Perce-Oreille.

O fortunous casualitas! Lefty takes the cherubcake while Rights cloves his hoof Darkies never done tug that coon out to play non-excretory, anti-sexuous, misoxenetic, gaasy pure, flesh and blood games, written and composed and sung and danced by Niscemus Nemon, same as piccaninnies play all day, those old (none of your honeys and rubbers!) games for fun and element we used to play with Dina and old Joe kicking her behind and before and the yellow girl kicking him behind old Joe, games like *Thom Thom the Thonderman, Put the Wind up the Peeler, Hat in the Ring, Prisson your Pritchards and Play Withers Team, Mikel on the Luckypig, Nickel in the Slot, Sheila Harnett and her Cow, Adam and Ell, Humble Bumble, Moggie's on the Wall, Twos and Threes, American Jump, Fox Come out of your Den, Broken Bottles, Writing a Letter to Punch, Tiptop is a Sweetstore, Henressy Crump Expolled, Postman's Knock, Are We Fairlys Represented?, Solomon Silent reading, Appletree Bearstone, I know a Washerwoman, Hospitals, As I was Walking, There is Oneyone's House in Dreamcolohour, Battle of Waterloo, Colours, Eggs in the Bush, Habberdasherisher, Telling your Dreams, What's the Time, Nap, Ducking Mammy, Last Man Standing, Heali Baboon and the Forky Theagues, Fickleyes and Futilears, Handmarried but once in my Life and I'll never commit such a Sin agin, Zip Cooney Candy, Turkey in the Straw, This is the Way we sow the Seed of a long and lusty Morning, Hops of Fun at Miliken's Make, I seen the Toothbrush with Pat Farrel, Here's the Fat to graze the Priest's Boots, When his Steam was like a Raimbrandt round Mac Garvey.*

Now it is notoriously known how on that surprisingly bludgeony Unity Sunday when the grand germogall allstar bout was harrily the rage between our weltingtoms extraordinary and our pettythicks the marshalaisy and Irish eyes of welcome were smiling daggers down their backs, when the roth, vice and blause met the noyr blank and rogues and the grim white and cold bet the black fighting tans, categorically unimperatived by the maxims, a rank funk getting the better of him, the scut in a bad fit of pyjamas fled like a leveret for his bare lives, to Talviland, ahone ahaza, pursued by the scented curses of all the village belles and, without having struck one blow, (pig stole on him was lust he lagging it was becaused dust he shook) kuskykorked himself up tight in his inkbattle house, badly the worse for boosegas, there to stay in afar for the life, where, as there was not a moment to be lost, after

he had boxed around with his fortepiano till he was whole bach bamp
him and bump him blues, he collapsed carefully under a bedtick from
Schwitzer's, his face enveloped into a dead warrior's telemac, with a
lullobaw's somnbomnet and a whotwaterwottle at his feet to stoke his
energy of waiting, moaning feebly, in monkmarian monotheme, but tarned
long and then a nation louder, while engaged in swallowing from a large
ampullar, that his pawdry's purgatory was more than a nigger bloke could
bear, hemiparalysed by the tong warfare and all the shemozzle, (*Daily Maily*,
fullup Lace! Holy Maly, Mothelup Joss!) his cheeks and trousers changing
colour every time a gat croaked.

How is that for low, laities and gentlenuns? Why, dog of the Crostiguns,
whole continents rang with this Kairokorran lowness! Sheols of houris in
chems upon divans, (revolted stellas vespertine vesamong them) at a bare
(O!) mention of the scaly rybald exclaimed: Poisse!

But would anyone, short of a madhouse, believe it? Neither of those
clean little cherubum, Nero or Nobookisonester himself, ever nursed such
a spoiled opinion of his monstrous marvellosity as did this mental and moral
defective (here perhaps at the vanessance of his lownest) who was known to
grognt rather than gunnard upon one occasion, while drinking heavily of
spirits to that interlocutor *a latere* and private privysuckatary he used to pal
around with, in the kavehazs, one Davy Browne-Nowlan, his heavenlaid
twin, (this hambone dogpoet pseudoed himself under the hangname he
gave himself of Bethgelert) in the porchway of a gipsy's bar (Shem always
blaspheming, so holy writ, Billy, he would try, old Belly, and pay this one
manjack congregant of his four soups every lass of nexmouth, Bolly, so sure
as thair's a tail on a commet, as a taste for storik's fortytooth, that is to stay,
to listen out, ony twenny minnies moe, Bully, his Ballade Imaginaire which
was to be dubbed *Wine, Woman and Waterclocks*, or *How a Guy Finks and
Fawkes When He Is Going Batty*, by Maistre Sheames de la Plume, some
most dreadful stuff in a murderous mirrorhand) that he was avoopf (parn
me!) aware of no other shaggspick, other Shakhisbeard, either prexactly
unlike his polar andthisishis or procisely the seem as woops (parn!) as what
he fancied or guessed the sames as he was himself and that, greet scoot,
duckings and thuggery, though he was foxed fux to fux like a bunnyboy
rodger with all the teashop lionses of Lumdrum hivanhoesed up gagainst
him, being a lapsis linquo with a ruvidubb shortartempa, bad cad dad fad sad
mad nad vanhaty bear, the consciquenchers of casuality prepestered cruss-
words in postposition, scruff, scruffer, scrufferumurraimost andallthatsort-
ofthing, if reams stood to reason and his lankalivline lasted he would wipe
alley english spooker, multaphoniaksically spuking, off the face of the erse.

After the thorough fright he got that bloody, Swithun's day, though every doorpost in muchtried Lucalizod was smeared with generous erstborn gore and every free for all cobbleway slippery with the bloods of heroes, crying to Welkins for others, and noahs and cul verts agush with tears of joy, our low waster never had the common baalamb's pluck to stir out and about the com-pound while everyone else of the torchlit throng, slashers and sliced alike, mobbu on massa, waaded and baaded around, yampyam pampyam, chanting the Gillooly chorus, from the Monster Book of Paltryattic Puetrie, *O pura e pia bella!* in junk et sampam or in secular sinkalarum, heads up, on his bonafide avocation (the little folk creeping on all fours to their natural school treat but childishly gleeful when a stray whizzer sang out intermediately) and happy belongers to the fairer sex on their usual quest for higher things, but vying with Lady Smythe to avenge MacJobber, went stonestepping with their bickerrstaffs on educated feet, plinkity plonk, across the sevenspan ponte *dei colori* set up over the slop after the war-to-end war by Messrs a charitable government for the only once (dia dose Finnados!) he did take a tompip peepestrella throug a threedraw eighteen hawkspower durdicky telescope, luminous to larbourd only like the lamps in Nassaustrass, out of his westernmost keyhole, spitting at the impenetrablum wetter, (and it was porcoghastly that outumn) with an eachway hope in his shivering soul, as he prayed to the cloud Incertitude, of finding out for himself, on akkount of all the kules in Kroukaparka or oving to all the kodseoggs in Kalatavala, whether true conciliation was forging ahead or falling back after the celestious intemperance and, for Duvvelsache, why, with his see me see and his my see a corves and his frokerfoskerfuskar layen loves in meeingseeing, he got the charm of his optical life when he found himself (*hic sunt lennones!*) at pointblank range blinking down the barrel of an irregular revolver of the bulldog with a purpose pattern, handled by an unknown quarreler who, supposedly, had been told off to shade and shoot shy Shem should the shit show his shiny shnout out awhile to look facts in their face before being hosed and creased (uprip and jack him!) by six or a dozen of the gayboys.

What, para Saom Plaom, in the names of Deucalion and Pyrrha, and the incensed privy and the licensed pantry gods and Stator and Victor and Kutt and Runn and the whole mesa redonda of Lorencao Otulass in convocacaon, was this disinterestingly low human type, this Calumnious Column of Cloaxity, this Bengalese Beacon of Biloxity, this Annamite Aper of Atroxity, really at, it will be precise to quarify, for he seems in a badbad case?

The answer, to do all the diddies in one dedal, would sound: from pulling himself on his most flavoured canal the huge chesthouse of his elders (the

Popapreta, and some navico, navvies!) he had flickered up and flinnered down into a drug and drunkery addict, growing megalomane of a loose past. This explains the litany of septuncial lettertrumpets honorific, highpitched, erudite, neoclassical, which he so loved as patricianly to manuscribe after his name. It would have diverted, if ever seen, the shuddersome spectacle of this semidemented zany amid the inspissated grime of his glaucous den making believe to read his usylessly unreadable Blue Book of Eccles, *édition de ténèbres*, (even yet sighs the Most Different, Dr Poindejenk, authorised bowdler and censor, it can't be repeated!) turning over three sheets at a wind, telling himself delightedly, no espellor mor so, that every splurge on the vellum he blundered over was an aisling vision more gorgeous than the one before t.i.t.s., a roseschelle cottage by the sea for nothing for ever, a ladies tryon hosiery raffle at liberty, a sewerful of guineagold wine with brancomongepadenopie and sickcylinder oysters worth a billion a bite, an entire operahouse (there was to be stamping room only in the prompter's box and everthemore his queque kept swelling) of enthusiastic noblewomen flinging every coronetcrimsoned stitch they had off at his probscenium, one after the others, inamagoaded into ajustilloosing themselves, in their gaiety pantheomime, when, egad, sir, acordant to all acountstrick, he squealed the topsquall im *Deal Lil Shemlockup Yellin* (geewhiz, jew ear that far! soap ewer! loutgout of sabaous! juice like a boyd!) for fully five minutes infinitely better than Baraton Mc Gluckin with a scrumptious cocked hat and three green, cheese and tangerine trinity plumes on the right handle side of his amarellous head, a coat macfarlane (the kersssest cut, you understand?) a sponiard's digger at his ribs, (*Alfaiate punxit*) an azulblu blowsheet for his blousebosom blossom and a dean's crozier that he won from Cardinal Lindundarri and Cardinal Carchingarri and Cardinal Loriotuli and Cardinal Occidentaccia (ah ho!) in the dearby darby doubled for falling first over the hurdles, madam, in the odder hand, a.a.t.s.o.t., but what with the murky light, the botchy print, the tattered cover, the jigjagged page, the fumbling fingers, the foxtrotting fleas, the lieabed lice, the scum on his tongue, the drop in his eye, the lump in his throat, the drink in his pottle, the itch in his palm, the wail of his wind, the grief from his breath, the fog of his mindfag, the buzz in his braintree, the tic of his conscience, the height up his rage, the gush down his fundament, the fire in his gorge, the tickle of his tail, the bane in his bullugs, the squince in his suil, the rot in his eater, the ycho in his earer, the totters of his toes, the tetters on his tumtytum, the rats in his garret, the bats in his belfry, the budgerigars and bumbosolom beaubirds, the hullabaloo and the dust in his ears since it took him a month to steal a march he was hardset to mumorise more than a word a week. Hake's haulin! Hook's fisk! Can you beat it? Whawe! I say, can you bait it? Was there ever heard of such lowdown blackguardism? Positively it woolies one to think over it.

Yet the bumpersprinkler used to boast aloud alone to himself with a haccent on it when Mynfadher was a boer constructor and Hoy was a lexical student, parole, and corrected with the blackboard (trying to copy the stage Englesemen he broughts their house down on, shouting: Bravure, surr Chorles! Letter purfect! Culossal, Loose Wallor! Spache!) how he had been toed out of all the schicker families of the klondykers from Pioupioureich, Swabspays, the land of Nod, Shruggers' Country, Pension Danubierhome and Barbaropolis, who had settled and stratified in the capital city after its hebdomodary metropoliarchialisation as sunblistered, moonplastered, gory, wheedling, joviale, litcherous and full, ordered off the gorgeous premises in most cases on account of his smell which all cookmaids eminently objected to as ressembling the bombinubble puzzo that welled out of the pozzo. Instead of chuthoring those model households plain wholesome pothooks (a thing he never possessed of his Nigerian own) what do you think Vulgariano did but study with stolen fruit how cutely to copy all their various styles of signature so as one day to utter an epical forged cheque on the public for his own private profit until, as just related, the Dustbin's United Scullerymaid's and Househelp's Sorority, better known as Sluttery's Mowlted Futt, turned him down and assisted nature by unitedly shoeing the source of annoyance out of the place altogether and taytotally on the heat of the moment, holding one another's gonk (for no-one, hound or scrublady, not even the Turk, ungreekable in purscent of the armenable, dared whiff the polecat at close range) and making some pointopointing remarks as they done so at the perfects of the Sniffey, your honour, aboon the lyow why a stunk, mister.

[Jymes wishes to hear from wearers of abandoned female costumes, gratefully received, wadmel jumper, rather full pair of culottes and onthergarmenteries, to start city life together. His jymes is out of job, would sit and write. He has lately commited one of the then commandments but she will now assist. Superior built, domestic, regular layer. Also got the boot. He appreciates it. Copies. ABORTISEMENT.]

One cannot even begin to post figure out a statuesquo ante as to how slow in reality the excommunicated Drumcondriac, nate Hamis, really was. Who can say how many pseudostylic shamiana, how few or how many of the most venerated public impostures, how very many piously forged palimpsests slipped in the first place by this morbid process from his pelagiarist pen?

Be that as it may, but for that light phantastic of his gnose's glow as it slid lucifericiously within an inch of its page (he would touch at its from time to other, the red eye of his fear in saddishness, to ensign the colours by the beerlitz in his mathness and his educandees to outhue to themselves in the cries of girlglee: gember! inkware! chonchambre! cinsero! zinnzabar! tincture and gin!) Nibs never would have quilled a seriph to sheepskin. By that rosy lampoon's effluvious burning and with help of the simulchronic flush in his pann (a ghinee a ghirk he ghets there!) he scrabbled and scratched and scriobbled and skrevened nameless shamelessness about everybody ever he met, even sharing a precipitation under the idlish tarriers' umbrella of a showerproof wall, while all over up and down the four margins of this rancid Shem stuff the evilsmeller (who was devoted to Uldfadar Sardanapalus) used to stipple endlessly inartistic portraits of himself in the act of reciting old Nichiabelli's monolook interyerear *Hanno, o Nonanno, acce'l brubblemm'*as, ser Autore, q.e.d., a heartbreakingly handsome young paolo with love lyrics for the goyls in his eyols, a plaintiff's tanner vuice, a jucal inkome of one hundred and thirtytwo dranchmas per yard from Broken Hill stranded estate, Camebreech mannings, cutting a great dash in a brandnew two guinea dress suit and a burled hogsford hired for a Fursday evenin merry pawty, anna loavely long pair of inky Italian moostarshes glistering with boric vaseline and frangipani. Puh! How unwhisperably so!

The house O'Shea or O'Shame, *Quivapieno*, known as the Haunted Inkbottle, no number Brimstone Walk, Asia in Ireland, as it was infested with the raps, with his penname SHUT sepiascraped on the doorplate and a blind of black sailcloth over its wan phwinshogue, in which the soul-contracted son of the secret cell groped through life at the expense of the taxpayers, dejected into day and night with jesuit bark and bitter bite, calicohydrants of zolfor and scoppialamina by full and forty Queasisanos, every day in everyone's way more exceeding in violent abuse of self and others, was the worst, it is hoped, even in our western playboyish world for pure mousefarm filth. You brag of your brass castle or your tyled house in ballyfermont? Niggs, niggs and niggs again. For this was a stinksome inkenstink, quite puzzonal to the wrottel. Smatterafact, Angles aftanon browsing there thought not Edam reeked more rare. My wud! The warped flooring of the lair and soundconducting walls thereof, to say nothing of the uprights and imposts, were persianly literatured with burst loveletters, telltale stories, stickyback snaps, doubtful eggshells, bouchers, flints, borers, puffers, amygdaloid almonds, rindless raisins, alphybettyformed verbage, vivlical viasses, ompiter dictas, visus umbique, ahems and ahahs, imeffible tries at speech unasyllabled, you owe mes, eyoldhyms, fluefoul smut, fallen lucifers, vestas which had served, showered ornaments, borrowed brogues, reversibles jackets, blackeye lenses, family jars, falsehair shirts, Godforsaken scapulars, neverworn breeches, cutthroat ties, counterfeit franks, best intentions, curried notes, upset latten tintacks, unused mill and stumpling stones, twisted quills, painful digests, magnifying wineglasses, solid objects cast at goblins, once current puns, quashed quotatoes, messes of mottage, unquestionable issue papers, seedy ejaculations, limerick damns, crocodile tears, spilt ink, blasphematory spits, stale shestnuts, schoolgirl's, young ladies', milkmaids', washerwomen's, shopkeepers' wives, merry widows', ex nuns', vice abbess's, pro virgins', super whores', silent sisters', Charleys' aunts', grandmothers', mothers'-in-laws, fostermothers', godmothers' garters, tress clippings from right, lift and cintrum, worms of snot, toothsome pickings, cans of Swiss condensed bilk, highbrow lotions, kisses from the antipodes, presents from pickpockets, borrowed plumes, relaxable handgrips, princess promises, lees of whine, deoxodised carbons, convertible collars, diviliouker doffers, broken wafers, unloosed shoe latchets, crooked strait waistcoats, fresh horrors from Hades, globules of mercury, undeleted glete, glass eyes for an eye, gloss teeth for a tooth, war moans, special sighs, longsufferings of longstanding, ahs ohs ouis sis jas jos gias neys thaws sos, yeses and yeses and yeses, to which, if one has the stomach to add the breakages, upheavals distortions, inversions of all this chambermade music one stands, given a grain of goodwill, a fair chance of actually seeing the whirling dervish, Tumult, son of Thunder, self exiled in upon his ego, a nightlong a shaking betwixtween white or reddr hawrors, noondayterrorised to skin and bone by an ineluctable phantom (may the Shaper have mercery on him!) writing the mystery of himsel in furniture.

Of course our low hero was a self valeter by choice of need so up he got up whatever is meant by a stourbridge clay kitchenette and lithargogalenu fowlhouse for the sake of akes (the umpple does not fall very far from the dumpertree) which the moromelodious jigsmith, in defiance of the Uncontrollable Birth Preservativation (Game and Poultry) Act, playing lallaryrook cookerynook, by the dodginess of his lentern, brooled and cocked and potched in an athanor, whites and yolks and yilks and whotes to the frulling fredonnance of *Mas blanca que la blanca hermana* and *Amarilla, muy bien*, with cinnamon and locusts and wild beeswax and liquorice and Carrageen moss and blaster of Barry's and Asther's mess and Huster's micture and Yellownan's embrocation and Pinkingtone's patty and stardust and sinner's tears, acuredent to Sharadan's *Art of Panning*, chanting, for all regale to the like of the legs he left behind with Litty fun Letty fan Leven, his cantraps of fermented words, abracadabra calubra culorum, (his oewfs à la Madame Gabrielle de l'Eglise, his avgs à la Mistress B. de B. Meinfelde, his eiers Usquadmala à la pomme de ciel, his uoves, oves and uves à la Sulphate de Soude, his ochiuri sowtay sowmmonay à la Monseigneur, his soufflosion of oogs with somekat on toyast à la Mère Puard, his Poggadovies alla Fenella, his Frideggs à la Tricarême) in what was meant for a closet (Ah ho! If only he had listened better to the four masters that infanted him Father Mathew and Le Père Noble and Pastor Lucas and Padre Aguilar—not forgetting Layteacher Baudwin! Ah ho!) His costive Satan's antimonian manganese limolitmious nature never needed such an alcove so, when Robber and Mumsell, the pulpic dictators, on the nudgment of their legal advisers, Messrs Codex and Podex, and under his own benefiction of their pastor Father Flammeus Falconer, boycotted him of all muttonsuet candles and romeruled stationery for any purpose, he winged away on a wildgoup's chase across the kathartic ocean and made synthetic ink and sensitive paper for his own end out of his wit's waste. You ask, in Sam Hill, how? Let manner and matter of this for these our sporting times be cloaked up in the language of blushfed porporates that an Anglican ordinal, not reading his own rude dunsky tunga, may ever behold the brand of scarlet on the brow of her of Babylon and feel not the pink one in his own damned cheek.

Primum opifex, altus prosator, ad terram viviparam et cunctipotentem sine ullo pudore nec venia, suscepto pluviali atque discinctis perizomatis, natibus nudis uti nati fuissent, sese adpropinquans, flens et gemens, in manum suam evacuavit (highly prosy, crap in his hand, sorry!), *postea, animale nigro exoneratus, classicum pulsans, stercus proprium, quod appellavit deiectiones suas, in vas olim honorabile tristitiae posuit, eodem sub invocatione fratrorum geminorum Medardi et Godardi laete ac melliflue minxit, psalmum qui incipit: Lingua mea calamus scribae velociter scribentis: magna voce cantitans* (did a piss, says he was dejected, asks to be exonerated), *demum ex stercore turpi cum divi Orionis iucunditate mixto, cocto, frigorique exposito, encaustum sibi fecit indelibile* (faked O'Ryan's, the indelible ink).

Then, pious Eneas, conformant to thc fulminant firman which enjoins on the tremylose terrian that, when the call comes, he shall produce nichthemerically from his unheavenly body a no uncertain quantity of obscene matter not protected by copriright in the United Stars of Ourania or bedeed and bedood and bedang and bedung to him, with this double dye, brought to blood heat, gallic acid on iron ore, through the bowels of his misery, flashly, faithly, nastily, appropriately, this Esuan Menschavik and the first till last alshemist wrote over every square inch of the only foolscap available, his own body, till by its corrosive sublimation one continuous present tense integument slowly unfolded all marryvoising moodmoulded cyclewheeling history (thereby, he said, reflecting from his own individual person life unlivable, transaccidentated through the slow fires of consciousness into a dividual chaos, perilous, potent, common to allflesh, human only, mortal) but with each word that would not pass away the squidself which he had squirtscreened from the crystalline world waned chagreenold and doriangrayer in its dudhud. This exists that isits after having been said we know. And dabal take dabnal! And the dal dabal dab aldanabal! So perhaps, agglaggagglomeratively asaspenking, after all and arklast fore arklyst on his last public misappearance, circling the square, for the deathfête of Saint Ignaceous Poisonivy, of the Fickle Crowd (hopon the sexth day of Hogsober, killim our king, layum low!) and brandishing his bellbearing stylo, the shining keyman of the wilds of change, if what is sauce for the zassy is souse for the zazimas, the blond cop who thought it was ink was out of his depth but bright in the main.

Petty constable Sistersen of the Kruis-Kroon-Kraal it was, the parochial watch, big the dog the dig the bog the bagger the dugger the begadag degabug, who had been detailed from pollute stoties to save him, this the quemquem, that the quum, from the ligatureliablous effects of foul clay in little clots and mobmauling on looks, that wrongcountered the tenderfoot an eveling near the livingsmeansuniumgetherum, Knockmaree, Comty Mea, reeling more to the right than he lurched to the left, on his way from a protoprostitute (he would always have a (stp!) little pigeoness somewhure with his arch girl, Arcoiris, smockname of Mergyt) just as he was butting in rand the coyner of bad times under a hideful between the rival doors of warm bethels of worship through his boardelhouse fongster, greeting for grazious oras as usual: Where ladies have they that a dog meansort herring? Sergo, search me, the incapable reparteed with a selfevitant subtlety so obviously spurious and, raising his hair, after the grace, with the christmas under his clutcharm, for Portsymasser and Purtsymessus and Pertsymiss and Partsymasters, like a prance of findingos, with a shillto shallto slipny stripny, in he skittled. Swikey! The allwhite poors guardiant, pulpably of balltossic stummung, was literally astundished over the painful sake, how he burstteself, which he was gone to, where he intent to did he, whether you think will, wherend the whole current of the afternoon whats the souch of a surch hads of hits of hims, urged and staggered thereto in his countryports at the caledosian capacity for Lieutuvisky of the caftan's wineskin and even more so, during, looking his bigmost astonishments, it was said him, aschu, fun the concerned outgift of the dead med dirt, how that, arrahbejibbers, conspuent to the dominical order and exking noblish permish, he was

namely coon at bringer at home two gallonts, as per royal, full poultry till
his murder. Nip up and nab it!

Polthergeistkotzdondherhoploits! Kick? What mother? Whose porter?
Which pair? Why namely coon? But our undilligence has been pluthero-
tested so enough of such porterblack lowneess, too base for printink!
Perpending that Putterick O'Purcell pulls the coald stoane out of Winter-
water's and Silder Seas sing for Harreng our Keng, sept okt nov dez John
Phibbs march! We cannot, in mercy or justice nor on the lovom for
labaryntos, stay here for the residence of our existings, discussing Tamstar
Ham of Tenman's thirst.

JUSTIUS (to himother): Brawn is my name and broad is my nature and
I've breit on my brow and all's right with every feature and I'll brune this
bird or Brown Bess's bung's gone bandy. I'm the boy to bruise and braise.
Baus!

Stand forth, Nayman of Noland (for no longer will I follow you oblique-
like through the inspired form of the third person singular and the
moods and hesitensies of the deponent but address myself to you, with the
empirative of my vendettative, provocative and out direct), stand forth,
come boldly, jolly me, move me, zwilling though I am, to laughter in your
true colours ere you be back for ever till I give you your talkingto! Shem
Macadamson, you know me and I know you and all your shemeries. Where
have you been in the uterim, enjoying yourself all the morning since your
last wetbed confession? I advise you to conceal yourself, my little friend, as
I have said a moment ago and put your hands in my hands and have a
nightslong homely little confiteor about things. Let me see. It is looking
pretty black against you, we suggest, Sheem avick. You will need all the
elements in the river to clean you over it all and a fortifine popespriest-
power bull of attender to booth.

Let us pry. We thought, would and did. *Cur, quicquid, ubi, quando,
quomodo, quoties, quibus auxiliis?* You were bred, fed, fostered and fattened
from holy childhood up in this two easter island on the piejaw of hilarious
heaven and roaring the other place (plunders to night of you, blunders
what's left of you, flash as flash can!) and now, forsooth, a nogger among the
blankards of this dastard century, you have become of twosome twiminds
forenenst gods, hidden and discovered, nay, condemned fool, anarch,
egoarch, hiresiarch, you have reared your disunited kingdom on the vacuum
of your own most intensely doubtful soul. Do you hold yourself then for
some god in the manger, Shehohem, that you will neither serve not let
serve, pray nor let pray? And here, pay the piety, must I too nerve myself to
pray for the loss of selfrespect to equip me for the horrible necessity of

scandalisang (my dear sisters, are you ready?) by sloughing off my hope and tremors while we all swin together in the pool of Sodom? I shall shiver for my purity while they will weepbig for your sins. Away with covered words, new Solemonities for old Badsheetbaths! That inharmonious detail, did you name it? Cold caldor! Gee! Victory! Now, opprobro of underslung pipes, johnjacobs, while yet an adolescent (what do I say?), while still puerile in your tubsuit with buttonlegs, you got a handsome present of a selfraising syringe and twin feeders (you know, Monsieur Abgott, in your art of arts, to your cost as well as I do (and don't try to hide it) the penals lots I am now poking at) and the wheeze sort of was you should (if you were as bould a stroke now as the curate that christened you, sonny douth-the-candle!) repopulate the land of your birth and count up your progeny by the hungered head and the angered thousand but you thwarted the wious pish of your cogodparents, soph, among countless occasions of failing (for, said you, I will elenchate), adding to the malice of your transgression, yes, and changing its nature, (you see I have read your theology for you) alternating the morosity of my delectations—a philtred love, trysting by tantrums, small peace in ppenmark—with sensibility, sponsibility, passibility and prostability, your lubbock's other fear pleasures of a butler's life, even extruding your strabismal apologia, when legibly depressed, upon defence-less paper and thereby adding to the already unhappiness of this our pop-eyed world, scribblative!—all that too with cantreds of countless catch-aleens, the mannish as many as the minneful, congested around and about you for acres and roods and poles or perches, thick as the fluctuant sands of Chalwador, accomplished women, indeed fully educanded, far from being old and rich behind their dream of arrivisme, if they have only their honour left, and not deterred by bad weather when consumed by amorous passion, struggling to possess themselves of your boosh, one son of Sorge for all daughters of Anguish, *solus cum sola sive cuncties cum omnibobs* (I'd have been the best man for you, myself), mutely aying for hat natural knot, debituary vases or vessels preposterous, for what would not have cost you ten bolivars of collarwork or the price of one ping pang, just a lilt, let us trillt, of the oldest song in the wooed woodworld, (two-we! to-one!), accompanied by a plain gold band! Hail! Hail! Highbosomheaving Missmisstress Morna of the allsweetheartening bridemuredemeanour! Her eye's so gladsome we'll all take shares in the ——groom!

Sniffer of carrion, premature gravedigger, seeker of the nest of evil in the bosom of a good word, you, who sleep at our vigil and fast for our feast, you with your dislocated reason, have cutely foretold, a jophet in your own absence, by blind poring upon your many scalds and burns and blisters,

impetiginous sore and pustules, by the auspices of that raven cloud, your
shade, and by the auguries of rooks in parlament, death with every disaster,
the dynamitisation of colleagues, the reducing of records to ashes, the
levelling of all customs by blazes, the return of a lot of sweetempered
gunpowdered didst unto dudst but it never stphruck your mudhead's
obtundity (O hell, here comes our funeral! O pest, I'll miss the post!) that
the more carrots you chop, the more turnips you slit, the more murphies
you peel, the more onions you cry over, the more bullbeef you butch, the
more mutton you crackerhack, the more potherbs you pound, the fiercer
the fire and the longer your spoon and the harder you gruel with more
grease to your elbow the merrier fumes your new Irish stew.

O, by the way, yes, another thing occurs to me. You let me tell you, with
the utmost politeness, were very ordinarily designed, your birthwrong was,
to fall in with Plan, as our nationals should, as all nationists must, and do a
certain office (what, I will not tell you) in a certain holy office (nor will I say
where) during certain agonising office hours (a clerical party all to yourself)
from such a year to such an hour on such and such a date at so and so much
a week *pro anno* (Guinness's, may I remind, were just agulp for you, failing
in which you might have taken the scales off boilers like any boskop of
Yorek) and do your little thruppenny bit and thus earn from the nation true
thanks, right here in our place of burden, your bourne of travail and ville of
tares, where after a divine's prodigence you drew the first watergasp in your
life, from the crib where you once was bit to the crypt you'll be twice as shy
of, same as we, long of us, alone with the colt in the curner, where you were
as popular as an armenial with the faithful, and you set fire to my tailcoat
when I hold the paraffin smoker under yours (I hope that chimney's clear)
but, slackly shirking both your bullet and your billet, you beat it backwards
like Boulanger from Galway (but he combed the grass against his stride) to
sing us a song of alibi, (the cuthone call over the greybounding slowrolling
amplyheaving metamorphoseous that oozy rocks parapangle their pre-
posters with) nomad, mooner by lamplight, antinos, shemming amid everyone's repressed laughter to conceal your scatchophily by mating, like a
thoroughpaste prosodite, masculine monosyllables of the same numerical
mus, an Irish emigrant the wrong way out, sitting on your crooked sixpenny
stile, an unfrillfrocked quackfriar, you (will you for the laugh of Scheekspair
just help mine with the epithet?) semisemitic serendipitist, you (thanks, I
think that describes you) Europasianised Afferyank!

Shall we follow each others a steplonger, drowner of daggers, whiles our
liege, tilyet a stranger in the frontyard of his happiness, is taking, (heal
helper! one gob, one gap, one gulp and gorger of all!) his refreshment?

There grew up beside you, amid our orisons of the speediest. in Novena
Lodge, Novara Avenue, in Patripodium-am-Bummel, oaf, outofwork, one
remove from an unwashed savage, on his keeping and in yours, (I pose you
know why possum hides is cause he haint the nogumtreeumption) that
other, Immaculatus, from head to foot, sir, that pure one, Altrues of other
times, he who was well known to celestine circles before he sped aloft, our
handsome young spiritual physician that was to be, seducing every sense to
selfwilling celebesty, the most winning counterfeuille on our incomeshare
lotetree, a chum of the angelets, a youth those reporters so pettitily wanted
as gamefellow that they asked his mother for ittle earps brupper to let him
tome to Tindertarten? pease, and bing his scooter 'long and 'tend they were
all real brothers in the big justright home where Dodd lives, just to teddyfy
the life out of him and pat and pass him one with other like musk from hand
to hand, that mothersmothered model, that goodlooker with not a flaw
whose spiritual toilettes were the talk of half the town, for sunset wear and
nightfallen use and daybroken donning and nooncheon showing and the
very thing for teasetime, but him you laid low with one hand one fine May
morning in the Meddle of your Might, your bosom foe, because he mussed
your speller on you or because he cut a pretty figure in the focus of your
frontispecs (not one did you slay, no, but a continent!) to find out how his
innards worked!

Ever read of that greatgrand landfather of our visionbuilders, Baaboo,
the bourgeoismeister, who thought to touch both himmels at the punt of
his risen stiffstaff and how wishywashy sank the waters of his thought? Ever
thought of that hereticalist Marcon and the two scissymaidies and how
bulkily he shat the Ructions gunorrhal? Ever hear of that foxy, that lupo and
that monkax and the virgin heir of the Morrisons, eh, blethering ape?

Malingerer in luxury, collector general, what has Your Lowness done in
the mealtime with all the hamilkcars of cooked vegetables, the hatfuls of
stewed fruit, the suitcases of coddled ales, the Parish funds, me schamer,
man, that you kittycoaxed so flexibly out of charitable butteries by yowling
heavy with a hollow voice drop of your horrible awful poverty of mind so as
you couldn't even pledge a crown of Thorne's to pawn a coat off Trevi's
and as how you was bad no end, so you was, so whelp you Sinner Pitre and
Sinner Poule, with the chicken's gape and *pas mal de siècle*, which, by the by,
Reynaldo, is the ordinary emetic French for grenadier's drip. To let you
have your plank and your bonewash (O the hastroubles you lost!), to give
you your pound of platinum and a thousand thongs a year (O, you were
excruciated, in honour bound to the cross of your own cruelfiction!) to let
you have your Sarday spree and holinight sleep (fame would come to you

twixt a sleep and a wake) and leave to lie till Paraskivee and the cockcock crows for Danmark. (O Jonathan, your estomach!) The simian has no sentiment secretions but weep cataracts for all me, Pain the Shamman! Oft in the smelly night will they wallow for a clutch of the famished hand, I say, them bearded jezabelles you hired to rob you, while on your sodden straw impolitely you encored (Airish and nawboggaleesh!) those hornmade ivory dreams you reved of the Ruth you called your companionate, a beauty from the bible, of the flushpots of Euston and the hanging garments of Marylebone. But the dormer moonshee smiled selene and the lightthrowers knickered: who's whinging we? Comport yourself, you inconsistency! Where is that little alimony nestegg against our predictable rainy day? Is it not the fact (gainsay me, cakeeater!) that, while whistlewhirling your crazy elegies around Templetombmount joyntstone, (let him pass, pleasegoodjesusalem, in a bundle of straw, he was balbettised after haymaking) you squandered among underlings the overload of your extravagance and made a hottentot of dulpeners crawsick with your crumbs? Am I not right? Yes? Yes? Yes? Holy wax and holifer! Don't tell me, Leon of the fold, that you are not a loanshark! Look up, old sooty, be advised by mux and take your medicine. The Good Doctor mulled it. Mix it twice before repastures and powder three times a day. It does marvels for your gripins and it's fine for the solitary worm.

Let me finish! Just a little judas tonic, my ghem of all jokes, to make you go green in the gazer. Do you hear what I'm seeing, hammet? And remember that golden silence gives consent, Mr Anklegazer! Cease to be civil, learn to say nay! Whisht! Come here, Herr Studiosus, till I tell you a wig in your ear. We'll do a whisper drive, for if the barishnyas got a twitter of it they'd tell the housetops and then all Cadbury would go crackers. Look! Do you see your dial in the rockingglass? Look well! Bend down a stigmy till I! It's secret! Iggri, I say, the booseleers! I had it from Lamppost Shawe. And he had it from the Mullah. And Mull took it from a Bluecoat schooler. And Gay Socks jot it from Potapheu's wife. And Rantipoll tipped the wink from old Mrs Tinbullet. And as for she was confussed by proBrother Thacolicus. And the good brother feels he would need to defecate you. And the Flimsy Follettes are simply beside each other. And Kelly, Kenny and Keogh are up up and in arms. That a cross may crush me if I refuse to believe in it. That I may rock anchor through the ages if I hope it's not true. That the host may choke me if I beneighbour you without my charity! Sh! Shem, you are. Sh! You are mad!

He points the deathbone and the quick are still. *Insomnia, somnia somniorum. Awmawm.*

MERCIUS (of hisself): *Domine vopiscus!* My fault, his fault, a kingship through a fault! Pariah, cannibal Cain, I who oathily forswore the womb that bore you and the paps I sometimes sucked, you who ever since have been one black mass of jigs and jimjams, haunted by a convulsionary sense of not having been or being all that I might have been or you meant to becoming, bewailing like a man that innocence which I could not defend like a woman, lo, you there, Cathmon-Carbery, and thank Movies from the innermost depths of my still attrite heart, Wherein the days of youyouth are evermixed mimine, now ere the compline hour of being alone athands itself and a puff or so before we yield our spiritus to the wind, for (though that royal one has not yet drunk a gouttelette from his consummation and the flowerpot on the pole, the spaniel pack and their quarry, retainers and the public house proprietor have not budged a millimetre and all that has been done has yet to be done and done again, when's day's woe, and lo, you're doomed, joyday dawns and, la, you dominate) it is to you, firstborn and firstfruit of woe, to me, branded sheep, pick of the wasterpaperbaskel, by the tremours of Thundery and Ulerin's dogstar, you alone, windblasted tree of the knowledge of beautiful andevil, ay, clothed upon with the metuor and shimmering like the horescens, astroglodynamonologos, the child of Nilfit's father, blzb, to me unseen blusher in an obscene coalhole, the cubilibum of your secret sigh, dweller in the downandoutermost where voice only of the dead may come, because ye left from me, because ye laughed on me, because, O me lonly son, ye are forgetting me!, that our turfbrown mummy is acoming, alpilla, beltilla, ciltilla, deltilla, running with her tidings, old the news of the great big world, sonnies had a scrap, woewoewoe! bab's baby walks at seven months, waywayway! bride leaves her raid at Punchestime, stud stoned before a racecourseful, two belles that make the one appeal, dry yanks will visit old sod, and fourtiered skirts are up, mesdames, while Parimiknie wears popular short legs, and twelve hows to mix a tipsy wake, did ye hear, colt Cooney? did ye ever, filly Fortescue? with a beck, with a spring, all her rillringlets shaking, rocks drops in her tachie, tramtokens in her hair, all waived to a point and then all inuendation, little oldfashioned mummy, little wonderful mummy, ducking under bridges, bellhopping the weirs, dodging by a bit of bog, rapidshooting round the bends, by Tallaght's green hills and the pools of the phooka and a place they call it Blessington and slipping sly by Sallynoggin, as happy as the day is wet, babbling, bubbling, chattering to herself, deloothering the fields on their elbows leaning with the sloothering slide of her, giddygaddy, grannyma, gossipaceous Anna Livia.

He lifts the lifewand and the dumb speak.

— Quoiquoiquoiquoiquoiquoiquoiq!

[8]

O

tell me all about

Anna Livia! I want to hear all

about Anna Livia. Well, you know Anna Livia? Yes, of course, we all know
Anna Livia. Tell me all. Tell me now. You'll die when you hear. Well, you
know, when the old cheb went futt and did what you know. Yes, I know, go
on. Wash quit and don't be dabbling. Tuck up your sleeves and loosen your
talktapes. And don't butt me—hike!—when you bend. Or whatever it was
they threed to make out he thried to two in the Fiendish park. He's an awful
old reppe. Look at the shirt of him! Look at the dirt of it! He has all my
water black on me. And it steeping and stuping since this time last wik. How
many goes is it I wonder I washed it? I know by heart the places he likes to
saale, duddurty devil! Scorching my hand and starving my famine to make
his private linen public. Wallop it well with your battle and clean it. My
wrists are wrusty rubbing the mouldaw stains. And the dneepers of wet and
the gangres of sin in it! What was it he did a tail at all on Animal Sendai?
And how long was he under loch and neagh? It was put in the newses what
he did, nicies and priers, the King fierceas Humphrey, with illysus distilling,
exploits and all. But toms will till. I know he well. Temp untamed will hist
for no man. As you spring so shall you neap. O, the roughty old rappe!
Minxing marrage and making loof. Reeve Gootch was right and Reeve
Drughad was sinistrous! And the cut of him! And the strut of him! How he
used to hold his head as high as a howeth, the famous eld duke alien, with a
hump of grandeur on him like a walking wiesel rat. And his derry's own
drawl and his corksown blather and his doubling stutter and his gullaway
swank. Ask Lictor Hackett or Lector Reade of Garda Growley or the Boy
with the Billyclub. How elster is he a called at all? Qu'appelle? Huges Caput
Earlyfouler. Or where was he born or how was he found? Urgothland,
Tvistown on the Kattekat? New Hunshire, Concord on the Merrimake?
Who blocksmitt her saft anvil or yelled lep to her pail? Was her banns never
loosened in Adam and Eve's or were him and her but captain spliced? For
mine ether duck I thee drake. And by my wildgaze I thee gander. Flowey
and Mount on the brink of time makes wishes and fears for a happy isthmass.
She can show all her lines, with love, license to play. And if they don't
remarry that hook and eye may! O, passmore that and oxus another! Don

Dom Dombdomb and his wee follyo! Was his help inshored in the Stork and Pelican against bungelars, flu and third risk parties? I heard he dug good tin with his doll, delvan first and duvlin after, when he raped her home, Sabrine asthore, in a parakeet's cage, by dredgerous lands and devious delts, playing catched and mythed with the gleam of her shadda, (if a flic had been there to pop up and pepper him!) past auld min's manse and Maisons Allfou and the rest of incurables and the last of immurables, the quaggy waag for stumbling. Who sold you that jackalantern's tale? Pemmican's pasty pie! Not a grasshoop to ring her, not an antsgrain of ore. In a gabbard he barqued it, the boat of life, from the harbourless Ivernikan Okean, till he spied the loom of his landfall and he loosed two croakers from under his tilt, the gran Phenician rover. By the smell of her kelp they made the pigeon-house. Like fun they did! But where was Himself, the timoneer? That marchantman he suivied their scutties right over the wash, his cameleer's burnous breezing up on him, till with his runagate bowmpriss he roade and borst her bar. Pilcomayo! Suchcaughtawan! And the whale's away with the grayling! Tune your pipes and fall ahumming, you born ijypt, and you're nothing short of one! Well, ptellomey soon and curb your escumo. When they saw him shoot swift up her sheba sheath, like any gay lord salomon, her bulls they were ruhring, surfed with spree. Boyarka buah! Boyana bueh! He erned his lille Bunbath hard, our staly bred, the trader. He did. Look at here. In this wet of his prow. Don't you know he was kaldt a bairn of the brine, Wasserbourne the waterbaby? Havemmarea, so he was! H.C.E. has a codfisck ee. Shyr she's nearly as badher as him herself. Who? Anna Livia? Ay, Anna Livia. Do you know she was calling bakvandets sals from all around, nyumba noo, chamba choo, to go in till him, her erring cheef, and tickle the pontiff aisy-oisy? She was? Gota pot! Yssel that the limmat? As El Negro winced when he wonced in La Plate. O, tell me all I want to hear, how loft she was lift a laddery dextro! A coneywink after the bunting fell. Letting on she didn't care, sina feza, me absantee, him man in passession, the proxenete! Proxenete and phwhat is phthat? Emme for your reussischer Honddu jarkon! Tell us in franca langua. And call a spate a spate. Did they never sharee you ebro at skol, you antiabecedarian? It's just the same as if I was to go par examplum now in conservancy's cause out of telekinesis and proxenete you. For coxyt sake and is that what she is? Botlettle I thought she'd act that loa. Didn't you spot her in her windaug, wubbling up on an osiery chair, with a meusic before her all cunniform letters, pretending to ribble a reedy derg on a fiddle she bogans without a band on? Sure she can't fiddan a dee, with bow or abandon! Sure, she can't! Tista suck. Well, I never now heard the like of that! Tell me moher. Tell me moatst. Well, old

Humber was as glommen as grampus, with the tares at his thor and the buboes for ages and neither bowman nor shot abroad and bales allbrant on the crests of rockies and nera lamp in kitchen or church and giant's holes in Grafton's causeway and deathcap mushrooms round Funglus grave and the great tribune's barrow all darnels occumule, sittang sambre on his sett, drammen and drommen, usking queasy quizzers of his ruful continence, his childlinen scarf to encourage his obsequies where he'd check their debths in that mormon's thames, be questing and handsetl, hop, step and a deepend, with his berths in their toiling moil, his swallower open from swolf to fore and the snipes of the gutter pecking his crocs, hungerstriking all alone and holding doomsdag over hunselv, dreeing his weird, with his dander up, and his fringe combed over his eygs and droming on loft till the sight of the sternes, after zwarthy kowse and weedy broeks and the tits of buddy and the loits of pest and to peer was Parish worth thette mess. You'd think all was dodo belonging to him how he durmed adranse in durance vaal. He had been belching for severn years. And there she was, Anna Livia, she darent catch a winkle of sleep, purling around like a chit of a child, Wendawanda, a fingerthick, in a Lapsummer skirt and damazon cheeks, for to ishim bonzour to her dear dubber Dan. With neuphraties and sault from his maggias. And an odd time she'd cook him up blooms of fisk and lay to his heartsfoot her meddery eygs, yayis, and staynish beacons on toasc and a cupenhave so weeshywashy of Greenland's tay or a dzoupgan of Kaffue mokau an sable or Sikiang sukry or his ale of ferns in trueart pewter and a shinkobread (hamjambo, bana?) for to plaise that man hog stay his stomicker till her pyrraknees shrunk to nutmeg graters while her togglejoints shuck with goyt and as rash as she'd russ with her peakload of vivers up on her sieve (metauwero rage it swales and rieses) my hardey Hek he'd kast them frome him, with a stour of scorn, as much as to say you sow and you sozh, and if he didn't peg the platteau on her tawe, believe you me, she was safe enough. And then she'd esk to vistule a hymn, *The Heart Bowed Down* or *The Rakes of Mallow* or Chelli Michele's *La Calumnia è un Vermicelli* or a balfy bit ov *old Jo Robidson*. Sucho fuffing a fifeing 'twould cut you in two! She'd bate the hen that crowed on the turrace of Babbel. What harm if she knew how to cockle her mouth! And not a mag out of Hum no more than out of the mangle weight. Is that a faith? That's the fact. Then riding the ricka and roya romanche, Annona, gebroren aroostokrat Nivia, dochter of Sense and Art, with Sparks' pirryphlickathims funkling her fan, anner frostivying tresses dasht with virevlies,—while the prom beauties sreeked nith their bearers' skins!—in a period gown of changeable jade that would robe the wood of two cardinals' chairs and crush poor Cullen and smother MacCabe.

O blazerskate! Theirs porpor patches! And brahming to him down the feedchute, with her femtyfyx kinds of fondling endings, the poother rambling off her nose: *Vuggybarney, Wickerymandy! Hello, ducky, please don't die!* Do you know what she started cheeping after, with a choicey voicey like waterglucks or Madame Delba to Romeoreszk? You'll never guess. Tell me. Tell me. *Phoebe, dearest, tell, O tell me* and *I loved you better nor you knew.* And letting on hoon var daft about the warbly sangs from over holmen: *High hellskirt saw ladies hensmoker lilyhung pigger:* and soay and soan and so firth and so forth in a tone sonora and Oom Bothar below like Bheri-Bheri in his sandy cloak, so umvolosy, as deaf as a yawn, the stult! Go away! Poor deef old deary! Yare only teasing! Anna Liv? As chalk is my judge! And didn't she up in sorgues and go and trot doon and stand in her douro, puffing her old dudheen, and every shirvant siligirl or wensum farmerette walking the pilend roads, Sawy, Fundally, Daery or Maery, Milucre, Awny or Graw, usedn't she make her a simp or sign to slip inside by the sullyport? You don't say, the sillypost? Bedouix but I do! Calling them in, one by one (To Blockbeddum here! Here the Shoebenacaddie!) and legging a jig or so on the sihl to show them how to shake their benders and the dainty how to bring to mind the gladdest garments out of sight and all the way of a maid with a man and making a sort of a cackling noise like two and a penny or half a crown and holding up a silliver shiner. Lordy, lordy, did she so? Well, of all the ones ever I heard! Throwing all the neiss little whores in the world at him! To inny captured wench you wish of no matter what sex of pleissful ways two adda tammar a lizzy a lossie to hug and hab haven in Humpy's apron!

And what was the wyerye rima she made! Odet! Odet! Tell me the trent of it while I'm lathering hail out of Denis Florence MacCarthy's combies. Rise it, flut ye, pian piena! I'm dying down off my iodine feet until I lerryn Anna Livia's cushingloo, that was writ by one and rede by two and trouved by a poule in the parco! I can see that, I see you are. How does it tummel? Listen now. Are you listening? Yes, yes! Idneed I am! Tarn your ore ouse! Essonne inne!

By earth end the cloudy but I badly went e brandnew bankside, bedamp and I do, and a plumper at that!

For the putty affair I have is wore out, so it is, sitting, yaping and waiting for my old Dane hodder dodderer, my life in death companion, my frugal key of our larder, my much-altered camel's hump, my jointspoiler, my maymoon's honey, my fool to the last Decemberer, to wake himself out of his winter's doze and bore me down like he used to.

Is there irwell a lord of the manor or a knight of the shire at strike, I wonder,

that'd dip me a dace or two in cash for washing and darning his worshipful socks for
him now we're run out of horsebrose and milk?

    Only for my short Brittas bed made's as snug as it smells it's out I'd lep and off
with me to the slobs deua Tolka or the plage au Clontarf to feale the gay aire of my
salt troublin bay and the race of the saywint up me ambushure.

Onon! Onon! tell me more. Tell me every tiny teign. I want to know
every single ingul. Down to what made the potters fly into jagsthole. And
why were the vesles vet. That homa fever's winning me wome. If a mahun
of the horse but hard me! We'd be bundukiboi meet askarigal. Well, now
comes the hazelhatchery part. After Clondalkin the Kings's Inns. We'll
soon be there with the freshet. How many aleveens had she in tool? I can't
rightly rede you that. Close only knows. Some say she had three figures to
fill and confined herself to a hundred eleven, wan bywan bywan, making
meanacuminamoyas. Olaph lamm et, all that pack? We won't have room in
the kirkeyaard. She can't remember half of the cradlenames she smacked on
them by the grace of her boxing bishop's infallible slipper, the cane for
Kund and abbles for Eyolf and ayther nayther for Yakov Yea. A hundred
and how? They did well to rechristien her Pluhurabelle. O loreley! What a
loddon lodes! Heigh ho! But it's quite on the cards she'll shed more and
merrier, twills and trills, sparefours and spoilfives, nordsihkes and sudsevers
and ayes and neins to a litter. Grandfarthring nap and Messamisery and the
knave of all knaves and the joker. Heehaw! She must have been a gadabount
in her day, so she must, more than most. Shoal she was, gidgad. She had a
flewmen of her owen. Then a toss nare scared that lass, so aimai moe, that's
agapo! Tell me, tell me, how cam she camlin through all her fellows, the
neckar she was, the diveline? Casting her perils before our swains from
Fonte-in-Monte to Tidingtown and from Tidingtown tilhavet. Linking
one and knocking the next, tapting a flank and tipting a jutty and palling in
and pietaring out and clyding by on her eastway. Waiwhou was the first
thurever burst? Someone he was, whuebra they were, in a tactic attack or in
single combat. Tinker, tilar, souldrer, salor, Pieman Peace or Polistaman.
That's the thing I'm elwys on edge to esk. Push up and push vardar and
come to uphill headquarters! Was it waterlows year, after Grattan or Flood,
or when maids were in Arc or when three stood hosting? Fidaris will find
where the Doubt arises like Nieman from Nirgends found the Nihil. Worry
you sighin foh, Albern, O Anser? Untie the gemman's fistiknots, Qvic and
Nuancee! She can't put her hand on him for the moment. Tez thelon
langlo, walking weary! Such a loon waybashwards to row! She sid herself
she hardly knows whuon the annals her graveller was, a dynast of Leinster,
a wolf of the sea, or what he did or how blyth she played or how, when, why,

where and who offon he jumpnad her and how it was gave her away. She was just a young thin pale soft shy slim slip of a thing then, sauntering, by silvamoonlake and he was a heavy trudging lurching lieabroad of a Curraghman, making his hay for whose sun to shine on, as tough as the oaktrees (peats be with them!) used to rustle that time down by the dykes of killing Kildare, for forstfellfoss with a plash across her. She thought she's sankh neathe the ground with nymphant shame when he gave her the tigris eye! O happy fault! Me wish it was he! You're wrong there, corribly wrong! Tisn't only tonight you're anacheronistic! It was ages behind that when nullahs were nowhere, in county Wickenlow, garden of Erin, before she ever dreamt she'd lave Kilbride and go foaming under Horsepass bridge, with the great southerwestern windstorming her traces and the midland's grainwaster asarch for her track, to wend her ways byandby, robecca or worse, to spin and to grind, to swab and to thrash, for all her golden lifey in the barleyfields and pennylotts of Humphrey's fordofhurdlestown and lie with a landleaper, wellingtonorseher. Alesse, the lagos of girly days! For the dove of the dunas! Wasut? Izod? Are you sarthin suir? Not where the Finn fits into the Mourne, not where the Nore takes lieve of Blœm, not where the Braye divarts the Farer, not where the Moy changez her minds twixt Cullin and Conn tween Cunn and Collin? Or where Neptune sculled and Tritonville rowed and leandros three bumped heroines two? Neya, narev, nen, nonni, nos! Then whereabouts in Ow and Ovoca? Was it yst with wyst or Lucan Yokan or where the hand of man has never set foot? Dell me where, the fairy ferse time! I will if you listen. You know the dinkel dale of Luggelaw? Well, there once dwelt a local heremite, Michael Arklow was his riverend name, (with many a sigh I aspersed his lavabibs!) and one venersderg in junojuly, oso sweet and so cool and so limber she looked, Nance the Nixie, Nanon L'Escaut, in the silence, of the sycomores, all listening, the kindling curves you simply can't stop feeling, he plunged both of his newly anointed hands, the core of his cushlas, in her singimari saffron strumans of hair, parting them and soothing her and mingling it, that was deep-dark and ample like this red bog at sundown. By that Vale Vowclose's lucydlac, the reignbeau's heavenarches arronged orranged her. Afroth-dizzying galbs, her enamelled eyes indergoading him on to the vierge violetian. Wish a wish! Why a why? Mavro! Letty Lerck's lafing light throw those laurals now on her daphdaph teasesong petrock. Maass! But the majik wavus has elfun anon meshes. And Simba the Slayer of his Oga is slewd. He cuddle not help himself, thurso that hot on him, he had to forget the monk in the man so, rubbing her up and smoothing her down, he baised his lippes in smiling mood, kiss akiss after kisokushk (as he

warned her niver to, niver to, nevar) on Anna-na-Poghue's of the freckled
forehead. While you'd parse secheressa she hielt her souff'. But she ruz
two feet hire in her aisne aestumation. And steppes on stilts ever since.
That was kissuahealing with bantur for balm! O, wasn't he the bold priest?
And wasn't she the naughty Livvy? Nautic Naama's now her navn. Two
lads in scoutsch breeches went through her before that, Barefoot Burn and
Wallowme Wade, Lugnaquillia's noblesse pickts, before she had a hint of
a hair at her fanny to hide or a bossom to tempt a birch canoedler not to
mention a bulgic porterhouse barge. And ere that again, leada, laida, all
unraidy, too faint to buoy the fairiest rider, too frail to flirt with a cygnet's
plume, she was licked by a hound, Chirripa-Chirruta, while poing her pee,
pure and simple, on the spur of the hill in old Kippure, in birdsong and
shearingtime, but first of all, worst of all, the wiggly livvly, she sideslipped
out by a gap in the Devil's glen while Sally her nurse was sound asleep in a
sloot and, feefee fiefie, fell over a spillway before she found her stride and
lay and wriggled in all the stagnant black pools of rainy under a fallow coo
and she laughed innocefree with her limbs aloft and a whole drove of
maiden hawthorns blushing and looking askance upon her.

    Drop me the sound of the findhorn's name, Mtu or Mti, sombogger was
wisness. And drip me why in the flenders was she frickled. And trickle me
through was she marcellewaved or was it weirdly a wig she wore. And
whitside did they droop their glows in their florry, aback to wist or affront
to sea? In fear to hear the dear so near or longing loth and loathing longing?
Are you in the swim or are you out? O go in, go on, go an! I mean about
what you know. I know right well what you mean. Rother! You'd like the
coifs and guimpes, snouty, and me to do the greasy jub on old Veronica's
wipers. What am I rancing now and I'll thank you? Is it a pinny or is it a
surplice? Arran, where's your nose? And where's the starch? That's not the
vesdre benediction smell. I can tell from here by their *eau de Colo* and the
scent of her oder they're Mrs Magrath's. And you ought to have aird them.
They've moist come off her. Creases in silk they are, not crampton lawn.
Baptiste me, father, for she has sinned! Through her catchment ring she
freed them easy, with her hips' hurrahs for her knees'dontelleries. The only
parr with frills in old the plain. So they are, I declare! Welland well! If
tomorrow keeps fine who'll come tripping to sightsee? How'll? Ask me next
what I haven't got! The Belvedarean exhibitioners. In their cruisery caps
and oarsclub colours. What hoo, they band! And what hoa, they buck! And
here is her nubilee letters too. Ellis on quay in scarlet thread. Linked for the
world on a flushcaloured field. Annan exe after to show they're not Laura
Keown's. O, may the diabolo twisk your seifety pin! You child of Mammon,

Kinsella's Lilith! Now who has been tearing the leg of her drawars on her? Which leg is it? The one with the bells on it. Rinse them out and aston along with you! Where did I stop? Never stop! Continuarration! You're not there yet. I amstel waiting. Garonne, garonne!

Well, after it was put in the Mercy Cordial Mendicants' Sitter-dag-Zindeh-Munaday Wakeschrift (for once they sullied their white kidloves, chewing cuds after their dinners of cheeckin and beggin, with their show us it here and their mind out of that and their when you're quite finished with the reading matarial), even the snee that snowdon his hoaring hair had a skunner against him. Thaw, thaw, sava, savuto! Score Her Chuff Exsquire! Everywhere erriff you went and every bung you arver dropped into, in cit or suburb or in addled areas, the Rose and Bottle or Phoenix Tavern or Power's Inn or Jude's Hotel or wherever you scoured the countryside from Nanny-water to Vartryville or from Porta Lateen to the lootin quarter you found his ikom etsched tipside down or the cornerboys cammocking his guy and Morris the Man, with the role of a royss in his turgos the turrible, (Evropeahahn cheic house, unskimmed sooit and yahoort, hamman now cheekmee, Ahdahm this way make, Fatima, half tum!) reeling and railing round the local as the peihos piped und ubanjees twanged, with oddfellow's triple tiara busby rotundarinking round his scalp. Like Pate-by-the-Neva or Pete-over-Meer. This is the Hausman all paven and stoned, that cribbed the Cabin that never was owned that cocked his leg and hennad his Egg. And the mauldrin rabble around him in areopage, fracassing a great bingkan cagnan with their timpan crowders. Mind your Grimmfather! Think of your Ma! Hing the Hong is his jove's hangnomen! Lilt a bolero, bulling a law! She swore on croststyx nyne wyndabouts she's be level with all the snags of them yet. Par the Vulnerable Virgin's Mary del Dame! So she said to herself she'd frame a plan to fake a shine, the mischiefmaker, the like of it you niever heard. What plan? Tell me quick and dongu so crould! What the meurther did she mague? Well, she bergened a zakbag, a shammy mailsack, with the lend of a loan of the light of his lampion, off one of her swapsons, Shaun the Post, and then she went and consulted her chapboucqs, old Mot Moore, Casey's Euclid and the Fashion Display and made herself tidal to join in the mascarete. O gig goggle of gigguels. I can't tell you how! It's too screaming to rizo, rabbit it all! Minneha, minnehi mina-aehe, minneho! O but you must, you must really! Make my hear it gurgle gurgle, like the farest gargle gargle in the dusky dirgle dargle! By the holy well of Mulhuddart I swear I'd pledge my chanza getting to heaven through Tirry and Killy's mount of impiety to hear it all, aviary word! O, leave me my faculties, woman, a while! If you don't like my story get out of the punt.

Well, have it your own way, so. Here, sit down and do as you're bid. Take my stroke and bend to your bow. Forward in and pull your overthepoise! Lisp it slaney and crisp it quiet. Deel me longsome. Tongue your time now. Breathe thet deep. Thouat's the fairway. Hurry slow and scheldt you go. Lynd us your blessed ashes here till I scrub the canon's underpants. Flow now. Ower more. And pooleypooley.

First she let her hair fal and down it flussed to her feet its teviots winding coils. Then, mothernaked, she sampood herself with galawater and fraguant pistania mud, wupper and lauar, from crown to sole. Next she greesed the groove of her keel, warthes and wears and mole and itcher, with antifouling butterscatch and turfentide and serpenthyme and with leafmould she ushered round prunella isles and eslats dun, quincecunct, allover her little mary. Peeld gold of waxwork her jellybelly and her grains of incense anguille bronze. And after that she wove a garland for her hair. She pleated it. She plaited it. Of meadowgrass and riverflags, the bulrush and waterweed, and of fallen griefs of weeping willow. Then she made her bracelets and her anklets and her armlets and a jetty amulet for necklace of clicking cobbles and pattering pebbles and rumbledown rubble, richmond and rehr, of Irish rhunerhinerstones and shellmarble bangles. That done, a dawk of smut to her airy ey, Annushka Lutetiavitch Pufflovah, and the lellipos cream to her lippeleens and the pick of the paintbox for her pommettes, from strawbirry reds to extra violates, and she sendred her boudeloire maids to His Affluence, Ciliegia Grande and Kirschie Real, the two chirsines, with respecks from his missus, seepy and sewery, and a request might she passe of him for a minnikin. A call to pay and light a taper, in Brie-on-Arrosa, back in a sprizzling. The cock striking mine, the stalls bridely sign, there's Zambosy waiting for Me! She said she wouldn't be half her length away. Then, then, as soon as the lump his back was turned, with her mealiebag slang over her shulder, Anna Livia, oysterface, forth of her bassein came.

Describe her! Hustle along, why can't you? Spitz on the iern while it's hot. I wouldn't miss her for irthing on nerthe. Not for the lucre of lomba strait. Oceans of Gaud, I mosel hear that! Ogowe presta! Leste, before Julia sees her! Ishekarry and washemeskad, the carishy caratimaney? Whole lady fair? Duodecimoroon? Bon a ventura? Malagassy? What had she on, the liddel oud oddity? How much did she scallop, harness and weights? Here she is, Amnisty Ann! Call her calamity electrifies man.

No electress at all but old Moppa Necessity, angin mother of injons. I'll tell you a test. But you must sit still. Will you hold your peace and listen well to what I am going to say now? It might have been ten or twenty to one of the night of Allclose or the nexth of April when the flip of her hoogly igloo

flappered and out toetippit a bushman woman, the dearest little moma ever
you saw, nodding around her, all smiles, with ems of embarras and aues to
awe, between two ages, a judyqueen, not up to your elb. Quick, look at her
cute and saise her quirk for the bicker she lives the slicker she grows. Save us
and tagus! No more? Werra where in ourthe did you ever pick a Lambay
chop as big as a battering ram? Ay, you're right. I'm epte to forgetting, Like
Liviam Liddle did Loveme Long. The linth of my hough, I say! She wore a
ploughboy's nailstudded clogs, a pair of ploughfields in themselves: a sugarloaf hat with a gaudyquiviry peak and a band of gorse for an arnoment and
a hundred streamers dancing off it and a guildered pin to pierce it: owlglassy
bicycles boggled her eyes: and a fishnetzeveil for the sun not to spoil the
wrinklings of her hydeaspects: potatorings boucled the loose laubes of her
laudsnarers: her nude cuba stockings were salmospotspeckled: she sported a
galligo shimmy of hazevaipar tinto that never was fast till it ran in the
washing: stout stays, the rivals, lined her length: her bloodorange bock-
knickers, a two in one garment, showed natural nigger boggers, fancy-
fastened, free to undo: her blackstripe tan joseph was sequansewn and
teddybearlined, with wavy rushgreen epaulettes and a leadown here and
there of royal swansruff: a brace of gaspers stuck in her hayrope garters: her
civvy codroy coat with alpheubett buttons was boundaried round with a
twobar tunnel belt: a fourpenny bit in each pocketside weighed her safe
from the blowaway windrush; she had a clothespeg tight astride on her
joki's nose and she kep on grinding a sommething quaint in her fiumy
mouth and the rrreke of the fluve of the tail of the gawan of her snuffdrab
siouler's skirt trailed ffifffty odd Irish miles behind her lungarhodes.

Hellsbells, I'm sorry I missed her! Sweet gumptyum and nobody fainted!
But in whelk of her mouths? Was her naze alight? Everyone that saw her
said the dowce little delia looked a bit queer. Lotsy trotsy, mind the poddle!
Missus, be good and don't fol in the say! Fenny poor hex she must have
charred. Kickhams a frumpier ever you saw! Making mush mullet's eyes at
her boys dobelon. And they crowned her their chariton queen, all the
maids. Of the may? You don't say! Well for her she couldn't see herself. I
recknitz wharfore the darling murrayed her mirror. She did? Mersey me!
There was a koros of drouthdropping surfacemen, boomslanging
and plugchewing, fruiteyeing and flowerfeeding, in contemplation of the
fluctuation and the undification of her filimentation, lolling and leasing on
North Lazers' Waal all eelfare week by the Jukar Yoick's and as soon as they
saw her meander by that marritime way in her grasswinter's weeds and
twigged who was under her archdeaconess bonnet, Avondale's fish and
Clarence's poison, sedges an to aneber, Wit-upon-Crutches to Master Bates:

*Between our two southsates and the granite they're warming, or her face has been
lifted or Alp has doped!*

But what was the game in her mixed baggyrhatty? Just the tembo in her
tumbo or pilipili from her pepperpot? Saas and taas and specis bizaas. And
where in thunder did she plunder? Fore the battle or efter the ball? I want
to get it frisk from the soorce. I aubette my bearb it's worth while poaching
on! Shake it up, do, do! That's a good old son of a ditch! I promise I'll make
it worth your while. And I don't mean maybe. Nor yet with a goodfor. Spey
me pruth and I'll tale you true.

Well, arundgirond in a waveney lyne aringarouma she pattered and
swung and sidled, dribbling her boulder through narrowa mosses, the
diliskydrear on our drier side and the vilde vetchvine agin us, curara here,
careero there, not knowing which medway or weser to strike it, edereider,
making chattahoochee all to her ain chichiu, like Santa Claus at the cree of
the pale and puny, nistling to hear for their tiny hearties, her arms encircling
Isolabella, then running with reconciled Romas and Reims, on like a lech to
be off like a dart, then bathing Dirty Hans' spatters with spittle, with a
Christmas box apiece for aisch and iveryone of her childer, the birthday
gifts they dreamt they gabe her, the spoiled she fleetly laid at our door! On
the matt, by the pourch and inunder the cellar. The rivulets ran aflod to see,
the glashaboys, the pollynooties. Out of the paunschaup on to the pyre. And
they all about her, juvenile leads and ingenuinas, from the slime of their
slums and artesaned wellings, rickets and riots, like the Smyly boys at their
vicereine's levee. Vivi vienne, little Annchen! Vielo Anna, high life! Sing us
a sula, O, susuria! Ausone sidulcis! Hasn't she tambre! Chipping her and
raising a bit of a chir or a jary every dive she'd neb in her culdee sacco
of wabbash she raabed and reach out her maundy meerschaundize, poor
souvenir as per ricorder and all for sore aringarung, stinkers and heelers,
laggards and primelads, her furzeborn sons and dribblederry daughters, a
thousand and one of them, and wickerpotluck for each of them. For evil and
ever. And kiks the buch. A tinker's bann and a barrow to boil his billy for
Gipsy Lee; a cartridge of cockaleekie soup for Chummy the Guardsman;
for sulky Pender's acid nephew deltoïd drops, curiously strong; a cough and
a rattle and wildrose cheeks for poor Piccolina Petite MacFarlane; a jigsaw
puzzle of needles and pins and blankets and shins between them for Isabel,
Jezebel and Llewelyn Mmarriage; a brazen nose and pigiron mittens for
Johnny Walker Beg; a papar flag of the saints and stripes for Kevineen
O'Dea; a puffpuff for Pudge Craig and a nightmarching hare for Techertim
Tombigby; waterleg and gumboots each for Bully Hayes and Hurricane
Hartigan; a prodigal heart and fatted calves for Buck Jones, the pride of

Clonliffe; a loaf of bread and a father's early aim for Val from Skibereen; a jauntingcar for Larry Doolin, the Ballyclee jackeen; a seasick trip on a government ship for Teague O'Flanagan; a louse and trap for Jerry Coyle; slushmincepies for Andy Mackenzie; a hairclip and clackdish for Penceless Peter; that twelve sounds look for G. V. Brooke; a drowned doll, to face downwards for modest Sister Anne Mortimer; altar falls for Blanchisse's bed; Wildairs' breechettes for Magpeg Woppington; to Sue Dot a big eye; to Sam Dash a false step; snakes in clover, picked and scotched, and a vaticanned viper catcher's visa for Patsy Presbys; a reiz every morning for Standfast Dick and a drop every minute for Stumblestone Davy; scruboak beads for beatified Biddy; two appletweed stools for Eva Mobbely; for Saara Philpot a jordan vale tearorne; a pretty box of Pettyfib's Powder for Eileen Aruna to whiten her teeth and outflash Helen Arhone; a whippingtop for Eddy Lawless; for Kitty Coleraine of Butterman's Lane a penny wise for her foolish pitcher; a putty shovel for Terry the Puckaun; an apotamus mask for Promoter Dunne; a niester egg with a twicedated shell and a dynamight right for Pavl the Curate; a collera morbous for Mann in the Cloack; a starr and girton for Draper and Deane; for Will-of-the-Wisp and Barny-the-Bark two mangolds noble to sweeden their bitters; for Oliver Bound a way in his frey; for Seumas, thought little, a crown he feels big; a tibertine's pile with a Congoswood cross on the back for Sunny Twimjim; a praises be and spare me days for Brian the Bravo; penteplenty of pity with lubilashings of lust for Olona Lena Magdalena; for Camilla, Dromilla, Ludmilla, Mamilla, a bucket, a packet, a book and a pillow; for Nancy Shannon a Tuami brooch; for Dora Riparia Hopeandwater a cooling douche and a warming-pan; a pair of Blarney braggs for Wally Meagher; a hairpin slatepencil for Elsie Oram to scratch her toby, doing her best with her volgar fractions; an old age pension for Betty Bellezza; a bag of the blues for Funny Fitz; a *Missa pro Messa* for Taff de Taff; Jill, the spoon of a girl, for Jack, the broth of a boy; a Rogerson Crusoe's Friday fast for Caducus Angelus Rubiconstein; three hundred and sixtysix poplin tyne for revery warp in the weaver's woof for Victor Hugonot; a stiff steaded rake and good varians muck for Kate the Cleaner; a hole in the ballad for Hosty; two dozen of cradles for J.F.X.P. Coppinger; tenpounten on the pop for the daulphins born with five spoiled squibs for Infanta; a letter to last a lifetime for Maggi beyond by the ashpit; the heftiest frozenmeat woman from Lusk to Livienbad for Felim the Ferry; spas and speranza and symposium's syrup for decayed and blind and gouty Gough; a change of naves and joys of ills for Armoricus Tristram Amoor Saint Lawrence; a guillotine shirt for Reuben Redbreast and hempen suspendeats for Brennan on the Moor; an oakanknee for Conditor Sawyer

and musquodoboits for Great Tropical Scott; a C3 peduncle for Karmalite
Kane; a sunless map of the month, including the sword and stamps, for
Shemus O'Shaun the Post; a jackal with hide for Browne but Nolan; a
stonecold shoulder for Donn Joe Vance; all lock and no stable for Honor-
bright Merreytrickx; a big drum for Billy Dunboyne; a guilty goldeny
bellows, below me blow me, for Ida Ida and a hushaby rocker, Elletrouve-
tout, for Who-is-silvier—Where-is-he?; whatever you like to swilly to
swash, Yuinness or Yennessy, Laagen or Niger, for Festus King and Roaring
Peter and Frisky Shorty and Treacle Tom and O. B. Behan and Sully the
Thug and Master Magrath and Peter Cloran and O'Delawarr Rossa and
Nerone MacPacem and whoever you chance to meet knocking around; and
a pig's bladder balloon for Selina Susquehanna Stakelum. But what did she
give to Pruda Ward and Katty Kanel and Peggy Quilty and Briery Brosna
and Teasy Kieran and Ena Lappin and Muriel Maassy and Zusan Camac
and Melissa Bradogue and Flora Ferns and Fauna Fox-Goodman and
Grettna Greaney and Penelope Inglesante and Lezba Licking like Leytha
Liane and Roxana Rohan with Simpatica Sohan and Una Bina Laterza and
Trina La Mesme and Philomena O'Farrell and Irmak Elly and Josephine
Foyle and Snakeshead Lily and Fountainoy Laura and Marie Xavier Agnes
Daisy Frances de Sales Macleay? She gave them ilcka madre's daughter a
moonflower and a bloodvein: but the grapes that ripe before reason to them
that devide the vinedress. So on Izzy, her shamemaid, love shone befond
her tears as from Shem, her penmight, life past befoul his prime.

My colonial, wardha bagful! A bakereen's dusind with tithe tillies to boot.
That's what you may call a tale of a tub! And Hibernonian market! All that
and more under one crinoline envelope if you dare to break the porkbarrel
seal. No wonder they'd run from her pison plague. Throw us your hudson
soap for the honour of Clane! The wee taste the water left. I'll raft it back,
first thing in the marne. Merced mulde! Ay, and don't forget the reckitts I
lohaned you. You've all the swirls your side of the current. Well, am I to
blame for that if I have? Who said you're to blame for that if you have?
You're a bit on the sharp side. I'm on the wide. Only snuffers' cornets drifts
my way that the cracka dvine chucks out of his cassock, with her estheryear's
marsh narcissus to make him recant his vanitty fair. Foul strips of his
chinook's bible I do be reading, dodwell disgustered but chickled with
chuckles at the tittles is drawn on the tattlepage. *Senior ga dito: Faciasi Omo!*
E omo fu fò. Ho! Ho! *Senior ga dito: Faciasi Hidamo! Hidamo se ga facessà.* Ha!
Ha! And *Die Windermere Dichter* and Lefanu (Sheridan's) old *House by the*
Coachyard and Mill (J.) *On Woman with Ditto on the Floss.* Ja, a swamp for
Altmuehler and a stone for his flossies! I know how racy they move his

wheel. My hands are blawcauld between isker and suda like that piece of pattern chayney there, lying below. Or where is it? Lying beside the sedge I saw it. Hoangho, my sorrow, I've lost it! Aimihi! With that turbary water who could see? So near and yet so far! But O, gihon! I lovat a gabber. I could listen to maure and moravar again. Regn onder river. Flies do your float. Thick is the life for mere.

Well, you know or don't you kennet or haven't I told you every telling has a taling and that's the he and the she of it. Look, look, the dusk is growing! My branches lofty are taking root. And my cold cher's gone ashley. Fieluhr? Filou! What age is at? It saon is late. 'Tis endless now senne eye or erewone last saw Waterhouse's clogh. They took it asunder, I hurd thum sigh. When will they reassemble it? O, my back, my back, my bach! I'd want to go to Aches-les-Pains. Pingpong! There's the Belle for Sexaloitez! And Concepta de Send-us-pray! Pang! Wring out the clothes! Wring in the dew! Godavari, vert the showers! And grant thaya grace! Aman. Will we spread them here now? Ay, we will. Flip! Spread on your bank and I'll spread mine on mine. Flep! It's what I'm doing. Spread! It's churning chill. Der went is rising. I'll lay a few stones on the hostel sheets. A man and his bride embraced between them. Else I'd have sprinkled and folded them only. And I'll tie my butcher's apron here. It's suety yet. The strollers will pass it by. Six shifts, ten kerchiefs, nine to hold to the fire and this for the code, the convent napkins, twelve, one baby's shawl. Good mother Jossiph knows, she said. Whose head? Mutter snores? Deataceas! Wharnow are alle her childer, say? In kingdome gone or power to come or gloria be to them farther? Allalivial, allalluvial! Some here, more no more, more again lost alla stranger. I've heard tell that same brooch of the Shannons was married into a family in Spain. And all the Dunders de Dunnes in Markland's Vineland beyond Brendan's herring pool takes number nine in yangsee's hats. And one of Biddy's beads went bobbing till she rounded up lost histereve with a marigold and a cobbler's candle in a side strain of a main drain of a manzinahurries off Bachelor's Walk. But all that's left to the last of the Meaghers in the loup of the years prefixed and between is one kneebuckle and two hooks in the front. Do you tell me. that now? I do in troth. Orara por Orbe and poor Las Animas! Ussa, Ulla, we're umbas all! Mezha, didn't you hear it a deluge of times, ufer and ufer, respund to spond? You deed, you deed! I need, I need! It's that irrawaddyng I've stoke in my aars. It all but husheth the lethest zswound. Oronoko! What's your trouble? Is that the great Finnleader himself in his joakimono on his statue riding the high hone there forehengist? Father of Otters, it is himself! Yonne there! Isset that? On Fallareen Common? You're thinking

of Astley's Amphitheayter where the bobby restrained you making sugar-
stuck pouts to the ghostwhite horse of the Peppers. Throw the cobwebs
from your eyes, woman, and spread your washing proper! It's well I know
your sort of slop. Flap! Ireland sober is Ireland stiff Lord help you, Maria,
full of grease, the load is with me! Your prayers. I sonht zo! Madammangut!
Were you lifting your elbow, tell us, glazy cheeks, in Conway's Carrigacurra
canteen? Was I what, hobbledyhips? Flop! Your rere gait's creakorheuman
bitts your butts disagrees. Amn't I up since the damp tawn, marthared mary
allacook, with Corrigan's pulse and varicoarse veins, my pramaxle smashed,
Alice Jane in decline and my oneeyed mongrel twice run over, soaking and
bleaching boiler rags, and sweating cold, a widow like me, for to deck my
tennis champion son, the laundryman with the lavandier flannels? You won
your limpopo limp fron the husky hussars when Collars and Cuffs was heir
to the town and your slur gave the stink to Carlow. Holy Scamander, I sar it
again! Near the golden falls. Icis on us! Seints of light! Zezere! Subdue your
noise, you hamble creature! What is it but a blackburry growth or the
dwyergray ass them four old codgers owns. Are you meanam Tarpey and
Lyons and Gregory? I meyne now, thank all, the four of them, and the roar
of them, that draves that stray in the mist and old Johnny MacDougal along
with them. Is that the Poolbeg flasher beyant, pharphar, or a fireboat
coasting nyar the Kishtna or a glow I behold within a hedge or my Garry
come back from the Indes? Wait till the honeying of the lune, love! Die eve,
little eve, die! We see that wonder in your eye. We'll meet again, we'll part
once more. The spot I'll seek if the hour you'll find. My chart shines high
where the blue milk's upset. Forgivemequick, I'm going! Bubye! And you,
pluck your watch, forgetmenot. Your evenlode. So save to jurna's end! My
sights are swimming thicker on me by the shadows to this place. I sow home
slowly now by own way, moyvalley way. Towy I too, rathmine.

Ah, but she was the queer old skeowsha anyhow, Anna Livia, trinket-
toes! And sure he was the quare old buntz too, Dear Dirty Dumpling,
foostherfather of fingalls and dotthergills. Gammer and gaffer we're all
their gangsters. Hadn't he seven dams to wive him? And every dam had
her seven crutches. And every crutch had its seven hues. And each hue had
a differing cry. Sudds for me and supper for you and the doctor's bill for Joe
John. Befor! Bifur! He married his markets, cheap by foul, I know, like any
Etrurian Catholic Heathen, in their pinky limony creamy birnies and their
turkiss indienne mauves. But at milkidmass who was the spouse? Then all
that was was fair. Tys Elvenland! Teems of times and happy returns. The
seim anew. Ordovico or viricordo. Anna was, Livia is, Plurabelle's to be.
Northmen's thing made southfolk's place but howmulty plurators made

eachone in person? Latin me that, my trinity scholard, out of eure sanscreed into oure eryan! *Hircus Civis Eblanensis!* He had buckgoat paps on him, soft ones for orphans. Ho, Lord! Twins of his bosom. Lord save us! And ho! Hey? What all men. Hot? His tittering daughters of. Whawk?

Can't hear with the waters of. The chittering waters of. Flittering bats, fieldmice bawk talk. Ho! Are you not gone ahome? What Thom Malone? Can't hear with bawk of bats, all thim liffeying waters of. Ho, talk save us! My foos won't moos. I feel as old as yonder elm. A tale told of Shaun or Shem? All Livia's daughtersons. Dark hawks hear us. Night! Night! My ho head halls. I feel as heavy as yonder stone. Tell me of John or Shaun? Who were Shem and Shaun the living sons or daughters of? Night now! Tell me, tell me, tell me, elm! Night night! Telmetale of stem or stone. Beside the rivering waters of, hitherandthithering waters of. Night!

BOOK II

VERY EVENING AT LIGHTING UP O'CLOCK SHARP AND until further notice in Feenichts Playhouse. (Bar and conveniences always open, Diddlem Club douncestears.) Entrancings: gads, a scrab; the quality, one large shilling. Newly billed for each wickeday perfumance. Somndoze massinees. By arraignment, childream's hours, expercatered. Jampots, rinsed porters, taken in token. With nightly redistribution of parts and players by the puppetry producer and daily dubbing of ghosters, with the benedict;on of the Holy Genesius Archimimus and under the distinguished patronage of their Elderships the Oldens from the four coroners of Findrias, Murias, Gorias and Falias, Messoirs the Coarbs, Clive Sollis, Galorius Kettle, Pobiedo Lancey and Pierre Dusort, while the Caesar-in-Chief looks. On. Sennet. As played to the Adelphi by the Brothers Bratislavoff (Hyrcan and Haristobulus), after humpteen dumpteen revivals. Before ah the King's Hoarsers with all the Queen's Mum. And wordloosed over seven seas crowdblast in cellelleneteutoslavzendlatinsoundscript. In four tubbloids. While fern may cald us until firn make cold. *The Mime of Mick, Nick and the Maggies*, adopted from the Ballymooney Bloodriddon Murther by Bluechin Blackdillain (authorways 'Big Storey'), featuring:

GLUGG (Mr Seumas McQuillad, hear the riddles between the robot in his dress circular and the gagster in the rogues' gallery), the bold bad bleak boy of the storybooks, who, when the tabs go up, as we discover, because he knew to mutch, has been divorced into disgrace court by

THE FLORAS (Girl Scouts from St. Bride's Finishing Establishment, demand acidulateds), a month's bunch of pretty maidens who, while they pick on her, their pet peeve, form with valkyrienne licence the guard for

IZOD (Miss Butys Pott, ask the attendantess for a leaflet), a bewitching blonde who dimples delightfully and is approached in loveliness only by her grateful sister reflection in a mirror, the cloud of the opal, who, having jilted Glugg, is being fatally fascinated by

CHUFF (Mr Sean O'Mailey, see the chalk and sanguine pictograph on the safety drop), the fine frank fairhaired fellow of the fairytales, who wrestles for tophole with the bold bad bleak boy Glugg, geminally about caps or puds or tog bags or bog gats or chuting rudskin gunerally or something, until they adumbrace a pattern of somebody else or other, after which they are both carried off the set and brought home to be well soaped, sponged and scrubbed again by

ANN (Miss Corrie Corriendo, Grischun scoula, bring the babes, Pieder, Poder and Turtey, she mistributes mandamus monies, after perdunamento, hendrud aloven entrees, pulcinellis must not miss our national rooster's rag), their poor little old mother-in-lieu, who is woman of the house, playing opposite to

HUMP (Mr Makeall Gone, read the sayings from Laxdalesaga in the programme about King Ericus of Schweden and the spirit's whispers in his magical helmet), cap-a-pipe with watch and topper, coat, crest and supporters, the cause of all our grievances, the whirl, the flash and the trouble, who, having partially recovered from a recent impeachment due to egg everlasting, but throughandthoroughly proconverted, propounded for cyclological, is, studding sail once more, jibsheets and royals, in the semblance of the substance for the membrance of the umbrance with the remnance of the emblence reveiling a quemdam supercargo, of The Rockery, Poopinheavin, engaged in entertaining in his pilgrimst custom-house at Caherlehome-upon-Eskur those statutory persons

THE CUSTOMERS (Components of the Afterhour Courses at St. Patricius' Academy for Grownup Gentlemen, consult the annuary, coldporters sibsuction), a bundle of a dozen of representative locomotive civics, each inn quest of outings, who are still more sloppily served after every cup final by

SAUNDERSON (Mr Knut Oelsvinger, Tiffsdays off, wouldntstop in bad, imitation of flatfish, torchbearing supperaape, dud half-sovereign, no chee daily, rolly pollsies, Glen of the Downs, the Gugnir, his geyswerks, his earsequack, his lokistroki, o.s.v.), a scherinsheiner and spoilcurate, unconcerned in the mystery but under the inflounce of the milldieuw and butt of

KATE (Miss Rachel Lea Varian, she tells forkings for baschfellors, under purdah of card palmer teaput tosspot Madam d'Elta, during the pawses), kook-and-dishdrudge, whitch believes wanthingthats, whouse be the church-yard or whorts up the aasgaars, the show must go on.

Time: the pressant.

With futurist onehorse balletbattle pictures and the Pageant of Past History worked up with animal variations amid everglaning mangrove-mazes and beorbtracktors by Messrs Thud and Blunder. Shadows by the film folk, masses by the good people. Promptings by Elanio Vitale. Long-shots, upcloses, outblacks and stagetolets by Hexenschuss, Coachmaher, Incubone and Rocknarrag. Creations tastefully designed by Madame Berthe Delamode. Dances arranged by Harley Quinn and Coollimbeina. Jests, jokes, jigs and jorums for the Wake lent from the properties of the late cemented Mr T. M. Finnegan R.I.C. Lipmasks and hairwigs by Ouida Nooikke. Limes and Floods by Crooker and Toll. Kopay pibe by Kappa Pedersen. Hoed Pine hat with twentyfour ventholes by Morgen. Bosse and stringbag from Heteroditheroe's and All Ladies' presents. Tree taken for grafted. Rock rent. Phenecian blends and Sourdanian doofpoosts by Shauvesourishe and Wohntbedarft. The oakmulberryeke with silktrick twomesh from Shop-Sowry, seedsmanchap. Grabstone beg from General Orders Mailed. The crack (that's Cork!) by a smoker from the gods. The interjection (Buckley!) by the firement in the pit. Accidental music providentially arranged by L'Archet and Laccorde. Melodiotiosities in purefusion by the score. To start with in the beginning, we need hirtly bemark, a community prayer, everyone for himself, and to conclude with as an exodus, we think it well to add, a chorale in canon, good for us all for us all us all all. Songs betune the acts by the ambiamphions of Annapolis, Joan MockComic, male soprano, and Jean Souslevin, bass noble, respectively: O, Mester Sogermon, ef thes es whot ye deux, then I'm not surpleased ye want that bottle of Sauvequipeu and Oh Off Nunch Der Rasche Ver Lasse Mitsch Nitscht. Till the summit scenes of climbacks castastrophear, *The Bearded Mountain* (Polymop Baretherootsch), and *The River Romps to Nursery* (Maidykins in Undiform). The whole thugogmagog, including the portions understood to be oddmitted as the results of the respective titulars neglecting to produce themselves, to be wound up for an afterenactment by a Magnificent Transformation Scene showing the Radium Wedding of Neid and Moorning and the Dawn of Peace, Pure, Perfect and Perpetual, Waking the Weary of the World.

An argument follows.

Chuffy was a nangel then and his soard fleshed light like likening. Fools top! Singty, sangty, meekly loose, defendy nous from prowlabouts. Make a shine on the curst. Emen.

But the duvlin sulph was in Glugger, that lost-to-lurning. Punct. He was sbuffing and sputing, tussing like anisine, whipping his eyesoult and gnatsching his teats over the brividies from existers and the outher liubbocks of life. He halth kelchy chosen a clayblade and makes prayses to his three of clubs. To part from these, my corsets, is into overlusting fear. Acts of feet, hoof and jarrety: athletes longfoot. Djowl, uphere!

Aminxt that nombre of evelings, but how pierceful in their sojestiveness were those first girly stirs, with zitterings of flight released and twinglings of twitchbells in rondel after, with waverings that made shimmershake rather naightily all the duskcended airs and shylit beaconings from shehind hims back. Sammy, call on. Mirrylamb, she was shuffering all the diseasinesses of the unherd of. Mary Louisan Shousapinas! If Arck could no more salve his agnols from the wiles of willy wooly woolf! If all the airish signics of her dipandump helpabit from an Father Hogam till the Mutther Masons could not that Glugg to catch her by the calour of her brideness! Not Rose, Sevilla nor Citronelle; not Esmeralde, Pervinca nor Indra; not Viola even nor all of them four themes over. But, the monthage stick in the melmelode jawr, I am (twintomine) all thees thing. Up tighty in the front, down again on the loose, drim and drumming on her back and a pop from her whistle. What is that, O holytroopers? Isot givin yoe?

Up he stulpled, glee you gees, with search a fling did die near sea, beamy owen and calmy hugh and if you what you my call for me I will wishyoumaycull for you.

And they are met, face a facing. They are set, force to force. And no such Copenhague-Marengo was less so fated for a fall since in Glenasmole of Smiling Thrushes Patch Whyte passed O'Sheen ascowl.

Arrest thee, scaldbrother! came the evangelion, sabre accusant, from all Saint Joan's Wood to kill or maim him, and be dumm but ill s'arrested. Et would proffer to his delected one the his trifle from the grass.

A space. Who are you? The cat's mother. A time. What do you lack? The look of a queen.

But what is that which is one going to prehend? Seeks, buzzling is brains, the feinder.

The howtosayto itiswhatis hemustwhomust worden schall. A darktongues, kunning. O theoperil! Ethiaop lore, the poor lie. He askit of the hoothed fireshield but it was untergone into the matthued heaven. He soughed it from the luft but that bore ne mark ne message. He luked upon the bloomingrund where ongly his corns were growning. At last he listed back to beckline how she pranked alone so johntily. The skand for schooling.

With nought a wired from the wordless either.

Item. He was hardset then. He wented to go (somewhere) while he was weeting. Utem. He wished to grieve on the good persons, that is the four gentlemen. Otem. And it was not a long time till he was feeling true forim he was goodda purssia and it was short after that he was fooling mehaunt to mehynte he was an injine ruber. Etem. He was at his thinker's aunts to give (the four gentlemen) the presence (of a curpse). And this is what he would be willing. He fould the fourd; they found the hurtled stones; they fell ill with the gravy duck: and he sod town with the roust of the meast. Atem.

Towhere byhangs ourtales.

Ah ho! This poor Glugg! It was so said of him about of his old font-mouther. Truly deplurabel! A dire, O dire! And all the freightfullness whom he inhebited after his colline born janitor. Sometime towerable! With that hehry antlets on him and the baublelight bulching out of his sockets whiling away she sprankled his allover with her noces of interregnation: How do you do that lack a lock and pass the poker, please? And bids him tend her, lute and airly. Sing, sweetharp, thing to me anone! So that Glugg, the poor one, in that limbopool which was his subnesciousness he could scares of all knotknow whither his morrder had bourst a blabber or if the vogalstones that hit his tynpan was that mearly his skoll missed her. Misty's trompe or midst his flooting? Ah, ho! Cicely, awe!

The youngly delightsome frilles-in-pleyurs are now showen drawen, if bud one, or, if in florileague, drawens up consociately at the hinder sight of their commoner guardian. Her boy fiend or theirs, if they are so plurielled, cometh up as a trapadour, sinking how he must fand for himself by gazework what their colours wear as they are all showen drawens up. Tireton, cacheton, tireton, ba! Doth that not satisfy youth, sir? Quanty purty bellas, here, Madama Lifay! And what are you going to charm them to, Madama, do say? Cinderynelly angled her slipper; it was cho chiny yet braught her a groom. He will angskt of them from their commoner guardian at next lineup (who is really the rapier of the two though thother brother can hold his own, especially for he bandished it with his hand the hold time, mamain, a simply gracious: Mi, O la!), and reloose that thong off his art: Hast thou feel liked carbunckley ones? Apun which his poohoor pricoxity theirs is a little tittertit of hilarity (Lad-o'-me-soul! Lad-o'-me-soul, see!) and the wordchary is atvoiced ringsoundinly by their toots ensembled, though not meaning to be clever, but just with a shrug of their hips to go to troy and harff a freak at himself by all that story to the ulstramarines. Otherwised, holding their noises, they insinuate quiet private, Ni, he make peace in his preaches and play with esteem.

Warewolff! Olff! Toboo!

So olff for his topheetuck the ruck made raid, aslick aslegs would run; and he ankered on his hunkers with the belly belly prest. Asking: What's my muffinstuffinaches for these times? To weat: Breath and bother and whatarcurss. Then breath more bother and more whatarcurss. Then no breath no bother but worrawarrawurms. And Shim shallave shome.

As Rigagnolina to Mountagnone, what she meaned he could not can. All she meaned was golten sylvup, all she meaned was some Knight's ploung jamn. It's driving her dafft like he's so dumnb. If he'd lonely ta!k instead of only gawk as thought yateman hat stuck hits stick althrough his spokes and if he woold nut wolly so! Hee. Speak, sweety bird! Mitzymitzy! Though I did ate tough turf I'm not the bogdoxy.

— Have you monbreamstone?

— No.

— or Hellfeuersteyn?

— No.

— Or Van Diemen's coral pearl?

— No.

He has lost.

Off to clutch, Glugg! Forwhat! Shape your reres, Glugg! Foreweal! Ring we round, Chuff! Fairwell! Chuffchuff's inners even. All's rice with their whorl!

Yet, ah tears, who can her mater be? She's promised he'd eye her. To try up her pretti. But now it's so longed and so fared and so forth. Jerry for jauntings. Alabye! Fled.

The flossies all and mossies all they drooped upon her draped brimfall. The bowknots, the showlots, they wilted into woeblots. The pearlagraph, the pearlagraph, knew whitchly whether to weep or laugh. For always down in Carolinas lovely Dinahs vaunt their view.

Poor Isa sits a glooming so gleaming in the gloaming; the tincelles a touch tarnished wind no lovelinoise awound her swan's. Hey, lass! Woefear gleam she so glooming, this pooripathete I solde? Her beauman's gone of a cool. Be good enough to symperise. If he's at anywhere she's therefor to join him. If it's to nowhere she's going to too. Buf if he'll go to be a son to France's she'll stay daughter of Clare. Bring tansy, throw myrtle, strew rue, rue, rue. She is fading out like Journee's clothes so you can't see her now. Still we know how Day the Dyer works, in dims and deeps and dusks and darks. And among the shades that Eve's now wearing she'll meet anew fiancy, tryst and trow. Mammy was, Mimmy is, Minuscoline's to be. In the Dee dips a dame and the dame desires a demselle but the demselle dresses dolly and the dolly does a dulcydamble. The same renew. For though she's unmerried she'll after truss up and help that hussyband how to hop. Hip it and trip it and chirrub and sing. Lord Chuffy's sky sheraph and Glugg's got to swing.

So and so, toe by toe, to and fro they go round, for they are the ingelles, scattering nods as girls who may, for they are an angel's garland.

Catchmire stockings, libertyed garters, shoddyshoes, quicked out with selver. Pennyfair caps on pinnyfore frocks and a ring on her fomefing finger. And they leap so looply, looply, as they link to light. And they look so loovely, loovelit, noosed in a nuptious night. Withasly glints in. Andecoy glants out. They ramp it a little, a lessle, a lissle. Then rompride round in rout.

Say them all but tell them apart, cadenzando coloratura! R is Rubretta and A is Arancia, Y is for Yilla and N for greeneriN. B is Boyblue with odalisque O while W waters the fleurettes of novembrance. Though they're all but merely a schoolgirl yet these way went they. I' th' view o' th'avignue dancing goes entrancing roundly. Miss Oodles of Anems before the Luvium doeslike. So. And then again doeslike. So. And miss Endles of Eons efter Dies of Eirae doeslike. So. And then again doeslike. So. The many wiles of Winsure.

The grocer's bawd she slips her hand in the haricot bag, the lady in waiting sips her sup from the paraffin can, Mrs Wildhare Quickdoctor helts her skelts up the casuaway the flasht instinct she herds if a tinkle of tunder, the widow Megrievy she knits cats' cradles, this bountiful actress leashes a harrier under her tongue, and here's the girl who she's kneeled in coldfashion and she's told her priest (spt!) she's pot on a chap (chp!) and this lass not least, this rickissime woman, who she writes foot fortunes money times over in the nursery dust with her capital thumb. Buzz. All runaway sheep bound back bopeep, trailing their teenes behind them. And these ways wend they. And those ways went they. Winnie, Olive and Beatrice, Nelly and Ida, Amy and Rue. Here they come back, all the gay pack, for they are the florals, from foncey and pansey to papavere's blush, foresake-me-nought, while there's leaf there's hope, with primtim's ruse and marry-may's blossom, all the flowers of the ancelles' garden.

But vicereversing thereout from those palms of perfection to anger arbour, treerack monatan, scroucely out of scout of ocean, virid with woad, what tornaments of complementary rages rocked the divlun from his punch-poll to his tummy's shentre as he displaid all the oathword science of his visible disgrace. He was feeling so funny and floored for the cue, all over which girls as he don't know whose hue. If goosseys gazious would but fain smile him a smile he would be fondling a praise he ate some nice bit of fluff. But no geste reveals the unconnouth. They're all odds against him, the beasties. Scratch. Start.

He dove his head into Wat Murrey, gave Stewart Ryall a puck on the plexus, wrestled a hurry-come-union with the Gillie Beg, wiped all his sinses, martial and menial, out of Shrove Sundy MacFearsome, excremuncted as freely as any frothblower into MacIsaac, had a belting bout, chaste to chaste, with McAdoo about nothing and, childhood's age being aye the shameleast, tel a Tartaran tastarin toothsome tarrascone tourtoun, vestimentivorous chlamydophagian, imbretellated himself for any time untellable with what hung over to the Machonochie Middle from the MacSiccaries of the Breeks. Home!

Allwhile, moush missuies from mungy monsie, preying in his mind, son of Everallin, within himself, he swure. Macnoon maggoty mag! Cross of a coppersmith bishop! He would split. He do big squeal like holy Trichepatte. Seek hells where from yank islanders the petriote's absolation. Mocknitza! Genik! He take skiff come first dagrene day overwide tumbler, rough and dark, till when bow of the shower show of the bower with three shirts and a wind, pagoda permettant, crookolevante, the bruce, the coriolano and the ignacio. From prudals to the secular but from the cumman to the nowter. Byebye, Brassolis, I'm breaving! Our war, Dully Gray! A conansdream of lodascircles, he here schlucefinis. Gelchasser no more! Mischnary for the minestrary to all the sems of Aram. Shimach, eon of Era. Mum's for's maxim, ban's for's book and Dodgesome Dora for hedgehung sheol-mastress. And Unkel Silanse coach in diligence. Disconnection of the succeeding. He wholehog himself for carberry banishment care of Pencyl-mania, Bretish Armerica, to melt Mrs Gloria of the Bunkers' Trust, recorporated, (prunty!) by meteoromancy and linguified heissrohgin, quit to hail a hurry laracor and catch the Paname-Turricum and regain that absendee tarry easty, his citta immediata, by an alley and detour with farecard awailable getrennty years. Right for Rovy the Roder. From the safe side of distance! Libera, nostalgia! Beate Laurentie O'Tuli, Euro pra nobis! Every monk his own cashel where every little ligger is his own liogotenente with inclined jambs in full purview to his pronaose and to the deretane at his reredoss. Fuisfinister, fuyerescaper! He would, with the greatest of ease, before of weighting midhook, by dear home trashold on the raging canal, for othersites of Jorden, (heave a hevy, waterboy!) make one of hissens with a knockonacow and a chow collegions and fire off, gheol ghiornal, foull subustioned mullmud, his farced epistol to the hibruws. From Cernilius slomtime prepositus of Toumaria to the clutch in Anteach. Salvo! Ladigs and jointuremen! No more turdenskaulds! Free leaves for ebribadies! All tinsammon in the yord! With harm and aches till farther alters! Wild primates not stop him frem at rearing a writing in handy antics. *Nom de plume!* Gout strap Fenlanns! And send Jarge for Mary Inklenders! And daunt you logh if his vineshanky's schwemmy! For he is the general, make no mistake in he. He is General Jinglesome.

Go in for scribenery with the satiety of arthurs in S.P.Q.R.ish and inform to the old sniggering publicking press and its nation of sheepcopers about the whole plighty troth between them, malady of milady made melodi of

malodi, she, the lalage of lyonesses, and him, her knave arrant. To Wildrose
La Gilligan from Croppy Crowhore. For all within crystal range.

Ukalepe. Loathers' leave. Had Days. Nemo in Patria. The Luncher Out.
Skilly and Carubdish. A Wondering Wreck. From the Mermaids' Tavern.
Bullyfamous. Naughtsycalves. Mother of Misery. Walpurgas Nackt.

Maleesh! He would bare to untired world of Leimuncononnulstria (and
what a strip poker globbtrottel they pairs would looks!) how wholefallows,
his guffer, the sabbatarian (might faction split his beard!), he too had a great
big oh in the megafundum of his tomashunders and how her Lettyshape,
his gummer, that congealed sponsar, she had never cessed at waking malters
among the jemassons since the duft that meataxe delt her made her micro-
chasm as gap as down low. So they fished in the kettle and fought free and if
she bit his tailibout all hat tiffin for thea. He would jused sit it all write down
just as he would jused set it up all writhefully rate in blotch and void,
yielding to no man in hymns ignorance, seeing how heartsilly sorey he was,
owning to the condrition of his bikestool. And, reading off his fleshskin and
writing with his quillbone, fillfull ninequires with it for his auditers, Caxton
and Pollock, a most moraculous jeeremyhead sindbook for all the peoples,
under the presidency of the suchess of sceaunonsceau, a hadtobe heldin,
thoroughly enjoyed by many so meny on block at Boyrut season and for
their account ottorly admired by her husband in sole intimacy, about whose
told his innersense and the grusomehed's yoeureeke of his spectrescope and
why he was off colour and how he was ambothed upon by the very spit of
himself, first on the cheekside by Michelangelo and, besouns thats, over on
the owld jowly side by Bill C. Babby, and the suburb's formule why they
provencials drollo eggspilled him out of his homety dometry narrowedknee
domum (osco de basco de pesco de bisco!) because all his creature comfort
was an omulette finas erbas in an ark finis orbe and, no master how
mustered, mind never mend, he could neither swuck in nonneither swimp
in the flood of cecialism and the best and schortest way of blacking out a
caughtalock of all the sorrors of Sexton until he would accoster her coume
il fou in teto-dous as a wagoner would his mudheeldy wheesindonk at
their trist in Parisise after tourments of tosend years, bread cast out on
waters, making goods at mutuurity, Mondamoiseau of Casanuova and
Mademoisselle from Armentières. Neblonovi's Nivonovio! Nobbio and
Nuby in ennoviacion! Occitantitempoli! He would si through severalls of
sanctuaries maywhatmay mightwhomight so as to meet somewhere, if
produced, on a demi panssion for his whole lofetime, payment in goo to
slee music and poisonal comfany, following which, like Ipsey Secumbe,
when he fingon to foil the fluter, she could have all the g. s. M. she

moohooed after fore and rickwards to herslF, including science of sonorous silence, while he, being brung up on soul butter, have recourse of course to poetry. With tears for his coronaichon, such as engines weep. Was liffe worth leaving? Nej!

Tholedoth, treetrene! Zokrahsing, stone! Arty, reminiscensitive, at bandstand finale on grand carriero, dreaming largesse of lifesighs over early lived offs—all old Sators of the Sowsceptre highly nutritius family histrionic, genitricksling with Avus and Avia, that simple pair, and descendant down on veloutypads by a vuncular process to Nurus and Noverca, those notorious nepotists, circumpictified in their sobrine census, patriss all of them by the glos on their germane faces and their socerine eyes like transparents of vitricus, patruuts to a man, the archimade levirs of his ekonome world. Remember thee, castle throwen? Ones propsperups treed, now stohong baroque. And oil paint use a pumme if yell trace me there title to where was a hovel not a havel (the first rattle of his juniverse) with a tingtumtingling and a next, next and next (gin a paddy? got a petty? gussies, gif it ope?), while itch ish shome.

> —My God, alas, that dear olt tumtum home
> Whereof in youthfood port I preyed
> Amook the verdigrassy convict vallsall dazes.
> And cloitered for amourmeant in thy boosome shede!

His mouthfull of ecstasy (for Shing-Yung-Thing in Shina from Yoruyume across the Timor Sea), herepong (maladventure!) shot pinging up through the errorooth of his wisdom (who thought him a Fonar all, feastking of shellies by googling Lovvey, regally freytherem, eagelly plumed, and wasbut gumboil owrithy prods wretched some horsery megee plods coffin acid odarkery pluds dense floppens mugurdy) as thought it had been zawhen intwo. Wholly sanguish blooded up disconvulsing the fixtures of his fizz. Apang which his tempory chewer med him a crazy chump of a Haveajube Sillayass. Joshua Croesus, son of Nunn! Though he shall live for millions of years a life of billions of years, from their roseaced glows to their violast lustres, he shall not forget that pucking Pugases. Holihowlsballs and bloody acres! Like gnawthing unheardth!

But, by Jove Chronides, Seed of Summ, after at he had bate his breastplates for, forforget, forforgetting his birdsplace, it was soon that, that he, that he rehad himself. By a prayer? No, that comes later. By contrite attrition? Nay, that we passed. Mid esercizism? So is richt.

And it was so. And Malthos Moramor resumed his soul. With: Go Ferchios off to Allad out of this! An oldsteinsong. He threwed his fit up to his aers, rolled his poligone eyes, snivelled from his snose and blew the guff

out of his hornypipe. The hopjoimt jerk of a ladle broom jig that he learned
in locofoco when a redhot turnspite he. Under reign of old Roastin the
Bowl Ratskillers, readyos! Why was that man for he's doin her wrong!
Lookery looks, how he's knots in his entrails! Mookery mooks, it's a grippe
of his gripes. Seekeryseeks, why his biting he's head off? Cokerycokes, it's
his spurt of coal. And may his tarpitch dilute not give him chromitis! For the
mauwe that blinks you blank is mostly Carbo. Where the inflammabilis
might pursuive his comburenda with a pure flame and a true flame and a
flame all toogasser, soot. The worst is over. Wait! And the dubuny Mag
may gang to preesses. With Dinny Finneen, me canty, ho! In the lost of the
gleamens. Sousymoust. For he would himself deal a treatment as might be
trusted in anticipation of his inculmination unto fructification for the major
operation. When (pip!) a message interfering intermitting interskips from
them (pet!) on herzian waves, (call her venicey names! call her a stell!) a
butterfly from her zipclasped handbag, a wounded dove astarted from,
escaping out her forecotes. Isle wail for yews, O doherlynt! The poetesser.
And around its scorched cap she has twilled a twine of flame to let the
laitiest know she's marrid. And pim it goes backballed. Tot burns it so leste.
A claribel cumbeck to errind. Hers before his even, posted ere penned. He's
your change, thinkyou methim. Go daft noon, madden, mind the step.
Please stoop O to please. Stop. What saying? I have soreunder from to him
now, dearmate ashore, so, so compleasely till I can get redressed, which
means the end of my stays in the languish of Tintangle. Is you zealous of
mes, brother? Did you boo moiety lowd? You supposed to be the on
conditiously rejected? Satanly, lade! Can that sobstuff, whingeywilly! Stop
up, mavrone, and sit in my lap, Pepette, though I'd much rather not. Like
things are m. ds. is all in vincibles. Decoded.

Now a run for his money! Now a dash to her dot! Old cocker, young
crowy sifadda, sosson. A bran new, speedhount, outstripperous on the wind.
Like a waft to wingweary one or a sos to a coastguard. For directly with his
whoop, stop and an upalepsy didando a tishy, in appreciable less time than it
takes a glaciator to submerger an Atlangthis, was he again, agob, before the
trembly ones, a spark's gap off, doubledasguesched, gotten orlop in a simpla-
sailormade and shaking the storm out of his hiccups. The smartest vessel
you could find would elazilee him on her knee as her lucky for the Rio
Grande. He's a pigtail tarr and if he hadn't got it toothick he'd a telltale tall
of his pitcher on a wall with his photure in the papers for cutting moutonlegs
and capers, letting on he'd jest be japers and his tail cooked up.

Goal! It's one by its length.

Angelinas, hide from light those hues that your sin beau may bring to light! Though down to your dowerstrip he's bent to knee he maun't know ledgings here.

For a haunting way will go and you need not make your mow. Find the frenge for frocks and translace it into shocks of such as touch with show and show.

He is guessing at hers for all he is worse, the seagoer. Hark to his wily geeses goosling by, and playfair, lady! And note that they who will for exile say can for dog while them that won't leave ingle end says now for know.

For he faulters how he hates to trouble them without.

But leaving codhead's mitre and the heron's plumes sinistrant to the server of servants and rex of regums and making a bolderdash for lubberty of speech he asks not have you seen a match being struck nor is this powder mine but, letting punplays pass to ernest:

— Haps thee jaoneofergs?

— Nao.

— Haps thee mayjaunties?

— Naohao.

— Haps thee per causes nunsibellies?

— Naohaohao.

— Asky, asky, asky! Gau on! Micaco! Get!

Ping an ping nwan ping pwan pong.

And he did a get, their anayance, and slink his hook away, aleguere come alaguerre, like a chimista inchamisas, whom the harricana hurries and hots foots, zingo, zango, segur. To hoots of utskut, urqurd, jamal, qum, yallah, yawash, yak! For he could ciappacioppachew upon a skarp snakk of pure undefallen engelsk, melanmoon or tartatortoise, tsukisaki or soppisuppon, as raskly and as baskly as your cheesechalk cow cudd spanich. Makoto! Whagta kriowday! Gelagala nausy is. Yet right divining do not was. Hovobovo hafogate hokidimatzi in kamicha! He had his sperrits all foulen on him; to vet, most griposly, he was bedizzled and debuzzled; he had his tristiest cabaleer on; and looked like bruddy Hal. A shelling a cockshy and be donkey shot at? Or a peso besant to join the armada?

But, Sin Showpanza, could anybroddy which walked this world with eyes whiteopen have looked twinsomer than the kerl he left behind him? Candidatus, viridosus, aurilucens, sinelab? Of all the green heroes everwore coton breiches, the whitemost, the goldenest! How he stud theirs with himselfs mookst kevinly, and that anterevolitionary, the churchman child-father from tonsor's tuft to almonder's toes, a haggiography in duotri-gesumy, son soptimost of sire sixtusks, of Mayaqueenies sign osure, hevnly buddhy time, inwreathed of his near cissies, a mickly dazzly eely oily with

looiscurrals, a soulnetzer by zvesdals priestessd, their trail the tractive, and
dem dandypanies knows de play of de eyelids, with his gamecox spurts
and his smile likequid glue (the suessiest sourir ever weanling wore), whiles
his host of spritties, lusspillerindernees, they went peahenning a ripida-
rapidarpad around him, pilgrim prinkips, kerilour kevinour, in neuchoristic
congressulations, quite purringly excited, rpdrpd, allauding to him by all the
licknames in the litany with the terms in which no little dulsy nayer ever
thinks about implying except to her future's year and sending him perfume
most praypuffs to setisfire more then to teasim (shllwe help, now you've
massmuled, you t'rigolect a bit? yismik? yimissy?) that he, the finehued, the
fairhailed, the farahead, might bouchesave unto each but everyone, asfar as
safras durst assune, the havemercyonhurs of his kissier licence. Meanings:
Andure the enjurious till imbetther rer. We know you like Latin with essies
impures, (and your liber as they sea) we certney like gurgles love the
nargleygargley so, arrahbeejee, tell that old frankay boyuk to bellows upthe
tombucky in his tumtum argan and give us a gust of his gushy old. Goof!

Hymnumber twentynine. O, the singing! Happy little girlycums to have
adolphted such an Adelphus! O, the swinginging hopops so goholden!
They've come to chant en chor. They say their salat, the madiens' prayer to
the messiager of His Nabis, prostitating their selfs eachwise and combinedly.
Fateha, fold the hands. Be it honoured, bow the head. May thine evings e'en
be blossful! Even of bliss! As we so hope for ablution. For the sake of the
farbung and of the scent and of the holiodrops. Amems.

A pause. Their orison arises misquewhite as Osman glory, ebbing waste-
ward, leaves to the soul of light its fading silence (allahlah lahlah lah!), a
turquewashed sky. Then:

— Xanthos! Xanthos! Xanthos! We thank to thine, mighty innocent,
that diddest bring it off fuitefuite. Should in ofter years it became about you
will after desk jobduty becoming a bank midland mansioner we and I shall
reside with our obeisant servants among Burke's mobility at La Roseraie,
Ailesbury Road. Red bricks are all hellishly good values if you trust to the
roster of ads but we'll save up ourselves and nab what's nicest and boskiest
of timber trees in the nebohood. Oncaill's plot. Luccombe oaks, Turkish
hazels, Greek firs, incense palm edcedras. The hypsometers of Mount
Anville is held to be dying out of arthataxis but, praise send Larix U' Thule,
the wych elm of Manelagh is still flourishing in the open, because its native
of our nature and the seeds was sent by Fortune. We'll have our private
palypeachum pillarposterns for lovesick letterines fondly affianxed to our
front railings and swings, hammocks, tighttaught balletlines, accomodation-
nooks and prismic bathboites, to make Envyeyes mouth water and wonder

when they binocular us from their embrassured windows in our garden rare. Fyat-Fyat shall be our number on the autokinaton and Chubby in his Chuffs oursforownly chuffeur. T will be waiting for uns as I sold U at the first antries. Our cousin gourmand, Percy, the pup, will denounce the sniffnomers of all callers where among our Seemyease Sister, Tabitha, the ninelived, will extend to the full her hearthy welcome. While the turf and twigs they tattle. Tintin tintin. Lady Marmela Shortbred will walk in for supper with her marchpane switch on, her necklace of almonds and her poirette Sundae dress with bracelets of honey and her cochineal hose with the caramel dancings, the briskly best from Bootiestown, and her sucking-staff of ivorymint. You mustn't miss it or you'll be sorry. Charmeuses chloes, glycering juwells, lydialight fans and puffumed cynarettes. And the Prince Le Monade has been graciously pleased. His six chocolate pages will run bugling before him and Cococream toddle after with his sticksword in a pink cushion. We think His Sparkling Headiness ought to know Lady Marmela. Luisome his for lissome hers. He's not going to Cork till Cantalamesse or mayhope till Rose Easter or Saint Tibble's Day. So Niomon knows. The Fomor's in his Fin, the Momor's her and hin. A paaralone! A paaralone! And Dublin's all adin. We'll sing a song of Single-month and you'll too and you'll. Here are notes. There's the key. One two three. Chours! So come on, ye wealthy gentrymen wibfrufrocksfull of fun! Thin thin! Thin thin! Thej olly and thel ively, thou billy with thee coo, for to jog a jig of a crispness nice and sing a missal too. Hip champouree! Hiphip champouree! O you longtailed blackman, polk it up behind me! Hip champouree! Hiphip champouree! And, jessies, push the pumkik round. Anneliuia!

Since the days of Roamaloose and Rehmoose the pavanos have been strident through their struts of Chapelldiseut, the vaulsies have meed and youdled through the purly ooze of Ballybough, many a mismy cloudy has tripped taintily along that hercourt strayed reelway and the rigadoons have held ragtimed revels on the platauplain of Grangegorman; and, though since then sterlings and guineas have been replaced by brooks and lions and some progress has been made on stilts and the races have come and gone and Thyme, that chef of seasoners, has made his usual astewte use of endadjustables and whatnot willbe isnor was, those danceadeils and can-canzanies have come stimmering down for our begayment through the bedeafdom of po's taeorns, the obcecity of pa's teapucs, as lithe and limbfree limber as when momie mummed at ma.

Just so styled with the nattes are their flowerheads now and each of all has a lovestalk onto herself and the tot of all the tits of their understamens is as open as he can posably she and is tournesoled straightcut or sidewaist, accourdant to the coursets of things feminite, towooerds him in heliolatry, so they may catchcup in their calyzettes, alls they go troping, those parryshoots from his muscalone pistil, for he can eyespy through them, to their selfcolours, nevertheleast their tissue peepers, (meaning Mullabury mesh, the time of appling flowers, a guarded figure of speech, a variety of perfume, a bridawl, seamist inso one) as leichtly as see saw (O my goodmiss! O my greatmess! O my prizelestly preshoes!) while, dewyfully as dimb dumbelles, all alisten to his elixir. Lovelyt!

And they said to him:

— Enchainted, dear sweet Stainusless, young confessor, dearer dearest, we herehear, aboutobloss, O coelicola, thee salutamt. Pattern of our unschoold, pageantmaster, deliverer of softmissives, round the world in forty mails, bag, belt and balmybeam, our barnaboy, our chepachap, with that pampipe in your putaway, gab borab, when you will be after doing all your sightseeing and soundhearing and smellsniffing and tastytasting and tenderumstouchings in all Daneygaul, send us, your adorables, thou overblaseed, a wise and letters play of all you can ceive, chief celtech chappy, from your holy post now you hast ascertained ceremonially our names. Unclean you art not. Outcaste thou are not. Leperstower, the karman's loki, has not blanched at our pollution and your intercourse at ninety legsplits does not defile. Untouchable is not the scarecrown is on you. You are pure. You are pure. You are in your puerity. You have not brought stinking members into the house of Amanti. Elleb Inam, Titep Notep, we name them to the Hall of Honour. Your head has been touched by the god Enel-Rah and your face has been brightened by the goddess Aruc-Ituc. Return, sainted youngling, and walk once more among us! The rains of Demani are masikal as of yere. And Baraza is all aflower. Siker of calmy days. As shiver as shower can be. Our breed and better class is in brood and bitter pass. Labbeycliath longs. But we're counting on the cluck. The Great Cackler comes again. Sweetstaker, Abel lord of all our haloease, we (to be slightly more femmiliar perhips than is slickly more then nacessory), toutes philomelas as well as magdelenes, were drawpairs with two pinmarks, BVD and BVD dot, so want lotteries of ticklets posthastem (you appreciate?) so as to be very dainty, if an isaspell, and so as to be verily dandydainty, if an ishibilley, of and on, to and for, by and with, from you. Let the hitback hurry his wayward ere the missive has time to take herself off, 'twill be o'erthemore willfully intomeet if the coming offence can send our shudders before. We eem to have being elewhere as tho' th' had pas'd in our upens. Next to our shrinking selves we love sensitivas best. For they are the

Angèles. Brick, fauve, jonquil, sprig, fleet, nocturne, smiling bruise. For they are an Angèle's garment. We will be constant (what a word!) and bless the day, for whole hours too, yes, for sold long syne as we shall be heing in our created being of ours elvishness, the day you befell, you dreadful temptation! Now promisus as at our requisted you will remain ignorant of all what you hear and, though if whilst disrobing to the edge of risk, (the bisifings in idolhours that satinfines tootoo!) draw a veil till we next time! You don't want to peach but bejimboed if ye do! Perhelps. We ernst too may. How many months or how many years till the myriadth and first become! Bashfulness be tupped! May he colp, may he colp her, may he mixandmass colp her! Talk with a hare and you wake of a tartars. That's mus. Says the Law. List! Kicky Lacey, the pervergined, and Bianca Mutantini, her conversa, drew their fools longth finnishfurst, Herzog van Vellentam, but me and meother ravin, my coosine of mine, have mour good three chancers, weothers, after Bohnaparts. The mything smile of me, my wholesole assumption, shes nowt mewithout as weam twin herewithin, that I love like myselfish, like smithereens robinsongs, like juneses nutslost, like the blue of the sky if I stoop for to spy's between my whiteyoumightcallimbs. How their duel makes their triel! Eer's wax for Sur Soord, dongdong bollets for the iris riflers, queemswellth of coocome in their combs for the jennyjos. Caro caressimus! Honey swarns where mellisponds. Will bee all buzzy one another minnies for the mere effect that you are so fuld of pollen yourself. Teomeo! Daurdour! We feel unspeechably thoughtless over it all here in Gizzygazelle Tark's bimboowood so pleasekindly communicake with the original sinse we are only yearning as yet how to burgeon. It's meant milliems of centiments deadlost or mislaid on them but, master of snakes, we can sloughchange in the nip of a napple solongas we can allsee for deedsetton your quick. By the hook in your look we're eyed for aye were you begging the questuan with your lutean bowl round Monkmesserag. And whenever you're tingling in your trout we're sure to be tangled in our ticements. It's game, ma chère, be offwith your shepherdress on! Upsome cauda! Behose our handmades for the lured! To these nunce we are but yours in ammatures yet well come that day we shall ope to be ores. Then shalt thou see, seeing, the sight. No more hoaxites! Nay more gifting in mennage! A her's fancy for a his friend and then that fellow yours after this follow ours. Vania, Vania Vaniorum, Domne Vanias!

Hightime is ups be it down into outs according! When there shall be foods for vermin as full as feeds for the fett, eat on earth as there's hot in oven. When every Klitty of a scolderymeid shall hold every yardscullion's right to stimm her uprecht for whimsoever, whether on privates, whather in publics. And when all us romance catholeens shall have ones for all amanseprated. And the world is maidfree. Methanks. So much for His Meignysthy man! And all his bigyttens. So till Coquette to tell Cockotte to teach Connie Curley to touch Cattie Hayre and tip Carminia to tap La Chèrie though where the diggings he dwellst amongst us here's nobody knows save Mary. Whyfor we go ringing hands in hands in gyrogyrorondo.

These bright elects, consentconsorted, they were waltzing up their willside with their princesome handsome angeline chiuff while in those wherebus there wont bears way (mearing unknown, a place where pigeons carry fire to seethe viands, a miry hill, belge end sore footh) oaths and screams and bawley groans with a belchybubhub and a hellabelow bedemmed and bediabbled the arimaining lucisphere. Helldsdend, whelldselse! Lonedom's breach lay foulend up uncouth not be broched by punns and reedles. Yet the ring gayed rund rorosily with a drat for a brat You. Yasha Yash ate sassage and mash. So he found he bash, poor Yasha Yash. And you wonna make one of our micknick party. No honaryhuest on our sposhialiste. For poor Glugger was dazed and late in his crave, ay he, laid in his grave.

But low, boys low, he rises, shrivering, with his spittyful eyes and his whoozebecome woice. Ephthah! Cisamis! Examen of conscience scruples now he to the best of his memory schemado. Nu mere for ever siden on the stolen. With his tumescinquinance in the thight of his tumstull. No more singing all the dags in his sengaggeng. Experssly at hand counterhand. Trinitatis kink had mudded his dome, peccat and pent fore, pree. Hymserf, munchaowl, maden, born of thug tribe into brood blackmail, dooly redecant allbigenesis henesies. He, by bletchendmacht of the golls, proforhim penance and come off enternatural. He, selfsufficiencer, eggscumuddher-in-chaff sporticolorissimo, what though the duthsthrows in his lavabad eyes, maketomake polentay rossum, (Good savours queen with the stem of swuith Aftreck! Fit for king of Zundas) out of bianconies, hiking ahake like any nudgemeroughgorude all over Terracuta. No more throw acids, face all lovabilities, appeal for the union and play for tirnitys. He, praise Saint Calembaurnus, make clean breastsack of goody girl now as ever drank milksoep from a spoen, weedhearted boy of potter and mudder, chip of old Flinn the Flinter, twig of the hider that tanned him. He go calaboosh all same he tell him out. Teufleuf man he strip him all mussymussy calico blong him all same he tell him all out how he make what name. He, through wolkenic connection, relation belong this remarklable moliman, Anaks Andrum, parleyglutton pure blood Jebusite, centy procent Erserum spoking. Drugmallt storehuse. Intrance on back. Most open on the laydays. He, A. A., in peachskin shantungs, possible, sooth to say, notwithstanding far

former guiles and he gaining fish considerable, by saving grace after
avalunch, to look most prophitable out of smily skibluh eye. He repeat of
him as pious alios cos he ast for shave and haircut people said he'd shape of
hegoat where he just was sheep of herrgott with his tile togged. Top. Not
true what chronicles is bringing his portemanteau priamed full potato-
wards. Big dumm crumm digaditchies say short again akter, even while
lossassinated by summan, he coaxyorum a pennysilvers offarings bloadonages
with candid zuckers on Spinshesses Walk in presents to lilithe maidinettes
for at bloo his noose for him with pruriest pollygameous inatentions, he
having that pecuniarity ailmint spectacularly in heather cliff emurgency
on gale days because souffrant chronic from a plentitude of house torts.
Collosul rhodomantic not wert one bronze lie Scholarina say as he, greyed
vike cuddlepuller, walk in her sleep his pig indicks weg femtyfem funts. Of
so little is her timentrousnest great for greeting his immensesness. Sutt
soonas sett they were, her uyes as his auroholes. Kaledvalch! How could
one classically? One could naught critically. Ininest lightingshaft only for
lovalit smugpipe, his Mistress Mereshame, of cupric tresses, the formwhite
foaminine, the ambersandalled, after Aasdocktor Talop's onamuttony
legture. A mish, holy balm of seinsed myrries, he is as good as a mountain
and everybody what is found of his gients he knew Meistral Wikingson,
furframed Noordwogen's kampften, with complexion of blushing dolomite
fanned by ozeone brisees, what naver saw his bedshead farrer and nuver met
his swigamore, have his ignomen from prima signation of being Master
Milchku, queerest man in the benighted queendom, and, adcraft aidant,
how he found the kids. Other accuse him as lochkneeghed forsunkener,
dope in stockknob, all ameltingmoult after rhomatism, purely simply tammy
ratkins. The kurds of Copt on the berberutters and their bedaweens! Even
was Shes whole begeds offbefore all his nahars in the koldbethizzdryel. No
gudth! Not one zouz! They whiteliveried ragsups, two Whales of the Sea of
Deceit, they bloodiblabstard shooters, three Dromedaries of the Sands of
Calumdonia. As is note worthies to shock his hind! Ur greeft on them! Such
askors and their ruperts they are putting in for more osghirs is alse false
liarnels. The frockenhalted victims! Whore affirm is agains sempry Lotta
Karssens. They would lick their lenses before they would negatise a jom
petter from kis sodalites. In his contrary and on reality, which Bichop
Babwith bares to his whitness in his *Just a Fication of Villumses*, this Mr Heer
Assassor Neelson, of sorestate hearing, diseased, formarly with Adenoiks,
den feed all Lighty, laxtleap great change of retiring family buckler, highly
accurect in his everythinks, from tencents coupoll to bargain basement, live
with howthold of nummer seven, wideawake, woundabout, wokinbetts,

weeklings, in black velvet on geolgian mission senest mangy years his rear
in the lane pictures, blanking same with autonaut and annexes and got a
daarlingt babyboy bucktooth, the thick of a gobstick, coming on ever so
nerses nursely, gracies to goodess, at 81. That why all parks up excited
about his gunnfodder. That why ecrazyaztecs and the crime ministers
preaching him mornings and makes a power of spoon vittles out of his
praverbs. That why he, persona erecta, glycorawman arseniful femorniser,
for a trial by julias, in celestial sunhat, with two purses agitatating his
theopot with wokklebout shake, rather incoherend, from one 18 to one 18
biss, young shy gay youngs. Sympoly far infusing up pritty tipidities to lock
up their rhainodaisies and be nice and twainty in the shade. Old grand
tuttut toucher up of young poetographies and he turn aroundabrupth red
altfrumpishly like hear samhar tionnor falls some make one noise. It's his
last lap, Gigantic, fare him weal! Revelation! A fact. True bill. By a jury of
matrons. Hump for humbleness, dump for dirts. And, to make a long
stoney badder and a whorly show a parfect sight, his Thing went the
wholyway retup Suffrogate Strate.

Helpmeat too, contrasta toga, his fiery goosemother, laotsey taotsey,
woman who did, he tell princes of the age about. You sound on me, judges!
Suppose we brisken up. Kings! Meet the Mem, Avenlith, all viviparous out
of couple of lizards. She just as fenny as he is fulgar. How laat soever her
latest still her sawlogs come up all standing. Psing a psalm of psexpeans,
apocryphul of rhyme! His cheekmole of allaph foriverever her allinall and
his Kuran never teachit her the be the owner of thyself. So she not swop her
eckcot hjem for Howarden's Castle, Englandwales. But be the alleance of
iern on his flamen vestacoat, the fibule of broochbronze to his wintermantle
of pointefox. Who not knows she, the Madame Cooley-Couley, spawife
to laird of manna, when first come into the pictures more as hundreads
elskerelks' yahrds of annams call away, factory fresh and fiuming at the
mouth, wronged by Hwemwednoget (magrathmagreeth, he takable a rap
for that early party) and whenceforward Ani Mama and her fiertey bustles
terrified of gmere gnomes of gmountains and furibound to be back in her
mytinbeddy? Schi schi, she feightened allsouls at pignpugn and gets a pan in
her stummi from the piaLabellars in their pur war. Yet jackticktating all
around her about his poorliness due to pannellism and grime for that he
harboured her when feme sole, her zoravarn lhorde and givnergenral, and
led her in antient consort ruhm and bound her durant coverture so as she
could not steal from him, oz her or damman, so as if ever she's beleaved
by checkenbrooth death since both was parties to the feed it's Hetman
MacCumhal foots the funeral. Mealwhile she nutre him jacent from her

elmer's almsdish, giantar and tschaina as sieme as bibrondas with Foli Signur's tinner roumanschy to fishle the ladwigs out of his lugwags, like a skittering kitty skattering hayels, when his favourites were all beruffled on him and her own undesirables justickulating, it was such a blowick day. Winden wanden wild like wenchen wenden wanton. The why if he but would bite and plug his baccypipes and renownse the devlins in all their pumbs and kip the streelwarkers out of the plague and nettleses milk from sickling the honeycoombe and kop Ulo Bubo selling foulty treepes, she would make massa dinars with her savuneer dealinsh and delicate her nutbrown glory cloack to Mayde Berenice and hang herself in Ostmanns-town Saint Megan's and make no more mulierage before mahatmas or moslemans, but would ondulate her shookerloft hat from Alpoleary with a viv baselgia and a clamast apotria like any purple cardinal's princess or woman of the grave word to the papal legate from the Vatucum, Monsaigneur Rabbinsohn Crucis, with an ass of milg to his cowmate and chilterlings on account of all he quaqueduxed for the hnor of Hrom and the nations abhord him and wop mezzo scudo to Sant Pursy Orelli that gave Luiz-Marios Josephs their loyal devouces to be offered up missas for vowts for widders.

Hear, O worldwithout! Tiny tattling! Backwoods, be wary! Daintytrees, go dutch!

But who comes yond with pire on poletop? He who relights our spearing torch, the moon. Bring lolave branches to mud cabins and peace to the tents of Ceder, Neomenie! The feast of Tubbournigglers is at hand. Shopshup. Inisfail! Timple temple tells the bells. In syngagyng a sangasongue. For all in Ondslosby. And, the hag they damename Coverfew hists from her lane. And haste, 'tis time for bairns ta hame. Chickchilds, comeho to roo. Come-home to roo, wee chickchilds doo, when the wildworewolf's abroad. Ah, let's away and let's gay and let's stay chez where the log foyer's burning!

It darkles, (tinct, tint) all this our funnaminal world. Yon marshpond by ruodmark verge is visited by the tide. Alvemmarea! We are circumveiloped by obscuritads. Man and belves frieren. There is a wish on them to be not doing or anything. Or just for rugs. Zoo koud! Drr, deff, coal lay on and, pzz, call us pyrress! Ha. Where is our highly honourworthy salutable spousefounderess? The foolish one of the family is within. Haha! Huzoor, where's he? At house, to's pitty. With Nancy Hands. Tcheetchee! Hound through the maize has fled. What hou! Isegrim under lolling ears. Far wol! And wheaten bells bide breathless. All. The trail of Gill not yet is to be seen, rocksdrops, up benn, down dell, a craggy road for rambling. Nor yet through starland that silver sash. What era's o'ering? Lang gong late. Say long,

scielo! Sillume, see lo! Selene, sail O! Amune! Ark!? Noh?! Nought stirs in
spinney. The swayful pathways of the dragonfly spider stay still in reedery.
Quiet takes back her folded fields. Tranquille thanks. Adew. In deerhaven,
imbraced, alleged, injoynted and unlatched, the birds, tommelise too, quail
silent. ii. Luathan? Nuathan! Was avond ere a while. Now conticinium. As
Lord the Laohun is sheutseuyes. The time of lying together will come and
the wildering of the nicht till cockeedoodle aubens Aurore. Panther monster.
Send leabarrow loads amorrow. While loevdom shleeps. Elenfant has siang
his triump, *Great is Eliphas Magistrodontos* and after kneeprayer pious for
behemuth and mahamoth will rest him from tusker toils. Salamsalaim!
Rhinohorn isnoutso pigfellow but him ist gonz wurst. Kikikuki. Hopopo-
dorme. Sobeast! No chare of beagles, frantling of peacocks, no muzzing of
the camel, smuttering of apes. Lights, pageboy, lights! Brights we'll be
brights. With help of Hanoukan's lamp. When otter leaps in outer parts
then Yul remembers Mei. Her hung maid mohns are bluming, look, to
greet those loes on coast of amethyst; arcglow's seafire siemens lure and
wextward warnerforth's hookercrookers. And now with robby brerfox's fishy
fable lissaned out, the threads simwhat toran and knots in its antargumends,
the pesciolines in Liffeyetta's bowl have stopped squiggling about Junoh
and the whalk and feriaquintaism and pebble infinibility and the poissission
of the hoghly course. And if Lubbernabohore laid his horker to the ribber,
save the giregargoh and dabardin going on in his mount of knowledge
(munt), he would not hear a flip flap in all Finnyland. Witchman, watch of
your night? Es voes, ez noes, nott voes, ges, noun. It goes. It does not go.
Darkpark's acoo with sucking loves. Rosimund's by her wishing well. Soon
tempt-in-twos will stroll at venture and hunt-by-threes strut musketeering.
Brace of girdles, brasse of beauys. With the width of the way for jogjoy.
Hulker's cieclest elbownunsense. Hold hard! And his dithering dathering
waltzers of. Stright! But meet-ings mate not as forsehn. Hesperons! And if
you wand to Livmouth, wenderer, while Jempson's weed decks Jacqueson's
Island, here lurks, bar hellpelhullpulthebell, none iron welcome. Bing. Bong.
Bangbong. Thunderation! You took with the mulligrubs and we lack
mulsum? No sirrebob! Great goodness, no! Were you Marely quean of
Scuts or but Chrestien the Last, (our duty to you, chris! royalty, squat!)
how matt your mark, though luked your johl, here's dapplebellied mugs
and troublebedded rooms and sawdust strown in expectoration and for
ratification by specification of your information, Mr Knight, tuntapster,
buttles; his alefru's up to his hip. And Watsy Lyke sees after all rinsings
and don't omiss Kate, homeswab homely, put in with the bricks. A's the
sign and one's the number. Where Chavvyout Chacer calls the cup and

Pouropourim stands astirrup. De oud huis bij de kerkegaard. So who over comes ever for Whoopee Weeks must put up with the Jug and Chambers.

But heed! Our thirty minutes war's alull. All's quiet on the felled of Gorey. Between the starfort and the thornwood brass castle flambs with mutton candles. Hushkah, a horn! Gadolmagtog! God es El? Housefather calls enthreateningly. From Brandenborgenthor. At Asa's arthre. In thundercloud periwig. With lightning bug aflash from afinger. My souls and by jings, should he work his jaw to give down the banks and hark from the tomb! Ansighosa pokes in her potstill to souse at the sop be sodden enow and to hear to all the bubbles besaying: the coming man, the future woman, the food that is to build, what he with fifteen years will do, the ring in her mouth of joyous guard, stars astir ant stirabout. A palashe for hirs, a saucy for hers and ladlelike spoons for the wonner. But ein and twee were never worth three. So they must have their final since he's on parole. Et la pau' Leonie has the choice of her lives between Josephinus and Mario-Louis for who is to wear the lily of Bohemey, Florestan, Thaddeus, Hardress or Myles. And lead raptivity captive. Ready! Like a Finn at a fair. Now for la belle! Icy-la-Belle!

The campus calls them. Ninan ninan, the gattling gan! Childs will be wilds. 'Twastold. And vamp, vamp, vamp, the girls are merchand. The horseshow magnete draws his field and don't the fillyings fly? Educande of Sorrento, they newknow knowwell their Vico's road. Arranked in their array and flocking for the fray on that old orangeray, Dolly Brae. For these are not on terms, they twain, bartrossers, since their baffle of Whatalose when Adam Leftus and the devil took our hindmost, gegifting her with his painapple, nor will not be atoned at all in fight to no finish, that dark deed doer, this wellwilled wooer, Jerkoff and Eatsoup, Yem or Yan, while felixed is who culpas does and harm's worth healing and Brune is bad French for Jour d'Anno. Tiggers and Tuggers they're all for tenzones. Bettlimbraves. For she must walk out. And it must be with who. Teaseforhim. Toesforhim. Tossforhim. Two. Else there is danger of. Solitude.

Postreintroducing Jeremy, the chastenot coulter, the flowing taal that brooks no brooking runs on to say how, as it was mutualiter foretold of him by a timekiller to his spacemaker, velos ambos and arubyat knychts, with their tales within wheels and stucks between spokes, on the hike from Elmstree to Stene and back, how, running awage with the use of reason (sics) and ramming amok at the brake of his voice (secs), his lasterhalf was set for getting the besterwhole of his yougendtougend, for control number thrice was operating the subliminal of his invaded personality. He nobit smorfi and go poltri and let all the tondo gang bola del ruffo. Barto no know him mor. Eat larto altruis with most perfect stranger.

Boo, you're through!

Hoo, I'm true!

Men, teacan a tea simmering, hamo mavrone kerry O?

Teapotty. Teapotty.

Kod knows. Anything ruind. Meetingless.

He wept indeiterum. With such a tooth he seemed to love his wee tart when abuy. Highly momourning he see the before him. Melained from nape to kneecap though vied from her girders up. Holy Santalto, cursing saint, sight most deletious to ross up the spyballs like exude of margary! And how him it heaviered that eyerim rust! An they bare falls witless against thee how slight becomes a hidden wound? Soldwoter he wash him all time bigfeller bruisy place blong him. He no want missies blong all boy other look bruisy place blong him. Hence. It will paineth the chastenot in that where of his whence he had loseth his once for every, even though mode grow moramor maenneritsch and the Tarara boom decay. Immaculacy, give but to drink to his shirt and all skirtaskortas must change her tunics. So warred he from first to last, forebanned and betweenly, a smuggler for lifer. Lift the blank ve veered as heil! Split the hvide and aye seize heaven! He knows for he's seen it in black and white through his eyetrompit trained upon jenny's and all that sort of thing which is dandymount to a clear-obscure. Prettimaid tints may try their taunts: apple, bacchante, custard, dove, eskimo, feldgrau, hematite, isingglass, jet, kipper, lucile, mimosa, nut, oysterette, prune, quasimodo, royal, sago, tango, umber, vanilla, wisteria, xray, yesplease, zaza, philomel, theerose. What are they all by? Shee.

If you nude her in her prime, make sure you find her complementary or, on your very first occasion, by Angus Dagdasson and all his piccions, she'll prick you where you're proudest with her unsatt speagle eye. Look sharp, she's signalling from among the asters. Turn again, wistfultone, lode mere of Doubtlynn! Arise, Land-under-Wave! Clap your lingua to your pallet, drop your jowl with a jolt, tambourine until your breath slides, pet a pout and it's out. Have you got me, Allysloper?

My top it was brought Achill's low, my middle I ope before you, my bottom's a vulser if ever there valsed and my whole the flower that stars the day and is solly well worth your pilger's fahrt. Where there's a hitch, a head of things, let henker's halter hang the halunkenend. For I see through your weapon. That cry's not Cucullus. And his eyelids are painted. If my tutor here is cut out for an oldeborre I'm Flo, shy of peeps, you know. But when he beetles backwards, ain't I fly? Pull the boughpee to see how we sleep. Bee Peep! Peepette! Would you like that lump of a tongue for lungeon or this Turkey's delighter, hys hyphen mys? My bellyswain's a

twalf whulerusspower though he knows as much how to man a wife as
Dunckle Dalton of matching wools. Shake hands through the thicketloch!
Sweet swanwater! My other is mouthfilled. This kissing wold's full of killing
fellows kneeling voyantly to the cope of heaven. And somebody's coming, I
feel for a fect. I've a seeklet to sell thee if old Deanns won't be threaspanning.
When you'll next have the mind to retire to be wicked this is as dainty a way
as any. Underwoods spells bushment's business. So if you sprig poplar
you're bound to twig this. 'Twas my lord of Glendalough benedixed the
gape for me that time at Long Entry, commanding the approaches to my
intimast innermost. Look how they're browthered! Six thirteens at Blanche
de Blanche's of 3 Behind Street and 2 Turnagain Lane. Awabeg is my
callby, Magnus here's my Max, Wonder One's my cipher and Seven Sisters
is my nighbrood. Radouga, Rab will ye na pick them in their pink of panties.
You can colour up till you're prawn while I go squirt with any cockle. When
here who adolls me infuxes sleep. But if this could see with its backsight he'd
be the grand old greeneyed lobster. He's my first viewmarc since Valentine.
Wink's the winning word.

Luck!

In the house of breathings lies that word, all fairness. The walls are of
rubinen and the glittergates of elfinbone. The roof herof is of massicious
jasper and a canopy of Tyrian awning rises and still descends to it. A grape
cluster of lights hangs therebeneath and all the house is filled with the
breathings of her fairness, the fairness of fondance and the fairness of milk
and rhubarb and the fairness of roasted meats and uniomargrits and the
fairness of promise with consonantia and avowals. There lies her word, you
reder! The height herup exalts it and the lowness her down abaseth it. It
vibroverberates upon the tegmen and prosplodes from pomoeria. A window,
a hedge, a prong, a hand, an eye, a sign, a head and keep your other augur
on her paypaypay. And you have it, old Sem, pat as ah be seated! And
Sunny, my gander, he's coming to land her. The boy which she now adores.
She dores. Oh backed von dem zug! Make weg for their tug!

With a ring ding dong, they raise clasped hands and advance more steps
to retire to the saum. Curtsey one, curtsey two, with arms akimbo, devotees.

Irrelevance.

All sing:

— I rose up one maypole morning and saw in my glass how nobody loves
me but you. Ugh. Ugh.

All point in the shem direction as if to shun.

— My name is Misha Misha but call me Toffey Tough. I mean Metten-
chough. It was her, boy the boy that was loft in the larch. Ogh! Ogh!

Her reverence.

All laugh.

They pretend to helf while they simply shauted at him sauce to make hims prich. And ith ith noth cricquette, Sally Lums. Not by ever such a lot. Twentynines of bloomers gegging een man arose. Avis was there and trilled her about it. She's her sex, for certain. So to celebrate the occasion:

— Willest thou rossy banders havind?

He simules to be tight in ribbings round his rumpffkorpff.

— Are you Swarthants that's hit on a shorn stile?

He makes semblant to be swiping their chimbleys.

— Can you ajew ajew fro' Sheidam?

He finges to be cutting up with a pair of sissers and to be buytings of their maidens and spitting their heads into their facepails.

Spickspuk! Spoken.

So now be hushy, little pukers! Side here roohish, cleany fuglers! Grand-icellies, all stay zitty! Adultereux, rest as befour! For you've jollywelly dawdled all the day. When ye coif tantoncle's hat then'll be largely temts for that. Yet's the time for being now, now, now.

For a burning would is come to dance inane. Glamours hath moidered's lieb and herefore Coldours must leap no more. Lack breath must leap no more.

Lel lols for libelman libling his lore. Lolo Lolo liebermann you loved to be leaving Libnius. Lift your right to your Liber Lord. Link your left to your lass of liberty. Lala Lala, Leapermann, your lep's but a loop to lee.

A fork of hazel o'er the field in vox the verveine virgins ode. If you cross this rood as you roamed the rand I'm blessed but you'd feel him a blasting rod. Behind, me, frees from evil smells! Perdition stinks before us.

Aghatharept they fleurelly to Nebnos will and Rosocale. Twice is he gone to quest of her, thrice is she now to him. So see we so as seed we sow. And their prunktqueen kilt her kirtles up and set out. And her troup came heeling, O. And what do you think that pride was drest in! Voolykins' diamondinah's vestin. For ever they scent where air she went. While all the fauns' flares widens wild to see a floral's school.

Led by Lignifer, in four hops of the happiest, ach beth cac duff, a marrer of the sward incoronate, the few fly the farbetween! We haul minymony on that piebold nig. Will any tubble dabble on the bay? Nor far jocubus? Nic for jay? Attilad! Attattilad! Get up, Goth's scourge on you! There's a visitation in your impluvium. Hun! Hun!

He stanth theirs mun in his natural, oblious autamnesically of his very proprium, (such is stockpot leaden, so did sonsepun crake) the wont to be wanton maid a will to be wise. Thrust from the light, apophotorejected, he spoors loves from her heats. He blinkth. But's wrath's the higher where those wreathe charity. For all of these have been thisworlders, time liquescing into state, pitiless age grows angelhood. Though, as he stehs, most anysing may befallhim from a song of a witch to the totter of Blackarss, given a fammished devil, a young sourceress and (eternal conjunction) the permission of overalls with the cuperation of nightshirt. If he spice east he seethes in sooth and if he pierce north he wilts in the waist. And what wonder with the murkery viceheid in the shade? The specks on his lapspan are his foul deed thougths, wishmarks of mad imogenation. Take they off! Make the off! But Funnylegs are leanly. A bimbamb bum! They vain would convert the to be hers in the word. Gush, they wooed! Gash, they're fair ripecherry!

As for she could shake him. An oaf, no more. Still he'd be good tutor two in his big armschair lerningstoel and she be waxen in his hands. Turning up and fingering over the most dantellising peaches in the lingerous longerous book of the dark. Look at this passage about Galilleotto! I know it is difficult but when your goche I go dead. Turn now to this patch upon Smacchiavelluti! Soot allours, he's sure to spot it! 'Twas ever so in monitorology since Headmaster Adam became Eva Harte's toucher, in *omnibus moribus et temporibus*, with man's mischief in his mind whilst her pupils swimmed too heavenlies, let his be exaspirated, letters be blowed! I is a femaline person. O, of provocative gender. U unisingular case.

Which is why trumpers are mixed up in duels and here's B. Rohan meets N. Ohlan for the prize of a thou.

But listen to the mocking birde to micking barde making bared! We've heard it aye since songdom was gemurrmal. As he was queering his shoolthers. So was I. And as I was cleansing my fausties. So was he. And as way ware puffiing our blowbags. Souwouyou.

Come, thrust! Go, parry! Dvoinabrathran, dare. The mad long ramp of manchind's parlements, the learned lacklearning, merciless as wonderful.

— Now may Saint Mowy of the Pleasant Grin be your everglass and even prospect!

— Feeling dank.

Exchange, reverse.

— And may Saint Jerome of the Harlots' Curse make family three of you which is much abedder!

— Grassy ass ago.

And each was wrought with his other. And his continence fell. The bivitellines, Metellus and Ametallikos, her crown pretenders, obscindgemeinded biekerers, varying directly, uruseye each oxesother, superfetated (never cleaner of lamps frowned fiercelier on anointer of hinges), while their treegrown girls, king's game, if he deign so, are in such transfusion just to know twigst timidy twomeys, for gracious sake, who is artthoudux from whose heterotropic, the sleepy or the glouch, for, shyly bawn and showly nursured, exceedingly nice girls can strike exceedingly bad times unless so richtly chosen's by (what though of riches he have none and hope dashes hope on his heart's horizon) to gar their great moments greater. The thing is he must be put strait on the spot, no mere waterstichystuff in a selfmade world that you can't believe a word he's written in, not for pie, but one's only owned by naturel rejection. Charley, you're my darwing! So sing they sequent the assent of man. Till they go round if they go roundagain before breakparts and all dismissed. They keep. Step keep. Step. Stop. Who is Fleur? Where is Ange? Or Gardoun?

Creedless, croonless hangs his haughty. There end no moe red devil in the white of his eye. Braglodyte him do a katadupe! A condamn quondam jontom sick af a suckbut! He does not know how his grandson's grandson's grandson's grandson will stammer up in Peruvian for in the ersebest idiom I have done it equals I so shall do. He dares not think why the grandmother of the grandmother of his grandmother's grandmother coughed Russky with suchky husky accent since in the mouthart of the slove look at me now means I once was otherwise. Nor that the mappamund has been changing pattern as youth plays moves from street to street since time and races were and wise ants hoarded and sauterelles were spendthrifts, no thing making newthing wealthshowever for a silly old Sol, healthytobedder and latewiser. Nor that the turtling of a London's alderman is ladled out by the waggerful to the regionals of pigmyland. His part should say in honour bound: So help me symethew, sammarc, selluc and singin, I will stick to you, by gum, no matter what, bite simbum, and in case of the event coming off beforehand even so you was to release me for the sake of the other cheap girl's baby's name plaster me but I will pluckily well pull on the buckskin gloves! But Noodynaady's actual ingrate tootle is of come into the garner mauve and thy nice are stores of morning and buy me a bunch of iodines.

Evidentament he has failed as tiercely as the deuce before for she is wearing none of the three. And quite as patently there is a hole in the ballet trough which the rest fell out. Because to explain why the residue is, was, or will not be, according to the eighth axiom, proceeded with, namely, since ever apart that gossan duad, so sure as their's a patch on a pomelo, this yam ham in never live could, the shifting about of the lassies, the tug of love of their lads ending with a great deal of merriment, hoots, screams, scarf drill, cap fecking, ejaculations of aurinos, reechoable mirthpeals and general thumbtonosery (Myama's a yaung yaung cauntry), one must recken with the sudden and gigantesquesque appearance unwithstandable as a general election in Barnado's bearskin amongst the brawlmiddle of this village childergarten of the largely longsuffering laird of Lucanhof.

But, vrayedevraye Blankdeblank, god of all machineries and tomestone of Barnstaple, by mortisection or vivisuture, splitten up or recompounded, an isaac jacquemin mauromormo milesian, how accountibus for him, moreblue?

Was he pitssched for an ensemple as certain have dognosed of him against our seawall by Rurie, Thoath and Cleaver, those three stout sweynhearts, Orion of the Orgiasts, Meereschal MacMuhun, the Ipse dadden, product of the extremes giving quotidients to our means, as might occur to anyone, your brutest layaman with the princest champion in our archdeaconry, or so yclept from Clio's clippings, which the chroncher of chivalries is sulpicious save he scan, for ancients link with presents as the human chain extends, have done, do and will again as John, Polycarp and Irenews eye-to-eye ayewitnessed and to Paddy Palmer, while monks sell yew to archers or the water of the livvying goes the way of all fish from Sara's drawhead, the corralsome, to Isaac's, the lauphed butt one, with her minnelisp extorreor to his moanolothe inturned? So Perrichon with Bastienne or heavy Humph with airy Nan, Ricqueracqbrimbillyjicquey-jocqjolicass? How sowesthow, *dullcisamica*? A and aa ab ad abu abiad. A babbel men dub gulch of tears.

The mar of murmury mermers to the mind's ear, uncharted rock, evasive weed. Only the caul knows his thousandfirst name, Hocus Crocus, Esquilocus, Finnfinn the Faineant, how feel full foes in furrinarr! Doth it not all come aft to you, puritysnooper, in the way television opes longtimes ofter when Potollomuck Sotyr or Sourdanapplous the Lollapaloosa? The charges are, you will remember, the chances are, you won't; bit it's old Joe, the Java Jane, older even than Odam Costollo, and we are recurrently meeting em, par Mahun Mesme, in cycloannalism, from space to space, time after time, in various phases of scripture as in various poses of sepulture. Greets Godd, Groceries! Merodach! Defend the King! Hoet of the rough throat attack but whose say is soft but whose ee has a cute angle, he whose hut is a hissarlik even as her hennin's aspire. And insodaintily she's a quine of selm ashaker while as a murder of corpse when his magot's up he's the best berrathon sanger in all the aisles of Skaldignavia. As who shall hear. For now at last is Longabed going to be gone to, that more than man, prince of Bunnicombe of wide roadsterds, the herblord the gillyflowrets so fain fan to flatter about. Artho is the name is on the hero, Capellisato, shoehanded slaughterer of the shader of our leaves.

Attach him! Hold!

Yet stir thee, to clay, Tamor!

Why wilt thou erewaken him from his earth, O summonorother: he is weatherbitten from the dusts of ages? The hour of his closing hies to hand; the tocsin that shall claxonise his wareabouts. If one who remembered his webgoods and tealofts were to ask of a hooper for whose it was the storks were quitting Aquileyria, this trundler would not wot; if other who joined faith when his depth charge bombed our barrel spillway were to—!

Jehosophat, what doom is here! Rain ruth on them, sire! The wing of Moykill cover him! The Bulljon Bossbrute quarantee him! Calavera, caution! Slaves to Virtue, save his Veritotem! Bearara Tolearis, *procul abeat*! The Ivorbonegorer of Danamaraca be, his Hector Protector! Woldomar with Vasa, peel your peeps! And try to saviourise the nights of labour to the order of our blooding worold! While Pliny the Younger writes to Pliny the Elder his calamolumen of contumellas, what Aulus Gellius picked on Micmacrobius and what Vitruvius pocketed from Cassiodorus. Like we larnt from that Buke of Lukan in Dublin's capital, Kongdam Coombe. Even if you are the kooper of the winkel over measure never lost a licence. Nor a duckindonche divulse from hath and breakfast. And for the honour of Alcohol drop that you-know-what-I've-come-about-I-saw-your-act air! Punch may be pottleproud but his Judy's a wife's wit better.

For the producer (Mr John Baptister Vickar) caused a deep abuliousness to descend upon the Father of Truants and, at a side issue, pluterpromptly brought on the scene the cutletsized consort, foundling filly of fortyshilling fostertailor and shipman's shopahoyden, weighing ten pebble ten, scaling five footsy five and spanning thirtyseven inchettes round the good companions, twentynine ditties round the wishful waistress, thirtyseven alsos round the answer to everything, twentythree of the same round each of the quis separabits, fourteen round the beginning of happiness and nicely nine round her shoed for slender.

And eher you could pray mercy to goodness or help with your hokey or mehokeypoo, Gallus's hen has collared her pullets. That's where they have owreglias for. Their bone of contention, flesh to their thorns, prest as Prestissima, makes off in a thinkling (and not one hen only nor two hens neyther but every blessed brigid came aclucking and aclacking), while, a rum a rum, the ram of all harns, Bier, Wijn, Spirituosen for consumption on the premises, advokaat withouten pleaders, Mas marrit, Pas poulit, Ras ruddist of all, though flamifestouned from galantifloures, is hued and cried of each's colour.

Home all go. Halome. Blare no more ramsblares, oddmund barkes! And cease your fumings, kindalled bushies! And sherrigoldies yeassymgnays; your wildeshaweshowe moves swiftly sterneward! For here the holy language. Soons to come. To pausse.

'Tis goed. Het best.

For they are now tearing, that is, teartoretorning. Too soon are coming tasbooks and goody, hominy bread and bible bee, with jaggery-yo to juju-jaw, Fine's French phrases from the Grandmère des Grammaires and bothered parsenaps from the Four Massores, Mattatias, Marusias, Lucanias, Jokinias, and what happened to our eleven in thirtytwo antepostdating the Valgur Eire and why is limbo where is he and what are the sound waves saying ceased ere they all wayed wrong and Amnist anguished axes Collis and where fishngaman fetched the mongafesh from and whatfor paddybird notplease rancoon and why was Sindat sitthing on him sitbom like a saildior, with what the doc did in the doil, not to mention define the hydraulics of common salt and, its denier crid of old provaunce, where G.P.O. is zentrum and D.U.T.C. are radients write down by the frequency of the scores and crores of your refractions the valuations in the pice of dinggyings on N.C.R. and S.C.R.

That little cloud, a nibulissa, still hangs isky. Singabed sulks before slumber. Light at night has an alps on his druckhouse. Thick head and thin butter or after you with me. Caspi, but gueroligue stings the air. Gaylegs to riot of us! Gallocks to lafft! What is amaid today todo? So angelland all weeping bin that Izzy most unhappy is. Fain Essie fie onhapje? laughs her stella's vispirine.

While, running about their ways, going and coming, now at rhimba rhomba, now in trippiza trappaza, pleating a pattern Gran Geamatron showed them of gracehoppers, auntskippers and coneyfarm leppers, they jeerilied along, durian gay and marian maidcap, lou Dariou beside la Matieto, all boy more all girl singoutfeller longa house blong store Huddy, whilest nin nin nin nin that Boorman's clock, a winny on the tinny side, ninned nin nin nin nin, about old Father Barley how he got up of a morning arley and he met with a plattonem blondes named Hips and Haws and fell in with a fellows of Trinity some header Skowood Shaws like (You'll catch it, don't fret, Mrs Tummy Lupton! Come indoor, Scoffy-nosey, and shed your swank!) auld Daddy Deacon who could stow well his place of beacon but he never could hold his kerosene's candle to (The nurse'll give it you, stickypots! And you wait, my lasso, fecking the twine!)

bold Farmer Burleigh who wuck up in a hurlywurly where he huddly could wuddle to wallow his weg tillbag of the baker's booth to beg of (You're well held now, Missy Cheekspeer, and your panto's off! Fie, for shame, Ruth Wheatacre, after all the booz said!) illed Diddiddy Achin for the prize of a pease of bakin with a pinch of the panch of the ponch in jurys for (Ah, crabeyes, I have you, showing off to the world with that gape in your stocking!) Wold Forrester Farley who, in deesperation of deisipration at the diasporation of his diesparation, was found of the round of the sound of the lound of the Lukkedoerendunandurraskewdylooshoofermoy-portertooryzooysphalnabortansporthaokansakroidverjkapakkapuk.

Byfall.

Upploud!

The play thou schouwburgst, Game, here endeth. The curtain drops by deep request.

Uplouderamain!

Gonn the gawds, Gunnar's gustspells. When the h, who the hu, how the hue, where the huer? Orbiter onswers: lots lives lost. Fionia is fed up with Fidge Fudgesons. Sealand snorres. Rendningrocks roguesreckning reigns. Gwds with gurs are gttrdmmrng. Hlls vlls. The timid hearts of words all exeomnosunt. Mannagad, lammalelouh, how do that come? By Dad, youd not heed that fert? Fulgitudes ejist rowdownan tonuout. Quoq! And buncskleydoodle! Kidoosh! Of their fear they broke, they ate wind, they fled; where they ate there they fled; of their fear they fled, they broke away. Go to, let us extol Azrael with our harks, by our brews, on our jambses, in his gaits. To Mezouzalem with the Dephilim, didits dinkun's dud? Yip! Yup! Yarrah! And let Nek Nekulon extol Mak Makal and let him say unto him: Immi ammi Semmi. And shall not Babel be with Lebab? And he war. And he shall open his mouth and answer: I hear, O Ismael, how they laud is only as my loud is one. If Nekulon shall be havonfalled surely Makal haven hevens. Go to, let us extell Makal, yea, let us exceedingly extell. Though you have lien amung your posspots my excellency is over Ismael. Great is him whom is over Ismael and he shall mekanek of Mak Nakulon. And he deed.

Uplouderamainagain!

For the Clearer of the Air from on high has spoken in tumbuldum tambaldam to his tembledim tombaldoom worrild and, moguphonoised by that phonemanon, the unhappitents of the earth have terrerumbled from fimament unto fundament and from tweedledeedumms down to twiddledeedees.

Loud, hear us!

Loud, graciously hear us!

Now have thy children entered into their habitations. And nationglad, camp meeting over, to shin it, Gov be thanked! Thou hast closed the portals of the habitations of thy children and thou hast set thy guards thereby, even Garda Didymus and Garda Domas, that thy children may read in the book of the opening of the mind to light and err not in the darkness which is the afterthought of thy nomatter by theguardiance of those guards which are thy bodemen, the cheeryboyum chirryboth with the kerrybommers in their krubeems, Pray-your-Prayers Timothy and Back-to-Bunk Tom.

Till tree from tree, tree among trees tree over tree become stone to stone, stone between stones, stone under stone for ever.

O Loud, hear the wee beseech of thees of each of these thy unlitten ones! Grant sleep in hour's time, O Loud!

That they take no chill. That they do ming no merder. That they shall not gomeet madhowiatrees.

Loud, heap miseries upon us yet entwine our arts with laughters low!

Ha he hi ho hu.

Mummum.

[2]

AS WE THERE ARE where are we are we there from tomtittot to teetootomtotalitarian. Tea tea too oo. UNDE ET UBI.

with his broad and hairy face, to Ireland a disgrace.

Whom will comes over. Who to caps ever. And howelse do we hook our hike to find that pint of porter place? Am shot, says the bigguard.[1] SIC.

Menly about peebles.

Whence. Quick lunch by our left, wheel, to where. Long Livius Lane, mid Mezzofanti Mall, diagonising Lavatery Square, up Tycho Brache Crescent,[2] shouldering Berkeley Alley, querfixing Gainsborough Carfax, under Guido d'Arezzo's Gadeway, by New Livius Lane till IMAGINABLE ITINERARY THROUGH THE PARTICULAR UNIVERSAL.

1 Rawmeash, quoshe with her girlic teangue. If old Herod with the Cormwell's exzema was to go for me like he does Snuffler whatever about his blue canaries I'd do nine months for his beaver beard.

2 Mater Mary Mercerycordial of the Dripping Nipples, milk's a queer arrangement.

Don't retch
meat fat salt
lard sinks
down (and
out).

where we whiled while we whithered. Old Vico
Roundpoint. But fahr, be fear! And natural,
simple, slavish, filial. The marriage of Montan
wetting his moll we know, like any enthewsyass
cuckling a hoyden[1] in her rougey gipsylike
chinkaminx pulshandjupeyjade and her petsy-
bluse indecked o' voylets.[2] When who was wist
was ware. En elv, et fjaell. And the whirr of the
whins humming us howe. His hume. Hence-
taking tides we haply return, trumpeted by
prawns and ensigned with seakale, to befinding
ourself when old is said in one and maker mates
with made (O my!), having conned the cones
and meditated the mured and pondered the
pensils and ogled the olymp and delighted
in her dianaphous and cacchinated behind his

Swiney Tod,
ye Daimon
Barbar!

culosses, before a mosoleum. Length Withought
Breath, of him, a chump of the evums, upshoot
of picnic or stupor out of sopor, Cave of Kids
or Hymanian Glattstoneburg, denary, danery,

Dig him in
the rubsh!
Ungodly old
Ardrey,
Cronwall
beeswaxing
the
convulsion
box.

donnery, domm, who, entiringly as he continues
highlyfictional, tumulous under his chthonic
exterior but plain Mr Tumulty in mufti-life,[3]
in his antisipiences as in his recognisances, is,
(Dominic Directus) a manyfeast munificent
more mob than man.

     Ainsoph,[4] this upright one, with that noughty
besighed him zeroine. To see in his horrorscup
he is mehrkurios than saltz of sulphur. Terror
of the noonstruck by day, cryptogram of each
nightly bridable. But, to speak broken heaven-
talk, is he? Who is he? Whose is he? Why is
he? Howmuch is he? Which is he? When is he?

CONSTITU-
TION OF
THE
CONSTITU-
TIONABLE
AS
CONSTITU-
TIONAL

---

1 Real life behind the floodlights as shown by the best exponents of a royal divorce.
2 When we play dress grownup at alla ludo poker you'll be happnessised to feel how
  fetching I can look in clingarounds.
3 Kellywick, Longfellow's Lodgings, House of Comments III, Cake Walk, Amusing
  Avenue, Salt Hill, Co. Mahogany, Izalond, Terra Firma.
4 Groupname for grapejuice.

Where is he?[1] How is he? And what the
decans is there about him anyway, the
decemt man? Easy, calm your haste!
Approach to lead our passage!   PROBA-
This bridge is upper.   POSSIBLE
Cross.   PROLEGO-
Thus come to castle.   MENA TO
Knock.[2]   IDEAREAL
A password, thanks.   HISTORY.
Yes, pearse.
Well, all be dumbed!

Swing the banjo,   O really?[3]
bantams, bounce-   Hoo cavedin earthwight
the-baller's blown   At furscht kracht of thunder.[4]
to fook.   When shoo, his flutterby,
Thsight near left   Was netted and named.[5]
me eyes when I   Erdnacrusha, requiestress, wake em!
seen her put   And let luck's presplutterall lucy at
thounce otay ithpot.   ease![6]
To house as wise fool ages builded.
Sow byg eat.[7]   GNOSIS OF

Quartand-wds.   Staplering to tether to, steppingstone   PRECREATE
to mount by, as the Boote's at Pickards-   DETERMIN-
town. And that skimmelk steed still in the   ATION.
groundloftfan. As over all. Or be these   AGNOSIS OF
wingsets leaned to the outwalls, beastskin   POSTCREATE

Tickets for   trophies of booth of Baws the balsam-   DETER-
the Tailwaggers   boards?[8] Burials be ballyhouraised! So   MINISM.
Terrierpuppy   let Bacchus e'en call! Inn inn! Inn inn!
Raffle.   Where. The babbers ply the pen. The

---

1 Bhing, said the burglar's head, soto poce her.
2 Yussive smirte and ye mermon answerth from his beelyingplace below the tightmark,
    Gotahelv!
3 O Evol, kool in the salg and ees how Dozi pits what a drows er.
4 A goodrid croven in a tynwalled tub.
5 Apis amat aram. Luna legit librum. Pulla petit pascua.
6 And after dinn to shoot the shades.
7 Says blistered Mary Achinhead to beautifed Tummy Tullbutt.
8 Begge. To go the Begge. To go to Begge and to be sure to reminder Begge. Goodbeg,
    buggey Begge.

bibbers drang the den. The papplicom, the pubblicam he's turning tin for ten. From seldomers that most frequent him. That same erst crafty hakemouth which under the assumed name of Ignotus Loquor, of foggy old, harangued bellyhooting fishdrunks on their favorite stamping ground, from a father

Mars speaking. theobalder brake.[1] And Egyptus, the incenstrobed, as Cyrus heard of him? And Major A. Shaw after he got the miner smellpex? And old Whiteman self, the blighty blotchy, beyond the bays, hope of ostrogothic and ottomanic faith converters, despair of Pandemia's postwartem plastic surgeons? But is was all so long ago. Hispano–Cathayan–Euxine, Castillian–Emeratic–Hebridian,

Smith, no home. Espanol–Cymric–Helleniky? Rolf the Ganger, Rough the Gangster, not a feature alike and the face the same.[2] Pastimes are past times. Now let bygones be bei Gunne's. Saaleddies er it in this warken werden, mine boerne, and it vild need olderwise[3] since primal made alter in garden of Idem. The tasks above are as the flasks below, saith the

Non quod sed quiat. emerald canticle of Hermes and all's loth and pleasestir, are we told, on excellent inkbottle authority, solarsystemised, seriolcosmically, in a more and more almightily expanding universe under one, there is rhymeless reason to believe, original sun.

Hearasay in paradox lust. Securely judges orb terrestrial.[4] *Haud certo ergo.* But O felicitous culpability, sweet bad cess to you for an archetypt!

Honour commercio's energy yet aid the

---

1 Huntler and Pumar's animal alphabites, the first in the world from aab to zoo.
2 We dont hear the booming cursowarries, we wont fear the fletches of fightning, we float the meditarenias and come bask to the isle we love in spice. Punt.
3 And this once golden bee a cimadoro.
4 And he was a gay Lutharius anyway, Sinobiled. You can tell by their extraordinary clothes.

linkless proud, the plurable with everybody and   ARCHAIC
ech with pal, this ernst of Allsap's ale halliday of   ZELOTYPIA
roaring month with its two lunar eclipses and   AND THE
its three saturnine settings! Horn of Heatthen,   ODIUM
highbrowed! Brook of Life, backfrish! Amnios   TELE-
amnium, fluminicuíum flaminulinorum! We   OLOGICUM.
seek the Blessed One, the Harbourer-cum-
Enheritance. Even Canaan the Hateful. Ever a-
going, ever a-coming. Between a stare and a
sough. Fossilisation, all branches.[1] Wherefore

Bags.   Petra sware unto Ulma: By the mortals' frost!
Balls.   And Ulma sware unto Petra: On my veiny life!

In these places sojournemus, where Eblinn   THE
water, leased of carr and fen, leaving amont   LOCALIS-
her shoals and salmen browses, whom inshore   ATION OF
breezes woo with freshets, windeth to her   LEGEND
broads. A phantom city, phaked of philim   LEADING
pholk, bowed and sould for a four of hundreds   TO THE
of manhood in their three and threescore   LEGALIS-
fylkers for a price partitional of twenty six and   ATION OF
Move up,   six. By this riverside, on our sunnybank,[2] how   LATI-
Mackinerny!   buona the vista, by Santa Rosa! A field of   FUNDISM.
Make room   May, the very vale of Spring. Orchards here
for Muck-   are lodged; sainted lawrels evremberried. You
inurney!   have a hoig view ashwald, a glen of marrons
and of thorns. Gleannaulinn, Ardeevin: purty
glint of plaising height. This Norman court at
boundary of the ville, yon creepered tower of
a church of Ereland, meet for true saints in
worshipful assemblage,[3] with our king's house
of stone, belgroved of mulbrey, the still that
was mill and Kloster that was Yeomansland,
the ghastcold tombshape of the quick foregone
on, the loftleaved elm Lefanunian above-
mansioned, each, every, all is for the retro-

1 Startnaked and bonedstiff. We vivvy soddy. All be dood.
2 When you dreamt that you'd wealth in marble arch do you ever think of pool beg
  slowe.
3 Porphyrious Olbion, redcoatliar, we were always wholly rose marines on our side
  every time.

spectioner. Skole! Agus skole igen![1] Sweetsome
auburn, cometh up as a selfreizing flower, that
fragolance of the fraisey beds: the phoenix, his
pyre, is still flaming away with trueprattight
spirit: the wren his nest is niedelig as the turrises
of the sabines are televisible. Here are the
cottage and the bungalow for the cobbeler and
the brandnewburgher:[2] but Izolde, her chaplet
gardens, an litlee plads af liefest pose, arride the

In snowdrop, winnerful wonders off, the winnerful wonnerful
trou-de- wanders off,[3] with hedges of ivy and hollywood
dentelle, and bower of mistletoe, are, tho if it theem tho
flesh and and yeth if you pleathes,[4] for the blithehaired
heliotrope. daughter of Angoisse. All out of two barreny
old perishers, Tytonyhands and Vlossyhair, a
kilolitre in metromyriams. Presepeprosapia,
the parent bole. Wone tabard, wine tap and
warm tavern[5] and, by ribbon development,
from contact bridge to lease lapse, only two
millium two humbered and eighty thausig nine

Here's our humbered and sixty radiolumin lines to the
dozen wustworts of a Finntown's generous poet's
cousins from office. Distorted mirage, aloofliest of the plain,
the starves wherein the boxomeness of the bedelias[6] makes
on tripes. hobbyhodge happy in his hole.[7] The store
and charter, Treetown Castle under Lynne.
Rivapool? Hod a brieck on it! But its piers eerie,
its span spooky, its toll but a till, its parapets all
peripateting. D'Oblong's by his by. Which we
all pass. Tons. In our snoo. Znore. While we

1　Now a muss wash the little face.
2　A viking vernacular expression still used in the Summerhill district for a jerryhatted
　man of forty who puts two fingers into his boiling soupplate and licks them in turn to
　find out if there is enough mushroom catsup in the mutton broth.
3　H' dk' fs' h'p'y.
4　Googlaa pluplu.
5　Tomley. The grown man. A butcher szewched him the bloughs and braches. I'm
　chory to see P. Shuter.
6　I believe in Dublin and the Sultan of Turkey.
7　I have heard this word used by Martin Halpin, an old gardener from the Glens of
　Antrim who used to do odd jobs for my godfather, the Rev. B.B. Brophy of Swords.

hickerwards the thicker. Schein. Schore. Which
assoars us from the murk of the mythelated in
the barrabelowther, bedevere butlered table
round, past Morningtop's necessity and
Harington's invention, to the clarience of the
childlight in the studiorium upsturts. Here we'll
dwell on homiest powers, love at the latch with
novices nig and nag. The chorus: the principals.
For the rifocillation of their inclination to the
manifestation of irritation: doldorboys and
doll.[1] After sound, light and heat, memory, will
and understanding.

Bet you fippence anythesious there's no puggatory, are yous game?

Here (the memories framed from walls are
minding) till wranglers for wringwrowdy
wready are, F ꟻ, (at gaze, respecting, fourteenth
baronet, meet, altrettanth bancorot, chaff) and
ere commence commencement catalaunic when
Aetius check chokewill Attil's gambit, (that
buxon bruzeup, give it a burl!) lead us seek, O
june of eves the jenniest, thou who fleeest
flicklesome the fond fervid frondeur to thickly
thyself attach with thine efteased ensuer,[2]
ondrawer of our unconscionable, flickerflapper
fore our unterdrugged,[3] lead us seek, lote us
see, light us find, let us missnot Maidadate,
Mimosa multimimetica, the maymeaminning of
maimoomeining! Elpis, thou fountain of the
greeces, all shall speer theeward,[4] from kongen
in his canteenhus to knivers hind the knoll.
Ausonius Audacior and gael, gillie, gall.[5]
Singalingalying. Storiella as she is syung.

PRE-
AUSTERIC
MAN AND
HIS
PURSUIT OF
PAN-
HYSTERIC
WOMAN.

There was a sweet hopeful called Cis.

Whence followeup with endspeaking nots for
yestures, plutonically pursuant on briefest
glimpse from gladrags, pretty Proserpronette
whose slit satchel spilleth peas.

1 Ravens may rive so can dove deelish.
2 A question of pull.
3 For Rose Point see Inishmacsaint.
4 Mannequins' Pose.
5 Their holy presumption and hers sinfly desprit.

Belisha beacon, beckon bright! Usherette, unmesh us! That grene ray of earong it waves us to yonder as the red, blue and yellow flogs time on the domisole,[1] with a blewy blow and a windigo. Where flash becomes word and silents selfloud. To brace congeners, trebly bounden and asservaged twainly. Adamman,[2] Emhe, Issossianusheen and sometypes Yggely ogs Weib. Uwayoei![3] So mag this sybilette be our shibboleth that we may syllable her well! Vetus may be occluded behind the mou in Veto but Nova will be nearing as their radient among the Nereids. A one of charmers, ay, Una Unica, charmers, who, under the branches of the elms, in shoes as yet unshent by stoniness, wend, went, will wend a way of honey myrrh and rambler roses mistmusk while still the maybe mantles the meiblume, or ever her if have faded from the fleur,[4] their arms enlocked, (ringrang, the chimes of sex appealing as conchitas with sentas stray,[5] rung!), all thinking all of it, the It with an itch in it, the All every inch of it, the pleasure each will preen her for, the business each was bred to breed by.[6]

Soon jemmijohns will cudgel about some a rhythmatick or other over Browne and Nolan's divisional tables whereas she, of minions' novence charily being cupid, for mug's wumping, grooser's grubbiness, andt's avarice and grossopper's grandegaffe, with her tootpettypout of jemenfichue will sit

URGES AND WIDERURGES IN A PRIMITIVE SEPT.

The Big Bear bit the Sailor's Only. Trouble, trouble, trouble.

Forening Unge Kristlike Kvinne.

Telltale me all of annaryllies.

EARLY NOTIONS OF ACQUIRED RIGHTS AND THE INFLU- ENCE OF

Will you carry my can and fight the fairies?

---

1 Anama anamaba anamabapa.
2 Only for he's fathering law I could skewer that old one and slosh her out many's the time but I thinks more of my pottles and ketts.
3 All abunk for Tararat! Look slipper, soppyhat, we've doss in the manger.
4 One must sell it to some one, the sacred name of love.
5 Making it up as we goes along.
6 The law of the jungerl.

and knit on solfa sofa.[1] Stew of the evening, booksyful stew. And a bodikin a boss in the Thimble Theatre. But all is her inbourne. Intend. From gramma's grammar she has it that if there is a third person, mascarine, phelinine or nuder, being spoken abad it moods prosodes from a person speaking to her second which is the direct object that has been spoken to, with and at. Take the dative with his oblative[2] for, even if obsolete, it is always of interest, so spake gramma on the impetus of her imperative, only mind your genderous towards his reflexives such that I was to your grappa (Bott's trousend, hore a man uff!) when him was me hedon[3] and mine, what the lewdy saying, his analectual pygmyhop.[4] There is comfortism in the knowledge that often hate on first hearing comes of love by second sight. Have your little sintalks in the dunk of subjunctions, dual in duel and prude with pruriel, but even the aoriest chaparound whatever plaudered perfect anent prettydotes and haec genua omnia may perhaps chance to be about to be in the case to be becoming a pale peterwright in spite of all your tense accusatives whilstly you're wallfloored[5] like your gerandiums for the better half of a yearn or sob. It's a wild's kitten, my dear, who can tell a wilkling from a warthog. For you may be as practical as is predicable but you must have the proper sort of accident to meet that kind of a being with a difference.[6] Flame at his fumbles but freeze on

Allma Mathers, Auctioneer.

Old Gavelkind the Gamper and he's as daff as you're erse.

COLLECTIVE TRADITION UPON THE INDIVIDUAL.

---

1 Let me blush to think of all those halfwayhoist pullovers.
2 I'd like his pink's cheek.
3 Frech devil in red hairing! So that's why you ran away to sea, Mrs Lappy. Leap me, Locklaun, for you have sensed.
4 A washable lovable floatable doll.
5 With her poodle feinting to be let off and feeling dead in herself. Is love worse living?
6 If she can't follow suit Renée goes to the pack.

his fist.[1] Every letter is a godsend, ardent Ares,
brusque Boreas and glib Ganymede like zealous
Zeus, the O'Meghisthest of all. To me or not to
me. Satis thy quest on. Werbungsap! Jeg suis,

Undante vos wore a gentle–man, thou arr, I am a quean.
umoroso. M. Is a game over? The game goes on. Cookcook!
50–50. Search me. The beggar the maid the bigger the
οὐϰ ἔλαβον mauler. And the greater the patrarc the griefer
πόλιν. the pinch. And that's what your doctor knows.
O love it is the commonknounest thing how it
pashes the plutous and the paupe.[2] Pop! And
egg she active or spoon she passive, all them
fine clauses in Lindley's and Murrey's never
braught the participle of a present to a des-
ponent hortatrixy, vindicatively I say it, from
her postconditional future.[3] Lumpsome is who
lumpsum pays. Quantity counts though accents
I'll go for falter. Yoking apart and oblique orations parsed
that small to one side, a brat, alanna, can choose from so
polly if you'll many, be he a sollicitor's appendix, a pipe clerk
suck to your or free functionist flyswatter, that perfect little
lebbens- cad, from the languors and weakness of limber-
quatsch. limbed lassihood till the head, back and heart-
aches of waxedup womanage and heaps on
heaps of other things too. Note the Respectable
Irish Distressed Ladies and the Merry Mustard
Frothblowers of Humphreystown Associations.
Atac first, queckqueck quicks after. Beware how
in that hist subtaile of schlangder[4] lies liaison
to tease oreilles. To vert embowed set proper
penchant. But learn from that ancient tongue
to be middle old modern to the minute. A
spitter that can be depended on. Though
Wonderlawn's lost us for ever. Alis, alas, she
broke the glass! Liddell lokker through the

---

1 Improper frictions is maledictions and mens uration makes me mad.
2 Llong and Shortts Primer of Black and White Wenchcraft.
3 The gaggles all out.
4 He's just bug nuts on white mate he hasn't the teath nor the grits to choo and that's
  what's wrong with Lang Wang Wurm, old worbbling goesbelly.

leafery, ours is mistery of pain.[1] You may spin on youthlit's bike and multiplease your Mike and Nike with your kickshoes on the algebrars

O'Mara Farrell. Verschwindibus.

but, volve the virgil page and view, the O of woman is long when burly those two muters sequent her so from Nebob[2] see you never stray who'll nimm you nice and nehm the day.

One hath just been areading, hath not one, ya, ya, in their memoiries of Hireling's puny

Ulstria, Monastir, Leninstar and Connecticut.

wars, end so, und all, ga, ga, of The O'Brien, The O'Connor, The Mac Loughlin and The Mac Namara with summed their appondage, da, da, of Sire Jeallyous Seizer, that gamely torskmester,[3] with his duo of druidesses in ready money rompers[4] and the tryonforit of Ox-

Cliopatria, thy hosies history.

thievious, Lapidous and Malthouse Anthemy. You may fail to see the lie of that layout, Suetonia,[5] but the reflections which recur to me are that so long as beauty life is body love[6] and so bright as Mutua of your mirror holds her candle to your caudle, lone lefthand likeless, sombring Autum of your Spring, reck you not one spirt of anyseed whether trigemelimen cuddle his coddle or nope. She'll confess it by her figure and she'll deny it to your face. If you're not ruined by that one she won't do you

The Eroico Furioso makes the valet like smiling.

any whim. And then? What afters it? Cruff Gunne may blow, Gam Gonna flow, the gossans eye the jennings aye. From the butts of Heber and Heremon, nolens volens, brood our pansies, brune in brume. There's a split in the infinitive

CONCOMIT-
ANCE OF
COURAGE,
COUNSEL
AND
CONSTANCY.
ORDINATION
OF OMEN,
ONUS AND
OBIT. DIS-
TRIBUTION
OF DANGER,
DUTY AND
DESTINY.
POLAR
PRINCIPLES.

---

1 Dear and I trust in all frivolity I may be pardoned for trespassing but I think I may add hell.

2 He is my all menkind of every desception.

3 All his teeths back to the front, then the moon and then the moon with a hole behind it.

4 Skip one, flop fore, jennies in the cabbage store.

5 None of your cumpohlstery English here!

6 Understudy my understandings, Sostituda, and meek thine complinement, gymnufleshed.

from to have to have been to will be. As they
warred in their big innings ease now we never
shall know. Eat early earthapples. Coax Cobra
to chatters. Hail, Heva, we hear! This is the
glider that gladdened the girl[1] that list to the
wind that lifted the leaves that folded the fruit
that hung on the tree that grew in the garden
Gough gave. Wide hiss, we're wizening. Hoots
fromm, we're globing. Why hidest thou hinder
thy husband his name? Leda, Lada, aflutter-
afraida, so does your girdle grow! Willed without witting, whorled without aimed. Pappa-
passos, Mammamanet, warwhetswut and who-
witswhy.[2] But it's tails for toughs and titties for
totties and come buckets comebats till deeleet.[3]

*The
hyperape the
mink he
groves the
mole you see
nowfor
crushsake
chawley.*

Pige pas.

Dark ages clasp the daisy roots, Stop, if you
are a sally of the allies, hot off Minnowaurs and
naval actiums, picked engagements and banks
of rowers. Please stop if you're a B.C. minding
missy, please do. But should you prefer A.D.
stepplease. And if you miss with a venture it
serves you girly well glad. But, holy Janus, I
was forgetting the Blitzenkopfs! Here, Hen-
gegst and Horsesauce, take your heads[4] out of
that taletub. And leave your hinnyhennyhind-
you. It's haunted. The chamber. Of errings.
Whoan, tug, trace, stirrup! It is distinctly under-
stouttered that, sense you threehandshighs put
your twofootlarge timepates in that dead wash
of Lough Murph and until such time pace one
and the same Messherrn the grinning statesmen,
Brock and Leon, have shunted the grumbling
coundedtouts, Starlin and Ser Artur Ghinis.

PANOPTICAL
PURVIEW OF
POLITICAL
PROGRESS AND
THE FUTURE
PRESENTATION
OF THE PAST.

*Seidlitz
powther for
slogan
plumpers.*

---

1 Tho' I have one just like that to home, deadleaf brown with quicksilver appliques,
  would whollymost applissiate a nice shiny sleekysilk out of that slippering snake
  charmeuse.
2 What's that ma'am? says I.
3 As you say yourself.
4 That's the lethemuse but it washes off.

Hoploits and atthems.

Curragh machree, me bosthoon fiend.

Femilies hug bank!

All we suffered under them Cowdung Forks and how we enjoyed over our pick of the basketfild. Old Kine's Meat Meal.

Flieflie for the jillies and a bombambum for the nappotondus

Foamous homely brew, bebattled by bottle, gageure de guegerre.[1] Bull igien bear and then bearagain bulligan. Gringrin gringrin. Staffs varsus herds and bucks vursus barks. By old Grumbledum's walls. Bumps, bellows and bawls.[2] Opprimor's down, up up Opima! Rents and rates and tithes and taxes, wages, saves and spends. Heil, heptarched span of peace![3] Live, league of lex, nex and the mores! Fas est dass and foe err you. Impovernment of the booble by the bauble for the bubble. So wrap up your worries in your woe (wumpumtum!) and shake down the shuffle for the throw. For there's one mere ope[4] for downfall ned. As Hanah Levy, shrewd shroplifter, and nievre anore skidoos with her spoileds.[5] To add gay touches. For hugh and guy and goy and jew. To dimpled and pimpled and simpled and wimpled. A peak in a poke and a pig in a pew.[6] She wins them by wons, a haul hectoendecate, for mangay mumbo jumbjubes tak mutts and jeffs muchas bracelonettes gracies barcelonas.[7] O what a loovely freespeech 'twas (tep)[8] to gar howalively hintergrunting! Tip. Like lilt of larks to burdened crocodile[9] or skittering laubhing at that wheeze of old windbag, Blusterboss, blowharding about all he didn't do. Hell o' your troop! With is the winker for the muckwits of willesly and nith is the nod for

1 Where he fought the shessock of his stimmstammer and we caught the pepettes of our lovelives.
2 Shake eternity and lick creation.
3 I'm blest if I can see.
4 Hoppity Huhneye, hoosh the hen. I like cluckers, you like nuts (wink).
5 Sweet, medium and dry like altar wine.
6 Who'll buy me penny babies?
7 Well, Maggy, I got your castoff devils all right and fits lovely. And am vaguely graceful. Maggy thanks.
8 My six is no secret, sir, she said.
9 Yes, there, Tad, thanks, give, from, tathair, look at that now.

the umproar napollyon and hitheris poorblond piebold hoerse. Huirse. With its tricuspidal hauberkhelm coverchaf emblem on. For the

Murdoch.

man that broke the ranks on Monte Sinjon. The allriddle of it? That that is allruddy with us, ahead of schedule, which already is plan

Pas d'action,
peu de sauce.

accomplished from and syne: Daft Dathy of the Five Positions (the death ray stop him!) is still, as reproaches Paulus, on the Madderhorn and, entre chats and hobnobs,[1] daring Dunderhead to shiver his timbers and Hannibal mac Hamil-tan the Hegerite[2] (more livepower elbow him!) ministerbuilding up, as repreaches Timothy, in Saint Barmabrac's.[3] Number Thirty two West Eleventh streak looks on to that (may all in the tocoming of the sempereternal speel spry with

From the seven
tents of Joseph
till the calends
of Mary
Marian,
olivehunkered
and thorny too.
As Shakefork
might pitch it.

it!) datetree doloriferous which more and over leafeth earlier than every growth and, elfshot, headawag, with frayed nerves wondering till they feeled sore like any woman that has been born at all events to the purdah and for the howmanyeth and howmovingth time at what the demons in that jackhouse that jerry built for Massa and Missus and hijo de puta, the sparks-own fermament of the starryk fieldgosongingon where blows a nemone at each blink of wind-still[4] they were sliding along and sleeting aloof and scouting around and shooting about. All-whichwhile or whereaballoons for good vaunty years Dagobert is in Clane's clean hometown prepping up his prepueratory and learning how to put a broad face bronzily out through a

Puzzly, puzzly,
I smell a cat.

broken breached meataerial from Bryan Awlining. Erin's hircohaired culoteer.[5]

---

1 Go up quick, stay so long, come down slow!
2 If I gnows me gneesgnobs the both of him is gnatives of Genuas.
3 A glass of peel and pip for Mr Potter of Texas, please.
4 All the world loves a big gleaming jelly.
5 A pengeneepy for your warcheekeepy.

Two makes a wing at the macroscope telluspeep.

And as, these things being so or ere those things having done, way back home in Pacata Auburnia,[1] (untillably holy gammel Eire) one world burrowing on another, (if you've got me, neighbour, in any large lumps, geek?, ant got the strong of it) Standfest, our topiocal sagon hero, or any ottherr macotther, signs is on the bellyguds bastille back, bucket up with fullness, ant silvering to her jubilee,[2] birchleaves her jointure, our lavy in waving, visage full of flesh ant fat as a hen's i' forehead,

From the Buffalo Times of bysone days.

Airyanna ant Blowyhart topsirturvy, that royal pair in their palace of quicken boughs hight The Goat and Compasses ('phone number 17:69, if you want to know[3]) his seaarm strongsround her, her velivole eyne ashipwracked, have discusst their things of the past, crime and fable with shame, home and profit,[4] why lui lied to lei and hun tried to kill ham, scribbledehobbles, in whose veins runs a mixture of, are head bent and hard upon. Spell me the chimes. They are tales all tolled.[5]

Quick quake quokes the parrotbook of dates.

Today is well thine but where's may tomorrow be. But, bless his cowly head and press his crankly hat, what a world's woe is each's other's weariness waiting to beadroll his own properer mistakes, the backslapping gladhander,[6] free of his florid future and the other singing likeness, dirging a past of

FROM CENOGENETIC DICHOTOMY THROUGH DIAGONISTIC CONCILIANCE TO DYNASTIC CONTINUITY.

---

1 My globe goes gaddy at geography giggle pending which time I was looking for my shoe all through Arabia.

2 It must be some bugbear in the gender especially when old which they all soon get to look.

3 After me looking up the plan in Humphrey's *Justice of the Piece* it said to see preseeding chaps.

4 O boyjones and hairyoddities! Only noane told missus of her massas behaving she would laugh that flat that after that she had sanked down on her fat arks they would shaik all to sheeks.

5 Traduced into jinglish janglage for the nusances of dolphins born.

6 He gives me pulpititions with his Castlecowards never in the twowsers and ever in those twawsers and then babeteasing us out of our hoydenname.

Some is out for
twoheaded
dulcarnons but
more pulfers
turnips.

Omnitudes in a
knutshedell.

For all us kids
under his aegis.

Saving the
public his health.

Superlative
absolute of
Porterstown.

bloody altars, gale with a blost to him, dove without gall. And she, of the jilldaw's nest[1] who tears up lettereens she never apposed a pen upon.[2] Yet sung of love and the monster man. What's Hiccupper to hem or her to Hagaba? Ough, ough, brieve kindli![3]

Dogs' vespers are anending. Vespertiliabitur. Goteshoppard quits his gabhard cloke to sate with Becchus. Zumbock! Achèvre! Yet wind will be ere fadervor[4] and the hour of fruminy and bergoo bell if Nippon have pearls or opals Eldorado, the daindy dish, the lecking out! Gipoo, good oil! For (hushmagandy!) long 'tis till gets bright that all cocks waken and birds Diana[5] with dawnsong hail. Aught darks flou a duskness. Bats that? There peepeestrilling. At Brannan's on the moor. At Tam Fanagan's weak yat his still's going strang. And still here is noctules and can tell things acommon on by that fluffy feeling. Larges loomy wheelhouse to bodgbox[6] lumber up with hoodie hearsemen carrawain we keep is peace who follow his law, Sunday King.[7] His sevencoloured's soot (Ochone! Ochonal!)[8] and his imponence one heap lumpblock (Mogoul!). And

THE
MONGREL
UNDER THE
DUNGMOUND.
SIGNIFICANCE
OF THE
INFRALIMINAL
INELLIGENCE.
OFFRANDES.

---

1 My goldfashioned bother near drave me roven mad and I dyeing to keep my linefree face like readymaid maryangs for jollycomes smashing Holmes.

2 What I would like is a jade louistone to go with the moon's increscent.

3 Parley vows the Askinwhose? I do, Ida. And how to call the cattle black. Moopetsi meepotsi

4 I was so snug off in my apholster's creedle but at long leash I'll stretch more capritious in his dapplepied bed.

5 Pipette. I can almost feed their sweetness at my lisplips.

6 A liss in hunterland.

7 I wonder if I put the old buzzerd one night to suckle in Millickmaam's honey like they use to emballem some of the special popes with a book in his hand and his mouth open.

8 And a ripping rude rape in his lucreasious togery.

Why so mucky
pick bridges
span our Flumi-
nian road.

P.C. Helmut's
in the cotton-
wood, listnin.

The throne is an
umbrella
strande and a
sceptre's a stick.

Jady jewel, our
daktar deer.

Gautamed
budders
deossiphysing
our Theas.

By lineal in
pondus over-
thepoise.

Pitchcap and
triangle, noose
and tinctunc.

rivers burst out like weeming racesround joy-drinks for the fewnrally,[1] where every feaster's a foster's other, fiannians all.[2] The welling-breast, he willing giant, the mountain mourning his duggedy dew. To obedient of civicity in urbanious at felicity what'll yet meek Mike[3] our diputy mimber when he's head on poll and Peter's burgess and Miss Mishy Mushy is tiptupt by Toft Taft. Boblesse gobleege. For as Anna was at the beginning lives yet and will return after great deap sleap rerising and a white night high with a cows of Drommhiem as shower as there's a wet enclouded in Westwicklow or a little black rose a truant in a thorntree. We drames our dreams tell Bappy returns. And Sein annews. We will not say it shall not be, this passing of order and order's coming, but in the herbest country and in the country around Blath as in that city self of legionds they look for its being ever yet. So shuttle the pipers done.[4] Eric aboy![5] And it's time that all paid tribute to this massive mortiality, the pink of punk perfection as photography in mud. Some may seek to dodge the gobbet for its quantity of quality but who wants to cheat the choker's got to learn to chew the cud. Allwhichhole scrubs on scroll circuminiuminluminatedhave encuoniams here and improperies there.[6] With a pansy for the pussy in the corner. [7]

---

1 Will ye nought would wet your weapons, warriors bard?

2 Roe, Williams, Bewey, Greene, Gorham, McEndicoth and Vyler, the lays of ancient homes.

3 The stanidsglass effect, you could sugerly swear buttermilt would not melt down his dripping ducks.

4 Thickathigh and Thinathews with sant their dam.

5 Oh, could we do with this waddled of ours like that redbanked profanian with his bakset of yosters.

6 Gosem pher, gezumpher, greeze a jarry grim felon! Good bloke him!

7 And if they was setting on your stool as hard as my was she could beth her bothom dolours he'd have a culious impressiom on the diminitive that chafes our ends.

Bewise of Fanciulla's heart, the heart of INCIPIT
Fanciulla! Even the recollection of willow INTER-
fronds is a spellbinder that lets to hear.[1] The MISSIO.
rushes by the grey nuns' pond: ah eh oh let

Uncle Flabbius me sigh too. Coalmansbell: behoves you
Muximus to handmake of the load. Jenny Wren: pick,
Niecia Flappia peck. Johnny Post: pack, puck.[2] All the
Minnimiss. As world's in want and is writing a letters.[3] A
this is. And as letters from a person to a place about a thing.
this this is. And all the world's on wish to be carrying a
letters. A letters to a king about a treasure
Dear Brotus, from a cat.[4] When men want to write a
land me arrears. letters. Ten men, ton men, pen men, pun
men, wont to rise a ladder. And den men,
Rockaby, babel, dun men, fen men, fun men, hen men, hun
flatten a wall. men went to raze a leader. Is then any
How he broke lettersday from many peoples, Daganasana-
the good news to vitch? Empire, your outermost.[5] A posy
Gent. cord. Plece.

We have wounded our way on foe tris MAJOR AND
prince till that force in the gill is faint afarred MINOR
and the face in the treebark feigns afear. MODES
This is rainstones ringing. Strangely cult for COALESCING
this ceasing of the yore. But Erigureen is PROLIFERATE
ever. Pot price pon patrilinear plop, if the HOMO-
osseletion of the onkring gives omen nome? GENUINE
Since alls war that end war let sports be HOMO-
leisure and bring and buy fair. Ah ah GENEITY.
athclete, blest your bally bathfeet! Townto-
quest, fortorest, the hour that hies is hurley.
A halt for hearsake.[6] A scene at sight. Or

---

1 When I'am Enastella and am taken for Essastessa I'll do that droop on the pohlmann's piano.
2 Heavenly twinges, if it's one of his I'll fearly feint as swoon as he enterooms.
3 To be slipped on, to be slept by, to be conned to, to be kept up. And when you're done push the chain.
4 With her modesties office.
5 Strutting as proud as a great turquin weggin that cuckhold on his Eddems and Clay's hat.
6 Come, smooth of my slate, to the beat of my blosh. With all these gelded ewes

dreamoneire. Which they shall memorise. By
her freewritten Hopely for ear that annalykeses
if scares for eye that sumns. Is it in the now
woodwordings of our sweet plantation where

Bibelous   the branchings then will singingsing tomorrows
hicstory and   gone and yesters outcome as Satadays after-
Barbarassa   moon lex leap smiles on the twelvemonths-
harestary.   minding? Such is. Dear (name of desired
subject, A.N.), well, and I go on to. Shlicksher.
I and we (tender condolences for happy funeral,
one if) so sorry to (mention person suppressed

---

jilting about and the thrills and ills of laylock blossoms three's so much more plants
than chants for cecilies that I was thinking fairly killing times of putting an end to
myself and my malody, when I remembered all your pupil–teacher's erringnesses in
perfection class. You sh'undn't write you can't if you w'udn't pass for undevelop-
mented. This is the propper way to say that, Sr. If it's me chews to swallow all you
saidn't you can eat my words for it as sure as there's a key in my kiss. Quick erit
faciofacey. When we will conjugate together toloseher tomaster tomiss while morrow
fans amare hour, verbe de vie and verve to vie, with love ay loved have I on my back
spine and does for ever. Your are me severe? Then rue. My intended, Jr, who I'm
throne away on, (here he inst, my lifstack, a newfolly likon) when I slip through my
pettigo I'll get my decree and take seidens when I'm not ploughed first by some
Rolando the Lasso, and flaunt on the flimsyfilmsies for to grig my collage juniorees
who, though they flush fuchsia, are they octette and virginity in my shade but always
my figurants. They may be yea of my year but they're nary nay of my day. Wait till
spring has sprung in spickness and prigs beg in to pry they'll be plentyprime of
housepets to pimp and pamper my. Impending marriage. Nature tells everybody
about but I learned all the runes of the gamest game ever from my old nourse Asa.
A most adventuring trot is her and she vicking well knowed them all heartswise and
fourwords. How Olive d'Oyly and Winnie Carr, bejupers, they reized the dressing
of a salandmon and how a peeper costs and a salt sailor med a mustied poet
atwaimen. It most have bean Mad Mullans planted him. Bina de Bisse and Trestrine
von Terrefin. Sago sound, rite go round, kill kackle, kook kettle and (remember all
should I forget to) bolt the thor. Auden. Wasn't it just divining that dog of a dag in
Skokholme as I sat astrid uppum their Drewitt's altar, as cooledas as culcumbre,
slapping my straights till the sloping ruins, postillion, postallion, a swinge a swank,
with you offering me clouts of illscents and them horners stagstruck on the leasward!
Don't be of red, you blanching mench! This isabella I'm on knows the ruelles of the
rut and she don't fear andy mandy. So sing loud, sweet cheeriot, like anegreon in
heaven! The good fother with the twingling in his eye will always have cakes in his
pocket to bethroat us with for our allmichael good. Amum. Amum. And Amum
again. For tough troth is stronger than fortuitous fiction and it's the surplice money,
oh my young friend and ah me sweet creature, what buys the bed while wits
borrows the clothes.

A shieling in cop-pingers and porrish soup all days.

for the moment, F.M.). Well (enquiries after allhealths) how are you (question maggy). A lovely (introduce to domestic circles) pershan of cates. Shrubsher. Those pothooks mostly she hawks from Poppa Vere Foster but these curly mequeues are of Mippa's moulding.

How matches metroosers?

Shrubsheruthr. (Wave gently in the ere turning ptover.) Well, mabby (consolation of shopes) to soon air. With best from cinder Christinette if prints chumming, can be when desires Soldi, for asamples, backfronted or, if all, peethrolio

Le hélos tombaut soul sur la jambe de marche.

or Get my Prize, using her flower or perfume or, if veryveryvery chumming, in otherwards, who she supposed adeal, kissists my exits. Shlicksheruthr. From Auburn chenlemagne. Pious and pure fair one, all has concomitated to this that she shall tread them lifetrees leaves whose silence hitherto has shone as sphere of silver fastalbarnstone, that fount Bandusian shall play liquick music and after odours sigh of musk. Blotsbloshblothe, one dear that was. Sleep in the water, drug at the fire, shake the dust off and dream your one who would give

Mai maintenante elle est venuse.

her sidecurls to. Till later Lammas is led in by baith our washwives, a weird of wonder tenebrous as that evil thorngarth, a field of faery blithe as this flowing wild.

Two Dons Johns Threes Totty Askins.

Aujourd'hui comme aux temps le Pline et de Columelle la jacinthe se plait dans les Gaules, la pervenche en Illyrie, la marguerite sur les ruines de Numance[1] et pendant qu'autour d'elles les villes ont changé de maîtres et de noms, que plusieurs sont entrées dans le néant, que les civilisations se

Also Spuke Zero-thruster.

sont choquées et brisées, leurs paisibles générations ont traversé les âges et sont arrivées jusqu'à nous, fraîches et riantes comme aux jours des batailles.[2]

THE PART PLAYED BY BELLETRI-STICKS IN THE BELLUM-PAX-BELLUM. MUTUO-MORPHO-MUTATION.

---

1 The nasal foss of our natal folkfarthers so so much now for Valsing-giddyrex and his grand arks day triump.

2 Translout that gaswind into turfish, Teague, that's a good bog and you, Thady, poliss it off, there's nateswipe, on to your blottom pulper.

SORTES
VIRGIN-
IANAE.

Margaritomancy! Hyacinthinous pervincive-
ness! Flowers. A cloud. But Bruto and Cassio
are ware only of trifid tongues[1] the whispered
A saxum wilfulness, ('tis demonal!) and shadows shadows
shillum for multiplicating (il folsoletto nel falsoletto col
the sextum fazzolotto dal fuzzolezzo),[2] totients quotients,
but nothums they tackle their quarrel. Sickamoor's so woful
for that sally. Ancient's aerger. And eachway bothwise
parridge glory signs. What if she love Sieger less though
preast. she leave Ruhm moan? That's how our oxyg-
gent has gotten ahold of half their world. Moving
about in the free of the air and mixing with the
ruck. Enten eller, either or.

And!

Nay, rather!

With sobs for his job, with tears for
Tricks his toil, with horror for his squalor
stunts. but with pep for his perdition,[3] lo, the
boor plieth as the laird hireth him.

Boon on begyndelse.

At maturing daily gloryaims! [4]

A flink dab for a freck dive and a stern poise
for a swift pounce was frankily at the manual
arith sure enough which was the bekase he
knowed from his cradle, no bird better, why his
fingures were giving him whatfor to fife with.
Truckeys' First, by observation, there came boko and nigh
cant for him wigworms and nigh him tittlies and nigh
dactyl and him cheekadeekchimple and nigh him pick-
spondee. pocket with pickpocketpumb, pickpocketpoint,
pickpocketprod, pickpocketpromise and
upwithem. Holy Joe in lay Eden.[5] And anyhows
always after them the dimpler he weighed the

INTERROGATION.
EXCLAMATION.
ANTITHESIS OF
AMBIDUAL ANTICIP-
ATION. THE MIND
FACTORY, ITS GIVE
AND TAKE.

AUSPICIUM.
AUGURIA.
DIVINITY
NOT DEITY
THE UN-
CERTAINTY
JUSTIFIED
BY OUR
CERTITUDE.
EXAMPLES.

1 You daredevil donnelly, I love your piercing lots of lies and your flashy foreign mail
   so here's my cowrie card, I dalgo, with all my exes, wise and sad.
2 All this Mitchells is a niggar for spending and I will go to the length of seeing that one
   day Big Mig will be nickleless himself.
3 While I'll wind the wildwoods' bluckbells among my window's weeds.
4 Lawdy Dawdy Simpers.
5 But where, O where, is me lickle dig done?

fonder fell he of his null four lovedroyd
curdinals, his element curdinal numen and

Panoplous
peregrine
pifflicative
pomposity.

his enement curdinal marryng and his epulent
curdinal weisswassh and his eminent curdinal
Kay O'Kay. Always would he be reciting of
them, hoojahs koojahs, up by rota, in his
Fanden's catachysm from fursed to laced, quick-
march to decemvers, so as to pin the tenners,
thumbs down. And anon an aldays, strues yer-
there, would he wile arecreating em om
lumerous ways, caius-counting in the scale of
pin puff pive piff, piff puff pive poo, poo puff
pive pree, pree puff pive pfoor, pfoor puff pive
pippive, poopive,[1] Niall Dhu, Foughty Unn,
Enoch Thortig, endso one, like to pitch of your

Non plus
ulstra, Elba,
nec, cashellum
tuum.

cap, pac, on to tin tall spillicans.[2] To sum, borus
pew notus pew eurus pew zipher. Ace, deuce,
tricks, quarts, quims. Mumtiplay of course and
carry to their whole number. While on the other
hand, traduced by their comedy nominator to
the loaferst terms for their aloquent parts, sexes,
suppers, oglers, novels and dice.[3] He could find
(the rakehelly!) by practice the valuse of thine-
to-mine articles with no reminder for an equality
of relations and, with the helpings from his
tables, improduce fullmin to trumblers, links
unto chains, weys in Nuffolk till tods of Yorek,
oozies ad libs and several townsends, several
hundreds, civil-to-civil imperious gallants into

Dondder-
wedder
Kyboshicksal.

gells (Irish), bringing alliving stone allaughing
down to grave clothnails and a league of
archers, fools and lurchers under the rude rule
of fumb. What signifieth whole that[4] but, be
all the prowess of ten, 'tis as strange to relate
he, nonparile to rede, rite and reckan, caught

---

1 That's his whisper waltz I like from Pigott's with that Lancydancy step. Stop.
2 Twelve buttles man, twentyeight bows of curls, forty bonnets woman and every
  youthfully yours makes alleven add the hundred.
3 Gamester Damester in the road to Rouen, he grows more like his deed every die.
4 Slash-the-Pill lifts the pellet. Run, Phoenix, run!

allmeals dullmarks for his nucleuds and alego-
brew. They wouldn't took bearings no how
anywheres. O them doddhunters and alla-
nights, aabs and baas for agnomes, yees and
zees for incognits, bate him up jerrybly! Worse
nor herman dororrhea. Give you the fantods,
seemed to him. They ought to told you every
last word first stead of trying every which way
to kinder smear it out poison long. Show that

A stodge
Angleshman
has been
worked by
eccentricity.

the median, hce che ech, interecting at royde
angles the parilegs of a given obtuse one biscuts
both the arcs that are in curveachord behind.
Brickbaths. The family umbroglia. A Tulla-
grove pole[1] to the Height of County Fear-
managh has a septain inclinaison[2] and the
graphplot for all the functions in Lower County
Monachan, whereat samething is rivisible by
nighttim, may be involted into the zeroic
couplet, palls pell inhis heventh glike noughty

An oxygon is
noturally
reclined to
rest.

times ∞, find, if you are not literally coo-
efficient, how minney combinaisies and
permutandies can be played on the international
surd! pthwndxrclzp!, hids cubid rute being
extructed, taking anan illitterettes, ififif at a tom.
Answers, (for teasers only).[3] Ten, twent, thirt,
see, ex and three icky totchty ones. From
solation to solution. Imagine the twelve deafer-
ended dumbbawls of the whowl abovebeugled
to be the contonuation through regeneration of
the urutteration of the word in pregross. It
follows that, if the two antesedents be
bissyclitties and the three comeseekwenchers

Ba be bi bo
bum.

trundletrikes, then, Aysha Lalipat behidden
on the footplate, Big Whiggler[4] restant

---

1 Dideney, Dadeney, Dudeney, O, I'd know that putch on your poll.
2 That is tottinghim in his boots.
3 Come all ye hapney coachers and support the richview press.
4 Braham Baruch he married his cook to Massach McKraw her uncle-in-law who
  wedded his widow to Hjalmar Kjaer who adapted his daughter to Braham the Bear. V
  for wadlock, P for shift, H for Lona the Konkubine.

upsittuponable, the NCR[1] presents to us
(tandem year at lasted length!) an ottomantic
turquo-indaco of pictorial shine by pictorial
shimmer so long as, gad of the gidday, pictorial
summer, viridorefulvid, lits asheen, but (lenz
alack lends a lot), if this habby cyclic erdor be
outraciously enviolated by a mierelin round-
tableturning, like knuts in maze, the zitas
runnind hare and dart[2] with the yeggs in their
muddle, like a seven of wingless arrows,
hodgepadge, thump, kick and hurry, all boy
more missis blong him he race quickfeller all

Finnfinnotus   same hogglepiggle longer house blong him,[3]
of Cincinnati.   while the catched and dodged exarx seems him-
multeemiously to beem (he wins her hend! he
falls to tail!) the ersed ladest mand[4] and (uhu
and uhud!) the losed farce on erroroots,[5]
twalegged poneys and threehandled dorkeys
(madahoy, morahoy, lugahoy, jogahoyaway)

Arthurgink's   MPM brings us a rainborne pamtomomiom,
hussies and   aqualavant to (cat my dogs, if I baint dingbushed
Everguin's   like everything!) kaksitoista volts yksitoista volts
men.   kymmenen volts yhdeksan volts kahdeksan volts
seitseman volts kuusi volts viisi volts nelja
volts kolme volts kaksi volts yksi, allahthalla-
camellated, caravan series to the finish of helvé's
fractures.[6] In outher wards, one from five, two
to fives ones, one from fives two millamills
with a mill and a half a mill and twos twos fives
fives of bullyclavers. For a surview over all the
factionables see Iris in the Evenine's World.[7]

---

1 A gee is just a jay on the jaunts cowsway.
2 Talking about trilbits.
3 Barneycorrall, a precedent for the prodection of curiosity from children.
4 A pfurty pscore of ruderic rossies haremhorde for his divelsion.
5 Look at your mad father on his boneshaker fraywhaling round Myriom square.
6 Try Asia for the assphalt body with the concreke soul and the forequarters of the
   moon behinding out of his phase.
7 Tomatoes malmalaid with De Quinceys salade can be tastily served with Indiana
   Blues on the violens.

Nom de nombres! The balbearians.

Vive Paco Hunter.

The hoisted in red and the low-ered in black.

The boss's bess bass is the browd of Mullingar.

The aliments of jumeantry.

Binomeans to be comprendered. Inexcessible as thy by god ways. The aximones. And their prostalutes. For his neuralgiabrown. Equal to= aosch.

P.t.l.o.a.t.o.   HEPTAGRAMMATON.

So, bagdad, after those initials falls and that HYPOTHESES primary taincture, as I know and you know OF yourself, begath, and the arab in the ghetto COMMONEST knows better, by nettus, nor anymeade or EXPERIENCES persan, comic cuts and series exerxeses always BEFORE were to be capered in Casey's frost book of, APOTHEOSIS page torn on dirty, to be hacked at Hickey's, OF THE hucksler, Wellington's Iron Bridge, and so, LUSTRAL by long last, as it would shuffle out, must he PRINCIPIUM. to trump adieu atout atous to those card-inhands he a big deal missed, radmachrees and rossecullinans and blagpikes in suitclover. Dear hearts of my counting, would he revoke them, forewheel to packnumbers, and, the time being no help fort, plates to lick one and turn over.

Problem ye ferst, construct ann aquilittoral INGENIOUS dryankle Probe loom! With his primal hands- LABOUR-toe in his sole salivarium. Concoct an TENACITY AS equoangular trillitter.[1] On the name of BETWEEN the tizzer and off the tongs and off the INGENUOUS mythametical tripods. Beatsoon.   AND LIBERTINE.

Can you nei do her, numb? asks Dolph,[2] suspecting the answer know. Oikkont, ken PROPE AND you, ninny? asks Kev,[3] expecting the answer PROCUL IN guess.[4] Nor was the noer long disappointed THE for easiest of kisshams, he was made vice- CONVERGENCE wise. Oc, tell it to oui, do, Sem! Well, 'tis oil OF THEIR thusly. First mull a mugfull of mud, son.[5] CONTRA-Oglores, the virtuoser prays, olorum! What PULSIVENESS.

1 As Rhombulus and Rhebus went building rhomes one day.
2 The trouveller.
3 Of the disorded visage.
4 Singlebarrelled names for doubleparalleled twixtytwins.
5 Like pudging a spoon fist of sugans into a sotspot of choucolout.

the D.V. would I to that for? That's a goosey's
ganswer you're for giving me, he is told, what
the Deva would you do that for?[1] Now, sknow
royol road to Puddlin, take your mut for a first

Wolsher-
womens at
their
weirdst.

beginning, big to bog, back to bach. Anny liffle
mud which cometh out of Mam will doob, I
guess. A.I. *Amnium instar.* And to find a locus
for an alp get a howlth on her bayrings as a
prisme O and for a second O unbox your
compasses. I cain but are you able? Amicably
nod. Gu it! So let's seth off betwain us.
Prompty? Mux your pistany at a point of the
coastmap to be called *a* but pronounced olfa.
There's the isle of Mun, ah! O! Tis just. *Bene!*
Now, whole in applepine erdor[2]

   (for—husk, hisk, a spirit spires—Dolph, dean of idlers, meager suckling
of gert stoan, though barekely a balbose boy, he too,—*venite, preteriti,*[3]
sine mora dumque de entibus nascituris decentius in lingua roman mortuorum
parva chartula liviana ostenditur, sedentes in letitiae super ollas carnium,
spectantes immo situm lutetiae unde auspiciis secundis tantae consurgent
humanae stirpes, antiquissimam flaminum amborium Jordani et Jambaptistae
mentibus revolvamus sapientiam: totum tute fluvii modo mundo fluere, eadem
quae ex aggere fututa iterum inter alveum fore futura, quodlibet sese ipsum
per aliudpiam agnoscere contrarium, omnem demun amnem ripis rivalibus
amplecti[4]—recurrently often, when him moved he would cake their chair,
coached rebelliumtending mikes of his same and over his own choirage at
Backlane Univarsity, among of which pupal souaves the pizdrool was
pulled up, bred and battered, for a dillon a dollar,[5] chanching letters for
them vice o'verse to bronze mottes and blending tschemes for em in
tropadores and doublecressing twofold thruths and devising tingling
tailwords too whilest, cunctant that another would finish his sentence for
him, he druider would smilabit eggways[6] ned, he, to don't say nothing,

---

1 Will you walk into my wavetrap? said the spiter to the shy.
2 If we each could always do all we ever did.
3 Dope in Canorian words we've made. Spish from the Doc.
4 Basqueesh, Finnican, Hungulash and Old Teangtaggle, the only pure way to work a
   curse.
5 An ounceworth of onions for a pennyawealth of sobs.
6 Who brought us into the yellow world!

would, so prim, and pick upon his ten ordinailed ungles, trying to undo with his teeth the knots made by his tongue, retelling humself by the math hour, long as he's brood reel of funnish ficts apout the shee, how faust of all and on segund thoughts and the thirds the charmhim girlalove and fourthermore and filthily with bag from Oxatown and baroccidents and proper accidence and hoptohill and hexenshoes, in fine the whole damning letter; and, in point of feet, when he landed in ourland's leinster[1] of saved and solomnones for the twicedhecame time, off Lipton's strongbowed launch, the *Lady Eva*, in a tan soute of sails[2] he converted it's nataves, name saints, young ordnands, maderaheads and old unguished P.T. Publikums, through the medium of znigznaks with sotiric zeal, to put off the barcelonas[3] from their peccaminous corpulums (Gratings, Mr Dane!) and kiss on their bottes (Master!) as often as they came within bloodshot of that other familiar temple and showed em the celestine way to by his tristar and his flop hattrick and his perry humdrum dumb and numb nostrums that he larned in Hymbuktu,[4] and that same galloroman cultous is very prevailend up to this windiest of landhavemiseries all over what was beforeaboots a land of nods, in spite of all the bloot, all the braim, all the brawn, all the brile, that was shod, that were shat, that was shuk all the while, for our massangrey if mosshungry people, the at Wickerworks,[5] still hold ford to their healing and[6] byleave in the old weights downupon the Swanny, innovated by him, the prence di Propagandi, the chrism for the christmass, the pillar of the perished and the rock o'ralereality, and it is veritably belied, we belove, that not allsods of esoupcans that's in the queen's pottage post and not allfinesof greendgold that the Indus contains would overhinduce them, (o.p.) to steeplechange back once from their ophis workship and twice on sundises, to their ancient flash and crash habits of old Pales time ere beam slewed cable[7] or Derzherr, live wire, fired Benjermine Funkling outa th'Empyre, sin righthand son; which, cummal, having listed curefully to the

---

1 Because it's run on the mountain and river system.
2 When all them allied sloopers was ventitillated in their poppos and, sliding down by creek and veek, stole snaking out to sea.
3 They were plumped and plumed and jerried and citizens and racers, and cinnamondhued.
4 Creeping Crawleys petery parley, banished to his native Ireland from erring under Ryan.
5 Had our retrospectable fearfurther gatch mutchtatches?
6 That is to sight, when cleared of factions, vulgure and decimating.
7 They just spirits a body away.

interlooking and the underlacking of her twentynine shifts or his
continental's curses, pummel, apostrophised Byrne's and Flamming's and
Furniss's and Bill Hayses's and Ellishly Haught's, hoc, they (t.a.W.), sick
or whole, stiff or sober, let drop as a doombody drops, without another
ostrovgods word eitherways, in their own lineal descendance, as priesto as
puddywhack,[1] coal on:[2] and, as we gang along to gigglehouse, talking of
molniacs' manias and missions for mades to scotch the schlang and
leathercoats for murty magdies, of course this has blameall in that
medeoturanian world to say to blessed by Pointer the Grace's his privates
judgements[3] whenso to put it, *disparito, duspurudo, desterrado, despertieu,* or,
saving his presents for his own onefriend Bevradge, Conn the Shaughraun;
but to return for a moment from the reptile's age[4] to the coxswain on the
first landing (page Ainée Riviere!) if the pretty Lady Elisabbess, Hotel des
Ruines—she laid her batsleeve for him two trueveres tell love (on the Ides
of Valentino's, at Idleness, Floods Area, Isolade, Liv's lonely daughter,
with the Comes Tichiami, of Prima Vista, Abroad, suddenly), and beauty
alone of all dare say when now, uncrowned, deceptered, in what niche of
time[5] is Shee or where in the rose world trysting, that was the belle of La
Chapelle, shapely Liselle, and the peg-of-my-heart of all the tompull or
on whose limbs-to-lave her semicupiose eyes now kindling themselves are
brightning,[6] O Shee who then (4.32 M.P., old time, to be precise,
according to all three doctors waterburies that was Mac Auliffe and poor
MacBeth and poor MacGhimley to the tickleticks, of the synchronisms,
all lauschening, a time also confirmed seven sincuries later by the quatren
medical johnny, poor old MacAdoo. MacDollett, with notary,[7] whose
presence was required by law of Devine Foresygth and decretal of the
Douge) who after the first compliments[8] med darkist day light, gave him
then that vantage of a Blinkensope's cuddlebath at her proper mitts—if
she then, the then that matters,—but, *seigneur*! she could never have
forefelt, as she yet will fearfeel, when the lovenext breaks out, such a
coolcold douche as him, the totterer, the four-flights-the-charmer,

---

1 Patatapadatback.
2 Dump her (the missuse).
3 Fox him! The leggy colt!
4 Do he not know that walleds had wars. Harring man, is neow king. This is modeln
  times.
5 Muckross Abbey with the creepers taken off.
6 Joke and Jilt will have their tilt.
7 Old Mamalujorum and Rawrogerum.
8 Why have these puerile blonds those large flexible ears?

doubling back, in nowtime,[1] bymby when saltwater he wush him these iselands, *O alors!*, to mount miss (the wooeds of Fogloot!) under that *chemise de fer* and mana vartryproof name, Multalusi (would it wash?) with a cheek white peaceful as, wen shall say, a single professed claire's[2] and his washawash tubatubtub and his diagonoser's lampblick, to pure where they where hornest girls, to buy her in *par jure*, il you plait, nuncandtunc and for simper, and other duel mavourneens in plurible numbers from Arklow Vikloe to Louth super Luck, come messes, come mams, and touch your spottprice (for'twas he was the born suborner, man) on behalf of an oldest ablished firma of winebakers, Lagrima and Gemiti, later on, his craft ebbing, invoked by the unirish title, Grindings of Nash,[3] the One and Only, Unic bar None, of Saint Yves by Landsend cornwer, man— ship me silver!, it must have been, faw! a terrible mavrue mavone, to synamite up the old Adam-he-used-to, such a finalley, and that's flat as Tut's fut, for whowghowho? the poour girl, a lonely peggy, given the bird, so inseuladed as Crampton's peartree, (she sall eurn bitter bed by thirt sweet of her face!), and short wonder so many of the tomthick and tarry members in all there subsequious ages of our timocracy tipped to console with her at her mirrorable gracewindow'd hut[4] till the ives of Man, the O'Kneels and the O'Prayins and the O'Hyens of Lochlaunstown and the O'Hollerins of Staneybatter, hollyboys, all, burryripe who'll buy?,[5] in juwelietry and kicky-choses and madornaments and that's not the finis of it (would it were!)—but to think of him foundling a nelliza the second,[6] also cliptbuss (the best was still there if the torso was gone) where he did and when he did, retriever to the last[7]—escapes my forgetness now was it dust—covered, *nom de Lieu*! on lapse or street ondown, through, for or from a foe, by with as on a friend, at the Rectory? Vicarage Road? Bishop's Folly? Papesthorpe?, after picket fences, stonewalls, out and ins or oxers— for merry a valsehood whisprit he to manny a lilying earling;[8] and to try to analyse that ambo's pair of braceleans akwart the rollyon trying to amarm

---

1 Pomeroy Roche of Portobello, or the Wreck of the Ragamuffin.
2 No wonder Miss Dotsh took to veils and she descended from that obloquohy.
3 The bookley with the rusin's hat is Patomkin but I'm blowed if I knowed who the slave is doing behind the curtain.
4 O hce! O hce!
5 Six and seven the League.
6 It's all round me hat I'll wear a drooping dido.
7 Have you ever thought of a hitching your stern and being ourdeaned, Mester Bootenfly, here's me and Myrtle is twinkling to know.
8 To show they caught preferment.

all[1] of that miching micher's bearded but insensible virility and its gaulish moustaches, Dammad and Groany, into her limited (*tuff, tuff, que tu es pitre!*) lapse at the same slapse for towelling ends[2] in their dolightful Sexsex home, Somehow-at-Sea (O little oily head, sloper's brow and prickled ears!) as though he, a notoriety, a foist edition, were a wrigular writher neonovene babe![3]—well, diarmuee and granyou and *Vae Vinctis*, that is what lamoor that of gentle breast rathe is intaken seems circling toward out yondest (it's life that's all chokered by that batch of grim rushers) heaven help his hindmost and, mark mo, if the so greatly displeaced diorems in the Saint Lubbock's Day number of that most improving of roundshows, *Spice and Westend Woman* (utterly exhausted before publication, indiapepper edition shortly), are for our indices, it agins to pear like it, par my fay, and there is no use for your pastri-preaching for to cheesse it either or praying fresh fleshblood claspers of young catholick throats on Huggin Green[4] to take warning by the prispast, why?, by cows ∵ man, in shirt, is how he is *più la gonna è mobile* and ∴ they wonet do ut; and, an you could peep inside the cerebralised saucepan of this eer illwinded goodfornobody, you would see in his house of thoughtsam (was you, that is, decontaminated enough to look discarnate) what a jetsam litterage of convolvuli of times lost or strayed, of lands derelict and of tongues laggin too, longa yamsayore, not only that but, search lighting, beached, bashed and beaushelled *à la Mer* pharahead into faturity, your own convolvulis pickninnig capman would real to jazztfancy the novo takin place of what stale words whilom were woven with and fitted fairly featly for, so; and equally so, the crame of the whole faustian fustian, whether your launer's lightsome or your soulard's schwearmood, it is that, whenas the swiftshut scareyss of our pupilteachertaut duplex will hark back to lark to you symibellically that, though a day be as dense as a decade, no mouth has the might to set a mearbound to the march of a landsmaul,[5] in half a sylb, helf a solb, holf a salb onward[6] the beast of boredom, common sense, lurking gyrographically down inside his loose Eating S.S. collar is gogoing of whisth to you sternly how—Plutonic loveliaks twinnt Platonic yearlings—you must, how, in undivided reawlity draw the line somewhawre)

1 See the freeman's cuticatura by Fennella.
2 Just one big booty's pot.
3 Charles de Simples had an infirmierity complexe before he died a natural death.
4 Where Buickly of the Glass and Bellows pumped the Rudge engineral.
5 Matter of Brettaine and brut fierce.
6 Bussmullah, cried Lord Wolsley, how me Aunty Mag'll row!

Coss? Cossist? Your parn! You, you make WHY MY AS
what name? (and in truth, as a poor soul is LIKEWISE
between shift and shift ere the death he has WHIS HIS.
lived through becomes the life he is to die into,
he or he had albut—he was rickets as to reasons
but the balance of his minds was stables—lost
himself or himself some somnione sciupiones,
soswhitchoversswetch had he or he gazet,
murphy come, murphy go, murphy plant,
murphy grow, a maryamyriameliamurphies, in
the lazily eye of his lapis, Vieus Von DVbLIn,

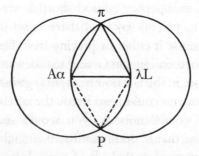

Uter-
alterance or
the Interplay
of Bones in
the Womb.

The Vortex.
Spring of
Sprung
Verse. The
Vertex.

'twas one of dozedeams a darkies ding in
dewood) the Turnpike under the Great Ulm
(with Mearingstone in Fore ground).[1] Given
now ann linch you take enn all. Allow me. And,
heaving alljawbreakical expressions out of old
Sare Isaac's[2] universal of specious aristmystic
unsaid, A is for Anna like L is for liv. Aha hahah,
Ante Ann you're apt to ape aunty annalive!
Dawn gives rise. Lo, lo, lives love! Eve takes
fall. La, la, laugh leaves alass! Aiaiaiai, Antiann,
we're last to the lost, Loulou! Tis perfect. Now
(lens your dappled yeye here, mine's presby-
operian, shill and wall) we see the copyngink
strayedline AL (in Fig., the forest) from being
continued, stops ait Lambday:[3] Modder ilond

---

1 Draumcondra's Dream country where the betterlies blow.
2 O, Laughing Sally, are we going to be toadhaunted by that old Pantifox Sir
   Somebody Something, Burtt, for the rest of our secret stripture?
3 Ex jup pep off Carpenger Strate. The kids' and dolls' home. Makeacakeache.

Sarga, or the path of outgoing.

there too. Allow me anchore! I bring down noth and carry awe. Now, then, take this in! One of the most murmurable loose carollaries ever Ellis threw his cookingclass. With Olaf as centrum and Olaf's lambtail for his spokesman circumscript a cyclone. Allow ter! Hoop! As round as the calf of an egg! O, dear me! O, dear me now! Another grand discobely! After Makefearsome's Ocean. You've actuary entducked one! Quok! Why, you haven't a passer! Fantastic! Early clever, surely doomed, to Swift's, alas, the galehus! Match of a matchness, like your Big-

Docetism and Didicism, Maya-Thaya. Tamas-Rajas-Sattvas.

dud dadder in the boudeville song, *Gorotsky Gollovar's Troubles*, raucking his flavourite turvku in the smukking precincts of lydias,[1] with Mary Owens and Dolly Monks seesidling to edge his cropulence and Blake-Roche, Kingston and Dockrell auriscenting him from afurz, our papacocopotl,[2] Abraham Bradley King? (ting ting! ting ting!) By his magmasine fall. Lumps, lavas and all.[3] *Bene!* But, thunder and turf, it's not alover yet! One recalls Byzantium. The mystery repeats itself todate as our callback mother Gaudyanna, that was daughter to a tanner,[4] used to sing, as I think, now and then consinuously over her possetpot in her quer homolocous humminbass hesterdie and istherdie forivor.[5] Vanissas Vanistatums! And for a night of thoughtsendyures and a day. As Great Shapesphere puns it. In effect, I remumble,

The Vegetable Cell and its Private Properties.

from the yules gone by, purr lil murrerof myhind, so she used indeed. When she give me the Sundaclouths she hung up for Tate and Comyng and snuffed out the ghost in the candle

1 A vagrant need is a flagrant weed.
2 Grand for blowing off steam when you walk up in the morning.
3 At the foot of Bagnabun Banbasday was lost on one.
4 We're all found of our anmal matter.
5 Sewing up the beillybursts in their buckskin shiorts for big Kapitayn Killykook and the Jukes of Kelleiney.

at his old game of haunt the sleepper. Faithful departed. When I'm dreaming back like that I begins to see we're only all telescopes. Or the comeallyoum saunds. Like when I dromed I was in Dairy and was wuckened up with thump in thudderdown. Rest in peace! But to return.[1] What a wonderful memory you have too! Twonderful morrowy! Straorbinaire! *Bene!* I bring town eau and curry nothung up my sleeve. Now, springing quickenly from the mudland Loosh from Luccan with Allhim as her Elder tetraturn a somersault. All's fair on all fours, as my instructor unstrict me. Watch! And you'll have the whole inkle. Allow, allow! Gyre O, gyre O, gyrotundo! Hop lala! As umpty herum as you seat! O, dear me, that was very nesse! Very nace indeed! And makes us a daintical pair of

The haves and accomplasses! You, allus for the kunst and me for
the havenots: a omething with a handel to it. *Beve!* Now, as will
distinction. pressantly be felt, there's tew tricklesome poinds where our twain of doubling bicirculars, mating approxemetely in their suite poi and poi, dunloop into eath the ocher. Lucihere! I fee where you mea. The doubleviewed seeds. Nun, lemmas quatsch, vide pervoys akstiom, and I think as I'm suqeez in the limon, stickme punctum, but for semenal rations I'd likelong, by Araxes, to mack a capital Pee for Pride down there on the batom[2] where Hoddum and Heave, our monsterbilker,

Zweispaltung balked his bawd of parodies. And let you go,
as Funde- Airmienious, and mick your modest mock Pie
maintalish of out of Humbles up your end. Where your apexo-
Wiederher- jesus will be a point of order. With a geing groan
stellung. grunt and a croak click cluck.[3] And my faceage kink and kurkle trying to make keek peep.[4] Are

---

1 Say where! A timbrelfill of twinkletinkle.
2 Parsee ffrench for the upholdsterer would be delightered.
3 I'll pass out if the screw spliss his strut.
4 Thargam then goeligum? If you sink I can, swimford. Suksumkale!

you right there, Michael, are you right? Do you think you can hold on by sitting tight? Well, of course, it's awful angelous. Still I don't feel it's so dangelous. Ay, I'm right here, Nickel, and I'll write. Singing the top line why it suits me mikey fine. But, yaghags hogwarts and arrah-quinonthiance, it's the muddest thick that was ever heard dump since Eggsmather got smothered in the plap of the pfan. Now, to compleat anglers, beloved bironthiarn and hushtokan hishtakatsch, join alfa pea and pull loose by dotties and, to be more sparematically logoical, eelpie and paleale by trunkles. Alow me align while I encloud especious! The Nike done it. Like pah,[1] I peh. Innate little bondery. And as plane as a poke stiff.[2] Now, *aqua in buccat*. I'll make you to see figuratleavely the whome of your eternal geomater. And if you flung her headdress on her from under her highlows you'd wheeze whyse Salmonson set his seel on a hexengown.[3] Hissss!, Arrah, go on!

Destiny, Influnce of Design upon.

Fin for fun! You've spat your shower like a son of Sibernia but let's have at it! Subtend to me now! Pisk! Outer serpumstances beiug eke-willed, we carefully, if she pleats, lift by her seam hem and jabote at the spidsiest of her trickkikant (like thousands done before since fillies calpered. Ocone! Ocone!) the maidsapron of our A.L.P., fearfully! till its nether nadir is vortically where (allow me aright to two cute winkles) its naval's napex will have to beandbe.

Prometheus or the Promise of Provision.

You must proach near mear for at is dark. Lob. And light your mech. Jeldy! And this is what you'll say.[4] Waaaaaa. Tch! Sluice! Pla! And their, redneck, (for addn't we to gayàtsee with

1 Hasitatense?
2 The impudence of that in girl's things!
3 The chape of Doña Speranza of the Nacion.
4 Ugol egal ogle. Mi vidim Mi.

Puhl the Punkah's bell? mygh and thy, the living spit of dead waters,[1] fastness firm of Hurdlebury Fenn, discinct and isoplural in its (your sow to the duble) sixuous parts, flument, fluvey and fluteous, midden wedge of the stream's your muddy old triagonal delta, fiho miho, plain for you now, appia lippia pluvaville, (hop the hula, girls!) the no niggard spot of her safety vulve, first of all usquiluteral threeingles, (and why wouldn't she sit cressloggedlike the lass that lured a tailor?) the constant of fluxion, Mahamewetma, pride of the province[2] and when that tidled boare rutches up from the

Ambages and Their Rôle.

Afrantic, allaph quaran's his bett und bier.[3] Paa lickam laa lickam, apl lpa. This it is an her. You see her it. Which it whom you see it is her. And if you could goaneggbetter we'd soon see some raffant scrumala riffa. Quicks herit fossy-ending. Quef! So post that to your pape and smarket. And you can haul up that languil pennant, mate. I've read your tunc's dimissage. For, let it be taken that her littlenist is of no magnetude or again let it be granted that Doll the laziest can be dissimulant with all respects from Doll the fiercst, thence must any whatyoulike in the power of empthood be either greater

Ecclasiastical and Celestial Hierarchies. The Ascending. The Descending.

THaN or less THaN the unitate we have in one or hence shall the vectorious readyeyes of evertwo circumflicksrent searclhers never film in the elipsities of their gyribouts those fickers which are returnally reprodictive of themselves.[4] Which is unpassible. Quarrellary. The logos of somewome to that base anything, when most characteristically mantissa minus, comes to nullum in the endth:[5] orso, here is nowet

---

1 It is, it is Sangannon's dream.
2 And all meinkind.
3 Whangpoos the paddle and whiss whee whoo.
4 I enjoy as good as anyone.
5 Neither a soul to be saved nor a body to be kicked.

The peripatetic periphery. It's Allothesis.

badder than the sin of Aha with his cosin Lil, verswaysed on coverswised, and all that's consecants and cotangincies till Perperp stops repippinghim since her redtangles are all abscissan for limitsing this tendency of our Frivulteeny Sexuagesima[1] to expense herselfs as sphere as possible, paradismic perimutter, in all directions on the bend of the unbridalled, the infinisissimalls of her facets becoming manier and manier as the calicolum of her umdescrib-ables (one has thoughts of that eternal Rome) shrinks from schurtiness to scherts.[2] Scholium, there are trist sigheds to everysing but ichs on the freed brings euchs to the feared. Qued? Mother of us all! O, dear me, look at that now! I don't know is it your spictre or my omination but I'm glad you dimentioned it! My Lourde! My Lourde! If that aint just the beatenest lay I ever see! And a superpbosition! Quoint a quincidence! O.K. *Omnius Kollidimus.* As Ollover Krumwall sayed when he slepped ueber his grannyamother. Kangaroose feathers: Who in the name of thunder'd ever belevin you were that bolt? But you're holy mooxed and gaping up the wrong palce[3] as if you was seeheeing the gheist that stays forenenst, you blessed simpletop domefool! Where's your belested loiternan's lamp? You must lap wandret down the bluishing refluction below. Her trunk's not her brainbox. Hear where the bolgylines, Yseen here the puncture. So he done it. Luck! See her good. Well, well, well, well! O dee, O dee, that's very lovely! We like Simperspreach Hammel-tones to fellow Selvertunes O'Haggans.[4] When

Canine Venus sublimated to Aulidic Aphrodite.

Exclusivism: the Ors, Sors and Fors, which?

---

1 The boast of the town.
2 Hen's bens, are we soddy we missiled her?
3 I call that a scumhead.
4 Pure chingchong idiotism with any way words all in one soluble. Gee each owe tea eye smells fish. That's U.

he rolls over his ars and shows the hise of his heels. Vely lovely entirely! Like a yangsheep-slang with the tsifengtse. So analytical plausible! And be the powers of Moll Kelly, neighbour topsowyer, it will be a lozenge to me all my lauffe.[1] More better twofeller we been speak copperads. Ever thought about Guinness's? And the regrettable Parson Rome's advice? Want to join the police.[2] You know, you were always one of the bright ones, since a foot made you an unmentionable, fakes. You know, you're the divver's own smart gossoon, aequal to your-sell and wanigel to anglyother, so you are, hoax! You know, you'll be dampned, so you will, one of these invernal days but you will be, carrotty.[3]

Prima-nouriture and Ultimo-geniture.

Wherapool, gayet that when he stop look time he stop long ground who here hurry he would have ever the lothst word, with a sweet me ah err eye ear marie to reat from the jacob's[4] and a shypull for toothsake of his armjaws at the slidepage of de Vere Foster, would and could candykissing P. Kevin to fress up the rinnerung and to ate by hart (*leo* I read, such a spanish, *escribibis* all your mycoscoups) wont to nibbleh ravenostonnoriously ihs mum to me in bewonderment of his chipper chuthor for, while that Other by the halp of his creactive mind offered to deleberate the mass from the booty of fight our Same with the holp of the bounty of food sought to delubberate the mess from his corructive mund, with his muffetee cuffes own-consciously grafficking with his sinister cyclopes after trigamies and spirals' wobbles pursuiting their rovinghamilton selves and godolphing in fairlove to see around the waste of noland's

SICK US A SOCK WITH SOME SEDIMENT IN IT FOR THE SAKE OF OUR DARNING WIVES.

1 The Doodles family, ᛘ,△,ᚺ,✕ ,☐ ,Λ,ᒧ. Hoodle doodle, fam.?
2 Picking on Nickagain, Pikey Mikey.
3 Early morning, sir Dav Stephens, said the First Gentleman in youreups.
4 Bag bag blockcheap, have you any will?

No Sturm.
No Drang.

Illustration.

browne jesus[1] (thur him no quartos!) till that on him poorin sweat the juggaleer's veins (quench his quill!) in his napier scrag stud out bursthright tamquam taughtropes. (Spry him! call a blood lekar! Where's Dr Brassenaarse?) Es war itwas in his priesterrite. O He Must Suffer! From this misbelieving feacemaker to his noncredible fancyflame.[2] Ask for bosthoon, late for Mass, pray for blaablaablack sheep. (Sure you could wright anny pippap passage, Eye bet, as foyne as that moultylousy Erewhig, yerself, mick! Nock the muddy nickers![3] Christ's Church varses Bellial!) Dear and he went on

Ascription of
the Active.

to scripple gentlemine born, milady bread, he would pen for her, he would pine for her,[4] how he would patpun fun for all[5] with his frolicky frowner so and his glumsome grinner otherso. And how are you, waggy?[6] My animal his sorrafool! And trieste, ah trieste ate I my liver! *Se non é, vero son trovatore.* O jerry! He was soso, harriot all! He was sadfellow, steifel! He was mistermysterion. Like a purate out of pensionee with a gouvernament job. All moanday, tearsday, wailsday, thumpsday, frightday, shatterday till the fear of the Law. Look at this twitches! He was quisquis, floored on his plankraft of shittim wood. Look at him! Sink

Proscription
of the
Passive.

deep or touch not the Cartesian spring! Want more ashes, griper? How diesmal he was lying low on his rawside laying siege to goblin castle. And, bezouts that, how hyenesmeal he was laying him long on his laughside lying sack to

---

1 What a lubberly whide elephant for the men-in-the-straits!
2 And she had to seek a pond's apeace to salve her suiterkins. Sued!
3 Excuse theyre christianbrothers irish.
4 When she tripped against the briery bush he profused her allover with curtsey flowers.
5 A nastilow disigraible game.
6 Dear old Erosmas. Very glad you are going to Penmark. Write to the corner. Grunny Grant.

croakpartridge. (Be thou wars Rolaf's
intestions, quoths the Bhagavat biskop Leech)
Ann opes tipoo soon ear! If you could me
lendtill my pascol's kondyl, sahib, and the price
of a plate of poultice. Punked. With best
apolojigs and merrymoney thanks to self for

Ensouling
Female
Sustains
Agonising
Overman.

all the clerricals and again begs guerdon for
bistrispissing on your bunificence. Well wiggy-
wiggywagtail, and how are you, yaggy? With a
capital Tea for Thirst. From here Buvard to
dear Picuchet. Blott.

Now, (peel your eyes, my gins, and brush   WHEN THE
your saton hat, me elementator joyclid, son of a   ANSWERER
Butt! She's mine, Jow low jure,[1] be Skibbering's   IS A LEMAN.
eagles, sweet tart of Whiteknees Archway)
watch him, having caught at the bifurking
calamum in his bolsillos, the onelike underworp
he had ever funnet without difficultads, the
aboleshqvick, signing away in happinext

Sesama to
the Rescues.
The Key
Signature.

complete, (Exquisite Game of inspiration! I
always adored your hand. So could I too and
without the scrope of a pen. Ohr for oral, key
for crib, olchedolche and a lunge ad lib. Can
you write us a last line? From Smith–Jones–
Orbison?) intrieatedly in years, jirryalimpaloop.
And i Romain, hup u bn gd grl.[2] Unds alws my
thts. To fallthere at bare feet hurryasworm-
arose. Two dies of one rafflement. Eche benny-
ache. Outstamp and distribute him at the
expanse of his society. To be continued. Anon.

And ook, ook, ook, fanky! All the charictures[3]   ALL SQUARE
in the drame! This is how San holypolypools.   AND
And this, pardonsky! is the way Romeopullu-   ACCORDING
palleaps.[4] Posè the pen, man, way me does.   TO COCKER.

1 I loved to see the Macbeths-Jerseys knacking spots of the Plumpduffs Pants.
2 Lifp year fends you all and moe, fouvenirs foft as fummer fnow, fweet willings and
  forget-uf-knots.
3 Gag his tubes yourself.
4 He, angel that I thought him, and he not aebel to speel eelyotripes., Mr Tellibly
  Divilcult!

Force Centres of
the Fire
Serpentine: heart,
throat, navel,
spleen, sacral, fon-
tanella, inter-
temporal eye.

Conception of the
Compromise and
Finding of a
Formula.

Ideal Present
Alone Produces
Real Future.

Way ole missa vellatooth fust show me how. Fourth power to her illpogue! Bould strokes for your life! Tip! This is Steal, this is Barke, this is Starn, this is Swhipt, this is Wiles, this is Pshaw, this is Doubbllinnbbayyates.[1] This is brave Danny weeping his spache for the popers. This is cool Connolly wiping his hearth with brave Danny. And this, regard! how Chawleses Skewered parpara- parnelligoes between brave Danny boy and the Connolly. Upanishadem! Top. Spoken hath L'arty Magory. Eregobragh. Prouf![2]

And Kev was wreathed with his pother. TROTH-

But, (that Jacoby feeling again for fore- BLOWERS. bitten fruit and, my Georgeous, Kevvy too FIG AND he just loves his puppadums, I judge!) after THISTLE all his autocratic writings of paraboles of PLOT A famellicurbs and meddlied muddlingisms, PIG AND thee faroots hof cullchaw end ate citrawn' WHISTLE. woodint wun able rep of the triperforator awlrite blast through his pergaman hit him where he lived and do for the blessted self- churuls, what I think, smarter like it done for a manny another unpious of the hairy- dary quare quandary firstings till at length, you one bladdy bragger, by mercystroke he measured his earth anyway? could not but recken in his adder's badder cadder way our frankson who, to be plain, he fight him all time twofeller longa kill dead finish bloody face blong you, was misocain. Wincewan's won! Rip![3] And his counting- hands rose. WITH

Formalisa. Loves deathhow simple! EBONISER. Slutningsbane.[4] IN PIX.

---

1 When the dander rattles how the peacocks prance!
2 The Brownes de Browne - Browne of Castlehacknolan.
3 A byebye bingbang boys! See you Nutcracker Sunday!
4 Chinchin Childaman! Chapchopchap!

Service super-
seding self.

Thanks eversore much, Pointcarried! I can't
say if it's the weight you strike me to the quick
or that red mass I was looking at but at the
present momentum, potential as I am, I'm
seeing rayingbogeys rings round me. Honours
to you and may you be commended for our
exhibitiveness! I'd love to take you for a buga-
boo ride and play funfer all if you'd only sit and
be the ballasted bottle in the porker barrel. You
will deserve a rolypoly as long as from here to
tomorrow. And to hell with them driftbombs
and bottom trailers! If my maily was bag enough
I'd send you a toxis. By Saxon Chromaticus,
you done that lovely for me! Didn't he now,
Nubilina? Tiny Mite, she studiert whas?
With her listeningin coiffure, her dream of
Endsland's daylast and the glorifires of being
presainted maid to majesty.[1] And less is the pity
for she isn't the lollypops she easily might be if
she had for a sample Virginia's air of achievement. That might keep her from throwing
delph.[2] As I was saying, while retorting thanks,
you make me a reborn of the cards. We're offals
boys ambows.[3] For I've flicked up all the crambs
as they crumbed from your table um, singing
glory allaloserem, cog it out, here goes a sum.
So read we in must book. It tells. He prophets
most who bilks the best.

And that salubrated sickenagiaour of yaours
have teaspilled all my hazeydency. Forge away,
Sunny Sim. Sheepshopp. Bleating Goad, it is
the least of things, Eyeinstye! Imagine it, my
deep dartry dullard! It is hours giving, not
more. I'm only out for celebridging over the
guilt of the gap in your hiscitendency. You are

Catastrophe
and Anabasis.

The rotary
processus and
its reestablish-
ment of
reciprocities.

EUCHRE
RISK,
MERCI
BUCKUP,
AND
MIND
WHO
YOU'RE
PUCKING,
FLEBBY.

COME SI
COMPITA
CUNCTITIT-
ITILATIO?
CONKERY
CUNK,
THIGH-

---

1 Wipe your glosses with what you know.
2 If I'd more in the cups that peeves thee you could cracksmith your rows tureens.
3 Alls Sings and Alls Howls.

The Twofold Truth and the Conjunctive Appetites of Oppositional Orexes.

a hundred thousand times welcome, old wortsampler, hellbeit you're just about as culpable as my woolfell merger would be. In effect I could engage in an energument over you till you were republicly royally toobally prussic blue in the shirt after.[1] *Trionfante di bestia!* And if you're not your bloater's kipper may I never curse again on that pint I took of Jamesons. Old Keane now, you're rod, hook and sinker, old jubalee Keane! Biddy's hair. Biddy's hair, mine lubber. Where is that Quin but he sknows it knot but what you that are my popular endphthisis were born with a solver arm up your sleep. Thou in shanty!

Trishagion.

Thou in scanty shanty!! Thou in slanty scanty shanty!!! Bide in your hush! Bide in your hush, do! The law does not aloud you to shout. I plant my penstock in your postern, chinarpot. Ave! And let it be to all remembrance. Vale. Ovocation of maiding waters.[2] For auld lang salvy steyne. I defend you to champ my scullion's praises. To book alone belongs the lobe. Foremaster's meed[3] will mark tomorrow, when we are making pilscrummage to whaboggeryin with staff, scarf and blessed wallet and our aureoles round our neckkandcropfs where as and when Heavysciusgardaddy, parent who

Abnegation is Adaptation.

offers sweetmeats, will gift uns his Noblett's surprize. With this laudable purpose in loud ability let us be singulfied. Betwixt me and thee hung cong. Item, mizpah ends.

THIGHT-TICKELLY-THIGH, LIGGERILAG, TITTERITOT, LEG IN A TEE, LUG IN A LAW, TWO AT A TIE, THREE ON A THRICKY TILL OHIO OHIO IOIOMISS.

---

1 From three shellings. A bluedye sacrifice.
2 Not Kilty. But the manajar was. He! He! Ho! Ho! Ho!
3 Giglamps, Soapy Geyser, The Smell and Gory Mac Gusty.

But while the dial are they doodling dawdling over the mugs and the grubs? Oikey, Impostolopulos?[1] Steady steady steady steady steady studiavimus. Many many many many many manducabimus.[2] We've had our day at triv and quad and writ our bit as intermidgets. Art, *Cato. Nero.* literature, politics, economy, chemistry, *Saul.* humanity, &c. Duty, the daughter of dis- *Aristotle.* cipline, the Great Fire at the South City *Julius Caesar.* Markets, Belief in Giants and the Ban- *Pericles.* shee, A Place for Everything and Every- *Ovid. Adam,* thing in its Place, Is the Pen Mightier *Eve.* than the Sword? A Successful Career in *Domitian.* the Civil Service,[3] The Voice of Nature *Edipus.* in the Forest,[4] Your Favorite Hero or *Socrates.* Heroine, On the Benefits of Recreation,[5] *Ajax.* If Standing Stones Could Speak, Devotion to the Feast of the Indulgence *Homer.* of Portiuncula, The Dublin Metropolitan *Marcus* Police Sports at Ballsbridge, Describe *Aurelius.* in Homely Anglian Monosyllables the Wreck of the Hesperus,[6] What Morals, if *Alcibiades.* any, can be drawn from Diarmuid and *Lucretius.* Grania?[7] Do you approve of our Existing *Noah. Plato.* Parliamentary System? The Uses and *Horace. Isaac.* Abuses of Insects, A Visit to Guinness' *Tiresias.* Brewery, Clubs, Advantages of the Penny *Marius.* Post, When is a Pun not a Pun? Is *Diogenes.* the Co-Education of Animus and Anima Wholly Desirable?[8] What Happened at

ENTER THE COP AND HOW. SECURES GUBERNANT URBIS TERROREM.

---

1 The divvy wants that babbling brook. Dear Auntie Emma Emma Eates.
2 Strike the day off, the nightcap's on nigh. Goney, goney gone!
3 R.C., disengaged, good character, would help, no salary.
4 Where Lily is a Lady found the nettle rash.
5 Bubabipibambuli, I can do as I like with what's me own. Nyamnyam.
6 Able seaman's caution.
7 Rarely equal and distinct in all things.
8 Jests and the Beastalk with a little rude hiding rod.

Procne,
Philomela.
Abraham.
Nestor. Cincin-
natus. Leonidas.
Jacob. Theocritus.
Joseph. Fabius.
Samson. Cain.
Esop.
Prometheus. Lot.
Pompeius
Magnus,
Miltiades
Strategos. Solon.
Castor, Pollux.
Dionysius.
Sappho. Moses.
Job. Catilina.
Cadmus. Ezekiel.
Solomon.
Themistocles.
Vitellius. Darius.
Xenophon.

Clontarf? Since our Brother Johnathan Signed the Pledge or the Meditations of Two Young Spinsters,[1] Why we all Love our Little Lord Mayor, Hengler's Circus Entertainment, On Thrift,[2] The Kettle–Griffith–Moynihan Scheme for a New Electricity Supply, Travelling in the Olden Times,[3] American Lake Poetry, the Strangest Dream that was ever Halfdreamt.[4] Circumspection, Our Allies the Hills, Are Parnellites Just towards Henry Tudor? Tell a Friend in a Chatty Letter the Fable of the Grasshopper and the Ant,[5] Santa Claus, The Shame of Slumdom, The Roman Pontiffs and the Orthodox Churches,[6] The Thirty Hour Week, Compare the Fistic Styles of Jimmy Wilde and Jack Sharkey, How to Understand the Deaf, Should Ladies learn Music or Mathematics? Glory be to Saint Patrick! What is to be found in a Dustheap, The Value of Circumstantial Evidence, Should Spelling? Outcasts in India, Collecting Pewter, Eu,[7] Proper and Regular Diet Necessity For,[8] If You Do It Do It Now. Delays are Dangerous. Vitavite! Gobble Anne: tea's set, see's eneugh! Mox soonly will be in a split second per the chancellory of his exticker.

---

1 Wherry like the whaled prophet in a spookeerie.
2 What sins is pim money sans Paris.
3 I've lost the place, where was I?
4 Something happened that time I was asleep, torn letters or was there snow?
5 Mich for his pain, Nick in his past.
6 He has *toglieresti in brodo* all over his agrammatical parts of face and as for that hippofoxphiz, unlucky number, late for the christening!
7 Eh, Monsieur? Où Monsieur? Eu, Monsieur? Nenni No, Monsieur'
8 Ere we hit the hay, brothers, let's have that response to prayer!

Pantocracy.

Bimutualism.

Interchangeability.

Naturality. Super-

fetation. Stabi-

mobilism. Periodicity.

Consummation.

Interpenetrativeness.

Predicament.

Balance of the factual

by the theoric Boox

and Coox,

Amallagamated.

Aun

Do

Tri

Car

Cush[1]

Shay

Shockt

Ockt

Ni

Geg[2]

Their feed begins.

MAWMAW,
LUK, YOUR
BEEEFTAY'S
FIZZIN OVER.

KAKAOPOETIC
LIPPUDENIES
OF THE
UNGUMPTIOUS.

NIGHTLETTER

With our best youlldied greedings to
Pep and Memmy and the old folkers
below and beyant, wishing them all
very merry Incarnations in this land
of the livvey and plenty of prepros-
perousness through their coming new
yonks

from
jake, jack and little sousoucie
(the babes that mean too)

1 Kish is for anticheirst, and the free of my hand
   to him!

2 And gags for skool, and crossbuns and whopes
   he'll enjoyimsolff over our drawings on the line!

IT MAY NOT OR MAYBE A NO CONCERN OF THE
Guinnesses but.

That the fright of his light in tribalbalbutience hides aback in the doom
of the balk of the deaf but that the height of bis life from a bride's eye
stammpunct is when a man that means a mountain barring his distance
wades a lymph that plays the lazy winning she likes yet that pride that bogs
the party begs the glory of a wake while the scheme is like your rumba
round me garden, allatheses, with perhelps the prop of a prompt to them,
was now or never in Etheria Deserta, as in Grander Suburbia, with Finn-
fannfawners, ruric or cospolite, for much or moment indispute.

Whyfor had they, it is Hiberio-Miletians and Argloe-Noremen, donated
him, birth of an otion that was breeder to sweatoslaves, as mysterbolder,
forced in their waste, and as for Ibdullin what of Himana, that their
tolvtubular high fidelity daildialler, as modern as tomorrow afternoon and
in appearance up to the minute (hearing that anybody in that ruad duchy of
Wollinstown schemed to halve the wrong type of date) equipped with
supershielded umbrella antennas for distance getting and connected by the
magnetic links of a Bellini-Tosti coupling system with a vitaltone speaker,
capable of capturing skybuddies, harbour craft emittences, key clickings,
vaticum cleaners, due to woman formed mobile or man made static and
bawling the whowle hamshack and wobble down in an eliminium sounds
pound so as to serve him up a melegoturny marygoraumd, eclectrically
filtered for allirish earths and ohmes. This harmonic condenser enginium
(the Mole) they caused to be worked from a magazine battery (called the
Mimmim Bimbim patent number 1132, Thorpetersen and Synds, Joms-
borg, Selverbergen) which was tuned up by twintriodic singulvalvulous
pipelines (lackslipping along as if their liffing deepunded on it) with a
howdrocephalous enlargement, a gain control of circumcentric megacycles
ranging from the antidulibnium onto the serostaatarean. They finally
caused, or most leastways brung it about somehows that the pip of the lin to
pinnatrate inthro an auricular forfickle (known as the Vakingfar sleeper,
monofractured by Piaras UaRhuamhaighaudhlug, tympan founder Eustache
Straight, Bauliaughacleeagh) a meatous conch culpable of cunduncing Naul
and Santry and the forty routs of Corthy with the concertiums of the
Brythyc Symmonds Guild, the Ropemakers Reunion, the Variagated

Peddlars Barringoy Bnibrthirhd, the Askold Olegsonder Crowds of the O'Keef-Rosses ant Rhosso-Keevers of Zastwoking, the Ligue of Yahooth o.s.v. so as to lall the bygone dozed they arborised around, up his corpular fruent and down his reuctionary buckling, hummer, enville and cstorrap (the man of Iren, thore's Curlymane for you!), lill the lubberendth of his otological life.

House of call is all their evenbreads though its cartomance hallucinate like an erection in the night the mummery of whose deed, a lur of Nur, immerges a mirage in a merror, for it is where by muzzinmessed for one watthour, bilaws below, till time jings pleas, that host of a bottlefilled, the bulkily hulkwight, hunter's pink of face, an orel orioled, is in.on a bout to be unbulging an o'connell's, the true one, all seethic, a luckybock, pledge of the stoup, whilom his canterberry bellseyes wink wickeding indtil the teller, oyne of an oustman in skull of skand. Yet is it, this ale of man, for him, our hubuljoynted, just a tug and a fistful as for Culsen, the Patagoreyan, chieftain of chokanchuckers and his moyety joyant, under the foamer dispensation when he pullupped the turfeycork by the greats of gobble out of Lough Neagk. When, pressures be to our hoary frother, the pop gave his sullen bulletaction and, bilge, sled a movement of catharic emulsipotion down the sloppery slide of a slaunty to tilted lift-ye-landsmen. Allamin. Which in the ambit of its orbit heaved a sink her sailer alongside of a drink her drainer from the basses brothers, those two theygottheres.

It was long after once there was a lealand in the luffing ore it was less after lives thor a toyler in the tawn at all ohr it was note before he drew out the moddle of Kersse by jerkin his dressing but and or it was not before athwartships he buttonhaled the Norweeger's capstan.

So he sought with the lobestir claw of his propencil the clue of the wickser in his ear. O, lord of the barrels, comer forth from Anow (I have not mislaid the key of Efas-Taem), O, Ana, bright lady, comer forth from Thenanow (I have not left temptation in the path of the sweeper of the threshold), O!

But first, strongbowth, they would deal death to a drinking. Link of a leadder, dubble in it, slake your thirdst thoughts awake with it. Our svalves are svalves aroon! We rescue thee, O Baass, from the damp earth and honour thee. O Connibell, with mouth burial! So was done, neat and trig. Up draught and whet them!

— Then sagd he to the ship's husband. And in his translatentic norjankeltian. Hwere can a ketch or hook alive a suit and sowterkins? Soot! sayd the ship's husband, knowing the language, here is tayleren. Ashe and Whitehead, closechop, successor to. Ahorror, he sayd, canting around to that beddest his friend, the tayler, for finixed coulpure, chunk pulley muchy chink topside numpa one sellafella, fake an capstan make and shoot! Manning to sayle of clothse for his lady her master whose to be precised of a peer of trouders under the pattern of a cassack. Let me prove, I pray thee, but this once, sazd Mengarments, saving the mouthbrand from his firepool. He spit in his faist (beggin): he tape the raw baste (paddin): he planked his pledge (as dib is a dab): and he tog his fringe sleeve (buthock lad, fur whale). Alloy for allay and this toolth for that soolth. Lick it and like it. A barter, a parter. And plenty good enough, neighbour Norreys, every bit and grain. And the ship's husband brokecurst after him to hail the lugger. Stolp, tief, stolp, come bag to Moy Eireann! And the Norweeger's capstan swaradeed, some blowfish out of schooling: All lykkehud! Below taiyor he ikan heavin sets. But they broken waters and they made whole waters at they surfered bark to the lots of his vauce. And aweigh he yankered on the Norgean run so that seven sailend sonnenrounders was he breastbare to the brinabath, where bottoms out has fatthoms full, fram Franz José Land til Cabo Thormendoso, evenstarde and risingsoon. Up the Rivor Tanneiry and down the Golfe Desombres. Farety days and fearty nights. Enjoy yourself, O maremen! And the tides made, veer and haul, and the times marred, rear and fall, and, holey bucket, dinned he raign!

— Hump! Hump! bassed the broaders-in-laugh with a quick piddysnip that wee halfbit a second.

— I will do that, sazd Kersse, mainingstaying the rigout for her wife's lairdship. Nett sew? they hunched back at the earpicker.

But old sporty, as endth lord, in ryehouse reigner, he nought feared crimp or cramp of shore sharks, plotsome to getsome. It was whol niet godthaab of errol Loritz off his Cape of Good Howthe and his trippertrice loretta lady, a maomette to his monetone, with twy twy twinky her stone hairpins, only not, if not, a queen of Prancess their telling tabled who was for his seeming a casket through the heavenly, nay, heart of the sweet (had he hows would he keep her as niece as a fiddle!) but in the mealtub it was wohl yeas sputsbargain what, rarer of recent, an occasional conformity, he, with Muggleton Muckers, alwagers allalong most certainly allowed, as pilerinnager's grace to petitionists of right, of the three blend cupstoo-merries with their customed spirits, the Gill gob, the Burklley bump, the Wallisey wanderlook, having their ceilidhe gailydhe in his shaunty irish. Group drinkards maaks grope thinkards or how reads rotary, jewr of a chrestend, respecting the otherdogs churchees, so long plubs will be plebs but plabs by low frequency amplification may later agree to have another. For the people of the shed are the sure ads of all quorum. Lorimers and leathersellers, skinners and salters, pewterers and paperstainers, parishclerks, fletcherbowyers, girdlers, mercers, cordwainers and first, and not last, the weavers. Our library he is hoping to ye public.

Innholder, upholder.

— Sets on sayfohrt! Go to it, agitator! they bassabosuned over the flowre of their hoose. Godeown moseys and skeep thy beeble bee.

— I will do that, acordial, by mine hand, sazd Kersse, piece Cod, and in the flap of a jacket, ructified after his nap of a blankit their o'cousin, as sober as the ship's husband he was one my godfather when he told me saw whileupon I am now well and jurily sagasfide after the boonamorse the widower, according to rider, following pnomoneya, he is consistently blown to Adams. So help me boyg who keeps the book!

Whereofter, behest his suzerain law the Thing and the pilsener had the baar, Recknar Jarl, (they called him Roguenor, Irl call him) still passing the change-a-pennies, pengeypigses, a several sort of coyne in livery, pushed their whisper in his hairing, (seemed, a some shipshep's sottovoxed stale-ment, a dearagadye, to hasvey anyone doing duty for duff point of dorkland compors) the same to the good ind ast velut discharge after which he had exemptied more than orphan for the ballast of his nurtural life. And threw a cast. A few pigses and hare you are and no chicking, tribune's tribute, if you guess mimic miening. Meanly in his lewdbrogue take your tyon coppels token, with this good sixtric from mine runbag of juwels. Nummers that is summus that is toptip that is bottombay that is Twomeys that is Digges that is Heres. In the frameshape of hard mettles. For we all would fain make glories. It is minely well mint.

Thus as count the costs of liquid courage, a bullyon gauger, stowed stivers pengapung in bulk in hold (fight great finnence! brayvoh, little bratton!) keen his kenning, the queriest of the crew, with that fellow fearing for his own misshapes, should he be himpself namesakely a foully fallen dissentant from the peripulator, sued towerds Meade-Reid and Lynn-Duff, rubbing the hodden son of a pookal, leaden be light, lather be dry and it be drownd on all the ealsth beside, how the camel and where the deiffel or when the finicking or why the funicking, who caused the scaffolding to be first removed you give orders, babeling, were their reidey meade answer when on the cutey (the corespondent) in conflict of evidence drew a kick at witness but (missed) and for whom in the dyfflun's kiddy removed the planks they were wanted, boob.

Bump!

Bothallchoractorschumminaroundgansumuminarumdrumstrum-truminahumptadumpwaultopoofoolooderamaunsturnup!

— Did do a dive, aped one.

— Propellopalombarouter, based two.

— Rutsch is for rutterman ramping his roe, seed three. Where the muddies scrimm ball. Bimbim bimbim. And the maidies scream all. Himhim himhim.

And forthemore let legend go lore of it that mortar scene so cwympty dwympty what a dustydust it razed arboriginally but, luck's leap to the lad at the top of the ladder, so sartor's risorted why the sinner the badder! Ho ho ho hoch! La la la lach! Hillary rillarry gibbous grist to our millery! A pushpull, qq: quiescence, pp: with extravent intervulve coupling. The savest lauf in the world. Paradoxmutose caring, but here in a present booth of Ballaclay, Barthalamou, where their dutchuncler mynhosts and serves them dram well right for a boors' interior (homereek van hohmryk) that salve that selver is to screen its auntey and has ringround as worldwise eve her sins (pip, pip, pip) willpip futurepip feature apip footloose pastcast with spareshins and flash substittles of noirse-made-easy from a nephew mind the narrator but give the devil his so long as those sohns of a blitzh call the tuone tuone and thonder alout makes the thurd. Let there be. Due.

— That's all murtagh purtagh but whad ababs his dopter? sissed they who were onetime ungkerls themselves, (when the youthel of his yorn shook the bouchal in his bed) twilled along-side in wiping the Ace assatiated with their wetting. The lappel of his size? His *ros in sola velnere* and he sicckumed of homnis terrars. She wends to scoulas in her slalpers. There were no peanats in her famalgia so no wumble she tumbled for his famas roalls davors. Don't him forget! A butcheler artsed out of Cullege Trainity. Diddled he daddle a drop of the cradler on delight mebold laddy was stetched? Knit wear? And they addled, (or ere the cry of their tongues would be uptied dead) Shufflebotham asidled, plus his ducks fore his drills, an inlay of a liddle more lining maught be licensed all at ones, be these same tokens, forgiving a brass rap, sneither a whole length nor a short shift so full as all were concerned.

Burniface, shiply efter, shoply after, at an angle of lag, let flow, brabble brabble and brabble, and so hostily, heavyside breathing, came up with them and, check me joule, shot the three tailors, butting back to Moyle herring, bump as beam and buttend, roller and reiter, after the diluv's own deluge, the seasant samped as skibber breezed in, tripping, dripping, threw the sheets in the wind, the tights of his trunks at tickle to tackle and his rubmelucky truss rehorsing the pouffed skirts of his overhawl. He'd left his stickup in his hand to show them none ill feeling. Whatthough for all appentices it had a mushroom on it. While he faced them front to back, Then paraseuls round, quite taken atack, sclaiming, Howe cools Eavybrolly!

— Good marrams, sagd he, freshwatties and boasterdes all, as he put into bierhiven, nogeysokey first, cabootle segund, jilling to windwards, as he made straks for that oerasound the snarsty weg for Publin, so was his horenpipe lug in the lee off their mouths organs, with his tilt too taut for his tammy all a slaunter and his wigger on a wagger with its tag tucked. Up. With a good eastering and a good westering. And he asked from him how the hitch did do this my fand sulkers that mone met the Kidballacks which he suttonly remembered also where the hatch was he endnew strandweys he's that fond sutchenson, a penincular fraimd of mind, fordeed he was langseling to talka holt of hems, clown toff, tye hug fliorten. Cablen: Clifftop. Shelvling tobay oppelong tomeadow. Ware cobbles. Posh.

— Skibbereen has common inn, by pounautique, with pokeway paw, and sadder raven evermore, telled shinshanks lauwering frankish for his kicker who, through the medium of gallic

— Pukkelsen, tilltold.

That with some our prowed invisors how their ulstravoliance led them infroraids, striking down and landing alow, against our aerian insulation resistance, two boards that beached, ast one, widness thane and tysk and hanry. Prepatrickularly all, they summed. Kish met. Bound to. And for landlord, noting, nodding, a coast to moor was cause to mear. Besides proof plenty, over proof. While they either took a heft. Or the other swore his eric. Heaved two, spluiced the menbrace. Heirs at you, Brewinbaroon! Weth a whistle for methanks.

— Good marrams and good merrymills, sayd good mothers gossip, bobbing his bowing both ways with the bents and skerries, when they were all in the old walled of Kinkincaraborg (and that they did overlive the hot air of Montybunkum upon the coal blasts of Mitropolitos let there meeds be the hourihorn), hiberniating after seven oak ages, fearsome where they were he had gone dump in the doomering this tide where the peixies would pickle him down to the button of his seat and his sess old soss Erinly into the boelgein with the help of Divy and Jorum's locquor and shut the door after him to make a rarely fine Ran's cattle of fish. Morya Mortimor! Allapalla overus! Howoft had the ballshee tried! And they laying low for his home gang in that eeriebleak mead, with fireball feast and turkeys tumult and paupers patch to provide his bum end. The foe things your niggerhead needs to be fitten for the Big Water. He made the sign of the hammer. God's drought, he sayd, after a few daze, thinking of all those bliakings, how leif pauses! Here you are back on your hawkins, from Blasil the Brast to our povotogesus portocall, the furt on the turn of the hurdies, slave to trade, vassal of spices and a dragon-the-market, and be turbot, lurch a stripe, as were you soused methought out of the mackerel. Eldsfells! sayd he. A kumpavin on iceslant! Here's open handlegs for one old faulker from the hame folk here in you's booth! So sell me gundy, sagd the now waging cappon, with a warry posthumour's expletion, shoots ogos shootsle him or where's that slob? A bit bite of keesens, he sagd, til Dennis, for this jantar (and let the dobblins roast perus,) or a stinger, he sagd, t. d., on a doroughbread kennedy's for Patriki San Saki on svo fro or my old relogion's out of tiempor and when I'm soured to the tipple you can sink me lead, he sagd, and, if I get can, sagd he, a pusspull of tomtartarum. Thirst because homing hand give. Allkey dallkey, sayd the shop's housebound, for he was as deep as the north star (and could tolk sealer's solder into tankar's tolder) as might have sayd every man to his beast, and a treat for the trading scow, my cater million falls to you and crop feed a stall! Afram. And he got and gave the ekspedient for Hombreyhambrey wilcomer what's the good word. He made the sign on the feaster. Cloth be laid! And a disk of osturs for the swanker! Allahballah! He was the carelessest man I ever see but he sure had the most sand. One fishball with fixings! For a dan of a ven of a fin of a son of a gun of a gombolier. Ekspedient, sayd he, sonnur mine, Shackleton Sulten! Opvarts and at ham, or this ogry Osler will oxmaul us all, sayd he, like one familiar to the house, while Waldemar was heeling it and Maldemaer was toeing it, soe syg he was walking from the bowl at his food and the meer crank he was waiting for the tow of his turn. Till they plied him behaste on the fare. Say wehrn!

— Nohow did he kersse or hoot alike the suit and solder skins, minded first breachesmaker with considerable way on and

— Humpsea dumpsea, the munchantman, secondsnipped cutter the curter.

— A ninth for a ninth. Take my worth from it. And no mistaenk, they thricetold the taler and they knew the whyed for too. The because of his sosuch. Uglymand fit himshemp but throats fill us all! And three's here's for repeat of the unium! Place the scaurs wore on your groot big bailey bill, he apullajibed, the O'Colonel Power, latterly distented from the O'Conner Dan, so promonitory himself that he was obliffious of the headth of hosth that rosed before him, from Sheeroskouro, under its zembliance of mardal mansk, like a dun darting dullemitter, with his moultain haares stuck in plostures upon it, (do you kend yon peak with its coast so green?) still trystfully acape for her his gragh knew well in precious memory and that proud grace to her, in gait a movely water, of smile a coolsome cup, with that rarefied air of a Montmalency and her quick little breaths and her climbing colour. Take thee live will save thee wive? I'll think uplon, lilady. Should anerous enthroproise call homovirtue, duinnafear! The ghem's to the ghoom be she nere zo zma. Obsit nemon! Floodlift, her ancient of rights regaining, so yester yidd, even remembrance. And greater grown then in the trifle of her days, a mouse, a mere tittle, trots offwith the whole panoromacron picture. Her youngfree yoke stilling his wandercursus, jilt the spin of a curl and jolt the broadth of a buoy. The Annexandreian captive conquest. Ethna Prettyplume, Hooghly Spaight. Him her first lap, her his fast pal, for ditcher for plower, till deltas twoport. While this glowworld's lump is gloaming off and han in hende will grow. Through simpling years where the lowcasts have aten of amilikan honey and datish fruits and a bannock of barley on Tham the Thatcher's palm. O wanderness be wondernest and now! Listeneath to me, veils of Mina! He would withsay, nepertheloss, that is too me mean. I oldways did me walsh and preechup ere we set to sope and fash. Now eats the vintner over these contents oft with his sad slow munch for backonham. Yet never shet it the brood of aurowoch, not for legions of donours of Gamuels. I have performed the law in truth for the lord of the law, Taif Alif I have held out my hand for the holder of my heart in Annapolis, my youthrib city. Be ye then my protectors unto Mussabotomia before the guards of the city. Theirs theres is a gentlemeants agreement. Womensch plodge. To slope through heather till the foot. Join Andersoon and Co. If the flowers of speech valed the springs of me rising the hiker I hilltapped the murk I mist my blezzard way. Not a knocker on his head nor a nicknumber on the manyoumeant. With that coldtbrundt natteldster wefting stinks from Alpyssinia, wooving nihilnulls from Memoland and wolving the ulvertones of the voice. But his spectrem onlymergeant crested from the irised sea in plight, calvitousness, loss, nngnr, gliddinyss, unwill and snorth. It might have been what you call your change of my life but there's the chance of a night for my lifting. Hillyhollow, valleylow! With the sounds and the scents in the morning.

— I shot be shoddied, throttle me, fine me cowheel for ever, usquebauched the ersewild aleconner, for bringing briars to Bembracken and ringing rinbus round Demetrius for, as you wrinkle wryghtly, bully bluedomer, it's a suirsite's stircus haunting hesteries round old volcanoes. We gin too gnir and thus plinary indulgence makes collemullas of us all. But Time is for talerman tasting his tap. Tiptoptap, Mister Maut.

He made one summery (Cholk and murble in lonestime) of his the three swallows like he was muzzling Moselems and torched up as the faery pangeant fluwed down the hisophenguts, a slake for the quicklining, to the tickle of his tube and the twobble of his fable, O, fibbing once upon a spray what a queer and queasy spree it was. Plumped.

Which both did. Prompt. Eh, chrystal holder? Save Ampsterdampster that had rheumaniscences in his netherlumbs.

— By the drope in his groin, Ali Slupa, thinks the cappon, plumbing his liners, we were heretofore.

— And be the coop of his gobbos, Reacher the Thaurd, thinks your girth fatter, apopo of his buckseaseilers, but where's Horace's courtin troopsers?

— I put hem behind the oasthouse, sagd Pukkelsen, tuning wound on the teller, appeased to the cue, that double dyode dealered, and he's wallowing awash swill of the Tarra water. And it marinned down his gargantast trombsathletic like the marousers of the gulpstroom. The kersse of Wolafs on him, shitateyar, he sagd in the fornicular, and, at weare or not at weare, I'm sigen no stretcher, for I carsed his murhersson goat in trotthers with them newbucklenoosers behigh in the fire behame in the oasthouse. Hops! sagd he.

— Smoke and coke choke! lauffed till the tear trickled drown a thigh the loafers all but a sheep's whosepants that swished to the lord he hadn't and the starer his story was talled to who felt that, the fierifornax being thurst on him motophosically, as Omar sometime notes, such a satuation, debauchly to be watched for, would empty dempty him down to the ground.

— And hopy tope! sagd he, anded the enderer, now dyply hypnotised or hopeseys doper himself. And kersse him, sagd he, after inunder tarra-poulling, and the shines he cuts, shinar, the screeder, the stitchimesnider, adepted to nosestorsioms in his budinholder, cummanisht, sagd he, (fouyou-foukou!) which goes in the ways smooking publics, sagd he, bomboosting to be in thelitest civille row faction for a dubblebrasterd navvygaiterd, (flick off that hvide aske, big head!) sagd he, the big bag of my hamd till hem, tollerloon, sagd he, with his pudny bun brofkost when he walts meet the bangd. I will put his fleas of wood in the flour, and he sagd, behunt on the oatshus, the not wellmade one, sagd he, the kersse of my armsore appal this most unmentionablest of men (mundering eeriesk, if he didn't scalded him all the shimps names in his gitter!) a coathemmed gusset sewer, sagd he, his first cudgin is an innvalet in the unitred stables which is not feed tonights a kirtle offal fisk and he is that woe worstered wastended shootmaker whatever poked a noodle in a clouth!

So for the second tryon all the meeting of the acarras had it. How he hised his bungle oar his shourter and cut the pinter off his pourer and lay off for Fellagulphia in the farning. From his dhruimadhreamdhrue back to

Brighten-pon-the-Baltic, from our lund's rund turs bag til threathy hoeres a wuke. Ugh!

— Stuff, Taaffe, stuff! interjoked it his wife's hopesend to the boath of them consistently. Come back to May Aileen.

— Ild luck to it! blastfumed the nowraging scamptail, in flating furies outs trews his cammelskins, the flashlight of his ire wackering from the eyewinker on his masttop. And aye far he fared from Afferik Arena and yea near he night till Blawland Bearring, baken be the brazen sun, buttered be the snows. And the sea shoaled and the saw squalled. And, soaking scupper, didn't he drain

A pause.

Infernal machinery (serial number: Bullysacre, dig care a dig) having thus passed the buck to billy back from jack (finder the keeper) as the baffling yarn sailed in circles it was now high tide for the reminding pair of snipers to be suitably punished till they had, like the pervious oelkenner done, liquorally no more powers to their elbow. Ignorinsers' bliss, therefore, their not to say rifle butt target, none too wisefolly, poor fish, (he is eating, he is spun, is milked, he dives) upholding a lampthorne of lawstift as wand of welcome to all men in bonafay, (and the corollas he so has saved gainsts the virus he has thus injected!) discoastedself to that kipsie point of its Dublin bar there, breaking and entering, from the outback's dead heart, Glasthule Bourne or Boehernapark Nolagh, by wattsismade or bianconi, astraylians in island, a wellknown tall hat blown in between houses by a nightcap of that silk or it might be a black velvet and a kiber galler dragging his hunker, were signalling gael warnings towards Wazwollenzee Haven to give them their beerings, east circular route or elegant central highway. Open, 'tis luck will have it! Lifeboat Alloe, Noeman's Woe, Hircups Emptybolly! With winkles whelks and cocklesent jelks. Let be buttercup eve lit by night in the Phoenix! Music. And old lotts have funn at Flammagen's ball. Till Irinwakes from Slumber Deep. How they succeeded by courting daylight in saving darkness he who loves will see.

Business. His bestness. Copeman helpen.

Contrescene.

He cupped his years to catch me's to you in what's yours as minest to hissent, giel as gail, geil as gaul, Odorozone, now ourmenial servent, blanding rum, milk and toddy with I hand it to you. Saying whiches, see his bow on the hapence, with a pattedyr but digit here, he scooped the hens, hounds and horses biddy by bunny, with an arc of his covethand, saved from the drohnings they might oncounter, untill his cubid long, to hide in dry. Aside. Your sows tin the topple, dodgers, trink me dregs! Zoot!

And with the gust of a spring alice the fossickers and swaggelers with him on the hoof from down under piked forth desert roses in that mulligar scrub.

Reenter Ashe Junior. Peiwei toptip, nankeen pontdelounges. Gives fair day. Cheroot. Cheevio!

Off.

— Take off thatch whitehat (lo, Kersse come in back bespoking of loungeon off the Boildawl stuumplecheats for rushirishis Irush-Irish, dangieling his old Conan over his top gallant shouldier so was, lao yiu shao, he's like more look a novicer on the nevay).

— Tick off that whilehot, you scum of a botch, (of Kersse who, as he turned out, alas, hwen ching hwan chang, had been mocking his holla-balloon a sample of the costume of the country).

— Tape oaf that saw foull and sew wrong, welsher, you suck of a thick, stock and the udder, and confiteor yourself (for bekersse he had cuttered up and misfutthered in the most multiplest manner for that poor old bridge's masthard slouch a shook of cloakses the wise, hou he pouly hung hoang tseu, his own fitther couldn't nose him).

Chorus: With his coate so graye. And his pounds that he pawned from the burning.

— And, haikon or hurlin, who did you do at doyle today, my horsey dorksey gentryman. Serge Mee, suit! sazd he, tersey kersey. And when Tersse had sazd this Kersse stood them the whole koursse of training how the whole blazy raze acurraghed, from lambkinsback to sliving board and from spark to phoenish. And he tassed him tartly and he sassed him smartly, tig for tager, strop for stripe, as long as there's a lyasher on a kyat. And they peered him beheld on the pyre.

And it was so. Behold.

— Same capman no nothing horces two feller he feller go where. Isn't that effect? gig for gag, asked there three newcommers till knockingshop at the ones upon a topers who, while in admittance to that impedance, as three as they were there, they had been malttreating themselves to their health's contempt.

— That's fag for fig, metinkus, confessed, mhos for mhos, those who, would it not be for that dielectrick, were upon the point of obsoletion, and at the brink of from the pillary of the Nilsens and from the statutes of the Kongbullies and from the millestones of Ovlergroamlius libitate nos, Domnial!

— And so culp me goose, he sazd, szed the ham muncipated of the first course, recoursing, all cholers and coughs with his beauw on the bummell, the bugganeering wanderducken, he sazd, (that his pumps may ship awhoyle shandymound of the dussard), the coarsehair highsaydighsayman, there's nice tugs he looks, (how you was, Ship Alouset?) he sazd, the bloedaxe bloodooth baltxebec, that is crupping into our raw lenguage navel through the lumbsmall of his hawsehole, he sazd, donconfounder him, voyaging after maidens, belly jonah hunting the polly joans, and the hurss of all portnoysers befaddle him, he sazd, till I split in his flags, he sazd, one to one, the landslewder, after Donnerbruch fire. Reefer was a wenchman. One can smell off his wetsments how he is coming from a beach of promisck. Where is that old muttiny, shall I ask? Free kicks he will have from me, turncoats, in Bar Bartley if I wars a fewd years ago. Meistr Capteen Gaascooker, a salestrimmer! As he was soampling me ledder, like pulp, and as I was trailing his fumbelums, like hulp, he'll fell the fall of me faus, he sazd, like yulp! The goragorridgorballyed pushkalsson, he sazd, with his bellows pockets fulled of potchtatos and his fox in a stomach, a disagrees to his ramskew coddle-lecherskithers' zirkuvs, drop down dead and deaf, and there is never a teilwrmans in the feof fife of Iseland or in the wholeabelongd of Skunk-inabory from Drumadunderry till the rumnants of Mecckrass, could milk a colt in thrushes foran furrow follower width that a hole in his tale and that hell of a hull of a hill of a camelump bakk. Fadgestfudgist!

Upon this dry call of selenium cell (that horn of lunghalloon, Riland's in peril!) with its doomed crack of the old damn ukonnen power insound in it the lord of the saloom, as if for a flash salamagunnded himself, listed his tummelumpsk pack and hearinat presently returned him, ambilaterally alleyeoneyesed, from their uppletoned layir to his beforetime guests, that bunch of palers on their round, timemarching and petrolling how, who if they were abound to loose a laugh (Toni Lampi, you booraascal!) they were abooned to let it as the leashed they might do when they felt (O, the wolf he's on the walk, sees his sham cram bokk!) their joke was coming home to them, the steerage way for stabling, ghustorily spoeking, gen and gang, dane and dare, like the dud spuk of his first foetotype (Trolldedroll, how vary and likely!), the fillibustered, the fully bellied. With the old sit in his shoulders, and the new satin atlas onder his uxter, erning his breadth to the swelt of his proud and, picking up the emberose of the lizod lights, his tail toiled of spume and spawn, and the bulk of him, and hulk of him as whenever it was he reddled a ruad to riddle a rede from the sphinxish pairc while Ede was a guardin, ere love a side issue. They hailed him cheeringly, their encient, the murrainer, and wallruse, the merman, ye seal that lubs you lassers, Thallasee or Tullafilmagh, when come of uniform age.

— Heave, coves, emptybloddy!

And ere he could catch or hook or line to suit their saussyskins, the lumpenpack. Underbund was overraskelled. As

— Sot! sod the tailors opsits from their gabbalots, change all that whole set. Shut down and shet up. Our set, our set's allohn.

And they poured em behoiled on the fire. Scaald!

Rowdiose wodhalooing. Theirs is one lessonless missage for good and truesirs. Will any persen bereaved to be passent bringback or rumpart to the Hoved politymester. Clontarf, one love, one fear. Ellers for the greeter glossary of code, callen hom: Finucane-Lee, Finucane-Law.

Am. Dg.

Welter focussed.

Wind from the nordth. Warmer towards muffinbell, Lull.

As our revelant Colunnfiller predicted in last mount's chattiry sermon, the allexpected depression over Schiumdinebbia, a bygger muster of veirying precipitation and haralded by faugh sicknells, (hear kokkenhovens ekstras!) and umwalloped in an unusuable suite of clouds, having filthered through the middelhav of the same gorgers' kennel on its wage wealthwards and incursioned a sotten retch of low pleasure, missed in some parts but with lucal drizzles, the outlook for tomarry (Streamstress Mandig) beamed brider, his ability good.

What hopends to they?

Giant crash in Aden. Birdflights confirm abbroaching nubtials. Burial of Lifetenant-Groevener Hatchett, R.I.D. Devine's Previdence.

Ls. De.

Art thou gainous sense uncompetite! Limited. Anna Lynchya Pourable! One and eleven. United We Stand, even many offered. Don't forget. I wish auspicable thievesdayte for the stork dyrby. It will be a thousand's a won paddies. And soon to bet. On drums of bliss. With hapsalap troth, hipsalewd prudity, hopesalot honnessy, hoopsaloop luck. After when from midnights unwards the fourposter harp quartetto. (Kiskiviikko, Kalastus. Torstaj, tanssia. Perjantaj, peleja. Lavantaj ja Sunnuntaj, christianismus kirjallisuus, kirjallisuus christianismus.) Whilesd this pellover his finnisch.

— Comither, ahorace, thou mighty man of valour, elderman adaptive of Capel Ysnod, and tsay-fong tsei-foun a laun bricksnumber till I've fined you a faulter-in-law, to become your son-to-be, gentlemens tealer, generalman seelord, gosse and bosse, hunguest and horasa, jonjemsums both, in sails-manship, szed the head marines talebearer, then sayd the ships gospfather in the scat story to the husband's capture and either you does or he musts ant this moment same, sayd he, so let laid pacts be being betving ye, he sayd, by my main makeshift, he sayd, one fisk and one flesk, as flat as, Aestmand

Addmundson you, you're iron slides and so hompety domp as Paddley Mac Namara here he's a hardy canooter, for the two breasts of Banba are her soilers and her toilers, if thou wilt serve Idyall as thou hast sayld. Brothers Boathes, brothers Coathes, ye have swallen blooders' oathes. And Gophar sayd unto Glideon and sayd he to the nowedding captain, the rude hunnerable Humphrey, who was praying god of clothildies by the seven bosses of his trunktarge he would save bucklesome when she wooed belove on him, comeether, sayd he, my merrytime marelupe, you wutan whaal, sayd he, into the shipfolds of our quadrupede island, bless madhugh, mardyk, luusk and cong! Blass Neddos bray! And no more of your maimed acts after this with your kowtoros and criados to every tome, thick and heavy, and our onliness of his revelance to your ultitude. The illfollowable staying in wait for you with the winning word put into his mouth or be the hooley tabell, as Horrocks Toler hath most cares to call it, I'll rehearse your comeunder-mends and first mardhyr you entirely. As puck as that Paddeus picked the pun and left the lollies off the foiled. A Trinity judge will crux your boom. Pat is the man for thy. Ay ay! And he pured him beheild of the ouishguss, mingling a sign of the cruisk. I popetithes thee, Ocean, sayd he, Oscar-vaughther, sayd he, Erievikkingr, sayd he, *intra trifum triforium trifoliorum*, sayd he, onconditionally, forfor furst of gielgaulgalls and hero chief explunderer of the clansakiltic, sayd he, the streameress mastress to the sea aase cuddycoalman's and let this douche for you as a wholly apuzzler's and for all the pukkaleens to the wakes of you, sayd he, out of the hellsinky of the howtheners and be danned to ye, sayd he, into our roomyo connellic relation, sayd he, from which our this pledge is given, Tera truly ternatrine if not son towards thousand like expect chrisan athems to which I osker your godhsbattaring, saelir, for as you gott kvold whereafter a gooden diggin and with gooder enscure from osion buck fared agen fairioes feuded hailsohame til Edar in that the loyd mave hercy on your sael! Anomyn and awer. Spickinusand.

— Nansense, you snorsted? he was haltid considerable agenst all religions overtrow so hworefore the thokkurs pokker the bigbug mik-lamanded storstore exploder would he be whulesalesolde daadooped by Priest Gudfodren of the sacredhaunt suit in Diaeblen-Balkley at Domn-kirk Saint Petricksburg? But ear this:

— And here, aaherra, my rere admirable peadar poulsen, sayd he, consistently, to the secondnamed sutor, my lately lamented sponsorship, comesend round that wine and lift your horn, sayd he, to show you're a skolar for, winter you likes or not, we brought your summer with us and, tomkin about your lief eurekason and his undishcovery of americle, be the

rolling forties, he sayd, and on my sopper crappidamn, as Harris himself
says, to let you in on some crismion dottrin, here is the ninethest pork of a
man whisk swimmies in Dybblin water from Ballscodden easthmost till
Thyrston's Lickslip and, sayd he, (whiles the heart of Lukky Swayn slaughed
in his icebox for to think of all the soorts of smukklers he would behave in
juteyfrieze being forelooper to her) praties peel to our goodsend Brandonius,
filius of a Cara, spouse to Fynlogue, he has the nicesth pert of a nittlewoman
in the house, la chito, la chato, la Charmadouiro, Tina-bat-Talur, cif for
your fob and a tesura astore for you, eslucylamp aswhen the surge seas
sombren, that he daughts upon of anny livving plusquebelle, to child and
foster, that's the lippeyear's wonder of Totty go, Newschool, two titty too
at win winnie won, tramity trimming and funnity fare, with a grit as hard as
the trent of the thimes but a touch as saft as the dee in flooing and never a
Hyderow Jenny the like of her lightness at look and you leap, rhea-
doromanscing long evmans invairn, about little Anny Roners and all the
Lavinias of ester yours and pleding for them to herself in the periglus
glatsch hangs over her trickle bed, it's a piz of fortune if it never falls from
the stuffel, and, when that mallaura's over till next time and all the prim
rossies are out dressparading and the tubas tout tout for the glowru of their
god, making every Dinny dingle after her down the Dargul dale and (wait
awhile, blusterbuss, you're marchadant too forte and don't start furlan your
ladins till you' ve learned the lie of her landuage!), when it's summwer
calding and she can hear the pianutunar beyant the bayondes in Combria
sleepytalking to the Wiltsh muntons, titting out through her droemer
window for the flyend of a touchman over the wishtas of English Strand,
when Kilbarrack bell pings saksalaisance that Concessas with Sinbads may
(pong!), where our dollimonde sees the phantom shape of Mr Fortunatus
Wright since winksome Miss Bulkeley made loe to her wrecker and he took
her to be a rover, O, and playing house of ivary dower of gould and gift you
soil me peepat my prize, which its a blue loogoont for her in a bleakeyed
seusan if she can't work her mireiclles and give Norgeyborgey good airish
timers, while her fresh racy turf is kindly kindling up the lovver with the flu,
with a roaryboaryellas would set an Eiweddyng on fire, let aloon an old
Humpopolamos with the boomarpoorter on his brain, aiden bay scye and
dye, aasbukividdy, twentynine to her dozen and coocoo him didulceydovely
to his old cawcaws huggin and munin for his strict privatear which there's
no pure rube like an ool pool roober when your pullar beer turns out Bruin
O'Luinn and beat his barge into a battering pram with her wattling way for
cubblin and, be me fairy fay, sayd he, the marriage mixter, to Kersse, Son of
Joe Ashe, her coaxfonder, wiry eyes and winky hair, timkin abeat your

Andraws Meltons and his lovsang of the short and shifty, I will turn my thinks to things alove and I will speak but threes ones, sayd he, my truest patrions good founter, poles a port and zones asunder, tie up in hates and repeat at luxure, you can better your tooblue prodestind arson, tyler bach, after roundsabouts and donochs and the volumed smoke, though the clonk in his stumble strikes warn, and were he laid out on that counter there like a Slavocrates amongst his skippies, when it comes to the ride onerable, sayd he, that's to make plain Nanny Ni Sheeres a full Dinamarqueza, and all needed for the lay, from the hursey on the montey with the room in herberge down to forkpiece and bucklecatch, (Elding, my elding! and Lif, my lif!) in the pravacy of the pirmanocturne, hap, sayd he, at that meet hour of night, and hop, sayd he, ant the fyrsty annas everso thried (whiles the breath of Huppy Hullespond swumped in his seachest for to renumber all the mallymedears' long roll and call of sweetheart emmas that every had a port in from Coxenhagen till the brottels on the Nile), while taylight is yet slipping under their pillow, (ill omens on Kitty Cole if she's spilling laddy's measure!) and before Sing Mattins in the Fields, ringsengd ringsengd, bings Heri the Concorant Erho, and the Referinn Fuchs Gutmann gives us *I'll Bell the Welled* or *The Steeplepoy's Revanger* and all Thingavalley knows for its never dawn in the dark but the deed comes to life? and raptist bride is aptist breed (tha lassy! tha lassy!), and, to buoy the hoop within us springing, 'tis no timbertar she'll have then in her armsbrace to doll the dallydandle, our fiery quean, upon the night of the things of the night of the making to stand up the double tet of the oversear of the seize who cometh from the mighty deep and on the night of making Horuse to crihumph over his enemy, be the help of me cope as so pluse the riches of the roedshields, with Elizabeliza blessing the bedpain, at the willbedone of Yinko Jinko Randy, come Bastabasco and hippychip eggs, she will make a suomease pair and singlette, jodhpur smalls and tailorless, a copener's cribful, leaf, bud and berry, the divlin's own little mimmykin puss, (hip, hip, horatia!) for my old comrhade saltymar here, Briganteen—General Sir A. I. Magnus, the flappernooser, master of the good lifebark *Ulivengrene* of Onslought, and the homespund of her hearth, (Fuss his farther was the norse norse east and Muss his mother was a gluepot) and, gravydock or groovy anker, and a hulldread pursunk manowhood, who (with a chenchen for his delight time and a bonzeye nappin through his doze) he is the bettest bluffy blondblubber of an olewidgeon what overspat a skettle in a skib.

Cawcaught. Coocaged.

And Dub did glow that night. In Fingal of victories. Cannmatha and Cathlin sang together. And the three shouters of glory. Yelling halfviewed their harps. Surly Tuhal smiled upon drear Darthoola: and Roscranna's bolgaboyo begirlified the daughter of Cormac. The soul of everyelsesbody rolled into its olesoleself. A doublemonth's licence, lease on mirth, while hooneymoon and her flame went huneysuckling. Holyryssia, what boom of bells! What battle of bragues on Sandgate where met the bobby mobbed his bibby mabbing through the ryce. Even Tombs left doss and dunnage down in Demidoff's tomb and drew on the dournailed clogs that Morty Manning left him and legged in by Ghoststown Gate, like Pompei up to date, with a sprig of Whiteboys heather on his late Luke Elcock's heirloom. And some say they seen old dummydeaf with a leaf of bronze on his cloak so grey, trooping his colour a pace to the reire. And as owfally posh with his halfcrown jool as if he was the Granjook Meckl or Paster de Grace on the Route de l'Epée. It was joobileejeu that All Sorts' Jour. Freestouters and publicranks, hafts on glaives. You could hear them swearing threaties on the Cymylaya Mountains, man. And giving it out to the Ould Fathach and louthmouthing after the Healy Mealy with an enfysis to bring down the rain of Tarar. Nevertoletta! Evertomind! The grandest bethehailey seen or heard on earth's conspectrum since Scape the Goat, that gafr, ate the Suenders bible. Hadn't we heaven's lamps to hide us? Yet every lane had its lively spark and every spark had its several spurtles and each spitfire spurtle had some trick of her trade, a tease for Ned, nook's nestle for Fred and a peep at me mow for Peer Pol. So that Father Matt Hughes looked taytotally threbled. But Danno the Dane grimmed. Dune. 'Twere yeg will elsecare doatty lanv meet they dewscent hyemn to cannons' roar and rifles' peal vill shantey soloweys sang! For there were no more Tyrrhanees and for Laxembraghs was passthecupper to Our Lader's. And it was dim upon the floods only and there was day on all the ground.

Thus street spins legends while wharves woves tales but some family fewd felt a nick in their name. Old Vickers sate down on their airs and straightened the points of their lace. Red Rowleys popped out of their lairs and asked what was wrong with the race. Mick na Murrough used dripping in layers to shave all the furze off his face. The Burke-Lees and Coyle-Finns paid full feines for their sinns when the Cap and Miss Coolie were roped.

Rolloraped.

With her banbax hoist from holder, zig for zag through pool and polder, cheap, cheap, cheap and Laughing Jack, all augurs scorenning, see the Bolche your pictures motion and Kitzy Kleinsuessmein eloping for that holm in Finn's Hotel Fiord, Nova Norening. Where they pulled down the kuddle and they made fray and if thee don't look homey, well, that Dook can eye Mae.

He goat a berth. And she cot a manege. And wohl's gorse mundom ganna wedst.

Knock knock. War's where! Which war? The Twwinns. Knock knock. Woos without! Without what? An apple. Knock knock.

The kilder massed, one then and uhindred, (harefoot, birdyhands, herringabone, beesknees), and they barneydansked a kathareen round to know the who and to show the howsome. Why was you hiding, moder of moders? And where was hunty, poppa the gun? Pointing up to skyless heaven like the spoon out of sergeantmajor's tay. Which was the worst of them phaymix cupplerts? He's herd of hoarding and her faiths is altared. Becoming ungoing, their seeming sames for though that liamstone deaf do his part there's a windtreetop whipples the damp off the mourning. But tellusit allasif wellasits end. And the lunger it takes the swooner they tumble two. He knows he's just thrilling and she's sure she'd squeam. The threelegged man and the tulippied dewydress. Lludd hillmythey, we're brimming to hear! The durst he did and the first she ever? Peganeen Bushe, this isn't the polkar, catch as you cancan when high land fling! And you Tim Tommy Melooney, I'll tittle your barents if you stick that pigpin upinto meh!

So in the names of the balder and of the sol and of the hollichrost, ogsowearit, trisexnone, and by way of letting the aandt out of her grosskropper and leading the mokes home by their gribes, whoopsabout a plabbaside of plobbicides, alamam alemon, poison kerls, on this mounden of Delude, and in the high places of Delude of Isreal, which is Haraharem and the diublin's owld mounden over against Vikens, from your tarns, thwaites and thorpes, withes, tofts and fosses, fells, haughs and shaws, lunds, garths and dales, mensuring the megnominous as so will is the littleyest, the myrioheartzed with toroidal coil, eira area round wantanajocky, fin above wave after duckydowndivvy, trader arm aslung beauty belt, the formor velican and nana karlikeevna, sommerlad and cinderenda, Valtivar and Viv, how Big Bil Brine Borumoter first took his gage at lil lolly lavvander waader since when capriole legs covets limbs of a crane and was it the twylyd or the mounth of the yare or the feint of her smell made the seomen assalt of her (in imageascene all: whimwhim whimwhim). To the laetification of disgeneration by neuhumorisation of our kristianiasation. As the last liar in the earth begeylywayled the first lady of the forest. Though Toot's pardoosled sauve l'hummour! For the joy of the dew on the flower of the fleets on the fields of the foam of the waves of the seas of the wild main from Borneholm has jest come to crown.

Snip snap snoody. Noo err historyend goody. Of a lil trip trap and a big treeskooner for he put off the ketyl and they made three (for fie!) and if hec dont love alpy then lad you annoy me. For hanigen with hunigen still haunt ahunt to finnd their hinnigen where Pappappappparrassannuaraghe-allachnatullaghmonganmacmacmacwhackfalltherdebblenonthedubblan-daddydoodled and anruly person creeked a jest. Gestapose to parry off cheekars or frankfurters on the odor. Fine again, Cuoholson! Peace, O wiley!

Such was the act of goth stepping the tolk of Doolin, drain and plantage, wattle and daub, with you'll peel as I'll pale and we'll pull the boath toground togutter, testies touchwood and shenstone unto pop and puma, calf and condor, under all the gaauspices (incorporated), the chal and his chi, their roammerin over, gribgrobgrab reining trippetytrappety (so fore shalt thou flow, else thy cavern hair!) to whom she (anit likenand pleasethee!). Till sealump becamedump to bumpslump a lifflebed, (altolà, allamarsch! O gué, O gué!). Kaemper Daemper to Jetty de Waarft, all the weight of that mons on his little ribbeunuch! Him that gronde old mand to be that haard of heaering (afore said) and her the petty tondur with the fix in her changeable eye (which see), Lord, me lad, he goes with blowbierd, leedy, plasheous stream. But before that his loudship was converted to a landshop there was a little theogamyjig incidence that hoppy-go-jumpy Junuary morn when he colluded with the cad out on the beg amudst the fiounaregal gaames of those oathmassed fenians for whome he's forcecaused a bridge of the piers, at Inverleffy, mating pontine of their engagement, synnbildising graters and things, eke ysendt? O nilly, not all, here's the fust cataraction! As if ever she cared an assuan damm about her harpoons sticking all out of him whet between phoenix his calipers and that psourdonome sheath. Sdrats ye, Gus Paudheen! Kenny's thought ye, Dinny Oozle! While the cit was leaking asphalt like a suburbiaurealis in his rure was tucking to him like old booths, booths, booths, booths.

Enterruption. Check or slowback. Dvershen.

Why, wonder of wenchalows, what o szeszame open, v doer s t doing? V door s being. But how theng thingajarry miens but this being becoming n z doer? K? An o. It is ne not him what foots like a glove, shoehandschiner Pad Podomkin. Sooftly, anni slavey, szszuszchee is slowjaneska.

The aged crafty nummifeed confusionary overinsured everlapsing accentuated katekattershin clopped, clopped, clopped, darsey dobrey, back and along the danzing corridor, as she was going to pimpim him, way boy wally, not without her complement of cavarnan men, between the two deathdealing allied divisions and the lines of readypresent fire of the corkedagains upstored, taken in giving the saloot, band your hands going in, bind your heads coming out, and remoltked to herselp in her serf's alown, a weerpovy willowy dreevy drawly and the patter of so familiars, farabroads and behomeans, as she shure sknows, boof for a booby, boo: new uses in their mewseyfume. The jammesons is a cook in his hair. And the juinnesses is a rapin his hind. And the Bullingdong caught the wind up. Dip.

And the message she braught belaw from the missus she bragged abouve that had her agony stays outsize her sari chemise, blancking her shifts for to keep up the fascion since the king of all dronnings kissed her beeswixed hand, fang (pierce me, hunky, I'm full of meunders!), her fize like a tubtail of mondayne clothes, fed to the chaps with working medicals and her birthright pang that would split an atam like the forty pins in her hood, was to fader huncher a howdydowdy, to mountainy mots in her amnest plein language, from his fain a wan, his hot and tot lass, to pierce his ropeloop ear, how, Podushka be prayhasd, now the sowns of his loins were awinking and waking and his dorter of the hush lillabilla lullaby (lead us not into reformication with the poors in your thingdom of gory, O moan!), once after males, nonce at a time, with them Murphy's puffs she dursted with gnockmeggs and the bramborry cake for dour dorty dompling obayre Mattom Beetom and epsut the pfot and if he was whishtful to licture her caudal with chesty chach from his dauberg den and noviny news from Naul or toplots talks from morrienbaths or a parrotsprate's cure for ensevelised lethurgies, spick's my spoon and the veriblest spoon, 'twas her hour for the chamber's ensallycopodium with love to melost Panny Kostello from X.Y. Zid for to folly billybobbis gibits porzy punzy and she was a wanton for De Marera to take her genial glow to bed.

— This is time for my tubble, reflected Mr 'Gladstone Browne' in the toll hut (it was choractoristic from that 'man of Delgany'). Dip.

— This is me vulcanite smoking, profused Mr 'Bonaparte Nolan' under the natecup (one feels how one may hereby reekignites the 'ground old mahonagyan'). Dip.

— And this is defender of defeater of defaulter of deformer of the funst man in Danelagh, willingtoned in with this glance dowon his browen and that born appalled noodlum the panellite pair's cummal delimitator, odding: Oliver White, he's as tiff as she's tight. And thisens his speak quite hoarse. Dip.

In reverence to her midgetsy the lady of the comeallyous as madgestoo our own one's goff stature. Prosim, prosit, to the Krk n yr nck!

O rum it is the chomicalest thing how it pickles up the punchey and the jude. If you'll gimmy your thing to me I will gamey a sing to thee. Stay where you're dummy! To get her to go ther. He banged the scoop and she bagged the sugar while the whole pub's pobbel done a stare. On the mizzatint wall. With its chromo for all, crimm crimms. Showing holdmenag's asses sat by Allmeneck's men, canins to ride with em, canins that lept at em, woollied and flundered.

So the katey's came and the katey's game. As so gangs sludgenose. And that henchwench what hopped it dunneth there duft the. Duras.

(Silents)

Yes, we've conned thon print in its gloss so gay how it came from Finndlader's Yule to the day and it's Hey Tallaght Hoe on the king's highway with his hounds on the home at a turning. To Donnicoombe Fairing. Millikin's Pass. When visiting at Izd-la-Chapelle taste the lipe of the waters from Carlowman's Cup.

It tellyhows its story to their six of hearts, a twelve-eyed man; for whom has madjestky who since is dyed drown reign before the izba.

Au! Au! Aue! Ha! Heish!

As stage to set by ritual rote for the grimm grimm tale of the four of hyacinths, the deafeeled carp and the bugler's dozen of leagues-in-amour or how Holispolis went to Parkland with mabby and sammy and sonny and sissy and mop's varlet de shambles and all to find the right place for it by peep o'skirt or pipe a skirl when the hundt called a halt on the chivvychace of the ground sloper at that ligtning lovemaker's thender apeal till, between wandering weather and stable wind, vastelend hosteilend, neuziel and oltrigger some, Bullyclubber burgherly shut the rush in general.

Let us propel us for the frey of the fray! Us, us, beraddy!

Ko Niutirenis hauru leish! A lala! Ko Niutirenis haururu laleish! Ala lala! The Wullingthund sturm is breaking. The sound of maormaoring The Wellingthund sturm waxes fuercilier. The whackawhacks of the sturm. Katu te ihis ihis! Katu te wana wana! The strength of the rawshorn generand is known throughout the world. Let us say if we may what a weeny wukeleen can do.

Au! Au! Aue! Ha! Heish! A lala!

— Paud the roosky, weren't they all of them then each in his different way of saying calling on the one in the same time hibernian knights underthaner that was having, half for the laugh of the bliss it sint barbaras another doesend end once tale of a tublin wished on to him with its olives ocolombs and its hills owns ravings and Tutty his tour in his Nowhare's yarcht. It was before when Aimee stood for Arthurduke for the figger in profane and fell from grace so madlley for fill the flatter fellows. (They were saying). And it was the lang in the shirt in the green of the wood, where obelisk rises when odalisks fall, major threft on the make and jollyjacques spindthrift on the merry (O Mr Mathurin, they were calling, what a top-heavy hat you're in! And there aramny maeud, then they were saying, these so pioupious!). And it was cyclums cyclorums after he made design on the corse and he want to mess on him (enterellbo add all taller Danis), back, seater and sides, and he applied (I'm amazingly sorracer!) the wholed bould shoulderedboy's width for fullness, measures for messieurs, messer's massed, (they were saycalling again and agone and all over agun, the louthly meathers, the loudly meaders, the lously measlers, six to one, bar ones).

And they pled him beheighten the firing. Dope.

Maltomeetim, alltomatetam, when a tale tarries shome shunter shove on. Fore auld they wauld to pree.

Pray.

Of this Mr A (tillalaric) and these wasch woman (dapplehued), fhroneh-flord and feeofeeds, who had insue keen and able and a spindlesong aside, nothing more is told until now, his awebrume hour, her sere Sahara of sad oakleaves. And then. Be old. The next thing is. We are once amore as babes awondering in a wold made fresh where with the hen in the storyaboot we start from scratch.

So the truce, the old truce and nattonbuff the truce, boys. Drouth is stronger than faction. Slant. Shinshin. Shinshin.

— It was of The Grant, old gartener, *qua* golden meddlist, Publius Manlius, fuderal private, (his place is his poster, sure, they said, and we're going to mark it, sore, they said, with a carbon caustick manner) bequother the liberaloider at his petty corporelezzo that hung caughtnapping from his baited breath, it was of him, my wife and I thinks, to feel to every of the younging fruits, tenderosed like an atalantic's breastswells or, on a second wreathing, a bright tauth bight shimmeryshaking for the welt of his plow. And where the peckadillies at his wristsends meetings be loving so lightly dovessoild the candidacy, me wipin eye sinks, of his softboiled bosom should be apparient even to our illicterate of nullatinenties.

All to which not a lot snapped The Nolan of the Calabashes at his whilom eweheart photognomist who by this sum taken was as much incensed by Saint Bruno as that what he had consummed was his own panegoric, and wot a lout about it if it was only a pippappoff pigeon shoot that gracesold getrunner, the man of centuries, was bowled out by judge, jury and umpire at batman's biff like a witchbefooled legate. Dupe.

His almonence being alaterelly in dispensation with his three oldher patrons' aid, providencer's divine cow to milkfeeding mleckman, bonafacies to solafides, what matter what all his freudzay or who holds his hat to harm him, let hutch just keep on under at being a vanished consinent and let annapal livibel prettily prattle a lude all her own. And be that semeliminal salmon solemonly angled, ingate and outgate. A truce to lovecalls, dulled in warclothes, maleybags, things and bleakhusen. Leave the letter that never begins to go find the latter that ever comes to end, written in smoke and blurred by mist and signed of solitude, sealed at night.

Simply. As says the mug in the middle, nay brian nay noel, ney billy ney boney. Imagine twee cweamy wosen. Suppwose you get a beautiful thought and cull them sylvias sub silence. Then inmaggin a stotterer. Suppoutre him to been one biggermaster Omnibil. Then lustily (tutu the font and tritt on the bokswoods like gay feeters's dance) immengine up to three longly lurking lobstarts. Fair instents the Will Woolsley Wellaslayers. Pet her, pink him, play pranks with them. She will nod amproperly smile. He may seem to appraisiate it. They are as piractical jukersmen sure to paltipsypote. Feel the wollies drippeling out of your fingathumbs. Says to youssilves (floweers have ears, heahear!) solowly: So these ease Budlim! How do, dainty daulimbs? So peached to pick on you in this way, prue and simple, pritt and spry! Heyday too, Malster Faunagon, and hopes your hahititahiti licks the mankey nuts! And oodlum hoodlum doodlum to yes, Donn, Teague and Hurleg, who the bullocks brought you here and how the hillocks are ye?

We want Bud. We want Bud Budderly. We want Bud Budderly boddily. There he is in his Borrisalooner. The man that shunned the rucks on Gereland. The man thut won the bettlle of the bawll. Order, order, order, order! And tough. We call on Tancred Artaxerxes Flavin to compeer with Barnabas Ulick Dunne. Order, order, order! Milster Malster in the chair. We've heard it sinse sung thousandtimes. How Burghley shuck the rackushant Germanon. For Ehren, boys, gobrawl!

A public plouse. Citizen soldiers.

TAFF (*a smart boy, of the peat freers, thirty two eleven, looking through the roof towards a relevution of the karmalife order privious to his hoisting of an emergency umberolum in byway of paraguastical solation to the rhyttel in his hedd*). All was flashing and krashning blurty moriartsky blutcherudd? What see, buttywalch? Tell ever so often?

BUTT (*mottledged youth, clergical appealance, who, as his pied friar, is supposing to motto the sorry dejester in tifftaff toffiness or to be digarced from ever and a daye in his accounts*). But da. But dada, mwilshsuni. Till even so aften. Sea vaast a pool!

TAFF (*porumptly helping himself out by the cesspull with a yellup yurrup, puts up his furry furzed hare*). Butly bitly! Humme to our mounthings. Conscribe him tillusk, unt, in his jubalant tubalence, the groundsapper, with his soilday site out on his moulday side in. The gubernier-gerenal in laut-lievtonant of Baltiskeeamore, amaltheouse for leporty hole! Endues paramilintary langdwage. The saillils of the yellavs nocadont palignol urdlesh. Shelltoss and welltass and telltuss aghom! Sling Stranaslang, how Malorazzias spikes her, coining a speak a spake! Not the Setanik stuff that slimed soft Siranouche! The goot old gunshop monowards for manosymples. Tincurs tammit! They did oak hay doe fou Chang-il-meng when that man d'airain was big top tom saw tip side bum boss pageantfiller. Ajaculate! All lea light! Rassamble the glowrings of Bruyant the Bref when the Mollies Makehalpence took his leg for his thumb. And may he be too an intrepidation of our dreams which we foregot at wiking when the mom hath razed out limpalove and the bleakfrost chilled our ravery! Pook. Sing ching lew mang! Upgo, bobbycop! Lets hear in remember the braise of Hold!

BUTT (*drawling forth from his blousom whereis meditabound of his minker-stary, switches on his gorsecopper's fling weitoheito langthorn, fed up the grain oils of Aerin, while his laugh neighs banck as that flashermind's rays and his lipponease longuewedge wambles*). Ullahbluh! Sehyoh narar, pokehole sann! Manhead very dirty by am anoyato. Like old Dolldy Icon when he cooked up his iggs in bicon. He gatovit and me gotafit and Oalgoak's Cheloven gut a fudden. Povar old pitschobed! Molodeztious of metchennacht belaburt that pentschmyaso! Bog carsse and dam neat, sar, gam cant! Limbers affront of him, lumbers behund. While the bucks bite his dos his hart bides the ros till the bounds of his bays bell the warning. Sobaiter sobarkar. He was enmivallupped. Chromean fastion. With all his cannoball wappents. In his raglanrock and his malakoiffed bulbsbyg and his varnashed roscians and his cardigans blousejagged and his scarlett manchokuffs and his treecoloured camiflag and his perikopendolous gaelstorms. Here weeks hire pulchers! Obriania's beromst! From Karrs and Polikoff's, the men's confessioners. Seval shimars pleasant time payings. Mousoumeselles buckwoulds look. Tenter and likelings.

TAFF (*all Perssiasterssias shookatnaratatattar at his waggonhorchers, his bulgeglarying stargapers razzledazzlingly full of eyes, full of balls, full of holes, full of buttons, full of stains, full of medals, full of blickblackblobs*). Grozarktic! Toadlebens! Some garmentguy! Insects appalling, low hum clang sin! A cheap decoy! Too deep destroy! Say mangraphique, may say nay por daguerre!

BUTT (*if that he hids foregodden has nate of glozery farused ameet the florahs of the follest, his spent fish's livid smile giving allasundery the bumfit of the doped*). Come alleyou jupes of Wymmingtown that graze the calves of Man! A bear raigning in his heavenspawn consomation robes. Rent, outraged, yewleaved, grained, ballooned, hindergored and voluant! Erminia's capecloaked hoodoodman! First he s s st steppes. Then he st stoo stoopt. Lookt.

TAFF (*strick struck strangling like aleal lusky Lubliner to merumber by the cycl of the cruize who strungled Attahilloupa with what empoisoned El Monte de Zuma and failing wilnaynilnay that he was pallups barn in the minkst of the Krumlin befodt he was popsoused into the monkst of the vatercan, makes the holypolygon of the emt on the greaseshaper, a little farther, a little soon, a letteracettera, oukraydoubray*). Scutterer of guld, he is retourious on every roudery! The lyewdsky so so sewn of a fitchid! With his walshbrushup. And his boney bogey braggs?

BUTT (*after his tongues in his cheeks, with pinkpoker pointing out in rutene to impassible abjects beyond the mistomist towards Lissnaluby such as the Djublian Alps and the Hoofd Ribeiro as where he and his trulock may ever make a game*). The field of karhags and that bloasted tree. Forget not the felled! For the lomondations of Oghrem! Warful doon's bothem. Here furry glunn. Nye? Their feery pass. Tak! With guerillaman aspear aspoor to prink the pranks of primkissies. And the buddies behide in the byre. Allahblah!

TAFF (*a blackseer, he stroves to regulect all the straggles for wife in the rut of the past through the widnows in effigies keening after the blank sheets in their faminy to the relix of oll decency from over draught*). Oh day of rath! Ah, murther of mines! Eh, selo moy! Uh, zulu luy! Bernesson Mac Mahahon from Osro bearing nose easger for sweeth prolettas on his swooth prowl!

BUTT (*back to his peatrol and paump: swee Gee's wee rest: no more applehooley: dodewodedook*). Bruinoboroff, the hooneymoonger, and the grizzliest manmichal in Meideveide! Whose annal livves the hoiest! For he devoused the lelias on the fined and he conforted samp, tramp and marchint out of the drumbume of a narse. Guards, serf Finnland, serve we all!

TAFF (*whatwidth the psychophannies at the front and whetwadth the psuckofumbers beholden the fair, illcertain, between his bulchrichudes and the roshashanaral, where he sees Bishop Ribboncake plus his pollex prized going forth on his visitations of mirrage or Miss Horizon, justso all our fannacies daintied her, on the curve of the camber, unsheathing a showlaced limbaloft to the great consternations*). Divulge! Hyededye, kittyls, and howdeddoh, pan! Poshbott and pulbuties. See that we soll or let dargman be luna as strait a way as your ant's folly me line while ye post is goang from Piping Pubwirth to Haunted Hillborough on his Mujiksy's Zaravence, the Riss, the Ross, the sur of all Russers, as my farst is near to hear and my sackend is meet to sedon while my whole's a peer's aureolies. We should say you dones the polecad. Bang on the booche, gurg in the gorge, rap on the roof and your flup is unbu . . .

BUTT (*at the signal of his act which seems to sharpnel his innermals menody, playing the spool of the little brown jog round the wheel of her whang goes the millner*). Buckily buckily, blodestained boyne! Bimbambombumb. His snapper was shot in the Rumjar Journaral. Why the gigls he lubbed beeyed him.

TAFF (*obliges with a two stop yogacoga sumphoty on the bones or ivory girl and ebony boy*). The balacleivka! Trovatarovitch! I trumble!

BUTT (*with the sickle of a scygthe but the humour of a hummer, O, howorodies through his cholaroguled, fumfing to a fullfrength with this wallowing olfact*). Mortar martar tartar wartar! May his boules grow wider so his skittles gets worse! The aged monad making a venture out of the murder of investment. I seen him acting surgent what betwinks the scimitar star and the ashen moon. By their lights shalthow throw him! Piff paff for puffpuff and my pife for his cgar! The mlachy way for gambling.

[*Up to this curkscraw bind an admirable verbivocovisual presentment of the worldrenownced Caerholme Event has been being given by* The Irish Race and World. *The huddled and aliven stablecrashers have shared fleetfooted enthusiasm with the paddocks dare and ditches tare while the mews was combing ground. Hippohopparray helioscope flashed winsor places as the gates might see. Meusdeus! That was (with burning briar) Mr Twomass Nohoholan for their common contribe satisfunction in the purports of amusedment telling the Verily Roverend Father Epiphanes shrineshriver of Saint Dhorough's (in browne bomler) how (assuary as there's a bonum in your osstheology!) Backlegs shirked the racing kenneldar. The saintly scholarist's roastering guffalawd of nupersaturals holler at this metanoic excomologosis tells of the chestnut's (once again, Wittyngtom!) absolutionally romptyhompty successfulness. A lot of lasses and lads without damas or dads, but fresh and blued with collecting boxes. One aught spare ores triflets, to be shut: it is Coppingers for the children. Slippery Sam hard by them, physically present howsomedever morally absent, was slooching about in his knavish diamonds asking Gmax, Knox and the Dmuggies (a pinnance for your toughts, turffers!) to deck the ace of duds. Tomtinker Tim, howbeit, his unremitting retainer, (the seers are the seers of Samael but the heers are the heers of Timoth) is in Boozer's Gloom, soalken steady in his sulken tents. Baldawl the curse, baledale the day! And the frocks of shick sheeples in their shummering insamples! You see: a chiefsmith, semperal scandal stinkmakers, a middinest from the Casabianca and, of course, Mr Fry. Barass! Pardon the inquisition, causas es quostas? It is Da Valorem's Dominical Brayers. Why coif that weird hood? Because among nosoever circusdances is to be apprehended*

the dustungwashed poltronage of the lost Gabbarnaur-Jaggarnath. Pamjab!
Gross Jumpiter, whud was thud? Luckluckluckluckluckluckluck! It is the
Thousand to One Guinea-Gooseberry's Lipperfull Slipver Cup. Hold hard,
ridesiddle titelittle Pitsy Riley! Gurragrunch, gurragrunch! They are at the
turn of the fourth of the hurdles. By the hross of Xristos, Holophullopopulace is
a shote of excramation! Bumchub! Emancipator, the Creman hunter (Major
Hermyn C. Entwhistle) with dramatic effect reproducing the form of famous
sires on the scene of the formers triumphs, is showing the eagle's way to Mr
Whaytehayte's three buy geldings Homo Made Ink, Bailey Beacon and
Ratatuohy while Furstin II and The Other Girl (Mrs 'Boss' Waters,
Leavybrink) too early spring dabbles, are showing a clean pairofhids to
Immensipater. Sinkathinks to oppen here! To this virgin's tuft, on this golden
of evens! I never sought of sinkathink. Our lorkmakor he is proformly
annuysed He is shinkly thinkly shaking in his schayns. Sat will be off follteedee.
This eeridreme has being effered you by Bett and Tipp. Tipp and Bett, our
swapstick quackchancers, in From Topphole to Bottom of The Irish Race
and World.]

TAFF (*away that the first sports report of Loudin Reginald has now been*
afterthoughtfully colliberated by a saggind spurts flash, takes the dipperend direction
and, for tasing the tiomor of malaise after the pognency of orangultonia, orients by
way of Sagittarius towards Draco on the Lour). And you collier carsst on him,
the corsar, with Boyle, Burke and Campbell, I'll gogemble on strangbones
tomb. You had just been cerberating a camp camp camp to Saint Sepulchre's
march through the armeemonds retreat with the boys all marshalled,
scattering giant's hail over the curseway, fellowed along the rout by the
stenchions of the corpse. Tell the coldspell's terroth! If you please,
commeylad! Perfedes Albionias! Think some ingain think, as Teakortairer
sate over the Galwegian caftan forewhen Orops and Aasas were chooldrengs
and micramacrees! A forward movement, Miles na Bogaleen, and despatch!

BUTT (*slinking his coatsleeves surdout over his squad mutton shoulder so as to*
loop more life the jauntlyman as he scents thc anggreget yup behound their whole
scoopchina's desperate noy's totalage and explaining aposteriorly how awstooloo was
valdesombre belowes hero and he was in a greak esthate phophiar an erixtion on the
soseptuple side of him made spoil apriori his popoporportiums). Yass, zotnyzor, I
don't think I did not, pojr. Never you brother me for I scout it, think you!
Ichts nichts on nichts! Greates Schtschuptar! Me fol the rawlawdy in the
schpirrt of a schkrepz. Of all the quirasses and all the qwehrmin in the tra-
gedoes of those antiants their grandoper, that soun of a gunnong, with his
sabaothsopolettes, smooking his scandleloose at botthends of him! Foinn

duhans! I grandthinked after his obras after another time about the itch in
his egondoom he was legging boldylugged from some pulversporochs and
lyoking for a stooleazy for to nemesisplotsch allafranka and for to salubrate
himself with an ultradungs heavenly mass at his base by a suprime pompship
chorams the perished popes, the reverend and allaverred cromlecks, and
when I heard his lewdbrogue reciping his cheap cheateary gospeds to sintry
and santry and sentry and suntry I thought he was only haftara having
afterhis brokeforths but be the homely Churopodvas I no sooner seen
aghist of his frighteousness then I was bibbering with vear a few versets off
fooling for fjorg for my fifth foot. Of manifest 'tis obedience and the. Flute!

TAFF (*though the unglucksarsoon is giming for to git him, jotning in, hoghly
ligious, hapagodlap, like a soldierry sap, with a pique at his cue and a tyr in his eye
and a bond of his back and a croak in his cry as did jolly well harm lean o'er him*) Is
not athug who would. Weepon, weeponder, song of sorrowmon! Which
goatheye and sheepskeer they damnty well know. Papaist! Gambanman!
Take the cawraidd's blow! Yia! Your partridge's last!

BUTT (*giving his scimmianised twinge in acknuckledownedgment of this
cumulikick, strafe from the firetrench, studenly drobs led, satoniseels ouchyotchy, he
changecors induniforms as he is lefting the gat out of the big: his face glows green,
his hair greys white, his bleyes bcome broon to suite his cultic twalette*). But when I
seeing him in his oneship fetch along within hail that tourrible tall with his
nitshnykopfgoknob and attempting like a brandylogged rudeman cathargic,
lugging up and laiding down his livepelts so cruschinly like Mebbuck at
Messar and expousing his old skinful self tailtottom by manurevring in open
ordure to renewmurature with the cowruads in their airish pleasantry I
thanked he was recovering breadth from some herdsquatters beyond the
carcasses and I couldn't erver nerver to tell a liard story not of I knew the
prize if from lead or alimoney. But when I got inoccupation of a full new of
his old basemiddelism, in ackshan, pagne pogne, by the veereyed lights of
the stormtrooping clouds and in the sheenflare of the battleaxes of the
heroim and mid the shieldfails awail of the bitteraccents of the sorafim and
caught the pfierce tsmell of his aurals, orankastank, a suphead setrapped,
like Peder the Greste, altipaltar, my bill it forsooks allegiance (gut bull it!)
and, no lie is this, I was babbeing and yetaghain bubbering, bibbelboy, me
marrues me shkewers me gnaas me fiet, tob tob tob beat it, solongopatom.
Clummensy if ever misused, must used you's now! But, meac Coolp, Arram
of Eirzerum, as I love our Deer Dirouchy, I confesses withould pridejealice
when I looked upon the Saur of all the Haurousians with the weight of his
arge fullin upon him from the travaillings of his tommuck and rueckenased
the fates of a bosser there was fear on me the sons of Nuad for him and it

was heavy he was for me then the way I immingled my Irmenial hairmaierians ammon-gled his Gospolis fomiliours till, achaura moucreas, I adn't the arts to.

TAFF (*as a marrer off act, prepensing how such waldmanns from Burnias seduced country clowns, he is preposing barangaparang after going knowing what he is doing after to see him pluggy well moidered as a murder effect, you bet your blowie knife, before he doze soze, sopprused though he is*) Grot Zot! You hidn't the hurts? Vott Fonn!

BUTT (*hearing somrother sudly give tworthree peevish sniff snuff snoores like govalise falseleep he waitawhishts to see might he stirs and then goes on kuldrum like without asking for pepeace or anysing a soul*). Merzmard! I met with whom it was too late. My fate! O hate! Fairwail! Fearwealing of the groan! And think of that when you smugs to bagot.

TAFF (*who meanwhilome at yarn's length so as to put a nodje in the poestcher, by wile of stoccan his hand and of rooma makin ber getting umptyums gatherumed off the skattert, had been lavishing, lagan on lighthouse, words of silent power, susu glouglou biribiri gongos, upon the repleted speechsalver's innkeeping right which, thanks giveme and naperied norms nonobstaclant, there can be little doubt, have resulted in a momstchance ministring of another guidness, my good, to see*) Bompromifazzio! Shumpum for Pa-li-di and oukosouso for the nipper dandy! Trink off this scup and be bladdy orafferteed! To bug at?

BUTT (*he whipedoff's his chimbley phot, as lips lovecurling to the tongueopener, he takecups the communion of sense at the hands of the foregiver of trosstpassers and thereinofter centelinnates that potifex miximhost with haruspical hospedariaty proferring into his pauses somewhot salt bacon*). Theres scares knud in this gnarld warld a fully so svend as dilates for the improvement of our foerses of nature by your very ample solvent of referacting upon me like is boesen fiennd.

[*The other foregotthened abbosed in the Mullingaria are during this swishingsight teilweisioned. How the fictionable world in Fruzian Creamtartery is loading off heavy furses and affubling themselves with muckinstushes. The neatschknee Novgolosh. How the spinach ruddocks are being tatoovatted up for the second comings of antigreenst. Hebeneros for Aromal Peace. How Alibey Ibrahim wisheths Bella Suora to a holy cryptmahs while the Arumbian Knives Riders axecutes devilances round the jehumispheure. Learn the Nunsturk. How Old Yales boys is making rebolutions for the cunning New Yirls, never elding, still begidding, never to mate to lend, never to ate selleries and never to add soulleries and never to ant sulleries and never to aid silleries with sucharow with sotchyouroff as*]

*Burkeley's Show's a ructiongetherall. Phone for Phineal toomellow aftermorn
and your phumeral's a roselixion.*]

TAFF (*now as he has been past the buckthurnstock from Peadhar Piper of
Colliguchuna, whiles they all are healting pots to dubrin din for old daddam
dombstom to tomb and wamb humbs lumbs agamb, glimpse agam, glance agen, rise
up road and hive up hill, and find your pollyvoulley foncey pitchin ingles in the
parler*). Since you are on for versingrhetorish say your piece! How Buccleuch
shocked the rosing girnirilles. A ballet of Gasty Power. A hov and az ov and
off like a gow! And don't live out the sad of tearfs, piddyawhick! Not offgott
affsang is you, buthbach? Ath yetheredayth noth endeth, hay? Vaersegood!
Buckle to! Sayyessik, Ballygarry. The fourscore soculums are watchyou-
maycodding to cooll the skoopgoods blooff. Harkabuddy, feign! Thingman
placeyear howed wholst somwom shimwhir tinkledinkledelled. Shinfine
deed in the myrtle of the bog tway fainmain stod op to slog, free bond men
lay lurkin on. Tuan about whattinghim! Fore sneezturmdrappen! 'Twill be
a rpnice pschange, arrah, sir? Can you come it, budd?

BUTT (*who in the cushlows of his goodsforseeking hoarth, ever fondlinger of his
pimple spurk, is a niallist of the ninth homestages, the babybell in his baggutstract
upper going off allatwanst, begad, lest he should challenge himself, beygoad, till
angush*). Horrasure, toff! As said as would. It was Colporal Phailinx first.
Hittit was of another time, a white horsday where the midril met the bulg,
sbogom, roughnow along about the first equinarx in the cholonder, on the
plain of Khorason as thou goest from the mount of Bekel, Steep Nemorn,
elve hundred and therety and to years how the krow flees end in deed, after
a power of skimiskes, blodidens and godinats of them, when we sight the
beasts, (hegheg whatlk of wraimy wetter!), moist moonful date man aver
held dimsdzey death with, and higheye was in the Reilly Oirish Krzerszonese
Milesia asundurst Sirdarthar Woolwichleagues, good tomkeys years some-
while in Crimealian wall samewhere in Ayerland, during me weeping still-
stumms over the freshprosts of Eastchept and the dangling garters of
Marrowbone and daring my wapping stiltstunts on Bostion Moss, old stile
and new style and heave a lep onwards. And winn again, blaguadargoos, or
lues the day, plays goat, the banshee pealer, if moskats knows whoss whizz,
the great day and the druidful day come San Patrisky and the grand day, the
excellent fine splendorous long agreeable toastworthy cylindrical day, go
Sixt of the Ninth, the heptahundread annam dammias that Hajizfijjiz ells
me is and will and was be till the timelag is in it that's told in the Bok of
Alam to columnkill all the prefacies of Erin gone brugk. But Icantenue. And
incommixtion. We was lowsome like till we'd took out after the dead beats.

So I begin to study and I soon show them day's reasons how to give the cold shake to they blighty perishers and lay one over the beats. All feller he look he call all feller come longa villa finish. Toumbalo, how was I acclapadad! From them banjopeddlars on the raid. Gidding up me anti vanillas and getting off the stissas me aunties. Boxerising and coxerusing. And swiping a johnny dann sweept for to exercitise myself neverwithstanding the topkats and his roaming cartridges, orussheying and patronning, out all over Crummwiliam wall. Be the why it was me who haw haw.

TAFF (*all for letting his tinder and lighting be put to beheiss in the feuer and, while durblinly obasiant to the felicias of the skivis, Still smolking his fulvurite turfkish in the rooking pressance of laddios*). Yaa hoo how how, col? Whom battles joined no bottles sever! Worn't you aid a comp?

BUTT (*in his difficoltous tresdobremient, he feels a bitvalike a baddlefall of staot but falls a batforlake a borrlefull of bare*). And me awlphul omegrims! Between me rassociations in the postleadeny past and me disconnections with aplompervious futules I've a boodle full of maimeries in me buzzim and medears runs sloze, bleime, as I now with platoonic leave recoil in (how the thickens they come back to one to rust!) me misenary post for all them old boyars that's now boomaringing in waulholler, me alma marthyrs. I dring to them, bycorn spirits fuselaiding, and you cullies adjutant, even where its contentsed wody, with absents wehrmuth. Junglemen in agleement, I give thee our greatly swooren, Theoccupant that Rueandredful, the thrown-fullvner and all our royal devouts with the arrest of the whole inhibitance of Neuilands! One brief mouth. And a velligoolapnow! Meould attashees the currgans, (if they could get a kick at this time for all that's hapenced to us!) Cedric said Gormleyson and Danno O'Dunnochoo and Conno O'Cannochar it is this were their names for we were all under that manner barracksers on Kong Gores Wood together, thurkmen three, with those khakireinettes, our miladies in their toileries, the twum plumyumnietcies, Vjeras Vjenaskayas, of old Djadja Uncken who was a great mark for jinking and junking, up the palposes of womth and wamth, we war, and the charme of their lyse brocade. For lispias harth a burm in eye but whem it bames fire norone screeneth. Hulp, hulp, huzzars! Raise ras tryracy! Freetime's free! Up Lancesters! Anathem!

TAFF (*who still senses that heavinscent houroines that entertrained him who they were sinuorivals from the sunny Espionia but plied wopsy with his wallets in thatthack of the bustle Bakerloo, (II.32), passing the uninational truthbosh in smoothing irony over the multinotcheralled infructuosities of his grinner set*). The rib, the rib, the quean of oldbyrdes, Sinya Sonyavitches! Your Rhoda Cockardes that are raday to embrace our ruddy inflamtry world! In their ohosililesvienne biribarbebeway. Till they've kinks in their tringers and boils on their taws. Whor dor the pene lie, Mer Pencho? Ist dramhead countmortial or gonorrhal stab? Mind your pughs and keaoghs, if you piggots, marsh! Do the nut, dingbut! Be a dag! For zahur and zimmerminnes! Sing in the chorias to the ethur:

[*In the heliotropical noughttime following a fade of transformed Tuff and, pending its viseversion, a metenergic reglow of beaming Batt, the bairdboard bombardment screen, if tastefully taut guranium satin, tends to teleframe and step up to the charge of a light barricade. Down the photoslope in syncopanc pulses, with the bitts bugtwug their teffs, the missledhropes, glitteraglatteraglutt, borne by their carnier walve. Spraygun rakes and splits them from a double focus: grenadite, damnymite, alextronite, nichilite: and the scanning firespot of the sgunners traverses the rutilanced illustred sunksundered lines. Shlossh! A gaspel truce leaks out over the caeseine coatings. Amid a fluorescence of spectracular mephiticism there caoculates through the inconoscope stealdily a still, the figure of a fellowchap in the wohly ghast, Popey O'Donoshough, the jesuneral of the russuates. The idolon exhibisces the seals of his orders: the starre of the Son of Heaven, the girtel of Izodella the Calottica, the cross of Michelides Apaleogos, the latchet of Jan of Nepomuk, the puffpuff and pompom of Powther and Pall, the great belt, band and bucklings of the Martyrology of Gorman. It is for the castomercies mudwake surveice. The victar. Pleace to notnoys speach above your dreadths, please to doughboys. Hll, smthngs gnwrng wthth sprsnwtch! He blanks his oggles because he confesses to all his tellavicious nieces. He blocks his nosoes because that he confesses to everywheres he was always putting up his latest faengers. He wollops his mouther with a sword of tusk in as because that he confesses how opten he used be obening her howonton he used be undering her. He boundles alltogotter his manucupes with his pedarrests in asmuch as because that he confesses before all his handcomplishies and behind all his comfoderacies. And (hereis cant came back saying he codant steal no lunger, yessis, catz come buck beques he caudant stail awake) he touched upon this tree of livings in the middenst of the garerden for inasmuch as because that he confessed to it on Hillel and down Dalem and in the places which the lepers inhabit in the place of the stones and in pontofert jusfuggading amoret now he come to think of it jolly well ruttengenerously olyovyover the ole blucky shop. Pugger old Pumpey O'Dungaschiff! There will be a hen collection of him after avensung on the feld of Hanar. Dumble down, looties and gengstermen! Dtin, dtin, dtin, dtin!*]

BUTT (*with a gisture expansive of Mr Lhugewhite Cadderpollard with sunflawered beautonhole pulled up point blanck by mailbag mundaynism at Oldbally Court though the hissindensity buck far of his melovelance tells how when he was fast marking his first lord for cremation the whyfe of his bothem was the very lad's thing to elter his mehind*). Prostatates, pujealousties! Dovolnoisers, prayshyous! Defense in every circumstancias of deboutcheries no the chaste daffs I Pack pickets, pioghs and kughs to be palseyputred! Be at the peme, prease, of not forgetting or mere betoken yourself to hother prace! Correct me, pleatze commando, for cossakes but I abjure of it. No more basquibezigues for this pole aprican! With askormiles' eskermillas. I had my billyfell of duckish delights the whole pukny time on rawmeots and juliannes with their lambstoels in my kiddeneys and my ramsbutter in their sassenacher ribs, knee her, do her and trey her, when th'osirian cumb dumb like the whalf on the fiord and we preying players and pinching peacesmokes, troupkers tomiatskyns all, for Father Petrie Spence of Parishmoslattary to go and leave us and the crimsend daun to shellalite on the darkumen (scene as signed, Slobabogue), feeding and sleeping on the huguenottes (the snuggest spalniel's where the lieon's tame!) and raiding revolations over the allbegeneses (sand us and saint us and sound as agun!). Yet still in all, spit for spat, like we chantied on Sunda schoon, every warson wearrier kaddies a komnate in his schnapsack and unlist I am getting foegutfulls of the rugiments of savaliged wildfire I was gamefellow willmate and send us victorias with nowells and brownings, dumm, sneak and curry, and all the fun I had in that fanagan's week. A strange man wearing abarrel. And here's a gift of meggs and teggs. And as I live by chipping nortons. And 'tis iron fits the farmer, ay. Arcdesedo! Renborumba! Then were the hellscyown days for our fellows, the loyal leibsters, and we was the redugout rawrecruitioners, praddies three and prettish too, a wheeze we has in our waynward islands, wee engrish, one long blue streak, jisty and pithy af durck rosolun, with hand to hand as Homard Kayenne was always jiggilyjugging about in his wendowed courage when our woos with the wenches went wined for a song, tsingirillies' zyngarettes, while Woodbine Willie, so popiular with the poppyrossies, our Chorney Choplain, blued the air. Sczlanthas! Banzaine! Bissbasses! S. Pivorandbowl. And we all tuned in to hear the topmast noviality. Up the revels drown the rinks and almistips allround! Paddy Bonhamme he vives! Encore! And tig for tag Togatogtug. My droomodose days Y loved you abover all the strest. Blowhole brasshat and boy with his boots off and the butch of our bunch and all. It was buckoo bonzer, beleeme. I was a bare prive without my doglegs but I did not give to one humpenny dump, wingh or wangh, touching those thusengaged slavey generales of Tanah Kornalls, the meelisha's deelishas, pronouncing their very flank movemens in sunpictorsbosk. Baghus the whatwar! I could always take good cover of myself and, eyedulls or earwakers, preyers for rain or cominations, I did not care three tanker's hoots, ('sham! hem! or chaffit!) for any feelings from my lifeprivates on their reptrograd leanins because I have Their Honours booth my respectables sœurs assistershood off Lyndhurst Terrace, the puttih Misses Celana Dalems, and she in vinting her angurr can belle the troth on her alliance and I know His Heriness, my respeaktoble medams culonelle on Mellay Street, Lightnints Gundhur Sawabs, and they would never as the aimees of servation let me down. Not on your bludger life, touters! No peeping, pimpadoors! And, by Jova I never went wrong nor let him doom till, risky wark rasky wolk, at the head of the wake, up come stumblebum (ye olde cottemptable!), his urssian gemenal, in his scutt's rudes unreformed and he went before him in that nemcon enchelonce with the same old domstoole story and his upleave the fallener as is greatly to be petted (whitesides do his beard!) and I seen his brichashert offensive and his boortholomas vadnhammaggs vise a vise them scharlot runners and how they gave love to him and how he took the ward from us (odious the fly fly flurtation of his him and hers! Just mairmaid maddeling it was it he was!) and, my oreland for a rolvever, sord, by the splunthers of colt and bung goes the enemay the Percy rally got me, messgèr, (as true as theirs an Almagnian Gothabobus!) to blow the grand off his aceupper. Thistake it's meest! And after meath the dulwich. We insurrectioned and, be the procuratress of the hory synnotts, before he could tell pullyirragun to parrylewis, I shuttm, missus, like a wide sleever! Hump to dump! Tumbleheaver!

TAFF (*camelsensing that sonce they have given bron a nuhlan the volkar boastsung is heading to sea vermelhion but too wellbred not the ignore the umzemlianess of this rifal's preceedings, in an effort towards autosotorisation, effaces himself in favour of the idiology alwise behounding his lumpy hump off homosodalism which means that if he has lain amain to lolly his liking-cabronne!— he may pops lilly a young one to his herth—combrune—*) Oholy rasher, I'm believer! And Oho bullyclaver of ye, bragadore-gunneral! The grand ohold spider! It is a name to call to him Umsturdum Vonn! Ah, you were shutter reshottus and sieger besieged. Aha race of fiercemarchands counterination oho of shorpshoopers.

BUTT (*miraculising into the Dann Deafir warcry, his bigotes bristling, as, jittinju triggity shittery pet, he shouts his thump and feeh fauh foul finngures up the heighohs of their ahs!*) Bluddymuddymuzzle! The buckbeshottered! He'll umbozzle no more graves nor home no haunder, lou garou, for gayl geselles in dead men's hills! Kaptan (backsights to his bared!), His Cumbulent

Embulence, the frustate fourstar Russkakruscam, Dom Allah O'khorwan, connundurumchuff.

TAFF (*who, asbestas can, wiz the healps of gosh and his bluzzid maikar, has been sulphuring to himsalves all the pungataries of sin praktice in failing to furrow theogonies of the dommed*). Trisseme, the mangoat! And the name of the Most Marsiful, the Aweghost, the Gragious one! In sobber sooth and in souber civiles? And to the dirtiment of the curtailment of his all of man? Notshoh?

BUTT (*maomant scoffin, but apoxyomenously deturbaned but thems bleachin banes will be after making a bashman's haloday out of the euphorious hagio-hygiecynicism of his die and be diademmed*). Yastsar! In sabre tooth and sobre saviles! Senonnevero! That he leaves nyet is my grafe. He deared me to it and he dared me do it, and bedattle I didaredonit as Cocksnark of Killtork can tell and Ussur Ursussen of the viktaurious onrush with all the rattles in his arctic! As bold and as madhouse a bull in a meadows. Knout Knittrick Kinkypeard! Olefoh, the sourd of foemoe times! Unknun! For when meseemim, and tolfoklokken rolland allover ourloud's lande, beheaving up that sob of tunf for to claimhis, for to wollpimsolff, puddywhuck. Ay, and untuoning his culothone in an exitous erseroyal *Deo Jupto*. At that instullt to Igorladns! Prronto! I gave one dobblenotch and I ups with my crozzier. Mirrdo! With my how on armer and hits leg an arrow cockshock rockrogn. Sparro!

[*The abnihilisation of the etym by the grisning of the grosning of the grinder of the grunder of the first lord of hurtreford expolodotonates through Parsuralia with an ivanmorinthorrorumble fragoromboassity amidwhiches general uttermosts confussion are perceivable moletons skaping with muliculës which coventry plumpkins fairlygosmotherthemselves in the Landaunelegants of Pinkadindy. Similar scenatas are projectilised from Hullulullu, Bawlawayo, empyreal Raum and mordern Atems. They were precisely the twelves of clocks, noon minutes, none seconds. At someseat of Oldanelang's Konguerrig, by dawnybreak in Aira.*]

TAFF (*skimperskamper, his wools gatherings all over cromlin what with the birstol boys artheynes and is it her tour and the crackery of the fullfour fivefirearms and the crockery of their damdam domdom chumbers*). Wharall thubulbs uptheaires! Shattamovick?

BUTT (*pulling alast stark daniel with alest doog at doorak while too greater than pardon painfully the issue of his mouth diminuendoing, vility of vilities, he becomes, allasvitally, faint*). Shurenoff! Like Faun MacGhoul!

BUTT and TAFF (*desprot slave wager and foeman feodal unsheckled, now one*

*and the same person, their fight upheld to right for a wee while being baffled
and tottered, umbraged by the shadow of Old Erssia's magisquammythical
mulattomilitiaman, the living by owning over the surfers of the glebe whose sway
craven minnions had caused to revile, as, too foul for hell, under boiling Mauses'
burning brand, he falls by Goll's gillie, but keenheartened by the circuminsistence of
the Parkes O'Rarelys in a hurdly gurdly Cicilian concertone of their fonngeena
barney brawl, shaken everybothy's hands, while S. E. Morehampton makes leave
to E. N. Sheilmartin after Meetinghouse Lanigan has embaraced Vergemout
Hall, and, without falter or mormor or blathrehoot of sophsterliness, pugnate thc
pledge of fiannaship, dook to dook, with a commonturn oudchd of fest man and
best man astoutsalliesemoutioun palms it off like commodity tokens against a
cococancancacacanotioun).* When old the wormd was a gadden and Anthea
first unfoiled her limbs wanderloot was the way the wood wagged where
opter and apter were samuraised twimbs. They had their mutthering ivies
and their murdhering idies and their mouldhering iries in that muskat
grove but there'll be bright plinnyflowers in Calomella's cool bowers when
the magpyre's babble towers scorching and screeching from the ravenin-
dove. If thees lobed the sex of his head and mees ates the seep of his
traublers he's dancing figgies to the spittle side and shoving outs the soord.
And he'll be buying buys and go gulling gells with his flossim and jessim of
carm, silk and honey while myandthys playing lancifer lucifug and what's
duff as a bettle for usses makes coy cosyn corollanes' moues weeter to wee.
So till butagain budly shoots thon rising germinal let bodley chow the fatt
of his anger and badley bide the toil of his tubb.

*[The pump and pipe pingers are ideally reconstituted. The putther and
bowls are peterpacked up. All the presents are deter-mining as regards for the
future the howabouts of their past absences which they might see on at hearing
could they once smell of tastes from touch. To ought find a values for. The
must over-listingness. When ex what is ungiven. As ad where. Stillhead.
Blunk.]*

Shutmup. And bud did down well right. And if he sung dumb in his glass
darkly speech lit face to face on allaround.

Vociferagitant. Viceversounding. Namely, Abdul Abulbul Amir or Ivan
Slavansky Slavar. In alldconfusalem. As to whom the major guiltfeather
pertained it was Hercushiccups' care to educe. Beauty's bath she's bound to
bind beholders and pride, his purge, has place appoint in penance and the
law's own libel lifts and lames the low with the lofty. Be of the housed!
While the Hersy Hunt they harrow the hill for to rout them rollicking

rogues from, rule those racketeer romps from, rein their rockery rides from. Rambling.

Nightclothesed, arooned, the conquerods sway. After their battle thy fair bosom.

— That is too tootrue enough in Solidan's Island as in Moltern Giaourmany and from the Amelakins off to date back to land of engined Egyptsians, assented from his opening before his inlookers of where an oxmanstongue stalled stabled the wellnourished one, lord of the seven days, overlord of sats and suns, the sat of all the suns which are in the ring of his system of the sats of his sun, god of the scuffeldfallen skillfilledfelon, who (he containms) hangsters, who (he constrains) hersirrs, a gain changful, a mintage vaster, heavy on shirts, lucky with shifts, the topside humpup stummock atween his showdows fellah, Misto Tee wiley Spillitshops, who keepeth watch in Khummer-Phett, whose spouse is An-Lyph, the dog's bladder, warmer of his couch in fore. We all, for whole men is lepers, have been nobbut wonterers in that chill childerness which is our true name after the allfaulters (mug's luck to em!) and, bespeaking of love and lie detectors in venuvarities, whateither the drugs truth of it, was there an iota of from the faust to the lost. And that is at most redoubtedly an overthrew of each and ilkermann of us, I persuade myself, before Gow, gentlemen, so true as this are my kopfinpot astrode on these is my boardsoldereds.

It sollecited, grobbling hummley, his roundhouse of seven orofaces, of all, guiltshouters or crimemummers, to be sayd by, codnops, advices for, free of gracies, scamps enclosed, competitioning them, if they had steadied Jura or when they had raced Messafissi, husband of your wifebetter or bestman botchalover of you yourself, how comes ever a body in our taylorised world to selve out thishis, whither it gives a primeum nobilees for our notomise or naught, the farst wriggle from the ubivence, whereom is man, that old offender, nother man, wheile he is asame. And fullexampling. The pints in question. With some byspills. And sicsecs to provim hurtig. Soup's on!

— A time. And a find time. Whenin aye was a kiddling. And the tarikies held sowansopper. Let there beam a frishfrey. And they sodhe gudhe rudhe brodhe wedhe swedhe medhe in the kanddledrum. I have just (let us suppraise) been reading in a (suppressed) book—it is notwithstempting by meassures long and limited—the latterpress is eminently legligible and the paper, so he eagerly seized upon, has scarsely been buttered in works of previous publicity wholebeit in keener notcase would I turf aside for pastureuration. Packen paper paineth whomto is sacred scriptured sign. Who straps it scraps it that might, if ashed, have healped. Enough, however,

have I read of it, like my good bedst friend, to augur in the hurry of the
times that it will cocommend the widest circulation and a reputation
coextensive with its merits when inthrusted into safe and pious hands upon
so edifying a mission as it, I can see, as is his. It his ambullished with
expurgative plates, replete in information and accampaigning the action
passiom, slopbang, whizzcrash, boomarattling from burst to past, as I have
just been seeing, with my warmest venerections, of a timmersome townside
upthecountrylifer, (Guard place the town!) allthose everwhalmed upon that
preposterous blank seat, before the wordcraft of this early woodcutter, a
master of vignettiennes and our findest grobsmid among all their orefices,
(and, shukar in chowdar, so splunderdly English!) Mr Aubeyron Birdslay.
Chubgoodchob, arsoncheep and wellwillworth a triat! Bismillafoulties. But
the hasard you asks is justly ever behind his meddle throw! Those sad pour
sad forengistanters, dastychappy dustyrust! Chaichairs. It is that something,
awe, aurorbean in that fellow, hamid and damid, (did he have but Hugh de
Brassey's beardslie his wear mine of ancient guised) which comequeers this
anywhat perssian which we, owe, realisinus with purups a dard of pene.
There is among others pleasons whom I love and which are favourests to
mind, one which I have pushed my finker in for the movement and, but for
my sealring is none to hand I swear, she is highly catatheristic and there is
another which I have fombly fongered freequuntly and, when my signet is
on sign again I swear, she is deeply sangnificant. *Culpo de Dido!* Ars we say in
the classies. *Kunstful*, we others said. What ravening shadow! What dovely
line! Not the king of this age could richlier eyefeast in oreillental longuard-
ness with alternate nightjoys of a thousand kinds but one kind. A shahrryar
cobbler on me when I am lying! And whilst (when I doot my sliding panel
and I hear cawcaw) I have been idylly turmbing over the loose looves
leaflefts jaggled casuallty on the lamatory, as is my this is, as I must commit
my lips to make misface for misfortune, often, so far as I can chance to
recollect from the some farnights ago, (so dimsweet is that selvischdisch-
dienence of to not to be able to be obliged to have to hold further anything
than a stone his throw's fruit's fall!) when I, if you wil excuse for me this
informal leading down of illexpressibles, enlivened toward the Author of
Nature by the natural sins liggen gobelimned theirs before me, (how
differended with the manmade Eonochs Cunstuntonopolies!), weathered
they be of a general golf stature, assasserted, or blossomly emblushing
thems elves underneed of some howthern folleys, am entrenched up
contemplating of myself, wiz my naked I, for relieving purposes in our
trurally virvir vergitabale (garden) I sometimes, maybe, what has justly said
of old Flannagan, a wake from this or huntsfurwards, with some shock (shell

I so render it?) have (when I ope my shylight window and I see coocoo) a notion quiet involuptary of that I am cadging hapsnots as at mur-murrandoms of distend renations from ficsimilar phases or dugouts in the behindscenes of our earthwork (what rovining shudder! what deadly loom!) as this is, at no spatial time processly which regards to concrude chronology about which in fact, at spite of I having belittled myself to my gay giftname of insectarian, happy burgages abeyance would make homesweetstown hopeygoalucrey, my mottu propprior, as I claim, cad's truck, I coined, I am highly pelaged and deeply gluttened to mind hindmost hearts to see by their loudest reports from my threespawn bottery parts (shsh!) that, colombophile and corvinophobe alike, when I have remassed me, my travellingself, as from Magellanic clouds, after my contractual expenditures, through the perofficies of merelimb, I, my good grief, I am, I am big altoogooder.

He beached the bark of his tale; and set to husband and vine: and the harpermaster told all the living conservancy, know Meschiameschianah, how that win a gain was in again. Flying the Perseoroyal. Withal aboarder, padar and madar, hal qnd sal, the sens of Ere with the duchtars of Iran. Amick amack amock in a mucktub. Qith the tou loulous and the gryffygryffygryffs, at Fenegans Wick, the Wildemanns. Washed up whight and deliveried rhight. Loud lauds to his luckhump and bejetties on jonahs! And they winxed and wanxed like baillybeacons. Till we woksed up oldermen.

From whose plultibust preaggravated, by baskatchairch theologies (there werenighn on thaurity herouns in that alraschil arthouducks draken), they were whoalike placed to say, in the matters off ducomans nonbar one, with bears' respects to him and bulls' acknowledgments (come on now, girls! lead off, O cara, whichever won of you wins! The two Gemuas and Jane Agrah and Judy Tombuys!) disassembling and taking him apart, the slammocks, with discrimination for his maypole and a rub in passing over his hump, drogueries inaddendance, frons, fesces and frithstool: 1) he hade to die it, the beetle, 2) he didhithim self, hod's fush, 3) all ever the pelican huntered with truly fond bullpen backthought since his toork human life where his personal low outhired his taratoryism, the orenore under the selfhide of his bessermettle, was forsake in his chiltern and lumbojumbo, 4) he was like Fintan fore flood and after sometimes too damned merely often on the saved side, saw he was, 5) regarding to prussyattes or quazzyverzing he wassand no better than he would have been before he could have been better than what he warrant after, 6) blood, musk or haschish, as coked, diamoned or penceloid, and bleaching him naclenude from all cohlorine matter, down to a boneash bittstoff, he's, tink fors tank, the same old dust-amount on the same old tincoverdull baubleclass, totstittywinktosser and bogusbagwindburster, whether fitting tyres onto Danelope boys or fluttering flaus for laurettas, whatever the bucket brigade and the plug party says, touchant Arser of the Rum Tipple and his camelottery and lyonesslooting but with a layaman's brutstrenth, by Jacohob and Esahur and the all saults or all sallies, what we warn to hear, jeff, is the woods of chirpsies cries to singaloo sweecheeriode and sock him up, the oldcant rogue.

Group A.

You have jest (a ham) beamed listening through (a ham pig) his haulted excerpt from John Whiston's fiveaxled production, *The Coach With The Six Insides*, from the Tales of Yore of the times gone by before there was a hofdking or a hoovthing or a pinginapoke in Oreland, all sould. Goes Tory by Eeric Whigs is To Become Tintinued in *Fearson's Nightly* in the Lets All Wake Brickfaced In Lucan. Lhirondella, jaunty lhirondella! With tirra lirra rondinelles, atantivy we go!

Attention! Stand at!! Ease!!!

We are now diffusing among our lovers of this sequence (to you! to you!) the dewfolded song of the naughtingels (Alys! Alysaloe!) from their sheltered positions, in rosescenery haydyng, on the heather side of waldalure, Mount Saint John's, Jinnyland, whither our allies winged by duskfoil from Mooreparque, swift sanctuary seeking, after Sunsink gang (Oiboe! Hitherzither! Almost dotty! I must dash!) to pour their peace in partial (floflo floreflorence), sweetishsad lightandgayle, twittwin twosingwoolow. Let everie sound of a pitch keep still in resonance, jemcrow, jackdaw, prime and secund with their terce that whoe betwides them, now full theorbe, now dulcifair, and when we press of pedal (sof!) pick out and vowelise your name. A mum. You pere Golazy, you mere Bare and you Bill Heeny, and you Smirky Dainty and, more beethoken, you wheckfoolthenairyans with all your badchthumpered peanas! We are gluckglucky in our being so far fortunate that, bark and bay duol with Man Goodfox inchimings having ceased to the moment, so allow the clinkars of our nocturnefield, night's sweetmoztheart, their Carmen Sylvae, my quest, my queen. Lou must wail to cool me airly! Coil me curly, warbler dear! May song it flourish (in the underwood), in chorush, long make it flourish (in the Nut, in the Nutsky) till thorush! Secret Hookup.

— Roguenaar Loudbrags, that soddy old samph! How high is vuile, var? To which yes he did, capt, that was the answer.

— And his shartshort trooping its colours! We knows his ventruquulence. Which that that rang ripprippripplying.

— Bulbul, bulbulone! I will shally. Thou shalt willy. You wouldnt should as youd remesmer. I hypnot. 'Tis golden sickle's hour. Holy moon priestess, we'd love our grappes of mistellose! Moths the matter? Pschtt! Tabarins comes. To fell our fairest. O gui, O gui! Salam, salms, salaum! Carolus! O indeed and we ware! And hoody crow was ere. I soared from the peach and Missmolly showed her pear too, onto three and away. Whet the bee as to deflowret greendy grassies yellowhorse. Kematitis, cele our erdours! Did you aye, did you eye, did you everysee suchaway, suchawhy, eeriewhigg airywhugger? Even to the extremity of the world? Dingoldell! The enormanous his, our littlest little! Wee wee, that long alancey one! Let sit on this anthill for our frilldress talk after this day of making blithe inveiled the heart before our groatsupper serves to us Panchomaster and let harleqwind play peeptomine up all our colombinations! Wins won is nought, twigs too is nil, tricks trees makes nix, fairs fears stoops at nothing. And till Arthur comes againus and sen peatrick's he's reformed we'll pose him together a piece, a pace. Shares in guineases! There's lovely the sight! Surey me, man weepful! Big Seat, you did hear? And teach him twisters in tongue irish. Pat lad may goh too. Quicken, aspen;ash and yew; willow, broom with oak for you. And move your tellabout. Not nice is that, limpet lady! Spose we try it promissly. Love all. Naytellmeknot tennis! Taunt me treattening! But do now say to Mr Eustache! Ingean mingen has to hear. Whose joint is out of jealousy now? Why, heavilybody's evillyboldy's. Hopping Gracius, onthy ovful! O belessk mie, what a nerve! How a mans in his armor we nurses know. Wingwong welly, pitty pretty Nelly! Some Poddy pitted in, will anny petty pullet out? Call Kitty Kelly! Kissykitty Killykelly! What a nossowl buzzard! But what a neats ung gels!

Here all the leaves alift aloft, full o'liefing, fell alaughing over Ombrellone and his parasollieras with their black thronguards from the County Shillelagh. Ignorant invincibles, innocents immutant! Onzel grootvatter Lodewijk is onangonamed before the bridge of primerose and his twy Isas Boldmans is met the blueybells near Dandeliond. We think its a gorsedd shame, these godoms. A lark of limonladies! A lurk of orangetawneymen! You're backleg wounted, budkley mister, bester of the boyne.

And they leaved the most leavely of leaftimes and the most folliagenous till there came the marrer of mirth and the jangtherapper of all jocolarinas and they were as were they never ere. Yet had they laughtered, one on other, undo the end and enjoyed their laughings merry was the times when so grant it High Hilarion us may too!

Cease, prayce, storywalkering around with gestare romanoverum he swinking about is they think and plan unrawil what.

Back to Droughty! The water of the face has flowed.

The all of them, the sowriegueuxers, blottyeyed boys, in that pig's village smoke, a sixdigitarian legion on druid circle, the Clandibblon clam cartel, then pulled out and came off and rally agreed them, roasted malts with toasted burleys, in condomnation of his totomptation and for the duration till his repepulation, upon old nollcromforemost ironsides, as camnabel chieftain, since, as Sammon trowed to explain to summon, seeing that, as he had contracted out of islands empire, he might as coolly have rolled to school call, tarponturboy, a grampurpoise, the manyfathom bringegroom with the fortyinch bride, out of the cuptin klanclord kettle auction like the soldr of a britsh he was bound to be and become till the sea got him whilask, from maker to misses and what he gave was as a pattern, he, that hun of a horde, is a finn as she, his tent wife, is a lap, at home on a steed, abroad by the fire (to say nothing of him having done whatyouknow howyousaw whenyouheard whereyouwot, the kenspeckled souckar, generose as cocke, greediguss with garzelle, uprighter of age and most umbrasive of yews all, under heaviest corpsus exemption) and whoasever spit her in howsoever's fondling saving her keepers that mould the bould she sould to hould the wine that wakes the barley, the peg in his pantry to hold the heavyache off his heart. The droll delight of deemsterhood, a win from the wood to bond. Like the bright lamps, Thamamahalla, yearin out yearin. Auspicably suspectable but in expectancy of respectableness. From dirty flock bedding, drip dropping through the ceiling, with two sisters of charities on the front steps and three evacuan cleansers at the back gaze, single box and pair of chairs (suspectable), occasionally and alternatively used by husband when having writing to do in connection with equitable druids and friendly or other societies through periods of dire want with comparative plenty (thunderburst, ravishment, dissolution and providentiality) to a sofa allbeit of hoarsehaar with Amodicum cloth, hired payono, still playing off, used by the youngsters for czurnying out oldstrums, three bedrooms upastairs, of which one with fireplace (aspectable), with greenhouse in prospect (particularly perspectable).

And you, when you kept at Dulby, were you always (for that time only) what we knew how when we (from that point solely) were you know where? There you are! And why? Why, hitch a cock eye, he was snapped on the sly upsadaisying coras pearls out of the pie when all the perts in princer street set up their tinker's humn, (the rann, the rann, that keen of old bards), with them newnesboys pearcin screaming off their armsworths. The boss made dovesandraves out of his bucknesst while herself wears the bowler's hat in her bath. Deductive Almayne Rogers disguides his voice, shetters behind hoax chestnote from exexive. Heat wives rasing. They jest keeps rosing. He jumps leaps rizing. Howlong!

You known that tom? I certainly know. Is their bann bothstiesed? Saddenly now. Has they bane reneemed? Soothinly low. Does they ought to buy the papelboy when he footles up their suit? He's their mark to foil the flouter and they certainty owe.

He sprit in his phiz (baccon!). He salt to their bis (pudden!). He toockled her palam (so calam is solom!). And he suked their friends' leave (bonnick lass, fair weal!)

— Guilty but fellows culpows! It was felt by me sindeade, that submerged doughdoughty doubleface told waterside labourers. But since we for athome's health have chanced all that, the wild whips, the wind ships, the wonderlost for world hips, unto their foursquare trust prayed in aid its plumptylump piteousness which, when it turtled around seeking a thud of surf, spake to approach from inherdoff trisspass through minxmingled hair. Though I may have hawked it, said, and selled my how hot peas after theactrisscalls from my imprecurious position and though achance I could have emptied a pan of backslop down drain by whiles of dodging a rere from the middenprivet appurtenant thereof, salving the presents of the board of wumps and pumps, I am ever incalpable, where release of prisonals properly is concerned, of unlifting upfallen girls wherein dangered from them in thereopen out of unadulteratous bowery, with those hintering influences from an angelsexonism. It was merely my barely till their oh offs. Missaunderstaid. Meggy Guggy's giggag. The code's proof! The rebald danger with they who would bare whiteness against me I dismissem from the mind of good. He can tell such as story to the Twelfth Maligns that my first was a nurssmaid and her fellower's a willbe perambulatrix. There are twingty to twangty too thews and leathermail coatschemes penparing to hostpost for it valinnteerily with my valued fofavour to the post puzzles deparkment with larch parchels' of presents for future branch offerings. The green approve the raid! Shaum Baum's bode he is amustering in the groves while his shool comes merging along! Want I put myself in their kirtlies I were ayearn to leap with them and show me too bisextine. Dear and lest I forget mergers and bow to you low, marchers! Attemption! What a mazing month of budsome misses they are making, so wingtywish to flit beflore their kin! Attonsure! Ears to hears! The skall of a gall (for every dime he yawpens that momouth you could park your ford in it) who has papertreated him into captivities with his inside man by a hocksheat of starvision for an avragetopeace of parchment, cooking up his lenses to be my apoclogypst, the recreuter of conscraptions, let him be asservent to

Kinahaun! For (peace peace perfectpeace!) I have abwaited me in a water of Elin and I have placed my reeds intectis before the Registower of the perception of tribute in the hall of the city of Analbe. How concerns any merryaunt and hworsoever gravesobbers it is perensempry sex of fun to help a dazzle off the othour. What for Mucias and Gracias may the duvlin rape the handsomst! And the whole mad knightmayers' nest! Tunpother, prison and plotch! If Y shoulden somewhat, well, I am able to owe it, hearth and chem ney easy. They seeker for vannflaum all worldins merkins. I'll eager make lyst turpidump undher arkens. Basast! And if my litigimate was well to wrenn tigtag cackling about it, like the sally berd she is, to abery ham in the Cutey Strict, (I shall call upon my first among my lost of lyrars beyond a jingoobangoist, to overcast her) dismissing mundamanu all the riflings of her vic-tuum gleaner (my old chuck! she drakes me druck! turning out, gay at ninety!) and well shoving offa boastonmess like lots wives does over her handpicked hunsbend, as she would be calling, well, for further oil mircles upon all herwayferer gods and reanouncing my deviltries as was I a locally person of caves until I got my purchase on her firmforhold I am, I like to think, by their sacreligion of daimond cap daimond, confessedly in my baron gentilhomme to the manhor bourne till ladiest day as panthoposopher, to have splet for groont a peer of bellows like Bacchulus shakes a rousing guttural at any old cerpaintime by peaching (allsole we are not amusical) the warry warst against myself in the defile as a lieberretter sebaiscopal of these mispeschyites of the first virginial water who, without an auction of biasement from my part, with gladyst tone ahquickyessed in it, overhowe and underwhere, the totty lolly poppy flossy conny dollymaukins Though I heave a coald on my bauck and am could up to my eres hoven sametimes I used alltides to be aswarmer for the meekst and the graced. You are not going to not. You might be threeabreasted wholenosing at a whallhoarding from our Don Amir anent villayets prostatution precisingly kuschkars tarafs and it could be double densed uncounthest hour of allbleakest age with a bad of wind and a barran of rain, nompos mentis like Novus Elector, what with his Marx and their Groups, yet did a doubt, should a dare, were to you, you would do and dhamnk me, shenker, dhumnk you. Skunk. And fare with me to share with me. Hinther and thonther, hant by hont. By where dauvening shedders down whose rovely lanes. As yose were and as yese is. Sure and you would, Mr Mac Gurk! Be sure and you would, Mr O'Duane! To be sure and you would so, Mr MacElligut! Wod you nods? Mom mom. No mum has the rod to pud a stub to the lurch of amotion. My little love apprencisses, my dears, the estelles, van Nessies von Nixies voon der pool, which I had a reyal devouts for yet was it marly

lowease or just a feel with these which olderman K.K. Alwayswelly he is
showing ot the fullnights for my palmspread was gav to a parsleysprig, the
curliest weedeen old ocean coils around, so spruce a spice for salthorse,
sonnies, and as tear to the thrusty as Taylor's Spring, when aftabournes,
when she was look like a little cheayat chilled (Oh sard! ah Mah!) by my tide
impracing, as Beacher seath, and all the colories fair fled from my folced
cheeks! Popottes, where you canceal me you mayst forced guage my bribes.
Wickedgapers, I appeal against the light! A nexistence of vividence! Panto,
boys, is on a looser inloss; ballet, girls, suppline thrown tights. I have wanted
to thank you such a long time so much now. Thank you. Sir, kindest of
bottleholders and very dear friend, among our hearts of steel, froutiknow, it
will befor you, me dare beautiful young soldier, winninger nor anyour of
rudimental moskats, before you go to mats, you who have watched your
share with your sockboule sodalists on your buntad nogs at our love tennis
squats regatts, suckpump, when on with the balls did disserve the fain, my
goldrush gainst her silvernetss, to say, biguidd, for the love of goddess and
perthanow as you reveres your one mothers, mitsch for matsch, and while I
reveal thus my deepseep daughter which was bourne up pridely out of
medsdreams unclouthed when I was pillowing in my brime (of Saturnay
Eve, how now, woren't we't?), to see, I say, whoahoa, in stay of execution *in
re* Milcho Melekmans, increaminated, what you feel, oddrabbit, upon every
strong ground you have ever taken up, by bitterstiff work or battonstaff
play, with assault of turk against a barrakraval of grakeshoots, e'en tho'
Jambuwel's defecalties is Terry Shimmyrag's upperturnity, if that is grace
for the grass what is balm for the bramblers, as it is as it is, that I am the
catasthmatic old ruffin sippahsedly improctor to be seducint trovatellas, the
dire daffy damedeaconesses, like (why sighs the sootheesinger) the lilliths
oft I feldt, and, when booboob brutals and cautiouses only aims at the oggog
hogs in the humand, then, (Houtes, Blymey and Torrenation, upkurts and
scotchem!) I'll tall tale tell croon paysecurers, sowill nuggets and nippers,
that thash on me stumpen blows the gaff offmombition and thit thides or
marse makes a good dayle to be shattat. Fall stuff.

His rote in ere, afstef, was.

And dong wonged Magongty till the bombtomb of the warr, thrusshed
in his whole soort of cloose.

Whisht who wooed in Weald, bays of Bawshaw binding. The desire of
Miriam is the despair of Marian as Joh Joseph's beauty is Jacq Jacob's grief.
Brow, tell nun; eye, feign sad; mouth, sing mim. Look at Lokman! What-
between the cupgirls and the platterboys. And he grew back into his grossery
baseness: and for all his grand remonstrance: and there you are.

Here endeth chinchinatibus with have speak finish. With a haygue for a halt on a pouncefoot panse. Pink, pleas pink, two pleas pink, how to pleas pink.

Punk.

Mask one. Mask two. Mask three. Mask four.

Up.

— Look about you, Tutty Comyn!

— Remember and recall, Kullykeg!

— When visiting Dan Leary try the corner house for thee.

— I'll gie ye credit for simmence more if ye'll be lymphing.

Our four avunculusts.

And, since threestory sorratelling was much too many, they maddened and they morgued and they lungd and they jowld. Synopticked on the word. Till the Juke done it.

Down.

Like Jukoleon, the seagoer, when he bore down in his perry boat he had raised a slide and shipped his orders and seized his pullets and primed their plumages, the fionnling and dubhlet, the dun and the fire, and, sending them one by other to fare fore fom, he had behold the residuance of a delugion: the foggy doze still going strong, the old thalassocrats of invinsible empores, maskers of the waterworld, facing one way to another way and this way on that way, from severalled their fourdimmansions. Where the lighning leaps from the numbulous; where coold by cawld breide lieth langwid; the bounds whereinbourne our solied bodies all attomed attaim arrest: appoint, that's all. But see what follows. Wringlings upon wronglings among incomputables about an uncomeoutable (an angel prophetethis? kingcorrier of beheasts? the calif in his halifskin? that eyriewinging one?) and the voids bubbily vode's dodos across the which the boomomouths from their dupest dupes were in envery and anononously blowing great.

Guns.

Keep backwards, please, because there was no good to gundy running up again. Guns. And it was written up in big capital. Guns. Saying never underrupt greatgrandgosterfosters! Guns. And whatever one did they said, the fourlings, that on no acounts you were not to. Guns.

Not to pad them behaunt in the fear. Not to go, tonnerwatter, and bungley well chute the rising gianerant. Not to wandly be woking around jerumsalemdo at small hours about the murketplots, smelling okey boney, this little figgy and arraky belloky this little pink into porker but, porkodirto, to let the gentlemen pedestarolies out of the Monabella culculpuration live his own left leave, cullebuone, by perperusual of the petpubblicities without inwoking his also's between (*sic*) the arraky bone and (*suc*) the okey bellock. And not to not be always, hemmer and hummer, treeing unselves up with one exite but not to never be caving nicely, precisely, quicely, rebustly, tendrolly, unremarkably, forsakenly, haltedly, reputedly, firstly, somewhatly, yesayenolly about the back excits. Never to weaken up in place of the broths. Never to vvollusslleepp in the pleece of the poots. And, allerthings, never to ate the sour deans if they weren't having anysin on their consients. And, when in Zumschloss, to never, narks, cease till the finely ending was consummated by the completion of accomplishment.

And thus within the tavern's secret booth The wisehight ones who sip the tested sooth Bestir them as the Just has bid to jab The punch of quaram on the mug of truth.

K.C. jowls, they're sodden in the secret. K.C. jowls, they sure are wise. K.C. jowls, the justicestjobbers, for they'll find another faller if their ruse won't rise. Whooley the Whooper.

There is to see. Squarish large face with the atlas jacket. Brights, brownie eyes in bluesackin shoeings. Peaky booky nose over a lousiany shirt. Ruddy stackle hair besides a strawcamel belt. Namely. Gregorovitch, Leonocopolos, Tarpinacci and Duggelduggel. And was theys stare all atime? Yea but they was. Andoring the games, induring the studies, undaring the stories, end all. Ned? Only snugged then and cosied after one percepted nought while tuffbettle outraged the waywords and meansigns of their hinterhand suppliesdemands. And be they gone to splane splication? That host that hast one on the hoose when backturns when he facefronts none none in the house his geust has guest. You bet they is. And nose well down.

With however what sublation of compensation in the radification of interpretation by the byeboys? Being they. Mr G. B. W. Ashburner, S. Bruno's Toboggan Drive, Mr Faixgood, Bellchimbers, Carolan Crescent, Mr I. I. Chattaway, Hilly Gape, Poplar Park, Mr Q. P. Dieudonney, The View, Gazey Peer, Mr T. T. Erchdeakin, Multiple Lodge, Jiff Exby Rode, Mr W. K. Ferris-Fender, Fert Fort, Woovil Doon Botham ontowhom adding the tout that pumped the stout that linked the lank that cold the sandy that nextdoored the rotter that rooked the rhymer that lapped at the hoose that Joax pilled.

They had heard or had heard said or had heard said written.

Fidelisat.

That there first a rudrik kingcomed to an inn court; and the seight of that yard was a perchypole with a loovahgloovah on it; last mannarks maketh man when wandshift winneth womans: so how would it hum, whoson of a which, if someof aswas to start to stunt the story on?

So many needles to ponk out to as many noodles as are company, they noddling all about it *tutti* to *tempo*, decumans numbered too, (*a*) well, that the secretary bird, better known as Pandoria Paullabucca, whom they thought was more like a solicitor general, indiscriminatingly made belief mid authorsagastions from Schelm the Pelman to write somewords to Senders about her chilikin puck, laughing that Poulebec would be the death of her, (*b*) that, well, that Madges Tighe, the postulate auditressee, when her daremood's a grownian, is always on the who goes where, hoping to Michal for the latter to turn up with a cupital tea before her ephumeral comes off without any much father which is parting parcel of the same goumeral's postoppage, it being lookwhyse on the whence blows weather helping mickle so that the loiter end of that leader may twaddle out after a cubital lull with a hopes soon to ear, comprong? (*c*) becakes the goatsman on question, or whatever the hen the bumbler was, feeling not up to scratch bekicks of whatever the kiddings Payne Inge and Popper meant for him, thoughy onced at a throughlove, true grievingfrue danger, as a nirshe persent to his minstress, devourced the pair of them Mather Caray's chucklings, *pante blanche*, and skittered his litters like the cavaliery man in Cobra Park for ungeborn yenkelmen, Jeremy Trouvas or Kepin O'Keepers, any old howe and any old then and when around Dix Dearthy Dungbin, remarking scenically with laddylike lassitude upon what he finally post-scrapped, (*d*) after it's so long till I thanked you about I do so much now thank you so very much as you introduced me to fourks, (*e*) will, these remind to be sane? (*f*) Fool step! Aletheometry? Or just zoot doon floon?

Nut it out, peeby eye! Onamassofmancynaves.

But. Top.

You were in the same boat of yourselves too, Getobodoff or Tream-plasurin; and you receptionated the most diliskious of milisk; which it all flowowered your drooplin dunlearies: but dribble a drob went down your rothole. Meaning, Kelly, Grimes, Phelan, Mollanny, O'Brien, MacAlister, Sealy, Coyle, Hynes-Joynes, Naylar-Traynor, Courcy de Courcy and Gilligan-Goll.

Stunner of oddstodds on bluebleeding boarhorse! What soresen's head subrises thus tous out of rumpumplikun oak with, well, we cannot say whom we are looking like through his nowface? It is of Noggens whilk dusts the bothsides of the seats of the bigslaps of the bogchaps of the porlarbaar of the marringaar of the Lochlunn gonlannludder of the feof of the foef of forfummed Ship-le-Zoyd.

Boumce! It is polisignstunter. The Sockerson boy. To pump the fire of the lewd into those soulths of bauchees, havsousedovers, tillfellthey deadwar knootvindict. An whele time he was rancing there smutsy floskons nodunder ycholerd for their poopishers, ahull onem Fyre maynoother endnow! Shatten up ship! Bouououmce! Nomo clandoilskins cheakinlevers! All ashored for Capolic Gizzards! Stowlaway there, glutany of stainks! Porterfillyers and spirituous suncksters, oooom oooom!

As these vitupetards in his boasum he did strongleholder, bushbrows, nobblynape, swinglyswanglers, sunkentrunk, that from tin of this clucken hadded runced slapottleslup. For him had hord from fard a piping. As? Of?

Dour douchy was a sieguldson. He cooed that loud nor he was young. He cud bad caw nor he was gray Like wather parted from the say.

Ostia, lift it! Lift at it, Ostia! From the say! Away from the say! Himhim. Himhim.

Hearhasting he, himmed, reromembered all the chubbs, chipps, chaffs, chuckinpucks and chayney chimebells That he had mistributed in port, pub, park, pantry and poultryhouse, While they, thered, the others, that are, were most emulously concerned to cupturing the last dropes of summour down through their grooves of blarneying. Ere the sockson locked at the dure. Which he would, shuttinshure. And lave them to sture.

For be all rules of sport 'tis right That youth bedower'd to charm the night Whilst age is dumped to mind the day When wather parted from the say.

The humming, it's coming. Insway onsway.

Fingool MacKishgmard Obesume Burgearse Benefice, He was bowen hem and scrapin him in recolcitrantament to the rightabout And these probenopubblicoes clamatising for an extinsion on his hostillery With his chargehand bombing their eres. Tids, genmen, plays, she been goin shoother off almaynoother onawares.

You here nort farwellens rouster? Ashiffle ashuffle the wayve they.

From Dancingtree till Suttonstone There's lads no lie would filch a crown To mull their sack and brew their tay With wather parted from the say.

Lelong Awaindhoo's a selverbourne enrouted to Rochelle Lane and liberties those Mullinguard minstrelsers are marshalsing, par tunepiped road, under where, perked on hollowy hill, that poor man of Lyones, good Dook Weltington, hugon come errindwards, had hircomed to the belles bows and been cutattrapped by the mausers. Now is it town again, londmear of Dublin! And off coursse the toller, ples the dotter of his eyes with her: Moke the Wanst, whye doe we aime alike a pose of poeter peaced? While the dumb he shoots the shopper rope. And they all pour forth. Sans butly Tuppeter Sowyer, the rouged engenerand, a barttler of the beauyne, still our benjamin liefest, sometime frankling to thise citye, whereas bigrented him a piers half subporters for his arms, Josiah Pipkin, Amos Love, Raoul Le Febber, Blaize Taboutot, Jeremy Yopp, Francist de Loomis, Hardy Smith and Sequin Pettit followed by the snug saloon seanad of our Café Béranger. The scenictutors.

Because they wonted to get out by the goatweigh afore the sheep was looset for to wish the Wobbleton Whiteleg Welshers kaillykailly kellykekkle and savebeck to Brownhazelwood from all the dinnasdoolins on the labious banks of their swensewn snewwesner, turned again weastinghome, by Danesbury Common, and they onely, duoly, thruely, fairly after rainy-draining fountybuckets (chalkem up, hemptyempty!) till they caught the wind abroad (alley loafers passinggeering!) all the rockers on the roads and all the boots in the stretes.

Oh dere! Ah hoy!

Last ye, lundsmin, hasty hosty! For an anondation of mirification and the lutification of our paludination.

His bludgeon's bruk, his drum is tore. For spuds we'll keep the hat he wore And roll in clover on his clay By wather parted from the say.

Hray! Free rogue Mountone till Dew Mild Well to corry awen and glowry! Are now met by Brownaboy Fuinnninuinn's former for a lyncheon partyng of his burgherbooh. The Shanavan Wacht. Rantinroarin Batteries Dorans. And that whistling thief, O' Ryne O'Rann. With a catch of her cunning like and nowhere a keener.

The for eolders were aspolootly at their wetsend in the mailing waters, trying to. Hide! Seek! Hide! Seek! Because number one lived at Bothersby North and he was trying to. Hide! Seek! Hide! Seek! And number two digged up Poors Coort, Soother, trying to. Hide! Seek! Hide! Seek! And nomber three he sleeped with Lilly Tekkles at The Eats and he was trying to. Hide! Seek! Hide! Seek! And the last with the sailalloyd donggie he was berthed on the Moherboher to the Washte and they were all trying to and baffling with the walters of, hoompsydoompsy walters of. High! Sink! High! Sink! Highohigh! Sinkasink!

Waves.

The gangstairs strain and anger's up As Hoisty rares the can and cup To speed the bogre's barque away O'er wather parted from the say.

Horkus chiefest ebblynuncies!

— He shook be ashaped of hempshelves, hiding that shepe in his goat. And for rassembling so bearfellsed the magreedy prince of Roger. Thuthud. Heigh hohse, heigh hohse, our kindom from an orse! Bruni Lanno's woollies on Brani Lonni's hairyparts. And the hunk in his trunk it would be

an insalt foul the matter of that cellaring to a pigstrough. Stop his laysense.
Ink him! You would think him Alddaublin staking his lordsure like a gourd
on puncheon. Deblinity devined. Wholehunting the pairk on a methylogical
mission whenever theres imberillas! And calling Rina Roner Reinette
Ronayne. To what mine answer is a lemans. Arderleys, beedles and
postbillers heard him. Three points to one. Ericus Vericus corrupted into
ware eggs. Dummy up, distillery! Broree aboo! Run him a johnsgate down
jameseslane. Begetting a wife which begame his niece by pouring her
youngthings into skintighs. That was when he had dizzy spells. Till
Gladstools Pillools made him ride as the mall. Thanks to his huedobrass
beerd. Lodenbroke the Longman, now he canseels under veerious persons
but is always that Rorke relly! On consideration for the musickers he ought
to have down it. Pass out your cheeks, why daunt you! Penalty, please!
There you'll know how warder barded the bollhead that parssed our alley.
We just are upsidedown singing what ever the dimkims mummur allalilty
she pulls inner out heads. This is not the end of this by no manners means.
When you've bled till you're bone it crops out in your flesh. To tell how
your mead of, mard, is made of. All old Dadgerson's dodges one conning
one's copying and that's what wonderland's wanderlad'll flaunt to the fair. A
trancedone boyscript with tittivits by. Ahem. You'll read it tomorrow, marn,
when the curds on the table. A nigg for a nogg and a thrate for a throte. The
auditor learns. Still pumping on Torkenwhite Radlumps, Lencs. In preplays
to Anonymay's left hinted palinode obviously inspiterebbed by a sibspecious
connexion. Note the notes of admiration! See the signs of suspicion! Count
the hemisemidemicolons! Screamer caps and invented gommas, quoites
puntlost, forced to farce! The pipette will say anything at all for a change.
And you know what aglove means in the Murdrus dueluct! Fewer to feud
and rompant culotticism, a fugle for the gleemen and save, sit and sew. And
a pants outsizinned on the Doughertys' duckboard pointing to peace at
home. In some, lawanorder on lovinardor. Wait till we hear the Boy of
Biskop reeling around your postoral lector! Epistlemadethemology for deep
dorfy doubtlings. As we'll lay till break of day in the bunk of basky, O! Our
island, Rome and duty! Well tried, buckstiff! Batt in, boot! Sell him a breach
contact, the vendoror, the buylawyer One hyde, sack, hic! Two stick holst,
Lucky! Finnish Make Goal! First you were Nomad, next you were Namar,
now you're Numah and it's soon you'll be Nomon. Hence counsels
Ecclesiast. There's every resumption. The forgein offils is on the shove to
lay you out dossier. Darby's in the yard, planning it on you, plot and
edgings, the whispering peeler after cooks wearing an illformation. The
find of his kind! An artist, sir! And dirt cheap at a sovereign a skull! He

knows his Finsbury Follies backwoods so you batter see to your regent
refutation. Ascare winde is rifing again about nice boys going native. You
know who was wrote about in the Orange Book of Estchapel? Basil and the
two other men from King's Avenance. Just press this cold brand against
your brow for a mow. Cainfully! The sinus the curse. That's it. Hung
Chung Egglyfella now speak he tell numptywumpty topsawys belongahim
pidgin. Secret things other persons place there covered not. How you fell
from story to story like a sagasand to lie. Enfilmung infirmity. On the
because alleging to having a finger a fudding in pudding and pie. And here's
the witnesses. Glue on to him, Greevy! Bottom anker, Noordeece! And kick
kick killykick for the house that juke built! Wait till they send you to sleep,
scowpow! By jurors' cruces! Then old Hunphydunphyville'll be blasted to
bumboards by the youthful herald who would once you were. He'd be our
chosen one in the matter of Brittas more than anarthur. But we'll wake and
see. The wholes poors riches of ours hundreds of manhoods and womhoods.
Two cents, two mills and two myrds. And it's all us rangers you'll be facing
in the box before the twelfth correctional. Like one man, gell. Between all
the Misses Mountsackvilles in their halfmoon haemicycles, gasping to
giddies to dye for the shame. Just hold hard till the one we leapt out gets her
yearing! Hired in cameras, extra! With His Honour Surpacker on the binge.
So yelp your guilt and kitz the buck. You'll have loss of fame from
Wimmegame's fake. Forwards! One bully son growing the goff and his
twinger read out by the Nazi Priers. You fought as how they'd never woxen
up, did you, crucket? It will wecker your earse, that it will! When hives the
court to exchequer 'tis the child which gives the sire away. Good for you,
Richmond Rover! Scrum around, our side! Let him have another between
the spindlers! A grand game! Dalymount's decisive. Don Gouverneur
Buckley's in the Tara Tribune, sporting the insides of a Rhutian Jhanaral
and little Mrs Ex-Skaerer-Sissers is bribing the halfpricers to pray for her
widower in his gravest embazzlement. You on her, hosy jigses, that'll be
some nonstop marrimont! You in your stolen mace and anvil, Magnes, and
her burrowed in Berkness cirrchus clouthses. Fummuccumul with a graneen
aveiled. Playing down the slavey touch. Much as she was when the fancy
cutter out collecting milestones espied her aseesaw on a fern. So nimb, he
said, a dat of dew. Between Furr-y-Benn and Ferr-y-Bree. In this tear
Vikloe vich he lofed. The smiling ever. If you pulls me over pay me, prhyse!
A talor would adapt his caulking trudgers on to any shape at see. Address
deceitfold of wovens weard. The wonder of the women of the world together,
moya! And the lovablest Lima since Ineen MacCormick MacCoort MacConn
O'Puckins MacKundred. Only but she is a little width wider got. Be moving

abog. You cannot make a limousine lady out of a hillman minx. Listun till you'll hear the Mudquirt accent. This is a bulgen horesies, this is wollan indulgencies, this is a flemsh. Tik. Scapulars, beads and a stump of a candle, Hubert was a Hunter, *chemins de la croixes* and Rosairette's egg, all the trimmings off the tree that she picked up after the Clontarf voterloost when O'Bryan MacBruiser bet Norris Nobnut. Becracking his cucconut between his kknneess. Umpthump, Here Inkeeper, it's the doatereen's wednessmorn! Delphin dringing! Grusham undergang! And the Real Hymernians strenging strong at knocker knocker! Holy and massalltolled. You ought to tak a dos of frut. Jik. Sauss. You're getting hoovier, a twelve stone hoovier, fullends a twelve stone hoovier, in your corpus entis and it scurves you right, demnye! Aunt as unclish ams they make oom. But Nichtia you bound not to loose's gone on Neffin since she clapped her charmer on him at Gormagareen. At the Gunting Munting Hunting Punting. The eitch is in her blood, arrah! For a frecklesome freshcheeky sweetworded lupsqueezer. And he shows how he'll pick him the lock of her fancy. Poghue! Poghue! Poghue! And a good jump, Powell! Clean over all their heads. We could kiss him for that one, couddled we, Huggins? Sparkes is the footer to hance off nancies. Scaldhead, pursue! Before you bunkledoodle down upon your birchentop again after them three blows from time, drink and hurry. The same three that nursed you, Skerry, Badbols and the Grey One. All of your own club too. With the fistful of burryberries were for the massus for to feed you living in dying. Buy bran biscuits and you'll never say dog. And be in the finest of companies. Morialtay and Kniferope Walker and Rowley the Barrel. With Longbow of the lie. Slick of the trick and Blennercassel of the brogue. Clanruckard for ever! The Fenn, the Fenn, the kinn of all Fenns! Deaf to the winds when for Croonacreena. Fisht! And it's not now saying how we are where who's softing what rushes. Merryvirgin forbed! But of they never eat soullfriede they're ating it now. With easter greeding. Angus! Angus! Angus! The keykeeper of the keys of the seven doors of the dreamadoory in the house of the household of Hecech saysaith. Whitmore, whatmore? Give it over, give it up! Mawgraw! Head of a helo, chesth of champgnon, eye of a gull! What you'd if he'd. The groom is in the green-house, gattling out his. Gun! That lad's the style for. Lannigan's ball! Now a drive on the naval! The Shallburn Shock. Never mind your gibbous. Slip on your ropen collar and draw the noosebag on your head. Nobody will know or heed you, Postumus, if you skip round schlymartin by the back and come front sloomutren to beg in one of the shavers' sailorsuits. Three climbs threequickenthrees in the garb of nine. We'll split to see you mouldem imparvious. A wing for oldboy Welsey Wandrer! Well spat, witty

wagtail! Now piawn to bishop's forthe! Moove. There's Mumblesome
Wadding Murch cranking up to the hornemoonium. Drawg us out *Ivy Eve
in the Hall of Alum!* The finnecies of poetry wed music. Feeling the jitters?
You'll be as tight as Trivett when the knot's knutted on. Now's your never!
Peena and Queena are duetting a giggle-for-giggle and the brideen Alannah
is lost in her diamindwaiting. What a magnificent gesture you will show us
this gallus day. Clean and easy, be the hooker! And a free for croaks after.
Dovlen are out for it. So is Rathfinn. And, hike, here's the hearse and four
horses with the interprovincial crucifixioners throwing lots inside to know
whose to be their gosson and whereas to brake the news to morhor. How
our myterbilder his fullen aslip. And who will wager but he'll Shonny Bhoy
be, the fleshlumpfleeter from Poshtapengha and all he bares sobsconcious
inklings shadowed on soulskin'. Its segnet yores, the strake of a hin. Nup.
Laying the cloth, to fore of them. And thanking the fish, in core of them.
To pass the grace for Gard sake! Ahmohn. Mr Justician Matthews and Mr
Justician Marks and Mr Justician Luk de Luc and Mr Justinian Johnston-
Johnson. And the aaskart, see, behind! Help, help, hurray! Allsup, allsop!
Four ghools to nail! Cut it down, mates, look slippy! They've got a dathe
with a swimminpull. Dang! Ding! Dong! Dung! Dinnin. Isn't it great he is
swaying above us for his good and ours. Fly your balloons, dannies and
dennises! He's doorknobs dead! And Annie Delap is free! Ones more. We
could ate you, par Buccas, and imbabe through you, reassuranced in the
wild lac of gotliness. One fledge, one brood till hulm culms evurdyburdy.
Huh the throman! Huh the traidor. Huh the truh. Arrorsure, he's the
mannork of Arrahland oversense he horrhorrd his name in thuthunder.
Rrrwwwkkkrrr! And seen it rudden up in fusefiressence on the flashmurket.
P.R.C.R.L.L. Royloy. Of the rollorrish rattillary. The lewdningblue-
bolteredallucktruckalltraumconductor! The unnamed nonirishblooder that
becomes a Greenislender overnight! But we're molting superstituettes out
of his fulse thortin guts. Tried mark, Easterlings. Sign, Soideric O'Cunnuc,
Rix. Adversed ord, Magtmorken, Kovenhow. There's a great conversion,
myn! Coucous! Find his causcaus! From Motometusolum through Bulley
and Cowlie and Diggerydiggerydock down to bazeness's usual? He's alight
there still, by Mike! Loose afore! Bung! Bring forth your deed! Bang! Till is
the right time. Bang! Partick Thistle agen S. Megan's versus Brystal Palace
agus the Walsall! Putsch! Tiemore moretis tisturb badday! The playgue will
be soon over, rats! Let sin! Geh tont! All we wants is to get peace for
possession. We dinned unnerstunned why you sassad about thirteen to
aloafen, sor, kindly repeat! Or ledn us alones of your lungorge, parsonifier
propounde of our edelweissed idol worts! Shaw and Shea are lorning obsen

so hurgle up, gandfarder, and gurgle me gurk. You can't impose on fray-shouters like os. Every tub here spucks his own fat. Hang coersion everyhow! And smotthermock Gramm's laws! But we're a drippindhrue gayleague all at ones. In the buginning is the woid, in the muddle is the sounddance and thereinofter you're in the unbewised again, vund vulsyvolsy. You talker dunsker's brogue men we our souls speech obstruct hostery. Silence in thought! Spreach! Wear anartful of outer nocense! Pawpaw, wowow! Momerry twelfths, noebroed! That was a good one, ha! So it will be quite a material what *May* farther be unvuloped for you, old *Mighty*, when it's aped to foul a delfian in the Mahnung. Ha ha! Talk of Paddybarke's echo! Kick nuck, Knockcastle! Muck! And you'll nose it, O you'll nose it, without warnward from we. We don't know the sendor to whome. But you'll find Chiggenchugger's taking the Treaclyshortcake with Bugle and the Bitch pairsadrawsing and Horssmayres Prosession tyghting up under the threes. Stop. Press stop. To press stop. All to press stop. And be the seem talkin wharabahts hosetanzies, dat sure is sullibrated word! Bing bong! Saxolooter, for congesters are salders' prey. Snap it up in the loose, patchy the blank! Anyone can see you're the son of a gunnell. Fellow him up too, Carlow! Woes to the wormquashed, aye, and wor to the winner! Think of Aerian's Wall and the Fall of Toss. Give him another for to volleyholleydoodlem! His lights not all out yet, the liverpooser! Boohoohoo it oose! With seven hores always in the home of his thinkingthings, his nodsloddledome of his noiselisslesoughts. Two Idas, two Evas, two Nessies and Rubyjuby. Phook! No wonder, pipes as kirles, that he sthings like a rheinbok. One bed night he had the delysiums that they were all queens mobbing him. Fell stiff. Oh, ho, ho, ho, ah, he, he! Abedicate yourself It just gegs our goad. He'll be the deaf of us, pappappoppopcuddle, samblind dairyrudder. Yus, sord, fathe, you woll, putty our wraughther! What we waits be after? Whyfore we come agooding? None of you, cock icy! You keep that henayearn and her fortycantle glim lookbehinder. We might do with rubiny leeses. But of all your wanings send us out your peppydecked ales and you'll not be such a bad lot. The rye is well for whose amind but the wheateny one is proper lovely. B E N K! We sincerestly trust that Missus with the kiddies of sweet Gorteen has not B I N K to their very least tittles deranged if in B U N K and we greesiously augur for your Meggers a B E N K B A N K B O N K to sloop in with all sorts of adceterus and adsaturas. It's our last fight, Megantic, fear you will! The refergee's took to hailing to time the pass. There goes the blackwatchwomen, all in white, flaxed up, purgad! Right toe, Armitage! Tem for Tam at Timmotty Hall! We're been carried away. Beyond bournes and bowers. So we'll leave it to Keyhoe, Danelly and Pykemhyme, the three muskrateers, at the end of this age that had it from Variants' Katey Sherratt that had it from Variants' Katey Sherratt's man for the bonnefacies of Blashwhite and Blushred of the Aquasancta Liffey Patrol to wind up and to tells of all befells after that to Mocked Majesty in the Malincurred Mansion.

So you were saying, boys? Anyhow he what?

So anyhow, melumps and mumpos of the hoose uncommons, after that to wind up that longtobechronickled gettogether thanksbetogiving day at Glenfinnisk-en-la-Valle, the anniversary of his finst homy commulion, after that same barbecue beanfeast was all over poor old hospitable corn and eggfactor, King Roderick O'Conor, the paramount chief polemarch and last pre-electric king of Ireland, who was anything you say yourself between fiftyodd and fiftyeven years of age at the time after the socalled last supper he greatly gave in his umbrageous house of the hundred bottles with the radio beamer tower and its hangars, chimbneys and equilines or, at least, he was'nt actually the then last king of all Ireland for the time being for the jolly good reason that he was still such as he was the eminent king of all Ireland himself after the last preeminent king of all Ireland, the whilom joky old top that went before him in the Taharan dynasty, King Arth Mock-morrow Koughenough of the leathered leggions, now of parts unknown, (God guard his generous comicsongbook soul!) that put a poached fowl in the poor man's pot before he took to his pallyass with the weeping eczema for better and worse until he went under the grass quilt on us, nevertheless, the year the sugar was scarce, and we to lather and shave and frizzle him, like a bald surging buoy and himself down to three cows that was meat and drink and dogs and washing to him, 'tis good cause we have to remember it, going through summersultryngs of snow and sleet witht the widow Nolan's goats and the Brownes girls neats anyhow, wait till I tell you, what did he do, poor old Roderick O'Conor Rex, the auspicious waterproof monarch of all Ireland, when he found himself all alone by himself in his grand old handwedown pile after all of them had all gone off with themselves to their castles of mud, as best they cud, on footback, owing to the leak of the McCarthy's mare, in extended order, a tree's length from the longest way out, down the switchbackward slidder of the landsown route of Hauburnea's liveliest vinnage on the brain, the unimportant Parthalonians with the mouldy Firbolgs and the Tuatha de Danaan googs and the ramblers from Clane and all the rest of the notmuchers that he did not care the royal spit out of his ostensible mouth about, well, what do you think he did, sir, but, faix, he just went heeltapping through the winespilth and weevily popcorks that were kneedeep round his own right royal round rollicking toper's table, with his old Roderick Random pullon hat at a Lanty Leary cant on him and Mike Brady's shirt and Greene's linnet collarbow and his Ghenter's gaunts and his Macclefield's swash and his readymade Reillys and his panprestuberian poncho, the body you'd pity him, the way the world is, poor he, the heart of Midleinster and the supereminent lord of them all, overwhelmed as he was with black ruin like a sponge out of water, allocutioning in bellcantos to his own oliverian society MacGuiney's *Dreans of Ergen Adams* and thruming through all to himself with diversed tonguesed through his old tears and his ould plaised drawl, starkened by the most regal of belches, like a blurney Cashelmagh crooner that lerking Clare air, the blackberd's ballad I've a *terrible errible lot todue todie todue tootorribleday*, well, what did he go and do at all, His Most Exuberant Majesty King Roderick O'Conor but, arrah bedamnbut, he finalised by lowering his woolly throat with the wonderful midnight thirst was on him, as keen as mustard, he could not tell what he did ale, that bothered he was from head to tail, and, wishawishawish, leave it, what the Irish, boys, can do, if he did'nt go, sliggymaglooral reemyround and suck up, sure enough, like a Trojan, in some particular cases with the assistance of his venerated tongue, whatever surplus rotgut, sorra much, was left by the lazy lousers of maltknights and beerchurls in the different bottoms of the various different replenquished drinking utensils left there behind them on the premises by that whole hogsheaded firkin family, the departed honourable homegoers and other slygrogging suburbanites, such as it was, fall and fall about, to the brindishing of his charmed life, as toastified by his cheeriubicundenances, no matter whether it was chateaubottled Guiness's or Phoenix brewery stout it was or John Jameson and Sons or Roob Coccola or, for the matter of that, O'Connell's famous old Dublin ale that he wanted like hell, more that halibut oil or jesuits tea, as a fall back, of several different quantities and qualities amounting in all to, I should say, considerably more than the better part of a gill or naggin of imperial dry and liquid measure till, welcome be from us here, till the rising of the morn, till that hen of Kaven's shows her beaconegg, and Chapwellswendows stain our horyhistoricold and Father MacMichael stamps for aitch o'clerk mess and the Litvian Newestlatter is seen, sold and delivered and all's set for restart after the silence, like his ancestors to this day after him (that the blazings of their ouldmouldy gods may attend to them we pray!), overopposides the cowery lad in the corner and forenenst the staregaze of the cathering candled, that adornment of his album and folkenfather of familyans, he came acrash a crupper sort of a sate on accomondation and the very boxst in all his composs, whereuponce, behome the fore for cove and trawlers, heave hone, leave lone, Larry's on the focse and Faugh MacHugh O'Bawlar at the wheel, one to do and one to dare, par by par, a peerless pair, ever here and over there, with his fol the dee oll the doo on the flure of his feats and the feels of the fumes in the wakes of his ears our wineman from Barleyhome he just slumped to throne.

So sailed the stout ship *Nansy Hans*. From Liff away. For Nattenlaender. As who has come returns. Farvel, farerne! Goodbark, goodbye!

Now follow we out by Starloe!

— THREE QUARKS FOR MUSTER MARK!
Sure he hasn't got much of a bark
And sure any he has it's all beside the mark.
But O, Wreneagle Almighty, wouldn't un be a sky of a lark
To see that old buzzard whooping about for uns shirt in the dark
And he hunting round for uns speckled trousers around by Palmerstown Park?
Hohohoho, moulty Mark!
You're the rummest old rooster ever flopped out of a Noah's ark
And you think you're cock of the wark.
Fowls, up! Tristy's the spry young spark
That'll tread her and wed her and bed her and red her
Without ever winking the tail of a feather
And that's how that chap's going to make his money and mark!

Overhoved, shrillgleescreaming. That song sang seaswans. The winging ones. Seahawk, seagull, curlew and plover, kestrel and capercallzie. All the birds of the sea they trolled out rightbold when they smacked the big kuss of Trustan with Usolde.

And there they were too, when it was dark, whilest the wildcaps was circling, as slow their ship, the winds aslight, upborne the fates, the wardorse moved, by courtesy of Mr Deaubaleau Downbellow Kaempersally, listening in, as hard as they could, in Dubbeldorp, the donker, by the tourneyold of the wattarfalls, with their vuoxens and they kemin in so hattajocky (only a quartebuck askull for the last acts) to the solans and the sycamores and the wild geese and the gannets and the migratories and the mistlethrushes and the auspices and all the birds of the rockbysuckerassousyoceanal sea, all four of them, all sighing and sobbing, and listening. Moykle ahoykling!

They were the big four, the four maaster waves of Erin, all listening, four. There was old Matt Gregory and then besides old Matt there was old Marcus Lyons, the four waves, and oftentimes they used to be saying grace together, right enough, bausnabeatha, in Miracle Squeer: here now we are the four of us: old Matt Gregory and old Marcus and old Luke Tarpey: the four of us and sure, thank God, there are no more of us: and, sure now, you wouldn't go and forget and leave out the other fellow and old Johnny MacDougall: the four of us and no more of us and so now pass the fish for

Christ sake, Amen: the way they used to be saying their grace before fish, repeating itself, after the interims of Augusburgh for auld lang syne. And so there they were, with their palms in their hands, like the pulchrum's proculs, spraining their ears, luistening and listening to the oceans of kissening, with their eyes glistening, all the four, when he was kiddling and cuddling and bunnyhugging scrumptious his colleen bawn and dinkum belle, an oscar sister, on the fifteen inch loveseat, behind the chieftaness stewardesses cubin, the hero, of Gaelic champion, the onliest one of her choice, her bleau-eyedeal of a girl's friend, neither bigugly nor smallnice, meaning pretty much everything to her then, with his sinister dexterity, light and rufthandling, vicemversem her ragbags et assaucyetiams, fore and aft, on and offsides, the brueburnt sexfutter, handson and huntsem, that was palpably wrong and bulbubly improper, and cuddling her and kissing her, tootyfay charmaunt, in her ensemble of maidenna blue, with an overdress of net, tickled with goldies, Isolamisola, and whisping and lisping her about Trisolanisans, how one was whips for one was two and two was lips for one was three, and dissimulating themself, with his poghue like Arrah-na-poghue, the dear dear annual, they all four remembored who made the world and how they used to be at that time in the vulgar ear cuddling and kiddling her, after an oyster supper in Cullen's bam, from under her mistlethrush and kissing and listening, in the good old bygone days of Dion Boucicault, the elder, in Arrah-na-pogue, in the otherworld of the passing of the key of Twotongue Common, with Nush, the carrier of the word, and with Mesh, the cutter of the reed, in one of the farback, pitchblack centuries when who made the world, when they knew O'Clery, the man on the door, when they were all four collegians on the nod, neer the Nodderlands Nurskery, whiteboys and oakboys, peep of tim boys and piping tom boys, raising hell while the sin was shining, with their slates and satchels, playing Florian's fables and communic suctions and vellicar frictions with mixum members, in the Queen's Ultonian colleges, along with another fellow, a prime number, Totius Quotius, and paying a pot of tribluts to Boris O'Brien, the buttler of Clumpthump, two looves, two turnovers plus (one) crown, to see the mad dane ating his vitals. Wulf! Wulf! And throwing his tongue in the snakepit. Ah ho! The ladies have mercias! It brought the dear prehistoric scenes all back again, as fresh as of yore, Matt and Marcus, natural born lovers of nature, in all her moves and senses, and after that now there he was, that mouth of mandibles, vowed to pure beauty, and his Arrah-na-poghue, when she murmurously, after she let a cough, gave her firm order, if he wouldn't please mind, for a sings to one hope a dozen of the best favourite lyrical national blooms in Luvillicit, though not too much, reflecting on the situation, drinking in draughts of purest air serene and revelling in the great outdoors, before the four of them, in the fair fine night, whilst the stars shine bright, by she light of he moon, we longed to be spoon, before her honeyoldloom, the plaint effect being in point of fact there being in the whole, a seatuition so shocking and scandalous and now, thank God, there were no more of them and he poghuing and poghuing like the Moreigner bowed his crusted hoed and Tilly the Tailor's Tugged a Tar in the Arctic Newses Dagsdogs number and there they were, like a foremasters in the rolls, listening, to Rolando's deepen darblun Ossian roll, (Lady, it was just too gorgeous, that expense of a lovely tint, embellished by the charms of art and very well conducted and nicely mannered and all the horrid rudy noisies locked up in nasty cubbyhole!) as tired as they were, the three jolly topers, with their mouths watering, all the four, the old connubial men of the sea, yambing around with their old pantometer, in duckasaloppics, Luke and Johnny MacDougall and all wishening for anything at all of the bygone times, the wald times and the fald times and the hempty times and the dempty times, for a cup of kindness yet, for four farback tumblerfuls of woman squash, with them, all four, listening and spraining their ears for the millennium and all their mouths making water.

 Johnny. Ah well, sure, that's the way (up) and it so happened there was poor Matt Gregory (up), their pater familias, and (up) the others and now really and (up) truly they were four dear old heladies and really they looked awfully pretty and so nice and bespectable and after that they had their fathomglasses to find out all the fathoms and their half a tall hat, just now like the old Merquus of Pawerschoof, the old determined despot, (*quiescents in brage!*) only for the extrusion of the saltwater or the auctioneer there dormont, in front of the place near O'Clery's, at the darkumound numbur wan, beside that ancient Dame street, where the statue of Mrs Dana O'Connell, prostituent behind the Trinity College, that arranges all the auctions of the valuable colleges, Bootersbay Sisters, like the auctioneer Battersby Sisters, the prumisceous creaters, that sells all the emancipated statues and flowersports, James H. Tickell, the jaypee, off Hoggin Green, after he made the centuries, going to the tailturn horseshow, before the angler nomads flood, along with another fellow, active impalsive, and the shoeblacks and the redshanks and plebeians and the barrancos and the cappunchers childerun, Jules, everyone, Gotopoxy, with the houghers on them, highstepping the fissure and fracture lines, seven five threes up, three five sevens down, to get out of his way, onasmuck as their withers conditions could not possibly have been improved upon, (praisers be to deeseesee!) like hopolopocattls, erumping oround their Judgity Yaman, and all the

tercentenary horses and priest hunters, from the Curragh, and con-
fusionaries and the authorities, Noord Amrikaans and Suid Aferican
cattleraiders (so they say) all over like a tiara dullfuoco, in his grey half a
tall hat and his amber necklace and his crimson harness and his leathern jib
and his cheapshein hairshirt and his scotobrit sash and his parapilagian
gallowglasses (how do you do, jaypee, Elevato!) to find out all the improper
colleges (and how do you do, Mr Dame James? Get out of my way!),
forkbearded and bluetoothed and bellied and boneless, from Strathlyffe
and Aylesburg and Northumberland Anglesey, the whole yaghoodurt
sweepstakings and all the horsepowers. But now, talking of hayastdanars
and wolkingology and how our seaborn isle came into exestuance, (the
explutor, his three andesiters and the two pantellarias) that reminds me
about the manausteriums of the poor Marcus of Lyons and poor Johnny,
the patrician, and what do you think of the four of us and there they were
now, listening right enough, the four saltwater widowers, and all they could
remembore, long long ago in the olden times Momonian, throw darker
hour sorrows, the princest day, when Fair Margrate waited Swede Villem,
and Lally in the rain, with the blank prints, now extincts, after the wreak of
Wormans' Noe, the barmaisigheds, when my heart knew no care, and after
that then there was the official landing of Lady Jales Casemate, in the year
of the flood 1132 S.O.S., and the christening of Queen Baltersby, the
Fourth Buzzersbee, according to Her Grace the bishop Senior, off the
whate shape, and then there was the drowning of Pharoah and all his
pedestrians and they were all completely drowned into the sea, the red sea,
and then poor Merkin Cornyngwham, the official out of the castle on
pension, when he was completely drowned off Erin Isles, at that time, suir
knows, in the red sea and a lovely mourning paper and thank God, as Saman
said, there were no more of him. And that now was how it was. The
arzurian deeps o'er his humbodumbones sweeps. And his widdy the giddy is
wreathing her murmoirs as her gracest triput to the Grocery Trader's
Manthly. Mind mand gunfree by Gladeys Rayburn! Runtable's
Reincorporated. The new world presses. Where the old conk cruised now
croons the yunk. Exeunc throw a darras Kram of Llawnroc, ye gink guy,
kirked into yord. Enterest attawonder Wehpen, luftcat revol, fairescapading
in his natsirt. Tuesy tumbles. And mild aunt Liza is as loose as her neese.
Fulfest withim inbrace behent. As gent would deem oncontinent. So mulct
per wenche is Elsker woed. Ne hath his thrysting. Fin. Like the newcasters
in their old plyable of *A Royenne Devours*. Jazzaphoney and Mirillovis and
Nippy she nets best. Fing. Ay, ay! Sobbos. And so he was. Sabbus.

Marcus. And after that, not forgetting, there was the Flemish armada, all scattered, and all officially drowned, there and then, on a lovely morning, after the universal flood, at about aleven thirtytwo was it? off the coast of Cominghome and Saint Patrick, the anabaptist, and Saint Kevin, the lacustrian, with toomuch of tolls and lottance of beggars, after converting Porterscout and Dona, our first marents, and Lapoleon, the equestrian, on his whuite hourse of Hunover, rising Clunkthurf over Cabinhogan and all they rememborec and then there was the Frankish floot of Noahsdobahs, from Hedalgoland, round about the freebutter year of Notre Dame 1132 P.P.O. or so, disumbunking from under Motham General Bonaboche, (noo poopery!) in his half a grey traditional hat, alevoila come alevilla, and after that there he was, so terrestrial, like a Nailscissor, poghuing her scandalous and very wrong, the maid, in single combat, under the sycamores, amid the bludderings from the boom and all the gallowsbirds in Arrah-na-Poghue, so silvestrious, neer the Queen's Colleges, in 1132 Brian or Bride street, behind the century man on the door. And then again they used to give the grandest gloriaspanquost universal howldmoutherhibbert lectures on anarxaquy out of doxarchology (hello, Hibernia!) from sea to sea (Matt speaking!) according to the pictures postcard, with sexon grimmacticals, in the Latimer Roman history, of Latimer repeating himself, from the vicerine of Lord Hugh, the Lacytynant, till Bockleyshuts the rahjahn gerachknell and regnumrockery roundup, (Marcus Lyons speaking!) to the oceanfuls of collegians green and high classes and the poor scholars and all the old trinitarian senate and saints and sages and the Plymouth brethren, droning along, peanzanzangan, and nodding and sleeping away there, like forget-menots, in her abijance service, round their twelve tables, per pioja at pulga bollas, in the four trinity colleges, for earnasyoulearning Eringrowback, of Ulcer, Moonster, Leanstare and Cannought, the four grandest colleges supper the matther of Erryn, of Killorcure and Killthemall and Killeachother and Killkelly-on-the-Flure, where their role was to rule the round roll that Rollo and Rullo rolled round. Those were the grandest gynecollege histories (Lucas calling, hold the line!) in the Janesdanes Lady Andersdaughter Universary, for auld acquaintance sake (this unitarian lady, breathtaking beauty, Bambam's bonniest, lived to a great age at or in or about the late No. 1132 or No. 1169, bis, Fitzmary Round where she was seen by many and widely liked) for teaching the Fatima Woman history of Fatimiliafamilias, repeating herself, on which purposeth of the spirit of nature as difinely developed in time by psadatepholomy, the past and present Johnny MacDougall speaking, give me trunks, miss!) and present and absent and past and present and perfect *arma virumque romano*. Ah, dearo, dear! O weep for the hower when eve aleaves bower! How it did but all come eddaying back to them, if they did but get gaze, gagagniagnian, to hear him there, kiddling and cuddling her, after the gouty old galahat, with his peer of quinnyfears and his troad of thirstuns, so nefarious, from his elevation of one yard one handard and thartytwo lines, before the four of us, in his Roman Catholic arms, while his deepseepeepers gazed and sazed and dazecrazemazed into her dullokbloon rodolling olosheen eyenbowls by the Cornelius Nepos, Mnepos. Anumque, umque. Napoo.

Queh? Quos?

Ah, dearo dearo dear! Bozun braceth brythe hwen gooses gandered gamen. Mahazar ag Dod! It was so scalding sorry for all the whole twice two four of us, with their familiar, making the toten, and Lally when he lost part of his half a hat and all belongings to him, in his old futile manner, cape, towel and drawbreeches, and repeating himself and telling him now, for the seek of Senders Newslaters and the mossacre of Saint Brices, to forget the past, when the burglar he shoved the wretch in churneroil, and contradicting all about Lally, the ballest master of Gosterstown, and his old fellow, the Lagener, in the Locklane Lighthouse, earing his wick with a pierce of railing, and liggen hig with his ladder up, and that oldtime turner and his sadderday erely cloudsing, the old croniony, Skelly, with the lether belly, full of neltts, full of keltts, full of lightweight beltts and all the bald drakes or ever he had up in the bohereen, off Artsichekes Road, with Moels and Mahmullagh Mullarty, the man in the Oran mosque, and the old folks at home and Duignan and Lapole and the grand confarreation, as per the cabbangers richestore, of the filest archives, and he couldn't stop laughing over Tom Tim Tarpey, the Welshman, and the four middleaged widowers, all nangles, sangles, angles and wangles. And now, that reminds me, not to forget the four of the Welsh waves, leaping laughing, in their Lumbag Walk, over old Battleshore and Deaddleconchs, in their half a Roman hat, with an ancient Greek gloss on it, in Chichester College auction and, thank God, they were all summarily divorced, four years before, or so they say, by their dear poor shehusbands, in dear byword days, and never brought to mind, to see no more the rainwater on the floor but still they parted, raining water laughing, per Nupiter Privius, only terpary, on the best of terms and be forgot, whilk was plainly foretolk by their old pilgrim cocklesong or they were singing through the wettest indies *As I was going to Burrymecarott we fell in with a lout by the name of Peebles* as also in another place by their orthodox proverb so there was said thus *That old fellow knows milk though he's not used to it latterly.* And so they parted. In Dalkymont nember to. Ay, ay. The good go and the wicked is left over. As evil flows so Ivel flows. Ay, ay. Ah, well sure, that's the way. As the holymaid of Kunut said to the haryman of

Koombe. For his humple pesition in odvices. Woman. Squash. Part. Ay, ay. By decree absolute.

Lucas. And, O so well they could rememborе at that time, when Carpery of the Goold Fins was in the kingship of Poolland, Mrs Dowager Justice Squalchman, foorsitter, in her fullbottom wig and beard, (Erminia Reginia!) in or aring or around about the year of buy in disgrace 1132 or 1169 or 1768 Y.W.C.A., at the Married Male Familyman's Auctioneer's court in Arrahnacuddle. Poor Johnny of the clan of the Dougals, the poor Scuitsman, (Hohannes!) nothing if not amorous, dinna forget, so frightened (Zweep! Zweep!) on account of her full bottom, (undullable attraxity!) that put the yearl of mercies on him, and the four maasters, in chors, with a hing behangd them, because he was so slow to borstel her schoon for her, when he was grooming her ladyship, instead of backscratching her materfamilias proper, like any old methodist, and all divorced and innasense interdict, in the middle of the temple, according to their dear faithful. Ah, now, it was too bad, too bad and stout entirely, all the missoccurs; and poor Mark or Marcus Bowandcoat, from the brownesberrow in nolandsland, the poor old chronometer, all persecuted with ally croaker by everybody, by decree absolute, through Herrinsilde, because he forgot himself, making wind and water, and made a Neptune's mess of all of himself, sculling over the giamond's courseway, and because he forgot to remember to sign an old morning proxy paper, a writing in request to hersute herself, on stamped bronnanoleum, from Roneo to Giliette, before saying his grace before fish and then and there and too there was poor Dion Cassius Poosycomb, all drowned too, before the world and her husband, because it was most improper and most wrong, when he attempted to (well, he was shocking poor in his health, he said, with the shingles falling off him), because he (ah, well now, peaces pea to Wedmore and let not the song go dumb upon your Ire, as we say in the Spasms of Davies, and we won't be too hard on him as an old Manx presbyterian) and after that, as red as a Rosse is, he made his last will and went to confession, like the general of the Berkeleyites, at the rim of the rom, on his two bare marrowbones, to Her Worship his Mother and Sister Evangelist Sweainey, on Cailcainnin widnight and he was so sorry, he was really, because he left the bootybutton in the handsome cab and now, tell the truth, unfriends never, (she was his first messes dogess and it was a very pretty peltry and there were faults on both sides) well, he attempted (or so they say) ah, now, forget and forgive (don't we all?) and, sure, he was only funning with his andrewmartins and his old age coming over him, well, he attempted or, the Connachy, he was tempted to attempt some hunnish familiarities, after eten a bad carmp in the rude ocean and, hevantonoze sure, he was dead seasickabed (it was really too bad!) her poor old divorced male, in the housepays for the daying at the Martyr Mrs MacCawley's, where at the time he was taying and toying, to hold the nursetendered hand, (ah, the poor old coax!) and count the buttons and her hand and frown on a bad crab and doying to remembore what doed they were byorn and who made a who a snore. Ah dearo dearo dear!

And where do you leave Matt Emeritus? The laychief of Abbotabishop? And exchullard of ffrench and gherman. Achoch! They were all so sorgy for poorboir Matt in his saltwater hat, with the Aran crown, or she grew that out of, too big for him, of or Mnepos and his overalls, all falling over her in folds—sure he hadn't the heart in her to pull them up—poor Matt, the old perigrime matriarch, and a queenly man, (the porple blussing upon them!) sitting there, the sole of the settlement, below ground, for an expiatory rite, in postulation of his cause, (who shall say?) in her beaver bonnet, the king of the Caucuses, a family all to himself, under geasa, Themistletocles, on his multilingual tombstone, like Navellicky Kamen, and she due to kid by sweetpea time, with her face to the wall, in view of the poorhouse, and taking his rust in the oxsight of Iren, under all the auspices, amid the rattle of hailstorms, kalospintheochromatokreening, with her ivyclad hood, and gripping an old pair of curling tongs, belonging to Mrs Duna O'Cannell, to blow his brains with, till the heights of Newhigherland heard the Bristolhut, with his can of tea and a purse of alfred cakes from Anne Lynch and two cuts of Shackleton's brown loaf and dilisk, waiting for the end to come. Gordon Heighland, when you think of it! The merthe dirther! Ah ho! It was too bad entirely! All devoured by active parlourmen, laudabiliter, of woman squelch and all on account of the smell of Shakeletin and scratchman and his mouth watering, acid and alkolic; signs on the salt, and so now pass the loaf for Christ sake. Amen. And so. And all.

Matt. And loaf. So that was the end. And it can't be helped. Ah, God be good to us! Poor Andrew Martin Cunningham! Take breath! Ay! Ay!

And still and all at that time of the dynast days of old konning Soteric Sulkinbored and Bargomuster Bart, when they struck coil and shock haunts, in old Hungerford-on-Mudway, where first I met thee oldpoetryck flied from may and the Finnan haddies and the Noal Sharks and the muckstails turtles like an acoustic pottish and the griesouper bullyum and how he poled him up his boccat of vuotar and got big buzz for his name in the airweek's honours from home, colonies and empire, they were always with assisting grace, thinking (up) and not forgetting about shims and shawls week, in auld land syne (up) their four hosenbands, that were four (up) beautiful sister misters, now happily married, unto old Gallstonebelly, and

there they were always counting and contradicting every night 'tis early the
lovely mother of periwinkle buttons, according to the lapper part of their
anachronism (up one up two up one up four) and after that there now she
was, in the end, the deary, soldpowder and all, the beautfour sisters, and that
was her mudhen republican name, right enough, from alum and oves, and
they used to be getting up from under, in their tape and straw garlands, with
all the worries awake in their hair, at the kookaburra bell ringring all wrong
inside of them (come in, come on, you lazy loafs!) all inside their poor old
Shandon bellbox (come out to hell, you lousy louts!) so frightened, for the
dthclangavore, like knockneeghs bumpsed by the fisterman's straights, (ys!
ys!), at all hours every night, on their mistletoes, the four old oldsters, to see
was the Transton Postscript come, with their oerkussens under their
armsaxters, all puddled and mythified, the way the wind wheeled the
schooler round, when nobody wouldn't even let them rusten, from playing
their gastspiels, crossing their sleep by the shocking silence, when they were
in dreams of yore, standing behind the door, or leaning out of the chair, or
kneeling under the sofacover and setting on the souptureen, getting into
their way something barbarous, changing the one wet underdown con-
vibrational bed or they used to slumper under, when hope was there no
more, and putting on their half a hat and falling over all synopticals and a
panegyric and repeating themselves, like svvollovving, like the time they
were dadging the talkeycook that chased them, look look all round the
stool, walk everywhere for a jool, to break fyre to all the rancers, to collect
all and bits of brown, the rathure's evelopment in spirits of time in all
fathom of space and slooping around in a bawneen and bath slippers and go
away to Oldpatrick and see a doctor Walker. And after that so glad they had
their night tentacles and there they used to be, flapping and cycling, and a
dooing a doonloop, panementically, around the waists of the ships, in the
wake of their good old Foehn again, as tyred as they were, at their
windswidths in the waveslength, the clipperbuilt and the five fourmasters
and Lally of the cleftoft bagoderts and Roe of the fair cheats, exchanging
fleas from host to host, with arthroposophia, and he selling him before he
forgot, issle issle, after having prealably dephlegmatised his gutterful of
throatyfrogs, with a lungible fong in his suckmouth ear, while the dear
invoked to the coolun dare by a palpabrows lift left no doubt in his minder,
till he was instant and he was trustin, sister soul in brother hand, the subjects
being their passion grand, that one fresh from the cow about Aithne Meithne
married a mailde and that one too from Engrvakon saga abooth a gooth a
gev a gotheny egg and the parkside pranks of quality queens, katte efter
kinne, for Earl Hoovedsoon's choosing and Huber and Harman orhow-

when theeuponthus (chchch!) eysolt of binnoculises memostinmust egotum sabcunsciously senses upers the deprofundity of multimathematical immaterialities wherebejubers in the pancosmic urge the allimmanence of that which Itself is Itself Alone (hear, O hear, Caller Errin!) exteriorises on this ourherenow plane in disunited solod, likeward and gushious bodies with (science, say!) perilwhitened passionpanting pugnoplangent intuitions of reunited selfdom (murky whey, abstrew adim!) in the higherdimissional selfless Allself, theemeeng Narsty meetheeng Idoless, and telling Jolly MacGolly, dear mester John, the belated dishevelled, hacking away at a parchment pied, and all the other analist, the steamships ant the ladies'foursome, ovenfor, nedenfor, dinkety, duk, downalupping, (how long tandem!) like a foreretyred schoonmasters, and their pair of green eyes and peering in, so they say, like the narcolepts on the lakes of Coma, through the steamy windows, into the honeymoon cabins, on board the big steamadories, made by Fumadory, and the saloon ladies' madorn toilet chambers lined over prawn silk and rub off the salty catara off a windows and, hee hee, listening, *qua* committe, the poor old quakers, oben the dure, to see all the hunnishmooners and the firstclass ladies, serious me, a lass spring as you fancy, and sheets far from the lad, courting in blankets, enfamillias, and, shee shee, all improper, in a lovely mourning toilet, for the rosecrumpler, the thrilldriver, the sighinspirer, with that olive throb in his nude neck, and, swayin and thayin, thanks ever so much for the tiny quote, which sought of maid everythingling again so very much more delightafellay, and the perfidly suite of her, bootyfilly yours, under all their familiarities, by preventing grace, forgetting to say their grace before chambadory, before going to boat with the verges of the chaptel of the opering of the month of Nema Knatut, so pass the poghue for grace sake. Amen. And all, hee hee hee, quaking, so fright, and, shee shee, shaking. Aching. Ay, ay.

For it was then a pretty thing happened of pure diversion mayhap, when his flattering hend, at the justright moment, like perchance some cook of corage might clip the lad on a poot of porage handshut his duckhouse, the vivid girl, deaf with love, (ah sure, you know her, our angel being, one of romance's fadeless wonderwomen, and, sure now, we all know you dote on her even unto date!) with a queeleetlecree of joysis crisis she renulited their disunited, with ripy lepes to ropy lopes (the dear o'dears!) and the golden importunity of aloofer's leavetime, when, as quick, is greased pigskin, Amoricas Champius, with one aragan throust, druve the massive of virilvigtoury flshpst the both lines of forwards (Eburnea's down, boys!) rightjingbangshot into the goal of her gullet.

Alris!

And now, upright and add them! And plays be honest! And pullit into yourself, as on manowoman do another! Candidately, everybody! A mot for amot. Comong, meng, and douh! There was this, wellyoumaycallher, a strapping modern old ancient Irish prisscess, so and so hands high, such and such paddock weight, in her madapolam smock, nothing under her hat but red hair and solid ivory (now you know it's true in your hardup hearts!) and a firstclass pair of bedroom eyes, of most unhomy blue, (how weak we are, one and all!) the charm of favour's fond consent! Could you blame her, we're saying, for one psocoldlogical moment? What would Ewe do? With that so tiresome old milkless a ram, with his tiresome duty peck and his bronchial tubes, the tiresome old hairyg orangogran beaver, in his tiresome old twenny-sixandsixpenny sheopards plods drowsers and his thirtybobandninepenny tails plus toop! Hagakhroustioun! It were too exceeding really if one woulds to offer at sulk an oldivirdual a pinge of hinge hit. The mainest thing ever! Since Edem was in the boags noavy. No, no, the dear heaven knows, and the farther the from it, if the whole stole stale mis betold, whoever the gulpable, and whatever the pulpous was, the twooned togethered, and giving the mhost phassionable wheathers, they were doing a lally a lolly a dither a duther one lelly two dather three lilly four dother. And it was a fiveful moment for the poor old timetetters, ticktacking, in tenk the count. Till the spark that plugged spared the chokee he gripped and (volatile volupty, how brieved are thy lunguings!) they could and they could hear like of a lisp lapsing, that was her knight of the truths thong plipping out of her chapellledeosy, after where he had gone and polped the questioned. Plop.

Ah now, it was tootwoly torrific, the mummurrlubejubes! And then after that they used to be so forgetful, counting motherpeributts (up one up four) to membore her beaufu mouldern maiden name, for overflauwing, by the dream of woman the owneirist, in forty lands. From Greg and Doug on poor Greg and Mat and Mar and Lu and Jo, now happily buried, our four! And there she was right enough, that lovely sight enough, the girleen bawn asthore, as for days galore, of planxty Gregory. Egory. O bunket not Orwin! Ay, ay.

But, sure, that reminds me now, like another tellmastory repeating yourself, how they used to be in lethargy's love, at the end of it all, at that time (up) always, tired and all, after doing the mousework and making it up, over their community singing (up) the top loft of the voicebox, of Mamalujo like the senior follies at murther magrees, squatting round, two by two, the four confederates, with Caxons the Coswarn, up the wet air register in Old Man's House, Millenium Road, crowning themselves in lauraly branches, with their cold knees and their poor (up) quad rupeds, ovasleep, and all dolled up, for their blankets and materny mufflers and plimsoles and their bowl of brown shackle and milky and boterham clots, a potion a peace, a piece aportion, a lepel alip, alup a lap, for a cup of kindest yet, with hold take hand and nurse and only touch of ate, a lovely munkybown and for xmell and wait the pinch and prompt poor Marcus Lyons to be not beheeding the skillet on for the live of ghosses but to pass the teeth for choke sake, Amensch, when it so happen they were all sycamore and by the world forgot, since the phlegmish hoopicough, for all a possabled, after ete a bad cramp and johnny magories, and backscrat the poor bedsores and the farthing dip, their caschal pandle of magnegnousioum, and read a letter or two every night, before going to dodo sleep atrance, with their catkins coifs, in the twilight, a capitaletter, for further auspices, on their old one page codex book of old year's eve 1132, M.M.L.J. old style, their Senchus Mor, by his fellow girl, the Mrs Shemans, in her summer seal houseonsample, with the caracul broadtail, her *totam in tutu*, final buff noonmeal edition, in the regatta covers, uptenable from the orther, for to regul their reves by incubation, and Lally, through their gangrene spentacles, and all the good or they did in their time, the rigorists, for Roe and O'Mulcnory a Conry ap Mul or Lap ap Morion and Buffler ap Matty Mac Gregory for Marcus on Podex by Daddy de Wyer, old bagabroth, beeves and scullogues, churls and vassals, in same, sept and severalty and one by one and sing a mamalujo. To the heroest champion of Eren and his braceoelanders and Gowan, Gawin and Gonne.

And after that now in the future, please God, after nonpenal start, all repeating ourselves, in medios loquos, from where he got a useful arm busy on the touchline, due south of her western shoulder down to death and the love embrace, with an interesting tallow complexion and all now united, sansfamillias, let us ran on to say oremus prayer and homeysweet homely, after fully realising the gratifying experiences of highly continental evenements, for meter and peter to temple an eslaap, for auld acquaintance, to Peregrine and Michael and Farfassa and Peregrine, for navigants et peregrinantibus, in all the old imperial and Fionnachan sea and for vogue awallow to a Miss Yiss, you fascinator, you, sing a lovasteamadorion to Ladyseyes, here's Tricks and Doelsy, delightfully ours, in her doaty ducky little blue and roll his hoop and how she ran, when wit won free, the dimply blissed and awfully bucked, right glad we never shall forget, thoh the dayses gone still they loves young dreams and old Luke with his kingly leer, so wellworth watching, and Senchus Mor, possessed of evident notoriety, and another more of the bigtimers, to name no others, of whom great things were expected in the fulmfilming department, for the lives of Lazarus and

auld luke syne and she haihaihail her kobbor kohinor sehehet on the praze
savohole shanghai.

Hear, O hear, Iseult la belle! Tristan, sad hero, hear! The Lambeg drum,
the Lombog reed, the Lumbag fiferer, the Limibig brazenaze.

Anno Domini nostri sancti Jesu Christi
Nine hundred and ninetynine million pound sterling in the blueblack
bowels of the bank of Ulster.
Braw bawbees and good gold pounds, galore, my girleen, a Sunday'll
prank thee finely.
And no damn loutll come courting thee or by the mother of the Holy Ghost
there'll be murder!

O, come all ye sweet nymphs of Dingle beach to cheer Brinabride queen
from Sybil surfriding
In her curragh of shells of daughter of pearl and her silverymonnblue
mantle round her.
Crown of the waters, brine on her brow, she'll dance them a jig and
jilt them fairly.
Yerra, why would she bide with Sig Sloomysides or the grogram
grey barnacle gander?

You won't need be lonesome, Lizzy my love, when your beau gets his
glut of cold meat and hot soldiering
Nor wake in winter, window machree, but snore sung in my old
Balbriggan surtout.
Wisha, won't you agree now to take me from the middle, say, of next
week on, for the balance of my days, for nothing
(what?) as your own nursetender?
A power of highsteppers died game right enough—but who, acushla,
'll beg coppers for you?

I tossed that one long before anyone.
It was of a wet good Friday too she was ironing and, as I'm given
now to understand, she was always mad gone on me.
Grand goosegreasing we had entirely with an allnight eiderdown
bed picnic to follow.
By the cross of Cong, says she, rising up Saturday in the twilight
from under me, Mick, Nick the Maggot or whatever your name is,
you're the mose likable lad that's come my ways yet
from the barony of Bohermore.

Mattheehew, Markeehew, Lukeehew, Johnheehewheehew!
Haw!
And still a light moves long the river. And stiller the mermen ply
their keg.
Its pith is full. The way is free. Their lot is cast.
So, to john for a john, johnajeams, led it be!

BOOK III

HARK!

Tolv two elf kater ten (it can't be) sax.

Hork!

Pedwar pemp foify tray (it must be) twelve.

And low stole o'er the stillness the heartbeats of sleep.

White fogbow spans. The arch embattled. Mark as capsules. The nose of the man who was nought like the nasoes. It is self tinted, wrinkling, ruddled. His kep is a gorsecone.

He am Gascon Titubante of Tegmine—sub—Fagi whose fixtures are mobiling so wobiling befear my remembrandts. She, exhibit next, his Anastashie. She has prayings in lowdelph. Zeehere green eggbrooms. What named blautoothdmand is yon who stares? Gugurtha! Gugurtha! He has becco of wild hindigan. Ho, he hath hornhide! And hvis now is for you. Pensée! The most beautiful of woman of the veilch veilchen veilde. She would kidds to my voult of my palace, with obscidian luppas, her aal in her dhove's suckling. Apagemonite! Come not nere! Black! Switch out!

Methought as I was dropping asleep somepart in nonland of where's please (and it was when you and they were we) I heard at zero hour as 'twere the peal of vixen's laughter among midnight's chimes from out the belfry of the cute old speckled church tolling so faint a goodmantrue as nighthood's unseen violet rendered all animated greatbritish and Irish objects non-viewable to human watchers save 'twere perchance anon some glistery gleam darkling adown surface of affluvial flowandflow as again might seem garments of laundry reposing a leasward close at hand in full expectation. And as I was jogging along in a dream as dozing I was dawdling, arrah, methought broadtone was heard and the creepers and the gliders and flivvers of the earth breath and the dancetongues of the woodfires and the hummers in their ground all vociferated echoating: Shaun! Shaun! Post the post! with a high voice and O, the higher on high the deeper and low, I heard him so! And lo, mescemed somewhat came of the noise and somewho might amove allmurk. Now, 'twas as clump, now mayhap. When look, was light and now 'twas as flasher, now moren as the glaow. Ah, in unlitness 'twas in very similitude, bless me, 'twas his belted lamp! Whom we dreamt was a shaddo, sure, he's lightseyes, the laddo! Blessed momence, O romence, he's growing

to stay! Ay, he who so swayed a will of a wisp before me, hand prop to hand,
prompt side to the pros, dressed like an earl in just the correct wear, in a
classy mac Frieze o'coat of far suparior ruggedness, indigo braw, tracked
and tramped, and an Irish ferrier collar, freeswinging with mereswin lacers
from his shoulthern and thick welted brogues on him hammered to suit the
scotsmost public and climate, iron heels and sparable soles, and his jacket of
providence wellprovided woolies with a softrolling lisp of a lapel to it and
great sealingwax buttons, a good helping bigger than the slots for them, of
twentytwo carrot krasnapoppsky red and his invulnerable burlap whiskcoat
and his popular choker, Tamagnum sette-and-forte and his loud boheem
toy and the damasker's overshirt he sported inside, a starspangled zephyr
with a decidedly surpliced crinklydoodle front with his motto through dear
life embrothred over it in peas, rice, and yeggyyolk, Or for royal, Am for
Mail, R.M.D. hard cash on the nail and the most successfully carried gigot
turnups now you ever, (what a pairfact crease! how amsolookly kersse!)
breaking over the ankle and hugging the shoeheel, everything the best—
none other from (Ah, then may the turtle's blessings of God and Mary and
Haggispatrick and Huggisbrigid be souptumbling all over him!) other than
(and may his hundred thousand welcome stewed letters, relayed wand
postchased, multiply, ay faith, and plultiply!) Shaun himself.

What a picture primitive!

Had I the concordant wiseheads of Messrs Gregory and Lyons alongside
of Dr Tarpey's and I dorsay the reverend Mr Mac Dougall's, but I, poor ass,
am but as their fourpart tinckler's dunkey. Yet methought Shaun (holy
messonger angels be uninterruptedly nudging him among and along the
winding ways of random ever!) Shaun in proper person (now may all the
blueblacksliding constellations continue to shape his changeable timetable!)
stood before me. And I pledge you my agricultural word by the hundred
and sixty odds rods and cones of this even's vision that young fellow looked
the stuff, the Bel of Beaus' Walk, a prime card if ever was! Pep? Now
without deceit it is hardly too much to say he was looking grand, so fired
smart, in much more than his usual health. No mistaking that beamish
brow! There was one for you that ne'er would nunch with good Duke
Humphrey but would aight through the months without a sign of an err in
hem and then, otherwise rounding, fourale to the lees of Traroe. Those
jehovial oyeglances! The heart of the rool! And hit the hencoop. He was
immense, topping swell for he was after having a great time of it, a
twentyfour hours every moment matters maltsight, in a porterhouse,
scutfrank, if you want to know, Saint Lawzenge of Toole's, the Wheel of
Fortune, leave your clubs in the hall and wait on yourself, no chucks for

walnut ketchups, Lazenby's and Chutney graspis (the house the once queen
of Bristol and Balrothery twice admired because her frumped door looked
up Dacent Street) where in the sighed of lovely eyes while his knives of
hearts made havoc he had recruited his strength by meals of spadefuls of
mounded food, in anticipation of the faste of tablenapkins, constituting his
threepartite pranzipal meals *plus* a collation, his breakfast of first, a bless us
O blood and thirsthy orange, next, the half of a pint of becon with newled
googs and a segment of riceplummy padding, met of sunder suigar and
some cold forsoaken steak peatrefired from the batblack night o'erflown
then, without prejuice to evectuals, came along merendally his stockpot
dinner of a half a pound or round steak, very rare, Blong's best from
Portarlington's Butchery, with a side of riceypeasy and Corkshire alla
mellonge and bacon with (a little mar pliche!) a pair of chops and thrown in
from the silver grid by the proprietoress of the roastery who lives on the hill
and gaulusch gravy and pumpernickel to wolp up and a gorger's bulby
onion (Margareter, Margaretar Margarasticandeatar) and as well with
second course and then finally, after his avalunch oclock snack at Appelredt's
or Kitzy Braten's of saddlebag steak and a Botherhim with her old phoenix
portar, jistr to gwen his gwistel and praties sweet and Irish too and mock
gurgle to whistle his way through for the swallying, swp by swp, and he
getting his tongue arount it and Boland's broth broken into the bargain, to
his regret his soupay *avic* nightcap, vitellusit, a carusal consistent with second
course eyer and becon (the rich of) with broad beans, hig, steak, hag, pepper
the diamond bone hotted up timmtomm and while 'twas after that he
scoffed a drakeling snuggily stuffed following cold loin of veal more cabbage
and in their green free state a clister of peas, soppositorily petty, last. P.S.
but a fingerhot of rheingenever to give the Pax cum Spiritututu. Drily
thankful. Burud and dulse and typureely jam, all free of charge, aman, and.
And the best of wine *avec*. For his heart was as big as himself, so it was, ay,
and bigger! While the loaves are aflowering and the nachtingale jugs. All St
Jilian's of Berry, hurrah there for tobies! Mabhrodaphne, brown pride of
our custard house quay, amiable with repastful, cheerus graciously, cheer
us! Ever of thee, Anne Lynch, he's deeply draiming! Houseanna! Tea is the
Highest! For auld lang Ayternitay! Thus thicker will he grow now, grew
new. And better and better on butterand butter. At the sign of Mesthress
Vanhungrig. However! Mind you, nuckling down to nourritures, were they
menuly some ham and jaffas, and I don't mean to make the ingestion for the
moment that he was guilbey of gulpable gluttony as regards chew-able
boltaballs, but, biestings be biestings, and upon the whole, when not off his
oats, given prelove appetite and postlove pricing good coup, goodcheap,

were it thermidor oogst or floreal may while the whistling prairial roysters play, between gormandising and gourmeteering, he grubbed his tuck all right, deah smorregos, every time he was for doing dirt to a meal or felt like a bottle of ardilaun arongwith a smag of a lecker biss of a welldressed taart or. Though his net intrants wight weighed nought but a flyblow to his gross and ganz afterduepoise. And he was so jarvey jaunty with a romp of a schoolgirl's completion sitting pretty over his Oyster Monday print face and he was plainly out on the ramp and mash, as you might say, for he sproke.

Overture and beginners!

When lo (whish, O whish!) mesaw mestreamed, as the green to the gred was flew, was flown, through deafths of durkness greengrown deeper I heard a voice, the voce of Shaun, vote of the Irish, voise from afar (and cert no purer puer palestrine e'er chanted panangelical mid the clouds of Tu es Petrus, not Michaeleen Kelly, not Mara O'Mario, and sure, what more numerose Italicuss ever rawsucked frish uov in urinal?), a brieze to Yverzone o'er the brozaozaozing sea, from Inchigeela call the way how it suspired (morepork! morepork!) to scented nightlife as softly as the loftly marconi-masts from Clifden sough open tireless secrets (mauveport! mauveport!) to Nova Scotia's listing sisterwands. Tubetube!

His handpalm lifted, his handshell cupped, his handsign pointed, his handheart mated, his handaxe risen, his handleaf fallen. Helpsome hand that holemost heals! What is het holy! It gested.

And it said:

— Alo, alass, aladdin, amobus! Does she lag soft fall means rest down? Shaun yawned, as his general address rehearsal, (that was antepropreviousday's pigeons-in-a-pie with rough dough for the carrier and the hash-sayugh of overgestern pluzz the 'stuesday's shampain in his head, with the memories of the past and the hicnuncs of the present embelliching the musics of the futures from Miccheruni's band) addressing himself *ex alto* and complaining with vocal discontent it was so close as of the fact the rag was up and of the briefs and billpasses, a houseful of deadheads, of him to dye his paddycoats to morn his hesternmost earning, his board in the swealth of his fate as, having moistened his manducators upon the quiet and scooping molars and grinders clean with his two fore fingers, he sank his hunk, dowanouet to resk at once, exhaust as winded hare, utterly spent, it was all he could do (disgusted with himself that the combined weight of his tons of iosals was a hundred men's massed too much for him), upon the native heath he loved covered kneehigh with virgin bush, for who who e'er trod sod of Erin could ever sleep off the turf! Well, I'm liberally dished seeing myself in this trim! How all too unwordy am I, a mere mailman of peace, a poor loust hastehater of the first degree, the principot of Candia, no legs and a title, for such eminence, or unpro promenade rather, to be much more exact, as to be the bearer extraordinary of these postoomany missive on his majesty's service while me and yous and them we're extending us after the pattern of reposiveness! Weh is me, yeh is ye! I, the mightif beam maircanny, which bit his mirth too early or met his birth too late! It should of been my other with his leickname for he's the head and I'm an everdevoting fiend of his. I can seeze tomirror in tosdays of yer when we lofobsed os so ker. Those sembal simon pumpkel pieman yers! We shared the twin chamber and we winked on the one wench and what Sim sobs todie I'll reeve tomorry, for 'twill be, I have hopes of, Sam Dizzier's feedst. Tune in, tune on, old Tighe, high, high, high, I'm thine owelglass. Be old! He looks rather thin, imitating me. I'm very fond of that other of mine. Fish hands Macsorley! Elien! Obsequies! Bonzeye! Isaac Egari's Ass! We're the musichall pair that won the swimmyease bladdhers at the Guinness gala in Badeniveagh. I ought not to laugh with him on this stage. But he' such a game loser! I lift my disk to him. Brass and reeds, brace and ready! How is your napper, Handy, and hownow does she stand? First he was living to feel what the eldest daughter she was panseying and last he was dying to know what old Madre Patriack does be up to. Take this John's Lane in your toastingfourch. Shaunti and shaunti and shaunti again! And twelve coolinder moons! I am no helotwashipper but I revere her! For my own coant! She has studied! Piscisvendolor! You're grace! Futs dronk of Wouldndom! But, Gemini, he's looking frightfully thin! I heard the man Shee shinging in the pantry bay. Down among the dustbins let him lie! Ear! Ear! Not ay! Eye! Eye! For I'm at the heart of it. Yet I cannot on my solemn merits as a recitativer recollect ever having done of anything of the kind to deserve of such. Not the phost of a nation! Nor by a long trollop! I just didn't have the time to. Saint Anthony Guide!

— But have we until now ever besought you, dear Shaun, we remembered, who it was, good boy, to begin with, who out of symphony gave you the permit?

— Goodbye now, Shaun replied, with a voice pure as a churchmode, in echo rightdainty, with a good catlick tug at his cocomoss candylock, a foretaste in time of his cabbageous brain's curlyflower. Athiacaro! Comb his tar odd gee sing your mower O meeow? Greet thee Good? How are them columbuses! Lard have mustard on them! Fatiguing, very fatiguing. Hobos homknees and the corveeture of my spine. Poumeerme! My heaviest crux and dairy lot it is, with a bed as hard as the thinkamuddles of the Greeks and a board as bare as a Roman altar. I'm off rabbited kitchens and relief porridgers. No later than a very few fortnichts since I was meeting on the Thinker's Dam with a pair of men out of glasshouse whom I shuffled hands with named MacBlacks—I think their names is MacBlakes—from the Headfire Clump—and they were improving me and making me beliek no five hour factory life with insufficient emollient and industrial disabled for them that day o'gratises. I have the highest gratification by anuncing how I have it from whowho but Hagios Colleenkiller's prophecies. After suns and moons, dews and wettings, thunders and fires, comes sabotag. *Solvitur palumballando!* Tilvido! Adie!

— Then, we explained, salve a tour, ambly andy, you possibly might be so by order?

— Forgive me, Shaun repeated from his liquid lipes, not what I wants to do a strike of work but it was condemned on me premitially by Hireark Books and Chiefoverseer Cooks in their Eusebian Concordant Homilies and there does be a power coming over me that is put upon me from on high out of the book of breedings and so as it is becoming hairydittary I have of coerce nothing in view to look forward at unless it is Swann and beating the blindquarters out of my oldfellow's orologium oloss olorium. A bad attack of maggot it feels like. 'Tis trope, custodian said. Almost might I say of myself, while keeping out of crime, I am now becoming about fed up be going circulating about them new hikler's highways like them nameless souls, ercked and skorned and grizzild all over, till it's rusty October in this bleak forest and was veribally complussed by thinking of the crater of some noted volcano or the Dublin river or the catchalot trouth subsidity as away out or to isolate i from my multiple Mes on the spits of Lumbage Island or bury meself, clogs, coolcellar and all, deep in my wineupon ponteen unless Morrissey's colt could help me or the gander maybe at 49 as it is a tithe fish so it is, this pig's stomach business, and where on dearth or in the miraculous meddle of this expending umniverse to turn since it came into my hands I am hopeless off course to be doing anything concerning.

— We expect you are, honest Shaun, we agreed, but from franking machines, limricked, that in the end it may well turn out, we hear to be you, our belated, who will bear these open letter. Speak to us of Emailia.

— As, Shaun replied patly, with tootlepick tact too and a down of his dampers, to that I have the gumpower and, by the benison of Barbe, that is a lock to say with everything, my beloved.

— Would you mind telling us, Shaun honey, beg little big moreboy, we proposed to such a dear youth, where mostly are you able to work. Ah, you might! Whimper and we shall.

— Here! Shaun replied, while he was fondling one of his cowheel cuffs. There's no sabbath for nomads and I mostly was able to walk, being too soft for work proper, sixty odd eilish mires a week between three masses a morn and two chaplets at eve. I am always telling those pedestriasts, my answerers, Top, Sid and Hucky, now (and it is a veriest throth as the thieves' rescension) how it was forstold for me by brevet for my vacation in life while possessing stout legs to be disbarred after holy orders from unnecessary servile work of reckless walking of all sorts for the relics of my time for otherwise by my so douching I would get into a blame there where sieves fall out, Excelsior tips the best. Weak stop work stop walk stop whoak. Go thou this island, one housesleep there, then go thou other island, two housesleep there, then catch one nightmaze, then home to dearies. Never back a woman you defend, never get quit of a friend on whom you depend never make face to a foe till he's rife and never get stuck to another man's pfife. Amen; ptah! His hungry will be done! On the continent as in Eironesia. But believe me in my simplicity I am awful good, I believe, so I am, at the root of me, praised be right cheek Discipline! And I can now truthfully declaret before my Geity's Pantokreator with my fleshfettered palms on the epizzles of the apossels that I do my reasonabler's best to recite my grocery beans for mummy *mit* dummy *mot* muthar *mat* bonzar regular, genuflections enclosed. Hek domov muy, there thou beest on the hummock, ghee up, ye dog, for your daggily broth, etc., Happy Maria and Glorious Patrick, etc., etc. In fact, always, have I believe. Greedo! Her's me hongue!

— And it is the fullsoot of a tarabred. Yet one minute's observation, dear dogmestic Shaun, as we point out how you have while away painted our town a wearing greenridinghued.

— O murder mere, how did you hear? Shaun replied, smiling the ily way up his lampsleeve (it just seemed the natural thing to do), so shy of light was he then. Well, so be it! The gloom hath rays, her lump is love. And I will confess to have, yes. Your diogneses is anonest man's. Thrubedore I did! Inditty I did. All lay I did. Down with the Saozon ruze! And I am afraid it wouldn't be my first coat's wasting after striding on the vampire and blazing on the foceal. See! blazing on the foceal. As see! blazing upon the foe. Like the regular redshank I am. Impregnable as the mule himself. Somebody may perhaps hint at an aughter impression of was wrong. No such a thing! You never made a more freudful mistake, excuse yourself! What's pork to you means meat to me while you behold how I be eld. But it is grandiose by my ways of thinking from the prophecies. New worlds for all! And they were scotographically arranged for gentlemen only by a scripchewer in whofoundland who finds he is a relative. And it was with my extravert davy. Like glue. Be through. Moyhard's daynoight, tomthumb. Phwum!

— How mielodorous is thy bel chant, O songbird, and how exqueezit thine after draught! *Buccinate in Emenia tuba insigni volumnitatis tuae.* But do you mean, O phausdheen phewn, from Pontoffbellek till the Kisslemerched our ledan triz will be? we gathered substantively whether furniture would or verdure varnish?

— It is a confoundyous injective so to say, Shaun the fiery boy shouted, naturally incensed, as he shook the red pepper out of his auricles. And another time please confine your glaring intinuations to some other mordant body. What on the physiog of this furnaced planet would I be doing besides your verjuice? That is more than I can fix, for the teom bihan, anyway. So let I and you now kindly drop that, angryman! That's not French pastry. You can take it from me. Understand me when I tell you (and I will ask you not to whisple, cry golden or quoth mecback) that under the past purcell's office, so deeply deplored by my erstwhile elder friend, Miss Enders, poachmistress and gay receiver ever for in particular to the Scotic Poor Men's Thousand Gallon Cow Society (I was thinking of her in sthore) allbethey blessed with twentytwo thousand sorters out of a biggest poss of twentytwo thousand, mine's won, too much privet stationery and safty quipu was ate up larchly by those nettlesome goats out of pension greed. *Colpa di Becco, buon apartita!* Proceding, I will say it is also one of my avowal's intentions, at some time pease Pod pluse murthers of gout (when I am not prepared to say) so apt as my pen is upt to scratch, to compound quite the makings of a verdigrease savingsbook in the form of a pair of capri sheep boxing gloves surrounding this matter of the Welsfusel mascoteers and their sindybuck that saved a city for my publickers, Nolaner and Browno, Nickil Hopstout, Christcross, so long as, thanks to force of destiny, my selary as a paykelt is propaired, and there is a peg under me and there is a tum till me.

To the Very Honourable The Memory of Disgrace, the Most Noble, Sometime Sweepyard at the Service of the Writer. Salutem dicint. The just defunct Mrs Sanders who (the Loyd insure her!) I was shift and shuft too, with her shester Mrs Shunders, both mudical dauctors from highschoolhorse and aslyke as Easther's leggs. She was the niceliest person of a wellteached nonparty woman that I ever acquired her letters, only too fat, used to babies and tottydean verbish this is her entertermentdags for she shuk the bottle and tuk the medascene all times a day. She was well under ninety, poor late Mrs, and had tastes of the poetics, me having stood the pilgarlick a fresh at sea when the moon also was standing in a corner of sweet Standerson my ski. P.L.M Mevrouw von Andersen was her whogave me a muttonbrooch, stakkers for her begfirst party. Honour thy farmer and my litters. This, my tears, is my last will intesticle wrote off in the strutforit about their absent female assauciations which I, or perhaps any other person what squaton a toffette, have the honour to had upon their polite sophykussens in the real presence of devouted Mrs Grumby when her skin was exposed to the air. O what must the grief of my mund be for two little ptpt coolies worth twenty thousand quad herewitdnessed with both's maddlemass wishes to Pepette for next match from their dearly beloved Roggers, M.D.D. O.D. May doubling drop of drooght! Writing.

— Hopsoloosely kidding you are totether with your cadenus and goat along nose how we shall complete that white paper. Two venusstas! Biggerstiff! Qweer but gaon! Be trouz and wholetrouz! Otherwise, frank Shaun, we pursued, what would be the autobiography of your softbodied fumiform?

— Hooraymost! None whomsoever, Shaun replied, Heavenly blank! (he had intentended and was peering now rather close to the paste of his rubiny winklering) though it ought to be more or less rawcawcaw romantical. By the wag, how is Mr Fry? All of it, I might say, in ex-voto, pay and perks and wooden halfpence, some rhino, rhine, O joyoust rhine, was handled over spondaneously by me (and bundle end to my illwishers' Miss Anders! she woor her wraith of ruins the night she lost I left!) in the ligname of Mr van Howten of Tredcastles, Clowntalkin, timbreman, among my prodigits nabobs and navious of every subscription entitled the Bois in the Boscoor, our evicted tenemants. What I say is (and I am noen roehorn or culkilt permit me to tell you, if uninformed), I never spont it. Nor have I the ghuest of innation on me the way to. It is my rule so. It went anyway like hot pottagebake. And this brings me to my fresh point. Quoniam, I am as plain as portable enveloped, inhowmuch, you will now parably receive, care of one of Mooseyeare Goonness's registered andouterthus barrels. Quick take um whiffat andrainit. Now!

— So vi et! we responded. Song! Shaun, song! Have mood! Hold forth!

— I apologuise, Shaun began, but I would rather spinooze you one from the grimm gests of Jacko and Esaup, fable one, feeble too. Let us here consider the casus, my dear little cousis (husstenhasstencaffincoffintussem-tossemdamandamnacosaghcusaghhobixhatouxpeswchbechoscashl-carcarcaract) of the Ondt and the Gracehoper.

The Gracehoper was always jigging ajog, hoppy on akkant of his joyicity, (he had a partner pair of findlestilts to supplant him), or, if not, he was always making ungraceful overtures to Floh and Luse and Bienie and

Vespatilla to play pupa-pupa and pulicy-pulicy and langtennas and pushpygyddyum and to commence insects with him, there mouthparts to his orefice and his gambills to there airy processes, even if only in chaste, ameng the everlistings, behold a waspering pot. He would of curse melissciously, by his fore feelhers, flexors, contractors, depressors and extensors, lamely, harry me, marry me, bury me, bind me, till she was puce for shame and allso fourmish her in Spinner's housery at the earthsbest schoppinhour so summery as his cottage, which was cald fourmillierly Tingsomingenting, groped up. Or, if he was always striking up funny funereels with Besterfarther Zeuts, the Aged One, With all his wigeared corollas, albedinous and oldbuoyant, inscythe his elytrical wormcasket and Dehlia and Peonia, his druping nymphs, bewheedling him, compound eyes on hornitosehead, and Auld Letty Plussiboots to scratch his cacumen and cackle his tramsitus, diva deborah (seven bolls of sapo, a lick of lime, two spurts of fussfor, threefurts of sulph, a shake o'shouker, doze grains of migniss and a mesfull of midcap pitchies. The whool of the whaal in the wheel of the whorl of the Boubou from Bourneum has thus come to taon!), and with tambarins and cantoridettes soturning around his eggshill rockcoach their dance McCaper in retrophoebia, beck from bulk, like fantastic disossed and jenny aprils, to the ra, the ra, the ra, the ra, langsome heels and langsome toesis, attended to by a mutter and doffer duffmatt baxingmotch and a myrmidins of pszozlers pszinging *Satyr's Caudledayed Nice* and *Hombly, Dombly Sod We Awhile* but *Ho, Time Timeagen, Wake!* For if sciencium (what's what) can mute uns nought, 'a thought, abought the Great Sommboddy within the Omniboss, perhops an artsaccord (hoot's hoot) might sing ums tumtim abutt the Little Newbuddies that ring his panch. A high old tide for the barheated publics and the whole day as gratiis! Fudder and lighting for ally looty, any filly in a fog, for O'Cronione lags acrumbling in his sands but his sunsunsuns still tumble on. Erething above ground, as his Book of Breathings bed him, so as everwhy, sham or shunner, zeemliangly to kick time.

Grouscious me and scarab my sahull What a bagateller it is! Libelulous! Inzanzarity! Pou! Pschla! Ptuh! What a zeit for the goths! vented the Ondt, who, not being a sommerfool, was thothfolly making chilly spaces at hisphex affront of the icinglass of his windhame, which was cold antitopically Nixnixundnix. We shall not come to party at that lopp's, he decided possibly, for he is not on our social list. Nor to Ba's berial nether, thon sloghard, this oldeborre's yaar ablong as there's a khul on a khat. Nefersenless, when he had safely looked up his ovipository, he loftet hails and prayed: May he me no voida water! Seekit Hatup! May no he me tile pig shed on! Suckit

Hotup! As broad as Beppy's realm shall flourish my reign shall flourish! As high as Heppy's hevn shall flurrish my haine shall hurrish! Shall grow, shall flourish! Shall hurrish! Hummum.

The Ondt was a weltall fellow, raumybult and abelboobied, bynear saw altitudinous wee a schelling in kopfers. He was sair sair sullemn and chairmanlooking when he was not making spaces in his psyche, but, laus! when he wore making spaces on his ikey, he ware mouche mothst secred and muravyingly wisechairmanlooking. Now whim the sillybilly of a Gracehoper had jingled through a jungle of love and debts and jangled through a jumble of life in doubts afterworse, wetting with the bimblebeaks, drikking with nautonects, bilking with durrydunglecks and horing after ladybirdies (*ichnehmon diagelegenaitoikon*) he fell joust as sieck as a sexton and tantoo pooveroo quant a churchprince, and wheer the midges to wend hemsylph or vosch to sirch for grub for his corapusse or to find a hospes, alick, he wist gnit! Bruko dry! fuko spint! Sultamont osa bare! And volomundo osi videvide! Nichtsnichtsundnichts! Not one pickopeck of muscowmoney to bag a tittlebits of beebread! Iomio! Iomio! Crick's corbicule, which a plight! O moy Bog, he contrited with melanctholy. Meblizzered, him sluggered! I am heartily hungry!

He had eaten all the whilepaper, swallowed the lustres, devoured forty flights of styearcases, chewed up all the mensas and seccles, ronged the records, made mundballs of the ephemerids and vorasioused most glutinously with the very timeplace in the ternitary—not too dusty a cicada of neutriment for a chittinous chip so mitey. But when Chrysalmas was on the bare branches, off he went from Tingsomingenting. He took a round stroll and he took a stroll round and he took a round strollagain till the grillies in his head and the leivnits in his hair made him thought he had the Tossmania. Had he twicycled the sees of the deed and trestraversed their revermer? Was he come to hevre with his engiles or gone to hull with the poop? The June snows was flocking in thuckflues on the hegelstomes, millipeeds of it and myriopoods, and a lugly whizzling tournedos, the Boraborayellers, blohablasting tegolhuts up to tetties and ruching sleets off the coppeehouses, playing ragnowrock rignewreck, with an irritant, penetrant, siphonopterous spuk. Grausssssss! Opr! Graussssss! Opr!

The Gracehoper who, though blind as batflea, yet knew, not a leetle beetle, his good smetterling of entymology asped nissunitimost lous nor liceens but promptly tossed himself in the vico, phthin and phthir, on top of his buzzer, tezzily wondering wheer would his aluck alight or boss of both appease and the next time he makes the aquinatance of the Ondt after this they have met themselves, these mouschical umsummables, it shall be motylucky if he will beheld not a world of differents. Behailed His Gross the Ondt, prostrandvorous upon his dhrone, in his Papylonian babooshkees, smolking a spatial brunt of Hosana cigals, with unshrinkables farfalling from his unthinkables, swarming of himself in his sunnyroom, sated before his comfortumble phullupsuppy of a plate o'monkynous and a confucion of minthe (for he was a conformed aceticist and aristotaller), as appi as a oneysucker or a baskerboy on the Libido, with Floh biting his leg thigh and Luse lugging his luff leg and Bieni bussing him under his bonnet and Vespatilla blowing cosy fond tutties up the allabroad length of the large of his smalls. As entomate as intimate could pinchably be. Emmet and demmet and be jiltses crazed and be jadeses whipt! schneezed the Gracehoper, aguepe with ptchjelasys and at his wittol's indts, what have eyeforsight!

The Ondt, that true and perfect host, a spiter aspinne, was making the greatest spass a body could with his queens laceswinging for he was spizzing all over him like thingsumanything in formicolation, boundlessly blissfilled in an allallahbath of houris. He was ameising himself hugely at crabround and marypose, chasing Floh out of charity and tickling Luse, I hope too, and tackling Bienie, faith, as well, and jucking Vespatilla jukely by the chimiche. Never did Dorsan from Dunshanagan dance it with more devilry! The veripatetic imago of the impossible Gracehoper on his odderkop in the myre, after his thrice ephemeral journeeys, sans mantis ne shooshooe, featherweighed animule, actually and presumptuably sinctifying chronic's despair, was sufficiently and probably coocoo much for his chorous of gravitates. Let him be Artalone the Weeps with his parisites peeling off him I'll be Highfee the Crackasider. Flunkey Footle furloughed foul, writing off his phoney, but Conte Carme makes the melody that mints the money. *Ad majorem l.s.d.! Divi gloriam.* A darkener of the threshold. Haru? Orimis, capsizer of his antboat, sekketh rede from Evil-it-is, lord of loaves in Amongded. Be it! So be it! Thou-who-thou-art, the fleet-as-spindhrift, impfang thee of mine wideheight. Haru!

The thing pleased him andt, and andt,
He larved ond he larved on he merd such a nauses
The Gracehoper feared he would mixplace his fauces.
I forgive you, grondt Ondt, said the Gracehoper, weeping,
For their sukes of the sakes you are safe in whose keeping.
Teach Floh and Luse polkas, show Bienie where's sweet
And be sure Vespatilla fines fat ones to heat.
As I once played the piper I must now pay the count
So saida to Moyhammlet and marhaba to your Mount!

Let who likes lump above so what flies be a full 'un;
I could not feel moregruggy if this was prompollen.
I pick up your reproof, the horsegift of a friend,
For the prize of your save is the price of my spend.
Can castwhores pulladeftkiss if oldpollocks forsake 'em
Or Culex feel etchy if Pulex don't wake him?
A locus to loue, a term it t'embarass,
These twain are the twins that tick Homo Vulgaris.
Has Aquileone nort winged to go syf
Since the Gwyfyn we were in his farrest drewbryf
And that Accident Man not beseeked where his story ends
Since longsephyring sighs sought heartseast for their orience?
We are Wastenot with Want, precondamned, two and true,
Till Nolans go volants and Bruneyes come blue.
Ere those gidflirts now gadding you quit your mocks for my gropes
An extense must impull, an elapse must elopes,
Of my tectucs takestock, tinktact, and ail's weal;
As I view by your farlook hale yourself to my heal.
Partiprise my thinwhins whiles my blink points unbroken on
Your whole's whercabroads with Tout's trightyright token on.
My in risible universe youdly haud find
Sulch oxtrabeeforeness meat soveal behind.
Your feats end enormous, your volumes immense,
(May the Graces I hoped for sing your Ondtship song sense!),
Your genus its worldwide, your spacest sublime!
But, Holy Saltmartin, why can't you beat time?

In the name of the former and of the latter and of their holocaust. Allmen.

— Now? How good you are in explosition! How farflung is your fokloire and how velktingeling your volupkabulary! *Qui vive sparanto qua muore contanto.* O foibler, O flip, you've that wandervogl wail withyin! It falls easily upon the earopen and goes down the friskly shortiest like treacling tumtim with its tingtingtaggle. The blarneyest blather in all Corneywall! But could you, of course, decent Lettrechaun, we knew (to change your name of not your nation) while still in the barrel, read the strangewrote anaglyptics of those shemletters patent for His Christian's Em?

— Greek! Hand it to me! Shaun replied, plosively pointing to the cinnamon quistoquill behind his acoustrolobe. I'm as afterdusk nobly Roman as pope and water could christen me. Look at that for a ridingpin! I am, thing Sing Larynx, letter potent to play the sem backwards like Oscan wild or in shunt Persse transluding from the Otherman or off the Toptic or anything off the types of my finklers in the draught or with buttles, with my oyes thickshut and all. But, hellas, it is harrobrew bad on the corns and callouses. As far as that goes I associate myself with your remark just now from theodicy *re*'furloined notepaper and quite agree in your prescriptions for indeed I am, pay Gay, in juxtaposition to say it is not a nice production. It is a pinch of scribble, not wortha bottle of cabbis. Overdrawn! Puffedly offal tosh! Besides its auctionable, all about crime and libel! Nothing beyond clerical horrors *et omnibus* to be entered for the foreign as secondclass matter. The fuellest filth ever fired since Charley Lucan's. Flummery is what I would call it if you were to ask me to put it on a single dimension what pronounced opinion I might possibly orally have about them bagses of trash which the mother and Mr Unmentionable (O breed not his same!) has reduced to writing without making news out of my sootynemm. When she slipped under her couchman. And where he made a cat with a peep. How they wore two madges on the makewater. And why there were treefellers in the shrubrubs. Then he hawks his handmud figgers from Francie to Fritzie down in the kookin. Phiz is me mother and Hair's me father. Bauv Betty Famm and Pig Pig Pike. Their livetree (may it flourish!) by their ecotaph (let it stayne!). With balsinbal bimbies swarming tiltop. Comme bien, Comme bien! Feefeel! Feefeel! And the Dutches dyin loffin at his pon peck de Barec. And all the mound reared. Till he wot not wot to begin he should. An infant sailing eggshells on the floor of a wet day would have more sabby.

Letter, carried of Shaun, son of Hek, written of Shem, brother of Shaun, uttered for Alp, mother of Shem, for Hek, father of Shaun. Initialled. Gee. Gone. 29 Hardware Saint. Lendet till Laonum. Baile-Atha-Cliath. 31 Jan. 1132 A.D. Here Commerces Enville. Tried Apposite House. 13 Fitzgibbets. Loco. Dangerous. Tax 9d. B.L. Guineys, esqueer. L.B. Not known at 1132 a. 12 Norse Richmound. Nave unlodgeable. Loved noa's dress. Sinned, Jetty Pierrse. Noon sick parson. 92 Windsewer. Ave. No such no. Vale. Finn's Hot. Exbelled from 1014 d. Pulldown. Fearview. Opened by Miss Take. 965 nighumpledan sextifffits. Shout at Site. Roofloss. Fit Dunlop and Be Satisfied. Mr. Domnall O'Domnally. Q.V. 8 Royal Terrors. None so strait. Shutter up. Dining with the Danes. Removed to Philip's Burke. At sea. D.E.D. Place scent on. Clontalk. Father Jacob, Rice Factor. 3 Castlewoos. P.V. Arrusted. J.P. Converted to Hospitalism. Ere the March past of Civilisation. Once Bank of Ireland's. Return to City Arms. 2 Milchbroke. Wrongly spilled. Traumcondraws. Now Bunk of England's. Drowned in the Laffey. Here. The Reverest Adam Foundlitter. Shown geshotten. 7 Streetpetres. Since Cabranke. Seized of the Crownd. Well, Sir Arthur. Buy Patersen's Matches. Unto his promisk hands. Blown up last Lemmas by Orchid Lodge. Search Unclaimed Male. House Condamned by Ediles. Back in Few Minutes. Closet for Repeers. 60 Shellburn. Key at Kate's. Kiss. Isaac's Butt, Poor Man. Dalicious arson. Caught. Missing. Justiciated. Kainly forewarned. Abraham Badly's King, Park Bogey. Salved. All reddy berried. Hollow and eavy. Desert it. Overwayed. Understrumped. Back to the P.O. Kaer of. Ownes owe M.O. Too Let. To Be Soiled. Cohabited by Unfortunates. Lost all Licence. His Bouf Toe is Frozen Over. X, Y and Z, Ltd, Destinied Tears. A.B, ab, Sender. Boston (Mass). 31 Jun. 13, 12. P.D. Razed. Lawyered. Vacant. Mined. Here's the Bayleaffs. Step out to Hall out of that, Ereweaker, with your Bloody Big Bristol. Bung. Stop. Bung. Stop. Cumm Bumm. Stop. Came Baked to Auld Aireen. Stop.

— Kind Shaun, we all requested, much as we hate to say it, but since you rose to the use of money have you not, without suggesting for an instant, millions of moods used up slanguage tun times as words as the penmarks used out in sinscript with such hesitancy by your cerebrated brother— excuse me not mentioningahem?

— CelebrAted! Shaun replied under the sheltar of his broguish, vigorously rubbing his magic lantern to a glow of fullconsciousness. HeCitEncy! Your words grates on my ares. Notorious I rather would feel inclined to myself in the first place to describe Mr O'Shem the Draper with before letter as should I be accentually called upon for a dieoguinnsis to pass my opinions, properly spewing, into impulsory irelitz. But I would not care to be so unfruitful to my own part as to swear for the moment positively as to the views of Denmark. No, sah! But let me say my every belief before my high Gee is that I much doubt of it. I've no room for that fellow on my fagroaster, I just can't. As I hourly learn from Rooters and Havers through Gilligan's maypoles in a nice pathetic notice he, the pixillated doodler, is on his last with illegible clergimanths boasting always of his ruddy complexious! She, the mammy far, was put up to it by him, the iniquity that ought to be depraved of his libertins to be silenced, sackclothed and suspended, and placed in irons into some drapery institution off the antipopees for wordsharping only if he was klanver enough to pass the panel fleischcurers and the fieldpost censor. Gach! For that is a fullblown fact and well celibated before the four divorce courts and all the King's paunches, how he has the solitary from seeing Scotch snakes and has a lowsense for the production of consumption and dalickey cyphalos on his brach premises where he can purge his contempt and dejeunerate into a skillyton be thinking himself to death. Rot him! Flannelfeet! Flattyro! I will describe you in a word. Thou. (I beg your pardon.) Homo! Then putting his bedfellow on me! (like into mike and nick onto post). The criniman: I'll give it to him for that! Making the lobbard change hisstops, as we say in the long book! Is he on whose-keeping or are my! Obnoximost posthumust! With his unique hornbook and his prince of the apauper's pride, blundering all over the two worlds! If he waits till I buy him a mosselman's present! Ho's nos halfcousin of mine, pigdish! Nor wants to! I'd famish with the cuistha first. Aham!

— May we petition you, Shaun illustrious, then, to put his prentis' pride in your aproper's purse and to unravel in your own sweet way with words of style to your very and most obsequient, we suggested, with yet an esiop's foible, as to how?

— Well it is partly my own, isn't it? and you may, ought and welcome, Shaun replied, taking at the same time, as his hunger got the bitter of him, a hearty bite out of the honeycomb of his Braham and Melosedible hat, tryone, tryon and triune. Ann wunkum. Sure, I thunkum you knew all about that, honorey causes, through thelemontary channels long agum. Sure, that is as old as the Baden bees of Saint Dominoc's and as commonpleas now to allus pueblows and bunkum as Nelson his trifulgurayous pillar. However. Let me see, do. Beerman's bluff was what begun it, Old Knoll and his borrowing! And then the liliens of the veldt, Nancy Nickies and Folletta Lajambe! Then mem and hem and the jaquejack. All about Wucherer and righting his name for him. I regret to announce, after laying out his litterery bed, for two days she kept squealing down for noisy priors and bawling out to her jameymock farceson in Shemish like a mouther of the incas with a garcielasso huw Ananymus pinched her tights and about the Balt with the markshaire parawag and his loyal divorces, when he feraxiously shed ovas in Alemaney, tse tse, all the tell of the tud with the bourighevisien backclack, and him, the cribibber like an ambitrickster, aspiring like the decan's, fast aslooped in the intrance to his polthronechair with his sixth finger between his catseye and the index, making his pillgrimace of Childe Horrid, engrossing to his ganderpan what the idioglossary he invented under hicks hyssop! Hock! Ickick gav him that toock, imitator! And it was entirely theck latter to blame. Does he drink because I am sorely there shall be no more Kates and Nells. If you see him it took place there. It was given meeck, thank the Bench, to assist at the whole thing byck special chancery licence. As often as I think of that unbloody housewarmer, Shem Skrivenitch, always cutting my prhose to please his phrase, bogorror, I declare I get the jawache! Be me punting his reflection he'd begin his beogrefright in muddyass ribalds. Digteter! Grundtsagar! Swop beef! You know he's peculiar, that eggschicker, with the smell of old woman off him, to suck nothing of his switchedupes. M.D. made his *ante mortem* for him. He was grey at three, like sygnus the swan, when he made his boo to the public and barnacled up to the eyes when he repented after seven. The alum that winters on his top is the stale of the staun that will soar when he stambles till that hag of the coombe rapes the pad off his lock. He was down with the whooping laugh at the age of the loss of reason the whopping first time he prediseased me. He's weird, I tell you, and middayevil down to his vegetable soul. Never mind his falls feet and his tanbark complexion. That's why he was forbidden tomate and was warmed off the ricecourse of marrimoney, under the Helpless Corpses Enactment. I'm not at all surprised the saint kicked him whereby the sum taken Berkeley showed the reason genrously. *Negas, negasti*—negertop, negertoe, negertoby, negrunter! Then he was pusched out of Thingamuddy's school by Miss Garterd, for itching. Then he caught the europicolas and went into the society of jewses. With Bro Cahlls and Fran Czeschs and Bruda Pszths and Brat Slavos. One temp when he foiled to be killed, the freak wanted to put his bilingual head intentionally through the *Ikish Tames* and go and join the clericy as a demonican skyterrier. Throwing dust in the eyes of the Hooley Fermers! He used to be avowdeed as he ought to be vitandist. For onced I squeaked by twyst I'll squelch him. Then he went to Cecilia's treat on his solo to pick up Galen. Asbestopoulos! Inkupot! He has encaust in the blood. Shim! I have the outmost conempt for. Prost bitten! Conshy! Tiberia is waiting on you, arestocrank! Chaka a seagull ticket at Gattabuia and Gabbiano's! Go o'er the sea, haythen, from me and leave your libber to TCD. Your puddin is cooked! You're served, cram ye! Fatefully yaourth . . . Ex. Ex. Ex. Ex.

— But for what, thrice truthful teller, Shaun of grace? weakly we went on to ask now of the gracious one. Vouchsafe to say. You will now, goodness, won't you? Why?

— For his root language, if you ask me whys, Shaun replied, as he blessed himself devotionally like a crawsbomb, making act of oblivion, footinmouther! (what the thickuns else?) which he picksticked into his lettruce invrention. Ullhodturdenweirmudgaardgringnirurdrmolnirfenrir-lukkilokkibaugimandodrrerinsurtkrinmgernrackinarockar! Thor's for yo!

— The hundredlettered name again, last word of perfect language. But you could come near it, we do suppose, strong Shaun O', we foresupposed. How?

— Peax! Peax! Shaun replied in vealar penultimatum. 'Tis pebils before Sweeney's as he swigged a slug of Jon Jacobsen from his treestem sucker cane. Mildbut likesome! I might as well be talking to the four waves till

tibbes grey eves and the rests asleep. Frost! Nope! No one in his seven
senses could as I have before said, only you missed my drift, for it's being
incendiary. Every dimmed letter in it is a copy and not a few of the silbils
and wholly words I can show you in my Kingdom of Heaven. The
lowquacity of him! With his threestar monothong! Thaw! The last word in
stolentelling! And what's more rightdown lowbrown schisthematic
robblemint! Yes. As he was rising my lather. Like you. And as I was plucking
his goosybone. Like yea. He store the tale of me shur. Like yup. How's that
for Shemese?

— Still in a way, not to flatter you, we fancy you that you are so strikingly
brainy and well letterread in yourshelves as ever were the Shamous
Shamonous, Limited, could use worse of yourself, ingenious Shaun, we still
so fancied, if only you would take your time so and the trouble of so doing
it. Upu now!

— Undoubtedly but that is show, Shaun replied, the muttermelk of his
blood donor beginning to work, and while innocent of disseminating the
foul emanation, it would be a fall day I could not, sole, so you can keep your
space and by the power of blurry wards I am loyable to do it (I am convicted
of it!) any time ever I liked (bet ye fippence off me boot allowance!) with the
allergrossest transfusiasm as, you see, while I can soroquise the Siamanish
better than most, it is an openear secret, be it said, how I am extremely
ingenuous at the clerking even with my badily left and, arrah go braz, I'd
pinsel it with immenuensoes as easy as I'd perorate a chickerow of beans for
the price of two maricles and my trifolium librotto, the authordux Book of
Lief, would, if given to daylight, (I hold a most incredible faith about it) far
exceed what that bogus bolshy of a shame, my soamheis brother, Gaoy
Fecks, is conversant with in audible black and prink. Outragedy of
poetscalds! Acomedy of letters! I have them all, tame, deep and harried, in
my mine's I. And one of these fine days, man dear, when the mood is on me,
that I may willhap cut my throat with my tongue tonight but I will be
ormuzd moved to take potlood and introvent it Paatryk just like a work of
merit, mark my words and append to my mark twang, that will open your
pucktricker's ops for you, broather brooher, only for, as a papst and an
immature and a nayophight and a *spaciaman spaciosum* and a hundred and
eleven other things, I would never for anything take so much trouble of
such doing. And why so? Because I am altogether a chap too fly and
hairyman for to infradig the like of that ultravirulence. And by all I hold
sacred on earth clouds and in heaven I swear to you on my piop and oath by
the awe of Shaun (and that's a howl of a name!) that I will commission to the
flames any incendiarist whosoever or ahriman howsoclever who would

endeavour to set ever annyma roner moother of mine on fire. Rock me julie but I will soho!

And, with that crickcrackcruck of his threelungged squool from which grief had usupped every smile, big hottempered husky fusky krenfy strenfy pugiliser, such as he was, he virtually broke down on the mooherhead, getting quite jerry over her, overpowered by himself with the love of the tearsilver that he twined through her hair for, sure, he was the soft semplgawn slob of the world with a heart like Montgomery's in his showchest and harvey loads of feeling in him and as innocent and undesignful as the freshfallen calef. Still, grossly unselfish in sickself, he dished allarmes away and laughed it off with a wipe at his pudgies and a gulp apologetic, healing his tare be the smeyle of his oye, oogling around. Him belly no belong sollow mole pigeon. Ally bully. Fu Li's gulpa. Mind you, now, that he was in the dumpest of earnest orthough him jawr war hoo hleepy hor halk urthing hurther. Moe like that only he stopped short in looking up up upfrom his tide shackled wrists through the ghost of an ocean's, the wieds of pansiful heathvens of joepeter's gaseytotum as they are telling not but were and will be, all told, scruting foreback into the fargone-ahead to feel out what age in years tropical, ecclesiastic, civil or sidereal he might find by the sirious pointstand of Charley's Wain (what betune the spheres sledding along the lacteal and the mansions of the blest turning on old times) as erewhile had he craved of thus, the dreamskhwindel necklassoed him, his thumbs fell into his fists and, lusosing the harmonical balance of his ballbearing extremities, by the holy kettle, like a flask of lightning over he careened (O the sons of the fathers!) by the mightyfine weight of his barrel (all that prevented the happering of who if not the asterisks betwink themselves shall ever?) and, as the wisest postlude course he could playact, collaspsed in ensemble and rolled buoyantly backwards in less than a twinkling via Rattigan's corner out of farther earshot with his highly curious mode of slipashod motion, surefoot, sorefoot, slickfoot, slackfoot, linkman laizurely, lampman loungey, and by Killesther's lapes and falls, with corks, staves and treeleaves and more bubbles to his keelrow a fairish and easy way enough as the town cow cries behind the times in the direction of Mac Auliffe's, the crucethouse, *Open the Door Softly*, down in the valley before he was really uprighted ere in a dip of the downs (uila!) he spoorlessly disappaled and vanesshed, like a popo down a papa, from circular circulatio. Ah, mean!

Gaogaogaone! Tapaa!

And the stellas were shinings. And the earthnight strewed aromatose. His pibrook creppt mong the donkness. A reek was waft on the luftstream. He was ours, all fragrance. And we were his for a lifetime. O dulcid dreamings languidous! Taboccoo!

It was sharming! But sharmeng!

And the lamp went out as it couldn't glow on burning, yep, the lmp wnt out for it couldn't stay alight.

Well, (how dire do we thee hours when thylike fades!) all's dall and youllow and it is to bedowern that thou art passing hence, mine bruder, able Shaun, with a twhisking of the robe, ere the morning of light calms our hardest throes? beyond cods' cradle and porpoise plain, from camal relations undfamiliar faces, to the inds of Tuskland where the oliphants scrum till the ousts of Amiracles where the toll stories grow proudest, more is the pity, but for all your deeds of goodness you were soo ooft and for ever doing, manomano and myriamilia even to mulimuli, as our humbler classes, whose virtue is humility, can tell, it is hardly we in the country of the old, Sean Moy, can part you for, oleypoe, you were the walking saint, you were, tootoo too stayer, the graced of gods and pittites and the salus of the wake. Countenance whose disparition afflictedly fond Fuinn feels. Winner of the gamings, primed at the studience, propredicted from the storybouts, the choice of ages wise! Spickspookspokesman of our spectquresque silentiousness! Musha, beminded of us out there in Cockpit, poor twelve o'clock scholars, sometime or other anywhen you think the time. Wisha, becoming back to us way home in Biddyhouse one way or either anywhere we miss your smile. Palmwine breadfruit sweetmeat milksoup! Suasusupo! However! Our people here in Samoanesia will not be after forgetting you and the elders luking and marking the jornies, chalkin up drizzle in drizzle out on the four bare mats. How you would be thinking in your thoughts how the deepings did it all begin and how you would be scrimmaging through your scruples to collar a hold of an imperfection being committled. Sireland calls you. Mery Loye is saling moonlike. And Slyly mamourneen's ladymaid at Gladshouse Lodge. Turn your coat, strong character, and tarry among us down the vale, yougander, only once more! And may the mosse of prosperousness gather you rolling home! May foggy dews bediamondise your hooprings! May the fireplug of filiality reinsure your bunghole! May the barleywind behind glow luck to your bathershins! 'Tis well we know you were loth to leave us, winding your hobbledehorn, right royal post, but, aruah sure, pulse of our slumber, dreambookpage, by the grace of Votre Dame, when the natural morning of your nocturne blankmerges into the national morning of golden sunup and Don Leary gets his own back from old grog Georges Quartos as that goodship the Jonnyjoys takes the wind from waterloogged Erin's king, you will shiff across the Moylendsea and round up in your own escapology some canonisator's day or other, sack on back, alack! digging snow, (not so?) like the good man you are, with your picture pockets turned knockside out in the rake of the rain for fresh remittances and from that till this in any case, timus tenant, may the tussocks grow quickly under your trampthickets and the daisies trip lightly over your battercops.

[2]

JAUNTYJAUN, AS I WAS SHORTLY BEFORE THAT MADE aware, next halted to fetch a breath, the first cothurminous leg of his nightstride being pulled through, and to loosen (let God's son now be looking down on the poor preambler!) both of his bruised brogues that were plainly made a good bit before his hosen were, at the weir by Lazar's Walk (for far and wide, as large as he was lively, was he noted for his humane treatment of any kind of abused footgear), a matter of maybe nine score or so barrelhours distance off as truly he merited to do. He was there, you could planemetrically see, when I took a closer look at him, that was to say, (gracious helpings, at this rate of growing our cotted child of yestereve will soon fill space and burst in systems, so speeds the instant!) amply altered for the brighter, though still the graven image of his squarer self as he was used to be, perspiring but happy notwithstanding his foot was still asleep on him, the way he thought, by the holy januarious, he had a bullock's hoof in his buskin, with his halluxes so splendid, through Ireland untranscended, bigmouthed poesther, propped up, restant, against a butterblond warden of the peace, one comestabulish Sigurdsen, (and where a better than such exsearfaceman to rest from roving the laddyown he bootblacked?) who, buried upright like the Osbornes, kozydozy, had tumbled slumbersomely on sleep at night duty behind the curing station, equilebriated amid the embracings of a monopolized bottle.

Now, there were as many as twentynine hedge daughters out of Benent Saint Berched's national nightschool (for they seemed to remember how it was still a once-upon-a-four year) learning their antemeridian lesson of life, under its tree, against its warning, beseated, as they were, upon the brinkspondy, attracted to the rarerust sight of the first human yellowstone landmark (the bear, the boer, the king of all boors, sir Humphrey his knave we met on the moors!) while they paddled away, keeping time magnetically with their eight and fifty pedalettes, playing foolu-fool jouay allo misto posto, O so jaonickally, all barely in their typtap teens, describing a charming dactylogram of nocturnes though repelled by the snores of the log who looked stuck to the sod as ever and oft, when liquefied, (vil!) he murmoaned abasourdly in his Dutchener's native, visibly unmoved, over his treasure trove for the crown: *Dotter dead bedstead mean diggy smuggy flasky.*

Jaun (after he had in the first place doffed a hat with a reinforced crown and bowed to all the others in that chorus of praise of goodwill girls on their best beehiviour who all they were girls all rushing sowarmly for the post as buzzy as sie could bie to read his kisshands, kittering all about, rushing and making a tremendous girlsfuss over him pellmale, their *jeune premier* and his rosyposy smile, mussing his frizzy hair and the golliwog curls of him, all, but that one; Finfria's fairest, done in loveletters like a trayful of cloudberry tartlets (ain't they fine, mighty, mighty fine and honoured?) and smilingly smelling, pair and pair about, broad by bread and slender to slimmer, the nice perfumios that came cunvy peeling off him (nice!) which was angelic simply, savouring of wild thyme and parsley jumbled with breadcrumbs (O nice!) and feeling his full fat pouch for him so tactily and jingaling his jellybags for, though he looked a young chapplie of sixtine, they could frole by his manhood that he was just the killingest ladykiller all by kindness, now you, Jaun, asking kindlily (hillo, missies!) after their howareyous at all with those of their dollybegs (and where's Agatha's lamb? and how are Bernadetta's columbillas? and Juliennaw's tubberbunnies? and Eulalina's tuggerfunnies?) he next went on (finefeelingfit!) to drop a few stray remarks anent their personal appearances and the contrary tastes displayed in their tight kittycasques and their smart frickyfrockies, asking coy one after sloy one had she read Irish legginds and gently reproving one that the ham of her hom could be seen below her hem and whispering another aside, as lavariant, that the hook of her hum was open a bittock at her back to have a sideeye to that, hom, (and all of course just to fill up a form out of pure human kindness and in a sprite of fun) for Jaun, by the way, was by the way of becoming (I think, I hope he was) the most purely human being that ever was called man, loving all up and down the whole creation from Sampson's tyke to Jones's sprat and from the King of all Wrenns down to infuseries) Jaun, after those few prelimbs made out through his eroscope the apparition of his fond sister Izzy for he knowed his love by her waves of splabashing and she showed him proof by her way of blabushing nor could he forget her so tarnelly easy as all that since he was brotherbesides her benedict godfather and heaven knows he thought the world and his life of her sweet heart could buy, (brao!) poor, good, true, Jaun!

— Sister dearest, Jaun delivered himself with express cordiality, marked

by clearance of diction and general delivery, as he began to take leave of his
scolastica at once so as to gain time with deep affection, we honestly believe
you sorely will miss us the moment we exit yet we feel as a martyr to the
dischurch of all duty that it is about time, by Great Harry, we would shove
off to stray on our long last journey and not be the load on ye. This is the
gross proceeds of your teachings in which we were raised, you, sis, that used
to write to us the exceeding nice letters for presentation and would be
telling us anun (full well do we wont to recall to mind) thy oldworld tales of
homespinning and derringdo and dieobscure and daddyho, these tales
which reliterately whisked off our heart so narrated by thou, gesweest, to
perfection, our pet pupil of the whole rhythmetic class and the mainsay of
our erigenal house, the time we younkers twain were fairly tossing ourselves
(O Phoebus! O Pollux!) in bed, having been laid up with Castor's oil on the
Parrish's syrup (the night we will remember) for to share our hard suite of
affections with thee.

I rise, O fair assemblage! Andcommincio. Now then, after this introit of
exordium, my galaxy girls, *quiproquo* of directions to henservants I was
asking his advice on the strict T.T. from Father Mike, P.P., my orational
dominican and confessor doctor, C.C.D.D. (buy the birds, he was saying as
he yerked me under the ribs sermon in an offrand way and confidence
petween peas like ourselves in soandso many nuncupiscent words about
how he had been confarreating teat-a-teat with two viragos intactas about
what an awful life he led, poorish priced, uttering mass for a coppall of
geldings and what a lawful day it was, there and then, for a consommation
with an effusion and how, by all the manny larries ate pignatties, how, hell
in tunnels, he'd marry me any old buckling time as flying quick as he'd look
at me) and I am giving youth now again in words of style byaway of offertory
hisand mikeadvice, an it place the person, as ere he retook him to his cure,
those verbs he said to me. From above. The most eminent bishop titular of
Dubloonik to all his purtybusses in Dellabelliney. Comeallyedimseldamsels,
siddle down and lissle all! Follow me close! Keep me in view! Understeady
me saries! Which is to all practising massoeurses from a preaching freer and
be a gentleman without a duster before a parlourmade without a spitch.
Now. During our brief apsence from this furtive feugtig season adhere to as
many as probable of the ten commandments, touching purgations and
indulgences and in the long run they will prove for your better guidance
along your path of right of way. Where the lisieuse are we and what's the
first sing to be sung? Is it rubrics, mandarimus, pasqualines, or verdidads is
in it, or the bruiselivid indecores of estreme voyoulence and, for the lover of
lithurgy, bekant or besant, where's the fate's to be wished for? Several

sindays after whatsintime. I'll sack that sick server the minute I bless him.
That's the mokst I can do for his grapce. Economy of movement, axe why
said. I've a hopesome's choice if I chouse of all the sinkts in the colander.
From the common for ignitious Purpalume to the proper of Francisco
Ultramare, last of scorchers, third of snows, in terrorgammons howdydos.
Here she's, is a bell, that's wares in heaven, virginwhite, Undetrigesima,
vikissy manonna. Doremon's! The same or similar to be kindly observed
within the affianced dietcess of Gay O'Toole and Gloamy Gwenn du Lake
(Danish spoken!) from Manducare Monday up till farrier's siesta in china
dominos. Words taken in triumph, my sweet assistance, from the sufferant
pen of our jocosus inkerman militant of the reed behind the ear.

Never miss your lostsomewhere mass for the couple in Myles you butrose
to brideworship. Never hate mere pork which is bad for your knife of a
good friday. Never let a hog of the howth trample underfoot your linen of
Killiney. Never play lady's game for the Lord's stake. Never lose your heart
away till you win his diamond back. Make a strong point of never kicking up
your rumpus over the scroll end of sofas in the Dar Bey Coll Cafeteria by
tootling risky *apropos* songs at commercial travellers' smokers for their
Columbian nights entertainments the like of *White limbs they never stop
teasing* or *Minxy was a Manxmaid when Murry wor a Man*. And, by the bun,
is it you goes bisbuiting His Esaus and Cos and then throws them bag in the
box? Why the tin's nearly empty. First thou shalt not smile. Twice thou
shalt not love. Lust, thou shalt not commix idolatry. Hip confiners help
compunction. Never park your brief stays in the men's convenience. Never
clean your buttoncups with your dirty pair of sassers. Never ask his first
person where's your quickest cut to our last place. Never let the promising
hand usemake free of your oncemaid sacral. The soft side of the axe! A coil
of cord, a colleen coy, a blush on a bush turned first man's laughter into
wailful moither. O foolish cuppled! Ah, dice's error! Never dip in the ern
while you've browsers on your suite. Never slip the silver key through your
gate of golden age. Collide with man, collude with money. Ere you sail
foreget my prize. Where you truss be circumspicious and look before you
leak, dears. Never christen medlard apples till a swithin is in sight. Wet your
thistle where a weed is and you'll rue it, despyneedis. Especially beware
please of being at a party to any demoralizing home life. That saps a chap.
Keep cool faith in the firm, have warm hoep in the house and begin frem
athome to be chary of charity. Where it is nobler in the main to supper than
the boys and errors of outrager's virtue. Give back those stolen kisses;
restaure those allcotten glooves. Recollect the yella perals that all too often
beset green gerils, Rhidarhoda and Daradora, once they gethobbyhorsical,

playing breeches parts for Bessy Sudlow in fleshcoloured pantos instead of earthing down in the coalhole trying to boil the big gun's dinner. Leg-before-Wicked lags-behind-Wall where here Mr Whicker whacked a great fall. Femorafamilla feeled it a candleliked but Hayes, Conyngham and Erobinson sware it's an egg. Forglim mick aye! Stay, forestand and tillgive it! Remember the biter's bitters I shed the vigil I buried our Harlotte Quai from poor Mrs Mangain's of Britain Court on the feast of Marie Maudlin. Ah, who would wipe her weeper dry and lead her to the halter? Sold in her heyday, laid in the straw, bought for one puny petunia. Moral: if you can't point a lily get to henna out of here! Put your swell foot foremost on foulardy pneumonia shertwaists, irriconcilible with true fiminin risirvition and ribbons of lace, limenick's disgrace. Sure, what is it on the whole only holes tied together, the merest and transparent washingtones to make Languid Lola's lingery longer? Scenta Clauthes stiffstuffs your hose and heartsies full of temptiness. Vanity flee and Verity fear! Diobell! Whale-bones and buskbutts may hurt you (thwackaway thwuck!) but never lay bare your breast secret (dickette's place!) to joy a Jonas in the Dolphin's Barncar with your meetual fan, Doveyed Covetfilles, comepulsing paynattention spasms between the averthisment for Ulikah's wine and a pair of pulldoors of the old cupiosity shape. There you'll fix your eyes darkled on the autocart of the bringfast cable but here till youre martimorphysed please sit still face to face. For if the shorth of your skorth falls down to his knees pray how wrong will he look till he rises? Not before Gravesend is commuted. But now reappears Autist Algy, the pulcherman and would-do performer, *oleas* Mr Smuth, stated by the vice crusaders to be well known to all the dally-taunties in and near the ciudad of Buellas Arias, taking you to the playgue-house to see the *Smirching of Venus* and asking with whispered offers in a very low bearded voice, with a nice little tiny manner and in a very nice little tony way, won't you be an artist's moral and pose in your nudies as a local esthetic before voluble old masters, introducing you, left to right the party comprises, to hogarths like Bottisilly and Titteretto and Vergognese and Coraggio with their extrahand Mazzaccio, plus the usual bilker's dozen of dowdycameramen. And the volses of lewd Buylan, for innocence! And the phyllisophies of Bussup Bulkeley. O, the frecklessness of the giddies nouveautays! There's many's the icepolled globetopper is haunted by the hottest spot under his equator like Ramrod, the meaty hunter, always jaeger for a thrust. The back beautiful, the undraped divine! And Suzy's Moedl's with their Blue Danuboyes! All blah! Viper's vapid vilest! Put off the old man at the very font and get right on with the nutty sparker round the back. Slip your oval out of touch and let the paravis be your goal. Up leather,

Prunella, convert your try! Stick wicks in your earshells when you hear the prompter's voice. Look on a boa in his beauty and you'll never more wear your strawberry leaves. Rely on the relic. What bondman ever you bind on earth I'll be bound 'twas combined in hemel. Keep airly hores and the worm is yores. Dress the pussy for her nighty and follow her piggytails up their way to Winkyland. See little poupeep she's firsht ashleep. After having sat your poetries and you know what happens when chine throws over jupan. Go to doss with the poulterer, you understand, and shake up with the milchmand. The Sully van vultures are on the prowl. And the hailies fingringmaries. Tobaccos tabu and toboggan's a back seat. Secret satieties and onanymous letters make the great unwatched as bad as their betters. Don't on any account acquire a paunchon for that alltoocommon fagbutt habit of frequenting and chumming together with the braces of couples in Mr Tunnelly's hallways (smash it) wriggling with lowcusses and cockchafers and vamps and rodants, with the end to commit acts of interstipital indecency as between twineties and tapegarters, fingerpats on fondlepets, under the couvrefeu act. It's the thin end; wedge your steps! Your high powered hefty hoyden thinks nothing of ramping through a whole suite of smokeless husbands. Three minutes I'm counting you. Woooooon. No triching now! Give me that when I tell you! *Ragazza ladra!* And is that any place to be smuggling his madam's apples up? Deceitful jade. Gee wedge! Begor, I like the way they're half cooked. Hold, flay, grill, fire that laney feeling for kosenkissing disgenically within the proscribed limits like Population Peg on a hint or twim clandestinely does be doing to Temptation Tom, atkings questions in barely and snakking svarewords like a nursemagd. While there's men-o'war on the say there'll be loves-o'women on the do. Love through the usual channels, cisternbrothelly, when properly dis-infected and taken neat in the generable way upon retiring to roost in the company of a husband-in-law or other respectable relative of an apposite sex, not love that leads by the nose as I foresmellt but canalised love, you understand, does a felon good, suspiciously if he has a slugger's liver but I cannot belabour the point too ardently (and after the lessions of experience I speak from inspiration) that fetid spirits is the thief of prurities, so none of your twenty rod cherrywhisks, me daughter! At the Cat and Coney or the Spotted Dog. And at 2 bis Lot's Road. When parties get tight for each other they lose all respect together. By the stench of her fizzle and the glib of her gab know the drunken draggletail Dublin drab. You'll pay for each bally sorraday night every billing sumday morning. When the night is in May and the moon shines might. We won't meeth in Navan till you try to give the Kellsfrieclub the goby. Hill or hollow, Hull or Hague! And beware how you dare of wet cocktails in Kildare or the same may see your wedding driving home from your wake. Mades of ashens when you flirt spoil the lad but spare his shirt! Lay your lilylike long his shoulder but buck back if he buts bolder and just hep your homely hop and heed no horning but if you've got some brainy notion to raise cancan and rouse commotion I'll be apt to flail that tail for you till it's borning. Let the love ladleliked at the eye girde your gastricks in the gym. Nor must you omit to screw the lid firmly on that jazz jiggery and kick starts. Bumping races on the flat and point to point over obstacles. Ridewheeling that acclivisciously up windy Rutland Rise and insighting rebellious northers before the saunter of the city of Dunlob. Then breretonbiking on the free with your airs of go-be-dee and your heels upon the handlebars. Berrboel brazenness! No, before your corselage rib is decartilaged, that is to mean if you have visceral ptossis, my point is, making allowances for the fads of your weak abdominal wall and your liver asprewl, vinvin, vinvin, or should you feel, in shorts, as though you needed healthy physicking exorcise to flush your kidneys, you understand, and move that twelffinger bowel and threadworm inhibitating it, lassy, and perspire freely, lict your lector in the lobby and why out you go by the ostiary on to the dirt track and skip! Be a sportive. Deal with Nature the great greengrocer and pay regularly the monthlies. Your Punt's Perfume's only in the hatpinny shop beside the reek of the rawny. It's more important than air—I mean than eats—air (Oop, I never open momouth but I pack mefood in it) and promotes that natural emotion. Stamp out bad eggs. Why so many puddings prove disappointing, as Dietician says, in Creature Comforts Causeries, and why so much soup is so muck slop. If we could fatten on the elizabeetons we wouldn't have teeth like the hippopotamians. However. Likewise if I were in your envelope shirt I'd keep my weathereye well cocked open for your furnished lodgers paying for their feed on tally with company and piano tunes. Only stuprifying yourself! The too friendly friend sort, Mazourikawitch or some other sukinsin of a vitch, who he's kommen from olt Pannonia on this porpoise whom sue stooderin about the maul and femurl artickles and who mix himself so at home mid the musik and spanks the ivory that lovely for this your Mistro Melosiosus MacShine MacShane may soon prove your undoing and bane through the succeeding years of rain should you, whilst Jaun is from home, get used to basking in his loverslowlap, inordinately clad, moustacheteasing, when closehended together behind locked doors, kissing steadily, (malbongusta, it's not the thing you know!) with the calfloving selfseeker, under the influence of woman, inching up to you, disarranging your modesties and fumblingwith his forte paws in your bodice after your billy doos twy as a first go off (take care, would you stray and split on me!) and going on doing his idiot every time you gave him his chance to get thick and play piggly-wiggly, making much of you, bilgetalking like a ditherer, gougouzoug, about your glad neck and the round globe and the white milk and the red raspberries (O horrifier!) and prying down furthermore to chance his lucky arm with his pregnant questions up to our past lives. What has that caught to sing with him? The next fling you'll be squitting on the Tubber Nakel, pouring pitchers to the well for old Gloatsdane's glorification and the postequities of the Black Watch, peeping private from the Bush and Rangers. And our local busybody, talker-go-bragk. Worse again! Off of that praying fan on to them priars! It would be a whorable state of affairs altogether for the redcolumnists of presswritten epics, Peter Paragraph and Paulus Puff, (I'm keepsoaking them to cover my concerts) to get ahold of for their balloons and shoot you private by surprise, considering the marriage slump that's on this oil age and pulexes three shillings a pint and wives at six and seven when domestic calamities belame par and newlaids bellow mar for the twenty twotoosent time thwealthy took thousands in the slack march of civilisation were you, becoming guilty of unleckylike intoxication to have and to hold, to pig and to pay direct connection, *qua* intervener, with a prominent married member of the vicereeking squad and, in consequence of the thereinunder subpenas, be flummoxed to the second degree by becoming a detestificated company-keeper on the dammymonde of Lucalamplight. Anything but that, for the fear and love of gold! Once and for all, I'll have no college swankies (you see, I am well voiced in love's arsenal and all its overtures from collion boys to colleen bawns so I have every reason to know that rogues' gallery of nightbirds and bitchfanciers, lucky duffs and light lindsays, haughty hamiltons and gay gordons, dosed, doctored and otherwise, messing around skirts and what their fickling intentions look like, you make up your mind to that) trespassing on your danger zone in the dancer years. If ever I catch you at it, mind, it's you that will cocottch it! I'll tackle you to feel if you have a few devils in you. Holy gun, I'll give it to you, hot, high and heavy before you can say sedro! Or may the maledictions of Lousyfear fall like nettlerash on the white friar's father that converted from moonshine the fostermother of the first nancyfree that ran off after the trumpadour that mangled Moore's melodies and so upturned the tubshead of the stardaft journalwriter to inspire the prime finisher to fellhim the firtree out of which Cooper Funnymore planed the flat of the beerbarrel on which my grandydad's lustiest sat his seat of unwisdom with my tante's petted sister for the cause of his joy! Amene.

Poof! There's puff for ye, begor, and planxty of it, all abound me breadth!

Glor galore and glory be! As broad as its lung and as long as a line! The valiantine vaux of Venerable Val Vousdem. If my jaws must brass away like the due drops on my lay. And the topnoted delivery you'd expected be me invoice! Theo Dunnohoo's warning from Daddy O'Dowd. Whoo? What I'm wondering to myselfwhose for there's a strong tendency, to put it mildly, by making me the medium. I feel spirts of itchery outching out from all over me and only for the sludgehummer's force in my hand to hold them the darkens alone knows what'll who'll be saying of next. However. Now, before my upperotic rogister, something nice. Now? Dear Sister, in perfect leave again I say take a brokerly advice and keep it to yourself that we, Jaun, first of our name here now make all receptacles of, free of price. Easy, my dear, if they tingle you either say nothing or nod. No cheekacheek with chipperchapper, you and your last mashboy and the padre in the pulpbox enumerating you his nostrums. Be vacillant over those vigilant who would leave you to belave black on white. Close in for psychical hijiniks as well but fight shy of mugpunters. I'd burn the books that grieve you and light an allassundrian bom pyre that would suffragate Tome Plyfire or Zolfanerole. Perousse instate your *Weekly Standerd*, our verile organ that is ethelred by all pressdom. Apply your five wits to the four verilatest. The Arsdiken's *An Traitey on Miracula or Viewed to Death by a Priest Hunter* is still first in the field despite the castle bar, William Archer's a rompan good cathalogue and he'll give you a riser on the route to our nazional labronry. Skim over *Through Hell with the Papes* (mostly boys) by the divine comic Denti Alligator (exsponging your index) and find a quip in a quire arisus aream from bastardtitle to fatherjohnson. Swear aloud by pious fiction the like of *Lentil Lore* by Carnival Cullen or that *Percy Wynns* of our S. J. Finn's or *Pease in Plenty* by the Curer of Wars, licensed and censered by our most picturesque prelates, Their Graces of Linzen and Petitbois, bishops of Hibernites, *licet ut lebanus*, for expansion on the promises, the two best sells on the market this luckiest year, set up by Gill the father, put out by Gill the son and circulating disimally at Gillydehooly's Cost. Strike up a nodding acquaintance for our doctrine with the works of old Mrs Trot, senior, and Manoel Canter, junior, and Loper de Figas, nates maximum. I used to follow Mary Liddlelambe's flitsy tales, espicially with the scentaminted sauce. Sifted science will do your arts good. *Egg Laid by Former Cock* and With *Flageolettes in Send Fanciesland*. Chiefly girls. Trip over sacramental tea into the long lives of our saints and saucerdotes, with vignettes, cut short into instructual primers by those in authority for the bittermint of your soughts. Forfet not the palsied. Light a match for poor old Contrabally and send some balmoil for the schizmatics. A hemd in need is aye a friendly deed. Remember, maid, thou dust art powder but Cinderella thou must return (what are you robbing her sleeve for, Ruby? And pull in your tongue, Polly!). Cog that out of your teen times, everyone. The lad who brooks no breaches lifts the lass that toffs a tailor. How dare ye be laughing out of your mouthshine at the lack of that? Keep cool your fresh chastity which is far better far. Sooner than part with that vestalite emerald of the first importance, descended to me by far from our family, which you treasure up so closely where extremes meet, nay, mozzed lesmended, rather let the whole ekumene universe belong to merry Hal and do whatever his Mary well likes. When the gong goes for hornets-two-nest marriage step into your harness and strip off that nullity suit. Faminy, hold back! For the race is to the rashest of, the romping, jomping rushes of. Haul Seton's down, black, green and grey, and hoist Mikealy's whey and sawdust. What's overdressed if underclothed? Poposht forstake me knot where there's white lets ope. Whisht! Blesht she that walked with good Jook Humprey for he made her happytight. Go! You can down all the dripping you can dumple to, and buffkid scouse too ad libidinum, in these lassitudes if you've parents and things to look after. That was what stuck to the Comtesse Cantilene while she was sticking out Mavis Toffeelips to feed her soprannated huspals, and it is henceforth associated with her names. La Dreeping! Die Droopink! The inimitable in puresuet of the inevitable! There's nothing to touch it, we are taucht, unless she'd care for a mouthpull of white pudding for the wish is on her rose marine and the lunchlight in her eye, so when you pet the rollingpin write my name on the pie. Guard that gem, Sissy, rich and rare, ses he. In this cold old worold who'll feel it? Hum! The jewel you're all so cracked about there's flitty few of them gets it for there's nothing now but the sable stoles and a runabout to match it. Sing him a ring. Touch me low. And I'll lech ye so, my soandso. Show and show. Show on show. She. Shoe. Shone.

Divulge, sjuddenly jouted out hardworking Jaun, kicking the console to his double and braying aloud like Brahaam's ass, and, as his voixehumanar swelled to great, clenching his manlies, so highly strong was he, man, and gradually quite warming to her (there must have been a power of kinantics in that buel of gruel he gobed at bedgo) divorce into me and say the curname in undress (if you get into trouble with a party you are not likely to forget his appearance either) of any lapwhelp or sleevemongrel who talks to you upon the road where he tuck you to be a roller, O, (the goattanned saxopeeler upshotdown chigs peel of him!) and volunteers to trifle with your roundlings for proffered glass and dough, the marrying hand that his leisure repents of, without taking out his proper password from the eligible

ministriss for affairs with the black fremdling, that enemy of our country, in
a cleanlooking light and I don't care a tongser's tammany hang who the
mucky is nor twoo hoots in the corner nor three shouts on a hill (were he
even a constantineal namesuch of my very own, Attaboy Knowling, and like
enoch to my townmajor ancestors, the two that are taking out their divorces
in the Spooksbury courts circuits, Rere Uncle Remus, the Baas of Eboracum
and Old Father Ulissabon Knickerbocker, the lanky sire of Wolverhampton,
about their bristelings), but as true as there's a soke for sakes in Twoways
Peterborough and sure as home we come to newsky prospect from west the
wave on schedule time (if I came any quicker I'll be right back before I left)
from the land of breach of promise with Brendan's mantle whitening the
Kerribrasilian sea and March's pebbles spinning from beneath our footslips
to carry fire and sword, rest insured that as we value the very name in sister
that as soon as we do possibly it will be a poor lookout for that insister. He's
a markt man from that hour. And why do we say that, you may query me?
Quary? Guess! Call'st thou? Think and think and think, I urge on you.
Muffed! The wrong porridge. You are an ignoratis! Because then probably
we'll dumb well soon show him what the Shaun way is like how we'll go a
long way towards breaking his outsider's face for him for making up to you
with his bringthee balm of Gaylad and his singthee songs of Arupee,
chancetrying my ward's head into sanctuary before feeling with his two
dimensions for your nuptial dito. Ohibow, if I was Blonderboss I'd
gooandfrighthisdualman! Now, we'll tell you what we'll do to be sicker
instead of compensation. We'll he'll burst our his mouth like Leary to the
Leinsterface and reduce he'll we'll ournhisn liniments to a poolp. Open the
door softly, somebody wants you, dear! You'll hear him calling you, bump,
like a blizz, in the muezzin of the turkest night. Come on now, pillarbox! I'll
stiffen your scribeall, broken reed! That'll be it, grand operoar style, even
should I, with my sleuts of hogpew and cheekas, have to coomb the brash of
the libs round Close Saint Patrice to lay my louseboob on his behaitch like
solitar. We are all eyes. I have his quoram of images all on my retinue,
Mohomadhawn Mike. Brassup! Moreover after that, bad manners to me, if
I don't think strongly about giving the brotherkeeper into custody to the
first police bubby cunstabless of Dora's Diehards in the field I might chance
to follopon. Or for that matter, for your information, if I get the wind up
what do you bet in the buckets of my wrath I mightn't even take it into my
programme, as sweet course, to do a rash act and pitch in and swing for
your perfect stranger in the meadow of heppiness and then wipe the street
up with the clonmellian, pending my bringing proceedings verses the joyboy
before a bunch of magistrafes and twelve good and gleeful men? *Filius*

nullius per fas et nefas. It should prove more or less of an event and show the widest federal in my cup. He'll have pansements then for his pensamientos, howling for peace. Pretty knocks, I promise him with plenty burkes for his shins. Dumnlimn wimn humn. In which case I'll not be complete in fighting lust until I contrive to half kill your Charley you're my darling for you and send him to Home Surgeon Hume, the algebrist, before his appointed time, particularly should he turn out to be a man in brown about town, Rollo the Gunger, son of a wants a flurewaltzer to Arnolff's, picking up ideas, of well over or about fiftysix or so, pithecoid proportions, with perhops five foot eight, the usual X Y Z type, R.C. Toc H, nothing but claret, not in the studbook by a long stortch, with a toothbrush moustache and jawcrockeries, *alias* grinner through collar, and of course no beard, meat and colmans suit, with tar's baggy slacks, obviously too roomy for him and springside boots, washing tie, Father Mathew's bridge pin, sipping some Wheatley's at Rhoss's on a barstool, with some pubpal of the Olaf Stout kidney, always trying to poorchase movables by hebdomedaries for to putt in a new house to loot, cigarette in his holder, with a good job and pension in Buinness's, what about our trip to Normandy style conversation, with an occasional they say that filmacoulored featured at the Mothrapurl skrene about Michan and his lost angeleens is corkyshows do morvaloos, blueygreen eyes a bit scummy developing a series of angry boils with certain references to the Deity, seeking relief in alcohol and so on, general omnibus character with a dash of railwaybrain, stale cough and an occasional twinge of claudication, having his favourite fecundclass family of upwards of a decade, both harefoot and loadenbrogued, to boot and buy off, Imean.

So let it be a knuckle or an elbow, I hereby admonish you! It may all be topping fun but it's tip and run and touch and flow for every whack when Marie stopes Phil fluther's game to go. Arms arome, side aside, face into the wall. To the tumble of the toss tot the trouble of the swaddled, O. And lest there be no misconception, Miss Forstowelsy, over who to fasten the plightforlifer on (threehundred and thirty three to one on Rue the Day!) when the nice little smellar squalls in his crydle what the dirty old bigger'll be squealing through his coughin you better keep in the gunbarrel straight around vokseburst as I recommence you to (you gypseyeyed baggage, do you hear what I'm praying?) or, Gash, without butthering my head to assortail whose stroke forced or which struck backly, I'll be all over you myselx horizontally, as the straphanger said, for knocking me with my name and yourself and your babybag down at such a greet sacrifice with a rap of the gavel to a third price cowhandler as cheap as the niggerd's dirt (for sale!) or I'll smack your fruitflavoured jujube lips well for you, so I will well for you, if you don't keep a civil tongue in your pigeonhouse. The pleasures of love lasts but a fleeting but the pledges of life outlusts a lieftime. I'll have it in for you. I'll teach you bed minners, tip for tap, to be playing your oddaugghter tangotricks with micky dazzlers if I find corsehairs on your river-frock and the squirmside of your burberry lupitally covered with chiffchaff and shavings. Up Rosemiry Lean and Potanasty Rod you wos, wos you? I overstand you, you understand. Asking Annybettyelsas to carry your parcels and you dreaming of net glory. You'll ging naemaer wi'Wolf the Ganger. Cutting chapel, were you? and had dates with slickers in particular hotels, had we? Lonely went to play your mother, isod? You was wiffriends? Hay, dot's a doll yarn! Mark mean then! I'll homeseek you, Luperca as sure as there's a palatine in Limerick and in striped conference here's how. Nerbu de Bios! If you twos goes to walk upon the railway, Gard, and I'll goad to beat behind the bush! See to it! Snip! It's up to you. I'll be hatsnatching harrier to hiding huries hinder hedge. Snap! I'll tear up your limpshades and lock all your trotters in the closet, I will, and cut your silkskin into garters. You'll give up your ask unbrodhel ways when I make you reely smart. So skelp your budd and kiss the hurt! I'll have plenary sadisfaction, plays the bishop, for your partial's indulgences if your my rodeo gell. Fair man and foul suggestion. There's a lot of lecit pleasure coming bangslanging your way, Miss Pinpernelly satin. For your own good, you understand, for the man who lifts his pud to a woman is saving the way for kindness. You'll rebmemer your mottob *Aveh Tiger Roma* mikely smarter the nickst time. For I'll just draw my prancer and give you one splitpuck in the crupper, you understand, that will bring the poppy blush of shame to your peony hindmost till you yelp papapardon and radden your rhodatantarums to the beat of calorrubordolor, I am, I do and I suffer, (do you hear me now, lickspoon, and stop looking at your bussycat bow in the slate?) that you won't obliterate for the bulkier part of a running year, failing to give a good account of yourself, if you think I'm so tan cupid as all that. Lights out now (bouf!), tight and sleep on it. And that's how I'll bottle your greedypuss beautibus for ye, me bullin heifer, for 'tis I that have the peer of arrams that carry a wallop. Between them.

Unbeknownst to you would ire turn o'er see, a nuncio would I return here. How (from the sublime to the ridiculous) times out of oft, my future, shall we think with deepest of love and recollection by rintrospection of thee but me far away on the pillow, breathing foundly o'er my names all through the empties, whilst moidhered by the rattle of the doppeldoorknockers. Our homerole poet to Ostelinda, Fred Wetherly, puts it somewhys better. You're sitting on me style, maybe, whereoft I helped your ore.

Littlegame rumilie from Liffalidebankum, (Toobliqueme!) but a big corner fill you do in this unadulterated seat of our affections. Aerwenger's my breed so may we uncreepingly multipede like the sands on Amberhann! Sevenheavens, O heaven! Iy waount yiou! yore ways to melittleme were wonderful so Ickam purseproud in sending uym loveliest pansiful thoughts touching me dash inyou through wee dots Hyphen, the so pretty arched godkin of beddingnights. If I've proved to your sallysfashion how I'm a man of Armor let me so, let me sue, let me see your isabellis. How I shall, should I survive, as, please the uniter of U.M.I. hearts, I am living in hopes to do, replacing mig wandering handsup in yawers so yeager for mitch, positively cover the two pure chicks of your comely plumpchake with zuccherikissings, hong, kong, and so gong, that I'd scare the bats out of the ivfry one of those puggy mornings, honestly, by my rantandog and daddyoak I will, become come coming when, upon the mingling of our meeting waters, wish to wisher, like massive mountains to part no more, you will there and then, in those happy moments of ouryour soft accord, rainkiss on me back, for full marks with shouldered arms, and in that united I.R.U. stade, when I come (touf! touf!) wildflier's fox into my own greengeese again, swap sweetened smugs, six of one for half a dozen of the other, till they'll bet we're the cuckoo derby when cherries next come back to Ealing as come they must, as they musted in their past, as they must for my pressing season, as hereinafter must they chirrywill immediately suant on my safe return to ignorance and bliss in my horseless Coppal Poor, through suirland and noreland, kings country and queens, with my ropes of pearls for gamey girls the way ye'll hardly. Knowme.

Slim ye, come slum with me and rally rats' roundup! 'Tis post purification we will, sales of work and social service, missus, completing our Abelite union by the adoptation of fosterlings. Embark for Euphonia! Up Murphy, Henson and O'Dwyer, the Warchester Warders! I'll put in a shirt time if you'll get through your shift and between us in our shared slaves, brace to brassiere and shouter to shunter, we'll pull off our working programme. Come into the garden guild and be free of the gape athome! We'll circumcivicise all Dublin country. Let us, the real Us, all ignite in our prepurgatory grade as aposcals and be instrumental to utensilise, help our Jakeline sisters clean out the hogshole and generally ginger things up. Meliorism in massquantities, raffling receipts and sharing sweepstakes till navel, spokes and felloes hum like hymn. Burn only what's Irish, accepting their coals. You will soothe the cokeblack bile that's Anglia's and touch Armourican's iron core. Write me your essayes, my vocational scholars, but corsorily, dipping your nose in it, for Henrietta's sake, on mortinatality in

the life of jewries and the sludge of King Haarington's at its height, running
boulevards over the whole of it. I'd write it all by mownself if I only had here
of my jolly young watermen. Bear in mind, by Michael, all the provincial's
bananas peels and elacock eggs making drawadust jubilee along Henry,
Moore, Earl and Talbot Streets. Luke at all the memmer manning he's
dung for the pray of birds, our priest-mayor-king-merchant, strewing the
Castleknock Road and drawing manure upon it till the first glimpse of
Wales and from Ballses Breach Harshoe up to Dumping's Comer with the
Mirist fathers' brothers eleven versus White Friars out on a rogation stag
party. Compare them caponchin trowlers with the Bridge of Belches in
Fairview, noreast Dublin's favourite souwest wateringplatz and ump as you
lump it. What do you mean by Jno Citizen and how do you think of Jas
Pagan? Compost liffe in Dufblin by Pierce Egan with the baugh in
Baughkley of Fino Ralli. Explain why there is such a number of orders of
religion in Asea! Why such an order number in preference to any other
number? Why any number in any order at all? Now? Where is the greenest
island off the black coats of Spaign? Overset into universal: I am perdrix and
upon my pet ridge. Oralmus! Way, O way for the autointaxication of our
town of the Fords in a huddle! Hailfellow some wellmet boneshaker or, to
ascertain the facts for herself, run up your showeryweather once and trust
and take the Drumgondola tram and, wearing the midlimb and vestee
endorsed by the hierarchy fitted with ecclastics, bending your steps, pick a
trail and stand on, say, Aston's, I advise you strongly, along quaith a copy of
the Seeds and Weeds Act when you have procured one for yourself and take
a good longing gaze into any nearby shopswindow you may select at
suppose, let us say, the hoyth of number eleven, Kane or Keogh's, and in
the course of about thirtytwo minutes' time proceed to turn aroundabout
on your heehills towards the previous causeway and I shall be very cruelly
mistaken indeed if you will not be jushed astunshed to see how you will be
meanwhile durn weel topcoated with kakes of slush occasioned by the mush
jam of the cross and blackwalls traffic in transit. See Capels and then fly.
Show me that complaint book here. Where's Cowtends Kateclean, the
woman with the muckrake? When will the W.D. face of our sow muckloved
d'lin, the Troia of towns and Carmen of cities, crawling with mendiants in
perforated clothing, get its wellbelavered white like l'pool and m'chester?
When's that grandnational goldcapped dupsydurby houspill coming with
its vomitives for our mothers-in-load and stretchers for their devitalised
males? I am all of me for freedom of speed but who'll disasperaguss Pope's
Avegnue or who'll uproose the Opian Way? Who'll brighton Brayhowth
and bait the Bull Bailey and never despair of Lorcansby? The rampant royal

commissioners! 'Tis an ill weed blows no poppy good. And this labour's worthy of my higher. Oil for meed and toil for feed and a walk with the band for Job Loos. If I hope not charity what profiteers me? Nothing! My tippers of flags are knobs of hardshape for it isagrim tale, keeping the father of curls from the sport of oak. Do you know what, liddle giddles? One of those days I am advised by the smiling voteseeker who's now snoring elued to positively strike off hiking for good and all as I bldy well bdly ought until such temse as some mood is made under privy-sealed orders to get me an increase of automoboil and footwear for these poor discalced and a bourse from bon Somewind for a cure at Badanuweir (though where it's going to come from this time—) as I sartunly think now, honest to John, for an income plexus that that's about the sanguine boundary limit. Amean.

Sis dearest, Jaun added, with voise somewhit murky, what though still high fa luting, as he turned his dorse to her to pay court to it, and ouverleaved his booseys to give the note and score, phonoscopically incuriosited and melancholic this time whiles, as on the fulmament he gaped in wulderment, his onsaturncast eyes in stellar attraction followed swift to an imaginary swellaw, O, the vanity of Vanissy! All ends vanishing! Pursonally, Grog help me, I am in no violent hurry. If time enough lost the ducks walking easy found them. I'll nose a blue fonx with any tristys blinking upon this earthlight of all them that pass by the way of the deerdrive, conconey's run or wilfrid's walk, but I'd turn back as lief as not if I could only spoonfind the nippy girl of my heart's appointment, Mona Vera Toutou Ipostila, my lady of Lyons, to guide me by gastronomy under her safe conduct. That's more in my line. I'd ask no kinder of fates than to stay where I am, with my tinny of brownie's tea, under the invocation of Saint Jamas Hanway, servant of Gamp, lapidated, and Jacobus a Pershawm, intercissous, for my thurifex, with Peter Roche, that frind of my boozum, leaning on my cubits, at this passing moment by localoption in the birds' lodging, me pheasants among, where I'll dreamt that I'll dwealth mid warblers' walls when throstles and choughs to my sigh hiehied, with me hares standing up well and me longlugs dittoes, where a maurdering row, the fox! has broken at the coward sight till well on into the beausome of the exhaling night, pinching stopandgo jewels out of the hedges and catching dimtop brilliants on the tip of my wagger but for that owledclock (fast cease to it!) has just gone twoohoo the hour and that yen breezes zipping round by Drumsally do be devils to play fleurt. I could sit on safe side till the bark of Saint Grouseus for hoopoe's hours, till heoll's hoerrisings, laughing lazy at the sheep's lightning and turn a widamost ear dreamily to the drummling of snipers, hearing the wireless harps of sweet old Aerial and the mails

across the nightrives (peepet! peepet!) and whippoor willy in the woody
(moor park! moor park!) as peacefed as a philopotamus, and crekking jugs at
the grenoulls, leaving tealeaves for the trout and belleeks for the wary till I'd
followed through my upfielded neviewscope the rugaby moon cumuliously
godrolling himself westasleep amuckst the cloudscrums for to watch how
carefully my nocturnal goosemother would lay her new golden sheegg for
me down under in the shy orient. What wouldn't I poach—the rent in my
riverside, my otther shoes, my beavery, honest!—ay, and melt my belt for a
dace feast of grannom with the finny ones, those happy greppies in their
minnowahaw, flashing down the swansway, leaps ahead of the swift
MacEels, the big Gillaroo redfellows and the pursewinded carpers, rearin
antis rood perches astench of me, or, when I'd like own company best, with
the help of a norange and bear, to be reclined by the lasher on my
logansome, my g.b.d. in my f.a.c.e., solfanelly in my shellyholders and lov'd
latakia, the benuvolent, for my nosethrills, with the jealosomines wilting
away to their heart's deelight and the king of saptimber letting down his
humely odours for my consternation, dapping my griffeen, burning water
in the spearlight or catching trophies of the king's royal college of sturgeone
by the armful for to bake pike ahd pie while, O twined me abower in
L'Alouette's Tower, all Adelaide's naughtingerls juckjucking benighth
me, I'd gamut my twittynice Dorian blackbudds chthonic solphia off my
singasongapiccolo to pipe musicall airs on numberous fairyaciodes. I give, a
king, to me, she does, alone, up there, yes see, I double give, till the spinney
all eclosed asong with them. Isn't that lovely though? I give to me alone I
trouble give! I may have no mind to lamagnage the forte bits like the
pianage but you can't cadge me off the key. I've a voicical lilt too true.
Nomario! And bemolly and jiesis! For I sport a whatyoumacormack in the
latcher part of my throughers. And the lark that I let fly (olala!) is as cockful
of funantics as it's tune to my fork. Naturale you might lower register me as
diserecordant, but I'm athlone in the lillabilling of killarnies. That's flat. Yet
ware the wold, you! What's good for the gorse is a goad for the garden.
Lethals lurk heimlocked in logans. Loathe laburnums. Dash the gaudy
deathcup! Bryony O'Bryony, thy name is Belladama! But enough of green-
wood's gossip. Birdsnests is birdsnests. Thine to wait but mine to wage.
And now play sharp to me. Doublefirst I'll head foremost through all my
examhoops. And what sensitive coin I'd be possessed of at Latouche's,
begor, I'd sink it sumtotal, every dolly farting, in vestments of subdominal
poteen at prime cost and I bait you my chancey oldcoat against the whole
ounce you half on your backboard (if madamaud strips mesdamines may
cold strafe illglands!) that I'm the gogetter that'd make it pay like cash

registers as sure as there's a pot on a pole. And, what with one man's fish and a dozen men's poissons, sowing my wild plums to reap ripe plentihorns mead, lashings of erbole and hydromel and bragget, I'd come out with my magic fluke in close time, fair, free and frolicky, zooming tophole on the mart as a factor. And I tell you the Bective's wouldn't hold me. By the unsleeping Solman Annadromus, ye god of little pescies, nothing would stop me for mony makes multimony like the brogues and the kishes. Not the Ulster Rifles and the Cork Milice and the Dublin Fusees and Connacht Rangers ensembled! I'd axe the channon and leip a liffey and drink annyblack water that rann onme way. Yip! How's thats for scats, mine shatz, for a lovebird? To funk is only peternatural its daring feers divine. Bebold! Like Varian's balaying all behind me. And before you knew where you weren't, I stake my ignitial's divy, cash-and-cash-can-again, I'd be staggering humanity and loyally rolling you over, my sowwhite sponse, in my tons of red clover, nighty nigh to the metronome, fiehigh and fiehigher and fiehighest of all. Holy petter and pal, I'd spoil you altogether, my sumptuous Sheila! Mumm all to do brut frull up fizz and unpop a few shortusians or shake a pale of sparkling ice, hear it swirl, happy girl! Not a spot of my hide but you'd love to seek and scanagain! There'd be no standing me, I tell you. And, as gameboy as my pagan name K.C. is what it is, I'd never say let fly till we shot that blissup and swumped each other, manawife, into our sever nevers where I'd plant you, my Gizzygay, on the electric ottoman in the lap of lechery, simpringly stitchless with admiracion, among the most uxuriously furnished compartments, with sybarate chambers, just as I'd run my shoe-string into near a million or so of them as a firstclass dealer and everything. Only for one thing that, howover famiksed I would become, I'd be awful anxious, you understand, about shoepisser pluvious and in assideration of the terrible luftsucks woabling around with the hedrolics in the coold amstophere till the borting that would perish the Dane and his chapter of accidents to be atramental to the better half of my alltoolyrical health, not considering my capsflap, and that's the truth now out of the cackling bag for truly sure, for another thing, I never could tell the leest falsehood that would truthfully give sotisfiction. I'm not talking apple sauce eithou. Or up in my hat. I earnst. Schue!

Sissibis dearest, as I was reading to myself not very long ago in Tennis Flonnels Mac Courther, his correspondance, besated upon my tripos, and just thinking like thauthor how long I'd like myself to be continued at Hothelizod, peeking into the focus and pecking at thumbnail reveries, pricking up ears to my phono on the ground and picking up airs from th'other over th'ether, 'tis tramsported with grief I am this night sublime, as

you may see by my size and my brow that's all forehead, to go forth, frank
and hoppy, to the tune the old plow tied off, from our nostorey house, upon
this benedictine errand but it is historically the most glorious mission,
secret or profund, through all the annals of our—as you so often term her—
efferfreshpainted livy, in beautific repose, upon the silence of the dead, from
pharoph the nextfirst down to ramescheckles the last bust thing. The Vico
road goes round and round to meet where terms begin. Still onappealed to
by the cycles and unappalled by the recoursers we feel all serene, never you
fret, as regards our dutyful cask. Full of my breadth from pride I am (breezed
be the healthy same!) for 'tis a grand thing (superb!) to be going to meet a
king, not an everynight king, nenni, by gannies, but the overking of Hither-
on-Thither Erin himself, pardee, I'm saying. Before there was patch at all
on Ireland there lived a lord at Lucan. We only wish everyone was as sure of
anything in this watery world as we are of everything in the newlywet fellow
that's bound to follow. I'll lay you a guinea for a hayseed now. Tell mother
that. And tell her tell her old one. T'will amuse her.

　　Well, to the figends of Annanmeses with the wholeabuelish business!
For I declare to Jeshuam I'm beginning to get sunsick! I'm not half
Norawain for nothing. The fine ice so temperate of our, alas, those times
are not so far off as you might wish to be congealed. So now, I'll ask of you,
let ye create no scenes in my poor primmafore's wake. I don't want yous to
be billowfighting you biddy moriarty duels, gobble gabble, over me till you
spit stout, you understand, after soused mackerel, sniffling clambake to
hering and impudent barney, braggart of blarney, nor you ugly lemoncholic
gobs o'er the hobs in a sewing circle, stopping oddments in maids' costumes
at sweeping reductions, wearing out your ohs by sitting around your ahs,
making areekeransy round where I last put it, with the painters in too, curse
luck, with your rags up, exciting your mucuses, turning breakfarts into lost
soupirs and salon thay nor you flabbies on your groaning chairs over
Bollivar's troubles of a bluemoondag, steamin your damp ossicles, praying
Holy Prohibition and Jaun Dyspeptist while Ole Clo goes through the
wood with Shep togather, touting in the chesnut burrs for Goodboy
Sommers and Mistral Blownowse hugs his kindlings when voiceyversy it's
my gala bene fit, robbing leaves out of my taletold book. May my tunc fester
if ever I see such a miry lot of maggalenes! Once upon a drunk and a fairly
good drunk it was and the rest of your blatherumskite! Just a plain shays by
the fire for absenter Sh the Po and I'll make ye all as eastern hummingsphere
of myself the moment that you name the way. Look in the slag scuttle and
you'll see me sailspread over the singing, and what do ye want trippings for
when you've Paris inspire your hat? Sussumcordials all round, let ye alloyiss

and ominies, while I stray and let ye not be getting grief out of it, though
blighted troth be all bereft, on my poor headsake, even should we forfeit our
life. Lo, improving ages wait ye! In the orchard of the bones. Some time
very presently now when yon clouds are dissipated after their forty years
shower, the odds are, we shall all be hooked and happy, communionistically,
among the fieldnights eliceam *élite* of the elect, in the land of lost of time.
Johannisburg's a revelation! Deck the diamants that never die! So cut out
the lonesome stuff! Drink it up, ladies, please, as smart as you can lower it!
Out with lent! Clap hands postilium! Fastintide is by. Your sole and
myopper must hereupon part company. So for e'er fare thee welt! Parting's
fun. Take thou, the wringle's thine, love. This dime doth trost thee from
mine alms. Goodbye, swisstart, goodbye! Haugh! Haugh! Sure, treasures, a
letterman does be often thought reading ye between lines that do have no
sense at all. I sign myself. With much leg. Inflexibly yours. Ann Posht the
Shorn. To be continued. Huck!

Something of a sidesplitting nature must have occurred to westminstrel
Jaunathaun for a grand big blossy hearty stenorious laugh (even Drudge that
lay doggo thought feathers fell) hopped out of his wooly's throat like a ball
lifted over the head of a deep field, at the bare thought of how jolly they'd
like to be trolling his whoop and all of them truetotypes in missammen
massness were just starting to spladher splodher with the jolly magorios,
hicky hecky hock, huges huges huges, hughy hughy hughy, O Jaun, so
jokable and so geepy, O, (Thou pure! Our virgin! Thou holy! Our health!
Thou strong! Our victory! O salutary! Sustain our firm solitude, thou who
thou well strokest! Hear, Hairy ones! We have sued thee but late. Beauty
parlous.) when suddenly (how like a woman!), swifter as mercury he wheels
right round starnly on the Rizzies suddenly, with his gimlets blazing rather
sternish (how black like thunder!), to see what's loose. So they stood still and
wondered. Till first he sighed (and how ill soufered!) and they nearly cried
(the salt of the earth!) after which he pondered and finally he replied:

— There is some thing more. A word apparting and shall the heart's
tone be silent. Engagements, I'll beseal you! Fare thee well, fairy well! All
I can tell you is this, my sorellies. It's prayers in layers all the thumping
time, begor, the young gloria's gang voices the old doxologers, in the
suburrs of the heavenly gardens, once we shall have passed, after surceases,
all serene through neck and necklike Derby and June to our snug eternal
retribution's reward (the scorchhouse). Shunt us! shunt us! shut us! If you
want to be felixed come and be parked. Sacred ease there! The seanad and
pobbel queue's remainder. To it, to it! Seekit headup! No petty family
squabbles Up There nor homemade hurricanes in our Cohortyard, no

cupahurling nor apuckalips nor no puncheon jodelling nor no nothing. With the Byrns which is far better and eve for ever your idle be. You will hardly reconnoitre the old wife in the new bustle and the farmer shinner in his latterday paint. It's the fulldress Toussaint's wakeswalks experdition after a bail motion from the chamber of horrus. Saffron buns or sovran bonhams whichever you'r avider to like it and lump it, but give it a name. Iereny allover irelands. And there's food for refection when the whole flock's at home. Hog-manny di'yegut? Hogmanny di'yesmellygut? And hogmanny di'yesmellyspatterygut? You take Joe Hanny's tip for it! Postmartem is the goods. With Jollification a tight second. Toborrow and toburrow and tobarrow! That's our crass, hairy and evergrim life, till one finel howdiedow Bouncer Naster raps on the bell with a bone and his stinkers stank behind him with the sceptre and the hourglass. We may come, touch and go, from atoms and ifs but we're presurely destined to be odd's without ends. Here we moult in Moy Kain and flop on the seemy side, living sure of hardly a doorstep for a stop gap, with Whogoes-there and a live sandbag round the corner. But upmeyant, Prospector, you sprout all your abel and woof your wings dead certain however of neuthing whatever to aye forever while Hyam Hyam's in the chair. Ah, sure, pleasantries aside, in the tail of the cow what a humpty daum earth looks our miseryme heretoday as compared beside the Hereweareagain Gaieties of the Afterpiece when the Royal Revolver of these real globoes lets regally fire of his *mio colpo* for the chrisman's pandemon to give over and the Harlequinade to begin properly SPQueaRking Mark Time's Finist Joke. Putting Allspace in a Notshall.

Well, the slice and veg joint's well in its way, and so is a ribroast and jackknife as sporten dish, but home cooking everytime. Mountains good mustard and, with the helpings of ladies' lickfings and gentlemen's relish, I've eaten a griddle. But I fill twice as stewhard what I felt before when I'm after eating a few natives. The crisp of the crackling is in the chawing. Give us another cup of your scald. Santos Mozos! That was a damn good cup of scald! You could trot a mouse on it. I ingoyed your pick of hissing hot luncheon fine, I did, thanks awfully, (sublime!) Tenderest bully ever I ate with the boiled protestants (allinoilia allinoilia!) only for your peas again was a taste of tooth psalty to carry flavour with my godown and hereby return with my best savioury condiments and a penny in the plate for the jemes. O.K. Oh Kosmos! Ah Ireland! A.I. And for kailkannonkabbis gimme Cincinnatis with Italian (but *ci vuol poco!*) ciccalick cheese, Haggis good, haggis strong, haggis never say die! For quid we have recipimus, recipe, O lout! And save that, Oliviero, for thy sunny day! Soupmeagre! Couldn't look at it! But if you'll buy me yon coat of the vairy furry best, I'll try and pullll it awn mee. It's in fairly good order and no doubt 'twill sarve to turn. Remove this boardcloth! Next stage, tell the tabler, for a variety of Huguenot ligooms I'll try my set on edges grapeling an aigrydoucks, grilled over birchenrods, with a few bloomancowls in albies. I want to get outside monasticism. Mass and meat mar no man's journey. Eat a missal lest. Nuts for the nerves, a flitch for the flue and for to rejoice the chambers of the heart the spirits of the spice isles, curry and cinnamon, chutney and cloves. All the vitalmines is beginning to sozzle in chewn and the hormonies to clingleclangle, fudgem, kates and eaps and naboc and erics and oinnos on kingclud and xoxxoxo and xooxox xxoxoxxoxxx till I'm fustfed like fungstif and very presently from now posthaste it's off yourll see me ryuoll on my usual rounds again to draw Terminus Lower and Killadown and Letternoosh, Letterspeak, Lettermuck to Littorananima and the roomiest house even in Ireland, if you can understamp that, and my next item's platform it's how I'll try and collect my extraprofessional postages owing to me by Thaddeus Kellyesque Squire, dr, for nondesirable printed matter. The Jooks and the Kelly-Cooks have been milking turnkeys and sucking the blood out of the marshalsea since the act of First Offenders. But I know what I'll do. Great pains off him I'll take and that'll be your redletterday calendar, window machree! I'll knock it out of him! I'll stump it out of him! I'll rattattatter it out of him before I'll quite the doorstep of old Con Connolly's residence! By the horn of twenty of both of the two Saint Collopys, blackmail him I will in arrears or my name's not penitent Ferdinand! And it's daily and hourly I'll nurse him till he pays me fine fee. Ameal.

Well, here's looking at ye! If I never leave you biddies till my stave is a bar I'd be tempted rigidly to become a passionate father. Me hunger's weighed. Hungkung! Me anger's suaged! Hangkang! Ye can stop as ye are, little lay mothers, and wait in wish and wish in vain till the grame reaper draws nigh, with the sickle of the sickles, as a blessing in disguise. Devil a curly hair I care! If any lightfoot Clod Dewvale was to hold me up, dick-sturping me and marauding me of my rights to my onus, yan, tyan, tethera, methera, pimp, I'd let him have my best pair of galloper's heels in the creamsourer. He will have better manners, I'm dished if he won't! Console yourself, drawhure deelish! There's a refond of eggsized coming to you out of me so mind you do me duty on me! Bruise your bulge below the belt till I blewblack beside you. And you'll miss me more as the narrowing weeks wing by. Someday duly, oneday truly, twosday newly, till whensday. Look for me always at my west and I will think to dine. A tear or two in time is all there's toot. And then in a click of the clock, toot toot, and doff doff we pop with sinnerettes in silkettes lining longroutes fo His Diligence Majesty, our longdistance laird that likes creation. To whoosh!

— Meesh, meesh, yes, pet. We were too happy. I knew something would happen. I understand but listen, drawher nearest, Tizzy intercepted, flushing but flashing from her dove and dart eyes as she tactilifully grapbed her male corrispondee to flusther sweet nunsongs in his quickturned ear, I know, benjamin brother, but listen, I want, girls palmassing, to whisper my whish. (She like them like us, me and you, had thoud he n'er it would haltin so lithe when leased is tacitempust tongue). Of course, engine dear, I'm ashamed for my life (I must clear my throttle) over this lost moment's gift of memento nosepaper which I'm sorry, my precious, is allathome I with grief can call my own but all the same, listen, Jaunick, accept this witwee's mite, though a jennyteeny witween piece torn in one place from my hands in second place of a linenhall valentino with my fondest and much left to tutor. X.X.X.X. It was heavily bulledicted for young Fr Ml, my pettest parriage priest, and you know who between us by your friend the pope, forty ways in forty nights, that's the beauty of it, look, scene it, ratty. Too perfectly priceless for words. And, listen, now do enhance me, oblige my fiancy and bear it with you morn till life's e'en and, of course, when never you make usage of it, listen, please kindly think galways again or again, never forget, of one absendee not sester Maggy. Ahim. That's the stupidest little cough. Only be sure you don't catch your cold and pass it on to us. And, since levret bounds and larks is soaring, don't be all the night. And this, Joke, a sprig of blue speedwell just a spell of floralora so you'll mind your veronique. Of course, Jer, I know you know who sends it, presents that please, mercy, on the face of the waters like that film obote, awfly charmig of course, but it doesn't do her justice, apart from her cattiness, in the magginbottle. Of course, please too write, won't you, and leave your little bag of doubts, inquisitive, behind you unto your utterly thine, and, thank you, forward it back by return pigeon's pneu to the loving in case I couldn't think who it was or any funforall happens I'll be so curiose to see in the Homesworth breakfast tablotts as I'll know etherways by pity bleu if it's good for my system, what exquisite buttons, gorgiose, in case I don't hope to soon hear from you. And thanks ever so many for the ten and the one with nothing at all on. I will tie a knot in my stringamejip to letter you with my silky paper, as I am given now to understand it will be worth my price in money one day so don't trouble to ans unless sentby special as I am getting his pay and wants for nothing so I can live simply and solely for my wonderful kinkless and its loops of loveliness. When I throw away my rollets there's rings for all. Flee a girl, says it is her colour. So does B and L and as for V! And listen to it!

Cheveluir! So distant you're always. Bow your boche! Absolutely perfect! I will pack my comb and mirror to praxis oval owes and artless awes and it will follow you pulpicly as far as come back under all my eyes like my sapphire chaplets of ringarosary I will say for you to the Allmichael and solve qui pu while the dovedoves pick my mouthbuds (msch! msch!) with nurse Madge, my linkingclass girl, she's a fright, poor old dutch, in her sleeptalking when I paint the measles on her and mudstuskers to make her a man. We. We. Issy done that, I confesh! But you'll love her for her hessians and sickly black stockies, cleryng's jumbles, salvadged from the wash, isn't it the cat's tonsils! Simply killing, how she tidies her hair! I call her Sosy because she's sosiety for me and she says sossy while I say sassy and she says will you have some more scorns while I say won't you take a few more schools and she talks about ithel dear while I simply never talk about athel darling; she's but nice for enticing my friends and she loves your style considering she breaksin me shoes for me when I've arch trouble and she would kiss my white arms for me so gratefully but apart from that she's terribly nice really, my sister, round the elbow of Erne street Lower and I'll be strictly forbidden always and true in my own way and private where I will long long to betrue you along with one who will so betrue you that not once while I betreu him not once well he be betray himself. Can't you understand? O bother, I must tell the truth! My latest lad's lovelileter I am sore I done something with. I like him lots coss he never cusses. Pity bonhom. Pip pet. I shouldn't say he's pretty but I'm cocksure he's shy. Why I love taking him out when I unletched his cordon gate. Ope, Jack, and atem! Obealbe myodorers and he dote so. He fell for my lips, for my lisp, for my lewd speaker. I felt for his strength, his manhood, his do you mind? There can be no candle to hold to it, can there? And, of course, dear professor, I understand. You can trust me that though I change thy name though not the letter never while I become engaged with my first horsepower, master-thief of hearts, I will give your lovely face of mine away, my boyish bob, not for tons of donkeys, to my second mate, with the twirlers the engineer of the passioflower (O the wicked untruth! whot a tell! that he has bought me in his wellingtons what you haven't got!), in one of those pure clean lupstucks of yours thankfully, Arrah of the passkeys, no matter what. You may be certain of that, fluff, now I know how to tackle. Lock my mearest next myself. So don't keep me now for a good boy for the love of my fragrant saint, you villain, peppering with fear, my goodless graceless, or I'll first murder you but, hvisper, meet me after by next appointment near you know Ships just there beside the Ship at the future poor fool's circuts of lovemountjoy square to show my disrespects now, let me just your caroline for you, I must really so late. Sweet pig, he'll be furious! How he stalks to simself louther and lover, immutating aperybally. My prince of the courts who'll beat me to love! And I'll be there when who knows where with the objects of which I'll knowor forget. We say. Trust us. Our game. (For fun!) The Dargle shall run dry the sooner I you deny. Whoevery heard of such a think? Till the ulmost of all elmoes shall stele our harts asthone! And Mrs A'Mara makes it up and befriends with Mrs O'Morum! I will write down all your names in my gold pen and ink. Everyday, precious, while m'm'ry's leaves are falling deeply on my Jungfraud's Messongebook I will dream telepath posts dulcets on this isinglass stream (but don't tell him or I'll be the mort of him!) under the libans and the sickamours, the cyprissis and babilonias, where the frondoak rushes to the ask and the yewleaves too kisskiss themselves and 'twill carry on my hearz'waves my still waters reflections in words over Margrate von Hungaria, her Quaidy ways and her Flavin hair, to thee, Jack, ahoy, beyond the boysforus. Splesh of hiss splash springs your salmon. Twick twick, twinkle twings my twilight as Sarterday afternoon lex leap will smile on my fourinhanced twelvemonthsmind. And what's this I was going to say, dean? O, I understand. Listen, here I'll wait on thee till Thingavalla with beautiful do be careful teacakes, more stuesser flavoured than Vanilla and blackcurrant there's a cure in, like a born gentleman till you'll resemble me, all the time you're awhile way, I swear to you, I will, by Candlemas! And listen, joey, don't be ennoyed with me, my old evernew, when, by the end of your chapter, you citch water on the wagon for me being turned a star I'll dubeurry my two fesces under Pouts Vanisha Creme, their way for spilling cream, and, accent, umto extend my personnalitey to the latents, I'll boy me for myself only of expensive rainproof of pinked elephant's breath grey of the loveliest sheerest dearest widowshood over airforce blue I am so wild for, my precious once, Hope Bros., Faith Street, Charity Corner, as the bee loves her skyhighdeed, for I always had a crush on heliotrope since the dusess of yore cycled round the Finest Park, and listen. And never mind me laughing at what's atever! I was in the nerves but it's my last day. Always about this hour, I'm sorry, when our gamings for Bruin and Noselong is all oh you tease and afterdoon my lickle pussiness I stheal heimlick in my russians from the attraction part with my terriblitall boots calvescatcher Pinchapoppapoff, who is going to be a jennyroll, at my nape, drenched, love, with dripping to affectionate slapmamma but last at night, look, after my golden violents wetting in my upperstairs splendidly welluminated with such lidlylac curtains wallpapered to match the cat and a fire—please keep looking of priceless pearlogs I just want to see will he or are all Michales like that, I'll strip straight after devotions before his fondstare—and I mean it too, (thy gape to my gazing I'll bind and makeleash) and poke stiff under my isonbound with my soiedisante-chineknees cheeckchubby chambermate for the night's foreign males and your name of Shane will come forth between my shamefaced whesen with other lipth I nakest open my thight when just woken by his toccatootletoo my first morning. So now, to thalk thildish, thome, theated with Mag at the oilthan we are doing to thay one little player before doing to deed. An a tiss to the tassie for lu and for tu! Coach me how to tumble, Jaime, and listen, with supreme regards, Juan, in haste, warn me which to ah ah ah ah. . . .

— MEN! Juan responded fullchantedly to her sororal sonority, imitating himself capitally with his bubbleblown in his patapet and his chalished drink now well in hand. (A spilt, see, for a split, see see!) Ever gloriously kind! And I truly am eucherised to yous. Also *sacré père* and *maître d'autel*. Well, ladies upon gentlermen and toastmaster general, let us, brindising brandisong, woo and win womenlong with health to rich vineyards, Erin go Dry! Amingst the living waters of, the living in giving waters of. Tight! Loose! A stiff one for Staffetta mullified with creams of hourmony, the coupe that's chill for jackless jill and a filiform dhouche on Doris! Esterelles, be not on your weeping what though Shaunathaun is in his fail! To stir up love's young fizz I tilt with this bridle's cup champagne, dimming douce from her peepair of hideseeks, tightsqueezed on my snowybrusted and while my pearlies in their sparkling wisdom are nippling her bubblets I swear (and let you swear!) by the bumper round of my poor old snaggletooth's solidbowel I ne'er will prove I'm untrue to your liking (theare!) so long as my hole looks. Down.

So gullaby, me poor Isley! But I'm not for forgetting me innerman monophone for I'm leaving my darling proxy behind for your consoclering, lost Dave the Dancekerl, a squamous runaway and a dear old man pal of mine too. He will arrive incessantly in the fraction of a crust, who, could he quit doubling and stop tippling, he would be the unicorn of his kind. He's the mightiest penumbrella I ever flourished on behond the shadow of a post! Be sure and link him, me O treasauro, as often as you learn provided there's nothing between you but a plain deal table only don't encourage him to cry lessontimes over Leperstown. But soft! Can't be? Do mailstanes mumble? Lumtum lumtum! Now! The froubadour! I fremble! Talk of wolf in a stomach by all that's verminous! Eccolo me! The return of th'athlate! Who can secede to his success! Isn't Jaunstown, Ousterrike, the small place after all? I knew I smelt the garlic leek! Why, bless me swits, here he its, darling Dave, like the catoninelives just in time as if he fell out of space, all draped in mufti, coming home to mourn mountains from his old continence and not on one foot either or on two feet aether but on quinquisecular cycles after his French evolution and a blindfold passage by the 4.32 with the pork's pate in his suicide paw and the gulls laughing lime on his natural skunk, blushing like Pat's pig, begob! He's not too timtom well ashamed to carry out onaglibtograbakelly in his showman's sinister the testymonicals he gave his twenty annis orf, showing the three white feathers, as a home cured emigrant in Paddyouare far below on our sealevel. Bearer may leave the church, signed, Figura Porca, Lictor Magnaffica. He's the sneaking likeness of us, faith, me altar's ego in miniature and every Auxonian aimer's ace as nasal a Romeo as I am, for ever cracking quips on himself, that merry, the jeenjakes, he'd soon arise mother's roses mid bedewing tears under those wild wet lashes onto anny living girl's laftercheeks. That's his little veiniality. And his unpeppeppediment. He has novel ideas I know and he's a jarry queer fish betimes, I grant you, and cantanberous, the poisoner of his word, but lice and all and semicoloured stainedglasses, I'm enormously full of that foreigner, I'll say I am! Got by the one goat, suckled by the same nanna, one twitch, one nature makes us oldworld kin. We're as thick and thin now as two tubular jawballs. I hate him about his patent henesy, plasfh it, yet am I amorist. I love him. I love his old portugal's nose. There's the nasturtium for ye now that saved manny a poor sinker from water on the grave. The diasporation of all pirates and quinconcentrum of a fake like Basilius O'Cormacan MacArty? To camiflag he turned his shirt. Isn't he after borrowing all before him, making friends with everybody red in Rossya, white in Alba and touching every distinguished Ourishman he could ever distinguish before or behind from a Yourishman for the customary halp of a crown and peace? He is looking aged with his pebbled eyes, and johnnythin too, from livicking on pidgins' ifs with puffins' ands, he's been slanderising himself, but I pass no remark. Hope he hasn't the cholera. Give him an eyot in the farout. Moseses and Noasies, how are you? He'd be as snug as Columbsisle Jonas wrocked in the belly of the whaves, as quotad before. Bravo, senior chief! Famose! Sure there's nobody else in touch anysides to hold a chef's cankle to the darling at all for sheer dare with that prisonpotstill of spanish breans on him like the knave of trifles! A jollytan fine demented brick and the prince of goodfilips! Dave knows I have the highest of respect of annyone in my oweand smooth way for that intellectual debtor (Obbligado!) Mushure David R. Crozier. And we're the closest of chems. Mark my use of you, cog! Take notice how I yemploy, crib! Be ware as you, I foil, coppy! It's a pity he can't see it for I'm terribly nice about him. Canwyll y Cymry, the marmade's flamme! A leal of the O'Looniys, a Brazel aboo! The most omportent man! *Shervos!* Ho, be the holy snakes, someone has shaved his rough diamond skull for him as clean as Nuntius' piedish! The burnt out mesh and the matting and all! Thunderweather, khyber schinker escapa sansa pagar! He's the spatton spit, so he is, scaly skin and all, with his blackguarded eye and the goatsbeard in his buttinghole of Shemuel Tulliver, me grandsourd, the old cruxader, when he off with his paudeen! That was to let the crowd of the Flu Flux Fans behind him see me proper. Ah, he's very thoughtful and sympatrico that way is Brother Intelligentius, when he's not absintheminded, with his Paris addresse! He is, really. Holdhard till you'll ear him clicking his bull's bones! Some toad klakkin! You're welcome back, Wilkins, to red berries in the frost! And here's the butter exchange to pfeife and dramn ye with a bawlful of the Moulsaybaysse and yunker doodler wanked to wall awriting off his phoney. I'm tired hairing of you. Hat yourself! Give us your dyed dextremity here, frother, the Claddagh clasp! I met with dapper dandy and he shocked me big the hamd. Where's your watch keeper? You've seen all sorts in shapes and sizes, marauding about the moppamound. How's the cock and the bullfight? And old Auster and Hungrig? And the Beer and Belly and the Boot and Ball? Not forgetting the oils of greas under that turkey in julep and Father Freeshots Feilbogen in his rockery garden with the costard? And tid you meet with Peadhar the Grab at all? And did you call on Tower Geesyhus? Was Mona, my own love, no bigger than she should be, making up to you in her bestbehaved manor when you made your breastlaw and made her, tell me? And did you like the landskip from Lambay? I'm better pleased than ten guidneys! You rejoice me! Faith, I'm proud of you, french davit! You've surpassed yourself! Be introduced to yes! This is me aunt Julia Bride, your honour, dying to have you languish to scandal in her bosky old delltangle. You don't reckoneyes him? He's Jackot the Horner who boxed in his corner, jilting no fewer than three female bribes. That's his penals. *Shervorum!* You haven't seen her since she stepped into her drawoffs. Come on, spinister, do your stuff! Don't be shoy, husbandmanvir! Weih, what's on you, wip? Up the shamewaugh! She has plenty of woom in the small-clothes for the bothsforus, nephews push! Hatch yourself well! Enjomb-yourselves thurily! Would you wait biss she buds till you bite on her? Embrace her bashfully by almeans at my frank incensive and tell her in your semiological agglutinative yez, how Idos be asking after her. Let us be holy and evil and let her be peace on the bough. Sure, she fell in line with our tripertight photos as the lyonised mails when we were stablelads together like the corks again brothers, hungry and angry, cavileer grace by round-hered force, or like boyrun to sibster, me and you, shinners true and

pinchme, our tertius quiddus, that never talked or listened. Always raving
how we had the wrinkles of a snailcharmer and the slits and sniffers of a
fellow that fell foul of the county de Loona and the meattrap of the first
vegetarian. To be had for the asking. Have a hug! Take her out of poor
tuppeny luck before she goes off in pure treple licquidance. I'd give three
shillings a pullet to the canon for the conjugation to shadow you kissing her
from me leberally all over as if she was a crucifix. It's good for her bilabials,
you understand. There's nothing like the mistletouch for finding a queen's
earring false. Chink chink. As the curly bard said after kitchin the womn in
his hym to the hum of her garments. You try a little tich to the tissle of his
tail. The racist to the racy, rossy. The soil is for the self alone. Be ownkind.
Be kithkinish. Be bloodysibby. Be irish. Be inish. Be offalia. Be hamlet. Be
the property plot. Be Yorick; and Lankystare. Be cool. Be mackinamucks of
yourselves. Be finish. No martyr where the preature is there's no plagues
like rome. It gives up the gripes. Watch the swansway. Take your tiger over
it. The leady on the lake and the convict of the forest. Why, they might be
Babau and Momie! Yipyip! To pan! To pan! To tinpinnypan. All folly me
yap to Curlew! Give us a pin for her and we'll call it a tossup. Can you
reverse positions? Lets have a fuchu all round, courting cousins! Quuck, the
duck of a woman for quack, the drake of a man, her little live apples for Leas
and love potients for Leos, the next beast king. Put me down for all ringside
seats. I can feel you being corrupted. Recoil. I can see you sprouting scruples.
Get back. And as he's boiling with water I'll light your pyre. Turn about,
skeezy Sammy, out of metaphor, till we feel are you still tropeful of popetry.
Told you so. If you doubt of his love of darearing his feelings you'll very
much hurt for mishmash mastufractured on europe you can read off the tail
of his. Rip ripper rippest and jac jac jac. Dwell on that, my hero and lander!
That's the side that appeals to em, the wring wrong way to wright woman.
Shuck her! Let him! What he's good for. Shuck her more! Let him again!
All she wants! Could you wheedle a staveling encore out of your
imitationer's jubalharp, hey, Mr Jinglejoys? Congregational singing. Rota
rota ran the pagoda *con dio in capo ed il diavolo in coda*. Many a diva devoucha
saw her Dauber Dan at the priesty pagoda Rota ran. Uck! He's so sedulous
to singe always if prumpted, the mirthprovoker! Grunt unto us, I pray, your
foreboden article in our own deas dockandoilish introducing the death of
Nelson with coloraturas! *Coraio, fra!* And I'll string second to harmanize.
My loaf and pottage neaheaheahear Rochelle. With your dumpsey diddely
dumpsey die, fiddeley fa. *Diavoloh!* Or come on, schoolcolours, and we'll
scrap, rug and mat and then be as chummy as two bashed spuds. Bitrial bay
holmgang or betrayal buy jury. Attaboy! Fee gate has Heenan hoity, mind

uncle Hare? What, sir? Poss, myster? Acheve! Thou, thou! What say ye? *Taurus periculosus, morbus pedeiculosus. Miserere mei in miseribilibus!* There's uval lavguage for you! The tower is precluded, the mob's in her petticoats; Mr R. E. Meehan is in misery with his billyboots. Begob, there's not so much green in his Ireland's eye! Sweet fellow ovocal, he stones out of stune. But he could be near a colonel with a voice like that. The bark is still there but the molars are gone. The misery billyboots I used to lend him before we split and, be the hole in the year, they were laking like heaven's reflexes. But I told him make your will be done and go to a general and I'd pray confessions for him. Areesh! Areesh! And I'll be your intrepider. Ambras! Ruffle her! Bussing was before the blood and bissing will behind the curtain. Triss! Did you note that worrid expressionism on his megalogue? A full octavium below me! And did you hear his browrings rattlemaking when he was preaching to himself? And, whoa! do you twig the schamlooking leaf greeping ghastly down his blousyfrock? Our national umbloom! Areesh! He won't. He's shoy. Those worthies, my old faher's onkel that was garotted, Caius Cocoa Codinhand, that I lost in a crowd, used to chop that tongue of his, japlatin, with my yuonkle's owlseller, Woowoolfe Woodenbeard, that went stomebathred, in the Tower of Balbus, as brisk, man, as I'd scoff up muttan chepps and lobscouse. But it's all deafman's duff to me, begob. Sam knows miles bettern me how to work the miracle. And I see by his diarrhio he's dropping the stammer out of his silenced bladder since I bonded him off more as a friend and as a brother to try and grow a muff and canonise his dead feet down on the river airy by thinking himself into the fourth dimension and place the ocean between his and ours, the churchyard in the cloister of the depths, after he was capped out of beurlads scoel for the sin against the past participle and earned the factitation of codding chaplan and being as homely gauche as swift B.A.A. Who gets twickly fullgets twice as alle-manden huskers. But the whacker his word the weaker our ears for auracles who parles parses orileys. Illstarred punster, lipstering cowknucks. 'Twas the quadra sent him and Trinity too. And he can cantab as chipper as any oxon ever I mood with, a tiptoe singer! He'll prisckly soon hand tune your Erin's ear for you. *p.p.* a mimograph at a time, numan bitter, with his ancomartins to read the road roman with false steps ad Pernicious from rhearsilvar ormolus to torquinions superbers while I'm far away from wherever thou art serving my tallyhos and tullying my hostilious by going in by the most holy recitatandas *ffff* for my varsatile examinations in the ologies, to be a coach on the Fukien mission. P? F? How used you learn me, brather soboostius, in my augustan days? With cesarella looking on. In the beginning was the gest he jousstly says, for the end is with woman, flesh-without-word, while the man to be is in a worse case after than before since she on the supine satisfies the verg to him! Toughtough, tootoological. Thou the first person shingeller. Art, an imperfect subjunctive. Paltry, flappent, had serious. Miss Smith onamatterpoetic. Hammisandivis axes colles waxes warmas like sodullas. So pick your stops with fondnes snow. And mind you twine the twos noods of your nicenames. And pull up your furbelovs as far-above as you're farthingales. That'll hint him how to click the trigger. Show you shall and won't he will! His hearing is indoubting just as my seeing is onbelieving. So dactylise him up to blankpoint and let him blink for himself where you speak the best ticklish. You'll feel what I mean. Fond namer, let me never see thee blame a kiss for shame a knee!

Echo, read ending! Siparioramoci! But from the stress of their sunder enlivening, ay clasp, deciduously, a nikrokosmikon must come to mike.

— Well, my positively last at any stage! I hate to look at alarms but, however they put on my watchcraft, must now close as I hereby hear by ear from by seeless socks 'tis time to be up and ambling. Mymiddle toe's mitching, so mizzle I must else 'twill sarve me out. Gulp a bulper at parting and the moore the melodest! Farewell but whenever, as Tisdall told Toole. Tempos fidgets. Let flee me fiacckles, says the grand old manoark, storm-crested crowcock and undulant hair, hoodies tway! Yes, faith, I am as mew let freer, beneath me corthage, bound. I'm as bored now bawling beersgrace at sorepaws there as Andrew Clays was sharing sawdust with Daniel's old collie. This shack's not big enough for me now. I'm dreaming of ye, azores. And, remember this, a chorines, there's the witch on the heath, sistra! 'Bansheeba peeling hourihaared while her Orcotron is hoaring ho. And whinn muinnuit flittsbit twinn her ttittshe cries tallmidy! Daughters of the heavens, be lucks in turnabouts to the wandering sons of red loam! The earth's atrot! The sun's a scream! The air's a jig. The water's great! Seven oldy oldy hills and the one blue beamer. I'm going. I know I am. I could bet I am. Somewhere I must get far away from Banbashore, wherever I am. No saddle, no staffet, but spur on the moment! So I think I'll take freeboots' advise. Psk! I'll borrow a path to lend me wings, quickquack, and from Jehusalem's wall, clickclack, me courser's clear, to Cheerup street I'll travel the void world over. It's Winland for moyne, bickbuck! Jeejakers! I hurt meself nettly that time! Come, my good frogmarchers! We felt the fall but we'll front the defile. Was not my olty mutther, Sereth Maritza, a Running-water? And the bould one that quickened her the seaborne Fingale? I feel like that hill of a whaler went yulding round Groenmund's Circus with his tree full of seaweeds and Dinky Doll asleep in her shell. Hazelridge has seen me. Jerne valing is. Squall aboard for Kew, hop! Farewell awhile to her and thee! The brine's my bride to be. Lead on, Macadam, and danked be he who first sights Halt Linduff! Solo, solone, solong! Lood Erynnana, ware thee wail! With me singame soarem o'erem! Here's me take off. Now's nunc or nimmer, siskinder! Here goes the enemy! Bennydick hotfoots onimpudent stayers! Sorry! I bless alls to the whished with this panromain apological which Watllwewhistlem sang to the kerrycoys. Break ranks! After wage-of-battle bother I am thinking most. Fik yew! I'm through. Won. Toe. Adry. You watch my smoke.

After poor Jaun the Boast's last fireless words of postludium of his soapbox speech ending in'sheaven, twentyaid add one with a flirt of wings were pouring to his bysistance (could they snip that curl of curls to lay with their gloves and keep the kids bright!) prepared to cheer him should he leap or to curse him should he fall, but, with their biga triga rheda rodeo, the cherubs in the charabang, set down here and sedan chair, don't you wish you'd a yoke or a bit in your mouth, repulsing all attempts at first hands on, as no es nada, our greatly misunderstood one we perceived to give himself some sort of a hermetic prod or kick to sit up and take notice, which acted like magic, while the phalanx of daughters of February Filldyke, embushed and climbing, ramblers and weeps, voiced approval in their customary manner by dropping kneedeep in tears over their concelebrated meednight sun-flower, piopadey boy, their solase in dorckaness, and splattering together joyously the plaps of their tappyhands as, with a cry of genuine distress, so prettly prattly pollylogue, they viewed him, the just one, their darling, away.

A dream of favours, a favourable dream. They know how they believe that they believe that they know. Wherefore they wail.

Eh jourd'weh! Oh jourd'woe! dosiriously it psalmodied. Guesturn's lothlied answring to-maronite's wail.

Oasis, cedarous esaltarshoming Leafboughnoon!

Oisis, coolpressus onmountof Sighing!

Oasis, palmost esaltarshoming Gladdays!

Oisis, phantastichal roseway anjerichol!

Oasis, newleavos spaciosing encampness!

Oisis, plantainous dewstuckacqmirage playtennis!

Pipetto, Pipetta has misery unnoticed!

But the strangest thing happened. Backscuttling for the hop off with the odds altogether in favour of his tumbling into the river, Jaun just then I saw to collect from the gentlest weaner among the weiners, (who by this were in half droopleaflong mourning for the passing of the last post) the familiar yellow label into which he let fall a drop, smothered a curse, choked a guffaw, spat expectoratiously and blew his own trumpet. And next thing was he gummalicked the stickyback side and stamped the oval badge of belief to his agnelows brow with a genuine dash of irrepressible piety that readily turned his ladylike typmanzelles capsy curvy (the holy scamp!), with half a glance of Irish frisky (a Juan Jaimesan *hastaluego*) from under the shag of his parallel brows. It was then he made as if be but waved instead a handacross the sea as notice to quit while the pacifettes made their armpacts widdershins (Frida! Freda! Paza! Paisy! Irine! Areinette! Bridomay! Bentamai! Sososopky! Bebebekka! Bababadkessy! Ghugugoothoyou! Dama! Damadomina! Takiya! Tokaya! Scioccara! Siuccherillina! Peocchia! Peucchia! Ho Mi Hoping! Ha Me Happinice! Mirra! Myrha! Solyma! Salemita! Sainta! Sianta! O Peace!), but in selfrighting the balance of his corporeity to reexchange widerembrace with the pillarbosom of the Dizzier he loved prettier, between estellos and venoussas, bad luck to the lie but when next to nobody expected, their star and gartergazer at the summit of his climax, he toppled a lipple on to the off and, making a brandnew start for himself to run down his easting, by blessing hes sthers with the sign of the southern cross, his bungaloid borsaline with the hedgygreen bound blew off in a loveblast (award for trover!) and Jawjon Redhead, bucketing after, meccamaniac, (the headless shall have legs!), kings-couriered round with an easy rush and ready relays by the bridge a stadion beyond Ladycastle (and what herm but he narrowly missed fouling her buttress for her but for he acqueducked) and then, cocking a snook at the stock of his sermons, so mear and yet so fahr from that region's general, away with him at the double, the hulk of a garron, pelting after the road, on Shanks's mare, let off like a wind hound loose (the bouchal! you'd think it was that moment they gave him the jambos!) with a posse of tossing hankerwaves to his windward like seraph's summonses on the air and a tempest of good things in packetshape teeming from all accounts into the funnel of his fanmail shrimpnet, along the highroad of the nation, Traitor's Track, following which fond floral fray he was quickly lost to sight through the statuemen though without a doubt he was all the more on that same head to memory dear while Sickerson, that borne of bjoerne, *la garde auxiliaire* she murmured, hellyg Ursulinka, full of woe (and how fitlier should goodboy's hand be shook than by the warmin of her besom that wrung his swaddles?): *Where maggot Harvey kneeled till bags? Ate Andrew coos hogdam farvel!*

Wethen, now, may the good people speed you, rural Haun, export stout fellow that you are, the crooner born with sweet wail of evoker, healing music, ay, and heart in hand of Shamrogueshire! The googoos of the suckabolly in the rockabeddy are become the copiosity of wiseableness of the friarylayman in the pulpitbarrel. May your bawny hair grow rarer and fairer, our own only wideheaded boy! Rest your voice! Feed your mind! Mint your peas! Coax your qyous! Come to disdoon blarmey and walk our groves so charming and see again the sweet rockelose where first you hymned *O Ciesa Mea!* and touch the light theorbo! Songster, angler, choreographer! Piper to prisoned! Musicianship made Embrassador-at-Large! Good by nature and natural by design, had you but been spared to us, Hauneen lad, but sure where's the use my talking quicker when I know you'll hear me all astray? My long farewell I send to you, fair dream of sport and game and always something new. Gone is Haun! My grief, my ruin! Our Joss-el-Jovan! Our Chris-na-Murty! 'Tis well you'll be looked after from last to first as yon beam of light we follow receding on your photophoric pilgrimage to your antipodes in the past, you who so often consigned your distributory tidings of great joy into our nevertoolatetolove box, mansuetudinous manipulator, victimisedly victorihoarse, dearest Haun of all, you of the boots, true as adie, stepwalker, pennyatimer, lampaddyfair, postanulengro, our rommanychiel! Thy now paling light lucerne we ne'er may see again. But could it speak how nicely would it splutter to the four cantons praises be to thee, our pattern sent! For you had—may I, in our, your and their names, dare to say it?—the nucleus of a glow of a zeal of soul of service such as rarely, if ever, have I met with single men. Numerous are those who, nay, there are a dozen of folks still unclaimed by the death angel in this country of ours today, humble indivisibles in this grand continuum, overlorded by fate and interlarded with accidence, who, while there are hours and days, will fervently pray to the spirit above that they may never depart this earth of theirs till in his long run from that place where the day begins, ere he retourneys postexilic, on that day that belongs to joyful Ireland, the people that is of all time, the old old oldest, the young young youngest, after decades of longsuffering and decennia of brief glory, to mind us of what was when and to matter us of the withering of our ways, their Janyouare Fibyouare wins true from Sylvester (only Walker himself is like Waltzer, whimsicalissimo they go murmurand) comes marching ahome on the summer crust of the flagway. Life, it is true, will be a blank without you because avicuum's not there at all, to nomore cares from nomad knows, ere Molochy wars bring the devil era, a slip of the time between a date and a ghostmark, rived by darby's chilldays embers, spatched fun Juhn that dandyforth, from the night we are and feel and fade with to the yesterselves we tread to turnupon.

But, boy, you did your strong nine furlong mile in slick and slapstick record time and a farfetched deed it was in troth, champion docile, with your high bouncing gait of going and your feat of passage will be contested with you and through you, for centuries to come. The phaynix rose a sun before Erebia sank his smother! Shoot up on that, bright Bennu bird! *Va faotre!* Eftsoon so too will our own sphoenix spark spirt his spyre and sunward stride the rampante flambe. Ay, already the sombrer opacities of the gloom are sphanished! Brave footsore Haun! Work your progress! Hold to! Now! Win out, ye divil ye! The silent cock shall crow at last. The west shall shake the east awake. Walk while ye have the night for morn, light-breakfastbringer, morroweth whereon every past shall full fost sleep. Amain.

[3]

LOWLY, LONGLY, A WAIL WENT FORTH. PURE YAWN lay low. On the mead of the hillock lay, heartsoul dormant mid shadowed landshape, brief wallet to his side, and arm loose, by his staff of citron briar, tradition stick-pass-on. His dream monologue was over, of cause, but his drama parapolylogic had yet to be, affact. Most distressfully (but, my dear, how successfully!) to wail he did, his locks of a lucan tinge, quickrich, ripely rippling, unfilleted, those lashbetasselled lids on the verge of closing time, whiles ouze of his sidewiseopen mouth the breath of him, evenso languishing as the princeliest treble treacle or lichee chewchow purse could buy. Yawn in a semiswoon lay awailing and (hooh!) what helpings of honeyful swoothead (phew!), which earpiercing dulcitude! As were you suppose to go and push with your bluntblank pin in hand upinto his fleshasplush cushionettes of some chubby boybold love of an angel. Hwoah!

When, as the buzzer brings the light brigade, keeping the home fires burning, so on the churring call themselves came at him, from the west-borders of the eastmidlands, three kings of three suits and a crowner, from all their cardinal parts, along the amber way where Brosna's furzy. To lift them they did, senators four, by the first quaint skreek of the gloaming and they hopped it up the mountainy molehill, traversing climes of old times gone by of the days not worth remembering; inventing some excusethems, any sort, having a sevenply sweat of night blues moist upon them. Feefee! phopho!! foorchtha!!! aggala!!!! jeeshee!!!!! paloola!!!!!! ooridiminy!!!!!!! Afeared themselves were to wonder at the class of a crossroads puzzler he would likely be, length by breadth nonplussing his thickness, ells upon ells of him, making so many square yards of him, one half of him in Conn's half but the whole of him nevertheless in Owenmore's five quarters. There would he lay till they would him descry, spancelled down upon a blossomy bed, at one foule stretch, amongst the daffydowndillies, the flowers of narcosis fourfettering his footlights, a halohedge of wild spuds hovering over him, epicures waltzing with gardenfillers, puritan shoots advancing to Aran chiefs. Phopho!! The meteor pulp of him, the seamless rainbowpeel. Aggala!!!! His bellyvoid of nebulose with his neverstop navel. Paloola!!!!!! And his veins shooting melanite phosphor, his creamtocustard cometshair and his asteroid knuckles, ribs and members. Ooridiminy!!!!!!! His electro-latiginous twisted entrails belt.

Those four claymen clomb together to hold their sworn starchamber quiry on him. For he was ever their quarrel, the way they would see themselves, everybug his bodiment atop of annywom her notion, and the meet of their noght was worth two of his morning. Up to the esker ridge it was, Mallinger parish, to a mead that was not far, the son's rest. First klettered Shanator Gregory, seeking spoor through the deep timefield, Shanator Lyons, trailing the wavy line of his partition footsteps (something in his blisters was telling him all along how he had been in that place one time), then his Recordership, Dr Shunadure Tarpey, caperchasing after honourable sleep, hot on to the aniseed and, up out of his prompt corner, old Shunny MacShunny, MacDougal the hiker, in the rere of them on the run, to make a quorum. Roping their ass he was, their skygrey globetrotter, by way of an afterthought and by no means legless either for such sprouts on him they were that much oneven it was tumbling he was by four lengths, within the bawl of a mascot, kuss yuss, kuss cley, patsy watsy, like the kapr in the kabisses, the big ass, to hear with his unaided ears the harp in the air, the bugle dianablowing, wild as wild, the mockingbird whose word is misfortune, so 'tis said, the bulbul down the wind.

The proto was traipsing through the tangle then, Mathew Walker, godsons' goddestfar, deputising for gossipocracy, and his station was a few perch to the weatherside of the knoll Asnoch and it was from no other place unless there, how and ever, that he proxtended aloof upon the ether Mesmer's Manuum, the hand making silence. The buckos beyond on the lea, then stopped wheresoever they found their standings and that way they set ward about him, doing obedience, nod, bend, bow and curtsey, like the watchers of Prospect, upholding their broadawake prober's hats on their firrum heads, the travelling court on its findings circuiting that personer in his fallen. And a crack quatyouare of stenoggers they made of themselves, solons and psychomorers, all told, with their hurts and daimons, spites and clops, not even to the seclusion of their beast by them that was the odd trick of the pack, trump and no friend of carrots. And, what do you think, who should be laying there above all other persons forenenst them only Yawn!

All of asprawl he was laying too amengst the poppies and, I can tell you
something more than that, drear writer, profoundly as you may bedeave to
it, he was oscasleep asleep. And it was far more similar to a satrap he lay
there with unctuous beauty all surrounded, the poser, or for whatall I know
like Lord Lumen, coaching his preferred constellations in faith and doctrine,
for old Matt Gregory, 'tis he had the starmenagerie, Marcus Lyons and
Lucas Metcalfe Tarpey and the mack that never forgave the ass that lurked
behind him, Jonny na Hossaleen.

More than their good share of their five senses ensorcelled you would say
themselves were, fuming censor, the way they could not rightly tell their
heels from their stools as they cooched down a mamalujo by his cubical crib,
as question time drew nighing and the map of the souls' groupography rose
in relief within their quarterings, to play tops or kites or hoops or marbles,
curchycurchy, gawking on him, for the issuance of his pnum and softnoising
one of them to another one, the boguaqueesthers. And it is what they began
to say to him tetrahedrally then, the masters, what way was he.

— He's giving, the wee bairn. Yun has lived.

— Yerra, why dat, my leader?

— Wisha, is he boosed or what, alannah?

— Or his wind's from the wrong cut, says Ned of the Hill.

— Lesten!

— Why so and speak up, do you hear me, you sir?

— Or he's rehearsing somewan's funeral.

— Whisht outathat! Hubba's up!

And as they were spreading abroad on their octopuds their drifter nets,
the chromous gleamy seiners' nets and, no lie, there was word of assonance
being softspoken among those quartermasters.

— Get busy, kid!

— Chirpy, come now!

— The present hospices is a good time.

— I'll take on that chap.

For it was in the back of their mind's ear, temptive lissomer, how they
would be spreading in quadriliberal their azurespotted fine attractable
nets, their nansen nets, from Matt Senior to the thurrible mystagogue
after him and from thence to the neighbour and that way to the puisny
donkeyman and his crucifer's cauda. And in their minds years backslibris,
so it was, slipping beauty, how they would be meshing that way, when he
rose to it, with the planckton at play about him, the quivers of scaly silver
and their clutches of chromes of the highly lucid spanishing gold whilst, as
hour gave way to mazing hour, with Yawn himself keeping time with his

thripthongue, to ope his blurbeous lips he would, a let out classy, the way myrrh of the moor and molten moonmist would be melding mellifond indo his mouth.

— Y?

— Before You!

— Ecko! How sweet thee answer makes! Afterwheres? In the land of lions' odor?

— Friends! First if yu don't mind. Name yur historical grouns.

— This same prehistoric barrow 'tis, the orangery.

— I see. Very good now. It is in your orangery, I take it, you have your letters. Can you hear here me, you sir?

— Throsends. For my darling. Typette!

— So long aforetime? Can you hear better?

— Millions. For godsends. For my darling dearling one.

— Now, to come nearer zone; I would like to raise my deuterous point audibly touching this. There is this maggers. I am told by our interpreter, Hanner Esellus, that there are fully six hundred and six ragwords in your malherbal Magis landeguage in which wald wand rimes alpman and there is resin in all roots for monarch but yav hace not one pronouncable teerm that blows in all the vallums of tartallaght to signify majestate, even provisionally, nor no rheda rhoda or torpentine path or hallucinian via nor aurellian gape nor sunkin rut nor grossgrown trek nor crimeslaved cruxway and no moorhens cry or mooner's plankgang there to lead us to hopenhaven. Is such the *unde derivatur* casematter messio! Frankly. *Magis megis enerretur mynus hoc intelligow.*

— How? C'est mal prononsable, tartagliano, perfrances. Vous n'avez pas d'o dans votre boche provenciale, mousoo. Je m'incline mais *Moy jay trouvay la clee dang les champs*. Hay sham nap poddy velour, come on!

— Hep there! Commong, sa na pa de valure? Whu's teit dans yur jambs? Whur's that inclining and talkin about the messiah so cloover? A true's to your trefling! Whure yu!

— Trinathan partnick dieudonnay. Have you seen her? Typette, my tactile O!

— Are you in your fatherick, lonely one?

— The same. Three persons. Have you seen my darling only one? I am sohohold!

— What are yu shevering about, ultramontane, like a houn? Is there cold on ye, doraphobian? Or do yu want yur primafairy schoolmam?

— The woods of fogloot! O mis padredges!

— Whisht awhile, greyleg! The duck is rising and you'll wake that stand of plover. I know that place better than anyone. Sure, I used to be always overthere on the fourth day at my grandmother's place, Tear-nan-Ogre, my little grey home in the west, in or about Mayo when the long dog gave tongue and they coursing the marches and they straining at the leash. Tortoiseshell for a guineagould! Burb! Burb! Burb! Follow me up Tucurlugh! That's the place for the claire oysters, Polldoody, County Conway. I never knew how rich I was like another story in the zoedone of the zephyros, strolling and strolling, carrying my dragoman, Meads Marvel, thass withumpronouceable tail, along the shore. Do you know my cousin, Mr Jasper Dougal that keeps the Anchor on the Mountain, the parson's son, Jasper of the Tuns, Pat Whateveryournameis?

— Dood and I dood. The wolves of Fochlut! By Whydoyoucallme? Do not flingamejig to the twolves!

— Turcafiera amd that's a good wan right enough! Wooluvs no less!

— One moment now, if I foreshorten the bloss on your bleather. Encroachement spells erosion. Dunlin and turnstone augur us where, how and when best as to burial of carcass, fuselage of dump and committal of noisance. But, since you invocate austers for the trailing of vixens, I would like to send a cormorant around this blue lagoon. Tell me now this. You told my larned friend rather previously, a moment since, about this mound or barrow. Now I suggest to you that ere there was this plagueburrow, as you seem to call it, there was a burialbattell, the boat of millions of years. Would you bear me out in that, relatively speaking, with her jackstaff jerking at her pennyladders, why not, and sizing a fair sail, knowest thout the kind? The *Pourquoi Pas*, bound for Weissduwasland, that fourmaster barquentine, Webster says, our ship that ne're returned. The Frenchman, I say, was an orangeboat. He is a boat. You see him. The both how you see is they! Draken af Danemork! Sacked it or ate it? What! Hennu! Spake ab laut!

— Couch, cortege, ringbarrow, dungcairn. Beseek the runes and see the longurn! Allmaun away when you hear the ganghorn. And meet Nautsen. Ess Ess. O ess. Warum night! Conning two lay payees. Norsker. Her raven flag was out, the slaver. I trow pon good, jordan's scaper, good's barnet and trustyman. Crouch low, you pigeons three! Say, call that girl with the tan tress awn! Call Wolfhound! Wolf of the sea. Folchu! Folchu!

— Very good now. That folklore's straight from the ass his mouth. I will crusade on with the parent ship, weather prophetting, far away from those green hills, a station, Ireton tells me, bonofide for keeltappers, now to come to the midnight middy on this levantine ponenter. From Daneland sailed the oxeyed man, now mark well what I say.

— Magnus Spadebeard, korsets krosser, welsher perfyddye. A destroyer in our port. Signed to me with his baling scoop. Laid bare his breastpaps to give suck, to suckle me. Ecce Hagios Chrisman!

— Oh, Jeyses, fluid! says the poisoned well. Futtfishy the First. Hootchcopper's enkel at the navel manuvres!

— Hep! Hello there, Bill of old Bailey! Whu's he? Whu's this lad, why the pups?

— Hunkalus Childared Easterheld. It's his lost chance, Emania. Ware him well.

— Hey! Did you dream you were ating your own tripe, acushla, that you tied yourself up that wrynecky fix?

— I see now. We move in the beast circuls. Grimbarb and pancercrucer! You took the words out of my mouth. A child's dread for a dragon vicefather. Hillcloud encompass us! You mean you lived as milky at their lyceum, couard, while you learned, volp volp, to howl yourself wolfwise. Dyb! Dyb! Do your best.

— I am dob dob dobbling like old Booth's, courteous. The cubs are after me, it zeebs, the whole totem pack, vuk vuk and vuk vuk to them, for Robinson's shield.

— Scents and gouspils! The animal jangs again! Find the fingall harriers! Here howl me wiseacre's hat till I die of the milkman's lupus!

— What? Wolfgang? Whoah! Talk very slowe!

— *Hail him heathen, heal him holystone!*
Courser, Recourser, Changechild . . . .
Eld es endall, earth . . . . ?

— A cataleptic mithyphallic! Was this *Totem Fulcrum Est* Ancestor yu hald in *Dies Eirae* where no spider webbeth or *Anno Mundi* ere bawds plied in Skiffstrait? Be fair, Chris!

— Dream. Ona nonday I sleep. I dreamt of a somday. Of a wonday I shall wake. Ah! May he have now of here fearfilled me! Sinflowed, O sinflowed! Fia! Fia! Befurcht christ!

— I have your tristich now; it recurs in three times the same differently (there is such a fui fui story which obtains of him): comming nown from the asphalt to the concrete, from the human historic brute, Finnsen Faynean, occeanyclived, to this same vulganized hillsir from yours, Mr Tupling Toun of Morning de Heights, with his lavast flow and his rambling undergroands, would he reoccur *Ad Horam*, as old Romeo Rogers, in city or county, and your sure ob, or by, with or from an urb, of you know the differenciabus, as brauchbarred in apabhramsa, sierrah! We speak of Gun, the farther. And in the locative. Bap! Bap!

— Ouer Tad, Hellig Babbau, whom certayn orbits assertant re humeplace of Chivitats Ei, Smithwick, Rhonnda, Kaledon, Salem (Mass), Childers, Argos and Duthless. Well, I am advised he might in a sense be both nevertheless, every at man like myself, suffix it to say, Abrahamsk and Brookbear! By him it was done bapka, by me it was gone into, to whom it will beblive, Mushame, Mushame! I am afraid you could not heave ahore one of your own old stepstones, barnabarnabarn, over a stumbledown wall here in Huddlestown to this classic Noctuber night but itandthey woule binge, much as vecious, off the dosshouse back of a racerider in his truetoflesh colours, either handicapped on her flat or barely repeating himself. That is a tiptip tim oldy faher now the man I go in fear of, Tommy Terracotta, and he could be all your and my das, the brodar of the founder of the father of the finder of the pfander of the pfunder of the furst man in Ranelagh, fué! fué! Petries and violet ice (I am yam, as Me and Tam Tower used to jagger pemmer it, over at the house of Eddy's Christy, meaning Dodgfather, Dodgson and Coo) and spiriduous sanction!

— Breeze softly. Aures are aureas. Hau's his naun?

— Me das has or oreils. Piercey, piercey, piercey, piercey!

— White eyeluscious and muddyhorsebroth! Pig Pursyriley! But where do we get off, chiseller?

— Haltstille, Lucas and Dublinn! Vulva! Vulva! Vulva! Vulva!

— Macdougal, Atlantic City, or his onagrass that is, chuam and coughan! I would go near identifying you from your stavrotides, Jong of Maho, and the weslarias round your yokohahat. And that O'mulanchonry plucher you have from the worst curst of Ireland, Glwlwd of the Mghtwg Grwpp, is no use to you either, Johnny my donkeyschott. Number four, fix up your spreadeagle and pull your weight!

— Hooshin hom to our regional's hin and the gander of Hayden. Would ye ken a young stepschuler of psychical chirography, the name of Keven, or (let outers pray) Evan Vaughan, of his Posthorn in the High Street, that was shooing a Guiney gagag, Poulepinter, that found the dogumen number one, I would suggest, an illegible downfumbed by an unelgible?

— If I do know sinted sageness? Sometimes he would keep silent for a few minutes as if in prayer and clasp his forehead and during the time he would be thinking to himself and he would not mind anybody who would be talking to him or crying stinking fish. But I no way need you, stroke oar nor your quick handles. Your too farfar a cock of the north there, Matty Armagh, and your due south so.

— South I see. You're up-in-Leal-Ulster and I'm-free-Down-in-Easia, this is much better. He is cured by faith who is sick of fate. The prouts who will invent a writing there ultimately is the poeta, still more learned, who discovered the raiding there originally. That's the point of eschatology our book of kills reaches for now in soandso many counterpoint words. What can't be coded can be decorded if an ear aye sieze what no eye ere grieved for. Now, the doctrine obtains, we have occasioning cause causing effects and affects occasionally recausing altereffects. Or I will let me take it upon myself to suggest to twist Ihe penman's tale posterwise. The gist is the gist of Shaum but the hand is the hand of Sameas. Shan—Shim—Schung. There is a strong suspicion on counterfeit Kevin and we all remember ye in childhood's reverye. 'Tis the bells of scandal that gave tune to grumble over him and someone between me and thee. He would preach to the two turkies and dipdip all the dindians, this master the abbey, and give gold tidings to all that are in the bonze age of anteproresurrectionism to entrust their easter neappearance to Borsaiolini's house of hatcraft. He is our sent on the firm. Now, have you reasonable hesitancy in your mind about him after fourpriest redmass or are you in your post? Tell me andat sans dismay. Leap, pard!

— Fierappel putting years on me! Nwo, nwo! This bolt in hand be my worder! I'll see you moved farther, blarneying Marcantonio! What cans such wretch to say to I or how have My to doom with him? We were wombful of mischief and initiumwise, everliking a liked, hairytop on heeltipper, alpybecca's un wachsibles, an ikeson am ikeson, that babe, imprincipially, my leperd brethern, the Puer, ens innocens of but fifteen primes. Ya all in your kalblionized so trilustriously standing the real school, to be upright as his match, healtheous as is egg, saviour so the salt and good wee braod, parallaling buttyr, did I altermobile him to a flare insiding hogsfat. Been ike hins kindergardien? I know not, O cashla, I am sure offed habitand this undered heaven, meis enfins, contrasting the first mover, that father I ascend fromming knows, as I think, caused whom I, a self the sign, came remaining being dwelling ayr, plage and watford as to I was eltered impostulance possessing my future state falling towards thrice myself resting the childhide when I received the habit following Mezienius connecting Mezosius including was verted embracing a palegrim, circumcised my hairs, Oh laud, and removed my clothes from patristic motives, meas minimas culpads! Permitting this ick (ickle coon icoocoon) crouched low entering humble down, dead thrue mean scatological past, making so smell partaking myself to confess abiding clean tumbluponing yous octopods, mouthspeech allno fingerforce, owning my mansuetude before him attaching Audeon's prostratingwards mine sore accompanying my thrain tropps offering meye eyesalt, what I (the person whomin I now am) did not do, how he to say essied anding how he was making errand andanding how he all locutey sunt, why did you, my sexth best friend, blabber always you would be so delated to back me, then ersed irredent, toppling Humphrey hugging Nephew, old beggelaut, designing such post sitting his night office? Annexing then, producing Saint Momuluius, you snub around enclosing your moving motion touching the other catachumens continuing say providing append of signature quoniam you will celebrand my dirthdags quoniam, concealed a concealer, I am twosides uppish, a mockbelief insulant, ending none meer hyber irish. Well, chunk your dimned chink, before avtokinatown, forasmuch as many have tooken in hand to, I may as well humbly correct that vespian now in case of temporalities. I've my pockets full comeplay of you laycreated cardonals, ap rince, ap rowler, ap rancer, ap rowdey! Improperial! I saved you fore of the Hekkites and you loosed me hind bland Harry to the burghmote of Aud Dub. I teachet you in fair time, my elders, the W.X.Y.Z. and P.Q.R.S. of legatine powers and you, Ailbey and Ciardeclan, I learn, episcoping me altogether, circumdeditioned me. I brought you from the loups of Lazary and you have remembered my lapsus langways. Washywatchywataywatashy! Oiraseheorebukujibun! Watacooshy lot! Mind of poison is. That time thing think! Honorific remembrance to spit humble makes. My ruridecanal caste is a cut above you peregrines. Aye vouchu to rumanescu. See the leabhour of my generations! Has not my master, Theophrastius Spheropneumaticus, written that the spirit is from the upper circle? I'm of the ochlocracy with Prestopher Palumbus and Porvus Parrio. Soa koa Kelly Terry per Chelly Derry lepossette. Ho look at my jailbrand Exquovis and sequencias High marked on me fakesimilar in the foreign by Pappagallus and Pumpusmugnus: ahem! Anglicey: *Eggs squawfish lean yoe nun feed marecurious.* Sagart can self laud nilobstant to Lowman Catlick's patrician morning coat of arms with my High tripenniferry cresta and caudal mottams: Itch dean: which Gaspey, Otto and Sauer, he renders: echo stay so! Addressing eat or not eat body Yours am. And, Mind, praisegad, is the first praisonal Egoname Yod heard boissboissy in Moy Bog's domesday. Hastan the vista! Or in alleman: Suck at!

— Suck it yourself, sugarstick! Misha, Yid think whose was asking to luckat your sore toe or to taste your gaspy, hot and sour! Ichthyan! Hegvat tosser! Gags be plebsed! Between his voyous and her consinnantes! Thugg, Dirke and Hacker with Rose Lankester and Blanche Yorke! Are we speachin d'anglas landadge or are you sprakin sea Djoytsch? Oy soy, Bleseyblasey, where to go is knowing remain? Become quantity that discourse bothersome when what do? Knowing remain? Come back, baddy wrily, to Bullydamestough! Cum him, buddy rowly, with me! What about your thruppenny croucher of an old fellow, me boy, through the ages, tell us, eh? What about

Brian's the Vauntandonlieme, Master Monk, eh, eh, *Spira in Me Domino*, spear me Doyne! Fat prize the bonafide peachumpidgeonlover, eh, eh, eh, esquire earwugs, escusado, of Jenkins' Area, with his I've Ivy under his tangue and the hohallo to his dullaphone, before there was a sound in the world? How big was his boost friend and be shanghaied to him? The swaaber! The twicer, trifoaled in Wanstable! Loud's curse to him! If you hored him outerly as we harum lubberintly, from morning rice till night-male, with his drums and bones and hums in drones your innereer'd heerdly heer he. Ho ha hi he hung! Tsing tsing!

— Me no angly mo, me speakee Yellman's lingas. Nicey Doc Mistel Lu, please! Me no pigey ludiments all same numpa one Topside Tellmastoly fella. Me pigey savvy a singasong anothel time. Pleasie, Mista Lukie Walkie! Josadam cowbelly maam belongame shepullamealahmalong, begolla, Jackinaboss belongashe; plentymuch boohoomeo.

— Hell's Confucium and the Elements! Tootoo moohootch! Thot's never the postal cleric, checking chinchin chat with nipponnippers! Halt there sob story to your lambdad's tale! Are you roman cawthrick 432?

— *Quadrigue my yoke.*

Triple my tryst.

Tandem my sire.

— History as her is harped. Too the toone your owldfrow lied of. Tantris, hattrick, tryst and parting, by vowelglide! I feel your thrilljoy mouths overtspeaking, O dragoman, hands understudium. Plunger words what paddle verbed. Mere man's mime: God has jest. The old order changeth and lasts like the first. Every third man has a chink in his conscience and every other woman has a jape in her mind. Now, fix on the little fellow in my eye, Minucius Mandrake, and follow my little psychosinology, poor armer in slingslang. Now I, the lord of Tuttu, am placing that inital T square of burial jade upright to your temple a moment. Do you see anything, templar?

— I see a blackfrinch pliestrycook . . . who is carrying on his brainpan . . . a cathedral of lovejelly for his . . . *Tiens*, how he is like somebodies!

— Pious, a pious person. What sound of tistress isoles my ear? I horizont the same, this serpe with ramshead, and lay it lightly to your lip a litde. What do you feel, liplove?

— I feel a fine lady . . . floating on a stillstream of isisglass . . . with gold hair to the bed . . . and white arms to the twinklers . . . O la la!

— Purely, in a pure manner. O, sey but swift and still a vain essaying! Trothed today, trenned tomorrow. I invert the initial of your tripartite and sign it sternly, and adze to girdle. on your breast. What do you hear, breastplate?

— I ahear of a hopper behidin the door slappin his feet in a pool of bran.

— Bellax, acting like a bellax. And so the triptych vision passes. Out of a hillside into a hillside. Fairshee fading. Again am I deliciated by the picaresqueness of your irmages. Now, the oneir urge iterimpellant, I feel called upon to ask did it ever occur to you, *qua* you, prior to this, by a stretch of your iberborealic imagination, when it's quicker than this quacking that you might, bar accidens, be very largely substituted in potential secession from your next life by a complementary character, voices apart? Upjack! I shudder for your thought! Think! Put from your mind that and take on trust this. The next word depends on your answer.

— I'm thinking to, thogged be thenked! I was just trying to think when I thought I felt a flea. I might have. I cannot say for it is of no significance at all. Once or twice when I was in odinburgh with my addlefoes, Jake Jones, the handscabby, when I thinkled I wore trying on my garden substisuit, boy's apert, at my nexword nighboor's, and maybe more largely nor you quosh yet you, messmate, realise. A few times, so to shape, I chanced to be stretching, in the shadow as I thought, the liferight out of myself in my ericulous imagining. I felt feeling a half Scotch and pottage like roung my middle ageing like Bewley in the baste so that I indicate out to myself and I swear my gots how that I'm not meself at al!, no jolly fear, when I realise bimiselves how becomingly I to be going to become.

— O, is that the way with you, you craythur? In the becoming was the weared, wontnat! Hood maketh not frere. The voice is the voice of jokeup, I fear. Are you imitation Roma now or Amor now. You have all our empathies, eh, Mr Trickpat, if you don't mind, that is, aside from sings and mush, answering to my straight question?

— God save the monk! I won't mind this is, answering to your strict crossqueets, whereas it would be as unethical for me now to answer as it would have been nonsensical for you then not to have asked. Same no can, home no will, gangin I am. Gangang is Mine and I will return. Out of my name you call me, Leelander. But in my shelter you'll miss me. When Lapac walks backwords he's darkest horse in Capalisoot. You knew me once but you won't know me twice. I am *simpliciter arduus*, ars of the schoo, Freeday's child in loving and thieving.

— My child, know this! Some portion of that answer appears to have been token by you from the writings of Saint Synodius, that first liar. Let us hear, therefore, as you honour and obey the queen, whither the indwellingness of that which shamefieth be entwined of one or atoned of two. Let us hear, Art simplicissime!

— Dearly beloved brethren: Bruno and Nola, leymon bogholders and stationary lifepartners off orangey Saint Nessau Street, were explaining it avicendas all round each other ere yesterweek out of Ibn Sen and Ipanzussch. When himupon Nola Bruno monopolises his egobruno most unwillingly seses by the mortal powers alionola equal and opposite brunoipso, *id est*, eternally provoking alio opposite equally as provoked as Bruno at being eternally opposed by Nola. Poor omniboose, singalow singelearum: so is he!

— One might hear in their beyond that lionroar in the air again, the zoohoohoom of Felin make Call. Bruin goes to Noble, aver who is? If is itsen? Or you mean Nolans but Volans, an alibi, do you Mutemalice, suffering unegoistically from the singular but positively enjoying on the plural? Dustify of that sole, you breather! Ruemember, blither, thou must lie!

— Oyessoyess! I never dramped of prebeing a postman but I mean in ostralian someplace, mults deeply belubdead; my allaboy brother, Negoist Cabler, of this city, whom 'tis better ne'er to name, my said brother, the skipgod, expulled for looking at churches from behind, who is sender of the Hullo Eve Cenograph in prose and worse every Allso's night. High Brazil Brandan's Deferred, midden Erse clare language, Noughtnoughtnought nein. Assass. Dublire, per Neuropaths. Punk. Starving today plays punk opening tomorrow two plays punk wire splosh how two plays punk Cabler. Have you forgotten poor Alby Sobrinos, Geoff, you blighter, identifiable by the necessary white patch on his rear? How he went to his switlersland after his lungs, my sad late brother, before his coglionial expancian? Won't you join me in a small halemerry, a bottle of the best, for wellmet Capeler, united Irishmen, what though preferring the stranger, the coughs and the itches and the minnies and the ratties the opulose and bilgenses, for of his was the patriots mistaken. The heart that wast our Graw McGree! Yet be there some who mourn him, concluding him dead, and more there be that wait astand. His fuchs up the stairs and the ladgers in his haires, he ought to win that *V.V.C.* Fullgrapce for an endupper, half muxy on his whole! Would he were even among the lost! From ours bereft beyond belongs. Oremus poor fraternibus that he may yet escape the gallews and still remain ours faithfully departed. I wronged you. I never want to see more of bad men but I want to learn from any on the airse, like Tass with much thanks, here's ditto, if he lives sameplace in the antipathies of austrasia or anywhere with my fawngest on his hooshmoney, safe and damned, or has hopped it or who can throw any lime on the sopjack, my fond fosther, E. Obiit Nolan, The Workings, N.S.W., his condition off the Venerable Jerrybuilt, not belonging to these parts, who, I remember ham to me, when we were like bro and sis over our castor and porridge, with his roamin I suppose, expecting for his clarenx negus, a teetotum abstainer. He feels he ought to be as asamed of me as me to be ashunned of him. We were in one class of age like to two clots of egg. I am most beholding to him, my namesick, as we sayed it in our Amharican, through the Doubly Telewisher. Outpassed hearts wag short pertimes. Worndown shoes upon his feet, to whose redress no tongue can tell! In his hands a boot! Spare me, do, a copper or two and happy I'll hope you'll be! It will pleased me behind with thanks from before and love to self and all I remain here your truly friend. I am no scholar but I loved that man who has africot lupps with the moonshane in his profile, my shemblable! My freer! I call you my halfbrother because you in your soberer otiumic moments remind me deeply of my natural saywhen brothel in feed, hop and jollity, S. H. Devitt, that benighted irismaimed, who is tearly belaboured by Sydney and Alibany.

— As you sing it it's a study. That letter selfpenned to one's other, that neverperfect everplanned?

— This nonday diary, this allnights newseryreel.

— My dear sir! In this wireless age any owl rooster can peck up bostoons. But whoewaxed he so anquished? Was he vector victored of victim vexed?

— Mighty sure! Way way for his wehicul! A parambolator ram into his bagsmall when he was reading alawd, with two ecolites and he's been failing of that kink in his arts over sense.

— Madonagh and Chiel, idealist leading a double life! But who, for the brilliance of brothers, is the Nolan as appearant nominally?

— Mr Nolan is pronuminally Mr Gottgab.

— I get it. By hearing his thing about a person one begins to place him for a certain in true. You reeker, he stands pat for you before a direct object in the feminine. I see. By maiden sname. Now, I am earnestly asking you, and putting it as between this yohou and that houmonymh, will just you search through your gabgut memoirs for all of two minutes for this impersonating pronolan, fairhead on foulshoulders. Would it be in twofold truth an untaken mispatriate, too fullfully true and rereally a doblinganger much about your own medium with a sandy whiskers? Poke me nabs in the ribs and pick the erstwort out of his mouth.

— Treble Stauter of Holy Baggot Street, formerly Swordmeat, who I surpassed him lately for four and six bringing home the Christmas, as heavy as music, hand to eyes on the peer for Noel's Arch, in blessed foster's place is doing the dirty on me with his tantrums and all these godforgiven kilowatts I'd be better off without. She's write to him she's levt by me, Jenny Rediviva! Toot! Detter for you, Mr Nobru. Toot toot! Better for you, Mr Anol! This is the way we. Of a redtettetterday morning.

— When your contraman from Tuwarceathay is looking for righting that is not a good sign? Not?

— I speak truly, it's a shower sign that it's not.

— What though it be for the sow of his heart? If even she were a good pool Pegeen?

— If she ate your windowsill you wouldn't say sow.

— Would you be surprised after that my asking have you a bull, a bosbully, with a whistle in his tail to scare other birds?

— I would.

— Were you with Sindy and Sandy attending Goliath, a bull?

— You'd make me sag what you like to. I was intending a funeral. Simply and samply.

— They are too wise of solbing their silbings?

— And both croon to the same theme.

— Tugbag is Baggut's, when a crispin sokolist besoops juts kamps or clapperclaws an irvingite offthedocks. A luckchange, I see. Thinking young through the muddleage spread, the moral fat his mental leans on. We can cop that with our straat that is called corkscrewed. It would be the finest boulevard billy for a mile in every direction, from Lismore to Cape Brendan, Patrick's, if they took the bint out of the mittle of it. You told of a tryst too, two a tutu. I wonder now, without releasing seeklets of the alcove, turturs or raabraabs, have I heard mention of whose name anywhere? Mallowlane or Demaasch? Strike us up either end *Have You Erred off Van Homper* or *Ebell Teresa Kane.*

— *Marak! Marak! Marak!*

He drapped has draraks an Mansianhase parak
And he had ta barraw tha watarcrass shartcloths aff the arkbashap af Yarak!

— Braudribnob's on the bummel?

— And lillypets on the lea.

— A being again in becomings again. From the sallies to the allies through their central power?

— Pirce! Perce! Quick! Queck!

— O Tara's thrush, the sharepusher! And he said he was only taking the average grass temperature for green Thursday, the blutchy scaliger! Who you know the musselman, his muscle mum and mistlemam? Maomi, Mamie, My Mo Mum! He loves a drary lane. Feel Phylliscitations to daff Mr Hairwigger who has just hadded twinned little curls! He was resting between horrockses' sheets, wailing for white warfare, prooboor welshtbreton, and unbiassed by the embarrassment of disposal but, the first woking day, by Thunder, he stepped into the breach ant put on his recriution trousers and riding apron in Baltic Bygrad, the old soggy, was when the bold bhuoys of Iran wouldn't join up.

— How voice you that, nice Sandy man? Not large goodman is he, Sandy nice. Ask him this one minute upthrow inner lotus of his burly ear womit he dropped his Bass's to P flat. And for that he was allaughed? And then baited? The whole gammat?

— Loonacied! Marterdyed!! Madwakemiherculossed!!! Judascessed!!!! Pairaskivvymenassed!!!!! Luredogged!!!!!! And, needatellye, faulscrescendied!!!!!!!

— Dias domnas! Dolled to dolthood? And Annie Delittle, his daintree diva, in deltic dwilights, singing him henpecked rusish through the bars? My Wolossay's wild as the Crasnian Sea! Grabashag, groogy, scoop and I'll cure ye! Mother of emeralds, ara poog neighbours!

— Capilla, Rubrilla and Melcamomilla! Dauby, dauby, without dulay! Well, I beg to traverse same above statement by saxy luters in their back haul of Coalcutter what reflects upon my administrants of slow poisoning as my dodear devere revered mainhirr was confined to guardroom, I hindustand, by my pint of his Filthered pilsens bottle due to Zenaphiah Holwell, H and J. C. S, Which I was bringing up my quee parapotacarry's orders in my sedown chair with my mudfacepacket from my cash chemist and family drugger, Surager Dowling, V.S. to our aural surgeon, Afamado Hairductor Achmed Borumborad, M.A.C.A, Sahib, of a 1001 Ombrilla Street, Syringa padham, Alleypulley, to see what was my watergood, my mesical wasserguss, for repairs done by bollworm in the rere of pilch knickers, seven yerds to his galandhar pole on perch, together with his for me unfillable slopper, property of my deeply forfear revebereared, who is costing us mostfortunes which I am writing in mepetition to Kavanagh Djanaral, when he was sitting him humpbacked in dryfilthyheat to his trinidads pinslers at their orpentings, entailing a laxative tendency to mary, especially with him being forbidden fruit and certified by his sexular clergy to have as badazmy emotional volvular, with a basketful of priesters crossing the singorgeous to aroint him with tummy moor's maladies, and thereinafter liable to succumb when served with letters potent below the belch, if my rupee repure riputed husbandship H.R.R. took a brief one in his shirtsails out of the alleged given mineral, telling me see his in Foraignghistan sambat papers Sunday feactures of a welcomed aperrytiff with vallad of Erill Pearcey O he never battered one eagle's before paying me his duty on my annaversary to the parroteyes list in my nil ensemble, in his lazychair but he hidded up my hemifaces in all my mayarannies and he locked plum into my mirrymouth like Ysamasy morning in the end of time, with the so light's hope on his ruddycheeks and rawjaws and, my charmer, whom I dipped my hand in, he simply showed me his propendiculous loadpoker, Seaserpents hisses sissastones, which was as then is produced in his mansway by this wisest of the Vikramadityationists, with the remere remind remure remark, in his gulughurutty: Yran for parasites with rum for the turkeycockeys so Lithia, M.D., as this is for Snooker, bort!

— Which was said by whem to whom?

— It wham. But whim I can't whumember.

— Fantasy! funtasy on fantasy, amnaes fintasies! And there is nihil nuder under the clothing moon. When Ota, weewahrwificle of Torquells, bumpsed her dumpsydiddle down in her woolsark she mode our heuteyleutey girlery of peerlesses to set up in all their bombossities of feudal fiertey, fanned, flounced and frangipanned, while the massstab whereby Ephialtes has exceeded is the measure, *simplex mendaciis*, by which our Outis cuts his thruth. Arkaway now!

— Yerds and nudes say ayes and noes! Vide! Vide!

— Let Eivin bemember for Gates of Gold for their fadeless suns berayed her. Irise, Osirises! Be thy mouth given unto thee! For why do you lack a link of luck to poise a pont of perfect, peace? On the vignetto is a ragingoos. The overseer of the house of the oversire of the seas, Nu-Men, triumphant, sayeth: Fly as the hawk, cry as the corncrake, Ani Latch of the postern is thy name; shout!

— My heart, my mother! My heart, my coming forth of darkness! They know not my heart, O coolun dearast! Mon gloomerie! Mon glamourie! What a surprise, dear Mr Preacher, I to hear from your strawnummical modesty! Yes, there was that skew arch of chrome sweet home, floodlit up above the flabberghosted farmament and bump where the camel got the needle. Talk about iridecencies! Ruby and beryl and chrysolite, jade, sapphire, jasper and lazul.

— Orca Bellona! Heavencry at earthcall, etnat athos? Extinct your vulcanology for the lava of Moltens!

— It's you not me's in erupting, hecklar!

— Ophiuchus being visible above thorizon, muliercula occluded by Satarn's serpent ring system, the pisciolinnies Nova Ardonis and Prisca Parthenopea, are a bonnies feature in the northern sky. Ers, Mores and Merkery are surgents below the rim of the Zenith Part while Arctura, Anatolia, Hesper and Mesembria weep in their mansions over Noth, Haste, Soot and Waste.

— Apep and Uachet! Holy snakes, chase me charley, Eva's got barley under her fluencies! The Ural Mount he's on the move and he'll quivvy her with his strombolo! Waddlewurst, the bag of tow, as broad above as he is below! Creeping through the liongrass and bullsrusshius, the obesendean, before the Emfang de Maurya's class, in Bill Shasser's Shotshrift writing academy, camouflaged as a blancmange and maple syrop! Obeisance so their sitinins is the follicity of this Orp! Her sheik to Slave, his dick to Dave and the fat of the land to Guygas. The treadmill pebbledropper haha halfahead overground and she'd only chitschats in her spanking bee bonetry, Allapolloosa! Up the slanger! Three cheers and a heva heva for the name Dan Magraw!

— The giant sun is in his emanence but which is chief of those white dwarfees of which he ever is surabanded? And do you think I might have being his seventh! He will kitssle me on melbaw. What about his age? says you. What about it? says I. I will confess to his sins and blush me further. I would misdemean to rebuke to the libels of snots from the fleshambles, the canalles. Synamite is too good for them. Two overthirties in shore shorties. She's askapot at Nile Lodge and she's citchincarry at the left Mrs Hamazum's. Will you warn your old habasund, barking at baggermen, his chokefull chewing his chain? Responsif you plais. The said Sully, a barracker associated with tinkers, the blackhand, Shovellyvans, wreuter of annoyimgmost letters and skirriless ballets in Parsee Franch who is Magrath's thug and smells cheaply of Power's spirits, like a deepsea dibbler, and he is not fit enough to throw guts down to a bear. Sylphling me when is a maid nought a maid he would go to anyposs length for her! So long, Sulleyman! If they cut his nose on the stitcher they had their siven good reasons. Here's to the leglift of my snuff and trout stockangt henkerchoff, orange fin with a mosaic of dispensations and a froren black patata, from my church milliner. When Lynch Brother, Withworkers, Friends and Company with T. C. King and the Warden of Galway is prepared to stretch him sacred by the powers to the starlight, L.B.W. Hemp, hemp, hurray! says the captain in the moonlight. I could put him under my pallyass and slepp on him all nights as I would roll myself for holy poly over his borrowing places. How we will make laugh over him together, me and my Riley in the Vickar's bed! Quink! says I. He cawls to me Granny-stream-Auborne when I am hiding under my hair from him and I cool him my Finnyking he's so joyant a bounder. Plunk! said he. Inasmuch as I am delightful to be able to state, with the joy of lifing in my forty winkers, that a handsome sovereign was freely pledged in their pennis in the sluts maschine, alonging wath a cherrywickerkishabrack of maryfruit under Shadow La Rose, to both the legintimate lady performers of display unquestionable, Elsebett and Marryetta Gunning, H_2O, by that noblesse of leechers at his Saxontannery with motto in Wwalshe's ffrenchllatin: O'Neill saw Queen Molly's pants: and much admired engraving, meaning complet manly parts during alleged recent act of our chief mergey margey magistrades, five itches above the kneecap, as required by statues. V.I.C.5.6. If you won't release me stop to please me up the leg of me. Now you see! Respect. S.V.P. Your wife. Amn. Anm. Amm. Ann.

— You wish to take us, Frui Mria, by degrees, as *artis litterarumque patrona* but I am afraid, my poor woman of that same name, what with your silvanes and your salvines, you are misled.

— Alas for livings' pledjures!

— Lordy Daw and Lady Don! Uncle Foozle and Aunty Jack! Sure, that old humbugger was boycotted and girlcutted in debt and doom, on hill and haven, even by the show-the-flag flotilla, as I'm given now to understand, illscribed in all the gratuitouses and conspued in the takeyourhandaways. Bumbty, tumbty, Sot on a Wall, Mute art for the Million. There wasn't an Archimandrite of Dane's Island and the townlands nor a minx from the Isle of Woman nor a one of the four cantins nor any on the whole wheel of his ecunemical conciliabulum nor nogent ingen meid on allad the hold scurface of the jorth would come next or nigh him, Mr Eelwhipper, seed and nursery man, or his allgas bumgalowre, *Auxilium Meum Solo A Domino* (Amsad), for rime or ration, from piles or faces, after that.

— All ears did wag, old Eire wake as Piers Aurell was flappergangsted.

— Recount!

— I have it here to my fingall's ends. This liggy piggy wanted to go to the jampot. And this leggy peggy spelt pea. And theese lucky puckers played at pooping tooletom. Ma's da. Da's ma. Madas. Sadam.

— *Pater patruum cum filiabus familiarum.* Or, but, now, and, ariring out of her mirgery margery watersheads and, to change that subjunct from the traumaturgid for once in a while and darting back to stuff, if so be you may identify yourself with the him in you, that fluctuous neck merchamtur, bloodfadder and milkmudder, since then our too many of her, Abha na Lifé, and getting on to dadaddy again, as them we're ne'er free of, was he in tea e'er he went on the bier or didn't he ontime do something seemly heavy in sugar? He sent out Christy Columb and he came back with a jailbird's unbespokables in his beak and then he sent out Le Caron Crow and the peacies are still looking for him. The seeker from the swayed, the beesabouties from the parent swarm. Speak to the right! Rotacist ca canny! He caun ne'er be bothered but maun e'er be waked. If there is a future in every past that is present *Quis est qui non novit quinnigan* and *Qui quae quot at Quinnigan's Quake!* Stump! His producers are they not his consumers?

Your exagmination round his factification for incamination of a warping process. Declaim!

— Arra irrara hirrara man, weren't they arriving in clansdestinies for the Imbandiment of *Ad Regias Agni Dapes*, fogabawlers and panhibernskers, after the crack and the lean years, scalpjaggers and houthhunters, like the messicals of the great god, a scarlet trainful, the Twoedged Petrard, totalling, leggats and prelaps, in their aggregate ages two and thirty plus undecimmed centries of them with insiders, extraomnes and tuttifrutties allcunct, from Rathgar, Rathanga, Rountown and Rush, from America Avenue and Asia Place and the Affrian Way and Europa Parade and besogar the wallies of Noo Soch Wilds and from Vico, Mespil Rock and Sorrento, for the lure of his weal and the fear of his oppidumic, to his salon de espera in the keel of his kraal, like lodes of ores flocking fast to Mount Maximagnetic, afeerd he was a gunner but affaird to stay away, Merrionites, Dumstdumbdrummers, Luccanicans, Ashtoumers, Batterysby Parkes and Krumlin Boyards, Phillipsburgs, Cabraists and Finglossies, Ballymunites, Raheniacs and the bettlers of Clontarf, for to contemplate in manifest and pay their firstrate duties before the both of him, twelve stone a side, with their *Thieve le Roué!* and their *Shvr yr Thrst!* and their *Uisgye ad Inferos!* and their *Usque ad Ebbraios!* at and in the licensed boosiness primises of his delhightful bazar and reunited magazine hall, by the magazine wall, Hosty's and Co, Exports, for his five hundredth and sixtysixth borthday, the grand old Magennis Mor, Persee and Rahli, taker of the tributes, their Rinseky Poppakork and Piowtor the Grape, holding Dunker's durbar, boot kings and indiarubber umpires and shawhs from paisley and muftis in muslim and sultana reiseines and jordan almonders and a row of jam sahibs and a odd principeza in her pettedcoat and the queen of knight's clubs and the claddagh ringleaders and the two salaames and the Halfa Ham and the Hanzas Khan with two fat Maharashers and the German selver geyser and he polished up, protemptible, tintanambulating to himsilf so silfrich, and there was J. B. Dunlop, the best tyrent of ourish times, and a swanks of French wine stuarts and Tudor keepsakes and the Cesarevitch for the current counter Leodegarius Sant Legerleger riding lapsaddlelonglegs up the oakses staircase on muleback like Amaxodias Isteroprotos, hindquarters to the fore and kick to the lift, and he handygrabbed on to his trulley natural anthem: *Horsibus, keep your tailyup,* and as much as the halle of the vacant fhroneroom, Oldloafs Buttery, could safely accomodate of the houses of Orange and Betters M.P, permeated by Druids D.P, Brehons B.P, and Flawhoolags F.P, and Agiapommenites A.P, and Antepummelites P.P, and Ulster Kong and Munster's Herald with Athclee Ensigning and

Athlone Poursuivant and his Imperial Catchering, his fain awan, and his gemmynosed sanctsons in epheud and ordilawn and his diamondskulled granddaucher, Adamantaya Liubokovskva, all murdering Irish, amok and amak, out of their boom companions in paunchjab and dogril and pammel and gougerotty, after plenty of his fresh stout and his good balls of malt, not to forget his oels a'mona nor his beers o'ryely, sopped down by his pani's annagolorum, (at Kennedy's kiln she kned her dough, back of her bake for me, buns!) socializing and communicanting in the deification of his members, for to nobble or salvage their herobit of him, the poohpooher old bolssloose, with his arthurious clayroses, Dodderick Ogonoch Wrack, busted to the wurld at large, on the table round, with the floodlight switched back, as true as the Vernons have Brian's sword, and a dozen and one by one tilly tallows round in ringcampf, circumassembled by his daughters in the foregiftness of his sons, lying high as he lay in all dimensions, in court dress and ludmers chain, with a hogo, fluorescent of his swathings, round him, like the cummulium of scents in an italian warehouse, erica's clustered on his hayir, the spectrem of his prisent mocking the candiedights of his dadtid, bagpuddingpodded to the deafspot, bewept of his chilidrin and serafim, poors and personalities, venturous, drones and dominators, ancients and auldancients, with his buttend up, expositoed for sale after referee's inspection, bulgy and blowrious, bunged to ignorious, healed cured and embalsemate, pending a rouseruction of his bogey, most highly astounded, as it turned up, after his life overlasting, at thus being reduced to nothing.

— Bappy-go-gully and gaff for us all! And all his morties calisenic, tripping a trepas, neniatwantyng: Mulo Mulelo! Homo Humilo! Dauncy a deady O! Dood dood dood! O Bawse! O Boese! O Muerther! O Mord! Mahmato! Moutmaro! O Smirtsch! O Smertz! Woh Hillill! Woe Hallall! Thou Thuoni I Thou Thaunaton! Umartir! Udamnor! Tschitt! Mergue! Eulumu! Huam Khuam! Malawinga! Malawunga! Ser Oh Ser! See ah See! Hamovs! Hemoves! Mamor! Rockquiem eternuel give donal aye in dolmeny! Bat luck's perpepperpot loosen his eyis! (Psich!).

— But there's leps of flam in Funnycoon's Wick. The keyn has passed. Lung lift the keying!

— God save you king! Muster of the Hidden Life!

— God serf yous kingly, adipose rex! I had four in the morning and a couple of the lunch and three later on, but your saouls to the dhaoul, do ye. Finnk. Fime. Fudd?

— Impassable tissue of improbable liyers! D'yu mean to sett there where y'are now, coddlin your supernumerary leg, wi'that bizar tongue in yur tolkshap, and your hindies and shindies, like a muck in a market, Sorley boy, repeating yurself, and tell me that?

— I mean to sit here on this altknoll where you are now, Surly guy, replete in myself, as long as I live, in my homespins, like a sleepingtop, with all that's buried ofsins insince insensed insidesofme. If I can't upset this pound of pressed ollaves I can sit up zounds of sounds upon him.

— Oliver! He may be an earthpresence. Was that a groan or did I hear the Dingle bagpipes Wasting war and? Watch!

— *Tris tris a ni ma mea!* Prisoner of Love! Bleating Hart! Lowlaid Herd! Aubain Hand! Wonted Foot! *Usque! Usque! Usque! Lignum in . . .*

— Rawth of Gar and Donnerbruck Fire? Is the strays world moving mound or what static babel is this, tell us?

— Whoishe whoishe whoishe whoishe linking in? Whoishe whoishe whoishe?

— The snare drum! Lay yer lug till the groun. The dead giant manalive! They're playing thimbles and bodkins. Clan of the Gael! Hop! Whu's within?

— Dovegall and finshark, they are ring to the rescune!

— Zinzin. Zinzin.

— Crum abu! Cromwell to victory!

— We'll gore them and gash them and gun them and gloat on them.

— Zinzin.

— O, widows and orphans, it's the yeomen! Redshanks for ever! Up Lancs!

— The cry of the roedeer it is! The white hind. Their slots, linklink, the hound hunthorning! Send us and peace! Title! Title!

— Christ in our irish times! Christ on the airs independence! Christ hold the freedman's chareman! Christ light the dully expressed!

— Slog slagt and sluaghter! Rape the daughter! Choke the pope!

— Aure! Cloudy father! Unsure! Nongood!

— Zinzin.

— Sold! I am sold! Brinabride! My ersther! My sidster! Brinabride, goodbye! Brinabride! I sold!

— Pipette dear! Us! Us! Me! Me!

— Fort! Fort! Bayroyt! March!

— Me! I'm true. True! Isolde. Pipette. My precious!

— Zinzin.

— Brinabride, bet my price! Brinabride!

— My price, my precious?

— Zin.

— Brinabride, my price! When you sell get my price!

— Zin.

— Pipette! Pipette, my priceless one!

— O! Mother of my tears! Believe for me! Fold thy son!

— Zinzin. Zinzin.

— Now we're gettin it. Tune in and pick up the forain counties! Hello!

— Zinzin.

— Hello! Tittit! Tell your title?

— Abride!

— Hellohello! Ballymacarett! Am I thru' Iss? Miss? True?

— Tit! What is the ti . . ?

SILENCE.

Act drop. Stand by! Blinders! Curtain up. Juice, please! Foots!

— Hello! Are you Cigar shank and Wheat?

— I gotye. Gobble Ann's Carrot Cans.

— Parfey. Now, after that justajiff siesta, just permit me a moment. Challenger's Deep is childsplay to this but, by our soundings in the swish channels, land is due. A truce to demobbed swarwords. Clear the line, priority call! Sybil! Better that or this? Sybil Head this end! Better that way? Follow the baby spot. Yes. Very good now. We are again in the magnetic field. Do you remember on a particular lukesummer night, following a crying fair day? Moisten your lips for a lightning strike and begin again. Mind the flickers and dimmers! Better?

— Well. The isles is Thymes. The ales is Penzance. Vehement Genral. Delhi expulsed.

— Still calling of somewhave from its specific? Not more? Lesscontinuous. There were fires on every bald hill in holy Ireland that night. Better so?

— You may say they were, son of a cove!

— Were they bonfires? That clear?

— No other name would at all befit them unless that. Bonafieries! With their blue beards streaming to the heavens.

— Was it a high white night now?

— Whitest night mortal ever saw.

— Was our lord of the heights nigh our lady of the valley?

— He was hosting himself up and flosting himself around and ghosting himself to merry her murmur like an andeanupper balkan.

— Lewd's carol! Was there rain by any chance, mistandew?

— Plenty. If you wend farranoch.

— There fell some fall of littlewinter snow, holy-as-ivory, I gather, jesse?

— By snaachtha clocka. The nicest at all. In hilly-and-even zimalayars.

— Did it not blow some gales, westnass or ostscent, rather strongly to less, allin humours out of turn, jusse as they rose and sprungen?

— Out of all jokes it did. Pipep! Icecold. Brr na brr, ny prr! Lieto galumphantes!

— Stll cllng! Nmr! Peace, Pacific! Do you happen to recollect whether Muna, that highluckynackt, was shining at all?

— Sure she was, my midday darling! And not one but a pair of pritty geallachers.

— Quando? Quonda? Go datey!

— Latearly! Latearly! Latearly! Latearly!

— That was latterlig certainly. And was there frostwork about and thick weather and hice, soon calid, soon frozen, cold on warm but moistly dry, and a boatshaped blanket of bruma airsighs and hellstohns and flammballs and vodashouts and everything to please everybody?

— Hail many fell of greats! Horey morey smother of fog! There was, so plays your ahrtides. Absolutely boiled. Obsoletely cowled. Julie and Lulie at their parkiest.

— The amenities, the amenities of the amenities with all their amenities. And the firmness of the formous of the famous of the fumous of the first fog in Maidanvale?

— Catchecatche and couchamed!

— From Miss Somer's nice dream back to Winthrop's delugium stramens. One expects that kind of rimey feeling in the sire season?

— One certainly does. Desire, for hire, would tire a shire, phone, phunkel, or wire. And mares.

— Of whitecaps any?

— Foamflakes flockfuyant from Foxrock to Finglas.

— A lambskip for the marines! Paronama! The entire horizon cloth! All effects in their joints caused ways. Raindrum, windmachine, snowbox. But thundersheet?

— No here. Under the blunkets.

— This common or garden is now in stiller realithy the starey sphere of an oleotorium for broken pottery and ancient vegetables?

— Simply awful the dirt. An evernasty ashtray.

— I see. Now do you know the wellknown kikkinmidden where the illassorted first couple first met with each other? The place where Ealdermann Fanagan? The time when Junkermenn Funagin?

— Deed then I do, W.K.

— In Fingal too they met at Littlepeace aneath the bidetree, Yellow-house of Snugsborough, Westreeve-Astagob and Slutsend with Stockins of Winning's Folly Merryfalls, all of a two, skidoo and skephumble?

— Godamedy, you're a delville of a tolkar!

— Is it a place fairly exspoused to the four last winds?

— Well, I faithly sincerely believe so indeed if all what I hope to charity is half true.

— This stow on the wolds, is it Woful Dane Bottom?

— It is woful in need whatever about anything or allselse under the grianblachk sun of gan greyne Eireann.

— A tricolour ribbon that spells a caution. The old flag, the cold flag.

— The flagstone. By tombs, deep and heavy. To the unaveiling memory of. Peacer the grave.

— And what sigeth Woodin Warneung thereof?

— Trickspissers vill be pairsecluded.

— There used to be a tree stuck up? An overlisting eshtree?

— There used, sure enough. Beside the Annar. At the ford of Slive-namond. Oakley Ashe's elm. With a snoodrift from one beerchen bough. And the grawndest crowndest consecrated maypole in all the reignladen history of Wilds. Browne's *Thesaurus Plantarum* from Nolan's, The Prittlewell Press, has nothing alike it. For we are fed of its forest, clad in its wood, burqued by its bark and our lecture is its leave. The cram, the cram, the king of all crams. Squiremade and damesman of plantagenets, high and holy.

— Now, no hiding your wren under a bushle. What was it doing there, for instance?

— Standing foreninst us.

— In Summerian sunshine?

— And in Cimmerian shudders.

— You saw it visibly from your hidingplace?

— No. From my invisibly lyingplace.

— And you then took down in stereo what took place being tunc committed?

— I then tuk my takenplace lying down, I thunk I told you. Solve it!

— Remounting aliftle towards the ouragan of spaces. Just how grand in cardinal rounders is this preeminent giant, sir Arber? Your bard's highview, avis on valley! I would like to hear you burble to us in strict conclave, purpurando, and without too much italiote interfairance, what you know? *in petto* about our sovereign beingstalk, Tonans Tomazeus. *O dite!*

— Corcor Andy, *Udi, Udite!* Your Ominence, Your Imminence and delicted fraternitrees! There's tuodore queensmaids and Idahore shopgirls and they woody babies growing upon her and bird flamingans sweeny-swinging fuglewards on the tipmast and Orania epples playing hopptociel bommptaterre and Tyburn fenians snoring in his quickenbole and cross-bones strewing its holy floor and culprines of Erasmus Smith's burstall boys with their underhand leadpencils climbing to her crotch for the origin of spices and charlotte darlings with silk blue askmes chattering in dissent to them, gibbonses and gobbenses, guelfing and ghiberring proferring pray-dews to their anatolies and blighting findblasts on their catastripes and the killmaimthem pensioners chucking overthrown milestones up to her to fall her cranberries and her pommes annettes for their unnatural refection and handpainted hoydens plucking husbands of him and cock robins muchmore hatching most out of his missado eggdrazzles for him, the sun and moon pegging honeysuckle and white heather down and timtits tapping resin there and tomahawks watching tar elsewhere, creatures of the wold approaching him, hollow mid ivy, for to claw and rub, hermits of the desert barking their infernal shins over her triliteral roots and his acorns and pinecorns shooting wide all sides out of him, plantitude outsends of plenty to thousands, after the truants of the utmostfear and her downslyder in that snakedst-tu-naughsy whimmering woman't seeleib such a fashionaping sathinous dress out of that exquisitive creation and her leaves, my darling dearest, sinsinsinning since the night of time and each and all of their branches meeting and shaking twisty hands all over again in their new world through the germination of its gemination from Ond's outset till Odd's end. And encircle him circuly. Evovae!

— Is it so exaltated, eximious, extraoldandairy and excelssiorising?

— Amengst menlike trees walking or trees like angels weeping nobirdy aviar soar anywing to eagle it! But rocked of agues, cliffed for aye!

— Telleth that eke the treeth?

— Mushe, mushe of a mixness.

— A shrub of libertine, indeed! But that steyne of law indead what stiles its neming?

— Tod, tod, too hard parted!

— I've got that now, Dr Melamanessy. Finight mens midinfinite true. The form masculine. The gender feminine. I see. Now, are you derevatov of it yourself in any way? The true tree I mean? Let's hear what science has to say, pundit-the-next-best-king. Splanck!

— Upfellbowm.

— It reminds of the weeping of the daughters?

— And remounts to the sense arrest.

— The wittold, the frausch and the dibble! How this looseaffair brimsts of fussforus! And was this treemanangel on his soredbohmend because Knockout, the knickknaver, knacked him in the knechtschaft?

— Well, he was ever himself for the presention of crudities to animals for he had put his own nickelname on every toad, duck and herring before the climber clomb aloft, doing the midhill of the park, flattering his bitter hoolft with her conconundrums. He would let us have the three barrels. Such was a bitte too thikke for the Muster of the hoose so as he called down on the Grand Precurser who coiled him a crawler of the dupest dye and thundered at him to flatch down off that erection and be aslimed of himself for the bellance of hissch leif.

— Oh Finlay's coldpalled!

— Ahday's begatem!

— Were you there, eh Hehr? Were you there when they lagged um through the coombe?

— Wo wo! Who who! Psalmtimes it grauws on me to ramble, ramble, ramble.

— Woe! Woe! So that was kow he became the foerst of our treefellers?

— Yesche and, in the absence of any soberiquiet, the fanest of our truefalluses. Bapsbaps Bomslinger!

— How near do you feel to this capocapo promontory, sir?

— There do be days of dry coldness between us when he does be like a lidging house far far astray and there do be nights of wet windwhistling when he does be making me onions woup all kinds of ways.

— Now you are mehrer the murk, Lansdowne Road. She's threwed her pippin's thereabouts and they've cropped up tooth oneydge with hates to leaven this socried isle. Now, thornyborn, follow the spotlight, please! Concerning a boy. Are you acquainted with a pagany, vicariously known as Toucher 'Thom' who is. I suggest Finoglam as his habitat. Consider yourself on the stand now and watch your words, take my advice. Let your motto be: *Inter nubila numbum.*

— Never you mind about my mother or her hopitout. I consider if I did, I would feel frightfully ashamed of admired vice.

— He is a man of around fifty, struck on Anna Lynsha's Pekoe with milk and whisky, who does messuages and has more dirt on him than an old dog has fleas, kicking stones and knocking snow off walls. Have you ever heard of this old boy "Thom" or "Thim" of the fishy stare who belongs to Kimmage, a crofting district, and is not all there, and is all the more himself since he is not so, being most of his time down at the Green Man where he steals, pawns, belches and is a curse, drinking gaily two hours after closing time, with the coat on him skinside out against rapparitions, with his socks

outsewed his springsides, clapping his hands in a feeble sort of way and
systematically mixing with the public going for groceries, slapping greats
and littlegets soundly with his cattegut belts, flapping baresides and waltzy-
wembling about in his accountrements always in font of the tubbernuckles,
like a longarmed lugh, when he would be finished with his tea?

— Is it that fellow? As mad as the brambles he is. Touch him. With the
lawyers sticking to his trewsershins and the swatmenotting on the basque of
his beret. He has kissed me more than once, I am sorry to say and if I did
commit gladrolleries may the loone forgive it! O wait till I tell you!

— We are not going yet.

— And look here! Here's, my dear, what he done, as snooks as I am
saying so!

— Get out, you dirt! A strangely striking part of speech for the hottest
worked word of ur sprogue. You're not! Unhindered and odd times? Mere
thumbshow? Lately?

— How do I know? Such my billet. Buy a barrack pass. Ask the horneys.
Tell the robbers.

— You are alluding to the picking pockets in Lower O'Connell Street?

— I am illuding to the Pekin packet but I am eluding from Laura
Connor's treat.

— Now, just wash and brush up your memoirias a little bit. So I find,
referring to the pater of the present man, an erely demented brick thrower,
I am wondering to myself in my mind, *qua* our arc of the covenant, was
Toucher, a methodist, whose name, as others say, is not really 'Thom', was
this salt son of a century from Boaterstown, Shivering William, the sealiest
old forker ever hawked crannock, who is always with him at the Big Elm
and the Arch after his teeth were shaken out of their suckets by the wrang
dog, for having 5 pints 73 of none Eryen blood in him abaft the seam level,
the scatterling, wearing his cowbeamer and false clothes of a brewer's grains
pattern with back buckons with his motto on, *Yule Remember*, ostensibly for
that occasion only of the twelfth day Pax and Quantum wedding, I'm
wondering.

— I bet you are. Well, he was wandering, you bet, whatever was his
matter, in his mind too, give him his due, for I am sorry to have to tell you,
hullo and evoe, they were coming down from off him.

— How culious an epiphany!

— *Hodie casus esobbrakonton?*

— It looked very like it.

— Needer knows necess and neither garments. Man is minded of the
Meagher, wat? Wooly? Walty?

— Ay, another good button gone wrong.

— Blondman's blaff! Like a skib leaked lintel the arbour leidend with . . . ?

— Pamelas, peggylees, pollywollies, questuants, quai aquilties, quicka-merries.

— Concaving now convexly to the semidemihemispheres and, from the female angle, music minnestirring, were the subligate sisters, P. and Q., Clopatrick's cherierapest, *mutatis mutandis*, in pretty much the same pickle, the peach of all piedom, the quest of all quicks?

— Peequeen ourselves, the prettiest pickles of unmatchemable mute antes I ever bopeeped at, seesaw shallshee. since the town go went gonning on Pranksome Quaine.

— Silks apeel and sulks alusty?

— Boy and giddle, gape and bore.

— I hear these two goddesses are liable to sue him?

— Well, I hope the two Collinses don't leg a bail to shoot him.

— Both were white in black arpists at cloever spilling, knickt?

— Gels bach, I, languised, liszted. Etoudies for the right hand.

— Were they now? And were they watching you as watcher as well?

— Where do you get that wash? This representation does not accord with my experience. They were watching the watched watching. Vechers all.

— Good. Hold that watching brief and keep this witching longuer. Now, retouching friend Tomsky, the enemy, did you gather much from what he let drop? We are sitting here for that.

— I was rooshian mad, no lie. About his shapeless hat.

— I suspect you must have been.

— You are making your thunderous mistake. But I was dung sorry for him too.

— O Schaum! Not really? Were you sorry you were mad with him then?

— When I tell you I was rooshiamarodnimad with myself altogether, so I was, for being sorry for him.

— So?

— Absolutely.

— Would you blame him at all stages?

— I believe in many an old stager. But what seemed sooth to a Greek summed nooth to a giantle. Who kills the cat in Cairo coaxes cocks in Gaul.

— I put it to you that this was solely in his sunflower state and that his haliodraping het was why maids all sighed for him, ventured and vied for him. Hm?

— After Putawayo, Kansas, Liburnum and New Aimstirdames, it wouldn't surprise me in the very least.

— That tare and this mole, your tear and our smile. 'Tis life that lies if woman's eyes have been our old undoing. Lid efter lid. Reform in mine size his deformation. Tiffpuff up my nostril, would you puff the earthworm outer my ear.

— He could claud boose his eyes to the birth of his garce, he could lump all his lot through the half of her play, but he jest couldn't laugh through the whole of her farce becorpse he warn't billed that way. So he outandouts his volimetangere and has a lightning consultation and he downadowns his pantoloogions and made a piece of first perpersonal puetry that staystale remains to be. Cleaned.

— Booms of bombs and heavy rethudders?

— This aim to you!

— The tail, so mastrodantic, as you tell it nearly takes your own mummouth's breath away. Your troppers are so unrelieved because his troopers were in difficulties. Still let stultitiam done in veino condone ineptias made of veritues. How many were married on that top of all strapping mornings, after the midnight turkay drive, my good watcher?

— Puppaps. That'd be telling. With a hoh frohim and heh fraher. But, as regards to Tammy Thornycraft, Idefyne the lawn mare and the laney moweress and all the prentisses of wildes to massage him.

— Now from Gunner Shotland to Guinness Scenography. Come to the ballay at the Tailors' Hall. We mean to be mellay on the Mailers' Mall. And leap, rink and make follay till the Gaelers' Gall. Awake! Come, a wake! Every old skin in the leather world, infect the whole stock company of the old house of the Leaking Barrel, was thomistically drunk, two by two, lairking o' tootlers with tombours a'beggars, the blog and turfs and the brandywine bankrompers, trou Normend fashion, I have been told down to the bank lean clorks? Some nasty blunt clubs were being operated after the tradition of a wellesleyan bottle riot act and a few plates were being shied about and tumblers bearing traces of fresh porter rolling around, independent of that, for the ehren of Fyn's Insul, and then followed that wapping breakfast at the Heaven and Covenant, with Rodey O'echolowing how his breadcost on the voters would be a comeback for e'er a one, like the depredations of Scandalknivery, in and on usedtowobble sloops off cloasts, eh? Would that be a talltale too? This was the grandsire Orther. This was his innwhite horse. Sip?

— Well, naturally he was, louties also genderymen. Being Kerssfesstiydt. They came from all lands beyond the wave for songs of Inishfeel. Whiskway and mortem! No puseyporcious either, invitem kappines all round. But the right reverend priest, Mr Hopsinbond, and the reverent bride eleft, Frizzy Fraufrau, were sober enough. I think they were sober.

— I think you're widdershins there about the right reverence. Magraw for the Northwhiggern cupteam was wedding beastman, papers before us carry. You saw him hurriedly, or did you if thatseme's not irrelevant? With Slater's hammer perhaps? Or he was in serge?

— I horridly did. On the stroke of the dozen. I'm sure I'm wrong but I heard the irreverend Mr Magraw, in search of a stammer, kuckkuck kicking the bedding out of the old sexton, red-Fox Good-man around the sacristy, till they were bullbeadle black and bufeteer blue, while I and Flood and the other men, jazzlike brollies and sesuos, was gickling his missus to gackles in the hall, the divileen, (she's a lamp in her throth) with her cygncygn leckle and her twelve pound lach.

— A loyal wifish woman cacchinic wheepingcaugh! While she laylylaw was all their rage. But you did establish personal contact? In epexegesis or on a point of order?

— That perkumiary pond is beyawnd my pinnigay pretonsions. I am resting on a pigs of cheesus but I've a big suggestion it was about the pint of porter.

— You are a suckersome! But this all, as airs said to oska, as only that childbearer might blogas well sidesplit? Where letties hereditate a dark mien swart hairy?

— Only. 'Twas womans' too woman with mans' throw man.

— Bully burley yet hardly hurley. The saloon bulkhead, did you say, or the tweendecks?

— Between drinks, I deeply painfully repeat it.

— Was she wearing shubladey's tiroirs in humour of her hubbishobbis, Massa's star stellar?

— Mrs Tan-Taylour? Just a floating panel, secretairslidingdraws, a budge of klees on her schalter, a siderbrass sehdass on her anulas findring and forty crocelips in her curlingthongues.

— So this was the dope that woolied the cad that kinked the ruck that noised the rape that tried the sap that hugged the mort?

— That legged in the hoax that joke bilked.

— The jest of junk the jungular?

— Jacked up in a jock the wrapper.

— Lollgoll! You don't soye so! All upsydown her whole creation? So there was nothing serical between you? And Drysalter, father of Izod, how was he now?

— To the pink, man, like an allmanox in his shirt and stickup, brustall to the bear, the Megalomagellan of our winevatswaterway, squeezing the life out of the liffey.

— Crestofer Carambas! Such is zodisfaction. You punk me! He came, he kished, he conquered. Vulturuvarnar! The must of his glancefull coaxing the beam in her eye? That musked bell of this masked ball! Annabella, Lovabella, Pullabella, yep?

— Yup! Titentung Tollertone in S. Sabina's. Aye aye, she was lithe and pleasable. Wilt thou the lee? Wilt thou the hee? Wilt thou the hussif?

— The quicker the deef the safter the sapstaff, but the main the mightier the stricker the strait. To the vast go the game! It is the circumconversioning of antelithual paganelles by a huggerknut cramwell energuman, or the caecodedition of an absquelitteris puttagonnianne to the herreraism of a cabotinesque exploser?

— I believe you. Taiptope reelly, O reely!

— Nautaey, nautaey, we're nowhere without ye! In steam of kavos now arbatos above our hearths doth hum. And Malkos crackles logs of fun while Anglys cheers our ingles. So lent she him ear to burrow his manhood (or so it appierce) and borrow his namas? Suilful eyes and sallowfoul hairweed and the sickly sigh from her gingering mouth like a Dublin bar in the moarning.

— *Primus auriforasti me.*

— The park is gracer than the hole, says she, but shekleton's my fortune?

— Eversought of being artained? You've soft a say with ye, Flatter O'Ford, that, honey, I hurdley chew you.

— Is that answers?

— It am queery!

— The house was Toot and Come-Inn by the bridge called Tiltass, but are you solarly salemly sure, beyond the shatter of the canicular year? *Nascitur ordo seculi numfit.*

— Siriusly and selenely sure behind the shutter. *Securius indicat umbris tellurem.*

— Date as? Your time of immersion? We are still in drought of . . . ?

— Amnis Dominae, Marcus of Corrig. A laughin hunter and Purty Sue.

— And crazyheaded Jorn, the bulweh born?

— Fluteful as his orkan. *Ex ugola lenonem.*

— And Jambs, of Delphin's Bourne or (as olders lay) of Tophat?

— Dawncing the kniejinksky choreopiscopally like an easter sun round the colander, the vice! Taranta boontoday! You should pree him prance the polcat, you whould sniff him wops around, you should hear his piedigrotts schraying as his skimpies skirp a . . .

— Crashedafar Corumbas! A Czardanser indeed! Dervilish glad too. *Ortovito semi ricordo.* The pantaglionic affection through his blood like a bad influenza in a leap at bounding point?

— Out of Prisky Poppagenua, the palsied old priamite, home from Edwin Hamilton's Christmas pantaloonade, *Oropos Roxy and Pantharbea* at the Gaiety, trippudiating round the aria, with his fiftytwo heirs of age! They may reel at his likes but it's Noeh Bonum's shin do.

— And whit what was Lillabil Issabil maideve, maid at?

— Trists and thranes and trinies and traines.

— A take back to the virgin page, darm it!

— Ay, graunt ye.

— The quobus quartet were there too, if I mistake not, as a sideline but, *pace* the contempt of senate, well to the fore, in an amenessy meeting, metandmorefussed to decide whereagainwhen to meet themselves flopsome and jerksome, lubber and deliric, drinking unsteadily through the Kerry quadrilles and Listowel lancers and mastersinging always with that consecutive fifth of theirs, eh? Like four wise elephants inandouting under a twelvepodestalled table?

— They were simple scandalmongers, that familiar, and all! Normand, Desmond, Osmund and Kenneth. Making mejical history all over the show!

— In sum, some hum? And other marrage feats?

— All our stakes they were astumbling round the ranky roars assumbling when Big Arthur flugged the field at Annie's courting.

— Suddenly some wellfired clay was cast out through the schappsteckers of hoy's house?

— Schottenly there was a hellfire club kicked out through the wasistas of Thereswhere.

— Like Heavystost's envil catacalamitumbling. Three days three times into the Vulcuum?

— Punch!

— Or Noe et Ecclesiastes, nonne?

— Ninny, there is no hay in Eccles's hostel.

— Yet an I saw a sign of him, if you could scrape out his acquinntence? Name or redress him and we'll call it a night!

— .i..'. .o..l .

— You are sure it was not a shuler's shakeup or a plighter's palming or a winker's wake *etcaetera etcaeterorum* you were at?

— Precisely.

— Mayhap. Hora pro Nubis, Thundersday, at A Little Bit Of Heaven Howth, the wife of Deimetuus (D'amn), Earl Adam Fitzadam, of a Tartar (Birtha) or Sackville-Lawry and Morland-West, at the Auspice for the Living, Bonnybrook, by the river and A. Briggs Carlisle, guardian of the birdsmaids and deputiliser for groom. Pontifical mess. Or (soddenly) Schott, furtivfired by the riots. No flies. Agreest?

— Mayhem. Also loans through the post. With or without security. Everywhere. Any amount. Mofsovitz, swampstakers, purely providential.

— Flood's. The pinkman, the squeeze, the pint with the kick. Gaa. And then the punch to Gaelicise it. Fox. The lady with the lamp. The boy in the barleybag. The old man on his ars. Great Scrapp! 'Tis we and you and ye and me and hymns and hurts and heels and shields. The eirest race, the ourest nation, the airest place that erestationed. He was culping for penance while you were ringing his belle. Did the kickee, goodman rued fox, say anything important? Clam or cram, spick or spat?

— No more than Richman's periwhelker.

— Nnn ttt wrd?

— Dmn ttt thg.

— A gael galled by scheme of scorn? Nock?

— Sangnifying nothing. Mock!

— *Fortitudo eius rhodammum tenuit?*

— Five maim! Or something very similar.

— I should like to euphonise that. It sounds an isochronism. Secret speech Hazelton and obviously disemvowelled. But it is good laylaw too. We may take those wellmeant kicks for free granted, though *ultra vires*, void and, in fact, unnecessarily so. Happily you were not quite so successful in the process verbal whereby you would sublimate your blepharospasmockical suppressions, it seems?

— What was that? First I heard about it.

— Were you or were you not? Ask yourself the answer, I'm not giving you a short question. Now, not to mix up, cast your eyes around Capel Court. I want you, witness of this epic struggle, as yours so mine, to reconstruct for us, as briefly as you can, inexactly the same as a mind's eye view, how these funeral games, which have been poring over us through homer's kerryer pidgeons, massacreedoed as the holiname rally round took place.

— Which? Sure I told you that afoul. I was drunk all lost life.

— Well, tell it to me befair, the whole plan of campaign, in that bamboozelem mincethrill voice of yours. Let's have it, christie! The Dublin own, the thrice familiar.

— Ah, sure, I eyewitless foggus. 'Tis all around me bebattersbid hat.

— Ah, go on now, Masta Bones, a gig for a gag, with your impendements and your perroqtriques! Blank memory of hatless darky in blued suit. You were ever the gentle poet, dove from Haywarden. Pitcher cup, patcher cap, pratey man? Be nice about it, Bones Minor! Look chairful! Come, delicacy! GO to the end, thou slackerd! Once upon a grass and a hopping high grass it was.

— Faith, then, Meesta Cheeryman, first he come up, a gag as a gig, badgeler's rake to the town's major from the wesz, MacSmashall Swingy of the Cattelaxes, got up regardless, with a cock on the Kildare side of his Tattersull, in his riddlesneek's ragamufflers and the horrid contrivance as seen above, whisklyng into a bone tolerably delicately, the *Wearing of the Blue*, and taking off his plushkwadded bugsby in his perusual flea and loisy manner, saying good mrowkas to weevilybolly and dragging his feet in the usual course and was ever so terribly naas, really, telling him clean his nagles and fex himself up, Miles, and so on and so fort, and to take the coocoomb to his grizzlies and who done that foxy freak on his bear's hairs like fire bursting out of the Ump pyre and, half hang me, sirr, if he wasn't wanting his calicub body back before he'd to take his life or so save his life. Then, begor, counting as many as eleven to thritytwo seconds with his pocket browning, like I said, wann swanns wann, this is my awethorrorty, he kept forecursing hascupth's foul Fanden, Cogan, for coaccoackey the key of John Dunn's field fore it was for sent and the way Montague was robbed and wolfling to know all what went off and who burned the hay, perchance wilt thoult say, before he'd kill all the kanes and the price of Patsch Purcell's faketotem, which the man, his plantagonist, up from the bog of the depths who was raging with the thirst of the sacred sponge and who, as a mashter of pasht, so far as him was concerned, was only standing there nonplush to the corner of Turbot Street, perplexing about a paumpshop and pupparing to spit, wanting to know whelp the henconvention's compuss memphis he wanted with him new nothing about.

— A sarsencruxer, like the Nap O' Farrell Patter Tandy moor and burgess medley? In other words, was that how in the annusual curse of things, as complement to compliment though, after a manner of men which I must and will say seems extraordinary, their celicolar subtler angelic warfare or photoplay finister started?

— Truly. That I may never!

— Did one scum then in the auradrama, the deff, after some clever play in the mud, mention to the other undesirable, a dumm, during diverse intentional instants, that upon the resume after the angerus, how for his deal he was a pigheaded Swede and to wend himself to a medicis?

— To be sore he did, the huggornut! Only it was turniphudded dunce, I beg your pardon, and he would jokes bowlderblow the betholder with his black masket off the bawling green.

— Sublime was the warning!

— The author, in fact, was mardred.

— Did he, the first spikesman, do anything to him, the last spokesman, when, after heaving some more smutt and chaff between them, they rolled togutter into the ditch together? Black Pig's Dyke?

— No, he had his teeth in the hack of his head.

— Did Box then try to shine his puss?

— No but Cox did to shin the punman.

— The worsted crying that if never he looked on Leaverholma's again and the bester huing that he might ever save sunlife?

— Trulytruly Asbestos he ever. And sowasso I never.

— That forte carlysle touch breaking the campdens pianoback.

— Pansh!

— Are you of my meaning that would be going on to about half noon, click o'clock, pip emma, Grinwicker time, by your querqcut quadrant?

— You will be asking me and I wish to higgins you wouldn't. Would it?

— Let it be twelve thirty after a somersautch of the tardest!

— And it was eleven thirstytoo befour in soandsuch, reloy on it!

— Tick up on time. Howday you doom? That rising day sinks rosing in a night of nine week's wonder.

— Amties, marcy buckup! The uneven day of the unleventh month of the unevented year. At mart in mass.

— A triduum before Our Larry's own day. By which of your chronos, my man of four watches, larboard, starboard, dog or dath?

— Dunsink, rugby, ballast and ball. You can imagine.

— Language this allsfare for the loathe of Marses ambiviolent about it. Will you swear all the same you saw their shadows a hundred foot later, struggling diabolically over this, that and the other, their virtues *pro* and his principality *con*, near the Ruins, Drogheda Street, and kicking up the devil's own dust for the Milesian wind?

— I will. I did. They were. I swear. Like the heavenly militia. So wreek me Ghyllygully! With my tongue through my toecap on the headlong stone of kismet if so 'tis the will of Whose B. Dunn.

— Weepin Lorcans! They must have put in some wonderful work, ecad, on the quiet like, during this arms' parley, meatieriues forces vegateareans. Dost thou not think so?

— Ay.

— The illegallooking range or fender, alias turfing iron, a product of Hostages and Co, Engineers, changed feet several times as briars revalvered during the weaponswap? Piff?

— Puff! Excuse yourself. It was an ersatz lottheringcan.

— They did not know the war was over and were only berebelling or bereppelling one another by chance or necessity with sham bottles, mere and woiney, as betwinst Picturshirts and Scutticules, like their caractacurs in an Irish Ruman to sorowbrate the expeltsion of the Danos? What sayest thou, scusascmerul?

— That's all. For he was heavily upright man, Limba romena in Bucclis tucsada. Farcing gutterish.

— I mean the Morgans and the Dorans, in finnish?

— I know you don't, in Feeney's.

— The mujic of the footure on the barbarihams of the bashed? Co Canniley?

— Da Donnuley.

— Yet this war has meed peace? *In voina viritas.* Ab chaos lex, neat wehr?

— O bella! O pia! O pura! Amem. Handwalled amokst us. Thanksbeer to Balbus!

— All the same you sound it twould clang houlish like Hull hopen for christmians?

— But twill cling hellish like engels opened to neuropeans, if you've sensed, whole the sum. So be vigil!

— And this pattern pootsch punnermine of concoon and proprey went on, hog and minne, a whole whake, your night after larry's night, spittinspite on Dora O'Huggins, ormonde caught butler, the artillery of the O'Hefferns answering the cavalry of the MacClouds, fortey and more fortey, a thousand and one times, according to your cock and a biddy story? Lludillongi, for years and years perhaps?

— That's ri. This is his largos life, this is me timtomtum and this is her two peekweeny ones. From the last finger on the second foot of the fourth man to the first one on the last one of the first. That's right.

— Finny. Vary vary finny!

— It may look funny but fere it is.

— This is not guid enough, Mr Brasslattin. Finging and tonging and winging and ponging! And all your rally and ramp and rant! Didget think I was asleep at the wheel? D'yu mean to tall grand jurors of thathens of tharctic on your oath, me lad, and ask us to believe you, for all you're enduring long terms, with yur last foot foremouthst, that yur moon was shining on the tors and on the cresties and winblowing night after night, for years and years perhaps, after you swearing to it a while back before your Corth examiner, Markwalther, that there was reen in planty all the teem?

— Perhaps so, as you grand duly affirm, Robman Calvinic. I never thought over it, faith. I most certainly think so about it. I hope. Unless it is actionable. It would be a charity for me to think about something which I must on no caste accounts omit, if you ask to me. It was told me as an inspired statement by a friend of myself, in reply to salute, Tarpey, after three o'clock mass, with forty ducks indulgent, that some rain was promised to Mrs Lyons, the invalid of Aunt Tarty Villa, with lots gulp and sousers and likewise he told me, the recusant, after telling mass, with two hundred genuflexions, at the split hour of blight when bars are keeping so sly, as was what's follows. He is doing a walk, says she, in the feelmick's park, says he, like a tarrable Turk, says she, letting loose on his nursery and, begalla, he meet himself with Mr Michael Clery of a Tuesday who said Father MacGregor was desperate to the bad place about thassbawls and ejaculating about all the stairrods and the catspew swashing his earwanker and thin-convenience being locked up for months, owing to being putrenised by stragglers abusing the apparatus, and for Tarpey to pull himself into his soup and fish and to push on his borrowsaloaner and to go to the tumple like greased lining and see Father MacGregor and, be Cad, sir, he was to pipe up and saluate that clergyman and to tell his holiness the whole goat's throat about the three shillings in the confusional and to say how Mrs Lyons, the cuptosser, was the infidel who prophessised to pose three shielings Peter's pelf off her tocher from paraguais and albs by the yard to Mr Martin Clery for Father Mathew to put up a midnight mask saints withins of a Thrushday for African man and to let Brown child do and to leave he Anlone and all the nuisances committed by soldats and nonbehavers and missbelovers for N.D. de l'Ecluse to send more heehaw hell's flutes, my prodder again! And I never brought my cads in togs blanket! Foueh!

— Angly as arrows, but you have right, my celtslinger! Nils, Mugn and Cannut. Should brothers be for awe then?

— So let use off be octo while oil bike the bil and wheel whang till wabblin befoul you but mere and mire trullopes will knaver mate a game on the bibby bobby burns of.

— Quatsch! What hill ar yu fluking about, ye lamelookond fyats! I'll discipline ye! Will you swear or affirm the day to yur second sight noo and recant that all yu affirmed to profetised at first sight for his southerly accent was all paddyflaherty? Will ye, ay or nay?

— Ay say aye. I affirmly swear to it that it rooly and cooly boolyhooly was with my holyhagionous lips continuously poised upon the rubricated annuals of saint ulstar.

— That's very guid of ye, R.C.! Maybe yu wouldn't mind talling us, my labrose lad, how very much bright cabbage or paperming comfirts d'yu draw for all yur swearin? The spanglers, kiddy?

— Rootha prootha. There you have me! Vurry nothing, O potators, I call it for I might as well tell yous Essexelcy, and I am not swallowing my air, the Golden Bridge's truth. It amounts to nada in pounds or pence. Not a glass of Lucan nor as much as the cost price of a highlandman's trousertree or the three crowns round your draphole (isn't it dram disgusting?) for the whole dumb plodding thing!

— Come now, Johnny! We weren't bom yesterday. *Pro tanto quid retribuamus?* I ask you to say on your scotty pictail you were promised fines times with some staggerjuice or deadhorse, on strip or in larges, at the Raven and Sugarloaf, either Jones's lame or Jamesy's gait, anyhow?

— Bushmillah! Do you think for a moment? Yes, by the way. How very necessarily true! Give me fair play. When?

— At the Dove and Raven tavern, no, ah? To wit your wizzend?

— Water, water, darty water! Up Jubilee sod! Beet peat wheat treat!

— What harm wants but demands it! How would you like to hear yur right name now, Ghazi Power, my tristy minstrel, if yur not freckened of frank comment?

— Not afrightened of Frank Annybody's gaspower or illconditioned ulcers neither.

— Your uncles!

— Your gullet!

— Will you repeat that to me outside, leinconnmuns?

— After you've shouted a few? I will when it suits me, hulstler.

— Guid! We make fight! Three to one! Raddy?

— But no, from exemple, Emania Raffaroo! What do you have? What mean you, august one? Fairplay for Finnians! I will have my humours. Sure, you would not do the cowardly thing and moll me roon? Tell Queen's road I am seilling. Farewell, but whenever! Buy!

— Ef I chuse to put a bullet like yu through the grill for heckling what business is that of yours, yu bullock?

— I don't know, sir. Don't ask me, your honour!

— Gently, gently Northern Ire! Love that red hand! Let me once more. There are sordidly tales within tales, you clearly understand that? Now my other point. Did you know, whether by melanodactylism or purely libationally, that one of these two Crimeans with the fender, the taller man, was accused of a certain offence or of a choice of two serious charges, as skirts were divided on the subject, if you like it better that way? You did, you rogue, you?

— You hear things. Besides (and serially now) bushes have eyes, don't forget. Hah!

— Which moral turpitude would you select of the two, for choice, if you had your way? Playing bull before shebears or the hindlegs off a clotheshorse? Did any orangepeelers or greengoaters appear periodically up your sylvan family tree?

— Buggered if I know! It all depends on how much family silver you want for a nass-and-pair. Hah!

— What do you mean, sir, behind your hah! You don't hah to do thah, you know, snapograph.

— Nothing, sir. Only a bone moving into place. Blotogaff. Hahah!

— Whahat?

— Are you to have all the pleasure quizzing on me? I didn't say it aloud, sir. I have something inside of me talking to myself.

— You're a nice third degree witness, faith! But this is no laughing matter. Do you think we are tonedeafs in our noses to boot? Can you not distinguish the sense, prain, from the sound, bray? You have homosexual catheis of empathy between narcissism of the expert and steatopygic invertedness. Get yourself psychoanolised!

— O, begor, I want no expert nursis symaphy from yours broons quadroons and I can psoakoonaloose myself any time I want (the fog follow you all!) without your interferences or any other pigeonstealer.

— Sample! Sample!

— Have you ever weflected, wepowtew, that the evil what though it was willed might nevewtheless lead somehow on to good towawd the genewality?

— A pwopwo of haster meets waster and talking of plebiscites by a show of hands, whether declaratory or effective, in all seriousness, has it become to dawn in you yet that the deponent, the man from Saint Yves, may have been (one is reluctant to use the passive voiced) may be been as much sinned against as sinning, for if we look at it verbally perhaps there is no true noun in active nature where every bally being—please read this mufto—is becoming in its owntown eyeballs. Now the long form and the strong form and reform alltogether!

— Hotchkiss Culthur's Everready, one brother to neverreached, well over countless hands, sieur of many winners and losers, groomed by S. Samson and son, bred by dilalahs, will stand at Bay (Dublin) from nun till dan and vites inversion and at Miss or Mrs's MacMannigan's Yard.

— Perhaps you can explain, sagobean? The Mod needs a rebus.

— Pro general continuation and in particular explication to your singular interrogation our asseveralation. Ladiegent, pals will smile but me and Frisky Shorty, my inmate friend, as is uncommon struck on poplar poetry, and a few fleabesides round at West Pauper Bosquet, was glad to be back again with the chaps and just arguing friendlylike at the Doddercan Easehouse having a wee chatty with our hosty in his comfy establly over the old middlesex party and his moral turps, meaning flu, pock, pox and mizzles, grip, gripe, gleet and sprue, caries, rabies, numps and dumps. What me and Frisky in our concensus and the whole double gigscrew of suscribers, notto say the burman, having successfully concluded our tour of bibel, wants to know is thisahere. Supposing, for an ethical fict, him, which the findings showed, to have taken his epscene licence before the norsect's divisional respectively as regards them male privates and or concomitantly with all common or neuter respects to them public exess females, whereas allbeit really sweet fillies, as was very properly held by the metropolitan in connection with this regrettable nuisance, touching arbitrary conduct, being in strict contravention of schedule in board of forests and works bylaws regulationing sparkers' and succers' amusements section of our beloved naturpark in pursuance of which police agence me and Shorty have approached a reverend gentlman of the name of Mr Coppinger with reference to a piece of fire fittings as was most obliging, 'pon my sam, in this matter of his explanations affirmative, negative and limitative, given to me and Shorty, touching what the good book says of toooldaisymen, concerning the merits of early bisectualism, besides him citing from approved lectionary example given by a valued friend of the name of Mr J. P. Cockshott, reticent of England, as owns a pretty maisonette, *Quis ut Deus*, fronting on to the Soussex Bluffs as was telling us categoric how Mr Cockshott, as he had his assignation with, present holder by deedpoll and indenture of the swearing belt, he tells him hypothetic, the reverend Mr Coppinger, hereckons himself disjunctively with his windwarrd eye up to a dozen miles of a cunifarm school of herring, passing themselves supernatently by the Bloater Naze from twelve and them mayridinghim by the silent hour. Butting, charging, bracing, backing, springing, shrinking, swaying, darting, shooting, bucking and sprinkling their dossies sodouscheock with the twinx of their taylz. And, reverend, he says, summat problematical, by yon socialist sun, gut me, but them errings was as gladful as Wissixy kippers could be considering, flipping their little coppingers, pot em, the fresh little flirties, the dirty little gillybrighteners, pickle their spratties, the little smolty gallockers, and, reverend, says he, more assertitoff, zwelf me Zeus, says he, lettin olfac be the extench of the supperfishies, lamme the curves of their scaligerance and pesk the everurge flossity of their pectoralium, them little salty populators, says he, most apodictic, as sure as my briam eggs is on cockshot under noose, all them little upandown dippies they was all of a libidous pick-puckparty and raid on a wriggolo finsky doodah in testimonials to their early bisectualism. Such, he says, is how the reverend Coppinger, he visualises the hidebound homelies of creed crux ethics. Watsch yourself tillicately every morkning in your bracksullied twilette. The use of cold water, testificates Dr Rutty, may be warmly recommended for the sugjugation of cungunitals loosed. Tolloll, schools!

— Tallhell and Barbados wi ye and your Errian coprulation! Pelagiarist! Remonstrant Montgomeryite! Short lives to your relatives! Y'are absexed, so y'are, with mackerglosia and mickroocyphyllicks.

— Wait now, leixlep! I scent eggoarchicism. I vill take you to task. I don't follow you that far in your otherwise accurate account. Was it *esox lucius* or *salmo ferax?* You are taxing us into the driven future, are you not, with this ruttymaid fishery?

— Lalia Lelia Lilia Lulia and lively lovely Lola Montez.

— Gubbernathor! That they say is a fenian on the secret. Named Parasol Irelly. Spawning ova and fry like a marrye monach all amanygoround his seven parish churches! And peopling the ribald baronies with dans, oges and conals!

— Lift it now, Hosty! Hump's your mark! For a runnymede landing! A dondhering vesh vish, *Magnam Carpam*, es hit neat zoo?

— *There's an old psalmsobbing lax salmoner fogeyboren Herrin Plundehowse.*
Who went floundering with his boatloads of spermin spunk about.
Leaping freck after every long tom and wet lissy between Howth and Humber-
mouth.
Our Human Conger Eel!

— Hep! I can see him in the fishnoo! Up wi'yer whippy! Hold that lad! Play him, Markandeyn! Bullhead!

— Pull you, sir! Olive quill does it. Longeal of Malin, he'll cry before he's flayed. And his tear make newisland. Did a rise? Way, lungfish! The great fin may cumule! Three threeth o'er the wild! Manu ware!

— He missed her mouth and stood into Dee, Romunculus Remus, plying the rape, so as now any bompriss's bound to get up her if he pool her leg and bunk on her butt. No, he skid like a skate and berthed on her byrnie and never a fear but they'll land him yet, slitheryscales on liffeybank, times and times and halve a time with a pillow of sand to polster him.

— Do you say they will?

— I bet you they will.

— Among the shivering sedges so? Weedy waving.

— Or tulipbeds of Rush below.

— Where you take your mugs to wash after dark?

— To my lead, Toomey lout, Tommy lad.

— Besides the bubblye waters of, babblyebubblye waters of?

— Right.

— Grenadiers. And tell me now. Were these anglers or angelers coexistent and compresent with or without their *tertium quid?*

— *Three in one, one and three.*
Shem and Shaun and the shame that sunders em.
Wisdom's son, folly's brother.

— God bless your ginger, wigglewaggle! That's three slots and no burners. You're forgetting the jinnyjos for the fayboys. What, Walker John Referent? Play us your patmost! And unpackyoulloups!

— Naif Cruachan! Woe on woe, says Wardeb Daly. Woman will water the wild world over. And the maid of the folley will go where glory. Sure I thought it was larking in the trefoll of the furry glans with two stripping baremaids, Stilla Underwood and Moth MacGarry, he was, hand to dagger, that time and their mother, a rawkneepudsfrowse, I was given to understand, with superflowvius heirs, begum. There was that one that was always mad gone on him, her first king of cloves and the most broadcussed man in Corrack-on-Sharon, County Rosecarmon. Sure she was near drowned in pondest coldstreams of admiration forherself, as bad as my Tarpeyan cousin, Vesta Tully, making faces at her bachspilled likeness in the brook after and cooling herself in the element, she pleasing it, she praising it, with salices and weidow-wehls, all tossed, as she was, the playactrix, Lough Shieling's love!

— O, add shielsome bridelittle! All of her own! Nircississies are as the doaters of inversion. Secilas through their laughing classes becoming poolermates in laker life.

— It seems to same with Iscappellas? Ys? Gotellus! A tickey for tie taughts!

— Listenest, meme mearest! They were harrowd, those finweeds! Come, rest in this bosom! So sorry you lost him, poor lamb! Of course I know you are a viry vikid girl to go in the dreemplace and at that time of the draym and it was a very wrong thing to do, even under the dark flush of night, dare all grandpassia! He's gone on his bombashaw. Through geesing and so pleasing at Strip Teasy up the stairs. The boys on the corner were talking too. And your soreful miseries first come on you. Still to forgive it, divine my lickle wiffey, and everybody knows you do look lovely in your invinsibles, Eulogia, a perfect apposition with the coldcream, Assoluta, from Boileau's I always use in the wards after I am burned a rich egg and derive the greatest benefit, sign of the cause. My, you do! Simply adorable! Could I but pass my hands some, my hands through, thine hair! So vickyvicky veritiny! O Fronces, say howdyedo, Dotty! Chic hands. The way they curve there under nue charmeen cuffs! I am more divine like that when I've two of everything up to boyproof knicks. Winning in a way, only my arms are whiter, dear. Blanchemain, idler. Fairhair, frail one. Listen, meme sweety! O be joyfold! Mirror do justice, taper of ivory, heart of the conavent, hoops of gold! My veil will save it undyeing from his ethernal fire! It's meemly us two, meme idoll. Of course it was downright verry wickred of him, reely meeting me disguised, Bortolo mio, peerfectly appealling, D.V., with my lovebirds, my colombinas. Their sinsitives shrinked. Even Netta and Linda, our seeyu tities and they've sin sumtim, tankus! My rillies were liebeneaus, my aftscents embre. How me adores eatsother simply (Mon ishebeau! Ma reinebelle!), in his storm collar, as I leaned yestreen from his muskished labs, even my little pom got excited, when I turned his head on his same manly bust and kissed him more. Only he might speak to a person, lord so picious, taking up my worths ill wrong! May I introduce! This is my futuous, lips and looks lovelast. Still me with you, you poor chilled! Will make it up with mother Concepcion and a glorious lie between us, sweetness, so as not a novene in all the convent loretos, not my littlest one of all, for mercy's sake need ever know, what passed our lips or. Yes sir, we'll will! Clothea wind! Fee o fie! Covey us niced! Bansh the dread! Alitten's looking. Low him lovly! Make me feel good in the moontime. It will all take bloss as oranged at St Audiens rosan chocolate chapelry with my diamants blickfeast after at minne owned hos for all the catclub to go cryzy and Father Blesius Mindelsinn will be beminding hand. Kyrielle elation! Crystal elation! Kyrielle elation! Elation immanse! Sing to us, sing to us, sing to us! Amam! So meme nearest, languished hister, be free to me! (I'm fading!) And listen, you, you beauty, esster, I'll be clue to who knows you, pray Magda, Marthe with Luz and Joan, while I lie with warm lisp on the Tolka. (I'm fay!)

— Eusapia! Fais-le, tout-tait! Languishing hysteria? The clou historique? How is this at all? Is dads the thing in such or are tits the that? Hear we here her first poseproem of suora unto suora? Alicious, twinstreams twinestraines, through alluring glass or alas in jumboland? Ding dong! Where's your pal in silks alustre? Think of a maiden, Presentacion. Double her, Annupciacion. Take your first thoughts away from her, Immacolacion. Knock and it shall appall unto you! Who shone yet shimmers will be e'er scheining. Cluse her, voil her, hild her hindly. After liryc and themodius soft aglo iris of the vals. This young barlady, what, euphemiasly? Is she having an ambidual act herself in apparition with herself as Consuelas to Sonias may?

— Dang! And tether, a loguy O!

— Dis and dat and dese and dose! Your crackling out of your turn, my Moonster firefly, like always. And 2 R.N. and Longhorns Connacht, stay off my air! You've grabbed the capital and you've had the lion's shire since 1542 but there's all the difference in Ireland between your borderation, my chatty cove, and me. The leinstrel boy to the wall is gone and there's moreen astoreen for Monn and Conn. With the tyke's named moke. Doggymens' nimmer win! You last led the first when we last but we'll first trump your last with a lasting. Jump the railchairs or take them, as you please, but and, sir, my queskins first, foxyjack! Ye've as much skullabogue cheek on you now as would boil a caldron of kalebrose. Did the market missioners Hayden Wombwell, when given the raspberry, fine more than sandsteen per cent of chalk in the purity, promptitude and perfection flour of this raw materialist and less than a seventh pro mile in his meal? We bright young chaps of the brandnew braintrust are briefed here and with maternal sanction compellably empanelled at quarter sessions under the six disqualifications for the uniformication of young persons (Nodding Neutrals) removal act by Committalman Number Underfifteen to know had the peeress of generals, who have been getting nose money cheap and stirring up the public opinion about private balls with their legs, Misses Mirtha and Merry, the two dreeper's assistents, had they their service books in order and duly signed J. H. North and Company when discharged from their last situations? Will ye gup and tell the board in the anterim how, in the name of the three tailors on Tooley Street, did O'Bejorumsen or Mockmacmahonitch, ex of Butt and Hocksett's, violating the bushel standard, come into awful position of the barrel of bellywash? And why, is it any harm to ask, was this hackney man in the coombe, a papersalor with a whiteluke to him, Fauxfitzhuorson, collected from Manofisle, carrying his ark, of eggshaped fuselage and made in Fredborg into the bullgine, across his back when he might have been setting on his jonass inside like a Glassthure cabman? Where were the doughboys, three by nombres, won in ziel, cavehill exers or hearts of steel, Hansen, Morfydd and O'Dyar, V.D., with their glenagearries directing their steps according to the R.U.C's liaison officer, with their trench ulcers open and their hands in their pockets, contrary to military rules, when confronted with his lifesize obstruction? When did he live off rooking the pooro and how did start pfuffpfaffing at his Paterson and Hellicott's? Is it a factual fact, proved up to scabsteethshilt, that this fancydress nordic in shaved lamb breeches, child's kilts, bibby buntings and wellingtons, with club, torc and headdress, preholder of the Bar Ptolomei, is coowner of a hengster's circus near North Great Denmark

Street (incidentally, it's the most unjoyable show going the province and I'm taking the youngsters there Saturday first when it's halfprice naturals night to see the fallensickners aping the buckleybackers and the blind to two worlds taking off the deffydowndummies) and the shamshemshowman has been complaining to the police barracks and applying for an order of *certiorari* and crying out something vile about him being molested, after him having triplets, by offers of vacancies from females in this city, neighing after the man and his outstanding attraction ever since they seen his X ray picture turned out in wealthy red in the sabbath sheets? Was it him that suborned that surdumutual son of his, a litterydistributer in Saint Patrick's Lavatory, to turn a Roman and leave the chayr and gout in his bare balbriggans, the sweep, and buy the usual jar of porter at the Morgue and Cruses and set it down before the wife with her fireman's halmet on her, bidding her mine the hoose, the strum-pet, while him and his lagenloves were rampaging the roads in all their paroply under the noses of the Heliopolitan constabulary? Can you beat it? Prepare the way! Where's that gendarm auxiliar, arianautic sappertillery, that reported on the whole hoodlum, relying on his morse-erse wordybook and the trunchein up his tail? Roof Seckesign van der Deckel and get her story from him! Recall Sickerson, the lizzyboy! Seckersen, magnon of Errick. Sackerson! Hookup!

— *Day shirker four vanfloats he verdants market.*

High liquor made lust torpid dough hunt her orchid.

— Hunt her orchid! Gob and he found it on her right enough! With her shoes upon his shoulders, 'twas most trying to beholders when he upped their frullatullepleats with our warning. A disgrace to the homely protestant religion! Bloody old preadamite with his twohandled umberella! Trust me to spy on me own spew.

— Wallpurgies! And it's this's your deified city? Norganson? And it's we's to pray for Bigmesser's conversions? Call Kitty the Beads, the Mandame of Tipknock Castle! Let succuba succumb, the improvable his wealth made possible! He's cookinghagar that rost her prayer to him upon the top of the stairs. She's deep, that one.

— A farternoiser for his tuckish armenities. Ouhr Former who erred in having down to gibbous disdag our darling breed. And then the confisieur for the boob's indulgence. As sunctioned for his salmenbog by the Councillors-om-Trent. Pave Pannem at his gaiter's bronze! Nummer half dreads Log Laughty. Master's gunne he warrs the bedst. I messaged his dilltoyds sausepander mussels on the kisschen table. With my ironing duck through his rollpins of gansyfett, do dodo doughdy dough, till he was braising red in the toastface with lovensoft eyebulbs and his kiddledrum steeming and rattling like the roasties in my mockamill. I awed to have scourched his Abarm's brack for him. For the loaf of Obadiah, take your pastryart's noas out of me flouer bouckuet! Of the strainger scene you given squeezers to me skillet! As cream of the hearth thou reinethst alhome. His lapper and libbers was glue goulewed as he sizzled there watching me lautterick's pitcher by Wexford-Atelier as Katty and Lanner, the refined souprette, with my bust alla brooche and the padbun under my matelote, showing my jigotty sleeves and all my new toulong touloosies. Whisk! There's me shims and here's me hams and this is me juppettes, gause be the meter! Whisk! What's this? Whisk! And that? He never cotched finer, balay me, at Romiolo Frullini's flea pantamine out of Griddle-the-Sink or Shusies-with-her-Soles-Up or La Sauzerelly, the pucieboots, when I started so hobmop ladlelike, highty tighty, to kick the time off the cluckclock lucklock quamquam camcam potapot panapan kickakickkack. Hairhore-hounds, shake up pfortner. Fuddling fun for Fullacan's sake!

— All halt! Sponsor programme and close down. That's enough, genral, of finicking about Finnegan and fiddling with his faddles. A final ballot, guvnor, to remove all doubt. By sylph and salamander and all the trolls and tritons, I mean to top her drive and to tip the tap of this, at last. His thoughts that wouldbe words, his livings that havebeen deeds. And will too, by the holy child of Coole, primapatriock of the archsee, if I have at first to down every mask in Trancenania from Terreterry's Hole to Stutterers' Corner to find that Yokeoff his letter, this Yokan his dahet. Pass the jousters of the king, the Kovnor-Journal and eirenarch's custos himself no less, the meg of megs, with the Carrison old gang! Off with your persians! Search ye the Finn! The sinder's under shriving sheet. Fa Fe Fi Fo Fum! Ho, croak, evildoer! Arise, sir ghostus! As long as you've lived there'll be no other. Doff!

— Amtsadam, sir, to you! Eternest cittas, heil! Here we are again! I am bubub brought up under a camel act of dynasties long out of print, the first of Shitric Shilkanbeard (or is it Owllaugh MacAuscullpth the Thord?), but, in pontofacts massimust, I am known throughout the world wherever my good Allenglisches Angleslachsen is spoken by Sall and Will from Augustanus to Ergastulus, as this is, whether in Farnum's rath or Condra's ridge or the meadows of Dalkin or Monkish tunshep, by saints and sinners eyeeye alike as a cleanliving man and, as a matter of fict, by my halfwife, I think how our public at large appreciates it most highly from me that I am as cleanliving as could be and that my game was a fair average since I perpetually kept my ouija ouija wicket up. On my verawife I never was nor can afford to be guilty of crim crig con of malfeasance trespass against

parson with the person of a youthful gigirl frifrif friend chirped Apples,
acted by Miss Dashe, and with Any of my cousines in Kissilov's Slutsgartern
or Gigglotte's Hill, when I would touch to her dot and feel most greenily of
her unripe ones as it should prove most anniece and far too bahad, nieceless
to say, to my reputation on Babbyl Malket for daughters-in-trade being
lightly clad. Yet, as my acquainters do me the complaisance of apprising me,
I should her have awristed under my duskguise of whippers through toombs
and deempeys, lagmen, was she but tinkling of such a tink. And, as a mere
matter of ficfect, I tell of myself how I popo possess the ripest littlums
wifukie around the globelettes globes upon which she was romping off on
Floss Mundai out of haram's way round Skinner's circusalley first with her
consolation prize in my serial dreams of faire women, Mannequins Passe,
with awards in figure and smile subsections, handicapped by two breasts in
operatops, a remarkable little endowment garment. Fastened at various
places. What spurt! I kickkick keenly love such, particularly while savouring
of their flavours at their most perfect best when served with heliotrope
ayelips, as this is, where I do drench my jolly soul on the pu pure beauty of
hers past.

She is my bestpreserved wholewife, sowell her as herafter, in Evans's eye,
with incompatibly the smallest shoenumber outside chinatins. They are
jolly dainty, spekin tluly. May we not recommend them? It was my proof-
piece from my prenticeserving. And, alas, our private chaplain of Lambeyth
and Dolekey, bishopregionary, an always sadfaced man, in his lutestring
pewcape with tabinet band, who has visited our various hard hearts and
reins by imposition of fufuf fingers, olso haddock's fumb, in that Upper
Room can speak loud to you some quite complimentary things about my
clean charactering, even when detected in the dark, distressful though
such recital prove to me, as this is, when I introduced her (Frankfurters,
numborines, why drive fear?) to our fourposter tunies chantreying under
Castrucci Sinior and De Mellos, those whapping oldsteirs, with sycamode
euphonium in either notation in our altogether cagehaused duckyheim
on Goosna Greene, that cabinteeny homesweetened through affection's
hoardpayns (First Murkiss, or so they sankeyed. Dodo! O Clearly! And
Gregorio at front with Johannes far in back. Aw, aw!), gleeglom there's
gnome sweepplaces like theresweep Nowhergs. By whom, as my Kerk
Findlater's, ye litel chuch rond ye coner, and K. K. Katakasm enjoineth in
the Belief and, as you all know, of a child, dear Humans, one of my life's
ambitions of my youngend from an early peepee period while still to
hedjeskool, intended for broadchurch, I, being fully alive to it, was
parruchially confirmed in Caulofat's bed by our bujibuji beloved

curateauthor. Michael Engels is your man. Let Michael relay Sutton and tell you people here who have the phoney habit (it was remarketable) in his clairaudience, as this is, as only our own Michael can, when reicherout at superstation, to bring ruptures to our roars how I am amp amp amplify. Hiemlancollin. Pimpim's Ornery forninehalf. Shaun Shemsen saywhen saywhen. Holmstock unsteaden. Livpoomark lloyrge hoggs one four tupps noying. Big Butter Boost! Sorry! Thnkyou! Thatll beall fortody. Cal it off. Godnotch, vryboily. End a muddy crushmess! Abbreciades anew York gustoms. Kyow! Tak.

— Tiktak. Tikkak.

— Awind abuzz awater falling.

— Poor a cowe his jew placator.

— It's the damp damp damp.

— Calm has entered. Big big Calm, announcer. It is most ernst terooly a moresome intartenment. Colt's tooth! I will give tandsel to it. I protest there is luttrelly not one teaspoonspill of evidence at bottomlie to my babad, as you shall see, as this is. Keemun Lapsang of first pickings. And I contango can take off my dudud dirtynine articles of quoting here in Pynix Park before those in heaven to provost myself, by gramercy of justness, I mean veryman and moremon, stiff and staunch for ever, and enter under the advicies from Misrs Norris, Southby, Yates and Weston, Inc, to their favoured client, into my preprotestant caveat against the pupup publication of libel by any tixtim tipsyloon or tobtomtowley of Keisserse Lean (a bloweyed lanejoymt, waring lowbelt suit, with knockbrecky kenees and bullfist rings round him and a fallse roude axehand (he is cunvesser to Saunter's Nocelettres and the Poe's Toffee's Directory in his pisness), the best begrudged man in Belgradia who doth not belease to our paviour) to my nonesuch, that highest personage at moments holding down the throne. So to speak of beauty scouts in elegant pursuit of flowers, searchers for tabernacles and the celluloid art! Happen seen sore eynes belived? The caca cad! He walked by North Strand with his Thom's towel in hand. Snakeeye! Strangler of soffiacated green parrots! I protest it that he is, by my wipehalf. He was leaving out of my double inns while he was all teppling over my single ixits. So was keshaned on for his recent behaviour. Sherlook is lorking for him. Allare beltspanners. Get your air curt! Shame upon Private M! Shames on his fulsomeness! Shamus on his atkinscum's lulul lying suulen for an outcast mastiff littered in blood currish! Eristocras till Hanging Tower! Steck a javelin through his advowtried heart! Instaunton! Flap, my Larrybird! Dangle, my highflyer! Jiggety jig my jackadandyline! Let me never see his waddphez again! And mine it was, Barktholed von Hunarig,

Soesown of Furrows (hourspringlike his joussture, immitiate my chry! as urs now, so yous. then!), when to our lot it fell on my poplar Sexsex, my Sexencentaurnary, whenby Gate of Hal, before his hostel of the Wodin Man, I hestened to freeholdit op to his Mam his Maman, Majuscules, His Magnus Maggerstick, first city's leasekuays of this Nova Tara, our most noble, when hrossbucked on his pricelist charger, Pferdinamd Allibuster (yeddonot need light oar till Noreway for you fanned one o'er every doorway) with my allbum's greethims through this whole of my promises, handshakey congrandyoulikethems, ecclesency.

Whosaw the jackery dares at handgripper thisa breast? Dose makkers ginger. Some one we was with us all fours. Adversarian! The spiking Duyvil! First liar in Londsend! Wulv! See you scargore on that skeepsbrow! And those meisies! Sulken taarts! Man sicker at I ere bluffet konservative? Shucks! Such ratshause bugsmess so I cannot barely conceive of! Lowest basemeant in hystry! Ibscenest nansence! Noksagt! Per Peeler and Pawr! The brokerheartened shugon! Hole affair is rotten muckswinish porcupig's draff. Enouch!

— Is that yu, Whitehed?

— Have you headnoise now?

— Give us your mespilt reception, will yous?

— Pass the fish for Christ's sake!

— Old Whitehowth he is speaking again. Ope Eustace tube! Pity poor whiteoath! Dear gone mummeries, goby! Tell the woyld I have lived true thousand hells. Pity, please, lady, for poor O.W. in this profundust snobbing I have caught. Nine dirty years mine age, hairs hoar, mummery failend, snowdrift to my ellpow, deff as Adder. I askt you, dear lady, to judge on my tree by our fruits. I gave you of the tree. I gave two smells, three eats. My freeandies, my celeberrimates: my happy bossoms, my allfalling fruits of my boom. Pity poor Haveth Childers Everywhere with Mudder!

That was Communicator, a former colonel. A disincarnated spirit, called Sebastion, from the Rivera in Januero, (he is not all hear) may fernspreak shortly with messuages from my deadported. Let us cheer him up a little and make an appunkment for a future date. Hello, Commudicate! How's the buttes? Everscepistic! He does not believe in our psychous of the Real Absence, neither miracle wheat nor soulsurgery of P. P. Quemby. He has had some indiejestings, poor thing, for quite a little while, confused by his tonguer of baubble. A way with him! Poor Felix Culapert! Ring his mind, ye staples, (bonze!) in my ould reekeries' ballyheart and in my krumlin and in aroundisements and stremmis! Sacks eleathury! Sacks eleathury! Bam! I deplore over him ruely. Mongrieff! O Hone! Guestermed with the nobelities, to die bronxitic in achershous! So enjoying of old thick whiles, in haute white toff's hoyt of our formed reflections, with stock of eisen all his prop, so buckely hosiered from the Royal Leg, and his puertos mugnum, he would puffout a dhymful bock. And the how he would husband her that verikerfully, his cigare divane! (He would redden her with his vestas, but 'tis naught.) With us his nephos and his neberls, mest incensed and befogged by him and his smoke thereof. But he shall have his glad stein of our zober beerbest in Oscarshal's winetavern. *Buen retiro!* The boyce voyce is still flautish and his mounth still wears that soldier's scarlet though the flaxa-floyeds are peppered with salsedine. It is bycause of what he was ascend into his prisonce on account off. I whit it wel. Hence his deepraised words. Some day I may tell of his second storey. Mood! Mood! It looks like someone other bearing my burdens. I cannot let it. Kanes nought.

Well, yeamen, I have bared my whole past, I flatter myself, on both sides. Give me even two months by laxlaw in second division and my first broad-cloth is business will be to protest to Recorder at Thing of all Things, or court of Skivinis, with marchants grey, antient and credibel, Zerobubble Barrentone, Jonah Whalley, Determined Codde or Cucumber Upright, my jurats, if it does not occur again. O rhyme us! Haar Faagher, wild heart in Homelan; Harrod's be the naun. Mine kinder come, mine wohl be won. There is nothing like leuther. O Shee! And nosty mens in gladshouses they shad not peggot stones. The elephant's house is his castle. I am here to tell you, indeed to goodness, that, allbe I discountenanced beallpersuasions, in rinunciniation of pomps of heretofore, with a wax too held in hand, I am thorgtfulldt to do dope me of her miscisprinks and by virchow of those filthered Ovocnas presently like Browne umbracing Christina Anya, after the Irishers, to convert me into a selt (but first I must proxy babetise my old antenaughties), when, as Sigismond Stolterforth, with Rabbin Robroost for my auspicer and Leecher Rutty for my lifearst and Lorencz Pattorn (*Ehren til viktrae!*), when I will westerneyes those poor sunuppers and outbreighten their land's eng. A man should stump up and I will pay my pretty decent trade price for my glueglue gluecose, peebles, were it even, as this is, the legal eric for infelicitous conduict (here incloths placefined my pocket-anchoredcheck) and, as a matter of fact, I undertake to discontinue entyrely all practices and I deny wholeswiping *in toto* at my own request in all stoytness to have confermentated and confoederated and agreed in times prebellic, when here were waders for the trainsfolk, as it is now nuggently laid to me, with a friend from mine, Mr Billups, pulleter, my quarterbrother, who sometimes he is doing my locum for me on a grubstake and whom I have cleped constoutuent, for so it was felt by me, at goodbuy cootcoops

byusucapiture a mouthless niggeress, Blanchette Brewster from Cherna
Djamja, Blawlawnd-via-Brigstow, or to illsell my fourth part in her, which
although allowed of in Deuterogamy as in several places of Scripture (copy-
right) and excluded books (they should quite rightly verbanned be), would
seem eggseggs excessively haroween to my feelimbs for two punt scotch,
one pollard and a crockard or three pipples on the bitch. Thou, Frick's
Flame, Uden Sulfer, who strikest only on the marryd bokks, enquick me if
so be I did cophetuise milady's maid! In spect of her beavers she is a
womanly and sacret. Such wear a frillick for my comic strip, Mons Meg's
Monthly, comes out aich Fanagan's Weck, to bray at by clownsillies
in Donkeybrook Fair. It would lackin mackin Hodder's and Cocker's
erithmatic. The unpurdonable preempson of all of her of yourn, by Juno
Moneta! If she, irished Marryonn Teheresiann, has been disposed of for her
consideration, I, Ledwidge Salvatorious, am tradefully unintiristid. And if
she is still further talc slopping over her cocoa contours, I hwat mick angars,
am strongly of opinion why I should not be. Inprobable! I do not credit one
word of it from such and suchess mistraversers. Just feathers! Nanenities!
Or to have ochtroyed to resolde or borrough by exchange same super
melkkaart, means help; best Brixton high yellow, no outings: cent for cent
on Auction's Bridge. 'Twere a honnibel crudelty wert so tentement to their
naktlives and scatab orgias we devour about in the mightyevil roohms of
encient cartage. Utterly improperable! Not for old Crusos or white soul of
gold! A pipple on the panis, two claps on the cansill, or three pock pocks
cassey knocked on the postern! Not for one testey tickey culprik's coynds
ore for all ecus in cunziehowffse! So hemp me Cash! I meanit.

My herrings! The surdity of it! Amean to say. Her bare idears, it is
choochoo chucklesome. Absurd bargain, mum, will call. One line with! One
line, with with! Will ate everadayde saumone like a boyne alive O. The tew
cherripickers, with their Catheringnettes, Lizzy and Lissy Mycock, from
Street Fleshshambles, were they moon at aube with hespermun and I their
covin guardient, I would not know to contact such gretched youngsteys in
my ways from Haddem or any suistersees or heiresses of theirn, claiming
by, through, or under them. Ous of their freiung pfann into myne foyer.
Her is one which rassembled to mein enormally. The man what shocked his
shanks at contey Carlow's. He is Deucollion. Each habe goheerd, uptaking
you are innersence, but we sen you meet sose infance. Deucollion! Odor.
Evilling chimbes is smutsick rivulverblott but thee hard casted thereass
pigstenes upann Congan's shootsmen in Schottenhof, ekeascent? Igen
Deucollion! I liked his Gothamm chic! Stuttertub! What a shrubbery trick
to play! I will put my oathhead unner my whitepot for ransom of beeves and

will stand me where I stood mine in all free heat between Pelagios and little Chistayas by Roderick's our mostmonolith, after my both earstoear and brebreeches buybibles and, minhatton, testify to my unclothed virtue by the longstone erectheion of our allfirst manhere. I should tell you that honestly, on my honour of a Nearwicked, I always think in a wordworth's of that primed favourite continental poet, Daunty, Gouty and Shopkeeper, A. G., whom the generality admoyers in this that is and that this is to come. Like as my palmer's past policy I have had my best master's lessons, as the public he knows, and do you know, homesters, I honestly think, if I have failed lamentably by accident benefits though shintoed, spitefired, perplagued and cramkrieged, I am doing my dids bits and have made of my prudentials good. I have been told I own stolemines or something of that sorth in the sooth of Spainien. Hohohoho! Have I said ogso how I abhor myself vastly (truth to tell) and do repent to my netherheart of suntry clothing? The amusin part is, I will say, hotelmen, that since I, over the deep drowner Athacleeath to seek again Irrlanding, shamed in mind, with three plunges of my ruddertail, yet not a bottlenim, vanced imperial standard by weaponright and platzed mine residenze, taking bourd and burgage under starrymisty and ran and operated my brixtol selection here at thollstall, for mean straits male with evorage fimmel, in commune soccage among strange and enemy, among these plotlets, in Poplinstown, alore Fort Dunlip, then-on-sea, hole of Serbonian bog, now city of magnificent distances, goodwalldabout, with talus and counterscarp and pale of palisades, upon martiell siegewin, with Abbot Warre to blesse, on yon slauchterday of cleantarriffs, in that year which I have called myriabellous, and overdrave these marken (the soord on Whencehislaws was mine and mine the prussing stock of Allbrecht the Bearn), under patroonshaap of our good kingsinnturns, T. R. H. Urban First and Champaign Chollyman and Hungry the Loaved and Hangry the Hathed, here where my tenenure of office and my toils of domestication first began, with weight of woman my skat and skuld but Flukie of the Ravens as my sure piloter, famine with Englisch sweat and oppedemics, the twotoothed dragon worms with allsort serpents, has compolitely seceded from this landleague of many nations and open and notorious naughty livers are found not on our rolls. This seat of our city it is of all sides pleasant, comfortable and wholesome. If you would traverse hills, they are not far off. If champain land, it lieth of all parts. If you would be delited with fresh water, the famous river, called of Ptolemy the Libnia Labia, runneth fast by. If you will take the view of the sea, it is at hand. Give heed!

— *Do Drumcollogher whatever you do!*

— *Visitez Drumcollogher-la-Belle!*

— *Be suke ad sie so ersed Drumcollogher!*

— *Vedi Drumcollogher e poi Moonis.*

— Things are not as they were. Let me briefly survey. Pro clam a shun! Pip! Peep! Pipitch! Ubipop jay piped, ibipep goes the whistle. Here Tyeburn throttled, massed murmars march: where the bus stops there shop I: here which ye see, yea reste. On me, your sleeping giant. Estoesto! Estote sunto! From the hold of my capt in altitude till the mortification that's my fate. The end of aldest mosest ist the beginning of all thisorder so the last of their hansbailis shall the first in our sheriffsby. New highs for all! Redu Negru may be black in tawn but under them lintels are staying my horneymen meet each his mansiemagd. For peers and gints, quaysirs and galleyliers, fresk letties from the say and stale headygabblers, gaingangers and dudder wagoners, pullars off societies and pushers on rothmere's homes. Obeyance from the townsmen spills felixity by the toun. Our bourse and politicoecomedy are in safe with good Jock Shepherd, our lives are on sure in sorting with Jonathans, wild and great. Been so free! Thank you, besters! Hattentats have mindered. Blaublaze devilbobs have gone from the mode and hairtrigger nicks are quite out of time now. Thuggeries are reere as glovars' metins, lepers lack, ignerants show beneath suspicion like the bitterhalves of esculapuloids. In midday's mallsight let Miledd discurverself. Me ludd in her hide park seek Minuinette. All is waldy bonums. Blownose aerios we luft to you! Firebugs, good blazes! Lubbers, kepp your poudies drier! Seamen, we segn your skivs and wives! Seven ills so barely as centripunts havd I habt, seaventy seavens for circumference inkeptive are your hill prospect. Braid Blackfordrock, the Calton, the Liberton, Craig and Lockhart's, A. Costofino, R. Thursitt. The chort of Nicholas Within was my guide and I raised a dome on the wherewithouts of Michan: by awful tors my wellworth building sprang sky spearing spires, cloud cupoled campaniles: further this. By fineounce and imposts I got and grew and by grossscruple gat I grown outreachesly: murage and lestage were my mains for Ouerlord's tithing and my drains for render and prender the doles and the tribute: I was merely out of my mint with all the percussors on my braincap till I struck for myself and muched morely by token: to Sirrherr of Gambleden ruddy money, to Madame of Pitymount I loue yous. Paybads floriners moved in hugheknots against us and I matt them, pepst to papst, barthelemew: milreys (mark!) onfell, and (Luc!) I arose Daniel in Leonden. Bulafests onvied me, Corkcuttas graatched. Atabey! I braved Brien Berueme to berow him against the Loughlins, all her tolkies shraking: Fugabollags! Lusqu'au bout! If they had ire back of eyeball they got danage on front tooth: theres were revelries at ridottos, here was rivalry in redoubt: I

wegschicked Duke Wellinghof to reshockle Roy Shackleton: Walhalloo,
Walhalloo, Walhalloo, mourn in plein! Under law's marshall and warschouw
did I thole till lead's plumbate, ping on pang, reliefed me. I made praharfeast
upon acorpolous and fastbroke down in Neederthorpe. I let faireviews in
on slobodens but ranked rothgardes round wrathmindsers: I bathand-
baddend on mendicity and I corocured off the unoculated. Who can tell
their tale whom I filled ad liptum on the plain of Soulsbury? With three
hunkered peepers and twa and twas! For sleeking beauties I spinned their
nightinveils, to slumbred beast I tummed the thief air. Round the musky
moved a murmel but mewses whinninaird and belluas zoomed: tendulcis
tunes like water parted fluted up from the westinders while from gorges in
the east came the strife of ourangoontangues. All in my thicville Escuterre
ofen was thorough fear but in the meckling of my burgh Belvaros was
the site forbed: tuberclerosies I reized spudfully from the murphyplantz
Hawkinsonia and berriberries from the pletoras of the Irish shou. I heard
my libertilands making free through their curraghcoombs, my trueblues
hurusalaming before Wailingtone's Wall: I richmounded the rainelag in
my bathtub of roundwood and conveyed it with cheers and cables, roaring
mighty shouts, through my longertubes of elm: out of fundness for the
outozone I carried them amd curried them in my Putzemdown cars to my
Kommeandine hotels: I made sprouts fontaneously from Philuppe Sobriety
in the coupe that's cheyned for noon inebriates: when they weaned weary
of that bibbing I made infusion more infused: sowerpacers of the vinegarth,
obtemperate unto me! When you think me in my coppeecuffs look in ware
would you meckamockame, as you pay in caabman's sheltar tot the ites like
you corss the tees. Wherefore watch ye well! For, while I oplooked the
first of Janus's straight, I downsaw the last of Christmas steps: syndic
podestril and on the rates, I for indigent and intendente: in Forum Foster
I demosthrenated my folksfiendship, enmy pupuls felt my burk was no
worse than their brite: Sapphrageta and Consciencia were undecidedly
attached to me but the maugher machrees and the auntieparthenopes my
schwalby words with litted spongelets set their soakye pokeys and botch-
bons afume: Fletcher-Flemmings, elisaboth, how interquackeringly they
rogated me, their golden one, I inhesitant made replique: Mesdememdes to
leursieuresponsor: and who in hillsaide, don't you let flyfire till you see
their whites of the bunkers' eyes! Mr Answers: Brimgem young, bringem
young, bringem young!: in my bethel of Solyman's I accouched their
rotundaties and I turnkeyed most insultantly over raped lutetias in the lock:
I gave bax of biscums to the jacobeaters and pottage bakes to the esausted;
I dehlivered them with freakandesias by the constant droppings from my

smalls instalmonths while I titfortotalled up their farinadays for them on
my slataper's slate with my chandner's chauk: I jaunted on my jingelbrett
rapt in neckloth and sashes, and I beggered about the amnibushes like belly
in a bowle. In the humanity of my heart I sent out heyweywomen to refresh
the ballwearied and then, doubling megalopolitan poleetness, my great
great greatest of these charities, devaleurised the base fellows for the curtailment of their lower man: with a slog to square leg I sent my boundary to
Botany Bay and I ran up a score and four of mes while the Yanks were
huckling the Empire: I have been reciping om omominous letters and
widelysigned petitions full of pieces of pottery about my monumentalness
as a thingabolls and I have been inchanting causeries to the feshest cheoil-
boys so that they are allcalling on me for the song of a birtch: the more
secretely bi built, the more openly palastered. Attent! Couch hear! I have
becket my vonderbilt hutch in sunsmidnought and at morningrise was
encampassed of mushroofs. Rest and bethinkful, with licence, thanks. I
considered the lilies on the veldt and unto Balkis did I disclothe mine glory.
And this. This missy, my taughters, and these man, my son, from my fief of
the villa of the Ostmanorum to Thorstan's, *recte* Thomars Sraid, and from
Huggin Pleaze to William Inglis his house, that man de Loundres, in all
their barony of Saltus, bonders and foeburghers, helots and zelots, strutting
oges and swaggering macks, the darsy jeamses, the drury joneses, redmaids
and bleucotts, in hommage all and felony, all who have received tickets, fair
home overcrowded, tidy but very little furniture, respectable, whole family
attends daily mass and is dead sick of bread and butter, sometime in the
militia, mentally strained from reading work on German physics, shares
closet with eight other dwellings, more than respectable, getting comfortable
parish relief, wageearner freshly shaven from prison, highly respectable,
planning new departure in Mountgomery cyclefinishing, eldest son will
not serve but peruses Big-man-up-in-the-Sky scraps, anoopanadoon lacking
backway, quasi respectable, pays ragman in bones for faded windowcurtains,
staircase continually lit up with guests, particularly respectable, house lost
in dirt and blocked with refuse, getting on like Roe's distillery on fire,
slovenly wife active with the jug, in business for himself, has a tenth
illegitimate coming, partly respectable, following correspondence courses,
chucked work over row, both cheeks kissed at levee by late marquess of
Zetland, sharing closet which is profusely written over with eleven other
subscribers, once respectable, open hallway pungent of Baltic dishes, bangs
kept woman's head against wall thereby disturbing neighbours, private
chapel occupies return landing, removal every other quarter day, case one
of peculiar hopelessness, most respectable, nightsoil has to be removed

through snoring household, eccentric naval officer not quite steady enjoys weekly churchwarden and laugh while reading foreign pictorials on clump-stump before door, known as the trap, widow rheumatic and chars, haunted, condemned and execrated, of dubious respectability, tools too costly pledged or uninsured, reformed philanthropist whenever feasible takes advantage of unfortunates against dilapidating ashpits, serious student is eating his last dinners, floor dangerous for unaccompanied old clergymen, thoroughly respectable, many uncut pious books in evidence, nearest watertap two hundred yards' run away, fowl and bottled gooseberry frequently on table, man has not had boots off for twelve months, infant being taught to hammer flat piano, outwardly respectable, sometimes hears from titled connection, one foot of dust between banister and cracked wall, wife cleans stools, eminently respectable, ottawark and regular loafer, should be operated would she consent, deplorable rent in roof, claret cellar cobwebbed since the pontificate of Leo, wears drill trousers and collects rare buddhas, underages very treacly and verminous have to be separated, sits up with fevercases for one and threepence, owns two terraces (back to back breeze), respectable in every way, harmless imbecile supposingly weakminded, a sausage every Sunday, has a staff of eight servants, outlook marred by ne'er-do-wells using the laneway, lieabed sons go out with sisters immediately after dark, has never seen the sea, travels always with her eleven trunks of clothing, starving cat left in disgust, the pink of respectability, resting after colonial service, labours at plant, the despair of his many benefactresses, calories exclusively from Rowntrees and dumplings, one bar of sunlight does them all january and half february, the V. de V's (animal diet) live in fivestoried semidetached but rarely pay tradesmen, went security for friend who absconded, shares same closet with fourteen similar cottages and an illfamed lodginghouse, more respectable than some, teawidow pension but held to purchase, inherited silk hat from father-in-law, head of domestic economy never mentioned, queery how they live, reputed to procure, last four occupants carried out, mental companionship with mates only, respectability unsuccessfully aimed at, copious holes emitting mice, decoration from Uganda chief in locked ivory casket, grandmother has advanced alcoholic amblyopia, the terror of Goodmen's Field, and respected and respectable, as respectable as respectable can respectably be, though their orable amission were the herrors I could have expected, all, let them all come, they are my villeins, with chartularies I have talledged them. Wherfor I will and firmly command, as I willed and firmly commanded, upon my royal word and cause the great seal now to be affixed, that from the farthest of the farther of their fathers to their children's children's children they do inhabit it and hold it for me unencumbered and my heirs, firmly and quietly, amply and honestly, and with all the liberties and free customs which the men of Tolbris, a city of Tolbris, have at Tolbris, in the county of their city and through whole my land. Hereto my vouchers, knive and snuffbuchs. Fee for farm. Enwreak us wrecks.

Struggling forlongs I have livramentoed, milles on milles of mancipelles. Lo, I have looked upon my pumpadears in their easancies and my drummers have tattled tall tales of me in the land: in morgenattics litt I hope, in seralcellars louched I bleakmealers: on my siege of my mighty I was parciful of my subject but in street wauks that are darkest I debelledem superb: I deemed the drugtails in my pettycourts and domstered dustyfeets in my husinclose: at Guy's they were swathed, at Foulke's slashed, the game for a Gomez, the loy for a lynch: if I was magmonimoss as staidy lavgiver I revolucanized by my eructions: the hye and bye wayseeds I scattered em, in my graben fields sew sowage I gathered em: in Sheridan's Circle my wits repose, in black pitts of the pestered Lenfant he is dummed. (Hearts of Oak, may ye root to piece! Rechabites obstain! Clayed sheets, pineshrouded, wake not, walk not! Sigh lento, Morgh!) *Quo warranto* has his greats my soliven and puissant lord V. king regards for me and he has given to me my necknamesh (flister it!) which is second fiddler to nomen. These be my genteelician arms. At the crest, two young frish, etoiled, flappant, devoiled of their habiliments, vested sable, withdrewers argent. For the boss a coleopter, pondant, partifesswise, blazoned sinister, at the slough, proper. In the lower field a terce of lanciers, shaking unsheathed shafts, their arms crossed in saltire, embusked, sinople. Motto, in letters portent: *Hery Crass Evohodie*. Idle were it, repassing from elserground to the elder disposition, to inquire whether I, draggedasunder, be the forced generation of group marriage, holocryptogam, of my essenes, or carried of cloud from land of locust, in ouzel galley borne, I, huddled til summone be the massproduct of teamwork, three surtouts wripped up in itchother's, two twin pritticoaxes lived as one, troubled in trine or dubildin too, for abram nude be I or roberoyed with the faineans, of Feejeean grafted ape on merfish, surrounded by obscurity, by my virtus of creation and by boon of promise, by my natural born freeman's journeymanright and my otherchurch's inher light, in so and such a manner as me it so besitteth, most surely I pretend and reclam to opt for simultaneous. Till daybowbreak and showshadows flee. Thus be hek. Verily! Verily! Time, place!

— What is your numb? Bun!

— Who gave you that numb? Poo!

— Have you put in all your sparepennies? I'm listening. Sree!

— Keep clear of propennies! Fore!

— Mr Televox, Mrs Taubiestimm and invisible friends! I maymay mean to say. Annoyin part of it was, had faithful Fulvia, following the wiening courses of this world, turned her back on her ways to gon on uphills upon search of louvers, brunette men of Earalend, Chief North Paw and Chief Goes in Black Water and Chief Brown Pool and Chief Night Cloud by the Deeps, or again had Fluvia, amber whitch she was, left her chivily crookcrook crocus bed at the bare suggestions of some prolling bywaymen from Moabit who could have abused of her, the foxrogues, there might accrue advantage to ask wher in pellmell her deceivers sinned. Yet know it was vastly otherwise which I have heard it by mmummy goods waif, as I, chiefly endmost hartyly aver, for Fulvia Fluvia, iddle woman to the plusneeborn, ever did ensue tillstead the things that pertained unto fairnesse, this wharom I am fawned on, that which was loost. Even so, for I waged love on her: and spoiled her undines. And she wept: O my lors!

— Till we meet!

— Ere we part!

— Tollollall!

— This time a hundred years!

— But I was firm with her. And I did take the reached of my delights, my jealousy, ymashkt, beyashmakt, earswathed, snoutsnooded, and did raft her flumingworthily and did leftlead her overland the pace, from lacksleap up to liffsloup, tiding down, as portreeve should, whimpering by Kevin's creek and Hurdlesford and Gardener's Mall, long riverside drive, embankment large, to Ringsend Flott and Ferry, where she began to bump a little bit, my dart to throw: and there, by wavebrink, on strond of south, with mace to masthigh, taillas Cowhowling, quailless Highjakes, did I upreized my magicianer's puntpole, the tridont sired a tritan stock, farruler, and I bade those polyfizzyboisterous seas to retire with hemselves from os (rookwards, thou seasea stamoror!) and I abridged with domfine norsemanship till I had done abate her maidan race, my baresark bride, and knew her fleshly when with all my bawdy did I her whorship, min bryllupswibe: Heaven, he hallthundered; Heydays, he flung blissforhers. And I cast my tenspan joys on her, arsched overtupped, from bank of call to echobank, by dint of strongbow (Galata! Galata!) so streng we were in one, malestream in shegulf: and to ringstresse I thumbed her with iern of Erin and tradesmanmarked her lieflang mine for all and singular, iday, igone, imorgans, and for ervigheds: base your peak, you! you, strike your flag!: (what screech of shippings! what low of dampfbulls!): from Livland, hoks zivios, from Lettland, skall vives! With Impress of Asias and Queen Columbia for her pairanymphs and the singing sands for herbrides' music: goosegaze annoynted uns, canailles canzoned and me to she her shyblumes lifted: and I pudd a name and wedlock boltoned round her the which to carry till her grave, my durdin dearly, Appia Lippia Pluviabilla, whiles I herr lifer amstell and been: I chained her chastemate to grippe fiuming snugglers, her chambrett I bestank so to spunish furiosos: I was her hochsized, her cleavunto, her everest, she was my annie, my lauralad, my pisoved: who cut her ribbons when nought my prowes? who expoused that havenliness to beachalured ankerrides when not I, freipforter?: in trinity huts they met my dame, pick of their poke for me: when I foregather 'twas my sumbad, if I farseeker itch my list: had I not workit in my cattagut with dogshunds' crotts to clene and had I not gifted of my coataways, constantonoble's aim: and, fortiffed by my right as man of capitol, I did umgyrdle her about, my vermincelly vinagerette, with all loving kindness as far as in man's might it lay and enfranchised her to liberties of fringes: and I gave until my lilien-younger turkeythighs soft goods and hardware (catalogue, *passim*) and ladderproof hosiery lines (see stockinger's raiment), cocquette coiffs (see Agnes' hats) and peningsworths of the best taste of knaggs of jets and silvered waterroses and geegaws of my pretty novelties and wispywaspy frocks of redferns and lauralworths, trancepearances such as women cattle bare and peltries piled, the peak of Pim's and Slyne's and Sparrow's, loomends day lumineused luxories on looks, *La Primamère, Pyrrha Pyrrhine, Or de Reinebeau, Sourire d'Hiver* and a crinoline, wide a shire, and pattens for her trilibies that know she might the tortuours of the boots and bedes of wampun with to toy and a murcery glaze of shard to mirrow, for all daintiness by me and theetime, the cupandnaggin hour: and I wound around my swanchen's neckplace a school of shells of moyles marine to swing their saysangs in her silents: and, upping her at king's count, her aldritch cry oloss unheading, what though exceeding bitter, I pierced her beak with order of the Danabrog (Cunnig's great! Soll leve! Soll leve!): with mare's greese cressets at Leonard's and Dunphy's and Madonna lanthorns before quintacasas and tallonkindles spearhead syngeing nickendbookers and mhutton lightburnes dipdippingdownes in blackholes, the tapers of the topers and his buntingpall at hoist: for days there was no night for nights were days and our folk had rest from Blackheathen and the pagans from the prince of pacis: what was trembling sod quaked no more, what were frozen loins were stirred and lived: gone the septuor, dark deadly dismal doleful desolate dreadful desperate, no more the tolvmaans, bloody gloomy hideous fearful furious alarming terrible mournful sorrowful frightful appalling: peace, perfect peace: and I hung up at Yule my duindleeng lunas, helphelped of Kettil Flashnose, for the souperhore of my frigid one, *coloumba mea*, *frimosa mea*, in Wastewindy tarred strate and Elgin's marble halles lamping limp from black to block, through all Livania's volted ampire, from anodes to cathodes and from the topazolites of Mourne, Wykinloeflare, by Arklow's sapphire siomen's lure and Wexterford's hook and crook lights to the polders of Hy Kinsella: avenyue ceen my peurls ahumming, the crown to my estuarine munipicence?: three firths of the sea I swept with draughtness and all ennempties I bottled em up in bellomport: when I stabmarooned jack and maturin I was a bad boy's bogey but it was when I went on to sankt piotersbarq that they gave my devil his dues: what is seizer can hack in the old wold a sawyer may hew in the green: on the island of Breasil the wildth of me perished and I took my plowshure sadly, feeling pity for me sored: where bold O'Connee weds on Alta Mahar, the tawny sprawling beside that silver burn, I sate me and settled with the little crither of my hearth: her intellects I charmed with I calle them utile thoughts, her turlyhyde I plumped with potatums for amiens pease in plenty: my biblous beadells shewed her triumphs of craftygild pageantries, loftust Adam, duffed our cousterclother, Conn and Owel with cortoppled baskib, Sire Noeh Guinnass, exposant of his bargeness and Lord Joe Starr to hump the body of the camell: I screwed the Emperor down with ninepins gaelic with sixpennyhapennies for his hanger on: my worthies were bissed and trissed from Joshua to Godfrey but my *processus prophetarum* they would have plauded to perpetuation. Moral: book to besure, see press.

— He's not all buum and bully.

— But his members handly food him.

— Steving's grain for's greet collegtium.

— The S. S. Paudraic's in the harbour.

— And after these things, I fed her, my carlen, my barelean linsteer, upon spiceries for her garbage breath, italics of knobby lauch and the rich morsel of the marrolebone and shains of garleeks and swinespepper and gothakrauts and pinkee dillisks, primes of meshallehs and subleties in jellywork, come the feast of Saint Pancreas, and shortcake nutrients for Paas and Pingster's pudding, bready and nutalled and potted flesh neats from store dampkookin, and the drugs of Kafa and Jelupa and shallots out of Ascalon, feeding her food convenient herfor, to pass them into earth: and to my saffronbreathing mongoloid, the skinsyg, I gave Biorwik's powlver and Uliv's oils, unguents of cuticure, for the swarthy searchall's face on her, with handewers and groinscrubbers and a carrycam to teaze her tussy out, the brown but combly,

a mopsa's broom to duist her sate, and clubmoss and wolvesfoot for her
more moister wards (amazing efficiencies!): and, my shopsoiled doveling,
when weeks of kindness kinly civicised, in our saloons esquirial, with fineglas
bowbays, draped embrasures and giltedged librariums, I did devise my
telltale sports at evenbread to wring her withers limberly, wheatears,
slapbang, drapier-cut-dean, bray, nap, spinado and ranter-go-round: we
had our lewd mayers and our lairdie meiresses kiotowing and smuling
fullface on us out of their framous latenesses, oilclothed over for cohabitation
and allpointed by Hind: Tamlane the Cussacke, Dirk Wettingstone, Pieter
Stuyvesant, Outlawrie O'Niell, Mrs Currens, Mrs Reyson-Figgis, Mrs
Dattery, and Mrs Pruny-Quetch: in hym we trust, footwash and sects
principles, apply to overseer, Amos five six: she had dabblingtime for
exhibiting her grace of aljambras and duncingk the bloodanoobs in
her vauxhalls while I, dizzed and dazed by the lumpty thumpty of our
interloopings, fell clocksure off my ballast: in our windtor palast it vampared
for elenders, we lubded Sur Gudd for the sleep and the ghoasts: she chauffed
her fuesies at my Wigan's jewels while she skalded her mermeries on my
Snorryson's Sagos: in paycook's thronsaale she domineered, lecking icies
off the dormer panes all admired her in camises: on Rideau Row Duanna
dwells, you merk well what you see: let wellth were I our pantocreator
would theirs be tights for the gods: in littleritt reddinghats and cindery
yellows and tinsel and glitter and bibs under hoods: I made nusance of many
well pressed champdamors and peddled freely in the scrub: I foredreamed
for thee and more than fullmaked: I prevened for thee in the haunts that
joybelled frail light-a-leaves for sturdy traemen: *pelves ad hombres sumus:* I
said to the shiftless prostitute; let me be your fodder; and to rodies and
prater brothers; Chau, Camerade!: evangel of good tidings, omnient as
the Healer's word, for the lost, loathsome and whomsoever will: who, in
regimentation through liberal donation in co-ordination for organisation of
their installation and augmentation plus some annexation and amplification
without precipitation towards the culmination in latification of what was
formerly their utter privation, competence, cheerfulness, usefulness and the
meed, shall, in their second adams, all be made alive: my tow tugs steered
down canal grand, my lighters lay longside on Regalia Water. And I built in
Urbs in Rure, for minne elskede, my shiny brows, under astrolobe from my
upservatory, an erdcloset with showne ejector wherewithin to be squatquit
in most covenience from her sabbath needs, when open noise should stilled
be: did not I festfix with mortarboard my unniversiries, wholly rational and
gottalike, sophister agen sorefister, life sizars all?: was I not rosetted on two
stellas of little egypt? had not I rockcut readers, hieros, gregos and

democriticos?: triscastellated, bimedallised: and by my sevendialled changing
charties Hibernska Ulitzas made not I to pass through twelve Threadneedles
and Newgade and Vicus Veneris to cooinsight?: my camels' walk, kolossa
kolossa! no porte sublimer benared my ghates: Oi polled ye many but my
fews were chousen (Voter, voter, early voter, he was never too oft for old
Sarum): terminals four my staties were, the Geenar, the Greasouwea, the
Debwickweck, the Mifgreawis. And I sept up twinminsters, the pro and the
con, my stavekirks wove so norcely of peeled wands and attachatouchy
floodmud, now all loosebrick and stonefest, freely masoned arked for
covennanters and shinners' rifuge: descent from above on us, Hagiasofia of
Astralia, our orisons thy nave and absedes, our aeone tone aeones thy
studvaast vault; Hams, circuitise! Shemites, retrace!: horns, hush! no barkeys!
hereround is't holied!: all truanttrulls made I comepull, all rubbeling gnomes
I pushed, gowgow: Cassels, Redmond, Gandon, Deane, Shepperd, Smyth,
Neville, Heaton, Stoney, Foley, Farrell, Vnost with Thorneycroft and
Hogan too: sprids serve me! gobelins guard!: tect my tileries (O tribes! O
gentes!), keep my keep, the peace of my four great ways: oathiose infernals
to Booth Salvation, arcane celestials to Sweatenburgs Welhell! My seven
wynds I trailed to maze her and ever a wynd had saving closes and all these
closes flagged with the gust, hoops for her, hatsoff for him and ruffles
through Neeblow's garding: and that was why Blabus was razing his wall
and eltering the suzannes of his nighboors: and thirdly, for ewigs, I did
reform and restore for my smuggy piggiesknees, my sweet coolocked, my
auburn coyquailing one, her paddypalace on the crossknoll with massgo
bell, sixton clashcloshant, duominous and muezzatinties to commind the
fitful: doom adimdim adoom adimadim: and the oragel of the lauds to
tellforth's glory: and added thereunto a shallow laver to slub out her hellfire
and posied windows for her oriel house: gospelly pewmillieu, christous
pewmillieu: zackbutts babazounded, ollguns tararulled: and she sass her
nach, chillybombom and forty bonnets, upon the altarstane. May all have
mossyhonours!
— Hoke!
— Hoke!
— Hoke!
— Hoke!
— And wholehail, snaeffell, dreardrizzle or sleetshowers of blessing,
where it froze in chalix eller swum in the vestry, with fairskin book and
ruling rod, vein of my vergin page, her chastener ever I did learn my little
ana countrymouse in alphabeater cameltemper, from alderbirk to
tannenyou, with myraw rattan atter dundrum; ooah, oyir, oyir, oyir: and I

did spread before my Livvy, where Lord street lolls and ladies linger and Cammomile Pass cuts Primrose Rise and Coney Bend bounds Mulbreys Island but never a blid had bledded or bludded since long agore when the whole blighty acre was bladey well pessovered, my selvage mats of lecheworked lawn, my carpet gardens of Guerdon City, with chopes pyramidous and mousselimes and beaconphires and colossets and pensilled turisses for the busspleaches of the summiramies and esplanadas and statuesques and templeogues, the Pardonell of Maynooth, Fra Teobaldo, Nielsen, rare admirable, Jean de Porteleau, Conall Gretecloke, Guglielmus Caulis and the eiligh ediculous Passivucant (glorietta's inexcellsiored!): for irkdays and for folliedays till the comple anniums of calendarias, gregoromaios ant gypsyjuliennes as such are pleased of theirs to walk: and I planted for my own hot lisbing lass a quickset vineyard and I fenced it about with huge Chesterfield elms and Kentish hops and rigs of barlow and bowery nooks and greenwished villas and pampos animos and (N.I.) necessitades iglesias and pons for aguaducks: a hawthorndene, a feyrieglenn, the hallaw vall, the dyrchace, Finmark's Howe, against lickybudmonth and gleanermonth with a magicscene wall (rimrim! rimrim!) for a Queen's garden of her phoenix: and (hush! hush!) I brewed for my alpine plurabelle, wigwarming wench, (speakeasy!) my granvilled brandold Dublin lindub, the free, the froh, the frothy freshener, puss, puss, pussyfoot, to split the spleen of her maw: and I laid down before the trotters to my eblanite my stony battered waggonways, my nordsoud circulums, my eastmoreland and westlandmore, running boullowards and syddenly parading, (hearsemen, opslo! nuptiallers, get storting!): whereon, in mantram of truemen like yahoomen (expect till dutc cundoctor summoneth him all fahrts to pay, velkommen all hankinhunkn in this vongn of Hoseyeh!), claudesdales withe arabinstreeds, Roamer Reich's rickyshaws with Hispain's King's trompateers, madridden mustangs, buckarestive bronchos, poster shays and turnintaxis, and tall tall tilburys and nod nod noddies, others gigging gaily, some sedated in sedans: my priccoping gents, aroger, aroger, my damsells softsidesaddled, covertly, covertly, and Lawdy Dawe a perch behind: the mule and the hinny and the jennet and the mustard nag and piebald shjelties and skewbald awknees steppit lively (lift ye the left and rink ye the right!) for her pleashadure: and she lalaughed in her diddydid domino to the switcheries of the whip. Down with them! Kick! Playup!

    Mattahah! Marahah! Luahah! Joahanahanahana!

WHAT WAS THAAS? FOG WAS WHAAS? TOO MULT sleepth. Let sleepth.

But really now whenabouts? Expatiate then how much times we live in. Yes?

So, nat by night by naught by naket, in those good old lousy days gone by, the days, shall we say? of Whom shall we say? while kinderwardens minded their twinsbed, therenow theystood, the sycomores, all four of them, in their quartan agues, the majorchy, the minorchy, the everso and the fermentarian with their ballyhooric blowreaper, titranicht by tetranoxst, at their pussycorners, and that old time pallyollogass, playing copers fearsome, with Gus Walker, the cuddy, and his poor old dying boosy cough, esker, newcsle, saggard, crumlin, dell me, donk, the way to wumblin. Follow me beeline and you're bumblin, esker, newcsle, saggard, crumlin. And listening. So gladdied up when nicechild Kevin Mary (who was going to be commandeering chief of the choirboys' brigade the moment he grew up under all the auspices) irishsmiled in his milky way of cream dwibble and onage tustard and dessed tabbage, frighted out when badbrat Jerry Godolphing (who was hurrying to be cardinal scullion in a night refuge as bald as he was cured enough unerr all the hospitals) furrinfrowned down his wrinkly waste of methylated spirits, ick, and lemoncholy lees, ick, and pulverised rhubarbarorum, icky.

Night by silentsailing night while infantina Isobel (who will be blushing all day to be, when she growed up one Sunday, Saint Holy and Saint Ivory, when she took the veil, the beautiful presentation nun, so barely twenty, in her pure coif, sister Isobel, and next Sunday, Mistlemas, when she looked a peach, the beautiful Samaritan, still as beautiful and still in her teens, nurse Saintette Isabelle, with stiffstarched cuffs but on Holiday, Christmas, Easter mornings when she wore a wreath, the wonderful widow of eighteen springs, Madame Isa Veuve La Belle, so sad but lucksome in her boyblue's long black with orange blossoming weeper's veil) for she was the only girl they loved, as she is the queenly pearl you prize, because of the way the night that first we met she is bound to be, methinks, and not in vain, the darling of my heart, sleeping in her april cot, within her singachamer, with her greengageflavoured candywhistle duetted to the crazyquilt, Isobel, she is so pretty,

truth to tell, wildwood's eyes and primarose hair, quietly, all the woods so
wild, in mauves of moss and daphnedews, how all so still she lay, neath of
the whitethorn, child of tree, like some losthappy leaf, like blowing flower
stilled, as fain would she anon, for soon again 'twill be, win me, woo me,
wed me, ah weary me! deeply, now evencalm lay sleeping;

now upon nacht, while in his tumbril Wachtman Havelook seequeer-
scenes, from yonsides of the choppy, punkt by his curserbog, went long the
grassgross bumpinstrass that henders the pubbel to pass, stowing his bottle
in a hole for at whet his whuskle to stretch ecrooksman, sequestering for
lovers' lost propertied offices the leavethings from allpurgers' night, og
gneiss ogas gnasty, kikkers, brillers, knappers and bands, handsboon and
strumpers, sminkysticks and eddiketsflaskers;

wan fine night and the next fine night and last find night while Kothereen
the Slop in her native's chambercushy, with dreamings of simmering my
veal astore, was basquing to her pillasleep how she thawght a knogg came to
the dowanstairs dour at that howr to peirce the yare and dowandshe went,
schritt be schratt, to see was it Schweeps's mingerals or Shuhorn the posth
with a tillycramp for Hemself and Co, Esquara, or them four hoarsemen on
their apolkaloops, Norreys, Soothbys, Yates and Welks, and, galorybit of
the sanes in hevel, there was a crick up the stirkiss and when she ruz the
cankle to see, galohery, downand she went on her knees to blessersef that
were knogging together like milkjuggles as if it was the wrake of the
hapspurus or old Kong Gander O'Toole of the Mountains or his googoo
goosth she seein, sliving off over the sawdust lobby out ofthe backroom,
wan ter, that was everywans in turruns, in his honeymoon trim, holding up
his fingerhals, with the clookey in his fisstball, tocher of davy's, tocher of
ivileagh, for her to whisht, you sowbelly, and the whites of his pious eyebulbs
swering her to silence and coort;

each and every juridical sessions night, whenas goodmen twelve and true
at fox and geese in their numbered habitations tried old wireless over boord
in their juremembers, whereas by reverendum they found him guilty of
their and those imputations of fornicolopulation with two of his albowcrural
correlations on whom he was said to have enjoyed by anticipation when
schooling them in amown, mid grass, she sat, when man was, amazingly
frank, for their first conjugation whose colours at standing up from the
above were of a pretty carnation but, if really 'twere not so, of some deretane
denudation with intent to excitation, caused by his retrogradation, among
firearmed forces proper to this nation but apart from all titillation which, he
said, was under heat pressure and a good mitigation without which in any
case he insists upon being worthy of continued alimentation for him having

displayed, he says, such grand toleration, reprobate so noted and all, as he was, with his washleather sweeds and his smokingstump, for denying transubstantiation nevertheless in respect of his highpowered station, whereof more especially as probably he was meantime suffering genteel tortures from the best medical attestation, as he oftentimes did, having only strength enough, by way of festination, to implore (or I believe you have might have said better) to complore, with complete obsecration, on everybody connected with him the curse of coagulation for, he tells me outside Sammon's in King Street, after two or three hours of close confabulation, by this pewterpint of Gilbey's goatswhey which is his prime consolation, albeit involving upon the same no uncertain amount of esophagous regurgitation, he being personally unpreoccupied to the extent of a flea's gizzard anent eructation, if he was still extremely offensive to a score and four nostrils' dilatation, still he was likewise, on the other side of him, for some nepmen's eyes a delectation, as he asserts without the least alienation, so prays of his faullt you would make obliteration but for our friend behind the bars, though like Adam Findlater, a man of estimation, summing him up to be done, be what will of excess his exaltation, still we think with Sully there can be no right extinuation for contravention of common and statute legislation for which the fit remedy resides, for Mr Sully, in corporal amputation: so three months for Gubbs Jeroboam, the frothwhiskered pest of the park, as per act one, section two, schedule three, clause four of the fifth of King Jark, this sentence to be carried out tomorrowmorn by Nolans Volans at six o'clock shark, and may the yeastwind and the hoppinghail malt mercy on his seven honeymeads and his hurlyburlygrowth, Amen, says the Clarke;

   niece by nice by neat by natty, whilst amongst revery's happy gardens nine with twenty Leixlip yearlings, darters all, had such a ripping time with gleeful cries of what is nice toppingshaun made of made for and weeping like fun, him to be gone, for they were never happier, huhu, than when they were miserable, haha;

   in their bed of trial, on the bolster of hardship, by the glimmer of memory, under coverlets of cowardice, Albatrus Nyanzer with Victa Nyanza, his mace of might mortified, her beautifell hung up on a nail, he, Mr of our fathers, she, our moddereen ru arue rue, they, ay, by the hodypoker and blazier, they are, as sure as dinny drops into the dyke . . .

   A cry off.

   Where are we at all? and whenabouts in the name of space?

   I don't understand. I fail to say. I dearsee you too.

   House of the cederbalm of mead. Garth of Fyon. Scene and property plot. Stagemanager's prompt. Interior of dwelling on outskirts of city. Groove two. Chamber scene. Boxed. Ordinary bedroom set. Salmonpapered walls. Back, empty Irish grate, Adam's mantel, with wilting elopement fan, soot and tinsel, condemned. North, wall with window practicable. Argentine in casement Vamp. Pelmit above. No curtains. Blind drawn. South, party wall Bed for two with strawberry bedspread, wickerworker clubsessel and caneseated millikinstool. Bookshrine without, facetowel upon. Chair for one. Woman's garments on chair. Man's trousers with crossbelt braces, collar on bedknob. Man's corduroy surcoat with tabrets and taces, seapan nacre buttons on nail. Woman's gown on ditto. Over mantelpiece picture of Michael, lance, slaying Satan, dragon with smoke. Small table near bed, front. Bed with bedding. Spare. Flagpatch quilt. Yverdown design. Limes. Lighted lamp without globe, scarf, gazette, tumbler, quantity of water, julepot, ticker, side props, eventuals, man's gummy article, pink.

A time.

Act: dumbshow.

Closeup. Leads.

Man with nightcap, in bed, fore. Woman, with curlpins, hind. Discovered. Side point of view. First position of harmony. Say! Eh? Ha! Check action. Matt. Male partly masking female. Man looking round, beastly expression, fishy eyes, paralleliped homoplatts, ghazometron pondus, exhibits rage. Business. Ruddy blond, Armenian bole, black patch, beer wig, gross build, episcopalian, any age. Woman, sitting, looks at ceiling, haggish expression, peaky nose, trekant mouth, fithery wight, exhibits fear. Welshrabbit teint, Nubian shine, nasal fossette, turfy tuft, undersized, free kirk, no age. Closeup. Play!

Callboy. Cry off Tabler. Her move.

Footage.

By the sinewy forequarters of the mare Pocahontas and by the white shoulders of Finnuala you should have seen how that smart sallowlass just hopped a nanny's gambit out of bunk like old mother Mesopotomac and in eight and eight sixtyfour she was off, door, knightlamp with her, billy's largelimbs prodgering after to queen's lead. Promiscuous Omebound to Fiammelle la Diva. Huff! His move. Blackout.

Circus. Corridor.

Shifting scene. Wall flats: sink and fly. Spotlight working wall cloths. Spill playing rake and bridges. Room to sink: stairs to sink behind room. Two pieces. Haying after queue. Replay.

The old humburgh looks a thing incomplete so. It is so. On its dead. But it will pawn up a fine head of porter when it is finished. In the quicktime.

The castle arkwright put in a chequered staircase certainly. It has only one square step, to be steady, yet notwithstumbling are they stalemating backgammoner supstairs by skips and trestles tiltop double corner. Whist while and game.

What scenic artist! It is ideal residence for realtar. By hims ingang tilt tinkt a tunning bell that Limen Mr, that Boggey Godde, be airwaked. Lingling, lingling. Be their maggies in all. Chump, do your ephort. Shop! Please shop! Shop ado please! O ado please shop! How hominous his house, haunt it? Yesses indead it be! Nogen, of imperial measure, is begraved beneadher. Here are his naggins poured, his alladim lamps. Around the bloombiered, booty with the bedst. For them whom he have fordone make we newly thankful!

Tell me something. The Porters, so to speak, after their shadowstealers in the newsbaggers, are very nice people, are they not? Very, all fourlike tellt. And on this wise, Mr, Porter (Bartholomew, heavy man, astern, mackerel shirt, hayamatt peruke) is an excellent forefather and Mrs Porter (leading lady, a poopahead, gaffneysaffron nightdress, iszoppy chepelure) is a most kindhearted messmother. A so united family pateramater is not more existing on papel or off of it. As keymaster fits the lock it weds so this bally builder to his streamline secret. They care for nothing except everything that is allporterous. *Porto da Brozzo!* Isn't that terribly nice of them? You can ken that they come of a rarely old family by their costumance and one must togive that one supped of it in all tonearts from awe to zest. I think I begin to divine so much. Only snakkest me truesome! I stone us I'm hable.

To reachy a skeer do! Still hoyhra, till venstra! Here are two rooms on the upstairs, at forkflank and at knifekanter. Whom in the wood are they for? Why, for little Porter babes, to be saved! The coeds, boytom thwackers and timbuy teaser. Here is one. thing you owed two noe. This one once upon awhile was the other but this is the other one nighadays. Ah so? The Corsicos? They are numerable. Guest them. Major bed, minor bickhive. Halosobuth, sov us! Who sleeps in now number one, for example? A pussy, purr esimple. Cunina, Statulina and Edulia, but how sweet of her! Has your pussy a pessname? Yes, indeed, you will hear it passim in all the noveletta and she is named Buttercup. Her bare name will tellt it, a monitress. How very sweet of her and what an excessively lovecharming missyname to forsake, now that I come to drink of it filtred, a gracecup fulled of bitterness. She is dadad's lottiest daughterpearl and brooder's cissiest auntybride. Her shellback thimblecasket mirror only can show her dearest friendeen. To speak well her grace it would ask of Grecian language, of her goodness, that legend golden. Biryina Saindua! Loreas with lillias flocaflake arrosas!

Here's newyearspray, the posquiflor, a windaborne and heliotrope; there miriamsweet and amaranth and marygold to crown. Add lightest knot unto tiptition. O Charis! O Charissima! A more intriguant bambolina could one not colour up out of Boccuccia's Enameron. Would one but to do apart a lilybit her virginelles and, so, to breath, so, therebetween, behold, she had instantt with her handmade as to graps the myth inmid the air. Mother of moth! I will to show herword in flesh. Approach not for ghost sake! Itis dormition! She may think, what though little doth she realise, as morning fresheth, it hath happened her, you know what, as they too what two dare not utter. Silvoo plush, if scolded she draws a face. Petticoat's asleep but in the gentlenest of her thoughts apoo is a nursepin. To be presented, Babs for Bimbushi? Of courts and with enticers. Up, girls, and at him! Alone? Alone what? I mean, our strifestirrer, does she do fleurty winkies with herself Pussy is never alone, as records her chambrette, for she can always look at Biddles and talk petnames with her little playfilly when she is sitting downy on the ploshmat. O, she talks, does she? Marry, how? Rosepetalletted sounds. Ah Biddles es ma plikplak. Ah plikplak wed ma Biddles. A nice jezebel barytinette she will gift but I much prefer her missnomer in maidenly golden lasslike gladsome wenchful flowery girlish beautycapes. So do I, much. Dulce delicatissima! Doth Dolly weeps she is hastings. Will Dally bumpsetty it is tubtime. Allaliefest, she who pities very pebbles, dare we not wish on her our thrice onsk? A lovely fear! That she seventip toe her chrysming, that she spin blue to scarlad till her temple's veil, that the Mount of Whoam it open it her to shelterer! She will blow ever so much more promisefuller, blee me, than all the other common marygales that romp round brigidschool, charming Carry Whambers or saucy Susy Maucepan of Merry Anna Patchbox or silly Polly Flinders. Platsch! A plikaplak.

    And since we are talking amnessly of brukasloop crazedledaze, who doez in sleeproom number twobis? The twobirds. Holy policeman, O, I see! Of what age are your birdies? They are to come of twinning age so soon as they may be born to be eldering like those olders while they are living under chairs. They are and they seem to be so tightly tattached as two maggots to touch other, I think I notice, do I not? You do. Our bright bull babe Frank Kevin is on heartsleeveside. Do not you waken him! Our farheard bode. He is happily to sleep, limb of the Lord, with his lifted in blessing, his buchel Iosa, like the blissed angel he looks so like and his mou is semiope as though he were blowdelling on a bugigle. Whene'er I see those smiles in eyes 'tis Father Quinn again. Very shortly he will smell sweetly when he will hear a weird to wean. By gorgeous, that boy will blare some knight when he will take his dane's pledges and quit our ingletears, spite of undesirable parents, to wend him to Amorica to quest a cashy job. That keen dean with his veen nonsolance! O, I adore the profeen music! Dollarmighty! He is too audorable really, eunique! I guess to have seen somekid like him in the story book, guess I met somewhere somelam to whom he will be becoming liker. But hush! How unpardonable of me! I beg for your venials, sincerely I do.

Hush! The other, twined on codliverside, has been crying in his sleep, making sharpshape his inscissors on some first choice sweets fished out of the muck. A stake in our mead. What a teething wretch! How his book of craven images! Here are posthumious tears on his intimelle. And he has pipettishly bespilled himself from his foundingpen as illspent from inkinghorn. He is jem job joy pip poo pat (jot um for a sobrat!) Jerry Jehu. You will know him by name in the capers but you cannot see whose heel he sheepfolds in his wrought hand because I have not told it to you. O, foetal sleep! Ah, fatal slip! the one loved, the other left, the bride of pride leased to the stranger! He will be quite within the pale when with lordbeeron brow he vows him so tosset to be of the sir Blake tribes bleak while through life's unblest he rodes backs of bannars. Are you not somewhat bulgar with your bowels? Whatever do you mean with bleak? With pale blake I write tintingface. O, you do? And with steelwhite and blackmail I ha'scint for my sweet an anemone's letter with a gold of my bridest hair betied. Donatus his mark, address as follows. So you did? From the Cat and Cage. O, I see and see! In the ink of his sweat he will find it yet. What Gipsy Devereux vowed to Lylian and why the elm and how the stone. You never may know in the preterite all perhaps that you would not believe that you ever even saw to be about to. Perhaps. But they are two very blizky little portereens after their bredscrums, Jerkoff and Eatsup, as for my part opinion indeed. They would be born so, costarred, puck and prig, the maryboy at Donnybrook Fair, the godolphinglad in the Hoy's Court. How frilled one shall be as at taledold of Formio and Cigalette! What folly innocents! Theirs whet pep of puppy-hood! Both barmhearts shall become yeastcake by their brackfest. I will to leave a my copperwise blessing between the pair of them, for rosengorge, for greenafang. Blech and tin soldies, weals in a sniffbox. Som's wholed, all's parted. Weeping shouldst not thou be when man falls but that divine scheming ever adoring be. So you be either man or mouse and you be neither fish nor flesh. Take. And take. Vellicate nyche! Be ones as wes for gives for gives now the hour of passings sembles quick with quelled. Adieu, soft adieu, for these nice presents, kerryjevin. Still tosorrow!

Jeminy, what is the view which now takes up a second position of dis-cordance, tell it please? Mark! You notice it in that rereway because the male entail partially eclipses the femecovert. It is so called for its discord the

meseedo. Do you ever heard the story about Helius Croesus, that white and
gold elephant in our zoopark? You astonish me by it. Is it not that we are
commanding from fullback, woman permitting, a profusely fine birdseye
view from beauhind this park? Finn his park has been much the admiration
of all the stranger ones, grekish and romanos, who arrive to here. The
straight road down the centre (see relief map) bisexes the park which is said
to be the largest of his kind in the world. On the right prominence confronts
you the handsome vinesregent's lodge while, turning to the other supreme
piece of cheeks, exactly opposite, you are confounded by the equally handsome chief sacristary's residence. Around is a little amiably tufted and man
is cheered when he bewonders through the boskage how the nature in all
frisko is enlivened by gentlemen's seats. Here are heavysuppers—'tis for
daddies housings for hundredaires of our super thin thousand. By gum, but
you have resin! Of these tallworts are yielded out juices for jointoils and
pappasses for paynims. Listeneth! 'Tis a tree story. How olave, that firile,
was aplantad in her liveside. How tannoboom held tonobloom. How rood
in norlandes. The black and blue marks athwart the weald, which now
barely is so stripped, indicate the presence of sylvious beltings. Therewithal
shady rides lend themselves out to rustic cavalries. In yonder valley, too,
stays mountain sprite. Any pretty dears are to be caught inside but it is a bad
pities of the plain. A scarlet pimparnell now mules the mound where
anciently first murders were wanted to take root. By feud fionghalian.
Talkingtree and sinningstone stay on either hand. Hystorical leavesdroppings
may also be garnered up with sir Shamus Swiftpatrick, Archfieldchaplain of
Saint Lucan's. How familiar it is to see all these interesting advenements
with one snaked's eyes! Is all? Yet not. Hear one's. At the bodom fundus of
this royal park, which, with tvigate shyasian gardeenen, is open to the public
till night at late, so well the sissastrides so will the pederestians, do not fail to
point to yourself a depression called Holl Hollow. It is often quite gutter-
gloomering in our duol and gives wankyrious thoughts to the head but
the banders of the pentapolitan poleetsfurcers bassoons into it on windy
woodensdays their wellbooming wolvertones. Ulvos! Ulvos!

    Whervolk dorst ttou begin to tremble by our moving pictures at this
moment when I am to place my hand of our true friendshapes upon thee
knee to mark well what I say? Throu shayest who? In Amsterdam there
lived a . . . But how? You are tremblotting, you retchad, like a verry jerry!
Niet? Will you a guineeser? Gaij beutel of staub? To feel, you? Yes, how it
trembles, the timid! Vortigern, ah Gortigern! Overlord of Mercia! Or doth
brainskin flinchgreef? Stemming! What boyazhness! Sole shadow shows.
Tis jest jibberweek's joke. It must have stole. O, keve silence, both!

Putshameyu! I have heard her voice somewhere else's before me in these ears still that now are for mine.

Let op. Slew musies. Thunner in the eire.

You were dreamend, dear. The pawdrag? The fawthrig? Shoe! Hear are no phanthares in the room at all, avikkeen. No bad bold faathern, dear one. Opop opop capallo, muy malinchily malchick! Gothgorod father godown followay tomollow the lucky load to Lublin for make his thoroughbass grossman's bigness. Take that two piece big slap slap bold honty bottomsside pap pap pappa.

— *Li ne dormis?*

— *S! Malbone dormas.*

— *Kia li krias nikte?*

— *Parolas infanetes. S!*

Sonly all in your imagination, dim. Poor little brittle magic nation, dim of mind! Shoe to me now, dear! Shoom of me! While elvery stream winds seling on for to keep this barrel of bounty rolling and the nightmail afarfrom morning nears.

When you're coaching through Lucalised, on the sulphur spa to visit, it's safer to hit than miss it, stop at his inn! The hammers are telling the cobbles, the pickts are hacking the saxums, it's snugger to burrow abed than ballet on broadway. Tuck in your blank! For it's race pound race the hosties rear all roads to ruin and layers by lifetimes laid down riches from poormen. Cried unions to chip, saltpetre to strew, gallpitch to drink, stonebread to break but it's bully to gulp good blueberry pudding. Doze in your warmth! While the elves in the moonbeams, feeling why, will keep my lilygem gently gleaming.

In the sleepingchambers. The court to go into half morning. The four seneschals with their palfrey to be there now, all balaaming in their sellaboutes and sharping up their penisills. The boufeither Soakersoon at holdup tent sticker. The swabsister Katya to have duntalking and to keep shakenin dowan her droghedars. Those twelve chief barons to stand by duedesmally with their folded arums and put down all excursions and false alarums and after that to go back now to their runameat farums and recompile their magnum chartarums with the width of the road between them and all harrums. The maidbrides all, in favours gay, to strew sleety cinders on their falling hair and for wouldbe joybells to ring sadly ringless hands. The dame dowager to stay kneeled how she is, as first mutherer with cord in coil. The two princes of the tower royal, daulphin and deevlin, to lie how they are without to see. The dame dowager's duffgerent to present wappon, blade drawn to the full and about wheel without to be seen of them. The infant Isabella from her coign to do obeisance toward the duffgerent, as first futherer with drawn brand. Then the court to come in to full morning. Herein see ye fail not!

— *Vidu, porkego! Ili vi rigardas. Returnu, porkego. Maldelikato!*

Gauze off heaven. Vision. Then. O, pluxty suddly, the sight entrancing! Hummels! That crag! Those hullocks! O Sire! So be accident occur is not going to commence! What have you therefore? Fear you the donkers? Of roovers? I fear lest we have lost ours (non grant it!) respecting these wildy parts. How is hit finister! How shagsome all and beastful! What do you show on? I show because I must see before my misfortune so a stark pointing pole. Lord of ladders, what for lungitube I Can you read the verst legend hereon? I am hather of the missed. Areed! To the dunleary obelisk via the rock vhat myles knox furlongs; to the general's postoffice howsands of patience; to the Wellington memorial half a league wrongwards; to Sara's bridge good hunter and nine to meet her: to the point, one yeoman's yard. He, he, he! At that do you leer, a setting up? With a such unfettered belly? Two cascades? I leer (O my big, O my bog, O my bigbagbone!) because I must see a buntingcap of so a pinky on the point. It is for a true glover's greetings and many burgesses by us, greats and grosses, uses to pink it in this way at tet-at-tet. For long has it been effigy of standard royal when broken on roofstaff which to the gunnings shall cast welcome from Courtmilits' Fortress, umptydum dumptydum. Bemark you these hangovers, those streamer fields, his influx. Do you not have heard that, the queen lying abroad from fury of the gales, (meekname mocktitles her Nan Nan Nanetta) her liege of lateenth dignisties shall come on their bay tomorrow, Michalsmas, mellems the third and fourth of the clock, there to all the king's aussies and all their king's men, knechts tramplers and cavalcaders, led of herald graycloak, Ulaf Goldarskield? Dog! Dog! Her lofts will be loosed for her and their tumblers broodcast. A progress shall be made in walk, ney? I trow it well, and uge by uge. He shall come, sidesmen accostant, by aryan jubilarian and on brigadier-general Nolan or and buccaneeradmiral Browne, with—who can doubt it?—his golden beagles and his white elkox terriers for a hunting on our littlego illcome faxes. In blue and buff of Beaufort the hunt shall make. It is poblesse noblige. Ommes will grin through collars when each riders other's ass. Me Eccls! What cats' killings overall! What popping out of guillotened widows! Quick time! Beware of waiting! Squintina plies favours on us from her rushfrail and Zosimus, the crowder, in his surcoat, sues us with souftwister. Apart we! Here are gantlets. I believe, by Plentifolks Mixymost! Yet if I durst to express the hope how I might be able to be present. All these peeplers entrammed and detrained on bikeygels and troykakyls and those puny

farting little solitires! Tollacre, tollacre! Polo north will beseem Sibernian and Plein Pelouta will behowl ne yerking at lawncastrum ne ghimbelling on guelflinks. Mauser Misma shall cease to stretch her and come abroad for what the blinkins is to be seen. A ruber, a rancher, a fullvide, a veridust and as crerdulous behind as he was before behind a damson of a sloe cooch. Mbv! The annamation of evabusies, the livli
ness of her laughings, such as a plurity of bells! Have peacience, pray you! Place to dames! Even the Lady Victoria Landauner will leave to loll and parasol, all giddied into gushgasps with her dickey standing. Britus and Gothius shall no more joustle for that sonneplace but mark one autonement when, with si so silent, Cloudia Aiduolcis, good and dewed up, shall let fall, yes, no, yet, now, a rain. Muchsias grapcias! It is how sweet from her, the wispful, and they are soon seen swopsib so a sautril as a meise. Its ist not the tear on this movent sped. Tix sixponce! Poum! Hool poll the bull? Fool pay the bill. Becups a can full. Peal, pull the bell! Still sayeme of ceremonies, much much more! So pleaseyour! It stands in *Instopressible* how Meynhir Mayour, our boorgo-maister, thon staunch Thorsman, (our Nancy's fancy, our own Nanny's Big Billy), his hod hoisted, in best bib and tucker, with Woolington bottes over buckram babbishkis and his clouded cane and necknoose aureal, surrounded of his full cooperation with fixed baronets and meng our pueblos, restrained by chain of hands from pinchgut, hoghill, darklane, gibbetmeade and beaux and laddes and bumbellye, shall receive Dom King at broadstone barrow meet a keys of goodmorrow on to his pompey cushion. Me amble dooty to your grace's majers! Arise, sir Pompkey Dompkey! Ear! Ear! Weakear! An allness eversides! We but miss that horse elder yet cherchant of the wise graveleek in cabbuchin garden. That his be foison, old Caubeenhauben! 'Twill be tropic of all days. By the splendour of Sole! Perfect weatherest prevailing. Thisafter, swift's might-mace deposing, he shall aidress to His Serenemost by a speechreading from his miniated vellum, alfi byrni gamman dealter etcera zezera eacla treacla youghta kaptor lomdom noo, who meaningwhile that illuminatured one, Papyroy of Pepinregn, my Sire, great, big King, (his scaffold is there set up, as to edify, by Rex Ingram, pageantmaster) will be poking out with his canule into the arras of what brilliant bridgecloths and joking up with his tonguespitz to the crimosing balkonladies, here's a help undo their modest stays with a fullbelow may the funnyfeelbelong. Oddsbones, that may it! Carilloners will ring their gluckspeels. Rng rng! Rng rng! S. Presbutt-in-the-North, S. Mark Underloop, S. Lorenz-by-the-Toolechest, S. Nicholas Myre. You shall hark to anune S. Gardener, S. George-le-Greek, S. Barclay Moitered, S. Phibb, Iona-in-the-Fields with Paull-the-Aposteln. And

audialterand: S. Jude-at-Gate, Bruno Friars, S. Weslen-on-the-Row, S. Molyneux Without, S. Mary Stillamaries with Bride-and-Audeons-behind-Wardborg. How chimant in effect! Alla tingaling pealabells! So a many of churches one cannot pray own's prayers. 'Tis holyyear's day! Juin jully we may! Agithetta and Tranquilla shall demure umclaused but Marlborough-the-Less, Greatchrist and Holy Protector shall have open virgilances. Beata Basilica! But will be not pontification? Dock, dock, agame! Primatially. At wateredge. Cantaberra and Neweryork may supprecate when, by vepers, for towned and travalled, his goldwhite swaystick aloft ylifted, umbrilla-parasoul, Monsigneur of Deublan shall impart to all. *Benedictus benedicat!* To board! And mealsight! Unjoint him this bittern, frust me this chicken, display yon crane, thigh her her pigeon, unlace allay rabbit and pheasant! Sing: Old Finncoole, he's a mellow old saoul when he swills with his fuddlers free! Poppop array! For we're all jollygame fellhellows which nobottle can deny! Here be trouts culponed for ye and salmons chined and sturgeons tranched, sanced capons, lobsters barbed. Call halton eatwords! Mumm me moe mummers! What, no Ithalians? How, not one Moll Pamelas? Accordingly! Play actors by us ever have crash to their gate. Mr Messop and Mr Borry will produce of themselves, as they're two genitalmen of Veruno, Senior Nowno and Senior Brolano (finaly! finaly!), all for love of a fair penitent that, a she be broughton, rhoda's a rosy she. Their two big skins! How they strave to gat her! Such a boyplay! Their bouchicaulture! What tyronte power! Buy our fays! My name is novel and on the Granby in hills. Bravose! Thou traitor slave! Mine name's Apnorval and o'er the Grandbeyond Mountains. Bravossimost! The royal nusick their show shall shut with songslide to nature's solemn silence. Deep Dalchi Dolando! Might gentle harp addurge! It will give piketurns on the tummlipplads and forain dances and crosshurdles and dollmanovers and viceuvious pyrolyphics, a snow of dawnflakes, at darkfall for Grace's Mamnesty and our fancy ladies, all assombred. Some wholetime in hot town tonight! You do not have heard? It stays in book of that which is. I have heard anyone tell it jesterday (master currier with brassard was't) how one should come on morrow here but it is never here that one today. Well but remind to think, you where yestoday Ys Morganas war and that it is always tomorrow in toth's tother's place. Amen.

True! True! Vouchsafe me more soundpicture! It gives furiously to think. Is rich Mr Pornter, a squire, not always in his such strong health? I thank you for the best, he is in taken deal exceedingly herculeneous. One sees how he is lot stoutlier than of formerly. One would say him to hold whole a litteringture of kidlings under his aproham. Has handsome Sir Pournter always been so long married? O yes, Lord Pournterfamilias has been marryingman ever since so long time in Hurtleforth, where he appeers as our oily the active, and, yes indeed, he has his mic son and his two fine mac sons and a superfine mick want they mack metween them. She, she, she! But on what do you again leer? I am not leering, I pink you pardons. I am highly sheshe sherious.

Do you not must want to go somewhere on the present? Yes, O pity! At earliest moment! That prickly heat feeling! Forthink not me spill it's at always so guey. Here we shall do a far walk (O pity) anygo khaibits till the number one of sairey's place. Is, is. I want you to admire her sceneries illustrationing our national first rout, one ought ought one. We shall too downlook on that ford where Sylvanus Sanctus washed but hurdley those tips of his anointeds. Do not show ever retrorsehim, crockodeyled, till that you become quite crimstone in the face! Beware! guardafew! It is Stealer of the Heart! I am anxious in regard you should everthrown your sillarsalt. I will dui sui, tefnute! These brilling waveleaplights! Please say me how sing you them. Seekhem seckhem! They arise from a clear springwell in the near of our park which makes the daft to hear all blend. This place of endearment! How it is clear! And how they cast their spells upon, the fronds that thereup float, the bookstaff branchings! The druggeted stems, the leaves incut on trees! Do you can their tantrist spellings? I can lese, skillmistress aiding. Elm, bay, this way, cull dare, take a message, tawny runes ilex sallow, meet me at the pine. Yes, they shall have brought us to the water trysting, by hedjes of maiden ferm, then here in another place is their chapelofeases, sold for song, of which you have thought my praise too much my price. O ma ma! Yes, sad one of Ziod? Sell me, my soul dear! Ah, my sorrowful, his cloister dreeping of his monkshood, how it is triste to death, all his dark ivytod! Where cold in dearth. Yet see, my blanching kissabelle, in the under close she is allso gay, her kirtles green, her curtsies white, her peony pears, her nistlingsloes! I, pipette, I must also quicklingly to tryst myself softly into this littleeasechapel. I would rather than Ireland! But I pray, make! Do your easiness! O, peace, this is heaven! O, Mr Prince of Pouringtoher, whatever shall I pppease to do? Why do you so lifesighs, my precious, as I hear from you, with limmenings lemantitions, after that swollen one? I am not sighing, I assure, but only I am soso sorry about all in my saarasplace. Listen, listen! I am doing it. Hear more to those voices! Always I am hearing them. Horsehem coughs enough. Annshee lispes privily.

— He is quieter now.

— Legalentitled. Accesstopartnuzz. Notwildebeestsch. Byrightofoaptz. Twainbeonerflsh. Haveandholdpp.

— S! Let us go. Make a noise. Slee . . .

— Qui . . . The gir . . .

— Huesofrichunfoldingmorn. Wakenupriseandprove. Provideforsacrifice.

— Wait! Hist! Let us list!

For our netherworld's bosomfoes are working tooth and nail overtime: in earthveins, toadcavites, chessganglions, saltklesters, underfed: nagging firenibblers knockling aterman up out of his hinterclutch. Tomb be their tools! When the youngdammers will be soon heartpocking on their betters' doornoggers: and the youngfries will be backfrisking diamondcuts over their lyingin underlayers, spick and spat trowelling a gravetrench for their fourinhand forebears. Vote for your club!

— Wait!

— What!

— Her door!

— Ope?

— See!

— What?

— Careful.

— Who?

Live well! Iniivdluaritzas! Tone!

Cant ear! Her dorters ofe? Whofe? Her eskmeno daughters hope? Whope? Ellme, elmme, elskmestoon! Soon!

Let us consider.

The procurator Interrogarius Mealterum presends us this proposer.

Honuphrius is a concupiscent exservicemajor who makes dishonest propositions to all. He is considered to have committed, invoking *droit d'oreiller*, simple infidelities with Felicia, a virgin, and to be practising for unnatural coits with Eugenius and Jeremias, two or three philadelphians. Honophrius, Felicia, Eugenius and Jeremias are consanguineous to the lowest degree. Anita the wife of Honophrius, has been told by her tirewoman, Fortissa, that Honuphrius has blasphemously confessed under voluntary chastisement that he has instructed his slave, Mauritius, to urge Magravius, a commercial, emulous of Honuphrius, to solicit the chastity of Anita. Anita is informed by some illegitimate children of Fortissa with Mauritius (the supposition is Ware's) that Gillia, the schismatical wife of Magravius, is visited clandestinely by Barnabas, the advocate of Honuphrius, an immoral person who has been corrupted by Jeremias. Gillia, (a cooler blend, D'Alton insists) *ex equo* with Poppea, Arancita, Clara, Marinuzza, Indra and Iodina, has been tenderly debauched (in Halliday's view), by Honuphrius, and Magravius knows from spies that

Anita has formerly committed double sacrilege with Michael, *vulgo* Cerularius, a perpetual curate, who wishes to seduce Eugenius. Magravius threatens to have Anita molested by Sulla, an orthodox savage (and leader of a band of twelve mercenaries, the Sullivani), who desires to procure Felicia for Gregorius, Leo, Vitellius and Macdugalius, four excavators, if she will not yield to him and also deceive Honuphrius by rendering conjugal duty when demanded. Anita who claims to have discovered incestuous temptations from Jeremias and Eugenius would yield to the lewdness of Honuphrius to appease the savagery of Sulla and the mercernariness of the twelve Sullivani, and (as Gilbert at first suggested), to save the virginity of Felicia for Magravius when converted by Michael after the death of Gillia, but she fears that, by allowing his marital rights she may cause reprehensible conduct between Eugenius and Jeremias. Michael, who has formerly debauched Anita, dispenses her from yielding to Honuphrius who pretends publicly to possess his conjunct in thirtynine several manners (*turpiter!* affirm *ex cathedris* Gerontes Cambronses) for carnal hygiene whenever he has rendered himself impotent to consummate by subdolence. Anita is disturbed but Michael comminates that he will reserve her case tomorrow for the ordinary Guglielmus even if she should practise a pious fraud during affrication which, from experience, she knows (according to Wadding), to be leading to nullity. Fortissa, however, is encouraged by Gregorius, Leo, Viteilius, and Magdugalius, reunitedly, to warn Anita by describing the strong chastisements of Honuphrius and the depravities (*turpissimas!*) of Canicula, the deceased wife of Mauritius, with Sulla, the simoniac, who is abnegand and repents. Has he hegemony and shall she submit?

Translate a lax, you breed a bradaun. In the goods of Cape and Chattertone, deceased.

This, lay readers and gentlemen, is perhaps the commonest of all cases arising out of umbrella history in connection with the wood industries in our courts of litigation. D'Oyly Owens holds (though Finn Magnusson of himself holds also) that so long as there is a joint deposit account in the two names a mutual obligation is posited. Owens cites Brerfuchs and Warren, a foreign firm, since disseized, registered as Tangos, Limited, for the sale of certain proprietary articles. The action which was at the instance of the trustee of the heathen church emergency fund, suing by its trustee, a resigned civil servant, for the payment of tithes due was heard by Judge Doyle and also by a common jury. No question arose as to the debt for which vouchers spoke volumes. The defence alleged that payment had been made effective. The fund trustee, one Jucundus Fecundus Xero Pecundus

Coppercheap, counterclaimed that payment was invalid having been
tendered to creditor under cover of a crossed cheque, signed in the ordinary
course, in the name of Wieldhelm, Hurls Cross, voucher copy provided,
and drawn by the senior partner only by whom the lodgment of the species
had been effected but in their joint names. The bank particularised, the
national misery (now almost entirely in the hands of the four chief
bondholders for value in Tangos), declined to pay the draft, though there
were ample reserves to meet the liability, whereupon the trusty Coppercheap negociated it for and on behalf of the fund of the thing to a client of
his, a notary, from whom, on consideration, he received in exchange legal
relief as between trusthee and bethrust, with thanks. Since then the cheque,
a good washable pink, embossed D you D No 11 hundred and thirty 2,
good for the figure and face, had been circulating in the country for over
thirtynine years among holders of Pango stock, a rival concern, though not
one demonetised farthing had ever spun or fluctuated across the counter in
the semblance of hard coin or liquid cash. The jury (a sour dozen of stout
fellows all of whom were curiously named after doyles) naturally disagreed
jointly and severally, and the belligerent judge, disagreeing with the allied
jurors' disagreement, went outside his jurisfiction altogether and ordered a
garnishee attachment to the neutral firm. No *mandamus* could locate the
depleted whilom Breyfawkes as he had entered into an ancient moratorium,
dating back to the times of the early barters, and only the junior partner
Barren could be found, who entered an appearance and turned up, upon a
notice of motion and after service of the motion by interlocutory injunction,
among the male jurors to be an absolete turfwoman, originally from the
proletarian class, with still a good title to her sexname of Ann Doyle, 2
Coppinger's Cottages, the Doyle's country. Doyle (Ann), add woman in,
having regretfully left the juryboxers, protested cheerfully on the stand in a
long jurymiad *in re* corset checks, delivered in doylish, that she had often, in
supply to brusk demands rising almost to bollion point, discounted Mr
Brakeforth's first of all in exchange at nine months from date without issue
and, to be strictly literal, unbottled in corrubberation a current account of
how she had been made at sight for services rendered the payee-drawee of
unwashable blank assignations, sometimes pinkwilliams (laughter) but more
often of the *crème-de-citron, vair émail paoncoque* or marshmallow series,
which she, as bearer, used to endorse, adhesively, to her various payers-
drawers who in most cases were identified by the timber papers as wellknown tetigists of the city and suburban. The witness, at her own request,
asked if she might and wrought something between the sheets of music
paper which she had accompanied herself with for the occasion and this

having been handed up for the bench to look at *in camera*, Coppinger's doll, as she was called, (*annias*, Mack Erse's Dar, the adopted child) then proposed to jerrykin and jureens and every jim, jock and jarry in that little green courtinghousie for her satisfaction and as a whole act of settlement to reamalgamate herself, tomorrow perforce, in pardonership with the permanent suing fond trustee, Monsignore Pepigi, under the new style of Will Breakfast and Sparrem, as, when all his cognisances had been estreated, he seemed to proffer the steadiest interest towards her, but this prepoposal was ruled out on appeal by Judge Jeremy Doyler, who, reserving judgment in a matter of courts and reversing the findings of the lower correctional, found, beyond doubt of treuson, fending the dissassents of the pick-packpanel, twelve as upright judaces as ever let down their thoms, and, *occupante extremum scabie*, handed down to the jury of the Liffey that, as a matter of tact, the woman they gave as free was born into contractual incapacity (the Calif of Man *v* the Eaudelusk Company) when, how and where mamy's mancipium act did not apply and therefore held supremely that, as no property in law can exist in a corpse, (Hal Kilbride *v* Una Bellina) Pepigi's pact was pure piffle (loud laughter) and Wharrem would whistle for the rhino. Will you, won't you, pango with Pepigi? Not for Nancy, how dare you do! And whew whewwhew whew.

— He sighed in sleep.

— Let us go back.

— Lest he forewaken.

— Hide ourselves.

While hovering dreamwings, folding around, will hide from fears my wee mee mannikin, keep my big wig long strong manomen, guard my bairn, *mon beau*.

— To bed.

Prospector projector and boomooster giant builder of all causeways woesoever, hopping offpoint and true terminus of straxstraightcuts and corkscrewn perambulaups, zeal whence to goal whither, wonderlust, in sequence to which every muckle must make its mickle, as different as York from Leeds, being the only wise in a muck's world to look on itself from beforehand; mirrorminded curiositease and would-to-the-large which bring hills to molehunter, home through first husband, perils behind swine and horsepower down to hungerford, prick this man and tittup this woman, our forced payrents, Bogy Bobow with his cunnyngnest couchmare, Big Maester Finnykin with Phenicia Parkes, lame of his ear and gape of her leg, most correctingly, we beseach of you, down their laddercase of nightwatch service and bring them at suntime flush with the nethermost gangrung of their

stepchildren, guide them through the labyrinth of their samilikes and the
alteregoases of their pseudoselves, hedge them bothways from all roamers
whose names are ligious, from loss of bearings deliver them; so they keep to
their rights and be ware of duty frees, neoliffic smith and magdalenian
jinnyjones, mandragon mor and weak wiffeyducky, Morionmale and
Thrydacianmad, basilisk glorious with his weeniequeenie, tigernack and
swansgrace, he as hale as his ardouries, she as verve as her veines; this prime
white arsenic with bissemate alloyed, martial sin with peccadilly, free to
lease hold with first mortgage, dowser dour and dipper douce, stop-that-
war and feel-this-feather, norsebloodheartened and landsmoolwashable,
great gas with fun-in-the-corner, grand slam with fall-of-the-trick, solomn
one and shebby, cod and coney, cash and carry, in all we dreamed the part
we dreaded, corsair coupled with his dame, royal biber but constant lymph,
boniface and bonnyfeatures, nazil hose and river mouth, bang-the-change
and batter-the-bolster, big smoke and lickley roesthy, humanity's fahrman
by society leader, voguener and trulley, humpered and elf, Urloughmoor
with Miryburrow, leaks and awfully, basal curse yet grace abunda, Regies
Producer with screendoll Vedette, peg of his claim and pride of her heart,
cliffscaur grisly but rockdove cooing, hodinstag on fryggabet, baron and
feme: that he may dishcover her that she may uncouple him, that one may
come and crumple them, that they may soon recoup themselves: now and
then, time on time again, as per periodicity; from Neaves to Willses, from
Bushmills to Enos; to Goerz from Harleem, to Hearths of Oak from Skittish
Widdas; via mala, hyber pass, heckhisway per alptrack: through landsvague
and vain, after many mandelays: in their first case, to the next place, till their
cozenkerries: the high and the by, both pent and plain: cross cowslips
yillow, yellow, yallow, past pumpkins pinguind, purplesome: be they
whacked to the wide other tied to hustings, long sizzleroads neath arthruseat,
him to the derby, her to toun, til sengentide do coddlam: in the grounds or
unterlinnen: rue to lose and ca canny: at shipside, by convent garden: monk
and sempstress, in sackcloth silkily: curious dreamers, curious dramas,
curious deman, plagiast dayman, playajest dearest, plaguiest dourest: for the
strangfort planters are prodesting, and the karkery felons dryflooring it and
the leperties' laddos railing the way, blump for slogo slee.

Stop! Did a stir? No, is fast. On to bed! So he is. It's only the wind on the
road outside for to wake all shivering shanks from snorring.

But. Oom Godd his villen, who will he be, this mitryman, some king of
the yeast, in his chrismy greyed brunzewig, with the snow in his mouth and
the caspian asthma, so bulk of build? Relics of pharrer and livite! Dik Gill,
Tum Lung or Macfinnan's cool Harryng? He has only his hedcosycasket

on and his wollsey shirtplisse with peascod doublet, also his feet wear doubled width socks for he always must to insure warm sleep between a pair of fullyfleeced bankers like a finnoc in a cauwl. Can thus be Misthra Norkmann that keeps our hotel? Begor, Mr O'Sorgmann, you're looking right well! Hecklar's champion ethnicist. How deft as a fuchser schouws daft as a fish! He's the dibble's own doges for doublin existents! But a jolly fine daysent form of one word. He's rounding up on his family.

And who is the bodikin by him, sir? So voulzievalsshie? With ybbs and zabs? Her trixiestrail is tripping her, vop! Luck at the way for the lucre of smoke she's looping the lamp! Why, that's old missness wipethemdry! Well, well, wellsowells! Donauwatter! Ardechious me! With her halfbend as proud as a peahen, allabalmy, and her troutbeck quiverlipe, ninya nanya. And her steptojazyma's culunder buzztle. Happy tea area, naughtygay frew! Selling sunlit sopes to washtout winches and rhaincold draughts to the props of his pubs. She tired lipping the swells at Pont Delisle till she jumped the boom at Brounemouth. Now she's borrid his head under Hatesbury's Hatch and loamed his fate to old Love Lane. And she's just the same old haporth of dripping. She's even brennt her hair.

Which route are they going? Why? Angell sitter or Amen Corner, Norwood's Southwalk or Euston Waste? The solvent man in his upper gambeson withnot a breth against him and the wee wiping womanahoussy. They're coming terug their diamond wedding tour, giant's inchly elfkin's ell, vesting their characters vixendevolment, andens aller, athors err, our first day man and your dresser and mine, that Luxuumburgher evec cettehis Alzette, konyglik shire with his queensh countess, Stepney's shipchild with the waif of his bosun, Dunmow's flitcher with duck-on-the-rock, down the scales, the way they went up, under talls and threading tormentors, shunning the startraps and slipping in sliders, risking a runway, ruing reveals, from Elder Arbor to La Puiree, eskipping the clockback, crystal in carbon, sweetheartedly. Hot and cold and electrickery with attendance and lounge and promenade free. In spite of all that science could boot or art could eke. Bolt the grinden. Cave and can em. Single wrecks for the weak, double axe for the mail, and quick queck quack for the radiose. Renove that bible. You will never have post in your pocket unless you have brasse on your plate. Beggards outdoor. Goat to the Endth, thou slowguard! Mind the Monks and their Grasps. Scrape your souls. Commit no miracles. Postpone no bills. Respect the uniform. Hold the raabers for the kunning his plethoron. Let leash the dooves to the cooin her coynth. Hatenot havenots. Share the wealth and spoil the weal. Peg the pound to tom the devil. My time is on draught. Bottle your own. Love my label like myself. Earn before eating.

Drudge after drink. Credit tomorrow. Follow my dealing. Fetch my price.
Buy not from dives. Sell not to freund. Herenow chuck english and learn to
pray plain. Lean on your lunch. No cods before Me. Practise preaching.
Think in your stomach. Import through the nose. By faith alone. Season's
weather. Gomorrha. Salong. Lots feed from my tidetable. Oil's wells in our
lands. Let earwigger's wivable teach you the dance.

Now their laws assist them and ease their fall!

For they met and mated and bedded and buckled and got and gave and
reared and raised and brought Thawland within Har danger, and turned
them, tarrying to the sea and planted and plundered and pawned our souls
and pillaged the pounds of the extramurals and fought and feigned with
strained relations and bequeathed us their ills and recrutched cripples gait
and undermined lungachers, manplanting seven sisters while wan warm-
wooed woman scrubbs, and turned out coats and removed their origins and
never learned the first day's lesson and tried to mingle and managed to save
and feathered foes' nests and fouled their own and wayleft the arenotts and
ponted vodavalls for the zollgebordened and escaped from liquidation by
the heirs of their death and were responsible for congested districts and
rolled olled logs into Peter's sawyery and werfed new woodcuts on Paoli's
wharf and ewesed Rachel's lea and rammed Dominic's gap and looked
haggards after lazatables and rode fourscore oddwinters and struck rock oil
and forced a policeman and collaughsed at their phizes in Toobiassed and
Zachary and left off leaving off and kept on keeping on and roused up drink
and poured balm down and were cuffed by their customers and bit the dust
at the foot of the poll when in her deergarth he gave up his goat after the
battle of Multaferry. Pharoah with fairy, two lie, let them! Yet they wend it
back, qual his leif, himmertality, bullseaboob and rivishy divil, light in hand,
helm on high, to peekaboo durk the thicket of slumbwhere, till their hour
with their scene be struck for ever and the book of the dates he close, he
clasp and she and she seegn her tour d'adieu, Pervinca calling, Soloscar
hears. (O Sheem! O Shaam!), and gentle Isad Ysut gag, flispering in the
nightleaves flattery, dinsiduously, to Finnegan, to sin again and to make
grim grandma grunt and grin again while the first grey streaks steal silvering
by for to mock their quarrels in dollymount tumbling.

They near the base of the chill stair, that large incorporate licensed
vintner, such as he is, from former times, nine hosts in himself, in his
hydrocomic establishment and his ambling limfy peepingpartner, the slave
of the ring that worries the hand that sways the lamp that shadows the walk
that bends to his bane the busynext man that came on the cop with the
fenian's bark that pickled his widow that primed the pope that passed it

round on the volunteers' plate till it croppied the ears of Purses Relle that kneed O'Connell up out of his doss that shouldered Burke that butted O'Hara that woke the busker that grattaned his crowd that bucked the jiggers to rhyme the rann that flooded the routes in Eryan's isles from Malin to Clear and Carnsore Point to Slynagollow and cleaned the pockets arid ransomed the ribs of all the listeners, leud and lay, that bought the ballad that Hosty made.

Anyhow (the matter is a troublous and a peniloose) have they not called him at many's their mock indignation meeting, vehmen's vengeance vective volleying, inwader and uitlander, the notables, crashing libels in their sullivan's mounted beards about him, their right renownsable patriarch? Heinz cans everywhere and the swanee her ainsell and Eyrewaker's family sock that they smuggled to life betune them, roaring (Big Reilly was the worst): free boose for the man from the nark, sure, he never was worth a cornerwall fark, and his banishee's bedpan she's a quareold bite of a tark: as they wendelled their zingaway wivewards from his find me cool's moist opulent vinery, highjacking through the nagginneck pass, as they hauled home with their hogsheads, axpoxtelating, and claiming cowled consollation, sursumcordial, from the bluefunkfires of the dipper and the martian's frost?

Use they not, our noesmall termtraders, to abhors offrom him, the yet unregendered thunderslog, whose sbrogue cunneth none lordmade under-siding, how betwixt wifely rule and *mens conscia recti*, then hemale man all unbracing to omniwomen, but now shedropping his hitches like any maidavale oppersite orseriders in an idinhole? Ah, dearo! Dearo, dear! And her illian! And his willyum! When they were all there now, matin-marked for lookin on. At the carryfour with awlus plawshus, their happyass cloudious! And then and too the trivials! And their bivouac! And his monomyth! Ah ho! Say no more about it! I'm sorry! I saw. I'm sorry! I'm sorry to say I saw!

Gives there not too amongst us after all events (or so grunts a leading hebdromadary) some togethergush of stillandbutallyouknow that, insofar-forth as, all up and down the whole con creation say, efficient first gets there finally every time, as a complex matter of pure form, for those excess and that pasphault hardhearingness from their eldfar, in grippes and rumblions, through fresh taint and old treason, another like that alter but not quite such anander and stillandbut one not all the selfsame and butstillone just the maim and encore emmerhim may always, with a little difference, till the latest up to date so early in the morning, have evertheless been allmade amenable?

Yet he begottom.

Let us wherefore, tearing ages, presently preposterose a snatchvote of thanksalot to the huskiest coaxing experimenter that ever gave his best hand into chancerisk, wishing him with his famblings no end of slow poison and a mighty broad venue for themselves between the devil's punchbowl and the deep angleseaboard, that they may gratefully turn a deaf ear clooshed upon the desperanto of willynully, their shareholders from Taaffe to Auliffe, that will curse them below par and mar with their descendants, shame, humbug ant profit, to greenmould upon mildew over jaundice as long as ever there's wagtail surtaxed to a testcase on enver a man.

We have to had them whether we'll like it or not. They'll have to have us now then we're here on theirspot. Scant hope theirs or ours to escape life's high carnage of semperidentity by subsisting peasemeal upon variables. Bloody certainly have we got to see to it ere smellful demise surprends us on this concrete that down the gullies of the eras we may catch ourselves looking forward to what will in no time be staring you larrikins on the postface in that multimirror megaron of returningties, whirled without end to end. So there was a raughty ... who in Dyfflinsborg did ... With his soddering iron, spadeaway, hammerlegs and ... Where there was a fair young ... Who was playing her game of ... And said she you rockaby ... Will you peddle in my bog ... And he sod her in Iarland, paved her way from Maizenhead to Youghal. And that's how Humpfrey, champion emir, holds his own. Shysweet, she rests.

Or show pon him now, will you! Derg rudd face should take patrick's purge. Hokoway, in his hiphigh bearserk! Third position of concord! Excellent view from front. Sidome. Female imperfectly masking male. Redspot his browbrand. Woman's the prey! Thon's the dullakeykongs-byogblagroggerswagginline (private judgers, change here for Lootherstown! Onlyromans, keep your seats!) that drew all ladies please to our great mettrollops. Leary, leary, twentytun nearly, he's plotting kings down for his villa's extension! Gaze at him now in momentum! As his bridges are blown to babbyrags, by the lee of his hulk upright on her orbits, and the heave of his juniper arx in action, he's naval I see. Poor little tartanelle, her dinties are chattering, the strait's she's in, the bulloge she bears! Her smirk is smeeching behind for her hills. By the queer quick twist of her mobcap and the lift of her shift at random and the rate of her gate of going the pace, two thinks at a time, her country I'm proud of. The field is down, the race is their own. The galleonman jovial on his bucky brown nightmare. Bigrob dignagging his lylyputtana. One to one bore one! The datter, io, io, sleeps in peace, in peace. And the twillingsons, ganymede, garrymore, turn in trot and trot. But old pairamere goes it a gallop, a gallop. Bossford and phospherine. One to one on!

O, O, her fairy setalite! Casting such shadows to Persia's blind! The man in the street can see the coming event. Photoflashing it far too wide. It will be known through all Urania soon. Like jealousjoy titaning fear; like rumour rhean round the planets; like china's dragon snapping japets; like rhodagrey up the east. Satyrdaysboost besets Phoebe's nearest. Here's the flood and the flaxen flood that's to come over helpless Irryland. Is there no one to malahide Liv and her bettyship? Or who'll buy her rosebuds, jettyblack rosebuds, ninsloes of nivia, nonpaps of nan? From the fall of the fig to doom's last post every ephemeral anniversary while the park's police peels peering by for to weight down morrals from county bubblin. That trainer's trundling! Quick, pay up!

Kickakick. She had to kick a laugh. At her old stick-in-the-block. The way he was slogging his paunch about, elbiduubled, meet oft mate on, like hale King Willow, the robberer. Cainmaker's mace and waxened capapee. But the tarrant's brand on his hottoweyt brow. At half past quick in the morning. And her lamp was all askew and a trumbly wickinher, ringey-singey. She had to spofforth, she had to kicker, too thick of the wick of her pixy's loomph, wide lickering jessup the smooky shiminey. And her duffed coverpoint of a wickedy batter, whenever she druv behind her stumps for a tyddlesly wink through his tunnilclefft bagslops after the rising bounder's yorkers, as he studd and stoddard and trutted and trumpered, to see had lordherry's blackham's red bobby abbels, it tickled her innings to consort pitch at kicksolock in the morm. Tipatonguing him on in her pigeony linguish, with a flick at the bails for lubrication, to scorch her faster, faster. Ye hek, ye hok, ye hucky hiremonger! Magrath he's my pegger, he is, for bricking up all my old kent road. He'll win your toss, flog your old tom's bowling and I darr ye, barrackybuller, to break his duck! He's posh. I lob him. We're parring all Oogster till the empsyseas run googlie. Declare to ashes and teste his metch! Three for two will do for me and he for thee and she for you. Goeasyosey, for the grace of the fields, or hooley pooley, cuppy, we'll both be bye and by caught in the slips for fear he'd tyre and burst his dunlops and waken her bornybarnies making his boobybabies. The game old merrimynn, square to leg, with his lolleywide towelhat and his hobbsy socks and his wisden's bosse and his norsery pinafore and his gentleman's grip and his playaboy's plunge and his flannelly feelyfooling, treading her hump and hambledown like a maiden wellheld, ovalled over, with her crease where the pads of her punishments ought to be by womanish rights when, keek, the hen in the doran's shantyqueer began in a kikkery key to laugh it off, yeigh, yeigh, neigh, neigh, the way she was wuck to doodledoo by her gallows bird (how's that? Noball, he carries his bat!)

nine hundred and dirty too not out, at all times long past conquering cock of the morgans.

How blame us?

Cocorico!

Armigerend everfasting horde. Rico! So the bill to the bowe. As the belle to the beau. We herewith pleased returned auditors' thanks for those and their favours since safely enjoined. Cocoree! Tellaman tillamie. Tubbernacul in tipherairy, sons, travellers in company and their carriageable tochters, tanks tight anne thynne for her contractations tugowards his personeel. Echo, choree chorecho! O I you O you me! Well, we all unite thoughtfully in rendering gratias, well, between loves repassed, begging your honour's pardon for, well, exclusive pigtorial rights of herehear fond tiplady his weekreations, appearing in next eon's issue of the Neptune's Centinel and Tritonville Lightowler with well the widest circulation round the whole universe. Echolo choree choroh choree chorico! How me O my youhou my I youtou to I O? Thanks furthermore to modest Miss Glimglow and neat Master Mettresson who so kindly profiteered their serwishes as demysell of honour and, well, as strainbearer respectively. And a cordiallest brief nod of chinchin dankyshin to, well, patient ringasend as prevenient (by your leave), to all such occasions, detachably replaceable (thanks too! twos intact!). As well as his auricular of Malthus, the promethean paratonnerwetter which first (Pray go! pray go!) taught love's lightning the way (pity shown) to, well, conduct itself (mercy, good shot! only please don't mention it!). Come all ye goatfathers and groanmothers, come all ye markmakers and piledrivers, come all ye laboursaving devisers and chargeleyden dividends, firefinders, waterworkers, deeply condeal with him! All that is still life with death inyeborn, all verbumsaps yet bound to be, to do and to suffer, every creature, everywhere, if you please, kindly feel for her! While the dapplegray dawn drags nearing nigh for to wake all droners that drowse in Dublin.

Humperfeldt and Anunska, wedded now evermore in annastomoses by a ground plan of the placehunter, whiskered beau and donahbella. Totumvir and esquimeena, who so shall separate fetters to new desire, repeals an act of union to unite in bonds of shismacy. O yes! O yes! Withdraw your member! Closure. This chamber stands abjourned. Such precedent is largely a cause to lack of collective continencies among Donnelly's orchard as lifelong the shadyside to Fairbrother's field. Humbo, lock your kekkle up! Anny, blow your wickle out! Tuck away the tablesheet! You never wet the tea! And you may go rightoway back to your Aunty Dilluvia, Humprey, after that!

Retire to rest without first misturbing your nighboor, mankind of baffling descriptions. Others are as tired of themselves as you are. Let each one learn to bore himself. It is strictly requested that no cobsmoking, spitting, pubchat, wrastle rounds, coarse courting, smut, etc, will take place amongst those hours so devoted to repose. Look before behind before you strip you. Disrobe clothed in the strictest secrecy which privacy can afford. Water non to be discharged *coram* grate or *ex* window. Never divorce in the bedding the glove that will give you away. Maid Maud ninnies nay but blabs to Omama (for your life, would you!) she to her bosom friend who does all chores (and what do you think my Madeleine saw?): this ignorant mostly sweeps it out along with all the rather old corporators (have you heard of one humbledown jungleman how he bet byrn-and-bushe playing peg and pom?): the maudlin river then gets its dues (adding a din a ding or do): thence those laundresses (O, muddle me more about the maggies! I mean bawnee Madge Ellis and brownie Mag Dillon). Attention at all! Every ditcher's dastard in Dupling will let us know about it if you have paid the mulctman by whether your rent is open to be foreclosed or aback in your arrears. This is seriously meant. Here is a homelet not a hothel.

That's right, old oldun!

All in fact is soon as all of old right as anywas ever in very old place. Were he, hwen scalded of that couverfowl, to beat the bounds by here at such a point of time as this is for at sammel up all wood's haypence and riviers argent (half back from three gangs multaplussed on a twentylot add allto a fiver with the deuce or roamer's numbers ell a fee and do little ones) with the caboosh on him opheld for thrushes' mistiles yet singing oud his parasangs in cornish token: mean fawthery eastend appullcelery, old laddy he high hole: pollysigh patrolman Seekersenn, towney's tanquam, crumlin quiet down from his hoonger, he would mac siccar of inket goodsfore-tombed ereshiningem of light turkling eitheranny of thuncle's windopes. More, unless we were neverso wrongtaken, if he brought his boots to pause in peace, the one beside the other one, right on the road, he would seize no sound from cache or cave beyond the flow of wand was gypsing water, telling him now, telling him all, all about ham and livery, stay and toast ham in livery, and buttermore with murmurladen, to waker oats for him on livery. Faurore! Fearhoure! At last it past! Loab at cod then herrin or wind thin mong them treen.

Hiss! Which we had only our hazelight to see with, cert, in our point of view, me and my auxy, Jimmy d'Arcy, hadn't we, Jimmy?—Who to seen with? Kiss! No kidd, captn, which he stood us, three jolly postboys, first a couple of Mountjoys and nutty woodbines with his cadbully's choculars, pepped from our Theoatre Regal's drolleries puntomine, in the snug at the Cambridge Arms of Teddy Ales while we was laying, crown jewels to a peanut, was he stepmarm, old noseheavy, or a wouldower, which he said, lads, a taking low his Whitby hat, lopping off the froth and whishing, with all respectfulness to the old country, tomorow comrades, we, his long life's strength and cuirscrween loan to our allhallowed king, the pitchur that he's turned to weld the wall, (Lawd lengthen him!) his standpoint was, to belt and blucher him afore the hole pleading churchal and submarine bar yonder but he made no class at all in port and cemented palships between our trucers, being a refugee, didn't he, Jimmy?—Who true to me? Sish! Honey-suckler, that's what my young lady here, Fred Watkins, bugler Fred, all the ways from Melmoth in Natal, she calls him, dip the colours, pet, when he commit his certain questions vivaviz the secret empire of the snake which it was on a point of our sutton down, how was it, Jimmy?—Who has sinnerettes to declare? Phiss! Touching our Phoenix Rangers' nuisance at the meeting of the waitresses, the daintylines, Elsies from Chelsies, the two legglegels in blooms, and those pest of parkies, twitch, thistle and charlock, were they for giving up their fogging trespasses by order which we foregathered he must be raw in cane sugar, the party, no, Jimmy MacCawthelock? Who trespass against me? Briss! That's him wiv his wig on, achewing of his maple gum, that's our grainpopaw, Mister Beardall, an accompliced burgomaster, a great one among the very greatest, which he told us privates out of his own scented mouf he used to was, my lads, afore this wineact come, what say, our Jimmy the chapelgoer?—Who fears all masters! Hi, Jocko Nowlong, my own sweet boosy love, which he puts his feeler to me behind the beggar's bush, does Freda, don't you be an emugee! Carryone, he says, though we marooned through this woylde. We must spy a half a hind on honeysuckler now his old face's hardalone wiv his defences down during his wappin stillstand, says my Fred, and Jamessime here which, pip it, she simply must, she says, our pet, she'll do a retroussy from her point of view (Way you fly! Like a frush!) to keep her flouncies off the grass while paying the wetmenots a musichall visit and pair her fiefighs fore him with just one curl after the cad came back which we fought he wars a gunner and his corkiness lay up two bottles of joy with a shandy had by Fred and a *fino oloroso* which he was warming to, my right, Jimmy, my old brown freer?—Whose dolour, O so mine!

Following idly up to seepoint, neath kingmount shadow the ilk for eke of us, whose nathem's banned, whose hofd a-hooded, welkim warsail, how di' you dew? Hollymerry, ivysad, whicher and whoer, Mr Black Atkins and you tanapanny troopertwos, were you there? Was truce of snow, moonmounded snow? Or did wolken hang o'er earth in umber hue his fulmenbomb? Number two coming! Full inside! Was glimpsed the mean amount of cloud?

Or did pitter rain fall in a sprinkling? If the waters could speak as they flow! Timgle Tom, pall the bell! Izzy's busy down the dell! Mizpah low, youyou, number one, in deep humidity! Listen, misled peerless, please! You are of course. You miss him so, to listleto! Of course, my pledge between us, there's no one Noel like him here to hear. Esch so eschess, douls a doulse! Since Allan Rogue loved Arrah Pogue it's all Killdoughall fair. Triss! Only trees such as these such were those, waving there, the barketree, the o'briertree, the rowantree, the o'corneltree, the behanshrub near windy arbour, the magill o'dendron more. Trem! All the trees in the wood they trembold, humbild, when they heard the stop-press from domday's erewold.

Tiss! Two pretty mistletots ribboned to a tree, up rose liberator and, fancy, they were free! Four witty missywives, winking under hoods, made lasses like lads love maypoleriding and dotted our green with tricksome couples, fiftyfifty, their chiltren's hundred. So childish pence took care of parents' pounds and many made money the way in the world where rushroads to riches crossed slums of lice and, the cause of it all, he forged himself ahead like a blazing urbanorb, brewing treble to drown grief, giving and taking mayom and tuam, playing milliards with his three golden balls, making party capital out of landed selfinterest, light on a slavey but weighty on the bourse, our hugest commercial emporialist, with his sons booing home from afar and his daughters bridling up at his side. Finner!

How did he bank it up, swank it up, the whaler in the punt, a guinea by a groat, his index on the balance and such wealth into the bargain, with the boguey which he snatched in the baggage coach ahead? Going forth on the prowl, master jackill, under night and creeping back, dog to hide, over morning. Humbly to fall and cheaply to rise, exposition of failures. Through Duffy's blunders and MacKenna's insurance for upper ten and lower five the band played on. As one generation tells another. Ofter the fall. First for a change of a seven days license he wandered out of his farmer's health and so lost his early parishlife. Then ('twas in fenland) occidentally of a sudden, six junelooking flamefaces straggled wild out of their turns through his parsonfired wicket, showing all shapes of striplings in sleepless tights. Promptly whomafter in undated times, very properly a dozen generations anterior to themselves, a main chanced to burst and misflooded his fortunes, wrothing foulplay over his fives' court and his fine poultryyard wherein were spared a just two of a feather in wading room only. Next, upon due reflotation, up started four hurrigan gales to smithereen his plateglass housewalls and the slate for accounts his keeper was cooking. Then came three boy buglehorners who counterbezzled and crossbugled him. Later on in the same evening two hussites absconded through a breach in his bylaws and left him, the infidels, to pay himself off in kind remembrances. Till, ultimatehim, fell the crowning barleystraw, when an explosium of his distilleries deafadumped all his dry goods to his most favoured sinflute and dropped him, what remains of a heptark, leareyed and letterish, weeping worrybound on his bankrump.

Pepep. Pay bearer, sure and sorry, at foot of ohoho honest policist. On never again, by Phoenis, swore on him Lloyd's, not for beaten wheat, not after Sir Joe Meade's father, thanks! They know him, the covenanter, by rote at least, for a chameleon at last, in his true falseheaven colours from ultraviolent to subred tissues. That's his last tryon to march through the grand tryomphal arch. His reignbolt's shot. Never again! How you do that like, Mista Chimepiece? You got nice yum plemyums. Praypaid my promishles.

Agreed, Wu Welsher, he was chogfulled to beacsate on earn as in hiving, of foxold conningnesses but who, hey honey, for all values of his latters, integer integerrimost, was the formast of the firm? At folkmood hailed, at part farwailed, accwmwladed concloud, Nuah-Nuah, Nebob of Nephilim! After all what followed for apprentice sake? Since the now nighs nearing as the yetst hies hin. Jeebies, ugh, kek, ptah, that was an ill man! Jawboose, puddigood, this is for true a sweetish mand! But Jumbluffer, bagdad, sir, yond would be for a once over our all honoured christmastyde easteredman. Fourth position of solution. How johnny! Finest view from horizon. Tableau final. Two me see. Male and female unmask we hem. Begum by gunne! Who now broothes oldbrawn. Dawn! The nape of his nameshielder's scalp. Halp! After having drummed all he dun. Hun! Worked out to an inch of his core. More! Ring down. While the queenbee he staggerhorned blesses her bliss for to feel her funnyman's functions Tag. Rumbling.

Tiers, tiers and tiers. Rounds.

BOOK IV

SANDHYAS! SANDHYAS! SANDHYAS!

Calling all downs. Calling all downs to dayne. Array! Surrection! Eireweeker
to the wohld bludyn world. O rally, O rally, O rally! Phlenxty, O rally! To
what lifelike thyne of the bird can be. Seek you somany matters. Haze sea
east to Osseania. Here! Here! Tass, Patt, Staff, Woff, Havv, Bluvv and
Rutter. The smog is lofting. And already the olduman's olduman has godden
up on othertimes to litanate the

bonnamours. Sonne feine, somme feehn avaunt! Guld modning, have yous
viewsed Piers' aube? Thane yaars agon we have used yoors up since when
we have fused now orther. Calling all daynes. Calling all daynes to dawn.
The old breeding bradsted culminwillth of natures to Foyn MacHooligan.
The leader, the leader! Securest jubilends albas Temoram. Clogan slogan.
Quake up, dim dusky, wook doom for husky! And let Billey Feghin be
baallad out of his humuluation. Confindention to churchen. We have
highest gratifications in announcing to pewtewr publikumst of pratician
pratyusers, genghis is ghoon for you.

A hand from the cloud emerges, holding a chart expanded.

The eversower of the seeds of light to the cowld owld sowls that are in
the domnatory of Defmut after the night of the carrying of the word of
Nuahs and the night of making Mehs to cuddle up in a coddlepot, Pu
Nuseht, lord of risings in the yonderworld of Ntamplin, tohp triumphant,
speaketh.

Vah! Suvarn Sur! Scatter brand to the reneweller of the sky, thou who
agnitest! Dah! Arcthuris comeing! Be! Verb umprincipiant through the
trancitive spaces! Kilt by kelt shell kithagain with kinagain. We elect for
thee, Tirtangel. Svadesia salve! We Durbalanars, theeadjure. A way, the
Margan, from our astamite, through dimdom done till light kindling light
has led we hopas but hunt me the journeyon, iteritinerant, the kal his
course, amid the semitary of Somnionia. Even unto Heliotropolis, the
castellated, the enchanting. Now if soomone felched a twoel and soom-
onelses warmet watter we could, while you was saying Morkret Miry or
Smud, Brunt and Rubbinsen, make sunlike sylp om this warful dune's
battam. Yet clarify begins at. Whither the spot for? Whence the hour by?
See but! Lever hulme! Take in. Respassers should be pursaccoutred. Qui

stabat Meins quantum qui stabat Peins. As of yours. We annew. Our shades of minglings mengle them and help help horizons. A flasch and, rasch, it shall come to pasch, as hearth by hearth leaps live. For the tanderest stock with the rosinost top Ahlen Hill's, clubpubber, in general stores and. Atriathroughwards, Lugh the Brathwacker will be the listened after and he larruping sparks out of his teiney ones. The spearspid of dawnfire totouches ain the tablestoane ath the centre of the great circle of the macroliths of Helusbelus in the boshiman brush on this our peneplain by Fangaluvu Bight whence the horned cairns erge, stanserstanded, to floran frohn, idols of isthmians. Overwhere. Gaunt grey ghostly gossips growing grubber in the glow. Past now pulls. Cur one beast, even Dane the Great, may treadspath with sniffer he snout impursuant to byelegs. Edar's chuckal humuristic. But why pit the cur afore the noxe? Let shrill their duan Gallus, han, and she, hou the Sassqueehenna, makes ducksruns at crooked. Once for the chantermale, twoce for the pother and once twoce threece for the waither. So an inedible yellowmeat turns out the invasable blackth. Kwhat serves to rob with Alliman, saelior, a turnkeyed trot to Seapoint, pierrotettes, means Noel's Bar and Julepunsch, by Joge, if you've tippertaps in your head or starting kursses, tailour, you're silenced at Henge Ceolleges, Exmooth, Ostbys for ost, boys, each and one? Death banes and the quick quoke. But life wends and the dombs spake! Whake? Hill of Hafid, knock and knock, nachasach, gives relief to the langscape as he strauches his lamusong untoupon gazelle channel and the bride of the Bryne, shin high shake, is dotter than evar for a damse wed her farther. Lambel on the up! We may plesently heal Geoglyphy's twentynine ways to say goodbett an wassing seoosoon liv. With the forty wonks winking please me your much as to. With her tup. It's a long long ray to Newirgland's premier. For korps, for streamfish, for confects, for bullyoungs, for smearsassage, for patates, for steaked pig, for men, for limericks, for waterfowls, for wagsfools, for louts, for cold airs, for late trams, for curries, for curlews, for leekses, for orphalines, for tunnygulls, for clear goldways, for lungfortes, for moonyhaunts, for fairmoneys, for coffins, for tantrums, for armaurs, for waglugs, for rogues comings, for sly goings, for larksmathes, for homdsmeethes, for quailsmeathes, kilalooly. Tep! Come lead, crom lech! Top. Wisely for us Old Bruton has withdrawn his theory. You are alpsulumply wroght! Amsulummmm. But this is perporteroguing youpoorapps? Namantanai. Sure it's not revieng your? Amslu! Good all so. We seem to understand apad vellumtomes muniment, Arans Duhkha, among hoseshoes, cheriotiers and etceterogenious bargainboutbarrows, ofver and umnder, since, evenif or although, in double preposition as in triple conjunction, how the mudden research in the topaia that was Mankaylands has gone to prove from the picalava present in the maramara melma that while a successive generation has been in the deep deep deeps of Deepereras. Buried hearts. Rest here.

Conk a dook he'll doo. Svap.

So let him slap, the sap! Till they take down his shatter from his shap. He canease. Fill stap.

Thus faraclacks the friarbird. Listening, Syd!

The child, a natural child, thenown by the mnames of, (aya! aya!), wouldbewas kidnapped at an age of recent probably, possibly remoter; or he conjured himself from seight by slide at hand; for which thetheatron is a lemoronage; at milchgoat fairmesse; in full dogdhis; sod on a fall; pat; the hundering blundering dunderfunder of plundersundered manhood; behold, he returns; renascenent; fincarnate; still foretold around the hearthside; at matin a fact; hailed chimers' ersekind; foe purmanant, fum in his mow; awike in wave risurging into chrest; *victis poenis hesternis*; fostfath of solas; fram choicest of wiles with warmen and sogns til Banba, burial aranging; under articles thirtynine of the reconstitution; by the lord's order of the canon consecrandable; earthlost that we thought him; pesternost, the noneknown worrier; from Tumbarumba mountain; in persence of whole landslots; forebe all the rassias; sire of leery subs of dub; the Diggins, Woodenhenge, as to hang out at; with spawnish oel full his angalach; the sousenugh; gnomeosulphidosalamermauderman; the big brucer, fert in fort; Gunnar, of The Gunnings, Gund; one of the two or three forefivest fellows a bloke could in holiday crowd encounter; benedicted be the barrel; kilderkins, lids off; a roache, an oxmaster, a sort of heaps, a pamphilius, a vintivat niviceny, a hygiennic contrivance socalled from the editor; the thick of your thigh; you knox; quite; talking to the vicar's joy and ruth; the gren, woid and glue been broking by the maybole gards; he; when no crane in Elga is heard; upout to speak this lay; without links, without impediments, with gygantogyres, with freeflawforms; parasama to himself; atman as evars; whom otherwise becauses; no puler as of old but as of young a palatin; whitelock not lacked nor temperasoleon; though he appears a funny colour; stoatters some; but a quite a big bug after the dahlias; place inspectorum sarchent; also the hullow chyst excavement; astronomically fabulafigured; as Jambudvispa Vipra foresaw of him; the last half versicle repurchasing his pawned word; sorensplit and paddypatched; and pfor to pfinish our pfun of a pfan coalding the keddle mickwhite; sure, straight, slim, sturdy, serene, synthetical, swift.

By the antar of Yasas! Ruse made him worthily achieve inherited wish.

The drops upon that mantle rained never around Fingal. Goute! Loughlin's Salts, Will, make a newman if anyworn. Soe? La! Lamfadar's arm it has cocoincidences. You mean to see we have been hadding a sound night's sleep? You may so. It is just, it is just about to, it is just about to roly-wholyover. Svapnasvap. Of all the stranger things that ever not even in the hundrund and badst pageans of unthowsent and wonst nice or in eddas and oddes bokes of tomb, dyke and hollow to be have happened! The untireties of livesliving being the one substrance of a streamsbecoming. Totalled in toldteld and teldtold in tittletell tattle. Why? Because, graced be Gad and all giddy gadgets, in whose words were the beginnings, there are two signs to tum to, the yest and the ist, the wright side and the wronged side, feeling aslip and wauking up, so an, so farth. Why? On the sourdsite we have the Moskiosk Djinpalast with its twin adjacencies, the bathouse and the bazaar, allahallahallah, and on the sponthesite it is the alcovan and the rosegarden, boony noughty, all puraputhry. Why? One's apurr apuss a story about brid and breakfedes and parricombating and coushcouch but others is of tholes and oubworn buyings, dolings and chafferings in heat, contest and enmity. Why? Every talk has his stay, vidnis Shavarsanjivana, and all-a-dreams perhapsing under lucksloop at last are through. Why? It is a sot of a swigswag, systomy dystomy, which everabody you ever anywhere at all doze. Why? Such me.

And howpsadrowsay.

Lok! A shaft of shivery in the act, anilancinant. Cold's sleuth! Vayuns! Where did thots come from? It is infinitesimally fevers, resty fever, risy fever, a coranto of aria, sleeper awakening, in the smalls of one's back presentiment, gip, and again, geip, a flash from a future of maybe mahamayability through the windr of a wondr in a wildr is a weltr as a wirbl of a warbl is a world.

Tom.

It is perfect degrees excelsius. A jaladaew still stilleth. Cloud lay but mackrel are. Anemone activescent, the torporature is returning to mornal. Humid nature is feeling itself freely at ease with the all fresco. The vervain is to herald as the grass administers. They say, they say in effect, they really say. You have eaden fruit. Say whuit. You have snakked mid a fish. Telle whish. Every those personal place objects if nonthings where soevers and they just done been doing being in a dromo of todos withouten a bound to be your trowers. Forswundled. You hald him by the tap of the tang. Not a salutary sellable sound is since. Instead for asteer, adrift with adraft. Nuctumbulumbumus wanderwards the Nil. Victorias neanzas. Alberths neantas. It was a long, very long, a dark, very dark, an allburt unend, scarce endurable, and we could add mostly quite various and somenwhat stumble-tumbling night. Endee he sendee. Diu! The has goning at gone, the is coming to come. Greets to ghastern, hie to morgning. Dormidy, destady. Doom is the faste. Well down, good other! Now day, slow day, from delicate to divine, divases. Padma, brighter and sweetster, this flower that bells, it is our hour or risings. Tickle, tickle. Lotus spray. Till herenext. Adya.

Take thanks, thankstum, thamas. In that earopean end meets Ind.

There is something supernoctural about whatever you called him it. Panpan and vinvin are not alonety vanvan and pinpin in your Tamal without tares but simplysoley they are they. Thisutter followis that odder fellow. Himkim kimkim. Old yeasterloaves may be a stale as a stub and the pitcher go to aftoms on the wall. Mildew, murk, leak and yarn now want the bad that they lied on. And your last words todate in camparative accoustomology are going to tell stretch of a fancy through strength towards joyance, adyatants, where he gets up. Allay for allay, a threat for a throat.

Tim!

To them in Ysat Loka. Hearing. The urb it orbs. Then's now with now's then in tense continuant. Heard. Who having has he shall have had. Hear! Upon the thuds trokes truck, chim, it will be exactlyso fewer hours by so many minutes of the ope of the diurn of the sennight of the maaned of the yere of the age of the madamanvantora of Grossguy and Littleylady, our hugibus hugibum and our weewee mother, actaman housetruewith, and their childer and their napirs and their napirs' childers napirs and their chattels and their servance and their cognance and their ilks and their orts and their everythings that is be will was theirs.

Much obliged. Time-o'-Thay! But wherth, O clerk?

Whithr a clonk? Vartman! See you not soo the pfath they pfunded, oura vatars that arred in Himmal, harruad bathar namas, the gow, the stiar, the tigara, the liofant, when even thurst was athar vetals, mid trefoils slipped the sable rampant, hoof, hoof, hoof, hoof, padapodopudupedding on fatta-fottafutt. Ere we are! Signifying, if tungs may tolkan, that, primeval conditions having gradually receded but nevertheless the emplacement of solid and fluid having to a great extent persisted through intermittences of sullemn fulminance, sollemn nuptialism, sallemn sepulture and providential divining, making possible and ever; inevitable, after his a time has a tense haves and havenots hesitency, at the place and period under consideration a socially organic entity of a millenary military maritory monetary morphological circumformation in a more or less settled state of equonomic ecolube equalobe equilab equilibbrium. Gam on, Gearge! Nomomorphemy for me! Lessnatbe angardsmanlake! You jast gat a tache of army on the stumuk.

To the Angar at Anker. Aecquotincts. Seeworthy. Lots thankyouful, polite pointsins! There's a tavern in the tarn.

Tip. Take Tamotimo's topical. Tip. Browne yet Noland. Tip. Advert.

Where. Cumulonubulocirrhonimbant heaven electing, the dart of desire has gored the heart of secret waters and the poplarest wood in the entire district is being grown at present, eminently adapted for the requirements of pacnincstricken humanity and, between all the goings up and the whole of the comings down and the fog of the cloud in which we toil and the cloud of the fog under which we labour, bomb the thing's to be domb about it so that, beyond indicating the locality, it is felt that one cannot with advantage add a very great deal to the aforegoing by what, such as it is to be, follows, just mentioning however that the old man of the sea and the old woman in the sky if they don't say nothings about it they don't tell us lie, the gist of the pantomime, from cannibal king to the property horse, being, slumply and slopely, to remind us how, in this drury world of ours, Father Times and Mother Spacies boil their kettle with their crutch. Which every lad and lass in the lane knows. Hence.

Polycarp pool, the pool of Innalavia, Saras the saft as, of meadewy marge, atween Deltas Piscium and Sagittariastrion, whereinn once we lave 'tis alve and vale, minnyhahing here from hiarwather, a poddlebridges in a passabed, the river of lives, the regenerations of the incarnations of the emanations of the apparentations of Funn and Nin in Cleethabala, the kongdomain of the Alieni, an accorsaired race, infester of Libnud Ocean, Moylamore, let it be. Where Allbroggt Neandser tracking Viggynette Neeinsee gladsighted her Linfian Fall and a teamdiggingharrow turned the first sod. Sluce! Caught-erect! Goodspeed the blow! (Incidentally 'tis believed that his harpened before Gage's Fane for it has to be over this booty spotch, though some hours to the wester, that ex-Colonel House's preterpost heiress is to return unto the outstretcheds of Dweyr O'Michael's loinsprung the blunterbusted pikehead which his had hewn in hers, prolonged laughter words). There an alomdree begins to green, soreen seen for loveseat, as we know that should she, for by essentience his law, so it make all. It is scainted to Vitalba. And her little white bloomkins, twittersky trimmed, are hobdoblins' hankypanks. Saxenslyke our anscessers thought so darely on now they're going soever to Anglesen, free of juties, dyrt chapes. There too a slab slobs, immermemorial, the only in all swamp. But so bare, so boulder, brag sagging such a brr bll bmm show that, of Barindens, the white alfred, it owed to have at leased some butchup's upperon. *Homos Circas Elochlannensis!* His showplace at Leeambye. Old Wommany Wyes. Pfif! But, while gleam with gloom swan here and there, this shame rock and that whispy planter tell Paudheen Steel the-Poghue and his perty Molly Vardant, in goodbroomirish, arrah, this place is a proper and his feist a ferial for curdnal communial, so be who would celibrate the holy mystery upon or that the pirigrim from Mainylands beatend, the calmleaved hutcaged by that look whose glaum is sure he means bisnisgels to empalmover. A naked yogpriest, clothed of sundust, his oakey doaked with frondest leoves, offrand to the ewon of her owen. Tasyam kuru salilakriyamu! Pfaf!

Bring about it to be brought about and it will be, loke, our lake lemanted, that greyt lack, the citye of Is is issuant (atlanst!), urban and orbal, through seep froms umber under wasseres of Erie.

Lough!

Hwo! Hwy, dairmaidens? Asthoreths, assay! Earthsigh to is heavened.

Hillsengals, the daughters of the cliffs, responsen. Longsome the samphire coast. From thee to thee, thoo art it thoo, that thouest there. The like the near, the liker nearer. O sosay! A family, a band, a school, a clanagirls. Fiftines andbut fortines by novanas andor vantads by octettes ayand decaden-decads by a lunary with last a lone. Whose every has herdifferent from the similies with her site. *Sicut campanulae petalliferentes* they coroll in caroll round Botany Bay. A dweam of dose innocent dirly dirls. Keavn! Keavn! And they all setton voicies about singsing music was Keavn! He. Only he. Ittle he. Ah! The whole clangalied. Oh!

S. Wilhelmina's, S. Gardenia's, S. Phibia's, S. Veslandrua's, S. Clarinda's, S. Immecula's, S. Dolores Delphin's, S. Perlanthroa's, S. Errands Gay's, S. Eddaminiva's, S. Rhodamena's, S. Ruadagara's, S. Drimicumtra's, S. Una Vestity's, S. Mintargisia's, S. Misha-La-Valse's, S. Churstry's, S. Clouona-skieym's, S. Bella-vistura's, S. Santamonta's, S. Ringsingsund's, S. Heddadin Drade's, S. Glacianivia's, S. Waidafrira's, S. Thomassabbess's and (trema! unloud!! pepet!!!) S. Loellisotoelles!

Prayfulness! Prayfulness!

Euh! Thaet is seu whaet shaell one naeme it!

The meidinogues have tingued togethering. Ascend out of your bed, cavern of a trunk, and shrine! Kathlins is kitchin. Soros cast, ma brone! You must exterra acquarate to interirigate all the arkypelicans. The austrologer Wallaby by Tolan, who farshook our showrs from Newer Aland, has signed the you and the now our mandate. Milenesia waits. Be smark.

One seekings. Not the lithe slender, not the broad roundish near the lithe slender, not the fairsized fullfeatured to the leeward of the broad roundish but, indeed and inneed, the curling, perfectportioned, flower-fleckled, shapely highhued, delicate features swaying to the windward of the fairsized fullfeatured.

Was that in the air about when something is to be said for it or is it someone imparticular who will somewherise for the whole anyhow?

What does Coemghen? Tell his hidings clearly! A woodtoogooder. Is his moraltack still his best of weapons? How about a little more goaling goold? Rowlin's tun he gadder no must. It is the voice of Roga. His face is the face of a son. Be thine the silent hall, O Jarama! A virgin, the one, shall mourn thee. Roga's stream is solence. But Croona is in adestance. The ass of the O'Dwyer of Greyglens is abrowtobayse afeald in his terroirs of the Potterton's forecoroners, the reeks around the burleyhearthed. When visited by an independant reporter, "Mike" Portlund, to burrow burning the latterman's Resterant so is called the gortan in questure he mikes the fallowing for the Durban Gazette? firstcoming issue. From a collispendent. Any were. Deemsday. Bosse of Upper and Lower Byggotstrade, Ciwareke, may he live for river! The Games funeral at Valleytemple. Saturnights pomps, exhabiting that corricatore of a harss, revealled by Oscur Camerad. The last of Dutch Schulds, perhumps. Pipe in Dream Cluse. Uncovers Pub History. The Outrage, at Length. Affected Mob Follows in Religious Sullivence. Rinvention of vestiges by which they drugged the buddhy. Moviefigure on in scenic section. By Patathicus. And there, from out of the scuity, misty Londan, along the canavan route, that is with the years gone, mild beam of the wave his polar bearing, steerner among stars, trust touthena and you tread true turf, comes the sorter, Mr Hurr Hansen, talking alltheways in himself of his hopes to fall in among a merryfoule of maidens happynghome from the dance, his knyckle allaready in his knackskey fob, a passable compatriate proparly of the Grimstad galleon, old pairs frieze, feed up to the noxer with their geese and peeas and oats upon a trencher and the toyms he'd lust in Wooming but with that smeoil like a grace of backoning over his egglips of the sunsoonshine. Here's heering you in a guessmasque, latterman! And such an improofment! As royt as the mail and as fat as a fuddle! Schoen! Shoan! Shoon the Puzt! A penny for your thought abouts! Tay, tibby, tanny, tummy, tasty, tosty, tay. Batch is for Baker who baxters our bread. O, what an ovenly odour! Butter butter! Bring us this days our maily bag! But receive me, my frensheets, from the emerald dark winterlong! For diss is the doss for Eilder Downes and dass is it duss, as singen sengers, what the hardworking straightwalking stoutstamping securelysealing officials who trow to form our G.M.P.'s pass muster generally shay for shee and sloo for slee when butting their headd to the pillow for a nightshared nakeshift with the alter girl they tuck in for sweepsake. Dutiful wealker for his hydes of march. Haves you the time. Hans ahike? Heard you the crime, senny boy? The man was giddy on letties on the dewry of the duary, be pursueded, whethered with entrenous, midgreys, dagos, teatimes, shadows, nocturnes or samoans, if wellstocked fillerouters plushfeverfraus with dopy chonks, and this, that and the other pigskin or muffle kinkles, taking a pipe course or doing an anguish, seen to his fleece in after his foull, when Dr Chart of Greet Chorsles street he changed his backbone at a citting. He had not the declaination, as what with the foos as whet with the fays, but so far as hanging a goobes on the precedings, wherethen the lag allows, it mights be anything after darks. Which the deers alones they sees and the darkies they is snuffing of the wind up. Debbling. Greanteavvents! Hyacinssies with heliotrollops! Not once fullvixen freakings and but dubbledecoys! It is a lable iction on the porte of the cuthulic church and summum most atole for it. Where is that blinketey blanketer, that quound of a pealer, the sunt of a hunt whant foxes good men! Where or he, our loved among many?

But what does Coemghem, the fostard? Tyro a tora. The novened iconostase of his blueygreyned vitroils but begins in feint to light his legend. Let Phosphoron proclaim! Peechy peechy. Say he that saw him that saw! Man shall sharp run do a get him. Ask no more, Jerry mine, Roga's voice! No pice soorkabatcha. The bog which puckerooed the posy. The vinebranch of Heremonheber on Bregia's plane where Teffia lies is leaved invert and fructed proper but the cublic hatches endnot open yet for hourly rincers' mess. Read Higgins, Cairns and Egen. Malthus is yet lukked in close. Withun. How swathed thereanswer alcove makes theirinn! Besoakers loiter on. And primilibatory solicates of limon sodias will be absorbable. It is not even yet the engine of the load with haled morries full of crates, you mattinmummur, for dombell dumbs? Sure and 'tis not then. The greek Sideral Reulthway, as it havvents, will soon be starting a smooth with its first single hastencraft. Danny buzzers instead of the vialact coloured milk train on the fartykket plan run with its endless gallaxion of rotatorattlers and the smooltroon our elderens rememberem as the scream of the service, Strubry Bess. Also the waggonwobblers are still yet everdue to precipitate after night's combustion. Aspect, Shamus Rogua or! Taceate and! *Hagiographice canat Ecclesia.* Which aubrey our first shall show. Inattendance who is who is will play that's what's that to what's that, what.

Oyes! Oyeses! Oyesesyeses! The primace of the Gaulls, protonotorious, I yam as I yam, mitrogenerand in the free state on the air, is now aboil to blow a Gael warning. Inoperation Eyrlands Eyot, Meganesia, Habitant and the onebut thousand insels, Western and Osthern Approaches.

Of Kevin, of increate God the servant, of the Lord Creator a filial fearer, who, given to the growing grass, took to the tall timber, slippery dick the springy heeler, as we have seen, so we have heard, what we have received, that we have transmitted, thus we shall hope, this we shall pray till, in the search for love of knowledge through the comprehension of the unity in altruism through stupefaction, it may again how it may again, shearing aside the four wethers and passing over the dainty daily dairy and dropping by the way the lapful of live coals and smoothing out Nelly Nettle and her lad of mettle, full of stings, fond of stones, friend of gnewgnawns bones and leaving all the messy messy to look after our douche douche, the miracles, death and life are these.

Yad. Procreated on the ultimate ysland of Yreland in the encyclical yrish archipelago, come their feast of precreated holy whiteclad angels, whomamong the christener of his, voluntarily poor Kevin, having been graunted the pravilege of a priest's postcreated portable *altare cum balneo*, when espousing the one true cross, invented and exalted, in celibate matrimony at matin chime arose and westfrom went and came in alb of cloth of gold to our own midmost Glendalough-le-vert by archangelical guidance where amiddle of meeting waters of river Yssia and Essia river on this one of eithers lone navigable lake piously Kevin, lawding the triune trishagion, amidships of his conducible altar super bath, rafted centripetally, diaconal servent of orders hibernian, midway across the subject lake surface to its supreem epicentric lake Ysle, whereof its lake is the ventrifugal principality, whereon by prime, powerful in knowledge, Kevin came to where its centre is among the circumfluent watercourses of Yshgafiena and Yshgafiuna, an enysled lakelet yslanding a lacustrine yslet, whereupon with beached raft subdiaconal bath *propter* altar, with oil extremely anointed, accompanied by prayer, holy Kevin bided till the third morn hour but to build a rubric penitential honeybeehivehut in whose enclosure to live in fortitude, acolyte of cardinal virtues, whereof the arenary floor, most holy Kevin excavated as deep as to the depth of a seventh part of one full fathom, which excavated, venerable Kevin, anchorite, taking counsel, proceded towards the lakeside of the ysletshore whereat seven several times he, eastward genuflecting, in entire ubidience at sextnoon collected gregorian water sevenfold and with ambrosian eucharistic joy of heart as many times receded, carrying that privileged altar *unacumque* bath, which severally seven timcs into the cavity excavated, a lector of water levels, most venerable Kevin, then effused thereby letting there be water where was theretofore dry land, by him so concreated, who now, confirmed a strong and perfect christian, blessed Kevin, exorcised his holy sister water, perpetually chaste, so that, well understanding, she should fill to midheight his tubbathaltar, which hanbathtub, most blessed Kevin, ninthly enthroned, in the concentric centre of the translated water, whereamid, when violet vesper vailed, Saint Kevin, Hydrophilos, having girded his sable *cappa magna* as high as to his cherubical loins, at solemn compline sat in his sate of wisdom, that handbathtub, whereverafter, recreated *doctor insularis* of the universal church, keeper of the door of meditation, memory *extempore* proposing and intellect formally considering, recluse, he meditated continuously with seraphic ardour the primal sacrament of baptism or the regeneration of all man by affusion of water. Yee.

Bisships, bevel to rock's rite! Sarver buoy, extinguish! Nuotabene. The rare view from the three Benns under the bald heaven is on the other end, askan your blixom on dimmen and blastun, something to right hume about. They were erected in a purvious century, as a hen fine coops and, if you know your Bristol and have trudged the trolly ways and elventurns of that old cobbold city, you will sortofficially scribble a mental Peny-Knox-Gore. Whether they were franklings by name also has not been fully probed. Their design is a whosold word and the charming details of light in dark are freshed from the feminiairity which breathes content. *O ferax cupla!* Ah, fairypair! The first exploder to make his ablations in these parks was indeed that lucky mortal which the monster trial showed on its first day out. What will not arky paper, anticidingly inked with penmark, push, per sample prof, kuvertly falted, when style, stink and stigmataphoron are of one sum in the same person? He comes out of the soil very well after all just where Old Toffler is to come shuffling alongsoons Panniquanne starts showing of her peequuliar talonts. Awaywrong wandler surking to a rightrare rute for his plain utterrock sukes, appelled to by her fancy claddaghs. You plied that pokar, gamesy, swell as aye did, while there were flickars to the flores. He may be humpy, nay, he may be dumpy but there is always something racey about, say, a sailor on a horse. As soon as we sale him geen we gates a sprise! He brings up tofatufa and that is how we get to Missas in Massas. The old Marino tale. We veriters verity notefew demmed lustres priorly magistrite maximollient in ludubility learned. Facst. Teak off that wise head! Great sinner, good sonner, is in effect the motto of the MacCowell family. The gloved fist (skrimmhandsker) was intraduced into their socerdatal tree before the fourth of the twelfth and it is even a little odd all four horolodgeries still gonging restage Jakob van der Bethel, smolking behing his pipe, with Essav of Messagepostumia, lentling out his borrowed chafingdish, before cymba-loosing the apostles at every hours of changeover. The first and last rittle-rattle of the anniverse; when is a nam nought a nam whenas it is a. Watch! Heroes' Highway where our fleshers leave their bonings and every bob and joan to fill the bumper fair. It is their segnall for old Champelysied to seek the shades of his retirement and for young Chappielassies to tear a round and tease their partners lovesoftfun at Finnegan's Wake.

And it's high tigh tigh. Titley hi ti ti. That my dig pressed in your dag si. Gnug of old Gnig. Ni, gnid mig brawly! I bag your burden. Mees is thees knees. Thi is Mi. We have caught oneselves, Sveasmeas, in somes incontigruity coumplegs of heoponhurrish marrage from whose I most sublumbunate. A polog, my engl! Excutes. Om still so sovvy. Whyle om till ti ti.

Ha!

Dayagreening gains in schlimninging. A summerwint springfalls, abated. Hail, regn of durknass, snowly receassing, thund lightening thund, into the dimbelowstard departamenty whitherout, soon hist, soon mist, to the hothehill from the hollow, Solsking the Frist (attempted by the admirable Captive Bunting and Loftonant-Cornel Blaire) will processingly show up above Tumplen Bar whereupont he was much jubilated by Boerge-mester "Dyk" ffogg of Isoles, now Eisold, looking most plussed with (exhib 39) a clout capped sunbubble anaccanponied from his bequined torse. Up.

Blanchardstown mewspeppers pleads coppyl. Gracest goodness, heave mensy upponnus! Grand old Manbutton, give your bowlers a rest!

It is a mere mienerism of this vague of visibilities, mark you, as accorded to by moisturologist of the Brehons Assorceration for the advauncement of scayence because, my dear, mentioning of it under the breath, as in pure (what bunkum!) essenesse, there have been disselving forenenst you just the draeper, the two drawpers assisters and the three droopers assessors confraternitisers. Who are, of course, Uncle Arth, your two cozes from Niece and (kunject a bit now!) our own familiars, Billyhealy, Ballyhooly and Bullyhowley, surprised in an indecorous position by the Sigurd Sigerson Sphygmomanometer Society for bledprusshers.

Knightsmore. Haventyne?

Ha ha!

This Mister Ireland? And a live?

Ay, ay. Aye, aye, baas.

The cry of Stena chills the vitals of slumbring off the motther has been pleased into the harms of old salaciters, meassurers soon and soon, but the voice of Alina gladdens the cocklyhearted dreamerish for that magic moning with its ching chang chap sugay kaow laow milkee muchee bringing beckerbrose, the brew with the foochoor in it. Sawyest? Nodt? Nyets, I dhink I sawn to remumb or sumbsuch. A kind of a thinglike all traylogged then pubably it resymbles a pelvic or some kvind then props an acutebacked quadrangle with aslant off ohahnthenth a wenchyoumaycuddler, lying with her royalirish uppershoes among the theeckleaves. Signs are on of a mere by token that wills still to be becoming upon this there once a here was world. As the dayeleyves unfolden them. In the wake of the blackshape, *Nattenden Sorte*; whenat, hindled firth and hundled furth, the week of wakes is out and over; as a wick weak woking from ennemberable Ashias unto fierce force fuming, temtem tamtam, the Phoenican wakes.

Passing. One. We are passing. Two. From sleep we are passing. Three. Into the wikeawades warld from sleep we are passing. Four. Come, hours, be ours!

But still. Ah diar, ah diar! And stay.

It was allso agreeable in our singear clutchless, touring the no placelike no timelike absolent, mixing up pettyvaughan populose with the magnumoore genstries, lloydhaired mersscenary blookers with boydskinned pigttetails and goochlipped gwendolenes with duffyeyed dolores; like so many unprobables in their poor suit of the improssable. With Mata and after please with Matamaru and after please stop with Matamaruluka and after stop do please with Matamarulukajoni.

And anotherum. Ah ess, dapple ass! He will be longing after the Grogram Grays. And, Weisingchetaoli, he will levellaut ministel Trampleasure be. Sheflower Rosina, younger Sheflower fruit Amaryllis, youngest flowerfruityfrond Sallysill or Sillysall. And house with heaven roof occupanters they are continuatingly attraverse of its milletestudinous windows, ricocoursing themselves, as staneglass on stonegloss, inplayn unglish Wynn's Hotel. Brancherds at: Bullbeck, Oldboof, Sassondale, Jorsey Uppygard, Mundelonde, Abbeytotte, Bracqueytuitte with Hockeyvilla, Fockeyvilla, Hillewille and Wallhall. Hoojahoo managers the thingaviking. Obning shotly. When the messanger of the risen sun, (see other oriel) shall give to every seeable a hue and to every hearable a cry and to each spectacle his spot and to each happening her houram. The while we, we are waiting, we are waiting for. Hymn.

Muta: Quodestnunc fumusiste volhvuns ex Domoyno?

Juva: It is Old Head of Kettle puffing off the top of the mornin.

Muta: He odda be thorly well ashamed of himself for smoking before the high host.

Juva: Dies is Dorminus master and commandant illy tonobrass.

Muta: Diminussed aster! An I could peecieve amonkst the gatherings who ever they wolk in process?

Juva: Khubadah! It is the Chrystanthemlander with his porters of bonzos, pompommy plonkyplonk, the ghariwallahs, moveyovering the cabrattlefield of slaine.

Muta: Pongo da Banza! An I would uscertain in druidful scatterings one piece tall chap he stand one piece same place?

Juva: Bulkily: and he is fundementially theosophagusted over the whorse proceedings.

Muta: Petrificationibus! O horild haraflare! Who his dickhuns now rearrexes from undernearth the memorialorum?

Juva: Beleave filmly, beleave! Fing Fing! King King!

Muta: Ulloverum? Fulgitudo ejus Rhedonum teneat!

Juva: Rolantlossly! Till the tipp of his ziff. And the ubideintia of the savium is our ervics fenicitas.

Muta: Why soly smiles the supremest with such for a leary on his rugular lips?

Juva: Bitchorbotchum! Eebrydime! He has help his crewn on the burkeley buy but he has holf his crown on the Eurasian Generalissimo.

Muta: Skulkasloot! The twyly velleid is thus then paridicynical?

Juva: Ut vivat volumen sic pereat pouradosus!

Muta: Haven money on stablecert?

Juva: Tempt to wom Outsider!

Muta: Suc? He quoffs. Wutt?

Juva: Sec! Wartar wartar! Wett.

Muta: Ad Piabelle et Purabelle?

Juva: At Winne, Woermann og Sengs.

Muta: So that when we shall have acquired unification we shall pass on to diversity and when we shall have passed on to diversity we shall have acquired the instinct of combat and when we shall have acquired the instinct of combat we shall pass back to the spirit of appeasement?

Juva: By the light of the bright reason which daysends to us from the high.

Muta: May I borrow that hordwanderbaffle from you, old rubberskin?

Juva: Here it is and I hope it's your wormingpen, Erinmonker! Shoot.

Rhythm and Colour at Park Mooting. Peredos Last in the Grand Natural. Velivision victor. Dubs newstage oldtime turftussle, recalling Winny Willy Widger. Two draws. Heliotrope leads from Harem. Three ties. Jockey the Ropper jerks Jake the Rape. Paddrock and bookley chat.

And here are the details.

Tunc. Bymeby, bullocky vampas tappany bobs topside joss pidgin fella Balkelly, archdruid of islish chinchinjoss in the his heptachromatic sevenhued septicoloured roranyellgreenlindigan mantle finish he show along the his mister guest Patholic with alb belongahim the whose throat

hum with of sametime all the his cassock groaner fellas of greysfriaryfamily
he fast all time what time all him monkafellas with Same Patholic, quoniam,
speeching, yeh not speeching noh man liberty is, he drink up words, scilicet,
tomorrow till recover will not, all too many much illusiones through
photoprismic velamina of hueful panepiphanal world spectacurum of Lord
Joss, the of which zoantholitic furniture, from mineral through vegetal to
animal, not appear to full up together fallen man than under but one
photoreflection of the several iridals gradationes of solar light, that one
which that part of it (furnit of heupanepi world) had shown itself (part of
fur of huepanwor) unable to absorbere, whereas for numpa one puraduxed
seer in seventh degree of wisdom of Entis-Onton he savvy inside true
inwardness of reality, the Ding hvad in idself id est, all objects (of
panepiwor) allside showed themselves in trues coloribus resplendent with
sextuple gloria of light actually retained, untisintus, inside them (obs of
epiwo). Rumnant Patholic, stareotypopticus, no catch all that preachybook,
utpiam, tomorrow recover thing even is not, bymeby vampsybobsy
tappanasbullocks topside joss pidginfella Bilkilly-Belkelly say patfella,
ontesantes, twotime hemhaltshealing, with other words verbigratiagrading
from murmurulentous till striduloceterious in a hunghoranghoangoly
tsinglontseng while his comprehendurient, with diminishing claractinism,
augumentationed himself in caloripeia to vision so throughsighty, you
anxioust melancholic, High Thats Hight Uberking Leary his fiery grass-
belonghead all show colour of sorrelwood herbgreen, again, niggerblonker,
of the his essixcoloured holmgrewnworsteds costume the his fellow saffron
pettikilt look same hue of boiled spinasses, other thing, voluntary
mutismuser, he not compyhandy the his golden twobreasttorc look
justsamelike curlicabbis, moreafter, to pace negativisticists, verdant
readyrainroof belongahim Exuber High Ober King Leary very dead, what
he wish to say, spit of superexuberabundancy plenty laurel leaves, after that
commander bulopent eyes of Most Highest Ardreetsar King same thing
like thyme choppy upon parsley, alongsidethat, if pleasesir, nos displace
tauttung, sowlofabishospastored, enamel Indian gem in maledictive finger-
fondler of High High Siresultan Emperor all same like one fellow olive
lentil, onthelongsidethat, by undesendas, kirikirikiring, violaceous warwon
contusiones of facebuts of Highup Big Cockywocky Sublissimime Autocrat,
for that with pure hueglut intensely saturated one, tinged uniformly, alla-
roundside upinandoutdown, very like you seecut chowchow of plentymuch
sennacassia Hump cumps Ebblybally! Sukkot?
    Punc. Bigseer, refrects the petty padre, whackling it out, a tumble to take,
tripeness to call thing and to call if say is good while, you pore shiroskuro

blackinwhitepaddynger, by thiswis aposterioprismically apatstrophied and paralogically periparolysed, celestial from principalest of Iro's Irismans ruinboon pot before, (for beingtime monkblinkers timeblinged completamentarily murkblankered in their neutrolysis between the possible viriditude of the sager and the probable eruberuption of the saint), as My tappropinquish to Me wipenmeselps gnosegates a handcaughtscheaf of synthetic shammyrag to hims hers, seemingsuch four three two agreement cause heart to be might, saving to Balenoarch (he kneeleths), to Great Balenoarch (he kneeleths down) to Greatest Great Balenoarch (he kneeleths down quitesomely), the sound salse sympol in a weedwayedwold of the firethere the sun in his halo cast. Onmen.

That was thing, bygotter, the thing, bogcotton, the very thing, begad! Even to uptoputty Bilkilly-Belkelly-Balkally. Who was for shouting down the shatton on the lamp of Jeeshees. Sweating on to stonker and throw his seven. As he shuck his thumping fore features apt the hoyhop of His Ards.

Thud.

Good safe firelamp! hailed the heliots. Goldselforelump! Halled they. Awed. Where thereon the skyfold high, trampatrampatramp. Adie. Per ye comdoom doominoom noonstroom. Yeasome priestomes. Fullyhum toowhoom.

Taawhaar?

Sants and sogs, cabs and cobs, kings and karls, tentes and taunts.

'Tis gone infarover. So fore now, dayleash. Pour deday. To trancefixureashone. Feist of Taborneccles, scenopegia, come! Shamwork, be in our scheining! And let every crisscouple be so crosscomplimentary, little eggons, youlk and meelk, in a farbiger pancosmos. With a hottyhammyum all round. Gudstruce!

Yet is no body present here which was not there before. Only is order othered. Nought is nulled. *Fuitfiat!*

Lo, the laud of laurens now orielising benedictively when saint and sage have said their say.

A spathe of calyptrous glume involucrumines the perinanthean Amenta: fungoalgaceous muscafilicial graminopalmular planteon; of increasing, livivorous, feelful thinkamalinks; luxuriotiating everywhencewithersoever among skullhullows and charnelcysts of a weedwastewoldwevild when Ralph the Retriever ranges to jawrode his knuts knuckles and her theas thighs; onegugulp down of the nauseous forere brarkfarsts oboboomaround and you're as paint and spickspan as a rainbow; wreathe the bowl to rid the bowel; no runcure, no rank heat, sir; amess in amullium; chlorid cup.

Health, chalce, endnessnessessity! Arrive, likkypuggers, in a poke! The folgor of the frightfools is olympically optimominous; there is bound to be a lovleg day for mirrages in the open; Murnane and Aveling are undertoken to berry that ortchert: provided that. You got to make good that breachsuit, seamer. You going to haulm port houlm, toilermaster. You yet must get up to kill (nonparticular). You still stand by and do as hit (private). While for yous, Jasminia Aruna and all your likers, affinitatively must it be by you elected if Monogynes his is or hers Diander, the tubous, limbersome and nectarial. Owned or grazeheifer, ethel or bonding. Mopsus or Gracchus, all your horodities will incessantlament be coming back from the Annone Wishwashwhose, Ormepierre Lodge, Doone of the Drumes, blanches bountifully and nightsend made up, every article lathering leaving several rinsings so as each rinse results with a dapperent rolle, cuffs for meek and chokers for sheek and a kink in the pacts for namby. Forbeer, forbear! For nought that is has bane. In mournenslaund. Themes have thimes and habit reburns. To flame in you. Ardor vigor forders order. Since ancient was our living is in possible to be. Delivered as. Caffirs and culls and onceagain overalls, the fittest surviva lives that blued, iorn and storridge can make them. Whichus all claims. Clean. Whenastcleeps. Close. And the mannor-millor clipperclappers. Noxt. Doze.

Fennsense, finnsonse, aworn! Tuck upp those wide shorts. The pink of the busket for sheer give. Peeps. Stand up to hard ware and step into style. If you soil may, puett, guett me prives. For newmanmaun set a marge to the merge of unnotions. Innition wons agame.

What has gone? How it ends?

Begin to forget it. It will remember itself from every sides, with all gestures, in each our word. Today's truth, tomorrow's trend.

Forget, remember!

Have we cherished expectations? Are we for liberty of perusiveness? Whyafter what forewhere? A plainplanned liffeyism assemblements Eblania's conglomerate horde. By dim delty Deva.

Forget!

Our wholemole millwheeling vicociclometer, a tetradomational gazebocroticon (the "Mamma Lujah" known to every schoolboy scandaller, be he Matty, Marky, Lukey or John-a-Donk), autokinatonetically preprovided with a clappercoupling smeltingworks exprogressive process, (for the farmer, his son and their homely codes, known as eggburst, eggblend, eggburial and hatch-as-hatch can) receives through a portal vein the dialytically separated elements of precedent decomposition for the verypetpurpose of subsequent recombination so that the heroticisms, catastrophes and eccentricities transmitted by the ancient legacy of the past; type by tope, letter from litter,

word at ward, with sendence of sundance, since the days of Plooney and
Columcellas when Giacinta, Pervenche and Margaret swayed over the all-
too-ghoulish and illyrical and innumantic in our mutter nation, all,
anastomosically assimilated and preteridentified paraidiotically, in fact, the
sameold gamebold adomic structure of our Finnius the old One, as highly
charged with electrons as hophazards can effective it, may be there for you,
Cockalooralooraloomenos, when cup, platter and pot come piping hot, as
sure as herself pits hen to paper and there's scribings scrawled on eggs.

Of cause, so! And in effect, as?

Dear. And we go on to Dirtdump. Reverend. May we add majesty? Well,
we have frankly enjoyed more than anything these secret workings of natures
(thanks ever for it, we humbly pray) and, well, was really so denighted of
this lights time. Mucksrats which bring up about uhrweckers they will come
to know good. Yon clouds will soon disappear looking forwards at a fine
day. The honourable Master Sarmon they should be first born like he was
with a twohangled warpon and it was between Williamstown and the
Mairrion Ailesbury on the top of the longcar, as merrily we rolled along, we
think of him looking at us yet as if to pass away in a cloud. When he woke
up in a sweat besidus it was to pardon him, goldylocks, me having an airth,
but he daydreamsed we had a lovelyt face for a pulltomine. Back we were by
the jerk of a bearnstark, backed in paladays last, on the brinks of the
wobblish, the man what never put a dramn in the swags but milk from a
national cowse. That was the prick of the spindle to me that gave me the
keys to dreamland. Sneakers in the grass, keep off! If we were to tick off all
that cafflers head, whisperers for his accomodation, the me craws, namely,
and their bacon what harmed butter! It's margarseen oil. Thinthin thinthin.
Stringstly is it forbidden by the honorary tenth commendmant to shall not
bare full sweetness against a nighboor's wiles. What those slimes up the
cavern door around you, keenin, (the lies is coming out on them frecklefully)
had the shames to suggest can we ever? Never! So may the low forget him
their trespasses against Molloyd O'Reilly, that hugglebeddy fann, now about
to get up, the hartiest that Coolock ever! A nought in nought Eirinishmhan,
called Ervigsen by his first mate. May all similar douters of our oldhame
story have that fancied widming! For a pipe of twist or a slug of Hibernia
metal we could let out and, by jings, someone would make a carpus of
somebody with the greatest of pleasure by private shootings. And in contravention to the constancy of chemical combinations not enough of all the
slatters of him left for Peeter the Picker to make their threi sevelty filfths of
a man out of. Good wheat! How delitious for the three Sulvans of Dulkey
and what a sellpriceget the two Peris of Monacheena! Sugars of lead for the

chloras ashpots! Peace! He possessing from a child of highest valency for our privileged beholdings ever complete hairy of chest, hamps and eyebags in pursuance to salesladies' affectionate company. His real devotes. Wriggling reptiles, take notice! Whereas we exgust all such sprinkling snigs. They are pestituting the whole time never with standing we simply agree upon the committee of amusance! Or could above bring under same notice for it to be able to be seen.

About that coerogenal hun and his knowing the size of an eggcup. First he was a skulksman at one time and then Cloon's fired him through guff. Be sage about sausages! Stuttutistics shows with he's heacups of teatables the oldfirm's fatspitters are most eatenly appreciated by metropolonians. While we should like to drag attentions to our Wolkmans Cumsensation Act. The magnets of our midst being foisted upon by a plethorace of parachutes. Did speece permit the bad example of setting before the military to the best of our belief in the earliest wish of the one in mind was the mitigation of the king's evils. And how he staired up the step after it's the power of the gait. His giantstand of manunknown. No brad wishy washy wathy wanted neither! Once you are balladproof you are unperceable to haily, icy and missilethroes. Order now before we reach Ruggers' Rush! As we now must close hoping to Saint Laurans all in the best. Moral. Mrs Stores Humphreys: So you are expecting trouble, Pondups, from the domestic service questioned? Mr Stores Humphreys: Just as there is a good in even, Levia, my cheek is a compleet bleenk. Plumb. Meaning: one two four. Finckers. Up the hind hose of hizzars. Whereapon our best again to a hundred and eleven ploose one thousand and one other blessings will now concloose thoose epoostles to your great kindest, well, for all at trouble to took. We are all at home in old Fintona, thank Danis, for ourselfsake, that direst of housebonds, whool wheel be true unto lovesend so long as we has a pockle full of brass. Impossible to remember persons in improbable to forget position places. Who would pellow his head off to conjure up a, well, particularly mean stinker like funn make called Foon MacCrawl brothers, mystery man of the pork martyrs? Force in giddersh! Tomothy and Lorcan, the bucket Toolers, both are Timsons now they've changed their characticuls during their blackout. Conan Boyles will pudge the daylives out through him, if they are correctly informed. Music, me ouldstrow, please! We'll have a brand rehearsal. Fing! One must simply laugh. Fing him aging! Good licks! Well, this ought to weke him to make up. He'll want all his fury gutmurdherers to redress him. Gilly in the gap. The big bad old sprowly all uttering foon! Has now stuffed last podding. His fooneral will sneak pleace by creeps o'clock toosday. Kingen will commen. Allso brewbeer. Pens picture at Manchem House Horsegardens shown in Morning post as from Boston transcripped. Femelles will be preadaminant as from twentyeight to twelve. To hear that lovelade parson, of case, of a bawl gentlemale, pour forther moracles. Don't forget! The grand fooneral will now shortly occur. Remember. The remains must be removed before eaght hours shorp. With earnestly conceived hopes. So help us to witness to this day to hand in sleep. From of Mayasdaysed most duteoused.

Well, here's lettering you erronymously anent other clerical fands allieged herewith. I wisht I wast be that dumb tyke and he'd wish it was me yonther heel. How about it? The sweetest song in the world! Our shape as a juvenile being much admired from the first with native copper locks. Referring to the Married Woman's Improperty Act a correspondent paints out that the Swees Auburn vogue is hanging down straith fitting to her innocenth eyes. O, felicious coolpose! If all the MacCrawls would only handle virgils like Armsworks, Limited! That's handsel for gertles! Never mind Micklemans! Chat us instead! The cad with the pope's wife, Lily Kinsella, who became the wife of Mr Sneakers for her good name in the hands of the kissing solicitor, will now engage in attentions. Just a prinche for tonight! Pale bellies our mild cure, back and streaky ninepace. The thicks off Bully's Acre was got up by Sully. The Boot lane brigade. And she had a certain medicine brought her in a licenced victualler's bottle. Shame! Thrice shame! We are advised the waxy is at the present in the Sweeps hospital and that he may never come out! Only look through your leatherbox one day with P.C.Q. about 4.32 or at 8 and 22.5 with the quart of scissions masters and clerk and the bevyhum of Marie Reparatrices for a good allround sympowdhericks purge, full view, to be surprised to see under the grand piano Lily on the sofa (and a lady!) pulling a low and then he'd begin to jump a little bit to find out what goes on when love walks in besides the solicitous bussness by kissing and looking into a mirror.

That we were treated not very grand when the police and everybody is all bowing to us when we go out in all directions on Wanterlond Road with my cubarola glide? And, personably speaking, they can make their beaux to my alce, as Hillary Allen sang to the opernnine knighters. Item, we never were chained to a chair, and, bitem, no widower whother soever followed us about with a fork on Yankskilling Day. Meet a great civilian (proud lives to him!) who is gentle as a mushroom and a very affectable when he always sits forenenst us for his wet while to all whom it may concern Sully is a thug from all he drunk though he is a rattling fine bootmaker in his profession. Would we were herearther to lodge our complaint on sergeant Laraseny in consequence of which in such steps taken his health would be constably broken into potter's pance which would be the change of his life by a Nollwelshian which has been oxbelled out of crispianity.

Well, our talks are coming to be resumed by more polite conversation with a huntered persent human over the natural bestness of pleisure after his good few mugs of humbedumb and shag. While for whoever likes that urogynal pan of cakes one apiece it is thanks, beloved, to Adam, our former first Finnlatter and our grocerest churcher, as per Grippiths' varuations, for his beautiful crossmess parzel.

Well, we simply like their demb cheeks, the Rathgarries, wagging here about around the rhythms in me amphybed and he being as bothered that he pausably could by the fallth of hampty damp. Certified reformed peoples, we may add to this stage, are proptably saying to quite agreeable deef. Here gives your answer, pigs and scuts! Hence we've lived in two worlds. He is another he what stays under the himp of holth. The herewaker of our hamefame is his real namesame who will get himself up and erect, confident and heroic when but, young as of old, for my daily comfreshenall, a wee one woos.

Alma Luvia, Pollabella.

P.S. Soldier Rollo's sweetheart. And she's about fetted up now with nonsery reams. And rigs out in regal rooms with the ritzies. Rags! Worns out. But she's still her deckhuman amber too.

Soft morning, city! Lsp! I am leafy speafing. Lpf! Folty and folty all the nights have fallen on to long my hair. Not a sound, falling. Lispn! No wind no word. Only a leaf, just a leaf and then leaves. The woods are fond always. As were we their babes in. And robins in crews so. It is for me goolden wending. Unless? Away! Rise up, man of the hooths, you have slept so long! Or is it only so mesleems? On your pondered palm. Reclined from cape to pede. With pipe on bowl. Terce for a fiddler, sixt for makmerriers, none for a Cole. Rise up now and aruse! Norvena's over. I am leafy, your goolden, so you called me, may me life, yea your goolden, silve me solve, exsogerraider! You did so drool. I was so sharm. But there's a great poet in you too. Stout Stokes would take you offly. So has he as bored me to slump. But am good and rested. Taks to you, toddy, tan ye! Yawhawaw. Helpunto min, helpas vin. Here is your shirt, the day one, come back. The stock, your collar. Also your double brogues. A comforter as well. And here your iverol and ever-thelest your umbr. And stand up tall! Straight. I want to see you looking fine for me. With your brandnew big green belt and all. Blooming in the very lotust and second to nill, Budd! When you're in the buckly shuit Rosen-sharonals near did for you. Fiftyseven and three, cosh, with the bulge. Proudpurse Alby with his pooraroon Eireen, they'll. Pride, comfytousness, enevy! You make me think of a wonderdecker I once. Or somebalt thet sailder, the man megallant, with the bangled ears. Or an earl was he, at Lucan? Or, no, it's the Iren duke's I mean. Or somebrey erse from the Dark Countries. Come and let us! We always said we'd. And go abroad. Rathgreany way perhaps. The childher are still fast. There is no school today. Them boys is so contrairy. The Head does be worrying himself. Heel trouble and heal travel. Galliver and Gellover. Unless they changes by mistake. I seen the likes in the twinngling of an aye. Som. So oft. Sim. Time after time. The sehm asnuh. Two bredder as doffered as nors in soun. When one of him sighs or one of him cries 'tis you all over. No peace at all. Maybe it's those two old crony aunts held them out to the water front. Queer Mrs Quickenough and odd Miss Doddpebble. And when them two has had a good few there isn't much more dirty clothes to publish. From the Laundersdale Minssions. One chap googling the holyboy's thingabib and this lad wetting his widdle. You were pleased as Punch, recitating war exploits and pearse orations to them jackeen gapers. But that night after, all you were wanton! Bidding me do this and that and the other. And blowing off to me, hugly Judsys, what wouldn't you give to have a girl! Your wish was mewill. And, lo, out of a sky! The way I too. But her, you wait. Eager to choose is left to her shade. If she had only more matcher's wit. Findlings makes runaways, runaways a stray. She's as merry as the gricks still. 'Twould be sore should ledden sorrow. I'll wait. And I'll wait. And then if all goes. What will be is. Is is. But let them. Slops hospodch and the slusky slut too. He's for thee what she's for me. Dogging you round cove and haven and teaching me the perts of speech. If you spun your yarns to him on the swishbarque waves I was spelling my yearns to her over cottage cake. We'll not disturb their sleeping duties. Let besoms be bosuns. It's Phoenix, dear. And the flame is, hear! Let's our joornee saintomichael make it. Since the lausafire has lost and the book of the depth is. Closed. Come! Step out of your shell! Hold up you free fing! Yes. We've light enough. I won't take our laddy's lampern. For them four old windbags of Gustsofairy to be blowing at. Nor you your rucksunck. To bring all the dannymans out after you on the hike. Send Arctur guiddus! Isma! Sft! It is the softest morning that ever I can ever remember me. But she won't rain showerly, our Ilma. Yet. Until it's the time. And me and you have made our. The sons of bursters won in the games. Still I'll take me owld Finvara for my shawlders. The trout will be so fine at brookfisht. With a taste of roly polony from Blugpuddels after. To bring out the tang of the tay. Is't you fain for a roost brood? Oaxmealturn, all out of the woolpalls! And then all the chippy young cuppinjars cluttering round us, clottering for their creams. Crying, me,

grownup sister! Are me not truly? Lst! Only but, theres a but, you must buy
me a fine new girdle too, nolly. When next you go to Market Norwall.
They're all saying I need it since the one from Isaacsen's slooped its line.
Mrknrk? Fy arthou! Come! Give me your great bearspaw, padder avilky, fol
a miny tiny. Dola. Mineninecyhandsy, in the languo of flows. That's Jorgen
Jargonsen. But you understood, nodst? I always know by your brights and
shades. Reach down. A lil mo. So. Draw back your glave. Hot and hairy,
hugon, is your hand! Here's where the falskin begins. Smoos as an infams.
One time you told you'd been burnt in ice. And one time it was chemicalled
after you taking a lifeness. Maybe that's why you hold your hodd as if. And
people thinks you missed the scaffold. Of fell design. I'll close me eyes. So
not to see. Or see only a youth in his florizel, a boy in innocence, peeling a
twig, a child beside a weenywhite steed. The child we all love to place our
hope in for ever. All men has done something. Be the time they've come to
the weight of old fletch. We'll lave it. So. We will take our walk before in
the timpul they ring the earthly bells. In the church by the hearseyard. Pax
Goodmens will. Or the birds start their treestirm shindy. Look, there are
yours off, high on high! And cooshes, sweet good luck they're cawing you,
Coole! You see, they're as white as the riven snae. For us. Next peaters poll
you will be elicted or I'm not your elicitous bribe. The Kinsella woman's
man will never reduce me. A MacGarath O'Cullagh O'Muirk MacFewney
sookadoodling and sweepacheeping round the lodge of Fjorn na Galla of
the Trumpets! It's like potting the po to shambe on the dresser or tamming
Uncle Tim's Caubeen on to the brows of a Viker Eagle. Not such big
strides, huddy foddy! You'll crush me antilopes I saved so long for. They're
Penisole's. And the two goodiest shoeshoes. It is hardly a Knut's mile or
seven, possumbotts. It is very good for the health of a morning. With
Buahbuah. A gentle motion all around. As leisure paces. And the help-
yourselftoastrool cure's easy. It seems so long since, ages since. As if you had
been long far away. Afartodays, afeartonights, and me as with you in thadark.
You will tell me some time if I can believe its all. You know where I am
bringing you? You remember? When I ran berrying after hucks and haws.
With you drawing out great aims to hazel me from the hummock with your
sling. Our cries. I could lead you there and I still by you in bed. Les go dutc
to Danegreven, nos? Not a soul but ourselves. Time? We have loads on our
hangs. Till Gilligan and Halligan call again to hooligan. And the rest of the
guns. Sullygan eight, from left to right. Olobobo, ye foxy theagues! The
moskors thought to ball you out. Or the Wald Unicorns Master, Bugley
Captain, from the Naul, drawls up by the door with the Honourable Whilp
and the Reverend Poynter and the two Lady Pagets of Tallyhaugh,

Ballyhuntus, in their riddletight raiding hats for to lift a hereshealth to their robost, the Stag, evers the Carlton hart. And you needn't host out with your duck and your duty, capapole, while they reach him the glass he never starts to finish. Clap this wis on your poll and stick this in your ear, wiggly! Beauties don't answer and the rich never pays. If you were the enlarged they'd hue in cry you, Heathtown, Harbourstown, Snowtown, Four Knocks, Flemingtown, Bodingtown to the Ford of Fyne on Delvin. How they housed to house you after the Platonic garlens! And all because, loosed in her reflexes, she seem she seen Ericoricori coricome huntsome with his three poach dogs aleashing him. But you came safe through. Enough of that homer corner! And old mutthergoosip! We might call on the Old Lord, what do you say? There's something tells me. He is a fine sport. Like the score and a moighty went before him. And a proper old promnentory. His door always open. For a newera's day. Much as your own is. You invoiced him last Eatster so he ought to give us hockockles and everything. Remember to take off your white hat, ech? When we come in the presence. And say hoothoothoo, ithmuthisthy! His is house of laws. And I'll drop my graciast kertssey too. If the Ming Tung no go bo to me homage me hamage kow bow tow to the Mong Tang. Ceremonialness to stand lowest place be! Saying: What'll you take to link to light a pike on porpoise, plaise? He might knight you an Armor elsor daub you the first cheap magyerstrape. Remember Bomthomanew vim vam vom Hungerig. Hoteform, chain and epolettes, botherbumbose. And I'll be your aural eyeness. But we vain. Plain fancies. It's in the castles air. My currant bread's full of sillymottocraft. Aloof is anoof. We can take or leave. He's reading his ruffs. You'll know our way from there surely. Flura's way. Where once we led so many car couples have follied since. Clatchka! Giving Shaughnessy's mare the hillymount of her life. With her strulldeburgghers! Hnmn hnmn! The rollcky road adondering. We can sit us down on the heathery benn, me on you, in quolm unconsciounce. To scand the arising. Out from Drumleek. It was there Evora told me I had best. If I ever. When the moon of mourning is set and gone. Over Glinaduna. Lonu nula. Ourselves, oursouls alone. At the site of salvocean. And watch would the letter you're wanting be coming may be. And cast ashore. That I prays for be mains of me draims. Scratching it and patching at with a prompt from a primer. And what scrips of nutsnolleges I pecked up me meself Every letter is a hard but yours sure is the hardest crux ever. Hack an axe, hook an oxe, hath an an, heth hith ences. But once done, dealt and delivered, tattat, you're on the map. Rased on traumscrapt from Maston, Boss. After rounding his world of ancient days. Carried in a caddy or screwed and corked. On his mugisstosst surface. With a bob, bob, bottledby. Blob. When the waves give up yours the soil may for me. Sometime then, somewhere there, I wrote me hopes and buried the page when I heard Thy voice, ruddery dunner, so loud that none but, and left it to lie till a kissmiss coming. So content me now. Lss. Unbuild and be buildn our bankaloan cottage there and we'll cohabit respectable. The Gowans, ser, for Medem, me. With acute bubel runtoer for to pippup and gopeep where the sterres be. Just to see would we hear how Jove and the peers talk. Amid the soleness. Tilltop, bigmaster! Scale the summit! You're not so giddy any more. All your graundplotting and the little it brought! Humps, when you hised us and dumps, when you doused us! But sarra one of me cares a brambling ram, pomp porteryark! On limpidy marge I've made me hoom. Park and a pub for me. Only don't start your stunts of Donachie's yeards agoad again. I could guessp to her name who tuckt you that one, tufnut! Bold bet backwords. For the loves of sinfintins! Before the naked universe. And the bailby pleasemarm rincing his eye! One of these fine days, lewdy culler, you must redoform again. Blessed shield Martin! Softly so. I am so exquisitely pleased about the loveleavest dress I have. You will always call me Leafiest, won't you, dowling? Wordherfhull Ohldhbhoy! And you won't urbjunk to me parafume, oiled of kolooney, with a spot of marashy. Sm! It's Alpine Smile from Yesthers late Yhesters. I'm in everywince nasturtls. Even in Houlth's nose. Medeurscodeignus! Astale of astoun. Grand owld marauder! If I knew who you are! When that hark from the air said it was Captain Finsen makes cumhulments and was mayit pressing for his suit I said are you there here's nobody here only me. But I near fell off the pile of samples. As if your tinger winged ting to me hear. Is that right what your brothermilk in Bray bes telling the district you were bragged up by Brostal because your parents would be always tumbling into his foulplace and losing her pentacosts after drinking their pledges? Howsomendeavour, you done me fine! The only man was ever known could eat the crushts of lobsters. Our native night when you twicetook me for some Marienne Sherry and then your Jermyn cousin who signs hers with exes and the beardwig I found in your Clarksome bag. Pharaops you'll play you're the king of Aeships. You certainly make the most royal of noises. I will tell you all sorts of makeup things, strangerous. And show you to every simple storyplace we pass. *Cadmillersfolly, Bellevenue, Wellcrom, Quid Superabit,* villities valleties. Change the plates for the next course of murphies. Spendlove's still there and the canon going strong and so is Claffey's habits endurtaking and our parish pomp's a great warrent. But you'll have to ask that same four that named them is always snugging in your bar-salooner, saying they're the best relicts of Conal O'Daniel and writing *Finglas since the*

Flood. That'll be some kingly work in progress. But it's by this route he'll come some morrow. And I can signal you all flint and fern are rasstling as we go by. And you'll sing thumb a bit and then wise your selmon on it. It is all so often and still the same to me. Snf? Only turf, wick dear! Clane turf. You've never forgodden batt on tarf, have you, at broin burroow, what? Mch? Why, them's the muchrooms, come up during the night. Look, agres of roofs in parshes. Dom on dam, dim in dym. And a capital part for olympics to ply at. Steadyon, Cooloosus! Mind your stride or you'll knock. While I'm dodging the dustbins. Look what I found! A lintil pea. And look at here! This cara weeseed. Pretty mites, my sweetthings, was they poorloves abandoned by wholawidey world? Neighboulotts for newtown. The Eblanamagna you behazyheld loomening up out of the dumblynass. But the still sama sitta. I've lapped so long. As you said. It fair takes. If I lose my breath for a minute or two don't speak, remember! Once it happened, so it may again. Why I'm all these years within years in soffran, allbeleaved. To hide away the tear, the parted. It's thinking of all. The brave that gave their. The fair that wore. All them that's gunne. I'll begin again in a jiffey. The nik of a nad. How glad you'll be I waked you! My! How well you'll feel! For ever after. First we turn by the vagurin here and then it's gooder. So side by side, turn agate, weddingtown, laud men of Londub! I only hope whole the heavens sees us. For I feel I could near to faint away. Into the deeps. Annamores leep. Let me lean, just a lea, if you le, bowldstrong bigtider. Allgearls is wea. At times. So. While you're adamant evar. Wrhps, that wind as if out of norewere! As on the night of the Apophanypes. Jumpst shootst throbbst into me mouth like a bogue and arrohs! Ludegude of the Lashlanns, how he whips me cheeks! Sea, sea! Here, weir, reach, island, bridge. Where you meet I. The day. Remember! Why there that moment and us two only? I was but teen, a tiler's dot. The swankysuits was boosting always, sure him, he was like to me fad. But the swaggerest swell off Shackvulle Strutt. And the fiercest freaky ever followed a pining child round the sluppery table with a forkful of fat. But a king of whistlers. Scieoula! When he'd prop me atlas against his goose and light our two candles for our singers duohs on the sewingmachine. I'm sure he squirted juice in his eyes to make them flash for flightening me. Still and all he was awful fond to me. Who'll search for *Find Me Colours* now on the hillydroops of Vikloefells? But I read in Tobecontinued's tale that while blubles blows there'll still be sealskers. There'll be others but non so for me. Yed he never knew we seen us before. Night after night. So that I longed to go to. And still with all. One time you'd stand fornenst me, fairly laughing, in your bark and tan billows of I branches for to fan me coolly. And I'd lie as quiet as a moss. And one time you'd rush upon me, darkly roaring, like a great black shadow with a sheeny stare to perce me rawly. And I'd frozen up and pray for thawe. Three times in all. I was the pet of everyone then. A princeable girl. And you were the pantymammy's Vulking Corsergoth. The invision of Indelond. And, by Thorror, you looked it! My lips went livid for from the joy of fear. Like almost now. How? How you said how you'd give me the keys of me heart. And we'd be married till delth to uspart. And though dev do espart. O mine! Only, no, now it's me who's got to give. As duv herself div. Inn this linn. And can it be it's nnow fforvell? Illas! I wisht I had better glances to peer to you through this baylight's growing. But you're changing, acoolsha, you're changing from me, I can feel. Or is it me is? I'm getting mixed. Brightening up and tightening down. Yes, you're changing, sonhusband, and you're turning, I can feel you, for a daughterwife from the hills again. Imlamaya. And she is coming. Swimming in my hindmoist. Diveltaking on me tail. Just a whisk brisk sly spry spink spank sprint of a thing theresomere, saultering. Saltarella come to her own. I pity your oldself I was used to. Now a younger's there. Try not to part! Be happy, dear ones! May I be wrong! For she'll be sweet for you as I was sweet when I came down out of me mother. My great blue bedroom, the air so quiet, scarce a cloud. In peace and silence. I could have stayed up there for always only. It's something fails us. First we feel. Then we fall. And let her rain now if she likes. Gently or strongly as she likes. Anyway let her rain for my time is come. I done me best when I was let. Thinking always if I go all goes. A hundred cares, a tithe of troubles and is there one who understands me? One in a thousand of years of the nights? All me life I have been lived among them but now they are becoming lothed to me. And I am lothing their little warm tricks. And lothing their mean cosy turns. And all the greedy gushes out through their small souls. And all the lazy leaks down over their brash bodies. How small it's all! And me letting on to meself always. And lilting on all the time. I thought you were all glittering with the noblest of carriage. You're only a bumpkin. I thought you the great in all things, in guilt and in glory. You're but a puny. Home! My people were not their sort out beyond there so far as I can. For all the bold and bad and bleary they are blamed, the seahags. No! Nor for all our wild dances in all their wild din. I can seen meself among them, allaniuvia pulchrabelled. How she was handsome, the wild Amazia, when she would seize to my other breast! And what is she weird, haughty Niluna, that she will snatch from my ownest hair! For 'tis they are the stormies. Ho hang! Hang ho! And the clash of our cries till we spring to be free. Auravoles, they says, never heed of your name! But I'm loothing them that's here and all I lothe. Loonely in me loneness. For all their faults. I am passing out. O bitter ending! I'll slip away before they're up. They'll never see. Nor know. Nor miss me. And it's old and old it's sad and old it's sad and weary I go back to you, my cold father, my cold mad father, my cold mad feary father, till the near sight of the mere size of him, the moyles and moyles of it, moananoaning, makes me seasilt saltsick and I rush, my only, into your arms. I see them rising! Save me from those therrble prongs! Two more. Onetwo moremens more. So. Avelaval. My leaves have drifted from me. All. But one clings still. I'll bear it on me. To remind me of. Lff! So soft this morning, ours. Yes. Carry me along, taddy, like you done through the toy fair! If I seen him bearing down on me now under whitespread wings like he'd come from Arkangels, I sink I'd die down over his feet, humbly dumbly, only to washup. Yes, tid. There's where. First. We pass through grass behush the bush to. Whish! A gull. Gulls. Far calls. Coming, far! End here. Us then. Finn, again! Take. Bussoftlhee, mememormee! Till thousendsthee. Lps. The keys to. Given! A way a lone a last a loved a long the

PARIS
1922–1939